SINCLAIR LEWIS

Sinclair Lewis

ARROWSMITH
ELMER GANTRY
DODSWORTH

THE LIBRARY OF AMERICA

The paper used in this publication meets the
minimum requirements of the American National Standard for
Information Sciences—Permanence of Paper for Printed
Library Materials, ANSI Z39.48—1984.

Distributed to the trade in the United States
by Penguin Putnam, Inc.
and in Canada by Penguin Books Canada Ltd.

Library of Congress Catalog Number: 2002019451
For cataloging information, see end of Notes.
ISBN 1–931082–08–1

First Printing
The Library of America—133

Manufactured in the United States of America

Richard Lingeman

wrote the notes for this volume

Sinclair Lewis's
Arrowsmith, Elmer Gantry, Dodsworth
is kept in print by a gift from

JOHN LOGAN

to the Guardians of American Letters Fund,
established by The Library of America
to ensure that every volume in the series
will be permanently available.

Contents

ARROWSMITH

To Dr. Paul H. DeKruif I am indebted not only for most of the bacteriological and medical material in this tale but equally for his help in the planning of the fable itself—for his realization of the characters as living people, for his philosophy as a scientist. With this acknowledgment I want to record our months of companionship while working on the book, in the United States, in the West Indies, in Panama, in London and Fontainebleau. I wish I could reproduce our talks along the way, and the laboratory afternoons, the restaurants at night, and the deck at dawn as we steamed into tropic ports.

SINCLAIR LEWIS

Chapter I

THE DRIVER of the wagon swaying through forest and swamp of the Ohio wilderness was a ragged girl of fourteen. Her mother they had buried near the Monongahela—the girl herself had heaped with torn sods the grave beside the river of the beautiful name. Her father lay shrinking with fever on the floor of the wagon-box, and about him played her brothers and sisters, dirty brats, tattered brats, hilarious brats.

She halted at the fork in the grassy road, and the sick man quavered, "Emmy, ye better turn down towards Cincinnati. If we could find your Uncle Ed, I guess he'd take us in."

"Nobody ain't going to take us in," she said. "We're going on jus' long as we can. Going West! They's a whole lot of new things I aim to be seeing!"

She cooked the supper, she put the children to bed, and sat by the fire, alone.

That was the great-grandmother of Martin Arrowsmith.

II

Cross-legged in the examining-chair in Doc Vickerson's office, a boy was reading "Gray's Anatomy." His name was Martin Arrowsmith, of Elk Mills, in the state of Winnemac.

There was a suspicion in Elk Mills—now, in 1897, a dowdy red-brick village, smelling of apples—that this brown-leather adjustable seat which Doc Vickerson used for minor operations, for the infrequent pulling of teeth and for highly frequent naps, had begun life as a barber's chair. There was also a belief that its proprietor must once have been called Doctor Vickerson, but for years he had been only The Doc, and he was scurfier and much less adjustable than the chair.

Martin was the son of J. J. Arrowsmith, who conducted the New York Clothing Bazaar. By sheer brass and obstinacy he had, at fourteen, become the unofficial, also decidedly unpaid, assistant to the Doc, and while the Doc was on a country call he took charge—though what there was to take charge of, no one could ever make out. He was a slender boy, not very tall; his hair and restless eyes were black, his skin unusually white, and the contrast gave him an air of passionate variability. The squareness of his head and a reasonable breadth of shoulders saved him from any appearance of effeminacy or of that querulous timidity which artistic young gentlemen call Sensitiveness. When he lifted his head to listen, his right eyebrow, slightly higher than the left, rose and quivered in his characteristic expression of energy, of independence, and a hint that he could fight, a look of impertinent inquiry which had been known to annoy his teachers and the Sunday School superintendent.

Martin was, like most inhabitants of Elk Mills before the Slavo-Italian immigration, a Typical Pure-bred Anglo-Saxon American, which means that he was a union of German, French, Scotch, Irish, perhaps a little Spanish, conceivably a little of the strains lumped together as "Jewish," and a great deal of English, which is itself a combination of Primitive Britain, Celt, Phœnician, Roman, German, Dane, and Swede.

It is not certain that, in attaching himself to Doc Vickerson, Martin was entirely and edifyingly controlled by a desire to become a Great Healer. He did awe his Gang by bandaging stone-bruises, dissecting squirrels, and explaining the astounding and secret matters to be discovered at the back of the physiology, but he was not completely free from an ambition to command such glory among them as was enjoyed by the son of the Episcopalian minister, who could smoke an entire cigar without becoming sick. Yet this afternoon he read steadily at the section on the lymphatic system, and he muttered the long and perfectly incomprehensible words in a hum which made drowsier the dusty room.

It was the central room of the three occupied by Doc Vickerson, facing on Main Street above the New York Clothing Bazaar. On one side of it was the foul waiting-room, on the other, the Doc's bedroom. He was an aged widower; for what he called "female fixings" he cared nothing; and the bedroom with its tottering bureau and its cot of frowsy blankets was cleaned only by Martin, in not very frequent attacks of sanitation.

This central room was at once business office, consultation-room, operating-theater, living-room, poker den, and warehouse for guns and fishing-tackle. Against a brown plaster wall was a cabinet of zoölogical collections and medical curiosities, and beside it the most dreadful and fascinating object known to the boy-world of Elk Mills—a skeleton with one gaunt gold tooth. On evenings when the Doc was away, Martin would acquire prestige among the trembling Gang by leading them into the unutterable darkness and scratching a sulfur match on the skeleton's jaw.

On the wall was a home-stuffed pickerel on a home-varnished board. Beside the rusty stove, a sawdust-box cuspidor rested on a slimy oilcloth worn through to the threads. On the senile table was a pile of memoranda of debts which the Doc was always swearing he would "collect from those deadbeats right now," and which he would never, by any chance, at any time, collect from any of them. A year or two—a decade or two—a century or two—they were all the same to the plodding doctor in the bee-murmuring town.

The most unsanitary corner was devoted to the cast-iron sink, which was oftener used for washing eggy breakfast plates than for sterilizing instruments. On its ledge were a broken test-tube, a broken fishhook, an unlabeled and forgotten bottle of pills, a nail-bristling heel, a frayed cigar-butt, and a rusty lancet stuck in a potato.

The wild raggedness of the room was the soul and symbol of Doc Vickerson; it was more exciting than the flat-faced stack of shoe-boxes in the New York Bazaar: it was the lure to questioning and adventure for Martin Arrowsmith.

III

The boy raised his head, cocked his inquisitive brow. On the stairway was the cumbersome step of Doc Vickerson. The Doc was sober! Martin would not have to help him into bed.

But it was a bad sign that the Doc should first go down the hall to his bedroom. The boy listened sharply. He heard the Doc open the lower part of the washstand, where he kept his bottle of Jamaica rum. After a long gurgle the invisible Doc put away the bottle and decisively kicked the doors shut. Still good. Only one drink. If he came into the consultation-room at once, he would be safe. But he was still standing in the bedroom. Martin sighed as the washstand doors were hastily opened again, as he heard another gurgle and a third.

The Doc's step was much livelier when he loomed into the office, a gray mass of a man with a gray mass of mustache, a form vast and unreal and undefined, like a cloud taking for the moment a likeness of humanity. With the brisk attack of one who wishes to escape the discussion of his guilt, the Doc rumbled while he waddled toward his desk-chair:

"What you doing here, young fella? What you doing here? I knew the cat would drag in something if I left the door unlocked." He gulped slightly; he smiled to show that he was being humorous—people had been known to misconstrue the Doc's humor.

He spoke more seriously, occasionally forgetting what he was talking about:

"Reading old Gray? That's right. Physician's library just three books: 'Gray's Anatomy' and Bible and Shakespeare. Study. You may become great doctor. Locate in Zenith and make five thousand dollars year—much as United States Senator! Set a high goal. Don't let things slide. Get training. Go college before go medical school. Study. Chemistry. Latin. Knowledge! I'm plug doc—got chick nor child—nobody—old drunk. But you—leadin' physician. Make five thousand dollars year.

"Murray woman's got endocarditis. Not thing I can do for her. Wants somebody hold her hand. Road's damn' disgrace. Culvert's out, beyond the grove. 'Sgrace.

"Endocarditis and—

"Training, that's what you got t' get. Fundamentals. Know chemistry. Biology. I nev' did. Mrs. Reverend Jones thinks she's got gastric ulcer. Wants to go city for operation. Ulcer, hell! She and the Reverend both eat too much.

"Why they don't repair that culvert— And don't be a booze-hoister like me, either. And get your basic science. I'll splain."

The boy, normal village youngster though he was, given to stoning cats and to playing pom-pom-pullaway, gained something of the intoxication of treasure-hunting as the Doc struggled to convey his vision of the pride of learning, the universality of biology, the triumphant exactness of chemistry. A fat old man and dirty and unvirtuous was the Doc; his grammar was doubtful, his vocabulary alarming, and his references to his rival, good Dr. Needham, were scandalous; yet he invoked in Martin a vision of making chemicals explode with much noise and stink and of seeing animalcules that no boy in Elk Mills had ever beheld.

The Doc's voice was thickening; he was sunk in his chair, blurry of eye and lax of mouth. Martin begged him to go to bed, but the Doc insisted:

"Don't need nap. No. Now you lissen. You don't appreciate but— Old man now. Giving you all I've learned. Show you collection. Only museum in whole county. Scientif' pioneer."

A hundred times had Martin obediently looked at the specimens in the brown, crackly-varnished bookcase: the beetles and chunks of mica; the embryo of a two-headed calf, the gallstones removed from a respectable lady whom the Doc enthusiastically named to all visitors. The Doc stood before the case, waving an enormous but shaky forefinger.

"Looka that butterfly. Name is *porthesia chrysorrhœa*. Doc Needham couldn't tell you that! He don't know what butterflies are called! He don't care if you get trained. Remember that name now?" He turned on Martin. "You payin' attention? You interested? *Huh?* Oh, the devil! Nobody wants to know about my museum—not a person. Only one in county but— I'm an old failure."

Martin asserted, "Honest, it's slick!"

"Look here! Look here! See that? In the bottle? It's an appendix. First one ever took out 'round here. I did it! Old Doc Vickerson, he did the first 'pendectomy in *this* neck of the woods, you bet! And first museum. It ain't—so big—but it's start. I haven't put away money like Doc Needham, but I started first c'lection—I started it!"

He collapsed in a chair, groaning, "You're right. Got to sleep. All in." But as Martin helped him to his feet he broke away, scrabbled about on his desk, and looked back doubtfully. "Want to give you something—start your training. And remember the old man. Will anybody remember the old man?"

He was holding out the beloved magnifying glass which for years he had used in botanizing. He watched Martin slip the lens into his pocket, he sighed, he struggled for something else to say, and silently he lumbered into his bedroom.

Chapter II

THE STATE of Winnemac is bounded by Michigan, Ohio, Illinois, and Indiana, and like them it is half Eastern, half Midwestern. There is a feeling of New England in its brick and sycamore villages, its stable industries, and a tradition which goes back to the Revolutionary War. Zenith, the largest city in the state, was founded in 1792. But Winnemac is Midwestern in its fields of corn and wheat, its red barns and silos, and, despite the immense antiquity of Zenith, many counties were not settled till 1860.

The University of Winnemac is at Mohalis, fifteen miles from Zenith. There are twelve thousand students; beside this prodigy Oxford is a tiny theological school and Harvard a select college for young gentlemen. The University has a baseball field under glass; its buildings are measured by the mile; it hires hundreds of young Doctors of Philosophy to give rapid instruction in Sanskrit, navigation, accountancy, spectacle-fitting, sanitary engineering, Provençal poetry, tariff schedules, rutabaga-growing, motor-car designing, the history of Voronezh, the style of Matthew Arnold, the diagnosis of *myohypertrophia kymoparalytica*, and department-store advertising. Its president is the best money-raiser and the best after-dinner speaker in the United States; and Winnemac was the first school in the world to conduct its extension courses by radio.

It is not a snobbish rich-man's college, devoted to leisurely nonsense. It is the property of the people of the state, and what they want—or what they are told they want—is a mill to turn out men and women who will lead moral lives, play bridge, drive good cars, be enterprising in business, and occasionally mention books, though they are not expected to have time to read them. It is a Ford Motor Factory, and if its products rattle a little, they are beautifully standardized, with perfectly interchangeable parts. Hourly the University of Winnemac grows in numbers and influence, and by 1950 one may expect it to have created an entirely new world-civilization, a civilization larger and brisker and purer.

II

In 1904, when Martin Arrowsmith was an Arts and Science Junior preparing for medical school, Winnemac had but five thousand students yet it was already brisk.

Martin was twenty-one. He still seemed pale, in contrast to his black smooth hair, but he was a respectable runner, a fair basket-ball center, and a savage hockey-player. The co-eds murmured that he "looked so romantic," but as this was before the invention of sex and the era of petting-parties, they merely talked about him at a distance, and he did not know that he could have been a hero of amours. For all his stubbornness he was shy. He was not entirely ignorant of caresses but he did not make an occupation of them. He consorted with men whose virile pride it was to smoke filthy corncob pipes and to wear filthy sweaters.

The University had become his world. For him Elk Mills did not exist. Doc Vickerson was dead and buried and forgotten; Martin's father and mother were dead, leaving him only enough money for his arts and medical courses. The purpose of life was chemistry and physics and the prospect of biology next year.

His idol was Professor Edward Edwards, head of the department of chemistry, who was universally known as "Encore." Edwards' knowledge of the history of chemistry was immense. He could read Arabic, and he infuriated his fellow chemists by asserting that the Arabs had anticipated all their researches. Himself, Professor Edwards never did researches. He sat before fires and stroked his collie and chuckled in his beard.

This evening Encore was giving one of his small and popular At Home's. He lolled in a brown-corduroy Morris chair, being quietly humorous for the benefit of Martin and half a dozen other fanatical young chemists, and baiting Dr. Norman Brumfit, the instructor in English. The room was full of heartiness and beer and Brumfit.

Every university faculty must have a Wild Man to provide thrills and to shock crowded lecture-rooms. Even in so energetically virtuous an institution as Winnemac there was one Wild Man, and he was Norman Brumfit. He was permitted, without restriction, to speak of himself as immoral, agnostic, and socialistic, so long as it was universally known that he remained pure, Presbyterian, and Republican. Dr. Brumfit was in form, to-night. He asserted that whenever a man showed genius, it could be proved that he had Jewish blood. Like all discussions of Judaism at Winnemac, this led to the mention of Max Gottlieb, professor of bacteriology in the medical school.

Professor Gottlieb was the mystery of the university. It was known that he was a Jew, born and educated in Germany, and that his work on immunology had given him fame in the East and in Europe. He rarely left his small brown weedy house except to return to his laboratory, and few students outside of his classes had ever identified him, but every one had heard of his tall, lean, dark aloofness. A thousand fables fluttered about him. It was believed that he was the son of a German prince, that he had immense wealth, that he lived as sparsely as the other professors only because he was doing terrifying and costly experiments which probably had something to do with human sacrifice. It was said that he could create life in the laboratory, that he could talk to the monkeys which he inoculated, that he had been driven out of Germany as a devil-worshiper or an anarchist, and that he secretly drank real champagne every evening at dinner.

It was the tradition that faculty-members did not discuss their colleagues with students, but Max Gottlieb could not be regarded as anybody's colleague. He was impersonal as the chill northeast wind. Dr. Brumfit rattled:

"I'm sufficiently liberal, I should assume, toward the claims of science, but with a man like Gottlieb— I'm prepared to believe that he knows all about material forces, but what astounds me is that such a man can be blind to the vital force that creates all others. He says that knowledge is worthless unless it is proven by rows of figures. Well, when one of you scientific sharks can take the genius of a Ben Jonson and measure it with a yardstick, then I'll admit that we literary chaps, with our doubtless absurd belief in beauty and loyalty and the world o' dreams, are off on the wrong track!"

Martin Arrowsmith was not exactly certain what this meant and he enthusiastically did not care. He was relieved when Professor Edwards from the midst of his beardedness and smokiness made a sound curiously like "Oh, hell!" and took the conversation away from Brumfit. Ordinarily Encore would have suggested, with amiable malice, that Gottlieb was a "crapehanger" who wasted time destroying the theories of other men instead of making new ones of his own. But to-night, in detestation of such literary playboys as Brumfit, he exalted Gottlieb's long, lonely, failure-burdened effort to synthesize antitoxin, and his diabolic pleasure in disproving his own contentions as he would those of Ehrlich or Sir Almroth Wright. He spoke of Gottlieb's great book, "Immunology," which had been read by seven-ninths of all the men in the world who could possibly understand it—the number of these being nine.

The party ended with Mrs. Edwards' celebrated doughnuts. Martin tramped toward his boarding-house through a veiled spring night. The discussion of Gottlieb had roused him to a reasonless excitement. He thought of working in a laboratory at night, alone, absorbed, contemptuous of academic success and of popular classes. Himself, he believed, he had never seen the man, but he knew that Gottlieb's laboratory was in the Main Medical Building. He drifted toward the distant medical campus. The few people whom he met were hurrying with midnight timidity. He entered the shadow of the Anatomy Building, grim as a barracks, still as the dead men lying up there in the dissecting-room. Beyond him was the turreted bulk of the Main Medical Building, a harsh and blurry mass, high up in its dark wall a single light. He started. The light had gone out abruptly, as though an agitated watcher were trying to hide from him.

On the stone steps of the Main Medical, two minutes after, appeared beneath the arc-light a tall figure, ascetic, self-contained, apart. His swart cheeks were gaunt, his nose high-bridged and thin. He did not hurry, like the belated home-bodies. He was unconscious of the world. He looked at Martin and through him; he moved away, muttering to himself, his shoulders stooped, his long hands clasped behind him. He was lost in the shadows, himself a shadow.

He had worn the threadbare top-coat of a poor professor yet Martin remembered him as wrapped in a black velvet cape with a silver star arrogant on his breast.

III

On his first day in medical school, Martin Arrowsmith was in a high state of superiority. As a medic he was more picturesque than other students, for medics are reputed to know secrets, horrors, exhilarating wickednesses. Men from the other departments go to their rooms to peer into their books. But also as an academic graduate, with a training in the basic sciences, he felt superior to his fellow medics, most of whom had but a high-school diploma, with perhaps one year in a ten-room Lutheran college among the cornfields.

For all his pride, Martin was nervous. He thought of operating, of making a murderous wrong incision; and with a more immediate, macabre fear, he thought of the dissecting-room and the stony, steely Anatomy Building. He had heard older medics mutter of its horrors: of corpses hanging by hooks, like rows of ghastly fruit, in an abominable tank of brine in the dark basement; of Henry the janitor, who was said to haul the cadavers out of the brine, to inject red lead into their veins, and to scold them as he stuffed them on the dumb-waiter.

There was prairie freshness in the autumn day but Martin did not heed. He hurried into the slate-colored hall of the Main Medical, up the wide stairs to the office of Max Gottlieb. He did not look at passing students, and when he bumped into them he grunted in confused apology. It was a portentous hour. He was going to specialize in bacteriology; he was going to discover enchanting new germs; Professor Gottlieb was going to recognize him as a genius, make him an assistant, predict for him— He halted in Gottlieb's private laboratory, a small, tidy apartment with racks of cotton-corked test-tubes on the bench, a place unimpressive and unmagical save for the constant-temperature bath with its tricky thermometer and electric bulbs. He waited till another student, a stuttering gawk of a student, had finished talking to Gottlieb, dark, lean, impassive at his desk in a cubbyhole of an office, then he plunged.

If in the misty April night Gottlieb had been romantic as a cloaked horseman, he was now testy and middle-aged. Near at hand, Martin could see wrinkles beside the hawk eyes.

Gottlieb had turned back to his desk, which was heaped with shabby note-books, sheets of calculations, and a marvelously precise chart with red and green curves descending to vanish at zero. The calculations were delicate, minute, exquisitely clear; and delicate were the scientist's thin hands among the papers. He looked up, spoke with a hint of German accent. His words were not so much mispronounced as colored with a warm unfamiliar tint.

"Vell? Yes?"

"Oh, Professor Gottlieb, my name is Arrowsmith. I'm a medic freshman, Winnemac B.A. I'd like awfully to take bacteriology this fall instead of next year. I've had a lot of chemistry—"

"No. It is not time for you."

"Honest, I know I could do it now."

"There are two kinds of students that the gods give me. One kind they dump on me like a bushel of potatoes. I do not like potatoes, and the potatoes they do not ever seem to have great affection for me, but I take them and teach them to kill patients. The other kind—they are very few!—they seem for some reason that is not at all clear to me to wish a liddle bit to become scientists, to work with bugs and make mistakes. Those, ah, those, I seize them, I denounce them, I teach them right away the ultimate lesson of science, which is to wait and doubt. Of the potatoes, I demand nothing; of the foolish ones like you, who think I could teach them something, I demand everything. No. You are too young. Come back next year."

"But honestly, with my chemistry—"

"Have you taken physical chemistry?"

"No, sir, but I did pretty well in organic."

"Organic chemistry! Puzzle chemistry! Stink chemistry! Drug-store chemistry! Physical chemistry is power, it is exactness, it is life. But organic chemistry—that is a trade for pot-washers. No. You are too young. Come back in a year."

Gottlieb was absolute. His talon fingers waved Martin to the door, and the boy hastened out, not daring to argue. He slunk off in misery. On the campus he met that jovial historian of chemistry, Encore Edwards, and begged, "Say, Professor, tell me, is there any value for a doctor in organic chemistry?"

"Value? Why, it seeks the drugs that allay pain! It produces the paint that slicks up your house, it dyes your sweetheart's dress—and maybe, in these degenerate days, her cherry lips! Who the dickens has been talking scandal about my organic chemistry?"

"Nobody. I was just wondering," Martin complained, and he drifted to the College Inn where, in an injured and melancholy manner, he devoured an enormous banana-split and a bar of almond chocolate, as he meditated:

"I want to take bacteriology. I want to get down to the bottom of this disease stuff. I'll learn some physical chemistry. I'll show old Gottlieb, damn him! Some day I'll discover the germ of cancer or something, and then he'll look foolish in the face! . . . Oh, Lord, I hope I won't take sick, first time I go into the dissecting-room. . . . I want to take bacteriology—now!"

He recalled Gottlieb's sardonic face; he felt and feared his quality of dynamic hatred. Then he remembered the wrinkles, and he saw Max Gottlieb not as a genius but as a man who had headaches, who became agonizingly tired, who could be loved.

"I wonder if Encore Edwards knows as much as I thought he did? What *is* Truth?" he puzzled.

IV

Martin was jumpy on his first day of dissecting. He could not look at the inhumanly stiff faces of the starveling gray men lying on the wooden tables. But they were so impersonal, these lost old men, that in two days he was, like the other medics, calling them "Billy" and "Ike" and "the Parson," and regarding them as he had regarded animals in biology. The dissecting-room itself was impersonal: hard cement floor, walls of hard plaster between wire-glass windows. Martin detested the reek of formaldehyde; that and some dreadful subtle other odor seemed to cling about him outside the dissecting-room; but he smoked cigarettes to forget it, and in a week he was exploring arteries with youthful and altogether unholy joy.

His dissecting partner was the Reverend Ira Hinkley, known to the class by a similar but different name.

Ira was going to be a medical missionary. He was a man of twenty-nine, a graduate of Pottsburg Christian College and of the Sanctification Bible and Missions School. He had played football; he was as strong and nearly as large as a steer, and no steer ever bellowed more enormously. He was a bright and happy Christian, a romping optimist who laughed away sin and doubt, a joyful Puritan who with annoying virility preached the doctrine of his tiny sect, the Sanctification Brotherhood, that to have a beautiful church was almost as damnable as the debaucheries of card-playing.

Martin found himself viewing "Billy," their cadaver—an undersized, blotchy old man with a horrible little red beard on his petrified, vealy face—as a machine, fascinating, complex, beautiful, but a machine. It damaged his already feeble belief in man's divinity and immortality. He might have kept his doubts to himself, revolving them slowly as he dissected out the nerves of the mangled upper arm, but Ira Hinkley would not let him alone. Ira believed that he could bring even medical students to bliss, which, to Ira, meant singing extraordinarily long and unlovely hymns in a chapel of the Sanctification Brotherhood.

"Mart, my son," he roared, "do you realize that in this, what some might call a sordid task, we are learning things that will enable us to heal the bodies and comfort the souls of countless lost unhappy folks?"

"Huh! Souls. I haven't found one yet in old Billy. Honest, do you believe that junk?"

Ira clenched his fist and scowled, then belched with laughter, slapped Martin distressingly on the back, and clamored, "Brother, you've got to do better than that to get Ira's goat! You think you've got a lot of these fancy Modern Doubts. You haven't—you've only got indigestion. What you need is exercise and faith. Come on over to the Y.M.C.A. and I'll take you for a swim and pray with you. Why, you poor skinny little agnostic, here you have a chance to see the Almighty's handiwork, and all you grab out of it is a feeling that you're real smart. Buck up, young Arrowsmith. You don't know how funny you are, to a fellow that's got a serene faith!"

To the delight of Clif Clawson, the class jester, who worked at the next table, Ira chucked Martin in the ribs, patted him, very painfully, upon the head, and amiably resumed work, while Martin danced with irritation.

V

In college Martin had been a "barb"—he had not belonged to a Greek Letter secret society. He had been "rushed," but he had resented the condescension of the aristocracy of men from the larger cities. Now that most of his Arts classmates had departed to insurance offices, law schools, and banks, he was lonely, and tempted by an invitation from Digamma Pi, the chief medical fraternity.

Digamma Pi was a lively boarding-house with a billiard table and low prices. Rough and amiable noises came from it at night, and a good deal of singing about When I Die Don't Bury Me at All; yet for three years Digams had won the valedictory and the Hugh Loizeau Medal in Experimental Surgery. This autumn the Digams elected Ira Hinkley, because they had been gaining a reputation for dissipation—girls were said to have been smuggled in late at night—and no company which included the Reverend Mr. Hinkley could possibly be taken by the Dean as immoral, which was an advantage if they were to continue comfortably immoral.

Martin had prized the independence of his solitary room. In a fraternity, all tennis rackets, trousers, and opinions are held in common. When Ira found that Martin was hesitating, he insisted, "Oh, come on in! Digam needs you. You do study hard—I'll say that for you—and think what a chance you'll have to influence The Fellows for good."

(On all occasions, Ira referred to his classmates as The Fellows, and frequently he used the term in prayers at the Y.M.C.A.)

"I don't want to influence anybody. I want to learn the doctor trade and make six thousand dollars a year."

"My boy, if you only knew how foolish you sound when you try to be cynical! When you're as old as I am, you'll understand that the glory of being a doctor is that you can teach folks high ideals while you soothe their tortured bodies."

"Suppose they don't want my particular brand of high ideals?"

"Mart, have I got to stop and pray with you?"

"No! Quit! Honestly, Hinkley, of all the Christians I ever met you take the rottenest advantages. You can lick anybody in the class, and when I think of how you're going to bully the poor heathen when you get to be a missionary, and make the kids put on breeches, and marry off all the happy lovers to the wrong people, I could bawl!"

The prospect of leaving his sheltered den for the patronage of the Reverend Mr. Hinkley was intolerable. It was not till Angus Duer accepted election to Digamma Pi that Martin himself came in.

Duer was one of the few among Martin's classmates in the academic course who had gone on with him to the Winnemac medical school. Duer had been the valedictorian. He was a silent, sharp-faced, curly-headed, rather handsome young man, and he never squandered an hour or a good impulse. So brilliant was his work in biology and chemistry that a Chicago surgeon had promised him a place in his clinic. Martin compared Angus Duer to a razor blade on a January morning; he hated him, was uncomfortable with him, and envied him. He knew that in biology Duer had been too busy passing examinations to ponder, to get any concept of biology as a whole. He knew that Duer was a tricky chemist, who neatly and swiftly completed the experiments demanded by the course and never ventured on original experiments which, leading him into a confused land of wondering, might bring him to glory or disaster. He was sure that Duer cultivated his manner of chill efficiency to impress instructors. Yet the man stood out so bleakly from a mass of students who could neither complete their experiments nor ponder nor do anything save smoke pipes and watch football-practice that Martin loved him while he hated him, and almost meekly he followed him into Digamma Pi.

Martin, Ira Hinkley, Angus Duer, Clif Clawson, the meaty class jester, and one "Fatty" Pfaff were initiated into Digamma Pi together. It was a noisy and rather painful performance, which included smelling asafetida. Martin was bored, but Fatty Pfaff was in squeaking, billowing, gasping terror.

Fatty was of all the new Freshmen candidates the most useful to Digamma Pi. He was planned by nature to be a butt. He looked like a distended hot-water bottle; he was magnificently imbecile; he believed everything, he knew nothing, he could memorize nothing; and anxiously he forgave the men who got through the vacant hours by playing jokes upon him. They persuaded him that mustard plasters were excellent for colds—solicitously they gathered about him, affixed an enormous plaster to his back, and afterward fondly removed it. They concealed the ear of a cadaver in his nice, clean, new pocket handkerchief when he went to Sunday supper at the house of a girl cousin in Zenith. . . . At supper he produced the handkerchief with a flourish.

Every night when Fatty retired he had to remove from his bed a collection of objects which thoughtful house-mates had stuffed between the sheets—soap, alarm clocks, fish. He was the perfect person to whom to sell useless things. Clif Clawson, who combined a brisk huckstering with his jokes, sold to Fatty for four dollars a History of Medicine which he had bought, second-hand, for two, and while Fatty never read it, never conceivably could read it, the possession of the fat red book made him feel learned. But Fatty's greatest beneficence to Digamma was his belief in spiritualism. He went about in terror of spooks. He was always seeing them emerging at night from the dissecting-room windows. His classmates took care that he should behold a great many of them flitting about the halls of the fraternity.

VI

Digamma Pi was housed in a residence built in the expansive days of 1885. The living-room suggested a recent cyclone. Knife-gashed tables, broken Morris chairs, and torn rugs were flung about the room, and covered with backless books, hockey shoes, caps, and cigarette stubs. Above, there were four men to a bedroom, and the beds were iron double-deckers, like a steerage.

For ash-trays the Digams used sawed skulls, and on the bedroom walls were anatomical charts, to be studied while dressing. In Martin's room was a complete skeleton. He and his roommates had trustingly bought it from a salesman who came out from a Zenith surgical supply house. He was such a genial and sympathetic salesman; he gave them cigars and told G.U. stories and explained what prosperous doctors they were all going to be. They bought the skeleton gratefully, on the instalment plan. . . . Later the salesman was less genial.

Martin roomed with Clif Clawson, Fatty Pfaff, and an earnest second-year medic named Irving Watters.

Any psychologist desiring a perfectly normal man for use in demonstrations could not have done better than to have engaged Irving Watters. He was always and carefully dull; smilingly, easily, dependably dull. If there was any cliché which he did not use, it was because he had not yet heard it. He believed in morality—except on Saturday evenings; he believed in the Episcopal Church—but not the High Church; he believed in the Constitution, Darwinism, systematic exercise in the gymnasium, and the genius of the president of the university.

Among them, Martin most liked Clif Clawson. Clif was the clown of the fraternity-house, he was given to raucous laughter, he clogged and sang meaningless songs, he even practised on the cornet, yet he was somehow a good fellow and solid, and Martin, in his detestation of Ira Hinkley, his fear of Angus Duer, his pity for Fatty Pfaff, his distaste for the amiable dullness of Irving Watters, turned to the roaring Clif as to something living and experimenting. At least Clif had reality; the reality of a plowed field, of a steaming manure-pile. It was Clif who would box with him; Clif who—though he loved to sit for hours smoking, grunting, magnificently loafing—could be persuaded to go for a five-mile walk.

And it was Clif who risked death by throwing baked beans at the Reverend Ira Hinkley at supper, when Ira was bulkily and sweetly corrective.

In the dissecting-room Ira was maddening enough with his merriment at such of Martin's ideas as had not been accepted in Pottsburg Christian College, but in the fraternity-house he was a moral pest. He never ceased trying to stop their profanity. After three years on a backwoods football team he still believed with unflinching optimism that he could sterilize young men by administering reproofs, with the nickering of a lady Sunday School teacher and the delicacy of a charging elephant.

Ira also had statistics about Clean Living.

He was full of statistics. Where he got them did not matter to him; figures in the daily papers, in the census report, or in the Miscellany Column of the *Sanctification Herald* were equally valid. He announced at supper table, "Clif, it's a wonder to me how as bright a fella as you can go on sucking that dirty old pipe. D'you realize that 67.9 per cent. of all women who go to the operating table have husbands who smoke tobacco?"

"What the devil would they smoke?" demanded Clif.

"Where'd you get those figures?" from Martin.

"They came out at a medical convention in Philadelphia in 1902," Ira condescended. "Of course I don't suppose it'll make any difference to a bunch of wise galoots like you that some day you'll marry a nice bright little woman and ruin her life with your vices. Sure, keep right on—fine brave virile bunch! A poor weakling preacher like me wouldn't dare do anything so brave as smoke a pipe!"

He left them triumphantly, and Martin groaned, "Ira makes me want to get out of medicine and be an honest harness-maker."

"Aw, gee now, Mart," Fatty Pfaff complained, "you oughtn't to cuss Ira out. He's awful sincere."

"Sincere? Hell! So is a cockroach!"

Thus they jabbered, while Angus Duer watched them in a superior silence that made Martin nervous. In the study of the profession to which he had looked forward all his life he found irritation and vacuity as well as serene wisdom; he saw no one clear path to Truth but a thousand paths to a thousand truths far-off and doubtful.

Chapter III

JOHN A. ROBERTSHAW, John Aldington Robertshaw, professor of physiology in the medical school, was rather deaf, and he was the only teacher in the University of Winnemac who still wore mutton-chop whiskers. He came from Back Bay; he was proud of it and let you know about it. With three other Brahmins he formed in Mohalis a Boston colony which stood for sturdy sweetness and decorously shaded light. On all occasions he remarked, "When I was studying with Ludwig in Germany—" He was too absorbed in his own correctness to heed individual students, and Clif Clawson and the other young men technically known as "hell-raisers" looked forward to his lectures on physiology.

They were held in an amphitheater whose seats curved so far around that the lecturer could not see both ends at once, and while Dr. Robertshaw, continuing to drone about blood circulation, was peering to the right to find out who was making that outrageous sound like a motor horn, far over on the left Clif Clawson would rise and imitate him, with sawing arm and stroking of imaginary whiskers. Once Clif produced the masterpiece of throwing a brick into the sink beside the platform, just when Dr. Robertshaw was working up to his annual climax about the effect of brass bands on the intensity of the knee-jerk.

Martin had been reading Max Gottlieb's scientific papers—as much of them as he could read, with their morass of mathematical symbols—and from them he had a conviction that experiments should be something dealing with the foundations of life and death, with the nature of bacterial infection, with the chemistry of bodily reactions. When Robertshaw chirped about fussy little experiments, standard experiments, maiden-aunt experiments, Martin was restless. In college he had felt that prosody and Latin Composition were futile, and he had looked forward to the study of medicine as illumination. Now, in melancholy worry about his own unreasonableness, he found that he was developing the same contempt for Robertshaw's rules of the thumb—and for most of the work in anatomy.

The professor of anatomy, Dr. Oliver O. Stout, was himself an anatomy, a dissection-chart, a thinly covered knot of nerves and blood vessels and bones. Stout had precise and enormous knowledge; in his dry voice he could repeat more facts about the left little toe than you would have thought anybody would care to learn regarding the left little toe.

No discussion at the Digamma Pi supper table was more violent than the incessant debate over the value to a doctor, a decent normal doctor who made a good living and did not worry about reading papers at medical associations, of remembering anatomical terms. But no matter what they thought, they all ground at learning the lists of names which enable a man to crawl through examinations and become an Educated Person, with a market value of five dollars an hour. Unknown sages had invented rimes which enabled them to memorize. At supper—the thirty piratical Digams sitting at a long and spotty table, devouring clam chowder and beans and codfish balls and banana layer-cake—the Freshmen earnestly repeated after a senior:

On old Olympus, topmost top
A fat-eared German viewed a hop.

Thus by association with the initial letters they mastered the twelve cranial nerves: olfactory, optic, oculomotor, trochlear, and the rest. To the Digams it was the world's noblest poem, and they remembered it for years after they had become practising physicians and altogether forgotten the names of the nerves themselves.

II

In Dr. Stout's anatomy lectures there were no disturbances, but in his dissecting-room were many pleasantries. The mildest of them was the insertion of a fire-cracker in the cadaver on which the two virginal and unhappy co-eds worked. The real excitement during Freshman year was the incident of Clif Clawson and the pancreas.

Clif had been elected class president, for the year, because he was so full of greetings. He never met a classmate in the hall of Main Medical without shouting, "How's your vermiform appendix functioning this morning?" or "I bid thee a lofty greeting, old pediculosis." With booming decorum he presided at class meetings (indignant meetings to denounce the proposal to let the "aggies" use the North Side Tennis Courts), but in private life he was less decorous.

The terrible thing happened when the Board of Regents were being shown through the campus. The Regents were the supreme rulers of the University; they were bankers and manufacturers and pastors of large churches; to them even the president was humble. Nothing gave them more interesting thrills than the dissecting-room of the medical school. The preachers spoke morally of the effect of alcohol on paupers, and the bankers of the disrespect for savings-accounts which is always to be seen in the kind of men who insist on becoming cadavers. In the midst of the tour, led by Dr. Stout and the umbrella-carrying secretary of the University, the plumpest and most educational of all the bankers stopped near Clif Clawson's dissecting-table, with his derby hat reverently held behind him, and into that hat Clif dropped a pancreas.

Now a pancreas is a damp and disgusting thing to find in your new hat, and when the banker did so find one, he threw down the hat and said that the students of Winnemac had gone to the devil. Dr. Stout and the secretary comforted him; they cleaned the derby and assured him that vengeance should be done on the man who could put a pancreas in a banker's hat.

Dr. Stout summoned Clif, as president of the Freshmen. Clif was pained. He assembled the class, he lamented that any Winnemac Man could place a pancreas in a banker's hat, and he demanded that the criminal be manly enough to stand up and confess.

Unfortunately the Reverend Ira Hinkley, who sat between Martin and Angus Duer, had seen Clif drop the pancreas. He growled, "This is outrageous! I'm going to expose Clawson, even if he is a frat-brother of mine."

Martin protested, "Cut it out. You don't want to get him fired?"

"He ought to be!"

Angus Duer turned in his seat, looked at Ira, and suggested, "Will you kindly shut up?" and, as Ira subsided,

Angus became to Martin more admirable and more hateful than ever.

III

When he was depressed by a wonder as to why he was here, listening to a Professor Robertshaw, repeating verses about fat-eared Germans, learning the trade of medicine like Fatty Pfaff or Irving Watters, then Martin had relief in what he considered debauches. Actually they were extremely small debauches; they rarely went beyond too much lager in the adjacent city of Zenith, or the smiles of a factory girl parading the sordid back avenues, but to Martin, with his pride in taut strength, his joy in a clear brain, they afterward seemed tragic.

His safest companion was Clif Clawson. No matter how much bad beer he drank, Clif was never much more intoxicated than in his normal state. Martin sank or rose to Clif's buoyancy, while Clif rose or sank to Martin's speculativeness. As they sat in a back-room, at a table glistening with beer-glass rings, Clif shook his finger and babbled, "You're only one 'at gets me, Mart. You know with all the hell-raising, and all the talk about bein' c'mmercial that I pull on these high boys like Ira Stinkley, I'm jus' sick o' c'mmercialism an' bunk as you are."

"Sure. You bet," Martin agreed with alcoholic fondness. "You're jus' like me. My God, do you get it—dough-face like Irving Watters or heartless climber like Angus Duer, and then old Gottlieb! Ideal of research! Never bein' content with what *seems* true! Alone, not carin' a damn, square-toed as a captain on the bridge, working all night, getting to the bottom of things!"

"Thash stuff. That's my idee, too. Lez have 'nother beer. Shake you for it!" observed Clif Clawson.

Zenith, with its saloons, was fifteen miles from Mohalis and the University of Winnemac; half an hour by the huge, roaring, steel interurban trolleys, and to Zenith the medical students went for their forays. To say that one had "gone into town last night" was a matter for winks and leers. But with Angus Duer, Martin discovered a new Zenith.

At supper Duer said abruptly, "Come into town with me and hear a concert."

For all his fancied superiority to the class, Martin was illimitably ignorant of literature, of painting, of music. That the bloodless and acquisitive Angus Duer should waste time listening to fiddlers was astounding to him. He discovered that Duer had enthusiasm for two composers, called Bach and Beethoven, presumably Germans, and that he himself did not yet comprehend all the ways of the world. On the interurban, Duer's gravity loosened, and he cried, "Boy, if I hadn't been born to carve up innards, I'd have been a great musician! To-night I'm going to lead you right into Heaven!"

Martin found himself in a confusion of little chairs and vast gilded arches, of polite but disapproving ladies with programs in their laps, unromantic musicians making unpleasant noises below and, at last, incomprehensible beauty, which made for him pictures of hills and deep forests, then suddenly became achingly long-winded. He exulted, "I'm going to have 'em all—the fame of Max Gottlieb—I mean his ability—and the lovely music and lovely women— Golly! I'm going to do big things. And see the world. . . . Will this piece never quit?"

IV

It was a week after the concert that he rediscovered Madeline Fox.

Madeline was a handsome, high-colored, high-spirited, opinionated girl whom Martin had known in college. She was staying on, ostensibly to take a graduate course in English, actually to avoid going back home. She considered herself a superb tennis player; she played it with energy and voluble swoopings and large lack of direction. She believed herself to be a connoisseur of literature; the fortunates to whom she gave her approval were Hardy, Meredith, Howells, and Thackeray, none of whom she had read for five years. She had often reproved Martin for his inappreciation of Howells, for wearing flannel shirts, and for his failure to hand her down from street-cars in the manner of a fiction hero. In college, they had gone to dances together, though as a dancer Martin was more spirited than accurate, and his partners sometimes had difficulty in deciding just what he was trying to dance. He liked Madeline's tall comeliness and her vigor; he felt that with her energetic culture she was somehow "good for him." During this year, he had scarcely seen her. He thought of her late in the evenings, and planned to telephone to her, and did not telephone. But as he became doubtful about medicine he longed for her sympathy, and on a Sunday afternoon of spring he took her for a walk along the Chaloosa River.

From the river bluffs the prairie stretches in exuberant rolling hills. In the long barley fields, the rough pastures, the stunted oaks and brilliant birches, there is the adventurousness of the frontier, and like young plainsmen they tramped the bluffs and told each other they were going to conquer the world.

He complained, "These damn' medics—"

"Oh, Martin, do you think 'damn' is a nice word?" said Madeline.

He did think it was a very nice word indeed, and constantly useful to a busy worker, but her smile was desirable.

"Well—these darn' studes, they aren't trying to learn science; they're simply learning a trade. They just want to get the knowledge that'll enable them to cash in. They don't talk about saving lives but about 'losing cases'—losing dollars! And they wouldn't even mind losing cases if it was a sensational operation that'd advertise 'em! They make me sick! How many of 'em do you find that're interested in the work Ehrlich is doing in Germany—yes, or that Max Gottlieb is doing right here and now! Gottlieb's just taken an awful fall out of Wright's opsonin theory."

"Has he, really?"

"*Has* he! I should say he had! And do you get any of the medics stirred up about it? You do not! They say, 'Oh, sure, science is all right in its way; helps a doc to treat his patients,' and then they begin to argue about whether they can make more money if they locate in a big city or a town, and is it better for a young doc to play the good-fellow and lodge game, or join the church and look earnest. You ought to hear Irve Watters. He's just got one idea: the fellow that gets ahead in medicine, is he the lad that knows his pathology? Oh, no; the bird that succeeds is the one that gets an office on a northeast corner, near a trolley car junction, with a 'phone number that'll be easy for patients to remember! Honest! He said so! I swear, when I graduate I believe I'll be a ship's doctor. You see the world that way, and at least you aren't racing up and down the boat trying to drag patients away from some rival doc that has an office on another deck!"

"Yes, I know; it's dreadful the way people don't have ideals about their work. So many of the English grad students just want to make money teaching, instead of enjoying scholarship the way I do."

It was disconcerting to Martin that she should seem to think that she was a superior person quite as much as himself, but he was even more disconcerted when she bubbled:

"At the same time, Martin, one does have to be practical, doesn't one! Think how much more money—no, I mean how much more social position and power for doing good a successful doctor has than one of these scientists that just putter, and don't know what's going on in the world. Look at a surgeon like Dr. Loizeau, riding up to the hospital in a lovely car with a chauffeur in uniform, and all his patients simply worshiping him, and then your Max Gottlieb—somebody pointed him out to me the other day, and he had on a dreadful old suit, and I certainly thought he could stand a haircut."

Martin turned on her with fury, statistics, vituperation, religious zeal, and confused metaphors. They sat on a crooked old-fashioned rail-fence where over the sun-soaked bright plantains the first insects of spring were humming. In the storm of his fanaticism she lost her airy Culture and squeaked, "Yes, I see now, I see," without stating what it was she saw. "Oh, you do have a fine mind and such fine—such integrity."

"Honest? Do you think I have?"

"Oh, indeed I do, and I'm sure you're going to have a wonderful future. And I'm so glad you aren't commercial, like the others. Don't mind what they say!"

He noted that Madeline was not only a rare and understanding spirit but also an extraordinarily desirable woman—fresh color, tender eyes, adorable slope from shoulder to side. As they walked back, he perceived that she was incredibly the right mate for him. Under his training she would learn the distinction between vague "ideals" and the hard sureness of science. They paused on the bluff, looking down at the muddy Chaloosa, a springtime Western river wild with floating branches. He yearned for her; he regretted the casual affairs of a student and determined to be a pure and extremely industrious young man, to be, in fact, "worthy of her."

"Oh, Madeline," he mourned, "you're so darn' lovely!"

She glanced at him, timidly.

He caught her hand; in a desperate burst he tried to kiss her. It was very badly done. He managed only to kiss the point of her jaw, while she struggled and begged, "Oh, don't!" They did not acknowledge, as they ambled back into Mohalis, that the incident had occurred, but there was softness in their voices and without impatience now she heard his denunciation of Professor Robertshaw as a phonograph, and he listened to her remarks on the shallowness and vulgarity of Dr. Norman Brumfit, that sprightly English instructor. At her boarding-house she sighed, "I wish I could ask you to come in, but it's almost suppertime and— Will you call me up some day?"

"You bet I will!" said Martin, according to the rules for amorous discourse in the University of Winnemac.

He raced home in adoration. As he lay in his narrow upper bunk at midnight, he saw her eyes, now impertinent, now reproving, now warm with trust in him. "I love her! I *love* her! I'll 'phone her— Wonder if I dare call her up as early as eight in the morning?"

But at eight he was too busy studying the lacrimal apparatus to think of ladies' eyes. He saw Madeline only once, and in the publicity of her boarding-house porch, crowded with co-eds, red cushions, and marshmallows, before he was hurled into hectic studying for the year's final examinations.

V

At examination-time, Digamma Pi fraternity showed its value to urgent seekers after wisdom. Generations of Digams had collected test-papers and preserved them in the sacred Quiz Book; geniuses for detail had labored through the volume and marked with red pencil the problems most often set in the course of years. The Freshmen crouched in a ring about Ira Hinkley in the Digam living-room, while he read out the questions they were most likely to get. They writhed, clawed their hair, scratched their chins, bit their fingers, and beat their temples in the endeavor to give the right answer before Angus Duer should read it to them out of the textbook.

In the midst of their sufferings they had to labor with Fatty Pfaff.

Fatty had failed in the mid-year anatomical, and he had to pass a special quiz before he could take the finals. There was a certain fondness for him in Digamma Pi; Fatty was soft, Fatty was superstitious, Fatty was an imbecile, yet they had for him the annoyed affection they might have had for a second-hand motor or a muddy dog. All of them worked on him; they tried to lift him and thrust him through the examination as through a trap-door. They panted and grunted and moaned at the labor, and Fatty panted and moaned with them.

The night before his special examination they kept him at it till two, with wet towels, black coffee, prayer, and profanity. They repeated lists—lists—lists to him; they shook their fists in his mournful red round face and howled, "Damn you, *will* you remember that the bicuspid valve is the SAME as the mitral valve and NOT another one?" They ran about the room, holding up their hands and wailing, "Won't he never remember nothing about nothing?" and charged back to purr with fictive calm, "Now no use getting fussed, Fatty. Take it easy. Just listen to this, quietly, will yuh, and try," coaxingly, "do try to remember *one* thing, anyway!"

They led him carefully to bed. He was so filled with facts that the slightest jostling would have spilled them.

When he awoke at seven, with red eyes and trembling lips, he had forgotten everything he had learned.

"There's nothing for it," said the president of Digamma Pi. "He's got to have a crib, and take his chance on getting caught with it. I thought so. I made one out for him yesterday. It's a lulu. It'll cover enough of the questions so he'll get through."

Even the Reverend Ira Hinkley, since he had witnessed the horrors of the midnight before, went his ways ignoring the crime. It was Fatty himself who protested: "Gee, I don't like to cheat. I don't think a fellow that can't get through an examination had hardly ought to be allowed to practise medicine. That's what my Dad said."

They poured more coffee into him and (on the advice of Clif Clawson, who wasn't exactly sure what the effect might be but who was willing to learn) they fed him a potassium bromide tablet. The president of Digamma, seizing Fatty with some firmness, growled, "I'm going to stick this crib in your pocket—look, here in your breast pocket, behind your handkerchief."

"I won't use it. I don't care if I fail," whimpered Fatty.

"That's all right, but you keep it there. Maybe you can absorb a little information from it through your lungs, for God knows—" The president clenched his hair. His voice rose, and in it was all the tragedy of night watches and black draughts and hopeless retreats. "—God knows you can't take it in through your head!"

They dusted Fatty, they stood him right side up, and pushed him through the door, on his way to Anatomy Building. They watched him go: a balloon on legs, a sausage in corduroy trousers.

"Is it possible he's going to be honest?" marveled Clif Clawson.

"Well, if he is, we better go up and begin packing his trunk. And this ole frat'll never have another goat like Fatty," grieved the president.

They saw Fatty stop, remove his handkerchief, mournfully blow his nose—and discover a long thin slip of paper. They saw him frown at it, tap it on his knuckles, begin to read it, stuff it back into his pocket, and go on with a more resolute step.

They danced hand in hand about the living-room of the fraternity, piously assuring one another, "He'll use it—it's all right—he'll get through or get hanged!"

He got through.

VI

Digamma Pi was more annoyed by Martin's restless doubtings than by Fatty's idiocy, Clif Clawson's raucousness, Angus Duer's rasping, or the Reverend Ira Hinkley's nagging.

During the strain of study for examinations Martin was peculiarly vexing in regard to "laying in the best quality medical terms like the best quality sterilizers—not for use but to impress your patients." As one, the Digams suggested, "Say, if you don't like the way we study medicine, we'll be tickled to death to take up a collection and send you back to Elk Mills, where you won't be disturbed by all us lowbrows and commercialists. Look here! We don't tell you how you ought to work. Where do you get the idea you got to tell us? Oh, turn it off, will you!"

Angus Duer observed, with sour sweetness, "We'll admit we're simply carpenters, and you're a great investigator. But there's several things you might turn to when you finish science. What do you know about architecture? How's your French verbs? How many big novels have you ever read? Who's the premier of Austro-Hungary?"

Martin struggled, "I don't pretend to know anything—except I do know what a man like Max Gottlieb means. He's got the right method, and all these other hams of profs, they're simply witch doctors. You think Gottlieb isn't religious, Hinkley. Why, his just being in a lab is a prayer. Don't you idiots realize what it means to have a man like that here, making new concepts of life? Don't you—"

Clif Clawson, with a chasm of yawning, speculated, "Praying in the lab! I'll bet I get the pants took off me, when I take bacteriology, if Pa Gottlieb catches me praying during experiment hours!"

"Damn it, listen!" Martin wailed. "I tell you, you fellows are the kind that keep medicine nothing but guess-work diagnosis, and here you have a man—"

So they argued for hours, after their sweaty fact-grinding.

When the others had gone to bed, when the room was a muck-heap of flung clothing and weary young men snoring in iron bunks, Martin sat at the splintery long pine study-table, worrying. Angus Duer glided in, demanding, "Look here, old son. We're all sick of your crabbing. If you think medicine is rot, the way we study it, and if you're so confoundedly honest, why don't you get out?"

He left Martin to agonize, "He's right. I've got to shut up or get out. Do I really mean it? What *do* I want? What *am* I going to do?"

VII

Angus Duer's studiousness and his reverence for correct manners were alike offended by Clif's bawdy singing, Clif's howling conversation, Clif's fondness for dropping things in people's soup, and Clif's melancholy inability to keep his hands washed. For all his appearance of nerveless steadiness, during the tension of examination-time Duer was as nervous as Martin, and one evening at supper, when Clif was bellowing, Duer snapped, "Will you kindly not make so much racket?"

"I'll make all the damn' racket I damn' please!" Clif asserted, and a feud was on.

Clif was so noisy thereafter that he almost became tired of his own noise. He was noisy in the living-room, he was noisy in the bath, and with some sacrifice he lay awake pretending to snore. If Duer was quiet and book-wrapped, he was not in the least timid; he faced Clif with the eye of a magistrate, and cowed him. Privily Clif complained to Martin, "Darn him, he acts like I was a worm. Either he or me has got to get out of Digam, that's a cinch, and it won't be me!"

He was ferocious and very noisy about it, and it was he who got out. He said that the Digams were a "bunch of bum sports; don't even have a decent game of poker," but he was fleeing from the hard eyes of Angus Duer. And Martin resigned from the fraternity with him, planned to room with him the coming autumn.

Clif's blustering rubbed Martin as it did Duer. Clif had no reticences; when he was not telling slimy stories he was demanding, "How much chuh pay for those shoes—must think you're a Vanderbilt!" or "D'I see you walking with that Madeline Fox femme—what chuh tryin' to do?" But Martin was alienated from the civilized, industrious, nice young men of Digamma Pi, in whose faces he could already see prescriptions, glossy white sterilizers, smart enclosed motors, and glass office-signs in the best gilt lettering. He preferred a barbarian loneliness, for next year he would be working with Max Gottlieb, and he could not be bothered.

That summer he spent with a crew installing telephones in Montana.

He was a lineman in the wire-gang. It was his job to climb the poles, digging the spurs of his leg-irons into the soft and silvery pine, to carry up the wire, lash it to the glass insulators, then down and to another pole.

They made perhaps five miles a day; at night they drove into little rickety wooden towns. Their retiring was simple—they removed their shoes and rolled up in a horse-blanket. Martin wore overalls and a flannel shirt. He looked like a farm-hand. Climbing all day long, he breathed deep, his eyes cleared of worry, and one day he experienced a miracle.

He was atop a pole and suddenly, for no clear cause, his eyes opened and he saw; as though he had just awakened he saw that the prairie was vast, that the sun was kindly on rough pasture and ripening wheat, on the old horses, the easy, broad-beamed, friendly horses, and on his red-faced jocose companions; he saw that the meadow larks were jubilant, and blackbirds shining by little pools, and with the living sun all life was living. Suppose the Angus Duers and Irving Watterses were tight tradesmen. What of it? "I'm *here!*" he gloated.

The wire-gang were as healthy and as simple as the west wind; they had no pretentiousness; though they handled electrical equipment they did not, like medics, learn a confusion of scientific terms and pretend to the farmers that they were scientists. They laughed easily and were content to be themselves, and with them Martin was content to forget how noble he was. He had for them an affection such as he had for no one at the University save Max Gottlieb.

He carried in his bag one book, Gottlieb's "Immunology." He could often get through half a page of it before he bogged down in chemical formulæ. Occasionally, on Sundays or rainy days, he tried to read it, and longed for the laboratory; occasionally he thought of Madeline Fox, and became certain that he was devastatingly lonely for her. But week slipped into careless and robust week, and when he awoke in a stable, smelling the sweet hay and the horses and the lark-ringing prairie that crept near to the heart of these shanty towns, he cared only for the day's work, the day's hiking, westward toward the sunset.

So they straggled through the Montana wheatland, whole duchies of wheat in one shining field, through the cattle-country and the sagebrush desert, and suddenly, staring at a persistent cloud, Martin realized that he beheld the mountains.

Then he was on a train; the wire-gang were already forgotten; and he was thinking only of Madeline Fox, Clif Clawson, Angus Duer, and Max Gottlieb.

Chapter IV

PROFESSOR MAX GOTTLIEB was about to assassinate a guinea pig with anthrax germs, and the bacteriology class were nervous.

They had studied the forms of bacteria, they had handled Petri dishes and platinum loops, they had proudly grown on potato slices the harmless red cultures of *Bacillus prodigiosus*, and they had come now to pathogenic germs and the inoculation of a living animal with swift disease. These two beady-eyed guinea pigs, chittering in a battery jar, would in two days be stiff and dead.

Martin had an excitement not free from anxiety. He laughed at it, he remembered with professional scorn how foolish were the lay visitors to the laboratory, who believed that sanguinary microbes would leap upon them from the mysterious centrifuge, from the benches, from the air itself. But he was conscious that in the cotton-plugged test-tube between the instrument-bath and the bichloride jar on the demonstrator's desk were millions of fatal anthrax germs.

The class looked respectful and did not stand too close. With the flair of technique, the sure rapidity which dignified the slightest movement of his hands, Dr. Gottlieb clipped the hair on the belly of a guinea pig held by the assistant. He soaped the belly with one flicker of a hand-brush, he shaved it and painted it with iodine.

(And all the while Max Gottlieb was recalling the eagerness of his first students, when he had just returned from working with Koch and Pasteur, when he was fresh from enormous beer seidels and Korpsbrüder and ferocious arguments. Passionate, beautiful days! *Die goldene Zeit!* His first classes in America, at Queen City College, had been awed by the sensational discoveries in bacteriology; they had crowded about him reverently; they had longed to know. Now the class was a mob. He looked at them—Fatty Pfaff in the front row, his face vacant as a doorknob; the co-eds emotional and frightened; only Martin Arrowsmith and Angus Duer visibly intelligent. His memory fumbled for a pale blue twilight in

Munich, a bridge and a waiting girl, and the sound of music.)

He dipped his hands in the bichloride solution and shook them—a quick shake, fingers down, like the fingers of a pianist above the keys. He took a hypodermic needle from the instrument-bath and lifted the test-tube. His voice flowed indolently, with German vowels and blurred W's:

"This, gentlemen, iss a twenty-four-hour culture of *Bacillus anthracis.* You will note, I am sure you will have noted already, that in the bottom of the tumbler there was cotton to keep the tube from being broken. I cannot advise breaking tubes of anthrax germs and afterwards getting the hands into the culture. You *might* merely get anthrax boils—"

The class shuddered.

Gottlieb twitched out the cotton plug with his little finger, so neatly that the medical students who had complained, "Bacteriology is junk; urinalysis and blood tests are all the lab stuff we need to know," now gave him something of the respect they had for a man who could do card tricks or remove an appendix in seven minutes. He agitated the mouth of the tube in the Bunsen burner, droning, "Every time you take the plug from a tube, flame the mouth of the tube. Make that a rule. It is a necessity of the technique, and technique, gentlemen, is the beginning of all science. It iss also the least-known thing in science."

The class was impatient. Why didn't he get on with it, on to the entertainingly dreadful moment of inoculating the pig?

(And Max Gottlieb, glancing at the other guinea pig in the prison of its battery jar, meditated, "Wretched innocent! Why should I murder him, to teach *Dummköpfe*? It would be better to experiment on that fat young man.")

He thrust the syringe into the tube, he withdrew the piston dextrously with his index finger, and lectured:

"Take one half c.c. of the culture. There are two kinds of M.D.'s—those to whom c.c. means cubic centimeter and those to whom it means compound cathartic. The second kind are more prosperous."

(But one cannot convey the quality of it: the thin drawl, the sardonic amiability, the hiss of the S's, the D's turned into blunt and challenging T's.)

The assistant held the guinea pig close; Gottlieb pinched up the skin of the belly and punctured it with a quick down thrust of the hypodermic needle. The pig gave a little jerk, a little squeak, and the co-eds shuddered. Gottlieb's wise fingers knew when the peritoneal wall was reached. He pushed home the plunger of the syringe. He said quietly, "This poor animal will now soon be dead as Moses." The class glanced at one another uneasily. "Some of you will think that it does not matter; some of you will think, like Bernard Shaw, that I am an executioner and the more monstrous because I am cool about it; and some of you will not think at all. This difference in philosophy iss what makes life interesting."

While the assistant tagged the pig with a tin disk in its ear and restored it to the battery jar, Gottlieb set down its weight in a note-book, with the time of inoculation and the age of the bacterial culture. These notes he reproduced on the blackboard, in his fastidious script, murmuring, "Gentlemen, the most important part of living is not the living but pondering upon it. And the most important part of experimentation is not doing the experiment but making notes, ve-ry accurate *quantitative* notes—in ink. I am told that a great many clever people feel they can keep notes in their heads. I have often observed with pleasure that such persons do not have heads in which to keep their notes. This iss very good, because thus the world never sees their results and science is not encumbered with them. I shall now inoculate the second guinea pig, and the class will be dismissed. Before the next lab hour I shall be glad if you will read Pater's 'Marius the Epicurean,' to derife from it the calmness which is the secret of laboratory skill."

II

As they bustled down the hall, Angus Duer observed to a brother Digam, "Gottlieb is an old laboratory plug; he hasn't got any imagination; he sticks here instead of getting out into the world and enjoying the fight. But he certainly is handy. Awfully good technique. He might have been a first-rate surgeon, and made fifty thousand dollars a year. As it is, I don't suppose he gets a cent over four thousand!"

Ira Hinkley walked alone, worrying. He was an extraordinarily kindly man, this huge and bumbling parson. He reverently accepted everything, no matter how contradictory to everything else, that his medical instructors told him, but this killing of animals—he hated it. By a connection not evident to him he remembered that the Sunday before, in the slummy chapel where he preached during his medical course, he had exalted the sacrifice of the martyrs and they had sung of the blood of the lamb, the fountain filled with blood drawn from Emmanuel's veins, but this meditation he lost, and he lumbered toward Digamma Pi in a fog of pondering pity.

Clif Clawson, walking with Fatty Pfaff, shouted, "Gosh, ole pig certainly did jerk when Pa Gottlieb rammed that needle home!" and Fatty begged, "Don't! Please!"

But Martin Arrowsmith saw himself doing the same experiment and, as he remembered Gottlieb's unerring fingers, his hands curved in imitation.

III

The guinea pigs grew drowsier and drowsier. In two days they rolled over, kicked convulsively, and died. Full of dramatic expectation, the class reassembled for the necropsy. On the demonstrator's table was a wooden tray, scarred from the tacks which for years had pinned down the corpses. The guinea pigs were in a glass jar, rigid, their hair ruffled. The class tried to remember how nibbling and alive they had been. The assistant stretched out one of them with thumb-tacks. Gottlieb swabbed its belly with a cotton wad soaked in lysol, slit it from belly to neck, and cauterized the heart with a red-hot spatula—the class quivered as they heard the searing of the flesh. Like a priest of diabolic mysteries, he drew out the blackened blood with a pipette. With the distended lungs, the spleen and kidneys and liver, the assistant made wavy smears on glass slides which were stained and given to the class for examination. The students who had learned to look through the microscope without having to close one eye were proud and professional, and all of them talked of the beauty of identifying the bacillus, as they twiddled the brass thumb-screws to the right focus and the cells rose from cloudiness to sharp distinctness on the slides before them. But they were uneasy, for Gottlieb remained with them that day, stalking behind them, saying nothing, watching them always, watching the disposal of the remains of the guinea pigs, and along the benches ran nervous rumors about a bygone student who had died from anthrax infection in the laboratory.

IV

There was for Martin in these days a quality of satisfying delight; the zest of a fast hockey game, the serenity of the prairie, the bewilderment of great music, and a feeling of creation. He woke early and thought contentedly of the day; he hurried to his work, devout, unseeing.

The confusion of the bacteriological laboratory was ecstasy to him—the students in shirt-sleeves, filtering nutrient gelatine, their fingers gummed from the crinkly gelatine leaves; or heating media in an autoclave like a silver howitzer. The roaring Bunsen flames beneath the hot-air ovens, the steam from the Arnold sterilizers rolling to the rafters, clouding the windows, were to Martin lovely with activity, and to him the most radiant things in the world were rows of test-tubes filled with watery serum and plugged with cotton singed to a coffee brown, a fine platinum loop leaning in a shiny test-glass, a fantastic hedge of tall glass tubes mysteriously connecting jars, or a bottle rich with gentian violet stain.

He had begun, perhaps in youthful imitation of Gottlieb, to work by himself in the laboratory at night. . . . The long room was dark, thick dark, but for the gas-mantle behind his microscope. The cone of light cast a gloss on the bright brass tube, a sheen on his black hair, as he bent over the eyepiece. He was studying trypanosomes from a rat—an eight-branched rosette stained with polychrome methylene blue; a cluster of organisms delicate as a narcissus, with their purple nuclei, their light blue cells, and the thin lines of the flagella. He was excited and a little proud; he had stained the germs perfectly, and it is not easy to stain a rosette without breaking the petal shape. In the darkness, a step, the weary step of Max Gottlieb, and a hand on Martin's shoulder. Silently Martin raised his head, pushed the microscope toward him. Bending down, a cigarette stub in his mouth—the smoke would have stung the eyes of any human being—Gottlieb peered at the preparation.

He adjusted the gas light a quarter inch, and mused, "Splendid! You have craftsmanship. Oh, there is an art in science—for a few. You Americans, so many of you—all full with ideas, but you are impatient with the beautiful dullness of long labors. I see already—and I watch you in the lab before—perhaps you may try the trypanosomes of sleeping sickness. They are very, very interesting, and very, very ticklish to handle. It is quite a nice disease. In some villages in Africa, fifty per cent. of the people have it, and it is invariably fatal. Yes, I think you might work on the bugs."

Which, to Martin, was getting his brigade in battle.

"I shall have," said Gottlieb, "a little sandwich in my room at midnight. If you should happen to work so late, I should be very pleast if you would come to have a bite."

Diffidently, Martin crossed the hall to Gottlieb's immaculate laboratory at midnight. On the bench were coffee and sandwiches, curiously small and excellent sandwiches, foreign to Martin's lunch-room taste.

Gottlieb talked till Clif had faded from existence and Angus Duer seemed but an absurd climber. He summoned forth London laboratories, dinners on frosty evenings in Stockholm, walks on the Pincio with sunset behind the dome of San Pietro, extreme danger and overpowering disgust from excreta-smeared garments in an epidemic at Marseilles. His reserve slipped from him and he talked of himself and of his family as though Martin were a contemporary.

The cousin who was a colonel in Uruguay and the cousin, a rabbi, who was tortured in a pogrom in Moscow. His sick wife—it might be cancer. The three children—the youngest girl, Miriam, she was a good musician, but the boy, the fourteen-year-old, he was a worry; he was saucy, he would not study. Himself, he had worked for years on the synthesis of antibodies; he was at present in a blind alley, and at Mohalis there was no one who was interested, no one to stir him, but he was having an agreeable time massacring the opsonin theory, and that cheered him.

"No, I have done nothing except be unpleasant to people that claim too much, but I have dreams of real discoveries some day. And— No. Not five times in five years do I have students who understand craftsmanship and precision and maybe some big imagination in hypotheses. I t'ink perhaps you may have them. If I can help you— So!

"I do not t'ink you will be a good doctor. Good doctors are fine—often they are artists—but their trade, it is not for us lonely ones that work in labs. Once, I took an M.D. label. In Heidelberg that was—Herr Gott, back in 1875! I could not get much interested in bandaging legs and looking at tongues. I was a follower of Helmholtz—what a wild blithering young fellow! I tried to make researches into the physics of sound—I was bad, most unbelievable, but I learned that in this wale of tears there is nothing certain but the quantitative method. And I was a chemist—a fine stink-maker was I. And so into biology and much trouble. It has been good. I have found one or two things. And if sometimes I feel an exile, cold— I had to get out of Germany one time for refusing to sing *Die Wacht am Rhein* and trying to kill a cavalry captain—he was a stout fellow—I had to choke him—you see I am boasting, but I was a lifely *Kerl* thirty years ago! Ah! So!

"There is but one trouble of a philosophical bacteriologist. Why should we destroy these amiable pathogenic germs? Are we too sure, when we regard these oh, most unbeautiful young students attending Y.M.C.A.'s and singing dinkle-songs and wearing hats with initials burned into them—iss it worth while to protect them from the so elegantly functioning *Bacillus typhosus* with its lovely flagella? You know, once I asked Dean Silva would it not be better to let loose the pathogenic germs on the world, and so solve all economic questions. But he did not care for my met'od. Oh, well, he is older than I am; he also gives, I hear, some dinner parties with bishops and judges present, all in nice clothes. He would know more than a German Jew who loves Father Nietzsche and Father Schopenhauer (but damn him, he was teleological-minded!) and Father Koch and Father Pasteur and Brother Jacques Loeb and Brother Arrhenius. Ja! I talk foolishness. Let us go look at your slides and so good-night."

When he had left Gottlieb at his stupid brown little house, his face as reticent as though the midnight supper and all the rambling talk had never happened, Martin ran home, altogether drunk.

Chapter V

THOUGH bacteriology was all of Martin's life now, it was the theory of the university that he was also studying pathology, hygiene, surgical anatomy, and enough other subjects to swamp a genius.

Clif Clawson and he lived in a large room with flowered wall-paper, piles of filthy clothes, iron beds, and cuspidors. They made their own breakfasts; they dined on hash at the Pilgrim Lunch Wagon or the Dew Drop Inn. Clif was occasionally irritating; he hated open windows; he talked of dirty socks; he sang "Some Die of Diabetes" when Martin was studying; and he was altogether unable to say anything directly. He had to be humorous. He remarked, "Is it your combobulatory concept that we might now feed the old faces?" or "How about ingurgitating a few calories?" But he had for Martin a charm that could not be accounted for by his cheerfulness, his shrewdness, his vague courage. The whole of Clif was more than the sum of his various parts.

In the joy of his laboratory work Martin thought rarely of his recent associates in Digamma Pi. He occasionally protested that the Reverend Ira Hinkley was a village policeman and Irving Watters a plumber, that Angus Duer would walk to success over his grandmother's head, and that for an idiot like Fatty Pfaff to practise on helpless human beings was criminal, but mostly he ignored them and ceased to be a pest. And when he had passed his first triumphs in bacteriology and discovered how remarkably much he did not know, he was curiously humble.

If he was less annoying in regard to his classmates, he was more so in his classrooms. He had learned from Gottlieb the trick of using the word "control" in reference to the person or animal or chemical left untreated during an experiment, as a standard for comparison; and there is no trick more infuriating. When a physician boasted of his success with this drug or that electric cabinet, Gottlieb always snorted, "Where was your control? How many cases did you have under identical conditions, and how many of them did not get the treatment?" Now Martin began to mouth it—control, control, control, where's your control? where's your control?—till most of his fellows and a few of his instructors desired to lynch him.

He was particularly tedious in materia medica.

The professor of materia medica, Dr. Lloyd Davidson, would have been an illustrious shopkeeper. He was very popular. From him a future physician could learn that most important of all things: the proper drugs to give a patient, particularly when you cannot discover what is the matter with him. His classes listened with zeal, and memorized the sacred hundred and fifty favorite prescriptions. (He was proud that this was fifty more than his predecessor had required.)

But Martin was rebellious. He inquired, and publicly, "Dr. Davidson, how do they know ichthyol is good for erysipelas? Isn't it just rotten fossil fish—isn't it like the mummy-dust and puppy-ear stuff they used to give in the olden days?"

"How do they know? Why, my critical young friend, because thousands of physicians have used it for years and found their patients getting better, and that's how they know!"

"But honest, Doctor, wouldn't the patients maybe have gotten better anyway? Wasn't it maybe a *post hoc, propter hoc*? Have they ever experimented on a whole slew of patients together, with controls?"

"Probably not—and until some genius like yourself, Arrowsmith, can herd together a few hundred people with exactly identical cases of erysipelas, it probably never will be tried! Meanwhile I trust that you other gentlemen, who perhaps lack Mr. Arrowsmith's profound scientific attainments and the power to use such handy technical terms as 'control,' will, merely on my feeble advice, continue to use ichthyol!"

But Martin insisted, "Please, Dr. Davidson, what's the use of getting all these prescriptions by heart, anyway? We'll forget most of 'em, and besides, we can always look 'em up in the book."

Davidson pressed his lips together, then:

"Arrowsmith, with a man of your age I hate to answer you as I would a three-year-old boy, but apparently I must. Therefore, you will learn the properties of drugs and the contents of prescriptions *because I tell you to!* If I did not hesitate to waste the time of the other members of this class, I would try to convince you that my statements may be accepted, not on my humble authority, but because they are the conclusions of wise men—men wiser or certainly a little older than you, my friend—through many ages. But as I have no desire to indulge in fancy flights of rhetoric and eloquence, I shall merely say that you will accept, and you will study, and you will memorize, because I tell you to!"

Martin considered dropping his medical course and specializing in bacteriology. He tried to confide in Clif, but Clif had become impatient of his fretting, and he turned again to the energetic and willowy Madeline Fox.

II

Madeline was at once sympathetic and sensible. Why not complete his medical course, then see what he wanted to do?

They tramped, they skated, they skied, they went to the University Dramatic Society play. Madeline's widowed mother had come to live with her, and they had taken a top-floor flat in one of the tiny apartment-houses which were beginning to replace the expansive old wooden houses of Mohalis. The flat was full of literature and decoration: a bronze Buddha from Chicago, a rubbing of Shakespeare's epitaph, a set of Anatole France in translation, a photograph of Cologne cathedral, a wicker tea-table with a samovar whose operation no one in the university understood, and a souvenir post-card album. Madeline's mother was a Main Street dowager duchess. She was stately and white-haired but she attended the Methodist Church. In Mohalis she was flustered by the chatter of the students; she longed for her home-town, for the church sociables and the meetings of the women's club—they were studying Education this year and she hated to lose all the information about university ways.

With a home and a chaperone, Madeline began to "entertain": eight-o'clock parties with coffee, chocolate cake, chicken salad, and word-games. She invited Martin, but he was jealous of his evenings, beautiful evenings of research. The first affair to which she enticed him was her big New Year's Party in January. They "did advertisements"—guessed at tableaux representing advertising pictures; they danced to the phonograph; and they had not merely a lap-supper but little tables excessively covered with doilies.

Martin was unaccustomed to such elegance. Though he had come in sulky unwillingness, he was impressed by the supper, by the frocks of the young women; he realized that his dancing was rusty, and he envied the senior who could do the new waltz called the "Boston." There was no strength, no grace, no knowledge, that Martin Arrowsmith did not covet, when consciousness of it had pierced through the layers of his absorption. If he was but little greedy for possessions, he was hungry for every skill.

His reluctant wonder at the others was drowned in his admiration for Madeline. He had known her as a jacketed outdoor girl, but this was an exquisite indoor Madeline, slender in yellow silk. She seemed to him a miracle of tact and ease as she bullied her guests into an appearance of merriment. She had need of tact, for Dr. Norman Brumfit was there, and it was one of Dr. Brumfit's evenings to be original and naughty. He pretended to kiss Madeline's mother, which vastly discomforted the poor lady; he sang a strongly improper negro song containing the word hell; he maintained to a group of women graduate students that George Sand's affairs might perhaps be partially justified by their influence on men of talent; and when they looked shocked, he pranced a little, and his eye-glasses glittered.

Madeline took charge of him. She trilled, "Dr. Brumfit, you're terribly learned and so on and so forth, and sometimes in English classes I'm simply scared to death of you, but other times you're nothing but a bad small boy, and I won't have you teasing the girls. You can help me bring in the sherbet, that's what you can do."

Martin adored her. He hated Brumfit for the privilege of disappearing with her into the closet-like kitchen of the flat. Madeline! She was the one person who understood him! Here, where every one snatched at her and Dr. Brumfit beamed on her with almost matrimonial fondness, she was precious, she was something he must have.

On pretense of helping her set the tables, he had a moment with her, and whimpered, "Lord, you're so lovely!"

"I'm glad you think I'm a wee bit nice." She, the rose and the adored of all the world, gave him her favor.

"Can I come call on you to-morrow evening?"

"Well, I— Perhaps."

III

It cannot be said, in this biography of a young man who was in no degree a hero, who regarded himself as a seeker after truth yet who stumbled and slid back all his life and bogged himself in every obvious morass, that Martin's intentions toward Madeline Fox were what is called "honorable." He was not a Don Juan, but he was a poor medical student who would have to wait for years before he could make a living. Certainly he did not think of proposing marriage. He wanted—like most poor and ardent young men in such a case, he wanted all he could get.

As he raced toward her flat, he was expectant of adventure. He pictured her melting; he felt her hand glide down his cheek. He warned himself, "Don't be a fool now! Probably nothing doing at all. Don't go get all worked up and then be disappointed. She'll probably cuss you out for something you did wrong at the party. She'll probably be sleepy and wish you hadn't come. Nothing!" But he did not for a second believe it.

He rang, he saw her opening the door, he followed her down the meager hall, longing to take her hand. He came into the over-bright living-room—and he found her mother, solid as a pyramid, permanent-looking as sunless winter.

But of course Mother would obligingly go, and leave him to conquest.

Mother did not.

In Mohalis, the suitable time for young men callers to depart is ten o'clock, but from eight till a quarter after eleven Martin did battle with Mrs. Fox; talked to her in two languages, an audible gossip and a mute but furious protest, while Madeline—she was present; she sat about and looked pretty. In an equally silent tongue Mrs. Fox answered him, till the room was thick with their antagonism, while they seemed to be discussing the weather, the university, and the trolley service into Zenith.

"Yes, of course, some day I guess they'll have a car every twenty minutes," he said weightily.

("Darn her, why doesn't she go to bed? Cheers! She's doing up her knitting. Nope. Damn it! She's taking another ball of wool.")

"Oh, yes, I'm sure they'll have to have better service," said Mrs. Fox.

("Young man, I don't know much about you, but I don't believe you're the right kind of person for Madeline to go with. Anyway, it's time you went home.")

"Oh, yes, sure, you bet. Lot better service."

("I know I'm staying too long, and I know you know it, but I don't care!")

It seemed impossible that Mrs. Fox should endure his stolid persistence. He used thought-forms, will-power, and hypnotism, and when he rose, defeated, she was still there, extremely placid. They said good-by not too warmly. Madeline took him to the door; for an exhilarating half-minute he had her alone.

"I wanted so much—I wanted to talk to you!"

"I know. I'm sorry. Some time!" she muttered.

He kissed her. It was a tempestuous kiss, and very sweet.

IV

Fudge parties, skating parties, sleighing parties, a literary party with the guest of honor a lady journalist who did the social page for the Zenith *Advocate-Times*—Madeline leaped into an orgy of jocund but extraordinarily tiring entertainments, and Martin obediently and smolderingly followed her. She appeared to have trouble in getting enough men, and to the literary evening Martin dragged the enraged Clif Clawson. Clif grumbled, "This is the damnedest zoo of sparrows I ever did time in," but he bore off treasure—he had heard Madeline call Martin by her favorite name of "Martykins." That was very valuable. Clif called him Martykins. Clif told others to call him Martykins. Fatty Pfaff and Irving Watters called him Martykins. And when Martin wanted to go to sleep, Clif croaked:

"Yuh, you'll probably marry her. She's a dead shot. She can

hit a smart young M.D. at ninety paces. Oh, you'll have one fine young time going on with science after that skirt sets you at tonsil-snatching. . . . She's one of these literary birds. She knows all about lite'ature except maybe how to read. . . . She's not so bad-looking, now. She'll get fat, like her Ma."

Martin said that which was necessary, and he concluded, "She's the only girl in the graduate school that's got any pep. The others just sit around and talk, and she gets up the best parties—"

"Any kissing parties?"

"Now you look here! I'll be getting sore, first thing you know! You and I are roughnecks, but Madeline Fox—she's like Angus Duer, some ways. I realize all the stuff we're missing: music and literature, yes, and decent clothes, too—no harm to dressing well—"

"That's just what I was tellin' you! She'll have you all dolled up in a Prince Albert and a boiled shirt, diagnosing everything as rich-widowitis. How you can fall for that four-flushing dame— *Where's your control?*"

Clif's opposition stirred him to consider Madeline not merely with a sly and avaricious interest but with a dramatic conviction that he longed to marry her.

V

Few women can for long periods keep from trying to Improve their men, and To Improve means to change a person from what he is, whatever that may be, into something else. Girls like Madeline Fox, artistic young women who do not work at it, cannot be restrained from Improving for more than a day at a time. The moment the urgent Martin showed that he was stirred by her graces, she went at his clothes—his corduroys and soft collars and eccentric old gray felt hat—at his vocabulary and his taste in fiction, with new and more patronizing vigor. Her sketchy way of saying, "Why, of course everybody knows that Emerson was the greatest thinker" irritated him the more in contrast to Gottlieb's dark patience.

"Oh, let me alone!" he hurled at her. "You're the nicest thing the Lord ever made, when you stick to things you know about, but when you spring your ideas on politics and chemotherapy— Darn it, quit bullying me! I guess you're right about slang. I'll cut out all this junk about 'feeding your face' and so on. But I will not put on a hard-boiled collar! I won't!"

He might never have proposed to her but for the spring evening on the roof.

She used the flat roof of her apartment-house as a garden. She had set out one box of geraniums and a cast-iron bench like those once beheld in cemetery plots; she had hung up two Japanese lanterns—they were ragged and they hung crooked. She spoke with scorn of the other inhabitants of the apartment-house, who were "so prosaic, so conventional, that they never came up to this darling hidey-place." She compared her refuge to the roof of a Moorish palace, to a Spanish patio, to a Japanese garden, to a "pleasaunce of old Provençal." But to Martin it seemed a good deal like a plain roof. He was vaguely ready for a quarrel, that April evening when he called on Madeline and her mother sniffily told him that she was to be found on the roof.

"Damned Japanese lanterns. Rather look at liver-sections," he grumbled, as he trudged up the curving stairs.

Madeline was sitting on the funereal iron bench, her chin in her hands. For once she did not greet him with flowery excitement but with a noncommittal "Hello." She seemed spiritless. He felt guilty for his scoffing; he suddenly saw the pathos in her pretense that this stretch of tar-paper and slatted walks was a blazing garden. As he sat beside her he piped, "Say, that's a dandy new strip of matting you've put down."

"It is not! It's mangy!" She turned toward him. She wailed, "Oh, Mart, I'm so sick of myself, to-night. I'm always trying to make people think I'm somebody. I'm not. I'm a bluff."

"What is it, dear?"

"Oh, it's lots. Dr. Brumfit, hang him—only he was right—he as good as told me that if I don't work harder I'll have to get out of the graduate school. I'm not doing a thing, he said, and if I don't have my Ph.D., then I won't be able to land a nice job teaching English in some swell school, and I'd better land one, too, because it doesn't look to poor Madeline as if anybody was going to marry her."

His arm about her, he blared, "I know exactly who—"

"No, I'm not fishing. I'm almost honest, to-night. I'm no good, Mart. I tell people how clever I am. And I don't suppose they believe it. Probably they go off and laugh at me!"

"They do not! If they did— I'd like to see anybody that tried laughing—"

"It's awfully sweet and dear of you, but I'm not worth it. The poetic Madeline! With her ree-fined vocabulary! I'm a— I'm a—Martin, I'm a tin-horn sport! I'm everything your friend Clif thinks I am. Oh, you needn't tell me. I know what he thinks. And— I'll have to go home with mother, and I can't stand it, dear, I can't stand it! I won't go back! That town! Never anything doing! The old tabbies, and the beastly old men, always telling the same old jokes. I won't!"

Her head was in the hollow of his arm; she was weeping, hard; he was stroking her hair, not covetously now but tenderly, and he was whispering:

"Darling! I almost feel as if I dared to love you. You're going to marry me and— Take me couple more years to finish my medical course and couple in hospital, then we'll be married and— By thunder, with you helping me, I'm going to climb to the top! Be big surgeon! We're going to have everything!"

"Dearest, do be wise. I don't want to keep you from your scientific work—"

"Oh. Well. Well, I would like to keep up *some* research. But thunder, I'm not just a lab-cat. Battle o' life. Smashing your way through. Competing with real men in real he-struggle. If I can't do that and do some scientific work too, I'm no good. Course while I'm with Gottlieb, I want to take advantage of it, but afterward— Oh, Madeline!"

Then was all reasoning lost in a blur of nearness to her.

VI

He dreaded the interview with Mrs. Fox; he was certain that she would demand, "Young man, how do you expect to support my Maddy? And you use bad language." But she took his hand and mourned, "I hope you and my baby will be happy. She's a dear good girl, even if she is a little flighty sometimes, and I know you're nice and kind and hard-working. I shall pray you'll be happy—oh, I'll pray so hard! You young people don't seem to think much of prayer, but if you knew how it helped me— Oh, I'll petition for your sweet happiness!"

She was weeping; she kissed Martin's forehead with the dry, soft, gentle kiss of an old woman, and he was near to weeping with her.

At parting Madeline whispered, "Boy, I don't care a bit, myself, but Mother would love it if we went to church with her. Don't you think you could, just once?"

The astounded world, the astounded and profane Clif Clawson, had the spectacle of Martin in shiny pressed clothes, a painful linen collar, and an arduously tied scarf, accompanying Mrs. Fox and the chastely chattering Madeline to the Mohalis Methodist Church, to hear the Reverend Dr. Myron Schwab discourse on "The One Way to Righteousness."

They passed the Reverend Ira Hinkley, and Ira gloated with a holy gloating at Martin's captivity.

VII

For all his devotion to Max Gottlieb's pessimistic view of the human intellect, Martin had believed that there was such a thing as progress, that events meant something, that people could learn something, that if Madeline had once admitted she was an ordinary young woman who occasionally failed, then she was saved. He was bewildered when she began improving him more airily than ever. She complained of his vulgarity and what she asserted to be his slack ambition. "You think it's terribly smart of you to feel superior. Sometimes I wonder if it isn't just laziness. You like to day-dream around labs. Why should *you* be spared the work of memorizing your materia medica and so on and so forth? All the others have to do it. No, I won't kiss you. I want you to grow up and listen to reason."

In fury at her badgering, in desire for her lips and forgiving smile, he was whirled through to the end of the term.

A week before examinations, when he was trying to spend twenty-four hours a day in making love to her, twenty-four in grinding for examinations, and twenty-four in the bacteriological laboratory, he promised Clif that he would spend that summer vacation with him, working as a waiter in a Canadian hotel. He met Madeline in the evening, and with her walked through the cherry orchard on the Agricultural Experiment Station grounds.

"You know what I think of your horrid Clif Clawson," she complained. "I don't suppose you care to hear my opinion of him."

"I've had your opinion, my beloved." Martin sounded mature, and not too pleasant.

"Well, I can tell you right now you haven't had my opinion of your being a waiter! For the life of me I can't understand why you don't get some gentlemanly job for vacation, instead of hustling dirty dishes. Why couldn't you work on a newspaper, where you'd have to dress decently and meet nice people?"

"Sure. I might edit the paper. But since you say so, I won't work at all this summer. Fool thing to do, anyway. I'll go to Newport and play golf and wear a dress suit every night."

"It wouldn't hurt you any! I do respect honest labor. It's like Burns says. But waiting on table! Oh, Mart, why are you so proud of being a roughneck? Do stop being smart, for a minute. Listen to the night. And smell the cherry blossoms. . . . Or maybe a great scientist like you, that's so superior to ordinary people, is too good for cherry blossoms!"

"Well, except for the fact that every cherry blossom has been gone for weeks now, you're dead right."

"Oh, they have, have they! They may be faded but— Will you be so good as to tell me what that pale white mass is up there?"

"I will. It looks to me like a hired-man's shirt."

"Martin Arrowsmith, if you think for one moment that I'm ever going to marry a vulgar, crude, selfish, microbe-grubbing smart aleck—"

"And if you think I'm going to marry a dame that keeps nag-nag-naggin' and jab-jab-jabbin' at me all day long—"

They hurt each other; they had pleasure in it; and they parted forever, twice they parted forever, the second time very rudely, near a fraternity-house where students were singing heart-breaking summer songs to a banjo.

In ten days, without seeing her again, he was off with Clif to the North Woods, and in his sorrow of losing her, his longing for her soft flesh and for her willingness to listen to him, he was only a little excited that he should have led the class in bacteriology, and that Max Gottlieb should have appointed him undergraduate assistant for the coming year.

Chapter VI

THE WAITERS at Nokomis Lodge, among the Ontario pines, were all of them university students. They were not supposed to appear at the Lodge dances—they merely appeared, and took the prettiest girls away from the elderly and denunciatory suitors in white flannels. They had to work but seven hours a day. The rest of the time they fished, swam, and tramped the shadowy trails, and Martin came back to Mohalis placid—and enormously in love with Madeline.

They had written to each other, politely, regretfully, and once a fortnight; then passionately and daily. For the summer she had been dragged to her home town, near the Ohio border of Winnemac, a town larger than Martin's native Elk Mills but more sun-baked, more barren with little factories. She sighed, in a huge loose script dashing all over the page:

> Perhaps we shall never see each other again but I do want you to know how much I prize all the talks we had together about science & ideals & education, etc.—I certainly appreciate them here when I listen to these stick in the muds going on, oh, it is too dreadful, about their automobiles & how much they have to pay their maids and so on & so forth. You gave me so much but I did give you something didn't I? I cant always be in the wrong can I?

"My dear, my little girl!" he lamented. "'Can't always be in the wrong'! You poor kid, you poor dear kid!"

By midsummer they were firmly re-engaged and, though he was slightly disturbed by the cashier, a young and giggling Wisconsin school-teacher with ankles, he so longed for Madeline that he lay awake thinking of giving up his job and fleeing to her caresses—lay awake for minutes at a time.

The returning train was torturingly slow, and he dismounted at Mohalis fevered with visions of her. Twenty minutes after, they were clinging together in the quiet of her living-room. It is true that twenty minutes after that, she was sneering at Clif Clawson, at fishing, and at all school-teachers, but to his fury she yielded in tears.

II

His Junior year was a whirlwind. To attend lectures on physical diagnosis, surgery, neurology, obstetrics, and gynecology in the morning, with hospital demonstrations in the afternoon; to supervise the making of media and the sterilization of glassware for Gottlieb; to instruct a new class in the use of microscope and filter and autoclave; to read a page now and then of scientific German or French; to see Madeline constantly; to get through it all he drove himself to hysterical hurrying, and in the dizziest of it he began his first original research—his first lyric, his first ascent of unexplored mountains.

He had immunized rabbits to typhoid, and he believed that if he mixed serum taken from these immune animals with typhoid germs, the germs would die. Unfortunately—he felt—the germs grew joyfully. He was troubled; he was sure that his technique had been clumsy; he performed his experiment over and over, working till midnight, waking at dawn to ponder on his notes. (Though in letters to Madeline his writing was an inconsistent scrawl, in his laboratory notes it was precise.) When he was quite sure that Nature was persisting in doing something she ought not to, he went guiltily to Gottlieb, protesting, "The darn' bugs ought to die in this immune serum, but they don't. There's something wrong with the theories."

"Young man, do you set yourself up against science?" grated Gottlieb, flapping the papers on his desk. "Do you feel competent, huh, to attack the dogmas of immunology?"

"I'm sorry, sir. I can't help what the dogma is. Here's my protocols. Honestly, I've gone over and over the stuff, and I get the same results, as you can see. I only know what I observe."

Gottlieb beamed. "I give you, my boy, my episcopal blessings! That is the way! Observe what you observe, and if it does violence to all the nice correct views of science—out they go! I am very pleast, Martin. But now find out the Why, the underneath principle."

Ordinarily, Gottlieb called him "Arrowsmith" or "You" or "Uh." When he was furious he called him, or any other student, "Doctor." It was only in high moments that he honored him with "Martin," and the boy trotted off blissfully, to try to find (but never to succeed in finding) the Why that made everything so.

III

Gottlieb had sent him into Zenith, to the huge Zenith General Hospital, to secure a strain of meningococcus from an interesting patient. The bored reception clerk—who was interested only in obtaining the names, business addresses, and religions of patients, and did not care who died or who spat on the beautiful blue and white linoleum or who went about collecting meningococci, so long as the addresses were properly entered—loftily told him to go up to Ward D. Through the long hallways, past numberless rooms from which peered yellow-faced old women sitting up in bed in linty nightgowns, Martin wandered, trying to look important, hoping to be taken for a doctor, and succeeding only in feeling extraordinarily embarrassed.

He passed several nurses rapidly, half nodding to them, in the manner (or what he conceived to be the manner) of a brilliant young surgeon who is about to operate. He was so absorbed in looking like a brilliant young surgeon that he was completely lost, and discovered himself in a wing filled with private suites. He was late. He had no more time to go on being impressive. Like all males, he hated to confess ignorance by asking directions, but grudgingly he stopped at the door of a bedroom in which a probationer nurse was scrubbing the floor.

She was a smallish and slender probationer, muffled in a harsh blue denim dress, an enormous white apron, and a turban bound about her head with an elastic—a uniform as grubby as her pail of scrub-water. She peered up with the alert impudence of a squirrel.

"Nurse," he said, "I want to find Ward D."

Lazily, "Do you?"

"I do! If I can interrupt your work—"

"Doesn't matter. The damn' superintendent of nurses put me at scrubbing, and we aren't ever *supposed* to scrub floors, because she caught me smoking a cigarette. She's an old terror. If she found a child like you wandering around here, she'd drag you out by the ear."

"My *dear* young woman, it may interest you to know—"

"Oh! 'My dear young woman, it may—' Sounds exactly like our old prof, back home."

Her indolent amusement, her manner of treating him as though they were a pair of children making tongues at each other in a railroad station, was infuriating to the earnest young assistant of Professor Gottlieb.

"I am Dr. Arrowsmith," he snorted, "and I've been informed that even probationers learn that the first duty of a nurse is to stand when addressing doctors! I wish to find Ward D, to take a strain of—*it may interest you to know!*—a very dangerous microbe, and if you will kindly direct me—"

"Oh, gee, I've been getting fresh again. I don't seem to get along with this military discipline. All right. I'll stand up." She did. Her every movement was swiftly smooth as the running of a cat. "You go back, turn right, then left. I'm sorry I was fresh. But if you saw some of the old muffs of doctors that a nurse has to be meek to— Honestly, Doctor—if you *are* a doctor—"

"I don't see that I need to convince you!" he raged, as he stalked off. All the way to Ward D he was furious at her veiled derision. He was an eminent scientist, and it was outrageous that he should have to endure impudence from a probationer—a singularly vulgar probationer, a thin and slangy young woman apparently from the West. He repeated his rebuke: "I don't see that I need to convince you." He was proud of himself for having been lofty. He pictured himself telling Madeline about it, concluding, "I just said to her quietly, 'My dear young woman, I don't know that you are the person to whom I have to explain my mission here,' I said, and she wilted."

But her image had not wilted, when he had found the intern who was to help him and had taken the spinal fluid. She was before him, provocative, enduring. He had to see her again, and convince her— "Take a better man than she is, better man than I've ever met, to get away with being insulting to *me*!" said the modest young scientist.

He had raced back to her room and they were staring at each other before it came to him that he had not worked out the crushing things he was going to say. She had risen from her scrubbing. She had taken off her turban, and her hair was silky and honey-colored, her eyes were blue, her face childish. There was nothing of the slavey in her. He could imagine her running down hillsides, shinning up a stack of straw.

"Oh," she said gravely. "I didn't mean to be rude then. I was just— Scrubbing makes me bad-tempered. I thought you were awfully nice, and I'm sorry I hurt your feelings, but you did seem so young for a doctor."

"I'm not. I'm a medic. I was showing off."

"So was I!"

He felt an instant and complete comradeship with her, a relation free from the fencing and posing of his struggle with Madeline. He knew that this girl was of his own people. If she was vulgar, jocular, unreticent, she was also gallant, she was full of laughter at humbugs, she was capable of a loyalty too casual and natural to seem heroic. His voice was lively, though his words were only:

"Pretty hard, this training for nursing, I guess."

"Not so awful, but it's just as romantic as being a hired girl—that's what we call 'em in Dakota."

"Come from Dakota?"

"I come from the most enterprising town—three hundred and sixty-two inhabitants—in the entire state of North Dakota—Wheatsylvania. Are you in the U. medic school?"

To a passing nurse, the two youngsters would have seemed absorbed in hospital business. Martin stood at the door, she by her scrubbing pail. She had reassumed her turban; its bagginess obscured her bright hair.

"Yes, I'm a Junior medic in Mohalis. But— I don't know. I'm not much of a medic. I like the lab side. I think I'll be a bacteriologist, and raise Cain with some of the fool theories of immunology. And I don't think much of the bedside manner."

"I'm glad you don't. You get it here. You ought to hear some of the docs that are the sweetest old pussies with their patients—the way they bawl out the nurses. But labs—they seem sort of real. I don't suppose you can bluff a bacteria—what is it?—bacterium?"

"No, they're— What do they call you?"

"Me? Oh, it's an idiotic name—Leora Tozer."

"What's the matter with Leora? It's fine."

Sound of mating birds, sound of spring blossoms dropping in the tranquil air, the bark of sleepy dogs at midnight; who is to set them down and make them anything but hackneyed? And as natural, as conventional, as youthfully gauche, as eternally beautiful and authentic as those ancient sounds was the talk of Martin and Leora in that passionate half-hour when each found in the other a part of his own self, always vaguely missed, discovered now with astonished joy. They rattled like hero and heroine of a sticky tale, like sweat-shop operatives, like bouncing rustics, like prince and princess. Their words were silly and inconsequential, heard one by one, yet taken together they were as wise and important as the tides or the sounding wind.

He told her that he admired Max Gottlieb, that he had crossed her North Dakota on a train, and that he was an excellent hockey-player. She told him that she "adored" vaudeville, that her father, Andrew Jackson Tozer, was born in the East (by which she meant Illinois), and that she didn't particularly care for nursing. She had no especial personal ambition; she had come here because she liked adventure. She hinted, with debonair regret, that she was not too popular with the superintendent of nurses; she meant to be good but somehow she was always dragged into rebellions connected with midnight fudge or elopements. There was nothing heroic in her story but from her placid way of telling it he had an impression of gay courage.

He interrupted with an urgent, "When can you get away from the hospital for dinner? To-night?"

"Why—"

"Please!"

"All right."

"When can I call for you?"

"Do you think I ought to— Well, seven."

All the way back to Mohalis he alternately raged and rejoiced. He informed himself that he was a moron to make this long trip into Zenith twice in one day; he remembered that he was engaged to a girl called Madeline Fox; he worried the matter of unfaithfulness; he asserted that Leora Tozer was merely an imitation nurse who was as illiterate as a kitchen wench and as impertinent as a newsboy; he decided, several times he decided, to telephone her and free himself from the engagement.

He was at the hospital at a quarter to seven.

He had to wait for twenty minutes in a reception-room like that of an undertaker. He was in a panic. What was he doing here? She'd probably be agonizingly dull, through a whole long dinner. Would he even recognize her, in mufti? Then he leaped up. She was at the door. Her sulky blue uniform was gone; she was childishly slim and light in a princess frock that was a straight line from high collar and soft young breast to her feet. It seemed natural to tuck her hand under his arm as they left the hospital. She moved beside him with a little dancing step, shyer now than she had been in the dignity of her job but looking up at him with confidence.

"Glad I came?" he demanded.

She thought it over. She had a trick of gravely thinking over obvious questions; and gravely (but with the gravity of a child, not the ponderous gravity of a politician or an office-manager) she admitted, "Yes, I am glad. I was afraid you'd go and get sore at me because I was so fresh, and I wanted to apologize and— I liked your being so crazy about your bacteriology. I think I'm a little crazy, too. The interns here—they come bothering around a lot, but they're so sort of—so sort of *soggy*, with their new stethoscopes and their brand-new dignity. Oh—" Most gravely of all: "Oh, gee, yes, I'm glad you came. . . . Am I an idiot to admit it?"

"You're a darling to admit it." He was a little dizzy with her. He pressed her hand with his arm.

"You won't think I let every medic and doctor pick me up, will you?"

"Leora! And you don't think I try and pick up every pretty girl I meet? I liked—I felt somehow we two could be chums. Can't we? Can't we?"

"I don't know. We'll see. Where are we going for dinner?"

"The Grand Hotel."

"We are not! It's terribly expensive. Unless you're awfully rich. You aren't, are you?"

"No, I'm not. Just enough money to get through medic school. But I want—"

"Let's go to the Bijou. It's a nice place, and it isn't expensive."

He remembered how often Madeline Fox had hinted that it would be a tasty thing to go to the Grand, Zenith's most resplendent hotel, but that was the last time he thought of Madeline that evening. He was absorbed in Leora. He found in her a casualness, a lack of prejudice, a directness, surprising in the daughter of Andrew Jackson Tozer. She was feminine but undemanding; she was never Improving and rarely shocked; she was neither flirtatious nor cold. She was indeed the first girl to whom he had ever talked without self-consciousness. It is doubtful if Leora herself had a chance to say anything, for he poured out his every confidence as a disciple of Gottlieb. To Madeline, Gottlieb was a wicked old man who made fun of the sanctities of Marriage and Easter lilies, to Clif, he was a bore, but Leora glowed as Martin banged the table and quoted his idol: "Up to the present, even in the work of Ehrlich, most research has been largely a matter of trial and error, the empirical method, which is the opposite of the scientific method, by which one seeks to establish a general law governing a group of phenomena so that he may predict what will happen."

He intoned it reverently, staring across the table at her, almost glaring at her. He insisted, "Do you see where he leaves all these detail-grubbing, machine-made researchers buzzing in the manure heap just as much as he does the commercial docs? Do you get him? Do you?"

"Yes, I think I do. Anyway, I get your enthusiasm for him. But please don't bully me so!"

"Was I bullying? I didn't mean to. Only, when I get to thinking about the way most of these damned profs don't even know what he's up to—"

Martin was off again, and if Leora did not altogether understand the relation of the synthesis of antibodies to the work of Arrhenius, yet she listened with comfortable pleasure in his zeal, with none of Madeline Fox's gently corrective admonitions.

She had to warn him that she must be at the hospital by ten.

"I've talked too much! Lord, I hope I haven't bored you," he blurted.

"I loved it."

"And I was so technical, and so noisy— Oh, I *am* a chump!"

"I like having you trust me. I'm not 'earnest,' and I haven't any brains whatever, but I do love it when my menfolks think I'm intelligent enough to hear what they really think and— Good night!"

They dined together twice in two weeks, and only twice in that time, though she telephoned to him, did Martin see his honest affianced, Madeline.

He came to know all of Leora's background. Her bedridden grand-aunt in Zenith, who was her excuse for coming so far to take hospital training. The hamlet of Wheatsylvania, North Dakota; one street of shanties with the red grain-elevators at the end. Her father, Andrew Jackson Tozer, sometimes known as Jackass Tozer; owner of the bank, of the creamery, and an elevator, therefore the chief person in town; pious at Wednesday evening prayer-meeting, fussing over every penny he gave to Leora or her mother. Bert Tozer, her brother; squirrel teeth, a gold eye-glass chain over his ear, cashier and all the rest of the staff in the one-room bank owned by his father. The chicken salad and coffee suppers at the United Brethren Church; German Lutheran farmers singing ancient Teutonic hymns; the Hollanders, the Bohemians and Poles. And round about the village, the living wheat, arched above by tremendous clouds. He saw Leora, always an "odd child," doing obediently enough the flat household tasks but keeping snug the belief that some day she would find a youngster with whom, in whatever danger or poverty, she would behold all the colored world.

It was at the end of her hesitating effort to make him see her childhood that he cried, "Darling, you don't have to tell me about you. I've always known you. I'm not going to let you go, no matter what. You're going to marry me—"

They said it with clasping hands, confessing eyes, in that blatant restaurant. Her first words were:

"I want to call you 'Sandy.' Why do I? I don't know why. You're as unsandy as can be, but somehow 'Sandy' means you to me and— Oh, my dear, I do like you!"

Martin went home engaged to two girls at once.

IV

He had promised to see Madeline the next morning.

By any canon of respectable behavior he should have felt like a low dog; he assured himself that he must feel like a low dog; but he could not bring it off. He thought of Madeline's pathetic enthusiasms: her "Provençal pleasaunce" and the limp-leather volumes of poetry which she patted with fond finger-tips; of the tie she had bought for him, and her pride in his hair when he brushed it like the patent-leather heroes in magazine illustrations. He mourned that he had sinned against loyalty. But his agitation broke against the solidity of his union with Leora. Her companionship released his soul. Even when, as advocate for Madeline, he pleaded that Leora was a trivial young woman who probably chewed gum in private and certainly was careless about her nails in public, her commonness was dear to the commonness that was in himself, valid as ambition or reverence, an earthy base to her gaiety as it was to his nervous scientific curiosity.

He was absent-minded in the laboratory, that fatal next day. Gottlieb had twice to ask him whether he had prepared the new batch of medium, and Gottlieb was an autocrat, sterner with his favorites than with the ruck of students. He snarled, "Arrowsmith, you are a moon-calf! My God, am I to spend my life with *Dummköpfe*? I cannot be always alone, Martin! Are you going to fail me? Two, three days now you haf not been keen about work."

Martin went off mumbling, "I love that man!" In his tangled mood he catalogued Madeline's pretenses, her nagging, her selfishness, her fundamental ignorance. He worked himself up to a state of virtue in which it was agreeably clear to him that he must throw Madeline over, entirely as a rebuke. He went to her in the evening prepared to blaze out at her first complaining, to forgive her finally, but to break their engagement and make life resolutely simple again.

She did not complain.

She ran to him. "Dear, you're so tired—your eyes look tired. Have you been working frightfully hard? I've been so sorry you couldn't come 'round, this week. Dear, you mustn't kill yourself. Think of all the years you have ahead to do splendid things in. No, don't talk. I want you to rest. Mother's gone to the movies. Sit here. See, I'll make you so comfy with these pillows. Just lean back—go to sleep if you want to—and I'll read you 'The Crock of Gold.' You'll love it."

He was determined that he would not love it and, as he probably had no sense of humor whatever, it is doubtful whether he appreciated it, but its differentness aroused him. Though Madeline's voice was shrill and cornfieldish after Leora's lazy softness, she read so eagerly that he was sick ashamed of his intention to hurt her. He saw that it was she, with her pretenses, who was the child, and the detached and fearless Leora who was mature, mistress of a real world. The reproofs with which he had planned to crush her vanished.

Suddenly she was beside him, begging, "I've been so lonely for you, all week!"

So he was a traitor to both women. It was Leora who had intolerably roused him; it was really Leora whom he was caressing now; but it was Madeline who took his hunger to herself, and when she whimpered, "I'm so glad you're glad to be here," he could say nothing. He wanted to talk about Leora, to shout about Leora, to exult in her, his woman. He dragged out a few sound but unimpassioned flatteries; he observed that Madeline was a handsome young woman and a sound English scholar; and while she gaped with disappointment at his lukewarmness, he got himself away, at ten. He had finally succeeded very well indeed in feeling like a low dog.

He hastened to Clif Clawson.

He had told Clif nothing about Leora. He resented Clif's probable scoffing. He thought well of himself for the calmness with which he came into their room. Clif was sitting on the small of his back, shoeless feet upon the study table, reading a Sherlock Holmes story which rested on the powerful volume of Osler's Medicine which he considered himself to be reading.

"Clif! Want a drink. Tired. Let's sneak down to Barney's and see if we can rustle one."

"Thou speakest as one having tongues and who putteth the speed behind the ole rhombencephalon comprising the cerebellum and the medulla oblongata."

"Oh, cut out the cuteness! I'm in a bad temper."

"Ah, the laddy has been having a scrap with his chaste lil Madeline! Was she horrid to ickly Martykins? All right. I'll quit. Come on. Yoicks for the drink."

He told three new stories about Professor Robertshaw, all of them scurrilous and most of them untrue, on their way, and he almost coaxed Martin into cheerfulness. "Barney's" was a pool-room, a tobacco shop and, since Mohalis was dry by local option, an admirable blind-pig. Clif and the hairy-handed Barney greeted each other in a high and worthy manner:

"The benisons of eventide to you, Barney. May your circulation proceed unchecked and particularly the dorsal carpal branch of the ulnar artery, in which connection, comrade, Prof. Dr. Col. Egbert Arrowsmith and I would fain trifle with another bottle of that renowned strawberry pop."

"Gosh, Clif, you cer'nly got a swell line of jaw-music. If I ever need a' arm amputated when you get to be a doc, I'll come around and let you talk it off. Strawberry pop, gents?"

The front room of Barney's was an impressionistic painting in which a pool-table, piles of cigarettes, chocolate bars, playing cards, and pink sporting papers were jumbled in chaos. The back room was simpler: cases of sweet and thinly flavored soda, a large ice-box, and two small tables with broken chairs. Barney poured, from a bottle plainly marked Ginger Ale, two glasses of powerful and appallingly raw whisky, and Clif and Martin took them to the table in the corner. The effect was swift. Martin's confused sorrows turned to optimism. He told Clif that he was going to write a book exposing idealism, but what he meant was that he was going to do something clever about his dual engagement. He had it! He would invite Leora and Madeline to lunch together, tell them the truth, and see which of them loved him. He whooped, and had another whisky; he told Clif that he was a fine fellow, and Barney that he was a public benefactor, and unsteadily he retired to the telephone, which was shut off from public hearing in a closet.

At the Zenith General Hospital he got the night superintendent, and the night superintendent was a man frosty and suspicious. "This is no time to be calling up a probationer! Half-past eleven! Who are you, anyway?"

Martin checked the "I'll damn' soon tell you who I am!" which was his natural reaction, and explained that he was speaking for Leora's invalid grand-aunt, that the poor old lady was very low, and if the night superintendent cared to take upon himself the murder of a blameless gentlewoman—

When Leora came to the telephone he said quickly, and soberly now, feeling as though he had come from the menace of thronging strangers into the security of her presence:

"Leora? Sandy. Meet me Grand lobby to-morrow, twelve-thirty. Must! Important! Fix 't somehow—your aunt's sick."

"All right, dear. G' night," was all she said.

It took him long minutes to get an answer from Madeline's flat, then Mrs. Fox's voice sounded, sleepily, quaveringly:

"Yes, yes?"

"'S Martin."

"Who is it? Who is it? What is it? Are you calling the Fox apartment?"

"Yes, yes! Mrs. Fox, it's Martin Arrowsmith speaking."

"Oh, oh, my dear! The 'phone woke me out of a sound sleep, and I couldn't make out what you were saying. I was so frightened. I thought maybe it was a telegram or something. I thought perhaps something had happened to Maddy's brother. What is it, dear? Oh, I do hope nothing's happened!"

Her confidence in him, the affection of this uprooted old woman bewildered in a strange land, overcame him; he lost all his whisky-colored feeling that he was a nimble fellow, and in a melancholy way, with all the weight of life again upon him, he sighed that no, nothing had happened, but he'd forgotten to tell Madeline something—so shor—so sorry call so late—could he speak Mad just minute—

Then Madeline was bubbling, "Why, Marty dear, what is it? I do hope nothing has happened! Why, dear, you just left here—"

"Listen, d-dear. Forgot to tell you. There's a—there's a great friend of mine in Zenith that I want you to meet—"

"Who is he?"

"You'll see to-morrow. Listen, I want you come in and meet—come meet um at lunch. Going," with ponderous jocularity, "going to blow you all to a swell feed at the Grand—"

"Oh, how nice!"

"—so I want you to meet me at the eleven-forty interurban, at College Square. Can you?"

Vaguely, "Oh, I'd love to but—I have an eleven o'clock, and I don't like to cut it, and I promised May Harmon to go shopping with her—she's looking for some kind of shoes that you can wear with her pink crêpe de chine but that you can walk in—and we sort of thought maybe we might lunch at Ye Kollege Karavanserai—and I'd half planned to go to the movies with her or somebody, Mother says that new Alaska film is simply dandy, she saw it to-night, and I thought I might go see it before they take it off, though Heaven knows I ought to come right home and study and not go anywhere at all—"

"Now *listen!* It's important. Don't you trust me? Will you come or not?"

"Why, of course I trust you, dear. All right, I'll try to be there. The eleven-forty?"

"Yes."

"At College Square? Or at Bluthman's Book Shop?"

"At College Square!"

Her gentle "I trust you" and her wambling "I'll try to" were warring in his ears as he plunged out of the suffocating cell and returned to Clif.

"What's the grief?" Clif wondered. "Wife passed away? Or did the Giants win in the ninth? Barney, our wandering-boy-to-night looks like a necropsy. Slip him another strawberry pop, quick. Say, Doctor, I think you better call a physician."

"Oh, shut up," was all Martin had to say, and that without conviction. Before telephoning he had been full of little brightnesses; he had praised Clif's pool-playing and called Barney "old *Cimex lectularius*"; but now, while the affectionate Clif worked on him, he sat brooding save when he grumbled (with a return of self-satisfaction), "If you knew all the troubles I have—all the doggone mess a fellow can get into—*you'd* feel down in the mouth!"

Clif was alarmed. "Look here, old socks. If you've gotten in debt, I'll raise the cash, somehow. If it's— Been going a little too far with Madeline?"

"You make me sick! You've got a dirty mind. I'm not worthy to touch Madeline's hand. I regard her with nothing but respect."

"The hell you do! But never mind, if you say so. Gosh, wish there was *something* I could do for you. Oh! Have 'nother shot! Barney! Come a-runnin'!"

By several drinks Martin was warmed into a hazy carelessness, and Clif solicitously dragged him home after he had desired to fight three large academic sophomores. But in the morning he awoke with a crackling skull and a realization that he was going to face Leora and Madeline at lunch.

V

His half-hour journey with Madeline into Zenith seemed a visible and oppressing thing, like a tornado cloud. He had not merely to get through each minute as it came; the whole grim thirty minutes were present at the same time. While he was practising the tactful observation he was going to present two minutes from now, he could still hear the clumsy thing he had said two minutes before. He fought to keep her attention from the "great friend of his" whom they were to meet. With fatuous beaming he described a night at Barney's; without any success whatever he tried to be funny; and when Madeline lectured him on the evils of liquor and the evils of association with immoral persons, he was for once relieved. But he could not sidetrack her.

"Who is this man we're going to see? What are you so mysterious about? Oh, Martykins, is it a joke? Aren't we going to meet anybody? Did you just want to run away from Mama for a while and we have a bat at the Grand together? Oh, what fun! I've always wanted to lunch at the Grand. Of course I do think it's too sort of rococo, but still, it is impressive, and— Did I guess it, darling?"

"No, there's some one— Oh, we're going to meet somebody, all right!"

"Then why don't you tell me who he is? Honestly, Mart, you make me impatient."

"Well, I'll tell you. It isn't a Him; it's a Her."

"Oh!"

"It's— You know my work takes me to the hospitals, and some of the nurses at Zenith General have been awfully helpful." He was panting. His eyes ached. Since the torture of the coming lunch was inevitable, he wondered why he should go on trying to resist his punishment. "Especially there's one nurse there who's a wonder. She's learned so much about the care of the sick, and she puts me onto a lot of good stunts, and she seems like a nice girl—Miss Tozer, her name is—I think her first name is Lee or something like that—and she's so—her father is one of the big men in North Dakota—awfully rich—big banker—I guess she just took up nursing to do her share in the world's work." He had achieved Madeline's own tone of poetic uplift. "I thought you two might like to know each other. You remember you were saying how few girls there are in Mohalis that really appreciate—appreciate ideals."

"Ye-es." Madeline gazed at something far away and, whatever it was, she did not like it. "I shall be ver' pleased to meet her, of course. *Any* friend of yours— Oh, Mart! I do hope you don't flirt; I hope you don't get too friendly with all these nurses. I don't know anything about it, of course, but I keep hearing how some of these nurses are regular man-hunters."

"Well, let me tell you right now, Leora isn't!"

"No, I'm sure, but— Oh, Martykins, you won't be silly and let these nurses just amuse themselves with you? I mean, for your own sake. They have such an advantage. Poor Madeline, she wouldn't be allowed to go hanging around men's rooms learning—things, and you think you're so psychological, Mart, but honestly, any smart woman can twist you around her finger."

"Well, I guess I can take care of myself!"

"Oh, I mean—I don't mean— But I do hope this Tozer person— I'm sure I shall like her, if you do, but— I am your own true love, aren't I, always!"

She, the proper, ignored the passengers as she clasped his hand. She sounded so frightened that his anger at her reflections on Leora turned into misery. Incidentally, her thumb was gouging painfully into the back of his hand. He tried to look tender as he protested, "Sure—sure—gosh, honest, Mad, look out. That old duffer across the aisle is staring at us."

For whatever infidelities he might ever commit he was adequately punished before they had reached the Grand Hotel.

The Grand was, in 1907, the best hotel in Zenith. It was compared by traveling salesmen to the Parker House, the Palmer House, the West Hotel. It has been humbled since by the supercilious modesty of the vast Hotel Thornleigh; dirty now is its tessellated floor and all the wild gilt tarnished, and in its ponderous leather chairs are torn seams and stogie ashes and horse-dealers. But in its day it was the proudest inn between Chicago and Pittsburg; an oriental palace, the entrance a score of brick Moorish arches, the lobby towering from a black and white marble floor, up past gilt iron balconies, to the green, pink, pearl, and amber skylight seven stories above.

They found Leora in the lobby, tiny on an enormous couch built round a pillar. She stared at Madeline, quiet, waiting. Martin perceived that Leora was unusually sloppy—his own word. It did not matter to him how clumsily her honey-colored hair was tucked under her black hat, a characterless little mushroom of a hat, but he did see and resent the contrast between her shirtwaist, with the third button missing, her checked skirt, her unfortunate bright brown bolero jacket, and Madeline's sleekness of blue serge. The resentment was not toward Leora. Scanning them together (not haughtily, as the choosing and lofty male, but anxiously) he was more irritated than ever by Madeline. That she should be better dressed was an affront. His affection flew to guard Leora, to wrap and protect her.

And all the while he was bumbling:

"—thought you two girls ought know each other—Miss Fox, want t' make you 'quainted with Miss Tozer—little celebration—lucky dog have two Queens of Sheba—"

And to himself, "Oh, hell!"

While they murmured nothing in particular to each other he herded them into the famous dining-room of the Grand. It was full of gilt chandeliers, red plush chairs, heavy silverware, and aged negro retainers with gold and green waistcoats. Round the walls ran select views of Pompeii, Venice, Lake Como, and Versailles.

"Swell room!" chirped Leora.

Madeline had looked as though she intended to say the same thing in longer words, but she considered the frescoes all over again and explained, "Well, it's very large—"

He was ordering, with agony. He had appropriated four dollars for the orgy, strictly including the tip, and his standard of good food was that he must spend every cent of the four dollars. While he wondered what "Purée St. Germain" could be, and the waiter hideously stood watching behind his shoulder, Madeline fell to. She chanted with horrifying politeness:

"Mr. Arrowsmith tells me you are a nurse, Miss—Tozer."

"Yes, sort of."

"Do you find it interesting?"

"Well—yes—yes, I think it's interesting."

"I suppose it must be wonderful to relieve suffering. Of course my work—I'm taking my Doctor of Philosophy degree in English—" She made it sound as though she were taking her earldom—"it's rather dry and detached. I have to master the growth of the language and so on and so forth. With your practical training, I suppose you'd find that rather stupid."

"Yes, it must be—no, it must be very interesting."

"Do you come from Zenith, Miss—Tozer?"

"No, I come from— Just a little town. Well, hardly a town. . . . North Dakota."

"Oh! North Dakota!"

"Yes. . . . Way West."

"Oh, yes. . . . Are you staying East for some time?" It was precisely what a much-resented New York cousin had once said to Madeline.

"Well, I don't— Yes, I guess I may be here quite some time."

"Do you, uh, do you find you like it here?"

"Oh, yes, it's pretty nice. These big cities— So much to see."

"'Big'? Well, I suppose it all depends on the point of view, *doesn't* it? I always think of New York as big but— Of course— Do you find the contrast to North Dakota interesting?"

"Well, of course it's different."

"Tell me what North Dakota's like. I've always wondered about these Western states." It was Madeline's second plagiarism of her cousin. "What is the general impression it makes on you?"

"I don't think I know just how you mean."

"I mean what is the general effect? The—*impression.*"

"Well, it's got lots of wheat and lots of Swedes."

"But I mean— I suppose you're all terribly virile and energetic, compared with us Easterners."

"I don't— Well, yes, maybe."

"Have you met lots of people in Zenith?"

"Not so *awfully* many."

"Oh, have you met Dr. Birchall, that operates in your hospital? He's such a nice man, and not just a good surgeon but frightfully talented. He sings won-derfully, and he comes from the most frightfully nice family."

"No, I don't think I've met him yet," Leora bleated.

"Oh, you must. And he plays the slickest—the most gorgeous game of tennis. He always goes to all these millionaire parties on Royal Ridge. Frightfully smart."

Martin now first interrupted. "Smart? Him? He hasn't got any brains whatever."

"My dear child, I didn't mean 'smart' in that sense!" He sat alone and helpless while she again turned on Leora and ever more brightly inquired whether Leora knew this son of a corporation lawyer and that famous débutante, this hatshop and that club. She spoke familiarly of what were known as the Leaders of Zenith Society, the personages who appeared daily in the society columns of the *Advocate-Times*, the Cowxes and Van Antrims and Dodsworths. Martin was astonished by the familiarity; he remembered that she had once gone to a charity ball in Zenith but he had not known that she was so intimate with the peerage. Certainly Leora had appallingly never heard of these great ones, nor ever attended the concerts, the lectures, the recitals at which Madeline apparently spent all her glittering evenings.

Madeline shrugged a little, then, "Well— Of course with the fascinating doctors and everybody that you meet in the hospital, I suppose you'd find lectures frightfully tame. Well—" She dismissed Leora and looked patronizingly at Martin. "Are you planning some more work on the what-is-it with rabbits?"

He was grim. He could do it now, if he got it over quickly. "Madeline! Brought you two together because— Don't know whether you cotton to each other or not, but I wish you could, because I've— I'm not making any excuses for myself. I couldn't help it. I'm engaged to both of you, and I want to know—"

Madeline had sprung up. She had never looked quite so proud and fine. She stared at them, and walked away, wordless. She came back, she touched Leora's shoulder, and quietly kissed her. "Dear, I'm sorry for you. You've got a job! You poor baby!" She strode away, her shoulders straight.

Hunched, frightened, Martin could not look at Leora.

He felt her hand on his. He looked up. She was smiling, easy, a little mocking. "Sandy, I warn you that I'm never going to give you up. I suppose you're as bad as She says; I suppose I'm foolish—I'm a hussy. But you're mine! I warn you it isn't a bit of use your getting engaged to somebody else again. I'd tear her eyes out! Now don't think so well of yourself! I guess you're pretty selfish. But I don't care. You're mine!"

He said brokenly many things beautiful in their commonness.

She pondered, "I do feel we're nearer together than you and Her. Perhaps you like me better because you can bully me—because I tag after you and She never would. And I know your work is more important to you than I am, maybe more important than you are. But I am stupid and ordinary and She isn't. I simply admire you frightfully (Heaven knows why, but I do), while She has sense enough to make you admire Her and tag after Her."

"No! I swear it isn't because I can bully you, Leora—I swear it isn't—I don't think it is. Dearest, don't, *don't* think she's brighter than you are. She's glib but— Oh, let's stop talking! I've found you! My life's begun!"

Chapter VII

THE DIFFERENCE between Martin's relations to Madeline and to Leora was the difference between a rousing duel and a serene comradeship. From their first evening, Leora and he depended on each other's loyalty and liking, and certain things in his existence were settled forever. Yet his absorption in her was not stagnant. He was always making discoveries about the observations of life which she kept incubating in her secret little head while she made smoke rings with her cigarettes and smiled silently. He longed for the girl Leora; she stirred him, and with gay frank passion she answered him; but to another, sexless Leora he talked more honestly than to Gottlieb or his own worried self, while with her boyish nod or an occasional word she encouraged him to confidence in his evolving ambition and disdains.

II

Digamma Pi fraternity was giving a dance. It was understood among the anxiously whispering medics that so cosmopolitan was the University of Winnemac becoming that they were expected to wear the symbols of respectability known as "dress-suits." On the solitary and nervous occasion when Martin had worn evening clothes he had rented them from the Varsity Pantorium, but he must own them, now that he was going to introduce Leora to the world as his pride and flowering. Like two little old people, absorbed in each other and diffidently exploring new, unwelcoming streets of the city where their alienated children live, Martin and Leora edged into the garnished magnificence of Benson, Hanley and Koch's, the loftiest department store in Zenith. She was intimidated by the luminous cases of mahogany and plate glass, by the opera hats and lustrous mufflers and creamy riding breeches. When he had tried on a dinner suit and come out for her approval, his long brown tie and soft-collared shirt somewhat rustic behind the low evening waistcoat, and when the clerk had gone to fetch collars, she wailed:

"Darn it, Sandy, you're too grand for me. I just simply can't get myself to fuss over my clothes, and here you're going to go and look so spiffy I won't have a chance with you."

He almost kissed her.

The clerk, returning, warbled, "I think, Modom, you'll find that your husband will look vurry nice indeed in these wing collars."

Then, while the clerk sought ties, he did kiss her, and she sighed:

"Oh, gee, you're one of these people that get ahead. I never thought I'd have to live up to a man with a dress-suit and a come-to-Heaven collar. Oh, well, I'll tag!"

III

For the Digamma Ball, the University Armory was extremely decorated. The brick walls were dizzy with bunting, spotty with paper chrysanthemums and plaster skulls and wooden scalpels ten feet long.

In six years at Mohalis, Martin had gone to less than a score of dances, though the refined titillations of communal embracing were the chief delight of the co-educational university. When he arrived at the Armory, with Leora timorously brave in a blue crêpe de chine made in no recognized style, he did not care whether he had a single two-step, though he did achingly desire to have the men crowd in and ask Leora, admire her and make her welcome. Yet he was too proud to introduce her about, lest he seem to be begging his friends to dance with her. They stood alone, under the balcony, disconsolately facing the vastness of the floor, while beyond them flashed the current of dancers, beautiful, formidable, desirable. Leora and he had assured each other that, for a student affair, dinner jacket and black waistcoat would be the thing, as stated in the Benson, Hanley and Koch Chart of Correct Gents' Wearing Apparel, but he grew miserable at the sight of voluptuous white waistcoats, and when that embryo famous surgeon, Angus Duer, came by, disdainful as a greyhound and pushing on white gloves (which are the whitest, the most superciliously white objects on earth), then Martin felt himself a hobbledehoy.

"Come on, *we'll* dance," he said, as though it were a defiance to all Angus Duers.

He very much wanted to go home.

He did not enjoy the dance, though she waltzed easily and himself not too badly. He did not even enjoy having her in his arms. He could not believe that she was in his arms. As they revolved he saw Duer join a brilliance of pretty girls and distinguished-looking women about the great Dr. Silva, dean of the medical school. Angus seemed appallingly at home, and he waltzed off with the prettiest girl, sliding, swinging, deft. Martin tried to hate him as a fool, but he remembered that yesterday Angus had been elected to the honorary society of Sigma Xi.

Leora and he crept back to the exact spot beneath the balcony where they had stood before, to their den, their one safe refuge. While he tried to be nonchalant and talk up to his new clothes, he was cursing the men he saw go by laughing with girls, ignoring his Leora.

"Not many here yet," he fussed. "Pretty soon they'll all be coming, and then you'll have lots of dances."

"Oh, I don't mind."

("God, won't somebody come and ask the poor kid?")

He fretted over his lack of popularity among the dancing-men of the medical school. He wished Clif Clawson were present—Clif liked any sort of assembly, but he could not afford dress-clothes. Then, rejoicing as at sight of the best-beloved, he saw Irving Watters, that paragon of professional normality, wandering toward them, but Watters passed by, merely nodding. Thrice Martin hoped and desponded, and now all his pride was gone. If Leora could be happy—

"I wouldn't care a hoot if she fell for the gabbiest fusser in the whole U., and gave me the go-by all evening. Anything to let her have a good time! If I could coax Duer over— No, that's one thing I couldn't stand: crawling to that dirty snob— I will!"

Up ambled Fatty Pfaff, just arrived. Martin pounced on him lovingly. "H'lo, old Fat! You a stag to-night? Meet my friend Miss Tozer."

Fatty's bulbous eyes showed approval of Leora's cheeks and amber hair. He heaved, "Pleasedmeetch—dance starting—

have the honor?" in so flattering a manner that Martin could have kissed him.

That he himself stood alone through the dance did not occur to him. He leaned against a pillar and gloated. He felt gorgeously unselfish. . . . That various girl wallflowers were sitting near him, waiting to be asked, did not occur to him either.

He saw Fatty introduce Leora to a decorative pair of Digams, one of whom begged her for the next. Thereafter she had more invitations than she could take. Martin's excitement cooled. It seemed to him that she clung too closely to her partners, that she followed their steps too eagerly. After the fifth dance he was agitated. "Course! *She's* enjoying herself! Hasn't got time to notice that I just stand here—yes, by thunder, and hold her scarf! Sure! Fine for her. Fact I might like a little dancing myself— And the way she grins and gawps at that fool Brindle Morgan, the—the—the damnedest— Oh, you and I are going to have a talk, young woman! And those hounds trying to pinch her off me—the one thing I've ever loved! Just because they dance better than I can, and spiel a lot of foolishness— And that damn' orchestra playing that damn' peppery music— And she falling for all their damn' cheap compliments and— You and I are going to have one lovely little understanding!"

When she next returned to him, besieged by three capering medics, he muttered to her, "Oh, it doesn't *matter* about *me!*"

"Would you like this one? *Course* you shall have it!" She turned to him fully; she had none of Madeline's sense of having to act for the benefit of observers. Through a strained eternity of waiting, while he glowered, she babbled of the floor, the size of the room, and her "dandy partners." At the sound of the music he held out his arms.

"No," she said. "I want to talk to you." She led him to a corner and hurled at him, "Sandy, this is the last time I'm going to stand for your looking jealous. Oh, I know! See here! If we're going to stick together—and we are!—I'm going to dance with just as many men as I want to, and I'm going to be just as foolish with 'em as I want to. Dinners and those things—I suppose I'll always go on being a clam. Nothing to say. But I love dancing, and I'm going to do exactly what I want to, and if you had any sense whatever, you'd know I don't care a hang for anybody but you. Yours! Absolute. No matter what fool things you do—and they'll probably be a plenty. So when you go and get jealous on me again, you sneak off and get rid of it. Aren't you ashamed of yourself!"

"I wasn't jealous— Yes, I was. Oh, I can't help it! I love you so much. I'd be one fine lover, now wouldn't I, if I never got jealous!"

"All right. Only you've got to keep it under cover. Now we'll finish the dance."

He was her slave.

IV

It was regarded as immoral, at the University of Winnemac, to dance after midnight, and at that hour the guests crowded into the Imperial Cafeteria. Ordinarily it closed at eight, but to-night it kept open till one, and developed a spirit of almost lascivious mirth. Fatty Pfaff did a jig, another humorous student, with a napkin over his arm, pretended to be a waiter, and a girl (but she was much disapproved) smoked a cigarette.

At the door Clif Clawson was waiting for Martin and Leora. He was in his familiar shiny gray suit, with a blue flannel shirt.

Clif assumed that he was the authority to whom all of Martin's friends must be brought for judgment. He had not met Leora. Martin had confessed his double engagement; he had explained that Leora was unquestionably the most gracious young woman on earth; but as he had previously used up all of his laudatory adjectives and all of Clif's patience on the subject of Madeline, Clif failed to listen, and prepared to dislike Leora as another siren of morality.

He eyed her now with patronizing enmity. He croaked at Martin, behind her back, "Good-looking kid, I will say that for her—what's wrong with her?" When they had brought their own sandwiches and coffee and mosaic cake from the long counter, Clif rasped:

"Well, it's grand of a couple of dress-suit swells like you to assassinate with me 'mid the midmosts of sartorials and

Sassiety. Gosh, it's fierce I had to miss the select pleasures of an evening with Anxious Duer and associated highboys, and merely play a low game of poker—in which Father deftly removed the sum of six simolea, point ten, from the foregathered bums and yahoos. Well, Leory, I suppose you and Martykins here have now ratiocinated all these questions of polo and, uh, Monte Carlo and so on."

She had an immense power of accepting people as they were. While Clif waited, leering, she placidly investigated the inside of a chicken sandwich and assented, "Um-huh."

"Good boy! I thought you were going to pull that 'If you are a roughneck, I don't see why you think you've got to boast about it' stuff that Mart springs on me!"

Clif turned into a jovial and (for him) unusually quiet companion. . . . Ex-farmhand, ex-book-agent, ex-mechanic, he had so little money yet so scratching a desire to be resplendent that he took refuge in pride in poverty, pride in being offensive. Now, when Leora seemed to look through his boasting, he liked her as quickly as had Martin, and they buzzed with gaiety. Martin was warmed to benevolence toward mankind, including Angus Duer, who was at the end of the room at a table with Dean Silva and his silvery women. Without plan, Martin sprang up, raced down the room. Holding out his hand he clamored:

"Angus, old man, want to congratulate you on getting Sigma Xi. That's fine."

Duer regarded the outstretched hand as though it was an instrument which he had seen before but whose use he could not quite remember. He picked it up and shook it tentatively. He did not turn his back; he was worse than rude—he looked patient.

"Well, good luck," said Martin, chilled and shaky.

"Very good of you. Thanks."

Martin returned to Leora and Clif, to tell them the incident as a cosmic tragedy. They agreed that Angus Duer was to be shot. In the midst of it Duer came past, trailing after Dean Silva's party, and nodded to Martin, who glared back, feeling noble and mature.

At parting, Clif held Leora's hand and urged, "Honey, I think a lot of Mart, and one time I was afraid the old kid was going to get tied up to—to parties that would turn him into a hand-shaker. I'm a hand-shaker myself. I know less about medicine than Prof Robertshaw. But this boob has some conscience to him, and I'm so darn' glad he's playing around with a girl that's real folks and— Oh, listen at me fallin' all over my clumsy feet! But I just mean I hope you won't mind Uncle Clif saying he does by golly like you a lot!"

It was almost four when Martin returned from taking Leora home and sagged into bed. He could not sleep. The aloofness of Angus Duer racked him as an insult to himself, as somehow an implied insult to Leora, but his boyish rage had passed into a bleaker worry. Didn't Duer, for all his snobbishness and shallowness, have something that he himself lacked? Didn't Clif, with his puppy-dog humor, his speech of a vaudeville farmer, his suspicion of fine manners as posing, take life too easily? Didn't Duer know how to control and drive his hard little mind? Wasn't there a technique of manners as there was of experimentation. . . . Gottlieb's fluent bench-technique versus the clumsy and podgy hands of Ira Hinkley. . . . Or was all this inquiry a treachery, a yielding to Duer's own affected standard?

He was so tired that behind his closed eyelids were flashes of fire. His whirling mind flew over every sentence he had said or heard that night, till round his twisting body there was fevered shouting.

V

As he grumped across the medical campus next day, he came unexpectedly upon Angus and he was smitten with the guiltiness and embarrassment one has toward a person who has borrowed money and probably will not return it. Mechanically he began to blurt "Hello," but he checked it in a croak, scowled, and stumbled on.

"Oh, Mart," Angus called. He was dismayingly even. "Remember speaking to me last evening? It struck me when I was going out that you looked huffy. I was wondering if you thought I'd been rude. I'm sorry if you did. Fact is, I had a rotten headache. Look. I've got four tickets for 'As It Listeth,' in Zenith, next Friday evening—original New York cast! Like to see it? And I noticed you were with a peach, at the dance. Suppose she might like to go along with us, she and some friend of hers?"

"Why—gosh—I'll 'phone her—darn' nice of you to ask us—"

It was not till melancholy dusk, when Leora had accepted and promised to bring with her a probationer-nurse named Nelly Byers, that Martin began to brood:

"Wonder if he did have a headache last night?

"Wonder if somebody *gave* him the tickets?

"Why didn't he ask Dad Silva's daughter to go with us? Does he think Leora is some tart I've picked up?

"Sure, he never really quarrels with anybody—wants to keep us all friendly, so we'll send him surgical patients some day when we're hick G.P.'s and he's a Great and Only.

"Why did I crawl down so meekly?

"I don't care! If Leora enjoys it— Me personally, I don't care two hoots for all this trotting around— Though of course it isn't so bad to see pretty women in fine clothes, and be dressed as good as anybody— Oh, I don't *know!*"

VI

In the slightly Midwestern city of Zenith, the appearance of a play "with the original New York cast" was an event. (What play it was did not much matter.) The Dodsworth Theatre was splendid with the aristocracy from the big houses on Royal Ridge. Leora and Nelly Byers admired the bloods—graduates of Yale and Harvard and Princeton, lawyers and bankers, motor-manufacturers and inheritors of real estate, virtuosi of golf, familiars of New York—who with their shrill and glistening women occupied the front rows. Miss Byers pointed out the Dodsworths, who were often mentioned in *Town Topics*.

Leora and Miss Byers bounced with admiration of the hero when he refused the governorship; Martin worried because the heroine was prettier than Leora; and Angus Duer (who gave an appearance of knowing all about plays without having seen more than half a dozen in his life) admitted that the set depicting "Jack Vanduzen's Camp in the Adirondacks: Sunset, the Next Day" was really very nice.

Martin was in a mood of determined hospitality. He was going to give them supper and that was all there was to it. Miss Byers explained that they had to be in the hospital by a quarter after eleven, but Leora said lazily, "Oh, I don't care. I'll slip in through a window. If you're there in the morning, the Old Cat can't prove you got in late." Shaking her head at this lying wickedness, Miss Byers fled to a trolley car, while Leora, Angus, and Martin strolled to Epstein's Alt Nuremberg Café for beer and Swiss cheese sandwiches flavored by the sight of German drinking mottos and papier-mâché armor.

Angus was studying Leora, looking from her to Martin, watching their glances of affection. That a keen young man should make a comrade of a girl who could not bring him social advancement, that such a thing as the boy and girl passion between Martin and Leora could exist, was probably inconceivable to him. He decided that she was conveniently frail. He gave Martin a refined version of a leer, and set himself to acquiring her for his own uses.

"I hope you enjoyed the play," he condescended to her.

"Oh, yes—"

"Jove, I envy you two. Of course I understand why girls fall for Martin here, with his romantic eyes, but a grind like me, I have to go on working without a single person to give me sympathy. Oh, well, I deserve it for being shy of women."

With unexpected defiance from Leora: "When anybody says that, it means they're not shy, and they despise women."

"Despise them? Why, child, honestly, I long to be a Don Juan. But I don't know how. Won't you give me a lesson?" Angus's aridly correct voice had become lulling; he concentrated on Leora as he would have concentrated on dissecting a guinea pig. She smiled at Martin now and then to say, "Don't be jealous, idiot. I'm magnificently uninterested in this conceited hypnotist." But she was flustered by Angus's sleek assurance, by his homage to her eyes and wit and reticence.

Martin twitched with jealousy. He blurted that they must be going—Leora really had to be back— The trolleys ran infrequently after midnight and they walked to the hospital through hollow and sounding streets. Angus and Leora kept up a high-strung chatter, while Martin stalked beside them, silent, sulky, proud of being sulky. Skittering through a garage alley they came out on the mass of Zenith General Hospital, a block long, five stories of bleak windows with infrequent dim blotches of light. No one was about. The first floor was but five feet from the ground, and they lifted Leora up to the limestone ledge of a half-open corridor window. She slid in, whispering, "G' night! Thanks!"

Martin felt empty, dissatisfied. The night was full of a chill mournfulness. A light was suddenly flickering in a window above them, and there was a woman's scream breaking down into moans. He felt the tragedy of parting—that in the briefness of life he should lose one moment of her living presence.

"I'm going in after her; see she gets there safe," he said.

The frigid edge of the stone sill bit his hands, but he vaulted, thrust up his knee, crawled hastily through the window. Ahead of him, in the cork-floored hallway lit only by a tiny electric globe, Leora was tiptoeing toward a flight of stairs. He ran after her, on his toes. She squeaked as he caught her arm.

"We got to say good-night better than that!" he grumbled. "With that damn' Duer—"

"Ssssssh! They'd simply murder me if they caught you here. Do you want to get me fired?"

"Would you care, if it was because of me?"

"Yes—no—well— But they'd probably fire you from medic school, my lad. If—" His caressing hands could feel her shiver with anxiety. She peered along the corridor, and his quickened imagination created sneaking forms, eyes peering from doorways. She sighed, then, resolutely: "We can't talk here. We'll slip up to my room—roommate's away for the week. Stand there, in the shadow. If nobody in sight upstairs, I'll come back."

He followed her to the floor above, to a white door, then breathlessly inside. As he closed the door he was touched by this cramped refuge, with its camp-beds and photographs from home and softly wrinkled linen. He clasped her, but with hand against his chest she forbade him, as she mourned:

"You were jealous again! How can you distrust me so? With that fool! Women not like him? They wouldn't have a chance! Likes himself too well. And then you jealous!"

"I wasn't— Yes, I was, but I don't care! To have to sit there and grin like a hyena, with him between us, when I wanted to talk to you, to kiss you! All right! Probably I'll always be jealous. It's you that have got to trust me. I'm not easy-going; never will be. Oh, trust me—"

Their profound and unresisted kiss was the more blind in memory of that barren hour with Angus. They forgot that the superintendent of nurses might dreadfully come bursting in; they forgot that Angus was waiting. "Oh, curse Angus—let him go home!" was Martin's only reflection, as his eyes closed and his long loneliness vanished.

"Good night, dear love—my love forever," he exulted.

In the still ghostliness of the hall, he laughed as he thought of how irritably Angus must have marched away. But from the window he discovered Angus huddled on the stone steps, asleep. As he touched the ground, he whistled, but stopped short. He saw bursting from the shadow a bulky man, vaguely in a porter's uniform, who was shouting:

"I've caught yuh! Back you come into the hospital, and we'll find out what you've been up to!"

They closed. Martin was wiry, but in the watchman's clasp he was smothered. There was a reek of dirty overalls, of unbathed flesh. Martin kicked his shins, struck at his boulder of red cheek, tried to twist his arm. He broke loose, started to flee, and halted. The struggle, in its contrast to the aching sweetness of Leora, had infuriated him. He faced the watchman, raging.

From the awakened Angus, suddenly appearing beside him, there was a thin sound of disgust. "Oh, come *on!* Let's get out of this. Why do you dirty your hands on scum like him?"

The watchman bellowed, "Oh, I'm scum, am I? I'll show you!"

He collared Angus and slapped him.

Under the sleepy street-lamp, Martin saw a man go mad. It was not the unfeeling Angus Duer who stared at the watchman; it was a killer, and his eyes were the terrible eyes of the killer, speaking to the least experienced a message of death.

He gasped only, "He dared to touch me!" A pen-knife was somehow in his hands, he had leaped at the watchman, and he was busily and earnestly endeavoring to cut his throat.

As Martin tried to hold them he heard the agitated pounding of a policeman's night stick on the pavement. Martin was slim but he had pitched hay and strung telephone wire. He hit the watchman, judiciously, beside the left ear, snatched Angus's wrist, and dragged him away. They ran up an alley, across a courtyard. They came to a thoroughfare as an owl trolley glowed and rattled round the corner; they ran beside it, swung up on the steps, and were safe.

Angus stood on the back platform, sobbing. "My God, I wish I'd killed him! He laid his filthy hands on me! Martin! Hold me here on the car. I thought I'd got over that. Once when I was a kid I tried to kill a fellow— God, I wish I'd cut that filthy swine's throat!"

As the trolley came into the center of the city, Martin coaxed, "There's an all-night lunch up Oberlin Avenue where we can get some white mule. Come on. It'll straighten you up."

Angus was shaky and stumbling—Angus the punctilious. Martin led him into the lunch-room where, between catsup bottles, they had raw whisky in granite-like coffee cups. Angus leaned his head on his arm and sobbed, careless of stares, till he had drunk himself into obliteration, and Martin steered him home. Then to Martin, in his furnished room with Clif snoring, the evening became incredible and nothing more incredible than Angus Duer. "Well, he'll be a good friend of mine now, for always. Fine!"

Next morning, in the hall of the Anatomy Building, he saw Angus and rushed toward him. Angus snapped, "You were frightfully stewed last night, Arrowsmith. If you can't handle your liquor better than that, you better cut it out entirely."

He walked on, clear-eyed, unruffled.

Chapter VIII

AND ALWAYS Martin's work went on—assisting Max Gottlieb, instructing bacteriological students, attending lectures and hospital demonstrations—sixteen merciless hours to the day. He stole occasional evenings for original research or for peering into the stirring worlds of French and German bacteriological publications; he went proudly now and then to Gottlieb's cottage where, against rain-smeared brown wall-paper, were Blake drawings and a signed portrait of Koch. But the rest was nerve-gnawing.

Neurology, O.B., internal medicine, physical diagnosis; always a few pages more than he could drudge through before he fell asleep at his rickety study-table.

Memorizing of gynecology, of ophthalmology, till his mind was burnt raw.

Droning afternoons of hospital demonstrations, among stumbling students barked at by tired clinical professors.

The competitive exactions of surgery on dogs, in which Angus Duer lorded it with impatient perfection.

Martin admired the professor of internal medicine, T.J.H. Silva, known as "Dad" Silva, who was also dean of the medical faculty. He was a round little man with a little crescent of mustache. Silva's god was Sir William Osler, his religion was the art of sympathetic healing, and his patriotism was accurate physical diagnosis. He was a Doc Vickerson of Elk Mills, grown wiser and soberer and more sure. But Martin's reverence for Dean Silva was counterbalanced by his detestation for Dr. Roscoe Geake, professor of otolaryngology.

Roscoe Geake was a pedler. He would have done well with oil stock. As an otolaryngologist he believed that tonsils had been placed in the human organism for the purpose of providing specialists with closed motors. A physician who left the tonsils in any patient was, he felt, foully and ignorantly overlooking his future health and comfort—the physician's future health and comfort. His earnest feeling regarding the nasal septum was that it never hurt any patient to have part of it removed, and if the most hopeful examination could find nothing the matter with the patient's nose and throat except that he was smoking too much, still, in any case, the enforced rest after an operation was good for him. Geake denounced this cant about Letting Nature Alone. Why, the average well-to-do man appreciated attention! He really didn't think much of his specialists unless he was operated on now and then—just a little and not very painfully. Geake had one classic annual address in which, winging far above otolaryngology, he evaluated all medicine, and explained to grateful healers like Irving Watters the method of getting suitable fees:

"Knowledge is the greatest thing in the medical world but it's no good whatever unless you can sell it, and to do this you must first impress your personality on the people who have the dollars. Whether a patient is a new or an old friend, you must always use *salesmanship* on him. Explain to him, also to his stricken and anxious family, the hard work and thought you are giving to his case, and so make him feel that the good you have done him, or intend to do him, is even greater than the fee you plan to charge. Then, when he gets your bill, he will not misunderstand or kick."

II

There was, as yet, no vision in Martin of serene spaciousness of the mind. Beyond doubt he was a bustling young man, and rather shrill. He had no uplifted moments when he saw himself in relation to the whole world—if indeed he realized that there was a deal of the world besides himself. His friend Clif was boorish, his beloved Leora was rustic, however gallant she might be, and he himself wasted energy in hectic busyness and in astonishment at dullness. But if he had not ripened, yet he was close to earth, he did hate pretentiousness, he did use his hands, and he did seek iron actualities with a curiosity inextinguishable.

And at infrequent times he perceived the comedy of life; relaxed for a gorgeous hour from the intensity wearing to his admirers. Such was the hour before Christmas vacation when Roscoe Geake rose to glory.

It was announced in the *Winnemac Daily News* that Dr. Geake had been called from the chair of otolaryngology to the vice-presidency of the puissant New Idea Medical Instrument and Furniture Company of Jersey City. In celebration he gave a final address to the entire medical school on "The Art and Science of Furnishing the Doctor's Office."

He was a neatly finished person, Geake, eye-glassed and enthusiastic and fond of people. He beamed on his loving students and cried:

"Gentlemen, the trouble with too many doctors, even those splendid old pioneer war-horses who through mud and storm, through winter's chill blast and August's untempered heat, go bringing cheer and surcease from pain to the world's humblest, yet even these old Nestors not so infrequently settle down in a rut and never shake themselves loose. Now that I am leaving this field where I have labored so long and happily, I want to ask every man jack of you to read, before you begin to practise medicine, not merely your Rosenau and Howell and Gray, but also, as a preparation for being that which all good citizens must be, namely, practical men, a most valuable little manual of modern psychology, 'How to Put Pep in Salesmanship,' by Grosvenor A. Bibby. For don't forget, gentlemen, and this is my last message to you, the man worth while is not merely the man who takes things with a smile but also the man who's trained in philosophy, *practical* philosophy, so that instead of day-dreaming and spending all his time talking about 'ethics,' splendid though they are, and 'charity,' glorious virtue though that be, yet he never forgets that unfortunately the world judges a man by the amount of good hard cash he can lay away. The graduates of the University of Hard Knocks judge a physician as they judge a business man, not merely by his alleged 'high ideals' but by the horse-power he puts into carrying them out—and making them pay! And from a scientific standpoint, don't overlook the fact that the impression of properly remunerated competence which you make on a patient is of just as much importance, in these days of the new psychology, as the drugs you get into him or the operations he lets you get away with. The minute he begins to see that other folks appreciate and reward your skill, that minute he must begin to feel your power and so to get well.

"Nothing is more important in inspiring him than to have such an office that as soon as he steps into it, you have begun to sell him the idea of being properly cured. I don't care whether a doctor has studied in Germany, Munich, Baltimore, and Rochester. I don't care whether he has all science at his finger-tips, whether he can instantly diagnose with a considerable degree of accuracy the most obscure ailment, whether he has the surgical technique of a Mayo, a Crile, a Blake, an Ochsner, a Cushing. If he has a dirty old office, with hand-me-down chairs and a lot of second-hand magazines, then the patient isn't going to have confidence in him; he is going to resist the treatment—and the doctor is going to have difficulty in putting over and collecting an adequate fee.

"To go far below the surface of this matter into the fundamental philosophy and esthetics of office-furnishing for the doctor, there are to-day two warring schools, the Tapestry School and the Aseptic School, if I may venture to so denominate and conveniently distinguish them. Both of them have their merits. The Tapestry School claims that luxurious chairs for waiting patients, handsome hand-painted pictures, a bookcase jammed with the world's best literature in expensively bound sets, together with cut-glass vases and potted palms, produce an impression of that opulence which can come only from sheer ability and knowledge. The Aseptic School, on the other hand, maintains that what the patient wants is that appearance of scrupulous hygiene which can be produced only by furnishing the outer waiting-room as well as the inner offices in white-painted chairs and tables, with merely a Japanese print against a gray wall.

"But, gentlemen, it seems obvious to me, so obvious that I wonder it has not been brought out before, that the ideal reception-room is a combination of these two schools! Have your potted palms and handsome pictures—to the practical physician they are as necessary a part of his working equipment as a sterilizer or a Baumanometer. But so far as possible have everything in sanitary-looking white—and think of the color-schemes you can evolve, or the good wife for you, if she be one blessed with artistic tastes! Rich golden or red cushions, in a Morris chair enameled the purest white! A floor-covering of white enamel, with just a border of delicate rose! Recent and unspotted numbers of expensive magazines, with art covers, lying on a white table! Gentlemen, there is the idea of imaginative salesmanship which I wish to leave with you; there is the gospel which I hope to spread in my fresh field of endeavor, the New Ideal Instrument Company of Jersey City, where at any time I shall be glad to see and shake by the hand any and all of you."

III

Through the storm of his Christmas examinations, Martin had an intensified need of Leora. She had been summoned home to Dakota, perhaps for months, on the ground that her mother was unwell, and he had, or thought he had, to see her daily. He must have slept less than four hours a night. Grinding at examinations on the interurban car, he dashed in to her, looking up to scowl when he thought of the lively interns and the men patients whom she met in the hospital, scorning himself for being so primitive, and worrying all over again. To see her at all, he had to wait for hours in the lobby, or walk up and down in the snow outside till she could slip to a window and peep out. When they were together, they were completely absorbed. She had a genius for frank passion; she teased him, tantalized him, but she was tender and unafraid.

He was sick lonely when he saw her off at the Union Station.

His examination papers were competent but, save in bacteriology and internal medicine, they were sketchy. He turned emptily to the laboratory for vacation time.

He had so far displayed more emotion than achievement in his tiny original researches. Gottlieb was patient. "It iss a fine system, this education. All what we cram into the students, not Koch and two dieners could learn. Do not worry about the research. We shall do it yet." But he expected Martin to perform a miracle or two in the whole fortnight of the holidays and Martin had no stomach with which to think. He played in the laboratory; he spent his time polishing glassware, and when he transplanted cultures from his rabbits, his notes were incomplete.

Gottlieb was instantly grim. "*Wass giebt es dann?* Do you call these notes? Always when I praise a man must he stop working? Do you think that you are a Theobald Smith or a

Novy that you should sit and meditate? You have the ability of Pfaff!"

For once, Martin was impenitent. He mumbled to himself, as Gottlieb stamped out like a Grand Duke, "Rats, I've got *some* rest coming to me. Gosh, most fellows, why, they go to swell homes for vacation, and have dances and fathers and everything. If Leora was here, we'd go to a show to-night."

He viciously seized his cap (a soggy and doubtful object), sought Clif Clawson, who was spending the vacation in sleeping between poker games at Barney's, and outlined a project of going into town and getting drunk. It was executed so successfully that during vacation it was repeated whenever he thought of the coming torture-wheel of uninspiring work, whenever he realized that it was only Gottlieb and Leora who held him here. After vacation, in late January, he found that whisky relieved him from the frenzy of work, from the terror of loneliness—then betrayed him and left him the more weary, the more lonely. He felt suddenly old; he was twenty-four now, he reminded himself, and a schoolboy, his real work not even begun. Clif was his refuge; Clif admired Leora and would listen to his babbling of her.

But Clif and Martin came to the misfortune of Founder's Day.

IV

January thirtieth, the birthday of the late Dr. Warburton Stonedge, founder of the medical department of Winnemac, was annually celebrated by a banquet rich in fraternalism and speeches and large lack of wine. All the faculty reserved their soundest observations for the event, and all the students were expected to be present.

This year it was held in the large hall of the University Y.M.C.A., a moral apartment with red wall paper, portraits of whiskered alumni who had gone out to be missionaries, and long thin pine boxes intended to resemble exposed oak beams. About the famous guests—Dr. Rouncefield the Chicago surgeon, a diabetes specialist from Omaha, a Pittsburg internist—stood massed the faculty members. They tried to look festal, but they were worn and nervous after four months of school. They had wrinkles and tired eyes. They were all in business suits, mostly unpressed. They sounded scientific and interested; they used words like phlebarteriectasia and hepatocholangio-enterostomy, and they asked the guests, "So you just been in Rochester? What's, uh, what're Charley and Will doing in orthopedics?" But they were full of hunger and melancholy. It was half-past seven, and they who did not normally dine at seven, dined at six-thirty.

Upon this seedy gaiety entered a splendor, a tremendous black-bearded personage, magnificent of glacial shirt-bosom, vast of brow, wild-eyed with genius or with madness. In a marvelous great voice, with a flavor of German accent, he inquired for Dr. Silva, and sailed into the dean's group like a frigate among fishing-smacks.

"Who the dickens is that?" wondered Martin.

"Let's edge in and find out," said Clif, and they clung to the fast increasing knot about Dean Silva and the mystery, who was introduced as Dr. Benoni Carr, the pharmacologist.

They heard Dr. Carr, to the pale admiration of the school-bound assistant professors, boom genially of working with Schmiedeberg in Germany on the isolation of dihydroxypentamethylendiamin, of the possibilities of chemotherapy, of the immediate cure of sleeping sickness, of the era of scientific healing. "Though I am American-born, I have the advantage of speaking German from a child, and so perhaps I can better understand the work of my dear friend Ehrlich. I saw him receive a decoration from His Imperial Highness the Kaiser. Dear old Ehrlich, he was like a child!"

There was at this time (but it changed curiously in 1914 and 1915) an active Germanophile section of the faculty. They bent before this tornado of erudition. Angus Duer forgot that he was Angus Duer; and Martin listened with excited stimulation. Benoni Carr had all of Gottlieb's individuality, all his scorn of machine-made teachers, all his air of a great world which showed Mohalis as provincial, with none of Gottlieb's nervous touchiness. Martin wished Gottlieb were present; he wondered whether the two giants would clash.

Dr. Carr was placed at the speakers' table, near the dean. Martin was astonished to see the eminent pharmacologist, after a shocked inspection of the sour chicken and mishandled salad which made up most of the dinner, pour something into his water glass from a huge silver flask—and pour that something frequently. He became boisterous. He leaned across two men to slap the indignant dean on the shoulder; he contradicted his neighbors; he sang a stanza of "I'm Bound Away for the Wild Missourai."

Few phenomena at the dinner were so closely observed by the students as the manners of Dr. Benoni Carr.

After an hour of strained festivity, when Dean Silva had risen to announce the speakers, Carr lumbered to his feet and shouted, "Let's not have any speeches. Only fools make speeches. Wise men sing songs. Whoopee! Oh, tireolee, oh, tireolee, oh, tireolee a lady! You profs are the bunk!"

Dean Silva was to be seen beseeching him, then leading him out of the room, with the assistance of two professors and a football tackle, and in the hush of a joyful horror Clif grunted to Martin:

"Here's where I get mine! And the damn' fool promised to stay sober!"

"Huh?"

"I might of known he'd show up stewed and spill the beans. Oh, maybe the dean won't hand me hell proper!"

He explained. Dr. Benoni Carr was born Benno Karkowski. He had graduated from a medical school which gave degrees in two years. He had read vastly, but he had never been in Europe. He had been "spieler" in medicine shows, chiropodist, spiritualist medium, esoteric teacher, head of sanitariums for the diversion of neurotic women. Clif had encountered him in Zenith, when they were both drunk. It was Clif who had told Dean Silva that the celebrated pharmacologist, just back from Europe, was in Zenith for a few days and perhaps might accept an invitation—

The dean had thanked Clif ardently.

The banquet ended early, and there was inadequate attention to Dr. Rouncefield's valuable address on the Sterilization of Catgut.

Clif sat up worrying, and admitting the truth of Martin's several observations. Next day—he had a way with women when he deigned to take the trouble—he pumped the dean's girl secretary, and discovered his fate. There had been a meeting of a faculty committee; the blame for the Benoni Carr outrage had been placed on Clif; and the dean had said all the things Clif had imagined, with a number which he had not possessed the talent to conceive. But the dean was not going to summon him at once; he was going to keep him waiting in torture, then execute him in public.

"Good-by, old M.D. degree! Rats, I never thought much of the doctor business. Guess I'll be a bond salesman," said Clif to Martin. He strolled away, he went to the dean, and remarked:

"Oh, Dean Silva, I just dropped in to tell you I've decided to resign from the medic school. Been offered a big job in, uh, in Chicago, and I don't think much of the way you run the school, anyway. Too much memorizing and too little real spirit of science. Good luck, Doc. So long."

"Gggggg—" said Dean Silva.

Clif moved into Zenith, and Martin was left alone. He gave up the double room at the front of his boarding-house for a hall-room at the rear, and in that narrow den he sat and mourned in a desolation of loneliness. He looked out on a vacant lot in which a tattered advertisement of pork and beans flapped on a leaning billboard. He saw Leora's eyes and heard Clif's comfortable scoffing, and the quiet was such as he could not endure.

Chapter IX

THE PERSISTENT yammer of a motor horn drew Martin to the window of the laboratory, a late afternoon in February. He looked down on a startling roadster, all streamlines and cream paint, with enormous headlights. He slowly made out that the driver, a young man in coffee-colored loose motor coat and hectic checked cap and intense neckwear, was Clif Clawson, and that Clif was beckoning.

He hastened down, and Clif cried:

"Oh, boy! How do you like the boat? Do you diagnose this suit? Scotch heather—honest! Uncle Clif has nabbed off a twenty-five-buck-a-week job *with* commissions, selling autos. Boy, I was lost in your old medic school. I can sell anything to anybody. In a year I'll be making eighty a week. Jump in, old son. I'm going to take you in to the Grand and blow you to the handsomest feed you ever stuffed into your skinny organism."

The thirty-eight miles an hour at which Clif drove into Zenith was, in 1908, dismaying speed. Martin discovered a new Clif. He was as noisy as ever, but more sure, glowing with schemes for immediately acquiring large sums of money. His hair, once bushy and greasy in front, tending to stick out jaggedly behind, was sleek now, and his face had the pinkness of massage. He stopped at the fabulous Grand Hotel with a jar of brakes; before he left the car he changed his violent yellow driving-gauntlets for a pair of gray gloves with black stitching, which he immediately removed as he paraded through the lobby. He called the coat-girl "Sweetie," and at the dining-room door he addressed the head-waiter:

"Ah, Gus, how's the boy, how's the boy feeling to-night? How's the mucho famoso majordomoso? Gus, want to make you 'quainted with Dr. Arrowsmith. Any time the doc comes here I want you to shake a leg and hand him out that well-known service, my boy, and give him anything he wants, and if he's broke, you charge it to me. Now, Gus, I want a nice little table for two, with garage and hot and cold water, and wouldst fain have thy advice, Gustavus, on the oysters and hore duffers and all the ingredients fair of a Mæcenan feast."

"Yes, sir, right this way, Mr. Clawson," breathed the head-waiter.

Clif whispered to Martin, "I've got him like that in two weeks! You watch my smoke!"

While Clif was ordering, a man stopped beside their table. He resembled an earnest traveling-man who liked to get back to his suburban bungalow every Saturday evening. He was beginning to grow slightly bald, slightly plump. His rimless eye-glasses, in the midst of a round smooth face, made him seem innocent. He stared about as though he wished he had some one with whom to dine. Clif darted up, patted the man's elbow, and bawled:

"Ah, there, Babski, old boy. Feeding with anybody? Come join the Sporting Gents' Association."

"All right, be glad to. Wife's out of town," said the man.

"Shake hands with Dr. Arrowsmith. Mart, meet George F. Babbitt, the hoch-gecelebrated Zenith real-estate king. Mr. Babbitt has just adorned his thirty-fourth birthday by buying his first benzine buggy from yours truly and beg to remain as always."

It was, at least on the part of Clif and Mr. Babbitt, a mirthful affair, and when Martin had joined them in cocktails, St. Louis beer, and highballs, he saw that Clif was the most generous person now living, and Mr. George F. Babbitt a companion of charm.

Clif explained how certain he was—apparently his distinguished medical training had something to do with it—to be president of a motor factory, and Mr. Babbitt confided:

"You fellows are a lot younger than I am, eight-ten years, and you haven't learned yet, like I have, that where the big pleasure is, is in Ideals and Service and a Public Career. Now just between you and me and the gatepost, my vogue doesn't lie in real estate but in oratory. Fact, one time I planned to study law and go right in for politics. Just between ourselves, and I don't want this to go any farther, I've been making some pretty good affiliations lately—been meeting some of the rising young Republican politicians. Of course a fellow has got to start in modestly, but I may say, *sotto voce*, that I expect to run for alderman next fall. It's practically only a step from that to mayor and then to governor of the state, and if

I find the career suits me, there's no reason why in ten or twelve years, say in 1918 or 1920, I shouldn't have the honor of representing the great state of Winnemac in Washington, D.C.!"

In the presence of a Napoleon like Clif and a Gladstone like George F. Babbitt, Martin perceived his own lack of power and business skill, and when he had returned to Mohalis he was restless. Of his poverty he had rarely thought, but now, in contrast to Clif's rich ease, his own shabby clothes and his pinched room seemed shameful.

II

A long letter from Leora, hinting that she might not be able to return to Zenith, left him the more lonely. Nothing seemed worth doing. In that listless state he was mooning about the laboratory during elementary bacteriology demonstration hour, when Gottlieb sent him to the basement to bring up six male rabbits for inoculation. Gottlieb was working eighteen hours a day on new experiments; he was jumpy and testy; he gave orders like insults. When Martin came dreamily back with six females instead of males, Gottlieb shrieked at him, "You are the worst fool that was ever in this lab!"

The groundlings, second-year men who were not unmindful of Martin's own scoldings, tittered like small animals, and jarred him into raging, "Well, I couldn't make out what you said. And it's the first time I ever fell down. I won't stand your talking to me like that!"

"You will stand anything I say! Clumsy! You can take your hat and get out!"

"You mean I'm fired as assistant?"

"I am glad you haf enough intelligence to understand that, no matter how wretchet I talk!"

Martin flung away. Gottlieb suddenly looked bewildered and took a step toward Martin's retreating back. But the class, the small giggling animals, they stood delighted, hoping for more, and Gottlieb shrugged, glared them into terror, sent the least awkward of them for the rabbits, and went on, curiously quiet.

And Martin, at Barney's dive, was hotly drinking the first of the whiskys which sent him wandering all night, by himself. With each drink he admitted that he had an excellent chance to become a drunkard, and with each he boasted that he did not care. Had Leora been nearer than Wheatsylvania, twelve hundred miles away, he would have fled to her for salvation. He was still shaky next morning, and he had already taken a drink to make it possible to live through the morning when he received the note from Dean Silva bidding him report to the office at once.

The dean lectured:

"Arrowsmith, you've been discussed a good deal by the faculty council of late. Except in one or two courses—in my own I have no fault to find—you have been very inattentive. Your marks have been all right, but you could do still better. Recently you have also been drinking. You have been seen in places of very low repute, and you have been intimate with a man who took it upon himself to insult me, the Founder, our guests, and the University. Various faculty members have complained of your superior attitude—making fun of our courses right out in class! But Dr. Gottlieb has always warmly defended you. He insisted that you have a real flair for investigative science. Last night, however, he admitted that you had recently been impertinent to him. Now unless you immediately turn over a new leaf, young man, I shall have to suspend you for the rest of the year and, if that doesn't do the work, I shall have to ask for your resignation. And I think it might be a good thing for your humility—you seem to have the pride of the devil, young man!—it might be a good idea for you to see Dr. Gottlieb and start off your reformation by apologizing—"

It was the whisky spoke, not Martin:

"I'm damned if I will! He can go to the devil! I've given him my life, and then he tattles on me—"

"That's absolutely unfair to Dr. Gottlieb. He merely—"

"Sure. He merely let me down. I'll see him in hell before I'll apologize, after the way I've worked for him. And as for Clif Clawson that you were hinting at—him 'take it on himself to insult anybody'? He just played a joke, and you went after his scalp. I'm glad he did it!"

Then Martin waited for the words that would end his scientific life.

The little man, the rosy, pudgy, good little man, he stared and hummed and spoke softly:

"Arrowsmith, I could fire you right now, of course, but I believe you have good stuff in you. I decline to let you go. Naturally, you're suspended, at least till you come to your senses and apologize to me and to Gottlieb." He was fatherly; almost he made Martin repent; but he concluded, "And as for Clawson, his 'joke' regarding this Benoni Carr person—and why I never looked the fellow up is beyond me, I suppose I was too busy—his 'joke,' as you call it, was the action either of an idiot or a blackguard, and until you are able to perceive that fact, I don't think you will be ready to come back to us."

"All right," said Martin, and left the room.

He was very sorry for himself. The real tragedy, he felt, was that though Gottlieb had betrayed him and ended his career, ended the possibility of his mastering science and of marrying Leora, he still worshiped the man.

He said good-by to no one in Mohalis save his landlady. He packed, and it was a simple packing. He stuffed his books, his notes, a shabby suit, his inadequate linen, and his one glory, the dinner clothes, into his unwieldy imitation-leather bag. He remembered with drunken tears the hour of buying the dinner jacket.

Martin's money, from his father's tiny estate, came in bimonthly checks from the bank at Elk Mills. He had now but six dollars.

In Zenith he left his bag at the interurban trolley station and sought Clif, whom he found practising eloquence over a beautiful pearl-gray motor hearse, in which a beer-fed undertaker was jovially interested. He waited, sitting hunched and twisted on the steel running-board of a limousine. He resented but he was too listless to resent greatly the stares of the other salesmen and the girl stenographers.

Clif dashed up, bumbling, "Well, well, how's the boy? Come out and catchum little drink."

"I could use one."

Martin knew that Clif was staring at him. As they entered the bar of the Grand Hotel, with its paintings of lovely but absent-minded ladies, its mirrors, its thick marble rail along a mahogany bar, he blurted:

"Well, I got mine, too. Dad Silva's fired me, for general footlessness. I'm going to bum around a little and then get some kind of a job. God, but I'm tired and nervous! Say, can you lend me some money?"

"You bet. All I've got. How much you want?"

"Guess I'll need a hundred dollars. May drift around quite some time."

"Golly, I haven't got that much, but prob'ly I can raise it at the office. Here, sit down at this table and wait for me."

How Clif obtained the hundred dollars has never been explained, but he was back with it in a quarter-hour. They went on to dinner, and Martin had much too much whisky. Clif took him to his own boarding-house—which was decidedly less promissory of prosperity than Clif's clothes—firmly gave him a cold bath to bring him to, and put him to bed. Next morning he offered to find a job for him, but Martin refused and left Zenith by the northbound train at noon.

Always, in America, there remains from pioneer days a cheerful pariahdom of shabby young men who prowl causelessly from state to state, from gang to gang, in the power of the Wanderlust. They wear black sateen shirts, and carry bundles. They are not permanently tramps. They have home towns to which they return, to work quietly in the factory or the section-gang for a year—for a week—and as quietly to disappear again. They crowd the smoking cars at night; they sit silent on benches in filthy stations; they know all the land yet of it they know nothing, because in a hundred cities they see only the employment agencies, the all-night lunches, the blind-pigs, the scabrous lodging-houses. Into that world of voyageurs Martin vanished. Drinking steadily, only half-conscious of whither he was going, of what he desired to do, shamefully haunted by Leora and Clif and the swift hands of Gottlieb, he flitted from Zenith to the city of Sparta, across to Ohio, up into Michigan, west to Illinois. His mind was a shambles. He could never quite remember, afterward, where he had been. Once, it is clear, he was soda-fountain clerk in a Minnemagantic drug-store. Once he must have been, for a week, dishwasher in the stench of a cheap restaurant. He wandered by freight trains, on blind baggages, on foot. To his fellow prospectors he was known as "Slim," the worst-tempered and most restless of all their company.

After a time a sense of direction began to appear in his crazy drifting. He was instinctively headed westward, and to the west, toward the long prairie dusk, Leora was waiting. For a day or two he stopped drinking. He woke up feeling not like the sickly hobo called "Slim," but like Martin Arrowsmith, and he pondered, with his mind running clear, "Why shouldn't I go back? Maybe this hasn't been so bad for me. I was working too hard. I was pretty high-strung. Blew up. Like to, uh— Wonder what happened to my rabbits? . . . Will they ever let me do research again?"

But to return to the University before he had seen Leora was impossible. His need of her was an obsession, making the rest of earth absurd and worthless. He had, with blurry cunning, saved most of the hundred dollars he had taken from Clif; he had lived—very badly, on grease-swimming stews and soda-reeking bread—by what he earned along the way. Suddenly, on no particular day, in no particular town in Wisconsin, he stalked to the station, bought a ticket to Wheatsylvania, North Dakota, and telegraphed to Leora, "Coming 2:43 tomorrow Wednesday Sandy."

III

He crossed the wide Mississippi into Minnesota. He changed trains at St. Paul; he rolled into gusty vastnesses of snow, cut by thin lines of fence-wire. He felt free, in release from the little fields of Winnemac and Ohio, in relaxation from the shaky nerves of midnight study and midnight booziness. He remembered his days of wire-stringing in Montana and regained that careless peace. Sunset was a surf of crimson, and by night, when he stepped from the choking railroad coach and tramped the platform at Sauk Center, he drank the icy air and looked up to the vast and solitary winter stars. The fan of the Northern Lights frightened and glorified the sky. He returned to the coach with the energy of that courageous land. He nodded and gurgled in brief smothering sleep; he sprawled on the seat and talked with friendly fellow vagrants;

he drank bitter coffee and ate enormously of buckwheat cakes at a station restaurant; and so, changing at anonymous towns, he came at last to the squatty shelters, the two wheat-elevators, the cattle-pen, the oil-tank, and the red box of a station with its slushy platform, which composed the outskirts of Wheatsylvania. Against the station, absurd in a huge coon-skin coat, stood Leora. He must have looked a little mad as he stared at her from the vestibule, as he shivered with the wind. She lifted to him her two open hands, childish in red mittens. He ran down, he dropped his awkward bag on the platform and, unaware of the gaping furry farmers, they were lost in a kiss.

Years after, in a tropic noon, he remembered the freshness of her wind-cooled cheeks.

The train was gone, pounding out of the tiny station. It had stood like a dark wall beside the platform, protecting them, but now the light from the snowfields glared in on them and left them exposed and self-conscious.

"What—what's happened?" she fluttered. "No letters. I was so frightened."

"Off bumming. The dean suspended me—being fresh to profs. D' y' care?"

"Course not, if you wanted to—"

"I've come to marry you."

"I don't see how we can, dearest, but— All right. There'll be a lovely row with Dad." She laughed. "He's always so surprised and *hurt* when anything happens that he didn't plan out. It'll be nice to have you with me in the scrap, because you aren't supposed to know that he expects to plan out everything for everybody and— Oh, Sandy, I've been so lonely for you! Mother isn't really a bit sick, not the least bit, but they go on keeping me here. I think probably somebody hinted to Dad that folks were saying he must be broke, if his dear little daughter had to go off and learn nursing, and he hasn't worried it all out yet—it takes Andrew Jackson Tozer about a year to worry out anything. Oh, Sandy! You're here!"

After the clatter and jam of the train, the village seemed blankly empty. He could have walked around the borders of Wheatsylvania in ten minutes. Probably to Leora one building differed from another—she appeared to distinguish between the general store of Norblom and that of Frazier & Lamb—but to Martin the two-story wooden shacks creeping aimlessly along the wide Main Street were featureless and inappreciable. Then "There's our house, end of the next block," said Leora, as they turned the corner at the feed and implement store, and in a panic of embarrassment Martin wanted to halt. He saw a storm coming: Mr. Tozer denouncing him as a failure who desired to ruin Leora, Mrs. Tozer weeping.

"Say—say—say—have you told 'em about me?" he stammered.

"Yes. Sort of. I said you were a wonder in medic school, and maybe we'd get married when you finished your interneship, and then when your wire came, they wanted to know why you were coming, and why it was you wired from Wisconsin, and what color necktie you had on when you were sending the wire, and I couldn't make 'em understand I didn't know. They discussed it. Quite a lot. They do discuss things. All through supper. Solemn. Oh, Sandy, do curse and swear some at meals."

He was in a funk. Her parents, formerly amusing figures in a story, became oppressively real in sight of the wide, brown, porchy house. A large plate-glass window with a colored border had recently been cut through the wall, as a sign of prosperity, and the garage was new and authoritative.

He tagged after Leora, expecting the blast. Mrs. Tozer opened the door, and stared at him plaintively—a thin, faded, unhumorous woman. She bowed as though he was not so much unwelcome as unexplained and doubtful.

"Will you show Mr. Arrowsmith his room, Ory, or shall I?" she peeped.

It was the kind of house that has a large phonograph but no books, and if there were any pictures, as beyond hope there must have been, Martin never remembered them. The bed in his room was lumpy but covered with a chaste figured spread, and the flowery pitcher and bowl rested on a cover embroidered in red with lambs, frogs, water lilies, and a pious motto.

He took as long as he could in unpacking things which needed no unpacking, and hesitated down the stairs. No one was in the parlor, which smelled of furnace-heat and balsam pillows; then, from nowhere apparent, Mrs. Tozer was there, worrying about him and trying to think of something polite to say.

"Did you have a comfortable trip on the train?"

"Oh, yes, it was— Well, it was pretty crowded."

"Oh, was it crowded?"

"Yes, there were a lot of people traveling."

"Were there? I suppose— Yes. Sometimes I wonder where all the people can be going that you see going places all the time. Did you—was it very cold in the Cities—in Minneapolis and St. Paul?"

"Yes, it was pretty cold."

"Oh, was it cold?"

Mrs. Tozer was so still, so anxiously polite. He felt like a burglar taken for a guest, and intensely he wondered where Leora could be. She came in serenely, with coffee and a tremendous Swedish coffee-ring voluptuous with raisins and glistening brown sugar, and she had them talking, almost easily, about the coldness of winter and the value of Fords when into the midst of all this brightness slid Mr. Andrew Jackson Tozer, and they drooped again to politeness.

Mr. Tozer was as thin and undistinguished and sun-worn as his wife, and like her he peered, he kept silence and fretted. He was astonished by everything in the world that did not bear on his grain elevator, his creamery, his tiny bank, the United Brethren Church, and the careful conduct of an Overland car. It was not astounding that he should have become almost rich, for he accepted nothing that was not natural and convenient to Andrew Jackson Tozer.

He hinted a desire to know whether Martin "drank," how prosperous he was, and how he could possibly have come all this way from the urbanities of Winnemac. (The Tozers were born in Illinois, but they had been in Dakota since childhood, and they regarded Wisconsin as the farthest, most perilous rim of the Eastern horizon.) They were so blank, so creepily polite, that Martin was able to avoid such unpleasant subjects as being suspended. He dandled an impression that he was an earnest young medic who in no time at all would be making large and suitable sums of money for the support of their Leora, but as he was beginning to lean back in his chair he was betrayed by the appearance of Leora's brother.

Bert Tozer, Albert R. Tozer, cashier and vice-president of the Wheatsylvania State Bank, auditor and vice-president of the Tozer Grain and Storage Company, treasurer and vice-president of the Star Creamery, was not in the least afflicted by the listening dubiousness of his parents. Bertie was a very articulate and modern man of affairs. He had buck teeth, and on his eye-glasses was a gold chain leading to a dainty hook behind his left ear. He believed in town-boosting, organized motor tours, Boy Scouts, baseball, and the hanging of I.W.W.'s; and his most dolorous regret was that Wheatsylvania was too small—as yet—to have a Y.M.C.A. or a Commercial Club. Plunging in beside him was his fiancée, Miss Ada Quist, daughter of the feed and implement store. Her nose was sharp, but not so sharp as her voice or the suspiciousness with which she faced Martin.

"This Arrowsmith?" demanded Bert. "Huh! Well, guess you're glad to be out here in God's country!"

"Yes, it's fine—"

"Trouble with the Eastern states is, they haven't got the git, or the room to grow. You ought to see a real Dakota harvest! Look here, how come you're away from school this time of year?"

"Why—"

"I know all about school-terms. I went to business college in Grand Forks. How come you can get away now?"

"I took a little lay-off."

"Leora says you and her are thinking of getting married."

"We—"

"Got any cash outside your school-money?"

"I have not!"

"Thought so! How juh expect to support a wife?"

"I suppose I'll be practising medicine some day."

"Some day! Then what's the use of talking about being engaged till you can support a wife?"

"That," interrupted Bert's lady-love, Miss Ada Quist, "that's just what *I* said, Ory!" She seemed to speak with her pointed nose as much as with her button of a mouth. "If Bert and I can wait, I guess other people can!"

Mrs. Tozer whimpered, "Don't be too hard on Mr. Arrowsmith, Bertie. I'm sure he wants to do the right thing."

"I'm not being hard on anybody! I'm being sensible. If Pa and you would tend to things instead of standing around fussing, I wouldn't have to butt in. I don't believe in interfering with anybody else's doings, or anybody interfering with mine. Live and let live and mind your own business is my motto, and that's what I said to Alec Ingleblad the other day when I was in there having a shave and he was trying to get funny about our holding so many mortgages, but I'll be blamed if I'm going to allow a fellow that I don't know anything about to come snooping around My Sister till I find out something about his prospects!"

Leora crooned, "Bertie, lamb, your tie is climbing your collar again."

"Yes and *you*, Ory," shrieked Bert, "if it wasn't for me you'd have married Sam Petchek, two years ago!"

Bert further said, with instances and illustrations, that she was light-minded, and as for nursing— *Nursing!*

She said that Bert was what he was, and tried to explain to Martin the matter of Sam Petchek. (It has never yet been altogether explained.)

Ada Quist said that Leora did not care if she broke her dear parents' hearts and ruined Bert's career.

Martin said, "Look here, I—" and never got farther.

Mr. and Mrs. Tozer said they were all to be calm, and of course Bert didn't mean— But really, it was true; they had to be sensible, and how Mr. Arrowsmith could expect to support a wife—

The conference lasted till nine-thirty, which, as Mr. Tozer pointed out, was everybody's bedtime, and except for the five-minute discussion as to whether Miss Ada Quist was to stay to supper, and the debate on the saltiness of this last cornbeef, they clave faithfully to the inquiry as to whether Martin and Leora were engaged. All persons interested, which apparently did not include Martin and Leora, decided that they were not. Bert ushered Martin upstairs. He saw to it that the lovers should not have a chance for a good-night kiss; and until Mr. Tozer called down the hall, at seven minutes after ten, "You going to stay up and chew the rag the whole blessed night, Bert?" he made himself agreeable by sitting on Martin's bed, looking derisively at his shabby baggage, and demanding the details of his parentage, religion, politics, and attitude toward the horrors of card-playing and dancing.

At breakfast they all hoped that Martin would stay one more night in their home—plenty of room.

Bert stated that Martin would come down-town at ten and be shown the bank, creamery, and wheat elevator.

But at ten Martin and Leora were on the eastbound train. They got out at the county seat, Leopolis, a vast city of four thousand population, with a three-story building. At one that afternoon they were married, by the German Lutheran pastor. His study was a bareness surrounding a large, rusty wood-stove, and the witnesses, the pastor's wife and an old German who had been shoveling walks, sat on the wood-box and looked drowsy. Not till they had caught the afternoon train for Wheatsylvania did Martin and Leora escape from the ghostly apprehension which had haunted them all day. In the fetid train, huddled close, hands locked, innocently free of the alienation which the pomposity of weddings sometimes casts between lovers, they sighed, "Now what are we going to do—what *are* we going to do?"

At the Wheatsylvania station they were met by the whole family, rampant.

Bert had suspected elopement. He had searched half a dozen towns by long-distance telephone, and got through to the county clerk just after the license had been granted. It did not soften Bert's mood to have the clerk remark that if Martin and Leora were of age, there was nothing he could do, and he didn't "care a damn who's talking—I'm running this office!"

Bert had come to the station determined to make Martin perfect, even as Bert Tozer was perfect, and to do it right now.

It was a dreadful evening in the Tozer mansion.

Mr. Tozer said, with length, that Martin had undertaken responsibilities.

Mrs. Tozer wept, and said that she hoped Ory had not, for certain reasons, *had* to be married—

Bert said that if such was the case, he'd kill Martin—

Ada Quist said that Ory could now see what came of pride and boasting about going off to her old Zenith—

Mr. Tozer said that there was one good thing about it, anyway: Ory could see for herself that they couldn't let her go back to nursing school and get into more difficulties—

Martin from time to time offered remarks to the effect that he was a good young man, a wonderful bacteriologist, and able to take care of *his* wife; but no one save Leora listened.

Bert further propounded (while his father squeaked, "Now don't be *too* hard on the boy,") that if Martin *thought* for one single *second* that he was going to get one red *cent* out of the Tozers because he'd gone and butted *in* where nobody'd *invited* him, he, Bert, wanted to *know* about it, that was all, he certainly wanted to *know* about it!

And Leora watched them, turning her little head from one to another. Once she came over to press Martin's hand. In the roughest of the storm, when Martin was beginning to glare, she drew from a mysterious pocket a box of very bad cigarettes, and lighted one. None of the Tozers had discovered that she smoked. Whatever they thought about her sex morals, her infidelity to United Brethrenism, and her general dementia, they had not suspected that she could commit such an obscenity as smoking. They charged on her, and Martin caught his breath savagely.

During these fulminations Mr. Tozer had somehow made up his mind. He could at times take the lead away from Bert, whom he considered useful but slightly indiscreet, and unable to grasp the "full value of a dollar." (Mr. Tozer valued it at one dollar and ninety, but the progressive Bert at scarce more than one-fifty.) Mr. Tozer mildly gave orders:

They were to stop "scrapping." They had no proof that Martin was necessarily a bad match for Ory. They would see. Martin would return to medical school at once, and be a good boy and get through as quickly as he could and begin to earn money. Ory would remain at home and behave herself—and she certainly would never act like a Bad Woman again, and smoke cigarettes. Meantime Martin and she would have no, uh, relations. (Mrs. Tozer looked embarrassed, and the hungrily attentive Ada Quist tried to blush.) They could write to each other once a week, but that was all. They would in no way, uh, act as though they were married till he gave permission.

"Well?" he demanded.

Doubtless Martin should have defied them and with his bride in his arms have gone forth into the night. But it seemed only a moment to graduation, to beginning his practise. He had Leora now, forever. For her, he must be sensible. He would return to work, and be Practical. Gottlieb's ideals of science? Laboratories? Research? Rot!

"All right," he said.

It did not occur to him that their abstention from love began to-night; it did not come to him till, holding out his hands to Leora, smiling with virtue at having determined to be prudent, he heard Mr. Tozer cackling, "Ory, you go on up to bed now—in your own room!"

That was his bridal night; tossing in his bed, ten yards from her.

Once he heard a door open, and thrilled to her coming. He waited, taut. She did not come. He peeped out, determined to find her room. His deep feeling about his brother-in-law suddenly increased. Bert was parading the hall, on guard. Had Bert been more formidable, Martin might have killed him, but he could not face that buck-toothed and nickering righteousness. He lay and resolved to curse them all in the morning and go off with Leora, but with the coming of the three-o'clock depression he perceived that with him she would probably starve, that he was disgraced, that it was not at all certain he would not become a drunkard.

"Poor kid, I'm not going to spoil her life. God, I do love her! I'm going back, and the way I'm going to work— Can I stand this?"

That was his bridal night and the barren dawn.

Three days later he was walking into the office of Dr. Silva, dean of the Winnemac Medical School.

Chapter X

DEAN SILVA'S secretary looked up delightedly, she harkened with anticipation. But Martin said meekly, "Please, could I see the dean?" and meekly he waited, in the row of oak chairs beneath the Dawson Hunziker pharmaceutical calendar.

When he had gone solemnly through the ground-glass door to the dean's office, he found Dr. Silva glowering. Seated, the little man seemed large, so domed was his head, so full his rounding mustache.

"Well, sir!"

Martin pleaded, "I'd like to come back, if you'll let me. Honest, I do apologize to you, and I'll go to Dr. Gottlieb and apologize—though honest, I can't lay down on Clif Clawson—"

Dr. Silva bounced up from his chair, bristling. Martin braced himself. Wasn't he welcome? Had he no home, anywhere? He could not fight. He had no more courage. He was so tired after the drab journey, after restraining himself from flaring out at the Tozers. He was so tired! He looked wistfully at the dean.

The little man chuckled, "Never mind, boy. It's all right! We're glad you're back. Bother the apologies! I just wanted you to do whatever'd buck you up. It's good to have you back! I believed in you, and then I thought perhaps we'd lost you. Clumsy old man!"

Martin was sobbing, too weak for restraint, too lonely and too weak, and Dr. Silva soothed, "Let's just go over everything and find out where the trouble was. What can I do? Understand, Martin, the thing I want most in life is to help give the world as many good physicians, great healers, as I can. What started your nervousness? Where have you been?"

When Martin came to Leora and his marriage, Silva purred, "I'm delighted! She sounds like a splendid girl. Well, we must try and get you into Zenith General for your internship, a year from now, and make you able to support her properly."

Martin remembered how often, how astringently, Gottlieb had sneered at "dese merry vedding or jail bells." He went away Silva's disciple; he went away to study furiously; and the brilliant insanity of Max Gottlieb's genius vanished from his faith.

II

Leora wrote that she had been dropped from the school of nursing for over-absence and for being married. She suspected that it was her father who had informed the hospital authorities. Then, it appeared, she had secretly sent for a shorthand book and, on pretense of helping Bert, she was using the typewriter in the bank, hoping that by next autumn she could join Martin and earn her own living as a stenographer.

Once he offered to give up medicine, to take what work he could find and send for her. She refused.

Though in his service to Leora and to the new god, Dean Silva, he had become austere, denying himself whisky, learning page on page of medicine with a frozen fury, he was always in a vacuum of desire for her, and always he ran the last block to his boarding-house, looking for a letter from her. Suddenly he had a plan. He had tasted shame—this one last shame would not matter. He would flee to her in Easter vacation, he would compel Tozer to support her while she studied stenography in Zenith; he would have her near him through the last year. He paid Clif the borrowed hundred, when the bimonthly check came from Elk Mills, and calculated his finances to the penny. By not buying the suit he distressingly needed, he could manage it. Then for a month and more he had but two meals a day, and of those meals one was bread and butter and coffee. He washed his own linen in the bath-tub and, except for occasional fiercely delightful yieldings, he did not smoke.

His return to Wheatsylvania was like his first flight, except that he talked less with fellow tramps, and all the way, between uneasy naps in the red-plush seats of coaches, he studied the bulky books of gynecology and internal medicine. He had written certain instructions to Leora. He met her on the edge of Wheatsylvania and they had a moment's talk, a resolute kiss.

News spreads not slowly in Wheatsylvania. There is a certain interest in other people's affairs, and the eyes of citizens of whose existence Martin did not know had followed him from his arrival. When the culprits reached the bone-littered castle of the Tozer ogres, Leora's father and brother were already there, and raging. Old Andew Jackson cried out upon them. He said that conceivably it may not have been insane in Martin to have "run away from school once, but to go and sneak back this second time was absolutely plumb crazy." Through his tirade, Martin and Leora smiled confidently.

From Bert, "By God, sir, this is too much!" Bert had been reading fiction. "I object to the use of profanity, but when you come and annoy My Sister a second time, all I can say is, by God, sir, this is too blame much!"

Martin looked meditatively out of the window. He noticed three people strolling the muddy street. They all viewed the Tozer house with hopeful interest. Then he spoke steadily:

"Mr. Tozer, I've been working hard. Everything has gone fine. But I've decided I don't care to live without my wife. I've come to take her back. Legally, you can't prevent me. I'll admit, without any argument, I can't support her yet, if I stay in the University. She's going to study stenography. She'll be supporting herself in a few months, and meanwhile I expect you to be decent enough to send her money."

"This *is* too much," said Tozer, and Bert carried it on: "Fellow not only practically ruins a girl but comes and demands that we support her for him!"

"All right. Just as you want. In the long run it'll be better for her and for me and for you if I finish medic school and have my profession, but if you won't take care of her, I'll chuck school, I'll go to work. Oh, I'll support her, all right! Only you'll never see her again. If you go on being idiots, she and I will leave here on the night train for the Coast, and that'll be the end." For the first time in his centuries of debate with the Tozers, he was melodramatic. He shook his fist under Bert's nose. "And if you try to prevent our going, God help you! And the way this town will laugh at you! . . . How about it, Leora? Are you ready to go away with me—forever?"

"Yes," she said.

They discussed it, greatly. Tozer and Bert struck attitudes of defense. They couldn't, they said, be bullied by anybody. Also, Martin was an Adventurer, and how did Leora know he wasn't planning to live on the money they sent her? In the end they crawled. They decided that this new, mature Martin, this new, hard-eyed Leora were ready to throw away everything for each other.

Mr. Tozer whined a good deal, and promised to send her seventy dollars a month till she should be prepared for office-work.

At the Wheatsylvania station, looking from the train window, Martin realized that this anxious-eyed, lip-puckering Andrew Jackson Tozer did love his daughter, did mourn her going.

III

He found for Leora a room on the frayed northern edge of Zenith, miles nearer Mohalis and the University than her hospital had been; a square white and blue room, with blotchy but shoulder-wise chairs. It looked out on breezy, stubbly waste land reaching to distant glittering railroad tracks. The landlady was a round German woman with an eye for romance. It is doubtful if she ever believed that they were married. She was a good woman.

Leora's trunk had come. Her stenography books were primly set out on her little table and her pink felt slippers were arranged beneath the white iron bed. Martin stood with her at the window, mad with the pride of proprietorship. Suddenly he was so weak, so tired, that the mysterious cement which holds cell to cell seemed dissolved, and he felt that he was collapsing. But with knees rigidly straightening, his head back, his lips tight across his teeth, he caught himself, and cried, "Our first home!"

That he should be with her, quiet, none disturbing, was intoxication.

The commonplace room shone with peculiar light; the vigorous weeds and rough grass of the waste land were radiant under the April sun, and sparrows were cheeping.

"Yes," said Leora, with voice, then hungry lips.

IV

Leora attended the Zenith University of Business Administration and Finance, which title indicated that it was a large and quite reasonably bad school for stenographers, bookkeepers, and such sons of Zenith brewers and politicians as were unable to enter even state universities. She trotted daily to the car-line, a neat, childish figure with note-books and sharpened pencils, to vanish in the horde of students. It was six months before she had learned enough stenography to obtain a place in an insurance office.

Till Martin graduated they kept that room, their home, ever dearer. No one was so domestic as these birds of passage. At least two evenings a week Martin dashed in from Mohalis and studied there. She had a genius for keeping out of his way, for not demanding to be noticed, so that, while he plunged into his books as he never had done in Clif's rustling, grunting, expectorating company, he had ever the warm, half-conscious feeling of her presence. Sometimes, at midnight, just as he began to realize that he was hungry, he would find that a plate of sandwiches had by silent magic appeared at his elbow. He was none the less affectionate because he did not comment. She made him secure. She shut out the world that had pounded at him.

On their walks, at dinner, in the dissolute and deliciously wasteful quarter-hour when they sat on the edge of the bed with comforters wrapped about them and smoked an inexcusable cigarette before breakfast, he explained his work to her, and when her own studying was done, she tried to read whichever of his books was not in use. Knowing nothing, never learning much, of the actual details of medicine, yet she understood—better it may be than Angus Duer—his philosophy and the basis of his work. If he had given up Gottlieb-worship and his yearning for the laboratory as for a sanctuary, if he had resolved to be a practical and wealth-mastering doctor, yet something of Gottlieb's spirit remained. He wanted to look behind details and impressive-sounding lists of technical terms for the causes of things, for general rules which might reduce the chaos of dissimilar and contradictory symptoms to the orderliness of chemistry.

Saturday evening they went solemnly to the motion pictures—one and two-reel films with Cowboy Billy Anderson and a girl later to be famous as Mary Pickford—and solemnly they discussed the non-existent plots as they returned, unconscious of other people on the streets; but when they walked into the country on a Sunday (with four sandwiches and a bottle of ginger ale in his threadbare pockets), he chased her up-hill and down-gully, and they lost their solemnity in joyous childishness. He intended, when he came to her room in the evening, to catch the owl-car to Mohalis and be near his work when he woke in the morning. He was resolute about it, always, and she admired his efficiency, but he never caught the car. The crew of the six o'clock morning interurban became used to a pale, quick-moving young man who sat hunched in a back seat, devouring large red books, absently gnawing a rather dreadful doughnut. But in this young man there was none of the heaviness of workers dragged out of bed at dawn for another gray and futile day of labor. He appeared curiously determined, curiously content.

It was all so much easier, now that he was partly freed from the tyrannical honesty of Gottliebism, from the unswerving quest for causes which, as it drove through layer below layer, seemed ever farther from the bottommost principles, from the intolerable strain of learning day by day how much he did not know. It warmed him to escape from Gottlieb's ice-box into Dean Silva's neighborly world.

Now and then he saw Gottlieb on the campus. They bowed in embarrassment and passed in haste.

V

There seemed to be no division between his Junior and Senior years. Because of the time he had lost, he had to remain in Mohalis all summer. The year and a half from his marriage to his graduation was one whirling bewilderment, without seasons or dates.

When he had, as they put it, "cut out his nonsense and buckled down to work," he had won the admiration of Dr. Silva and all the Good Students, especially Angus Duer and the Reverend Ira Hinkley. Martin had always announced that he did not care for their approbation, for the applause of commonplace drudges, but now that he had it, he prized it. However much he scoffed, he was gratified when he was treated as a peer by Angus, who spent the summer as extern in the Zenith General Hospital, and who already had the unapproachable dignity of a successful young surgeon.

Through that hot summer Martin and Leora labored, panting, and when they sat in her room, over their books and a stout pot of beer, neither their costumes nor their language had the decorum which one ought to expect from a romantic pair devoted to science and high endeavor. They were not very modest. Leora came to use, in her casual way, such words, such ancient Anglo-Saxon monosyllables, as would have dismayed Angus or Bert Tozer. On their evenings off they went economically to an imitation Coney Island beside a scummy and stinking lake, and with grave pleasure they ate Hot Dogs, painstakingly they rode the scenic railway.

Their chief appetizer was Clif Clawson. Clif was never willingly alone or silent except when he was asleep. It is probable that his success in motor-salesmanship came entirely from his fondness for the enormous amounts of bright conversation which seem necessary in that occupation. How much of his attention to Martin and Leora was friendliness and how much of it was due to his fear of being alone cannot be determined, but certainly he entertained them and drew them out of themselves, and never seemed offended by the surly unwillingness with which Martin was sometimes guilty of greeting him.

He would come roaring up to the house in a motor, the muffler always cut out. He would shout at their window, "Come on, you guys! Come out of it! Shake a leg! Lez have a little drive and get cooled off, and then I'll buy you a feed."

That Martin had to work, Clif never comprehended. There was small excuse for Martin's occasional brutality in showing his annoyance but, now that he was fulfilled in Leora and quite thoroughly and selfishly careless as to what hungry need others might have of himself, now that he was in a rut of industry and satisfied companionship, he was bored by Clif's unchanging flood of heavy humor. It was Leora who was courteous. She had heard rather too often the seven jokes which, under varying guises, made up all of Clif's humor and philosophy, but she could sit for hours looking amiable while Clif told how clever he was at selling, and she sturdily reminded Martin that they would never have a friend more loyal or generous.

But Clif went to New York, to a new motor agency, and Martin and Leora were more completely and happily dependent on each other than ever before.

Their last agitation was removed by the complacence of Mr. Tozer. He was cordial now in all his letters, however much he irritated them by the parental advice with which he penalized them for every check he sent.

VI

None of the hectic activities of Senior year—neurology and pediatrics, practical work in obstetrics, taking of case-histories in the hospitals, attendance on operations, dressing wounds, learning not to look embarrassed when charity patients called one "Doctor"—was quite so important as the discussion of "What shall we do after graduation?"

Is it necessary to be an intern for more than a year? Shall we remain general practitioners all our lives, or work toward becoming specialists? Which specialties are the best—that is, the best paid? Shall we settle in the country or in the city? How about going West? What about the army medical corps; salutes, riding-boots, pretty women, travel?

This discussion they harried in the corridors of Main Medical, at the hospital, at lunch-rooms; and when Martin came home to Leora he went through it all again, very learnedly, very explanatorily. Almost every evening he "reached a decision" which was undecided again by morning.

Once when Dr. Loizeau, professor of surgery, had operated before a clinic which included several renowned visiting doctors—the small white figure of the surgeon below them, slashing between life and death, dramatic as a great actor taking his curtain-call—Martin came away certain that he was for surgery. He agreed then with Angus Duer, who had just won the Hugh Loizeau Medal in Experimental Surgery, that the operator was the lion, the eagle, the soldier among doctors. Angus was one of the few who knew without wavering precisely what he was going to do: after his internship he was to join the celebrated Chicago clinic headed by Dr. Rouncefield, the eminent abdominal surgeon. He would, he said briefly, be making twenty thousand a year as a surgeon within five years.

Martin explained it all to Leora. Surgery. Drama. Fearless nerves. Adoring assistants. Save lives. Science in devising new techniques. Make money—not be commercial, of course, but provide Leora with comforts. To Europe—they two together—gray London, Viennese cafés. Leora was useful to him during his oration. She blandly agreed; and the next evening, when he sought to prove that surgery was all rot and most surgeons merely good carpenters, she agreed more amiably than ever.

Next to Angus, and the future medical missionary, Ira Hinkley, Fatty Pfaff was the first to discover what his future was. He was going to be an obstetrician—or, as the medical students called it technically, a "baby-snatcher." Fatty had the soul of a midwife; he sympathized with women in their gasping agony, sympathized honestly and almost tearfully, and he was magnificent at sitting still and drinking tea and waiting. During his first obstetrical case, when the student with him was merely nervous as they fidgeted by the bed in the hard desolation of the hospital room, Fatty was terrified, and he longed as he had never longed for anything in his flabby yet wistful life to comfort this gray-faced, straining, unknown woman, to take her pains on himself.

While the others drifted, often by chance, often through relatives, into their various classes, Martin remained doubtful. He admired Dean Silva's insistence on the physician's immediate service to mankind, but he could not forget the cool ascetic hours in the laboratory. Toward the end of Senior year, decision became necessary, and he was moved by a speech in which Dean Silva condemned too much specialization and pictured the fine old country doctor, priest and father of his people, sane under open skies, serene in self-conquest. On top of this came urgent letters from Mr. Tozer, begging Martin to settle in Wheatsylvania.

Tozer loved his daughter, apparently, and more or less liked Martin, and he wanted them near him. Wheatsylvania was a "good location," he said: solid Scandinavian and Dutch and German and Bohemian farmers who paid their bills. The nearest doctor was Hesselink, at Groningen, nine and a half miles away, and Hesselink had more than he could do. If they would come, he would help Martin buy his equipment; he would even send him a check now and then during his two-year hospital internship. Martin's capital was practically gone. Angus Duer and he had received appointments to Zenith General Hospital, where he would have an incomparable training, but Zenith General gave its interns, for the first year, nothing but board and room, and he had feared that he could not take the appointment. Tozer's offer excited him. All night Leora and he sat up working themselves into enthusiasm about the freedom of the West, about the kind hearts and friendly hands of the pioneers, about the heroism and usefulness of country doctors, and this time they reached a decision which remained decided.

They would settle in Wheatsylvania.

If he ached a little for research and Gottlieb's divine curiosity—well, he would be such a country doctor as Robert Koch! He would not degenerate into a bridge-playing, duck-hunting drone. He would have a small laboratory of his own. So he came to the end of the year and graduated, looking rather flustered in his cap and gown. Angus stood first and Martin seventh in the class. He said good-by, with lamentations and considerable beer; he found a room for Leora nearer to the hospital; and he emerged as Martin L. Arrowsmith, M.D., house physician in the Zenith General Hospital.

Chapter XI

THE Boardman Box Factory was afire. All South Zenith was agitated by the glare on the low-hung clouds, the smell of scorched timber, the infernal bells of charging fire-apparatus. Miles of small wooden houses west of the factory were threatened, and shawled women, tousled men in trousers over nightshirts, tumbled out of bed and came running with a thick mutter of footsteps in the night-chilled streets.

With professional calmness, firemen in helmets were stoking the dripping engines. Policemen tramped in front of the press of people, swinging their clubs, shouting, "Get back there, you!" The fire-line was sacred. Only the factory-owner and the reporters were admitted. A crazy-eyed factory-hand was stopped by a police sergeant.

"My tools are in there!" he shrieked.

"That don't make no never-minds," bawled the strutting sergeant. "*Nobody* can't get through here!"

But one got through. They heard the blang-blang-blang of a racing ambulance, incessant, furious, defiant. Without orders, the crowd opened, and through them, almost grazing them, slid the huge gray car. At the back, haughty in white uniform, nonchalant on a narrow seat, was The Doctor—Martin Arrowsmith.

The crowd admired him, the policemen sprang to receive him.

"Where's the fireman got hurt?" he snapped.

"Over in that shed," cried the police sergeant, running beside the ambulance.

"Drive over closer. Nev' mind the smoke!" Martin barked at the driver.

A lieutenant of firemen led him to a pile of sawdust on which was huddled an unconscious youngster, his face bloodless and clammy.

"He got a bad dose of smoke from the green lumber and keeled over. Fine kid. Is he a goner?" the lieutenant begged.

Martin knelt by the man, felt his pulse, listened to his breathing. Brusquely opening a black bag, he gave him a hypodermic of strychnin and held a vial of ammonia to his nose. "He'll come around. Here, you two, getum into the ambulance—hustle!"

The police sergeant and the newest probationer patrolman sprang together, and together they mumbled, "All right, Doc."

To Martin came the chief reporter of the *Advocate-Times*. In years he was only twenty-nine, but he was the oldest and perhaps the most cynical man in the world. He had interviewed senators; he had discovered graft in charity societies and even in prize-fights. There were fine wrinkles beside his eyes, he rolled Bull Durham cigarettes constantly, and his opinion of man's honor and woman's virtue was but low. Yet to Martin, or at least to The Doctor, he was polite.

"Will he pull through, Doc?" he twanged.

"Sure, I think so. Suffocation. Heart's still going."

Martin yelped the last words from the step at the back of the ambulance as it went bumping and rocking through the factory yard, through the bitter smoke, toward the shrinking crowd. He owned and commanded the city, he and the driver. They ignored traffic regulations, they disdained the people, returning from theaters and movies, who dotted the streets which unrolled before the flying gray hood. Let 'em get out of the way! The traffic officer at Chickasaw and Twentieth heard them coming, speeding like the Midnight Express—urrrrrr—blang-blang-blang-blang—and cleared the noisy corner. People were jammed against the curb, threatened by rearing horses and backing motors, and past them hurled the ambulance, blang-blang-blang-blang, with The Doctor holding a strap and swinging easily on his perilous seat.

At the hospital the hall-man cried, "Shooting case in the Arbor, Doc."

"All right. Wait'll I sneak in a drink," said Martin placidly.

On the way to his room he passed the open door of the hospital laboratory, with its hacked bench, its lifeless rows of flasks and test-tubes.

"Huh! That stuff! Poking 'round labs! This is real sure-enough life," he exulted, and he did not permit himself to see the vision of Max Gottlieb waiting there, so gaunt, so tired, so patient.

II

The six interns in Zenith General, including Martin and Angus Duer, lived in a long dark room with six camp beds, and six bureaus fantastic with photographs and ties and undarned socks. They spent hours sitting on their beds, arguing surgery versus internal medicine, planning the dinners which they hoped to enjoy on their nights off, and explaining to Martin, as the only married man, the virtues of the various nurses with whom, one by one, they fell in love.

Martin found the hospital routine slightly dull. Though he developed the Intern's Walk, that quick corridor step with the stethoscope conspicuous in the pocket, he did not, he could not, develop the bedside manner. He was sorry for the bruised, yellowed, suffering patients, always changing as to individuals and never changing as a mass of drab pain, but when he had thrice dressed a wound, he had had enough; he wanted to go on to new experiences. Yet the ambulance work outside the hospital was endlessly stimulating to his pride.

The Doctor, and The Doctor alone, was safe by night in the slum called "the Arbor." His black bag was a pass. Policemen saluted him, prostitutes bowed to him without mockery, saloon-keepers called out, "Evenin', Doc," and hold-up men stood back in doorways to let him pass. Martin had power, the first obvious power in his life. And he was led into incessant adventure.

He took a bank-president out of a dive; he helped the family conceal the disgrace; he irritably refused their bribe; and afterward, when he thought of how he might have dined with Leora, he was sorry he had refused it. He broke into hotel-rooms reeking with gas and revived would-be suicides. He drank Trinidad rum with a Congressman who advocated prohibition. He attended a policeman assaulted by strikers, and a striker assaulted by policemen. He assisted at an emergency abdominal operation at three o'clock in the morning. The operating-room—white tile walls and white tile floor and glittering frosted-glass skylight—seemed lined with fire-lit ice, and the large incandescents glared on the glass instrument cases, the cruel little knives. The surgeon, in long white gown, white turban, and pale orange rubber gloves, made his swift incision in the square of yellowish flesh exposed between towels, cutting deep into layers of fat, and Martin looked on unmoved as the first blood menacingly followed the cut. And a month after, during the Chaloosa River flood, he worked for seventy-six hours, with half-hours of sleep in the ambulance or on a police-station table.

He landed from a boat at what had been the second story of a tenement and delivered a baby on the top floor; he bound up heads and arms for a line of men; but what gave him glory was the perfectly foolhardy feat of swimming the flood to save five children marooned and terrified on a bobbing church pew. The newspapers gave him large headlines, and when he had returned to kiss Leora and sleep twelve hours, he lay and thought about research with salty self-defensive scorn.

"Gottlieb, the poor old impractical fusser! I'd like to see him swim that current!" jeered Dr. Arrowsmith to Martin.

But on night duty, alone, he had to face the self he had been afraid to uncover, and he was homesick for the laboratory, for the thrill of uncharted discoveries, the quest below the surface and beyond the moment, the search for fundamental laws which the scientist (however blasphemously and colloquially he may describe it) exalts above temporary healing as the religious exalts the nature and terrible glory of God above pleasant daily virtues. With this sadness there was envy that he should be left out of things, that others should go ahead of him, ever surer in technique, more widely aware of the phenomena of biological chemistry, more deeply daring to explain laws at which the pioneers had but fumbled and hinted.

In his second year of internship, when the thrills of fires and floods and murder became as obvious a routine as bookkeeping, when he had seen the strangely few ways in which mankind can contrive to injure themselves and slaughter one another, when it was merely wearing to have to live up to the pretentiousness of being The Doctor, Martin tried to satisfy and perhaps kill his guilty scientific lust by voluntary scrabbling about the hospital laboratory, correlating the blood counts in pernicious anemia. His trifling with the drug of research was risky. Amid the bustle of operations he began to picture the rapt quietude of the laboratory. "I better cut this out," he said to Leora, "if I'm going to settle down in Wheatsylvania and 'tend to business and make a living—and I by golly am!"

Dean Silva often came to the hospital on consultations. He passed through the lobby one evening when Leora, returned from the office where she was a stenographer, was meeting Martin for dinner. Martin introduced them, and the little man held her hand, purred at her, and squeaked, "Will you children give me the pleasure of taking you to dinner? My wife has deserted me. I am a lone and misanthropic man."

He trotted between them, round and happy. Martin and he were not student and teacher, but two doctors together, for Dean Silva was one pedagogue who could still be interested in a man who no longer sat at his feet. He led the two starvelings to a chop-house and in a settle-walled booth he craftily stuffed them with roast goose and mugs of ale.

He concentrated on Leora, but his talk was of Martin:

"Your husband must be an Artist Healer, not a picker of trifles like these laboratory men."

"But Gottlieb's no picker of trifles," insisted Martin.

"No-o. But with him— It's a difference of one's gods. Gottlieb's gods are the cynics, the destroyers—crapehangers, the vulgar call 'em: Diderot and Voltaire and Elser; great men, wonder-workers, yet men that had more fun destroying other people's theories than creating their own. But my gods now, they're the men who took the discoveries of Gottlieb's gods and turned them to the use of human beings—made them come alive!

"All credit to the men who invented paint and canvas, but there's more credit, eh? to the Raphaels and Holbeins who used those discoveries! Laënnec and Osler, those are the men! It's all very fine, this business of pure research: seeking the truth, unhampered by commercialism or fame-chasing. Getting to the bottom. Ignoring consequences and practical uses. But do you realize if you carry that idea far enough, a man could justify himself for doing nothing but count the cobblestones on Warehouse Avenue—yes, and justify himself for torturing people just to see how they screamed—and then sneer at a man who was making millions of people well and happy!

"No, no! Mrs. Arrowsmith, this lad Martin is a passionate fellow, not a drudge. He must be passionate on behalf of mankind. He's chosen the highest calling in the world, but he's a feckless, experimental devil. You must keep him at it, my dear, and not let the world lose the benefit of his passion."

After this solemnity Dad Silva took them to a musical comedy and sat between them, patting Martin's shoulder, patting Leora's arm, choking with delight when the comedian stepped into the pail of whitewash. In midnight volubility Martin and Leora sputtered their affection for him, and saw their Wheatsylvania venture as glory and salvation.

But a few days before the end of Martin's internship and their migration to North Dakota, they met Max Gottlieb on the street.

Martin had not seen him for more than a year; Leora never. He looked worried and ill. While Martin was agonizing as to whether to pass with a bow, Gottlieb stopped.

"How is everything, Martin?" he said cordially. But his eyes said, "Why have you never come back to me?"

The boy stammered something, nothing, and when Gottlieb had gone by, stooped and moving as in pain, he longed to run after him.

Leora was demanding, "Is that the Professor Gottlieb you're always talking about?"

"Yes. Say! How does he strike you?"

"I don't— Sandy, he's the greatest man I've ever seen! I don't know how I know, but he is! Dr. Silva is a darling, but that was a *great* man! I wish—I wish we were going to see him again. There's the first man I ever laid eyes on that I'd leave you for, if he wanted me. He's so—oh, he's like a sword—no, he's like a brain walking. Oh, Sandy, he looked so wretched. I wanted to cry. I'd black his shoes!"

"God! So would I!"

But in the bustle of leaving Zenith, the excitement of the journey to Wheatsylvania, the scramble of his state examinations, the dignity of being a Practising Physician, he forgot Gottlieb, and on that Dakota prairie radiant in early June, with meadow larks on every fence post, he began his work.

Chapter XII

AT THE MOMENT when Martin met him on the street, Gottlieb was ruined.

Max Gottlieb was a German Jew, born in Saxony in 1850. Though he took his medical degree, at Heidelberg, he was never interested in practising medicine. He was a follower of Helmholtz, and youthful researches in the physics of sound convinced him of the need of the quantitative method in the medical sciences. Then Koch's discoveries drew him into biology. Always an elaborately careful worker, a maker of long rows of figures, always realizing the presence of uncontrollable variables, always a vicious assailant of what he considered slackness or lie or pomposity, never too kindly to well-intentioned stupidity, he worked in the laboratories of Koch, of Pasteur, he followed the early statements of Pearson in biometrics, he drank beer and wrote vitriolic letters, he voyaged to Italy and England and Scandinavia, and casually, between two days, he married (as he might have bought a coat or hired a housekeeper) the patient and wordless daughter of a Gentile merchant.

Then began a series of experiments, very important, very undramatic-sounding, very long, and exceedingly unappreciated. Back in 1881 he was confirming Pasteur's results in chicken cholera immunity and, for relief and pastime, trying to separate an enzyme from yeast. A few years later, living on the tiny inheritance from his father, a petty banker, and quite carelessly and cheerfully exhausting it, he was analyzing critically the ptomain theory of disease, and investigating the mechanism of the attenuation of virulence of microörganisms. He got thereby small fame. Perhaps he was over-cautious, and more than the devil or starvation he hated men who rushed into publication unprepared.

Though he meddled little in politics, considering them the most repetitious and least scientific of human activities, he was a sufficiently patriotic German to hate the Junkers. As a youngster he had a fight or two with ruffling subalterns; once he spent a week in jail; often he was infuriated by discriminations against Jews: and at forty he went sadly off to the America which could never become militaristic or anti-Semitic—to the Hoagland Laboratory in Brooklyn, then to Queen City University as professor of bacteriology.

Here he made his first investigation of toxin-anti-toxin reactions. He announced that antibodies, excepting antitoxin, had no relation to the immune state of an animal, and while he himself was being ragingly denounced in the small but hectic world of scientists, he dealt calmly and most brutally with Yersin's and Marmorek's theories of sera.

His dearest dream, now and for years of racking research, was the artificial production of antitoxin—its production *in vitro*. Once he was prepared to publish, but he found an error and rigidly suppressed his notes. All the while he was lonely. There was apparently no one in Queen City who regarded him as other than a cranky Jew catching microbes by their little tails and leering at them—no work for a tall man at a time when heroes were building bridges, experimenting with Horseless Carriages, writing the first of the poetic Compelling Ads, and selling miles of calico and cigars.

In 1899 he was called to the University of Winnemac, as professor of bacteriology in the medical school, and here he drudged on for a dozen years. Not once did he talk of results of the sort called "practical"; not once did he cease warring on the *post hoc propter hoc* conclusions which still make up most medical lore; not once did he fail to be hated by his colleagues, who were respectful to his face, uncomfortable in feeling his ironic power, but privily joyous to call him Mephisto, Diabolist, Killjoy, Pessimist, Destructive Critic, Flippant Cynic, Scientific Bounder Lacking in Dignity and Seriousness, Intellectual Snob, Pacifist, Anarchist, Atheist, Jew. They said, with reason, that he was so devoted to Pure Science, to art for art's sake, that he would rather have people die by the right therapy than be cured by the wrong. Having built a shrine for humanity, he wanted to kick out of it all mere human beings.

The total number of his papers, in a brisk scientific realm where really clever people published five times a year, was not more than twenty-five in thirty years. They were all exquisitely finished, all easily reduplicated and checked by the doubtfullest critics.

At Mohalis he was pleased by large facilities for work, by excellent assistants, endless glassware, plenty of guinea pigs, enough monkeys; but he was bored by the round of teaching, and melancholy again in a lack of understanding friends. Always he sought some one to whom he could talk without suspicion or caution. He was human enough, when he meditated upon the exaltation of doctors bold through ignorance, of inventors who were but tinkers magnified, to be irritated by his lack of fame in America, even in Mohalis, and to complain not too nobly.

He had never dined with a duchess, never received a prize, never been interviewed, never produced anything which the public could understand, nor experienced anything since his schoolboy amours which nice people could regard as romantic. He was, in fact, an authentic scientist.

He was of the great benefactors of humanity. There will never, in any age, be an effort to end the great epidemics or the petty infections which will not have been influenced by Max Gottlieb's researches, for he was not one who tagged and prettily classified bacteria and protozoa. He sought their chemistry, the laws of their existence and destruction, basic laws for the most part unknown after a generation of busy biologists. Yet they were right who called him "pessimist," for this man who, as much as any other, will have been the cause of reducing infectious diseases to almost-zero often doubted the value of reducing infectious diseases at all.

He reflected (it was an international debate in which he was joined by a few and damned by many) that half a dozen generations nearly free from epidemics would produce a race so low in natural immunity that when a great plague, suddenly springing from almost-zero to a world-smothering cloud, appeared again, it might wipe out the world entire, so that the measures to save lives to which he lent his genius might in the end be the destruction of all human life.

He meditated that if science and public hygiene did remove tuberculosis and the other major plagues, the world was grimly certain to become so overcrowded, to become such a universal slave-packed shambles, that all beauty and ease and wisdom would disappear in a famine-driven scamper for existence. Yet these speculations never checked his work. If the future became overcrowded, the future must by birth-control or otherwise look to itself. Perhaps it would, he reflected. But even this drop of wholesome optimism was lacking in his final doubts. For he doubted all progress of the intellect and the emotions, and he doubted, most of all, the superiority of divine mankind to the cheerful dogs, the infallibly graceful cats, the unmoral and unagitated and irreligious horses, the superbly adventuring sea-gulls.

While medical quacks, manufacturers of patent medicines, chewing-gum salesmen, and high priests of advertising lived in large houses, attended by servants, and took their sacred persons abroad in limousines, Max Gottlieb dwelt in a cramped cottage whose paint was peeling, and rode to his laboratory on an ancient and squeaky bicycle. Gottlieb himself protested rarely. He was not so unreasonable—usually—as to demand both freedom and the fruits of popular slavery. "Why," he once said to Martin, "should the world pay me for doing what I want and what they do not want?"

If in his house there was but one comfortable chair, on his desk were letters, long, intimate, and respectful, from the great ones of France and Germany, Italy and Denmark, and from scientists whom Great Britain so much valued that she gave them titles almost as high as those with which she rewarded distillers, cigarette-manufacturers, and the owners of obscene newspapers.

But poverty kept him from fulfilment of his summer longing to sit beneath the poplars by the Rhine or the tranquil Seine, at a table on whose checkered cloth were bread and cheese and wine and dusky cherries, those ancient and holy simplicities of all the world.

II

Max Gottlieb's wife was thick and slow-moving and mute; at sixty she had not learned to speak easy English; and her German was of the small-town bourgeois, who pay their debts and over-eat and grow red. If he was not confidential with her, if at table he forgot her in long reflections, neither was he unkind or impatient, and he depended on her housekeeping, her warming of his old-fashioned nightgown. She had not been well of late. She had nausea and indigestion, but she kept on with her work. Always you heard her old slippers slapping about the house.

They had three children, all born when Gottlieb was over thirty-eight: Miriam, the youngest, an ardent child who had a touch at the piano, an instinct about Beethoven, and hatred for the "ragtime" popular in America; an older sister who was nothing in particular; and their boy Robert—Robert Koch Gottlieb. He was a wild thing and a distress. They sent him, with anxiety over the cost, to a smart school near Zenith, where he met the sons of manufacturers and discovered a taste for fast motors and eccentric clothes, and no taste whatever for studying. At home he clamored that his father was a "tightwad." When Gottlieb sought to make it clear that he was a poor man, the boy answered that out of his poverty he was always sneakingly spending money on his researches—he had no right to do that and shame his son—let the confounded University provide him with material!

III

There were few of Gottlieb's students who saw him and his learning as anything but hurdles to be leaped as quickly as possible. One of the few was Martin Arrowsmith.

However harshly he may have pointed out Martin's errors, however loftily he may have seemed to ignore his devotion, Gottlieb was as aware of Martin as Martin of him. He planned vast things. If Martin really desired his help (Gottlieb could be as modest personally as he was egotistic and swaggering in competitive science), he would make the boy's career his own. During Martin's minute original research, Gottlieb rejoiced in his willingness to abandon conventional—and convenient—theories of immunology and in the exasperated carefulness with which he checked results. When Martin for unknown reasons became careless, when he was obviously drinking too much, obxiously mixed up in some absurd personal affair, it was tragic hunger for friends and flaming respect for excellent work which drove Gottlieb to snarl at him. Of the apologies demanded by Silva he had no notion. He would have raged—

He waited for Martin to return. He blamed himself: "Fool! There was a fine spirit. You should have known one does not use a platinum loop for shoveling coal." As long as he could (while Martin was dish-washing and wandering on improbable trains between impossible towns), he put off the appointment of a new assistant. Then all his wistfulness chilled to anger. He considered Martin a traitor, and put him out of his mind.

IV

It is possible that Max Gottlieb was a genius. Certainly he was mad as any genius. He did, during the period of Martin's internship in Zenith General, a thing more preposterous than any of the superstitions at which he scoffed.

He tried to become an executive and a reformer! He, the cynic, the anarch, tried to found an Institution, and he went at it like a spinster organizing a league to keep small boys from learning naughty words.

He conceived that there might, in this world, be a medical school which should be altogether scientific, ruled by exact quantitative biology and chemistry, with spectacle-fitting and most of surgery ignored, and he further conceived that such an enterprise might be conducted at the University of Winnemac! He tried to be practical about it; oh, he was extremely practical and plausible!

"I admit we should not be able to turn out doctors to cure village bellyaches. And ordinary physicians are admirable and altogether necessary—perhaps. But there are too many of them already. And on the 'practical' side, you gif me twenty years of a school that is precise and cautious, and we shall cure diabetes, maybe tuberculosis and cancer, and all these arthritis things that the carpenters shake their heads at them and call them 'rheumatism.' So!"

He did not desire the control of such a school, nor any credit. He was too busy. But at a meeting of the American Academy of Sciences he met one Dr. Entwisle, a youngish physiologist from Harvard, who would make an excellent dean. Entwisle admired him, and sounded him on his willingness to be called to Harvard. When Gottlieb outlined his new sort of medical school, Entwisle was fervent. "Nothing I'd like so much as to have a chance at a place like that," he fluttered, and Gottlieb went back to Mohalis triumphant. He was the more assured because (though he sardonically refused it) he was at this time offered the medical deanship of the University of West Chippewa.

So simple, or so insane, was he that he wrote to Dean Silva politely bidding him step down and hand over his school—his work, his life—to an unknown teacher in Harvard! A courteous old gentleman was Dad Silva, a fit disciple of Osler, but this incredible letter killed his patience. He replied that while he could see the value of basic research, the medical school belonged to the people of the state, and its task was to provide them with immediate and practical attention. For himself, he hinted, if he ever believed that the school would profit by his resignation he would go at once, but he needed a rather broader suggestion than a letter from one of his own subordinates!

Gottlieb retorted with spirit and indiscretion. He damned the People of the State of Winnemac. Were they, in their present condition of nincompoopery, worth any sort of attention? He unjustifiably took his demand over Silva's head to that great orator and patriot, Dr. Horace Greeley Truscott, president of the University.

President Truscott said, "Really, I'm too engrossed to consider chimerical schemes, however ingenious they may be."

"You are too busy to consider anything but selling honorary degrees to millionaires for gymnasiums," remarked Gottlieb.

Next day he was summoned to a special meeting of the University Council. As head of the medical department of bacteriology, Gottlieb was a member of this all-ruling body, and when he entered the long Council Chamber, with its gilt ceiling, its heavy maroon curtains, its somber paintings of pioneers, he started for his usual seat, unconscious of the knot of whispering members, meditating on far-off absorbing things.

"Oh, uh, Professor Gottlieb, will you please sit down there at the far end of the table?" called President Truscott.

Then Gottlieb was aware of tensions. He saw that out of the seven members of the Board of Regents, the four who lived in or near Zenith were present. He saw that sitting beside Truscott was not the dean of the academic department but Dean Silva. He saw that however easily they talked, they were looking at him through the mist of their chatter.

President Truscott announced, "Gentlemen, this joint meeting of the Council and the regents is to consider charges against Professor Max Gottlieb preferred by his dean and by myself."

Gottlieb suddenly looked old.

"These charges are: Disloyalty to his dean, his president, his regents, and to the State of Winnemac. Disloyalty to recognized medical and scholastic ethics. Insane egotism. Atheism. Persistent failure to collaborate with his colleagues, and such inability to understand practical affairs as makes it dangerous to let him conduct the important laboratories and classes with which we have entrusted him. Gentlemen, I shall now prove each of these points, from Professor Gottlieb's own letters to Dean Silva."

He proved them.

The chairman of the Board of Regents suggested, "Gottlieb, I think it would simplify things if you just handed us your resignation and permitted us to part in good feeling, instead of having the unpleasant—"

"I'm damned if I will resign!" Gottlieb was on his feet, a lean fury. "Because you all haf schoolboy minds, golf-links minds, you are twisting my expression, and perfectly accurate expression, of a sound revolutionary ideal, which would personally to me be of no value or advantage whatefer, into a desire to steal promotions. That fools should judge honor—!" His long forefinger was a fish-hook, reaching for President Truscott's soul. "No! I will not resign! You can cast me out!"

"I'm afraid, then, we must ask you to leave the room while we vote." The president was very suave, for so large and strong and hearty a man.

Gottlieb rode his wavering bicycle to the laboratory. It was by telephone message from a brusque girl clerk in the president's office that he was informed that "his resignation had been accepted."

He agonized, "Discharge me? They couldn't! I'm the chief glory, the only glory, of this shopkeepers' school!" When he comprehended that apparently they very much had discharged him, he was shamed that he should have given them a chance to kick him. But the really dismaying thing was that he should by an effort to be a politician have interrupted the sacred work.

He required peace and a laboratory, at once.

They'd see what fools they were when they heard that Harvard had called him!

He was eager for the mellower ways of Cambridge and Boston. Why had he remained so long in raw Mohalis? He wrote to Dr. Entwisle, hinting that he was willing to hear an offer. He expected a telegram. He waited a week, then had a long letter from Entwisle admitting that he had been premature in speaking for the Harvard faculty. Entwisle presented the faculty's compliments and their hope that some time they might have the honor of his presence, but as things were now—

Gottlieb wrote to the University of West Chippewa that, after all, he was willing to think about their medical deanship . . . and had answer that the place was filled, that they had not greatly liked the tone of his former letter, and they did not "care to go into the matter further."

At sixty-one, Gottlieb had saved but a few hundred dollars—literally a few hundred. Like any bricklayer out of work, he had to have a job or go hungry. He was no longer a genius impatient of interrupted creation but a shabby schoolmaster in disgrace.

He prowled through his little brown house, fingering papers, staring at his wife, staring at old pictures, staring at nothing. He still had a month of teaching—they had dated ahead the resignation which they had written for him—but he was too dispirited to go to the laboratory. He felt unwanted, almost unsafe. His ancient sureness was broken into self-pity. He waited from delivery to delivery for the mail. Surely there would be aid from somebody who knew what he was, what he meant. There were many friendly letters about research, but the sort of men with whom he corresponded did not listen to intercollegiate faculty tattle nor know of his need.

He could not, after the Harvard mischance and the West Chippewa rebuke, approach the universities or the scientific institutes, and he was too proud to write begging letters to the men who revered him. No, he would be business-like! He applied to a Chicago teachers' agency, and received a stilted answer promising to look about and inquiring whether he would care to take the position of teacher of physics and chemistry in a suburban high school.

Before he had sufficiently recovered from his fury to be able to reply, his household was overwhelmed by his wife's sudden agony.

She had been unwell for months. He had wanted her to see a physician, but she had refused, and all the while she was stolidly terrified by the fear that she had cancer of the stomach. Now when she began to vomit blood, she cried to him for help. The Gottlieb who scoffed at medical credos, at "carpenters" and "pill mongers," had forgotten what he knew of diagnosis, and when he was ill, or his family, he called for the doctor as desperately as any backwoods layman to whom illness was the black malignity of unknown devils.

In unbelievable simplicity he considered that, as his quarrel with Silva was not personal, he could still summon him, and this time he was justified. Silva came, full of excessive benignity, chuckling to himself, "When he's got something the matter, he doesn't run for Arrenhius or Jacques Loeb, but for me!" Into the meager cottage the little man brought strength, and Gottlieb gazed down on him trustingly.

Mrs. Gottlieb was suffering. Silva gave her morphine. Not without satisfaction he learned that Gottlieb did not even know the dose. He examined her—his pudgy hands had the sensitiveness if not the precision of Gottlieb's skeleton fingers. He peered about the airless bedroom: the dark green curtains, the crucifix on the dumpy bureau, the color-print of a virtuously voluptuous maiden. He was bothered by an impression of having recently been in the room. He remembered. It was the twin of the doleful chamber of a German grocer whom he had seen during a consultation a month ago.

He spoke to Gottlieb not as to a colleague or an enemy but as a patient, to be cheered.

"Don't think there's any tumorous mass. As of course you know, Doctor, you can tell such a lot by the differences in the shape of the lower border of the ribs, and by the surface of the belly during deep breathing."

"Oh, yesss."

"I don't think you need to worry in the least. We'd better hustle her off to the University Hospital, and we'll give her a test meal and get her X-rayed and take a look for Boas-Oppler bugs."

She was taken away, heavy, inert, carried down the cottage steps. Gottlieb was with her. Whether or not he loved her, whether he was capable of ordinary domestic affection, could not be discovered. The need of turning to Dean Silva had damaged his opinion of his own wisdom. It was the final affront, more subtle and more enervating than the offer to teach chemistry to children. As he sat by her bed, his dark face was blank, and the wrinkles which deepened across that mask may have been sorrow, may have been fear. . . . Nor is it known how, through the secure and uninvaded years, he had regarded his wife's crucifix, which Silva had spied on their bureau—a gaudy plaster crucifix on a box set with gilded shells.

Silva diagnosed it as probable gastric ulcer, and placed her on treatment, with light and frequent meals. She improved, but she remained in the hospital for four weeks, and Gottlieb wondered: Are these doctors deceiving us? Is it really cancer, which by Their mystic craft They are concealing from me who know naught?

Robbed of her silent assuring presence on which night by weary night he had depended, he fretted over his daughters, despaired at their noisy piano-practice, their inability to manage the slattern maid. When they had gone to bed he sat alone in the pale lamplight, unmoving, not reading. He was bewildered. His haughty self was like a robber baron fallen into the hands of rebellious slaves, stooped under a filthy load, the proud eye rheumy and patient with despair, the sword hand chopped off, obscene flies crawling across the gnawed wrist.

It was at this time that he encountered Martin and Leora on the street in Zenith.

He did not look back when they had passed him, but all that afternoon he brooded on them. "That girl, maybe it was she that stole Martin from me—from science! No! He was right. One sees what happens to the fools like me!"

On the day after Martin and Leora had started for Wheatsylvania, singing, Gottlieb went to Chicago to see the teachers' agency.

The firm was controlled by a Live Wire who had once been a county superintendent of schools. He was not much interested. Gottlieb lost his temper: "Do you make an endeavor to find positions for teachers, or do you merely send out circulars to amuse yourself? Haf you looked up my record? Do you know who I am?"

The agent roared, "Oh, we know about you, all right, all right! I didn't when I first wrote you, but— You seem to have a good record as a laboratory man, though I don't see that you've produced anything of the slightest use in medicine. We had hoped to give you a chance such as you nor nobody else ever had. John Edtooth, the Oklahoma oil magnate, has decided to found a university that for plant and endowment and individuality will beat anything that's ever been pulled off in education—biggest gymnasium in the world, with an ex-New York Giant for baseball coach! We thought maybe we might work you in on the bacteriology or the physiology—I guess you could manage to teach that, too, if you boned up on it. But we've been making some inquiries. From some good friends of ours, down Winnemac way. And we find that you're not to be trusted with a position of real responsibility. Why, they fired you for general incompetence! But now that you've had your lesson— Do you think you'd be competent to teach Practical Hygiene in Edtooth University?"

Gottlieb was so angry that he forgot to speak English, and as all his cursing was in student German, in a creaky dry voice, the whole scene was very funny indeed to the cackling bookkeeper and the girl stenographers. When he went from that place Max Gottlieb walked slowly, without purpose, and in his eyes were senile tears.

Chapter XIII

No one in the medical world had ever damned more heartily than Gottlieb the commercialism of certain large pharmaceutical firms, particularly Dawson T. Hunziker & Co., Inc., of Pittsburgh. The Hunziker Company was an old and ethical house which dealt only with reputable doctors—or practically only with reputable doctors. It furnished excellent antitoxins for diphtheria and tetanus, as well as the purest of official preparations, with the plainest and most official-looking labels on the swaggeringly modest brown bottles. Gottlieb had asserted that they produced doubtful vaccines, yet he returned from Chicago to write to Dawson Hunziker that he was no longer interested in teaching, and he would be willing to work for them on half time if he might use their laboratories, on possibly important research, for the rest of the day.

When the letter had gone he sat mumbling. He was certainly not altogether sane. "Education! Biggest gymnasium in the world! Incapable of responsibility. Teaching I can do no more. But Hunziker will laugh at me. I haf told the truth about him and I shall haf to— Dear Gott, what shall I do?"

Into this still frenzy, while his frightened daughters peered at him from doorways, hope glided.

The telephone rang. He did not answer it. On the third irascible burring he took up the receiver and grumbled, "Yes, yes, vot iss it?"

A twanging nonchalant voice: "This M. C. Gottlieb?"

"This is Dr. Gottlieb!"

"Well, I guess you're the party. Hola wire. Long distance wants yuh."

Then, "Professor Gottlieb? This is Dawson Hunziker speaking. From Pittsburgh. My dear fellow, we should be delighted to have you join our staff."

"I— But—"

"I believe you have criticized the pharmaceutical houses—oh, we read the newspaper clippings very efficiently!—but we feel that when you come to us and understand the Spirit of the Old Firm better, you'll be enthusiastic. I hope, by the way, I'm not interrupting something."

Thus, over certain hundreds of miles, from the gold and blue drawing-room of his Sewickley home, Hunziker spoke to Max Gottlieb sitting in his patched easy chair, and Gottlieb grated, with a forlorn effort at dignity:

"No, it iss all right."

"Well—we shall be glad to offer you five thousand dollars a year, for a starter, and we shan't worry about the half-time arrangement. We'll give you all the space and technicians and material you need, and you just go ahead and ignore us, and work out whatever seems important to you. Our only request is that if you do find any serums which are of real value to the world, we shall have the privilege of manufacturing them, and if we lose money on 'em, it doesn't matter. We like to make money, if we can do it honestly, but our chief purpose is to serve mankind. Of course if the serums pay, we shall be only too delighted to give you a generous commission. Now about practical details—"

II

Gottlieb, the placidly virulent hater of religious rites, had a religious-seeming custom.

Often he knelt by his bed and let his mind run free. It was very much like prayer, though certainly there was no formal invocation, no consciousness of a Supreme Being—other than Max Gottlieb. This night, as he knelt, with the wrinkles softening in his drawn face, he meditated, "I was asinine that I should ever scold the commercialists! This salesman fellow, he has his feet on the ground. How much more aut'entic the worst counter-jumper than frightened professors! Fine dieners! Freedom! No teaching of imbeciles! *Du Heiliger!*"

But he had no contract with Dawson Hunziker.

III

In the medical periodicals the Dawson Hunziker Company published full-page advertisements, most starchy and refined in type, announcing that Professor Max Gottlieb, perhaps the most distinguished immunologist in the world, had joined their staff.

In his Chicago clinic, one Dr. Rouncefield chuckled, "That's what becomes of these super-highbrows. Pardon me if I seem to grin."

In the laboratories of Ehrlich and Roux, Bordet and Sir David Bruce, sorrowing men wailed, "How could old Max have gone over to that damned pill-pedler? Why didn't he come to us? Oh, well, if he didn't want to— *Voila!* He is dead."

In the village of Wheatsylvania, in North Dakota, a young doctor protested to his wife, "Of all the people in the world! I wouldn't have believed it! Max Gottlieb falling for those crooks!"

"I don't care!" said his wife. "If he's gone into business, he had some good reason for it. I told you, I'd leave you for—"

"Oh, well," sighingly, "give and forgive. I learned a lot from Gottlieb and I'm grateful for— God, Leora, I wish *he* hadn't gone wrong!"

And Max Gottlieb, with his three young and a pale, slow-moving wife, was arriving at the station in Pittsburgh, tugging a shabby wicker bag, an immigrant bundle, and a Bond Street dressing-case. From the train he had stared up at the valiant cliffs, down to the smoke-tinged splendor of the river, and his heart was young. Here was fiery enterprise, not the flat land and flat minds of Winnemac. At the station-entrance every dingy taxicab seemed radiant to him, and he marched forth a conqueror.

IV

In the Dawson Hunziker building, Gottlieb found such laboratories as he had never planned, and instead of student assistants he had an expert who himself had taught bacteriology, as well as three swift technicians, one of them German-trained. He was received with acclaim in the private office of Hunziker, which was remarkably like a minor cathedral. Hunziker was bald and business-like as to skull but tortoise-spectacled and sentimental of eye. He stood up at his Jacobean desk, gave Gottlieb a Havana cigar, and told him that they had awaited him pantingly.

In the enormous staff dining-room Gottlieb found scores of competent young chemists and biologists who treated him with reverence. He liked them. If they talked too much of money—of how much this new tincture of cinchona ought to sell, and how soon their salaries would be increased—yet they were free of the careful pomposities of college instructors. As a youngster, the cap-tilted young Max had been a laughing man, and now in gusty arguments his laughter came back.

His wife seemed better; his daughter Miriam found an excellent piano teacher; the boy Robert entered college that autumn; they had a spacious though decrepit house; the relief from the droning and the annually repeated, inevitable routine of the classroom was exhilarating; and Gottlieb had never in his life worked so well. He was unconscious of everything outside of his laboratory and a few theaters and concert-halls.

Six months passed before he realized that the young technical experts resented what he considered his jolly thrusts at their commercialism. They were tired of his mathematical enthusiasms and some of them viewed him as an old bore, muttered of him as a Jew. He was hurt, for he liked to be merry with fellow workers. He began to ask questions and to explore the Hunziker building. He had seen nothing of it save his laboratory, a corridor or two, the dining-room, and Hunziker's office.

However abstracted and impractical, Gottlieb would have made an excellent Sherlock Holmes—if anybody who would have made an excellent Sherlock Holmes would have been willing to be a detective. His mind burned through appearances to actuality. He discovered now that the Dawson Hunziker Company was quite all he had asserted in earlier days. They did make excellent antitoxins and ethical preparations, but they were also producing a new "cancer remedy" manufactured from the orchid, pontifically recommended and possessing all the value of mud. And to various billboard-advertising beauty companies they sold millions of bottles of a complexion-cream guaranteed to turn a Canadian Indian guide as lily-fair as the angels. This treasure cost six cents a bottle to make and a dollar over the counter, and the name of Dawson Hunziker was never connected with it.

It was at this time that Gottlieb succeeded in his masterwork after twenty years of seeking. He produced antitoxin in the test-tube, which meant that it would be possible to immunize against certain diseases without tediously making sera by the inoculation of animals. It was a revolution, the revolution, in immunology . . . if he was right.

He revealed it at a dinner for which Hunziker had captured a general, a college president, and a pioneer aviator. It was an expansive dinner, with admirable hock, the first decent German wine Gottlieb had drunk in years. He twirled the slender green glass affectionately; he came out of his dreams and became excited, gay, demanding. They applauded him and for an hour he was a Great Scientist. Of them all, Hunziker was most generous in his praise. Gottlieb wondered if some one had not tricked this good bald man into intrigues with the beautifiers.

Hunziker summoned him to the office next day. Hunziker did his summoning very well indeed (unless it happened to be merely a stenographer). He sent a glossy morning-coated male secretary, who presented Mr. Hunziker's compliments to the much less glossy Dr. Gottlieb, and hinted with the delicacy of a lilac bud that if it was quite altogether convenient, if it would not in the least interfere with Dr. Gottlieb's experiments, Mr. Hunziker would be flattered to see him in the office at a quarter after three.

When Gottlieb rambled in, Hunziker motioned the secretary out of existence and drew up a tall Spanish chair.

"I lay awake half the night thinking about your discovery, Dr. Gottlieb. I've been talking to the technical director and sales-manager and we feel it's the time to strike. We'll patent your method of synthesizing antibodies and immediately put them on the market in large quantities, with a great big advertising campaign—you know—not circus it, of course—strictly high-class ethical advertising. We'll start with anti-diphtheria serum. By the way, when you receive your next check you'll find we've raised your honorarium to seven thousand a year." Hunziker was a large purring pussy, now, and Gottlieb death-still. "Need I say, my dear fellow, that if there's the demand I anticipate, you will have exceedingly large commissions coming!"

Hunziker leaned back with a manner of "How's that for glory, my boy?"

Gottlieb spoke nervously: "I do not approve of patenting serological processes. They should be open to all laboratories. And I am strongly against premature production or even announcement. I think I am right, but I must check my technique, perhaps improve it—be *sure.* Then, I should think, there should be no objection to market production, but in very small quantities and in fair competition with others, not under patents, as if this was a dinglebat toy for the Christmas tradings!"

"My dear fellow, I quite sympathize. Personally I should like nothing so much as to spend my whole life in just producing one priceless scientific discovery, without consideration of mere profit. But we have our duty toward the stockholders of the Dawson Hunziker Company to make money for them. Do you realize that they have—and many of them are poor widows and orphans—invested their Little All in our stock, and that we must keep faith? I am helpless; I am but their Humble Servant. And on the other side: I think we've treated you rather well, Dr. Gottlieb, and we've given you complete freedom. And we intend to go on treating you well! Why, man, you'll be rich; you'll be one of us! I don't like to make any demands, but on this point it's my duty to insist, and I shall expect you at the earliest possible moment to start manufacturing—"

Gottlieb was sixty-two. The defeat at Winnemac had done something to his courage. . . . And he had no contract with Hunziker.

He protested shakily, but as he crawled back to his laboratory it seemed impossible for him to leave this sanctuary and face the murderous brawling world, and quite as impossible to tolerate a cheapened and ineffective imitation of his antitoxin. He began, that hour, a sordid strategy which his old proud self would have called inconceivable; he began to equivocate, to put off announcement and production till he should have "cleared up a few points," while week on week Hunziker became more threatening. Meantime he prepared for disaster. He moved his family to a smaller house, and gave up every luxury, even smoking.

Among his economies was the reduction of his son's allowance.

Robert was a square-rigged, swart, tempestuous boy, arrogant where there seemed to be no reason for arrogance, longed for by the anemic, milky sort of girls, yet ever supercilious to them. While his father was alternately proud and amiably sardonic about his own Jewish blood, the boy conveyed to his classmates in college that he was from pure and probably noble German stock. He was welcomed, or half welcomed, in a motoring, poker-playing, country-club set, and he had to have more money. Gottlieb missed twenty dollars from his desk. He who ridiculed conventional honor had the honor, as he had the pride, of a savage old squire. A new misery stained his incessant bitterness at having to deceive Hunziker. He faced Robert with, "My boy, did you take the money from my desk?"

Few youngsters could have faced that jut of his hawk nose, the red-veined rage of his sunken eyes. Robert spluttered, then shouted:

"Yes, I did! And I've got to have some more! I've got to get some clothes and stuff. It's your fault. You bring me up to train with a lot of fellows that have all the cash in the world, and then you expect me to dress like a hobo!"

"Stealing—"

"Rats! What's stealing! You're always making fun of these preachers that talk about Sin and Truth and Honesty and all those words that've been used so much they don't mean a darn' thing and— I don't care! Daws Hunziker, the old man's son, he told me his dad said you could be a millionaire, and then you keep us strapped like this, and Mom sick— Let me tell you, back in Mohalis Mom used to slip me a couple of dollars almost every week and— I'm tired of it! If you're going to keep me in rags, I'm going to cut out college!"

Gottlieb stormed, but there was no force in it. He did not know, all the next fortnight, what his son was going to do, what himself was going to do.

Then, so quietly that not till they had returned from the cemetery did they realize her passing, his wife died, and the next week his oldest daughter ran off with a worthless laughing fellow who lived by gambling.

Gottlieb sat alone. Over and over he read the Book of Job. "Truly the Lord hath smitten me and my house," he whispered. When Robert came in, mumbling that he would be good, the old man lifted to him a blind face, unhearing. But as he repeated the fables of his fathers it did not occur to him to believe them, or to stoop in fear before their God of Wrath—or to gain ease by permitting Hunziker to defile his discovery.

He arose, in time, and went silently to his laboratory. His experiments were as careful as ever, and his assistants saw no change save that he did not lunch in hall. He walked blocks away, to a vile restaurant at which he could save thirty cents a day.

V

Out of the dimness which obscured the people about him, Miriam emerged.

She was eighteen, the youngest of his brood, squat, and in no way comely save for her tender mouth. She had always been proud of her father, understanding the mysterious and unreasoning compulsions of his science, but she had been in awe till now, when he walked heavily and spoke rarely. She dropped her piano lessons, discharged the maid, studied the cook-book, and prepared for him the fat crisp dishes that he loved. Her regret was that she had never learned German, for he dropped now and then into the speech of his boyhood.

He eyed her, and at length: "So! One is with me. Could you endure the poverty if I went away—to teach chemistry in a high school!"

"Yes. Of course. Maybe I could play the piano in a movie theater."

He might not have done it without her loyalty, but when Dawson Hunziker next paraded into the laboratory, demanding, "Now look here. We've fussed long enough. We got to put your stuff on the market," then Gottlieb answered, "No. If you wait till I have done all I can—maybe one year, probably three—you shall have it. But not till I am sure. No."

Hunziker went off huffily, and Gottlieb prepared for sentence.

Then the card of Dr. A. DeWitt Tubbs, Director of the McGurk Institute of Biology, of New York, was brought to him.

Gottlieb knew of Tubbs. He had never visited McGurk but he considered it, next to Rockefeller and McCormick, the soundest and freest organization for pure scientific research in the country, and if he had pictured a Heavenly laboratory in which good scientists might spend eternity in happy and thoroughly impractical research, he would have devised it in the likeness of McGurk. He was mildly pleased that its director should have called on him.

Dr. A. DeWitt Tubbs was tremendously whiskered on all visible spots save his nose and temples and the palms of his hands, short but passionately whiskered, like a Scotch terrier. Yet they were not comic whiskers; they were the whiskers of dignity; and his eyes were serious, his step an earnest trot, his voice a piping solemnity.

"Dr. Gottlieb, this is a great pleasure. I have heard your papers at the Academy of Sciences but, to my own loss, I have hitherto failed to have an introduction to you."

Gottlieb tried not to sound embarrassed.

Tubbs looked at the assistants, like a plotter in a political play, and hinted, "May we have a talk—"

Gottlieb led him to his office, overlooking a vast bustle of sidetracks, of curving rails and brown freight-cars, and Tubbs urged:

"It has come to our attention, by a curious chance, that you are on the eve of your most significant discovery. We all wondered, when you left academic work, at your decision to enter the commercial field. We wished that you had cared to come to us."

"You would have taken me in? I needn't at all have come here?"

"Naturally! Now from what we hear, you are not giving your attention to the commercial side of things, and that tempts us to wonder whether you could be persuaded to join us at McGurk. So I just sprang on a train and ran down here. We should be delighted to have you become a member of the institute, and chief of the Department of Bacteriology and Immunology. Mr. McGurk and I desire nothing but the advancement of science. You would, of course, have absolute freedom as to what researches you thought it best to pursue, and I think we could provide as good assistance and material as would be obtainable anywhere in the world. In regard to salary—permit me to be business-like and perhaps blunt, as my train leaves in one hour—I don't suppose we could equal the doubtless large emolument which the Hunziker people are able to pay you, but we can go to ten thousand dollars a year—"

"Oh, my God, do not talk of the money! I shall be wit' you in New York one week from to-day. You see," said Gottlieb, "I haf no contract here!"

Chapter XIV

ALL AFTERNOON they drove in the flapping buggy across the long undulations of the prairie. To their wandering there was no barrier, neither lake nor mountain nor factory-bristling city, and the breeze about them was flowing sunshine.

Martin cried to Leora, "I feel as if all the Zenith dust and hospital lint were washed out of my lungs. Dakota. Real man's country. Frontier. Opportunity. America!"

From the thick swale the young prairie chickens rose. As he watched them sweep across the wheat, his sun-drowsed spirit was part of the great land, and he was almost freed of the impatience with which he had started out from Wheatsylvania.

"If you're going driving, don't forget that supper is six o'clock sharp," Mrs. Tozer had said, smiling to sugar-coat it.

On Main Street, Mr. Tozer waved to them and shouted, "Be back by six. Supper at six o'clock sharp."

Bert Tozer ran out from the bank, like a country schoolmaster skipping from a one-room schoolhouse, and cackled, "Say, you folks better not forget to be back at six o'clock for supper or the Old Man'll have a fit. He'll expect you for supper at six o'clock sharp, and when he says six o'clock *sharp*, he means six o'clock *sharp*, and not five minutes *past* six!"

"Now that," observed Leora, "is funny, because in my twenty-two years in Wheatsylvania I remember three different times when supper was as late as seven minutes after six. Let's get out of this, Sandy. . . . I wonder were we so wise to live with the family and save money?"

Before they had escaped from the not very extensive limits of Wheatsylvania they passed Ada Quist, the future Mrs. Bert Tozer, and through the lazy air they heard her voice slashing: "Better be home by six."

Martin would be heroic. "We'll by golly get back when we're by golly good and ready!" he said to Leora; but on them both was the cumulative dread of the fussing voices, beyond every breezy prospect was the order, "Be back at six sharp"; and they whipped up to arrive at eleven minutes to six, as Mr. Tozer was returning from the creamery, full thirty seconds later than usual.

"Glad to see you among us," he said. "Hustle now and get that horse in the livery stable. Supper's at six—sharp!"

Martin survived it sufficiently to sound domestic when he announced at the supper-table:

"We had a bully drive. I'm going to like it here. Well, I've loafed for a day and a half, and now I've got to get busy. First thing is, I must find a location for my office. What is there vacant, Father Tozer?"

Mrs. Tozer said brightly, "Oh, I have such a nice idea, Martin. Why can't we fix up an office for you out in the barn? It'd be so handy to the house, for you to get to meals on time, and you could keep an eye on the house if the girl was out and Ory and I went out visiting or to the Embroidery Circle."

"In the barn!"

"Why, yes, in the old harness room. It's partly ceiled, and we could put in some nice tar paper or even beaver board."

"Mother Tozer, what the dickens do you think I'm planning to do? I'm not a hired man in a livery stable, or a kid looking for a place to put his birds' eggs! I was thinking of opening an office as a physician!"

Bert made it all easy: "Yuh, but you aren't much of a physician yet. You're just getting your toes in."

"I'm one hell of a good physician! Excuse me for cussing, Mother Tozer, but— Why, nights in the hospital, I've held hundreds of lives in my hand! I intend—"

"Look here, Mart," said Bertie. "As we're putting up the money—I don't want to be a tightwad but after all, a dollar is a dollar—if we furnish the dough, we've got to decide the best way to spend it."

Mr. Tozer looked thoughtful and said helplessly, "That's so. No sense taking a risk, with the blame' farmers demanding all the money they can get for their wheat and cream, and then deliberately going to work and not paying the interest on their loans. I swear, it don't hardly pay to invest in mortgages any longer. No sense putting on lugs. Stands to reason you can look at a fellow's sore throat or prescribe for an earache just as well in a nice simple little office as in some fool place all fixed up like a Moorhead saloon. Mother will see you have a comfortable corner in the barn—"

Leora intruded: "Look here, Papa. I want you to lend us one thousand dollars, outright, to use as we see fit." The sensation was immense. "We'll pay you six per cent—no, we won't; we'll pay you five; that's enough."

"And mortgages bringing six, seven, and eight!" Bert quavered.

"Five's enough. And we want our own say, absolute, as to how we use it—to fit up an office or anything else."

Mr. Tozer began, "That's a foolish way to—"

Bert took it away from him: "Ory, you're crazy! I suppose we'll have to lend you some money, but you'll blame well come to us for it from time to time, and you'll blame well take our advice—"

Leora rose. "Either you do what I say, just exactly what I say, or Mart and I take the first train and go back to Zenith, and I mean it! Plenty of places open for him there, with a big salary, so we won't have to be dependent on anybody!"

There was much conversation, most of which sounded like all the rest of it. Once Leora started for the stairs, to go up and pack; once Martin and she stood waving their napkins as they shook their fists, the general composition remarkably like the Laocoön.

Leora won.

They settled down to the most solacing fussing.

"Did you bring your trunk up from the depot?" asked Mr. Tozer.

"No sense leaving it there—paying two bits a day storage!" fumed Bert.

"I got it up this morning," said Martin.

"Oh, yes, Martin had it brought up this morning," agreed Mrs. Tozer.

"You had it brought? Didn't you bring it up yourself?" agonized Mr. Tozer.

"No. I had the fellow that runs the lumberyard haul it up for me," said Martin.

"Well, gosh almighty, you could just as well've put it on a wheelbarrow and brought it up yourself and saved a quarter!" said Bert.

"But a doctor has to keep his dignity," said Leora.

"Dignity, rats! Blame sight more dignified to be seen shoving a wheelbarrow than smoking them dirty cigarettes all the time!"

"Well, anyway— Where'd you put it?" asked Mr. Tozer.

"It's up in our room," said Martin.

"Where'd you think we better put it when it's unpacked? The attic is awful' full," Mr. Tozer submitted to Mrs. Tozer.

"Oh, I think Martin could get it in there."

"Why couldn't he put it in the barn?"

"Oh, not a nice new trunk like that!"

"What's the matter with the barn?" said Bert. "It's all nice and dry. Seems a shame to waste all that good space in the barn, now that you've gone and decided he mustn't have his dear little office there!"

"Bertie," from Leora, "I know what we'll do. You seem to have the barn on your brain. You move your old bank there, and Martin'll take the bank building for his office."

"That's entirely different—"

"Now there's no sense you two showing off and trying to be smart," protested Mr. Tozer. "Do you ever hear your mother and I scrapping and fussing like that? When do you think you'll have your trunk unpacked, Mart?" Mr. Tozer could consider barns and he could consider trunks but his was not a brain to grasp two such complicated matters at the same time.

"I can get it unpacked to-night, if it makes any difference—"

"Well, I don't suppose it really makes any special difference, but when you start to *do* a thing—"

"Oh, what difference does it make whether he—"

"If he's going to look for an office, instead of moving right into the barn, he can't take a month of Sundays getting unpacked and—"

"Oh, good Lord, I'll get it done to-night—"

"And I think we can get it in the attic—"

"I tell you it's jam full already—"

"We'll go take a look at it after supper—"

"Well now, I tell you when I tried to get that duck-boat in—"

Martin probably did not scream, but he heard himself screaming. The free and virile land was leagues away and for years forgotten.

II

To find an office took a fortnight of diplomacy, and of discussion brightening three meals a day, every day. (Not that office-finding was the only thing the Tozers mentioned. They went thoroughly into every moment of Martin's day; they commented on his digestion, his mail, his walks, his shoes that needed cobbling, and whether he had yet taken them to the farmer-trapper-cobbler, and how much the cobbling ought to cost, and the presumable theology, politics, and marital relations of the cobbler.)

Mr. Tozer had from the first known the perfect office. The Norbloms lived above their general store, and Mr. Tozer knew that the Norbloms were thinking of moving. There was indeed nothing that was happening or likely to happen in Wheatsylvania which Mr. Tozer did not know and explain. Mrs. Norblom was tired of keeping house, and she wanted to go to Mrs. Beeson's boarding house (to the front room, on the right as you went along the up-stairs hall, the room with the plaster walls and the nice little stove that Mrs. Beeson bought from Otto Krag for seven dollars and thirty-five cents—no, seven and a quarter it was).

They called on the Norbloms and Mr. Tozer hinted that "it might be nice for the Doctor to locate over the store, if the Norbloms were thinking of making any change—"

The Norbloms stared at each other, with long, bleached, cautious, Scandinavian stares, and grumbled that they "didn't *know*—of course it was the finest location in town—" Mr. Norblom admitted that if, against all probability, they ever considered moving, they would probably ask twenty-five dollars a month for the flat, unfurnished.

Mr. Tozer came out of the international conference as craftily joyful as any Mr. Secretary Tozer or Lord Tozer in Washington or London:

"Fine! Fine! We made him commit himself! Twenty-five, he says. That means, when the time's ripe, we'll offer him eighteen and close for twenty-one-seventy-five. If we just handle him careful, and give him time to go see Mrs. Beeson and fix up about boarding with her, we'll have him just where we want him!"

"Oh, if the Norbloms can't make up their minds, then let's try something else," said Martin. "There's a couple of vacant rooms behind the *Eagle* office."

"What? Go chasing around, after we've given the Norbloms reason to think we're serious, and make enemies of 'em for life? Now that would be a fine way to start building up a practise, wouldn't it! And I must say I wouldn't blame the Norbloms one bit for getting wild if you let 'em down like that. This ain't Zenith, where you can go yelling around expecting to get things done in two minutes!"

Through a fortnight, while the Norbloms agonized over deciding to do what they had long ago decided to do, Martin waited, unable to begin work. Until he should open a certified and recognizable office, most of the village did not regard him as a competent physician but as "that son-in-law of Andy Tozer's." In the fortnight he was called only once: for the sick-headache of Miss Agnes Ingleblad, aunt and housekeeper of Alec Ingleblad the barber. He was delighted, till Bert Tozer explained:

"Oh, so *she* called you in, eh? She's always doctorin' around. There ain't a thing the matter with her, but she's always trying out the latest stunt. Last time it was a fellow that come through here selling pills and liniments out of a Ford, and the time before that it was a faith-healer, crazy loon up here at Dutchman's Forge, and then for quite a spell she doctored with an osteopath in Leopolis—though I tell you there's something to this osteopathy—they cure a lot of folks that you regular docs can't seem to find out what's the matter with 'em, don't you think so?"

Martin remarked that he did not think so.

"Oh, you docs!" Bert crowed in his most jocund manner, for Bert could be very joky and bright. "You're all alike, especially when you're just out of school and think you know it all. You can't see any good in chiropractic or electric belts or bone-setters or anything, because they take so many good dollars away from you."

Then behold the Dr. Martin Arrowsmith who had once infuriated Angus Duer and Irving Watters by his sarcasm on medical standards upholding to a lewdly grinning Bert Tozer the benevolence and scientific knowledge of all doctors; proclaiming that no medicine had ever (at least by any Winnemac graduate) been prescribed in vain nor any operation needlessly performed.

He saw a good deal of Bert now. He sat about the bank, hoping to be called on a case, his fingers itching for bandages. Ada Quist came in with frequency and Bert laid aside his figuring to be coy with her:

"You got to be careful what you even think about, when the doc is here, Ade. He's been telling me what a whale of a lot of neurology and all that mind-reading stuff he knows. How about it, Mart? I'm getting so scared that I've changed the combination on the safe."

"Heh!" said Ada. "He may fool some folks but he can't fool me. Anybody can learn things in books, but when it comes to practising 'em— Let me tell you, Mart, if you ever have one-tenth of the savvy that old Dr. Winter of Leopolis has, you'll live longer than I expect!"

Together they pointed out that for a person who felt his Zenith training had made him so "gosh-awful' smart that he sticks up his nose at us poor hicks of dirt-farmers," Martin's scarf was rather badly tied.

All of his own wit and some of Ada's Bert repeated at the supper table.

"You oughtn't to ride the boy so hard. Still, that was pretty cute about the necktie—I guess Mart does think he's some punkins," chuckled Mr. Tozer.

Leora took Martin aside after supper. "Darlin', can you stand it? We'll have our own house, soon as we can. Or shall we vamoose?"

"I'm by golly going to stand it!"

"Um. Maybe. Dear, when you hit Bertie, do be careful—they'll hang you."

He ambled to the front porch. He determined to view the rooms behind the *Eagle* office. Without a retreat in which to be safe from Bert he could not endure another week. He could not wait for the Norbloms to make up their minds, though they had become to him dread and eternal figures whose enmity would crush him; prodigious gods shadowing this Wheatsylvania which was the only perceptible world.

He was aware, in the late sad light, that a man was tramping the plank walk before the house, hesitating and peering at him. The man was one Wise, a Russian Jew known to the village as "Wise the Polack." In his shack near the railroad he sold silver stock and motor-factory stock, bought and sold farmlands and horses and muskrat hides. He called out, "That you, Doc?"

"Yup!"

Martin was excited. A patient!

"Say, I wish you'd walk down a ways with me. Couple things I'd like to talk to you about. Or say, come on over to my place and sample some new cigars I've got." He emphasized the word "cigars." North Dakota was, like Mohalis, theoretically dry.

Martin was pleased. He had been sober and industrious so long now!

Wise's shack was a one-story structure, not badly built, half a block from Main Street, with nothing but the railroad track between it and open wheat country. It was lined with pine, pleasant-smelling under the stench of old pipe-smoke. Wise winked—he was a confidential, untrustworthy wisp of a man—and murmured, "Think you could stand a little jolt of first-class Kentucky bourbon?"

"Well, I wouldn't get violent about it."

Wise pulled down the sleazy window-shades and from a warped drawer of his desk brought up a bottle out of which they both drank, wiping the mouth of the bottle with circling palms. Then Wise, abruptly:

"Look here, Doc. You're not like these hicks; you understand that sometimes a fellow gets mixed up in crooked business he didn't intend to. Well, make a long story short, I guess I've sold too much mining stock, and they'll be coming down on me. I've got to be moving—curse it—hoped I could stay settled for couple of years, this time. Well, I hear you're looking for an office. This place would be ideal. Ideal! Two rooms at the back besides this one. I'll rent it to you, furniture and the whole shooting-match, for fifteen dollars a month, if you'll pay me one year in advance. Oh, this ain't phony. Your brother-in-law knows all about my ownership."

Martin tried to be very business-like. Was he not a young doctor who would soon be investing money, one of the most Substantial Citizens in Wheatsylvania? He returned home, and under the parlor lamp, with its green daisies on pink glass, the Tozers listened acutely, Bert stooping forward with open mouth.

"You'd be safe renting it for a year, but that ain't the point," said Bert.

"It certainly isn't! Antagonize the Norbloms, now that they've almost made up their minds to let you have their place? Make me a fool, after all the trouble I've taken?" groaned Mr. Tozer.

They went over it and over it till almost ten o'clock, but Martin was resolute, and the next day he rented Wise's shack.

For the first time in his life he had a place utterly his own, his and Leora's.

In his pride of possession this was the most lordly building on earth, and every rock and weed and doorknob was peculiar and lovely. At sunset he sat on the back stoop (a very interesting and not too broken soap-box) and from the flamboyant horizon the open country flowed across the thin band of the railroad to his feet. Suddenly Leora was beside him, her arm round his neck, and he hymned all the glory of their future:

"Know what I found in the kitchen here? A dandy old auger, hardly rusty a bit, and I can take a box and make a test-tube rack . . . of my own!"

Chapter XV

WITH none of the profane observations on "medical pedlers" which had annoyed Digamma Pi, Martin studied the catalogue of the New Idea Instrument and Furniture Company, of Jersey City. It was a handsome thing. On the glossy green cover, in red and black, were the portraits of the president, a round quippish man who loved all young physicians; the general manager, a cadaverous scholarly man who surely gave all his laborious nights and days to the advancement of science; and the vice-president, Martin's former preceptor, Dr. Roscoe Geake, who had a lively, eye-glassed, forward-looking modernity all his own. The cover also contained, in surprisingly small space, a quantity of poetic prose, and the inspiring promise:

Doctor, don't be buffaloed by the unenterprising. No reason why YOU should lack the equipment which impresses patients, makes practise easy, and brings honor and riches. All the high-class supplies which distinguish the Leaders of the Profession from the Dubs are within YOUR reach right NOW by the famous New Idea Financial System: "Just a little down and the rest FREE—out of the increased earnings which New Idea apparatus will bring you!"

Above, in a border of laurel wreaths and Ionic capitals, was the challenge:

Sing not the glory of soldiers or explorers or statesmen for who can touch the doctor—wise, heroic, uncontaminated by common greed. Gentlemen, we salute you humbly and herewith offer you the most up-to-the-jiffy catalogue ever presented by any surgical supply house.

The back cover, though it was less glorious with green and red, was equally arousing. It presented illustrations of the Bindledorf Tonsillectomy Outfit and of an electric cabinet, with the demand:

Doctor, are you sending your patients off to specialists for tonsil removal or to sanitoriums for electric, etc., treatment? If so, you are losing the chance to show yourself one of the distinguished powers in the domain of medical advancement in your locality, and losing a lot of big fees. Don't you WANT to be a high-class practitioner? Here's the Open Door.

The Bindledorf Outfit is not only useful but exquisitely beautiful, adorns and gives class to any office. We guarantee that by the installation of a Bindledorf Outfit and a New Idea Panaceatic Electro-Therapeutic Cabinet (see details on pp. 34 and 97) you can increase your income from a thousand to ten thousand annually and please patients more than by the most painstaking plugging.

When the Great Call sounds, Doctor, and it's time for you to face your reward, will you be satisfied by a big Masonic funeral and tributes from Grateful Patients if you have failed to lay up provision for the kiddies, and faithful wife who has shared your tribulations?

You may drive through blizzard and August heat, and go down into the purple-shadowed vale of sorrow and wrestle with the ebon-cloaked Powers of Darkness for the lives of your patients, but that heroism is incomplete without Modern Progress, to be obtained by the use of a Bindledorf Tonsillectomy Outfit and the New Idea Panaceatic Cabinet, to be obtained on small payment down, rest on easiest terms known in history of medicine!

II

This poetry of passion Martin neglected, for his opinion of poetry was like his opinion of electric cabinets, but excitedly he ordered a steel stand, a sterilizer, flasks, test-tubes, and a white-enameled mechanism with enchanting levers and gears which transformed it from examining-chair to operating-table. He yearned over the picture of a centrifuge while Leora was admiring the "stunning seven-piece Reception Room fumed oak set, upholstered in genuine Barcelona Longware Leatherette, will give your office the class and distinction of any high-grade New York specialist's."

"Aw, let 'em sit on plain chairs," Martin grunted.

In the attic Mrs. Tozer found enough seedy chairs for the reception-room, and an ancient bookcase which, when Leora had lined it with pink fringed paper, became a noble instrument-cabinet. Till the examining-chair should arrive, Martin would use Wise's lumpy couch, and Leora busily covered it with white oilcloth. Behind the front room of the tiny office-building were two cubicles, formerly bedroom and kitchen. Martin made them into consultation-room and laboratory.

Whistling, he sawed out racks for the glassware and turned the oven of a discarded kerosene stove into a hot-air oven for sterilizing glassware.

"But understand, Lee, I'm not going to go monkeying with any scientific research. I'm through with all that."

Leora smiled innocently. While he worked she sat outside in the long wild grass, sniffing the prairie breeze, her hands about her ankles, but every quarter-hour she had to come in and admire.

Mr. Tozer brought home a package at suppertime. The family opened it, babbling. After supper Martin and Leora hastened with the new treasure to the office and nailed it in place. It was a plate-glass sign; on it in gold letters, "M. Arrowsmith, M.D." They looked up, arms about each other, squealing softly, and in reverence he grunted, "There—by—jiminy!"

They sat on the back stoop, exulting in freedom from Tozers. Along the railroad bumped a freight train with a cheerful clanking. The fireman waved to them from the engine, a brakeman from the platform of the red caboose. After the train there was silence but for the crickets and a distant frog.

"I've never been so happy," he murmured.

III

He had brought from Zenith his own Ochsner surgical case. As he laid out the instruments he admired the thin, sharp, shining bistoury, the strong tenotome, the delicate curved needles. With them was a dental forceps. Dad Silva had warned his classes, "Don't forget the country doctor often has to be not only physician but dentist, yes, and priest, divorce lawyer, blacksmith, chauffeur, and road engineer, and if you are too lily-handed for those trades, don't get out of sight of a trolley line and a beauty parlor." And the first patient whom Martin had in the new office, the second patient in Wheatsylvania, was Nils Krag, the carpenter, roaring with an ulcerated tooth. This was a week before the glass sign was up, and Martin rejoiced to Leora, "Begun already! You'll see 'em tumbling in now."

They did not see them tumbling in. For ten days Martin

tinkered at his hot-air oven or sat at his desk, reading and trying to look busy. His first joy passed into fretfulness, and he could have yelped at the stillness, the inactivity.

Late one afternoon, when he was in a melancholy way preparing to go home, into the office stamped a grizzled Swedish farmer who grumbled, "Doc, I got a fish-hook caught in my thumb and it's all swole." To Arrowsmith, intern in Zenith General Hospital with its out-patient clinic treating hundreds a day, the dressing of a hand had been less important than borrowing a match, but to Dr. Arrowsmith of Wheatsylvania it was a hectic operation, and the farmer a person remarkable and very charming. Martin shook his left hand violently and burbled, "Now if there's anything, you just 'phone me—you just 'phone me."

There had been, he felt, a rush of admiring patients sufficient to justify them in the one thing Leora and he longed to do, the thing about which they whispered at night: the purchase of a motor car for his country calls.

They had seen the car at Frazier's store.

It was a Ford, five years old, with torn upholstery, a gummy motor, and springs made by a blacksmith who had never made springs before. Next to the chugging of the gas engine at the creamery, the most familiar sound in Wheatsylvania was Frazier's closing the door of his Ford. He banged it flatly at the store, and usually he had to shut it thrice again before he reached home.

But to Martin and Leora, when they had tremblingly bought the car and three new tires and a horn, it was the most impressive vehicle on earth. It was their own; they could go when and where they wished.

During his summer at a Canadian hotel Martin had learned to drive the Ford station wagon, but it was Leora's first venture. Bert had given her so many directions that she had refused to drive the family Overland. When she first sat at the steering wheel, when she moved the hand-throttle with her little finger and felt in her own hands all this power, sorcery enabling her to go as fast as she might desire (within distinct limits), she transcended human strength, she felt that she could fly like the wild goose—and then in a stretch of sand she killed the engine.

Martin became the demon driver of the village. To ride with him was to sit holding your hat, your eyes closed, waiting for death. Apparently he accelerated for corners, to make them more interesting. The sight of anything on the road ahead, from another motor to a yellow pup, stirred in him a frenzy which could be stilled only by going up and passing it. The village adored, "The Young Doc is quite some driver, all right." They waited, with amiable interest, to hear that he had been killed. It is possible that half of the first dozen patients who drifted into his office came because of awe at his driving . . . the rest because there was nothing serious the matter, and he was nearer than Dr. Hesselink at Groningen.

IV

With his first admirers he developed his first enemies.

When he met the Norbloms on the street (and in Wheatsylvania it is difficult not to meet every one on the street every day), they glared. Then he antagonized Pete Yeska.

Pete conducted what he called a "drug store," devoted to the sale of candy, soda water, patent medicines, fly paper, magazines, washing-machines, and Ford accessories, yet Pete would have starved if he had not been postmaster also. He alleged that he was a licensed pharmacist but he so mangled prescriptions that Martin burst into the store and addressed him piously.

"You young docs make me sick," said Pete. "I was putting up prescriptions when you was in the cradle. The old doc that used to be here sent everything to me. My way o' doing things suits me, and I don't figure on changing it for you or any other half-baked young string-bean."

Thereafter Martin had to purchase drugs from St. Paul, overcrowd his tiny laboratory, and prepare his own pills and ointments, looking in a homesick way at the rarely used test-tubes and the dust gathering on the bell glass of his microscope, while Pete Yeska joined with the Norbloms in whispering, "This new doc here ain't any good. You better stick to Hesselink."

V

So blank, so idle, had been the week that when he heard the telephone at the Tozers', at three in the morning, he rushed to it as though he were awaiting a love message.

A hoarse and shaky voice: "I want to speak to the doctor."

"Yuh—yuh— 'S the doctor speaking."

"This is Henry Novak, four miles northeast, on the Leopolis road. My little girl, Mary, she has a terrible sore throat. I think maybe it is croup and she look awful and— Could you come right away?"

"You bet. Be right there."

Four miles—he would do it in eight minutes.

He dressed swiftly, dragging his worn brown tie together, while Leora beamed over the first night call. He furiously cranked the Ford, banged and clattered past the station and into the wheat prairie. When he had gone six miles by the speedometer, slackening at each rural box to look for the owner's name, he realized that he was lost. He ran into a farm driveway and stopped under the willows, his headlight on a heap of dented milk-cans, broken harvester wheels, cordwood, and bamboo fishing-poles. From the barn dashed a woolly anomalous dog, barking viciously, leaping up at the car.

A frowsy head protruded from a ground-floor window. "What you want?" screamed a Scandinavian voice.

"This is The Doctor. Where does Henry Novak live?"

"Oh! The Doctor! Dr. Hesselink?"

"No! Dr. Arrowsmith."

"Oh. Dr. Arrowsmith. From Wheatsylvania? Um. Well, you went right near his place. You yoost turn back one mile and turn to the right by the brick schoolhouse, and it's about forty rods up the road—the house with a cement silo. Somebody sick by Henry's?"

"Yuh—yuh—girl's got croup—thanks—"

"Yoost keep to the right. You can't miss it."

Probably no one who has listened to the dire "you can't miss it" has ever failed to miss it.

Martin swung the Ford about, grazing a slashed chopping-block; he rattled up the road, took the corner that side of the schoolhouse instead of this, ran half a mile along a boggy trail between pastures, and stopped at a farmhouse. In the surprising fall of silence, cows were to be heard feeding, and a white horse, startled in the darkness, raised its head to wonder at him. He had to arouse the house with wild squawkings of his horn, and an irate farmer who bellowed, "Who's there? I've got a shotgun!" sent him back to the country road.

It was forty minutes from the time of the telephone call when he rushed into a furrowed driveway and saw on the doorstep, against the lamplight, a stooped man who called, "The Doctor? This is Novak."

He found the child in a newly finished bedroom of white plastered walls and pale varnished pine. Only an iron bed, a straight chair, a chromo of St. Anne, and a shadeless hand-lamp on a rickety stand broke the staring shininess of the apartment, a recent extension of the farmhouse. A heavy-shouldered woman was kneeling by the bed. As she lifted her wet red face, Novak urged:

"Don't cry now; he's here!" And to Martin: "The little one is pretty bad but we done all we could for her. Last night and to-night we steam her throat, and we put her here in our own bedroom!"

Mary was a child of seven or eight. Martin found her lips and finger-tips blue, but in her face no flush. In the effort to expel her breath she writhed into terrifying knots, then coughed up saliva dotted with grayish specks. Martin worried as he took out his clinical thermometer and gave it a professional-looking shake.

It was, he decided, laryngeal croup or diphtheria. Probably diphtheria. No time now for bacteriological examination, for cultures and leisurely precision. Silva the healer bulked in the room, crowding out Gottlieb the inhuman perfectionist. Martin leaned nervously over the child on the tousled bed, absent-mindedly trying her pulse again and again. He felt helpless without the equipment of Zenith General, its nurses and Angus Duer's sure advice. He had a sudden respect for the lone country doctor.

He had to make a decision, irrevocable, perhaps perilous. He would use diphtheria antitoxin. But certainly he could not obtain it from Pete Yeska's in Wheatsylvania.

Leopolis?

"Hustle up and get me Blassner, the druggist at Leopolis, on the 'phone," he said to Novak, as calmly as he could contrive. He pictured Blassner driving through the night, respectfully bringing the antitoxin to The Doctor. While Novak bellowed into the farm-line telephone, in the dining-room, Martin waited—waited—staring at the child; Mrs. Novak waited for him to do miracles; the child's tossing and hoarse gasping became horrible; and the glaring walls, the glaring lines of pale yellow woodwork, hypnotized him into sleepiness. It was too late for anything short of antitoxin or tracheotomy. Should he operate; cut into the wind-pipe that she might breathe? He stood and worried; he drowned in sleepiness and shook himself awake. He had to do something, with the mother kneeling there, gaping at him, beginning to look doubtful.

"Get some hot cloths—towels, napkins—and keep 'em around her neck. I wish to God he'd get that telephone call!" he fretted.

As Mrs. Novak, padding on thick slippered feet, brought in the hot cloths, Novak appeared with a blank "Nobody sleeping at the drug store, and Blassner's house-line is out of order."

"Then listen. I'm afraid this may be serious. I've got to have antitoxin. Going to drive t' Leopolis and get it. You keep up these hot applications and— Wish we had an atomizer. And room ought to be moister. Got 'n alcohol stove? Keep some water boiling in here. No use of medicine. B' right back."

He drove the twenty-four miles to Leopolis in thirty-seven minutes. Not once did he slow down for a cross-road. He defied the curves, the roots thrusting out into the road, though always one dark spot in his mind feared a blow-out and a swerve. The speed, the casting away of all caution, wrought in him a high exultation, and it was blessed to be in the cool air and alone, after the strain of Mrs. Novak's watching. In his mind all the while was the page in Osler regarding diphtheria, the very picture of the words: "In severe cases the first dose should be from 8,000 —" No. Oh, yes: "—from 10,000 to 15,000 units."

He regained confidence. He thanked the god of science for antitoxin and for the gas motor. It was, he decided, a Race with Death.

"I'm going to do it—going to pull it off and save that poor kid!" he rejoiced.

He approached a grade crossing and hurled toward it, ignoring possible trains. He was aware of a devouring whistle, saw sliding light on the rails, and brought up sharp. Past him, ten feet from his front wheels, flung the Seattle Express like a flying volcano. The fireman was stoking, and even in the thin clearness of coming dawn the glow from the fire-box was appalling on the under side of the rolling smoke. Instantly the apparition was gone and Martin sat trembling, hands trembling on the little steering-wheel, foot trembling like St. Vitus's dance on the brake. "That was an awful' close thing!" he muttered, and thought of a widowed Leora, abandoned to Tozers. But the vision of the Novak child, struggling for each terrible breath, overrode all else. "Hell! I've killed the engine!" he groaned. He vaulted over the side, cranked the car, and dashed into Leopolis.

To Crynssen County, Leopolis with its four thousand people was a metropolis, but in the pinched stillness of the dawn it was a tiny graveyard: Main Street a sandy expanse, the low shops desolate as huts. He found one place astir; in the bleak office of the Dakota Hotel the night clerk was playing poker with the 'bus-driver and the town policeman.

They wondered at his hysterical entrance.

"Dr. Arrowsmith, from Wheatsylvania. Kid dying from diphtheria. Where's Blassner live? Jump in my car and show me."

The constable was a lanky old man, his vest swinging open over a collarless shirt, his trousers in folds, his eyes resolute. He guided Martin to the home of the druggist, he kicked the door, then, standing with his lean and bristly visage upraised in the cold early light, he bawled, "Ed! Hey, you, Ed! Come out of it!"

Ed Blassner grumbled from the up-stairs window. To him, death and furious doctors had small novelty. While he drew on his trousers and coat he was to be heard discoursing to his drowsy wife on the woes of druggists and the desirability of moving to Los Angeles and going into real estate. But he did have diphtheria antitoxin in his shop, and sixteen minutes after Martin's escape from being killed by a train he was speeding to Henry Novak's.

VI

The child was still alive when he came bruskly into the house.

All the way back he had seen her dead and stiff. He grunted "Thank God!" and angrily called for hot water. He was no longer the embarrassed cub doctor but the wise and heroic physician who had won the Race with Death, and in the peasant eyes of Mrs. Novak, in Henry's nervous obedience, he read his power.

Swiftly, smoothly, he made intravenous injection of the antitoxin, and stood expectant.

The child's breathing did not at first vary, as she choked in the labor of expelling her breath. There was a gurgle, a struggle in which her face blackened, and she was still. Martin peered, incredulous. Slowly the Novaks began to glower, shaky hands at their lips. Slowly they knew the child was gone.

In the hospital, death had become indifferent and natural to Martin. He had said to Angus, he had heard nurses say one to another, quite cheerfully, "Well, fifty-seven has just passed out." Now he raged with desire to do the impossible. She *couldn't* be dead. He'd do something— All the while he was groaning, "I should've operated—I should have." So insistent was the thought that for a time he did not realize that Mrs. Novak was clamoring, "She is dead? Dead?"

He nodded, afraid to look at the woman.

"You killed her, with that needle thing! And not even tell us, so we could call the priest!"

He crawled past her lamentations and the man's sorrow, and drove home, empty of heart.

"I shall never practise medicine again," he reflected.

"I'm through," he said to Leora. "I'm no good. I should of operated. I can't face people, when they know about it. I'm through. I'll go get a lab job—Dawson Hunziker or some place."

Salutary was the tartness with which she protested, "You're the most conceited man that ever lived! Do you think you're the only doctor that ever lost a patient? I know you did everything you could." But he went about next day torturing himself, the more tortured when Mr. Tozer whined at supper, "Henry Novak and his woman was in town to-day. They say you ought to have saved their girl. Why didn't you give your mind to it and manage to cure her somehow? Ought to tried. Kind of too bad, because the Novaks have a lot of influence with all these Pole and Hunky farmers."

After a night when he was too tired to sleep, Martin suddenly drove to Leopolis.

From the Tozers he had heard almost religious praise of Dr. Adam Winter of Leopolis, a man of nearly seventy, the pioneer physician of Crynssen County, and to this sage he was fleeing. As he drove he mocked furiously his melodramatic Race with Death, and he came wearily into the dust-whirling Main Street. Dr. Winter's office was above a grocery, in a long "block" of bright red brick stores with an Egyptian cornice—of tin. The darkness of the broad hallway was soothing after the prairie heat and incandescence. Martin had to wait till three respectful patients had been received by Dr. Winter, a hoary man with a sympathetic bass voice, before he was admitted to the consultation-room.

The examining-chair was of doubtful superiority to that once used by Doc Vickerson of Elk Mills, and sterilizing was apparently done in a wash-bowl, but in a corner was an electric therapeutic cabinet with more electrodes and pads than Martin had ever seen.

He told the story of the Novaks, and Winter cried, "Why, Doctor, you did everything you could have and more too. Only thing is, next time, in a crucial case, you better call some older doctor in consultation—not that you need his advice, but it makes a hit with the family, it divides the responsibility, and keeps 'em from going around criticizing. I, uh, I frequently have the honor of being called by some of my younger colleagues. Just wait. I'll 'phone the editor of the *Gazette* and give him an item about the case."

When he had telephoned, Dr. Winter shook hands ardently. He indicated his electric cabinet. "Got one of those things yet? Ought to, my boy. Don't know as I use it very often, except with the cranks that haven't anything the matter with 'em, but say, it would surprise you how it impresses folks. Well, Doctor, welcome to Crynssen County. Married? Won't you and your wife come take dinner with us some Sunday noon? Mrs. Winter will be real pleased to meet you. And if I ever can be of service to you in a consultation— I only charge a very little more than my regular fee, and it looks so well, talking the case over with an older man."

Driving home, Martin fell into vain and wicked boasting:

"You bet I'll stick to it! At worst, I'll never be as bad as that snuffling old fee-splitter!"

Two weeks after, the *Wheatsylvania Eagle*, a smeary four-page rag, reported:

> Our enterprising contemporary, the *Leopolis Gazette*, had as follows last week to say of one of our townsmen who we recently welcomed to our midst.
>
> "Dr. M. Arrowsmith of Wheatsylvania is being congratulated, we are informed by our valued pioneer local physician, Dr. Adam Winter, by the medical fraternity all through the Pony River Valley, there being no occupation or profession more unselfishly appreciative of each other's virtues than the medical gentlemen, on the courage and enterprise he recently displayed in addition to his scientific skill.
>
> "Being called to attend the little daughter of Henry Norwalk of near Delft the well-known farmer and finding the little one near death with diphtheria he made a desperate attempt to save it by himself bringing antitoxin from Blassner our ever popular druggist, who had on hand a full and fresh supply. He drove out and back in his gasoline chariot, making the total distance of 48 miles in 79 minutes.
>
> "Fortunately our ever alert policeman, Joe Colby, was on the job and helped Dr. Arrowsmith find Mr. Blassner's bungalow on Red River Avenue and this gentleman rose from bed and hastened to supply the doctor with the needed article but unfortunately the child was already too low to be saved but it is by such incidents of pluck and quick thinking as well as knowledge which make the medical profession one of our greatest blessings."

Two hours after this was published, Miss Agnes Ingleblad came in for another discussion of her non-existent ailments, and two days later Henry Novak appeared, saying proudly:

"Well, Doc, we all done what we could for the poor little girl, but I guess I waited too long calling you. The woman is awful' cut up. She and I was reading that piece in the *Eagle* about it. We showed it to the priest. Say, Doc, I wish you'd take a look at my foot. I got kind of a rheumatic pain in the ankle."

Chapter XVI

WHEN he had practised medicine in Wheatsylvania for one year, Martin was an inconspicuous but not discouraged country doctor. In summer Leora and he drove to the Pony River for picnic suppers and a swim, very noisy, splashing, and immodest; through autumn he went duck-hunting with Bert Tozer, who became nearly tolerable when he stood at sunset on a pass between two slews; and with winter isolating the village in a sun-blank desert of snow, they had sleigh-rides, card-parties, "sociables" at the churches.

When Martin's flock turned to him for help, their need and their patient obedience made them beautiful. Once or twice he lost his temper with jovial villagers who bountifully explained to him that he was less aged than he might have been; once or twice he drank too much whisky at poker parties in the back room of the Coöperative Store; but he was known as reliable, skilful, and honest—and on the whole he was rather less distinguished than Alec Ingleblad the barber, less prosperous than Nils Krag, the carpenter, and less interesting to his neighbors than the Finnish garageman.

Then one accident and one mistake made him famous for full twelve miles about.

He had gone fishing, in the spring. As he passed a farmhouse a woman ran out shrieking that her baby had swallowed a thimble and was choking to death. Martin had for surgical kit a large jack-knife. He sharpened it on the farmer's oil-stone, sterilized it in the tea-kettle, operated on the baby's throat, and saved its life.

Every newspaper in the Pony River Valley had a paragraph, and before this sensation was over he cured Miss Agnes Ingleblad of her desire to be cured.

She had achieved cold hands and a slow circulation, and he was called at midnight. He was soggily sleepy, after two country drives on muddy roads, and in his torpor he gave her an overdose of strychnin, which so shocked and stimulated her that she decided to be well. It was so violent a change that it made her more interesting than being an invalid—people had of late taken remarkably small pleasure in her symptoms. She went about praising Martin, and all the world said, "I hear this Doc Arrowsmith is the only fellow Agnes ever doctored with that's done her a mite of good."

He gathered a practise small, sound, and in no way remarkable. Leora and he moved from the Tozers' to a cottage of their own, with a parlor-dining-room which displayed a nickeled stove on bright, new, pleasant-smelling linoleum, and a golden-oak sideboard with a souvenir match-holder from Lake Minnetonka. He bought a small Roentgen ray outfit; and he was made a director of the Tozer bank. He became too busy to long for his days of scientific research, which had never existed, and Leora sighed:

"It's fierce, being married. I did expect I'd have to follow you out on the road and be a hobo, but I never expected to be a Pillar of the Community. Well, I'm too lazy to look up a new husband. Only I warn you: when you become the Sunday School superintendent, you needn't expect me to play the organ and smile at the cute jokes you make about Willy's not learning his Golden Text."

II

So did Martin stumble into respectability.

In the autumn of 1912, when Mr. Debs, Mr. Roosevelt, Mr. Wilson, and Mr. Taft were campaigning for the presidency, when Martin Arrowsmith had lived in Wheatsylvania for a year and a half, Bert Tozer became a Prominent Booster. He returned from the state convention of the Modern Woodmen of America with notions. Several towns had sent boosting delegations to the convention, and the village of Groningen had turned out a motor procession of five cars, each with an enormous pennant, "Groningen for White Men and Black Dirt."

Bert came back clamoring that every motor in town must carry a Wheatsylvania pennant. He had bought thirty of them, and they were on sale at the bank at seventy-five cents apiece. This, Bert explained to every one who came into the bank, was exactly cost-price, which was within eleven cents of the truth. He came galloping at Martin, demanding that he be the first to display a pennant.

"I don't want one of those fool things flopping from my 'bus," protested Martin. "What's the idea, anyway?"

"What's the *idea*? To advertise your own town, of course!"

"What is there to advertise? Do you think you're going to make strangers believe Wheatsylvania is a metropolis like New York or Jimtown by hanging a dusty rag behind a second-hand tin lizzie?"

"You never did have any patriotism! Let me tell you, Mart, if you don't put on a banner I'll see to it that everybody in town notices it!"

While the other rickety cars of the village announced to the world, or at least to several square miles of the world, that Wheatsylvania was the "Wonder Town of Central N. D.," Martin's clattering Ford went bare; and when his enemy Norblom remarked, "I like to see a fellow have some public spirit and appreciate the place he gets his money outa," the citizenry nodded and spat, and began to question Martin's fame as a worker of miracles.

III

He had intimates—the barber, the editor of the *Eagle*, the garageman—to whom he talked comfortably of hunting and the crops, and with whom he played poker. Perhaps he was too intimate with them. It was the theory of Crynssen County that it was quite all right for a young professional man to take a timely drink providing he kept it secret and made up for it by yearning over the clergy of the neighborhood. But with the clergy Martin was brief, and his drinking and poker he never concealed.

If he was bored by the United Brethren minister's discourse on doctrine, on the wickedness of movies, and the scandalous pay of pastors, it was not at all because he was a distant and supersensitive young man but because he found more savor in the garageman's salty remarks on the art of remembering to ante in poker.

Through all the state there were celebrated poker players, rustic-looking men with stolid faces, men who sat in shirt-sleeves, chewing tobacco; men whose longest remark was "By me," and who delighted to plunder the gilded and condescending traveling salesmen. When there was news of a "big game on," the county sports dropped in silently and went to work—the sewing-machine agent from Leopolis, the undertaker from Vanderheide's Grove, the bootlegger from St. Luke, the red fat man from Melody who had no known profession.

Once (still do men tell of it gratefully, up and down the Valley), they played for seventy-two unbroken hours, in the office of the Wheatsylvania garage. It had been a livery-stable; it was littered with robes and long whips, and the smell of horses mingled with the reek of gasoline.

The players came and went, and sometimes they slept on the floor for an hour or two, but they were never less than four in the game. The stink of cheap feeble cigarettes and cheap powerful cigars hovered about the table like a malign spirit; the floor was scattered with stubs, matches, old cards, and whisky bottles. Among the warriors were Martin, Alec Ingleblad the barber, and a highway engineer, all of them stripped to flannel undershirts, not moving for hour on hour, ruffling their cards, eyes squinting and vacant.

When Bert Tozer heard of the affair, he feared for the good fame of Wheatsylvania, and to every one he gossiped about Martin's evil ways and his own patience. Thus it happened that while Martin was at the height of his prosperity and credit as a physician, along the Pony River Valley sinuated the whispers that he was a gambler, that he was a "drinking man," that he never went to church; and all the godly enjoyed mourning, "Too bad to see a decent young man like that going to the dogs."

Martin was as impatient as he was stubborn. He resented the well-meant greetings: "You ought to leave a little hooch for the rest of us to drink, Doc," or "I s'pose you're too busy playing poker to drive out to the house and take a look at the woman." He was guilty of an absurd and boyish tactlessness when he heard Norblom observing to the postmaster, "A fellow that calls himself a doctor just because he had luck with that fool Agnes Ingleblad, he hadn't ought to go getting drunk and disgracing—"

Martin stopped. "Norblom! You talking about me?"

The storekeeper turned slowly. "I got more important things to do 'n talk about you," he cackled.

As Martin went on he heard laughter.

He told himself that these villagers were generous; that their snooping was in part an affectionate interest, and inevitable in a village where the most absorbing event of the year was the United Brethren Sunday School picnic on Fourth of July. But he could not rid himself of twitchy discomfort at their unending and maddeningly detailed comments on everything. He felt as though the lightest word he said in his consultation-room would be megaphoned from flapping ear to ear all down the country roads.

He was contented enough in gossiping about fishing with the barber, nor was he condescending to meteorologicomania, but except for Leora he had no one with whom he could talk of his work. Angus Duer had been cold, but Angus had his teeth into every change of surgical technique, and he was an acrid debater. Martin saw that, unless he struggled, not only would he harden into timid morality under the pressure of the village, but be fixed in a routine of prescriptions and bandaging.

He might find a stimulant in Dr. Hesselink of Groningen.

He had seen Hesselink only once, but everywhere he heard of him as the most honest practitioner in the Valley. On impulse Martin drove down to call on him.

Dr. Hesselink was a man of forty, ruddy, tall, broad-shouldered. You knew immediately that he was careful and that he was afraid of nothing, however much he might lack in imagination. He received Martin with no vast ebullience, and his stare said, "Well, what do you want? I'm a busy man."

"Doctor," Martin chattered, "do you find it hard to keep up with medical developments?"

"No. Read the medical journals."

"Well, don't you—gosh, I don't want to get sentimental about it, but don't you find that without contact with the Big Guns you get mentally lazy—sort of lacking in inspiration?"

"I do not! There's enough inspiration for me in trying to help the sick."

To himself Martin was protesting, "All right, if you don't want to be friendly, go to the devil!" But he tried again:

"I know. But for the game of the thing, for the pleasure of increasing medical knowledge, how can you keep up if you don't have anything but routine practise among a lot of farmers?"

"Arrowsmith, I may do you an injustice, but there's a lot of you young practitioners who feel superior to the farmers, that are doing their own jobs better than you are. You think that if you were only in the city with libraries and medical meetings and everything, you'd develop. Well, I don't know of anything to prevent your studying at home! You consider yourself so much better educated than these rustics, but I notice you say 'gosh' and 'Big Guns' and that sort of thing. How much do you read? Personally, I'm extremely well satisfied. My people pay me an excellent living wage, they appreciate my work, and they honor me by election to the schoolboard. I find that a good many of these farmers think a lot harder and squarer than the swells I meet in the city. Well! I don't see any reason for feeling superior, or lonely either!"

"Hell, I don't!" Martin mumbled. As he drove back he raged at Hesselink's superiority about not feeling superior, but he stumbled into uncomfortable meditation. It was true; he was half-educated. He was supposed to be a college graduate but he knew nothing of economics, nothing of history, nothing of music or painting. Except in hasty bolting for examinations he had read no poetry save that of Robert Service, and the only prose besides medical journalism at which he looked nowadays was the baseball and murder news in the Minneapolis papers and Wild West stories in the magazines.

He reviewed the "intelligent conversation" which, in the desert of Wheatsylvania, he believed himself to have conducted at Mohalis. He remembered that to Clif Clawson it had been pretentious to use any phrase which was not as colloquial and as smutty as the speech of a truck-driver, and that his own discourse had differed from Clif's largely in that it had been less fantastic and less original. He could recall nothing save the philosophy of Max Gottlieb, occasional scoldings of Angus Duer, one out of ten among Madeline Fox's digressions, and the councils of Dad Silva which was above the level of Alec Ingleblad's barber-shop.

He came home hating Hesselink but by no means loving himself; he fell upon Leora and, to her placid agreement, announced that they were "going to get educated, if it kills us." He went at it as he had gone at bacteriology.

He read European history aloud at Leora, who looked interested or at least forgiving; he worried the sentences in a copy of "The Golden Bowl" which an unfortunate schoolteacher had left at the Tozers'; he borrowed a volume of Conrad from the village editor and afterward, as he drove the prairie roads, he was marching into jungle villages—sun helmets, orchids, lost temples of obscene and dog-faced deities, secret and sun-scarred rivers. He was conscious of his own mean vocabulary. It cannot be said that he became immediately and conspicuously articulate, yet it is possible that in those long intense evenings of reading with Leora he advanced a step or two toward the tragic enchantments of Max Gottlieb's world—enchanting sometimes and tragic always.

But in becoming a schoolboy again he was not so satisfied as Dr. Hesselink.

IV

Gustaf Sondelius was back in America.

In medical school, Martin had read of Sondelius, the soldier of science. He held reasonable and lengthy degrees, but he was a rich man and eccentric, and neither toiled in laboratories nor had a decent office and a home and a lacy wife. He roamed the world fighting epidemics and founding institutions and making inconvenient speeches and trying new drinks. He was a Swede by birth, a German by education, a little of everything by speech, and his clubs were in London, Paris, Washington, and New York. He had been heard of from Batoum and Fuchau, from Milan and Bechuanaland, from Antofagasta and Cape Romanzoff. Manson on Tropical Diseases mentions Sondelius's admirable method of killing rats with hydrocyanic acid gas, and *The Sketch* once mentioned his atrocious system in baccarat.

Gustaf Sondelius shouted, in high places and low, that most diseases could be and must be wiped out; that tuberculosis, cancer, typhoid, the plague, influenza, were an invading army against which the world must mobilize—literally; that public health authorities must supersede generals and oil kings. He was lecturing through America, and his exclamatory assertions were syndicated in the press.

Martin sniffed at most newspaper articles touching on science or health but Sondelius's violence caught him, and suddenly he was converted, and it was an important thing for him, that conversion.

He told himself that however much he might relieve the sick, essentially he was a business man, in rivalry with Dr. Winter of Leopolis and Dr. Hesselink of Groningen; that though they might be honest, honesty and healing were less their purpose than making money; that to get rid of avoidable disease and produce a healthy population would be the worst thing in the world for them; and that they must all be replaced by public health officials.

Like all ardent agnostics, Martin was a religious man. Since the death of his Gottlieb-cult he had unconsciously sought a new passion, and he found it now in Gustaf Sondelius's war on disease. Immediately he became as annoying to his patients as he had once been to Digamma Pi.

He informed the farmers at Delft that they had no right to have so much tuberculosis.

This was infuriating, because none of their rights as American citizens was better established, or more often used, than the privilege of being ill. They fumed, "Who does he think he is? We call him in for doctoring, not for bossing. Why, the damn' fool said we ought to burn down our houses—said we were committing a crime if we had the con. here! Won't stand for nobody talking to me like that!"

Everything became clear to Martin—too clear. The nation must make the best physicians autocratic officials, at once, and that was all there was to it. As to how the officials were to become perfect executives, and how people were to be persuaded to obey them, he had no suggestions but only a beautiful faith. At breakfast he scolded, "Another idiotic day of writing prescriptions for bellyaches that ought never to have happened! If I could only get into the Big Fight, along with men like Sondelius! It makes me tired!"

Leora murmured, "Yes, darling. I'll promise to be good. I won't have any little bellyaches or T.B. or anything, so please don't lecture me!"

Even in his irritability he was gentle, for Leora was with child.

V

Their baby was coming in five months. Martin promised to it everything he had missed.

"He's going to have a real education!" he gloated, as they sat on the porch in spring twilight. "He'll learn all this literature and stuff. We haven't done much ourselves—here we are, stuck in this two-by-twice crossroads for the rest of our lives—but maybe we've gone a little beyond our dads, and he'll go way beyond us."

He was worried, for all his flamboyance. Leora had undue morning sickness. Till noon she dragged about the house, pea-green and tousled and hollow-faced. He found a sort of maid, and came home to help, to wipe the dishes and sweep the front walk. All evening he read to her, not history now and Henry James but "Mrs. Wiggs of the Cabbage Patch," which both of them esteemed a very fine tale. He sat on the floor by the grubby second-hand couch on which she lay in her weakness; he held her hand and crowed:

"Golly, we— No, not 'golly.' Well, what *can* you say except 'golly'? Anyway: Some day we'll save up enough money for a couple months in Italy and all those places. All those old narrow streets and old castles! There must be scads of 'em that are couple hundred years old or older! And we'll take the boy . . . Even if he turns out to be a girl, darn him! . . . And he'll learn to chatter Wop and French and everything like a regular native, and his dad and mother'll be so proud! Oh, we'll be a fierce pair of old birds! We never did have any more morals 'n a rabbit, either of us, and probably when we're seventy we'll sit out on the doorstep and smoke pipes and snicker at all the respectable people going by, and tell each other scandalous stories about 'em till they want to take a shot at us, and our boy—he'll wear a plug hat and have a chauffeur—he won't dare to recognize us!"

Trained now to the false cheerfulness of the doctor, he shouted, when she was racked and ghastly with the indignity of morning sickness, "There, that's fine, old girl! Wouldn't be making a good baby if you weren't sick. Everybody is." He was lying, and he was nervous. Whenever he thought of her dying, he seemed to die with her. Barren of her companionship, there would be nothing he wanted to do, nowhere to go. What would be the worth of having all the world if he could not show it to her, if she was not there—

He denounced Nature for her way of tricking human beings, by every gay device of moonlight and white limbs and reaching loneliness, into having babies, then making birth as cruel and clumsy and wasteful as she could. He was abrupt and jerky with patients who called him into the country. With their suffering he was sympathetic as he had never been, for his eyes had opened to the terrible beauty of pain, but he must not go far from Leora's need.

Her morning sickness turned into pernicious vomiting. Suddenly, while she was torn and inhuman with agony, he sent for Dr. Hesselink, and that horrible afternoon when the prairie spring was exuberant outside the windows of the poor iodoform-reeking room, they took the baby from her, dead.

Had it been possible, he might have understood Hesselink's success then, have noted that gravity and charm, that pity and sureness, which made people entrust their lives to him. Not cold and blaming was Hesselink now, but an older and wiser brother, very compassionate. Martin saw nothing. He was not a physician. He was a terrified boy, less useful to Hesselink than the dullest nurse.

When he was certain that Leora would recover, Martin sat by her bed, coaxing, "We'll just have to make up our minds we never can have a baby now, and so I want— Oh, I'm no good! And I've got a rotten temper. But to you, I want to be everything!"

She whispered, scarce to be heard:

"He would have been such a sweet baby. Oh, I know! I saw him so often. Because I knew he was going to be like you, when you were a baby." She tried to laugh. "Perhaps I wanted him because I could boss him. I've never had anybody that would let me boss him. So if I can't have a real baby, I'll have to bring you up. Make you a great man that everybody will wonder at, like your Sondelius. . . . Darling, I worried so about your worrying—"

He kissed her, and for hours they sat together, unspeaking, eternally understanding, in the prairie twilight.

Chapter XVII

DR. COUGHLIN of Leopolis had a red mustache, a large heartiness, and a Maxwell which, though it was three years old this May and deplorable as to varnish, he believed to be the superior in speed and beauty of any motor in Dakota.

He came home in high cheerfulness, rode the youngest of his three children pickaback, and remarked to his wife:

"Tessie, I got a swell idea."

"Yes, and you got a swell breath, too. I wish you'd quit testing that old Spirits Frumentus bottle at the drug store!"

"'At a girl! But honest, listen!"

"I will not!" She bussed him heartily. "Nothing doing about driving to Los Angeles this summer. Too far, with all the brats squalling."

"Sure. All right. But I mean: Let's pack up and light out and spend a week touring 'round the state. Say to-morrow or next day. Got nothing to keep me now except that obstetrical case, and we'll hand that over to Winter."

"All right. We can try out the new thermos bottles!"

Dr. Coughlin, his lady, and the children started at four in morning. The car was at first too well arranged to be interesting, but after three days, as he approached you on the flat road that without an inch of curving was slashed for leagues through the grassy young wheat, you saw the doctor in his khaki suit, his horn-rimmed spectacles, and white linen boating hat; his wife in a green flannel blouse and a lace boudoir cap. The rest of the car was slightly confused. While you motored by you noticed a canvas Egyptian Water Bottle, mud on wheels and fenders, a spade, two older children leaning perilously out and making tongues at you, the baby's diapers hanging on a line across the tonneau, a torn copy of *Snappy Stories*, seven lollypop sticks, a jack, a fish-rod, and a rolled tent.

Your last impression was of two large pennants labeled "Leopolis, N.D.," and "Excuse Our Dust."

The Coughlins had agreeable adventures. Once they were stuck in a mud-hole. To the shrieking admiration of the family, the doctor got them out by making a bridge of fence rails.

Once the ignition ceased and, while they awaited a garageman summoned by telephone, they viewed a dairy farm with an electrical milking machine. All the way they were broadened by travel, and discovered the wonders of the great world: the movie theater at Roundup, which had for orchestra not only a hand-played piano but also a violin; the black fox farm at Melody; and the Severance water-tower, which was said to be the tallest in Central North Dakota.

Dr. Coughlin "dropped in to pass the time of day," as he said, with all the doctors. At St. Luke he had an intimate friend in Dr. Tromp—at least they had met twice, at the annual meetings of the Pony River Valley Medical Association. When he told Tromp how bad they had found the hotels, Tromp looked uneasy and conscientious, and sighed, "If the wife could fix it up somehow, I'd like to invite you all to stay with us to-night."

"Oh, don't want to impose on you. Sure it wouldn't be any trouble?" said Coughlin.

After Mrs. Tromp had recovered from her desire to call her husband aside and make unheard but vigorous observations, and after the oldest Tromp boy had learned that "it wasn't nice for a little gentleman to kick his wee guests that came from so far, far away," they were all very happy. Mrs. Coughlin and Mrs. Tromp bewailed the cost of laundry soap and butter, and exchanged recipes for pickled peaches, while the men, sitting on the edge of the porch, their knees crossed, eloquently waving their cigars, gave themselves up to the ecstasy of shop-talk:

"Say, Doctor, how do you find collections?"

(It was Coughlin speaking—or it might have been Tromp.)

"Well, they're pretty good. These Germans pay up first rate. Never send 'em a bill, but when they've harvested they come in and say, 'How much do I owe you, Doctor?' "

"Yuh, the Germans are pretty good pay."

"Yump, they certainly are. Not many dead-beats among the Germans."

"Yes, that's a fact. Say, tell me, Doctor, what do you do with your jaundice cases?"

"Well, I'll tell you, Doctor: if it's a persistent case I usually give ammonium chlorid."

"Do you? I've been giving ammonium chlorid but here the other day I see a communication in the *Journal of the A.M.A.* where a fellow was claiming it wasn't any good."

"Is that a fact! Well, well! I didn't see that. Hum. Well. Say, Doctor, do you find you can do much with asthma?"

"Well now, Doctor, just in confidence, I'm going to tell you something that may strike you as funny, but I believe that foxes' lungs are fine for asthma, and T.B. too. I told that to a Sioux City pulmonary specialist one time and he laughed at me—said it wasn't scientific—and I said to him, 'Hell!' I said, 'scientific!' I said,'I don't know if it's the latest fad and wrinkle in science or not,' I said, 'but I get results, and that's what I'm looking for 's results!' I said. I tell you a plug G.P. may not have a lot of letters after his name, but he sees a slew of mysterious things that he can't explain, and I swear I believe most of these damn' alleged scientists could learn a whale of a lot from the plain country practitioners, let me tell you!'

"Yuh, that's a fact. Personally I'd rather stay right here in the country and be able to do a little hunting and take it easy than be the classiest specialist in the cities. One time I kind of figured on becoming an X-ray specialist—place in New York where you can take the whole course in eight weeks—and maybe settling in Butte or Sioux Falls, but I figured that even if I got to making eight-ten thousand a year, 'twouldn't hardly mean more than three thousand does here and so— And a fellow has to consider his duty to his old patients."

"That's so. . . . Say, Doctor, say what sort of fellow is McMinturn, down your way?"

"Well, I don't like to knock any fellow practitioner, and I suppose he's well intentioned, but just between you and me he does too confounded much guesswork. Now you take you and me, we apply *science* to a case, instead of taking a chance and just relying on experience and going off half-cocked. But McMinturn, he doesn't know enough. And *say*, that wife of his, she's a caution—she's got the meanest tongue in four counties, and the way she chases around drumming up business for Mac— Well, I suppose that's their way of doing business."

"Is old Winter keeping going?"

"Oh, yes, in a sort of way. You know how he is. Of course

he's about twenty years behind the times, but he's a great hand-holder—keep some fool woman in bed six weeks longer than he needs to, and call around twice a day and chin with her—absolutely unnecessary."

"I suppose you get your biggest competition from Silzer, Doctor?"

"Don't you believe it, Doctor! He isn't beginning to do the practise he lets on to. Trouble with Silzer is, he's too brash—shoots off his mouth too much—likes to hear himself talk. Oh, say, by the way, have you run into this new fellow—will been located here about two years now—at Wheatsylvania—Arrowsmith?"

"No, but they say he's a good bright young fellow."

"Yes, they claim he's a brainy man—very well-informed—and I hear his wife is a nice brainy little woman."

"I hear Arrowsmith hits it up too much though—likes his booze awful' well."

"Yes, so they say. Shame, for a nice hustling young fellow. I like a nip myself, now and then, but a Drinking Man—! Suppose he's drunk and gets called out on a case! And a fellow from down there was telling me Arrowsmith is great on books and study, but he's a freethinker—never goes to church."

"Is that a fact! Hm. Great mistake for any doctor to not identify himself with some good solid religious denomination, whether he believes the stuff or not. I tell you a priest or a preacher can send you an awful lot of business."

"You bet he can! Well, this fellow said Arrowsmith was always arguing with the preachers—he told some Reverend that everybody ought to read this immunologist Max Gottlieb, and this Jacques Loeb—you know—the fellow that, well I don't recall just exactly what it was, but he claimed he could create living fishes out of chemicals."

"Sure! There you got it! That's the kind of delusions these laboratory fellows get unless they have some practical practise to keep 'em well balanced. Well, if Arrowsmith falls for that kind of fellow, no wonder people don't trust him."

"That's so. Hm. Well, it's too bad Arrowsmith goes drinking and helling around and neglecting his family and his patients. I can see his finish. Shame. Well—wonder what time o' night it's getting to be?"

II

Bert Tozer wailed, "Mart, what you been doing to Dr. Coughlin of Leopolis? Fellow told me he was going around saying you were a boose-hoister and so on."

"Did he? People do sort of keep an eye on one another around here, don't they."

"You bet your life they do, and that's why I tell you you ought to cut out the poker and the booze. You don't see *me* needing any liquor, do you?"

Martin more desperately than ever felt the whole county watching him. He was not a praise-eater; he was not proud that he should feel misplaced; but however sturdily he struggled he saw himself outside the picture of Wheatsylvania and trudging years of country practise.

Suddenly, without planning it, forgetting in his admiration for Sondelius and the health war his pride of the laboratory, he was thrown into a research problem.

III

There was blackleg among the cattle in Crynssen County. The state veterinarian had been called and Dawson Hunziker vaccine had been injected, but the disease spread. Martin heard the farmers wailing. He noted that the injected cattle showed no inflammation nor rise in temperature. He was roused by a suspicion that the Hunziker vaccine had insufficient living organisms, and he went yelping on the trail of his hypothesis.

He obtained (by misrepresentations) a supply of the vaccine and tested it in his stuffy closet of a laboratory. He had to work out his own device for growing anaërobic cultures, but he had been trained by the Gottlieb who remarked, "Any man dat iss unable to build a filter out of toot'-picks, if he has to, would maybe better buy his results along with his fine equipment." Out of a large fruit-jar and a soldered pipe Martin made his apparatus.

When he was altogether sure that the vaccine did not contain living blackleg organisms, he was much more delighted than if he had found that good Mr. Dawson Hunziker was producing honest vaccine.

With no excuse and less encouragement he isolated blackleg organisms from sick cattle and prepared an attenuated vaccine of his own. It took much time. He did not neglect his patients but certainly he failed to appear in the stores, at the poker games. Leora and he dined on a sandwich every evening and hastened to the laboratory, to heat the cultures in the improvised water-bath, an ancient and leaky oatmeal-cooker with an alcohol lamp. The Martin who had been impatient of Hesselink was of endless patience as he watched his results. He whistled and hummed, and the hours from seven to midnight were a moment. Leora, frowning placidly, the tip of her tongue at the corner of her mouth, guarded the temperature like a good little watchdog.

After three efforts with two absurd failures, he had a vaccine which satisfied him, and he injected a stricken herd. The blackleg stopped, which was for Martin the end and the reward, and he turned his notes and supply of vaccine over to the state veterinarian. For others, it was not the end. The veterinarians of the county denounced him for intruding on their right to save or kill cattle; the physicians hinted, "That's the kind of monkey-business that ruins the dignity of the profession. I tell you Arrowsmith's a medical nihilist and a notoriety-seeker, that's what he is. You mark my words, instead of his sticking to decent regular practise, you'll be hearing of his opening a quack sanitarium, one of these days!"

He commented to Leora:

"Dignity, hell! If I had my way I'd be doing research—oh, not this cold detached stuff of Gottlieb but really practical work—and then I'd have some fellow like Sondelius take my results and jam 'em down people's throats, and I'd make them and their cattle and their tabby-cats healthy whether they wanted to be or not, that's what I'd do!"

In this mood he read in his Minneapolis paper, between a half column on the marriage of the light middleweight champion and three lines devoted to the lynching of an I.W.W. agitator, the announcement:

> Gustave Sundelios, well-known authority on cholera prevention, will give an address on "Heroes of Health" at the University summer school next Friday evening.

He ran into the house gloating, "Lee! Sondelius going to lecture in Minneapolis. I'm going! Come on! We'll hear him and have a bat and everything!"

"No, you run down by yourself. Be fine for you to get away from the town and the family and me for a while. I'll go down with you in the fall. Honestly. If I'm not in the way, maybe you can manage to have a good long talk with Dr. Sondelius."

"Fat chance! The big city physicians and the state health authorities will be standing around him ten deep. But I'm going."

IV

The prairie was hot, the wheat rattled in a weary breeze, the day-coach was gritty with cinders. Martin was cramped by the hours of slow riding. He drowsed and smoked and meditated. "I'm going to forget medicine and everything else," he vowed. "I'll go up and talk to somebody in the smoker and tell him I'm a shoe-salesman."

He did. Unfortunately his confidant happened to be a real shoe-salesman, with a large curiosity as to what firm Martin represented, and he returned to the day coach with a renewed sense of injury. When he reached Minneapolis, in mid-afternoon, he hastened to the University and besought a ticket to the Sondelius lecture before he had even found a hotel, though not before he had found the long glass of beer which he had been picturing for a hundred miles.

He had an informal but agreeable notion of spending his first evening of freedom in dissipation. Somewhere he would meet a company of worthies who would succor him with laughter and talk and many drinks—not too many drinks, of course—and motor very rapidly to Lake Minnetonka for a moonlight swim. He began his search for the brethren by having a cocktail at a hotel bar and dinner in a Hennepin Avenue restaurant. Nobody looked at him, nobody seemed to desire a companion. He was lonely for Leora, and all his state of grace, all his earnest and simple-hearted devotion to carousal, degenerated into sleepiness.

As he turned and turned in his hotel bed he lamented,

"And probably the Sondelius lecture will be rotten. Probably he's simply another Roscoe Geake."

V

In the hot night desultory students wandered up to the door of the lecture-hall, scanned the modest Sondelius poster, and ambled away. Martin was half minded to desert with them, and he went in sulkily. The hall was a third full of summer students and teachers, and men who might have been doctors or school-principals. He sat at the back, fanning with his straw hat, disliking the man with side-whiskers who shared the row with him, disapproving of Gustaf Sondelius, and as to himself having no good opinions whatever.

Then the room was charged with vitality. Down the central aisle, ineffectively attended by a small fussy person, thundered a man with a smile, a broad brow, and a strawpile of curly flaxen hair—a Newfoundland dog of a man. Martin sat straight. He was strengthened to endure even the depressing man with side-whiskers as Sondelius launched out, in a musical bellow with Swedish pronunciation and Swedish singsong:

"The medical profession can have but one desire: to destroy the medical profession. As for the laymen, they can be sure of but one thing: nine-tenths of what they know about health is not so, and with the other tenth they do nothing. As Butler shows in 'Erewhon'—the swine stole that idea from me, too, maybe thirty years before I ever got it—the only crime for w'ich we should hang people is having toobercoolosis."

"Umph!" grunted the studious audience, doubtful whether it was fitting to be amused, offended, bored, or edified.

Sondelius was a roarer and a playboy, but he knew incantations. With him Martin watched the heroes of yellow fever, Reed, Agramonte, Carroll, and Lazear; with him he landed in a Mexican port stilled with the plague and famished beneath the virulent sun; with him rode up the mountain trails to a hill town rotted with typhus; with him, in crawling August, when babies were parched skeletons, fought an ice trust beneath the gilt and blunted sword of the law.

"That's what I want to do! Not just tinker at a lot of worn-out bodies but make a new world!" Martin hungered. "Gosh, I'd follow him through fire! And the way he lays out the crapehangers that criticize public health results! If I could only manage to meet him and talk to him for a couple o' minutes—"

He lingered after the lecture. A dozen people surrounded Sondelius on the platform; a few shooks hands; a few asked questions; a doctor worried, "But how about the danger of free clinics and all those things drifting into socialism?" Martin stood back till Sondelius had been deserted. A janitor was closing the windows, very firmly and suggestively. Sondelius looked about, and Martin would have sworn that the Great Man was lonely. He shook hands with him, and quaked:

"Sir, if you aren't due some place, I wonder if you'd like to come out and have a—a—"

Sondelius loomed over him in solar radiance and rumbled, "Have a drink? Well I think maybe I would. How did the joke about the dog and his fleas go to-night? Do you think they liked it?"

"Oh, sure, you bet."

The warrior who had been telling of feeding five thousand Tatars, of receiving a degree from a Chinese university and refusing a decoration from quite a good Balkan king, looked affectionately on his band of one disciple and demanded, "Was it all right—was it? Did they like it? So hot to-night, and I been lecturing nine time a week—Des Moines, Fort Dodge, LaCrosse, Elgin, Joliet (but he pronounced it Zho-lee-ay) and—I forget. Was it all right? Did they like it?"

"Simply corking! Oh, they just ate it up! Honestly, I've never enjoyed anything so much in my life!"

The prophet crowed, "Come! I buy a drink. As a hygienist, I war on alcohol. In excessive quantities it is almost as bad as coffee or even ice cream soda. But as one who is fond of talking, I find a nice long whisky and soda a great solvent of human idiocy. Is there a cool place with some Pilsener here in Detroit—no; where am I to-night?—Minneapolis?"

"I understand there's a good beer-garden. And we can get the trolley right near here."

Sondelius stared at him. "Oh, I have a taxi waiting."

Martin was abashed by this luxury. In the taxi-cab he tried to think of the proper things to say to a celebrity.

"Tell me, Doctor, do they have city health boards in Europe?"

Sondelius ignored him. "Did you see that girl going by? What ankles! What shoulders! Is it good beer at the beer-garden? Have they any decent cognac? Do you know Courvoisier 1865 cognac? Oof! Lecturing! I swear I will give it up. And wearing dress clothes a night like this! You know, I mean all the crazy things I say in my lectures, but let us now forget being earnest, let us drink, let us sing 'Der Graf von Luxemburg,' let us detach exquisite girls from their escorts, let us discuss the joys of 'Die Meistersinger,' which only I appreciate!"

In the beer-garden the tremendous Sondelius discoursed of the Cosmos Club, Halle's investigation of infant morality, the suitability of combining benedictine and apple-jack, Biarritz, Lord Haldane, the Doane-Buckley method of milk examination, George Gissing, and *homard thermidor*. Martin looked for a connection between Sondelius and himself, as one does with the notorious or with people met abroad. He might have said, "I think I met a man who knows you," or "I have had the pleasure of reading all your articles," but he fished with "Did you ever run into the two big men in my medical school—Winnemac—Dean Silva and Max Gottlieb?"

"Silva? I don't remember. But Gottlieb—you know him? Oh!" Sondelius waved his mighty arms. "The greatest! The spirit of science! I had the pleasure to talk with him at McGurk. He would not sit here bawling like me! He makes me like a circus clown! He takes all my statements about epidemiology and shows me I am a fool! Ho, ho, ho!" He beamed, and was off on a denunciation of high tariff.

Each topic had its suitable refreshment. Sondelius was a fantastic drinker, and zinc-lined. He mixed Pilsener, whisky, black coffee, and a liquid which the waiter asserted to be absinthe. "I should go to bed at midnight," he lamented, "but it is a cardinal sin to interrupt good talk. Yoost tempt me a little! I am an easy one to be tempted! But I must have five hours' sleep. Absolute! I lecture in—it's some place in Iowa—

to-morrow evening. Now that I am past fifty, I cannot get along with three hours as I used to, and yet I have found so many new things that I want to talk about."

He was more eloquent than ever; then he was annoyed. A surly-looking man at the next table listened and peered, and laughed at them. Sondelius dropped from Haffkine's cholera serum to an irate:

"If that fellow stares at me some more, I am going over and kill him! I am a peaceful man, now that I am not so young, but I do not like starers. I will go and argue with him. I will yoost hit him a little!"

While the waiters came rushing, Sondelius charged the man, threatened him with enormous fists, then stopped, shook hands repeatedly, and brought him back to Martin.

"This is a born countryman of mine, from Gottenborg. He is a carpenter. Sit down, Nilsson, sit down and have a drink. Herumph! VAI-ter!"

The carpenter was a socialist, a Swedish Seventh Day Adventist, a ferocious arguer, and fond of drinking aquavit. He denounced Sondelius as an aristocrat, he denounced Martin for his ignorance of economics, he denounced the waiter concerning the brandy; Sondelius and Martin and the waiter answered with vigor; and the conversation became admirable. Presently they were turned out of the beer-garden and the three of them crowded into the still waiting taxicab, which shook to their debating. Where they went, Martin could never trace. He may have dreamed the whole tale. Once they were apparently in a roadhouse on a long street which must have been University Avenue; once in a saloon on Washington Avenue South, where three tramps were sleeping at the end of the bar; once in the carpenter's house, where an unexplained man made coffee for them.

Wherever they might be, they were at the same time in Moscow and Curaçao and Murwillumbah. The carpenter created communistic states, while Sondelius, proclaiming that he did not care whether he worked under socialism or an emperor so long as he could bully people into being well, annihilated tuberculosis and by dawn had cancer fleeing.

They parted at four, tearfully swearing to meet again, in Minnesota or Stockholm, in Rio or on the southern seas, and

Martin started for Wheatsylvania to put an end to all this nonsense of allowing people to be ill.

And the great god Sondelius had slain Dean Silva, as Silva had slain Gottlieb, Gottlieb had slain "Encore" Edwards the playful chemist, Edwards had slain Doc Vickerson, and Vickerson had slain the minister's son who had a real trapeze in his barn.

Chapter XVIII

DR. WOESTIJNE of Vanderheide's Grove acted in spare time as Superintendent of Health for Crynssen County, but the office was not well paid and it did not greatly interest him. When Martin burst in and offered to do all the work for half the pay, Woestijne accepted with benevolence, assuring him that it would have a great effect on his private practise.

It did. It almost ruined his private practise.

There was never an official appointment. Martin signed Woestijne's name (spelling it in various interesting ways, depending on how he felt) to papers, and the Board of County Commissioners recognized Martin's limited power, but the whole thing was probably illegal.

There was small science and considerably less heroism in his first furies as a health officer, but a great deal of irritation for his fellow-townsmen. He poked into yards, he denounced Mrs. Beeson for her reeking ash-barrels, Mr. Norblom for piling manure on the street, and the schoolboard for the school ventilation and lack of instruction in tooth-brushing. The citizens had formerly been agitated by his irreligion, his moral looseness, and his lack of local patriotism, but when they were prodded out of their comfortable and probably beneficial dirt, they exploded.

Martin was honest and appallingly earnest, but if he had the innocence of the dove he lacked the wisdom of the serpent. He did not make them understand his mission; he scarce tried to make them understand. His authority, as Woestijne's *alter ego*, was imposing on paper but feeble in action, and it was worthless against the stubbornness which he aroused.

He advanced from garbage-spying to a drama of infection.

The community at Delft had a typhoid epidemic which slackened and continually reappeared. The villagers believed that it came from a tribe of squatters six miles up the creek, and they considered lynching the offenders, as a practical protest and an interesting break in wheat-farming. When Martin insisted that in six miles the creek would purify any waste and that the squatters were probably not the cause, he was amply denounced.

"He's a fine one, he is, to go around blatting that we'd ought to have more health precautions! Here we go and show him where there's some hellhounds that ought to be shot, and them only Bohunks anyway, and he doesn't do a darn' thing but shoot a lot of hot air about germicidal effect or whatever the fool thing is," remarked Kaes, the wheat-buyer at the Delft elevator.

Flashing through the county, not neglecting but certainly not enlarging his own practise, Martin mapped every recent case of typhoid within five miles of Delft. He looked into milk-routes and grocery deliveries. He discovered that most of the cases had appeared after the visits of an itinerant seamstress, a spinster virtuous and almost painfully hygienic. She had had typhoid four years before.

"She's a chronic carrier of the bugs. She's got to be examined," he announced.

He found her sewing at the house of an old farmer-preacher.

With modest indignation she refused to be examined, and as he went away she could be heard weeping at the insult, while the preacher cursed him from the doorstep. He returned with the township police officer and had the seamstress arrested and confined in the segregation ward of the county poor-farm. In her discharges he found billions of typhoid bacilli.

The frail and decent body was not comfortable in the board-lined whitewashed ward. She was shamed and frightened. She had always been well beloved, a gentle, shabby, bright-eyed spinster who brought presents to the babies, helped the overworked farmwives to cook dinner, and sang to the children in her thin sparrow voice. Martin was reviled for persecuting her. "He wouldn't dare pick on her if she wasn't so poor," they said, and they talked of a jail-delivery.

Martin fretted. He called upon the seamstress at the poor-farm, he tried to make her understand that there was no other place for her, he brought her magazines and sweets. But he was firm. She could not go free. He was convinced that she had caused at least one hundred cases of typhoid, with nine deaths.

The county derided him. Cause typhoid now, when she had been well for four years? The County Commissioners and the County Board of Health called Dr. Hesselink in from the next county. He agreed with Martin and his maps. Every meeting of the Commissioners was a battle now, and it was uncertain whether Martin would be ruined or throned.

Leora saved him, and the seamstress. "Why not take up a collection to send her off to some big hospital where she can be treated, or where they can keep her if she can't be cured?" said she.

The seamstress entered a sanitarium—and was amiably forgotten by everybody for the rest of her life—and his recent enemies said of Martin, "He's mighty smart, and right on the job." Hesselink drove over to inform him, "You did pretty well this time, Arrowsmith. Glad to see you're settling down to business."

Martin was slightly cocky, and immediately bounded after a fine new epidemic. He was so fortunate as to have a case of small-pox and several which he suspected. Some of these lay across the border in Mencken County, Hesselink's domain, and Hesselink laughed at him. "It's probably all chicken-pox, except your one case. Mighty rarely you get small-pox in summer," he chuckled, while Martin raged up and down the two counties, proclaiming the scourge, imploring every one to be vaccinated, thundering, "There's going to be all hell let loose here in ten or fifteen days!"

But the United Brethren parson, who served chapels in Wheatsylvania and two other villages, was an anti-vaccinationist and he preached against it. The villages sided with him. Martin went from house to house, beseeching them, offering to treat them without charge. As he had never taught them to love him and follow him as a leader, they questioned, they argued long and easily on doorsteps, they cackled that he was drunk. Though for weeks his strongest draft had been the acrid coffee of the countryside, they peeped one to another that he was drunk every night, that the United Brethren minister was about to expose him from the pulpit.

And ten dreadful days went by and fifteen, and all but the first case did prove to be chicken-pox. Hesselink gloated and the village roared and Martin was the butt of the land.

He had only a little resented their gossip about his wickedness, only in evenings of slow depression had he meditated upon fleeing from them, but at their laughter he was black furious.

Leora comforted him with cool hands. "It'll pass over," she said. But it did not pass.

By autumn it had become such a burlesque epic as peasants love through all the world. He had, they mirthfully related, declared that anybody who kept hogs would die of small-pox; he had been drunk for a week, and diagnosed everything from gall-stones to heart-burn as small-pox. They greeted him, with no meaning of offense in their snickering, "Got a pimple on my chin, Doc. What is 't—small-pox?"

More terrible than their rage is the people's laughter, and if it rend tyrants, with equal zest it pursues the saint and wise man and befouls their treasure.

When the neighborhood suddenly achieved a real epidemic of diphtheria and Martin shakily preached antitoxin, one-half of them remembered his failure to save Mary Novak and the other half clamored, "Oh, give us a rest! You got epidemics on the brain!" That a number of children quite adequately died did not make them relinquish their comic epic.

Then it was that Martin came home to Leora and said quietly, "I'm licked. I've got to get out. Nothing more I can do here. Take years before they'd trust me again. They're so damned *humorous*! I'm going to go get a real job—public health."

"I'm so glad! You're too good for them here. We'll find some big place where they'll appreciate your work."

"No, that's not fair. I've learned a little something. I've failed here. I've antagonized too many people. I didn't know how to handle them. We could stick it out, and I would, except that life is short and I think I'm a good worker in some ways. Been worrying about being a coward, about running away, 'turning my—' What is it? '—turning my hand from the plow.' I don't care now! By God, I know what I can do! Gottlieb saw it! And I want to get to work. On we go. All right?"

"Of course!"

II

He had read in the *Journal of the American Medical Association* that Gustaf Sondelius was giving a series of lectures at Harvard. He wrote asking whether he knew of a public health appointment. Sondelius answered, in a profane and blotty scrawl, that he remembered with joy their Minneapolis vacation, that he disagreed with Entwisle of Harvard about the nature of metathrombin, that there was an excellent Italian restaurant in Boston, and that he would inquire among his health-official friends as to a position.

Two days later he wrote that Dr. Almus Pickerbaugh, Director of Public Health in the city of Nautilus, Iowa, was looking for a second-in-command, and would probably be willing to send particulars.

Leora and Martin swooped on an almanac.

"Gosh! Sixty-nine thousand people in Nautilus! Against three hundred and sixty-six here—no, wait, it's three hundred and sixty-seven now, with that new baby of Pete Yeska's that the dirty swine called in Hesselink for. People! People that can talk! Theaters! Maybe concerts! Leora, we'll be like a pair of kids let loose from school!"

He telegraphed for details, to the enormous interest of the station agent, who was also telegraph operator.

The mimeographed form which was sent to him said that Dr. Pickerbaugh required an assistant who would be the only full-time medical officer besides Pickerbaugh himself, as the clinic and school doctors were private physicians working part-time. The assistant would be epidemiologist, bacteriologist, and manager of the office clerks, the nurses, and the lay inspectors of dairies and sanitation. The salary would be twenty-five hundred dollars a year—against the fifteen or sixteen hundred Martin was making in Wheatsylvania.

Proper recommendations were desired.

Martin wrote to Sondelius, to Dad Silva, and to Max Gottlieb, now at the McGurk Institute in New York.

Dr. Pickerbaugh informed him, "I have received very pleasant letters from Dean Silva and Dr. Sondelius about you, but the letter from Dr. Gottlieb is quite remarkable. He says you have rare gifts as a laboratory man. I take great pleasure in offering you the appointment kindly wire."

Not till then did Martin completely realize that he was leaving Wheatsylvania—the tedium of Bert Tozer's nagging—the spying of Pete Yeska and the Norbloms—the inevitability of turning, as so many unchanging times he had turned, south from the Leopolis road at the Two Mile Grove and following again that weary, flat, unbending trail—the superiority of Dr. Hesselink and the malice of Dr. Coughlin—the round which left him no time for his dusty laboratory—leaving it all for the achievement and splendor of the great city of Nautilus.

"Leora, we're going! We're really going!"

III

Bert Tozer said:

"You know by golly there's folks that would call you a traitor, after all we've done for you, even if you did pay back the thousand, to let some other doc come in here and get all that influence away from the Family."

Ada Quist said:

"I guess if you ain't any too popular with the folks around here you'll have one fine time in a big city like Nautilus! Well Bert and me are going to get married next year and when you two swells make a failure of it I suppose we'll have to take care of you at our house when you come sneaking back do you think we could get your house at the same rent you paid for it oh Bert why couldn't we take Mart's office instead it would save money well I've always said since we were in school together you couldn't stand a decent regular life Ory."

Mr. Tozer said:

"I simply can't understand it, with everything going so nice. Why, you'd be making three-four thousand a year some day, if you just stuck to it. Haven't we tried to treat you nice? I don't like to have my little girl go away and leave me alone, now I'm getting on in years. And Bert gets so cranky with me and Mother, but you and Ory would always kind of listen to us. Can't you fix it somehow so you could stay?"

Pete Yeska said:

"Doc, you could of knocked me down with a feather when I heard you were going! Course you and me have scrapped about this drug business, but Lord! I been kind of half thinking about coming around some time and offering you a partnership and let you run the drug end to suit yourself, and we could get the Buick agency, maybe, and work up a nice little business. I'm real sorry you're going to leave us. . . . Well, come back some day and we'll take a shot at the ducks, and have a good laugh about that bull you made over the smallpox. I never will forget that! I was saying to the old woman just the other day, when she had an ear-ache, 'Ain't got smallpox, have yuh, Bess!'"

Dr. Hesselink said:

"Doctor, what's this I hear? You're not going away? Why, you and I were just beginning to bring medical practise in this neck of the woods up to where it ought to be, so I drove over to-night— Huh? We panned you? Ye-es, I suppose we did, but that doesn't mean we didn't appreciate you. Small place like here or Groningen, you have to roast your neighbors to keep busy. Why, Doctor, I've been watching you develop from an unlicked cub to a real upstanding physician, and now you're going away—you don't know how I feel!"

Henry Novak said:

"Why, Doc, you ain't going to *leave* us? And we got a new baby coming, and I said to the woman, just the other day, 'It's a good thing we got a doctor that hands you out the truth and not all this guff we used to get from Doc Winter.'"

The wheat-buyer at Delft said:

"Doc, what's this I hear? You ain't going *away*? A fellow told me you was and I says to him, 'Don't be more of a damn' fool than the Lord meant you to be,' I says. But I got to worrying about it, and I drove over and— Doc, I fire off my mouth pretty easy, I guess. I was agin you in the typhoid epidemic, when you said that seamstress was carrying the sickness around, and then you showed me up good. Doc, if you'd like to be state senator, and if you'll stay—I got quite a little influence—believe me, I'll get out and work my shirt off for you!"

Alec Ingleblad said:

"You're a lucky guy!"

All the village was at the train when they left for Nautilus.

For a hundred autumn-blazing miles Martin mourned his neighbors. "I feel like getting off and going back. Didn't we used to have fun playing Five Hundred with the Fraziers! I hate to think of the kind of doctor they may get. I swear, if some quack settles there or if Woestijne neglects the health work again, I'll go back and run 'em both out of business! And be kind of fun to be state senator, some ways."

But as evening thickened and nothing in all the rushing world existed save the yellow Pinsch gas globes above them in the long car, they saw ahead of them great Nautilus, high honor and achievement, the making of a radiant model city, and the praise of Sondelius—perhaps even of Max Gottlieb.

Chapter XIX

MIDMOST of the black-soiled Iowa plain, watered only by a shallow and insignificant creek, the city of Nautilus bakes and rattles and glistens. For hundreds of miles the tall corn springs in a jungle of undeviating rows, and the stranger who sweatily trudges the corn-walled roads is lost and nervous with the sense of merciless growth.

Nautilus is to Zenith what Zenith is to Chicago.

With seventy thousand people, it is a smaller Zenith but no less brisk. There is one large hotel to compare with the dozen in Zenith, but that one is as busy and standardized and frenziedly modern as its owner can make it. The only authentic difference between Nautilus and Zenith is that in both cases all the streets look alike but in Nautilus they do not look alike for so many miles.

The difficulty in defining its quality is that no one has determined whether it is a very large village or a very small city. There are houses with chauffeurs and Baccardi cocktails, but on August evenings all save a few score burghers sit in their shirt-sleeves on front porches. Across from the ten-story office building, in which a little magazine of the New Prose is published by a young woman who for five months lived in the cafés of Montparnasse, is an old frame mansion comfortable with maples, and a line of Fords and lumber-wagons in which the overalled farmers have come to town.

Iowa has the richest land, the lowest illiteracy rate, the largest percentages of native-born whites and motor-car owners, and the most moral and forward-looking cities of all the States, and Nautilus is the most Iowan city in Iowa. One out of every three persons above the age of sixty has spent a winter in California, and among them are the champion horseshoe pitcher of Pasadena and the woman who presented the turkey which Miss Mary Pickford, the cinema princess, enjoyed at her Christmas dinner in 1912.

Nautilus is distinguished by large houses with large lawns and by an astounding quantity of garages and lofty church spires. The fat fields run up to the edge of the city, and the scattered factories, the innumerable railroad side-tracks, and the scraggly cottages for workmen are almost amid the corn. Nautilus manufactures steel windmills, agricultural implements, including the celebrated Daisy Manure Spreader, and such corn-products as Maize Mealies, the renowned breakfast-food. It makes brick, it sells groceries wholesale, and it is the headquarters of the Cornbelt Coöperative Insurance Company.

One of its smallest but oldest industries is Mugford Christian College, which has two hundred and seventeen students, and sixteen instructors, of whom eleven are ministers of the Church of Christ. The well-known Dr. Tom Bissex is football coach, health director, and professor of hygiene, chemistry, physics, French, and German. Its shorthand and piano departments are known far beyond the limits of Nautilus, and once, though that was some years ago, Mugford held the Grinnell College baseball team down to a score of eleven to five. It has never been disgraced by squabbles over teaching evolutionary biology—it never has thought of teaching biology at all.

II

Martin left Leora at the Sims House, the old-fashioned, second-best hotel in Nautilus, to report to Dr. Pickerbaugh, Director of the Department of Public Health.

The department was on an alley, in a semi-basement at the back of that large graystone fungus, the City Hall. When he entered the drab reception-office he was highly received by the stenographer and the two visiting nurses. Into the midst of their flutterings—"Did you have a good trip, Doctor? Dr. Pickerbaugh didn't hardly expect you till to-morrow, Doctor. Is Mrs. Arrowsmith with you, Doctor?"—charged Pickerbaugh, thundering welcomes.

Dr. Almus Pickerbaugh was forty-eight. He was a graduate of Mugford College and of the Wassau Medical School. He looked somewhat like President Roosevelt, with the same squareness and the same bristly mustache, and he cultivated the resemblance. He was a man who never merely talked; he either bubbled or made orations.

He received Martin with four "Well's," which he gave after the manner of a college cheer; he showed him through the Department, led him into the Director's private office, gave him a cigar, and burst the dam of manly silence:

"Doctor, I'm delighted to have a man with your scientific inclinations. Not that I should consider myself entirely without them. In fact I make it a regular practise to set aside a period for scientific research, without a certain amount of which even the most ardent crusade for health methods would scarcely make much headway."

It sounded like the beginning of a long seminar. Martin settled in his chair. He was doubtful about his cigar, but he found that it helped him to look more interested.

"But with me, I admit, it's a matter of temperament. I have often hoped that, without any desire whatever for mere personal aggrandizement, the powers above may yet grant me the genius to become at once the Roosevelt and the Longfellow of the great and universally growing movement for public health measures is your cigar too mild, Doctor? or perhaps it would be better to say the Kipling of public health rather than the Longfellow, because despite the beautiful passages and high moral atmosphere of the Sage of Cambridge, his poetry lacked the swing and punch of Kipling.

"I assume you agree with me, or you will when you have had an opportunity to see the effect our work has on the city, and the success we have in selling the idea of Better Health, that what the world needs is a really inspired, courageous, overtowering leader—say a Billy Sunday of the movement—a man who would know how to use sensationalism properly and wake the people out of their sloth. Sometimes the papers, and I can only say they flatter me when they compare me with Billy Sunday, the greatest of all evangelists and Christian preachers—sometimes they claim that I'm too sensational. Huh! If they only could understand it, trouble is I can't be sensational enough! Still, I try, I try, and— Look here. Here's a placard, it was painted by my daughter Orchid and the poetry is my own humble effort, and let me tell you it gets quoted around everywhere:

You can't get health
By a pussyfoot stealth,
So let's every health-booster
Crow just like a rooster.

"Then there's another—this is a minor thing; it doesn't try to drive home general abstract principles, but it'd surprise you the effect it's had on careless housewives, who of course don't mean to neglect the health of their little ones and merely need instruction and a little pep put into them, and when they see a card like this, it makes 'em think:

Boil the milk bottles or by gum
You better buy your ticket to Kingdom Come.

"I've gotten quite a lot of appreciation in my small way for some of these things that didn't hardly take me five minutes to dash off. Some day when you get time, glance over this volume of clippings—just to show you, Doctor, what you can do if you go at the Movement in the up-to-date and scientific manner. This one, about the temperance meeting I addressed in Des Moines—say, I had that hall, and it was jam-pack-full, lifting right up on their feet when I proved by statistics that ninety-three per cent. of all insanity is caused by booze! Then this—well, it hasn't anything to do with health, directly, but it'll just indicate the opportunity you'll have here to get in touch with all the movements for civic weal."

He held out a newspaper clipping in which, above a pen-and-ink caricature portraying him with large mustached head on a tiny body, was the headline:

DOC PICKERBAUGH BANNER BOOSTER
OF EVANGELINE COUNTY LEADS BIG
GO-TO-CHURCH DEMONSTRATION HERE

Pickerbaugh looked it over, reflecting, "That was a dandy meeting! We increased church attendance here seventeen per cent.! Oh, Doctor, you went to Winnemac and had your internship in Zenith, didn't you? Well, this might interest you then. It's from the *Zenith Advocate-Times*, and it's by Chum Frink, who, I think you'll agree with me, ranks with Eddie

Guest and Walt Mason as the greatest, as they certainly are the most popular, of all our poets, showing that you can bank every time on the literary taste of the American Public. Dear old Chum! That was when I was in Zenith to address the national convention of Congregational Sunday-schools, I happen to be a Congregationalist myself, on 'The Morality of A 1 Health.' So Chum wrote this poem about me:"

> Zenith welcomes with high hurraw
> A friend in Almus Pickerbaugh,
> The two-fisted fightin' poet doc
> Who stands for health like Gibraltar's rock.
> He's jammed with figgers and facts and fun,
> The plucky old, lucky old son—of—a—gun!

For a moment the exuberant Dr. Pickerbaugh was shy.

"Maybe it's kind of immodest in me to show that around. And when I read a poem with such originality and swing, when I find a genu-ine vest-pocket masterpiece like this, then I realize that I'm not a poet at all, no matter how much my jingles may serve to jazz up the Cause of Health. My brain-children may teach sanitation and do their little part to save thousands of dear lives, but they aren't literature, like what Chum Frink turns out. No, I guess I'm nothing but just a plain scientist in an office.

"Still, you'll readily see how one of these efforts of mine, just by having a good laugh and a punch and some melody in it, does gild the pill and make careless folks stop spitting on the sidewalks, and get out into God's great outdoors and get their lungs packed full of ozone and lead a real hairy-chested he-life. In fact you might care to look over the first number of a little semi-yearly magazine I'm just starting—I know for a fact that a number of newspaper editors are going to quote from it and so carry on the good work as well as boost my circulation."

He handed to Martin a pamphlet entitled *Pickerbaugh Pickings.*

In verse and aphorism, *Pickings* recommended good health, good roads, good business, and the single standard of morality. Dr. Pickerbaugh backed up his injunctions with statistics as impressive as those the Reverend Ira Hinkley had once used at Digamma Pi. Martin was edified by an item which showed that among all families divorced in Ontario, Tennessee, and Southern Wyoming in 1912, the appalling number of fifty-three per cent. of the husbands drank at least one glass of whisky daily.

Before this warning had sunk in, Pickerbaugh snatched *Pickings* from him with a boyish, "Oh, you won't want to read any more of my rot. You can look it over some future time. But this second volume of my clippings may perhaps interest you, just as a hint of what a fellow can do."

While he considered the headlines in the scrapbook, Martin realized that Dr. Pickerbaugh was vastly better known than he had realized. He was exposed as the founder of the first Rotary Club in Iowa; superintendent of the Jonathan Edwards Congregational Sunday School of Nautilus; president of the Moccasin Ski and Hiking Club, of the West Side Bowling Club, and the 1912 Bull Moose and Roosevelt Club; organizer and cheer-leader of a Joint Picnic of the Woodmen, Moose, Elks, Masons, Oddfellows, Turnverein, Knights of Columbus, B'nai B'rith, and the Y.M.C.A.; and winner of the prizes both for reciting the largest number of Biblical texts and for dancing the best Irish jig at the Harvest Moon Soiree of the Jonathan Edwards Bible Class for the Grown-ups.

Martin read of him as addressing the Century Club of Nautilus on "A Yankee Doctor's Trip Through Old Europe," and the Mugford College Alumni Association on "Wanted: A Man-sized Feetball Coach for Old Mugford." But outside of Nautilus as well, there were loud alarums of his presence.

He had spoken at the Toledo Chamber of Commerce Weekly Luncheon on "More Health—More Bank Clearings." He had edified the National Interurban Trolley Council, meeting at Wichita, on "Health Maxims for Trolley Folks." Seven thousand, six hundred Detroit automobile mechanics had listened to his observations on "Health First, Safety Second, and Booze Nowhere A-tall." And in a great convention at Waterloo he had helped organize the first regiment in Iowa of the Anti-rum Minute Men.

The articles and editorials regarding him, in newspapers, house organs, and one rubber-goods periodical, were accompanied by photographs of himself, his buxom wife, and his eight bounding daughters, depicted in Canadian winter costumes among snow and icicles, in modest but easy athletic costumes, playing tennis in the backyard, and in costumes of no known genus whatever, frying bacon against a background of Northern Minnesota pines.

Martin felt strongly that he would like to get away and recover.

He walked back to the Sims House. He realized that to a civilized man the fact that Pickerbaugh advocated any reform would be sufficient reason for ignoring it.

When he had gone thus far, Martin pulled himself up, cursed himself for what he esteemed his old sin of superiority to decent normal people. . . . Failure. Disloyalty. In medical school, in private practise, in his bullying health administration. Now again?

He urged, "This pep and heartiness stuff of Pickerbaugh's is exactly the thing to get across to the majority of people the scientific discoveries of the Max Gottliebs. What do I care how much Pickerbaugh gases before conventions of Sunday School superintendents and other morons, as long as he lets me alone and lets me do my work in the lab and dairy inspection?"

He pumped up enthusiasm and came quite cheerfully and confidently into the shabby, high-ceilinged hotel bedroom where Leora sat in a rocker by the window.

"Well?" she said.

"It's fine—gave me fine welcome. And they want us to come to dinner, to-morrow evening."

"What's he like?"

"Oh, he's awfully optimistic—he puts things over—he— Oh, Leora, am I going to be a sour, cranky, unpopular, rotten failure again?"

His head was buried in her lap and he clung to her affection, the one reality in a world of chattering ghosts.

III

When the maples fluttered beneath their window in the breeze that sprang up with the beginning of twilight, when the amiable citizens of Nautilus had driven home to supper in their shaky Fords, Leora had persuaded him that Pickerbaugh's flamboyance would not interfere with his own work, that in any case they would not remain in Nautilus forever, that he was impatient, and that she loved him dearly. So they descended to supper, an old-fashioned Iowa supper with corn fritters and many little dishes which were of interest after the loving but misinformed cooking of Leora, and they went to the movies and held hands and were not ill content.

The next day Dr. Pickerbaugh was busier and less buoyant. He gave Martin a notion of the details of his work.

Martin had thought of himself, freed from tinkering over cut fingers and ear-aches, as spending ecstatic days in the laboratory, emerging only to battle with factory-owners who defied sanitation. But he found that it was impossible to define his work, except that he was to do a little of everything that Pickerbaugh, the press, or any stray citizen of Nautilus might think of.

He was to placate voluble voters who came in to complain of everything from the smell of sewer-gas to the midnight beer parties of neighbors; he was to dictate office correspondence to the touchy stenographer, who was not a Working Girl but a Nice Girl Who Was Working; to give publicity to the newspapers; to buy paper-clips and floor-wax and report-blanks at the lowest prices; to assist, in need, the two part-time physicians in the city clinic; to direct the nurses and the two sanitary inspectors; to scold the Garbage Removal Company; to arrest—or at least to jaw at—all public spitters; to leap into a Ford and rush out to tack placards on houses in which were infectious diseases; to keep a learned implacable eye on epidemics from Vladivostok to Patagonia, and to prevent (by methods not very clearly outlined) their coming in to slay the yeomanry and even halt the business activities of Nautilus.

But there was a little laboratory work: milk tests, Wassermanns for private physicians, the making of vaccines, cultures in suspected diphtheria.

"I get it," said Leora, as they dressed for the dinner at Pickerbaugh's. "Your job will only take about twenty-eight hours a day, and the rest of the time you're perfectly welcome to spend in research, unless somebody interrupts you."

IV

The home of Dr. and Mrs. Almus Pickerbaugh, on the steeple-prickly West Side, was a Real Old-fashioned Home. It was a wooden house with towers, swings, hammocks, rather mussy shade trees, a rather mangy lawn, a rather damp arbor, and an old carriage-house with a line of steel spikes along the ridge-pole. Over the front gate was the name: UNEEDAREST.

Martin and Leora came into a shambles of salutations and daughters. The eight girls, from pretty Orchid aged nineteen to the five-year-old twins, surged up in a tidal wave of friendly curiosity and tried to talk all at once.

Their hostess was a plump woman with an air of worried trustfulness. Her conviction that everything was all right was constantly struggling with her knowledge that a great many things seemed to be all wrong. She kissed Leora while Pickerbaugh was pump-handling Martin. Pickerbaugh had a way of pressing his thumb into the back of your hand which was extraordinarily cordial and painful.

He immediately drowned out even his daughters by an oration on the Home Nest:

"Here you've got an illustration of Health in the Home. Look at these great strapping girls, Arrowsmith! Never been sick a day in their lives—practically—and though Mother does have her sick-headaches, that's to be attributed to the early neglect of her diet, because while her father, the old deacon—and a fine upstanding gentleman of the old school he was, too, if there ever was one, and a friend of Nathaniel Mugford, to whom more than any other we owe not only the foundation of Mugford College but also the tradition of integrity and industry which have produced our present prosperity—BUT he had no knowledge of diet or sanitation, and I've always thought—"

The daughters were introduced as Orchid, Verbena, Daisy, Jonquil, Hibisca, Narcissa, and the twins, Arbuta and Gladiola.

Mrs. Pickerbaugh sighed:

"I suppose it would be dreadfully conventional to call them My Jewels—I do so hate these conventional phrases that everybody uses, don't you?—but that's what they really are to their mother, and the Doctor and I have sometimes wished— Of course when we'd started giving them floral names we had to keep it up, but if we'd started with jewels, just think of all the darling names we might have used, like Agate and Cameo and Sardonyx and Beryl and Topaz and Opal and Esmeralda and Chrysoprase—it *is* Chrysoprase, isn't it, not Chrysalis? Oh, well, many people have congratulated us on their names as it is. You know the girls are getting quite famous—their pictures in so many papers, and we have a Pickerbaugh Ladies' Baseball Team all our own—only the Doctor has to play on it now, because I'm beginning to get a little stout."

Except by their ages, it was impossible to tell the daughters apart. They were all bouncing, all blond, all pretty, all eager, all musical, and not merely pure but clamorously clean-minded. They all belonged to the Congregational Sunday School, and to either the Y.W.C.A. or the Camp Fire Girls; they were all fond of picnicking; and they could all of them, except the five-year-old twins, quote practically without error the newest statistics showing the evils of alcohol.

"In fact," said Dr. Pickerbaugh, "*we* think they're a very striking brood of chickabiddies."

"They certainly are!" quivered Martin.

"But best of all, they are able to help me put over the doctrine of the *Mens Sana* in the *Corpus Sano*. Mrs. Pickerbaugh and I have trained them to sing together, both in the home and publicly, and as an organization we call them the Healthette Octette."

"Really?" said Leora, when it was apparent that Martin had passed beyond speech.

"Yes, and before I get through with it I hope to popularize the name Healthette from end to end of this old nation, and you're going to see bands of happy young women going around spreading their winged message into every dark corner. Healthette Bands! Beautiful and pure-minded and enthusiastic and good basket-ball players! I tell you, *they'll* make the lazy and wilful stir their stumps! They'll shame the filthy livers and filthy talkers into decency! I've already worked out a poem-slogan for the Healthette Bands. Would you like to hear it?

Winsome young womanhood wins with a smile
Boozers, spitters, and gamblers from things that are vile.
Our parents and teachers have explained the cause of life,
So against the evil-minded we'll also make strife.
We'll shame them, reclaim them, from bad habits, you bet!
Better watch out, Mr. Loafer, I am a Healthette!

"But of course an even more important Cause is—and I was one of the first to advocate it—having a Secretary of Health and Eugenics in the cabinet at Washington—"

On the tide of this dissertation they were swept through a stupendous dinner. With a hearty "Nonsense, nonsense, man, of course you want a second helping—this is Hospitality Hall!" Pickerbaugh so stuffed Martin and Leora with roast duck, candied sweet potatoes, and mince pie that they became dangerously ill and sat glassy-eyed. But Pickerbaugh himself did not seem to be affected. While he carved and gobbled, he went on discoursing till the dining-room, with its old walnut buffet, its Hoffmann pictures of Christ, and its Remington pictures of cowpunchers, seemed to vanish, leaving him on a platform beside a pitcher of ice-water.

Not always was he merely fantastic. "Dr. Arrowsmith, I tell you we're lucky men to be able to get a living out of doing our honest best to make the people in a he-town like this well and vital. I could be pulling down eight or ten thousand a year in private practise, and I've been told I could make more than that in the art of advertising, yet I'm glad, and my dear ones are glad with me, to take a salary of four thousand. Think of our having a job where we've got nothing to sell but honesty and decency and the brotherhood o' man!"

Martin perceived that Pickerbaugh meant it, and the shame of the realization kept him from leaping up, seizing Leora, and catching the first freight train out of Nautilus.

After dinner the younger daughters desired to love Leora, in swarms. Martin had to take the twins on his knees and tell them a story. They were remarkably heavy twins, but no heavier than the labor of inventing a plot. Before they went to bed, the entire Healthette Octette sang the famous Health Hymn (written by Dr. Almus Pickerbaugh) which Martin was to hear on so many bright and active public occasions in Nautilus. It was set to the tune of "The Battle Hymn of the Republic," but as the twins' voices were energetic and extraordinarily shrill, it had an effect all its own:

Oh, are you out for happiness or are you out for pelf?
You owe it to the grand old flag to cultivate yourself,
To train the mind, keep clean the streets, and ever guard
    your health,
        Then we'll all go marching on.

A healthy mind in A clean body,
A healthy mind in A clean body,
A healthy mind in A clean body,
    The slogan for one and all.

As a bedtime farewell, the twins then recited, as they had recently recited at the Congregational Festival, one of their father's minor lyrics:

What does little birdie say
On the sill at break o' day?
"Hurrah for health in Nautilus
For Pa and Ma and all of us,
    Hurray, hurray, hurray!"

"There, my popsywopsies, up to bed we go!" said Mrs. Pickerbaugh. "Don't you think, Mrs. Arrowsmith, they're natural-born actresses? They're not afraid of any audience, and the way they throw themselves into it—perhaps not Broadway, but the more refined theaters in New York would just love them, and maybe they've been sent to us to elevate the drama. Upsy go."

During her absence the others gave a brief musical program.

Verbena, the second oldest, played Chaminade. ("Of course we all love music, and popularize it among the neighbors, but Verby is perhaps the only real musical genius in the family.") But the unexpected feature was Orchid's cornet solo.

Martin dared not look at Leora. It was not that he was sniffily superior to cornet solos, for in Elk Mills, Wheatsylvania, and surprisingly large portions of Zenith, cornet solos were done by the most virtuous females. But he felt that he had been in a madhouse for dozens of years.

"I've never been so drunk in my life. I wish I could get at a drink and sober up," he agonized. He made hysterical and completely impractical plans for escape. Then Mrs. Pickerbaugh, returning from the still audible twins, sat down at the harp.

While she played, a faded woman and thickish, she fell into a great dreaming, and suddenly Martin had a picture of her as gay, good, dove-like maiden who had admired the energetic young medical student, Almus Pickerbaugh. She must have been a veritable girl of the late eighties and the early nineties, the naïve and idyllic age of Howells, when young men were pure, when they played croquet and sang Swanee River; a girl who sat on a front porch enchanted by the sweetness of lilacs, and hoped that when Almus and she were married they would have a nickel-plated baseburner stove and a son who would become a missionary or a millionaire.

For the first time that evening, Martin managed to put a respectable heartiness into his "Enjoyed that s' much." He felt victorious, and somewhat recovered from his weakness.

But the evening's orgy was only begun.

They played word-games, which Martin hated and Leora did very badly indeed. They acted charades, at which Pickerbaugh was tremendous. The sight of him on the floor in his wife's fur coat, being a seal on an ice-floe, was incomparable. Then Martin, Orchid, and Hibisca (aged twelve) had to present a charade, and there were complications.

Orchid was as full of simple affections, of smilings and pattings and bouncings, as her younger sisters, but she was nineteen and not altogether a child. Doubtless she was as pure-minded and as devoted to Clean and Wholesome Novels as Dr. Pickerbaugh stated, and he stated it with frequency, but she was not unconscious of young men, even though they were married.

She planned to enact the word *doleful*, with a beggar asking a dole, and a corncrib full. As they skipped upstairs to dress, she hugged Martin's arm, frisked beside him, and murmured, "Oh, Doctor, I'm so glad Daddy has you for assistant—somebody that's young and good-looking. Oh, was that dreadful of me? But I mean: you look so athletic and everything, and the other assistant director—don't tell Daddy I said so, but he was an old crank!"

He was conscious of brown eyes and unshadowed virginal lips. As Orchid put on her agreeably loose costume as a beggar, he was also conscious of ankles and young bosom. She smiled at him, as one who had long known him, and said loyally, "We'll show 'em! I know you're a dan-dy actor!"

When they bustled downstairs, as she did not take his arm, he took hers, and he pressed it slightly and felt alarmed and relinquished it with emphasis.

Since his marriage he had been so absorbed in Leora, as lover, as companion, as helper, that till this hour his most devastating adventure had been a glance at a pretty girl in a train. But the flushed young gaiety of Orchid disturbed him. He wanted to be rid of her, he hoped that he would not be altogether rid of her, and for the first time in years he was afraid of Leora's eyes.

There were acrobatic feats later, and a considerable prominence of Orchid, who did not wear stays, who loved dancing, and who praised Martin's feats in the game of "Follow the Leader."

All the daughters save Orchid were sent to bed, and the rest of the fête consisted of what Pickerbaugh called "a little quiet scientific conversation by the fireside," made up of his observations on good roads, rural sanitation, Ideals in politics, and methods of letter filing in health departments. Through this placid hour, or it may have been an hour and a half, Martin saw that Orchid was observing his hair, his jaw, his hands, and he had, and dismissed, and had again a thought about the innocent agreeableness of holding her small friendly paw.

He also saw that Leora was observing both of them, and he suffered a good deal, and had practically no benefit whatever from Pickerbaugh's notes on the value of disinfectants. When Pickerbaugh predicted for Nautilus, in fifteen years, a health department thrice as large, with many full-time clinic and school physicians and possibly Martin as director (Pickerbaugh himself having gone off to mysterious and interesting activities in a Larger Field), Martin merely croaked, "Yes, that'd be—be fine," while to himself he was explaining, "Damn that girl, I wish she wouldn't shake herself at me."

At half-past eight he had pictured his escape as life's highest ecstasy; at twelve he took leave with nervous hesitation.

They walked to the hotel. Free from the sight of Orchid, brisk in the coolness, he forgot the chit and pawed again the problem of his work in Nautilus.

"Lord, I don't know whether I can do it. To work under that gas-bag, with his fool pieces about boozers—"

"They weren't so bad," protested Leora.

"Bad? Why, he's probably the worst poet that ever lived, and he certainly knows less about epidemiology than I thought any one man could ever learn, all by himself. But when it comes to this—what was it Clif Clawson used to call it?—by the way, wonder what's ever become of Clif; haven't heard from him for a couple o' years—when it comes to this 'overpowering Christian Domesticity'— Oh, let's hunt for a blind-pig and sit around with the nice restful burglars."

She insisted, "I thought his poems were kind of cute."

"Cute! What a word!"

"It's no worse than the cuss-words you're always using! But the cornet yowling by that awful oldest daughter—Ugh!"

"Well, now she played darn' well!"

"Martin, the cornet is the kind of an instrument my brother would play. And you so superior about the doctor's poetry and my saying 'cute'! You're just as much a backwoods hick as I am, and maybe more so!"

"Why, gee, Leora, I never knew you to get sore about nothing before! And can't you understand how important—You see, a man like Pickerbaugh makes all public health work simply ridiculous by his circusing and his ignorance. If he said that fresh air was a good thing, instead of making me open my windows it'd make me or any other reasonable person close 'em. And to use the word 'science' in those flop-eared limericks or whatever you call 'em—it's sacrilege!"

"Well, if you want to *know*, Martin Arrowsmith, I'll have no more of these high jinks with that Orchid girl! Practically hugging her when you came downstairs, and then mooning at her all evening! I don't mind your cursing and being cranky and even getting drunk, in a reasonable sort of way, but ever since the lunch when you told me and that Fox woman, 'I hope you girls won't mind, but I just happen to remember that I'm engaged to both of you'— You're mine, and I won't have any trespassers. I'm a cavewoman, and you'd better learn it, and as for that Orchid, with her simper and her stroking your arm and her great big absurd feet— Orchid! She's no orchid! She's a bachelor's button!"

"But, honest, I don't even remember which of the eight she was."

"Huh! Then you've been making love to all of 'em, that's why. Drat her! Well, I'm not going to go on scrapping about it. I just wanted to warn you, that's all."

At the hotel, after giving up the attempt to find a short, jovial, convincing way of promising that he would never flirt with Orchid, he stammered, "If you don't mind, I think I'll stay down and walk a little more. I've got to figure this health department business out."

He sat in the Sims House office—singularly dismal it was, after midnight, and singularly smelly.

"That fool Pickerbaugh! I wish I'd told him right out that we know hardly anything about the epidemiology of tuberculosis, for instance.

"Just the same, she's a darling child. Orchid! She's like an orchid—no, she's too healthy. Be a great kid to go hunting with. Sweet. And she acted as if I were her own age, not an old doctor. I'll be good, oh, I'll be good, but— I'd like to kiss her once, *good!* She likes me. Those darling lips, like—like rosebuds!

"Poor Leora. I nev' was so astonished in my life. Jealous. Well, she's got a right to be! No woman ever stood by a man like— Lee, sweet, can't you see, idiot, if I skipped round the corner with seventeen billion Orchids, it'd be you I loved, and never anybody but you!

"I can't go round singing Healthette Octette Pantalette stuff. Even if it did instruct people, which it don't. Be almost better to let 'em die than have to live and listen to—

"Leora said I was a 'backwoods hick.' Let me tell you, young woman, as it happens I am a Bachelor of Arts, and you may recall the kind of books the 'backwoods hick' was reading to you last winter, and even Henry James and everybody and— Oh, she's right. I am. I do know how to make pipets and agar, but— And yet some day I want to travel like Sondelius—

"Sondelius! God! If it were he I was working for, instead of Pickerbaugh, I'd slave for him—

"Or does he pull the bunk, too?

"Now that's just what I mean. That kind of phrase. 'Pull the bunk'! Horrible!

"Hell! I'll use any kind of phrase I want to! I'm not one of your social climbers like Angus. The way Sondelius cusses, for instance, and yet he's used to all those highbrows—

"And I'll be so busy here in Nautilus that I won't even be able to go on reading. Still— I don't suppose they read much, but there must be quite a few of these rich men here that know about nice houses. Clothes. Theaters. That stuff.

"Rats!"

He wandered to an all-night lunch-wagon, where he gloomily drank coffee. Beside him, seated at the long shelf which served as table, beneath the noble red-glass window with a portrait of George Washington, was a policeman who, as he gnawed a Hamburger sandwich, demanded:

"Say, ain't you this new doctor that's come to assist Pickerbaugh? Seen you at City Hall."

"Yes. Say, uh, say how does the city like Pickerbaugh? How do you like him? Tell me honestly, because I'm just starting in, and, uh— You get me."

With his spoon held inside the cup by a brawny thumb, the policeman gulped his coffee and proclaimed, while the greasy friendly cook of the lunch-wagon nodded in agreement:

"Well, if you want the straight dope, he hollers a good deal, but he's one awful brainy man. He certainly can sling the Queen's English, and jever hear one of his poems? They're darn' bright. I'll tell you: There's some people say Pickerbaugh pulls the song and dance too much, but way I figure it, course maybe for you and me, Doctor, it'd be all right if he just looked after the milk and the garbage and the kids' teeth. But there's a lot of careless, ignorant, foreign slobs that need to be jollied into using their konks about these health biznai, so's they won't go getting sick with a lot of these infectious diseases and pass 'em on to the rest of us, and believe me, old Doc Pickerbaugh is the boy that gets the idea into their noodles!

"Yes, sir, he's a great old coot—he ain't a clam like some of these docs. Why, say, one day he showed up at the St. Patrick picnic, even if he is a dirty Protestant, and him and Father Costello chummed up like two old cronies, and darn' if he didn't wrestle a fellow half his age, and awful' near throw him, yes, you bet he did, he certainly give that young fellow a run for his money all right! We fellows on the Force all like him, and we have to grin, the way he comes around and soft-soaps us into doing a lot of health work that by law we ain't hardly supposed to do, you might say, instead of issuing a lot of fool orders. You bet. He's a real guy."

"I see," said Martin, and as he returned to the hotel he meditated:

"But think of what Gottlieb would say about him.

"Damn Gottlieb! Damn everybody except Leora!

"I'm not going to fail here, way I did in Wheatsylvania.

"Some day Pickerbaugh will get a bigger job— Huh! He's just the kind of jollying fourflusher that *would* climb! But anyway, I'll have my training then, and maybe I'll make a real health department here.

"Orchid said we'd go skating this winter—

"*Damn* Orchid!"

Chapter XX

MARTIN found in Dr. Pickerbaugh a generous chief. He was eager to have Martin invent and clamor about his own Causes and Movements. His scientific knowledge was rather thinner than that of the visiting nurses, but he had little jealousy, and he demanded of Martin only the belief that a rapid and noisy moving from place to place is the means (and possibly the end) of Progress.

In a two-family house on Social Hill, which is not a hill but a slight swelling in the plain, Martin and Leora found an upper floor. There was a simple pleasantness in these continuous lawns, these wide maple-shaded streets, and a joy in freedom from the peering whisperers of Wheatsylvania.

Suddenly they were being courted by the Nice Society of Nautilus.

A few days after their arrival Martin was summoned to the telephone to hear a masculine voice rasping:

"Hello. Martin? I bet you can't guess who this is!"

Martin, very busy, restrained his desire to observe, "You win—g' by!" and he buzzed, with the cordiality suitable to a new Assistant Director:

"No, I'm afraid I can't."

"Well, make a guess."

"Oh—Clif Clawson?"

"Nope. Say, I see you're looking fine. Oh, I guess I've got you guessing this time! Go on! Have another try!"

The stenographer was waiting to take letters, and Martin had not yet learned to become impersonal and indifferent in her presence. He said with a perceptible tartness:

"Oh, I suppose it's President Wilson. Look here—"

"Well, Mart, it's Irve Watters! What do you know about that!"

Apparently the jester expected large gratification, but it took ten seconds for Martin to remember who Irving Watters might be. Then he had it: Watters, the appalling normal medical student whose faith in the good, the true, the profitable, had annoyed him at Digamma Pi. He made his response as hearty as he could:

"Well, well, what you doing here, Irve?"

"Why, I'm settled here. Been here ever since internship. And got a nice little practise, too. Look, Mart, Mrs. Watters and I want you and your wife—I believe you are married, aren't you?—to come up to the house for dinner, to-morrow evening, and I'll put you onto all the local slants."

The dread of Watters's patronage enabled Martin to lie vigorously:

"Awfully sorry—awfully sorry—got a date for to-morrow evening and the next evening."

"Then come have lunch with me to-morrow at the Elks' Club, and you and your wife take dinner with us Sunday noon."

Hopelessly, "I don't think I can make it for lunch but—Well, we'll dine with you Sunday."

It is one of the major tragedies that nothing is more discomforting than the hearty affection of the Old Friends who never were friends. Martin's imaginative dismay at being caught here by Watters was not lessened when Leora and he reluctantly appeared on Sunday at one-thirty and were by a fury of Old Friendship dragged back into the days of Digamma Pi.

Watters's house was new, and furnished in a highly built-in and leaded-glass manner. He had in three years of practise already become didactic and incredibly married; he had put on weight and infallibility; and he had learned many new things about which to be dull. Having been graduated a year earlier than Martin and having married an almost rich wife, he was kind and hospitable with an emphasis which aroused a desire to do homicide. His conversation was a series of maxims and admonitions:

"If you stay with the Department of Public Health for a couple of years and take care to meet the right people, you'll be able to go into very lucrative practise here. It's a fine town—prosperous—so few dead beats.

"You want to join the country club and take up golf. Best opportunity in the world to meet the substantial citizens. I've picked up more than one high-class patient there.

"Pickerbaugh is a good active man and a fine booster but he's got a bad socialistic tendency. These clinics—outrageous—the people that go to them that can afford to pay! Pauperize people. Now this may startle you—oh, you had a lot of crank notions when you were in school, but you aren't the only one that does some thinking for himself!—sometimes I believe it'd be better for the general health situation if there weren't any public health departments at all, because they get a lot of people into the habit of going to free clinics instead of to private physicians, and cut down the earnings of the doctors and reduce their number, so there are less of us to keep a watchful eye on sickness.

"I guess by this time you've gotten over the funny ideas you used to have about being practical—'commercialism' you used to call it. You can see now that you've got to support your wife and family, and if you don't, nobody else is going to.

"Any time you want a straight tip about people here, you just come to me. Pickerbaugh is a crank—he won't give you the right dope—the people you want to tie up with are the good, solid, conservative, successful business men."

Then Mrs. Watters had her turn. She was meaty with advice, being the daughter of a prosperous person, none other than Mr. S. A. Peaseley, the manufacturer of the Daisy Manure Spreader.

"You haven't any children?" she sobbed at Leora. "Oh, you must! Irving and I have two, and you don't know what an interest they are to us, and they keep us so young."

Martin and Leora looked at each other pitifully.

After dinner, Irving insisted on their recalling the "good times we used to have together at the dear old U." He took no denial. "You always want to make folks think you're eccentric, Mart. You pretend you haven't any college patriotism, but I know better—I know you're showing off—you admire the old place and our profs just as much as anybody. Maybe I know you better than you do yourself! Come on, now; let's give a long cheer and sing 'Winnemac, Mother of Brawny Men.'"

And, "Don't be silly; of course you're going to sing," said Mrs. Watters, as she marched to the piano, with which she dealt in a firm manner.

When they had politely labored through the fried chicken and brick ice cream, through the maxims, gurglings, and memories, Martin and Leora went forth and spoke in tongues:

"Pickerbaugh must be a saint, if Watters roasts him. I begin to believe he has sense enough to come in when it rains."

In their common misery they forgot that they had been agitated by a girl named Orchid.

II

Between Pickerbaugh and Irving Watters, Martin was drafted into many of the associations, clubs, lodges, and "causes" with which Nautilus foamed; into the Chamber of Commerce, the Moccasin Ski and Hiking Club, the Elks' Club, the Oddfellows, and the Evangeline County Medical society. He resisted, but they said in a high hurt manner, "Why, my boy, if you're going to be a public official, and if you have the slightest appreciation of their efforts to make you welcome here—"

Leora and he found themselves with so many invitations that they, who had deplored the dullness of Wheatsylvania, complained now that they could have no quiet evenings at home. But they fell into the habit of social ease, of dressing, of going places without nervous anticipation. They modernized their rustic dancing; they learned to play bridge, rather badly, and tennis rather well; and Martin, not by virtue and heroism but merely by habit, got out of the way of resenting the chirp of small talk.

Probably they were never recognized by their hostesses as pirates, but considered a Bright Young Couple who, since they were protégés of Pickerbaugh, must be earnest and forward-looking, and who, since they were patronized by Irving and Mrs. Watters, must be respectable.

Watters took them in hand and kept them there. He had so thick a rind that it was impossible for him to understand that Martin's frequent refusals of his invitations could conceivably mean that he did not wish to come. He detected traces of heterodoxy in Martin, and with affection, diligence, and an extraordinarily heavy humor he devoted himself to the work of salvation. Frequently he sought to entertain other guests by urging, "Come on now, Mart, let's hear some of those crazy ideas of yours!"

His friendly zeal was drab compared with that of his wife. Mrs. Watters had been reared by her father and by her husband to believe that she was the final fruit of the ages, and she set herself to correct the barbarism of the Arrowsmiths. She rebuked Martin's damns, Leora's smoking, and both their theories of bidding at bridge. But she never nagged. To have nagged would have been to admit that there were persons who did not acknowledge her sovereignty. She merely gave orders, brief, humorous, and introduced by a strident "Now don't be silly," and she expected that to settle the matter.

Martin groaned, "Oh, Lord, between Pickerbaugh and Irve, it's easier to become a respectable member of society than to go on fighting."

But Watters and Pickerbaugh were not so great a compulsion to respectability as the charms of finding himself listened to in Nautilus as he never had been in Wheatsylvania, and of finding himself admired by Orchid.

III

He had been seeking a precipitation test for the diagnosis of syphilis which should be quicker and simpler than the Wassermann. His slackened fingers and rusty mind were becoming used to the laboratory and to passionate hypotheses when he was dragged away to help Pickerbaugh in securing publicity. He was coaxed into making his first speech: an address on "What the Laboratory Teaches about Epidemics" for the Sunday Afternoon Free Lecture Course of the Star of Hope Universalist Church.

He was flustered when he tried to prepare his notes, and on the morning of the affair he was chill as he remembered the dreadful thing he would do this day, but he was desperate with embarrassment when he came up to the Star of Hope Church.

People were crowding in; mature, responsible people. He quaked, "They're coming to hear *me*, and I haven't got a darn' thing to say to 'em!" It made him feel the more ridiculous that they who presumably wished to listen to him should not be aware of him, and that the usher, profusely shaking hands at the Byzantine portal, should bluster, "You'll find plenty room right up the side aisles, young man."

"I'm the speaker for the afternoon."

"Oh, oh, yes, oh, yes, Doctor. Right round to the Bevis Street entrance, if you please, Doctor."

In the parlors he was unctuously received by the pastor and a committee of three, wearing morning clothes and a manner of Christian intellectuality.

They held his hand in turn, they brought up rustling women to meet him, they stood about him in a polite and twittery circle, and dismayingly they expected him to say something intelligent. Then, suffering, ghastly frightened, dumb, he was led through an arched doorway into the auditorium. Millions of faces were staring at his apologetic insignificance—faces in the curving lines of pews, faces in the low balcony, eyes which followed him and doubted him and noted that his heels were run down.

The agony grew while he was prayed over and sung over.

The pastor and the lay chairman of the Lecture Course opened with suitable devotions. While Martin trembled and tried to look brazenly at the massed people who were looking at him, while he sat nude and exposed and unprotected on the high platform, the pastor made announcement of the Thursday Missionary Supper and the Little Lads' Marching Club. They sang a brief cheerful hymn or two—Martin wondering whether to sit or stand—and the chairman prayed that "our friend who will address us to-day may have power to put his Message across." Through the prayer Martin sat with his forehead in his hand, feeling foolish, and raving, "I guess this is the proper attitude—they're all gawping at me—gosh, won't he ever quit?—oh, damn it, now what was that point I was going to make about fumigation?—oh, Lord, he's winding up and I've got to shoot!"

Somehow, he was standing by the reading-desk, holding it for support, and his voice seemed to be going on, producing reasonable words. The blur of faces cleared and he saw individuals. He picked out a keen old man and tried to make him laugh and marvel.

He found Leora, toward the back, nodding to him, reassuring him. He dared to look away from the path of faces directly in front of him. He glanced at the balcony—

The audience perceived a young man who was being earnest about sera and vaccines but, while his voice buzzed on, that churchly young man had noted two silken ankles distinguishing the front row of the balcony, had discovered that they belonged to Orchid Pickerbaugh and that she was flashing down admiration.

At the end Martin had the most enthusiastic applause ever known—all lecturers, after all lectures, are gratified by that kind of applause—and the chairman said the most flattering things ever uttered, and the audience went out with the most remarkable speed ever witnessed, and Martin discovered himself holding Orchid's hand in the parlors while she warbled, in the most adorable voice ever heard, "Oh, Dr. Arrowsmith, you were just wonderful! Most of these lecturers are old stuffs, but you put it right over! I'm going to do a dash home and tell Dad. He'll be so tickled!"

Not till then did he find that Leora had made her way to the parlors and was looking at them like a wife.

As they walked home Leora was eloquently silent.

"Well, did you like my spiel?" he said, after a suitable time of indignant waiting.

"Yes, it wasn't bad. It must have been awfully hard to talk to all those stupid people."

"Stupid? What d'you mean by 'stupid'? They got me splendidly. They were fine."

"Were they? Well anyway, thank Heaven, you won't have to keep up this silly gassing. Pickerbaugh likes to hear himself talk too well to let you in on it very often."

"I didn't mind it. Fact, don't know but what it's a good thing to have to express myself publicly now and then. Makes you think more lucidly."

"As for instance the nice, lovely, lucid politicians!"

"Now you look here, Lee! Of course we know your husband is a mutt, and no good outside the laboratory, but I do think you might *pretend* to be a little enthusiastic over the first address he's ever made—the very first he's ev-er tackled—when it went off so well."

"Why, silly, I was enthusiastic. I applauded a lot. I thought you were terribly smart. It's just— There's other things I think you can do better. What shall we do to-night; have a cold snack at home or go to the cafeteria?"

Thus was he reduced from hero to husband, and he had all the pleasures of inappreciation.

He thought about his indignities the whole week, but with the coming of winter there was a fever of dully sprightly dinners and safely wild bridge and their first evening at home, their first opportunity for secure and comfortable quarreling, was on Friday. They sat down to what he announced as "getting back to some real reading, like physiology and a little of this fellow Arnold Bennett—nice quiet reading," but which consisted of catching up on the news notes in the medical journals.

He was restless. He threw down his magazine. He demanded:

"What're you going to wear at Pickerbaugh's snow-picnic to-morrow?"

"Oh, I haven't— I'll find something."

"Lee, I want to ask you: Why the devil did you say I talked too much at Dr. Strafford's last evening? I know I've got most of the faults going, but I didn't know talking too much was one of 'em."

"It hasn't been, till now."

"'Till now'!"

"You look here, Sandy Arrowsmith! You've been pouting like a bad brat, all week. What's the matter with you?"

"Well, I— Gosh, it makes me tired! Here everybody is so enthusiastic about my Star of Hope spiel—that note in the *Morning Frontiersman*, and Pickerbaugh says Orchid said it was a corker—and you never so much as peep!"

"Didn't I applaud? But— It's just that I hope you aren't going to keep up this drooling."

"You do, do you! Well, let me tell you I *am* going to keep it up! Not that I'm going to talk a lot of hot air. I gave 'em straight science, last Sunday, and they ate it up. I hadn't realized it isn't necessary to be mushy, to hold an audience. And the amount of good you can do! Why, I got across more Health Instruction and ideas about the value of the lab in that three-quarters of an hour than— I don't care for being a big gun but it's fine to have people where they have to listen to what you've got to say and can't butt in, way they did in Wheatsylvania. You bet I'm going to keep up what you so politely call my damn' fool drooling—"

"Sandy, it may be all right for some people, but not for you. I can't tell you—that's one reason why I haven't said more about your talk—I can't tell you how astonished I am to hear you, who're always sneering at what you call sentimentality, simply weeping over the Dear Little Tots!"

"I never said that—never used the phrase and you know it. And by God! *You* talk about sneering! Just let me tell you that the Public Health Movement, by correcting early faults in children, by looking after their eyes and tonsils and so on, can save millions of lives and make a future generation—"

"I know it! I love children much more than you do! But I mean all this ridiculous simpering—"

"Well, gosh, somebody has to do it. You can't work with people till you educate 'em. There's where old Pick, even if he is an imbecile, does such good work with his poems and all that stuff. Prob'ly be a good thing if I could write 'em—golly, wonder if I couldn't learn to?"

"They're horrible!"

"Now there's a fine consistency for you! The other evening you called 'em 'cute.'"

"I don't have to be consistent. I'm a mere woman. You, Martin Arrowsmith, you'd be the first to tell me so. And for Dr. Pickerbaugh they're all right, but not for you. You belong in a laboratory, finding out things, not advertising them. Do you remember once in Wheatsylvania for five minutes you almost thought of joining a church and being a Respectable Citizen? Are you going on for the rest of your life, stumbling into respectability and having to be dug out again? Will you never learn you're a barbarian?"

"By God, I am! And—what was that other lovely thing you called me?—I'm also, soul of my soul, a damn' backwoods hick! And a fine lot you help! When I want to settle down to a decent and useful life and not go 'round antagonizing people, you, the one that ought to believe in me, you're the first one to crab!"

"Maybe Orchid Pickerbaugh would help you better."

"She probably would! Believe me, she's a darling, and she did appreciate my spiel at the church, and if you think I'm going to sit up all night listening to you sneering at my work and my friends— I'm going to have a hot bath. Good *night!*"

In the bath he gasped that it was impossible he should have been quarreling with Leora. Why! She was the only person in the world, besides Gottlieb and Sondelius and Clif Clawson—by the way, where was Clif? still in New York? didn't Clif owe him a letter? but anyway— He was a fool to have lost his temper, even if she was so stubborn that she wouldn't adjust her opinions, couldn't see that he had a gift for influencing people. Nobody would ever stand by him as she had, and he loved her—

He dried himself violently; he dashed in with repentances; they told each other that they were the most reasonable persons living; they kissed with eloquence; and then Leora reflected:

"Just the same, my lad, I'm not going to help you fool yourself. You're not a booster. You're a lie-hunter. Funny, you'd think to hear about these lie-hunters, like Professor Gottlieb and your old Voltaire, they couldn't be fooled. But maybe they were like you: always trying to get away from the tiresome truth, always hoping to settle down and be rich, always selling their souls to the devil and then going and double-crossing the poor devil. I think—I think—" She sat up in bed, holding her temples in the labor of articulation. "You're different from Professor Gottlieb. He never makes mistakes or wastes time on—"

"He wasted time at Hunziker's nostrum factory all right, and his title is 'Doctor,' not 'Professor,' if you *must* give him a—"

"If he went to Hunziker's he had some good reason. He's a genius; he couldn't be wrong. Or could he, even he? But *anyway*: you, Sandy, you have to stumble every so often; have to learn by making mistakes. I will say one thing: you learn from your crazy mistakes. But I get a little tired, sometimes, watching you rush up and put your neck in every noose—like being a blinking orator or yearning over your Orchid."

"Well by golly! After I come in here trying to make peace!

It's a good thing *you* never make any mistakes! But one perfect person in a household is enough!"

He banged into bed. Silence. Soft sounds of "Mart—*Sandy!*" He ignored her, proud that he could be hard with her, and so fell asleep. At breakfast, when he was ashamed and eager, she was curt.

"I don't care to discuss it," she said.

In that wry mood they went on Saturday afternoon to the Pickerbaughs' snow picnic.

IV

Dr. Pickerbaugh owned a small log cabin in a scanty grove of oaks among the hillocks north of Nautilus. A dozen of them drove out in a bob-sled filled with straw and blue woolly robes. The sleigh bells were exciting and the children leaped out to run beside the sled.

The school physician, a bachelor, was attentive to Leora; twice he tucked her in, and that, for Nautilus, was almost compromising. In jealousy Martin turned openly and completely to Orchid.

He grew interested in her not for the sake of disciplining Leora but for her own rosy sweetness. She was wearing a tweed jacket, with a tam, a flamboyant scarf, and the first breeches any girl had dared to display in Nautilus. She patted Martin's knee, and when they rode behind the sled on a perilous toboggan, she held his waist, resolutely.

She was calling him "Dr. Martin" now, and he had come to a warm "Orchid."

At the cabin there was a clamor of disembarkation. Together Martin and Orchid carried in the hamper of food; together they slid down the hillocks on skiis. When their skiis were entangled, they rolled into a drift, and as she clung to him, unafraid and unembarrassed, it seemed to him that in the roughness of tweeds she was but the softer and more wonderful—eyes fearless, cheeks brilliant as she brushed the coating of wet snow from them, flying legs of a slim boy, shoulders adorable in their pretense of sturdy boyishness—

But "I'm a sentimental fool! Leora was right!" he snarled at himself. "I thought you had some originality! And poor little

Orchid—she'd be shocked if she knew how sneak-minded you are!"

But poor little Orchid was coaxing, "Come on, Dr. Martin, let's shoot off that high bluff. We're the only ones that have any pep."

"That's because we're the only young ones."

"It's because you're so young. I'm dreadfully old. I just sit and moon when you rave about your epidemics and things."

He saw that, with her infernal school physician, Leora was sliding on a distant slope. It may have been pique and it may have been relief that he was licensed to be alone with Orchid, but he ceased to speak to her as though she were a child and he a person laden with wisdom; ceased to speak to her as though he were looking over his shoulder. They raced to the high bluff. They skiied down it and fell; they had one glorious swooping slide, and wrestled in the snow.

They returned to the cabin together, to find the others away. She stripped off her wet sweater and patted her soft blouse. They ferreted out a thermos of hot coffee, and he looked at her as though he was going to kiss her, and she looked back at him as though she did not mind. As they laid out the food they hummed with the intimacy of understanding, and when she trilled, "Now hurry up, lazy one, and put those cups on that horrid old table," it was as one who was content to be with him forever.

They said nothing compromising, they did not hold hands, and as they rode home in the electric snow-flying darkness, though they sat shoulder by shoulder he did not put his arms about her except when the bob-sled slewed on sharp corners. If Martin was exalted with excitement, it was presumably caused by the wholesome exercises of the day. Nothing happened and nobody looked uneasy. At parting all their farewells were cheery and helpful.

And Leora made no comments, though for a day or two there was about her a chill air which the busy Martin did not investigate.

Chapter XXI

NAUTILUS was one of the first communities in the country to develop the Weeks habit, now so richly grown that we have Correspondence School Week, Christian Science Week, Osteopathy Week, and Georgia Pine Week.

A Week is not merely a week.

If an aggressive, wide-awake, live-wire, and go-ahead church or chamber of commerce or charity desires to improve itself, which means to get more money, it calls in those few energetic spirits who run any city, and proclaims a Week. This consists of one month of committee meetings, a hundred columns of praise for the organization in the public prints, and finally a day or two on which athletic persons flatter inappreciative audiences in churches or cinema theaters, and the prettiest girls in town have the pleasure of being allowed to talk to male strangers on the street corners, apropos of giving them extremely undecorative tags in exchange for the smallest sums which those strangers think they must pay if they are to be considered gentlemen.

The only variation is the Weeks in which the object is not to acquire money immediately by the sale of tags but by general advertising to get more of it later.

Nautilus had held a Pep Week, during which a race of rapidly talking men, formerly book-agents but now called Efficiency Engineers, went about giving advice to shopkeepers on how to get money away from one another more rapidly, and Dr. Almus Pickerbaugh addressed a prayer-meeting on "The Pep of St. Paul, the First Booster." It had held a Gladhand Week, when everybody was supposed to speak to at least three strangers daily, to the end that infuriated elderly traveling salesmen were backslapped all day long by hearty and powerful unknown persons. There had also been an Old Home Week, a Write to Mother Week, a We Want Your Factory in Nautilus Week, an Eat More Corn Week, a Go to Church Week, a Salvation Army Week, and an Own Your Own Auto Week.

Perhaps the bonniest of all was Y. Week, to raise eighty thousand dollars for a new Y.M.C.A. building.

On the old building were electric signs, changed daily, announcing "You Must Come Across," "Young Man Come Along" and "Your Money Creates 'Appiness." Dr. Pickerbaugh made nineteen addresses in three days, comparing the Y.M.C.A. to the Crusaders, the Apostles, and the expeditions of Dr. Cook—who, he believed, really had discovered the North Pole. Orchid sold three hundred and nineteen Y. tags, seven of them to the same man, who afterward made improper remarks to her. She was rescued by a Y.M.C.A. secretary, who for a considerable time held her hand to calm her.

No organization could rival Almus Pickerbaugh in the invention of Weeks.

He started in January with a Better Babies Week, and a very good Week it was, but so hotly followed by Banish the Booze Week, Tougher Teeth Week, and Stop the Spitter Week that people who lacked his vigor were heard groaning, "My health is being ruined by all this fretting over health."

During Clean-up Week, Pickerbaugh spread abroad a new lyric of his own composition:

Germs come by stealth
And ruin health,
So listen, pard,
Just drop a card
To some man who'll clean up your yard
And that will hit the old germs hard.

Swat the Fly Week brought him, besides the joy of giving prizes to the children who had slaughtered the most flies, the inspiration for two verses. Posters admonished:

Sell your hammer and buy a horn,
But hang onto the old fly-swatter.
If you don't want disease sneaking into the Home
Then to kill the fly you gotter!

It chanced that the Fraternal Order of Eagles were holding a state convention at Burlington that week, and Pickerbaugh telegraphed to them:

Just mention fly-prevention
At the good old Eagles' convention.

This was quoted in ninety-six newspapers, including one in Alaska, and waving the clippings Pickerbaugh explained to Martin, "Now you see the way a fellow can get the truth across, if he goes at it right."

Three Cigars a Day Week, which Pickerbaugh invented in midsummer, was not altogether successful, partly because an injudicious humorist on a local newspaper wanted to know whether Dr. Pickerbaugh really expected all babes in arms to smoke as many as three cigars a day, and partly because the cigar-manufacturers came around to the Department of Health with strong remarks about Common Sense. Nor was there thorough satisfaction in Can the Cat and Doctor the Dog Week.

With all his Weeks, Pickerbaugh had time to preside over the Program Committee of the State Convention of Health Officers and Agencies.

It was he who wrote the circular letter sent to all members:

Brother Males and Shemales:

Are you coming to the Health Bee? It will be the livest Hop-to-it that this busy lil ole planet has ever see. And it's going to be Practical. We'll kiss out on all these glittering generalities and get messages from men as kin talk, so we can lug a think or two (2) home wid us.

Luther Botts, the famous community-sing leader, will be there to put Wim an Wigor neverything into the program. John F. Zeisser, M.A., M.D., nall the rest of the alphabet (part your hair Jack and look cute, the ladies sure love you) will unlimber a coupla key-notes. (On your tootsies, fellers, thar she blows!) From time to time, if the brakes hold, we will, or shall in the infinitive, hie oursellufs from wherein we are at to thither, and grab a lunch with Wild Wittles.

Do it sound like a good show? It do! Barber, you're next. Let's have those cards saying you're coming.

This created much enthusiasm and merriment. Dr. Feesons of Clinton wrote to Pickerbaugh:

I figure it was largely due to your snappy come-on letter that we pulled such an attendance and with all modesty I think we may say it was the best health convention ever held in the world. I had to laugh at one old hen. Bostonian or somepun, who was howling that your letter was "undignified"! Can you beat it! I think people as hypercritical and lacking in humor as her should be treated with the dignified contempt they deserve, the damn fool!

II

Martin was enthusiastic during Better Babies Week. Leora and he weighed babies, examined them, made out diet charts, and in each child saw the baby they could never have. But when it came to More Babies Week, then he was argumentative. He believed, he said, in birth-control. Pickerbaugh answered with theology, violence, and the example of his own eight beauties.

Martin was equally unconvinced by Anti-Tuberculosis Week. He liked his windows open at night and he disliked men who spat tobacco juice on sidewalks, but he was jarred by hearing these certainly esthetic and possibly hygienic reforms proposed with holy frenzy and bogus statistics.

Any questioning of his fluent figures about tuberculosis, any hint that the cause of decline in the disease may have been natural growth of immunity and not the crusades against spitting and stale air, Pickerbaugh regarded as a criticism of his honesty in making such crusades. He had the personal touchiness of most propagandists; he believed that because he was sincere, therefore his opinions must always be correct. To demand that he be accurate in his statements, to quote Raymond Pearl's dictum: "As a matter of objective scientific fact, extremely little is known about why the mortality from tuberculosis has declined"—this was to be a scoundrel who really liked to befoul the pavements.

Martin was so alienated that he took an anti-social and probably vicious joy in discovering that though the death-rate in tuberculosis certainly had decreased during Pickerbaugh's administration in Nautilus, it had decreased at the same rate in most villages of the district, with no speeches about spitting, no Open Your Windows parades.

It was fortunate for Martin that Pickerbaugh did not expect him to take much share in his publicity campaigns but rather to be his substitute in the office during them. They stirred in Martin the most furious and complicated thoughts that had ever afflicted him.

Whenever he hinted criticism, Pickerbaugh answered, "What if my statistics aren't always exact? What if my advertising, my jollying of the public, does strike some folks as vulgar? It all does good; it's all on the right side. No matter what methods we use, if we can get people to have more fresh air and cleaner yards and less alcohol, we're justified."

To himself, a little surprised, Martin put it, "Yes, does it really matter? Does truth matter—clean, cold, unfriendly truth, Max Gottlieb's truth? Everybody says, 'Oh, you mustn't tamper with the truth,' and everybody is furious if you hint that they themselves are tampering with it. Does anything matter, except making love and sleeping and eating and being flattered?

"I think truth does matter to me, but if it does, isn't the desire for scientific precision simply my hobby, like another man's excitement about his golf? Anyway, I'm going to stick by Pickerbaugh."

To the defense of his chief he was the more impelled by the attitude of Irving Watters and such other physicians as attacked Pickerbaugh because they feared that he really would be successful, and reduce their earnings. But all the while Martin was weary of unchecked statistics.

He estimated that according to Pickerbaugh's figures on bad teeth, careless motoring, tuberculosis, and seven other afflictions alone, every person in the city had a one hundred and eighty per cent chance of dying before the age of sixteen, and he could not startle with much alarm when Pickerbaugh shouted, "Do you realize that the number of people who died from yaws in Pickens County, Mississippi, last year alone, was twenty-nine and that they might all have been saved, yes, sir, *saved*, by a daily cold shower?"

For Pickerbaugh had the dreadful habit of cold showers, even in winter, though he might have known that nineteen men between the ages of seventeen and forty-two died of cold showers in twenty-two years in Milwaukee alone.

To Pickerbaugh the existence of "variables," a word which Martin now used as irritatingly as once he had used "control," was without significance. That health might be determined by temperature, heredity, profession, soil, natural immunity, or by anything save health-department campaigns for increased washing and morality, was to him inconceivable.

"Variables! Huh!" Pickerbaugh snorted. "Why, every enlightened man in the public service *knows* enough about the causes of disease—matter now of acting on that knowledge."

When Martin sought to show that they certainly knew very little about the superiority of fresh air to warmth in schools, about the hygienic dangers of dirty streets, about the real danger of alcohol, about the value of face-masks in influenza epidemics, about most of the things they tub-thumped in their campaigns, Pickerbaugh merely became angry, and Martin wanted to resign, and saw Irving Watters again, and returned to Pickerbaugh with new zeal, and was in general as agitated and wretched as a young revolutionist discovering the smugness of his leaders.

He came to question what Pickerbaugh called "the proven practical value" of his campaigns as much as the accuracy of Pickerbaugh's biology. He noted how bored were most of the newspapermen by being galvanized into a new saving of the world once a fortnight, and how incomparably bored was the Man in the Street when the nineteenth pretty girl in twenty days had surged up demanding that he buy a tag to support an association of which he had never heard.

But more dismaying was the slimy trail of the dollar which he beheld in Pickerbaugh's most ardent eloquence.

When Martin suggested that all milk should be pasteurized, that certain tenements known to be tuberculosis-breeders should be burnt down instead of being fumigated in a fiddling useless way, when he hinted that these attacks would save more lives than ten thousand sermons and ten years of parades by little girls carrying banners and being soaked by the rain, then Pickerbaugh worried, "No, no, Martin, don't think we could do that. Get so much opposition from the dairymen and the landlords. Can't accomplish anything in this work unless you keep from offending people."

When Pickerbaugh addressed a church or the home circle he spoke of "the value of health in making life more joyful," but when he addressed a business luncheon he changed it to "the value in good round dollars and cents of having workmen who are healthy and sober, and therefore able to work faster at the same wages." Parents' associations he enlightened upon "the saving in doctors' bills of treating the child before maladjustments go too far," but to physicians he gave assurance that public health agitation would merely make the custom of going regularly to doctors more popular.

To Martin, he spoke of Pasteur, George Washington, Victor Vaughan, and Edison as his masters, but in asking the business men of Nautilus—the Rotary Club, the Chamber of Commerce, the association of wholesalers—for their divine approval of more funds for his department, he made it clear that they were his masters and lords of all the land, and fatly, behind cigars, they accepted their kinghood.

Gradually Martin's contemplation moved beyond Almus Pickerbaugh to all leaders, of armies or empires, of universities or churches, and he saw that most of them were Pickerbaughs. He preached to himself, as Max Gottlieb had once preached to him, the loyalty of dissent, the faith of being very doubtful, the gospel of not bawling gospels, the wisdom of admitting the probable ignorance of one's self and of everybody else, and the energetic acceleration of a Movement for going very slow.

III

A hundred interruptions took Martin out of his laboratory. He was summoned into the reception-room of the department to explain to angry citizens why the garage next door to them should smell of gasoline; he went back to his cubbyhole to dictate letters to school-principals about dental clinics; he drove out to Swede Hollow to see what attention the food and dairy inspector had given to the slaughter-houses; he ordered a family in Shantytown quarantined; and escaped at last into the laboratory.

It was well lighted, convenient, well stocked. Martin had little time for anything but cultures, blood-tests, and Wassermanns for the private physicians of the city, but the work rested him, and now and then he struggled over a precipitation test which was going to replace Wassermanns and make him famous.

Pickerbaugh apparently believed that this research would take six weeks; Martin had hoped to do it in two years; and with the present interruptions it would require two hundred, by which time the Pickerbaughs would have eradicated syphilis and made the test useless.

To Martin's duties was added the entertainment of Leora in the strange city of Nautilus.

"Do you manage to keep busy all day?" he encouraged her, and, "Any place you'd like to go this evening?"

She looked at him suspiciously. She was as easily and automatically contented by herself as a pussy cat, and he had never before worried about her amusement.

IV

The Pickerbaugh daughters were always popping into Martin's laboratory. The twins broke test-tubes, and made doll tents out of filter paper. Orchid lettered the special posters for her father's Weeks, and the laboratory, she said, was the quietest place in which to work. While Martin stood at his bench he was conscious of her, humming at a table in the corner. They talked, tremendously, and he listened with fatuous enthusiasm to opinions which, had Leora produced them, he would have greeted with "That's a damn' silly remark!"

He held a clear, claret-red tube of hemolyzed blood up to the light, thinking half of its color and half of Orchid's ankles as she bent over the table, absurdly patient with her paint-brushes, curling her legs in a fantastic knot.

Abruptly he asked her, "Look here, honey. Suppose you—suppose a kid like you were to fall in love with a married man. What d'you think she ought to do? Be nice to him? Or chuck him?"

"Oh, she ought to chuck him. No matter how much she suffered. Even if she liked him terribly. Because even if she liked him, she oughtn't to wrong his wife."

"But suppose the wife never knew, or maybe didn't care?" He had stopped his pretense of working; he was standing before her, arms akimbo, dark eyes demanding.

"Well, if she didn't know— But it isn't that. I believe marriages really and truly are made in Heaven, don't you? Some day Prince Charming will come, the perfect lover—" She was so young, her lips were so young, so very sweet! "—and of course I want to keep myself for him. It would spoil everything if I made light of love before my Hero came."

But her smile was caressing.

He pictured them thrown together in a lonely camp. He saw her parroted moralities forgotten. He went through a change as definite as religious conversion or the coming of insane frenzy in war; the change from shamed reluctance to be unfaithful to his wife, to a determination to take what he could get. He began to resent Leora's demand that she, who had eternally his deepest love, should also demand his every wandering fancy. And she did demand it. She rarely spoke of Orchid, but she could tell (or nervously he thought she could tell) when he had spent an afternoon with the child. Her mute examination of him made him feel illicit. He who had never been unctuous was profuse and hearty as he urged her, "Been home all day? Well, we'll just skip out after dinner and take in a movie. Or shall we call up somebody and go see 'em? Whatever you'd like."

He heard his voice being flowery, and he hated it and knew that Leora was not cajoled. Whenever he drifted into one of his meditations on the superiority of his brand of truth to Pickerbaugh's, he snarled, "You're a fine bird to think about truth, you liar!"

He paid, in fact, an enormous price for looking at Orchid's lips, and no amount of anxiety about the price kept him from looking at them.

In early summer, two months before the outbreak of the Great War in Europe, Leora went to Wheatsylvania for a fortnight with her family. Then she spoke:

"Sandy, I'm not going to ask you any questions when I come back, but I hope you won't look as foolish as you've been looking lately. I don't think that bachelor's button, that ragweed, that lady idiot of yours is worth our quarreling. Sandy darling, I do want you to be happy, but unless I up and die on you some day, I'm not going to be hung up like an old cap. I warn you. Now about ice. I've left an order for a hundred pounds a week, and if you want to get your own dinners sometimes—"

When she had gone, nothing immediately happened, though a good deal was always about to happen. Orchid had the flapper's curiosity as to what a man was likely to do, but she was satisfied by exceedingly small thrills.

Martin swore, that morning of June, that she was a fool and a flirt, and he "hadn't the slightest intention of going near her." No! He would call on Irving Watters in the evening, or read, or have a walk with the school-clinic dentist.

But at half-past eight he was loitering toward her house.

If the elder Pickerbaughs were there— Martin could hear himself saying, "Thought I'd just drop by, Doctor, and ask you what you thought about—" Hang it! Thought about what? Pickerbaugh never thought about anything.

On the low front steps he could see Orchid. Leaning over her was a boy of twenty, one Charley, a clerk.

"Hello, Father in?" he cried, with a carelessness on which he could but pride himself.

"I'm terribly sorry; he and Mama won't be back till eleven. Won't you sit down and cool off a little?"

"Well—" He did sit down, firmly, and tried to make youthful conversation, while Charley produced sentiments suitable, in Charley's opinion, to the aged Dr. Arrowsmith, and Orchid made little purry interested sounds, an art in which she was very intelligent.

"Been, uh, been seeing many of the baseball games?" said Martin.

"Oh, been getting in all I can," said Charley. "How's things going at City Hall? Been nailing a lot of cases of smallpox and winkulus pinkulus and all those fancy diseases?"

"Oh, keep busy," grunted old Dr. Arrowsmith.

He could think of nothing else. He listened while Charley and Orchid giggled cryptically about things which barred him out and made him feel a hundred years old: references to Mamie and Earl, and a violent "Yeh, that's all right, but any time you see me dancing with her you just tell me about it, will yuh!" At the corner, Verbena Pickerbaugh was yelping, and observing, "Now you quit!" to persons unknown.

"Hell! It isn't worth it! I'm going home," Martin sighed, but at the moment Charley screamed, "Well, ta, ta, be good; gotta toddle along."

He was left to Orchid and peace and a silence rather embarrassing.

"It's so nice to be with somebody that has brains and doesn't always try to flirt, like Charley," said Orchid.

He considered, "Splendid! She's going to be just a nice good girl. And I've come to my senses. We'll just have a little chat and I'll go home."

She seemed to have moved nearer. She whispered at him, "I was so lonely, especially with that horrid slangy boy, till I heard your step on the walk. I knew it the second I heard it."

He patted her hand. As his pats were becoming more ardent than might have been expected from the assistant and friend of her father, she withdrew her hand, clasped her knees, and began to chatter.

Always it had been so in the evenings when he had drifted to the porch and found her alone. She was ten times more incalculable than the most complex woman. He managed to feel guilty toward Leora without any of the reputed joys of being guilty.

While she talked he tried to discover whether she had any brains whatever. Apparently she did not have enough to attend a small Midwestern denominational college. Verbena was going to college this autumn, but Orchid, she explained, thought she "ought to stay home and help Mama take care of the chickabiddies."

"Meaning," Martin reflected, "that she can't even pass the Mugford entrance exams!" But his opinion of her intelligence was suddenly enlarged as she whimpered, "Poor little me, prob'ly I'll always stay here in Nautilus, while you—oh, with your knowledge and your frightfully strong will-power, I know you're going to conquer the world!"

"Nonsense, I'll never conquer any world, but I do hope to pull off a few good health measures. Honestly, Orchid honey, do you think I have much will-power?"

The full moon was spacious now behind the maples. The seedy Pickerbaugh domain was enchanted; the tangled grass was a garden of roses, the ragged grape-arbor a shrine to Diana, the old hammock turned to fringed cloth of silver, the bad-tempered and sputtering lawn-sprinkler a fountain, and over all the world was the proper witchery of moonstruck love. The little city, by day as noisy and busy as a pack of children, was stilled and forgotten. Rarely had Martin been inspired to perceive the magic of a perfect hour, so absorbed was he ever in irascible pondering, but now he was caught, and lifted in rapture.

He held Orchid's quiet hand—and was lonely for Leora.

The belligerent Martin who had carried off Leora had not thought about romance, because in his clumsy way he had been romantic. The Martin who, like a returned warrior scented and enfeebled, yearned toward a girl in the moonlight, now desirously lifted his face to romance and was altogether unromantic.

He felt the duty of making love. He drew her close, but when she sighed, "Oh, please don't," there was in him no ruthlessness and no conviction with which to go on. He considered the moonlight again, but also he considered being at the office early in the morning, and he wondered if he could without detection slip out his watch and see what time it was. He managed it. He stooped to kiss her good-night, and somehow didn't quite kiss her, and found himself walking home.

As he went, he was ruthless and convinced enough regarding himself. He had never, he raged, however stumbling he might have been, expected to find himself a little pilferer of love, a peeping, creeping area-sneak, and not even successful in his sneaking, less successful than the soda-clerks who swanked nightly with the virgins under the maples. He told himself that Orchid was a young woman of no great wisdom, a sigher and drawer-out of her M's and O's, but once he was in his lonely flat he longed for her, thought of miraculous and completely idiotic ways of luring her here to-night, and went to bed yearning, "Oh, Orchid—"

Perhaps he had paid too much attention to moonlight and soft summer, for quite suddenly, one day when Orchid came swarming all over the laboratory and perched on the bench with a whisk of stockings, he stalked to her, masterfully seized her wrists, and kissed her as she deserved to be kissed.

He immediately ceased to be masterful. He was frightened. He stared at her wanly. She stared back, shocked, eyes wide, lips uncertain.

"Oh!" she profoundly said.

Then, in a tone of immense interest and some satisfaction:

"Martin—oh—my dear—do you think you ought to have done that?"

He kissed her again. She yielded and for a moment there was nothing in the universe, neither he nor she, neither laboratory nor fathers nor wives nor traditions, but only the intensity of their being together.

Suddenly she babbled, "I know there's lots of conventional people that would say we'd done wrong, and perhaps I'd have thought so, one time, but— Oh, I'm terribly glad I'm liberal! Of course I wouldn't hurt dear Leora or do anything *really* wrong for the world, but isn't it wonderful that with so many bourgeois folks all around, we can rise above them and realize the call that strength makes to strength and— But I've simply *got* to be at the Y.W.C.A. meeting. There's a woman lawyer from New York that's going to tell us about the Modern Woman's Career."

When she had gone Martin viewed himself as a successful lover. "I've won her," he gloated. . . . Probably never has gloating been so shakily and badly done.

That evening, when he was playing poker in his flat with Irving Watters, the school-clinic dentist, and a young doctor from the city clinic, the telephone bell summoned him to an excited but saccharine:

"This is Orchid. Are you glad I called up?"

"Oh, yes, yes, mighty glad you called up." He tried to make it at once amorously joyful, and impersonal enough to beguile the three coatless, beer-swizzling, grinning doctors.

"Are you doing anything this evening, Marty?"

"Just, uh, couple fellows here for a little game cards."

"Oh!" It was acute. "Oh, then you— I was such a baby to call you up, but Daddy is away and Verbena and everybody, and it was such a lovely evening, and I just thought— *Do* you think I'm an awful little silly?"

"No—no—sure not."

"I'm so glad you don't. I'd hate it if I thought you thought I was just a silly to call you up. You don't, do you?"

"No—no—course not. Look, I've got to—"

"I know. I mustn't keep you. But I just wanted you to tell me whether you thought I was a silly to—"

"No! Honest! Really!"

Three fidgety minutes later, deplorably aware of masculine snickers from behind him, he escaped. The poker-players said all the things considered suitable in Nautilus: "Oh, you little Don Jewen!" and "Can you beat it—his wife only gone for a week!" and "Who is she, Doctor? Go on, you tightwad, bring her up here!" and "Say, I know who it is; it's that little milliner on Prairie Avenue."

Next noon she telephoned from a drug store that she had lain awake all night, and on profound contemplation decided that they "mustn't ever do that sort of thing again"—and would he meet her at the corner of Crimmins Street and Missouri Avenue at eight, so that they might talk it all over?

In the afternoon she telephoned and changed the tryst to half-past eight.

At five she called him up just to remind him—

In the laboratory that day Martin transplanted cultures no more. He was too confusedly human to be a satisfactory experimenter, too coldly thinking to be a satisfactory sinful male, and all the while he longed for the sure solace of Leora.

"I can go as far as I like with her to-night.

"But she's a brainless man-chaser.

"All the better. I'm tired of being a punk philosopher.

"I wonder if these other lucky lovers that you read about in all this fiction and poetry feel as glum as I do?

"I will *not* be middle-aged and cautious and monogamic and moral! It's against my religion. I demand the right to be free—

"Hell! These free souls that have to slave at being free are just as bad as their Methodist dads. I have enough sound natural immorality in me so I can afford to be moral. I want to keep my brain clear for work. I don't want it blurred by dutifully running around trying to kiss everybody I can.

"Orchid is too easy. I hate to give up the right of being a happy sinner, but my way was so straight, with just Leora and my work, and I'm not going to mess it. God help any man that likes his work and his wife! He's beaten from the beginning."

He met Orchid at eight-thirty, and the whole matter was unkind. He was equally distasteful of the gallant Martin of two days ago and the prosy cautious Martin of to-night. He went home desolately ascetic, and longed for Orchid all the night.

A week later Leora returned from Wheatsylvania.

He met her at the station.

"It's all right," he said. "I feel a hundred and seven years old. I'm a respectable, moral young man, and Lord how I'd hate it, if it wasn't for my precipitation test and you and—*Why* do you always lose your trunk check? I suppose I am a bad example for others, giving up so easily. No, no, darling, can't you *see*; that's the transportation check the conductor gave you!"

Chapter XXII

THIS SUMMER Pickerbaugh had shouted and hand-shaken his way through a brief Chautauqua tour in Iowa, Nebraska, and Kansas. Martin realized that though he seemed, in contrast to Gustaf Sondelius, an unfortunately articulate and generous lout, he was destined to be ten times better known in America than Sondelius could ever be, a thousand times better known than Max Gottlieb.

He was a correspondent of many of the nickel-plated Great Men whose pictures and sonorous aphorisms appeared in the magazines: the advertising men who wrote little books about Pep and Optimism, the editor of the magazine which told clerks how to become Goethes and Stonewall Jacksons by studying correspondence-courses and never touching the manhood-rotting beer, and the cornfield sage who was equally an authority on finance, peace, biology, editing, Peruvian ethnology, and making oratory pay. These intellectual rulers recognized Pickerbaugh as one of them; they wrote quippish letters to him: and when he answered he signed himself "Pick," in red pencil.

The *Onward March Magazine*, which specialized in biographies of Men Who Have Made Good, had an account of Pickerbaugh among its sketches of the pastor who built his own beautiful Neo-Gothic church out of tin cans, the lady who had in seven years kept 2,698 factory-girls from leading lives of shame, and the Oregon cobbler who had taught himself to read Sanskrit, Finnish, and Esperanto.

"Meet Ol' Doc Almus Pickerbaugh, a he-man whom Chum Frink has hailed as 'the two-fisted, fighting poet-doc,' a scientist who puts his remarkable discoveries right over third base, yet who, as a reg-lar old-fashioned Sunday-school superintendent, rebukes the atheistic so-called scientists that are menacing the foundations of our religion and liberties by their smart-aleck cracks at everything that is noble and improving," chanted the chronicler.

Martin was reading this article, trying to realize that it was actually exposed in a fabulous New York magazine, with a million circulation, when Pickerbaugh summoned him.

"Mart," he said, "do you feel competent to run this Department?"

"Why, uh—"

"Do you think you can buck the Interests and keep a clean city all by yourself?"

"Why, uh—"

"Because it looks as if I were going to Washington, as the next congressman from this district!"

"Really?"

"Looks that way. Boy, I'm going to take to the whole nation the Message I've tried to ram home here!"

Martin got out quite a good "I congratulate you." He was so astonished that it sounded fervent. He still had a fragment of his boyhood belief that congressmen were persons of intelligence and importance.

"I've just been in conference with some of the leading Republicans of the district. Great surprise to me. Ha, ha, ha! Maybe they picked me because they haven't anybody else to run this year. Ha, ha, ha!"

Martin also laughed. Pickerbaugh looked as though that was not exactly the right response, but he recovered and caroled on:

"I said to them, 'Gentlemen, I must warn you that I am not sure I possess the rare qualifications needful in a man who shall have the high privilege of laying down, at Washington, the rules and regulations for the guidance, in every walk of life, of this great nation of a hundred million people. However, gentlemen,' I said, 'the impulse that prompts me to consider, in all modesty, your unexpected and probably undeserved honor is the fact that it seems to me that what Congress needs is more forward-looking scientists to plan and more genu-ine trained business men to execute the improvements demanded by our evolving commonwealth, and also the possibility of persuading the Boys there at Washington of the preëminent and crying need of a Secretary of Health who shall completely control—' "

But no matter what Martin thought about it, the Republicans really did nominate Pickerbaugh for Congress.

II

While Pickerbaugh went out campaigning, Martin was in charge of the Department, and he began his reign by getting himself denounced as a tyrant and a radical.

There was no more sanitary and efficient dairy in Iowa than that of old Klopchuk, on the outskirts of Nautilus. It was tiled and drained and excellently lighted; the milking machines were perfect; the bottles were super-boiled; and Klopchuk welcomed inspectors and the tuberculin test. He had fought the dairymen's union and kept his dairy open-shop by paying more than the union scale. Once, when Martin attended a meeting of the Nautilus Central Labor Council as Pickerbaugh's representative, the secretary of the council confessed that there was no plant which they would so like to unionize and which they were so unlikely to unionize as Klopchuk's Dairy.

Now Martin's labor sympathies were small. Like most laboratory men, he believed that the reason why workmen found less joy in sewing vests or in pulling a lever than he did in a long research was because they were an inferior race, born lazy and wicked. The complaint of the unions was the one thing to convince him that at last he had found perfection.

Often he stopped at Klopchuk's merely for the satisfaction of it. He noted but one thing which disturbed him: a milker had a persistent sore throat. He examined the man, made cultures, and found hemolytic streptococcus. In a panic he hurried back to the dairy, and after cultures he discovered that there was streptococcus in the udders of three cows.

When Pickerbaugh had saved the health of the nation through all the smaller towns in the congressional district and had returned to Nautilus, Martin insisted on the quarantine of the infected milker and the closing of the Klopchuk Dairy till no more infection should be found.

"Nonsense! Why, that's the cleanest place in the city," Pickerbaugh scoffed. "Why borrow trouble? There's no sign of an epidemic of strep."

"There darn' well will be! Three cows infected. Look at what's happened in Boston and Baltimore, here recently. I've asked Klopchuk to come in and talk it over."

"Well, you know how busy I am, but—"

Klopchuk appeared at eleven, and to Klopchuk the affair was tragic. Born in a gutter in Poland, starving in New York, working twenty hours a day in Vermont, in Ohio, in Iowa, he had made this beautiful thing, his dairy.

Seamed, drooping, twirling his hat, almost in tears, he protested, "Dr. Pickerbaugh, I do everything the doctors say is necessary. I know dairies! Now comes this young man and he says because one of my men has a cold, I kill little children with diseased milk! I tell you, this is my life, and I would sooner hang myself than send out one drop of bad milk. The young man has some wicked reason. I have asked questions. I find he is a great friend from the Central Labor Council. Why, he go to their meetings! And they want to break me!"

To Martin the trembling old man was pitiful, but he had never before been accused of treachery. He said grimly:

"You can take up the personal charges against me later, Dr. Pickerbaugh. Meantime I suggest you have in some expert to test my results; say Long of Chicago or Brent of Minneapolis or somebody."

"I—I—I—" The Kipling and Billy Sunday of health looked as distressed as Klopchuk. "I'm sure our friend here doesn't really mean to make charges against you, Mart. He's overwrought, naturally. Can't we just treat the fellow that has the strep infection and not make everybody uncomfortable?"

"All right, if you want a bad epidemic here, toward the end of your campaign!"

"You know cussed well I'd do anything to avoid— Though I want you to distinctly understand it has nothing to do with my campaign for Congress! It's simply that I owe my city the most scrupulous performance of duty in safeguarding it against disease, and the most fearless enforcement—"

At the end of his oratory Pickerbaugh telegraphed to Dr. J. C. Long, the Chicago bacteriologist.

Dr. Long looked as though he had made the train journey in an ice-box. Martin had never seen a man so free from the poetry and flowing philanthropy of Almus Pickerbaugh. He was slim, precise, lipless, lapless, and eye-glassed, and his hair was parted in the middle. He coolly listened to Martin, coldly listened to Pickerbaugh, icily heard Klopchuk, made his inspection, and reported, "Dr. Arrowsmith seems to know his business perfectly, there is certainly a danger here, I advise closing the dairy, my fee is one hundred dollars, thank you no I shall not stay to dinner I must catch the evening train."

Martin went home to Leora snarling, "That man was just as lovable as a cucumber salad, but my God, Lee, with his freedom from bunk he's made me wild to get back to research; away from all these humanitarians that are so busy hollering about loving the dear people that they let the people die! I hated him, but— Wonder what Max Gottlieb's doing this evening? The old German crank! I'll bet—I'll bet he's talking music or something with some terrible highbrow bunch. Wouldn't you like to see the old coot again? You know, just couple minutes. D'I ever tell you about the time I made the dandy stain of the trypanosomes— Oh, did I?"

He assumed that with the temporary closing of the dairy the matter was ended. He did not understand how hurt was Klopchuk. He knew that Irving Watters, Klopchuk's physician, was unpleasant when they met, grumbling, "What's the use going on being an alarmist, Mart?" But he did not know how many persons in Nautilus had been trustily informed that this fellow Arrowsmith was in the pay of labor-union thugs.

III

Two months before, when Martin had been making his annual inspection of factories, he had encountered Clay Tredgold, the president (by inheritance) of the Steel Windmill Company. He had heard that Tredgold, an elaborate but easy-spoken man of forty-five, moved as one clad in purple on the loftiest planes of Nautilus society. After the inspection Tredgold urged, "Sit down, Doctor; have a cigar and tell me all about sanitation."

Martin was wary. There was in Tredgold's affable eye a sardonic flicker.

"What d'you want to know about sanitation?"

"Oh, all about it."

"The only thing I know is that your men must like you. Of course you haven't enough wash-bowls in that second-floor toilet room, and the whole lot of 'em swore you were putting in others immediately. If they like you enough to lie against their own interests, you must be a good boss, and I think I'll let you get away with it—till my next inspection! Well, got to hustle."

Tredgold beamed on him. "My dear man, I've been pulling that dodge on Pickerbaugh for three years. I'm glad to have seen you. And I think I really may put in some more bowls—just before your next inspection. Good-by!"

After the Klopchuk affair, Martin and Leora encountered Clay Tredgold and that gorgeous slim woman, his wife, in front of a motion-picture theater.

"Give you a lift, Doctor?" cried Tredgold.

On the way he suggested, "I don't know whether you're dry, like Pickerbaugh, but if you'd like I'll run you out to the house and present you with the noblest cocktail conceived since Evangeline County went dry. Does it sound reasonable?"

"I haven't heard anything so reasonable for years," said Martin.

The Tredgold house was on the highest knoll (fully twenty feet above the general level of the plain) in Ashford Grove, which is the Back Bay of Nautilus. It was a Colonial structure, with a sun-parlor, a white-paneled hall, and a blue and silver drawing-room. Martin tried to look casual as they were wafted in on Mrs. Tredgold's chatter, but it was the handsomest house he had ever entered.

While Leora sat on the edge of her chair in the manner of one likely to be sent home, and Mrs. Tredgold sat forward like a hostess, Tredgold flourished the cocktail-shaker and performed courtesies:

"How long you been here now, Doctor?"

"Almost a year."

"Try that. Look here, it strikes me you're kind of different from Salvation Pickerbaugh."

Martin felt that he ought to praise his chief but, to Leora's gratified amazement, he sprang up and ranted in something like Pickerbaugh's best manner:

"Gentlemen of the Steel Windmill Industries, than which there is no other that has so largely contributed to the prosperity of our commonwealth, while I realize that you are getting away with every infraction of the health laws that the inspector doesn't catch you at, yet I desire to pay a tribute to your high respect for sanitation, patriotism, and cocktails, and if I only had an assistant more earnest than young Arrowsmith, I should, with your permission, become President of the United States."

Tredgold clapped. Mrs. Tredgold asserted, "If that isn't exactly like Dr. Pickerbaugh!" Leora looked proud, and so did her husband.

"I'm glad you're free from this socialistic clap-trap of Pickerbaugh's," said Tredgold.

The assumption roused something sturdy and defensive in Martin:

"Oh, I don't care a hang how socialistic he is—whatever that means. Don't know anything about socialism. But since I've gone and given an imitation of him—I suppose it was probably disloyal—I must say I'm not very fond of oratory that's so full of energy it hasn't any room for facts. But mind you, Tredgold, it's partly the fault of people like your Manufacturers' Association. You encourage him to rant. I'm a laboratory man—or rather, I sometimes wish I were. I like to deal with exact figures."

"So do I. I was keen on mathematics in Williams," said Tredgold.

Instantly Martin and he were off on education, damning the universities for turning out graduates like sausages. Martin found himself becoming confidential about "variables," and Tredgold proclaimed that he had not wanted to take up the ancestral factory, but to specialize in astronomy.

Leora was confessing to the friendly Mrs. Tredgold how cautiously the wife of an assistant director has to economize, and with that caressing voice of hers Mrs. Tredgold comforted, "I know. I was horribly hard-up after Dad died. Have you tried the little Swedish dressmaker on Crimmins Street, two doors from the Catholic church? She's awfully clever, and so cheap."

Martin had found, for the first time since marriage, a house in which he was altogether happy; Leora had found, in a woman with the easy smartness which she had always feared and hated, the first woman to whom she could talk of God and the price of toweling. They came out from themselves and were not laughed at.

It was at midnight, when the charms of bacteriology and toweling were becoming pallid, that outside the house sounded a whooping, wheezing motor horn, and in lumbered a ruddy fat man who was introduced as Mr. Schlemihl, president of the Cornbelt Insurance Company of Nautilus.

Even more than Clay Tredgold was he a leader of the Ashford Grove aristocracy, but, while he stood like an invading barbarian in the blue and silver room, Schlemihl was cordial:

"Glad meet yuh, Doctor. Well, say, Clay, I'm tickled to death you've found another highbrow to gas with. Me, Arrowsmith, I'm simply a poor old insurance salesman. Clay is always telling me what an illiterate boob I am. Look here, Clay darling, do I get a cocktail or don't I? I seen your lights! I seen you in here telling what a smart guy you are! Come on! *Mix!*"

Tredgold mixed, extensively. Before he had finished, young Monte Mugford, great-grandson of the sainted but side-whiskered Nathaniel Mugford who had founded Mugford College, also came in, uninvited. He wondered at the presence of Martin, found him human, told him he was human, and did his rather competent best to catch up on the cocktails.

Thus it happened that at three in the morning Martin was singing to a commendatory audience the ballad he had learned from Gustaf Sondelius:

> She'd a dark and a roving eye,
> And her hair hung down in ringlets,
> A nice girl, a decent girl,
> But one of the rakish kind.

At four, the Arrowsmiths had been accepted by the most desperately Smart Set of Nautilus, and at four-thirty they were driven home, at a speed neither legal nor kind, by Clay Tredgold.

IV

There was in Nautilus a country club which was the axis of what they called Society, but there was also a tribe of perhaps twelve families in the Ashford Grove section who, though they went to the country club for golf, condescended to other golfers, kept to themselves, and considered themselves as belonging more to Chicago than to Nautilus. They took turns in entertaining one another. They assumed that they were all welcome at any party given by any of them, and to none of their parties was any one outside the Group invited except migrants from larger cities and occasional free lances like Martin. They were a tight little garrison in a heathen town.

The members of the Group were very rich, and one of them, Montgomery Mugford, knew something about his great-grandfather. They lived in Tudor manor houses and Italian villas so new that the scarred lawns had only begun to grow. They had large cars and larger cellars, though the cellars contained nothing but gin, whisky, vermouth, and a few sacred bottles of rather sweet champagne. Every one in the Group was familiar with New York—they stayed at the St. Regis or the Plaza and went about buying clothes and discovering small smart restaurants—and five of the twelve couples had been in Europe; had spent a week in Paris, intending to go to art galleries and actually going to the more expensive fool-traps of Montmartre.

In the Group Martin and Leora found themselves welcomed as poor relations. They were invited to choric dinners, to Sunday lunches at the country club. Whatever the event, it always ended in rapidly motoring somewhere, having a number of drinks, and insisting that Martin again "give that imitation of Doc Pickerbaugh."

Besides motoring, drinking, and dancing to the Victrola, the chief diversion of the Group was cards. Curiously, in this completely unmoral set, there were no flirtations; they talked with considerable freedom about "sex," but they all seemed monogamic, all happily married or afraid to appear unhappily married. But when Martin knew them better he heard murmurs of husbands having "times" in Chicago, of wives picking up young men in New York hotels, and he scented furious restlessness beneath their superior sexual calm.

It is not known whether Martin ever completely accepted as a gentleman-scholar the Clay Tredgold who was devoted to everything about astronomy except studying it, or Monte

Mugford as the highly descended aristocrat, but he did admire the Group's motor cars, shower baths, Fifth Avenue frocks, tweed plus-fours, and houses somewhat impersonally decorated by daffodillic young men from Chicago. He discovered sauces and old silver. He began to consider Leora's clothes not merely as convenient coverings, but as a possible expression of charm, and irritably he realized how careless she was.

In Nautilus, alone, rarely saying much about herself, Leora had developed an intense mute little life of her own. She belonged to a bridge club, and she went solemnly by herself to the movies, but her ambition was to know France and it engrossed her. It was an old desire, mysterious in source and long held secret, but suddenly she was sighing:

"Sandy, the one thing I want to do, maybe ten years from now, is to see Touraine and Normandy and Carcassonne. Could we, do you think?"

Rarely had Leora asked for anything. He was touched and puzzled as he watched her reading books on Brittany, as he caught her, over a highly simplified French grammar, breathing "J'ay—j'aye—damn it, whatever it is!"

He crowed, "Lee, dear, if you want to go to France—Listen! Some day we'll shoot over there with a couple of knap-sacks on our backs, and we'll see that ole country from end to end!"

Gratefully yet doubtfully: "You know, if you got bored, Sandy, you could go see the work at the Pasteur Institute. Oh, I would like to tramp, just once, between high plastered walls, and come to a foolish little café and watch the men with funny red sashes and floppy blue pants go by. Really, do you think maybe we could?"

Leora was strangely popular in the Ashford Grove Group, though she possessed nothing of what Martin called their "elegance." She always had at least one button missing. Mrs. Tredgold, best natured as she was least pious of women, adopted her complete.

Nautilus had always doubted Clara Tredgold. Mrs. Almus Pickerbaugh said that she "took no part in any movement for the betterment of the city." For years she had seemed content to grow her roses, to make her startling hats, to almond-cream her lovely hands, and listen to her husband's improper stories—and for years she had been a lonely woman. In Leora she perceived an interested casualness equal to her own. The two women spent afternoons sitting on the sun-porch, reading, doing their nails, smoking cigarettes, saying nothing, trusting each other.

With the other women of the Group Leora was never so intimate as with Clara Tredgold, but they liked her, the more because she was a heretic whose vices, her smoking, her indolence, her relish of competent profanity, disturbed Mrs. Pickerbaugh and Mrs. Irving Watters. The Group rather approved all unconventionalities—except such economic unconventionalities as threatened their easy wealth. Leora had tea, or a cocktail, alone with nervous young Mrs. Monte Mugford, who had been the lightest-footed débutante in Des Moines four years before and who hated now the coming of her second baby; and it was to Leora that Mrs. Schlemihl, though publicly she was rompish and serene with her porker of a husband, burst out, "If that man would only quit pawing me—reaching for me—slobbering on me! I hate it here! I *will* have my winter in New York—alone!"

The childish Martin Arrowsmith, so unworthy of Leora's old quiet wisdoms, was not content with her acceptance by the Group. When she appeared with a hook unfastened or her hair like a crow's nest, he worried, and said things about her "sloppiness" which he later regretted.

"Why can't you take a little time to make yourself attractive? God knows you haven't anything else to do! Great Jehoshaphat, can't you even sew on buttons?"

But Clara Tredgold laughed, "Leora, I do think you have the sweetest back, but do you mind if I pin you up before the others come?"

It happened after a party which lasted till two, when Mrs. Schlemihl had worn the new frock from Lucile's and Jack Brundidge (by day vice-president and sales-manager of the Maize Mealies Company) had danced what he belligerently asserted to be a Finnish polka, that when Martin and Leora were driving home in a borrowed Health Department car he snarled, "Lee, why can't you ever take any trouble with what you wear? Here this morning—or yesterday morning—you were going to mend that blue dress, and as far as I can figure out you haven't done a darn' thing the whole day but sit around and read, and then you come out with that ratty embroidery—"

"Will you stop the car!" she cried.

He stopped it, astonished. The headlights made ridiculously important a barbed-wire fence, a litter of milkweeds, a bleak reach of gravel road.

She demanded, "Do you want me to become a harem beauty? I could. I could be a floosey. But I've never taken the trouble. Oh, Sandy, I won't go on fighting with you. Either I'm the foolish sloppy wife that I am, or I'm nothing. What do you want? Do you want a real princess like Clara Tredgold, or do you want me, that don't care a hang where we go or what we do as long as we stand by each other? You do such a lot of worrying. I'm tired of it. Come on now. What do you want?"

"I don't want anything but you. But can't you understand—I'm not just a climber—I want us both to be equal to anything we run into. I certainly don't see why we should be inferior to this bunch, in *anything*. Darling, except for Clara, maybe, they're nothing but rich bookkeepers! But we're real soldiers of fortune. Your France that you love so much—some day we'll go there, and the French President will be at the N.P. depot to meet us! Why should we let anybody do anything better than we can? Technique!"

They talked for an hour in that drab place, between the poisonous lines of barbed wire.

Next day, when Orchid came into his laboratory and begged, with the wistfulness of youth, "Oh, Dr. Martin, aren't you ever coming to the house again?" he kissed her so briskly, so cheerfully, that even a flapper could perceive that she was unimportant.

V

Martin realized that he was likely to be the next Director of the Department. Pickerbaugh had told him, "Your work is very satisfactory. There's only one thing you lack, my boy: enthusiasm for getting together with folks and giving a long pull and a strong pull, all together. But perhaps that'll come to you when you have more responsibility."

Martin sought to acquire a delight in giving long strong pulls all together, but he felt like a man who has been dragooned into wearing yellow tights at a civic pageant.

"Gosh, I may be up against it when I become Director," he fretted. "I wonder if there's people who become what's called 'successful' and then hate it? Well, anyway, I'll start a decent system of vital statistics in the department before they get me. I won't lay down! I'll fight! I'll make myself succeed!"

Chapter XXIII

IT MAY have been a yearning to give one concentrated dose of inspiration so powerful that no citizen of Nautilus would ever again dare to be ill, or perhaps Dr. Pickerbaugh desired a little reasonable publicity for his congressional campaign, but certainly the Health Fair which the good man organized was overpowering.

He got an extra appropriation from the Board of Aldermen; he bullied all the churches and associations into coöperation; he made the newspapers promise to publish three columns of praise each day.

He rented the rather dilapidated wooden "tabernacle" in which the Reverend Mr. Billy Sunday, an evangelist, had recently wiped out all the sin in the community. He arranged for a number of novel features. The Boy Scouts were to give daily drills. There was a W.C.T.U. booth at which celebrated clergymen and other physiologists would demonstrate the evils of alcohol. In a bacteriology booth, the protesting Martin (in a dinky white coat) was to do jolly things with test-tubes. An anti-nicotine lady from Chicago offered to kill a mouse every half-hour by injecting ground-up cigarette paper into it. The Pickerbaugh twins, Arbuta and Gladiola, now aged six, were to show the public how to brush its teeth, and in fact they did, until a sixty-year-old farmer of whom they had lovingly inquired, "Do you brush your teeth daily?" made thunderous answer, "No, but I'm going to paddle your bottoms daily, and I'm going to start in right now."

None of these novelties was so stirring as the Eugenic Family, who had volunteered to give, for a mere forty dollars a day, an example of the benefits of healthful practises.

They were father, mother, and five children, all so beautiful and powerful that they had recently been presenting refined acrobatic exhibitions on the Chautauqua Circuit. None of them smoked, drank, spit upon pavements, used foul language, or ate meat. Pickerbaugh assigned to them the chief booth, on the platform once sacerdotally occupied by the Reverend Mr. Sunday.

There were routine exhibits: booths with charts and banners and leaflets. The Pickerbaugh Healthette Octette held song recitals, and daily there were lectures, most of them by Pickerbaugh or by his friend Dr. Bissex, football coach and professor of hygiene and most other subjects in Mugford College.

A dozen celebrities, including Gustaf Sondelius and the governor of the state, were invited to come and "give their messages," but it happened, unfortunately, that none of them seemed able to get away that particular week.

The Health Fair opened with crowds and success. There was a slight misunderstanding the first day. The Master Bakers' Association spoke strongly to Pickerbaugh about the sign "Too much pie makes pyorrhea" on the diet booth. But the thoughtless and prosperity-destroying sign was removed at once, and the Fair was thereafter advertised in every bakery in town.

The only unhappy participant, apparently, was Martin. Pickerbaugh had fitted up for him an exhibition laboratory which, except that it had no running water and except that the fire laws forbade his using any kind of a flame, was exactly like a real one. All day long he poured a solution of red ink from one test-tube into another, with his microscope carefully examined nothing at all, and answered the questions of persons who wished to know how you put bacterias to death once you had caught them swimming about.

Leora appeared as his assistant, very pretty and demure in a nurse's costume, very exasperating as she chuckled at his low cursing. They found one friend, the fireman on duty, a splendid person with stories about pet cats in the fire-house and no tendency to ask questions in bacteriology. It was he who showed them how they could smoke in safety. Behind the Clean Up and Prevent Fires exhibit, consisting of a miniature Dirty House with red arrows to show where a fire might start and an extremely varnished Clean House, there was an alcove with a broken window which would carry off the smoke of their cigarettes. To this sanctuary Martin, Leora, and the bored fireman retired a dozen times a day, and thus wore through the week.

One other misfortune occurred. The detective sergeant, coming in not to detect but to see the charming spectacle of the mouse dying in agony from cigarette paper, stopped before the booth of the Eugenic Family, scratched his head, hastened to the police station, and returned with certain pictures. He growled to Pickerbaugh:

"Hm. That Eugenic Family. Don't smoke or booze or anything?"

"Absolutely! And look at their perfect health."

"Hm. Better keep an eye on 'em. I won't spoil your show, Doc—we fellows at City Hall had all ought to stick together. I won't run 'em out of town till after the Fair. But they're the Holton gang. The man and woman ain't married, and only one of the kids is theirs. They've done time for selling licker to the Indians, but their specialty, before they went into education, used to be the badger game. I'll detail a plain-clothes man to keep 'em straight. Fine show you got here, Doc. Ought to give this city a lasting lesson in the value of up-to-date health methods. Good luck! Say, have you picked your secretary yet, for when you get to Congress? I've got a nephew that's a crackajack stenographer and a bright kid and knows how to keep his mouth shut about stuff that don't concern him. I'll send him around to have a talk with you. So long."

But, except that once he caught the father of the Eugenic Family relieving the strain of being publicly healthy by taking a long, gurgling, ecstatic drink from a flask, Pickerbaugh found nothing wrong in their conduct, till Saturday. There was nothing wrong with anything, till then.

Never had a Fair been such a moral lesson, or secured so much publicity. Every newspaper in the congressional district gave columns to it, and all the accounts, even in the Democratic papers, mentioned Pickerbaugh's campaign.

Then, on Saturday, the last day of the Fair, came tragedy.

There was terrific rain, the roof leaked without restraint, and the lady in charge of the Healthy Housing Booth, which also leaked, was taken home threatened with pneumonia. At noon, when the Eugenic Family were giving a demonstration of perfect vigor, their youngest blossom had an epileptic fit, and before the excitement was over, upon the Chicago anti-nicotine lady as she triumphantly assassinated a mouse charged an anti-vivisection lady, also from Chicago.

Round the two ladies and the unfortunate mouse gathered a crowd. The anti-vivisection lady called the anti-nicotine lady a murderer, a wretch, and an atheist, all of which the anti-nicotine lady endured, merely weeping a little and calling for the police. But when the anti-vivisection lady wound up, "And as for your pretensions to know anything about science, you're no scientist at all!" then with a shriek the anti-nicotine lady leaped from her platform, dug her fingers into the anti-vivisection lady's hair, and observed with distinctness, "I'll show you whether I know anything about science!"

Pickerbaugh tried to separate them. Martin, standing happily with Leora and their friend the fireman on the edge, distinctly did not. Both ladies turned on Pickerbaugh and denounced him, and when they had been removed he was the center of a thousand chuckles, in decided danger of never going to Congress.

At two o'clock, when the rain had slackened, when the after-lunch crowd had come in and the story of the anti ladies was running strong, the fireman retired behind the Clean Up and Prevent Fires exhibit for his hourly smoke. He was a very sleepy and unhappy little fireman; he was thinking about the pleasant fire-house and the unending games of pinochle. He dropped the match, unextinguished, on the back porch of the model Clean House. The Clean House had been so handsomely oiled that it was like kindling soaked in kerosene. It flared up, and instantly the huge and gloomy Tabernacle was hysterical with flames. The crowd rushed toward the exits.

Naturally, most of the original exits of the Tabernacle had been blocked by booths. There was a shrieking panic, and children were being trampled.

Almus Pickerbaugh was neither a coward nor slothful. Suddenly, coming from nowhere, he was marching through the Tabernacle at the head of his eight daughters, singing "Dixie," his head up, his eyes terrible, his arms wide in pleading. The crowd weakly halted. With the voice of a clipper captain he unsnarled them and ushered them safely out, then charged back into the spouting flames.

The rain-soaked building had not caught. The fireman, with Martin and the head of the Eugenic Family, was beating the flames. Nothing was destroyed save the Clean House, and the crowd which had fled in agony came back in wonder. Their hero was Pickerbaugh.

Within two hours the Nautilus papers vomited specials which explained that not merely had Pickerbaugh organized the greatest lesson in health ever seen, but he had also, by his courage and his power to command, saved hundreds of people from being crushed, which latter was probably the only completely accurate thing that has been said about Dr. Almus Pickerbaugh in ten thousand columns of newspaper publicity.

Whether to see the Fair, Pickerbaugh, the delightful ravages of a disaster, or another fight between the anti ladies, half the city struggled into the Tabernacle that evening, and when Pickerbaugh took the platform for his closing lecture he was greeted with frenzy. Next day, when he galloped into the last week of his campaign, he was overlord of all the district.

II

His opponent was a snuffy little lawyer whose strength lay in his training. He had been state senator, lieutenant governor, county judge. But the Democratic slogan, "Pickerbaugh the Pick-up Candidate," was drowned in the admiration for the hero of the health fair. He dashed about in motors, proclaiming, "I am not running because I want office, but because I want the chance to take to the whole nation my ideals of health." Everywhere was plastered:

For Congress
PICKERBAUGH
The two-fisted fighting poet doc

Just elect him for a term
And all through the nation he'll swat the germ.

Enormous meetings were held. Pickerbaugh was ample and vague about his Policies. Yes, he was opposed to our entering the European War, but he assured them, he certainly did assure them, that he was for using every power of our Government to end this terrible calamity. Yes, he was for high tariff, but it must be so adjusted that the farmers in his district could buy everything cheaply. Yes, he was for high wages for each and every workman, but he stood like a rock, like a boulder, like a moraine, for protecting the prosperity of all manufacturers, merchants, and real-estate owners.

While this larger campaign thundered, there was proceeding in Nautilus a smaller and much defter campaign, to reëlect as mayor one Mr. Pugh, Pickerbaugh's loving chief. Mr. Pugh sat nicely at desks, and he was pleasant and promissory to everybody who came to see him; clergymen, gamblers, G.A.R. veterans, circus advance-agents, policemen, and ladies of reasonable virtue—everybody except perhaps socialist agitators, against whom he staunchly protected the embattled city. In his speeches Pickerbaugh commended Pugh for "that firm integrity and ready sympathy with which His Honor had backed up every movement for the public weal," and when Pickerbaugh (quite honestly) begged, "Mr. Mayor, if I go to Congress you must appoint Arrowsmith in my place; he knows nothing about politics but he's incorruptible," then Pugh gave his promise, and amity abode in that land. . . . Nobody said anything at all about Mr. F. X. Jordan.

F. X. Jordan was a contractor with a generous interest in politics. Pickerbaugh called him a grafter, and the last time Pugh had been elected—it had been on a Reform Platform, though since that time the reform had been coaxed to behave itself and be practical—both Pugh and Pickerbaugh had denounced Jordan as a "malign force." But so kindly was Mayor Pugh that in the present election he said nothing that could hurt Mr. Jordan's feelings, and in return what could Mr. Jordan do but speak forgivingly about Mr. Pugh to the people in blind-pigs and houses of ill fame?

On the evening of the election, Martin and Leora were among the company awaiting the returns at the Pickerbaughs'. They were confident. Martin had never been roused by politics, but he was stirred now by Pickerbaugh's twitchy pretense of indifference, by the telephoned report from the newspaper office, "Here's Willow Grove township—Pickerbaugh leading, two to one!" by the crowds which went past the house howling, "Pickerbaugh, Pickerbaugh, Pickerbaugh!"

At eleven the victory was certain, and Martin, his bowels weak with unconfidence, realized that he was now Director of Public Health, with responsibility for seventy thousand lives.

He looked wistfully toward Leora and in her still smile found assurance.

Orchid had been airy and distant with Martin all evening, and dismayingly chatty and affectionate with Leora. Now she drew him into the back parlor and "So I'm going off to Washington—and you don't care a bit!" she said, her eyes blurred and languorous and undefended. He held her, muttering, "You darling child, I can't let you go!" As he walked home he thought less of being Director than of Orchid's eyes.

In the morning he groaned, "Doesn't anybody ever learn anything? Must I watch myself and still be a fool, all my life? Doesn't any story ever end?"

He never saw her afterward, except on the platform of the train.

Leora surprisingly reflected, after the Pickerbaughs had gone, "Sandy dear, I know how you feel about losing your Orchid. It's sort of Youth going. She really is a peach. Honestly, I can appreciate how you feel, and sympathize with you—I mean, of course, providin' you aren't ever going to see her again."

III

Over the *Nautilus Cornfield's* announcement was the vigorous headline:

ALMUS PICKERBAUGH WINS
First Scientist Ever Elected
to Congress

Side-kick of Darwin and Pasteur
Gives new Punch to Steering
Ship of State

Pickerbaugh's resignation was to take effect at once; he was, he explained, going to Washington before his term began, to study legislative methods and start his propaganda for the creation of a national Secretaryship of Health. There was a considerable struggle over the appointment of Martin in his stead. Klopchuk the dairyman was bitter; Irving Watters whispered to fellow doctors that Martin was likely to extend the socialistic free clinics; F. X. Jordan had a sensible young doctor as his own candidate. It was the Ashford Grove Group, Tredgold, Schlemihl, Monte Mugford, who brought it off.

Martin went to Tredgold worrying, "Do the people want me? Shall I fight Jordan or get out?"

Tredgold said balmily, "Fight? What about? I own a good share of the bank that's lent various handy little sums to Mayor Pugh. You leave it to me."

Next day Martin was appointed, but only as Acting Director, with a salary of thirty-five hundred instead of four thousand.

That he had been put in by what he would have called "crooked politics" did not occur to him.

Mayor Pugh called him in and chuckled:

"Doc, there's been a certain amount of opposition to you, because you're pretty young and not many folks know you. I haven't any doubt I can give you the full appointment later—if we find you're competent and popular. Meantime you better avoid doing anything brash. Just come and ask my advice. I know this town and the people that count better than you do."

IV

The day of Pickerbaugh's leaving for Washington was made a fiesta. At the Armory, from twelve to two, the Chamber of Commerce gave to everybody who came a lunch of hot wienies, doughnuts, and coffee, with chewing gum for the women and, for the men, Schweinhügel's Little Dandy Nautilus-made Cheroots.

The train left at three-fifty-five. The station was, to the astonishment of innocent passengers gaping from the train windows, jammed with thousands.

By the rear platform, on a perilous packing box, Mayor Pugh held forth. The Nautilus Silver Cornet Band played three patriotic selections, then Pickerbaugh stood on the platform, his family about him. As he looked on the crowd, tears were in his eyes.

"For once," he stammered, "I guess I can't make a speech. D-darn it, I'm all choked up! I meant to orate a lot, but all I can say is—I love you all, I'm mighty grateful, I'll represent you my level best, neighbors! God bless you!"

The train moved out, Pickerbaugh waving as long as he could see them.

And Martin to Leora, "Oh, he's a find old boy. He— No, I'm hanged if he is! The world's always letting people get away with asininities because they're kind-hearted. And here I've sat back like a coward, not saying a word, and watched 'em loose that wind-storm on the whole country. Oh, curse it, isn't anything in the world simple? Well, let's go to the office, and I'll begin to do things conscientiously and all wrong."

Chapter XXIV

IT CANNOT be said that Martin showed any large ability for organization, but under him the Department of Public Health changed completely. He chose as his assistant Dr. Rufus Ockford, a lively youngster recommended by Dean Silva of Winnemac. The routine work, examination of babies, quarantines, anti-tuberculosis placarding, went on as before.

Inspection of plumbing and food was perhaps more thorough, because Martin lacked Pickerbaugh's buoyant faith in the lay inspectors, and one of them he replaced, to the considerable displeasure of the colony of Germans in the Homedale district. Also he gave thought to the killing of rats and fleas, and he regarded the vital statistics as something more than a recording of births and deaths. He had notions about their value which were most amusing to the health department clerk. He wanted a record of the effect of race, occupation, and a dozen other factors upon the disease rate.

The chief difference was that Martin and Rufus Ockford found themselves with plenty of leisure. Martin estimated that Pickerbaugh must have used half his time in being inspirational and eloquent.

He made his first mistake in assigning Ockford to spend part of the week in the free city clinic, in addition to the two half-time physicians. There was fury in the Evangeline County Medical Society. At a restaurant, Irving Watters came over to Martin's table.

"I hear you've increased the clinic staff," said Dr. Watters.

"Yuh."

"Thinking of increasing it still more?"

"Might be a good idea."

"Now you see here, Mart. As you know, Mrs. Watters and I have done everything in our power to make you and Leora welcome. Glad to do anything I can for a fellow alumnus of old Winnemac. But at the same time, there are limits, you know! Not that I've got any objection to your providing free clinical facilities. Don't know but what it's a good thing to treat the damn', lazy, lousy pauper-class free, and keep the D.B.'s off the books of the regular physicians. But same *time*, when you begin to make a practise of encouraging a lot of folks, that can afford to pay, to go and get free treatment, and practically you attack the integrity of the physicians of this city, that have been giving God knows how much of their time to charity—"

Martin answered neither wisely nor competently: "Irve, sweetheart, you can go straight to hell!"

After that hour, when they met there was nothing said between them.

Without disturbing his routine work, he found himself able to sink blissfully into the laboratory. At first he merely tinkered, but suddenly he was in full cry, oblivious of everything save his experiment.

He was playing with cultures isolated from various dairies and various people, thinking mostly of Klopchuk and streptococcus. Accidentally he discovered the lavish production of hemolysin in sheep's blood as compared with the blood of other animals. Why should streptococcus dissolve the red blood corpuscles of sheep more easily than those of rabbits?

It is true that a busy health-department bacteriologist has no right to waste the public time in being curious, but the irresponsible sniffing beagle in Martin drove out the faithful routineer.

He neglected the examination of an ominously increasing number of tubercular sputums; he set out to answer the question of the hemolysin. He wanted the streptococcus to produce its blood-destroying poison in twenty-four-hour cultures.

He beautifully and excitedly failed, and sat for hours meditating. He tried a six-hour culture. He mixed the supernatant fluid from a centrifugated culture with a suspension of red blood corpuscles and placed it in the incubator. When he returned, two hours after, the blood cells were dissolved.

He telephoned to Leora: "Lee! Got something! C'n you pack up sandwich and come down here f'r evening?"

"Sure," said Leora.

When she appeared he explained to her that his discovery was accidental, that most scientific discoveries were accidental, and that no investigator, however great, could do anything more than see the value of his chance results.

He sounded mature and rather angry.

Leora sat in the corner, scratching her chin, reading a medical journal. From time to time she reheated coffee, over a doubtful Bunsen flame. When the office staff arrived in the morning they found something that had but rarely occurred during the régime of Almus Pickerbaugh: the Director of the Department was transplanting cultures, and on a long table was his wife, asleep.

Martin blared at Dr. Ockford, "Get t' hell out of this, Rufus, and take charge of the department for to-day—I'm out—I'm dead—and oh, say, get Leora home and fry her a couple o' eggs, and you might bring me a Denver sandwich from the Sunset Trail Lunch, will you?"

"You bet, chief," said Ockford.

Martin repeated his experiment, testing the cultures for hemolysin after two, four, six, eight, ten, twelve, fourteen, sixteen, and eighteen hours of incubation. He discovered that the maximum production of hemolysin occurred between four and ten hours. He began to work out the formula of production—and he was desolate. He fumed, raged, sweated. He found that his mathematics was childish, and all his science rusty. He pottered with chemistry, he ached over his mathematics, and slowly he began to assemble his results. He believed that he might have a paper for the *Journal of Infectious Diseases.*

Now Almus Pickerbaugh had published scientific papers—often. He had published them in the *Midwest Medical Quarterly*, of which he was one of fourteen editors. He had discovered the germ of epilepsy and the germ of cancer—two entirely different germs of cancer. Usually it took him a fortnight to make the discovery, write the report, and have it accepted. Martin lacked this admirable facility.

He experimented, he re-experimented, he cursed, he kept Leora out of bed, he taught her to make media, and was ill-pleased by her opinions on agar. He was violent to the stenographer; not once could the pastor of the Jonathan Edwards Congregational Church get him to address the Bible Class; and still for months his paper was not complete.

The first to protest was His Honor the Mayor. Returning from an extremely agreeable game of chemin de fer with F. X. Jordan, taking a short cut through the alley behind the City Hall, Mayor Pugh saw Martin at two in the morning drearily putting test-tubes into the incubator, while Leora sat in a corner smoking. Next day he summoned Martin, and protested:

"Doc, I don't want to butt in on your department—my specialty is never butting in—but it certainly strikes me that after being trained by a seventy-horse-power booster like Pickerbaugh, you ought to know that it's all damn' foolishness to spend so much time in the laboratory, when you can hire an A1 laboratory fellow for thirty bucks a week. What you ought to be doing is jollying along these sobs that are always panning the administration. Get out and talk to the churches and clubs, and help me put across the ideas that we stand for."

"Maybe he's right," Martin considered. "I'm a rotten bacteriologist. Probably I never will get this experiment together. My job here is to keep tobacco-chewers from spitting. Have I the right to waste the tax-payers' money on anything else?"

But that week he read, as an announcement issued by the McGurk Institute of Biology of New York, that Dr. Max Gottlieb had synthesized antibodies *in vitro*.

He pictured the saturnine Gottlieb not at all enjoying the triumph but, with locked door, abusing the papers for their exaggerative reports of his work; and as the picture became sharp Martin was like a subaltern stationed in a desert isle when he learns that his old regiment is going off to an agreeable Border war.

Then the McCandless fury broke.

II

Mrs. McCandless had once been a "hired girl"; then nurse, then confidante, then wife to the invalid Mr. McCandless, wholesale grocer and owner of real estate. When he died she inherited everything. There was a suit, of course, but she had an excellent lawyer.

She was a grim, graceless, shady, mean woman, yet a nymphomaniac. She was not invited into Nautilus society, but in her unaired parlor, on the mildewed couch, she entertained seedy, belching, oldish married men, a young policeman to whom she often lent money, and the contractor-politician, F. X. Jordan.

She owned, in Swede Hollow, the filthiest block of tenements in Nautilus. Martin had made a tuberculosis map of these tenements, and in conferences with Dr. Ockford and Leora he denounced them as murder-holes. He wanted to destroy them, but the police power of the Director of Public Health was vague. Pickerbaugh had enjoyed the possession of large power only because he never used it.

Martin sought a court decision for the demolition of the McCandless tenements. Her lawyer was also the lawyer of F. X. Jordan, and the most eloquent witness against Martin was Dr. Irving Watters. But it chanced, because of the absence of the proper judge, that the case came before an ignorant and honest person who quashed the injunction secured by Mrs. McCandless's lawyer and instructed the Department of Public Health that it might use such methods as the city ordinances provided for emergencies.

That evening Martin grumbled to young Ockford, "You don't suppose for a moment, do you, Rufus, that McCandless and Jordan won't appeal the case? Let's get rid of the tenements while it's comparatively legal, heh?"

"You bet, chief," said Ockford, and, "Say, let's go out to Oregon and start practise when we get kicked out. Well, we can depend on our sanitary inspector, anyway. Jordan seduced his sister, here 'bout six years back."

At dawn a gang headed by Martin and Ockford, in blue overalls, joyful and rowdyish, invaded the McCandless tenements, drove the tenants into the street, and began to tear down the flimsy buildings. At noon, when lawyers appeared and the tenants were in new flats commandeered by Martin, the wreckers set fire to the lower stories, and in half an hour the buildings had been annihilated.

F. X. Jordan came to the scene after lunch. A filthy Martin and a dusty Ockford were drinking coffee brought by Leora.

"Well, boys," said Jordan, "you've put it all over us. Only if you ever pull this kind of stunt again, use dynamite and save a lot of time. You know, I like you boys—I'm sorry for what I've got to do to you. But may the saints help you, because it's just a question of time when I learn you not to monkey with the buzz-saw."

III

Clay Tredgold admired their amateur arson and rejoiced, "Fine! I'm going to back you up in everything the D.P.H. does."

Martin was not too pleased by the promise, for Tredgold's set were somewhat exigent. They had decided that Martin and Leora were free spirits like themselves, and amusing, but they had also decided, long before the Arrowsmiths had by coming to Nautilus entered into authentic existence, that the Group had a monopoly of all Freedom and Amusingness, and they expected the Arrowsmiths to appear for cocktails and poker every Saturday and Sunday evening. They could not understand why Martin should desire to spend his time in a laboratory, drudging over something called "streptolysin," which had nothing to do with cocktails, motors, steel windmills, or insurance.

On an evening perhaps a fortnight after the destruction of the McCandless tenements, Martin was working late in the laboratory. He wasn't even doing experiments which might have diverted the Group—causing bacterial colonies to cloud liquids, or making things change color. He was merely sitting at a table, looking at logarithmic tables. Leora was not there, and he was mumbling, "Confound her, why did she have to go and be sick to-day?"

Tredgold and Schlemihl and their wives were bound for the Old Farmhouse Inn. They had telephoned to Martin's flat and learned where he was. From the alley behind City Hall they could peer in and see him, dreary and deserted.

"We'll take the old boy out and brighten him up. First, let's rush home and shake up a few cocktails and bring 'em down to surprise him," was Tredgold's inspiration.

Tredgold came into the laboratory, a half-hour later, with much clamor.

"This is a nice way to put in a moonlit spring evening, young Narrowsmith! Come on, we'll all go out and dance a little. Grab your hat."

"Gosh, Clay, I'd like to, but honestly I can't. I've got to work; simply got to."

"Rats! Don't be silly. You've been working too hard. Here—look what Father's brought. Be reasonable. Get outside of a nice long cocktail and you'll have a new light on things."

Martin was reasonable up to that point, but he did not have a new light. Tredgold would not take No. Martin continued to refuse, affectionately, then a bit tartly. Outside, Schlemihl pressed down the button of the motor horn and held it, producing a demanding, infuriating yawp which made Martin cry, "For God's sake go out and make 'em quit that, will you, and let me alone! I've got to work, I told you!"

Tredgold stared a moment. "I certainly shall! I'm not accustomed to force my attentions on people. Pardon me for disturbing you!"

By the time Martin sulkily felt that he must apologize, the car was gone. Next day and all the week, he waited for Tredgold to telephone, and Tredgold waited for him to telephone, and they fell into a circle of dislike. Leora and Clara Tredgold saw each other once or twice, but they were uncomfortable, and a fortnight later, when the most prominent physician in town dined with the Tredgolds and attacked Martin as a bumptious and narrow-visioned young man, both the Tredgolds listened and agreed.

Opposition to Martin developed all at once.

Various physicians were against him, not only because of the enlarged clinics, but because he rarely asked their help and never their advice. Mayor Pugh considered him tactless. Klopchuk and F. X. Jordan were assailing him as crooked. The reporters disliked him for his secrecy and occasional bruskness. And the Group had ceased to defend him. Of all these forces Martin was more or less aware, and behind them he fancied that doubtful business men, sellers of impure ice-cream and milk, owners of unsanitary shops and dirty tenements, men who had always hated Pickerbaugh but who had feared to attack him because of his popularity, were gathering to destroy the entire Department of Public Health. . . . He appreciated Pickerbaugh in those days, and loved soldier-wise the Department.

There came from Mayor Pugh a hint that he would save trouble by resigning. He would not resign. Neither would he go to the citizens begging for support. He did his work, and leaned on Leora's assurance, and tried to ignore his detractors. He could not.

News-items and three-line editorial squibs dug at his tyranny, his ignorance, his callowness. An old woman died after treatment at the clinic, and the coroner hinted that it had been the fault of "our almighty health-officer's pet cub assistant." Somewhere arose the name "the Schoolboy Czar" for Martin, and it stuck.

In the gossip at luncheon clubs, in discussions at the Parents' and Teachers' Association, in one frank signed protest sent to the Mayor, Martin was blamed for too strict an inspection of milk, for insufficiently strict inspection of milk; for permitting garbage to lie untouched, for persecuting the overworked garbage collectors; and when a case of small-pox appeared in the Bohemian section, there was an opinion that Martin had gone out personally and started it.

However vague the citizens were as to the nature of his wickedness, once they lost faith in him they lost it completely and with joy, and they welcomed an apparently spontaneously generated rumor that he had betrayed his benefactor, their beloved Dr. Pickerbaugh, by seducing Orchid.

At this interesting touch of immorality, he had all the fashionable churches against him. The pastor of the Jonathan Edwards Church touched up a sermon about Sin in High Places by a reference to "one who, while like a Czar he pretends to be safeguarding the city from entirely imaginary dangers, yet winks at the secret vice rampant in hidden places; who allies himself with the forces of graft and evil and the thugs who batten on honest but deluded Labor; one who cannot arise, a manly man among men, and say, 'I have a clean heart and clean hands.'"

It is true that some of the delighted congregation thought that this referred to Mayor Pugh, and others applied it to F. X. Jordan, but wise citizens saw that it was a courageous attack on that monster of treacherous lewdness, Dr. Arrowsmith.

In all the city there were exactly two ministers who defended him: Father Costello of the Irish Catholic Church, and Rabbi Rovine. They were, it happened, very good friends, and not at all friendly with the pastor of the Jonathan Edwards Church. They bullied their congregations; each of them asserted, "People come sneaking around with criticisms of our new Director of Health. If you want to make charges, make them openly. I will not listen to cowardly hints. And let me tell you that this city is lucky in having for health-officer a man who is honest and who actually knows something!"

But their congregations were poor.

Martin realized that he was lost. He tried to analyze his unpopularity.

"It isn't just Jordan's plotting and Tredgold's grousing and Pugh's weak spine. It's my own fault. I can't go out and soft-soap the people and get their permission to help keep them well. And I won't tell them what a hell of an important thing my work is—that I'm the one thing that saves the whole lot of 'em from dying immediately. Apparently an official in a democratic state has to do those things. Well, I don't! But I've got to think up something or they'll emasculate the whole Department."

One inspiration he did have. If Pickerbaugh were here, he could crush, or lovingly smother, the opposition. He remembered Pickerbaugh's farewell: "Now, my boy, even if I'm way off there in Washington, this Work will be as close to my heart as it ever was, and if you should really need me, you just send for me and I'll drop everything and come."

Martin wrote hinting that he was very much needed.

Pickerbaugh replied by return mail—good old Pickerbaugh!—but the reply was, "I cannot tell you how grieved I am that I cannot for the moment possibly get away from Washington but am sure that in your earnestness you exaggerate strength of opposition, write me freely, at any time."

"That's my last shot," Martin said to Leora. "I'm done. Mayor Pugh will fire me, just as soon as he comes back from his fishing trip. I'm a failure again, darling."

"You're not a failure, and you must eat some of this nice steak, and what shall we do now—time for us to be moving on, anyway—I hate staying in one place," said Leora.

"I don't know what we'll do. Maybe I could get a job at Hunziker's. Or go back to Dakota and try to work up a practise. What I'd like is to become a farmer and get me a big shotgun and drive every earnest Christian citizen off the place. But meantime I'm going to stick here. I might win yet—with just a couple of miracles and a divine intervention. Oh, God, I am so tired! Are you coming back to the lab with me this evening? Honest, I'll quit early—before eleven, maybe."

He had completed his paper on the streptolysin research, and he took a day off to go to Chicago and talk it over with an editor of the *Journal of Infectious Diseases.* As he left Nautilus he was confused. He had caught himself rejoicing that he was free of Wheatsylvania and bound for great Nautilus. Time bent back, progress was annihilated, and he was mazed with futility.

The editor praised his paper, accepted it, and suggested only one change. Martin had to wait for his train. He remembered that Angus Duer was in Chicago, with the Rouncefield Clinic—a private organization of medical specialists, sharing costs and profits.

The clinic occupied fourteen rooms in a twenty-story building constructed (or so Martin certainly remembered it) of marble, gold, and rubies. The clinic reception-room, focused on a vast stone fireplace, was like the drawing-room of an oil magnate, but it was not a place of leisure. The young woman at the door demanded Martin's symptoms and address. A page in buttons sped with his name to a nurse, who flew to the inner offices. Before Angus appeared, Martin had to wait a quarter-hour in a smaller, richer, still more abashing reception-room. But this time he was so awed that he would have permitted the clinic surgeons to operate on him for any ill which at the moment they happened to fancy.

In medical school and Zenith General Hospital, Angus Duer had been efficient enough, but now he was ten times as self-assured. He was cordial; he invited Martin to step out for a dish of tea as though he almost meant it; but beside him Martin felt young, rustic, inept.

Angus won him by pondering, "Irving Watters? He was Digam? I'm not sure I remember him. Oh, yes—he was one of these boneheads that are the curse of every profession."

When Martin had sketched his conflict at Nautilus, Angus suggested, "You better come join us here at Rouncefield, as pathologist. Our pathologist is leaving in a few weeks. You could do the job, all right. You're getting thirty-five hundred a year now? Well, I think I could get you forty-five hundred, as a starter, and some day you'd become a regular member of the clinic and get in on all the profits. Let me know if you want it. Rouncefield told me to dig up a man."

With this resource and with an affection for Angus, Martin returned to Nautilus and open war. When Mayor Pugh returned he did not discharge Martin, but he appointed over him, as full Director, Pickerbaugh's friend, Dr. Bissex, the football coach and health director of Mugford College.

Dr. Bissex first discharged Rufus Ockford, which took five minutes, went out and addressed a Y.M.C.A. meeting, then bustled in and invited Martin to resign.

"I will like hell!" said Martin. "Come on, be honest, Bissex. If you want to fire me, do it, but let's have things straight. I won't resign, and if you do fire me I think I'll take it to the courts, and maybe I can turn enough light on you and His Honor and Frank Jordan to keep you from taking all the guts out of the work here."

"Why, Doctor, what a way to talk! Certainly I won't fire you," said Bissex, in the manner of one who has talked to difficult students and to lazy football teams. "Stay with us as long as you like. Only, in the interests of economy, I reduce your salary to eight hundred dollars a year!"

"All right, reduce and be damned," said Martin.

It sounded particularly fine and original when he said it, but less so when Leora and he found that, with their rent fixed by their lease, they could not by whatever mean economies live on less than a thousand a year.

Now that he was free from responsibility he began to form his own faction, to save the Department. He gathered Rabbi Rovine, Father Costello, Ockford, who was going to remain in town and practise, the secretary of the Labor Council, a banker who regarded Tredgold as "fast," and that excellent fellow the dentist of the school clinic.

"With people like that behind me, I can do something," he gloated to Leora. "I'm going to stick by it. I'm not going to have the D.P.H. turned into a Y.M.C.A. Bissex has all of Pickerbaugh's mush without his honesty and vigor. I can beat him! I'm not much of an executive, but I was beginning to visualize a D.P.H. that would be solid and not gaseous—that would save kids and prevent epidemics. I won't give it up. You watch me!"

His committee made representations to the Commercial Club, and for a time they were certain that the chief reporter of the *Frontiersman* was going to support them, "as soon as he could get his editor over being scared of a row." But Martin's belligerency was weakened by shame, for he never had enough money to meet his bills, and he was not used to dodging irate grocers, receiving dunning letters, standing at the door arguing with impertinent bill-collectors. He, who had been a city dignitary a few days before, had to endure, "Come on now, you pay up, you dead beat, or I'll get a cop!" When the shame had grown to terror, Dr. Bissex suddenly reduced his salary another two hundred dollars.

Martin stormed into the mayor's office to have it out, and found F. X. Jordan sitting with Pugh. It was evident that they both knew of the second reduction and considered it an excellent joke.

He reassembled his committee. "I'm going to take this into the courts," he raged.

"Fine," said Father Costello; and Rabbi Rovine: "Jenkins, that radical lawyer, would handle the case free."

The wise banker observed, "You haven't got anything to take into the courts till they discharge you without cause. Bissex has a legal right to reduce your salary all he wants to. The city regulations don't fix the salary for anybody except the Director and the inspectors. You haven't a thing to say."

With a melodramatic flourish Martin protested, "And I suppose I haven't a thing to say if they wreck the Department!"

"Not a thing, if the city doesn't care."

"Well, I care! I'll starve before I'll resign!"

"You'll starve if you don't resign, and your wife, too. Now here's my plan," said the banker. "You go into private practise here—I'll finance your getting an office and so on—and when the time comes, maybe in five or ten years from now, we'll all get together again and have you put in as full Director."

"Ten years of waiting—in *Nautilus*? Nope. I'm licked. I'm a complete failure—at thirty-two! I'll resign. I'll wander on," said Martin.

"I know I'm going to love Chicago," said Leora.

IV

He wrote to Angus Duer. He was appointed pathologist in the Rouncefield Clinic. But, Angus wrote, "they could not at the moment see their way clear to pay him forty-five hundred a year, though they were glad to go to twenty-five hundred." Martin accepted.

V

When the Nautilus papers announced that Martin had resigned, the good citizens chuckled, "Resigned? He got kicked out, that's what happened." One of the papers had an innocent squib:

> Probably a certain amount of hypocrisy is inevitable in us sinful human critters, but when a public official tries to pose as a saint while indulging in every vice, and tries to cover up his gross ignorance and incompetence by pulling political wires, and makes a holy show of himself by not even doing a first-class job of wire-pulling, then even the cussedest of us old scoundrels begins to holler for the meat-ax.

Pickerbaugh wrote to Martin from Washington:

> I greatly regret to hear that you have resigned your post. I cannot tell you how disappointed I am, after all the pains I took in breaking you in and making you acquainted with my ideals. Bissex informs me that, because of crisis in city finances, he had to reduce your salary temporarily. Well personally I would rather work for the D.P.H. for nothing a year and earn my keep by being a night watchman than give up the fight for everything that is decent and constructive. I am

sorry. I had a great liking for you, and your defection, your going back to private practise merely for commercial gain, your selling out for what I presume is a very high emolument, is one of the very greatest blows I have recently had to sustain.

VI

As they rode up to Chicago Martin thought aloud:

"I never knew I could be so badly licked. I never want to see a laboratory or a public health office again. I'm done with everything but making money.

"I suppose this Rouncefield Clinic is probably nothing but a gilded boob-trap—scare the poor millionaire into having all the fancy kinds of examinations and treatments the traffic will bear. I hope it is! I expect to be a commercial-group doctor the rest of my life. I hope I have the sense to be!

"All wise men are bandits. They're loyal to their friends, but they despise the rest. Why not, when the mass of people despise them if they *aren't* bandits? Angus Duer had the sense to see this from the beginning, way back in medic school. He's probably a perfect technician as a surgeon, but he knows you get only what you grab. Think of the years it's taken me to learn what he savvied all the time!

"Know what I'll do? I'll stick to the Rouncefield Clinic till I'm making maybe thirty thousand a year, and then I'll get Ockford and start my own clinic, with myself as internist and head of the whole shooting-match, and collect every cent I can.

"All right, if what people want is a little healing and a lot of tapestry, they shall have it—and pay for it.

"I never thought I could be such a failure—to become a commercialist and not want to be anything else. And I don't want to be anything else, believe me! I'm through!"

Chapter XXV

THEN for a year with each day longer than a sleepless night, yet the whole year speeding without events or seasons or eagerness, Martin was a faithful mechanic in that most competent, most clean and brisk and visionless medical factory, the Rouncefield Clinic. He had nothing of which to complain. The clinic did, perhaps, give over-many roentgenological examinations to socially dislocated women who needed children and floor-scrubbing more than pretty little skiagraphs; they did, perhaps, view all tonsils with too sanguinary a gloom; but certainly no factory could have been better equipped or more gratifyingly expensive, and none could have routed its raw human material through so many processes so swiftly. The Martin Arrowsmith who had been supercilious toward Pickerbaugh and old Dr. Winters had for Rouncefield and Angus Duer and the other keen taut specialists of the clinic only the respect of the poor and uncertain for the rich and shrewd.

He admired Angus's firmness of purpose and stability of habit.

Angus had a swim or a fencing lesson daily; he swam easily and fenced like a still-faced demon. He was in bed before eleven-thirty; he never took more than one drink a day; and he never read anything or said anything which would not contribute to his progress as a Brilliant Young Surgeon. His underlings knew that Dr. Duer would not fail to arrive precisely on time, precisely well dressed, absolutely sober, very cool, and appallingly unpleasant to any nurse who made a mistake or looked for a smile.

Martin would without fear have submitted to the gilded and ardent tonsil-snatcher of the clinic, would have submitted to Angus for abdominal surgery or to Rouncefield for any operation of the head or neck, providing he was himself quite sure the operation was necessary, but he was never able to rise to the clinic's lyric faith that any portions of the body without which people could conceivably get along should certainly be removed at once.

The real flaw in his year of Chicago was that through all his working day he did not live. With quick hands, and one-tenth of his brain, he made blood counts, did urinalyses and Wassermanns and infrequent necropsies, and all the while he was dead, in a white-tiled coffin. Amid the blattings of Pickerbaugh and the peepings of Wheatsylvania, he had lived, had fought his environment. Now there was nothing to fight.

After hours, he almost lived. Leora and he discovered the world of book-shops and print-shops and theaters and concerts. They read novels and history and travel; they talked, at dinners given by Rouncefield or Angus, to journalists, engineers, bankers, merchants. They saw a Russian play, and heard Mischa Elman, and read Gottlieb's beloved Rabelais. Martin learned to flirt without childishness, and Leora went for the first time to a hair-dresser and to a manicure, and began her lessons in French. She had called Martin a "lie-hunter," a "truth-seeker." They decided now, talking it over in their tight little two-and-quarter room flat, that most people who called themselves "truth-seekers"—persons who scurry about chattering of Truth as though it were a tangible separable thing, like houses or salt or bread—did not so much desire to find Truth as to cure their mental itch. In novels, these truth-seekers quested the "secret of life" in laboratories which did not seem to be provided with Bunsen flames or reagents; or they went, at great expense and much discomfort from hot trains and undesirable snakes, to Himalayan monasteries, to learn from unaseptic sages that the Mind can do all sorts of edifying things if one will but spend thirty or forty years in eating rice and gazing on one's navel.

To these high matters Martin responded, "Rot!" He insisted that there is no Truth but only many truths; that Truth is not a colored bird to be chased among the rocks and captured by its tail, but a skeptical attitude toward life. He insisted that no one could expect more than, by stubbornness or luck, to have the kind of work he enjoyed and an ability to become better acquainted with the facts of that work than the average job-holder.

His mechanistic philosophy did not persuade him that he was progressing adequately. When he tried to match himself with the experts of the clinic or with their professional friends, he was even more uncomfortable than he had been under the disconcerting scorn of Dr. Hesselink of Groningen. At clinic luncheons he met surgeons from London, New York, Boston; men with limousines and social positions and the offensive briskness of the man who has numerous engagements, or the yet more offensive quietness of the person who is amused by his inferiors; master technicians, readers of papers at medical congresses, executives and controllers, unafraid to operate before a hundred peering doctors, or to give well-bred and exceedingly final orders to subordinates; captain-generals of medicine, never doubting themselves; great priests and healers; men mature and wise and careful and blandly cordial.

In their winged presences, Max Gottlieb seemed an aged fusser, Gustaf Sondelius a mountebank, and the city of Nautilus unworthy of passionate warfare. As their suave courtesy smothered him, Martin felt like a footman.

In long hours of increasing frankness and lucidity he discussed with Leora the question of "What is this Martin Arrowsmith and whither is he going?" and he admitted that the sight of the Famous Surgeons disturbed his ancient faith that he was somehow a superior person. It was Leora who consoled him:

"I've got a lovely description for your dratted Famous Surgeons. You know how polite and important they are, and they smile so carefully? Well, don't you remember you once said that Professor Gottlieb called all such people like that 'men of measured merriment'?"

He caught up the phrase; they sang it together; and they made of it a beating impish song:

"Men of measured merriment! Men of measured merriment! Damn the great executives, the men of measured merriment, damn the men with careful smiles, damn the men that run the shops, oh, damn their measured merriment, the men with measured merriment, oh, damn their measured merriment, and DAMN their careful smiles!"

II

While Martin developed in a jagged way from the boy of Wheatsylvania to mature man, his relations to Leora developed from loyal boy-and-girl adventurousness to lasting solidity. They had that understanding of each other known only to married people, a few married people, wherein for all their differences they were as much indissoluble parts of a whole as are the eye and hand. Their identification did not mean that they dwelt always in rosy bliss. Because he was so intimately fond of her and so sure of her, because anger and eager hot injustices are but ways of expressing trust, Martin was irritated by her and querulous with her as he would not have endured being with any other woman, any charming Orchid.

He stalked out now and then after a quarrel, disdaining to answer her, and for hours he left her alone, enjoying the knowledge that he was hurting her, that she was alone, waiting, perhaps weeping. Because he loved her and also was fond of her, he was annoyed when she was less sleek, less suave, than the women he encountered at Angus Duer's.

Mrs. Rouncefield was a worthy old waddler—beside her, Leora was shining and exquisite. But Mrs. Duer was of amber and ice. She was a rich young woman, she dressed with distinction, she spoke with finishing-school mock-melodiousness, she was ambitious, and she was untroubled by the possession of a heart or a brain. She was, indeed, what Mrs. Irving Watters believed herself to be.

In the simple gorgeousness of the Nautilus Smart set, Mrs. Clay Tredgold had petted Leora and laughed at her if she lacked a shoe-buckle or split an infinitive, but the gold-slippered Mrs. Duer was accustomed to sneer at carelessness with the most courteous and unresentable and unmistakable sneers.

As they returned by taxicab from the Duers', Martin flared:

"Don't you ever learn anything? I remember once in Nautilus we stopped on a country road and talked till—oh, darn' near dawn, and you were going to be so energetic, but here we are again to-night, with just the same thing— Good God, couldn't you even take the trouble to notice that you had a spot of soot on your nose to-night? Mrs. Duer noticed it, all right! Why are you so sloppy? Why can't you take a little care? And why can't you make an effort, anyway, to have something to say? You just sit there at dinner—you just sit and look healthy! Don't you want to help me? Mrs. Duer will probably help Angus to become president of the American Medical Association, in about twenty years, and by that time I suppose you'll have me back in Dakota as assistant to Hesselink!"

Leora had been snuggling beside him in the unusual luxury of a taxicab. She sat straight now, and when she spoke she had lost the casual independence with which she usually regarded life:

"Dear, I'm awfully sorry. I went out this afternoon, I went out and had a facial massage, so as to look nice for you, and then I knew you like conversation, so I got my little book about modern painting that I bought and I studied it terribly hard, but to-night I just couldn't seem to get the conversation around to modern painting—"

He was sobbing, with her head on his shoulder, "Oh, you poor, scared, bullied kid, trying to be grown-up with these dollar-chasers!"

III

After the first daze of white tile and bustling cleverness at the Rouncefield Clinic, Martin had the desire to tie up a few loose knots of his streptolysin research.

When Angus Duer discovered it he hinted, "Look here, Martin, I'm glad you're keeping on with your science, but if I were you I wouldn't, I think, waste too much energy on mere curiosity. Dr. Rouncefield was speaking about it the other day. We'd be glad to have you do all the research you want, only we'd like it if you went at something practical. Take for instance: if you could make a tabulation of the blood-counts in a couple of hundred cases of appendicitis and publish it, that'd get somewhere, and you could sort of bring in a mention of the clinic, and we'd all receive a little credit—and incidentally maybe we could raise you to three thousand a year then."

This generosity had the effect of extinguishing Martin's desire to do any research whatever.

"Angus is right. What he means is: as a scientist I'm finished. I am. I'll never try to do anything original again."

It was at this time, when Martin had been with the clinic for a year, that his streptolysin paper was published in the *Journal of Infectious Diseases.* He gave reprints to Rouncefield and to Angus. They said extremely nice things which showed that they had not read the paper, and again they suggested his tabulating blood-counts.

He also sent a reprint to Max Gottlieb, at the McGurk Institute of Biology.

Gottlieb wrote to him, in that dead-black spider-web script:

Dear Martin:

I have read your paper with great pleasure. The curves of the relation of hemolysin production to age of culture are illuminating. I have spoken about you to Tubbs. When are you coming to us—to me? Your laboratory and diener are waiting for you here. The last thing I want to be is a mystic, but I feel when I see your fine engraved letterhead of a clinic and a Rouncefield that you should be tired of trying to be a good citizen and ready to come back to work. We shall be glad, & Dr. Tubbs, if you can come.

Truly yours

M. Gottlieb

"I'm simply going to adore New York," said Leora.

Chapter XXVI

THE McGurk Building. A sheer wall, thirty blank stories of glass and limestone, down in the pinched triangle whence New York rules a quarter of the world.

Martin was not overwhelmed by his first hint of New York; after a year in the Chicago Loop, Manhattan seemed leisurely. But when from the elevated railroad he beheld the Woolworth Tower, he was exalted. To him architecture had never existed; buildings were larger or smaller bulks containing more or less interesting objects. His most impassioned architectural comment had been, "There's a cute bungalow; be nice place to live." Now he pondered, "Like to see that tower every day—clouds and storms behind it and everything—so sort of satisfying."

He came along Cedar Street, among thunderous trucks portly with wares from all the world; came to the bronze doors of the McGurk Building and a corridor of intemperately colored terra-cotta, with murals of Andean Indians, pirates booming up the Spanish Main, guarded gold-trains, and the stout walls of Cartagena. At the Cedar Street end of the corridor, a private street, one block long, was the Bank of the Andes and Antilles (Ross McGurk chairman of the board), in whose gold-crusted sanctity red-headed Yankee exporters drew drafts on Quito, and clerks hurled breathless Spanish at bulky women. A sign indicated, at the Liberty Street end, "Passenger Offices, McGurk Line, weekly sailings for the West Indies and South America."

Born to the prairies, never far from the sight of the cornfields, Martin was conveyed to blazing lands and portentous enterprises.

One of the row of bronze-barred elevators was labeled "Express to McGurk Institute." He entered it proudly, feeling himself already a part of the godly association. They rose swiftly, and he had but half-second glimpses of ground glass doors with the signs of mining companies, lumber companies, Central American railroad companies.

The McGurk Institute is probably the only organization for scientific research in the world which is housed in an office building. It has the twenty-ninth and thirtieth stories of the McGurk Building, and the roof is devoted to its animal house and to tiled walks along which (above a world of stenographers and bookkeepers and earnest gentlemen who desire to sell Better-bilt Garments to the golden dons of the Argentine) saunter rapt scientists dreaming of osmosis in Spirogyra.

Later, Martin was to note that the reception-room of the Institute was smaller, yet more forbiddingly polite, in its white paneling and Chippendale chairs, than the lobby of the Rouncefield Clinic, but now he was unconscious of the room, of the staccato girl attendant, of everything except that he was about to see Max Gottlieb, for the first time in five years.

At the door of the laboratory he stared hungrily.

Gottlieb was thin-cheeked and dark as ever, his hawk nose bony, his fierce eyes demanding, but his hair had gone gray, the flesh round his mouth was sunken, and Martin could have wept at the feebleness with which he rose. The old man peered down at him, his hand on Martin's shoulder, but he said only:

"Ah! Dis is good. . . . Your laboratory is three doors down the hall. . . . But I object to one thing in the good paper you send me. You say, 'The regularity of the rate at which the streptolysin disappears suggests that an equation may be found—"

"But it can, sir!"

"Then why did you not make the equation?"

"Well— I don't know. I wasn't enough of a mathematician."

"Then you should not have published till you knew your math!"

"I— Look, Dr. Gottlieb, do you really think I know enough to work here? I want terribly to succeed."

"Succeed? I have heard that word. It is English? Oh, yes, it is a word that liddle schoolboys use at the University of Winnemac. It means passing examinations. But there are no examinations to pass here. . . . Martin, let us be clear. You know something of laboratory technique; you have heard about dese bacilli; you are not a good chemist, and mathematics—pfui!—most terrible! But you have curiosity and you are stubborn. You do not accept rules. Therefore I t'ink you will either make a very good scientist or a very bad one, and if you are bad enough, you will be popular with the rich ladies who rule this city, New York, and you can gif lectures for a living or even become, if you get to be plausible enough, a college president. So anyvay, it will be interesting."

Half an hour later they were arguing ferociously, Martin asserting that the whole world ought to stop warring and trading and writing and get straightway into laboratories to observe new phenomena; Gottlieb insisting that there were already too many facile scientists, that the one thing necessary was the mathematical analysis (and often the destruction) of phenomena already observed.

It sounded bellicose, and all the while Martin was blissful with the certainty that he had come home.

The laboratory in which they talked (Gottlieb pacing the floor, his long arms fantastically knotted behind his thin back; Martin leaping on and off tall stools) was not in the least remarkable—a sink, a bench with racks of numbered test-tubes, a microscope, a few note-books and hydrogen-ion charts, a grotesque series of bottles connected by glass and rubber tubes on an ordinary kitchen table at the end of the room—yet now and then during his tirades Martin looked about reverently.

Gottlieb interrupted their debate: "What work do you want to do here?"

"Why, sir, I'd like to help you, if I can. I suppose you're cleaning up some things on the synthesis of antibodies."

"Yes, I t'ink I can bring immunity reactions under the mass action law. But you are not to help me. You are to do your own work. What do you want to do? This is not a clinic, wit' patients going through so neat in a row!"

"I want to find a hemolysin for which there's an antibody. There isn't any for streptolysin. I'd like to work with staphylolysin. Would you mind?"

"I do not care what you do—if you just do not steal my staph cultures out of the ice-box, and if you will look mysterious all the time, so Dr. Tubbs, our Director, will t'ink you are up to something big. So! I haf only one suggestion: when you get stuck in a problem, I have a fine collection of detective stories in my office. But no. Should I be serious—this once, when you are just come?

"Perhaps I am a crank, Martin. There are many who hate me. There are plots against me—oh, you t'ink I imagine it, but you shall see! I make many mistakes. But one thing I keep always pure: the religion of a scientist.

"To be a scientist—it is not just a different job, so that a man should choose between being a scientist and being an explorer or a bond-salesman or a physician or a king or a farmer. It is a tangle of ver-y obscure emotions, like mysticism, or wanting to write poetry; it makes its victim all different from the good normal man. The normal man, he does not care much what he does except that he should eat and sleep and make love. But the scientist is intensely religious—he is so religious that he will not accept quarter-truths, because they are an insult to his faith.

"He wants that everything should be subject to inexorable laws. He is equal opposed to the capitalists who t'ink their silly money-grabbing is a system, and to liberals who t'ink man is not a fighting animal; he takes both the American booster and the European aristocrat, and he ignores all their blithering. Ignores it! All of it! He hates the preachers who talk their fables, but he iss not too kindly to the anthropologists and historians who can only make guesses, yet they have the nerf to call themselves scientists! Oh, yes, he is a man that all nice good-natured people should naturally hate!

"He speaks no meaner of the ridiculous faith-healers and chiropractors than he does of the doctors that want to snatch our science before it is tested and rush around hoping they heal people, and spoiling all the clues with their footsteps; and worse than the men like hogs, worse than the imbeciles who have not even heard of science, he hates pseudo-scientists, guess-scientists—like these psycho-analysts; and worse than those comic dream-scientists he hates the men that are allowed in a clean kingdom like biology but know only one text-book and how to lecture to nincompoops all so popular! He is the only real revolutionary, the authentic scientist, because he alone knows how liddle he knows.

"He must be heartless. He lives in a cold, clear light. Yet dis is a funny t'ing: really, in private, he is not cold nor heartless—so much less cold than the Professional Optimists. The world has always been ruled by the Philanthropists: by the doctors that want to use therapeutic methods they do not understand, by the soldiers that want something to defend their country against, by the preachers that yearn to make everybody listen to them, by the kind manufacturers that love their workers, by the eloquent statesmen and soft-hearted authors—and see once what a fine mess of hell they haf made of the world! Maybe now it is time for the scientist, who works and searches and never goes around howling how he loves everybody!

"But once again always remember that not all the men who work at science are scientists. So few! The rest—secretaries, press-agents, camp-followers! To be a scientist is like being a Goethe: it is born in you. Sometimes I t'ink you have a liddle of it born in you. If you haf, there is only one t'ing—no, there is two t'ings you must do: work twice as hard as you can, and keep people from using you. I will try to protect you from Success. It is all I can do. So. . . . I should wish, Martin, that you will be very happy here. May Koch bless you!"

II

Five rapt minutes Martin spent in the laboratory which was to be his—smallish but efficient, the bench exactly the right height, a proper sink with pedal taps. When he had closed the door and let his spirit flow out and fill that minute apartment with his own essence, he felt secure.

No Pickerbaugh or Rouncefield could burst in here and drag him away to be explanatory and plausible and public; he would be free to work, instead of being summoned to the package-wrapping and dictation of breezy letters which men call work.

He looked out of the broad window above his bench and saw that he did have the coveted Woolworth Tower, to keep and gloat on. Shut in to a joy of precision, he would nevertheless not be walled out from flowing life. He had, to the north, not the Woolworth Tower alone but the Singer Building, the arrogant magnificence of the City Investing Building. To the west, tall ships were riding, tugs were bustling, all the world went by. Below his cliff, the streets were feverish. Suddenly he loved humanity as he loved the decent, clean rows of test-tubes, and he prayed then the prayer of the scientist:

"God give me unclouded eyes and freedom from haste. God give me a quiet and relentless anger against all pretense and all pretentious work and all work left slack and unfinished. God give me a restlessness whereby I may neither sleep nor accept praise till my observed results equal my calculated results or in pious glee I discover and assault my error. God give me strength not to trust to God!"

III

He walked all the way up to their inconsiderable hotel in the Thirties, and all the way the crowds stared at him—this slim, pale, black-eyed, beaming young man who thrust among them, half-running, seeing nothing yet in a blur seeing everything: gallant buildings, filthy streets, relentless traffic, soldiers of fortune, fools, pretty women, frivolous shops, windy sky. His feet raced to the tune of "I've found my work, I've found my work, I've found my work!"

Leora was awaiting him—Leora whose fate it was ever to wait for him in creaky rocking-chairs in cheapish rooms. As he galloped in she smiled, and all her thin, sweet body was illumined. Before he spoke she cried:

"Oh, Sandy, I'm so glad!"

She interrupted his room-striding panegyrics on Max Gottlieb, on the McGurk Institute, on New York, on the charms of staphylolysin, by a meek "Dear, how much are they going to pay you?"

He stopped with a bump. "Gosh! I forgot to ask!"

"Oh!"

"Now you look here! This isn't a Rouncefield Clinic! I hate these buzzards that can't see anything but making money—"

"I know, Sandy. Honestly, I don't care. I was just wondering what kind of a flat we'll be able to afford, so I can begin looking for it. Go on. Dr. Gottlieb said—"

It was three hours after, at eight, when they went to dinner.

IV

The city of magic was to become to Martin neither a city nor any sort of magic but merely a route: their flat, the subway, the Institute, a favorite inexpensive restaurant, a few streets of laundries and delicatessens and movie theaters. But to-night it was a fog of wonder. They dined at the Brevoort, of which Gustaf Sondelius had told him. This was in 1916, before the country had become wholesome and sterile, and the Brevoort was a tumult of French uniforms, caviar, Louis, dangling neckties, Nuits St. Georges, illustrators, Grand Marnier, British Intelligence officers, brokers, conversation, and Martell, V.O.

"It's a fine crazy bunch," said Martin. "Do you realize we can stop being respectable now? Irving Watters isn't watching us, or Angus! Would we be too insane if we had a bottle of champagne?"

He awoke next day to fret that there must be a trick somewhere, as there had been in Nautilus, in Chicago. But as he set to work he seemed to be in a perfect world. The Institute deftly provided all the material and facilities he could desire—animals, incubators, glassware, cultures, media—and he had a thoroughly trained technician—"garçon" they called him at the Institute. He really was let alone; he really was encouraged to do individual work; he really was associated with men who thought not in terms of poetic posters or of two-thousand-dollar operations but of colloids and sporulation and electrons, and of the laws and energies which governed them.

On his first day there came to greet him the head of the Department of Physiology, Dr. Rippleton Holabird.

Holabird seemed, though Martin had found his name starred in physiological journals, too young and too handsome to be the head of a department: a tall, slim, easy man with a trim mustache. Martin had been reared in the school of Clif Clawson; he had not realized, till he heard Dr. Holabird's quick greeting, that a man's voice may be charming without effeminacy.

Holabird guided him through the two floors of the Institute, and Martin beheld all the wonders of which he had ever dreamed. If it was not so large, McGurk ranked in equipment with Rockefeller, Pasteur, McCormick, Lister. Martin saw rooms for sterilizing glass and preparing media, for glass-blowing, for the polariscope and the spectroscope, and a steel-and-cement-walled combustion-chamber. He saw a museum of pathology and bacteriology to which he longed to add. There was a department of publications, whence were issued the Institute reports, and the *American Journal of Geographic Pathology*, edited by the Director, Dr. Tubbs; there was a room for photography, a glorious library, an aquarium for the Department of Marine Biology, and (Dr. Tubbs's own idea) a row of laboratories which visiting foreign scientists were invited to use as their own. A Belgian biologist and a Portuguese bio-chemist were occupying guest laboratories now, and once, Martin thrilled to learn, Gustaf Sondelius had been here.

Then Martin saw the Berkeley-Saunders centrifuge.

The principle of the centrifuge is that of the cream-separator. It collects as sediment the solids scattered through a liquid, such as bacteria in a solution. Most centrifuges are hand- or water-power contrivances the size of a large cocktail-shaker, but this noble implement was four feet across, electrically driven, the central bowl enclosed in armor plate fastened with levers like a submarine hatch, the whole mounted on a cement pillar.

Holabird explained, "There're only three of these in existence. They're made by Berkeley-Saunders in England. You know the normal speed, even for a good centrifuge, is about four thousand revolutions a minute. This does twenty thousand a minute—fastest in the world. Eh?"

"Jove, they do give you the stuff to work with!" gloated Martin. (He really did, under Holabird's handsome influence, say Jove, not Gosh.)

"Yes, McGurk and Tubbs are the most generous men in the scientific world. I think you'll find it very pleasant to be here, Doctor."

"I know I will—shall. And Jove, it's awfully nice of you to take me around this way."

"Can't you see how much I'm enjoying my chance to display my knowledge? There's no form of egotism so agreeable and so safe as being a cicerone. But we still have the real wonder of the Institute for to behold, Doctor. Down this way."

The real wonder of the Institute had nothing visible to do with science. It was the Hall, in which lunched the staff, and in which occasional scientific dinners were given, with Mrs. McGurk as hostess. Martin gasped and his head went back as his glance ran from glistening floor to black and gold ceiling. The Hall rose the full height of the two floors of the Institute. Clinging to the soaring wall, above the dais on which lunched the Director and the seven heads of departments, was a carved musicians'-gallery. Against the oak paneling of the walls were portraits of the pontiffs of science, in crimson robes, with a vast mural by Maxfield Parrish, and above all was an electrolier of a hundred globes.

"Gosh—*Jove!*" said Martin. "I never knew there was such a room!"

Holabird was generous. He did not smile. "Oh, perhaps it's almost too gorgeous. It's Capitola's pet creation—Capitola is Mrs. Ross McGurk, wife of the founder; she's really an awfully nice woman but she does love Movements and Associations. Terry Wickett, one of the chemists here, calls this 'Bonanza Hall.' Yet it does inspire you when you come in to lunch all tired and grubby. Now let's go call on the Director. He told me to bring you in."

After the Babylonian splendor of the Hall, Martin expected to find the office of Dr. A. DeWitt Tubbs fashioned like a Roman bath, but it was, except for a laboratory bench at one end, the most rigidly business-like apartment he had ever seen.

Dr. Tubbs was an earnest man, whiskered like a terrier, very scholarly, and perhaps the most powerful American exponent of coöperation in science, but he was also a man of the world, fastidious of boots and waistcoats. He had graduated from Harvard, studied on the Continent, been professor of pathology in the University of Minnesota, president of Hartford University, minister to Venezuela, editor of the *Weekly Statesman* and president of the Sanity League, finally Director of McGurk.

He was a member both of the American Academy of Arts and Letters and of the Academy of Sciences. Bishops, generals, liberal rabbis, and musical bankers dined with him. He was one of the Distinguished Men to whom the newspapers turned for authoritative interviews on all subjects.

You realized before he had talked to you for ten minutes that here was one of the few leaders of mankind who could discourse on any branch of knowledge, yet could control practical affairs and drive stumbling mankind on to sane and reasonable ideals. Though a Max Gottlieb might in his research show a certain talent, yet his narrowness, his sour and antic humor, kept him from developing the broad view of education, politics, commerce, and all other noble matters which marked Dr. A. DeWitt Tubbs.

But the Director was as cordial to the insignificant Martin Arrowsmith as though Martin were a visiting senator. He shook his hand warmly; he unbent in a smile; his baritone was mellow.

"Dr. Arrowsmith, I trust we shall do more than merely say you are welcome here; I trust we shall show you how welcome you are! Dr. Gottlieb tells me that you have a natural aptitude for cloistered investigation but that you have been looking over the fields of medical practise and public health before you settled down to the laboratory. I can't tell you how wise I consider you to have made that broad preliminary survey. Too many would-be scientists lack the tutored vision which comes from coördinating all mental domains."

Martin was dazed to discover that he had been making a broad survey.

"Now you'll doubtless wish to take some time, perhaps a year or more, in getting into your stride, Dr. Arrowsmith. I shan't ask you for any reports. So long as Dr. Gottlieb feels that you yourself are satisfied with your progress, I shall be content. Only if there is anything in which I can advise you, from a perhaps somewhat longer career in science, please believe that I shall be delighted to be of aid, and I am quite sure the same obtains with Dr. Holabird here, though he really ought to be jealous, because he is one of our youngest workers—in fact I call him my *enfant terrible*—but you, I believe, are only thirty-three, and you quite put the poor fellow's nose out!"

Holabird merrily suggested, "Oh, no, Doctor, it's been put out long ago. You forget Terry Wickett. He's under forty."

"Oh. *Him!*" murmured Dr. Tubbs.

Martin had never heard a man disposed of so poisonously with such politeness. He saw that in Terry Wickett there might be a serpent even in this paradise.

"Now," said Dr. Tubbs, "perhaps you might like to glance around my place here. I pride myself on keeping our card-indices and letter-files as unimaginatively as though I were an insurance agent. But there is a certain exotic touch in these charts." He trotted across the room to show a nest of narrow drawers filled with scientific blue-prints.

Just what they were charts of, he did not say, nor did Martin ever learn.

He pointed to the bench at the end of the room, and laughingly admitted:

"You can see there what an inefficient fellow I really am. I keep asserting that I have given up all the idyllic delights of pathological research for the less fascinating but so very important and fatiguing cares of the directorship. Yet such is the weakness of *genius homo* that sometimes, when I ought to be attending to practical details, I become obsessed by some probably absurd pathological concept, and so ridiculous am I that I can't wait to hasten down the hall to my regular laboratory—I must always have a bench at hand and an experiment going on. Oh, I'm afraid I'm not the moral man that I pose as being in public! Here I am married to executive procedure, and still I hanker for my first love, Milady Science!"

"I think it's fine you still have an itch for it," Martin ventured.

He was wondering just what experiments Dr. Tubbs had been doing lately. The bench seemed rather unused.

"And now, Doctor, I want you to meet the real Director of the Institute—my secretary, Miss Pearl Robbins."

Martin had already noticed Miss Robbins. You could not help noticing Miss Robbins. She was thirty-five and stately, a creamy goddess. She rose to shake hands—a firm, competent grasp—and to cry in her glorious contralto, "Dr. Tubbs is so complimentary only because he knows that otherwise I wouldn't give him his afternoon tea. We've heard so much about your cleverness from Dr. Gottlieb that I'm almost afraid to welcome you, Dr. Arrowsmith, but I do want to."

Then, in a glow, Martin stood in his laboratory looking at the Woolworth Tower. He was dizzy with these wonders—his own wonders, now! In Rippleton Holabird, so gaily elegant yet so distinguished, he hoped to have a friend. He found Dr. Tubbs somewhat sentimental, but he was moved by his kindness and by Miss Robbins's recognition. He was in a haze of future glory when his door was banged open by a hard-faced, red-headed, soft-shirted man of thirty-six or -eight.

"Arrowsmith?" the intruder growled. "My name is Wickett, Terry Wickett. I'm a chemist. I'm with Gottlieb. Well, I noticed the Holy Wren was showing you the menagerie."

"Dr. Holabird?"

"Him. . . . Well, you must be more or less intelligent, if Pa Gottlieb let you in. How's it starting? Which kind are you going to be? One of the polite birds that uses the Institute for social climbing and catches him a rich wife, or one of the roughnecks like me and Gottlieb?"

Terry Wickett's croak was as irritating a sound as Martin had ever heard. He answered in a voice curiously like that of Rippleton Holabird:

"I don't think you need to worry. I happen to be married already!"

"Oh, don't let that fret you, Arrowsmith. Divorces are cheap, in this man's town. Well, did the Holy Wren show you Gladys the Tart?"

"Huh?"

"Gladys the Tart, or the Galloping Centrifuge."

"Oh. You mean the Berkeley-Saunders?"

"I do, soul of my soul. Whajuh think of it?"

"It's the finest centrifuge I've ever seen. Dr. Holabird said—"

"Hell, he ought to say something! He went and got old Tubbs to buy it. He just loves it, Holy Wren does."

"Why not? It's the fastest—"

"Sure. Speediest centrifuge in the whole *Vereinigen*, and made of the best toothpick steel. The only trouble is, it always blows out fuses, and it spatters the bugs so that you need a gas-mask if you're going to use it. . . . And did you love dear old Tubbsy and the peerless Pearl?"

"I did!"

"Fine. Of course Tubbs is an illiterate jackass but still, at that, he hasn't got persecution-mania, like Gottlieb."

"Look here, Wickett—is it Dr. Wickett?"

"Uh-huh. . . . M.D., Ph.D., but a first-rate chemist just the same."

"Well, Dr. Wickett, it seems to me a shame that a man of your talents should have to associate with idiots like Gottlieb and Tubbs and Holabird. I've just left a Chicago clinic where everybody is nice and sensible. I'd be glad to recommend you for a job there!"

"Wouldn't be so bad. At least I'd avoid all the gassing at lunch in Bonanza Hall. Well, sorry I got your goat, Arrowsmith, but you look all right to me."

"Thanks!"

Wickett grinned obscenely—red-headed, rough-faced, wiry—and snorted, "By the way, did Holabird tell you about being wounded in the first month of the war, when he was a field marshal or a hospital orderly or something in the British Army?"

"He did not! He didn't mention the war!"

"He will! Well, Brer Arrowsmith, I look forward to many happy, happy years together, playing at the feet of Pa Gottlieb. So long. My lab is right next to yours."

"Fool!" Martin decided, and, "Well, I can stand him as long as I can fall back on Gottlieb and Holabird. But— The conceited idiot! Gosh, so Holabird was in the war! Invalided out, I guess. I certainly got back at Wickett on that! 'Did he tell you about his being a jolly old hero in the blinkin' war?' he said, and I came right back at him, 'I'm sorry to displease you,' I said, 'but Dr. Holabird did not mention the war.' The idiot! Well, I won't let him worry me."

And indeed, as Martin met the staff at lunch, Wickett was the only one whom he did not find courteous, however brief their greetings. He did not distinguish among them; for days most of the twenty researchers remained a blur. He confused Dr. Yeo, head of the Department of Biology, with the carpenter who had come to put up shelves.

The staff sat in Hall at two long tables, one on the dais, one below: tiny insect groups under the massy ceiling. They were not particularly noble of aspect, these possible Darwins and

Huxleys and Pasteurs. None of them were wide-browed Platos. Except for Rippleton Holabird and Max Gottlieb and perhaps Martin himself, they looked like lunching grocers: brisk featureless young men; thick mustached elders; and wimpish little men with spectacles, men whose collars did not meet. But there was a steady calm about them; there was, Martin believed, no anxiety over money in their voices nor any restlessness of envy and scandalous gossip. They talked gravely or frivolously of their work, the one sort of work that, since it becomes part of the chain of discovered fact, is eternal, however forgotten the worker's name.

As Martin listened to Terry Wickett (rude and slangy as ever, referring to himself as "the boy chemist," speaking of "this gaudy Institute" and "our trusting new lil brother, Arrowsmith") debating with a slight thin-bearded man—Dr. William T. Smith, assistant in bio-chemistry—the possibility of increasing the effects of all enzymes by doses of X-rays, as he heard one associate-member vituperate another for his notions of cell-chemistry and denounce Ehrlich as "the Edison of medical science," Martin perceived new avenues of exciting research; he stood on a mountain, and unknown valleys, craggy tantalizing paths, were open to his feet.

V

Dr. and Mrs. Rippleton Holabird invited them to dinner, a week after their coming.

As Holabird's tweeds made Clay Tredgold's smartness seem hard and pretentious, so his dinner revealed Angus Duer's affairs in Chicago as mechanical and joyless and a little anxious. Every one whom Martin met at the Holabirds' flat was a Somebody, though perhaps a minor Somebody: a goodish editor or a rising ethnologist; and all of them had Holabird's graceful casualness.

The provincial Arrowsmiths arrived on time, therefore fifteen minutes early. Before the cocktails appeared, in old Venetian glass, Martin demanded, "Doctor, what problems are you getting after now in your physiology?"

Holabird was transformed into an ardent boy. With a deprecatory "Would you really like to hear about 'em—you needn't be polite, you know!" he dashed into an exposition of his experiments, drawing sketches on the blank spaces in newspaper advertisements, on the back of a wedding invitation, on the fly-leaf of a presentation novel, looking at Martin apologetically, learned yet gay.

"We're working on the localization of brain functions. I think we've gone beyond Bolton and Flechsig. Oh, it's jolly exciting, exploring the brain. Look here!"

His swift pencil was sketching the cerebrum; the brain lived and beat under his fingers.

He threw down the paper. "I say, it's a shame to inflict my hobbies on you. Besides, the others are coming. Tell me, how is your work going? Are you comfortable at the Institute? Do you find you like people?"

"Everybody except— To be frank, I'm jarred by Wickett."

Generously, "I know. His manner is slightly aggressive. But you mustn't mind him; he's really an extraordinarily gifted bio-chemist. He's a bachelor—gives up everything for his work. And he doesn't really mean half the rude things he says. He detests me, among others. Has he mentioned me?"

"Why, not especially—"

"I have a feeling he goes around saying that I talk about my experiences in the war, which really isn't quite altogether true."

"Yes," in a burst, "he did say that."

"I do rather wish he wouldn't. So sorry to have offended him by going and getting wounded. I'll remember and not do it again! Such a fuss for a war record as insignificant as mine! What happened was: when the war broke out in '14 I was in England, studying under Sherrington. I pretended to be a Canadian and joined up with the medical corps and got mine within three weeks and got hoofed out, and that was the end of my magnificent career! Here's somebody arriving."

His easy gallantry won Martin complete. Leora was equally captivated by Mrs. Holabird, and they went home from the dinner in new enchantment.

So began for them a white light of happiness. Martin was scarce more blissful in his undisturbed work than in his life outside the laboratory.

All the first week he forgot to ask what his salary was to be. Then it became a game to wait till the end of the month. Evenings, in little restaurants, Leora and he would speculate about it.

The Institute would surely not pay him less than the twenty-five hundred dollars a year he had received at the Rouncefield Clinic, but on evenings when he was tired it dropped to fifteen hundred, and one evening when they had Burgundy he raised it to thirty-five hundred.

When his first monthly check came, neat in a little sealed envelope, he dared not look at it. He took it home to Leora. In their hotel room they stared at the envelope as though it was likely to contain poison. Martin opened it shakily; he stared, and whispered, "Oh, those decent people! They're paying me—this is for four hundred and twenty dollars—they're paying me five thousand a year!"

Mrs. Holabird, a white kitten of a woman, helped Leora find a three-room flat with a spacious living-room, in an old house near Gramercy Park, and helped her furnish it with good bits, second-hand. When Martin was permitted to look he cried, "I hope we stay here for fifty years!"

This was the Grecian isle where they found peace. Presently they had friends: the Holabirds, Dr. Billy Smith—the thin-bearded bio-chemist, who had an intelligent taste in music and German beer—an anatomist whom Martin met at a Winnemac alumni dinner, and always Max Gottlieb.

Gottlieb had found his own serenity. In the Seventies he had a brown small flat, smelling of tobacco and leather books. His son Robert had graduated from City College and gone bustlingly into business. Miriam kept up her music while she guarded her father—a dumpling of a girl, holy fire behind the deceptive flesh. After an evening of Gottlieb's acrid doubting, Martin was inspired to hasten to the laboratory and attempt a thousand new queries into the laws of microörganisms, a task which usually began with blasphemously destroying all the work he had recently done.

Even Terry Wickett became more tolerable. Martin perceived that Wickett's snarls were partly a Clif Clawson misconception of humor, but partly a resentment, as great as Gottlieb's, of the morphological scientists who ticket things with the nicest little tickets, who name things and rename them and never analyze them. Wickett often worked all night; he was to be seen in shirt-sleeves, his sulky red hair rumpled, sitting with a stop-watch before a constant temperature bath for hours. Now and then it was a relief to have the surly intentness of Wickett instead of the elegance of Rippleton Holabird, which demanded from Martin so much painful elegance in turn, at a time when he was sunk beyond sounding in his experimentation.

Chapter XXVII

HIS WORK began fumblingly. There were days when, for all the joy of it, he dreaded lest Tubbs stride in and bellow, "What are you doing here? You're the wrong Arrowsmith! Get out!"

He had isolated twenty strains of staphylococcus germs and he was testing them to discover which of them was most active in producing a hemolytic, a blood-disintegrating, toxin, so that he might produce an antitoxin.

There were picturesque moments when, after centrifuging, the organisms lay in coiling cloudy masses at the bottoms of the tubes; or when the red corpuscles were completely dissolved and the opaque brick-red liquid turned to the color of pale wine. But most of the processes were incomparably tedious: removing samples of the culture every six hours, making salt suspensions of corpuscles in small tubes, recording the results.

He never knew they were tedious.

Tubbs came in now and then, found him busy, patted his shoulder, said something which sounded like French and might even have been French, and gave vague encouragement; while Gottlieb imperturbably told him to go ahead, and now and then stirred him by showing his own notebooks (they were full of figures and abbreviations, stupid-seeming as invoices of calico) or by speaking of his own work, in a vocabulary as heathenish as Tibetan magic:

"Arrhenius and Madsen have made a contribution toward bringing immunity reactions under the mass action law, but I hope to show that antigen-antibody combinations occur in stoicheiometric proportions when certain variables are held constant."

"Oh, yes, I see," said Martin; and to himself: "Well, I darn' near a quarter understand that! Oh, Lord, if they'll only give me a little time and not send me back to tacking up diphtheria posters!"

When he had obtained a satisfactory toxin, Martin began his effort to find an antitoxin. He made vast experiments with no results. Sometimes he was certain that he had something, but when he rechecked his experiments he was bleakly certain that he hadn't. Once he rushed into Gottlieb's laboratory with the announcement of the antitoxin, whereupon with affection and several discomforting questions and the present of a box of real Egyptian cigarettes, Gottlieb showed him that he had not considered certain dilutions.

With all his amateurish fumbling, Martin had one characteristic without which there can be no science: a wide-ranging, sniffing, snuffling, undignified, unselfdramatizing curiosity, and it drove him on.

II

While he puttered his insignificant way through the early years of the Great European War, the McGurk Institute had a lively existence under its placid surface.

Martin may not have learned much in the matter of antibodies but he did learn the secret of the Institute, and he saw that behind all its quiet industriousness was Capitola McGurk, the Great White Uplifter.

Capitola, Mrs. Ross McGurk, had been opposed to woman suffrage—until she learned that women were certain to get the vote—but she was a complete controller of virtuous affairs. Ross McGurk had bought the Institute not only to glorify himself but to divert Capitola and keep her itching fingers out of his shipping and mining and lumber interests, which would not too well have borne the investigations of a Great White Uplifter.

Ross McGurk was at the time a man of fifty-four, second generation of California railroad men; a graduate of Yale; big, suave, dignified, cheerful, unscrupulous. Even in 1908, when he had founded the Institute, he had had too many houses, too many servants, too much food, and no children, because Capitola considered "that sort of thing detrimental to women with large responsibilities." In the Institute he found each year more satisfaction, more excuse for having lived.

When Gottlieb arrived, McGurk went up to look him over. McGurk had bullied Dr. Tubbs now and then; Tubbs was compelled to scurry to his office as though he were a messenger boy; yet when he saw the saturnine eyes of Gottlieb, McGurk looked interested; and the two men, the bulky, clothes-conscious, powerful, reticent American and the cynical, simple, power-despising European, became friends. McGurk would slip away from a conference affecting the commerce of a whole West Indian island to sit on a high stool, silent, and watch Gottlieb work.

"Some day when I quit hustling and wake up, I'm going to become your garçon, Max," said McGurk, and Gottlieb answered, "I don't know—you haf imagination, Ross, but I t'ink you are too late to get a training in reality. Now if you do not mind eating at Childs's, we will avoid your very expostulatory Regal Hall, and I shall invite you to lunch."

But Capitola did not join their communion.

Gottlieb's arrogance had returned, and with Capitola McGurk he needed it. She had such interesting little problems for her husband's pensioners to attack. Once, in excitement, she visited Gottlieb's laboratory to tell him that large numbers of persons die of cancer, and why didn't he drop this anti-whatever-it-was and find a cure for cancer, which would be ever so nice for all of them.

But her real grievance arose when, after Rippleton Holabird had agreed to give midnight supper on the roof of the Institute to one of her most intellectual dinner-parties, she telephoned to Gottlieb, merely asking, "Would it be too much trouble for you to go down and open your lab, so we can all enjoy just a tiny peep at it?" and he answered:

"It would! Good night!"

Capitola protested to her husband. He listened—at least he seemed to listen—and remarked:

"Cap, I don't mind your playing the fool with the footmen. They've got to stand it. But if you get funny with Max, I'll simply shut up the whole Institute, and then you won't have anything to talk about at the Colony Club. And it certainly does beat the deuce that a man worth thirty million dollars—at least a fellow that's got that much—can't find a clean pair of pajamas. No, I *won't* have a valet! Oh, please now, Capitola, please quit being high-minded and let me go to sleep, will you!"

But Capitola was uncontrollable, especially in the matter of the monthly dinners which she gave at the Institute.

III

The first of the McGurk Scientific Dinners which Martin and Leora witnessed was a particularly important and explanatory dinner, because the guest of honor was Major-General Sir Isaac Mallard, the London surgeon, who was in America with a British War Mission. He had already beautifully let himself be shown through the Institute; he had been Sir Isaac'd by Dr. Tubbs and every researcher except Terry Wickett; he remembered meeting Rippleton Holabird in London, or said he remembered; and he admired Gladys the Centrifuge.

The dinner began with one misfortune in that Terry Wickett, who hitherto could be depended upon to stay decently away, now appeared, volunteering to the wife of an ex-ambassador, "I simply couldn't duck this spread, with dear Sir Isaac coming. Say, if I hadn't told you, you wouldn't hardly think my dress-suit was rented, would you! Have you noticed that Sir Isaac is getting so he doesn't tear the carpet with his spurs any more? I wonder if he still kills all his mastoid patients?"

There was vast music, vaster food; there were uncomfortable scientists explaining to golden cooing ladies, in a few words, just what they were up to and what in the next twenty years they hoped to be up to; there were the cooing ladies themselves, observing in tones of pretty rebuke, "But I'm afraid you haven't yet made it as clear as you might." There were the cooing ladies' husbands—college graduates, manipulators of oil stocks or of corporation law—who sat ready to give to anybody who desired it their opinion that while antitoxins might be racy, what we really needed was a good substitute for rubber.

There was Rippleton Holabird, being charming.

And in the pause of the music, there suddenly was Terry Wickett, saying to quite an important woman, one of Capitola's most useful friends, "Yes, his name is spelled G-o-t-t-l-i-e-b but it's pronounced Gottdamn."

But such outsiders as Wickett and such silent riders as Martin and Leora and such totally absent members as Max

Gottlieb were few, and the dinner waxed magnificently to a love-feast when Dr. Tubbs and Sir Isaac Mallard paid compliments to each other, to Capitola, to the sacred soil of France, to brave little Belgium, to American hospitality, to British love of privacy, and to the extremely interesting things a young man with a sense of coöperation might do in modern science.

The guests were conducted through the Institute. They inspected the marine biology aquarium, the pathological museum, and the animal house, at sight of which one sprightly lady demanded of Wickett, "Oh, the poor little guinea pigs and darling rabbicks! Now honestly, Doctor, don't you think it would be ever so much nicer if you let them go free, and just worked with your test-tubes?"

A popular physician, whose practise was among rich women, none of them west of Fifth Avenue, said to the sprightly lady, "I think you're absolutely right. I never have to kill any poor wee little beasties to get my knowledge!"

With astounding suddenness Wickett took his hat and went away.

The sprightly lady said, "You see, he didn't dare stand up to a real argument. Oh, Dr. Arrowsmith, of course I know how wonderful Ross McGurk and Dr. Tubbs and all of you are, but I must say I'm disappointed in your laboratories. I'd expected there'd be such larky retorts and electric furnaces and everything but, honestly, I don't see a single thing that's interesting, and I do think all you clever people ought to do *something* for us, now that you've coaxed us all the way down here. Can't you or somebody create life out of turtle eggs, or whatever it is? Oh, please do! Pretty please! Or at least, do put on one of these cunnin' dentist coats that you wear."

Then Martin also went rapidly away, accompanied by a furious Leora, who in the taxicab announced that she had desired to taste the champagne-cup which she had observed on the buffet, and that her husband was little short of a fool.

IV

Thus, however satisfying his work, Martin began to wonder about the perfection of his sanctuary; to wonder why Gottlieb should be so insulting at lunch to neat Dr. Sholtheis, the industrious head of the Department of Epidemiology, and why Dr. Sholtheis should endure the insults; to wonder why Dr. Tubbs, when he wandered into one's laboratory, should gurgle, "The one thing for you to keep in view in all your work is the ideal of coöperation"; to wonder why so ardent a physiologist as Rippleton Holabird should all day long be heard conferring with Tubbs instead of sweating at his bench.

Holabird had, five years before, done one bit of research which had taken his name into scientific journals throughout the world: he had studied the effect of the extirpation of the anterior lobes of a dog's brain on its ability to find its way through the laboratory. Martin had read of that research before he had thought of going to McGurk; on his arrival he was thrilled to have it chronicled by the master himself; but when he had heard Holabird refer to it a dozen times he was considerably less thrilled, and he speculated whether all his life Holabird would go on being "the man—*you* remember—the chap that did the big stunt, whatever it was, with locomotion in dogs or something."

Martin speculated still more as he perceived that all his colleagues were secretly grouped in factions.

Tubbs, Holabird, and perhaps Tubbs's secretary, Pearl Robbins, were the ruling caste. It was murmured that Holabird hoped some day to be made Assistant Director, an office which was to be created for him. Gottlieb, Terry Wickett, and Dr. Nicholas Yeo, that long-mustached and rustic biologist whom Martin had first taken for a carpenter, formed an independent faction of their own, and however much he disliked the boisterous Wickett, Martin was dragged into it.

Dr. William Smith, with his little beard and a notion of mushrooms formed in Paris, kept to himself. Dr. Sholtheis, who had been born to a synagogue in Russia but who was now the most zealous high-church Episcopalian in Yonkers, was constantly in his polite small way trying to have his scientific work commended by Gottlieb. In the Department of Bio-Physics, the good-natured chief was reviled and envied by his own assistant. And in the whole Institute there was not one man who would, in all states of liquor, assert that the work of any other scientist anywhere was completely sound, or that there was a single one of his rivals who had not stolen ideas from him. No rocking-chair clique on a summer-hotel porch, no knot of actors, ever whispered more scandal or hinted more warmly of complete idiocy in their confrères than did these uplifted scientists.

But these discoveries Martin could shut out by closing his door, and he had that to do now which deafened him to the mutters of intrigue.

V

For once Gottlieb did not amble into his laboratory but curtly summoned him. In a corner of Gottlieb's office, a den opening from his laboratory, was Terry Wickett, rolling a cigarette and looking sardonic.

Gottlieb observed, "Martin, I haf taken the privilege of talking you over with Terry, and we concluded that you haf done well enough now so it is time you stop puttering and go to work."

"I thought I was working, sir!"

All the wide placidness of his halcyon days was gone; he saw himself driven back to Pickerbaughism.

Wickett intruded, "No, you haven't. You've just been showing that you're a bright boy who might work if he only knew something."

While Martin turned on Wickett with a "Who the devil are you?" expression, Gottlieb went on:

"The fact is, Martin, you can do nothing till you know a little mathematics. If you are not going to be a cookbook bacteriologist, like most of them, you must be able to handle some of the fundamentals of science. All living things are physico-chemical machines. Then how can you make progress if you do not know physical chemistry, and how can you know physical chemistry without much mathematics?"

"Yuh," said Wickett, "you're lawn-mowing and daisy-picking, not digging."

Martin faced them. "But rats, Wickett, a man can't know everything. I'm a bacteriologist, not a physicist. Strikes me a fellow ought to use his insight, not just a chest of tools, to make discoveries. A good sailor could find his way at sea even if he didn't have instruments, and a whole *Lusitania*-ful of junk wouldn't make a good sailor out of a dub. Man ought to develop his brain, not depend on tools."

"Ye-uh, but if there were charts and quadrants in existence, a sailor that cruised off without 'em would be a chump!"

For half an hour Martin defended himself, not too politely, before the gem-like Gottlieb, the granite Wickett. All the while he knew that he was sickeningly ignorant.

They ceased to take interest. Gottlieb was looking at his note-books, Wickett was clumping off to work. Martin glared at Gottlieb. The man meant so much that he could be furious with him as he would have been with Leora, with his own self.

"I'm sorry you think I don't know anything," he raged, and departed with the finest dramatic violence. He slammed into his own laboratory, felt freed, then wretched. Without volition, like a drunken man, he stormed to Wickett's room, protesting, "I suppose you're right. My physical chemistry is nix, and my math rotten. What am I going to do—what am I going to do?"

The embarrassed barbarian grumbled, "Well, for Pete's sake, Slim, don't worry. The old man and I were just egging you on. Fact is, he's tickled to death about the careful way you're starting in. About the math—probably you're better off than the Holy Wren and Tubbs right now; you've forgotten all the math you ever knew, and they never knew any. Gosh all fishhooks! Science is supposed to mean Knowledge—from the Greek, a handsome language spoken by the good old booze-hoisting Helleens—and the way most of the science boys resent having to stop writing little jeweled papers or giving teas and sweat at getting some knowledge certainly does make me a grand booster for the human race. My own math isn't any too good, Slim, but if you'd like to have me come around evenings and tutor you— Free, I mean!"

Thus began the friendship between Martin and Terry Wickett; thus began a change in Martin's life whereby he gave up three or four hours of wholesome sleep each night to grind over matters which every one is assumed to know, and almost every one does not know.

He took up algebra; found that he had forgotten most of it; cursed over the competition of the indefatigable A and the indolent B who walk from Y to Z; hired a Columbia tutor; and finished the subject, with a spurt of something like interest in regard to quadratic equations, in six weeks . . . while Leora listened, watched, waited, made sandwiches, and laughed at the tutor's jokes.

By the end of his first nine months at McGurk, Martin had reviewed trigonometry and analytic geometry and he was finding differential calculus romantic. But he made the mistake of telling Terry Wickett how much he knew.

Terry croaked, "Don't trust math too much, son," and he so confused him with references to the thermo-dynamical derivation of the mass action law, and to the oxidation reduction potential, that he stumbled again into raging humility, again saw himself an impostor and a tenth-rater.

He read the classics of physical science: Copernicus and Galileo, Lavoisier, Newton, LaPlace, Descartes, Faraday. He became completely bogged in Newton's "Fluxions"; he spoke of Newton to Tubbs and found that the illustrious Director knew nothing about him. He cheerfully mentioned this to Terry, and was shockingly cursed for his conceit as a "nouveau cultured," as a "typical enthusiastic convert," and so returned to the work whose end is satisfying because there is never an end.

His life did not seem edifying nor in any degree amusing. When Tubbs peeped into his laboratory he found a humorless young man going about his tests of hemolytic toxins with no apparent flair for the Real Big Thing in Science, which was coöperation and being efficient. Tubbs tried to set him straight with "Are you quite sure you're following a regular demarked line in your work?"

It was Leora who bore the real tedium.

She sat quiet (a frail child, only up to one's shoulder, not nine minutes older than at marriage, nine years before), or she napped inoffensively, in the long living-room of their flat, while he worked over his dreary digit-infested books till one, till two, and she politely awoke to let him worry at her, "But look here now, I've got to keep up my research at the same time. God, I am so tired!"

She dragged him away for an illegal five-day walk on Cape Cod, in March. He sat between the Twin Lights at Chatham, and fumed, "I'm going back and tell Terry and Gottlieb they can go to the devil with their crazy physical chemistry. I've had enough, now I've done math," and she commented, "Yes, I certainly would—though isn't it funny how Dr. Gottlieb always seems to be right?"

He was so absorbed in staphylolysin and in calculus that he did not realize the world was about to be made safe for democracy. He was a little dazed when America entered the war.

VI

Dr. Tubbs dashed to Washington to offer the services of the Institute to the War Department.

All the members of the staff, except Gottlieb and two others who declined to be so honored, were made officers and told to run out and buy nice uniforms.

Tubbs became a Colonel, Rippleton Holabird a Major, Martin and Wickett and Billy Smith were Captains. But the garçons had no military rank whatever, nor any military duties except the polishing of brown riding-boots and leather puttees, which the several warriors wore as pleased their fancies or their legs. And the most belligerent of all, Miss Pearl Robbins, she who at tea heroically slaughtered not only German men but all their women and viperine children, was wickedly unrecognized and had to make up a uniform for herself.

The only one of them who got nearer to the front than Liberty Street was Terry Wickett, who suddenly asked for leave, was transferred to the artillery, and sailed off to France.

He apologized to Martin: "I'm ashamed of chucking my work like this, and I certainly don't want to kill Germans—I mean not any more'n I want to kill most people—but I never could resist getting into a big show. Say, Slim, keep an eye on Pa Gottlieb, will you? This has hit him bad. He's got a bunch of nephews and so on in the German army, and the patriots like Big Foot Pearl will give an exhibit of idealism by persecuting him. So long, Slim, take care y'self."

Martin had vaguely protested at being herded into the army. The war was to him chiefly another interruption to his work, like Pickerbaughism, like earning his living at Wheatsylvania. But when he had gone strutting forth in uniform, it was so enjoyable that for several weeks he was a standard patriot. He had never looked so well, so taut and erect, as in khaki. It was enchanting to be saluted by privates, quite as enchanting to return the salute in the dignified, patronizing, all-comrades-together splendor which Martin shared with the other doctors, professors, lawyers, brokers, authors, and former socialist intellectuals who were his fellow-officers.

But in a month the pleasures of being a hero became mechanical, and Martin longed for soft shirts, easy shoes, and clothes with reasonable pockets. His puttees were a nuisance to wear and an inferno to put on; his collar pinched his neck and jabbed his chin; and it was wearing on a man who sat up till three, on the perilous duty of studying calculus, to be snappy at every salute.

Under the martinet eye of Col. Director Dr. A. DeWitt Tubbs he had to wear his uniform, at least recognizable portions of it, at the Institute, but by evening he slipped into the habit of sneaking into citizen clothes, and when he went with Leora to the movies he had an agreeable feeling of being Absent Without Leave, of risking at every street corner arrest by the Military Police and execution at dawn.

Unfortunately no M.P. ever looked at him. But one evening when in an estimable and innocent manner he was looking at the remains of a gunman who had just been murdered by another gunman, he realized that Major Rippleton Holabird was standing by, glaring. For once the Major was unpleasant:

"Captain, does it seem to you that this is quite playing the game, to wear mufti? We, unfortunately, with our scientific work, haven't the privilege of joining the Boys who are up against the real thing, but we are under orders just as if we were in the trenches—where *some* of us would so much like to be again! Captain, I trust I shall never again see you breaking the order about being in uniform, or—uh—"

Martin blurted to Leora, later:

"I'm sick of hearing about his being wounded. Nothing that I can see to prevent his going back to the trenches. Wound's all right now. I want to be patriotic, but my patriotism is chasing antitoxins, doing my job, not wearing a particular kind of pants and a particular set of ideas about the Germans. Mind you, I'm anti-German all right—I think they're probably just as bad as we are. Oh, let's go back and do some more calculus. . . . Darling, my working nights doesn't bore you too much, does it?"

Leora had cunning. When she could not be enthusiastic, she could be unannoyingly silent.

At the Institute Martin perceived that he was not the only defender of his country who was not comfortable in the garb of heroes. The most dismal of the staff-members was Dr. Nicholas Yeo, the Yankee sandy-mustached head of the Department of Biology.

Yeo had put on Major's uniform, but he never felt neighborly with it. (He knew he was a Major, because Col. Dr. Tubbs had told him he was, and he knew that this was a Major's uniform, because the clothing salesman said so.) He walked out of the McGurk Building in a melancholy, deprecatory way, with one breeches leg bulging over his riding-boots; and however piously he tried, he never remembered to button his blouse over the violet-flowered shirts which, he often confided, you could buy ever so cheap on Eighth Avenue.

But Major Dr. Yeo had one military triumph. He hoarsely explained to Martin, as they were marching to the completely militarized dining-hall:

"Say, Arrowsmith, do you ever get balled up about this saluting? Darn it, I never can figure out what all these insignia mean. One time I took a Salvation Army Lieutenant for a Y.M.C.A. General, or maybe he was a Portygee. But I've got the idea now!" Yeo laid his finger beside his large nose, and produced wisdom: "Whenever I see any fellow in uniform that looks older than I am, I salute him—my nephew, Ted, has drilled me so I salute swell now—and if he don't salute back, well, Lord, I just think about my work and don't fuss. If you look at it scientifically, this military life isn't so awful' hard after all!"

VII

Always, in Paris or in Bonn, Max Gottlieb had looked to America as a land which, in its freedom from Royalist tradition, in its contact with the realities of cornfields and blizzards and town-meetings, had set its face against the puerile pride of war. He believed that he had ceased to be a German, now, and become a countryman of Lincoln.

The European War was the one thing, besides his discharge from Winnemac, which had ever broken his sardonic serenity. In the war he could see no splendor nor hope, but only crawling tragedy. He treasured his months of work and good talk in France, in England, in Italy; he loved his French and English and Italian friends as he loved his ancient *Korpsbrüder*, and very well indeed beneath his mocking did he love the Germans with whom he had drudged and drunk.

His sister's sons—on home-craving vacations he had seen them, in babyhood, in boyhood, in ruffling youngmanhood—went out with the Kaiser's colors in 1914; one of them became an Oberst, much decorated, one existed insignificantly, and one was dead and stinking in ten days. This he sadly endured, as later he endured his son Robert's going out as an American lieutenant, to fight his own cousins. What struck down this man to whom abstractions and scientific laws were more than kindly flesh was the mania of hate which overcame the unmilitaristic America to which he had emigrated in protest against Junkerdom.

Incredulously he perceived women asserting that all Germans were baby-killers, universities barring the language of Heine, orchestras outlawing the music of Beethoven, professors in uniform bellowing at clerks, and the clerks never protesting.

It is uncertain whether the real hurt was to his love for America or to his egotism, that he should have guessed so grotesquely; it is curious that he who had so denounced the machine-made education of the land should yet have been surprised when it turned blithely to the old, old, mechanical mockeries of war.

When the Institute sanctified the war, he found himself regarded not as the great and impersonal immunologist but as a suspect German Jew.

True, the Terry who went off to the artillery did not look upon him dourly, but Major Rippleton Holabird became erect and stiff when they passed in the corridor. When Gottlieb insisted to Tubbs at lunch, "I am villing to admit every virtue of the French—I am very fond of that so individual people—but on the theory of probabilities I suggest that there must be some good Germans out of sixty millions," then Col. Dr. Tubbs commanded, "In this time of world tragedy, it does not seem to me particularly becoming to try to be flippant, Dr. Gottlieb!"

In shops and on the elevated trains, little red-faced sweaty people when they heard his accent glared at him, and growled one to another, "There's one of them damn' barb'rous well-poisoning Huns!" and however contemptuous he might be, however much he strove for ignoring pride, their nibbling reduced him from arrogant scientist to an insecure, raw-nerved, shrinking old man.

And once a hostess who of old time had been proud to know him, a hostess whose maiden name was Straufnabel and who had married into the famous old Anglican family of Rosemont, when Gottlieb bade her *"Auf Wiedersehen"* cried out upon him, "Dr. Gottlieb, I'm very sorry, but the use of that disgusting language is not permitted in this house!"

He had almost recovered from the anxieties of Winnemac and the Hunziker factory; he had begun to expand, to entertain people—scientists, musicians, talkers. Now he was thrust back into himself. With Terry gone, he trusted only Miriam and Martin and Ross McGurk; and his deep-set wrinkle-lidded eyes looked ever on sadness.

But he could still be tart. He suggested that Capitola ought to have in the window of her house a Service Flag with a star for every person at the Institute who had put on uniform.

She took it quite seriously, and did it.

VIII

The military duties of the McGurk staff did not consist entirely in wearing uniforms, receiving salutes, and listening to Col. Dr. Tubbs's luncheon lectures on "the part America will inevitably play in the reconstruction of a Democratic Europe."

They prepared sera; the assistant in the Department of Bio-Physics was inventing electrified wire entanglements; Dr. Billy Smith, who six months before had been singing

Student Lieder at Lüchow's, was working on poison gas to be used against all singers of *Lieder*; and to Martin was assigned the manufacture of lipovaccine, a suspension of finely ground typhoid and paratyphoid organisms in oil. It was a greasy job, and dull. Martin was faithful enough about it, and gave to it almost every morning, but he blasphemed more than usual and he unholily welcomed scientific papers in which lipovaccines were condemned as inferior to ordinary salt solutions.

He was conscious of Gottlieb's sorrowing and tried to comfort him.

It was Martin's most pitiful fault that he was not very kind to shy people and lonely people and stupid old people; he was not cruel to them, he simply was unconscious of them or so impatient of their fumbling that he avoided them. Whenever Leora taxed him with it he grumbled:

"Well, but— I'm too much absorbed in my work, or in doping stuff out, to waste time on morons. And it's a good thing. Most people above the grade of hog do so much chasing around after a lot of vague philanthropy that they never get anything done—and most of your confounded shy people get spiritually pauperized. Oh, it's so much easier to be good-natured and purring and self-congratulatory and generally footless than it is to pound ahead and keep yourself strictly for your own work, the work that gets somewhere. Very few people have the courage to be decently selfish—not answer letters—and demand the right to work. If they had their way, these sentimentalists would've had a Newton—yes, or probably a Christ!—giving up everything they did for the world to address meetings and listen to the troubles of cranky old maids. Nothing takes so much courage as to keep hard and clear-headed."

And he hadn't even that courage.

When Leora had made complaint, he would be forcibly kind to all sorts of alarmed stray beggars for a day or two, then drift back into his absorption. There were but two people whose unhappiness could always pierce him: Leora and Gottlieb.

Though he was busier than he had known any one could ever be, with lipovaccines in the morning, physical chemistry in the evening and, at all sorts of intense hours between, the continuation of his staphylolysin research, he gave what time he could to seeking out Gottlieb and warming his vanity by reverent listening.

Then his research wiped out everything else, made him forget Gottlieb and Leora and all his briskness about studying, made him turn his war work over to others, and confounded night and day in one insane flaming blur as he realized that he had something not unworthy of a Gottlieb, something at the mysterious source of life.

Chapter XXVIII

CAPTAIN MARTIN ARROWSMITH, M.R.C., came home to his good wife Leora, wailing, "I'm so rotten tired, and I feel kind of discouraged. I haven't accomplished a darn' thing in this whole year at McGurk. Sterile. No good. And I'm hanged if I'll study calculus this evening. Let's go to the movies. Won't even change to regular human clothes. Too tired."

"All right honey," said Leora. "But let's have dinner here. I bought a wonderful ole fish this afternoon."

Through the film Martin gave his opinion, as a captain and as a doctor, that it seemed improbable a mother should not know her daughter after an absence of ten years. He was restless and rational, which is not a mood in which to view the cinema. When they came blinking out of that darkness lit only from the shadowy screen, he snorted, "I'm going back to the lab. I'll put you in a taxi."

"Oh, let the beastly thing go for one night."

"Now that's unfair! I haven't worked late for three or four nights now!"

"Then take me along."

"Nope. I have a hunch I may be working all night."

Liberty Street, as he raced along it, was sleeping below its towers. It was McGurk's order that the elevator to the Institute should run all night, and indeed three or four of the twenty staff-members did sometimes use it after respectable hours.

That morning Martin had isolated a new strain of staphylococcus bacteria from the gluteal carbuncle of a patient in the Lower Manhattan Hospital, a carbuncle which was healing with unusual rapidity. He had placed a bit of the pus in broth and incubated it. In eight hours a good growth of bacteria had appeared. Before going wearily home he had returned the flask to the incubator.

He was not particularly interested in it, and now, in his laboratory, he removed his military blouse, looked down to the lights on the blue-black river, smoked a little, thought what a dog he was not to be gentler to Leora, and damned

Bert Tozer and Pickerbaugh and Tubbs and anybody else who was handy to his memory before he absent-mindedly wavered to the incubator, and found that the flask, in which there should have been a perceptible cloudy growth, had no longer any signs of bacteria—of staphylococci.

"Now what the hell!" he cried. "Why, the broth's as clear as when I seeded it! Now what the— Think of this fool accident coming up just when I was going to start something new!"

He hastened from the incubator, in a closet off the corridor, to his laboratory and, holding the flask under a strong light, made certain that he had seen aright. He fretfully prepared a slide from the flask contents and examined it under the microscope. He discovered nothing but shadows of what had been bacteria: thin outlines, the form still there but the cell substance gone; minute skeletons on an infinitesimal battlefield.

He raised his head from the microscope, rubbed his tired eyes, reflectively rubbed his neck—his blouse was off, his collar on the floor, his shirt open at the throat. He considered:

"Something funny here. This culture was growing all right, and now it's committed suicide. Never heard of bugs doing that before. I've hit something! What caused it? Some chemical change? Something organic?"

Now in Martin Arrowsmith there were no decorative heroisms, no genius for amours, no exotic wit, no edifyingly borne misfortunes. He presented neither picturesque elegance nor a moral message. He was full of hasty faults and of perverse honesty; a young man often unkindly, often impolite. But he had one gift: a curiosity whereby he saw nothing as ordinary. Had he been an acceptable hero, like Major Rippleton Holabird, he would have chucked the contents of the flask into the sink, avowed with pretty modesty, "Silly! I've made some error!" and gone his ways. But Martin, being Martin, walked prosaically up and down his laboratory, snarling, "Now there was some *cause* for that, and I'm going to find out what it was."

He did have one romantic notion: he would telephone to Leora and tell her that splendor was happening, and she wasn't to worry about him. He fumbled down the corridor, lighting matches, trying to find electric switches.

At night all halls are haunted. Even in the smirkingly new McGurk Building there had been a bookkeeper who committed suicide. As Martin groped he was shakily conscious of feet padding behind him, of shapes which leered from doorways and insolently vanished, of ancient bodiless horrors, and when he found the switch he rejoiced in the blessing and security of sudden light that recreated the world.

At the Institute telephone switchboard he plugged in wherever it seemed reasonable. Once he thought he was talking to Leora, but it proved to be a voice, sexless and intolerant, which said "Nummer pleeeeeze" with a taut alertness impossible to any one so indolent as Leora. Once it was a voice which slobbered, "Is this Sarah?" then, "I don't want *you*! Ring off, will yuh!" Once a girl pleaded, "Honestly, Billy, I did try to get there but the boss came in at five and he said—"

As for the rest it was only a burring; the sound of seven million people hungry for sleep or love or money.

He observed, "Oh, rats, I guess Lee'll have gone to bed by now," and felt his way back to the laboratory.

A detective, hunting the murderer of bacteria, he stood with his head back, scratching his chin, scratching his memory for like cases of microörganisms committing suicide or being slain without perceptible cause. He rushed up-stairs to the library, consulted the American and English authorities and, laboriously, the French and German. He found nothing.

He worried lest there might, somehow, have been no living staphylococci in the pus which he had used for seeding the broth—none there to die. At a hectic run, not stopping for lights, bumping corners and sliding on the too perfect tile floor, he skidded down the stairs and galloped through the corridors to his room. He found the remains of the original pus, made a smear on a glass slide, and stained it with gentian-violet, nervously dribbling out one drop of the gorgeous dye. He sprang to the microscope. As he bent over the brass tube and focused the objective, into the gray-lavender circular field of vision rose to existence the grape-like clusters of staphylococcus germs, purple dots against the blank plane.

"Staph in it, all right!" he shouted.

Then he forgot Leora, war, night, weariness, success, everything, as he charged into preparations for an experiment, his first great experiment. He paced furiously, rather dizzy. He shook himself into calmness and settled down at a table, among rings and spirals of cigarette smoke, to list on small sheets of paper all the possible causes of suicide in the bacteria—all the questions he had to answer and the experiments which should answer them.

It might be that alkali in an improperly cleaned flask had caused the clearing of the culture. It might be some anti-staph substance existing in the pus, or something liberated by the staphylococci themselves. It might be some peculiarity of this particular broth.

Each of these had to be tested.

He pried open the door of the glass-storeroom, shattering the lock. He took new flasks, cleaned them, plugged them with cotton, and placed them in the hot-air oven to sterilize. He found other batches of broth—as a matter of fact he stole them, from Gottlieb's private and highly sacred supply in the ice-box. He filtered some of the clarified culture through a sterile porcelain filter, and added it to his regular staphylococcus strains.

And, perhaps most important of all, he discovered that he was out of cigarettes.

Incredulously he slapped each of his pockets, and went the round and slapped them all over again. He looked into his discarded military blouse; had a cheering idea about having seen cigarettes in a drawer; did not find them; and brazenly marched into the room where hung the aprons and jackets of the technicians. Furiously he pilfered pockets, and found a dozen beautiful cigarettes in a wrinkled and flattened paper case.

To test each of the four possible causes of the flask's clearing he prepared and seeded with bacteria a series of flasks under varying conditions, and set them away in the incubator at body temperature. Till the last flask was put away, his hand was steady, his worn face calm. He was above all nervousness, free from all uncertainty, a professional going about his business.

By this time it was six o'clock of a fine wide August morning, and as he ceased his swift work, as taut nerves slackened, he looked out of his lofty window and was conscious of the world below: bright roofs, jubilant towers, and a high-decked Sound steamer swaggering up the glossy river.

He was completely fagged; he was, like a surgeon after a battle, like a reporter during an earthquake, perhaps a little insane; but sleepy he was not. He cursed the delay involved in the growth of the bacteria, without which he could not discover the effect of the various sorts of broths and bacterial strains, but choked his impatience.

He mounted the noisy slate stairway to the lofty world of the roof. He listened at the door of the Institute's animal house. The guinea pigs, awake and nibbling, were making a sound like that of a wet cloth rubbed on glass in window-cleaning. He stamped his foot, and in fright they broke out in their strange sound of fear, like the cooing of doves.

He marched violently up and down, refreshed by the soaring sky, till he was calmed to hunger. Again he went pillaging. He found chocolate belonging to an innocent technician; he even invaded the office of the Director and in the desk of the Diana-like Pearl Robbins unearthed tea and a kettle (as well as a lip-stick, and a love-letter beginning "My Little Ickles"). He made himself a profoundly bad cup of tea, then, his whole body dragging, returned to his table to set down elaborately, in a shabby, nearly-filled note-book, every step of his experiment.

After seven he worked out the operation of the telephone switchboard and called the Lower Manhattan Hospital. Could Dr. Arrowsmith have some more pus from the same carbuncle? What? It'd healed? Curse it! No more of that material.

He hesitated over waiting for Gottlieb's arrival, to tell him of the discovery, but determined to keep silence till he should have determined whether it was an accident. Eyes wide, too wrought up to sleep in the subway, he fled uptown to tell Leora. He had to tell some one! Waves of fear, doubt, certainty, and fear again swept over him; his ears rang and his hands trembled.

He rushed up to the flat; he bawled "Lee! Lee!" before he had unlocked the door. And she was gone.

He gaped. The flat breathed emptiness. He searched it again. She had slept there, she had had a cup of coffee, but she had vanished.

He was at once worried lest there had been an accident, and furious that she should not have been here at the great hour. Sullenly he made breakfast for himself. . . . It is strange that excellent bacteriologists and chemists should scramble eggs so waterily, should make such bitter coffee and be so casual about dirty spoons. . . . By the time he had finished the mess he was ready to believe that Leora had left him forever. He quavered, "I've neglected her a lot." Sluggishly, an old man now, he started for the Institute, and at the entrance to the subway he met her.

She wailed, "I was so worried! I couldn't get you on the 'phone. I went clear down to the Institute to see what'd happened to you."

He kissed her, very competently, and raved, "God, woman, I've got it! The real big stuff! I've found something, not a chemical you put in I mean, that eats bugs—dissolves 'em—kills 'em. May be a big new step in therapeutics. Oh, no, rats, I don't suppose it really is. Prob'ly just another of my bulls."

She sought to reassure him but he did not wait. He dashed down to the subway, promising to telephone to her. By ten, he was peering into his incubator.

There was a cloudy appearance of bacteria in all the flasks except those in which he had used broth from the original alarming flask. In these, the mysterious murderer of germs had prevented the growth of the new bacteria which he had introduced.

"Great stuff," he said.

He returned the flasks to the incubator, recorded his observations, went again to the library, and searched handbooks, bound proceedings of societies, periodicals in three languages. He had acquired a reasonable scientific French and German. It is doubtful whether he could have bought a drink or asked the way to the Kursaal in either language, but he understood the universal Hellenistic scientific jargon, and he pawed through the heavy books, rubbing his eyes, which were filled with salty fire.

He remembered that he was an army officer and had lipovaccine to make this morning. He went to work, but he was so twitchy that he ruined the batch, called his patient garçon a fool, and after this injustice sent him out for a pint of whisky.

He had to have a confidant. He telephoned to Leora, lunched with her expensively, and asserted, "It still looks as if there were something to it." He was back in the Institute every hour that afternoon, glancing at his flasks, but between he tramped the streets, creaking with weariness, drinking too much coffee.

Every five minutes it came to him, as a quite new and ecstatic idea, "Why don't I go to sleep?" then remembered, and groaned, "No, I've got to keep going and watch every step. Can't leave it, or I'll have to begin all over again. But I'm so sleepy! Why don't I go to sleep?"

He dug down, before six, into a new layer of strength, and at six his examination showed that the flasks containing the original broth still had no growth of bacteria, and the flasks which he had seeded with the original pus had, like the first eccentric flask, after beginning to display a good growth of bacteria cleared up again under the slowly developing attack of the unknown assassin.

He sat down, drooping with relief. He had it! He stated in the conclusions of his first notes:

"I have observed a principle, which I shall temporarily call the X Principle, in pus from a staphylococcus infection, which checks the growth of several strains of staphylococcus, and which dissolves the staphylococci from the pus in question."

When he had finished, at seven, his head was on his notebook and he was asleep.

He awoke at ten, went home, ate like a savage, slept again, and was in the laboratory before dawn. His next rest was an hour that afternoon, sprawled on his laboratory table, with his garçon on guard; the next, a day and a half later, was eight hours in bed, from dawn till noon.

But in dreams he was constantly upsetting a rack of test-tubes or breaking a flask. He discovered an X Principle which dissolved chairs, tables, human beings. He went about smearing it on Bert Tozers and Dr. Bissexes and fiendishly watching them vanish, but accidentally he dropped it on Leora and saw her fading, and he woke screaming to find the real Leora's arms about him, while he sobbed, "Oh, I couldn't do anything without you! Don't ever leave me! I do love you so, even if this damned work does keep me tied up. Stay with me!"

While she sat by him on the frowsy bed, gay in her gingham, he went to sleep, to wake up three hours later and start off for the Institute, his eyes blood-glaring and set. She was ready for him with strong coffee, waiting on him silently, looking at him proudly, while he waved his arms, babbling:

"Gottlieb better not talk any more about the importance of new observations! The X Principle may not just apply to staph. Maybe you can sic it on any bug—cure any germ disease by it. Bug that lives on bugs! Or maybe it's a chemical principle, an enzyme. Oh, I don't know. But I will!"

As he bustled to the Institute he swelled with the certainty that after years of stumbling he had arrived. He had visions of his name in journals and textbooks; of scientific meetings cheering him. He had been an unknown among the experts of the Institute, and now he pitied all of them. But when he was back at his bench the grandiose aspirations faded and he was the sniffing, snuffling beagle, the impersonal worker. Before him, supreme joy of the investigator, new mountain-passes of work opened, and in him was new power.

II

For a week Martin's life had all the regularity of an escaped soldier in the enemy's country, with the same agitation and the same desire to prowl at night. He was always sterilizing flasks, preparing media of various hydrogen-ion concentrations, copying his old notes into a new book lovingly labeled "X Principle, Staph," and adding to it further observations. He tried, elaborately, with many flasks and many reseedings, to determine whether the X Principle would perpetuate itself indefinitely, whether when it was transmitted from tube to new tube of bacteria it would reappear, whether, growing by cell-division automatically, it was veritably a germ, a sub-germ infecting germs.

During the week Gottlieb occasionally peered over his shoulder, but Martin was unwilling to report until he should have proof, and one good night's sleep, and perhaps even a shave.

When he was sure that the X Principle did reproduce itself indefinitely, so that in the tenth tube it grew to have as much effect as in the first, then he solemnly called on Gottlieb and laid before him his results, with his plans for further investigation.

The old man tapped his thin fingers on the report, read it intently, looked up and, not wasting time in congratulations, vomited questions:

Have you done dis? Why have you not done dat? At what temperature is the activity of the Principle at its maximum? Is its activity manifested on agar-solid medium?

"This is my plan for new work. I think you'll find it includes most of your suggestions."

"Huh!" Gottlieb ran through it and snorted, "Why have you not planned to propagate it on dead staph? That is most important of all."

"Why?"

Gottlieb flew instantly to the heart of the jungle in which Martin had struggled for many days: "Because that will show whether you are dealing with a living virus."

Martin was humbled, but Gottlieb beamed:

"You haf a big thing. Now do not let the Director know about this and get enthusiastic too soon. I am glad, Martin!"

There was that in his voice which sent Martin swanking down the corridor, back to work—and to not sleeping.

What the X Principle was—chemical or germ—he could not determine, but certainly the original Principle flourished. It could be transmitted indefinitely; he determined the best temperature for it and found that it did not propagate on dead staphylococcus. When he added a drop containing the Principle to a growth of staphylococcus which was a gray film on the solid surface of agar, the drop was beautifully outlined by bare patches, as the enemy made its attack, so that the agar slant looked like moth-eaten beeswax. But within a fortnight one of the knots of which Gottlieb warned him appeared.

Wary of the hundreds of bacteriologists who would rise to slay him once his paper appeared, he sought to make sure that his results could be confirmed. At the hospital he obtained pus from many boils, of the arms, the legs, the back; he sought to reduplicate his results—and failed, complete. No X Principle appeared in any of the new boils, and sadly he went to Gottlieb.

The old man meditated, asked a question or two, sat hunched in his cushioned chair, and demanded:

"What kind of a carbuncle was the original one?"

"Gluteal."

"Ah, den the X Principle may be present in the intestinal contents. Look for it, in people with boils and without."

Martin dashed off. In a week he had obtained the Principle from intestinal contents and from other gluteal boils, finding an especial amount in boils which were "healing of themselves"; and he transplanted his new Principle, in a heaven of triumph, of admiration for Gottlieb. He extended his investigation to the intestinal group of organisms and discovered an X Principle against the colon bacillus. At the same time he gave some of the original Principle to a doctor in the Lower Manhattan Hospital for the treatment of boils, and from him had excited reports of cures, more excited inquiries as to what this mystery might be.

With these new victories he went parading in to Gottlieb, and suddenly he was being trounced:

"Oh! So! Beautiful! You let a doctor try it before you finished your research? You want fake reports of cures to get into the newspapers, to be telegraphed about places, and have everybody in the world that has a pimple come tumbling in to be cured, so you will never be able to work? You want to be a miracle man, and not a scientist? You do not want to complete things? You wander off monkey-skipping and flap-doodeling with colon bacillus before you have finish with staph—before you haf really begun your work—before you have found what is the *nature* of the X Principle? Get out of my office! You are a—a—a college president! Next I know you will be dining with Tubbs, and get your picture in the papers for a smart cure-vendor!"

Martin crept out, and when he met Billy Smith in the corridor and the little chemist twittered, "Up to something big? Haven't seen you lately," Martin answered in the tone of Doc Vickerson's assistant in Elk Mills:

"Oh—no—gee—I'm just grubbing along, I guess."

III

As sharply and quite as impersonally as he would have watched the crawling illness of an infected guinea pig, Martin watched himself, in the madness of overwork, drift toward neurasthenia. With considerable interest he looked up the symptoms of neurasthenia, saw one after another of them twitch at him, and casually took the risk.

From an irritability which made him a thoroughly impossible person to live with, he passed into a sick nervousness in which he missed things for which he reached, dropped test-tubes, gasped at sudden footsteps behind him. Dr. Yeo's croaking voice became to him a fever, an insult, and he waited with his whole body clenched, muttering, "Shut up—shut up—oh, shut *up!*" when Yeo stopped to talk to some one outside his door.

Then he was obsessed by the desire to spell backward all the words which snatched at him from signs.

As he stood dragging out his shoulder on a subway strap, he pored over the posters, seeking new words to spell backward. Some of them were remarkably agreeable: No Smoking became a jaunty and agreeable "gnikoms on," and Broadway was tolerable as "yawdaorb," but he was displeased by his attempts on Punch, Health, Rough; while Strength, turning into "htgnerts" was abominable.

When he had to return to his laboratory three times before he was satisfied that he had closed the window, he sat down, coldly, informed himself that he was on the edge, and took council as to whether he dared go on. It was not very good council: he was so glorified by his unfolding work that his self could not be taken seriously.

At last Fear closed in on him.

It began with childhood's terror of the darkness. He lay awake dreading burglars; footsteps in the hall were a creeping cutthroat; an unexplained scratching on the fire-escape was a murderer with an automatic in his fist. He beheld it so clearly that he had to spring from bed and look timorously out, and when in the street below he did actually see a man standing still, he was cold with panic.

Every sky glow was a fire. He was going to be trapped in his bed, be smothered, die writhing.

He knew absolutely that his fears were absurd, and that knowledge did not at all keep them from dominating him.

He was ashamed at first to acknowledge his seeming cowardice to Leora. Admit that he was crouching like a child? But when he had lain rigid, almost screaming, feeling the cord of an assassin squeezing his throat, till the safe dawn brought back a dependable world, he muttered of "insomnia" and after that, night on night, he crept into her arms and she shielded him from the horrors, protected him from garroters, kept away the fire.

He made a checking list of the favorite neurasthenic fears: agoraphobia, claustrophobia, pyrophobia, anthropophobia, and the rest, ending with what he asserted to be "the most fool, pretentious, witch-doctor term of the whole bloomin' lot," namely, siderodromophobia, the fear of a railway journey. The first night, he was able to check against pyrophobia, for at the vaudeville with Leora, when on the stage a dancer lighted a brazier, he sat waiting for the theater to take fire. He looked cautiously along the row of seats (raging at himself the while for doing it), he estimated his chance of reaching an exit, and became easy only when he had escaped into the street.

It was when anthropophobia set in, when he was made uneasy by people who walked too close to him, that, sagely viewing his list and seeing how many phobias were now checked, he permitted himself to rest.

He fled to the Vermont hills for a four-day tramp—alone, that he might pound on the faster. He went at night, by sleeper, and was able to make the most interesting observations of siderodromophobia.

He lay in a lower berth, the little pillow wadded into a lump. He was annoyed by the waving of his clothes as they trailed from the hanger beside him, at the opening of the green curtains. The window-shade was up six inches; it left a milky blur across which streaked yellow lights, emphatic in the noisy darkness of his little cell. He was shivering with anxiety. Whenever he tried to relax, he was ironed back into apprehension. When the train stopped between stations and from the engine came a questioning, fretful whistle, he was aghast with certainty that something had gone wrong—a bridge was out, a train was ahead of them; perhaps another was coming just behind them, about to smash into them at sixty miles an hour—

He imagined being wrecked, and he suffered more than from the actual occurrence, for he pictured not one wreck but half a dozen, with assorted miseries. . . . The flat wheel just beneath him—surely it shouldn't pound like that—why hadn't the confounded man with the hammer detected it at the last big station?—the flat wheel cracking; the car lurching, falling, being dragged on its side. . . . A collision, a crash, the car instantly a crumpled, horrible heap, himself pinned in the telescoped berth, caught between seat and seat. Shrieks, death groans, the creeping flames. . . . The car turning, falling, plumping into a river on its side; himself trying to crawl through a window as the water seeped about his body. . . . Himself standing by the wrenched car, deciding whether to keep away and protect his sacred work or go back, rescue people, and be killed.

So real were the visions that he could not endure lying here, waiting. He reached for the berth light, and could not find the button. In agitation he tore a match-box from his coat pocket, scratched a match, snapped on the light. He saw himself, under the sheets, reflected in the polished wooden ceiling of his berth like a corpse in a coffin. Hastily he crawled out, with trousers and coat over his undergarments (he had somehow feared to show so much trust in the train as to put on pajamas), and with bare disgusted feet he paddled up to the smoking compartment.

The porter was squatting on a stool, polishing an amazing pile of shoes.

Martin longed for his encouraging companionship, and ventured, "Warm night."

"Uh-huh," said the porter.

Martin curled on the chill leather seat of the smoking compartment, profoundly studying a brass wash-bowl. He was conscious that the porter was disapproving, but he had comfort in calculating that the man must make this run thrice a week, tens of thousand of miles yearly, apparently without being killed, and there might be a chance of their lasting till morning.

He smoked till his tongue was raw and till, fortified by the calmness of the porter, he laughed at the imaginary catastrophes. He staggered sleepily to his berth.

Instantly he was tense again, and he lay awake till dawn.

For four days he tramped, swam in cold brooks, slept under trees or in straw stacks, and came back (but by day) with enough reserve of energy to support him till his experiment should have turned from overwhelming glory into sane and entertaining routine.

Chapter XXIX

When the work on the X Principle had gone on for six weeks, the Institute staff suspected that something was occurring, and they hinted to Martin that he needed their several assistances. He avoided them. He did not desire to be caught in any of the log-rolling factions, though for Terry Wickett, still in France, and for Terry's rough compulsion to honesty he was sometimes lonely.

How the Director first heard that Martin was finding gold is not known.

Dr. Tubbs was tired of being a Colonel—there were too many Generals in New York—and for two weeks he had not had an Idea which would revolutionize even a small part of the world. One morning he burst in, whiskers alive, and reproached Martin:

"What is this mysterious discovery you're making, Arrowsmith? I've asked Dr. Gottlieb, but he evades me; he says you want to be sure, first. I must know about it, not only because I take a very friendly interest in your work but because I am, after all, your Director!"

Martin felt that his one ewe lamb was being snatched from him but he could see no way to refuse. He brought out his note-books, and the agar slants with their dissolved patches of bacilli. Tubbs gasped, assaulted his whiskers, did a moment of impressive thinking, and clamored:

"Do you mean to say you think you've discovered an infectious disease of bacteria, and you haven't told me about it? My dear boy, I don't believe you quite realize that you may have hit on the supreme way to kill pathogenic bacteria. . . . And you didn't tell me!"

"Well, sir, I wanted to make certain—"

"I admire your caution, but you must understand, Martin, that the basic aim of this Institution is the conquest of disease, not making pretty scientific notes! You *may* have hit on one of the discoveries of a generation; the sort of thing that Mr. McGurk and I are looking for. . . . If your results are confirmed. . . . I shall ask Dr. Gottlieb's opinion."

He shook Martin's hand five or six times and bustled out. Next day he called Martin to his office, shook his hand some more, told Pearl Robbins that they were honored to know him, then led him to a mountain top and showed him all the kingdoms of the world:

"Martin, I have some plans for you. You have been working brilliantly, but without a complete vision of broader humanity. Now the Institute is organized on the most flexible lines. There are no set departments, but only units formed about exceptional men like our good friend Gottlieb. If any new man has the real right thing, we'll provide him with every facility, instead of letting him merely plug along doing individual work. I have given your results the most careful consideration, Martin; I have talked them over with Dr. Gottlieb—though I must say he does not altogether share my enthusiasm about immediate practical results. And I have decided to submit to the Board of Trustees a plan for a Department of Microbic Pathology, with you as head! You will have an assistant—a real trained Ph.D.—and more room and technicians, and you will report to me directly, talk things over with me daily, instead of with Gottlieb. You will be relieved of all war work, by my order—though you can retain your uniform and everything. And your salary will be, I should think, if Mr. McGurk and the other Trustees confirm me, ten thousand a year instead of five.

"Yes, the best room for you would be that big one on the upper floor, to the right of the elevators. That's vacant now. And your office across the hall.

"And all the assistance you require. Why, my boy, you won't need to sit up nights using your hands in this wasteful way, but just think things out and take up possible extensions of the work—cover all the possible fields. We'll extend this to everything! We'll have scores of physicians in hospitals helping us and confirming our results and widening our efforts. . . . We might have a weekly council of all these doctors and assistants, with you and me jointly presiding. . . . If men like Koch and Pasteur had only had such a system, how much more *scope* their work might have had! Efficient universal *coöperation*—that's the thing in science to-day—the time of this silly, jealous, fumbling individual research has gone by.

"My boy, we may have found the real thing—another salvarsan! We'll publish together! We'll have the whole world talking! Why, I lay awake last night thinking of our magnificent opportunity! In a few months we may be curing not only staph infections but typhoid, dysentery! Martin, as your colleague, I do not for a moment wish to detract from the great credit which is yours, but I must say that if you had been more closely allied with Me you would have extended your work to practical proofs and results long before this."

Martin wavered back to his room, dazzled by the view of a department of his own, assistants, a cheering world—and ten thousand a year. But his work seemed to have been taken from him, his own self had been taken from him; he was no longer to be Martin, and Gottlieb's disciple, but a Man of Measured Merriment, Dr. Arrowsmith, Head of the Department of Microbic Pathology, who would wear severe collars and make addresses and never curse.

Doubts enfeebled him. Perhaps the X Principle would develop only in the test-tube; perhaps it had no large value for human healing. He wanted to know—to *know*.

Then Rippleton Holabird burst in on him:

"Martin, my dear boy, the Director has just been telling me about your discovery and his splendid plans for you. I want to congratulate you with all my heart, and to welcome you as a fellow department-head—and you so young—only thirty-four, isn't it? What a magnificent future! Think, Martin"—Major Holabird discarded his dignity, sat astride a chair—"think of all you have ahead! If this work really pans out, there's no limit to the honors that'll come to you, you lucky young dog! Acclaim by scientific societies, any professorship you might happen to want, prizes, the biggest men begging to consult you, a ripping place in society!

"Now listen, old boy: Perhaps you know how close I am to Dr. Tubbs, and I see no reason why you shouldn't come in with us, and we three run things here to suit ourselves. Wasn't it simply too decent of the Director to be so eager to recognize and help you in every way! So cordial—and so helpful. Now you really understand him. And the three of us— Some day we might be able to erect a superstructure of coöperative science which would control not only McGurk but every institute and every university scientific department in the country, and so produce really efficient research. When Dr. Tubbs retires, I have—I'm speaking with the most complete confidence—I have some reason to suppose that the Board of Trustees will consider me as his successor. Then, old boy, if this work succeeds, you and I can do things together!

"To be ever so frank, there are very few men in our world (think of poor old Yeo!) who combine presentable personalities with first-rate achievement, and if you'll just get over some of your abruptness and your unwillingness to appreciate big executives and charming women (because, thank God, you do wear your clothes well—when you take the trouble!) why, you and I can become the dictators of science throughout the whole country!"

Martin did not think of an answer till Holabird had gone.

He perceived the horror of the shrieking bawdy thing called Success, with its demand that he give up quiet work and parade forth to be pawed by every blind devotee and mud-spattered by every blind enemy.

He fled to Gottlieb as to the wise and tender father, and begged to be saved from Success and Holabirds and A. De Witt Tubbses and their hordes of address-making scientists, degree-hunting authors, pulpit orators, popular surgeons, valeted journalists, sentimental merchant princes, literary politicians, titled sportsmen, statesmenlike generals, interviewed senators, sententious bishops.

Gottlieb was worried:

"I knew Tubbs was up to something idealistic and nasty when he came purring to me, but I did not t'ink he would try to turn you into a megaphone all so soon in one day! I will gird up my loins and go oud to battle with the forces of publicity!"

He was defeated.

"I have let you alone, Dr. Gottlieb," said Tubbs, "but hang it, I am the Director! And I must say that, perhaps owing to my signal stupidity, I fail to see the horrors of enabling Arrowsmith to cure thousands of suffering persons and to become a man of weight and esteem!"

Gottlieb took it to Ross McGurk.

"Max, I love you like a brother, but Tubbs is the Director, and if he feels he needs this Arrowsmith (is he the thin young fellow I see around your lab?) then I have no right to stop him. I've got to back him up the same as I would the master of one of our ships," said McGurk.

Not till the Board of Trustees, which consisted of McGurk himself, the president of the University of Wilmington, and three professors of science in various universities, should meet and give approval, would Martin be a department-head. Meantime Tubbs demanded:

"Now, Martin, you must hasten and publish your results. Get right to it. In fact you should have done it before this. Throw your material together as rapidly as possible and send a note in to the Society for Experimental Biology and Medicine, to be published in their next proceedings."

"But I'm not ready to publish! I want to have every loophole plugged up before I announce anything whatever!"

"Nonsense! That attitude is old-fashioned. This is no longer an age of parochialism but of competition, in art and science just as much as in commerce—coöperation with your own group, but with those outside it, competition to the death! Plug up the holes thoroughly, later, but we can't have somebody else stealing a march on us. Remember you have your name to make. The way to make it is by working with me—toward the greatest good for the greatest number."

As Martin began his paper, thinking of resigning but giving it up because Tubbs seemed to him at least better than the Pickerbaughs, he had a vision of a world of little scientists, each busy in a roofless cell. Perched on a cloud, watching them, was the divine Tubbs, a glory of whiskers, ready to blast any of the little men who stopped being earnest and wasted time on speculation about anything which he had not assigned to them. Back of their welter of coops, unseen by the tutelary Tubbs, the lean giant figure of Gottlieb stood sardonic on a stormy horizon.

Literary expression was not easy to Martin. He delayed with his paper, while Tubbs became irritable and whipped him on. The experiments had ceased; there was misery and pen-scratching and much tearing of manuscript paper in Martin's particular roofless cell.

For once he had no refuge in Leora. She cried:

"Why not? Ten thousand a year would be awfully nice, Sandy. Gee! We've always been so poor, and you do like nice flats and things. And to boss your own department— And you could consult Dr. Gottlieb just the same. He's a department-head, isn't he, and yet he keeps independent of Dr. Tubbs. Oh, I'm for it!"

And slowly, under the considerable increase in respect given to him at Institute lunches, Martin himself was "for it."

"We could get one of those new apartments on Park Avenue. Don't suppose they cost more than three thousand a year," he meditated. "Wouldn't be so bad to be able to entertain people there. Not that I'd let it interfere with my work. . . . Kind of nice."

It was still more kind of nice, however agonizing in the taking, to be recognized socially.

Capitola McGurk, who hitherto had not perceived him except as an object less interesting than Gladys the Centrifuge, telephoned: ". . . Dr. Tubbs so enthusiastic and Ross and I are so pleased. Be delighted if Mrs. Arrowsmith and you could dine with us next Thursday at eight-thirty."

Martin accepted the royal command.

It was his conviction that after glimpses of Angus Duer and Rippleton Holabird he had seen luxury, and understood smart dinner parties. Leora and he went without too much agitation to the house of Ross McGurk, in the East Seventies, near Fifth Avenue. The house did, from the street, seem to have an unusual quantity of graystone gargoyles and carven lintels and bronze grills, but it did not seem large.

Inside, the vaulted stone hallway opened up like a cathedral. They were embarrassed by the footmen, awed by the automatic elevator, oppressed by a hallway full of vellum folios and Italian chests and a drawing-room full of watercolors, and reduced to rusticity by Capitola's queenly white satin and pearls.

There were eight or ten Persons of Importance, male and female, looking insignificant but bearing names as familiar as Ivory Soap.

Did one give his arm to some unknown lady and "take her in," Martin wondered. He rejoiced to find that one merely straggled into the dining-room under McGurk's amiable basso herding.

The dining-room was gorgeous and very hideous, in stamped leather and hysterias of gold, with collections of servants watching one's use of asparagus forks. Martin was seated (it is doubtful if he ever knew that he was the guest of honor) between Capitola McGurk and a woman of whom he could learn only that she was the sister of a countess.

Capitola leaned toward him in her great white splendor.

"Now, Dr. Arrowsmith, just what is this you are discovering?"

"Why, it's—uh—I'm trying to figure—"

"Dr. Tubbs tells us that you have found such wonderful new ways of controlling disease." Her L's were a melody of summer rivers, her R's the trill of birds in the brake. "Oh, what—*what* could be more beau-tiful than relieving this sad old world of its burden of illness! But just precisely what *is* it that you're doing?"

"Why, it's awfully early to be sure but— You see, it's like this. You take certain bugs like staph—"

"Oh, how interesting science is, but how frightfully difficult for simple people like me to grasp! But we're all so humble. We're just waiting for scientists like you to make the world secure for friendship—"

Then Capitola gave all her attention to her other man. Martin looked straight ahead and ate and suffered. The sister of the countess, a sallow and stringy woman, was glowing at him. He turned with unhappy meekness (noting that she had one more fork than he, and wondering where he had got lost).

She blared, "You are a scientist, I am told."

"Ye-es."

"The trouble with scientists is that they do not understand beauty. They are so cold."

Rippleton Holabird would have made pretty mirth, but Martin could only quaver, "No, I don't think that's true," and consider whether he dared drink another glass of champagne.

When they had been herded back to the drawing-room, after masculine but achingly elaborate passings of the port, Capitola swooped on him with white devouring wings:

"Dear Dr. Arrowsmith, I really didn't get a chance at dinner to ask you just exactly *what* you are doing. . . . Oh! Have you seen my dear little children at the Charles Street settlement? I'm sure ever so many of them will become the most fascinating scientists. You must come lecture to them."

That night he fretted to Leora, "Going to be hard to keep up this twittering. But I suppose I've got to learn to enjoy it. Oh, well, think how nice it'll be to give some dinners of our own, with real people, Gottlieb and everybody, when I'm a department-head."

Next morning Gottlieb came slowly into Martin's room. He stood by the window; he seemed to be avoiding Martin's eyes. He sighed, "Something sort of bad—perhaps not altogether bad—has happened."

"What is it, sir? Anything I can do?"

"It does not apply to me. To you."

Irritably Martin thought, "Is he going into all this danger-of-rapid-success stuff again? I'm getting tired of it!"

Gottlieb ambled toward him. "It iss a pity, Martin, but you are not the discoverer of the X Principle."

"Wh-what—"

"Some one else has done it."

"They have not! I've searched all the literature, and except for Twort, not one person has even hinted at anticipating—Why, good Lord, Dr. Gottlieb, it would mean that all I've done, all these weeks, has just been waste, and I'm a fool—"

"Vell. Anyvay. D'Hérelle of the Pasteur Institute has just now published in the *Comptes Rendus, Académie des Sciences*, a report—it is your X Principle, absolute. Only he calls it 'bacteriophage.' So."

"Then I'm—"

In his mind Martin finished it, "Then I'm not going to be a department-head or famous or anything else. I'm back in the gutter." All strength went out of him and all purpose, and the light of creation faded to dirty gray.

"Now of course," said Gottlieb, "you could claim to be co-discoverer and spend the rest of your life fighting to get recognized. Or you could forget it, and write a nice letter congratulating D'Hérelle, and go back to work."

Martin mourned, "Oh, I'll go back to work. Nothing else to do. I guess Tubbs'll chuck the new department now. I'll have time to really finish my research—maybe I've got some points that D'Hérelle hasn't hit on—and I'll publish it to corroborate him. . . . Damn him! . . . Where is his report? . . . I suppose you're glad that I'm saved from being a Holabird."

"I ought to be. It is a sin against my religion that I am not. But I am getting old. And you are my friend. I am sorry you are not to have the fun of being pretentious and successful—for a while. . . . Martin, it iss nice that you will corroborate D'Hérelle. That is science: to work and not to care—too much—if somebody else gets the credit. . . . Shall I tell Tubbs about D'Hérelle's priority, or will you?"

Gottlieb straggled away, looking back a little sadly.

Tubbs came in to wail, "If you had only published earlier, as I told you, Dr. Arrowsmith! You have really put me in a most embarrassing position before the Board of Trustees. Of course there can be no question now of a new department."

"Yes," said Martin vacantly.

He carefully filed away the beginnings of his paper and turned to his bench. He stared at a shining flask till it fascinated him like a crystal ball. He pondered:

"Wouldn't have been so bad if Tubbs had let me alone. Damn these old men, damn these Men of Measured Merriment, these Important Men that come and offer you honors. Money. Decorations. Titles. Want to make you windy with authority. Honors! If you get 'em, you become pompous, and then when you're used to 'em, if you lose 'em you feel foolish.

"So I'm not going to be rich. Leora, poor kid, she won't have her new dresses and flat and everything. We— Won't be so much fun in the lil old flat, now. Oh, quit whining!

"I wish Terry were here.

"I love that man Gottlieb. He might have gloated—

"Bacteriophage, the Frenchman calls it. Too long. Better just call it *phage*. Even got to take his name for it, for my own X Principle. Well, I had a lot of fun, working all those nights. Working—"

He was coming out of his trance. He imagined the flask filled with staph-clouded broth. He plodded into Gottlieb's office to secure the journal containing D'Hérelle's report, and read it minutely, enthusiastically.

"There's a man, there's a scientist!" he chuckled.

On his way home he was planning to experiment on the Shiga dysentery bacillus with phage (as henceforth he called the X Principle), planning to volley questions and criticisms at D'Hérelle, hoping that Tubbs would not discharge him for a while, and expanding with relief that he would not have to do his absurd premature paper on phage, that he could be lewd and soft-collared and easy, not judicious and spied-on and weighty.

He grinned, "Gosh, I'll bet Tubbs was disappointed! He'd figured on signing all my papers with me and getting the credit. Now for this Shiga experiment— Poor Lee, she'll have to get used to my working nights, I guess."

Leora kept to herself what she felt about it—or at least most of what she felt.

Chapter XXX

FOR A YEAR broken only by Terry Wickett's return after the Armistice, and by the mockeries of that rowdy intelligence, Martin was in a grind of drudgery. Week on week he toiled at complicated phage experiments. His work—his hands, his technique—became more adept, and his days more steady, less fretful.

He returned to his evening studying. He went from mathematics into physical chemistry; began to understand the mass action law; became as sarcastic as Terry about what he called the "bedside manner" of Tubbs and Holabird; read much French and German; went canoeing on the Hudson on Sunday afternoons; and had a bawdy party with Leora and Terry to celebrate the day when the Institute was purified by the sale of Holabird's pride, Gladys the Centrifuge.

He suspected that Dr. Tubbs, now magnificent with the ribbon of the Legion of Honor, had retained him in the Institute only because of Gottlieb's intervention. But it may be that Tubbs and Holabird hoped he would again blunder into publicity-bringing miracles, for they were both polite to him at lunch—polite and wistfully rebuking, and full of meaty remarks about publishing one's discoveries early instead of dawdling.

It was more than a year after Martin's anticipation by D'Hérelle when Tubbs appeared in the laboratory with suggestions:

"I've been thinking, Arrowsmith," said Tubbs.

He looked it.

"D'Hérelle's discovery hasn't aroused the popular interest I thought it would. If he'd only been here with us, I'd have seen to it that he got the proper attention. Practically no newspaper comment at all. Perhaps we can still do something. As I understand it, you've been going along with what Dr. Gottlieb would call 'fundamental research.' I think it may now be time for you to use phage in practical healing. I want you to experiment with phage in pneumonia, plague, perhaps typhoid, and when your experiments get going, make some practical tests in collaboration with the hospitals. Enough of all this mere frittering and vanity. Let's really *cure* somebody!"

Martin was not free from a fear of dismissal if he refused to obey. And he was touched as Tubbs went on:

"Arrowsmith, I suspect you sometimes feel I lack a sense of scientific precision when I insist on practical results. I—Somehow I don't see the really noble and transforming results coming out of this Institute that we ought to be getting, with our facilities. I'd like to do something big, my boy, something fine for poor humanity, before I pass on. Can't you give it to me? Go cure the plague!"

For once Tubbs was a tired smile and not an earnestness of whiskers.

That day, concealing from Gottlieb his abandonment of the quest for the fundamental nature of phage, Martin set about fighting pneumonia, before attacking the Black Death. And when Gottlieb learned of it, he was absorbed in certain troubles of his own.

Martin cured rabbits of pleuro-pneumonia by the injection of phage, and by feeding them with it he prevented the spread of pneumonia. He found that phage-produced immunity could be as infectious as a disease.

He was pleased with himself, and expected pleasure from Tubbs, but for weeks Tubbs did not heed him. He was off on a new enthusiasm, the most virulent of his whole life: he was organizing the League of Cultural Agencies.

He was going to standardize and coördinate all mental activities in America, by the creation of a bureau which should direct and pat and gently rebuke and generally encourage chemistry and batik-making, poetry and Arctic exploration, animal husbandry and Bible study, negro spirituals and business-letter writing. He was suddenly in conference with conductors of symphony orchestras, directors of art-schools, owners of itinerant Chautauquas, liberal governors, ex-clergymen who wrote tasty philosophy for newspaper syndicates, in fact all the proprietors of American intellectuality—particularly including a millionaire named Minnigen who had recently been elevating the artistic standards of the motion pictures.

Tubbs was all over the Institute inviting the researchers to join him in the League of Cultural Agencies with its fascinating committee-meetings and dinners. Most of them grunted, "The Old Man is erupting again," and forgot him, but one ex-major went out every evening to confer with serious ladies who wore distinguished frocks, who sobbed over "the loss of spiritual and intellectual horse-power through lack of coördination," and who went home in limousines.

There were rumors. Dr. Billy Smith whispered that he had gone in to see Tubbs and heard McGurk shouting at him, "Your job is to run this shop and not work for that land-stealing, four-flushing, play-producing son of evil, Pete Minnigen!"

The morning after, when Martin ambled to his laboratory, he discovered a gasping, a muttering, a shaking in the corridors, and incredulously he heard:

"Tubbs has resigned!"

"No!"

"They say he's gone to his League of Cultural Agencies. This fellow Minnigen has given the League a scad of money, and Tubbs is to get twice the salary he had here!"

II

Instantly, for all but the zealots like Gottlieb, Terry, Martin, and the bio-physics assistant, research was halted. There was a surging of factions, a benevolent and winning buzz of scientists who desired to be the new Director of the Institute.

Rippleton Holabird, Yeo the carpenter-like biologist, Gillingham the joky chief in bio-physics, Aaron Sholtheis the neat Russian Jewish High Church Episcopalian, all of them went about with expressions of modest willingness. They were affectionate with everybody they met in the corridors, however violent they were in private discussions. Added to them were no few outsiders, professors and researchers in other institutes, who found it necessary to come and confer about rather undefined matters with Ross McGurk.

Terry remarked to Martin, "Probably Pearl Robbins and your garçon are pitching horseshoes for the Directorship. My garçon ain't—the only reason, though, is because I've just murdered him. At that, I think Pearl would be the best choice. She's been Tubbs's secretary so long that she's learned all his ignorance about scientific technique."

Rippleton Holabird was the most unctuous of the office-seekers, and the most hungry. The war over, he missed his uniform and his authority. He urged Martin:

"You know how I've always believed in your genius, Martin, and I know how dear old Gottlieb believes in you. If you would get Gottlieb to back me, to talk to McGurk— Of course in taking the Directorship I would be making a sacrifice, because I'd have to give up my research, but I'd be willing because I feel, really, that somebody with a Tradition ought to carry on the control. Tubbs is backing me, and if Gottlieb did—I'd see that it was to Gottlieb's advantage. I'd give him a lot more floor-space!"

Through the Institute it was vaguely known that Capitola was advocating the election of Holabird as "the only scientist here who is also a gentleman." She was seen sailing down corridors, a frigate, with Holabird a sloop in her wake.

But while Holabird beamed, Nicholas Yeo looked secret and satisfied.

The whole Institute fluttered on the afternoon when the Board of Trustees met in the Hall, for the election of a Director. They were turned from investigators into boarding-school girls. The Board debated, or did something annoying, for draining hours.

At four, Terry Wickett hastened to Martin with, "Say, Slim, I've got a straight tip that They've elected Silva, dean of the Winnemac medical school. That's your shop, isn't it? Wha's like?"

"He's a fine old— No! He and Gottlieb hate each other. Lord! Gottlieb'll resign, and I'll have to get out. Just when my work's going nice!"

At five, past doors made of attentive eyes, the Board of Trustees marched to the laboratory of Max Gottlieb.

Holabird was heard saying bravely, "Of course with me, I wouldn't give my research up for any administrative job." And Pearl Robbins informed Terry, "Yes, it's true—Mr. McGurk himself just told me—the Board has elected Dr. Gottlieb the new Director."

"Then they're fools," said Terry. "He'll refuse it, with wilence. 'Dot dey should ask me to go monkey-skipping mit committee meetings!' Fat chance!"

When the Board had gone, Martin and Terry flooded into Gottlieb's laboratory and found the old man standing by his bench, more erect than they had seen him for years.

"Is it true—they want you to be Director?" panted Martin.

"Yes, they have asked me."

"But you'll refuse? You won't let 'em gum up your work!"

"Vell. . . . I said my real work must go on. They consent I should appoint an Assistant Director to do the detail. You see— Of course nothing must interfere with my immunology, but dis gives me the chance to do big t'ings and make a free scientific institute for all you boys. And those fools at Winnemac that laughed at my idea of a real medical school, now maybe they will see— Do you know who was my rival for Director—do you know who it was, Martin? It was that man Silva! Ha!"

In the corridor Terry groaned, *"Requiescat in pace."*

III

To the dinner in Gottlieb's honor (the only dinner that ever was given in Gottlieb's honor) there came not only the men of impressive but easy affairs who attend all dinners of honor, but the few scientists whom Gottlieb admired.

He appeared late, rather shaky, escorted by Martin. When he reached the speakers' table, the guests rose to him, shouting. He peered at them, he tried to speak, he held out his long arms as if to take them all in, and sank down sobbing.

There were cables from Europe; ardent letters from Tubbs and Dean Silva bewailing their inability to be present; telegrams from college presidents; and all of these were read to admiring applause.

But Capitola murmured, "Just the same, we shall miss dear Dr. Tubbs. He was so forward-looking. Don't play with your fork, Ross."

So Max Gottlieb took charge of the McGurk Institute of Biology, and in a month that Institute became a shambles.

IV

Gottlieb planned to give only an hour a day to business. As Assistant Director he appointed Dr. Aaron Sholtheis, the epidemiologist, the Yonkers churchman and dahlia-fancier. Gottlieb explained to Martin that, though of course Sholtheis was a fool, yet he was the only man in sight who combined at least a little scientific ability with a willingness to endure the routine and pomposity and compromises of executive work.

By continuing his ancient sneers at all bustling managers, Gottlieb obviously felt that he excused himself for having become a manager.

He could not confine his official work to an hour a day. There were too many conferences, too many distinguished callers, too many papers which needed his signature. He was dragged into dinner-parties; and the long, vague, palavering luncheons to which a Director has to go, and the telephoning to straighten out the dates of these tortures, took nervous hours. Each day his executive duties crawled into two hours or three or four, and he raged, he became muddled by complications of personnel and economy, he was ever more autocratic, more testy; and the loving colleagues of the Institute, who had been soothed or bullied into surface peace by Tubbs, now jangled openly.

While he was supposed to radiate benevolence from the office recently occupied by Dr. A. DeWitt Tubbs, Gottlieb clung to his own laboratory and to his narrow office as a cat clings to its cushion under a table. Once or twice he tried to sit and look impressive in the office of the Director, but he fled from that large clean vacuity and from Miss Robbins's snapping typewriter to his own den that smelled not of forward-looking virtue but only of cigarettes and old papers.

To McGurk, as to every scientific institution, came hundreds of farmers and practical nurses and suburban butchers who had paid large fares from Oklahoma or Oregon to get recognition for the unquestionable cures which they had discovered: oil of Mississippi catfish which saved every case of tuberculosis, arsenic pastes guaranteed to cure all cancers. They came with letters and photographs amid the frayed clean linen in their shabby suit-cases—at any opportunity they would stoop over their bags and hopefully bring out testimonials from their Pastors; they begged for a chance to heal humanity, and for themselves only enough money to send The Girl to musical conservatory. So certain, so black-crapely beseeching were they that no reception-clerk could be trained to keep them all out.

Gottlieb found them seeping into his office. He was sorry for them. They did take his working hours, they did scratch his belief that he was hard-hearted, but they implored him with such wretched timorousness that he could not get rid of them without making promises, and admitting afterward that to have been more cruel would have been less cruel.

It was the Important People to whom he was rude.

The Directorship devoured enough time and peace to prevent Gottlieb from going on with the ever more recondite problems of his inquiry into the nature of specificity, and his inquiry prevented him from giving enough attention to the Institute to keep it from falling to pieces. He depended on Sholtheis, passed decisions on to him, but Sholtheis, since in any case Gottlieb would get all the credit for a successful Directorship, kept up his own scientific work and passed the decisions to Miss Pearl Robbins, so that the actual Director was the handsome and jealous Pearl.

There was no craftier or crookeder Director in the habitable world. Pearl enjoyed it. She so warmly and modestly assured Ross McGurk of the merits of Gottlieb and of her timorous devotion to him, she so purred to the flattery of Rippleton Holabird, she so blandly answered the hoarse hostility of Terry Wickett by keeping him from getting materials for his work, that the Institute reeled with intrigue.

Yeo was not speaking to Sholtheis. Terry threatened Holabird to "paste him one." Gottlieb constantly asked Martin for advice, and never took it. Joust, the vulgar but competent bio-physicist, lacking the affection which kept Martin and Terry from reproaching the old man, told Gottlieb that he was a "rotten Director and ought to quit," and was straightway discharged and replaced by a muffin.

Max Gottlieb had ever discoursed to Martin of "the jests of the gods." Among these jests Martin had never beheld one so pungent as this whereby the pretentiousness and fussy unimaginativeness which he had detested in Tubbs should have made him a good manager, while the genius of Gottlieb should have made him a feeble tyrant; the jest that the one thing worse than a too managed and standardized institution should be one that was not managed and standardized at all. He would once have denied it with violence, but nightly now he prayed for Tubbs's return.

If the business of the Institute was not more complicated thereby, certainly its placidity was the more disturbed by the appearance of Gustaf Sondelius, who had just returned from a study of sleeping sickness in Africa and who noisily took one of the guest laboratories.

Gustaf Sondelius, the soldier of preventive medicine whose lecture had sent Martin from Wheatsylvania to Nautilus, had remained in his gallery of heroes as possessing a little of Gottlieb's perception, something of Dad Silva's steady kindliness, something of Terry's tough honesty though none of his scorn of amenities, and with these a spicy, dripping richness altogether his own. It is true that Sondelius did not remember Martin. Since their evening in Minneapolis he had drunk and debated and flamboyantly ridden to obscure but vinuous destinations with too many people. But he was made to remember, and in a week Sondelius and Terry and Martin were to be seen tramping and dining, or full of topics and gin at Martin's flat.

Sondelius's wild flaxen hair was almost gray, but he had the same bull shoulders, the same wide brow, and the same tornado of plans to make the world aseptic, without neglecting to enjoy a few of the septic things before they should pass away.

His purpose was, after finishing his sleeping sickness report, to found a school of tropical medicine in New York.

He besieged McGurk and the wealthy Mr. Minnigen who was Tubbs's new patron, and in and out of season he besieged Gottlieb.

He adored Gottlieb and made noises about it. Gottlieb admired his courage and his hatred of commercialism, but his presence Gottlieb could not endure. He was flustered by Sondelius's hilarity, his compliments, his bounding optimism, his inaccuracy, his boasting, his oppressive bigness. It may be that Gottlieb resented the fact that though Sondelius was only eleven years younger—fifty-eight to Gottlieb's sixty-nine—he seemed thirty years younger, half a century gayer.

When Sondelius perceived this grudgingness he tried to overcome it by being more noisy and complimentary and enthusiastic than ever. On Gottlieb's birthday he gave him a shocking smoking-jacket of cherry and mauve velvet, and when he called at Gottlieb's flat, which was often, Gottlieb had to put on the ghastly thing and sit humming while Sondelius assaulted him with roaring condemnations of mediocre soup and mediocre musicians. . . . That Sondelius gave up surprisingly decorative dinner-parties for these calls, Gottlieb never knew.

Martin turned to Sondelius for courage as he turned to Terry for concentration. Courage and concentration were needed, in these days of an Institute gone insane, if a man was to do his work.

And Martin was doing it.

V

After a consultation with Gottlieb and a worried conference with Leora about the danger of handling the germs, he had gone on to bubonic plague, to the possibilities of preventing it and curing it with phage.

To have heard him asking Sondelius about his experience in plague epidemics, one would have believed that Martin found the Black Death delightful. To have beheld him infecting lean snaky rats with the horror, all the while clucking to them and calling them pet names, one would have known him mad.

He found that rats fed with phage failed to come down with plague; that after phage-feeding, *Bacillus pestis* disappeared from carrier rats which, without themselves being killed thereby, harbored and spread chronic plague; and that, finally, he could cure the disease. He was as absorbed and happy and nervous as in the first days of the X Principle. He worked all night. . . . At the microscope, under a lone light, fishing out with a glass pipette drawn fine as a hair one single plague bacillus.

To protect himself from infection by the rat-fleas he wore, while he worked with the animals, rubber gloves, high leather boots, straps about his sleeves. These precautions thrilled him, and to the others at McGurk they had something of the esoteric magic of the alchemists. He became a bit of a hero and a good deal of a butt. No more than hearty business men in offices or fussy old men in villages are researchers free from the tedious vice of jovial commenting. The chemists and biologists called him "The Pest," refused to come to his room, and pretended to avoid him in the corridors.

As he went fluently on from experiment to experiment, as the drama of science obsessed him, he thought very well of himself and found himself taken seriously by the others. He published one cautious paper on phage in plague, which was mentioned in numerous scientific journals. Even the harassed Gottlieb was commendatory, though he could give but little attention and no help. But Terry Wickett remained altogether cool. He showed for Martin's somewhat brilliant work only enough enthusiasm to indicate that he was not jealous; he kept poking in to ask whether, with his new experimentation, Martin was continuing his quest for the fundamental nature of all phage, and his study of physical chemistry.

Then Martin had such an assistant as has rarely been known, and that assistant was Gustaf Sondelius.

Sondelius was discouraged regarding his school of tropical medicine. He was looking for new trouble. He had been through several epidemics, and he viewed plague with affectionate hatred. When he understood Martin's work he gloated, "Hey, Yesus! Maybe you got the t'ing that will be better than Yersin or Haffkine or anybody! Maybe you cure all the world of plague—the poor devils in India—millions of them. Let me in!"

He became Martin's collaborator; unpaid, tireless, not very skilful, valuable in his buoyancy. As well as Martin he loved irregularity; by principle he never had his meals at the same hours two days in succession, and by choice he worked all night and made poetry, rather bad poetry, at dawn.

Martin had always been the lone prowler. Possibly the thing he most liked in Leora was her singular ability to be cheerfully non-existent even when she was present. At first he was annoyed by Sondelius's disturbing presence, however interesting he found his fervors about plague-bearing rats (whom Sondelius hated not at all but whom, with loving zeal, he had slaughtered by the million, with a romantic absorption in traps and poison gas). But the Sondelius who was raucous in conversation could be almost silent at work. He knew exactly how to hold the animals while Martin did intrapleural injections; he made cultures of *Bacillus pestis*; when Martin's technician had gone home at but a little after midnight (the garçon liked Martin and thought well enough of science, but he was prejudiced in favor of six hours daily sleep and sometimes seeing his wife and children in Harlem), then Sondelius cheerfully sterilized glassware and needles, and lumbered up to the animal house to bring down victims.

The change whereby Sondelius was turned from Martin's master to his slave was so unconscious, and Sondelius, for all his Pickerbaughian love of sensationalism, cared so little about mastery or credit, that neither of them considered that there had been a change. They borrowed cigarettes from each other; they went out at the most improbable hours to have flap-jacks and coffee at an all-night lunch; and together they handled test-tubes charged with death.

Chapter XXXI

FROM Yunnan in China, from the clattering bright bazaars, crept something invisible in the sun and vigilant by dark, creeping, sinister, ceaseless; creeping across the Himalayas down through walled market-places, across a desert, along hot yellow rivers, into an American missionary compound—creeping, silent, sure; and here and there on its way a man was black and stilled with plague.

In Bombay a new dock-guard, unaware of things, spoke boisterously over his family rice of a strange new custom of the rats.

Those princes of the sewer, swift to dart and turn, had gone mad. They came out on the warehouse floor, ignoring the guard, springing up as though (the guard said merrily) they were trying to fly, and straightway falling dead. He had poked at them, but they did not move.

Three days later that dock-guard died of the plague.

Before he died, from his dock a ship with a cargo of wheat steamed off to Marseilles. There was no sickness on it all the way; there was no reason why at Marseilles it should not lie next to a tramp steamer, nor why that steamer, pitching down to Montevideo with nothing more sensational than a discussion between the supercargo and the second officer in the matter of a fifth ace, should not berth near the S.S. *Pendown Castle*, bound for the island of St. Hubert to add cocoa to its present cargo of lumber.

On the way to St. Hubert, a Goanese seedie boy and after him the messroom steward on the *Pendown Castle* died of what the skipper called influenza. A greater trouble was the number of rats which, ill satisfied with lumber as diet, scampered up to the food-stores, then into the forecastle, and for no reason perceptible died on the open decks. They danced comically before they died, and lay in the scuppers stark and ruffled.

So the *Pendown Castle* came to Blackwater, the capital and port of St. Hubert.

It is a little isle of the southern West Indies, but St. Hubert supports a hundred thousand people—English planters and clerks, Hindu road-makers, negro cane-hands, Chinese merchants. There is history along its sands and peaks. Here the buccaneers careened their ships; here the Marquess of Wimsbury, when he had gone mad, took to repairing clocks and bade his slaves burn all the sugar-cane.

Hither that peasant beau, Gaston Lopo, brought Madame de Merlemont, and dwelt in fashionableness till the slaves whom he had often relished to lash came on him shaving, and straightway the lather was fantastically smeared with blood.

To-day, St. Hubert is all sugar-cane and Ford cars, oranges and plantains and the red and yellow pods of cocoa, bananas and rubber trees and jungles of bamboo, Anglican churches and tin chapels, colored washerwomen busy at the hollows in the roots of silk-cotton trees, steamy heat and royal palms and the immortelle that fills the valleys with crimson; to-day it is all splendor and tourist dullness and cabled cane-quotations, against the unsparing sun.

Blackwater, flat and breathless town of tin-roofed plaster houses and incandescent bone-white roads, of salmon-red hibiscus and balconied stores whose dark depths open without barrier from the stifling streets, has the harbor to one side and a swamp to the other. But behind it are the Penrith Hills, on whose wholesome and palm-softened heights is Government House, looking to the winking sails.

Here lived in bulky torpor His Excellency the Governor of St. Hubert, Colonel Sir Robert Fairlamb.

Sir Robert Fairlamb was an excellent fellow, a teller of messroom stories, one who in a heathen day never smoked till the port had gone seven times round; but he was an execrable governor and a worried governor. The man whose social rank was next to his own—the Hon. Cecil Eric George Twyford, a lean, active, high-nosed despot who owned and knew rod by snake-writhing rod some ten thousand acres of cane in St. Swithin's Parish—Twyford said that His Excellency was a "potty and snoring fool," and versions of the opinion came not too slowly to Fairlamb. Then, to destroy him complete, the House of Assembly, which is the St. Hubert legislature, was riven by the feud of Kellett the Red Leg and George William Vertigan.

The Red Legs were a tribe of Scotch-Irish poor whites who had come to St. Hubert as indentured servants two hundred years before. Most of them were still fishermen and plantation-foremen, but one of them, Kellett, a man small-mouthed and angry and industrious, had risen from office-boy to owner of a shipping company, and while his father still spread his nets on the beach at Point Carib, Kellett was the scourge of the House of Assembly and a hound for economy—particularly any economy which would annoy his fellow legislator, George William Vertigan.

George William, who was sometimes known as "Old Jeo Wm" and sometimes as "The King of the Ice House" (that enticing and ruinous bar), had been born behind a Little Bethel in Lancashire. He owned The Blue Bazaar, the hugest store in St. Hubert; he caused tobacco to be smuggled into Venezuela; he was as full of song and incaution and rum as Kellett the Red Leg was full of figures and envy and decency.

Between them, Kellett and George William split the House of Assembly. There could be, to a respectable person, no question as to their merits: Kellett the just and earnest man of domesticity whose rise was an inspiration to youth; George William the gambler, the lusher, the smuggler, the liar, the seller of shoddy cottons, a person whose only excellence was his cheap good nature.

Kellett's first triumph in economy was to pass an ordinance removing the melancholy Cockney (a player of oboes) who was the official rat-catcher of St. Hubert.

George William Vertigan insisted in debate, and afterward privily to Sir Robert Fairlamb, that rats destroy food and perhaps spread disease, and His Excellency must veto the bill. Sir Robert was troubled. He called in The Surgeon General, Dr. R. E. Inchcape Jones (but he preferred to be called Mister, not Doctor).

Dr. Inchcape Jones was a thin, tall, fretful, youngish man, without bowels. He had come out from Home only two years before, and he wanted to go back Home, to that particular part of Home represented by tennis-teas in Surrey. He remarked to Sir Robert that rats and their ever faithful fleas do carry diseases—plague and infectious jaundice and rat-bite fever and possibly leprosy—but these diseases did not and therefore could not exist in St. Hubert, except for leprosy, which was a natural punishment of outlandish Native Races. In fact, noted Inchcape Jones, nothing did exist in St. Hubert except malaria, dengue, and a general beastly dullness, and if Red Legs like Kellett longed to die of plague and rat-bite fever, why should decent people object?

So by the sovereign power of the House of Assembly of St. Hubert, and of His Excellency the Governor, the Cockney rat-catcher and his jiggling young colored assistant were commanded to cease to exist. The rat-catcher became a chauffeur. He drove Canadian and American tourists, who stopped over at St. Hubert for a day or two between Barbados and Trinidad, along such hill-trails as he considered most easy to achieve with a second-hand motor, and gave them misinformation regarding the flowers. The rat-catcher's assistant became a respectable smuggler and leader of a Wesleyan choir. And as for the rats themselves, they flourished, they were glad in the land, and each female produced from ten to two hundred offspring every year.

They were not often seen by day. "The rats aren't increasing; the cats kill 'em," said Kellett the Red Leg. But by darkness they gamboled in the warehouses and in and out of the schooners along the quay. They ventured countryward, and lent their fleas to a species of ground squirrels which were plentiful about the village of Carib.

A year and a half after the removal of the rat-catcher, when the *Pendown Castle* came in from Montevideo and moored by the Councillor Pier, it was observed by ten thousand glinty small eyes among the piles.

As a matter of routine, certainly not as a thing connected with the deaths from what the skipper had called influenza, the crew of the *Pendown Castle* put rat-shields on the mooring hawsers, but they did not take up the gang-plank at night, and now and then a rat slithered ashore to find among its kin in Blackwater more unctuous fare than hardwood lumber. The *Pendown* sailed amiably for home, and from Avonmouth came to Surgeon General Inchcape Jones a cable announcing that the ship was held, that others of the crew had died . . . and died of plague.

In the curt cablegram the word seemed written in bone-scorching fire.

Two days before the cable came, a Blackwater lighterman had been smitten by an unknown ill, very unpleasant, with delirium and buboes. Inchcape Jones said that it could not be plague, because there never was plague in St. Hubert. His confrère, Stokes, retorted that perhaps it couldn't be plague, but it damn' well *was* plague.

Dr. Stokes was a wiry, humorless man, the parish medical officer of St. Swithin Parish. He did not remain in the rustic reaches of St. Swithin, where he belonged, but snooped all over the island, annoying Inchcape Jones. He was an M.B. of Edinburgh; he had served in the African bush; he had had blackwater fever and cholera and most other reasonable afflictions; and he had come to St. Hubert only to recover his red blood corpuscles and to disturb the unhappy Inchcape Jones. He was not a nice man; he had beaten Inchcape Jones at tennis, with a nasty, unsporting serve—the sort of serve you'd expect from an American.

And this Stokes, rather a bounder, a frightful bore, fancied himself as an amateur bacteriologist! It was a bit thick to have him creeping about the docks, catching rats, making cultures from the bellies of their fleas, and barging in—sandy-headed and red-faced, thin and unpleasant—to insist that they bore plague.

"My dear fellow, there's always some *Bacillus pestis* among rats," said Inchcape Jones, in a kindly but airy way.

When the lighterman died, Stokes irritatingly demanded that it be openly admitted that the plague had come to St. Hubert.

"Even if it was plague, which is not certain," said Inchcape Jones, "there's no reason to cause a row and frighten everybody. It was a sporadic case. There won't be any more."

There was more, immediately. In a week three other waterfront workers and a fisherman at Point Carib were down with something which, even Inchcape Jones acknowledged, was uncomfortably like the description of plague in "Manson's Tropical Diseases": "a prodromal stage characterized by depression, anorexia, aching of the limbs," then the fever, the vertigo, the haggard features, the bloodshot and sunken eyes, the buboes in the groin. It was not a pretty disease. Inchcape Jones ceased being chattery and ever so jolly about picnics, and became almost as grim as Stokes. But publicly he still hoped and denied, and St. Hubert did not know . . . did not know.

II

To drinking men and wanderers, the pleasantest place in the rather dull and tin-roofed town of Blackwater is the bar and restaurant called the Ice House.

It is on the floor above the Kellett Shipping Agency and the shop where the Chinaman who is supposed to be a graduate of Oxford sells carved tortoise, and cocoanuts in the horrible likeness of a head shrunken by headhunters. Except for the balcony, where one lunches and looks down on squatting breech-clouted Hindu beggars, and unearthly pearl-pale English children at games in the savannah, all of the Ice House is a large and dreaming dimness wherein you are but half conscious of Moorish grills, a touch of gilt on white-painted walls, a heavy, amazingly long mahogany bar, slot machines, and marble-topped tables beyond your own.

Here, at the cocktail-hour, are all the bloodless, sun-helmeted white rulers of St. Hubert who haven't quite the caste to belong to the Devonshire Club: the shipping-office clerks, the merchants who have no grandfathers, the secretaries to the Inchcape Joneses, the Italians and Portuguese who smuggle into Venezuela.

Calmed by rum swizzles, those tart and commanding apéritifs which are made in their deadly perfection only by the twirling swizzle-sticks of the darkies at the Ice House bar, the exiles become peaceful, and have another swizzle, and grow certain again (as for twenty-four hours, since the last cocktail-hour, they have not been certain) that next year they will go Home. Yes, they will taper off, take exercise in the dawn coolness, stop drinking, become strong and successful, and go Home . . . the Lotus Eaters, tears in their eyes when in the dimness of the Ice House they think of Piccadilly or the heights of Quebec, of Indiana or Catalonia or the clogs of Lancashire. . . . They never go Home. But always they have new reassuring cocktail-hours at the Ice House, until they die, and the other lost men come to their funerals and whisper one to another that they *are* going Home.

Now of the Ice House, George William Vertigan, owner of the Blue Bazaar, was unchallenged monarch. He was a thick, ruddy man, the sort of Englishman one sees in the Midlands, the sort that is either very Non-Conformist or very alcoholic, and George William was not Non-Conformist. Each day from five to seven he was tilted against the bar, never drunk, never altogether sober, always full of melody and kindliness; the one man who did not long for Home, because outside the Ice House he remembered no home.

When it was whispered that a man had died of something which might be plague, George William announced to his court that if it were true, it would serve Kellett the Red Leg jolly well right. But every one knew that the West Indian climate prevented plague.

The group, quivering on the edge of being panicky, were reassured.

It was two nights afterward that there writhed into the Ice House a rumor that George William Vertigan was dead.

III

No one dared speak of it, whether in the Devonshire Club or the Ice House or the breeze-fluttered, sea-washed park where the negroes gather after working hours, but they heard, almost without hearing, of this death—and this—and another. No one liked to shake hands with his oldest friend; every one fled from every one else, though the rats loyally stayed with them; and through the island galloped the Panic, which is more murderous than its brother, the Plague.

Still there was no quarantine, no official admission. Inchcape Jones vomited feeble proclamations on the inadvisability of too-large public gatherings, and wrote to London to inquire about Haffkine's prophylactic, but to Sir Robert Fairlamb he protested, "Honestly, there's only been a few deaths, and I think it's all passed over. As for these suggestions of Stokes that we burn the village of Carib, merely because they've had several cases—why, it's barbarous! And it's been conveyed to me that if we were to establish a quarantine, the merchants would take the strongest measures against the administration. It would ruin the tourist and export business."

But Stokes of St. Swithin's secretly wrote to Dr. Max Gottlieb, Director of the McGurk Institute, that the plague was ready to flare up and consume all the West Indies, and would Dr. Gottlieb do something about it?

Chapter XXXII

THERE may have been in the shadowy heart of Max Gottlieb a diabolic insensibility to divine pity, to suffering humankind; there may have been mere resentment of the doctors who considered his science of value only as it was handy to advertising their business of healing; there may have been the obscure and passionate and unscrupulous demand of genius for privacy. Certainly he who had lived to study the methods of immunizing mankind against disease had little interest in actually using those methods. He was like a fabulous painter, so contemptuous of popular taste that after a lifetime of creation he should destroy everything he had done, lest it be marred and mocked by the dull eyes of the crowd.

The letter from Dr. Stokes was not his only intimation that plague was striding through St. Hubert, that to-morrow it might be leaping to Barbados, to the Virgin Islands . . . to New York. Ross McGurk was an emperor of the new era, better served than any cloistered satrap of old. His skippers looked in at a hundred ports; his railroads penetrated jungles; his correspondents whispered to him of the next election in Colombia, of the Cuban cane-crop, of what Sir Robert Fairlamb had said to Dr. R. E. Inchcape Jones on his bungalow porch. Ross McGurk, and after him Max Gottlieb, knew better than did the Lotus Eaters of the Ice House how much plague there was in St. Hubert.

Yet Gottlieb did not move, but pondered the unknown chemical structure of antibodies, interrupted by questions as to whether Pearl Robbins had enough pencils, whether it would be quite all right for Dr. Holabird to receive the Lettish scientific mission this afternoon, so that Dr. Sholtheis might attend the Anglican Conference on the Reservation of the Host.

He was assailed by inquirers: public health officials, one Dr. Almus Pickerbaugh, a congressman who was said to be popular in Washington, Gustaf Sondelius, and a Martin Arrowsmith who could not (whether because he was too big or too small) quite attain Gottlieb's concentrated indifference.

It was rumored that Arrowsmith of McGurk had something which might eradicate plague. Letters demanded of Gottlieb, "Can you stand by, with the stuff of salvation in your hands, and watch thousands of these unfortunate people dying in St. Hubert, and what is more, are you going to let the dreaded plague gain a foothold in the Western hemisphere? My dear man, this is the time to come out of your scientific reverie and act!"

Then Ross McGurk, over a comfortable steak, hinted, not too diffidently, that this was the opportunity for the Institute to acquire world-fame.

Whether it was the compulsion of McGurk or the demands of the public-spirited, or whether Gottlieb's own imagination aroused enough to visualize the far-off misery of the blacks in the canefields, he summoned Martin and remarked:

"It comes to me that there is pneumonic plague in Manchuria and bubonic in St. Hubert, in the West Indies. If I could trust you, Martin, to use the phage with only half your patients and keep the others as controls, under normal hygienic conditions but without the phage, then you could make an absolute determination of its value, as complete as what we have of mosquito transmission of yellow fever, and then I would send you down to St. Hubert. What do you t'ink?"

Martin swore by Jacques Loeb that he would observe test conditions; he would determine forever the value of phage by the contrast between patients treated and untreated, and so, perhaps, end all plague forever; he would harden his heart and keep clear his eyes.

"We will get Sondelius to go along," said Gottlieb. "He will do the big boom-boom and so bring us the credit in the newspapers which, I am now told, a Director must obtain."

Sondelius did not merely consent—he insisted.

Martin had never seen a foreign country—he could not think of Canada, where he had spent a vacation as hotel-waiter, as foreign to him. He could not comprehend that he was really going to a place of palm trees and brown faces and languid Christmas Eves. He was busy (while Sondelius was out ordering linen suits and seeking a proper new sun helmet) making anti-plague phage on a large scale: a hundred liters of it, sealed in tiny ampules. He felt like the normal Martin, but conferences and powers were considering him.

There was a meeting of the Board of Trustees to advise Martin and Sondelius as to their methods. For it the President of the University of Wilmington gave up a promising interview with a millionaire alumnus, Ross McGurk gave up a game of golf, and one of the three university scientists arrived by aeroplane. Called in from the laboratory, a rather young man in a wrinkled soft collar, dizzy still with the details of Erlenmeyer flasks, infusorial earth, and sterile filters, Martin was confronted by the Men of Measured Merriment, and found that he was no longer concealed in the invisibility of insignificance but regarded as a leader who was expected not only to produce miracles but to explain beforehand how important and mature and miraculous he was.

He was shy before the spectacled gravity of the five Trustees as they sat, like a Supreme Court, at the dais table in Bonanza Hall—Gottlieb a little removed, also trying to look grave and supreme. But Sondelius rolled in, enthusiastic and tremendous, and suddenly Martin was not shy, nor was he respectful to his one-time master in public health.

Sondelius wanted to exterminate all the rodents in St. Hubert, to enforce a quarantine, to use Yersin's serum and Haffkine's prophylactic, and to give Martin's phage to everybody in St. Hubert, all at once, all with everybody.

Martin protested. For the moment it might have been Gottlieb speaking.

He knew, he flung at them, that humanitarian feeling would make it impossible to use the poor devils of sufferers as mere objects of experiment, but he must have at least a few real test cases, and he was damned, even before the Trustees he was damned, if he would have his experiment so mucked up by multiple treatment that they could never tell whether the cures were due to Yersin or Haffkine or phage or none of them.

The Trustees adopted his plan. After all, while they desired to save humanity, wasn't it better to have it saved by a McGurk representative than by Yersin or Haffkine or the outlandish Sondelius?

It was agreed that if Martin could find in St. Hubert a district which was comparatively untouched by the plague, he should there endeavor to have test cases, one half injected with phage, one half untreated. In the badly afflicted districts, he might give the phage to every one, and if the disease slackened unusually, that would be a secondary proof.

Whether the St. Hubert government, since they had not asked for aid, would give Martin power to experiment and Sondelius police authority, the Trustees did not know. The Surgeon General, a chap named Inchcape Jones, had replied to their cables: "No real epidemic not need help." But McGurk promised that he would pull his numerous wires to have the McGurk Commission (Chairman, Martin Arrowsmith, B.A., M.D.) welcomed by the authorities.

Sondelius still insisted that in this crisis mere experimentation was heartless, yet he listened to Martin's close-reasoned fury with the enthusiasm which this bull-necked eternal child had for anything which sounded new and preferably true. He did not, like Almus Pickerbaugh, regard a difference of scientific opinion as an attack on his character.

He talked of going on his own, independent of Martin and McGurk, but he was won back when the Trustees murmured that though they really did wish the dear man wouldn't fool with sera, they would provide him with apparatus to kill all the rats he wanted.

Then Sondelius was happy:

"And you watch me! I am the captain-general of rat-killers! I yoost walk into a warehouse and the rats say, 'There's that damn' old Uncle Gustaf—what's the use?' and they turn up their toes and die! I am yoost as glad I have you people behind me, because I am broke—I went and bought some oil stock that don't look so good now—and I shall need a lot of hydrocyanic acid gas. Oh, those rats! You watch me! Now I go and telegraph I can't keep a lecture engagement next week—huh! me to lecture to a women's college, me that can talk rat-language and know seven beautiful deadly kind of traps!"

II

Martin had never known greater peril than swimming a flood as a hospital intern. From waking to midnight he was too busy making phage and receiving unsolicited advice from all the Institute staff to think of the dangers of a plague epidemic, but when he went to bed, when his brain was still revolving with plans, he pictured rather too well the chance of dying, unpleasantly.

When Leora received the idea that he was going off to a death-haunted isle, to a place of strange ways and trees and faces (a place, probably, where they spoke funny languages and didn't have movies or tooth-paste), she took the notion secretively away with her, to look at it and examine it, precisely as she often stole little foods from the table and hid them and meditatively ate them at odd hours of the night, with the pleased expression of a bad child. Martin was glad that she did not add to his qualms by worrying. Then, after three days, she spoke:

"I'm going with you."

"You are not!"

"Well. . . . I am!"

"It's not safe."

"Silly! Of course it is. You can shoot your nice old phage into me, and then I'll be absolutely all right. Oh, I have a husband who cures things, I have! I'm going to blow in a lot of money for thin dresses, though I bet St. Hubert isn't any hotter than Dakota can be in August."

"Listen! Lee, darling! Listen! I do think the phage will immunize against the plague—you bet I'll be mighty well injected with it myself!—but I don't *know*, and even if it were practically perfect, there'd always be some people it wouldn't protect. You simply can't go, sweet. Now I'm terribly sleepy—"

Leora seized his lapels, as comic fierce as a boxing kitten, but her eyes were not comic, nor her wailing voice; age-old wail of the soldiers' women:

"Sandy, don't you know I haven't any life outside of you? I might've had, but honestly, I've been glad to let you absorb me. I'm a lazy, useless, ignorant scut, except as maybe I keep you comfortable. If you were off there, and I didn't know you were all right, or if you died and somebody else cared for your body that I've loved so—haven't I loved it, dear?—I'd go mad. I mean it—can't you see I mean it—I'd go mad! It's just— I'm you, and I got to be with you. And I *will* help you!

Make your media and everything. You know how often I've helped you. Oh, I'm not much good at McGurk, with all your awful' complicated jiggers, but I did help you at Nautilus—I *did* help you, didn't I?—and maybe in St. Hubert"—her voice was the voice of women in midnight terror—"maybe you won't find anybody that can help you even my little bit, and I'll cook and everything—"

"Darling, don't make it harder for me. Going to be hard enough in any case—"

"Damn you, Sandy Arrowsmith, don't you dare use those old stuck-up expressions that husbands have been drooling out to wives forever and ever! I'm not a wife, any more'n you're a husband. You're a rotten husband! You neglect me absolutely. The only time you know what I've got on is when some doggone button slips—and how they can pull off when a person has gone over 'em and sewed 'em all on again is simply beyond me!—and then you bawl me out. But I don't care. I'd rather have you than any decent husband. . . . Besides. I'm going."

Gottlieb opposed it, Sondelius roared about it, Martin worried about it, but Leora went, and—his only act of craftiness as Director of the Institute—Gottlieb made her "Secretary and Technical Assistant to the McGurk Plague and Bacteriophage Commission to the Lesser Antilles," and blandly gave her a salary.

III

The day before the Commission sailed, Martin insisted that Sondelius take his first injection of phage. He refused.

"No, I will not touch it till you get converted to humanity, Martin, and give it to everybody in St. Hubert. And you will! Wait till you see them suffering by the thousand. You have not seen such a thing. Then you will forget science and try to save everybody. You shall not inject me till you will inject all my negro friends down there too."

That afternoon Gottlieb called Martin in. He spoke with hesitation:

"You're off for Blackwater to-morrow."

"Yes, sir."

"Hm. You may be gone some time. I— Martin, you are my oldest friend in New York, you and the good Miriam. Tell me: At first you and Terry t'ought I should not take up the Directorship. Don't you now t'ink I was wise?"

Martin stared, then hastily he lied and said that which was comforting and expected.

"I am glad you t'ink so. You have known so long what I have tried to do. I haf faults, but I t'ink I begin to see a real scientific note coming into the Institute at last, after the popoolarity-chasing of Tubbs and Holabird. . . . I wonder how I can discharge Holabird, that pants-presser of science? If only he dit not know Capitola so well—socially, they call it! But anyway—

"There are those that said Max Gottlieb could not do the child job of running an institution. Huh! Buying note-books! Hiring women that sweep floors! Or no—the floors are swept by women hired by the superintendent of the building, *nicht wahr*? But anyway—

"I did not make a rage when Terry and you doubted. I am a great fellow for allowing every one his opinion. But it pleases me—I am very fond of you two boys—the only real sons I have—" Gottlieb laid his withered hand on Martin's arm. "It pleases me that you see now I am beginning to make a real scientific Institute. Though I have enemies. Martin, you would t'ink I was joking if I told you the plotting against me—

"Even Yeo. I t'ought he was my friend. I t'ought he was a real biologist. But just to-day he comes to me and says he cannot get enough sea-urchins for his experiments. As if I could make sea-urchins out of thin air! He said I keep him short of all materials. Me! That have always stood for—I do not care what they *pay* scientists, but always I have stood, against that fool Silva and all of them, all my enemies—

"You do not know how many enemies I have, Martin! They do not dare show their faces. They smile to me, but they whisper— I will show Holabird—always he plot against me and try to win over Pearl Robbins, but she is a good girl, she knows what I am doing, but—"

He looked perplexed; he peered at Martin as though he did not quite recognize him, and begged:

"Martin, I grow old—not in years—it is a lie I am over seventy—but I have my worries. Do you mind if I give you advice as I have done so often, so many years? Though you are not a schoolboy now in Queen City—no, at Winnemac it was. You are a man and you are a genuine worker. But—

"Be sure you do not let anything, not even your own good kind heart, spoil your experiment at St. Hubert. I do not make funniness about humanitarianism as I used to; sometimes now I t'ink the vulgar and contentious human race may yet have as much grace and good taste as the cats. But if this is to be, there must be knowledge. So many men, Martin, are kind and neighborly; so few have added to knowledge. You have the chance! You may be the man who ends all plague, and maybe old Max Gottlieb will have helped, too, *hein*, maybe?

"You must not be just a good doctor at St. Hubert. You must pity, oh, so much the generation after generation yet to come that you can refuse to let yourself indulge in pity for the men you will see dying.

"Dying. . . . It will be peace.

"Let nothing, neither beautiful pity nor fear of your own death, keep you from making this plague experiment complete. And as my friend— If you do this, something will yet have come out of my Directorship. If but one fine thing could come, to justify me—"

When Martin came sorrowing into his laboratory he found Terry Wickett waiting.

"Say, Slim," Terry blurted, "just wanted to butt in and suggest, now for St. Gottlieb's sake keep your phage notes complete and up-to-date, and keep 'em in ink!"

"Terry, it looks to me as if you thought I had a fine chance of not coming back with the notes myself."

"Aw, what's biting you!" said Terry feebly.

IV

The epidemic in St. Hubert must have increased, for on the day before the McGurk Commission sailed, Dr. Inchcape Jones declared that the island was quarantined. People might come in, but no one could leave. He did this despite the fretting of the Governor, Sir Robert Fairlamb, and the protests of the hotel-keepers who fed on tourists, the ex-rat-catchers who drove the same, Kellett the Red Leg who sold them tickets, and all the other representatives of sound business in St. Hubert.

V

Besides his ampules of phage and his Luer syringes for injection, Martin made personal preparations for the tropics. He bought, in seventeen minutes, a Palm Beach suit, two new shirts, and, as St. Hubert was a British possession and as he had heard that all Britishers carry canes, a stick which the shop-keeper guaranteed to be as good as genuine malacca.

VI

They started, Martin and Leora and Gustaf Sondelius, on a winter morning, on the six-thousand-ton steamer *St. Buryan* of the McGurk Line, which carried machinery and flour and codfish and motors to the Lesser Antilles and brought back molasses, cocoa, avocados, Trinidad asphalt. A score of winter tourists made the round trip, but only a score, and there was little handkerchief-waving.

The McGurk Line pier was in South Brooklyn, in a district of brown anonymous houses. The sky was colorless above dirty snow. Sondelius seemed well content. As they drove upon a wharf littered with hides and boxes and disconsolate steerage passengers, he peered out of their crammed taxicab and announced that the bow of the *St. Buryan*—all they could see of it—reminded him of the Spanish steamer he had taken to the Cape Verde Isles. But to Martin and Leora, who had read of the drama of departure, of stewards darting with masses of flowers, dukes and divorcees being interviewed, and bands playing "The Star Spangled Banner," the *St. Buryan* was unromantic and its ferry-like casualness was discouraging.

Only Terry came to see them off, bringing a box of candy for Leora.

Martin had never ridden a craft larger than a motor launch. He stared up at the black wall of the steamer's side. As they mounted the gangplank he was conscious that he was cutting himself off from the safe, familiar land, and he was embarrassed by the indifference of more experienced-looking passengers, staring down from the rail. Aboard, it seemed to him that the forward deck looked like the backyard of an old-iron dealer, that the *St. Buryan* leaned too much to one side, and that even in the dock she swayed undesirably.

The whistle snorted contemptuously; the hawsers were cast off. Terry stood on the pier till the steamer, with Martin and Leora and Sondelius above him, their stomachs pressed against the rail, had slid past him, then he abruptly clumped away.

Martin realized that he was off for the perilous sea and the perilous plague; that there was no possibility of leaving the ship till they should reach some distant island. This narrow deck, with its tarry lines between planks, was his only home. Also, in the breeze across the wide harbor he was beastly cold, and in general God help him!

As the *St. Buryan* was warped out into the river, as Martin was suggesting to his Commission, "How about going downstairs and seeing if we can raise a drink?" there was the sound of a panicky taxicab on the pier, the sight of a lean, tall figure running—but so feebly, so shakily—and they realized that it was Max Gottlieb, peering for them, tentatively raising his thin arm in greeting, not finding them in the line at the rail, and turning sadly away.

VII

As representatives of Ross McGurk and his various works, evil and benevolent, they had the two suites de luxe on the boat deck.

Martin was cold off snow-blown Sandy Hook, sick off Cape Hatteras, and tired and relaxed between; with him Leora was cold, and in a ladylike manner she was sick, but she was not at all tired. She insisted on conveying information to him, from the West Indian guide-book which she had earnestly bought.

Sondelius was conspicuously all over the ship. He had tea with the Captain, scouse with the fo'c'sle, and intellectual conferences with the negro missionary in the steerage. He was to be heard—always he was to be heard: singing on the promenade deck, defending Bolshevism against the boatswain, arguing oil-burning with the First Officer, and explaining to the bar steward how to make a gin sling. He held a party for the children in the steerage, and he borrowed from the First Officer a volume of navigation to study between parties.

He gave flavor to the ordinary cautious voyage of the *St. Buryan*, but he made a mistake. He was courteous to Miss Gwilliam; he tried to cheer her on a seemingly lonely adventure.

Miss Gwilliam came from one of the best families in her section of New Jersey; her father was a lawyer and a churchwarden, her grandfather had been a solid farmer. That she had not married, at thirty-three, was due entirely to the preference of modern young men for jazz-dancing hussies; and she was not only a young lady of delicate reservations but also a singer; in fact, she was going to the West Indies to preserve the wonders of primitive art for reverent posterity in the native ballads she would collect and sing to a delighted public—if only she learned how to sing.

She studied Gustaf Sondelius. He was a silly person, not in the least like the gentlemanly insurance-agents and office-managers she was accustomed to meet at the country club, and what was worse, he did not ask her opinions on art and good form. His stories about generals and that sort of people could be discounted as lies, for did he not associate with grimy engineers? He needed some of her gentle but merry chiding.

When they stood together at the rail and he chanted in his ludicrous up-and-down Swedish sing-song that it was a fine evening, she remarked, "Well, Mr. Roughneck, have you been up to something smart again to-day? Or have you been giving somebody else a chance to talk, for once?"

She was placidly astonished when he clumped away with none of the obedient reverence which any example of cultured American womanhood has a right to expect from all males, even foreigners.

Sondelius came to Martin lamenting, "Slim—if I may call you so, like Terry—I think you and your Gottlieb are right. There is no use saving fools. It's a great mistake to be natural.

One should always be a stuffed shirt, like old Tubbs. Then one would have respect even from artistic New Jersey spinsters. . . . How strange is conceit! That I who have been cursed and beaten by so many Great Ones, who was once led out to be shot in a Turkish prison, should never have been annoyed by them as by this smug wench. Ah, smugness! That is the enemy!"

Apparently he recovered from Miss Gwilliam. He was seen arguing with the ship's doctor about sutures in negro skulls, and he invented a game of deck cricket. But one evening when he sat reading in the "social hall," stooped over, wearing betraying spectacles and his mouth puckered, Martin walked past the window and incredulously saw that Sondelius was growing old.

VIII

As he sat by Leora in a deck-chair, Martin studied her, really looked at her pale profile, after years when she had been a matter of course. He pondered on her as he pondered on phage; he weightily decided that he had neglected her, and weightily he started right in to be a good husband.

"Now I have a chance to be human, Lee, I realize how lonely you must have been in New York."

"But I haven't."

"Don't be foolish! Of course you've been lonely! Well, when we get back, I'll take a little time off every day and we'll—we'll have walks and go to the movies and everything. And I'll send you flowers, every morning. Isn't it a relief to just sit here! But I do begin to think and realize how I've prob'ly neglected— Tell me, honey, has it been too terribly dull?"

"Hunka. Really."

"No, but *tell* me."

"There's nothing to tell."

"Now hang it, Leora, here when I *do* have the first chance in eleven thousand years to think about you, and I come right out frankly and admit how slack I've been— And planning to send you flowers—"

"You look here, Sandy Arrowsmith! Quit bullying me! You want the luxury of harrowing yourself by thinking what a poor, bawling, wretched, story-book wife I am. You're working up to become perfectly miserable if you can't enjoy being miserable. . . . It would be terrible, when we got back to New York, if you did get on the job and devoted yourself to showing me a good time. You'd go at it like a bull. I'd have to be so dratted grateful for the flowers every day—the days you didn't forget!—and the way you'd sling me off to the movies when I wanted to stay home and snooze—"

"Well, by thunder, of all the—"

"No, please! You're dear and good, but you're so bossy that I've always got to be whatever *you* want, even if it's lonely. But— Maybe I'm lazy. I'd rather just snoop around than have to work at being well-dressed and popular and all those jobs. I fuss over the flat—hang it, wish I'd had the kitchen repainted while we're away, it's a *nice* little kitchen—and I make believe read my French books, and go out for a walk, and look in the windows, and eat an ice cream soda, and the day slides by. Sandy, I do love you awful' much; if I could, I'd be as ill-treated as the dickens, so you could enjoy it, but I'm no good at educated lies, only at easy little ones like the one I told you last week—I said I hadn't eaten any candy and didn't have a stomach-ache, and I'd eaten half a pound and I was sick as a pup. . . . Gosh, I'm a good wife I am!"

They rolled from gray seas to purple and silver. By dusk they stood at the rail, and he felt the spaciousness of the sea, of life. Always he had lived in his imagination. As he had blundered through crowds, an inconspicuous young husband trotting out to buy cold roast beef for dinner, his brain-pan had been wide as the domed sky. He had seen not the streets, but microörganisms large as jungle monsters, miles of flasks cloudy with bacteria, himself giving orders to his garçon, Max Gottlieb awesomely congratulating him. Always his dreams had clung about his work. Now, no less passionately, he awoke to the ship, the mysterious sea, the presence of Leora, and he cried to her, in the warm tropic winter dusk:

"Sweet, this is only the first of our big hikes! Pretty soon, if I'm successful in St. Hubert, I'll begin to count in science, and we'll go abroad, to your France and England and Italy and everywhere!"

"Can we, do you think? Oh, Sandy! Going *places*!"

IX

He never knew it but for an hour, in their cabin half-lighted from the lamps in their sitting-room beyond, she watched him sleeping.

He was not handsome; he was grotesque as a puppy napping on a hot afternoon. His hair was ruffled, his face was deep in the crumpled pillow he had encircled with both his arms. She looked at him, smiling, with the stretched corners of her lips like tiny flung arrows.

"I do love him so when he's frowsy! Don't you see, Sandy, I was wise to come! You're so worn out. *It* might get you, and nobody but me could nurse you. Nobody knows all your cranky ways—about how you hate prunes and everything. Night and day I'll nurse you—the least whisper and I'll be awake. And if you need ice bags and stuff— And I'll *have* ice, too, if I have to sneak into some millionaire's house and steal it out of his highballs! My dear!"

She shifted the electric fan so that it played more upon him, and on soft toes she crept into their stiff sitting-room. It did not contain much save a round table, a few chairs, and a Sybaritic glass and mahogany wall-cabinet whose purpose was never discovered.

"It's so sort of— Aah! Pinched. I guess maybe I ought to fix it up somehow."

But she had no talent for the composing of chairs and pictures which brings humanness into a dead room. Never in her life had she spent three minutes in arranging flowers. She looked doubtful, she smiled and turned out the light, and slipped in to him.

She lay on the coverlet of her berth, in the tropic languidness, a slight figure in a frivolous nightgown. She thought, "I like a small bedroom, because Sandy is nearer and I don't get so scared by things. What a dratted bully the man is! Some day I'm going to up and say to him: 'You go to the devil!' I will so! Darling, we will hike off to France together, just you and I, won't we!"

She was asleep, smiling, so thin a little figure—

Chapter XXXIII

MISTY MOUNTAINS they saw, and on their flanks the palm-crowned fortifications built of old time against the pirates. In Martinique were white-faced houses like provincial France, and a boiling market full of colored women with kerchiefs ultramarine and scarlet. They passed hot St. Lucia, and Saba that is all one lone volcano. They devoured paw-paws and breadfruit and avocados, bought from coffee-colored natives who came alongside in nervous small boats; they felt the languor of the isles, and panted before they approached Barbados.

Just beyond was St. Hubert.

None of the tourists had known of the quarantine. They were raging that the company should have taken them into danger. In the tepid wind they felt the plague.

The skipper reassured them, in a formal address. Yes, they would stop at Blackwater, the port of St. Hubert, but they would anchor far out in the harbor; and while the passengers bound for St. Hubert would be permitted to go ashore, in the port-doctor's launch, no one in St. Hubert would be allowed to leave—nothing from that pest-hole would touch the steamer except the official mail, which the ship's surgeon would disinfect.

(The ship's surgeon was wondering, the while, how you disinfected mail—let's see—sulfur burning in the presence of moisture, wasn't it?)

The skipper had been trained in oratory by arguments with wharf-masters, and the tourists were reassured. But Martin murmured to his Commission, "I hadn't thought of that. Once we go ashore, we'll be practically prisoners till the epidemic's over—if it ever does get over—prisoners with the plague around us."

"Why, of course!" said Sondelius.

II

They left Bridgetown, the pleasant port of Barbados, by afternoon. It was late night, with most of the passengers asleep, when they arrived at Blackwater. As Martin came out on the damp and vacant deck, it seemed unreal, harshly unfriendly, and of the coming battleground he saw nothing but a few shore lights beyond uneasy water.

About their arrival there was something timorous and illicit. The ship's surgeon ran up and down, looking disturbed; the captain could be heard growling on the bridge; the first officer hastened up to confer with him and disappeared below again; and there was no one to meet them. The steamer waited, rolling in a swell, while from the shore seemed to belch a hot miasma.

"And here's where we're going to land and *stay*!" Martin grunted to Leora, as they stood by their bags, their cases of phage, on the heaving, black-shining deck near the top of the accommodation-ladder.

Passengers came out in dressing-gowns, chattering, "Yes, this must be the place, those lights there. Must be fierce. *What?* Somebody going ashore? Oh, sure, those two doctors. Well, they got nerve. I certainly don't envy them!"

Martin heard.

From shore a pitching light made toward the ship, slid round the bow, and sidled to the bottom of the accommodation-ladder. In the haze of a lantern held by a steward at the foot of the steps, Martin could see a smart covered launch, manned by darky sailors in naval uniform and glazed black straw hats with ribbons, and commanded by a Scotch-looking man with some sort of a peaked uniform cap over a civilian jacket.

The captain clumped down the swinging steps beside the ship. While the launch bobbed, its wet canvas top glistening, he had a long and complaining conference with the commander of the launch, and received a pouch of mail, the only thing to come aboard.

The ship's surgeon took it from the captain with aversion, grumbling, "Now where can I get a barrel to disinfect these darn' letters in?"

Martin and Leora and Sondelius waited, without option.

They had been joined by a thin woman in black whom they had not seen all the trip—one of the mysterious passengers who are never noticed till they come on deck at landing. Apparently she was going ashore. She was pale, her hands twitching.

The captain shouted at them, "All right—all right—all right! You can go now. Hustle, please. I've got to get on. . . . Damn' nuisance."

The *St. Buryan* had not seemed large or luxurious, but it was a castle, steadfast among storms, its side a massy wall, as Martin crept down the swaying stairs, thinking all at once, "We're in for it; like going to the scaffold—they lead you along—no chance to resist," and, "You're letting your imagination run away with you; quit it now!" and, "Is it too late to make Lee stay behind, on the steamer?" and an agonized, "Oh, Lord, are the stewards handling that phage carefully?" Then he was on the tiny square platform at the bottom of the accommodation-ladder, the ship's side was high above him, lit by the round ports of cabins, and some one was helping him into the launch.

As the unknown woman in black came aboard, Martin saw in lantern light how her lips tightened once, then her whole face went blank, like one who waited hopelessly.

Leora squeezed his hand, hard, as he helped her in.

He muttered, while the steamer whistled, "Quick! You can still go back! You must!"

"And leave the pretty launch? Why, Sandy! Just look at the elegant engine it's got! . . . Gosh, I'm scared blue!"

As the launch sputtered, swung round, and headed for the filtering of lights ashore, as it bowed its head and danced to the swell, the sandy-headed official demanded of Martin:

"You're the McGurk Commission?"

"Yes."

"Good." He sounded pleased yet cold, a busy voice and humorless.

"Are you the port-doctor?" asked Sondelius.

"No, not exactly. I'm Dr. Stokes, of St. Swithin's Parish. We're all of us almost everything, nowadays. The port-doctor— In fact he died couple of days ago."

Martin grunted. But his imagination had ceased to agitate him.

"You're Dr. Sondelius, I imagine. I know your work in Africa, in German East—was out there myself. And you're Dr. Arrowsmith? I read your plague phage paper. Much impressed. Now I have just the chance to say before we go ashore— You'll both be opposed. Inchcape Jones, the S.G., has lost his head. Running in circles, lancing buboes—afraid to burn Carib, where most of the infection is. Arrowsmith, I have a notion of what you may want to do experimentally. If Inchcape balks, you come to me in my parish—if I'm still alive. Stokes, my name is. . . . Damn it, boy, what *are* you doing? Trying to drift clear down to Venezuela? . . . Inchcape and H.E. are so afraid that they won't even cremate the bodies—some religious prejudice among the blacks—obee or something."

"I see," said Martin.

"How many cases plague you got now?" said Sondelius.

"Lord knows. Maybe a thousand. And ten million rats. . . . I'm so sleepy! . . . Well, welcome, gentlemen—" He flung out his arms in a dry hysteria. "Welcome to the Island of Hesperides!"

Out of darkness Blackwater swung toward them, low flimsy barracks on a low swampy plain stinking of slimy mud. Most of the town was dark, dark and wickedly still. There was no face along the dim waterfront—warehouses, tram station, mean hotels—and they ground against a pier, they went ashore, without attention from customs officials. There were no carriages, and the hotel-runners who once had pestered tourists landing from the *St. Buryan*, whatever the hour, were dead now or hidden.

The thin mysterious woman passenger vanished, staggering with her suit-case—she had said no word, and they never saw her again. The Commission, with Stokes and the harbor-police who had manned the launch, carried the baggage (Martin weaving with a case of the phage) through the rutty balconied streets to the San Marino Hotel.

Once or twice faces, disembodied things with frightened lips, stared at them from alley-mouths; and when they came to the hotel, when they stood before it, a weary caravan laden with bags and boxes, the bulging-eyed manageress peered from a window before she would admit them.

As they entered, Martin saw under a street light the first stirring of life: a crying woman and a bewildered child following an open wagon in which were heaped a dozen stiff bodies.

"And I might have saved all of them, with phage," he whispered to himself.

His forehead was cold, yet it was greasy with sweat as he babbled to the manageress of rooms and meals, as he prayed that Leora might not have seen the Things in that slow creaking wagon.

"I'd have choked her before I let her come, if I'd known," he was shuddering.

The woman apologized, "I must ask you gentlemen to carry your things up to your rooms. Our boys— They aren't here any more."

What became of the walking stick which, in such pleased vanity, Martin had bought in New York, he never knew. He was too busy guarding the cases of phage, and worrying, "Maybe this stuff would save everybody."

Now Stokes of St. Swithin's was a reticent man and hard, but when they had the last bag up-stairs, he leaned his head against a door, cried "My God, Arrowsmith, I'm so glad you've got here," and broke from them, running. . . . One of the negro harbor-police, expressionless, speaking the English of the Antilles with something of the accent of Piccadilly, said, "Sar, have you any other command for I? If you permit, we boys will now go home. Sar, on the table is the whisky Dr. Stokes have told I to bring."

Martin stared. It was Sondelius who said, "Thank you very much, boys. Here's a quid between you. Now get some sleep."

They saluted and were not.

Sondelius made the novices as merry as he could for half an hour.

Martin and Leora woke to a broiling, flaring, green and crimson morning, yet ghastly still; awoke and realized that about them was a strange land, as yet unseen, and before them the work that in distant New York had seemed dramatic and joyful and that stank now of the charnel house.

III

A sort of breakfast was brought to them by a negress who, before she would enter, peeped fearfully at them from the door.

Sondelius rumbled in from his room, in an impassioned silk dressing-gown. If ever, spectacled and stooped, he had looked old, now he was young and boisterous.

"Hey, ya, Slim, I think we get some work here! Let me at those rats! This Inchcape—to try to master them with strychnin! A noble melon! Leora, when you divorce Martin, you marry me, heh? Give me the salt. Yey, I sleep fine!"

The night before, Martin had scarce looked at their room. Now he was diverted by what he considered its foreignness: the lofty walls of wood painted a watery blue, the wide furnitureless spaces, the bougainvillæa at the window, and in the courtyard the merciless heat and rattling metallic leaves of palmettoes.

Beyond the courtyard walls were the upper stories of a balconied Chinese shop, and the violent-colored skylight of the Blue Bazaar.

He felt that there should be a clamor from this exotic world, but there was only a rebuking stillness, and even Sondelius became dumb, though he had his moment. He waddled back to his room, dressed himself in surah silk last worn on the East Coast of Africa, and returned bringing a sun-helmet which secretly he had bought for Martin.

In linen jacket and mushroom helmet, Martin belonged more to the tropics than to his own harsh Northern meadows. But his pleasure in looking foreign was interrupted by the entrance of the Surgeon General, Dr. R. E. Inchcape Jones, lean but apple-cheeked, worried and hasty.

"Of course you chaps are welcome, but really, with all we have to do I'm afraid we can't give you the attention you doubtless expect," he said indignantly.

Martin sought for adequate answer. It was Sondelius who spoke of a non-existent cousin who was a Harley Street specialist, and who explained that all they wanted was a laboratory for Martin and, for himself, a chance to slaughter rats. How many times, in how many lands, had Gustaf Sondelius flattered pro-consuls, and persuaded the heathen to let themselves be saved!

Under his hands the Surgeon General became practically human; he looked as though he really thought Leora was pretty; he promised that he might perhaps let Sondelius tamper with his rats. He would return that afternoon and conduct them to the house prepared for them, Penrith Lodge, on the safe secluded hills behind Blackwater. And (he bowed gallantly) he thought that Mrs. Arrowsmith would find the Lodge a topping bungalow, with three rather decent servants. The butler, though a colored chap, was an old mess-sergeant.

Inchcape Jones had scarce gone when at the door there was a pounding and it opened on Martin's classmate at Winnemac, Dr. the Rev. Ira Hinkley.

Martin had forgotten Ira, that bulky Christian who had tried to save him during otherwise dulcet hours of dissection. He recalled him confusedly. The man came in, vast and lumbering. His eyes were staring and altogether mad, and his voice was parched:

"Hello, Mart. Yump, it's old Ira. I'm in charge of all the chapels of the Sanctification Brotherhood here. Oh, Mart, if you only knew the wickedness of the natives, and the way they lie and sing indecent songs and commit all manner of vileness! And the Church of England lets them wallow in their sins! Only us to save them. I heard you were coming. I have been laboring, Mart. I've nursed the poor plague-stricken devils, and I've told them how hellfire is roaring about them. Oh, Mart, if you knew how my heart bleeds to see these ignorant fellows going unrepentant to eternal torture! After all these years I know you can't still be a scoffer. I come to you with open hands, begging you not merely to comfort the sufferers but to snatch their souls from the burning lakes of sulfur to which, in His everlasting mercy, the Lord of Hosts hath condemned those that blaspheme against His gospel, freely given—"

Again it was Sondelius who got Ira Hinkley out, not too discontented, while Martin could only splutter, "Now how do you suppose that maniac ever got here? This is going to be awful!"

Before Inchcape Jones returned, the Commission ventured out for their first sight of the town. . . . A Scientific Commission, yet all the while they were only boisterous Gustaf and doubtful Martin and casual Leora.

The citizens had been told that in bubonic plague, unlike pneumonic, there is no danger from direct contact with people developing the disease, so long as vermin were kept away, but they did not believe it. They were afraid of one another, and the more afraid of strangers. The Commission found a street dying with fear. House-shutters were closed, hot slatted patches in the sun; and the only traffic was an empty trolley-car with a frightened motorman who peered down at them and sped up lest they come aboard. Grocery shops and drug-stores were open, but from their shady depths the shopkeepers looked out timidly, and when the Commission neared a fish-stall, the one customer fled, edging past them.

Once a woman, never explained, a woman with wild ungathered hair, ran by them shrieking, "My little boy—"

They came to the market, a hundred stalls under a long corrugated-iron roof, with stone pillars bearing the fatuous names of the commissioners who had built it—by voting bonds for the building. It should have been buzzing with jovial buyers and sellers, but in all the gaudy booths there were only one negress with a row of twig besoms, one Hindu in gray rags squatting before his wealth of a dozen vegetables. The rest was emptiness, and a litter of rotted potatoes and scudding papers.

Down a grim street of coal yards, they found a public square, and here was the stillness not of sleep but of ancient death.

The square was rimmed with the gloom of mango trees, which shut out the faint-hearted breeze and cooped in the heat—stale lifeless heat, in whose misery the leering silence was the more dismaying. Through a break in the evil mangoes they beheld a plaster house hung with black crape.

"It's too hot to walk. Perhaps we'd better go back to the hotel," said Leora.

IV

In the afternoon Inchcape Jones appeared with a Ford, whose familiarity made it the more grotesque in this creepy world, and took them to Penrith Lodge, on the cool hills behind Blackwater.

They traversed a packed native section of bamboo hovels, and shops that were but unpainted, black-weathered huts, without doors, without windows, from whose recesses dark faces looked at them resentfully. They passed, at their colored driver's most jerky speed, a new brick structure in front of which stately negro policemen with white gloves, white sun-helmets, and scarlet coats cut by white belts, marched with rifles at the carry.

Inchcape Jones sighed, "Schoolhouse. Turned it into pest-house. Hundred cases in there. Die every hour. Have to guard it—patients get delirious and try to escape."

After them trailed an odor of rotting.

Martin did not feel superior to humanity.

V

With broad porches and low roof, among bright flamboyants and the cheerful sago palms, the bungalow of Penrith Lodge lay high on a crest, looking across the ugly flat of the town to the wash of sea. At its windows the reed jalousies whispered and clattered, and the high bare rooms were enlivened by figured Carib scarfs. . . . It had belonged to the port-doctor, dead these three days.

Inchcape Jones assured the doubtful Leora that she would nowhere else be so safe; the house was rat-proofed, and the doctor had caught the plague at the pier, had died without ever coming back to this well-beloved bungalow in which he, the professional bachelor, had given the most clamorous parties in St. Hubert.

Martin had with him sufficient equipment for a small laboratory, and he established it in a bedroom with gas and running water. Next to it was his and Leora's bedroom, then an apartment which Sondelius immediately made homelike by dropping his clothes and his pipe ashes all over it.

There were two colored maids and an ex-soldier butler, who received them and unpacked their bags as though the plague did not exist.

Martin was perplexed by their first caller. He was a singularly handsome young negro, quick-moving, intelligent of eye. Like most white Americans, Martin had talked a great deal about the inferiority of negroes and had learned nothing whatever about them. He looked questioning as the young man observed:

"My name is Oliver Marchand."

"Yes?"

"Dr. Marchand—I have my M.D. from Howard."

"Oh."

"May I venture to welcome you, Doctor? And may I ask before I hurry off—I have three cases from official families isolated at the bottom of the hill—oh, yes, in this crisis they permit a negro doctor to practise even among the whites! But— Dr. Stokes insists that D'Hérelle and you are right in calling bacteriophage an organism. But what about Bordet's contention that it's an enzyme?"

Then for half an hour did Dr. Arrowsmith and Dr. Marchand, forgetting the plague, forgetting the more cruel plague of race-fear, draw diagrams.

Marchand sighed, "I must go, Doctor. May I help you in any way I can? It is a great privilege to know you."

He saluted quietly and was gone, a beautiful young animal.

"I never thought a negro doctor— I wish people wouldn't keep showing me how much I don't know!" said Martin.

VI

While Martin prepared his laboratory, Sondelius was joyfully at work, finding out what was wrong with Inchcape Jones's administration, which proved to be almost anything that could be wrong.

A plague epidemic to-day, in a civilized land, is no longer an affair of people dying in the streets and of drivers shouting "Bring out your dead." The fight against it is conducted like modern warfare, with telephones instead of foaming chargers. The ancient horror bears a face of efficiency. There are offices, card indices, bacteriological examinations of patients and of rats. There is, or should be, a lone director with superlegal powers. There are large funds, education of the public by placard and newspaper, brigades of rat-killers, a corps of disinfectors, isolation of patients lest vermin carry the germs from them to others.

In most of these particulars Inchcape Jones had failed. To have the existence of the plague admitted in the first place, he had had to fight the merchants controlling the House of Assembly, who had howled that a quarantine would ruin them, and who now refused to give him complete power and tried to manage the epidemic with a Board of Health, which was somewhat worse than navigating a ship during a typhoon by means of a committee.

Inchcape Jones was courageous enough, but he could not cajole people. The newspapers called him a tyrant, would not help win over the public to take precautions against rats and ground squirrels. He had tried to fumigate a few warehouses with sulfur dioxid, but the owners complained that the fumes stained fabrics and paint; and the Board of Health bade him wait—wait a little while—wait and see. He had tried to have the rats examined, to discover what were the centers of infection, but his only bacteriologists were the overworked Stokes and Oliver Marchand; and Inchcape Jones had often explained, at nice dinner-parties, that he did not trust the intelligence of negroes.

He was nearly insane; he worked twenty hours a day; he assured himself that he was not afraid; he reminded himself that he had an honestly won D.S.O.; he longed to have some one besides a board of Red Leg merchants give him orders; and always in the blur of his sleepless brain he saw the hills of Surrey, his sisters in the rose-walk, and the basket-chairs and tea-table beside his father's tennis-lawn.

Then Sondelius, that crafty and often lying lobbyist, that unmoral soldier of the Lord, burst in and became dictator.

He terrified the Board of Health. He quoted his own experiences in Mongolia and India. He assured them that if they did not cease being politicians, the plague might cling in St. Hubert forever, so that they would no more have the amiable dollars of the tourists and the pleasures of smuggling.

He threatened and flattered, and told a story which they had never heard, even at the Ice House; and he had Inchcape Jones appointed dictator of St. Hubert.

Gustaf Sondelius stood extremely close behind the dictator.

He immediately started rat-killing. On a warrant signed by Inchcape Jones, he arrested the owner of a warehouse who had declared that he was not going to have *his* piles of cocoa ruined. He marched his policemen, stout black fellows trained in the Great War, to the warehouse, set them on guard, and pumped in hydrocyanic acid gas.

The crowd gathered beyond the police line, wondering, doubting. They could not believe that anything was happening, for the cracks in the warehouse walls had been adequately stuffed and there was no scent of gas. But the roof was leaky. The gas crept up through it, colorless, diabolic, and suddenly a buzzard circling above the roof tilted forward, fell slantwise, and lay dead among the watchers.

A man picked it up, goggling.

"Dead, right enough," everybody muttered. They looked at Sondelius, parading among his soldiers, with reverence.

His rat-crew searched each warehouse before pumping in the gas, lest some one be left in the place, but in the third one a tramp had been asleep, and when the doors were anxiously opened after the fumigation, there were not only thousands of dead rats but also a dead and very stiff tramp.

"Poor fella—bury him," said Sondelius.

There was no inquest.

Over a rum swizzle at the Ice House, Sondelius reflected, "I wonder how many men I murder, Martin? When I was disinfecting ships at Antofagasta, always afterward we find two or three stowaways. They hide too good. Poor fellas."

Sondelius arbitrarily dragged bookkeepers and porters from their work, to pursue the rats with poison, traps, and gas, or to starve them by concreting and screening stables and warehouses. He made a violent red and green rat map of the town. He broke every law of property by raiding shops for supplies. He alternately bullied and caressed the leaders of the House of Assembly. He called on Kellett, told stories to his children, and almost wept as he explained what a good Lutheran he was—and consistently (but not at Kellett's) he drank too much.

The Ice House, that dimmest and most peaceful among saloons, with its cool marble tables, its gilt-touched white walls, had not been closed, though only the oldest topers and the youngest bravos, fresh out from Home and agonizingly lonely for Peckham or Walthamstow, for Peel Park or the Cirencester High Street, were desperate enough to go there, and of the attendants there remained only one big Jamaica barman. By chance he was among them all the most divine mixer of the planter's punch, the New Orleans fizz, and the rum swizzle. His masterpieces Sondelius acclaimed, he alone placid among the scary patrons who came in now not to dream but to gulp and flee. After a day of slaughtering rats and disinfecting houses he sat with Martin, with Martin and Leora, or with whomever he could persuade to linger.

To Gustaf Sondelius, dukes and cobblers were alike remarkable, and Martin was sometimes jealous when he saw Sondelius turning to a cocoa-broker's clerk with the same smile he gave to Martin. For hours Sondelius talked, of Shanghai and epistemology and the painting of Nevinson; for hours he sang scurrilous lyrics of the Quarter, and boomed, "Yey, how I kill the rats at Kellett's wharf to-day! I don't t'ink one little swizzle would break down too many glomeruli in an honest man's kidneys."

He was cheerful, but never with the reproving and infuriating cheerfulness of an Ira Hinkley. He mocked himself, Martin, Leora, and their work. At home dinner he never cared what he ate (though he did care what he drank), which at Penrith Lodge was desirable, in view of Leora's efforts to combine the views of Wheatsylvania with the standards of West Indian servants and the absence of daily deliveries. He shouted and sang—and took precautions for working among rats and the agile fleas: the high boots, the strapped wrists, and the rubber neck-band which he had invented and which is known in every tropical supply shop to-day as the Sondelius Anti-vermin Neck Protector.

It happened that he was, without Martin or Gottlieb ever understanding it, the most brilliant as well as the least pompous and therefore least appreciated warrior against epidemics that the world has known.

Thus with Sondelius, though for Martin there were as yet but embarrassment and futility and the fear of fear.

Chapter XXXIV

To persuade the shopkeeping lords of St. Hubert to endure a test in which half of them might die, so that all plague might—perhaps—be ended forever, was impossible. Martin argued with Inchcape Jones, with Sondelius, but he had no favor, and he began to meditate a political campaign as he would have meditated an experiment.

He had seen the suffering of the plague and he had (though he still resisted) been tempted to forget experimentation, to give up the possible saving of millions for the immediate saving of thousands. Inchcape Jones, a little rested now under Sondelius's padded bullying and able to slip into a sane routine, drove Martin to the village of Carib, which, because of its pest of infected ground squirrels, was proportionately worse smitten than Blackwater.

They sped out of the capital by white shell roads agonizing to the sun-poisoned eyes; they left the dusty shanties of suburban Yamtown for a land cool with bamboo groves and palmettos, thick with sugar-cane. From a hilltop they swung down a curving road to a beach where the high surf boomed in limestone caves. It seemed impossible that this joyous shore could be threatened by plague, the slimy creature of dark alleys.

The motor cut through a singing trade wind which told of clean sails and disdainful men. They darted on where the foam feathers below Point Carib and where, round that lone royal palm on the headland, the bright wind hums. They slipped into a hot valley, and came to the village of Carib and to creeping horror.

The plague had been dismaying in Blackwater; in Carib it was the end of all things. The rat-fleas had found fat homes in the ground squirrels which burrowed in every garden about the village. In Blackwater there had from the first been isolation of the sick, but in Carib death was in every house, and the village was surrounded by soldier police, with bayonets, who let no one come or go save the doctors.

Martin was guided down the stinking street of cottages palm-thatched and walled with cow-dung plaster on bamboo laths, cottages shared by the roosters and the goats. He heard men shrieking in delirium; a dozen times he saw that face of terror—sunken bloody eyes, drawn face, open mouth—which marks the Black Death; and once he beheld an exquisite girl child in coma on the edge of death, her tongue black and round her the scent of the tomb.

They fled away, to Point Carib and the trade wind, and when Inchcape Jones demanded, "After that sort of thing, can you really talk of experimenting?" then Martin shook his head, while he tried to recall the vision of Gottlieb and all their little plans: "half to get the phage, half to be sternly deprived."

It came to him that Gottlieb, in his secluded innocence, had not realized what it meant to gain leave to experiment amid the hysteria of an epidemic.

He went to the Ice House; he had a drink with a frightened clerk from Derbyshire; he regained the picture of Gottlieb's sunken, demanding eyes; and he swore that he would not yield to a compassion which in the end would make all compassion futile.

Since Inchcape Jones could not understand the need of experimentation, he would call on the Governor, Colonel Sir Robert Fairlamb.

II

Though Government House was officially the chief residence of St. Hubert, it was but a thatched bungalow a little larger than Martin's own Penrith Lodge. When he saw it, Martin felt more easy, and he ambled up to the broad steps, at nine of the evening, as though he were dropping in to call on a neighbor in Wheatsylvania.

He was stopped by a Jamaican man-servant of appalling courtesy.

He snorted that he was Dr. Arrowsmith, head of the McGurk Commission, and he was sorry but he must see Sir Robert at once.

The servant was suggesting, in his blandest and most annoying manner, that really Dr. Uh would do better to see the Surgeon General, when a broad red face and a broad red voice projected themselves over the veranda railing, with a rumble of, "Send him up, Jackson, and don't be a fool!"

Sir Robert and Lady Fairlamb were finishing dinner on the verandah, at a small round table littered with coffee and liqueurs and starred with candles. She was a slight, nervous insignificance; he was rather puffy, very flushed, undoubtedly courageous, and altogether dismayed; and at a time when no laundress dared go anywhere, his evening shirt was luminous.

Martin was in his now beloved linen suit, with a crumply soft shirt which Leora had been meanin' to wash.

Martin explained what he wanted to do—what he must do, if the world was ever to get over the absurdity of having plague.

Sir Robert listened so agreeably that Martin thought he understood, but at the end he bellowed:

"Young man, if I were commanding a division at the front, with a dud show, an awful show, going on, and a War Office clerk asked me to risk the whole thing to try out some precious little invention of his own, can you imagine what I'd answer? There isn't much I can do now—these doctor Johnnies have taken everything out of my hands—but as far as possible I shall certainly prevent you Yankee vivisectionists from coming in and using us as a lot of sanguinary—sorry, Evelyn—sanguinary corpses. Good night, sir!"

III

Thanks to Sondelius's crafty bullying, Martin was able to present his plan to a Special Board composed of the Governor, the temporarily suspended Board of Health, Inchcape Jones, several hearty members of the House of Assembly, and Sondelius himself, attending in the unofficial capacity which all over the world he had found useful for masking a cheerful tyranny. Sondelius even brought in the negro doctor, Oliver Marchand, not on the ground that he was the most intelligent person on the island (which happened to be Sondelius's reason) but because he "represented the plantation hands."

Sondelius himself was as much opposed to Martin's unemotional experiments as was Fairlamb; he believed that all experiments should be, by devices not entirely clear to him, carried on in the laboratory without disturbing the conduct of agreeable epidemics, but he could never resist a drama like the innocent meeting of the Special Board.

The meeting was set for a week ahead . . . with scores dying every day. While he waited for it Martin manufactured more phage and helped Sondelius murder rats, and Leora listened to the midnight debates of the two men and tried to make them acknowledge that it had been wise to let her come. Inchcape Jones offered to Martin the position of Government bacteriologist, but he refused lest he be sidetracked.

The Special Board met in Parliament House, all of them trying to look not like their simple and domestic selves but like judges. With them appeared such doctors of the island as could find the time.

While Leora listened from the back of the room, Martin addressed them, not unaware of the spectacle of little Mart Arrowsmith of Elk Mills taken seriously by the rulers of a tropic isle headed by a Sir Somebody. Beside him stood Max Gottlieb, and in Gottlieb's power he reverently sought to explain that mankind has ever given up eventual greatness because some crisis, some war or election or loyalty to a Messiah which at the moment seemed weighty, has choked the patient search for truth. He sought to explain that he could—perhaps—save half of a given district, but that to test for all time the value of phage, the other half must be left without it . . . though, he craftily told them, in any case the luckless half would receive as much care as at present.

Most of the Board had heard that he possessed a magic cure for the plague which, for unknown and probably discreditable reasons, he was withholding, and they were not going to have it withheld. There was a great deal of discussion rather unconnected with what he had said, and out of it came only the fact that everybody except Stokes and Oliver Marchand was against him; Kellett was angry with this American, Sir Robert Fairlamb was beefily disapproving, and Sondelius admitted that though Martin was quite a decent young man, he was a fanatic.

Into their argument plunged a fury in the person of Ira Hinkley, missionary of the Sanctification Brotherhood.

Martin had not seen him since the first morning in Blackwater. He gaped as he heard Ira pleading:

"Gentlemen, I know almost the whole bunch of you are Church of England, but I beg you to listen to me, not as a minister but as a qualified doctor of medicine. Oh, the wrath of God is upon you— But I mean: I was a classmate of Arrowsmith in the States. I'm onto him! He was such a failure that he was suspended from medical school. A scientist! And his boss, this fellow Gottlieb, he was fired from the University of Winnemac for incompetence! I know 'em! Liars and fools! Scorners of righteousness! Has anybody but Arrowsmith himself told you he's a qualified scientist?"

The face of Sondelius changed from curiosity to stolid Scandinavian wrath. He arose and shouted:

"Sir Robert, this man is crazy! Dr. Gottlieb is one of the seven distinguished living scientists, and Dr. Arrowsmith is his representative! I announce my agreement with him, complete. As you must have seen from my work, I'm perfectly independent of him and entirely at your service, but I know his standing and I follow him, quite humbly."

The Special Board coaxed Ira Hinkley out, for the meanest of reasons—in St. Hubert the whites do not greatly esteem the holy ecstasies of negroes in the Sanctification Brotherhood chapels—but they voted only to "give the matter their consideration," while still men died by the score each day, and in Manchuria as in St. Hubert they prayed for rest from the ancient clawing pain.

Outside, as the Special Board trudged away, Sondelius blared at Martin and the indignant Leora, "Yey, a fine fight!"

Martin answered, "Gustaf, you've joined me now. The first darn' thing you do, you come have a shot of phage."

"No. Slim, I said I will not have your phage till you give it to everybody. I mean it, no matter how much I make fools of your Board."

As they stood before Parliament House, a small motor possessing everything but comfort and power staggered up to them, and from it vaulted a man lean as Gottlieb and English as Inchcape Jones.

"You Dr. Arrowsmith? My name is Twyford, Cecil Twyford of St. Swithin's Parish. Tried to get here for the Special Board meeting, but my beastly foreman had to take the afternoon off and die of plague. Stokes has told me your plans. Quite right. All nonsense to go on having plague. Board refused? Sorry. Perhaps we can do something in St. Swithin's. Goo' day."

All evening Martin and Sondelius were full of language. Martin went to bed longing for the regularity of working all night and foraging for cigarettes at dawn. He could not sleep, because an imaginary Ira Hinkley was always bursting in on him.

Four days later he heard that Ira was dead.

Till he had sunk in coma, Ira had nursed and blessed his people, the humble colored congregation in the hot tin chapel which he had now turned into a pest-house. He staggered from cot to cot, under the gospel texts he had lettered on the whitewashed wall, then he cried once, loudly, and dropped by the pine pulpit where he had joyed to preach.

IV

One chance Martin did have. In Carib, where every third man was down with plague and one doctor to attend them all, he now gave phage to the entire village; a long strain of injections, not improved by the knowledge that one jaunty flea from any patient might bring him the plague.

The tedium of dread was forgotten when he began to find and make precise notes of a slackening of the epidemic, which was occurring nowhere except here at Carib.

He came home raving to Leora, "I'll show 'em! Now they'll let me try test conditions, and then when the epidemic's over we'll hustle home. It'll be lovely to be cold again! Wonder if Holabird and Sholtheis are any more friendly now? Be pretty good to see the little ole flat, eh?"

"Yes, won't it!" said Leora. "I wish I'd thought to have the kitchen painted while we're away. . . . I think I'll put that blue chair in the bedroom."

Though there was a decrease in the plague at Carib, Sondelius was worried, because it was the worst center for infected ground squirrels on the island. He made decisions quickly. One evening he explained certain things to Inchcape Jones and Martin, rode down their doubts, and snorted:

"Only way to disinfect that place is to burn it—burn th' whole thing. Have it done by morning, before anybody can stop us."

With Martin as his lieutenant he marshaled his troop of rat-catchers—ruffians all of them, with high boots, tied jacket sleeves, and ebon visages of piracy. They stole food from shops, tents and blankets and camp-stoves from the Government military warehouse, and jammed their booty into motor trucks. The line of trucks roared down to Carib, the rat-catchers sitting atop, singing pious hymns.

They charged on the village, drove out the healthy, carried the sick on litters, settled them all in tents in a pasture up the valley, and after midnight they burned the town.

The troops ran among the huts, setting them alight with fantastic torches. The palm thatch sent up thick smoke, dead sluggish white with currents of ghastly black through which broke sudden flames. Against the glare the palmettos were silhouetted. The solid-seeming huts were instantly changed into thin bamboo frameworks, thin lines of black slats, with the thatch falling in sparks. The flame lighted the whole valley; roused the terrified squawking birds, and turned the surf at Point Carib to bloody foam.

With such of the natives as had strength enough and sense enough, Sondelius's troops made a ring about the burning village, shouting insanely as they clubbed the fleeing rats and ground squirrels. In the flare of devastation Sondelius was a fiend, smashing the bewildered rats with a club, shooting at them as they fled, and singing to himself all the while the obscene chantey of Bill the Sailor. But at dawn he was nursing the sick in the bright new canvas village, showing mammies how to use their camp-stoves, and in a benevolent way discussing methods of poisoning ground squirrels in their burrows.

Sondelius returned to Blackwater, but Martin remained in the tent village for two days, giving them the phage, making notes, directing the amateur nurses. He returned to Blackwater one mid-afternoon and sought the office of the Surgeon General, or what had been the office of the Surgeon General till Sondelius had come and taken it away from him.

Sondelius was there, at Inchcape Jones's desk, but for once he was not busy. He was sunk in his chair, his eyes bloodshot.

"Yey! We had a fine time with the rats at Carib, eh? How is my new tent willage?" he chuckled, but his voice was weak, and as he rose he staggered.

"What is it? What is it?"

"I t'ink— It's got me. Some flea got me. Yes," in a shaky but extremely interested manner, "I was yoost thinking I will go and quarantine myself. I have fever all right, and adenitis. My strength— Huh! I am almost sixty, but the way I can lift weights that no sailor can touch— And I could fight five rounds! Oh, my God, Martin, I am so weak! Not scared! No!"

But for Martin's arms he would have collapsed.

He refused to return to Penrith Lodge and Leora's nursing. "I who have isolated so many—it is my turn," he said.

Martin and Inchcape Jones found for Sondelius a meager clean cottage—the family had died there, all of them, but it had been fumigated. They procured a nurse and Martin himself attended the sick man, trying to remember that once he had been a doctor, who understood ice-bags and consolation. One thing was not to be had—mosquito netting—and only of this did Sondelius complain.

Martin bent over him, agonized to see how burning was his skin, how swollen his face and his tongue, how weak his voice as he babbled:

"Gottlieb is right about these jests of God. Yey! His best one is the tropics. God planned them so beautiful, flowers and sea and mountains. He made the fruit to grow so well that man need not work—and then He laughed, and stuck in volcanoes and snakes and damp heat and early senility and the plague and malaria. But the nastiest trick He ever played on man was inventing the flea."

His bloated lips widened, from his hot throat oozed a feeble croaking, and Martin realized that he was trying to laugh.

He became delirious, but between spasms he muttered, with infinite pain, tears in his eyes at his own weakness:

"I want you to see how an agnostic can die!

"I am not afraid, but yoost once more I would like to see Stockholm, and Fifth Avenue on the day the first snow falls, and Holy Week at Sevilla. And one good last drunk! I am very peaceful, Slim. It hurts some, but life was a good game. And—I am a pious agnostic. Oh, Martin, give my people the phage! Save all of them— God, I did not think they could hurt me so!"

His heart had failed. He was still on his low cot.

V

Martin had an unhappy pride that, with all his love for Gustaf Sondelius, he could still keep his head, still resist Inchcape Jones's demand that he give the phage to every one, still do what he had been sent to do.

"I'm not a sentimentalist; I'm a scientist!" he boasted.

They snarled at him in the streets now; small boys called him names and threw stones. They had heard that he was wilfully withholding their salvation. The citizens came in committees to beg him to heal their children, and he was so shaken that he had ever to keep before him the vision of Gottlieb.

The panic was increasing. They who had at first kept cool could not endure the strain of wakening at night to see upon their windows the glow of the pile of logs on Admiral Knob, the emergency crematory where Gustaf Sondelius and his curly gray mop had been shoveled into the fire along with a crippled negro boy and a Hindu beggar.

Sir Robert Fairlamb was a blundering hero, exasperating the sick while he tried to nurse them; Stokes remained the Rock of Ages—he had only three hours' sleep a night, but he never failed to take his accustomed fifteen minutes of exercise when he awoke; and Leora was easy in Penrith Lodge, helping Martin prepare phage.

It was the Surgeon General who went to pieces.

Robbed of his dependence on the despised Sondelius, sunk again in a mad planlessness, Inchcape Jones shrieked when he thought he was speaking low, and the cigarette which was ever in his thin hand shook so that the smoke quivered up in trembling spirals.

Making his tour, he came at night on a sloop by which a dozen Red Legs were escaping to Barbados, and suddenly he was among them, bribing them to take him along.

As the sloop stood out from Blackwater Harbor he stretched his arms toward his sisters and the peace of the Surrey hills, but as the few frightened lights of the town were lost, he realized that he was a coward and came up out of his madness, with his lean head high.

He demanded that they turn the sloop and take him back. They refused, howling at him, and locked him in the cabin. They were becalmed; it was two days before they reached Barbados, and by then the world would know that he had deserted.

Altogether expressionless, Inchcape Jones tramped from the sloop to a waterfront hotel in Barbados, and stood for a long time in a slatternly room smelling of slop-pails. He would never see his sisters and the cool hills. With the revolver which he had carried to drive terrified patients back into the isolation wards, with the revolver which he had carried at Arras, he killed himself.

VI

Thus Martin came to his experiment. Stokes was appointed Surgeon General, vice Inchcape Jones, and he made an illegal assignment of Martin to St. Swithin's Parish, as medical officer with complete power. This, and the concurrence of Cecil Twyford, made his experiment possible.

He was invited to stay at Twyford's. His only trouble was the guarding of Leora. He did not know what he would encounter in St. Swithin's, while Penrith Lodge was as safe as any place on the island. When Leora insisted that, during his experiment, the cold thing which had stilled the laughter of Sondelius might come to him and he might need her, he tried to satisfy her by promising that if there was a place for her in St. Swithin's, he would send for her.

Naturally, he was lying.

"Hard enough to see Gustaf go. By thunder she's not going to run risks!" he vowed.

He left her, protected by the maids and the soldier butler, with Dr. Oliver Marchand to look in when he could.

VII

In St. Swithin's Parish the cocoa and bamboo groves and sharp hills of southern St. Hubert gave way to unbroken cane-fields. Here Cecil Twyford, that lean abrupt man, ruled every acre and interpreted every law.

His place, Frangipani Court, was a refuge from the hot humming plain. The house was old and low, of thick stone and plaster walls; the paneled rooms were lined with the china, the portraits, and the swords of Twyfords for three hundred years; and between the wings was a walled garden dazzling with hibiscus.

Twyford led Martin through the low cool hall and introduced him to five great sons and to his mother, who, since his wife's death, ten years ago, had been mistress of the house.

"Have tea?" said Twyford. "Our American guest will be down in a moment."

He would not have thought of saying it, but he had sworn that since for generations Twyfords had drunk tea here at a seemly hour, no panic should prevent their going on drinking it at that hour.

When Martin came into the garden, when he saw the old silver on the wicker table and heard the quiet voices, the plague seemed conquered, and he realized that, four thousand miles southwest of the Lizard, he was in England.

They were seated, pleasant but not too comfortable, when the American guest came down and from the door stared at Martin as strangely as he stared in turn.

He beheld a woman who must be his sister. She was perhaps thirty to his thirty-seven, but in her slenderness, her paleness, her black brows and dusky hair, she was his twin; she was his self enchanted.

He could hear his voice croaking, "But you're my sister!" and she opened her lips, yet neither of them spoke as they bowed at introduction. When she sat down, Martin had never been so conscious of a woman's presence.

He learned, before evening, that she was Joyce Lanyon, widow of Roger Lanyon of New York. She had come to St. Hubert to see her plantations and had been trapped by the quarantine. He had tentatively heard of her dead husband as a young man of wealth and family; he seemed to remember having seen in *Vanity Fair* a picture of the Lanyons at Palm Beach.

She talked only of the weather, the flowers, but there was a rising gaiety in her which stirred even the dour Cecil Twyford. In the midst of her debonair insults to the hugest of the huge sons, Martin turned on her:

"You *are* my sister!"

"Obviously. Well, since you're a scientist— Are you a good scientist?"

"Pretty good."

"I've met your Mrs. McGurk. And Dr. Rippleton Holabird. Met 'em in Hessian Hook. You know it, don't you?"

"No, I— Oh, I've heard of it."

"You know. It's that renovated old part of Brooklyn where writers and economists and all those people, some of them almost as good as the very best, consort with people who are almost as smart as the very smartest. You know. Where they dress for dinner but all of them have heard about James Joyce. Dr. Holabird is frightfully charming, don't you think?"

"Why—"

"Tell me. I really mean it. Cecil has been explaining what you plan to do experimentally. Could I help you—nursing or cooking or something—or would I merely be in the way?"

"I don't know yet. If I can use you, I'll be unscrupulous enough!"

"Oh, don't be earnest like Cecil here, and Dr. Stokes! They have no sense of play. Do you like that man Stokes? Cecil adores him, and I suppose he's simply infested with virtues, but I find him so dry and thin and unappetizing. Don't you think he might be a little gayer?"

Martin gave up all chance of knowing her as he hurled:

"Look here! You said you found Holabird 'charming.' It makes me tired to have you fall for his scientific tripe and not appreciate Stokes. Stokes is hard—thank God!—and probably he's rude. Why not? He's fighting a world that bellows for fake charm. No scientist can go through his grind and not come out more or less rude. And I tell you Stokes was born a researcher. I wish we had him at McGurk. Rude? Wish you could hear him being rude to me!"

Twyford looked doubtful, his mother looked delicately shocked, and the five sons beefily looked nothing at all, while Martin raged on, trying to convey his vision of the barbarian, the ascetic, the contemptuous acolyte of science. But Joyce

Lanyon's lovely eyes were kind, and when she spoke she had lost something of her too-cosmopolitan manner of a diner-out:

"Yes. I suppose it's the difference between me, playing at being a planter, and Cecil."

After dinner he walked with her in the garden and sought to defend himself against he was not quite sure what, till she hinted:

"My dear man, you're so apologetic about never being apologetic! If you really must be my twin brother, do me the honor of telling me to go to the devil whenever you want to. I don't mind. Now about your Gottlieb, who seems to be so much of an obsession with you—"

"Obsession! Rats! He—"

They parted an hour after.

Least of all things Martin desired such another peeping, puerile, irritable restlessness as he had shared with Orchid Pickerbaugh, but as he went to bed in a room with old prints and a four-poster, it was disturbing to know that somewhere near him was Joyce Lanyon.

He sat up, aghast with truth. Was he going to fall in love with this desirable and quite useless young woman? (How lovely her shoulders, above black satin at dinner! She had a genius of radiant flesh; it made that of most women, even the fragile Leora, seem coarse and thick. There was a rosy glow behind it, as from an inner light.)

Did he really want Leora here, with Joyce Lanyon in the house? (Dear Leora, who was the source of life! Was she now, off there in Penrith Lodge, missing him, lying awake for him?)

How could he, even in the crisis of an epidemic, invite the formal Twyfords to invite Leora? (How honest was he? That afternoon he had recognized the rigid though kindly code of the Twyfords, but could he not set it aside by being frankly an Outlander?)

Suddenly he was out of bed, kneeling, praying to Leora.

Chapter XXXV

THE PLAGUE had only begun to invade St. Swithin's, but it was unquestionably coming, and Martin, with his power as official medical officer of the parish, was able to make plans. He divided the population into two equal parts. One of them, driven in by Twyford, was injected with plague phage, the other half was left without.

He began to succeed. He saw far-off India, with its annual four hundred thousand deaths from plague, saved by his efforts. He heard Max Gottlieb saying, "Martin, you haf done your experiment. I am very glat!"

The pest attacked the unphaged half of the parish much more heavily than those who had been treated. There did appear a case or two among those who had the phage, but among the others there were ten, then twenty, then thirty daily victims. These unfortunate cases he treated, giving the phage to alternate patients, in the somewhat barren almshouse of the parish, a whitewashed cabin the meaner against its vaulting background of banyans and breadfruit trees.

He could never understand Cecil Twyford. Though Twyford had considered his hands as slaves, though he had, in his great barony, given them only this barren almshouse, yet he risked his life now in nursing them, and the lives of all his sons.

Despite Martin's discouragement, Mrs. Lanyon came down to cook, and a remarkably good cook she was. She also made beds; she showed more intelligence than the Twyford men about disinfecting herself; and as she bustled about the rusty kitchen, in a gingham gown she had borrowed from a maid, she so disturbed Martin that he forgot to be gruff.

II

In the evening, while they returned by Twyford's rattling little motor to Frangipani Court, Mrs. Lanyon talked to Martin as one who had shared his work, but when she had bathed and powdered and dressed, he talked to her as one who was afraid of her. Their bond was their resemblance as brother and sister. They decided, almost irritably, that they looked utterly alike, except that her hair was more patent-leather than his and she lacked his impertinent, cocking eyebrow.

Often Martin returned to his patients at night, but once or twice Mrs. Lanyon and he fled, as much from the family stolidity of the Twyfords as from the thought of fever-scorched patients, to the shore of a rocky lagoon which cut far in from the sea.

They sat on a cliff, full of the sound of the healing tide. His brain was hectic with the memory of charts on the white-washed broad planks of the almshouse, the sun cracks in the wall, the puffy terrified faces of black patients, how one of the Twyford sons had knocked over an ampule of phage, and how itchingly hot it had been in the ward. But to his intensity the lagoon breeze was cooling, and cooling the rustling tide. He perceived that Mrs. Lanyon's white frock was fluttering about her knees; he realized that she too was strained and still. He turned somberly toward her, and she cried:

"I'm so frightened, and so lonely! The Twyfords are heroic, but they're stone. I'm so marooned!"

He kissed her, and she rested against his shoulder. The softness of her sleeve was agitating to his hand. But she broke away with:

"No! You don't really care a hang about me. Just curious. Perhaps that's a good thing for me—to-night."

He tried to assure her, to assure himself, that he did care with peculiar violence, but languor was over him; between him and her fragrance were the hospital cots, a great weariness, and the still face of Leora. They were silent together, and when his hand crept to hers they sat unimpassioned, comprehending, free to talk of what they would.

He stood outside her door, when they had returned to the house, and imagined her soft moving within.

"No," he raged. "Can't do it. Joyce—women like her—one of the million things I've given up for work and for Lee. Well. That's all there is to it then. But if I were here two weeks—Fool! She'd be furious if you knocked! But—"

He was aware of the dagger of light under her door; the more aware of it as he turned his back and tramped to his room.

III

The telephone service in St. Hubert was the clumsiest feature of the island. There was no telephone at Penrith Lodge—the port-doctor had cheerfully been wont to get his calls through a neighbor. The central was now demoralized by the plague, and when for two hours Martin had tried to have Leora summoned, he gave up.

But he had triumphed. In three or four days he would drive to Penrith Lodge. Twyford had blankly assented to his suggestion that Leora be invited hither, and if she and Joyce Lanyon should become such friends that Joyce would never again turn to him in loneliness, he was willing, he was eager—he was almost eager.

IV

When Martin left her at the Lodge, in the leafy gloom high on the Penrith Hills, Leora felt his absence. They had been so little apart since he had first come on her, scrubbing a hospital room in Zenith.

The afternoon was unending; each time she heard a creaking she roused with the hope that it was his step, and realized that he would not be coming, all the blank evening, the terrifying night; would not be here anywhere, not his voice nor the touch of his hand.

Dinner was mournful. Often enough she had dined alone when Martin was at the Institute, but then he had been returning to her some time before dawn—probably—and she had reflectively munched a snack on the corner of the kitchen table, looking at the funnies in the evening paper. To-night she had to live up to the butler, who served her as though she were a dinner-party of twenty.

She sat on the porch, staring at the shadowy roofs of Blackwater below, sure that she felt a "miasm" writhing up through the hot darkness.

She knew the direction of St. Swithin's Parish—beyond that delicate glimmer of lights from palm huts coiling up the hills. She concentrated on it, wondering if by some magic she might not have a signal from him, but she could get no feeling of his looking toward her. She sat long and quiet. . . . She had nothing to do.

Her night was sleepless. She tried to read in bed, by an electric globe inside the misty little tent of the mosquito-netting, but there was a tear in the netting and the mosquitoes crept through. As she turned out the light and lay tense, unable to give herself over to sleep, unable to sink into security, while to her blurred eyes the half-seen folds of the mosquito netting seemed to slide about her, she tried to remember whether these mosquitoes might be carrying plague germs. She realized how much she had depended on Martin for such bits of knowledge, as for all philosophy. She recalled how annoyed he had been because she could not remember whether the yellow fever mosquito was *Anopheles* or *Stegomyia*—or was it *Aëdes*?—and suddenly she laughed in the night.

She was reminded that he had told her to give herself another injection of phage.

"Hang it, I forgot. Well, I must be sure to do that to-morrow."

"Do that t'morrow—do that t'morrow," buzzed in her brain, an irritating inescapable refrain, while she was suspended over sleep, conscious of how much she wanted to creep into his arms.

Next morning (and she did not remember to give herself another injection) the servants seemed twitchy, and her effort to comfort them brought out the news that Oliver Marchand, the doctor on whom they depended, was dead.

In the afternoon the butler heard that his sister had been taken off to the isolation ward, and he went down to Blackwater to make arrangements for his nieces. He did not return; no one ever learned what had become of him.

Toward dusk, when Leora felt as though a skirmish line were closing in on her, she fled into Martin's laboratory. It seemed filled with his jerky brimming presence. She kept away from the flasks of plague germs, but she picked up, because it was his, a half-smoked cigarette and lighted it.

Now there was a slight crack in her lips; and that morning, fumbling at dusting—here in the laboratory meant as a fortress against disease—a maid had knocked over a test-tube, which had trickled. The cigarette seemed dry enough, but in it there were enough plague germs to kill a regiment.

Two nights after, when she was so desperately lonely that she thought of walking to Blackwater, finding a motor, and fleeing to Martin, she woke with a fever, a headache, her limbs chilly. When the maids discovered her in the morning, they fled from the house. While lassitude flowed round her, she was left alone in the isolated house, with no telephone.

All day, all night, as her throat crackled with thirst, she lay longing for some one to help her. Once she crawled to the kitchen for water. The floor of the bedroom was an endless heaving sea, the hall a writhing dimness, and by the kitchen door she dropped and lay for an hour, whimpering.

"Got to—got to—can't remember what it was," her voice kept appealing to her cloudy brain.

Aching, fighting the ache, she struggled up, wrapped about her a shabby cloak which one of the maids had abandoned in flight, and in the darkness staggered out to find help. As she came to the highway she stumbled, and lay under the hedge, unmoving, like a hurt animal. On hands and knees she crawled back into the Lodge, and between times, as her brain went dark, she nearly forgot the pain in her longing for Martin.

She was bewildered; she was lonely; she dared not start on her long journey without his hand to comfort her. She listened for him—listened—tense with listening.

"You will come! I know you'll come and help me! I know. You'll come! Martin! Sandy! *Sandy!*" she sobbed.

Then she slipped down into the kindly coma. There was no more pain, and all the shadowy house was quiet but for her hoarse and struggling breath.

V

Like Sondelius, Joyce Lanyon tried to persuade Martin to give the phage to everybody.

"I'm getting to be good and stern, with all you people after me. Regular Gottlieb. Nothing can make me do it, not if they tried to lynch me," he boasted.

He had explained Leora to Joyce.

"I don't know whether you two will like each other. You're so darn' different. You're awfully articulate, and you like these 'pretty people' that you're always talking about, but she doesn't care a hang for 'em. She sits back—oh, she never misses anything, but she never says much. Still, she's got the best instinct for honesty that I've ever known. I hope you two'll get each other. I was afraid to let her come here—didn't know what I'd find—but now I'm going to hustle to Penrith and bring her here to-day."

He borrowed Twyford's car and drove to Blackwater, up to Penrith, in excellent spirits. For all the plague, they could have a lively time in the evenings. One of the Twyford sons was not so solemn; he and Joyce, with Martin and Leora, could slip down to the lagoon for picnic suppers; they would sing—

He came up to Penrith Lodge bawling, "Lee! Leora! Come on! *Here* we are!"

The veranda, as he ran up on it, was leaf-scattered and dusty, and the front door was banging. His voice echoed in a desperate silence. He was uneasy. He darted in, found no one in the living-room, the kitchen, then hastened into their bedroom.

On the bed, across the folds of the torn mosquito netting, was Leora's body, very frail, quite still. He cried to her, he shook her, he stood weeping.

He talked to her, his voice a little insane, trying to make her understand that he had loved her, and had left her here only for her safety—

There was rum in the kitchen, and he went out to gulp down raw full glasses. They did not affect him.

By evening he strode to the garden, the high and windy garden looking toward the sea, and dug a deep pit. He lifted her light stiff body, kissed it, and laid it in the pit. All night he wandered. When he came back to the house and saw the row of her little dresses with the lines of her soft body in them, he was terrified.

Then he went to pieces.

He gave up Penrith Lodge, left Twyford's, and moved into a room behind the Surgeon General's office. Beside his cot there was always a bottle.

Because death had for the first time been brought to him, he raged, "Oh, damn experimentation!" and, despite Stokes's dismay, he gave the phage to every one who asked.

Only in St. Swithin's, since there his experiment was so excellently begun, did some remnant of honor keep him from distributing the phage universally; but the conduct of this experiment he turned over to Stokes.

Stokes saw that he was a little mad, but only once, when Martin snarled, "What do I care for your science?" did he try to hold Martin to his test.

Stokes himself, with Twyford, carried on the experiment and kept the notes Martin should have kept. By evening, after working fourteen or fifteen hours since dawn, Stokes would hasten to St. Swithin's by motor-cycle—he hated the joggling and the lack of dignity and he found it somewhat dangerous to take curving hill-roads at sixty miles an hour, but this was the quickest way, and till midnight he conferred with Twyford, gave him orders for the next day, arranged his clumsy annotations, and marveled at his grim meekness.

Meantime, all day, Martin injected a line of frightened citizens, in the Surgeon General's office in Blackwater. Stokes begged him at least to turn the work over to another doctor and take what interest he could in St. Swithin's, but Martin had a bitter satisfaction in throwing away all his significance, in helping to wreck his own purposes.

With a nurse for assistant, he stood in the bare office. File on file of people, black, white, Hindu, stood in an agitated cue a block long, ten deep, waiting dumbly, as for death. They crept up to the nurse beside Martin and in embarrassment exposed their arms, which she scrubbed with soap and water and dabbled with alcohol before passing them on to him. He brusquely pinched up the skin of the upper arm and jabbed it with the needle of the syringe, cursing at them for jerking, never seeing their individual faces. As they left him they fluttered with gratitude—"Oh, may God bless you, Doctor!"—but he did not hear.

Sometimes Stokes was there, looking anxious, particularly when in the cue he saw plantation-hands from St. Swithin's, who were supposed to remain in their parish under strict control, to test the value of the phage. Sometimes Sir Robert Fairlamb came down to beam and gurgle and offer his aid. . . . Lady Fairlamb had been injected first of all, and next to her a tattered kitchen wench, profuse with Hallelujah's.

After a fortnight when he was tired of the drama, he had four doctors making the injections, while he manufactured phage.

But by night Martin sat alone, tousled, drinking steadily, living on whisky and hate, freeing his soul and dissolving his body by hatred as once hermits dissolved theirs by ecstasy. His life was as unreal as the nights of an old drunkard. He had an advantage over normal cautious humanity in not caring whether he lived or died, he who sat with the dead, talking to Leora and Sondelius, to Ira Hinkley and Oliver Marchand, to Inchcape Jones and a shadowy horde of blackmen with lifted appealing hands.

After Leora's death he had returned to Twyford's but once, to fetch his baggage, and he had not seen Joyce Lanyon. He hated her. He swore that it was not her presence which had kept him from returning earlier to Leora, but he was aware that while he had been chattering with Joyce, Leora had been dying.

"Damn' glib society climber! Thank God I'll never see *her* again!"

He sat on the edge of his cot, in the constricted and airless room, his hair ruffled, his eyes blotched with red, a stray alley kitten, which he esteemed his only friend, asleep on his pillow. At a knock he muttered, "I can't talk to Stokes now. Let him do his own experiments. Sick of experiments!"

Sulkily, "Oh, come in!"

The door opened on Joyce Lanyon, cool, trim, sure.

"What do you want?" he grunted.

She stared at him; she shut the door; silently she straightened the litter of food, papers, and instruments on his table. She coaxed the indignant kitten to a mat, patted the pillow, and sat by him on the frowsy cot. Then:

"Please! I know what's happened. Cecil is in town for an

hour and I wanted to bring— Won't it comfort you a little if you know how fond we are of you? Won't you let me offer you friendship?"

"I don't want anybody's friendship. I haven't any friends!"

He sat dumb, her hand on his, but when she was gone he felt a shiver of new courage.

He could not get himself to give up his reliance on whisky, and he could see no way of discontinuing the phage-injection of all who came begging for it, but he turned both injection and manufacture over to others, and went back to the most rigid observation of his experiment in St. Swithin's . . . blotted as it now was by the unphaged portion of the parish going in to Blackwater to receive the phage.

He did not see Joyce. He lived at the almshouse, but most evenings now he was sober.

VI

The gospel of rat-extermination had spread through the island; everybody from five-year-old to hobbling grandam was out shooting rats and ground squirrels. Whether from phage or rat-killing or Providence, the epidemic paused, and six months after Martin's coming, when the West Indian May was broiling and the season of hurricanes was threatened, the plague had almost vanished and the quarantine was lifted.

St. Hubert felt safe in its kitchens and shops, and amid the roaring spring the island rejoiced as a sick man first delivered from pain rejoices at merely living and being at peace.

That chaffering should be abusive and loud in the public market, that lovers should stroll unconscious of all save themselves, that loafers should tell stories and drink long drinks at the Ice House, that old men should squat cacking in the shade of the mangoes, that congregations should sing together to the Lord—this was no longer ordinary to them nor stupid, but the bliss of paradise.

They made a festival of the first steamer's leaving. White and black, Hindu and Chink and Caribbee, they crowded the wharf, shouting, waving scarfs, trying not to weep at the feeble piping of what was left of the Blackwater Gold Medal Band; and as the steamer, the *St. Ia* of the McGurk Line, was warped out, with her captain at the rail of the bridge, very straight, saluting them with a flourish but his eyes so wet that he could not see the harbor, they felt that they were no longer jailed lepers but a part of the free world.

On that steamer Joyce Lanyon sailed. Martin said good-by to her at the wharf.

Strong of hand, almost as tall as he, she looked at him without flutter, and rejoiced, "You've come through. So have I. Both of us have been mad, trapped here the way we've been. I don't suppose I helped you, but I did try. You see, I'd never been trained in reality. You trained me. Good-by."

"Mayn't I come to see you in New York?"

"If you'd really like to."

She was gone, yet she had never been so much with him as through that tedious hour when the steamer was lost beyond the horizon, a line edged with silver wire. But that night, in panic, he fled up to Penrith Lodge and buried his cheek in the damp soil above the Leora with whom he had never had to fence and explain, to whom he had never needed to say, "Mayn't I come to see you?"

But Leora, cold in her last bed, unsmiling, did not answer him nor comfort him.

VII

Before Martin took leave he had to assemble the notes of his phage experiment; add the observation of Stokes and Twyford to his own first precise figures.

As the giver of phage to some thousands of frightened islanders, he had become a dignitary. He was called, in the first issue of the *Blackwater Guardian* after the quarantine was raised, "the savior of all our lives." He was the universal hero. If Sondelius had helped to cleanse them, had Sondelius not been his lieutenant? If it was the intervention of the Lord, as the earnest old negro who succeeded Ira Hinkley in the chapels of the Sanctification Brotherhood insisted, had not the Lord surely sent him?

No one heeded a wry Scotch doctor, diligent but undramatic through the epidemic, who hinted that plagues have been known to slacken and cease without phage.

When Martin was completing his notes he had a letter from the McGurk Institute, signed by Rippleton Holabird.

Holabird wrote that Gottlieb was "feeling seedy," that he had resigned the Directorship, suspended his own experimentation, and was now at home, resting. Holabird himself had been appointed Acting Director of the Institute, and as such he chanted:

> The reports of your work in the letters from Mr. McGurk's agents which the quarantine authorities have permitted to get through to us apprize us far more than does your own modest report what a really sensational success you have had. You have done what few other men living could do, both established the value of bacteriophage in plague by tests on a large scale, and saved most of the unfortunate population. The Board of Trustees and I are properly appreciative of the glory which you have added, and still more will add when your report is published, to the name of McGurk Institute, and we are thinking, now that we may for some months be unable to have your titular chief, Dr. Gottlieb, working with us, of establishing a separate Department, with you as its head.

"Established the value—rats! I about half made the tests," sighed Martin, and: "Department! I've given too many orders here. Sick of authority. I want to get back to my lab and start all over again."

It came to him that now he would probably have ten thousand a year. . . . Leora would have enjoyed small extravagant dinners.

Though he had watched Gottlieb declining, it was a shock that he could be so unwell as to drop his work even for a few months.

He forgot his own self as it came to him that in giving up his experiment, playing the savior, he had been a traitor to Gottlieb and all that Gottlieb represented. When he returned to New York he would have to call on the old man and admit to him, to those sunken relentless eyes, that he did not have complete proof of the value of the phage.

If he could have run to Leora with his ten thousand a year—

VIII

He left St. Hubert three weeks after Joyce Lanyon.

The evening before his sailing, a great dinner with Sir Robert Fairlamb in the chair was given to him and to Stokes. While Sir Robert ruddily blurted compliments and Kellett tried to explain things, and all of them drank to him, standing, after the toast to the King, Martin sat lonely, considering that to-morrow he would leave these trusting eyes and face the harsh demands of Gottlieb, of Terry Wickett.

The more they shouted his glory, the more he thought about what unknown, tight-minded scientists in distant laboratories would say of a man who had had his chance and cast it away. The more they called him the giver of life, the more he felt himself disgraced and a traitor; and as he looked at Stokes he saw in his regard a pity worse than condemnation.

Chapter XXXVI

IT HAPPENED that Martin returned to New York, as he had come, on the *St. Buryan*. The ship was haunted with the phantoms of Leora dreaming, of Sondelius shouting on the bridge.

And on the *St. Buryan* was the country-club Miss Gwilliam who had offended Sondelius.

She had spent the winter importantly making notes on native music in Trinidad and Caracas; at least in planning to make notes. She saw Martin come aboard at Blackwater, and pertly noted the friends who saw him off—two Englishmen, one puffy, one rangy, and a dry-looking Scotsman.

"Your friends all seem to be British," she enlightened him, when she had claimed him as an old friend.

"Yes."

"You've spent the winter here."

"Yes."

"Hard luck to be caught by the quarantine. But I *told* you you were silly to go ashore! You must have managed to pick up quite a little money practising. But it must have been unpleasant, really."

"Ye-es, I suppose it was."

"I *told* you it would be! You ought to have come on to Trinidad. Such a fascinating island! And tell me, how is the Roughneck?"

"Who?"

"Oh, you know—that funny Swede that used to dance and everything."

"He is dead."

"Oh, I *am* sorry. You know, no matter what the others said, I never thought he was so bad. I'm sure he had quite a nice cultured mind, when he wasn't carousing around. Your wife isn't with you, is she?"

"No—she isn't with me. I must go down and unpack now."

Miss Gwilliam looked after him with an expression which said that the least people could do was to learn some manners.

II

With the heat and the threat of hurricanes, there were few first-class passengers on the *St. Buryan*, and most of these did not count, because they were not jolly, decent Yankee tourists but merely South Americans. As tourists do when their minds have been broadened and enriched by travel, when they return to New Jersey or Wisconsin with the credit of having spent a whole six months in the West Indies and South America, the respectable remnant studied one another fastidiously, and noted the slim pale man who seemed so restless, who all day trudged round the deck, who after midnight was seen standing by himself at the rail.

"That guy looks awful' restless to me!" said Mr. S. Sanborn Hibble of Detroit to the charming Mrs. Dawson of Memphis, and she answered, with the wit which made her so popular wherever she went, "Yes, don't he. I reckon he must be in love!"

"Oh, I know him!" said Miss Gwilliam. "He and his wife were on the *St. Buryan* when I came down. She's in New York now. He's some kind of a doctor—not awful' successful I don't believe. Just between ourselves, I don't think much of him or of her either. They sat and looked stupid all the way down."

III

Martin was itching to get his fingers on his test-tubes. He knew, as once he had guessed, that he hated administration and Large Affairs.

As he tramped the deck, his head cleared and he was himself. Angrily he pictured the critics who would soon be pecking at whatever final report he might make. For a time he hated the criticism of his fellow laboratory-grinds as he had hated their competition; he hated the need of forever looking over his shoulder at pursuers. But on a night when he stood at the rail for hours, he admitted that he was afraid of their criticism, and afraid because his experiment had so many loop-holes. He hurled overboard all the polemics with which he had protected himself: "Men who never have had the experience of trying, in the midst of an epidemic, to remain calm and keep experimental conditions, do not realize in the security of their laboratories what one has to contend with."

Constant criticism was good, if only it was not spiteful, jealous, petty—

No, even then it might be good! Some men had to be what easy-going workers called "spiteful." To them the joyous spite of crushing the almost-good was more natural than creation. Why should a great house-wrecker, who could clear the cumbered ground, be set at trying to lay brick?

"All right!" he rejoiced. "Let 'em come! Maybe I'll anticipate 'em and publish a roast of my own work. I have got something, from the St. Swithin test, even if I did let things slide for a while. I'll take my tables to a biometrician. He may rip 'em up. Good! What's left, I'll publish."

He went to bed feeling that he could face the eyes of Gottlieb and Terry, and for the first time in weeks he slept without terror.

IV

At the pier in Brooklyn, to the astonishment and slight indignation of Miss Gwilliam, Mr. S. Sanborn Hibble, and Mrs. Dawson, Martin was greeted by reporters who agreeably though vaguely desired to know what were these remarkable things he had been doing to some disease or other, in some island some place.

He was rescued from them by Rippleton Holabird, who burst through them with his hands out, crying, "Oh, my dear fellow! We know all that's happened. We grieve for you so, and we're so glad you were spared to come back to us."

Whatever Martin might, under the shadow of Max Gottlieb, have said about Holabird, now he wrung his hands and muttered, "It's good to be home."

Holabird (he was wearing a blue shirt with a starched blue collar, like an actor) could not wait till Martin's baggage had gone through the customs. He had to return to his duties as Acting Director of the Institute. He delayed only to hint that the Board of Trustees were going to make him full Director, and that certainly, my dear fellow, he would see that Martin had the credit and the reward he deserved.

When Holabird was gone, driving away in his neat coupé (he often explained that his wife and he could afford a chauffeur, but they preferred to spend the money on other things), Martin was conscious of Terry Wickett, leaning against a gnawed wooden pillar of the wharf-house, as though he had been there for hours.

Terry strolled up and snorted, "Hello, Slim. All O.K.? Lez shoot the stuff through the customs. Great pleasure to see the Director and you kissing."

As they drove through the summer-walled streets of Brooklyn, Martin inquired, "How's Holabird working out as Director? And how is Gottlieb?"

"Oh, the Holy Wren is no worse than Tubbs; he's even politer and more ignorant. . . . Me, you watch me! One of these days I'm going off to the woods—got a shack in Vermont—going to work there without having to produce results for the Director! They've stuck me in the Department of Bio-chemistry. And Gottlieb—" Terry's voice became anxious. "I guess he's pretty shaky— They've pensioned him off. Now look, Slim: I hear you're going to be a gilded department-head, and I'll never be anything but an associate member. Are you going on with me, or are you going to be one of the Holy Wren's pets—hero-scientist?"

"I'm with you, Terry, you old grouch." Martin dropped the cynicism which had always seemed proper between him and Terry. "I haven't got anybody else. Leora and Gustaf are gone and now maybe Gottlieb. You and I have got to stick together!"

"It's a go!"

They shook hands, they coughed gruffly, and talked of straw hats.

V

When Martin entered the Institute, his colleagues galloped up to shake hands and to exclaim, and if their praise was flustering, there is no time at which one can stomach so much of it as at home-coming.

Sir Robert Fairlamb had written to the Institute a letter

glorifying him. The letter arrived on the same boat with Martin, and next day Holabird gave it out to the press.

The reporters, who had been only a little interested at his landing, came around for interviews, and while Martin was sulky and jerky Holabird took them in hand, so that the papers were able to announce that America, which was always rescuing the world from something or other, had gone and done it again. It was spread in the prints that Dr. Martin Arrowsmith was not only a powerful witch-doctor and possibly something of a laboratory-hand, but also a ferocious rat-killer, village-burner, Special Board addresser, and snatcher from death. There was at the time, in certain places, a doubt as to how benevolent the United States had been to its Little Brothers—Mexico, Cuba, Haiti, Nicaragua—and the editors and politicians were grateful to Martin for this proof of their sacrifice and tender watchfulness.

He had letters from the Public Health service; from an enterprising Midwestern college which desired to make him a Doctor of Civil Law; from medical schools and societies which begged him to address them. Editorials on his work appeared in the medical journals and the newspapers; and Congressman Almus Pickerbaugh telegraphed him from Washington, in what the Congressman may conceivably have regarded as verse: "They got to go some to get ahead of fellows that come from old Nautilus." And he was again invited to dinner at the McGurks', not by Capitola but by Ross McGurk, whose name had never had such a whitewashing.

He refused all invitations to speak, and the urgent organizations which had invited him responded with meekness that they understood how intimidatingly busy Dr. Arrowsmith was, and if he ever *could* find the time, they would be most highly honored—

Rippleton Holabird was elected full Director now, in succession to Gottlieb, and he sought to use Martin as the prize exhibit of the Institute. He brought all the visiting dignitaries, all the foreign Men of Measured Merriment, in to see him, and they looked pleased and tried to think up questions. Then Martin was made head of the new Department of Microbiology at twice his old salary.

He never did learn what was the difference between microbiology and bacteriology. But none of his glorification could he resist. He was still too dazed—he was the more dazed when he had seen Max Gottlieb.

VI

The morning after his return he had telephoned to Gottlieb's flat, had spoken to Miriam and received permission to call in the late afternoon.

All the way up-town he could hear Gottlieb saying, "You were my son! I gave you eferyt'ing I knew of truth and honor, and you haf betrayed me. Get out of my sight!"

Miriam met him in the hall, fretting, "I don't know if I should have let you come at all, Doctor."

"Why? Isn't he well enough to see people?"

"It isn't that. He doesn't really seem ill, except that he's feeble, but he doesn't know any one. The doctors say it's senile dementia. His memory is gone. And he's just suddenly forgotten all his English. He can only speak German, and I can't speak it, hardly at all. If I'd only studied it, instead of music! But perhaps it may do him good to have you here. He was always so fond of you. You don't know how he talked of you and the splendid experiment you've been doing in St. Hubert."

"Well, I—" He could find nothing to say.

Miriam led him into a room whose walls were dark with books. Gottlieb was sunk in a worn chair, his thin hand lax on the arm.

"Doctor, it's Arrowsmith, just got back!" Martin mumbled.

The old man looked as though he half understood; he peered at him, then shook his head and whimpered, *"Versteh' nicht."* His arrogant eyes were clouded with ungovernable slow tears.

Martin understood that never could he be punished now and cleansed. Gottlieb had sunk into his darkness still trusting him.

VII

Martin closed his flat—their flat—with a cold swift fury, lest he yield to his misery in finding among Leora's possessions a thousand fragments which brought her back: the frock she had bought for Capitola McGurk's dinner, a petrified chocolate she had hidden away to munch illegally by night, a memorandum, "Get almonds for Sandy." He took a grimly impersonal room in a hotel, and sunk himself in work. There was nothing for him but work and the harsh friendship of Terry Wickett.

His first task was to check the statistics of his St. Swithin treatments and the new figures still coming in from Stokes. Some of them were shaky, some suggested that the value of phage certainly had been confirmed, but there was nothing final. He took his figures to Raymond Pearl the biometrician, who thought less of them than did Martin himself.

He had already made a report of his work to the Director and the Trustees of the Institute, with no conclusion except "the results await statistical analysis and should have this before they are published." But Holabird had run wild, the newspapers had reported wonders, and in on Martin poured demands that he send out phage; inquiries as to whether he did not have a phage for tuberculosis, for syphilis; offers that he take charge of this epidemic and that.

Pearl had pointed out that his agreeable results in first phaging the whole of Carib village must be questioned, because it was possible that when he began the curve of the disease had already passed its peak. With this and the other complications, viewing his hot work in St. Hubert as coldly as though it were the pretense of a man whom he had never seen, Martin decided that he had no adequate proof, and strode in to see the Director.

Holabird was gentle and pretty, but he sighed that if this conclusion were published, he would have to take back all the things he had said about the magnificence which, presumably, he had inspired his subordinate to accomplish. He was gentle and pretty, but firm; Martin was to suppress (Holabird did not say "suppress"—he said "leave to me for further consideration") the real statistical results, and issue the report with an ambiguous summary.

Martin was furious, Holabird delicately relentless. Martin hastened to Terry, declaring that he would resign—would denounce—would expose— Yes! He would! He no longer had to support Leora. He'd work as a drug-clerk. He'd go back right now and tell the Holy Wren—

"Hey! Slim! Wait a minute! Hold your horses!" observed Terry. "Just get along with Holy for a while, and we'll work out something we can do together, and be independent. Meanwhile you have got your lab here, and you still have some physical chemistry to learn! And, uh— Slim, I haven't said anything about your St. Hubert stuff, but you know and I know you bunged it up badly. Can you come into court with clean hands, if you're going to indict the Holy One? Though I do agree that aside from being a dirty, lying, social-climbing, sneaking, power-grabbing hypocrite, he's all right. Hold on. We'll fix up something. Why, son, we've just been learning our science; we're just beginning to work."

Then Holabird published officially, under the Institute's seal, Martin's original report to the Trustees, with such quaint revisions as a change of "the results should have analysis" to "while statistical analysis would seem desirable, it is evident that this new treatment has accomplished all that had been hoped."

Again Martin went mad, again Terry calmed him; and with a hard fury unlike his eagerness of the days when he had known that Leora was waiting for him he resumed his physical chemistry.

He learned the involved mysteries of freezing-point determinations, osmotic pressure determinations, and tried to apply Northrop's generalizations on enzymes to the study of phage.

He became absorbed in mathematical laws which strangely predicted natural phenomena; his world was cold, exact, austerely materialistic, bitter to those who founded their logic on impressions. He was daily more scornful toward the counters of paving stones, the renamers of species, the compilers of irrelevant data. In his absorption the pleasant seasons passed unseen.

Once he raised his head in astonishment to perceive that it was spring; once Terry and he tramped two hundred miles through the Pennsylvania hills, by summer roads; but it seemed only a day later when it was Christmas, and Holabird was being ever so jolly and yuley about the Institute.

The absence of Gottlieb may have been good for Martin, since he no longer turned to the master for solutions in tough queries. When he took up diffusion problems, he began to develop his own apparatus, and whether it was from inborn ingenuity or merely from a fury of labor, he was so competent that he won from Terry the almost overwhelming praise: "Why, that's not so darn' bad, Slim!"

The sureness to which Max Gottlieb seems to have been born came to Martin slowly, after many stumblings, but it came. He desired a perfection of technique in the quest for absolute and provable fact; he desired as greatly as any Pater to "burn with a hard gem-like flame," and he desired not to have ease and repute in the market-place, but rather to keep free of those follies, lest they confuse him and make him soft.

Holabird was as much bewildered as Tubbs would have been by the ramifications of Martin's work. What did he think he was anyway—a bacteriologist or a bio-physicist? But Holabird was won by the scientific world's reception of Martin's first important paper, on the effect of X-rays, gamma rays, and beta rays on the anti-Shiga phage. It was praised in Paris and Brussels and Cambridge as much as in New York, for its insight and for "the clarity and to perhaps be unscientifically enthusiastic, the sheer delight and style of its presentation," as Professor Berkeley Wurtz put it; which may be indicated by quoting the first paragraph of the paper:

> In a preliminary publication, I have reported a marked qualitative destructive effect of the radiations from radium emanations on Bacteriophage-anti-Shiga. In the present paper it is shown that X-rays, gamma rays, and beta rays produce identical inactivating effects on this bacteriophage. Furthermore, a quantitative relation is demonstrated to exist between this inactivation and the radiations that produce it. The results obtained from this quantitative study permit the statement that the percentage of inactivation, as measured by determining the units of bacteriophage remaining after irradiation by gamma and beta rays of a suspension of fixed virulence, is a function of the two variables, millicuries and hours. The following equation accounts quantitatively for the experimental results obtained:

$$K = \frac{\lambda \log e \dfrac{u_0}{u}}{E_0 (\epsilon - \lambda t_1)}$$

When Director Holabird saw the paper—Yeo was vicious enough to take it in and ask his opinion—he said, "Splendid, oh, I say, simply splendid! I've just had the chance to skim through it, old boy, but I shall certainly read it carefully, the first free moment I have."

Chapter XXXVII

MARTIN did not see Joyce Lanyon for weeks after his return to New York. Once she invited him to dinner, but he could not come, and he did not hear from her again.

His absorption in osmotic pressure determinations did not content him when he sat in his prim hotel room and was reduced from Dr. Arrowsmith to a man who had no one to talk to. He remembered how they had sat by the lagoon in the tepid twilight; he telephoned asking whether he might come in for tea.

He knew in an unformulated way that Joyce was rich, but after seeing her in gingham, cooking in the kitchen of St. Swithin's almshouse, he did not grasp her position; and he was uncomfortable when, feeling dusty from the laboratory, he came to her great house and found her the soft-voiced mistress of many servants. Hers was a palace, and palaces, whether they are such very little ones as Joyce's, with its eighteen rooms, or Buckingham or vast Fontainebleau, are all alike; they are choked with the superfluities of pride, they are so complete that one does not remember small endearing charms, they are indistinguishable in their common feeling of polite and uneasy grandeur, they are therefore altogether tedious.

But amid the pretentious splendor which Roger Lanyon had accumulated, Joyce was not tedious. It is to be suspected that she enjoyed showing Martin what she really was, by producing footmen and too many kinds of sandwiches, and by boasting, "Oh, I never do know what they're going to give me for tea."

But she had welcomed him, crying, "You look so much better. I'm frightfully glad. Are you still my brother? I was a good cook at the almshouse, wasn't I!"

Had he been suave then and witty, she would not have been greatly interested. She knew too many men who were witty and well-bred, ivory smooth and competent to help her spend the four or five million dollars with which she was burdened. But Martin was at once a scholar who made osmotic pressure determinations almost interesting, a taut swift man whom she could fancy running or making love, and a lonely youngster who naïvely believed that here in her soft security she was still the girl who had sat with him by the lagoon, still the courageous woman who had come to him in a drunken room at Blackwater.

Joyce Lanyon knew how to make men talk. Thanks more to her than to his own articulateness, he made living the Institute, the members, their feuds, and the drama of coursing on the trail of a discovery.

Her easy life here had seemed tasteless after the risks of St. Hubert, and in his contempt for ease and rewards she found exhilaration.

He came now and then to tea, to dinner; he learned the ways of her house, her servants, the more nearly intelligent of her friends. He liked—and possibly he was liked by—some of them. With one friend of hers Martin had a state of undeclared war. This was Latham Ireland, an achingly well-dressed man of fifty, a competent lawyer who was fond of standing in front of fireplaces and being quietly clever. He fascinated Joyce by telling her that she was subtle, then telling her what she was being subtle about.

Martin hated him.

In midsummer Martin was invited for a week-end at Joyce's vast blossom-hid country house at Greenwich. She was half apologetic for its luxury; he was altogether unhappy.

The strain of considering clothes, of galloping out to buy white trousers when he wanted to watch the test-tubes in the constant-temperature bath, of trying to look easy in the limousine which met him at the station, and of deciding which servants to tip and how much and when, was dismaying to a simple man. He felt rustic when, after he had blurted, "Just a minute till I go up and unpack my suit-case," she said gently, "Oh, that will have been done for you."

He discovered that a valet had laid out for him to put on, that first evening, all the small store of underclothes he had brought, and had squeezed out on his brush a ribbon of toothpaste.

He sat on the edge of his bed, groaning, "This is too rich for my blood!"

He hated and feared that valet, who kept stealing his clothes, putting them in places where they could not be found, then popping in menacingly when Martin was sneaking about the enormous room looking for them.

But his chief unhappiness was that there was nothing to do. He had no sport but tennis, at which he was too rusty to play with these chattering unidentified people who filled the house and, apparently with perfect willingness, worked at golf and bridge. He had met but few of the friends of whom they talked. They said, "You know dear old R.G.," and he said, "Oh, *yes*," but he never did know dear old R.G.

Joyce was as busily amiable as when they were alone at tea, and she found for him a weedy flapper whose tennis was worse than his own, but she had twenty guests—forty at Sunday lunch—and he gave up certain agreeable notions of walking with her in fresh lanes and, after excitedly saying this and that, perhaps kissing her. He had one moment with her. As he was going, she ordered, "Come here, Martin," and led him apart.

"You haven't really enjoyed it."

"Why, sure, course I—"

"Of course you haven't! And you despise us, rather, and perhaps you're partly right. I do like pretty people and gracious manners and good games, but I suppose they seem piffling after nights in a laboratory."

"No, I like 'em too. In a way. I like to look at beautiful women—at you! But— Oh, darn it, Joyce, I'm not up to it. I've always been poor, and horribly busy. I haven't learned your games."

"But, Martin, you could, with the intensity you put into everything."

"Even getting drunk in Blackwater!"

"And I hope in New York, too! Dear Roger, he did have such an innocent, satisfying time getting drunk at class-dinners! But I mean: if you went at it, you could play bridge and golf—and talking—better than any of them. If you only knew how frightfully recent most of the ducal class in America are! And Martin: wouldn't it be good for you? Wouldn't you work all the better if you got away from your logarithmic tables now and then? And are you going to admit there's anything you can't conquer?"

"No, I—"

"Will you come to dinner on Tuesday week, just us two, and we'll fight it out?"

"Be glad to."

For a number of hours, on the train to Terry Wickett's vacation place in the Vermont hills, Martin was convinced that he loved Joyce Lanyon, and that he was going to attack the art of being amusing as he had attacked physical chemistry. Ardently, and quite humorlessly, as he sat stiffly in a stale Pullman chair-car with his feet up on his suit-case, he pictured himself wearing a club-tie (presumably first acquiring the tie and the club), playing golf in plus-fours, and being entertaining about dear old R.G. and incredibly witty about dear old Latham Ireland's aged Rolls-Royce.

But these ambitions he forgot as he came to Terry's proud proprietary shanty, by a lake among oaks and maples, and heard Terry's real theories of the decomposition of quinine derivatives.

Being perhaps the least sentimental of human beings, Terry had named his place "Birdies' Rest." He owned five acres of woodland, two miles from a railroad station. His shanty was a two-room affair of logs, with bunks for beds and oilcloth for table-linen.

"Here's the layout, Slim," said Terry. "Some day I'm going to figure out a way of making a lab here pay, by manufacturing sera or something, and I'll put up a couple more buildings on the flat by the lake, and have one absolutely independent place for science—two hours a day on the commercial end, and say about six for sleeping and a couple for feeding and telling dirty stories. That leaves—two and six and two make ten, if I'm any authority on higher math—that leaves fourteen hours a day for research (except when you got something special on), with no Director and no Society patrons and no Trustees that you've got to satisfy by making fool reports. Of course there won't be any scientific dinners with ladies in candy-box dresses, but I figure we'll be able to afford plenty of salt pork and corncob pipes, and your bed will be made perfectly—if you make it yourself. Huh? Lez go and have a swim."

Martin returned to New York with the not very compatible plans of being the best-dressed golfer in Greenwich and of cooking beef-stew with Terry at Birdies' Rest.

But the first of these was the more novel to him.

II

Joyce Lanyon was enjoying a conversion. Her St. Hubert experiences and her natural variability had caused her to be dissatisfied with Roger's fast-motoring set.

She let the lady Mæcenases of her acquaintance beguile her into several of their Causes, and she enjoyed them as she had enjoyed her active and entirely purposeless war work in 1917, for Joyce Lanyon was to some degree an Arranger, which was an epithet invented by Terry Wickett for Capitola McGurk.

An Arranger and even an Improver was Joyce, but she was not a Capitola; she neither waved a feathered fan and spoke spaciously, nor did she take out her sex-passion in talking. She was fine and occasionally gorgeous, with tiger in her, though she was as far from perfumed-boudoir and black-lingerie passion as she was from Capitola's cooing staleness. Hers was sheer straight white silk and cherished skin.

Behind all her reasons for valuing Martin was the fact that the only time in her life when she had felt useful and independent was when she had been an almshouse cook.

She might have drifted on, in her world of drifters, but for the interposition of Latham Ireland, the lawyer-dilettante-lover.

"Joy," he observed, "there seems to be an astounding quantity of that Dr. Arrowsmith person about the place. As your benign uncle—"

"Latham, my sweet, I quite agree that Martin is too agressive, thoroughly unlicked, very selfish, rather a prig, absolutely a pedant, and his shirts are atrocious. And I rather think I shall marry him. I almost think I love him!"

"Wouldn't cyanide be a neater way of doing suicide?" said Latham Ireland.

III

What Martin felt for Joyce was what any widowed man of thirty-eight would feel for a young and pretty and well-spoken woman who was attentive to his wisdom. As to her wealth, there was no problem at all. He was no poor man marrying money! Why, he was making ten thousand a year, which was eight thousand more than he needed to live on!

Occasionally he was suspicious of her dependence on luxury. With tremendous craft he demanded that instead of their dining in her Jacobean hall of state, she come with him on his own sort of party. She came, with enthusiasm. They went to abysmal Greenwich Village restaurants with candles, artistic waiters, and no food; or to Chinatown dives with food and nothing else. He even insisted on their taking the subway—though after dinner he usually forgot that he was being Spartan, and ordered a taxicab. She accepted it all without either wincing or too much gurgling.

She played tennis with him in the court on her roof; she taught him bridge, which, with his concentration and his memory, he soon played better than she and enjoyed astonishingly; she persuaded him that he had a leg and would look well in golf clothes.

He came to take her to dinner, on a serene autumn evening. He had a taxi waiting.

"Why don't we stick to the subway?" she said.

They were standing on her doorstep, in a blankly expensive and quite unromantic street off Fifth Avenue.

"Oh, I hate the rotten subway as much as you do! Elbows in my stomach never did help me much to plan experiments. I expect when we're married I'll enjoy your limousine."

"Is this a proposal? I'm not at all sure I'm going to marry you. Really, I'm *not*! You have no sense of ease!"

They were married the following January, in St. George's Church, and Martin suffered almost as much over the flowers, the bishop, the relatives with high-pitched voices, and the top hat which Joyce had commanded, as he did over having Rippleton Holabird wring his hand with a look of, "At last, dear boy, you have come out of barbarism and become One of Us."

Martin had asked Terry to be his best man. Terry had refused, and asserted that only with pain would he come to the wedding at all. The best man was Dr. William Smith, with his beard trimmed for the occasion, and distressing morning clothes and a topper which he had bought in London eleven years before, but both of them were safe in charge of a cousin of Joyce who was guaranteed to have extra handkerchiefs and to recognize the Wedding March. He had understood that Martin was Groton and Harvard, and when he discovered that he was Winnemac and nothing at all, he became suspicious.

In their stateroom on the steamer Joyce murmured, "Dear, you were brave! I didn't know what a damn' fool that cousin of mine was. Kiss me!"

Thenceforth . . . except for a dreadful second when Leora floated between them, eyes closed and hands crossed on her pale cold breast . . . they were happy and in each other found adventurous new ways.

IV

For three months they wandered in Europe.

On the first day Joyce had said, "Let's have this beastly money thing over. I should think you are the least mercenary of men. I've put ten thousand dollars to your credit in London—oh, yes, and fifty thousand in New York—and if you'd like, when you have to do things for me, I'd be glad if you'd draw on it. No! Wait! Can't you see how easy and decent I want to make it all? You won't hurt me to save your own self-respect?"

V

They really had, it seemed, to stay with the Principessa del Oltraggio (formerly Miss Lucy Deemy Bessy of Dayton), Madame des Basses Loges (Miss Brown of San Francisco), and the Countess of Marazion (who had been Mrs. Arthur Snaipe of Albany, and several things before that), but Joyce did go with him to see the great laboratories in London, Paris, Copenhagen. She swelled to perceive how Nobel-prize winners received Her Husband, knew of him, desired to be violent with him about phage, and showed him their work of years. Some of them were hasty and graceless, she thought. Her Man was prettier than any of them, and if she would but be patient with him, she could make him master polo and clothes and conversation . . . but of course go on with his science . . . a pity he could not have a knighthood, like one or two of the British scientists they met. But even in America there were honorary degrees. . . .

While she discovered and digested Science, Martin discovered Women.

VI

Aware only of Madeline Fox and Orchid Pickerbaugh, who were Nice American Girls, of soon-forgotten ladies of the night, and of Leora who, in her indolence, her indifference to decoration and good fame, was neither woman nor wife but only her own self, Martin knew nothing whatever about Women. He had expected Leora to wait for him, to obey his wishes, to understand without his saying them all the flattering things he had planned to say. He was spoiled, and Joyce was not timorous about telling him so.

It was not for her to sit beaming and wordless while he and his fellow-researchers arranged the world. With many jolts he perceived that even outside the bedroom he had to consider the fluctuations and variables of his wife, as A Woman, and sometimes as A Rich Woman.

It was confusing to find that where Leora had acidly claimed sex-loyalty but had hummingly not cared in what manner he might say Good Morning, Joyce was indifferent as to how many women he might have fondled (so long as he did not insult her by making love to them in her presence) but did require him to say Good Morning as though he meant it. It was confusing to find how starkly she discriminated between his caresses when he was absorbed in her and his hasty interest when he wanted to go to sleep. She could, she said, kill a man who considered her merely convenient furniture, and she uncomfortably emphasized the "kill."

She expected him to remember her birthday, her taste in wine, her liking for flowers, and her objection to viewing the process of shaving. She wanted a room to herself; she insisted that he knock before entering; and she demanded that he admire her hats.

When he was so interested in the work at Pasteur Institute that he had a clerk telephone that he would not be able to meet her for dinner, she was tight-lipped with rage.

"Oh, you got to expect that," he reflected, feeling that he was being tactful and patient and penetrating.

It annoyed him, sometimes, that she would never impulsively start off on a walk with him. No matter how brief the jaunt, she must first go to her room for white gloves—placidly stand there drawing them on. . . . And in London she made him buy spats . . . and even wear them.

Joyce was not only an Arranger—she was a Loyalist. Like most American cosmopolites she revered the English peerage, adopted all their standards and beliefs—or what she considered their standards and beliefs—and treasured her encounters with them. Three and a half years after the War of 1914–18, she still said that she loathed all Germans, and the one complete quarrel between her and Martin occurred when he desired to see the laboratories in Berlin and Vienna.

But for all their differences it was a romantic pilgrimage. They loved fearlessly; they tramped through the mountains and came back to revel in vast bathrooms and ingenious dinners; they idled before cafés, and save when he fell silent as he remembered how much Leora had wanted to sit before cafés in France, they showed each other all the eagernesses of their minds.

Europe, her Europe, which she had always known and loved, Joyce offered to him on generous hands, and he who had ever been sensitive to warm colors and fine gestures—when he was not frenzied with work—was grateful to her and boyish with wonder. He believed that he was learning to take life easily and beautifully; he criticized Terry Wickett (but only to himself) for provincialism; and so in a golden leisure they came back to America and prohibition and politicians charging to protect the Steel Trust from the communists, to conversation about bridge and motors and to osmotic pressure determinations.

Chapter XXXVIII

DIRECTOR Rippleton Holabird had also married money, and whenever his colleagues hinted that since his first ardent work in physiology he had done nothing but arrange a few nicely selected flowers on the tables hewn out by other men, it was a satisfaction to him to observe that these rotters came down to the Institute by subway, while he drove elegantly in his coupé. But now Arrowsmith, once the poorest of them all, came by limousine with a chauffeur who touched his hat, and Holabird's coffee was salted.

There was a simplicity in Martin, but it cannot be said that he did not lick his lips when Holabird mooned at the chauffeur.

His triumph over Holabird was less than being able to entertain Angus Duer and his wife, on from Chicago; to introduce them to Director Holabird, to Salamon the king of surgeons, and to a medical baronet; and to have Angus gush, "Mart, do you mind my saying we're all awfully proud of you? Rouncefield was speaking to me about it the other day. 'It may be presumptuous,' he said, 'but I really feel that perhaps the training we tried to give Dr. Arrowsmith here in the Clinic did in some way contribute to his magnificent work in the West Indies and at McGurk.' What a lovely woman your wife is, old man! Do you suppose she'd mind telling Mrs. Duer where she got that frock?"

Martin had heard about the superiority of poverty to luxury, but after the lunch-wagons of Mohalis, after twelve years of helping Leora check the laundry and worry about the price of steak, after a life of waiting in the slush for trolleys, it was not at all dismaying to have a valet who produced shirts automatically; not at all degrading to come to meals which were always interesting, and, in the discretion of his car, to lean an aching head against softness and think how clever he was.

"You see, by having other people do the vulgar things for you, it saves your own energy for the things that only you can do," said Joyce.

Martin agreed, then drove to Westchester for a lesson in golf.

A week after their return from Europe, Joyce went with him to see Gottlieb. He fancied that Gottlieb came out of his brooding to smile on them.

"After all," Martin considered, "the old man did like beautiful things. If he'd had the chance, he might've liked a big Establishment, too, maybe."

Terry was surprisingly complaisant.

"I'll tell you, Slim—if you want to know. Personally I'd hate to have to live up to servants. But I'm getting old and wise. I figure that different folks like different things, and awful' few of 'em have the sense to come and ask me what they ought to like. But honest, Slim, I don't think I'll come to dinner. I've gone and bought a dress-suit—*bought* it!—got it in my room—damn' landlady keeps filling it with mothballs—but I don't think I could stand listening to Latham Ireland being clever."

It was, however, Rippleton Holabird's attitude which most concerned Martin, for Holabird did not let him forget that unless he desired to drift off and be merely a ghostly Rich Woman's Husband, he would do well to remember who was Director.

Along with the endearing manners which he preserved for Ross McGurk, Holabird had developed the remoteness, the inhuman quiet courtesy, of the Man of Affairs, and people who presumed on his old glad days he courteously put in their places. He saw the need of repressing insubordination, when Arrowsmith appeared in a limousine. He gave him one week after his return to enjoy the limousine, then blandly called on him in his laboratory.

"Martin," he sighed, "I find that our friend Ross McGurk is just a bit dissatisfied with the practical results that are coming out of the Institute and, to convince him, I'm afraid I really must ask you to put less emphasis on bacteriophage for the moment and take up influenza. The Rockefeller Institute has the right idea. They've utilized their best minds, and spent money magnificently, on such problems as pneumonia, meningitis, cancer. They've already lessened the terrors of meningitis and pneumonia, and yellow fever is on the verge of complete abolition through Noguchi's work, and I have no doubt that their hospital, with its enormous resources and splendidly coöperating minds, will be the first to find something to alleviate diabetes. Now, I understand, they're hot after the cause of influenza. They're not going to permit another great epidemic of it. Well, dear chap, it's up to us to beat them on the flu, and I've chosen you to represent us in the race."

Martin was at the moment hovering over a method of reproducing phage on dead bacteria, but he could not refuse, he could not risk being discharged. He was too rich! Martin the renegade medical student could flounder off and be a soda-clerk, but if the husband of Joyce Lanyon should indulge in such insanity, he would be followed by reporters and photographed at the soda handles. Still less could he chance becoming merely her supported husband—a butler of the boudoir.

He assented, not very pleasantly.

He began to work on the cause of influenza with a half-heartedness almost magnificent. In the hospitals he secured cultures from cases which might be influenza and might be bad colds—no one was certain just what the influenza symptoms were; nothing was clean cut. He left most of the work to his assistants, occasionally giving them sardonic directions to "put on another hundred tubes of the A medium—hell, make it another thousand!" and when he found that they were doing as they pleased, he was not righteous nor rebuking. If he did not guiltily turn his hand from the plow it was only because he never touched the plow. Once his own small laboratory had been as fussily neat as a New Hampshire kitchen. Now the several rooms under his charge were a disgrace, with long racks of abandoned test-tubes, many half-filled with mold, none of them properly labeled.

Then he had his idea. He began firmly to believe that the Rockefeller investigators had found the cause of flu. He gushed in to Holabird and told him so. As for himself, he was going back to his search for the real nature of phage.

Holabird argued that Martin must be wrong. If Holabird wanted the McGurk Institute—and the Director of McGurk Institute—to have the credit for capturing influenza, then it simply could not be possible that Rockefeller was ahead of them. He also said weighty things about phage. Its essential nature, he pointed out, was an academic question.

But Martin was by now too much of a scientific dialectician for Holabird, who gave up and retired to his den (or so Martin gloomily believed) to devise new ways of plaguing him. For a time Martin was again left free to wallow in work.

He found a means of reproducing phage on dead bacteria by a very complicated, very delicate use of partial oxygen-carbon dioxide tension—as exquisite as cameo-carving, as improbable as weighing the stars. His report stirred the laboratory world, and here and there (in Tokio, in Amsterdam, in Winnemac) enthusiasts believed he had proven that phage was a living organism; and other enthusiasts said, in esoteric language with mathematical formulæ, that he was a liar and six kinds of a fool.

It was at this time, when he might have become a Great Man, that he pitched over most of his own work and some of the duties of being Joyce's husband to follow Terry Wickett, which showed that he lacked common sense, because Terry was still an assistant while he himself was head of a department.

Terry had discovered that certain quinine derivatives when introduced into the animal body slowly decompose into products which are highly toxic to bacteria but only mildly toxic to the body. There was hinted here a whole new world of therapy. Terry explained it to Martin, and invited him to collaborate. Buoyant with great things they got leave from Holabird—and from Joyce—and though it was winter they went off to Birdies' Rest, in the Vermont hills. While they snowshoed and shot rabbits, and all the long dark evenings while they lay on their bellies before the fire, they ranted and planned.

Martin had not been so long silk-wrapped that he could not enjoy gobbling salt pork after the northwest wind and the snow. It was not unpleasant to be free of thinking up new compliments for Joyce.

They had, they saw, to answer an interesting question: Do the quinine derivatives act by attaching themselves to the bacteria, or by changing the body fluids? It was a simple, clear, definite question which required for answer only the inmost knowledge of chemistry and biology, a few hundred animals on which to experiment, and perhaps ten or twenty or a million years of trying and failing.

They decided to work with the pneumococcus, and with the animal which should most nearly reproduce human pneumonia. This meant the monkey, and to murder monkeys is expensive and rather grim. Holabird, as Director, could supply them, but if they took him into confidence he would demand immediate results.

Terry meditated, "'Member there was one of these Nobel-prize winners, Slim, one of these plumb fanatics that instead of blowing in the prize spent the whole thing on chimps and other apes, and he got together with another of those whiskery old birds, and they ducked up alleys and kept the anti-viv folks from prosecuting them, and settled the problem of the transfer of syphilis to lower animals? But we haven't got any Nobel Prize, I grieve to tell you, and it doesn't look to me—"

"Terry, I'll do it, if necessary! I've never sponged on Joyce yet, but I will now, if the Holy Wren holds out on us."

II

They faced Holabird in his office, sulkily, rather childishly, and they demanded the expenditure of at least ten thousand dollars for monkeys. They wished to start a research which might take two years without apparent results—possibly without any results. Terry was to be transferred to Martin's department as co-head, their combined salaries shared equally.

Then they prepared to fight.

Holabird stared, assembled his mustache, departed from his Diligent Director manner, and spoke:

"Wait a minute, if you don't mind. As I gather it, you are explaining to me that occasionally it's necessary to take some time to elaborate an experiment. I really must tell you that I was formerly a researcher in an Institute called McGurk, and learned several of these things all by myself! Hell, Terry, and you, Mart, don't be so egotistic! You're not the only scientists who like to work undisturbed! If you poor fish only knew how I long to get away from signing letters and get my fingers on a kymograph drum again! Those beautiful long hours of search for truth! And if you knew how I've fought the Trustees for the chance to keep you fellows free! All right. You shall have your monkeys. Fix up the joint department to suit yourselves. And work ahead as seems best. I doubt if in the whole scientific world there's two people that can be trusted as much as you two surly birds!"

Holabird rose, straight and handsome and cordial, his hand out. They sheepishly shook it and sneaked away, Terry grumbling, "He's spoiled my whole day! I haven't got a single thing to kick about! Slim, where's the catch? You can bet there is one—there always is!"

In a year of divine work, the catch did not appear. They had their monkeys, their laboratories and garçons, and their unbroken leisure; they began the most exciting work they had ever known, and decidedly the most nerve-jabbing. Monkeys are unreasonable animals; they delight in developing tuberculosis on no provocation whatever; in captivity they have a liking for epidemics; and they make scenes by cursing at their masters in seven dialects.

"They're so up-and-coming," sighed Terry. "I feel like lettin' 'em go and retiring to Birdies' Rest to grow potatoes. Why should we murder live-wires like them to save pasty-faced, big-bellied humans from pneumonia?"

Their first task was to determine with accuracy the tolerated dose of the quinine derivative, and to study its effects on the hearing and vision, and on the kidneys, as shown by endless determinations of blood sugar and blood urea. While Martin did the injections and observed the effect on the monkeys and lost himself in chemistry, Terry toiled (all night, all next day, then a drink and a frowsy nap and all night again) on new methods of synthesizing the quinine derivative.

This was the most difficult period of Martin's life. To work, staggering sleepy, all night, to drowse on a bare table at dawn and to breakfast at a greasy lunch-counter, these were natural and amusing, but to explain to Joyce why he had missed her dinner to a lady sculptor and a lawyer whose grandfather had been a Confederate General, this was impossible. He won a brief tolerance by explaining that he really had longed to kiss her good-night, that he did appreciate the basket of sandwiches which she had sent, and that he was about to remove pneumonia from the human race, a statement which he healthily doubted.

But when he had missed four dinners in succession; when she had raged, "Can you imagine how awful it was for Mrs. Thorn to be short a man at the last moment?" when she had wailed, "I didn't so much mind your rudeness on the other nights, but this evening when I had nothing to do and sat home alone and waited for you"—then he writhed.

Martin and Terry began to produce pneumonia in their monkeys and to treat them, and they had success which caused them to waltz solemnly down the corridor. They could save the monkeys from pneumonia invariably, when the infection had gone but one day, and most of them on the second day and the third.

Their results were complicated by the fact that a certain number of the monkeys recovered by themselves, and this they allowed for by simple-looking figures which took days of stiff, shoulder-aching sitting over papers . . . one wild-haired collarless man at a table, while the other walked among stinking cages of monkeys, clucking to them, calling them Bess and Rover, and grunting placidly, "Oh, you would bite me, would you, sweetheart!" and all the while, kindly but merciless as the gods, injecting them with the deadly pneumonia.

They came into a high upland where the air was thin with failures. They studied in the test-tube the break-down products of pneumococci—and failed. They constructed artificial body fluids (carefully, painfully, inadequately), they tried the effect of the derivative on germs in this artificial blood—and failed.

Then Holabird heard of their previous success, and came down on them with laurels and fury.

He understood, he said, that they had a cure for pneumonia. Very well! The Institute could do with the credit for curing that undesirable disease, and Terry and Martin would kindly publish their findings (mentioning McGurk) at once.

"We will not! Look here, Holabird!" snarled Terry, "I thought you were going to let us alone."

"I have! Nearly a year! Till you should complete your research. And now you've completed it. It's time to let the world know what you're doing."

"If I did, the world would know a doggone sight more'n I do! Nothing doing, Chief. Maybe we can publish in a year from now."

"You'll publish now or—"

"All right, Holy. The blessed moment has arrived. I quit! And I'm so gentlemanly that I do it without telling you what I think of you!"

Thus was Terry Wickett discharged from McGurk. He patented the process of synthesizing his quinine derivative and retired to Birdies' Rest, to build a laboratory out of his small savings and spend a life of independent research supported by a restricted sale of sera and of his drug.

For Terry, wifeless and valetless, this was easy enough, but for Martin it was not simple.

III

Martin assumed that he would resign. He explained it to Joyce. How he was to combine a town house and a Greenwich castle with flannel-shirt collaboration at Birdies' Rest he had not quite planned, but he was not going to be disloyal.

"Can you beat it! The Holy Wren fires Terry but doesn't dare touch me! I waited simply because I wanted to watch Holabird figure out what I'd do. And now—"

He was elucidating it to her in their—in her—car, on the way home from a dinner at which he had been so gaily charming to an important dowager that Joyce had crooned, "What a fool Latham Ireland was to say he couldn't be polite!"

"I'm free, by thunder at last I'm free, because I've worked up to something that's worth being free for!" he exulted.

She laid her fine hand on his, and begged, "Wait! I want to think. Please! Do be quiet a moment."

Then: "Mart, if you went on working with Mr. Wickett, you'd have to be leaving me constantly."

"Well—"

"I really don't think that would be quite nice—I mean especially now, because I fancy I'm going to have a baby."

He made a sound of surprise.

"Oh, I'm not going to do the weeping mother. And I don't know whether I'm glad or furious, though I do believe I'd like to have one baby. But it does complicate things, you know. And personally, I should be sorry if you left the Institute, which gives you a solid position, for a hole-and-corner existence. Dear, I have been fairly nice, haven't I? I really do like you, you know! I don't want you to desert me, and you would if you went off to this horrid Vermont place."

"Couldn't we get a little house near there, and spend part of the year?"

"Pos-sibly. But we ought to wait till this beastly job of bearing a Dear Little One is over, then think about it."

Martin did not resign from the Institute, and Joyce did not think about taking a house near Birdies' Rest to the extent of doing it.

Chapter XXXIX

WITH Terry Wickett gone, Martin returned to phage. He made a false start and did the worst work of his life. He had lost his fierce serenity. He was too conscious of the ordeal of a professional social life, and he could never understand that esoteric phenomenon, the dinner-party—the painful entertainment of people whom one neither likes nor finds interesting.

So long as he had had a refuge in talking to Terry, he had not been too irritated by well-dressed nonentities, and for a time he had enjoyed the dramatic game of making Nice People accept him. Now he was disturbed by reason.

Clif Clawson showed him how tangled his life had grown.

When he had first come to New York, Martin had looked for Clif, whose boisterousness had been his comfort among Angus Duers and Irving Watterses in medical school. Clif was not to be found, neither at the motor agency for which he had once worked nor elsewhere on Automobile Row. For fourteen years Martin had not seen him.

Then to his laboratory at McGurk was brought a black-and-red card:

CLIFFORD L. CLAWSON
(Clif)
Top Notch Guaranteed Oil Investments

Higham Block
Butte

"Clif! Good old Clif! The best friend a man ever had! That time he lent me the money to get to Leora! Old Clif! By golly I need somebody like him, with Terry out of it and all these tea-hounds around me!" exulted Martin.

He dashed out and stopped abruptly, staring at a man who was, not softly, remarking to the girl reception-clerk:

"Well, sister, you scientific birds certainly do lay on the agony! Never struck a sweller layout than you got here, except in crook investment-offices—and I've never seen a nicer cutie than you anywhere. How 'bout lil dinner one of these beauteous evenings? I expect I'll parley-vous with thou full often now—I'm a great friend of Doc Arrowsmith. Fact I'm a doc myself—honest—real sawbones—went to medic school and everything. Ah! *Here's* the boy!"

Martin had not allowed for the changes of fourteen years. He was dismayed.

Clif Clawson, at forty, was gross. His face was sweaty, and puffy with pale flesh; his voice was raw; he fancied checked Norfolk jackets, tight across his swollen shoulders and his beefy hips.

He bellowed, while he belabored Martin's back:

"Well, well, well, well, well, well! Old Mart! Why, you old son of a gun! Why, you old son of a gun! Why, you damn' old chicken-thief! Say, you skinny little runt, I'm a son of a gun if you look one day older'n when I saw you last in Zenith!"

Martin was aware of the bright leering of the once humble reception-clerk. He said, "Well, gosh, it certainly is good to see you," and hastened to get Clif into the privacy of his office.

"You look fine," he lied, when they were safe. "What you been doing with yourself? Leora and I did our best to look you up, when we first came to New York. Uh— Do you know about, uh, about her?"

"Yuh, I read about her passing away. Fierce luck. And about your swell work in the West Indies—where was it? I guess you're a great man now—famous plague-chaser and all that stuff, and world-renowned skee-entist. I don't suppose you remember your old friends now."

"Oh, don't be a chump! It's—it's—it's fine to see you."

"Well, I'm glad to observe you haven't got the *capitus enlargatus*, Mart. Golly, I says to meself says I, if I blew in and old Mart high-hatted me, I'd just about come nigh unto letting him hear the straight truth, after all the compliments he's been getting from the sassiety dames. I'm glad you've kept your head. I thought about writing you from Butte—been selling some bum oil-stock there and kind of got out quick to save the inspectors the trouble of looking over my books. 'Well,' I thought, 'I'll just sit down and write the whey-faced runt a letter, and make him feel good by telling him how tickled I am over his nice work.' But you know how it is—time kind of slips by. Well, this is excellentus! We'll have a chance to see a whole lot of each other now. I'm going in with a fellow on an investment stunt here in New York. Great pickings, old kid! I'll take you out and show you how to order a real feed, one of these days. Well, tell me what you been doing since you got back from the West Indies. I suppose you're laying your plans to try and get in as the boss or president or whatever they call it of this gecelebrated Institute."

"No—I, uh, well, I shouldn't much care to be Director. I prefer sticking to my lab. I— Perhaps you'd like to hear about my work on phage."

Rejoicing to discover something of which he could talk, Martin sketched his experiments.

Clif spanked his forehead with a spongy hand, and shouted:

"Wait! Say, I've got an idea—and you can come right in on it. As I apperceive it, the dear old Gen. Public is just beginning to hear about this bac—what is it?—bacteriophage junk. Look here! Remember that old scoundrel Benoni Carr, that I introduced as a great pharmacologist at the medical banquet? Had din-din with him last eventide. He's running a sanitarium out on Long Island—slick idea, too—practically he's a bootlegger; gets a lot of high-rollers out there and let's 'em have all the hooch they want, on prescriptions, absolutely legal and water-tight! The parties they throw at that joint, dames and everything! Believe me, Uncle Clif is sore stricken with tootelus bootelus and is going to the Carr Sanitarium for what ails him! But now look: Suppose we got him or somebody to rig up a new kind of cure—call it phageotherapy—oh, it takes Uncle Clif to invent the names that claw in the bounteous dollars! Patients sit in a steam cabinet and eat tablets made of phage, with just a little strychnin to jazz up their hearts! Bran-new! Million in it! What cha think?"

Martin was almost feeble. "No, I'm afraid I'm against it."

"Why?"

"Well, I— Honestly, Clif, if you don't understand it, I don't know how I can explain the scientific attitude to you. You know—that's what Gottlieb used to call it—scientific attitude. And as I'm a scientist—least I hope I am—I couldn't— Well, to be associated with a thing like that—"

"But, you poor louse, don't you suppose I understand the scientific attitude? Gosh, I've seen a dissecting-room myself!

Why, you poor crab, of course I wouldn't expect you to have your name associated with it! You'd keep in the background and slip us all the dope, and get a lot of publicity for phage in general so the Dee-ah People would fall easier, and we'd pull all the strong-arm work."

"But— I hope you're joking, Clif. If you weren't joking, I'd tell you that if anybody tried to pull a thing like that, I'd expose 'em and get 'em sent to jail, no matter who they were!"

"Well, gosh, if you feel that way about it—!"

Clif was peering over the fatty pads beneath his eyes. He sounded doubtful:

"I suppose you have the right to keep other guys from grabbing your own stuff. Well, all right, Mart. Got to be teloddeling. Tell you what you *might* do, though, if that don't hurt your tender conscience, too: you might invite old Clif up t' the house for dinner, to meet the new lil wifey that I read about in the sassiety journals. You might happen to remember, old bean, that there have been times when you were glad enough to let poor fat old Clif slip you a feed and a place to sleep!"

"Oh, I know. You bet there have! Nobody was ever decenter to me; nobody. Look. Where you staying? I'll find out from my wife what dates we have ahead, and telephone you to-morrow morning."

"So you let the Old Woman keep the work-sheet for you, huh? Well, I never butt into anybody's business. I'm staying at the Berrington Hotel, room 617—'member that, 617—and you might try and 'phone me before ten to-morrow. Say, that's one grand sweet song of a cutie you got on the door here. What cha think? How's chances on dragging her out to feed and shake a hoof with Uncle Clif?"

As primly as the oldest, most staid scientist in the Institute, Martin protested, "Oh, she belongs to a very nice family. I don't think I should try it. Really, I'd rather you didn't."

Clif's gaze was sharp, for all its fattiness.

With excessive cordiality, with excessive applause when Clif remarked, "You better go back to work and put some salt on a coupla bacteria's tails," Martin guided him to the reception-room, safely past the girl clerk, and to the elevator.

For a long time he sat in his office and was thoroughly wretched.

He had for years pictured Clif Clawson as another Terry Wickett. He saw that Clif was as different from Terry as from Rippleton Holabird. Terry was rough, he was surly, he was colloquial, he despised many fine and gracious things, he offended many fine and gracious people, but these acerbities made up the haircloth robe wherewith he defended a devotion to such holy work as no cowled monk ever knew. But Clif—

"I'd do the world a service by killing that man!" Martin fretted. "Phageotherapy at a yegg sanitarium! I stand him only because I'm too much of a coward to risk his going around saying that 'in the days of my Success, I've gone back on my old friends.' (Success! Puddling at work! Dinners! Talking to idiotic women! Being furious because you weren't invited to the dinner to the Portuguese minister!) No. I'll 'phone Clif we can't have him at the house."

Over him came remembrance of Clif's loyalty in the old barren days, and Clif's joy to share with him every pathetic gain.

"Why *should* he understand my feeling about phage? Was his scheme any worse than plenty of reputable drug-firms? How much was I righteously offended, and how much was I sore because he didn't recognize the high social position of the rich Dr. Arrowsmith?"

He gave up the question, went home, explained almost frankly to Joyce what her probable opinion of Clif would be, and contrived that Clif should be invited to dinner with only the two of them.

"My dear Mart," said Joyce, "why do you insult me by hinting that I'm such a snob that I'll be offended by racy slang, and by business ethics very much like those of dear Roger's grandpapa? Do you think I've never ventured out of the drawing-room? I thought you'd seen me outside it! I shall probably like your Clawson person very much indeed."

The day after Martin had invited him to dinner, Clif telephoned to Joyce:

"This Mrs. Arrowsmith? Well, say, this is old Clif."

"I'm afraid I didn't quite catch it."

"Clif! Old Clif!"

"I'm frightfully sorry but— Perhaps there's a bad connection."

"Why, it's Mr. *Clawson*, that's going to feed with you on—"

"Oh, of course. I *am* so sorry."

"Well, look: What I wanted to know is: Is this going to be just a homey grub-grabbing or a real soirée? In other words, honey, shall I dress natural or do I put on the soup-and-fish? Oh, I got 'em—swallow-tail and the whole darn' outfit!"

"I— Do you mean— Oh. Shall you dress for dinner? I think perhaps I would."

"Attaboy! I'll be there, dolled up like a new saloon. I'll show you folks the cutest lil line of jeweled studs you ever laid eyes on. Well, it's been a great pleezhure to meet Mart's Missus, and we will now close with singing 'Till We Meet Again' or 'Au Reservoir.'"

When Martin came home, Joyce faced him with, "Sweet, I can't do it! The man must be mad. Really, dear, you just take care of him and let me go to bed. Besides: you two won't want me—you'll want to talk over old times, and I'd only interfere. And with baby coming in two months now, I ought to go to bed early."

"Oh, Joy, Clif'd be awfully offended, and he's always been so decent to me and— And you've often asked me about my cub days. Don't you *want*," plaintively, "to hear about 'em?"

"Very well, dear. I'll try to be a little sunbeam to him, but I warn you I sha'n't be a success."

They worked themselves up to a belief that Clif would be raucous, would drink too much, and slap Joyce on the back. But when he appeared for dinner he was agonizingly polite and flowery—till he became slightly drunk. When Martin said "damn," Clif reproved him with, "Of course I'm only a hick, but I don't think a lady like the Princess here would like you to cuss."

And, "Well, I never expected a rube like young Mart to marry the real bon-ton article."

And, "Oh, maybe it didn't cost something to furnish this dining-room, oh, not a-tall!"

And, "Champagne, heh? Well, you're certainly doing poor old Clif proud. Your Majesty, just tell your High Dingbat to tell his valay to tell my secretary the address of your bootlegger, will you?"

In his cups, though he severely retained his moral and elegant vocabulary, Clif chronicled the jest of selling oil-wells unprovided with oil and of escaping before the law closed in; the cleverness of joining churches for the purpose of selling stock to the members; and the edifying experience of assisting Dr. Benoni Carr to capture a rich and senile widow for his sanitarium by promising to provide medical consultation from the spirit-world.

Joyce was silent through it all, and so superbly polite that every one was wretched.

Martin struggled to make a liaison between them, and he had no elevating remarks about the strangeness of a man's boasting of his own crookedness, but he was coldly furious when Clif blundered:

"You said old Gottlieb was sort of down on his luck now."

"Yes, he's not very well."

"Poor old coot. But I guess you've realized by now how foolish you were when you used to fall for him like seven and a half brick. Honestly, Lady Arrowsmith, this kid used to think Pa Gottlieb was the cat's pajamas—begging your pardon for the slanguageness."

"What do you mean?" said Martin.

"Oh, I'm onto Gottlieb! Of course you know as well as I do that he always was a self-advertiser, getting himself talked about by confidin' to the whole *ops terrara* what a strict scientist he was, and putting on a lot of dog and emitting these wise cracks about philosophy and what fierce guys the regular docs were. But what's worse than— Out in San Diego I ran onto a fellow that used to be an instructor in botany in Winnemac, and he told me that with all this antibody stuff of his, Gottlieb never gave any credit to—well, he was some Russian that did most of it before and Pa Gottlieb stole all his stuff."

That in this charge against Gottlieb there was a hint of truth, that he knew the great god to have been at times ungenerous, merely increased the rage which was clenching Martin's fist in his lap.

Three years before, he would have thrown something, but he was an adaptable person. He had yielded to Joyce's training in being quietly instead of noisily disagreeable; and his only comment was "No, I think you're wrong, Clif. Gottlieb has carried the antibody work 'way beyond all the others."

Before the coffee and liqueurs had come into the drawing-room, Joyce begged, at her prettiest, "Mr. Clawson, do you mind awfully if I slip up to bed? I'm so frightfully glad to have had the opportunity of meeting one of my husband's oldest friends, but I'm not feeling very well, and I do think I'd be wise to have some rest."

"Madam the Princess, I noticed you were looking peeked."

"Oh! Well— Good night!"

Martin and Clif settled in large chairs in the drawing-room, and tried to play at being old friends happy in meeting. They did not look at each other.

After Clif had cursed a little and told three sound smutty stories, to show that he had not been spoiled and that he had been elegant only to delight Joyce, he flung:

"Huh! So that is that, as the Englishers remark. Well, I could see your Old Lady didn't cotton to me. She was just as chummy as an iceberg. But gosh, I don't mind. She's going to have a kid, and of course women, all of 'em, get cranky when they're that way. But—"

He hiccuped, looked sage, and bolted his fifth cognac.

"But what I never could figure out— Mind you, I'm not criticizing the Old Lady. She's as swell as they make 'em. But what I can't understand is how after living with Leora, who was the real thing, you can stand a hoity-toity skirt like Joycey!"

Then Martin broke.

The misery of not being able to work, these months since Terry had gone, had gnawed at him.

"Look here, Clif. I won't have you discuss my wife. I'm sorry she doesn't please you, but I'm afraid that in this particular matter—"

Clif had risen, not too steadily, though his voice and his eyes were resolute.

"All right. I figured out you were going to high-hat me. Of course I haven't got a rich wife to slip me money. I'm just a plain old hobo. I don't belong in a place like this. Not smooth enough to be a butler. You are. All right. I wish you luck. And meanwhile you can go plumb to hell, my young friend!"

Martin did not pursue him into the hall.

As he sat alone he groaned, "Thank Heaven, that operation's over!"

He told himself that Clif was a crook, a fool, and a fat waster; he told himself that Clif was a cynic without wisdom, a drunkard without charm, and a philanthropist who was generous only because it larded his vanity. But these admirable truths did not keep the operation from hurting any more than it would have eased the removal of an appendix to be told that it was a bad appendix, an appendix without delicacy or value.

He had loved Clif—did love him and always would. But he would never see him again. Never!

The impertinence of that flabby blackguard to sneer at Gottlieb! His boorishness! Life was too short for—

"But hang it—yes, Clif is a tough, but so am I. He's a crook, but wasn't I a crook to fake my plague figures in St. Hubert—and the worse crook because I got praise for it?"

He bobbed up to Joyce's room. She was lying in her immense four-poster, reading "Peter Whiffle."

"Darling, it was all rather dreadful, wasn't it!" she said. "He's gone?"

"Yes. . . . He's gone. . . . I've driven out the best friend I ever had—practically. I let him go, let him go off feeling that he was a rotter and a failure. It would have been decenter to have killed him. Oh, why couldn't you have been simple and jolly with him? You were so confoundedly polite! He was uneasy and unnatural, and showed up worse than he really is. He's no tougher than—he's a lot better than the financiers who cover up their stuff by being suave. . . . Poor devil! I'll bet right now Clif's tramping in the rain, saying, 'The one man I ever loved and tried to do things for has turned against me, now he's—now he has a lovely wife. What's the use of ever being decent?' he's saying. . . . Why couldn't you be simple, and chuck your highfalutin' manners for once?"

"See here! You disliked him quite as much as I did, and I will not have you blame it on me! You've grown beyond him.

You that are always blaring about Facts—can't you face the fact? For once, at least, it's not my fault. You may perhaps remember, my king of men, that I had the good sense to suggest that I shouldn't appear to-night; not meet him at all."

"Oh—well—yes—gosh—but— Oh, I suppose so. Well, anyway— It's over, and that's all there is to it."

"Darling, I do understand how you feel. But isn't it good it is over! Kiss me good-night."

"*But*"—Martin said to himself, as he sat feeling naked and lost and homeless, in the dressing-gown of gold dragon-flies on black silk which she had bought for him in Paris—"but if it'd been Leora instead of Joyce— Leora would've known Clif was a crook, and she'd'd've accepted it as a fact. (Talk about your facing facts!) She wouldn't've insisted on sitting as a judge. She wouldn't've said, 'This is different from me, so it's wrong.' She'd've said, 'This is different from me, so it's interesting.' Leora—"

He had a sharp, terrifying vision of her, lying there coffinless, below the mold in a garden on the Penrith Hills.

He came out of it to growl, "What was it Clif said? 'You're not her husband—you're her butler—you're too smooth.' He was right! The whole point is: I'm not allowed to see who I want to. I've been so clever that I've made myself the slave of Joyce and Holy Holabird."

He was always going to, but he never did see Clif Clawson again.

II

It happened that both Joyce's and Martin's paternal grandfathers had been named John, and John Arrowsmith they called their son. They did not know it, but a certain John Arrowsmith, mariner of Devonport, had died in the matter of the Spanish Armada, taking with him five valorous Dons.

Joyce suffered horribly, and renewed all of Martin's love for her (he did love pitifully this slim, brilliant girl).

"Death's a better game than bridge—you have no partner to help you!" she said, when she was grotesquely stretched on a chair of torture and indignity; when before they would give her the anesthetic, her face was green with agony.

John Arrowsmith was straight of back and straight of limb—ten good pounds he weighed at birth—and he was gay of eye when he had ceased to be a raw wrinkled grub and become a man-child. Joyce worshiped him, and Martin was afraid of him, because he saw that this miniscule aristocrat, this child born to the self-approval of riches, would some day condescend to him.

Three months after child-bearing, Joyce was more brisk than ever about putting and back-hand service and hats and Russian emigrés.

III

For science Joyce had great respect and no understanding. Often she asked Martin to explain his work, but when he was glowing, making diagrams with his thumb-nail on the table-cloth, she would interrupt him with a gracious "Darling—do you mind—just a second— Plinder, isn't there any more of the sherry?"

When she turned back to him, though her eyes were kind his enthusiasm was gone.

She came to his laboratory, asked to see his flasks and tubes, and begged him to bully her into understanding, but she never sat back watching for silent hours.

Suddenly, in his bogged floundering in the laboratory, he touched solid earth. He blundered into the effect of phage on the mutation of bacterial species—very beautiful, very delicate—and after plodding months when he had been a sane citizen, an almost good husband, an excellent bridge-player, and a rotten workman, he knew again the happiness of high taut insanity.

He wanted to work nights, every night. During his uninspired fumbling, there had been nothing to hold him at the Institute after five, and Joyce had become used to having him flee to her. Now he showed an inconvenient ability to ignore engagements, to snap at delightful guests who asked him to explain all about science, to forget even her and the baby.

"I've *got* to work evenings!" he said. "I can't be regular and easy about it when I'm caught by a big experiment, any more than you could be regular and easy and polite when you were gestating the baby."

"I know but— Darling, you get so nervous when you're working like this. Heavens, I don't care how much you offend people by missing engagements—well, after all, I wish you wouldn't, but I do know it may be unavoidable. But when you make yourself so drawn and trembly, are you gaining time in the long run? It's just for your own sake. Oh, I have it! Wait! You'll see what a scientist I am! No, I won't explain—not yet!"

Joyce had wealth and energy. A week later, flushed, slim, gallant, joyous, she said to him after dinner, "I've got a surprise for you!"

She led him to the unoccupied rooms over the garage, behind their house. In that week, using a score of workmen from the most immaculate and elaborate scientific supply-house in the country, she had created for him the best bacteriological laboratory he had ever seen—white-tile floor and enameled brick walls, ice-box and incubator, glassware and stains and microscope, a perfect constant-temperature bath—and a technician, trained in Lister and Rockefeller, who had his bedroom behind the laboratory and who announced his readiness to serve Dr. Arrowsmith day or night.

"There!" sang Joyce. "Now when you simply must work evenings, you won't have to go clear down to Liberty Street. You can duplicate your cultures, or whatever you call 'em. If you're bored at dinner—all right! You can slip out here afterward, and work as late as ever you want. Is— Sweet, is it all right? Have I done it right? I tried so hard—I got the best men I could—"

While his lips were against hers he brooded, "To have done this for me! And to be so humble! . . . And now, curse it, I'll *never* be able to get away by myself!"

She so joyfully demanded his finding some fault that, to give her the novel pleasure of being meek, he suggested that the centrifuge was inadequate.

"You wait, my man!" she crowed.

Two evenings after, when they had returned from the opera, she led him to the cement-floored garage beneath his new laboratory, and in a corner, ready to be set up, was a second-hand but adequate centrifuge, a most adequate centrifuge, the masterpiece of the great firm of Berkeley-Saunders—in fact none other than Gladys, whose dismissal from McGurk for her sluttish ways had stirred Martin and Terry to go out and get bountifully drunk.

It was less easy for him, this time, to be grateful, but he worked at it.

IV

Through both the economico-literary and the Rolls-Royce sections of Joyce's set the rumor panted that there was a new diversion in an exhausted world—going out to Martin's laboratory and watching him work, and being ever so silent and reverent, except perhaps when Joyce murmured, "Isn't he adorable the way he teaches his darling bacteria to say 'Pretty Polly'!" or when Latham Ireland convulsed them by arguing that scientists had no sense of humor, or Sammy de Lembre burst out in his marvelous burlesque of jazz:

> Oh, Mistah Back-sil-lil-us, don't you gri-in at me;
> You mi-cro-bi-o-log-ic cuss, I'm o-on-to thee.
> When Mr. Dr. Arrowsmith's done looked at de clues,
> You'll sit in jail a-singin' dem Bac-ter-i-uh Blues.

Joyce's cousin from Georgia sparkled, "Mart is so cute with all those lil vases of his. But Ah can always get him so mad by tellin' him the trouble with *him* is, he don't go to church often enough!"

While Martin sought to concentrate.

They flocked from the house to his laboratory only once a week, which was certainly not enough to disturb a resolute man—merely enough to keep him constantly waiting for them.

When he sedately tried to explain this and that to Joyce, she said, "Did we bother you this evening? But they do admire you so."

He remarked, "Well," and went to bed.

V

R. A. Hopburn, the eminent patent-lawyer, as he drove away from the Arrowsmith-Lanyon mansion grunted at his wife:

"I don't mind a host throwing the port at you, if he thinks you're a chump, but I do mind his being bored at your daring to express any opinion whatever. . . . Didn't he look silly, out in his idiotic laboratory! . . . How the deuce do you suppose Joyce ever came to marry him?"

"I can't imagine."

"I can only think of one reason. Of course she may—"

"Now please don't be filthy!"

"Well, anyway— She who might have picked any number of well-bred, agreeable, intelligent chaps—and I *mean* intelligent, because this Arrowsmith person may know all about germs, but he doesn't know a symphony from a savory. . . . I don't think I'm too fussy, but I don't quite see why we should go to a house where the host apparently enjoys flatly contradicting you. . . . Poor devil, I'm really sorry for him; probably he doesn't even know when he's being rude."

"No. Perhaps. What hurts is to think of old Roger—so gay, so strong, real Skull and Bones—and to have this abrupt Outsider from the tall grass sitting in his chair, failing to appreciate his Pol Roger— What Joyce ever saw in him! Though he does have nice eyes and such funny strong hands—"

VI

Joyce's busyness was on his nerves. Why she was so busy it was hard to ascertain; she had an excellent housekeeper, a noble butler, and two nurses for the baby. But she often said that she was never allowed to attain her one ambition: to sit and read.

Terry had once called her The Arranger, and though Martin resented it, when he heard the telephone bell he groaned, "Oh, Lord, there's The Arranger—wants me to come to tea with some high-minded hen."

When he sought to explain that he must be free from entanglements, she suggested, "Are you such a weak, irresolute, *little* man that the only way you can keep concentrated is by running away? Are you afraid of the big men who can do big work, and still stop and play?"

He was likely to turn abusive, particularly as to her definition of Big Men, and when he became hot and vulgar, she turned *grande dame*, so that he felt like an impertinent servant and was the more vulgar.

He was afraid of her then. He imagined fleeing to Leora, and the two of them, frightened little people, comforting each other and hiding from her in snug corners.

But often enough Joyce was his companion, seeking new amusements as surprises for him, and in their son they had a binding pride. He sat watching little John, rejoicing in his strength.

It was in early winter, after she had royally taken the baby South for a fortnight, that Martin escaped for a week with Terry at Birdies' Rest.

He found Terry tired and a little surly, after months of working absolutely alone. He had constructed beside the home cabin a shanty for laboratory, and a rough stable for the horses which he used in the preparation of his sera. Terry did not, as once he would have, flare into the details of his research, and not till evening, when they smoked before the rough fireplace of the cabin, loafing in chairs made of barrels cushioned with elk skin, could Martin coax him into confidences.

He had been compelled to give up much of his time to mere housework and the production of the sera which paid his expenses. "If you'd only been with me, I could have accomplished something." But his quinine derivative research had gone on solidly, and he did not regret leaving McGurk. He had found it impossible to work with monkeys; they were too expensive, and too fragile to stand the Vermont winter; but he had contrived a method of using mice infected with pneumococcus and—

"Oh, what's the use of my telling you this, Slim? You're not interested, or you'd have been up here at work with me, months ago. You've chosen between Joyce and me. All right, but you can't have both."

Martin snarled, "I'm very sorry I intruded on you, Wickett," and slammed out of the cabin. Stumbling through the snow, blundering in darkness against stumps, he knew the agony of his last hour, the hour of failure.

"I've lost Terry, now (though I won't stand his impertinence!). I've lost everybody, and I've never really had Joyce. I'm completely alone. And I can only half work! I'm through! They'll never let me get to work again!"

Suddenly, without arguing it out, he knew that he was not going to give up.

He floundered back to the cabin and burst in, crying, "You old grouch, we got to stick together!"

Terry was as much moved as he; neither of them was far from tears; and as they roughly patted each other's shoulders they growled, "Fine pair of fools, scrapping just because we're tired!"

"I will come and work with you, somehow!" Martin swore. "I'll get a six-months' leave from the Institute, and have Joyce stay at some hotel near here, or do *some*thing. Gee! Back to real work. . . . *Work!* . . . Now tell me: When I come up here, what d'you say we—"

They talked till dawn.

Chapter XL

DR. and Mrs. Rippleton Holabird had invited only Joyce and Martin to dinner. Holabird was his most charming self. He admired Joyce's pearls, and when the squabs had been served he turned on Martin with friendly intensity:

"Now will Joyce and you listen to me most particularly? Things are happening, Martin, and I want you—no, Science wants you!—to take your proper part in them. I needn't, by the way, hint that this is absolutely confidential. Dr. Tubbs and his League of Cultural Agencies are beginning to accomplish marvels, and Colonel Minnigen has been extraordinarily liberal.

"They've gone at the League with exactly the sort of thoroughness and taking-it-slow that you and dear old Gottlieb have always insisted on. For four years now they've stuck to making plans. I happen to know that Dr. Tubbs and the council of the League have had the most wonderful conferences with college-presidents and editors and clubwomen and labor-leaders (the sound, sensible ones, of course) and efficiency-experts and the more advanced advertising-men and ministers, and all the other leaders of public thought.

"They've worked out elaborate charts classifying all intellectual occupations and interests, with the methods and materials and tools, and especially the goals—the aims, the ideals, the moral purposes—that are suited to each of them. Really tremendous! Why, a musician or an engineer, for example, could look at his chart and tell accurately whether he was progressing fast enough, at his age, and if not, just what his trouble was, and the remedy. With this basis, the League is ready to go to work and encourage all brain-workers to affiliate.

"McGurk Institute simply must get in on this coördination, which I regard as one of the greatest advances in thinking that has ever been made. We are at last going to make all the erstwhile chaotic spiritual activities of America really conform to the American ideal; we're going to make them as practical and supreme as the manufacture of cash-registers! I have certain reasons for supposing I can bring Ross McGurk and Minnigen together, now that the McGurk and Minnigen lumber interests have stopped warring, and if so I shall probably quit the Institute and help Tubbs guide the League of Cultural Agencies. Then we'll need a new Director of McGurk who will work with us and help us bring Science out of the monastery to serve Mankind."

By this time Martin understood everything about the League except what the League was trying to do.

Holabird went on:

"Now I know, Martin, that you've always rather sneered at Practicalness, but I have faith in you! I believe you've been too much under the influence of Wickett, and now that he's gone and you've seen more of life and of Joyce's set and mine, I believe I can coax you to take (oh! without in any way neglecting the severities of your lab work!) a broader view.

"I am authorized to appoint an Assistant Director, and I think I'm safe in saying he would succeed me as full Director. Sholtheis wants the place, and Dr. Smith and Yeo would leap at it, but I haven't yet found any of them that are quite Our Own Sort, and I offer it to you! I daresay in a year or two, you will be Director of McGurk Institute!"

Holabird was uplifted, as one giving royal favor. Mrs. Holabird was intense, as one present on an historical occasion, and Joyce was ecstatic over the honor to her Man.

Martin stammered, "W-why, I'll have to think it over. Sort of unexpected—"

The rest of the evening Holabird so brimmingly enjoyed himself picturing an era in which Tubbs and Martin and he would rule, coördinate, standardize, and make useful the whole world of intelligence, from trousers-designing to poetry, that he did not resent Martin's silence. At parting he chanted, "Talk it over with Joyce, and let me have your decision to-morrow. By the way, I think we'll get rid of Pearl Robbins; she's been useful but now she considers herself indispensable. But that's a detail. . . . Oh, I do have faith in you, Martin, dear old boy! You've grown and calmed down, and you've widened your interests so much, this past year!"

In their car, in that moving curtained room under the crystal dome-light, Joyce beamed at him.

"Isn't it too wonderful, Mart! And I do feel Rippleton can bring it off. Think of your being Director, head of that whole great Institute, when just a few years ago you were only a cub there! But haven't I perhaps helped, just a little?"

Suddenly Martin hated the blue-and-gold velvet of the car, the cunningly hid gold box of cigarettes, all this soft and smothering prison. He wanted to be out beside the unseen chauffeur—His Own Sort!—facing the winter. He tried to look as though he were meditating, in an awed, appreciative manner, but he was merely being cowardly, reluctant to begin the slaughter. Slowly:

"Would you really like to see me Director?"

"Of course! All that— Oh, you know; I don't just mean the prominence and respect, but the power to accomplish good."

"Would you like to see me dictating letters, giving out interviews, buying linoleum, having lunch with distinguished fools, advising men about whose work I don't know a blame' thing?"

"Oh, don't be so superior! Some one has to do these things. And that'd be only a small part of it. Think of the opportunity of encouraging some youngster who wanted a chance to do splendid science!"

"And give up my own chance?"

"Why need you? You'd be head of your own department just the same. And even if you did give up— You are so stubborn! It's lack of imagination. You think that because you've started in on one tiny branch of mental activity, there's nothing else in the world. It's just as when I persuaded you that if you got out of your stinking laboratory once a week or so, and actually bent your powerful intellect to a game of golf, the world of science wouldn't immediately stop! No imagination! You're precisely like these business men you're always cursing because they can't see anything in life beyond their soap-factories or their banks!"

"And you really would have me give up my work—"

He saw that with all her eager complaisances she had never understood what he was up to, had not comprehended one word about the murderous effect of the directorship on Gottlieb.

He was silent again, and before they reached home she said only, "You know I'm the last person to speak of money, but really, it's you who have so often brought up the matter of hating to be dependent on me, and you know as Director you would make so much more that— Forgive me!"

She fled before him into her palace, into the automatic elevator.

He plodded up the stairs, grumbling, "Yes, it is the first chance I've had to really contribute to the expenses here. Sure! Willing to take her money, but not to do anything in return, and then call it 'devotion to science!' Well, I've got to decide right now—"

He did not go through the turmoil of deciding; he leaped to decision without it. He marched into Joyce's room, irritated by its snobbishness of discreet color. He was checked by the miserable way in which she sat brooding on the edge of her day couch, but he flung:

"I'm not going to do it, even if I have to leave the Institute—and Holabird will just about make me quit. I will not get buried in this pompous fakery of giving orders and—"

"Mart! Listen! Don't you want your son to be proud of you?"

"Um. Well— *No,* not if he's to be proud of me for being a stuffed shirt, a sideshow barker—"

"Please don't be vulgar."

"Why not? Matter of fact, I haven't been vulgar enough lately. What I ought to do is to go to Birdies' Rest right now, and work with Terry."

"I wish I had some way of showing you— Oh, for a 'scientist' you do have the most incredible blind-spots! I wish I could make you see just how weak and futile that is. The wilds! The simple life! The old argument. It's just the absurd, cowardly sort of thing these tired highbrows do that sneak off to some Esoteric Colony and think they're getting strength to conquer life, when they're merely running away from it."

"No. Terry has his place in the country only because he can live cheaper there. If we—if he could afford it, he'd probably be right here in town, with garçons and everything, like McGurk, but with no Director Holabird by God—and no Director Arrowsmith!"

"Merely a cursing, ill-bred, intensely selfish Director Terry Wickett!"

"Now by God let me tell you—"

"Martin, do you need to emphasize your arguments by a 'by God' in every sentence, or have you a few other expressions in your highly scientific vocabulary?"

"Well, I have enough vocabulary to express the idea that I'm thinking of joining Terry."

"Look here, Mart. You feel so virtuous about wanting to go off and wear a flannel shirt, and be peculiar and very, very pure. Suppose everybody argued that way. Suppose every father deserted his children whenever his nice little soul ached? Just what would become of the world? Suppose I were poor, and you left me, and I had to support John by taking in washing—"

"It'd probably be fine for you but fierce on the washing! No! I beg your pardon. That was an obvious answer. But— I imagine it's just that argument that's kept almost everybody, all these centuries, from being anything but a machine for digestion and propagation and obedience. The answer is that very few ever do, under any condition, willingly leave a soft bed for a shanty bunk in order to be pure, as you very properly call it, and those of us that are pioneers— Oh, this debate could go on forever! We could prove that I'm a hero or a fool or a deserter or anything you like, but the fact is I've suddenly seen I must go! I want my freedom to work, and I herewith quit whining about it and grab it. You've been generous to me. I'm grateful. But you've never been mine. Good-by."

"Darling, darling— We'll talk it over again in the morning, when you aren't so excited. . . . And an hour ago I was so proud of you!"

"All right. Good-night."

But before morning, taking two suit-cases and a bag of his roughest clothes, leaving for her a tender note which was the hardest thing he had ever written, kissing his son and muttering, "Come to me when you grow up, old man," he went to a cheap side-street hotel. As he stretched on the rickety iron bed, he grieved for their love. Before noon he had gone to the Institute, resigned, taken certain of his own apparatus and notes and books and materials, refused to answer a telephone call from Joyce, and caught a train for Vermont.

Cramped on the red-plush seat of the day-coach (he who of late had ridden in silken private cars), he grinned with the joy of no longer having to toil at dinner-parties.

He drove up to Birdies' Rest in a bob-sled. Terry was chopping wood, in a mess of chip-littered snow.

"Hello, Terry. Come for keeps."

"Fine, Slim. Say, there's a lot of dishes in the shack need washing."

II

He had become soft. To dress in the cold shanty and to wash in icy water was agony; to tramp for three hours through fluffy snow exhausted him. But the rapture of being allowed to work twenty-four hours a day without leaving an experiment at its juiciest moment to creep home for dinner, of plunging with Terry into arguments as cryptic as theology and furious as the indignation of a drunken man, carried him along, and he felt himself growing sinewy. Often he meditated on yielding to Joyce so far as to allow her to build a better laboratory for them, and more civilized quarters.

With only one servant, though, or two at the very most, and just a simple decent bathroom—

She had written, "You have been thoroughly beastly, and any attempt at reconciliation, if that is possible now, which I rather doubt, must come from you."

He answered, describing the ringing winter woods and not mentioning the platform word Reconciliation.

III

They wanted to study further the exact mechanism of the action of their quinine derivatives. This was difficult with the mice which Terry had contrived to use instead of monkeys, because of their size. Martin had brought with him strains of *Bacillus lepisepticus*, which causes a pleuro-pneumonia in rabbits, and their first labor was to discover whether their original compound was effective against this bacillus as well as against pneumococcus. Profanely they found that it was not;

profanely and patiently they trudged into an infinitely complicated search for a compound that should be.

They earned their living by preparing sera which rather grudgingly they sold to physicians of whose honesty they were certain, abruptly refusing the popular drug-vendors. They thus received surprisingly large sums, and among all clever people it was believed that they were too coyly shrewd to be sincere.

Martin worried as much over what he considered his treachery to Clif Clawson as over his desertion of Joyce and John, but this worrying he did only when he could not sleep. Regularly, at three in the morning, he brought both Joyce and honest Clif to Birdies' Rest; and regularly, at six, when he was frying bacon, he forgot them.

Terry the barbarian, once he was free of the tittering and success-pawing of Holabird, was an easy campmate. Upper berth or lower was the same to him, and till Martin was hardened to cold and fatigue, Terry did more than his share of wood-cutting and supply-toting, and with great melody and skill he washed their clothes.

He had the genius to see that they two alone, shut up together season on season, would quarrel. He planned with Martin that the laboratory scheme should be extended to include eight (but never more!) maverick and undomestic researchers like themselves, who should contribute to the expenses of the camp by manufacturing sera, but otherwise do their own independent work—whether it should be the structure of the atom, or a disproof of the results of Drs. Wickett and Arrowsmith. Two rebels, a chemist now caught in a drug-firm and a university professor, were coming next autumn.

"It's kind of a mis'able return to monasteries," grumbled Terry, "except that we're not trying to solve anything for anybody but our own fool selves. Mind you! When this place becomes a shrine, and a lot of cranks begin to creep in here, then you and I got to beat it, Slim. We'll move farther back in the woods, or if we feel too old for that, we'll take another shot at professorships or Dawson Hunziker or even the Rev. Dr. Holabird."

For the first time Martin's work began definitely to draw ahead of Terry's.

His mathematics and physical chemistry were now as sound as Terry's, his indifference to publicity and to flowery hangings as great, his industry as fanatical, his ingenuity in devising new apparatus at least comparable, and his imagination far more swift. He had less ease but more passion. He hurled out hypotheses like sparks. He began, incredulously, to comprehend his freedom. He would yet determine the essential nature of phage; and as he became stronger and surer—and no doubt less human—he saw ahead of him innumerous inquiries into chemotherapy and immunity; enough adventures to keep him busy for decades.

It seemed to him that this was the first spring he had ever seen and tasted. He learned to dive into the lake, though the first plunge was an agony of fiery cold. They fished before breakfast, they supped at a table under the oaks, they tramped twenty miles on end, they had bluejays and squirrels for interested neighbors; and when they had worked all night, they came out to find serene dawn lifting across the sleeping lake.

Martin felt sun-soaked and deep of chest, and always he hummed.

And one day he peeped out, beneath his new horn-rimmed almost-middle-aged glasses, to see a gigantic motor crawling up their woods road. From the car, jolly and competent in tweeds, stepped Joyce.

He wanted to flee through the back door of the laboratory shanty. Reluctantly he edged out to meet her.

"It's a sweet place, really!" she said, and amiably kissed him. "Let's walk down by the lake."

In a stilly place of ripples and birch boughs, he was moved to grip her shoulders.

She cried, "Darling, I *have* missed you! You're wrong about lots of things, but you're right about this—you must work, and not be disturbed by a lot of silly people. Do you like my tweeds? Don't they look wildernessy? You see, I've come to stay! I'll build a house near here; perhaps right across the lake. Yes. That will make a sweet place, over there on that sort of little plateau, if I can get the land—probably some horrid tight-fisted old farmer owns it. Can't you just *see* it: a wide low house, with enormous verandas and red awnings—"

"And visitors coming?"

"I suppose so. Sometimes. Why?"

Desperately, "Joyce, I do love you. I want awfully, just now, to kiss you properly. But I will not have you bringing a lot of people—and there'd probably be a rotten noisy motor launch. Make our lab a joke. Roadhouse. New sensation. Why, Terry would go crazy! You *are* lovely! But you want a playmate, and I want to work. I'm afraid you can't stay. No."

"And our son is to be left without your care?"

"He— Would he have my care if I died? . . . He is a nice kid, too! I hope he won't be a Rich Man! . . . Perhaps ten years from now he'll come to me here."

"And live like *this*?"

"Sure—unless I'm broke. Then he won't live so well. We have meat practically every day now!"

"I see. And suppose your Terry Wickett should marry some waitress or some incredibly stupid rustic? From what you've told me, he rather fancies that sort of girl!"

"Well, either he and I would beat her, together, or it would be the one thing that could break me."

"Martin, aren't you perhaps a little insane?"

"Oh, absolutely! And how I enjoy it! Though you— You look here now, Joy! We're insane but we're not cranks! Yesterday an 'esoteric healer' came here because he thought this was a free colony, and Terry walked him twenty miles, and then I think he threw him in the lake. No. Gosh. Let me think." He scratched his chin. "I don't believe we're insane. We're farmers."

"Martin, it's too infinitely diverting to find you becoming a fanatic, and all the while trying to wriggle out of being a fanatic. You've left common sense. I *am* common sense. I believe in bathing! Good-by!"

"Now you look here. By golly—"

She was gone, reasonable and triumphant.

As the chauffeur manœuvered among the stumps of the clearing, for a moment Joyce looked out from her car, and they stared at each other, through tears. They had never been so frank, so pitiful, as in this one unarmored look which recalled every jest, every tenderness, every twilight they had known together. But the car rolled on unhalted, and he remembered that he had been doing an experiment—

IV

On a certain evening of May, Congressman Almus Pickerbaugh was dining with the President of the United States.

"When the campaign is over, Doctor," said the President, "I hope we shall see you a cabinet-member—the first Secretary of Health and Eugenics in the country!"

That evening, Dr. Rippleton Holabird was addressing a meeting of celebrated thinkers, assembled by the League of Cultural Agencies. Among the men of measured merriment on the platform were Dr. Aaron Sholtheis, the new Director of McGurk Institute, and Dr. Angus Duer, head of the Duer Clinic and professor of surgery in Fort Dearborn Medical College.

Dr. Holabird's epochal address was being broadcast by radio to a million ardently listening lovers of science.

That evening, Bert Tozer of Wheatsylvania, North Dakota, was attending mid-week prayer-meeting. His new Buick sedan awaited him outside, and with modest satisfaction he heard the minister gloat:

"The righteous, even the Children of Light, they shall be rewarded with a great reward and their feet shall walk in gladness, saith the Lord of Hosts; but the mockers, the Sons of Belial, they shall be slain betimes and cast down into darkness and failure, and in the busy marts shall they be forgot."

That evening, Max Gottlieb sat unmoving and alone, in a dark small room above the banging city street. Only his eyes were alive.

That evening, the hot breeze languished along the palm-waving ridge where the ashes of Gustaf Sondelius were lost among cinders, and a depression in a garden marked the grave of Leora.

That evening, after an unusually gay dinner with Latham Ireland, Joyce admitted, "Yes, if I do divorce him, I may marry you. I know! He's never going to see how egotistical it is to think he's the only man living who's always right!"

That evening, Martin Arrowsmith and Terry Wickett lolled in a clumsy boat, an extraordinarily uncomfortable boat, far out on the water.

"I feel as if I were really beginning to work now," said Martin. "This new quinine stuff may prove pretty good. We'll plug along on it for two or three years, and maybe we'll get something permanent—and probably we'll fail!"

[illegible] came, Margie Arrowsmith and Terry [illegible] [illegible] boat. [illegible] out of the water.

"[illegible] said [illegible]" said Marcia. "This new surprise stuff may prove very good! We'll plug along on it for two or three years and maybe we'll get some of the people [illegible] tall!"

ELMER GANTRY

To

H. L. MENCKEN

with profound admiration

No character in this book is
the portrait of any actual person.

S. L.

Chapter I

ELMER GANTRY was drunk. He was eloquently drunk, lovingly and pugnaciously drunk. He leaned against the bar of the Old Home Sample Room, the most gilded and urbane saloon in Cato, Missouri, and requested the bartender to join him in "The Good Old Summer Time," the waltz of the day.

Blowing on a glass, polishing it and glancing at Elmer through its flashing rotundity, the bartender remarked that he wasn't much of a hand at this here singing business. But he smiled. No bartender could have done other than smile on Elmer, so inspired and full of gallantry and hell-raising was he, and so dominating was his beefy grin.

"All right, old socks," agreed Elmer. "Me and my roommate'll show you some singing as is singing! Meet roommate. Jim Lefferts. Bes' roommate in world. Wouldn't live with him if wasn't! Bes' quarterback in Milwest. Meet roommate."

The bartender again met Mr. Lefferts, with protestations of distinguished pleasure.

Elmer and Jim Lefferts retired to a table to nourish the long, rich, chocolate strains suitable to drunken melody. Actually, they sang very well. Jim had a resolute tenor, and as to Elmer Gantry, even more than his bulk, his thick black hair, his venturesome black eyes, you remembered that arousing barytone. He was born to be a senator. He never said anything important, and he always said it sonorously. He could make "Good morning" seem profound as Kant, welcoming as a brass band, and uplifting as a cathedral organ. It was a 'cello, his voice, and in the enchantment of it you did not hear his slang, his boasting, his smut, and the dreadful violence which (at this period) he performed on singulars and plurals.

Luxuriously as a wayfarer drinking cool beer they caressed the phrases in linked sweetness long drawn out:

Strolling through the shaaaaady lanes, with your baby-mine,
You hold her hand and she holds yours, and that's a very
good sign
That she's your tootsey-wootsey in the good old summer time.

Elmer wept a little, and blubbered, "Lez go out and start a scrap. You're lil squirt, Jim. You get somebody to pick on you, and I'll come along and knock his block off. I'll show 'em!" His voice flared up. He was furious at the wrong about to be suffered. He arched his paws with longing to grasp the non-existent scoundrel. "By God, I'll knock the tar out of um! Nobody can touch *my* roommate! Know who I am? Elmer Gantry! Thash me! I'll show um!"

The bartender was shuffling toward them, amiably ready for homicide.

"Shut up, Hell-cat. What you need is 'nother drink. I'll get 'nother drink," soothed Jim, and Elmer slid into tears, weeping over the ancient tragic sorrows of one whom he remembered as Jim Lefferts.

Instantly, by some tricky sort of magic, there were two glasses in front of him. He tasted one, and murmured foolishly, "'Scuse me." It was the chaser, the water. But they couldn't fool him! The whisky would certainly be in that other lil sawed-off glass. And it was. He was right, as always. With a smirk of self-admiration he sucked in the raw Bourbon. It tickled his throat and made him feel powerful, and at peace with every one save that fellow—he could not recall who, but it was some one whom he would shortly chastise, and after that float into an Elysium of benevolence.

The barroom was deliciously calming. The sour invigorating stench of beer made him feel healthy. The bar was one long shimmer of beauty—glowing mahogany, exquisite marble rail, dazzling glasses, curiously shaped bottles of unknown liqueurs, piled with a craftiness which made him very happy. The light was dim, completely soothing, coming through fantastic windows such as are found only in churches, saloons, jewelry shops, and other retreats from reality. On the brown plaster walls were sleek naked girls.

He turned from them. He was empty now of desire for women.

"That damn' Juanita. Jus' wants to get all she can out of you. That's all," he grumbled.

But there was an interesting affair beside him. A piece of newspaper sprang up, apparently by itself, and slid along the floor. That was a very funny incident, and he laughed greatly.

He was conscious of a voice which he had been hearing for centuries, echoing from a distant point of light and flashing through ever-widening corridors of a dream.

"We'll get kicked out of here, Hell-cat. Come on!"

He floated up. It was exquisite. His legs moved by themselves, without effort. They did a comic thing once—they got twisted and the right leg leaped in front of the left when, so far as he could make out, it should have been behind. He laughed, and rested against some one's arm, an arm with no body attached to it, which had come out of the *Ewigkeit* to assist him.

Then unknown invisible blocks, miles of them, his head clearing, and he made grave announcement to a Jim Lefferts who suddenly seemed to be with him:

"I gotta lick that fellow."

"All right, all *right*. You might as well go find a nice little fight and get it out of your system!"

Elmer was astonished; he was grieved. His mouth hung open and he drooled with sorrow. But still, he was to be allowed one charming fight, and he revived as he staggered industriously in search of it.

Oh, he exulted, it was a great party. For the first time in weeks he was relieved from the boredom of Terwillinger College.

II

Elmer Gantry, best known to classmates as Hell-cat, had, this autumn of 1902, been football captain and led the best team Terwillinger College had known in ten years. They had won the championship of the East-middle Kansas Conference, which consisted of ten denominational colleges, all of them with buildings and presidents and chapel services and yells and colors and a standard of scholarship equal to the best high-schools. But since the last night of the football season, with the glorious bonfire in which the young gentlemen had burned up nine tar barrels, the sign of the Jew tailor, and the president's tabby-cat, Elmer had been tortured by boredom.

He regarded basket-ball and gymnasium antics as light-minded for a football gladiator. When he had come to college, he had supposed he would pick up learnings of cash-value to a lawyer or doctor or insurance man—he had not known which he would become, and in his senior year, aged twenty-two this November, he still was doubtful. But this belief he found fallacious. What good would it be in the courtroom, or at the operating table, to understand trigonometry, or to know (as last spring, up to the examination on European History, he remembered having known) the date of Charlemagne? How much cash would it bring in to quote all that stuff—what the dickens was it now?—all that rot about "The world is too much around us, early and soon" from that old fool Wordsworth?

Punk, that's what it was. Better be out in business. But still, if his mother claimed she was doing so well with her millinery business and wanted him to be a college graduate, he'd stick by it. Lot easier than pitching hay or carrying two-by-fours anyway.

Despite his invaluable voice, Elmer had not gone out for debating, because of the irritating library-grinding, nor had he taken to prayer and moral eloquence in the Y.M.C.A., for with all the force of his simple and valiant nature he detested piety and admired drunkenness and profanity.

Once or twice in the class in Public Speaking, when he had repeated the splendors of other great thinkers, Dan'l Webster and Henry Ward Beecher and Chauncey M. Depew, he had known the intoxication of holding an audience with his voice as with his closed hand, holding it, shaking it, lifting it. The debating set urged him to join them, but they were rabbit-faced and spectacled young men, and he viewed as obscene the notion of digging statistics about immigration and the products of San Domingo out of dusty spotted books in the dusty spotted library.

He kept from flunking only because Jim Lefferts drove him to his books.

Jim was less bored by college. He had a relish for the flavor of scholarship. He liked to know things about people dead these thousand years, and he liked doing canned miracles in chemistry. Elmer was astounded that so capable a drinker, a man so deft at "handing a girl a swell spiel and getting her going" should find entertainment in Roman chariots and the unenterprising amours of sweet-peas. But himself—no. Not on your life. He'd get out and finish law school and never open another book—kid the juries along and hire some old coot to do the briefs.

To keep him from absolutely breaking under the burden of hearing the professors squeak, he did have the joy of loafing with Jim, illegally smoking the while; he did have researches into the lovability of co-eds and the baker's daughter; he did revere becoming drunk and world-striding. But he could not afford liquor very often and the co-eds were mostly ugly and earnest.

It was lamentable to see this broad young man, who would have been so happy in the prize-ring, the fish-market, or the stock exchange, poking through the cobwebbed corridors of Terwillinger.

III

Terwillinger College, founded and preserved by the more zealous Baptists, is on the outskirts of Gritzmacher Springs, Kansas. (The springs have dried up and the Gritzmachers have gone to Los Angeles, to sell bungalows and delicatessen.) It huddles on the prairie, which is storm-racked in winter, frying and dusty in summer, lovely only in the grass-rustling spring or drowsy autumn.

You would not be likely to mistake Terwillinger College for an Old Folks' Home, because on the campus is a large rock painted with class numerals.

Most of the faculty are ex-ministers.

There is a men's dormitory, but Elmer Gantry and Jim Lefferts lived together in the town, in a mansion once the pride of the Gritzmachers themselves: a square brick bulk with a white cupola. Their room was unchanged from the days of the original August Gritzmacher; a room heavy with a vast bed of carved black walnut, thick and perpetually dusty brocade curtains, and black walnut chairs hung with scarves that dangled gilt balls. The windows were hard to open. There was about the place the anxious propriety and all the dead hopes of a second-hand furniture shop.

In this museum, Jim had a surprising and vigorous youthfulness. There was a hint of future flabbiness in Elmer's bulk, but there would never be anything flabby about Jim Lefferts. He was slim, six inches shorter than Elmer, but hard as ivory and as sleek. Though he came from a prairie village, Jim had fastidiousness, a natural elegance. All the items of his wardrobe, the "ordinary suit," distinctly glossy at the elbows, and the dark-brown "best suit," were ready-made, with faltering buttons, and seams that betrayed rough ends of thread, but on him they were graceful. You felt that he would belong to any set in the world which he sufficiently admired. There was a romantic flare to his upturned overcoat collar; the darned bottoms of his trousers did not suggest poverty but a careless and amused ease; and his thoroughly commonplace ties hinted of clubs and regiments.

His thin face was resolute. You saw only its youthful freshness first, then behind the brightness a taut determination, and his brown eyes were amiably scornful.

Jim Lefferts was Elmer's only friend; the only authentic friend he had ever had.

Though Elmer was the athletic idol of the college, though his occult passion, his heavy good looks, caused the college girls to breathe quickly, though his manly laughter was as fetching as his resonant speech, Elmer was never really liked. He was supposed to be the most popular man in college; every one believed that every one else adored him; and none of them wanted to be with him. They were all a bit afraid, a bit uncomfortable, and more than a bit resentful.

It was not merely that he was a shouter, a pounder on backs, an overwhelming force, so that there was never any refuge of intimacy with him. It was because he was always demanding. Except with his widow mother, whom he vaguely worshiped, and with Jim Lefferts, Elmer assumed that he was the center of the universe and that the rest of the system was valuable only as it afforded him help and pleasure.

He wanted everything.

His first year, as the only Freshman who was playing on the college football team, as a large and smiling man who was expected to become a favorite, he was elected president. In that office, he was not much beloved. At class-meetings he cut speakers short, gave the floor only to pretty girls and lads who toadied to him, and roared in the midst of the weightiest debates, "Aw, come on, cut out this chewing the rag and let's get down to business!" He collected the class-fund by demanding subscriptions as arbitrarily as a Catholic priest assessing his parishioners for a new church.

"He'll never hold any office again, not if I can help it!" muttered one Eddie Fislinger, who, though he was a meager and rusty-haired youth with protruding teeth and an uneasy titter, had attained power in the class by always being present at everything, and by the piety and impressive intimacy of his prayers in the Y.M.C.A.

There was a custom that the manager of the Athletic Association should not be a member of any team. Elmer forced himself into the managership in Junior year by threatening not to play football if he were not elected. He appointed Jim Lefferts chairman of the ticket committee, and between them, by only the very slightest doctoring of the books, they turned forty dollars to the best of all possible uses.

At the beginning of Senior year, Elmer announced that he desired to be president again. To elect any one as class-president twice was taboo. The ardent Eddie Fislinger, now president of the Y.M.C.A. and ready to bring his rare talents to the Baptist ministry, asserted after an enjoyable private prayer-meeting in his room that he was going to face Elmer and forbid him to run.

"Gwan! You don't dare!" observed a Judas who three minutes before had been wrestling with God under Eddie's coaching.

"I don't, eh? Watch me! Why, everybody hates him, the darn' hog!" squeaked Eddie.

By scurrying behind trees he managed to come face to face with Elmer on the campus. He halted, and spoke of football, quantitative chemistry, and the Arkansas spinster who taught German.

Elmer grunted.

Desperately, his voice shrill with desire to change the world, Eddie stammered:

"Say—say, Hell-cat, you hadn't ought to run for president again. Nobody's ever president twice!"

"Somebody's going to be."

"Ah, gee, Elmer, don't run for it. Ah, come on. Course all the fellows are crazy about you but— Nobody's ever been president twice. They'll vote against you."

"Let me catch 'em at it!"

"How can you stop it? Honest, Elm—Hell-cat—I'm just speaking for your own good. The voting's secret. You can't tell—"

"Huh! The nominations ain't secret! Now you go roll your hoop, Fissy, and let all the yellow coyotes know that anybody that nominates anybody except Uncle Hell-cat will catch it right where the chicken caught the ax. See? And if they tell me they didn't know about this, you'll get merry Hail Columbia for not telling 'em. Get me? If there's anything but an unanimous vote, you won't do any praying the rest of this year!"

Eddie remembered how Elmer and Jim had shown a Freshman his place in society by removing all his clothes and leaving him five miles in the country.

Elmer was elected president of the senior class—unanimously.

He did not know that he was unpopular. He reasoned that men who seemed chilly to him were envious and afraid, and that gave him a feeling of greatness.

Thus it happened that he had no friend save Jim Lefferts.

Only Jim had enough will to bully him into obedient admiration. Elmer swallowed ideas whole; he was a maelstrom of prejudices; but Jim accurately examined every notion that came to him. Jim was selfish enough, but it was with the selfishness of a man who thinks and who is coldly unafraid of any destination to which his thoughts may lead him. The little man treated Elmer like a large damp dog, and Elmer licked his shoes and followed.

He also knew that Jim, as quarter, was far more the soul of the team than himself as tackle and captain.

A huge young man, Elmer Gantry; six foot one, thick, broad, big handed; a large face, handsome as a Great Dane is handsome, and a swirl of black hair, worn rather long. His eyes were friendly, his smile was friendly—oh, he was always friendly enough; he was merely astonished when he found that you did not understand his importance and did not want to hand over anything he might desire. He was a barytone solo turned into portly flesh; he was a gladiator laughing at the comic distortion of his wounded opponent.

He could not understand men who shrank from blood, who liked poetry or roses, who did not casually endeavor to seduce every possibly seducible girl. In sonorous arguments with Jim he asserted that "these fellows that study all the time are just letting on like they're so doggone high and mighty, to show off to these doggone profs that haven't got anything but lemonade in their veins."

IV

Chief adornment of their room was the escritoire of the first Gritzmacher, which held their library. Elmer owned two volumes of Conan Doyle, one of E. P. Roe, and a priceless copy of "Only a Boy." Jim had invested in an encyclopedia which explained any known subject in ten lines, in a "Pickwick Papers," and from some unknown source he had obtained a complete Swinburne, into which he was never known to have looked.

But his pride was in the possession of Ingersoll's "Some Mistakes of Moses," and Paine's "The Age of Reason." For Jim Lefferts was the college freethinker, the only man in Terwillinger who doubted that Lot's wife had been changed into salt for once looking back at the town where, among the young married set, she had had so good a time; who doubted that Methuselah lived to nine hundred and sixty-nine.

They whispered of Jim all through the pious dens of Terwillinger. Elmer himself was frightened, for after giving minutes and minutes to theological profundities Elmer had concluded that "there must be something to all this religious guff if all these wise old birds believe it, and some time a fellow had ought to settle down and cut out the hell-raising." Probably Jim would have been kicked out of college by the ministerial professors if he had not had so reverent a way of asking questions when they wrestled with his infidelity that they let go of him in nervous confusion.

Even the President, the Rev. Dr. Willoughby Quarles, formerly pastor of the Rock of Ages Baptist Church of Moline, Ill., than whom no man had written more about the necessity of baptism by immersion, in fact in every way a thoroughly than-whom figure—even when Dr. Quarles tackled Jim and demanded, "Are you getting the best out of our instruction, young man? Do you believe with us not only in the plenary inspiration of the Bible but also in its verbal inspiration, and that it is the only divine rule of faith and practise?" then Jim looked docile and said mildly:

"Oh, yes, Doctor. There's just one or two little things that have been worrying me, Doctor. I've taken them to the Lord in prayer, but he doesn't seem to help me much. I'm sure you can. Now why did Joshua need to have the sun stand still? Of course it happened—it *says* so right in Scripture. But why did he need to, when the Lord always helped those Jews, anyway, and when Joshua could knock down big walls just by having his people yell and blow trumpets? And if devils cause a lot of the diseases, and they had to cast 'em out, why is it that good Baptist doctors today don't go on diagnosing devil-possession instead of T.B. and things like that? *Do* people have devils?"

"Young man, I will give you an infallible rule. Never question the ways of the Lord!"

"But why don't the doctors talk about having devils now?"

"I have no time for vain arguments that lead nowhere! If you would think a little less of your wonderful powers of reasoning, if you'd go humbly to God in prayer and give him a chance, you'd understand the true spiritual significances of all these things."

"But how about where Cain got his wife—"

Most respectfully Jim said it, but Dr. Quarles (he had a chin-whisker and a boiled shirt) turned from him and snapped, "I have no further time to give you, young man! I've told you what to do. Good morning!"

That evening Mrs. Quarles breathed, "Oh, Willoughby, did you 'tend to that awful senior—that Lefferts—that's trying to spread doubt? Did you fire him?"

"No," blossomed President Quarles. "Certainly not. There was no need. I showed him how to look for spiritual guidance and— Did that freshman come and mow the lawn? The idea of him wanting fifteen cents an hour!"

Jim was hair-hung and breeze-shaken over the abyss of hell, and apparently enjoying it very much indeed, while his wickedness fascinated Elmer Gantry and terrified him.

V

That November day of 1902, November of their Senior year, was greasy of sky, and slush blotted the wooden sidewalks of Gritzmacher Springs. There was nothing to do in town, and their room was dizzying with the stench of the stove, first lighted now since spring.

Jim was studying German, tilted back in an elegant position of ease, with his legs cocked up on the desk tablet of the escritoire. Elmer lay across the bed, ascertaining whether the blood would run to his head if he lowered it over the side. It did, always.

"Oh, God, let's get out and do something!" he groaned.

"Nothing to do, Useless," said Jim.

"Let's go over to Cato and see the girls and get drunk."

As Kansas was dry, by state prohibition, the nearest haven was at Cato, Missouri, seventeen miles away.

Jim scratched his head with a corner of his book, and approved:

"Well, that's a worthy idea. Got any money?"

"On the twenty-eighth? Where the hell would I get any money before the first?"

"Hell-cat, you've got one of the deepest intellects I know. You'll be a knock-out at the law. Aside from neither of us having any money, and me with a Dutch quiz tomorrow, it's a great project."

"Oh, well—" sighed the ponderous Elmer, feebly as a sick kitten, and lay revolving the tremendous inquiry.

It was Jim who saved them from the lard-like weariness into which they were slipping. He had gone back to his book, but he placed it, precisely and evenly, on the desk, and rose.

"I would like to see Nellie," he sighed. "Oh, man, I could give her a good time! Little devil! Damn these co-eds here. The few that'll let you love 'em up, they hang around trying to catch you on the campus and make you propose to 'em."

"Oh, gee! And I got to see Juanita," groaned Elmer. "Hey, cut out talking about 'em, will you! I've got a palpitating heart right now, just thinking about Juanny!"

"Hell-cat! I've got it. Go and borrow ten off this new instructor in chemistry and physics. I've got a dollar sixty-four left, and that'll make it."

"But I don't know him."

"Sure, you poor fish. That's why I suggested him! Do the check-failed-to-come. I'll get another hour of this Dutch while you're stealing the ten from him—"

"Now," lugubriously, "you oughtn't to talk like that!"

"If you're as good a thief as I think you are, we'll catch the five-sixteen to Cato."

They were on the five-sixteen for Cato.

The train consisted of a day coach, a combined smoker and baggage car, and a rusty old engine and tender. The train swayed so on the rough tracks as it bumped through the drooping light that Elmer and Jim were thrown against each other and gripped the arm of their seat. The car staggered like a freighter in a gale. And tall raw farmers, perpetually shuffling forward for a drink at the water-cooler, stumbled against them or seized Jim's shoulder to steady themselves.

To every surface of the old smoking-car, to streaked windows and rusty ironwork and mud-smeared cocoanut matting, clung a sickening bitterness of cheap tobacco fumes, and whenever they touched the red plush of the seat, dust whisked up and the prints of their hands remained on the plush. The car was jammed. Passengers came to sit on the arm of their seat to shout at friends across the aisle.

But Elmer and Jim were unconscious of filth and smell and crowding. They sat silent, nervously intent, panting a little, their lips open, their eyes veiled, as they thought of Juanita and Nellie.

The two girls, Juanita Klauzel and Nellie Benton, were by no means professional daughters of joy. Juanita was cashier of the Cato Lunch—Quick Eats; Nellie was assistant to a dressmaker. They were good girls but excitable, and they found a little extra money useful for red slippers and nut-center chocolates.

"Juanita—what a lil darling—she understands a fellow's troubles," said Elmer, as they balanced down the slushy steps at the grimy stone station of Cato.

When Elmer, as a Freshman just arrived from the pool-halls and frame high school of Paris, Kansas, had begun to learn the decorum of amour, he had been a boisterous lout who looked shamefaced in the presence of gay ladies, who blundered against tables, who shouted and desired to let the world know how valiantly vicious he was being. He was still rather noisy and proud of wickedness when he was in a state of liquor, but in three and a quarter years of college he had learned how to approach girls. He was confident, he was easy, he was almost quiet; he could look them in the eye with fondness and amusement.

Juanita and Nellie lived with Nellie's widow aunt—she was a moral lady, but she knew how to keep out of the way—in three rooms over a corner grocery. They had just returned from work when Elmer and Jim stamped up the rickety outside wooden steps. Juanita was lounging on a divan which even a noble Oriental red and yellow cover (displaying a bearded Wazir, three dancing ladies in chiffon trousers, a narghile, and a mosque slightly larger than the narghile) could never cause to look like anything except a disguised bed. She was curled up, pinching her ankle with one tired and nervous hand, and reading a stimulating chapter of Laura Jean Libbey. Her shirt-waist was open at the throat, and down her slim stocking was a grievous run. She was so un-Juanita-like—an ash-blonde, pale and lovely, with an ill-restrained passion in her blue eyes.

Nellie, a buxom jolly child, dark as a Jewess, was wearing a frowsy dressing-gown. She was making coffee and narrating her grievances against her employer, the pious dressmaker, while Juanita paid no attention whatever.

The young men crept into the room without knocking.

"You devils—sneaking in like this, and us not dressed!" yelped Nellie.

Jim sidled up to her, dragged her plump hand away from the handle of the granite-ware coffee-pot, and giggled, "But aren't you glad to see us?"

"I don't know whether I *am* or not! Now you quit! You behave, will you?"

Rarely did Elmer seem more deft than Jim Lefferts. But now he was feeling his command over women—certain sorts of women. Silent, yearning at Juanita, commanding her with hot eyes, he sank on the temporarily Oriental couch, touched her pale hand with his broad finger-tips, and murmured, "Why, you poor kid, you look so tired!"

"I am and— You hadn't ought to of come here this afternoon. Nell's aunt threw a conniption fit the last time you were here."

"Hurray for aunty! But *you*'re glad to see me?"

She would not answer.

"Aren't you?"

Bold eyes on hers that turned uneasily away, looked back, and sought the safety of the blank wall.

"Aren't you?"

She would not answer.

"Juanita! And I've longed for you something fierce, ever since I saw you!" His fingers touched her throat, but softly. "Aren't you a *little* glad?"

As she turned her head, for a second she looked at him with embarrassed confession. She sharply whispered, "No— don't!" as he caught her hand, but she moved nearer to him, leaned against his shoulder.

"You're so big and strong," she sighed.

"But, golly, you don't know how I need you! The president, old Quarles—quarrels is right, by golly, ha, ha, ha!— 'member I was telling you about him?—he's laying for me because he thinks it was me and Jim that let the bats loose in chapel. And I get so sick of that gosh-awful Weekly Bible Study—all about these holy old gazebos. And then I think about you, and gosh, if you were just sitting on the other side of the stove from me in my room there, with your cute lil red slippers cocked up on the nickel rail—gee, how happy I'd be! You don't think I'm just a bonehead, do you?"

Jim and Nellie were at the stage now of nudging each other and bawling, "Hey, quit, will yuh!" as they stood over the coffee.

"Say, you girls change your shirts and come on out and we'll blow you to dinner, and maybe we'll dance a little," proclaimed Jim.

"We can't," said Nellie. "Aunty's sore as a pup because we was up late at a dance night before last. We got to stay home, and you boys got to beat it before she comes in."

"Aw, come *on!*"

"No, we *can't!*"

"Yuh, fat chance you girls staying home and knitting! You got some fellows coming in and you want to get rid of us, that's what's the trouble."

"It is not, Mr. James Lefferts, and it wouldn't be any of your business if it was!"

While Jim and Nellie squabbled, Elmer slipped his hand about Juanita's shoulder, slowly pressed her against him. He believed with terrible conviction that she was beautiful, that she was glorious, that she was life. There was heaven in the softness of her curving shoulder, and her pale flesh was living silk.

"Come on in the other room," he pleaded.

"Oh—no—not now."

He gripped her arm.

"Well—don't come in for a minute," she fluttered. Aloud, to the others, "I'm going to do my hair. Looks just *ter*-ble!"

She slipped into the room beyond. A certain mature self-reliance dropped from Elmer's face, and he was like a round-faced big baby, somewhat frightened. With efforts to appear careless, he fumbled about the room and dusted a pink and gilt vase with his large crumpled handkerchief. He was near the inner door.

He peeped at Jim and Nellie. They were holding hands, while the coffee-pot was cheerfully boiling over. Elmer's heart thumped. He slipped through the door and closed it, whimpering, as in terror:

"Oh—Juanita—"

VI

They were gone, Elmer and Jim, before the return of Nellie's aunt. As they were not entertaining the girls, they dined on pork chops, coffee, and apple pie at the Maginnis Lunch.

It has already been narrated that afterward, in the Old Home Sample Room, Elmer became philosophical and misogynistic as he reflected that Juanita was unworthy of his generous attention; it has been admitted that he became drunk and pugnacious.

As he wavered through the sidewalk slush, on Jim's arm, as his head cleared, his rage increased against the bully who was about to be encouraged to insult his goo' frien' and roommate. His shoulders straightened, his fists clenched, and he began to look for the scoundrel among the evening crowd of mechanics and coal-miners.

They came to the chief corner of the town. A little way down the street, beside the red brick wall of the Congress Hotel, some one was talking from the elevation of a box, surrounded by a jeering gang.

"What they picking on that fella that's talking for? They better let him alone!" rejoiced Elmer, throwing off Jim's restraining hand, dashing down the side street and into the crowd. He was in that most blissful condition to which a powerful young man can attain—unrighteous violence in a righteous cause. He pushed through the audience, jabbed his elbow into the belly of a small weak man, and guffawed at the cluck of distress. Then he came to a halt, unhappy and doubting.

The heckled speaker was his chief detestation, Eddie Fislinger, president of the Terwillinger College Y.M.C.A., that rusty-haired gopher who had obscenely opposed his election as president.

With two other seniors who were also in training for the Baptist ministry, Eddie had come over to Cato to save a few souls. At least, if they saved no souls (and they never had saved any, in seventeen street meetings) they would have handy training for their future jobs.

Eddie was a rasping and insistent speaker who got results by hanging to a subject and worrying it, but he had no great boldness, and now he was obviously afraid of his chief heckler, a large, blond, pompadoured young baker, who bulked in front of Eddie's rostrum and asked questions. While Elmer stood listening, the baker demanded:

"What makes you think you know all about religion?"

"I don't pretend to know all about religion, my friend, but I do know what a powerful influence it is for clean and noble living, and if you'll only be fair now, my friend, and give me a chance to tell these other gentlemen what my experience of answers to prayer has been—"

"Yuh, swell lot of experience you've had, by your looks!"

"See here, there are others who may want to hear—"

Though Elmer detested Eddie's sappiness, though he might have liked to share drinks with the lively young baker-heckler, there was no really good unctuous violence to be had except by turning champion of religion. The packed crowd excited him, and the pressure of rough bodies, the smell of wet overcoats, the rumble of mob voices. It was like a foot-ball line-up.

"Here, you!" he roared at the baker. "Let the fellow speak! Give him a chance. Whyn't you pick on somebody your own size, you big stiff!"

At his elbow, Jim Lefferts begged, "Let's get out of this, Hell-cat. Good Lord! You ain't going to help a gospel-peddler!"

Elmer pushed him away and thrust his chest out toward the baker, who was cackling, "Heh! I suppose you're a Christer, too!"

"I would be, if I was worthy!" Elmer fully believed it, for that delightful moment. "These boys are classmates of mine, and they're going to have a chance to speak!"

Eddie Fislinger bleated to his mates, "Oh, fellows, Elm Gantry! Saved!"

Even this alarming interpretation of his motives could not keep Elmer now from the holy zeal of fighting. He thrust aside the one aged man who stood between him and the baker—bashing in the aged one's derby and making him tele-scope like a turtle's neck—and stood with his fist working like a connecting-rod by his side.

"If you're looking for trouble—" the baker suggested, clumsily wobbling his huge bleached fists.

"Not me," observed Elmer and struck, once, very judi-ciously, just at the point of the jaw.

The baker shook like a skyscraper in an earthquake and caved to the earth.

One of the baker's pals roared, "Come on, we'll kill them guys and—"

Elmer caught him on the left ear. It was a very cold ear, and the pal staggered, extremely sick. Elmer looked pleased. But he did not feel pleased. He was almost sober, and he realized that half a dozen rejoicing young workmen were about to rush him. Though he had an excellent opinion of himself, he had seen too much football, as played by denominational colleges with the Christian accompaniments of kneeing and gouging, to imagine that he could beat half a dozen workmen at once.

It is doubtful whether he would ever have been led to further association with the Lord and Eddie Fislinger had not Providence intervened in its characteristically mysterious way. The foremost of the attackers was just reaching for Elmer when the mob shouted, "Look out! The cops!"

The police force of Cato, all three of them, were wedging into the crowd. They were lanky, mustached men with cold eyes.

"What's all this row about?" demanded the chief.

He was looking at Elmer, who was three inches taller than any one else in the assembly.

"Some of these fellows tried to stop a peaceable religious assembly—why, they tried to rough-house the Reverend here—and I was protecting him," Elmer said.

"That's right, Chief. Reg'lar outrage," complained Jim.

"That's true, Chief," whistled Eddie Fislinger from his box.

"Well, you fellows cut it out now. What the hell! Ought to be ashamed yourselves, bullyragging a Reverend! Go ahead, Reverend!"

The baker had come to, and had been lifted to his feet. His expression indicated that he had been wronged and that he wanted to do something about it, if he could only find out what had happened. His eyes were wild, his hair was a muddy chaos, and his flat floury cheek was cut. He was too dizzy to realize that the chief of police was before him, and his fuming mind stuck to the belief that he was destroying all religion.

"Yah, so you're one of them wishy-washy preachers, too!" he screamed at Elmer—just as one of the lanky policemen reached out an arm of incredible length and nipped him.

The attention of the crowd warmed Elmer, and he expanded in it, rubbed his mental hands in its blaze.

"Maybe I ain't a preacher! Maybe I'm not even a good Christian!" he cried. "Maybe I've done a whole lot of things I hadn't ought to of done. But let me tell you, I respect religion—"

"Oh, amen, praise the Lord, brother," from Eddie Fislinger.

"—and I don't propose to let anybody interfere with it. What else have we got except religion to give us hope—"

"Praise the Lord, oh, bless his name!"

"—of *ever* leading decent lives, tell me that, will you, just tell me that!"

Elmer was addressing the chief of police, who admitted:

"Yuh, I guess that's right. Well now, we'll let the meeting go on, and if any more of you fellows interrupt—" This completed the chief's present ideas on religion and mob-violence. He looked sternly at everybody within reach, and stalked through the crowd, to return to the police station and resume his game of seven-up.

Eddie was soaring into enchanted eloquence:

"Oh, my brethren, now you see the power of the spirit of Christ to stir up all that is noblest and best in us! You have heard the testimony of our brother here, Brother Gantry, to the one and only way to righteousness! When you get home I want each and every one of you to dig out the Old Book and turn to the Song of Solomon, where it tells about the love of the Savior for the Church—turn to the Song of Solomon, the fourth chapter and the tenth verse, where it says—where Christ is talking about the church, and he says—Song of Solomon, the fourth chapter and the tenth verse—'How fair is thy love, my sister, my spouse! how much better is thy love than wine!'

"Oh, the unspeakable joy of finding the joys of salvation! You have heard our brother's testimony. We know of him as a man of power, as a brother to all them that are oppressed, and now that he has had his eyes opened and his ears unstopped, and he sees the need of confession and of humble surrender before the throne— Oh, this is a historic moment in the life of Hell-c—— of Elmer Gantry! Oh, Brother, be not afraid! Come! Step up here beside me, and give testimony—"

"God! We better get outa here quick!" panted Jim.

"Gee, yes!" Elmer groaned, and they edged back through the crowd, while Eddie Fislinger's piping pursued them like icy and penetrating rain:

"Don't be afraid to acknowledge the leading of Jesus! Are you boys going to show yourselves too cowardly to risk the sneers of the ungodly?"

They were safely out of the crowd, walking with severe countenances and great rapidity back to the Old Home Sample Room.

"That was a dirty trick of Eddie's!" said Jim.

"God, it certainly was! Trying to convert me! Right before those muckers! If I ever hear another yip out of Eddie, I'll knock his block off! Nerve of him, trying to lead *me* up to any mourners' bench! Fat chance! I'll fix him! Come on, show a little speed!" asserted the brother to all them that were oppressed.

By the time for their late evening train, the sound conversation of the bartender and the sound qualities of his Bourbon had caused Elmer and Jim to forget Eddie Fislinger and the horrors of undressing religion in public. They were the more shocked, then, swaying in their seat in the smoker, to see Eddie standing by them, Bible in hand, backed by his two beaming partners in evangelism.

Eddie bared his teeth, smiled all over his watery eyes, and caroled:

"Oh, fellows, you don't know how wonderful you were tonight! But, oh, boys, now you've taken the first step, why do you put it off—why do you hesitate—why do you keep the Savior suffering as he waits for you, longs for you? He needs you boys, with your splendid powers and intellects that we admire so—"

"This air," observed Jim Lefferts, "is getting too thick for me. I seem to smell a peculiar and a fishlike smell." He slipped out of the seat and marched toward the forward car.

Elmer sought to follow him, but Eddie had flopped into Jim's place and was blithely squeaking on, while the other two hung over them with tender Y.M.C.A. smiles very discomforting to Elmer's queasy stomach as the train bumped on.

For all his brave words, Elmer had none of Jim's resolute contempt for the church. He was afraid of it. It connoted his boyhood. . . . His mother, drained by early widowhood and drudgery, finding her only emotion in hymns and the Bible, and weeping when he failed to study his Sunday School lesson. The church, full thirty dizzy feet up to its curiously carven rafters, and the preachers, so overwhelming in their wallowing voices, so terrifying in their pictures of little boys who stole watermelons or indulged in biological experiments behind barns. The awe-oppressed moment of his second conversion, at the age of eleven, when, weeping with embarrassment and the prospect of losing so much fun, surrounded by solemn and whiskered adult faces, he had signed a pledge binding him to give up, forever, the joys of profanity, alcohol, cards, dancing, and the theater.

These clouds hung behind and over him, for all his boldness.

Eddie Fislinger, the human being, he despised. He considered him a grasshopper, and with satisfaction considered stepping on him. But Eddie Fislinger, the gospeler, fortified with just such a pebble-leather Bible (bookmarks of fringed silk and celluloid smirking from the pages) as his Sunday School teachers had wielded when they assured him that God was always creeping about to catch small boys in their secret thoughts—this armored Eddie was an official, and Elmer listened to him uneasily, never quite certain that he might not yet find himself a dreadful person leading a pure and boresome life in a clean frock coat.

"—and remember," Eddie was wailing, "how terribly dangerous it is to put off the hour of salvation! 'Watch therefore for you know not what hour your Lord doth come,' it says. Suppose this train were wrecked! Tonight!"

The train ungraciously took that second to lurch on a curve.

"You see? Where would you spend Eternity, Hell-cat? Do you think that any sportin' round is fun enough to burn in hell for?"

"Oh, cut it out. I know all that stuff. There's a lot of arguments— You wait'll I get Jim to tell you what Bob Ingersoll said about hell!"

"Yes! Sure! And you remember that on his deathbed Ingersoll called his son to him and repented and begged his son to hurry and be saved and burn all his wicked writings!"

"Well— Thunder— I don't feel like talking religion tonight. Cut it out."

But Eddie did feel like talking religion, very much so. He waved his Bible enthusiastically and found ever so many uncomfortable texts. Elmer listened as little as possible, but he was too feeble to make threats.

It was a golden relief when the train bumped to a stop at Gritzmacher Springs. The station was a greasy wooden box, the platform was thick with slush, under the kerosene lights. But Jim was awaiting him, a refuge from confusing theological questions, and with a furious "G'night!" to Eddie he staggered off.

"Why didn't you make him shut his trap?" demanded Jim.

"I did! Whadja take a sneak for? I told him to shut up and he shut up and I snoozed all the way back and— Ow! My head! Don't walk so fast!"

Chapter II

FOR YEARS the state of sin in which dwelt Elmer Gantry and Jim Lefferts had produced fascinated despair in the Christian hearts of Terwillinger College. No revival but had flung its sulphur-soaked arrows at them—usually in their absence. No prayer at the Y.M.C.A. meetings but had worried over their staggering folly.

Elmer had been known to wince when President the Rev. Dr. Willoughby Quarles was especially gifted with messages at morning chapel, but Jim had held him firm in the faith of unfaith.

Now, Eddie Fislinger, like a prairie seraph, sped from room to room of the elect with the astounding news that Elmer had publicly professed religion, and that he had endured thirty-nine minutes of private adjuration on the train. Instantly started a holy plotting against the miserable sacrificial lamb, and all over Gritzmacher Springs, in the studies of ministerial professors, in the rooms of students, in the small prayer-meeting room behind the chapel auditorium, joyous souls conspired with the Lord against Elmer's serene and zealous sinning. Everywhere, through the snowstorm, you could hear murmurs of "There is more rejoicing over one sinner who repenteth—"

Even collegians not particularly esteemed for their piety, suspected of playing cards and secret smoking, were stirred to ecstasy—or it may have been snickering. The football center, in unregenerate days a companion of Elmer and Jim but now engaged to marry a large and sanctified Swedish co-ed from Chanute, rose voluntarily in Y.M.C.A. and promised God to help him win Elmer's favor.

The spirit waxed most fervent in the abode of Eddie Fislinger, who was now recognized as a future prophet, likely, some day, to have under his inspiration one of the larger Baptist churches in Wichita or even Kansas City.

He organized an all-day and all-night prayer-meeting on Elmer's behalf, and it was attended by the more ardent, even at the risk of receiving cuts and uncivil remarks from instructors.

On the bare floor of Eddie's room, over Knute Halvorsted's paint-shop, from three to sixteen young men knelt at a time, and no 1800 revival saw more successful wrestling with the harassed Satan. In fact one man, suspected of Holy Roller sympathies, managed to have the jerks, and while they felt that this was carrying things farther than the Lord and the Baptist association would care to see, it added excitement to praying at three o'clock in the morning, particularly as they were all of them extraordinarily drunk on coffee and eloquence.

By morning they felt sure that they had persuaded God to attend to Elmer, and though it is true that Elmer himself had slept quite soundly all night, unaware of the prayer-meeting or of divine influences, it was but an example of the patience of the heavenly powers. And immediately after those powers began to move.

To Elmer's misery and Jim's stilled fury, their sacred room was invaded by hordes of men with uncombed locks on their foreheads, ecstasy in their eyes, and Bibles under their arms. Elmer was safe nowhere. No sooner had he disposed of one disciple, by the use of spirited and blasphemous arguments patiently taught to him by Jim, than another would pop out from behind a tree and fall on him.

At his boarding-house—Mother Metzger's, over on Beech Street—a Y.M.C.A. dervish crowed as he passed the bread to Elmer, "Jever study a kernel of wheat? Swonnerful! Think a wonnerful intricate thing like that created *itself*? Somebody must have created it. Who? God! Anybody that don't reconize God in Nature—and acknowledge him in repentance—is *dumm*. That's what he is!"

Instructors who had watched Elmer's entrance to class-rooms with nervous fury now smirked on him and with tenderness heard the statement that he wasn't quite prepared to recite. The president himself stopped Elmer on the street and called him My Boy, and shook his hand with an affection which, Elmer anxiously assured himself, he certainly had done nothing to merit.

He kept assuring Jim that he was in no danger, but Jim was alarmed, and Elmer himself more alarmed with each hour, each new greeting of: "We need you with us, old boy—the world needs you!"

Jim did well to dread. Elmer had always been in danger of giving up his favorite diversions—not exactly giving them up, perhaps, but of sweating in agony after enjoying them. But for Jim and his remarks about co-eds who prayed in public and drew their hair back rebukingly from egg-like foreheads, one of these sirens of morality might have snared the easy-going pangynistic Elmer by proximity.

A dreadful young woman from Mexico, Missouri, used to coax Jim to "tell his funny ideas about religion," and go off in neighs of pious laughter, while she choked, "Oh, you're just too cute! You don't mean a word you say. You simply want to show off!" She had a deceptive sidelong look which actually promised nothing whatever this side of the altar, and she might, but for Jim's struggles, have led Elmer into an engagement.

The church and Sunday School at Elmer's village, Paris, Kansas, a settlement of nine hundred evangelical Germans and Vermonters, had nurtured in him a fear of religious machinery which he could never lose, which restrained him from such reasonable acts as butchering Eddie Fislinger. That small pasty-white Baptist church had been the center of all his emotions, aside from hell-raising, hunger, sleepiness, and love. And even these emotions were represented in the House of the Lord, in the way of tacks in pew-cushions, Missionary Suppers with chicken pie and angel's-food cake, soporific sermons, and the proximity of flexible little girls in thin muslin. But the arts and the sentiments and the sentimentalities—they were for Elmer perpetually associated only with the church.

Except for circus bands, Fourth of July parades, and the singing of "Columbia, the Gem of the Ocean" and "Jingle Bells" in school, all the music which the boy Elmer had ever heard was in church.

The church provided his only oratory, except for campaign speeches by politicians ardent about Jefferson and the price of binding-twine; it provided all his painting and sculpture, except for the portraits of Lincoln, Longfellow, and Emerson in the school-building, and the two china statuettes of pink ladies with gilt flower-baskets which stood on his mother's bureau. From the church came all his profounder philosophy, except the teachers' admonitions that little boys who let garter-snakes loose in school were certain to be licked now and hanged later, and his mother's stream of opinions on hanging up his overcoat, wiping his feet, eating fried potatoes with his fingers, and taking the name of the Lord in vain.

If he had sources of literary inspiration outside the church—in McGuffey's Reader he encountered the boy who stood on the burning deck, and he had a very pretty knowledge of the Nick Carter Series and the exploits of Cole Younger and the James Boys—yet here too the church had guided him. In Bible stories, in the words of the great hymns, in the anecdotes which the various preachers quoted, he had his only knowledge of literature—

The story of Little Lame Tom who shamed the wicked rich man that owned the handsome team of grays and the pot hat and led him to Jesus. The ship's captain who in the storm took counsel with the orphaned but righteous child of missionaries in Zomballa. The Faithful Dog who saved his master during a terrific conflagration (only sometimes it was a snowstorm, or an attack by Indians) and roused him to give up horse-racing, rum, and playing the harmonica.

How familiar they were, how thrilling, how explanatory to Elmer of the purposes of life, how preparatory for his future usefulness and charm.

The church, the Sunday School, the evangelistic orgy, choir-practise, raising the mortgage, the delights of funerals, the snickers in back pews or in the other room at weddings—they were as natural, as inescapable a mold of manners to Elmer as Catholic processionals to a street gamin in Naples.

The Baptist Church of Paris, Kansas! A thousand blurred but indestructible pictures.

Hymns! Elmer's voice was made for hymns. He rolled them out like a negro. The organ-thunder of "Nicæa":

Holy, holy, holy! all the saints adore thee,
Casting down their golden crowns around the glassy sea.

The splendid rumble of the Doxology. "Throw Out the Lifeline," with its picture of a wreck pounded in the darkness by surf which the prairie child imagined as a hundred feet high. "Onward, Christian Soldiers," to which you could without rebuke stamp your feet.

Sunday School picnics! Lemonade and four-legged races and the ride on the hay-rack, singing "Seeing Nelly Home."

Sunday School text cards! True, they were chiefly a medium of gambling, but as Elmer usually won the game (he was the first boy in Paris to own a genuine pair of loaded dice) he had plenty of them in his gallery, and they gave him a taste for gaudy robes, for marble columns and the purple-broidered palaces of kings, which was later to be of value in quickly habituating himself to the more decorative homes of vice. The three kings bearing caskets of ruby and sardonyx. King Zedekiah in gold and scarlet, kneeling on a carpet of sapphire-blue, while his men-at-arms came fleeing and blood-stained, red blood on glancing steel, with tidings of the bannered host of Nebuchadnezzar, great king of Babylon. And all his life Elmer remembered, in moments of ardor, during oratorios in huge churches, during sunset at sea, a black-bearded David standing against raw red cliffs—a figure heroic and summoning to ambition, to power, to domination.

Sunday School Christmas Eve! The exhilaration of staying up, and publicly, till nine-thirty. The tree, incredibly tall, also incredibly inflammable, flashing with silver cords, with silver stars, with cotton-batting snow. The two round stoves red-hot. Lights and lights and lights. Pails of candy, and for every child in the school a present—usually a book, very pleasant, with colored pictures of lambs and volcanoes. The Santa Claus—he couldn't possibly be Lorenzo Nickerson, the house-painter, so bearded was he, and red-cheeked, and so witty in his comment on each child as it marched up for its present. The enchantment, sheer magic, of the Ladies' Quartette singing of shepherds who watched their flocks by nights . . . brown secret hilltops under one vast star.

And the devastating morning when the preacher himself, the Rev. Wilson Hinckley Skaggs, caught Elmer matching for Sunday School contribution pennies on the front steps, and led him up the aisle for all to giggle at, with a sharp and not very clean ministerial thumb-nail gouging his ear-lobe.

And the other passing preachers: Brother Organdy, who got you to saw his wood free; Brother Blunt, who sneaked behind barns to catch you on Halloween; Brother Ingle, who was zealous but young and actually human, and who made whistles from willow branches for you.

And the morning when Elmer concealed an alarm clock behind the organ and it went off, magnificently, just as the superintendent (Dr. Prouty, the dentist) was whimpering, "Now let us all be par*tic*ularly quiet as Sister Holbrick leads us in prayer."

And always the three chairs that stood behind the pulpit, the intimidating stiff chairs of yellow plush and carved oak borders, which, he was uneasily sure, were waiting for the Father, the Son, and the Holy Ghost.

He had, in fact, got everything from the church and Sunday School, except, perhaps, any longing whatever for decency and kindness and reason.

II

Even had Elmer not known the church by habit, he would have been led to it by his mother. Aside from his friendship for Jim Lefferts, Elmer's only authentic affection was for his mother, and she was owned by the church.

She was a small woman, energetic, nagging but kindly, once given to passionate caresses and now to passionate prayer, and she had unusual courage. Early left a widow by Logan Gantry, dealer in feed, flour, lumber, and agricultural implements, a large and agreeable man given to debts and whisky, she had supported herself and Elmer by sewing, trimming hats, baking bread, and selling milk. She had her own millinery and dressmaking shop now, narrow and dim but proudly set right on Main Street, and she was able to give Elmer the three hundred dollars a year which, with his summer earnings in harvest field and lumber-yard, was enough to support him—in Terwillinger, in 1902.

She had always wanted Elmer to be a preacher. She was jolly enough, and no fool about pennies in making change, but for a preacher standing up on a platform in a long-tailed coat she had gaping awe.

Elmer had since the age of sixteen been a member in good standing of the Baptist Church—he had been most satisfactorily immersed in the Kayooska River. Large though Elmer was, the evangelist had been a powerful man and had not only ducked him but, in sacred enthusiasm, held him under, so that he came up sputtering, in a state of grace and muddiness. He had also been saved several times, and once, when he had pneumonia, he had been esteemed by the pastor and all visiting ladies as rapidly growing in grace.

But he had resisted his mother's desire that he become a preacher. He would have to give up his entertaining vices, and with wide-eyed and panting happiness he was discovering more of them every year. Equally he felt lumbering and shamed whenever he tried to stand up before his tittering gang in Paris and appear pious.

It was hard even in college days to withstand his mother. Though she came only to his shoulder, such was her bustling vigor, her swift shrewdness of tongue, such the gallantry of her long care for him, that he was afraid of her as he was afraid of Jim Lefferts' scorn. He never dared honestly to confess his infidelity, but he grumbled, "Oh, gee, Ma, I don't know. Trouble is, fellow don't make much money preaching. Gee, there's no hurry. Don't have to decide yet."

And she knew now that he was likely to become a lawyer. Well, that wasn't so bad, she felt; some day he might go to Congress and reform the whole nation into a pleasing likeness of Kansas. But if he could only have become part of the mysteries that hovered about the communion table—

She had talked him over with Eddie Fislinger. Eddie came from a town twelve miles from Paris. Though it might be years before he was finally ordained as a minister, Eddie had by his home congregation been given a License to Preach as early as his Sophomore year in Terwillinger, and for a month, one summer (while Elmer was out in the harvest fields or the swimming hole or robbing orchards), Eddie had earnestly supplied the Baptist pulpit in Paris.

Mrs. Gantry consulted him, and Eddie instructed her with the dignity of nineteen.

Oh, yes, Brother Elmer was a fine young man—so strong—they all admired him—a little too much tempted by the vain gauds of This World, but that was because he was young. Oh, yes, some day Elmer would settle down and be a fine Christian husband and father and business man. But as to the ministry—no. Mrs. Gantry must not too greatly meddle with these mysteries. It was up to God. A fellow had to have a Call before he felt his vocation for the ministry; a real overwhelming mysterious knock-down Call, such as Eddie himself had ecstatically experienced, one evening in a cabbage patch. No, not think of that. Their task now was to get Elmer into a real state of grace and that, Eddie assured her, looked to him like a good deal of a job.

Undoubtedly, Eddie explained, when Elmer had been baptized, at sixteen, he had felt conviction, he had felt the invitation, and the burden of his sins had been lifted. But he had not, Eddie doubted, entirely experienced salvation. He was not really in a state of grace. He might almost be called unconverted.

Eddie diagnosed the case completely, with all the proper pathological terms. Whatever difficulties he may have had with philosophy, Latin, and calculus, there had never been a time since the age of twelve when Eddie Fislinger had had difficulty in understanding what the Lord God Almighty wanted, and why, all through history, he had acted thus or thus.

"I should be the last to condemn athaletics," said Eddie. "We must have strong bodies to endure the burden and the sweat of carrying the Gospel to the world. But at the same time, it seems to me that football tends to detract from religion. I'm a little afraid that just at *present* Elmer is not in a state of grace. But, oh, Sister, don't let us worry and travail! Let us trust the Lord. I'll go to Elmer myself, and see what I can do."

That must have been the time—it certainly was during that vacation between their Sophomore and Junior years—when Eddie walked out to the farm where Elmer was working, and looked at Elmer, bulky and hayseedy in a sleeveless undershirt, and spoke reasonably of the weather, and walked back again. . . .

Whenever Elmer was at home, though he tried affectionately to live out his mother's plan of life for him, though without very much grumbling he went to bed at nine-thirty, white-washed the hen-house, and accompanied her to church, yet Mrs. Gantry suspected that sometimes he drank beer and doubted about Jonah, and uneasily Elmer heard her sobbing as she knelt by her high-swelling, white-counterpaned, old-fashioned bed.

III

With alarmed evangelistic zeal, Jim Lefferts struggled to keep Elmer true to the faith, after his exposure to religion in defending Eddie at Cato.

He was, on the whole, rather more zealous and fatiguing than Eddie.

Nights, when Elmer longed to go to sleep, Jim argued; mornings, when Elmer should have been preparing his history, Jim read aloud from Ingersoll and Thomas Paine.

"How you going to explain a thing like this—how you going to explain it?" begged Jim. "It says here in Deuteronomy that God chased these Yids around in the desert for forty years and their shoes didn't even wear out. That's what it *says*, right in the Bible. You believe a thing like that? And do you believe that Samson lost all his strength just because his gal cut off his hair? Do you, eh? Think hair had anything to do with his strength?"

Jim raced up and down the stuffy room, kicking at chairs, his normally bland eyes feverish, his forefinger shaken in wrath, while Elmer sat humped on the edge of the bed, his forehead in his hands, rather enjoying having his soul fought for.

To prove that he was still a sound and freethinking stalwart, Elmer went out with Jim one evening and at considerable effort they carried off a small outhouse and placed it on the steps of the Administration Building.

Elmer almost forgot to worry after the affair of Eddie and Dr. Lefferts.

Jim's father was a medical practitioner in an adjoining village. He was a plump, bearded, bookish, merry man, very proud of his atheism. It was he who had trained Jim in the faith and in his choice of liquor; he had sent Jim to this denominational college partly because it was cheap and partly because it tickled his humor to watch his son stir up the fretful complacency of the saints. He dropped in and found Elmer and Jim agitatedly awaiting the arrival of Eddie.

"Eddie said," wailed Elmer, "he said he was coming up to see me, and he'll haul out some more of these proofs that I'm going straight to hell. Gosh, Doctor, I don't know what's got into me. You better examine me. I must have anemics or something. Why, one time, if Eddie Fislinger had smiled at me, damn him, think of *him* daring to smile at me!—if he'd said he was coming to my room, I'd of told him, 'Like hell you will!' and I'd of kicked him in the shins."

Dr. Lefferts purred in his beard. His eyes were bright.

"I'll give your friend Fislinger a run for his money. And for the inconsequential sake of the non-existent Heaven, Jim, try not to look surprised when you find your respectable father being pious."

When Eddie arrived, he was introduced to a silkily cordial Dr. Lefferts, who shook his hand with that lengthiness and painfulness common to politicians, salesmen, and the godly. The doctor rejoiced:

"Brother Fislinger, my boy here and Elmer tell me that you've been trying to help them see the true Bible religion."

"I've been seeking to."

"It warms my soul to hear you say that, Brother Fislinger! You can't know what a grief it is to an old man tottering to the grave, to one whose only solace now is prayer and Bible-reading"— Dr. Lefferts had sat up till four A.M., three nights ago, playing poker and discussing biology with his cronies, the probate judge and the English stock-breeder—"what a grief it is to him that his only son, James Blaine Lefferts, is not a believer. But perhaps you can do more than I can, Brother Fislinger. They think I'm a fanatical old fogy. Now let me see— You're a real Bible believer?"

"Oh, yes!" Eddie looked triumphantly at Jim, who was leaning against the table, his hands in his pockets, as expressionless as wood. Elmer was curiously hunched up in the Morris chair, his hands over his mouth.

The doctor said approvingly:

"That's splendid. You believe every word of it, I hope, from cover to cover?"

"Oh, yes. What *I* always say is, 'It's better to have the whole Bible than a Bible full of holes.' "

"Why, that's a real thought, Brother Fislinger. I must remember that, to tell any of these alleged higher critics, if I ever meet any! 'Bible whole—not Bible full of holes.' Oh, that's a fine thought, and cleverly expressed. You made it up?"

"Well, not exactly."

"I see, I see. Well, that's splendid. Now of course you believe in the premillennial coming—I mean the real, authentic, genuwine, immediate, bodily, premillennial coming of Jesus Christ?"

"Oh, yes, sure."

"And the virgin birth?"

"Oh, you bet."

"That's splendid! Of course there are doctors who question whether the virgin birth is quite in accordance with their experience of obstetrics, but I tell those fellows, 'Look here! How do I know it's true? Because it says so in the Bible, and if it weren't true, do you suppose it would say so in the Bible?' That certainly shuts them up! They have precious little to say after that!"

By this time a really beautiful, bounteous fellowship was flowing between Eddie and the doctor, and they were looking with pity on the embarrassed faces of the two heretics left out in the cold. Dr. Lefferts tickled his beard and crooned:

"And of course, Brother Fislinger, you believe in infant damnation."

Eddie explained, "No; that's not a Baptist doctrine."

"You—you—" The good doctor choked, tugged at his collar, panted, and wailed:

"It's not a Baptist doctrine? You don't believe in infant damnation?"

"W-why, no—"

"Then God help the Baptist church and the Baptist doctrine! God help us all, in these unregenerate days, that we should be contaminated by such infidelity!" Eddie sweat, while the doctor patted his plump hands and agonized: "Look you here, my brother! It's very simple. Are we not saved by being washed in the blood of the Lamb, and by that alone, by his blessed sacrifice alone?"

"W-why, yes, but—"

"Then either we *are* washed white, and saved, or else we are not washed, and we are not saved! That's the simple truth, and all weakenings and explanations and hemming and hawing about this clear and beautiful truth are simply of the devil, brother! And at what moment does a human being, in all his inevitable sinfulness, become subject to baptism and salvation? At two months? At nine years? At sixteen? At forty-seven? At ninety-nine? No! The moment he is born! And so if he be not baptized, then he must burn in hell forever. What does it say in the Good Book? 'For there is none other name under heaven given among men, whereby we must be saved.' It may seem a little hard of God to fry beautiful little babies, but then think of the beautiful women whom he loves to roast there for the edification of the saints! Oh, brother, brother, now I understand why Jimmy here, and poor Elmer, are lost to the faith! It's because professed Christians like you give them this emasculated religion! Why, it's fellows like you who break down the dike of true belief, and open a channel for higher criticism and sabellianism and nymphomania and agnosticism and heresy and Catholicism and Seventh-day Adventism and all those horrible German inventions! Once you begin to doubt, the wicked work is done! Oh, Jim, Elmer, I told you to listen to our friend here, but now that I find him practically a free-thinker—"

The doctor staggered to a chair. Eddie stood gaping.

It was the first time in his life that any one had accused him of feebleness in the faith, of under-strictness. He was smirkingly accustomed to being denounced as over-strict. He had almost as much satisfaction out of denouncing liquor as other collegians had out of drinking it. He had, partly from his teachers and partly right out of his own brain, any number of good answers to classmates who protested that he was old-fashioned in belaboring domino-playing, open communion, listening to waltz music, wearing a gown in the pulpit, taking a walk on Sunday, reading novels, transubstantiation, and these new devices of the devil called moving-pictures. He could frighten almost any Laodicean. But to be called shaky himself, to be called heretic and slacker—for that inconceivable attack he had no retort.

He looked at the agonized doctor, he looked at Jim and Elmer, who were obviously distressed at his fall from spiritual leadership, and he fled to secret prayer.

He took his grief presently to President Quarles, who explained everything perfectly.

"But this doctor quoted Scripture to prove his point!" bleated Eddie.

"Don't forget, Brother Fislinger, that 'the devil can quote Scripture to his purpose.'"

Eddie thought that was a very nice thought and very nicely expressed, and though he was not altogether sure that it was from the Bible, he put it away for future use in sermons. But before he was sufficiently restored to go after Elmer again, Christmas vacation had arrived.

When Eddie had gone, Elmer laughed far more heartily than Jim or his father. It is true that he hadn't quite understood what it was all about. Why, sure; Eddie had said it right; infant damnation *wasn't* a Baptist doctrine; it belonged to some of the Presbyterians, and everybody knew the Presbyterians had a lot of funny beliefs. But the doctor certainly had done something to squelch Eddie, and Elmer felt safer than for many days.

He continued to feel safe up till Christmas vacation. Then—

Some one, presumably Eddie, had informed Elmer's mother of his new and promising Christian status. He himself had been careful to keep such compromising rumors out of his weekly letters home. Through all the vacation he was conscious that his mother was hovering closer to him than usual, that she was waiting to snatch at his soul if he showed weakening. Their home pastor, the Reverend Mr. Aker—known in Paris as Reverend Aker—shook hands with him at the church door with approval as incriminating as the affection of his instructors at Terwillinger.

Unsupported by Jim, aware that at any moment Eddie might pop in from his neighboring town and be accepted as an ally by Mrs. Gantry, Elmer spent a vacation in which there was but little peace. To keep his morale up, he gave particularly earnest attention to bottle-pool and to the daughter of a near-by farmer. But he was in dread lest these be the last sad ashen days of his naturalness.

It seemed menacing that Eddie should be on the same train back to college. Eddie was with another exponent of piety, and he said nothing to Elmer about the delights of hell, but he and his companion secretly giggled with a confidence more than dismaying.

Jim Lefferts did not find in Elmer's face the conscious probity and steadfastness which he had expected.

Chapter III

EARLY in January was the Annual College Y.M.C.A. Week of Prayer. It was a countrywide event, but in Terwillinger College it was of especial power that year because they were privileged to have with them for three days none other than Judson Roberts, State Secretary of the Y.M.C.A., and a man great personally as well as officially.

He was young, Mr. Roberts, only thirty-four, but already known throughout the land. He had always been known. He had been a member of a star University of Chicago football team, he had played varsity baseball, he had been captain of the debating team, and at the same time he had commanded the Y.M.C.A. He had been known as the Praying Fullback. He still kept up his exercise—he was said to have boxed privily with Jim Jeffries—and he had mightily increased his praying. A very friendly leader he was, and helpful; hundreds of college men throughout Kansas called him "Old Jud."

Between prayer-meetings at Terwillinger, Judson Roberts sat in the Bible History seminar-room, at a long table, under a bilious map of the Holy Land, and had private conferences with the men students. A surprising number of them came edging in, trembling, with averted eyes, to ask advice about a secret practice, and Old Jud seemed amazingly able to guess their trouble before they got going.

He was very manly and jolly:

"Well, now, old boy, I'll tell you. Terrible thing, all right, but I've met quite a few cases, and you just want to buck up and take it to the Lord in prayer. Remember that he is able to help unto the uttermost. Now the first thing you want to do is to get rid of— I'm afraid that you have some pretty nasty pictures and maybe a juicy book hidden away, now haven't you, old boy?"

How could Old Jud have guessed? What a corker!

"That's right. I've got a swell plan, old boy. Make a study of missions, and think how clean and pure and manly you'd want to be if you were going to carry the joys of Christianity to a lot of poor gazebos that are under the evil spell of

Buddhism and a lot of these heathen religions. Wouldn't you want to be able to look 'em in the eye, and shame 'em? Next thing to do is to get a lot of exercise. Get out and run like hell! And then cold baths. Darn' cold. There now!" Rising, with ever so manly a handshake: "Now skip along and remember"—with a tremendous and fetching and virile laugh—"just run like hell!"

Jim and Elmer heard Old Jud in chapel. He was tremendous. He told them a jolly joke about a man who kissed a girl, yet he rose to feathered heights when he described the beatitude of real ungrudging prayer, in which a man was big enough to be as a child. He made them tearful over the gentleness with which he described the Christchild, wandering lost by his parents, yet the next moment he had them stretching with admiration as he arched his big shoulder-muscles and observed that he would knock the block off any sneering, sneaking, lying, beer-bloated bully who should dare to come up to *him* in a meeting and try to throw a monkey-wrench into the machinery by dragging out a lot of contemptible, quibbling, atheistic, smart-aleck doubts! (He really did, the young men glowed, use the terms "knock the block off," and "throw a monkey-wrench." Oh, he was a lulu, a real red-blooded regular fellow!)

Jim was coming down with the grippe. He was unable to pump up even one good sneer. He sat folded up, his chin near his knees, and Elmer was allowed to swell with hero-worship. Golly! He'd thought he had some muscle, but that guy Judson Roberts—zowie, he could put Elmer on the mat seven falls out of five! What a football player he must have been! Wee!

This Homeric worship he tried to explain to Jim, back in their room, but Jim sneezed and went to bed. The rude bard was left without audience and he was practically glad when Eddie Fislinger scratched at the door and edged in.

"Don't want to bother you fellows, but noticed you were at Old Jud's meeting this afternoon and, say, you gotta come out and hear him again tomorrow evening. Big evening of the week. Say, honest, Hell-cat, don't you think Jud's a real humdinger?"

"Yes, I gotta admit, he's a dandy fellow."

"Say, he certainly is, isn't he! He certainly is a dandy fellow, isn't he! Isn't he a peach!"

"Yes, he certainly is a peach—for a religious crank!"

"Aw now, Hell-cat, don't go calling him names! You'll admit he looks like some football shark."

"Yes, I guess he does, at that. I'd liked to of played with him."

"Wouldn't you like to meet him?"

"Well—"

At this moment of danger, Jim raised his dizzy head to protest, "He's a holy strikebreaker! One of these thick-necks that was born husky and tries to make you think he made himself husky by prayer and fasting. I'd hate to take a chance on any poor little orphan nip of Bourbon wandering into Old Jud's presence! Yeh! Chest-pounder! 'Why can't you hundred-pound shrimps be a big manly Christian like me!"

Together they protested against this defilement of the hero, and Eddie admitted that he had ventured to praise Elmer to Old Jud; that Old Jud had seemed enthralled; that Old Jud was more than likely—so friendly a Great Man was he—to run in on Elmer this afternoon.

Before Elmer could decide whether to be pleased or indignant, before the enfeebled Jim could get up strength to decide for him, the door was hit a mighty and heroic wallop, and in strode Judson Roberts, big as a grizzly, jolly as a spaniel pup, radiant as ten suns.

He set upon Elmer immediately. He had six other doubting Thomases or suspected smokers to dispose of before six o'clock.

He was a fair young giant with curly hair and a grin and with a voice like the Bulls of Bashan whenever the strategy called for manliness. But with erring sisters, unless they were too erring, he could be as lulling as woodland violets shaken in the perfumed breeze.

"Hello, Hell-cat!" he boomed. "Shake hands!"

Elmer had a playful custom of squeezing people's hands till they cracked. For the first time in his life his own paw felt limp and burning. He rubbed it and looked simple.

"Been hearing a lot about you, Hell-cat, and you, Jim. Laid out, Jim? Want me to trot out and get a doc?" Old Jud was sitting easily on the edge of Jim's bed, and in the light of that grin, even Jim Lefferts could not be very sour as he tried to sneer, "No, thanks."

Roberts turned to Elmer again, and gloated:

"Well, old son, I've been hearing a lot about you. Gee whillikins, that must have been a great game you played against Thorvilsen College! They tell me when you hit that line, it gave like a sponge, and when you tackled that big long Swede, he went down like he'd been hit by lightning."

"Well, it was—it was a good game."

"Course I read about it at the time—"

"Did you, honest?"

"—and course I wanted to hear more about it, and meet you, Hell-cat, so I been asking the boys about you, and say, they certainly do give you a great hand! Wish I could've had you with me on my team at U of Chi—we needed a tackle like you."

Elmer basked.

"Yes, sir, the boys all been telling me what a dandy fine fellow you are, and what a corking athlete, and what an A-1 gentleman. They all say there's just one trouble with you, Elmer lad."

"Eh?"

"They say you're a coward."

"Heh? *Who* says I'm a coward?"

Judson Roberts swaggered across from the bed, stood with his hand on Elmer's shoulder. "They all say it, Hell-cat! You see it takes a sure-enough dyed-in-the-wool brave man to be big enough to give Jesus a shot at him, and admit he's licked when he tries to fight God! It takes a man with guts to kneel down and admit his worthlessness when all the world is jeering at him! And you haven't got that kind of courage, Elmer. Oh, you think you're such a big cuss—"

Old Jud swung him around; Old Jud's hand was crushing his shoulder. "You think you're too husky, too good, to associate with the poor little sniveling gospel-mongers, don't you! You could knock out any of 'em, couldn't you! Well, I'm one of 'em. Want to knock me out?"

With one swift jerk Roberts had his coat off, stood with a striped silk shirt revealing his hogshead torso.

"You bet, Hell-cat! I'm willing to fight you for the glory of God! God needs you! Can you think of anything finer for a big husky like you than to spend his life bringing poor, weak, sick, scared folks to happiness? Can't you see how the poor little skinny guys and all the kiddies would follow you, and praise you and admire you, you old son of a gun? Am I a little sneaking Christian? Can you lick me? Want to fight it out?"

"No, gee, Mr. Roberts—"

"Judson, you big hunk of cheese, Old Jud!"

"No, gee, Judson, I guess you got me trimmed! I pack a pretty good wallop, but I'm not going to take any chance on you!"

"All right, old son. Still think that all religious folks are crabs?"

"No."

"And weaklings and pikers?"

"No."

"And liars?"

"Oh, no."

"All right, old boy. Going to allow me to be a friend of yours, if I don't butt in on your business?"

"Oh, gee, sure."

"Then there's just one favor I want to ask. Will you come to our big meeting tomorrow night? You don't have to do a thing. If you think we're four-flushers—all right; that's your privilege. Only will you come and not decide we're all wrong beforehand, but really use that big fine incisive brain of yours and study us as we are? Will you come?"

"Oh, yes, sure, you bet."

"Fine, old boy. Mighty proud to have you let me come butting in here in this informal way. Remember: if you honestly feel I'm using any undue influence on the boys, you come right after me and say so, and I'll be mighty proud of your trusting me to stand the gaff. So long, old Elm! So long, Jim. God bless you!"

"So long, Jud."

He was gone, a whirlwind that whisked the inconspicuous herb Eddie Fislinger out after it.

And *then* Jim Lefferts spoke.

For a time after Judson Roberts' curtain, Elmer stood glowing, tasting praise. He was conscious of Jim's eyes on his back, and he turned toward the bed, defiantly.

They stared, in a tug of war. Elmer gave in with a furious:

"Well, then, why didn't you say something while he was here?"

"To him? Talk to a curly wolf when he smells meat? Besides, he's intelligent, that fellow."

"Well, say, I'm glad to hear you say that, because—well, you see—I'll explain how I feel."

"Oh, no, you won't, sweetheart! You haven't got to the miracle-pulling stage yet. Sure he's intelligent. I never heard a better exhibition of bunco-steering in my life. Sure! He's just crazy to have you come up and kick him in the ear and tell him you've decided you can't give your imprimatur—"

"My *what*?"

"—to his show, and he's to quit and go back to hod-carrying. Sure. He read all about your great game with Thorvilsen. Sent off to New York to get the *Review of Reviews* and read more about it. Eddie Fislinger never told him a word. He read about your tackling in the *London Times*. You bet. Didn't he say so? And he's a saved soul—he couldn't lie. And he just couldn't stand it if he didn't become a friend of yours. He can't know more than a couple of thousand collidge boys to spring that stuff on! . . . You bet I believe in the old bearded Jew God! Nobody but him could have made all the idiots there are in the world!"

"Gee, Jim, honest, you don't understand Jud."

"No. I don't. When he could be a decent prize-fighter, and not have to go around with angleworms like Eddie Fislinger day after day!"

And thus till midnight, for all Jim's fevers.

But Elmer was at Judson Roberts' meeting next evening, unprotected by Jim, who remained at home in so vile a temper that Elmer had sent in a doctor and sneaked away from the room for the afternoon.

II

It was undoubtedly Eddie who wrote or telegraphed to Mrs. Gantry that she would do well to be present at the meeting. Paris was only forty miles from Gritzmacher Springs.

Elmer crept into his room at six, still wistfully hoping to have Jim's sanction, still ready to insist that if he went to the meeting he would be in no danger of conversion. He had walked miles through the slush, worrying. He was ready now to give up the meeting, to give up Judson's friendship, if Jim should insist.

As he wavered in, Mrs. Gantry stood by Jim's lightning-shot bed.

"Why, Ma! What you doing here? What's gone wrong?" Elmer panted.

It was impossible to think of her taking a journey for anything less than a funeral.

Cozily, "Can't I run up and see my two boys if I want to, Elmy? I declare, I believe you'd of killed Jim, with all this nasty tobacco air, if I hadn't come in and aired the place out. I *thought*, Elmer Gantry, you weren't supposed to smoke in Terwillinger! By the rules of the college! I thought, young man, that you lived up to 'em! But never mind."

Uneasily—for Jim had never before seen him demoted to childhood, as he always was in his mother's presence—Elmer grumbled, "But honest, Ma, what did you come up for?"

"Well, I read about what a nice week of prayer you were going to have, and I thought I'd just like to hear a real big bug preach. I've got a vacation coming, too! Now don't you worry one mite about me. I guess I can take care of myself after all these years! The first traveling I ever done with you, young man—the time I went to Cousin Adeline's wedding—I just tucked you under one arm—and how you squalled, the whole way!—mercy, you liked to hear the sound of your own voice then just like you do now!—and I tucked my old valise under the other, and off I went! Don't you worry one mite about me. I'm only going to stay over the night—got a sale on remnants starting—going back on Number Seven tomorrow. I left my valise at that boarding-house right across from the depot. But there's one thing you might do if 'tain't too much trouble, Elmy. You know I've only been up here at the college once before. I'd feel kind of funny, country bumpkin like me, going alone to that big meeting, with all those smart professors and everybody there, and I'd be glad if you could come along."

"Of course he'll go, Mrs. Gantry," said Jim.

But before Elmer was carried away, Jim had the chance to whisper, "God, do be careful! Remember I won't be there to protect you! Don't let 'em pick on you! Don't do one single doggone thing they want you to do, and then maybe you'll be safe!"

As he went out, Elmer looked back at Jim. He was shakily sitting up in bed, his eyes imploring.

III

The climactic meeting of the Annual Prayer Week, to be addressed by President Quarles, four ministers, and a rich trustee who was in the pearl-button business, with Judson Roberts as star soloist, was not held at the Y.M.C.A. but at the largest auditorium in town, the Baptist Church, with hundreds of town-people joining the collegians.

The church was a welter of brownstone, with Moorish arches and an immense star-shaped window not yet filled with stained glass.

Elmer hoped to be late enough to creep in inconspicuously, but as his mother and he straggled up to the Romanesque portico, students were still outside, chattering. He was certain they were whispering, "There he is—Hell-cat Gantry. Say, is it really true he's under conviction of sin? I thought he cussed out the church more'n anybody in college."

Meek though Elmer had been under instruction by Jim and threats by Eddie and yearning by his mother, he was not normally given to humility, and he looked at his critics defiantly. "I'll show 'em! If they think I'm going to sneak in—"

He swaggered down almost to the front pews, to the joy of his mother, who had been afraid that as usual he would hide in the rear, handy to the door if the preacher should become personal.

There was a great deal of decoration in the church, which had been endowed by a zealous alumnus after making his strike in Alaskan boarding-houses during the gold-rush. There were Egyptian pillars with gilded capitals, on the ceiling were gilt stars and clouds more woolen than woolly, and the walls were painted cheerily in three strata—green, watery blue, and khaki. It was an echoing and gaping church, and presently it was packed, the aisles full. Professors with string mustaches and dog-eared Bibles, men students in sweaters or flannel shirts, earnest young women students in homemade muslin with modest ribbons, over-smiling old maids of the town, venerable saints from the back-country with beards which partly hid the fact that they wore collars without ties, old women with billowing shoulders, irritated young married couples with broods of babies who crawled, slid, bellowed, and stared with embarrassing wonder at bachelors.

Five minutes later Elmer would not have had a seat down front. Now he could not escape. He was packed in between his mother and a wheezing fat man, and in the aisle beside his pew stood evangelical tailors and ardent school-teachers.

The congregation swung into "When the Roll Is Called Up Yonder" and Elmer gave up his frenzied but impractical plans for escape. His mother nestled happily beside him, her hand proudly touching his sleeve, and he was stirred by the march and battle of the hymn:

When the trumpet of the Lord shall sound, and time shall
be no more,
And the morning breaks eternal, bright and fair. . . .

They stood for the singing of "Shall We Gather at the River?" Elmer inarticulately began to feel his community with these humble, aspiring people—his own prairie tribe: this gaunt carpenter, a good fellow, full of friendly greetings; this farm-wife, so courageous, channeled by pioneer labor; this class-mate, an admirable basket-ball player, yet now chanting beatifically, his head back, his eyes closed, his voice ringing. Elmer's own people. Could he be a traitor to them, could he resist the current of their united belief and longing?

Yes, we'll gather at the river,
The beautiful, the beautiful river,
Gather with the saints at the river
That flows by the throne of God.

Could he endure it to be away from them, in the chill void of Jim Lefferts' rationalizing, on that day when they should be rejoicing in the warm morning sunshine by the river rolling to the imperishable Throne?

And his voice—he had merely muttered the words of the first hymn—boomed out ungrudgingly:

Soon our pilgrimage will cease;
Soon our happy hearts will quiver
With the melody of peace.

His mother stroked his sleeve. He remembered that she had maintained he was the best singer she had ever heard; that Jim Lefferts had admitted, "You certainly can make that hymn dope sound as if it meant something." He noted that people near by looked about with pleasure when they heard his Big Ben dominate the cracked jangling.

The preliminaries merely warmed up the audience for Judson Roberts. Old Jud was in form. He laughed, he shouted, he knelt and wept with real tears, he loved everybody, he raced down into the audience and patted shoulders, and for the moment everybody felt that he was closer to them than their closest friends.

"Rejoiceth as a strong man to run a race," was his text.

Roberts was really a competent athlete, and he really had skill in evoking pictures. He described the Chicago-Michigan game, and Elmer was lost in him, with him lived the moments of the scrimmage, the long run with the ball, the bleachers rising to him.

Roberts' voice softened. He was pleading. He was not talking, he said, to weak men who needed coddling into the Kingdom, but to strong men, to rejoicing men, to men brave in armor. There was another sort of race more exhilarating than any game, and it led not merely to a score on a big board but to the making of a new world—it led not to newspaper paragraphs but to glory eternal. Dangerous—calling for strong men! Ecstatic—brimming with thrills! The team captained by Christ! No timid Jesus did he preach, but the adventurer who had joyed to associate with common men, with reckless fishermen, with captains and rulers, who had dared to face the soldiers in the garden, who had dared the myrmidons of Rome and death itself! Come! Who was gallant? Who had nerve? Who longed to live abundantly? Let them come!

They must confess their sins, they must repent, they must know their own weakness save as they were reborn in Christ. But they must confess not in heaven-pilfering weakness, but in training for the battle under the wind-torn banners of the Mighty Captain. Who would come? Who would come? Who was for vision and the great adventure?

He was among them, Judson Roberts, with his arms held out, his voice a bugle. Young men sobbed and knelt; a woman shrieked; people were elbowing the standers in the aisles and pushing forward to kneel in agonized happiness, and suddenly they were setting relentlessly on a bewildered Elmer Gantry, who had been betrayed into forgetting himself, into longing to be one with Judson Roberts.

His mother was wringing his hand, begging, "Oh, won't you come? Won't you make your old mother happy? Let yourself know the joy of surrender to Jesus!" She was weeping, old eyes puckered, and in her weeping was his every recollection of winter dawns when she had let him stay in bed and brought porridge to him across the icy floor; winter evenings when he had awakened to find her still stitching; and that confusing intimidating hour, in the abyss of his first memories, when he had seen her shaken beside a coffin that contained a cold monster in the shape of his father.

The basket-ball player was patting his other arm, begging, "Dear old Hell-cat, you've never let yourself be happy! You've been lonely! Let yourself be happy with us! You know I'm no mollycoddle. Won't you know the happiness of salvation with us?"

A thread-thin old man, very dignified, a man with secret eyes that had known battles and mountain-valleys, was holding out his hands to Elmer, imploring with a humility utterly disconcerting, "Oh, come, come with us—don't stand there making Jesus beg and beg—don't leave the Christ that died for us standing out in the cold, begging!"

And, somehow, flashing through the crowd, Judson Roberts was with Elmer, honoring him beyond all the multitude, appealing for his friendship—Judson Roberts the gorgeous, beseeching:

"Are you going to hurt me, Elmer? Are you going to let me go away miserable and beaten, old man? Are you going to betray me like Judas, when I've offered you my Jesus as the most precious gift I can bring you? Are you going to slap me and defile me and hurt me? Come! Think of the joy of being rid of all those nasty little sins that you've felt so ashamed of! Won't you come kneel with me, won't you?"

His mother shrieked, "Won't you, Elmer? With him and me? Won't you make us happy? Won't you be big enough to not be afraid? See how we're all longing for you, praying for you!"

"Yes!" from around him, from strangers; and "Help *me* to follow you, Brother—I'll go if you will!" Voices woven, thick, dove-white and terrifying black of mourning and lightning-colored, flung around him, binding him— His mother's pleading, Judson Roberts' tribute—

An instant he saw Jim Lefferts, and heard him insist: "Why, sure, course they believe it. They hypnotize themselves. But don't let 'em hypnotize you!"

He saw Jim's eyes, that for him alone veiled their bright harshness and became lonely, asking for comradeship. He struggled; with all the blubbering confusion of a small boy set on by his elders, frightened and overwhelmed, he longed to be honest, to be true to Jim—to be true to himself and his own good honest sins and whatsoever penalties they might carry. Then the visions were driven away by voices that closed over him like surf above an exhausted swimmer. Volitionless, marveling at the sight of himself as a pinioned giant, he was being urged forward, forced forward, his mother on one arm and Judson on the other, a rhapsodic mob following.

Bewildered. Miserable. . . . False to Jim.

But as he came to the row kneeling in front of the first pew, he had a thought that made everything all right. Yes! He could have both! He could keep Judson and his mother, yet retain Jim's respect. He had only to bring Jim also to Jesus, then all of them would be together in beatitude!

Freed from misery by that revelation, he knelt, and suddenly his voice was noisy in confession, while the shouts of the audience, the ejaculations of Judson and his mother, exalted him to hot self-approval and made it seem splendidly right to yield to the mystic fervor.

He had but little to do with what he said. The willing was not his but the mob's; the phrases were not his but those of the emotional preachers and hysterical worshipers whom he had heard since babyhood:

"O God, oh, I have sinned! My sins are heavy on me! I am unworthy of compassion! O Jesus, intercede for me! Oh, let thy blood that was shed for me be my salvation! O God, I do truly repent of my great sinning and I do long for the everlasting peace of thy bosom!"

"Oh, praise God," from the multitude, and "Praise his holy name! Thank God, thank God, thank God! Oh, hallelujah, Brother, thank the dear loving God!"

He was certain that he would never again want to guzzle, to follow loose women, to blaspheme; he knew the rapture of salvation—yes, and of being the center of interest in the crowd.

Others about him were beating their foreheads, others were shrieking, "Lord, be merciful," and one woman—he remembered her as a strange, repressed, mad-eyed special student who was not known to have any friends—was stretched out, oblivious of the crowd, jerking, her limbs twitching, her hands clenched, panting rhythmically.

But it was Elmer, tallest of the converts, tall as Judson Roberts, whom all the students and most of the townpeople found important, who found himself important.

His mother was crying, "Oh, this is the happiest hour of my life, dear! This makes up for everything!"

To be able to give her such delight!

Judson was clawing Elmer's hand, whooping, "Liked to had you on the team at Chicago, but I'm a lot gladder to have you with me on Christ's team! If you knew how proud I am!"

To be thus linked forever with Judson!

Elmer's embarrassment was gliding into a robust self-satisfaction.

Then the others were crowding on him, shaking his hand, congratulating him: the football center, the Latin professor, the town grocer. President Quarles, his chin whisker vibrant and his shaven upper lip wiggling from side to side, was insisting, "Come, Brother Elmer, stand up on the platform and say a few words to us—you must—we all need it—we're thrilled by your splendid example!' "

Elmer was not quite sure how he got through the converts, up the steps to the platform. He suspected afterward that Judson Roberts had done a good deal of trained pushing.

He looked down, something of his panic returning. But they were sobbing with affection for him. The Elmer Gantry who had for years pretended that he relished defying the whole college had for those same years desired popularity. He had it now—popularity, almost love, almost reverence, and he felt overpoweringly his rôle as leading man.

He was stirred to more flamboyant confession:

"Oh, for the first time I know the peace of God! Nothing I have ever done has been right, because it didn't lead to the way and the truth! Here I thought I was a good church-member, but all the time I hadn't seen the real light. I'd never been willing to kneel down and confess myself a miserable sinner. But I'm kneeling now, and, oh, the blessedness of humility!"

He wasn't, to be quite accurate, kneeling at all; he was standing up, very tall and broad, waving his hands; and though what he was experiencing may have been the blessedness of humility, it sounded like his announcements of an ability to lick anybody in any given saloon. But he was greeted with flaming hallelujahs, and he shouted on till he was rapturous and very sweaty:

"Come! Come to him now! Oh, it's funny that I who've been so great a sinner could dare to give you his invitation, but he's almighty and shall prevail, and he giveth his sweet tidings through the mouths of babes and sucklings and the most unworthy, and, lo, the strong shall be confounded and the weak exalted in his sight!"

It was all, the Mithraic phrasing, as familiar as "Good morning" or "How are you?" to the audience, yet he must have put new violence into it, for instead of smiling at the recency of his ardor they looked at him gravely, and suddenly a miracle was beheld.

Ten minutes after his own experience, Elmer made his first conversion.

A pimply youth, long known as a pool-room tout, leaped up, his greasy face working, shrieked, "O God, forgive me!" butted in frenzy through the crowd, ran to the mourners' bench, lay with his mouth frothing in convulsion.

Then the hallelujahs rose till they drowned Elmer's accelerated pleading, then Judson Roberts stood with his arm about Elmer's shoulder, then Elmer's mother knelt with a light of paradise on her face, and they closed the meeting in a maniac pealing of

Draw me nearer, blessed Lord,
To thy precious bleeding side.

Elmer felt himself victorious over life and king of righteousness.

But it had been only the devoted, the people who had come early and taken front seats, of whom he had been conscious in his transports. The students who had remained at the back of the church now loitered outside the door in murmurous knots, and as Elmer and his mother passed them, they stared, they even chuckled, and he was suddenly cold. . . .

It was hard to give heed to his mother's wails of joy all the way to her boarding-house.

"Now don't you dare think of getting up early to see me off on the train," she insisted. "All I have to do is just to carry my little valise across the street. You'll need your sleep, after all this stirrin' up you've had tonight—I was so proud—I've never known anybody to really wrestle with the Lord like you did. Oh, Elmy, you'll stay true? You've made your old mother so happy! All my life I've sorrowed, I've waited, I've prayed, and now I shan't ever sorrow again! Oh, you will stay true?"

He threw the last of his emotional reserve into a ringing, "You bet I will, Ma!" and kissed her good-night.

He had no emotion left with which to face walking alone, in a cold and realistic night, down a street not of shining columns but of cottages dumpy amid the bleak snow and unfriendly under the bitter stars.

His plan of saving Jim Lefferts, his vision of Jim with reverent and beatific eyes, turned into a vision of Jim with extremely irate eyes and a lot to say. With that vanishment his own glory vanished.

"Was I," he wondered, "just a plain damn' fool?

"Jim warned me they'd nab me if I lost my head.

"Now I suppose I can't ever even smoke again without going to hell."

But he wanted a smoke. Right now!

He had a smoke.

It comforted him but little as he fretted on:

"There *wasn't* any fake about it! I really did repent all these darn' fool sins. Even smoking—I'm going to cut it out. I did feel the—the peace of God.

"But can I keep up this speed? Christ! I can't *do* it! Never take a drink or anything—

"I wonder if the Holy Ghost really was there and getting after me? I did feel different! I did! Or was it just because Judson and Ma and all those Christers were there whooping it up—

"Jud Roberts kidded me into it. With all his Big Brother stuff. Prob'ly pulls it everywhere he goes. Jim'll claim I— Oh, damn Jim, too! I got some rights! None of his business if I come out and do the fair square thing! And they *did* look up to me when I gave them the invitation! It went off fine and dandy! And that kid coming right up and getting saved. Mighty few fellows ever've pulled off a conversion as soon after their own conversion as I did! Moody or none of 'em! I'll bet it busts the records! Yes, sir, maybe they're right. Maybe the Lord has got some great use for me, even if I ain't always been all I might of been . . . some ways . . . but I was never mean or tough or anything like that . . . just had a good time.

"Jim—what right's he got telling me where I head in? Trouble with him is, he thinks he knows it all. I guess these wise old coots that've written all these books about the Bible, I guess they know more'n one smart-aleck Kansas agnostic!

"Yes, sir! The whole crowd! Turned to me like I was an All-American preacher!

"Wouldn't be so bad to be a preacher if you had a big church and— Lot easier than digging out law-cases and having to put it over a jury and another lawyer maybe smarter'n you are.

"The crowd have to swallow what you tell 'em in a pulpit, and no back-talk or cross-examination allowed!"

For a second he snickered, but:

"Not nice to talk that way. Even if a fellow don't do what's right himself, no excuse for his sneering at fellows that do, like preachers. . . . There's where Jim makes his mistake.

"Not worthy to be a preacher. But if Jim Lefferts thinks for one single solitary second that I'm afraid to be a preacher because *he* pulls a lot of guff— I guess *I* know how I felt when I stood up and had all them folks hollering and rejoicing— I guess *I* know whether I experienced salvation or not! And I don't require any James Blaine Lefferts to tell me, neither!"

Thus for an hour of dizzy tramping; now colder with doubt than with the prairie wind, now winning back some of the exaltation of his spiritual adventure, but always knowing that he had to confess to an inexorable Jim.

IV

It was after one. Surely Jim would be asleep, and by next day there might be a miracle. Morning always promises miracles.

He eased the door open, holding it with a restraining hand. There was a light on the washstand beside Jim's bed, but it was a small kerosene lamp turned low. He tiptoed in, his tremendous feet squeaking.

Jim suddenly sat up, turned up the wick. He was red-nosed, red-eyed, and coughing. He stared, and unmoving, by the table, Elmer stared back.

Jim spoke abruptly:

"You son of a sea-cook! You've gone and done it! You've been *saved!* You've let them hornswoggle you into being a Baptist witch-doctor! I'm through! You can go—to heaven!"

"Aw, say now, Jim, lissen!"

"I've listened enough. I've got nothing more to say. And now you listen to me!" said Jim, and he spoke with tongues for three minutes straight.

Most of the night they struggled for the freedom of Elmer's soul, with Jim not quite losing yet never winning. As Jim's face had hovered at the gospel meeting between him and the evangelist, blotting out the vision of the cross, so now the faces of his mother and Judson hung sorrowful and misty before him, a veil across Jim's pleading.

Elmer slept four hours and went out, staggering with weariness, to bring cinnamon buns, a wienie sandwich, and a tin pail of coffee for Jim's breakfast. They were laboring windily into new arguments, Jim a little more stubborn,

Elmer ever more irritable, when no less a dignitary than President the Rev. Dr. Willoughby Quarles, chin whisker, glacial shirt, bulbous waistcoat and all, plunged in under the fat soft wing of the landlady.

The president shook hands a number of times with everybody, he eyebrowed the landlady out of the room, and boomed in his throaty pulpit voice, with belly-rumblings and long-drawn R's and L's, a voice very deep and owlish, most holy and fitting to the temple which he created merely by his presence, rebuking to flippancy and chuckles and the puerile cynicisms of the Jim Leffertses—a noise somewhere between the evening bells and the morning jackass:

"Oh, Brother Elmer, that was a brave thing you did! I have never seen a braver! For a great strong man of your gladiatorial powers to not be afraid to humble himself! And your example will do a great deal of good, a grrrrrreat deal of good! And we must catch and hold it. You are to speak at the Y.M.C.A. tonight—special meeting to reënforce the results of our wonderful Prayer Week."

"Oh, gee, President, I can't!" Elmer groaned.

"Oh, yes, Brother, you must. You *must!* It's already announced. If you'll go out within the next hour, you'll be gratified to see posters announcing it all over town!"

"But I can't make a speech!"

"The Lord will give the words if you give the good will! I myself shall call for you at a quarter to seven. God bless you!"

He was gone.

Elmer was completely frightened, completely unwilling, and swollen with delight that after long dark hours when Jim, an undergraduate, had used him dirtily and thrown clods at his intellect, the president of Terwillinger College should have welcomed him to that starched bosom as a fellow-apostle.

While Elmer was making up his mind to do what he had made up his mind to do, Jim crawled into bed and addressed the Lord in a low poisonous tone.

Elmer went out to see the posters. His name was in lovely large letters.

For an hour, late that afternoon, after various classes in which every one looked at him respectfully, Elmer tried to prepare his address for the Y.M.C.A. and affiliated lady worshipers. Jim was sleeping, with a snore like the snarl of a leopard.

In his class in Public Speaking, a course designed to create congressmen, bishops, and sales-managers, Elmer had had to produce discourses on Taxation, the Purpose of God in History, Our Friend the Dog, and the Glory of the American Constitution. But his monthly orations had not been too arduous; no one had grieved if he stole all his ideas and most of his phrasing from the encyclopedia. The most important part of preparation had been the lubrication of his polished-mahogany voice with throat-lozenges after rather steady and totally forbidden smoking. He had learned nothing except the placing of his voice. It had never seemed momentous to impress the nineteen students of oratory and the instructor, an unordained licensed preacher who had formerly been a tax-assessor in Oklahoma. He had, in Public Speaking, never been a failure nor ever for one second interesting.

Now, sweating very much, he perceived that he was expected to think, to articulate the curious desires whereby Elmer Gantry was slightly different from any other human being, and to rivet together opinions which would not be floated on any tide of hallelujahs.

He tried to remember the sermons he had heard. But the preachers had been so easily convinced of their authority as prelates, so freighted with ponderous messages, while himself, he was not at the moment certain whether he was a missionary who had to pass his surprising new light on to the multitude, or just a sinner who—

Just a sinner! For keeps! Nothing else! Damned if he'd welsh on old Jim! No, *sir!* Or welsh on Juanita, who'd stood for him and merely kidded him, no matter how soused and rough and mouthy he might be! . . . Her hug. The way she'd get rid of that buttinsky aunt of Nell's; just wink at him and give Aunty some song and dance or other and send her out for chow—

God! If Juanita were only here! She'd give him the real dope. She'd advise him whether he ought to tell Prexy and the Y.M. to go to hell or grab this chance to show Eddie

Fislinger and all those Y.M. highbrows that he wasn't such a bonehead—

No! Here Prexy had said he was the whole cheese; gotten up a big meeting for him. Prexy Quarles and Juanita! Aber nit! Never get them two together! And Prexy had called on him—

Suppose it got into the newspapers! How he'd saved a tough kid, just as good as Judson Roberts could do. Juanita—find skirts like her any place, but where could they find a guy that could start in and save souls right off the bat?

Chuck all these fool thoughts, now that Jim was asleep, and figure out his spiel. What was that about sweating in the vineyard? Something like that, anyway. In the Bible. . . . However much they might rub it in—and no gink'd ever had a worse time, with that sneaking Eddie poking him on one side and Jim lambasting him on the other—whatever happened, he had to show those yahoos he could do just as good—

Hell! This wasn't buying the baby any shoes; this wasn't getting his spiel done. But—

What was the doggone thing to be *about*?

Let's see now. Gee, there was a bully thought! Tell 'em about how a strong husky guy, the huskier he was the more he could afford to admit that the power of the Holy Ghost had just laid him out cold—

No. Hell! That was what Old Jud had said. Must have something new—kinda new, anyway.

He shouldn't say "hell." Cut it out. Stay converted, no matter how hard it was. *He* wasn't afraid of— Him and Old Jud, they were husky enough to—

No, sir! It wasn't Old Jud; it was his mother. What'd she think if she ever saw him with Juanita? Juanita! That sloppy brat! No modesty!

Had to get down to brass tacks. Now!

Elmer grasped the edge of his work-table. The top cracked. His strength pleased him. He pulled up his dingy red sweater, smoothed his huge biceps, and again tackled his apostolic labors:

Let's see now: The fellows at the Y. would expect him to say—

He had it! Nobody ever amounted to a darn except as the—what was it?—as the inscrutable designs of Providence intended him to be.

Elmer was very busy making vast and unformed scrawls in a ten-cent note-book hitherto devoted to German. He darted up, looking scholarly, and gathered his library about him: his Bible, given to him by his mother; his New Testament, given by a Sunday School teacher; his text-books in Weekly Bible and Church History; and one-fourteenth of a fourteen-volume set of Great Orations of the World which, in a rare and alcoholic moment of bibliomania, he had purchased in Cato for seventeen cents. He piled them and repiled them and tapped them with his fountain-pen.

His original stimulus had run out entirely.

Well, he'd get help from the Bible. It was all inspired, every word, no matter what scoffers like Jim said. He'd take the first text he turned to and talk on that.

He opened on: "Now *therefore*, Tatnai, governor beyond the river, Shethar-boznai, and your companions the Apharsachites, which *are* beyond the river, be ye far from thence," an injunction spirited but not at present helpful.

He returned to pulling his luxuriant hair and scratching.

Golly. Must be something.

The only way of putting it all over life was to understand these Forces that the scientists, with their laboratories and everything, couldn't savvy, but to a real Christian they were just as easy as rolling off a log—

No. He hadn't taken any lab courses except Chemistry I, so he couldn't show where all these physicists and biologists were boobs.

Elmer forlornly began to cross out the lovely scrawls he had made in his note-book.

He was irritably conscious that Jim was awake, and scoffing:

"Having quite a time being holy and informative, Hell-cat? Why don't you pinch your first sermon from the heathen? You won't be the first up-and-coming young messiah to do it!"

Jim shied a thin book at him, and sank again into infidel sleep. Elmer picked up the book. It was a selection from the writings of Robert G. Ingersoll.

Elmer was indignant.

Take his speech from Ingersoll, that rotten old atheist that said—well, anyway, he criticized the Bible and everything! Fellow that couldn't believe the Bible, least he could do was not to disturb the faith of others. Darn' rotten thing to do! Fat nerve of Jim to suggest his pinching anything from Ingersoll! He'd throw the book in the fire!

But— Anything was better than going on straining his brains. He forgot his woes by drugging himself with heedless reading. He drowsed through page on page of Ingersoll's rhetoric and jesting. Suddenly he sat up, looked suspiciously over at the silenced Jim, looked suspiciously at Heaven. He grunted, hesitated, and began rapidly to copy into the German note-book, from Ingersoll:

> Love is the only bow on life's dark cloud. It is the Morning and the Evening Star. It shines upon the cradle of the babe, and sheds its radiance upon the quiet tomb. It is the mother of Art, inspirer of poet, patriot and philosopher. It is the air and light of every heart, builder of every home, kindler of every fire on every hearth. It was the first to dream of immortality. It fills the world with melody, for Music is the voice of Love. Love is the magician, the enchanter, that changes worthless things to joy, and makes right royal kings and queens of common clay. It is the perfume of the wondrous flower—the heart—and without that sacred passion, that divine swoon, we are less than beasts; but with it, earth is heaven and we are gods.

Only for a moment, while he was copying, did he look doubtful; then:

"Rats! Chances are nobody there tonight has ever read Ingersoll. Agin him. Besides I'll kind of change it around."

V

When President Quarles called for him, Elmer's exhortation was outlined, and he had changed to his Sunday-best blue serge double-breasted suit and sleeked his hair.

As they departed, Jim called Elmer back from the hall to whisper, "Say, Hell-cat, you won't forget to give credit to Ingersoll, and to me for tipping you off, will you?"

"You go to hell!" said Elmer.

VI

There was a sizable and extremely curious gathering at the Y.M.C.A. All day the campus had debated, "Did Hell-cat really sure-enough get saved? Is he going to cut out his hell-raising?"

Every man he knew was present, their gaping mouths dripping question-marks, grinning or doubtful. Their leers confused him, and he was angry at being introduced by Eddie Fislinger, president of the Y.M.C.A.

He started coldly, stammering. But Ingersoll had provided the beginning of his discourse, and he warmed to the splendor of his own voice. He saw the audience in the curving Y.M.C.A. auditorium as a radiant cloud, and he began to boom confidently, he began to add to his outline impressive ideas which were altogether his own—except, perhaps, as he had heard them thirty or forty times in sermons.

It sounded very well, considering. Certainly it compared well with the average mystical rhapsody of the pulpit.

For all his slang, his cursing, his mauled plurals and singulars, Elmer had been compelled in college to read certain books, to hear certain lectures, all filled with flushed, florid polysyllables, with juicy sentiments about God, sunsets, the moral improvement inherent in a daily view of mountain scenery, angels, fishing for souls, fishing for fish, ideals, patriotism, democracy, purity, the error of Providence in creating the female leg, courage, humility, justice, the agricultural methods of Palestine *circ.* 4 A.D., the beauty of domesticity, and preachers' salaries. These blossoming words, these organ-like phrases, these profound notions, had been rammed home till they stuck in his brain, ready for use.

But even to the schoolboy-wearied faculty who had done the ramming, who ought to have seen the sources, it was still astonishing that after four years of grunting, Elmer Gantry should come out with these flourishes, which they took perfectly seriously, for they themselves had been nurtured in minute Baptist and Campbellite colleges.

Not one of them considered that there could be anything comic in the spectacle of a large young man, divinely fitted for coal-heaving, standing up and wallowing in thick slippery words about Love and the Soul. They sat—young instructors not long from the farm, professors pale from years of napping in unaired pastoral studies—and looked at Elmer respectfully as he throbbed:

"It's awful' hard for a fellow that's more used to bucking the line than to talking publicly to express how he means, but sometimes I guess maybe you think about a lot of things even if you don't always express how you mean, and I want to—what I want to talk about is how if a fellow looks down deep into things and is really square with God, and lets God fill his heart with higher aspirations, he sees that—he sees that Love is the one thing that can really sure-enough lighten all of life's dark clouds.

"Yes, sir, just Love! It's the morning and evening star. It's—even in the quiet tomb, I mean those that are around the quiet tomb, you find it even there. What is it that inspires all great men, all poets and patriots and philosophers? It's Love, isn't it? What gave the world its first evidences of immortality? Love! It fills the world with melody, for what is music? What is music? Why! *Music is the voice of Love!*"

The great President Quarles leaned back and put on his spectacles, which gave a slight appearance of learning to his chin-whiskered countenance, otherwise that of a small-town banker in 1850. He was the center of a row of a dozen initiates on the platform of the Y.M.C.A. auditorium, a shallow platform under a plaster half-dome. The wall behind them was thick with diagrams, rather like anatomical charts, showing the winning of souls in Egypt, the amount spent on whisky versus the amount spent on hymn-books, and the illustrated progress of a pilgrim from Unclean Speech through Cigarette Smoking and Beer Saloons to a lively situation in which he beat his wife, who seemed to dislike it. Above was a large and enlightening motto: "Be not overcome of evil, but overcome evil with good."

The whole place had that damp-straw odor characteristic of places of worship, but President Quarles did not, seemingly, suffer in it. All his life he had lived in tabernacles and in rooms devoted to thin church periodicals and thick volumes of sermons. He had a slight constant snuffle, but his organism was apparently adapted now to existing without air. He beamed and rubbed his hands, and looked with devout joy on Elmer's long broad back as Elmer snapped into it, ever surer of himself; as he bellowed at the audience—beating them, breaking through their interference, making a touchdown:

"What is it makes us different from the animals? The passion of Love! Without it, we are—in fact we are nothing; with it, earth is heaven, and we are, I mean to some extent, like God himself! Now that's what I wanted to explain about Love, and here's how it applies. Prob'ly there's a whole lot of you like myself—oh, I been doing it, I'm not going to spare myself—I been going along thinking I was too good, too big, too smart, for the divine love of the Savior! Say! Any of you ever stop and think how much you're handing yourself when you figure you can get along without divine intercession? Say! I suppose prob'ly you're bigger than Moses, bigger than St. Paul, bigger than Pastewer, that great scientist—"

President Quarles was exulting, "It was a genuine conversion! But more than that! Here's a true discovery—my discovery! Elmer is a born preacher, once he lets himself go, and I can make him do it! O Lord, how mysterious are thy ways! Thou hast chosen to train our young brother not so much in prayer as in the mighty struggles of the Olympic field! I—thou, Lord, hast produced a born preacher. Some day he'll be one of our leading prophets!"

The audience clapped when Elmer hammered out his conclusion: "—and you Freshmen will save a lot of the time that I wasted if you see right now that until you know God you know—just nothing!"

They clapped, they made their faces to shine upon him. Eddie Fislinger won him by sighing, "Old fellow, you got me beat at my own game like you have at your game!" There was much hand-shaking. None of it was more ardent than that of his recent enemy, the Latin professor, who breathed:

"Where did you get all those fine ideas and metaphors about the Divine Love, Gantry?"

"Oh," modestly, "I can't hardly call them mine, Professor. I guess I just got them by praying."

VII

Judson Roberts, ex-football-star, state secretary of the Y.M.C.A., was on the train to Concordia, Kansas. In the vestibule he had three puffs of an illegal cigarette and crushed it out.

"No, really, it wasn't so bad for him, that Elmer what's-his-name, to get converted. Suppose there *isn't* anything to it. Won't hurt him to cut out some of his bad habits for a while, anyway. And how do we know? Maybe the Holy Ghost does come down. No more improbable than electricity. I do wish I could get over this doubting! I forget it when I've got 'em going in an evangelistic meeting, but when I watch a big butcher like him, with that damn' silly smirk on his jowls— I believe I'll go into the real estate business. I don't think I'm hurting these young fellows any, but I do wish I could be honest. Oh, Lordy, Lordy, Lordy, I wish I had a good job selling real estate!"

VIII

Elmer walked home firmly. "Just what right has Mr. James B. Lefferts got to tell me I mustn't use my ability to get a crowd going? And I certainly had 'em going! Never knew I could spiel like that. Easy as feetball! And Prexy saying I was a born preacher! Huh!"

Firmly and resentfully he came into their room, and slammed down his hat.

It awoke Jim. "How'd it go over? Hand 'em out the gospel guff?"

"I did!" Elmer trumpeted. "It went over, as you put it, corking. Got any objections?"

He lighted the largest lamp and turned it up full, his back to Jim.

No answer. When he looked about, Jim seemed asleep.

At seven next morning he said forgivingly, rather patronizingly, "I'll be gone till ten—bring you back some breakfast?"

Jim answered, "No, thanks," and those were his only words that morning.

When Elmer came in at ten-thirty, Jim was gone, his possessions gone. (It was no great moving: three suitcases of clothes, an armful of books.) There was a note on the table:

I shall live at the College Inn the rest of this year. You can probably get Eddie Fislinger to live with you. You would enjoy it. It has been stimulating to watch you try to be an honest roughneck, but I think it would be almost too stimulating to watch you become a spiritual leader.

J.B.L.

All of Elmer's raging did not make the room seem less lonely.

Chapter IV

PRESIDENT QUARLES urged him.

Elmer would, perhaps, affect the whole world if he became a minister. What glory for Old Terwillinger and all the shrines of Gritzmacher Springs!

Eddie Fislinger urged him.

"Jiminy! You'd go way beyond me! I can see you president of the Baptist convention!" Elmer still did not like Eddie, but he was making much now of ignoring Jim Lefferts (they met on the street and bowed ferociously), and he had to have some one to play valet to his virtues.

The ex-minister dean of the college urged him.

Where could Elmer find a profession with a better social position than the ministry—thousands listening to him—invited to banquets and everything. So much easier than—Well, not exactly easier; all ministers worked arduously—great sacrifices—constant demands on their sympathy—heroic struggle against vice—but same time, elegant and superior work, surrounded by books, high thoughts, and the finest ladies in the city or country as the case might be. And cheaper professional training than law. With scholarships and outside preaching, Elmer could get through the three years of Mizpah Theological Seminary on almost nothing a year. What other plans *had* he for a career? Nothing definite? Why, looked like divine intervention; certainly did; let's call it settled. Perhaps he could get Elmer a scholarship the very first year—

His mother urged him.

She wrote, daily, that she was longing, praying, sobbing—

Elmer urged himself.

He had no prospects except the chance of reading law in the dingy office of a cousin in Toluca, Kansas. The only things he had against the ministry, now that he was delivered from Jim, were the low salaries and the fact that if ministers were caught drinking or flirting, it was often very hard on them. The salaries weren't so bad—he'd go to the top, of course, and maybe make eight or ten thousand. But the diversions— He thought about it so much that he made a hasty trip to Cato, and came back temporarily cured forever of any desire for wickedness.

The greatest urge was his memory of holding his audience, playing on them. To move people— Golly! He wanted to be addressing somebody on something right now, and being applauded!

By this time he was so rehearsed in his rôle of candidate for righteousness that it didn't bother him (so long as no snickering Jim was present) to use the most embarrassing theological and moral terms in the presence of Eddie or the president; and without one grin he rolled out dramatic speeches about "the duty of every man to lead every other man to Christ," and "the historic position of the Baptists as the one true Scriptural Church, practising immersion, as taught by Christ himself."

He was persuaded. He saw himself as a white-browed and star-eyed young evangel, wearing a new frock coat, standing up in a pulpit and causing hundreds of beautiful women to weep with conviction and rush down to clasp his hand.

But there was one barrier, extremely serious. They all informed him that select though he was as sacred material, before he decided he must have a mystic experience known as a Call. God himself must appear and call him to service, and conscious though Elmer was now of his own powers and the excellence of the church, he saw no more of God about the place than in his worst days of unregeneracy.

He asked the president and the dean if they had had a Call. Oh, yes, certainly; but they were vague about practical tips as to how to invite a Call and recognize it when it came. He was reluctant to ask Eddie—Eddie would be only too profuse with tips, and want to kneel down and pray with him, and generally be rather damp and excitable and messy.

The Call did not come, not for weeks, with Easter past and no decision as to what he was going to do next year.

II

Spring on the prairie, high spring. Lilacs masked the speckled brick and stucco of the college buildings, spiræa made a flashing wall, and from the Kansas fields came soft airs and the whistle of meadow larks.

Students loafed at their windows, calling down to friends; they played catch on the campus; they went bareheaded and wrote a great deal of poetry; and the Terwillinger baseball team defeated Fogelquist College.

Still Elmer did not receive his divine Call.

By day, playing catch, kicking up his heels, belaboring his acquaintances, singing "The happiest days that ever were, we knew at old Terwillinger" on a fence fondly believed to resemble the Yale fence, or tramping by himself through the minute forest of cottonwood and willow by Tunker Creek, he expanded with the expanding year and knew happiness.

The nights were unadulterated hell.

He felt guilty that he had no Call, and he went to the president about it in mid-May.

Dr. Quarles was thoughtful, and announced:

"Brother Elmer, the last thing I'd ever want to do, in fairness to the spirit of the ministry, would be to create an illusion of a Call when there was none present. That would be like the pagan hallucinations worked on the poor suffering followers of Roman Catholicism. Whatever else he may be, a Baptist preacher must be free from illusions; he must found his work on good hard scientific *facts*—the proven facts of the Bible, and substitutionary atonement, which even pragmatically we know to be true, because it works. No, no! But at the same time I feel sure the voice of God is calling you, if you can but hear it, and I want to help you lift the veil of worldliness which still, no doubt, deafens your inner ear. Will you come to my house tomorrow evening? We'll take the matter to the Lord in prayer."

It was all rather dreadful.

That kindly spring evening, with a breeze fresh in the branches of the sycamores, President Quarles had shut the windows and drawn the blinds in his living-room, an apartment filled with crayon portraits of Baptist worthies, red-plush chairs, and leaded-glass unit bookcases containing the lay writings of the more poetic clergy. The president had gathered as assistants in prayer the more aged and fundamentalist ex-pastors on the faculty and the more milky and elocutionary of the Y.M.C.A. leaders, headed by Eddie Fislinger.

When Elmer entered, they were on their knees, their arms on the seats of reversed chairs, their heads bowed, all praying aloud and together. They looked up at him like old women surveying the bride. He wanted to bolt. Then the president nabbed him, and had him down on his knees, suffering and embarrassed and wondering what the devil to pray about.

They took turns at telling God what he ought to do in the case of "our so ardently and earnestly seeking brother."

"Now will you lift your voice in prayer, Brother Elmer? Just let yourself go. Remember we're all with you, all loving and helping you," grated the president.

They crowded near him. The president put his stiff old arm about Elmer's shoulder. It felt like a dry bone, and the president smelled of kerosene. Eddie crowded up on the other side and nuzzled against him. The others crept in, patting him. It was horribly hot in that room, and they were so close—he felt as if he were tied down in a hospital ward. He looked up and saw the long shaven face, the thin tight lips, of a minister . . . whom he was now to emulate.

He prickled with horror, but he tried to pray. He wailed, "O blessed Lord, help me to—help me to—"

He had an enormous idea. He sprang up. He cried, "Say, I think the spirit is beginning to work and maybe if I just went out and took a short walk and kinda prayed by myself, while you stayed here and prayed for me, it might help."

"I don't think that would be the way," began the president, but the most aged faculty-member suggested, "Maybe it's the Lord's guidance. We hadn't ought to interfere with the Lord's guidance, Brother Quarles."

"That's so, that's so," the president announced. "You have your walk, Brother Elmer, and pray hard, and we'll stay here and besiege the throne of grace for you."

Elmer blundered out into the fresh clean air.

Whatever happened, he was never going back! How he hated their soft, crawly, wet hands!

He had notions of catching the last train to Cato and getting solacingly drunk. No. He'd lose his degree, just a month off now, and be cramped later in appearing as a real, high-class, college-educated lawyer.

Lose it, then! Anything but go back to their crawling creepy hands, their aged breathing by his ear—

He'd get hold of somebody and say he felt sick and send him back to tell Prexy and sneak off to bed. Cinch! He just wouldn't get his Call, just pass it up, by Jiminy, and not have to go into the ministry.

But to lose the chance to stand before thousands and stir them by telling about divine love and the evening and morning star— If he could just stand it till he got through theological seminary and was on the job— Then, if any Eddie Fislinger tried to come into his study and breathe down his neck—throw him out, by golly!

He was conscious that he was leaning against a tree, tearing down twigs, and that facing him under a street-lamp was Jim Lefferts.

"You look sick, Hell-cat," said Jim.

Elmer strove for dignity, then broke, with a moaning, "Oh, I am! What did I ever get into this religious fix for?"

"What they doing to you? Never mind; don't tell me. You need a drink."

"By God, I do!"

"I've got a quart of first-rate corn whisky from a moonshiner I've dug up out here in the country, and my room's right in this block. Come along."

Through his first drink, Elmer was quiet, bewildered, vaguely leaning on the Jim who would guide him away from this horror.

But he was out of practice in drinking, and the whisky took hold with speed. By the middle of the second glass he was boasting of his ecclesiastical eloquence, he was permitting Jim to know that never in Terwillinger College had there appeared so promising an orator, that right now they were there praying for him, waiting for him, the president and the whole outfit!

"But," with a slight return of apology, "I suppose prob'ly you think maybe I hadn't ought to go back to 'em."

Jim was standing by the open window, saying slowly, "No. I think now— You'd better go back. I've got some peppermints. They'll fix your breath, more or less. Good-by, Hell-cat."

He had won even over old Jim!

He was master of the world, and only a very little bit drunk.

He stepped out high and happy. Everything was extremely beautiful. How high the trees were! What a wonderful drug-store window, with all those glossy new magazine covers! That distant piano—magic. What exquisite young women the co-eds! What lovable and sturdy men the students! He was at peace with everything. What a really good fellow he was! He'd lost all his meannesses. How kind he'd been to that poor lonely sinner, Jim Lefferts. Others might despair of Jim's soul—he never would.

Poor old Jim. His room had looked terrible—that narrow little room with a cot, all in disorder, a pair of shoes and a corncob pipe lying on a pile of books. Poor Jim. He'd forgive him. Go around and clean up the room for him.

(Not that Elmer had ever cleaned up their former room.)

Gee, what a lovely spring night! How corking those old boys were, Prexy and everybody, to give up an evening and pray for him!

Why was it he felt so fine? Of course! The Call had come! God had come to him, though just spiritually, not corporeally, so far as he remembered. It had come! He could go ahead and rule the world!

He dashed into the president's house; he shouted from the door, erect, while they knelt and looked up at him mousily, "It's come! I feel it in everything! God just opened my eyes and made me feel what a wonderful ole world it is, and it was just like I could hear his voice saying, 'Don't you want to love everybody and help them to be happy? Do you want to just go along being selfish, or have you got a longing to—to help everybody?' "

He stopped. They had listened silently, with interested grunts of "Amen, Brother."

"Honest, it was awful' impressive. Somehow, something has made me feel so much better than when I went away from here. I'm sure it was a real Call. Don't you think so, President?"

"Oh, I'm sure of it!" the president ejaculated, getting up hastily and rubbing his knees.

"I feel that all is right with our brother; that he has now, this sacred moment, heard the voice of God, and is entering upon the highest calling in the sight of God," the president observed to the dean. "Don't you feel so?"

"God be praised," said the dean, and looked at his watch.

III

On their way home, they two alone, the oldest faculty-member said to the dean, "Yes, it was a fine gratifying moment. And—herumph!—slightly surprising. I'd hardly thought that young Gantry would go on being content with the mild blisses of salvation. Herumph! Curious smell of peppermint he had about him."

"I suppose he stopped at the drug-store during his walk and had a soft drink of some kind. Don't know, Brother," said the dean, "that I approve of these soft drinks. Innocent in themselves, but they might lead to carelessness in beverages. A man who drinks ginger ale—how are you going to impress on him the terrible danger of drinking *ale*?"

"Yes, yes," said the oldest faculty-member (he was sixty-eight, to the dean's boyish sixty). "Say, Brother, how do you feel about young Gantry? About his entering the ministry? I know you did well in the pulpit before you came here, as I more or less did myself, but if you were a boy of twenty-one or -two, do you think you'd become a preacher now, way things are?"

"Why, Brother!" grieved the dean. "Certainly I would! What a question! What would become of all our work at Terwillinger, all our ideals in opposition to the heathenish large universities, if the ministry weren't the highest ideal—"

"I know. I know. I just wonder sometimes— All the new vocations that are coming up. Medicine. Advertising. World just going it! I tell you, Dean, in another forty years, by 1943, men will be up in the air in flying machines, going maybe a hundred miles an hour!"

"My dear fellow, if the Lord had meant men to fly, he'd have given us wings."

"But there are prophecies in the Book—"

"Those refer purely to spiritual and symbolic flying. No, no! Never does to oppose the clear purpose of the Bible, and

I could dig you out a hundred texts that show unquestionably that the Lord intends us to stay right here on earth till that day when we shall be upraised in the body with him."

"Herumph! Maybe. Well, here's my corner. Good night, Brother."

The dean came into his house. It was a small house.

"How'd it go?" asked his wife.

"Splendid. Young Gantry seemed to feel an unmistakable divine call. Something struck him that just uplifted him. He's got a lot of power. Only—"

The dean irritably sat down in a cane-seated rocker, jerked off his shoes, grunted, drew on his slippers.

"Only, hang it, I simply can't get myself to like him! Emma, tell me: If I were his age now, do you think I'd go into the ministry, as things are today?"

"Why, Henry! What in the world ever makes you say a thing like that? Of course you would! Why, if that weren't the case— What would our whole lives mean, all we've given up and everything?"

"Oh, I know. I just get to thinking. Sometimes I wonder if we've given up so much. Don't hurt even a preacher to face himself! After all, those two years when I was in the carpet business, before I went to the seminary, I didn't do very well. Maybe I wouldn't have made any more than I do now. But if I could— Suppose I could've been a great chemist? Wouldn't that (mind you, I'm just speculating, as a student of psychology)—wouldn't that conceivably be better than year after year of students with the same confounded problems over and over again—and always so pleased and surprised and important about them!—or year after year again of standing in the pulpit and knowing your congregation don't remember what you've said seven minutes after you've said it?"

"Why, Henry, I don't know what's gotten into you! I think you better do a little praying yourself instead of picking on this poor young Gantry! Neither you nor I could ever have been happy except in a Baptist church or a real cover-to-cover Baptist college."

The dean's wife finished darning the towels and went up to say good-night to her parents.

They had lived with her since her father's retirement, at seventy-five, from his country pastorate. He had been a missionary in Missouri before the Civil War.

Her lips had been moving, her eyebrows working, as she darned the towels; her eyebrows were still creased as she came into their room and shrieked at her father's deafness:

"Time to go to bed, Papa. And you, Mama."

They were nodding on either side of a radiator unheated for months.

"All right, Emmy," piped the ancient.

"Say, Papa— Tell me: I've been thinking: If you were just a young man today, would you go into the ministry?"

"Course I would! What an idea! Most glorious vocation young man could have. Idea! G'night, Emmy!"

But as his ancient wife sighingly removed her corsets, she complained, "Don't know as you would or not—if *I* was married to you—which ain't any too certain, a second time—and if I had anything to say about it!"

"Which *is* certain! Don't be foolish. Course I would."

"I don't know. Fifty years I had of it, and I never did get so I wa'n't just mad clear through when the ladies of the church came poking around, criticizing me for every little tidy I put on the chairs, and talking something terrible if I had a bonnet or a shawl that was the least mite tasty. ''Twa'n't suitable for a minister's wife.' Drat 'em! And I always did like a bonnet with some nice bright colors. Oh, I've done a right smart of thinking about it. You always were a powerful preacher, but's I've told you—"

"You have!"

"—I never could make out how, if when you were in the pulpit you really knew so much about all these high and mighty and mysterious things, how it was when you got home you never knew enough, and you never could learn enough, to find the hammer or make a nice piece of cornbread or add up a column of figures twice alike or find Oberammergau on the map of Austria!"

"Germany, woman! I'm sleepy!"

"And all these years of having to pretend to be so good when we were just common folks all the time! Ain't you glad you can just be simple folks now?"

"Maybe it is restful. But that's not saying I wouldn't do it over again." The old man ruminated a long while. "I think I would. Anyway, no use discouraging these young people from entering the ministry. Somebody got to preach the gospel truth, ain't they?"

"I suppose so. Oh, dear. Fifty years since I married a preacher! And if I could still only be sure about the virgin birth! Now don't you go explaining! Laws, the number of times you've explained! I know it's true—it's in the Bible. If I could only *believe* it! But—

"I would of liked to had you try your hand at politics. If I could of been, just once, to a senator's house, to a banquet or something, just once, in a nice bright red dress with gold slippers, I'd of been willing to go back to alpaca and scrubbing floors and listening to you rehearsing your sermons, out in the stable, to that old mare we had for so many years—oh, laws, how long is it she's been dead now? Must be—yes, it's twenty-seven years—

"Why is it that it's only in religion that the things you got to believe are agin all experience? Now drat it, don't you go and quote that 'I believe because it *is* impossible' thing at me again! Believe because it's impossible! Huh! Just like a minister!

"Oh, dear, I hope I don't live long enough to lose my faith. Seems like the older I get, the less I'm excited over all these preachers that talk about hell only they never saw it.

"Twenty-seven years! And we had that old hoss so long before that. My how she could kick— Busted that buggy—"

They were both asleep.

Chapter V

IN THE COTTONWOOD grove by the muddy river, three miles west of Paris, Kansas, the godly were gathered with lunch-baskets, linen dusters, and moist unhappy babies for the all-day celebration. Brothers Elmer Gantry and Edward Fislinger had been licensed to preach before, but now they were to be ordained as full-fledged preachers, as Baptist ministers.

They had come home from distant Mizpah Theological Seminary for ordination by their own council of churches, the Kayooska River Baptist Association. Both of them had another year to go out of the three-year seminary course, but by the more devout and rural brethren it is considered well to ordain the clerics early, so that even before they attain infallible wisdom they may fill backwoods pulpits and during week-ends do good works with divine authority.

His vacation after college Elmer had spent on a farm; during vacation after his first year in seminary he had been supervisor in a boys' camp; now, after ordination, he was to supply at the smaller churches in his corner of Kansas.

During his second year of seminary, just finished, he had been more voluminously bored than ever at Terwillinger. Constantly he had thought of quitting, but after his journeys to the city of Monarch, where he was in closer relation to fancy ladies and to bartenders than one would have desired in a holy clerk, he got a second wind in his resolve to lead a pure life, and so managed to keep on toward perfection, as symbolized by the degree of Bachelor of Divinity.

But if he had been bored, he had acquired professional training.

He was able now to face any audience and to discourse authoritatively on any subject whatever, for any given time to the second, without trembling and without any errors of speech beyond an infrequent "ain't" or "he don't." He had an elegant vocabulary. He knew eighteen synonyms for sin, half of them very long and impressive, and the others very short and explosive and minatory—minatory being one of his own best words, constantly useful in terrifying the as yet imaginary horde of sinners gathered before him.

He was no longer embarrassed by using the most intimate language about God; without grinning he could ask a seven-year-old boy, "Don't you want to give up your vices?" and without flinching he could look a tobacco salesman in the eye and demand, "Have you ever knelt before the throne of grace?"

Whatever worldly expressions he might use in *sub rosa* conversations with the less sanctified theological students, such as Harry Zenz, who was the most confirmed atheist in the school, in public he never so much as said "doggone," and he had on tap, for immediate and skilled use, a number of such phrases as "Brother, I am willing to help you find religion," "My whole life is a testimonial to my faith," "To the inner eye there is no trouble in comprehending the three-fold nature of divinity," "We don't want any long-faced Christians in this church—the fellow that's been washed in the blood of the Lamb is just so happy he goes 'round singing and hollering hallelujah all day long," and "Come on now, all get together, and let's make this the biggest collection this church has ever seen." He could explain foreordination thoroughly, and he used the words "baptizo" and "Athanasian."

He would, perhaps, be less orchestral, less Palladian, when he had been in practise for a year or two after graduation and discovered that the hearts of men are vile, their habits low, and that they are unwilling to hand the control of all those habits over to the parson. But he would recover again, and he was a promise of what he might be in twenty years, as a ten-thousand-dollar seer.

He had grown broader, his glossy hair, longer than at Terwillinger, was brushed back from his heavy white brow, his nails were oftener clean, and his speech was Jovian. It was more sonorous, more measured and pontifical; he could, and did, reveal his interested knowledge of your secret moral diabetes merely by saying, "How are we today, Brother?"

And though he had almost flunked in Greek, his thesis on "Sixteen Ways of Paying a Church Debt" had won the ten-dollar prize in Practical Theology.

II

He walked among the Kayooska Valley communicants, beside his mother. She was a small-town business woman; she was not unduly wrinkled or shabby; indeed she wore a good little black hat and a new brown silk frock with a long gold chain; but she was inconspicuous beside his bulk and sober magnificence.

He wore for the ceremony a new double-breasted suit of black broadcloth, and new black shoes. So did Eddie Fislinger, along with a funereal tie and a black wide felt hat, like a Texas congressman's. But Elmer was more daring. Had he not understood that he must show dignity, he would have indulged himself in the gaudiness for which he had a talent. He had compromised by buying a beautiful light gray felt hat in Chicago, on his way home, and he had ventured on a red-bordered gray silk handkerchief, which gave a pleasing touch of color to his sober chest.

But he had left off, for the day, the large opal ring surrounded by almost gold serpents for which he had lusted and to which he had yielded when in liquor, in the city of Monarch.

He walked as an army with banners, he spoke like a trombone, he gestured widely with his large blanched thick hand; and his mother, on his arm, looked up in ecstasy. He wafted her among the crowd, affable as a candidate for probate judgeship, and she was covered with the fringes of his glory.

For the ordination, perhaps two hundred Baptist laymen and laywomen and at least two hundred babies had come in from neighboring congregations by buckboard, democrat wagon, and buggy. (It was 1905; there was as yet no Ford nearer than Fort Scott.) They were honest, kindly, solid folk; farmers and blacksmiths and cobblers; men with tanned deep-lined faces, wearing creased "best suits"; the women, deep bosomed or work-shriveled, in clean gingham. There was one village banker, very chatty and democratic, in a new crash suit. They milled like cattle, in dust up to their shoe laces, and dust veiled them, in the still heat, under the dusty branches of the cottonwoods from which floated shreds to catch and glisten on the rough fabric of their clothes.

Six preachers had combined to assist the Paris parson in his ceremony, and one of them was no less than the Rev. Dr. Ingle, come all the way from St. Joe, where he was said to have a Sunday School of six hundred. As a young man—very thin and eloquent in a frock coat—Dr. Ingle had for six months preached in Paris, and Mrs. Gantry remembered him as her favorite minister. He had been so kind to her when she was ill; had come in to read "Ben Hur" aloud, and tell stories to a chunky little Elmer given to hiding behind furniture and heaving vegetables at visitors.

"Well, well, Brother, so this is the little tad I used to know as a shaver! Well, you always were a good little mannie, and they tell me that now you're a consecrated young man—that you're destined to do a great work for the Lord," Dr. Ingle greeted Elmer.

"Thank you, Doctor. Pray for me. It's an honor to have you come from your great church," said Elmer.

"Not a bit of trouble. On my way to Colorado—I've taken a cabin way up in the mountains there—glorious view—sunsets—painted by the Lord himself. My congregation have been so good as to give me two months' vacation. Wish you could pop up there for a while, Brother Elmer."

"I wish I could, Doctor, but I have to try in my humble way to keep the fires burning around here."

Mrs. Gantry was panting. To have her little boy discoursing with Dr. Ingle as though they were equals! To hear him talking like a preacher—just as *natural!* And some day—Elmer with a famous church; with a cottage in Colorado for the summer; married to a dear pious little woman, with half a dozen children; and herself invited to join them for the summer; all of them kneeling in family prayers, led by Elmer . . . though it was true Elmer declined to hold family prayers just now; said he'd had too much of it in seminary all year . . . too bad, but she'd keep on coaxing . . . and if he just *would* stop smoking, as she'd begged and besought him to do . . . well, perhaps if he didn't have a few naughtinesses left, he wouldn't hardly be her little boy any more. . . . How she'd had to scold once upon a time to get him to wash his hands and put on the nice red woolen wristlets she'd knitted for him!

No less satisfying to her was the way in which Elmer impressed all their neighbors. Charley Watley, the house-painter, commander of the Ezra P. Nickerson Post of the G.A.R. of Paris, who had always pulled his white mustache and grunted when she had tried to explain Elmer's hidden powers of holiness, took her aside to admit: "You were right, Sister; he makes a fine upstanding young man of God."

They encountered that town problem, Hank McVittle, the druggist. Elmer and he had been mates; together they had stolen sugar-corn, drunk hard cider, and indulged in haymow venery. Hank was a small red man, with a lascivious and knowing eye. It was certain that he had come today only to laugh at Elmer.

They met face on, and Hank observed, "Morning, Mrs. Gantry. Well, Elmy, going to be a preacher, eh?"

"I am, Hank."

"Like it?" Hank was grinning and scratching his cheek with a freckled hand; other unsanctified Parisians were listening.

Elmer boomed, "I do, Hank. I love it! I love the ways of the Lord, and I don't ever propose to put my foot into any others! Because I've tasted the fruit of evil, Hank—you know that. And there's nothing to it. What fun we had, Hank, was nothing to the peace and joy I feel now. I'm kind of sorry for you, my boy." He loomed over Hank, dropped his paw heavily on his shoulder. "Why don't you try to get right with God? Or maybe you're smarter than he is!"

"Never claimed to be anything of the sort!" snapped Hank, and in that testiness Elmer triumphed, his mother exulted.

She was sorry to see how few were congratulating Eddie Fislinger, who was also milling, but motherless, inconspicuous, meek to the presiding clergy.

Old Jewkins, humble, gentle old farmer, inched up to murmur, "Like to shake your hand, Brother Elmer. Mighty fine to see you chosen thus and put aside for the work of the Lord. Jiggity! T' think I remember you as knee-high to a grasshopper! I suppose you study a lot of awful learned books now."

"They make us work good and hard, Brother Jewkins. They give us pretty deep stuff: hermeneutics, chrestomathy, pericopes, exegesis, homiletics, liturgics, isagogics, Greek and

Hebrew and Aramaic, hymnology, apologetics—oh, a good deal."

"Well! I should *say* so!" worshiped old Jewkins, while Mrs. Gantry marveled to find Elmer even more profound than she had thought, and Elmer reflected proudly that he really did know what all but a couple of the words meant.

"My!" sighed his mother. "You're getting so educated, I declare t' goodness pretty soon I won't hardly dare to talk to you!"

"Oh, no. There'll never come a time when you and I won't be the best of pals, or when I won't need the inspiration of your prayers!" said Elmer Gantry melodiously, with refined but manly laughter.

III

They were assembling on benches, wagon-seats and boxes for the ceremony of ordination.

The pulpit was a wooden table with a huge Bible and a pitcher of lemonade. Behind it were seven rocking chairs for the clergy, and just in front, two hard wooden chairs for the candidates.

The present local pastor, Brother Dinger, was a meager man, slow of speech and given to long prayers. He rapped on the table. "We will, uh, we will now begin."

. . . Elmer, looking handsome on a kitchen chair in front of the rows of flushed hot faces. He stopped fretting that his shiny new black shoes were dust-gray. His heart pounded. He was in for it! No escape! He was going to be a pastor! Last chance for Jim Lefferts, and Lord knew where Jim was. He couldn't— His shoulder muscles were rigid. Then they relaxed wearily, as though he had struggled to satiety, while Brother Dinger went on:

"Well, we'll start with the usual, uh, examination of our young brothers, and the brethren have, uh, they've been good enough, uh, to let me, uh, in whose charge one, uh, one of these fine young brothers has always lived and made his home—to let me, uh, let me ask the questions. Now, Brother Gantry, do you believe fully and whole-heartedly in baptism by immersion?"

Elmer was thinking, "What a rotten pulpit voice the poor duck has," but aloud he was rumbling:

"I believe, Brother, and I've been taught, that possibly a man *might* be saved if he'd just been baptized by sprinkling or pouring, but only if he were ignorant of the truth. Of course immersion is the only Scriptural way—if we're really going to be like Christ, we must be buried with him in baptism."

"That's fine, Brother Gantry. Praise God! Now, Brother Fislinger, do you believe in the final perseverance of the saints?"

Eddie's eager but cracked voice explaining—on—on—somniferous as the locusts in the blazing fields across the Kayooska River.

As there is no hierarchy in the Baptist Church, but only a free association of like-minded local churches, so are there no canonical forms of procedure, but only customs. The ceremony of ordination is not a definite rite; it may vary as the local associations will, and ordination is conferred not by any bishop but by the general approval of the churches in an association.

The questions were followed by the "charge to the candidates," a tremendous discourse by the great Dr. Ingle, in which he commended study, light meals, and helping the sick by going and reading texts to them. Every one joined then in a tremendous basket-lunch on long plank tables by the cool river . . . banana layer cake, doughnuts, fried chicken, chocolate layer cake, scalloped potatoes, hermit cookies, cocoanut layer cake, pickled tomato preserves, on plates which skidded about the table, with coffee poured into saucerless cups from a vast tin pot, inevitably scalding at least one child, who howled. There were hearty shouts of "Pass the lemon pie, Sister Skiff," and "That was a fine discourse of Brother Ingle's," and "Oh, dear, I dropped my spoon and an ant got on it—well, I'll just wipe it on my apron—that was fine the way Brother Gantry explained how the Baptist Church has existed ever since Bible days." . . . Boys bathing, shrieking, splashing one another. . . . Boys getting into the poison ivy. . . . Boys becoming so infected with the poison ivy that they would turn spotty and begin to swell within seven hours. . . . Dr. Ingle enthusiastically telling the other clergy of his trip to the

Holy Land. . . . Elmer lying about his fondness for the faculty of his theological seminary.

Reassembled after lunch, Brother Tusker, minister of the largest congregation in the association, gave the "charge to the churches." This was always the juicest and most scandalous and delightful part of the ordination ceremony. In it the clergy had a chance to get back at the parishioners who, as large contributors, as guaranteed saints, had all year been nagging them.

Here were these fine young men going into the ministry, said Brother Tusker. Well, it was up to them to help. Brother Gantry and Brother Fislinger were leaping with the joy of sacrifice and learning. Then let the churches give 'em a chance, and not make 'em spend all the time hot-footing it around, as some older preachers had to do, raising their own salaries! Let folks quit criticizing; let 'em appreciate godly lives and the quickening word once in a while, instead of ham-ham-hammering their preachers all day long!

And certain of the parties who criticized the preachers' wives for idleness—funny the way some of *them* seemed to have so much time to gad around and notice things and spread scandal! T'wa'n't only the menfolks that the Savior was thinking of when he talked about them that were without sin being the only folks that were qualified to heave any rocks!

The other preachers leaned back in their chairs and tried to look casual, and hoped that Brother Tusker was going to bear down even a lee-tle heavier on that matter of raising salaries.

In his sermon and the concluding ordination prayer Brother Knoblaugh (of Barkinsville) summed up, for the benefit of Elmer Gantry, Eddie Fislinger, and God, the history of the Baptists, the importance of missions, and the perils of not reading the Bible before breakfast daily.

Through this long prayer, the visiting pastors stood with their hands on the heads of Elmer and Eddie.

There was a grotesque hitch at first. Most of the ministers were little men who could no more than reach up to Elmer's head. They stood strained and awkward and unecclesiastical, these shabby good men, before the restless audience. There was a giggle. Elmer had a dramatic flash. He knelt abruptly, and Eddie, peering and awkward, followed him.

In the powdery gray dust Elmer knelt, ignoring it. On his head were the worn hands of three veteran preachers, and suddenly he was humble, for a moment he was veritably being ordained to the priestly service of God.

He had been only impatient till this instant. In the chapels at Mizpah and Terwillinger he had heard too many famous visiting pulpiteers to be impressed by the rustic eloquence of the Kayooska Association. But he felt now their diffident tenderness, their unlettered fervor—these poverty-twisted parsons who believed, patient in their bare and baking tabernacles, that they were saving the world, and who wistfully welcomed the youths that they themselves had been.

For the first time in weeks Elmer prayed not as an exhibition but sincerely, passionately, savoring righteousness:

"Dear God—I'll get down to it—not show off but just think of thee—do good—God help me!"

Coolness fluttered the heavy dust-caked leaves, and as the sighing crowd creaked up from their benches, Elmer Gantry stood confident . . . ordained minister of the gospel.

Chapter VI

THE STATE of Winnemac lies between Pittsburgh and Chicago, and in Winnemac, perhaps a hundred miles south of the city of Zenith, is Babylon, a town which suggests New England more than the Middle West. Large elms shade it, there are white pillars beyond lilac bushes, and round about the town is a serenity unknown on the gusty prairies.

Here is Mizpah Theological Seminary, of the Northern Baptists. (There is a Northern and Southern convention of this distinguished denomination, because before the Civil War the Northern Baptists proved by the Bible, unanswerably, that slavery was wrong; and the Southern Baptists proved by the Bible, irrefutably, that slavery was the will of God.)

The three buildings of the seminary are attractive: brick with white cupolas, green blinds at the small-paned wide windows. But within they are bare, with hand-rubbings along the plaster walls, with portraits of missionaries and ragged volumes of sermons.

The large structure is the dormitory, Elizabeth J. Schmutz Hall—known to the less reverent as Smut Hall.

Here lived Elmer Gantry, now ordained but completing the last year of work for his Bachelor of Divinity degree, a commodity of value in bargaining with the larger churches.

There were only sixteen left now of his original class of thirty-five. The others had dropped out, for rural preaching, life insurance, or a melancholy return to plowing. There was no one with whom he wanted to live, and he dwelt sulkily in a single room, with a cot, a Bible, a portrait of his mother, and with a copy of "What a Young Man Ought to Know," concealed inside his one starched pulpit shirt.

He disliked most of his class. They were too rustic or too pious, too inquisitive about his monthly trips to the city of Monarch or simply too dull. Elmer liked the company of what he regarded as intellectual people. He never understood what they were saying, but to hear them saying it made him feel superior.

The group which he most frequented gathered in the room of Frank Shallard and Don Pickens, the large corner room on the second floor of Smut Hall.

It was not an esthetic room. Though Frank Shallard might have come to admire pictures, great music, civilized furniture, he had been trained to regard them as worldly, and to content himself with art which "presented a message," to regard "Les Miserables" as superior because the bishop was a kind man, and "The Scarlet Letter" as a poor book because the heroine was sinful and the author didn't mind.

The walls were of old plaster, cracked and turned deathly gray, marked with the blood of mosquitoes and bed-bugs slain in portentous battles long ago by theologians now gone forth to bestow their thus uplifted visions on a materialistic world. The bed was a skeleton of rusty iron bars, sagging in the center, with a comforter which was not too clean. Trunks were in the corners, and the wardrobe was a row of hooks behind a calico curtain. The grass matting was slowly dividing into separate strands, and under the study table it had been scuffed through to the cheap pine flooring.

The only pictures were Frank's steel engraving of Roger Williams, his framed and pansy-painted copy of "Pippa Passes," and Don Pickens' favorite, a country church by winter moonlight, with tinsel snow, which sparkled delightfully. The only untheological books were Frank's poets: Wordsworth, Longfellow, Tennyson, Browning, in standard volumes, fine-printed and dismal, and one really dangerous papist document, his "Imitation of Christ," about which there was argument at least once a week.

In this room, squatting on straight chairs, the trunks, and the bed, on a November evening in 1905, were five young men besides Elmer and Eddie Fislinger. Eddie did not really belong to the group, but he persisted in following Elmer, feeling that not even yet was everything quite right with the brother.

"A preacher has got to be just as husky and pack just as good a wallop as a prize-fighter. He ought to be able to throw out any roughneck that tries to interrupt his meetings, and still more, strength makes such a hit with the women in his congregation—of course I don't mean it in any wrong way," said Wallace Umstead.

Wallace was a student-instructor, head of the minute seminary gymnasium and "director of physical culture"; a young man who had a military mustache and who did brisk things on horizontal bars. He was a state university B.A. and graduate of a physical-training school. He was going into Y.M.C.A. work when he should have a divinity degree, and he was fond of saying, "Oh, I'm still one of the Boys, you know, even if I am a prof."

"That's right," agreed Elmer Gantry. "Say, I had—I was holding a meeting at Grauten, Kansas, last summer, and there was a big boob that kept interrupting, so I just jumped down from the platform and went up to him, and he says, 'Say, Parson,' he says, 'can you tell us what the Almighty wants us to do about prohibition, considering he told Paul to take some wine for his stomach's sake?' 'I don't know as I can,' I says, 'but you want to remember he also commanded us to cast out devils!' and I yanked that yahoo out of his seat and threw him out on his ear, and say, the whole crowd—well, there weren't so *awfully* many there, but they certainly did give him the ha-ha! You bet. And to be a husky makes a hit with the whole congregation, men's well as women. But there's more'n one high-toned preacher that got his pulpit because the deacons felt he could lick 'em. Of course praying and all that is all O.K., but you got to be practical! We're here to do good, but first you have to cinch a job that you can do good in!"

"You're commercial!" protested Eddie Fislinger, and Frank Shallard: "Good heavens, Gantry, is that all your religion means to you?"

"Besides," said Horace Carp, "you have the wrong angle. It isn't mere brute force that appeals to women—to congregations. It's a beautiful voice. I don't envy you your bulk, Elmer—besides, you're going to get fat—"

"I am like hell!"

"—but what I could do with that voice of yours! I'd have 'em all weeping! I'd read 'em poetry from the pulpit!"

Horace Carp was the one High Churchman in the Seminary. He was a young man who resembled a water spaniel, who concealed saints' images, incense, and a long piece of scarlet brocade in his room, and who wore a purple velvet smoking-jacket. He was always raging because his father, a wholesale plumber and pious, had threatened to kick him out if he went to an Episcopal seminary instead of a Baptist fortress.

"Yes, you prob'ly would read 'em poetry!" said Elmer. "That's the trouble with you high-falutin' guys. You think you can get people by a lot of poetry and junk. What gets 'em and holds 'em and brings 'em to their pews every Sunday is the straight gospel—and it don't hurt one bit to scare 'em into being righteous with the good old-fashioned Hell!"

"You bet—providing you encourage 'em to keep their bodies in swell shape, too," condescended Wallace Umstead. "Well, I don't want to talk as a prof—after all I'm glad I can still remain just one of the Boys—but you aren't going to develop any very big horse-power in your praying tomorrow morning if you don't get your sleep. And me to my little downy! G'night!"

At the closing of the door, Harry Zenz, the seminary iconoclast, yawned, "Wallace is probably the finest slice of tripe in my wide clerical experience. Thank God, he's gone! Now we can be natural and talk dirty!"

"And yet," complained Frank Shallard, "you encourage him to stay and talk about his pet methods of exercise! Don't you ever tell the truth, Harry?"

"Never carelessly. Why, you idiot, I want Wallace to run and let the dean know what an earnest worker in the vineyard I am. Frank, you're a poor innocent. I suspect you actually believe some of the dope they teach us here. And yet you're a man of some reading. You're the only person in Mizpah except myself who could appreciate a paragraph of Huxley. Lord, how I pity you when you get into the ministry! Of course, Fislinger here is a grocery clerk, Elmer is a ward politician, Horace is a dancing master—"

He was drowned beneath a surf of protests, not too jocose and friendly.

Harry Zenz was older than the others—thirty-two at least. He was plump, almost completely bald, and fond of sitting still; and he could look profoundly stupid. He was a man of ill-assorted but astonishing knowledge; and in the church ten miles from Mizpah which he had regularly supplied for two years he was considered a man of humorless learning and bloodless piety. He was a complete and cheerful atheist, but he admitted it only to Elmer Gantry and Horace Carp. Elmer regarded him as a sort of Jim Lefferts, but he was as different from Jim as pork fat from a crystal. He hid his giggling atheism—Jim flourished his; he despised women—Jim had a disillusioned pity for the Juanita Klauzels of the world; he had an intellect—Jim had only cynical guesses.

Zenz interrupted their protests:

"So you're a bunch of Erasmuses! You ought to know. And there's no hypocrisy in what we teach and preach! We're a specially selected group of Parsifals—beautiful to the eye and stirring to the ear and overflowing with knowledge of what God said to the Holy Ghost *in camera* at 9:16 last Wednesday morning. We're all just rarin' to go out and preach the precious Baptist doctrine of 'Get ducked or duck.' We're wonders. We admit it. And people actually sit and listen to us, and don't choke! I suppose they're overwhelmed by our nerve! And we have to have nerve, or we'd never dare to stand in a pulpit again. We'd quit, and pray God to forgive us for having stood up there and pretended that we represent God, and that we can explain what we ourselves say are the unexplainable mysteries! But I still claim that there are preachers who haven't our holiness. Why is it that the clergy are so given to sex crimes?"

"That's not true!" from Eddie Fislinger.

"Don't talk that way!" Don Pickens begged. Don was Frank's roommate: a slight youth, so gentle, so affectionate, that even that raging lion of righteousness, Dean Trosper, was moved to spare him.

Harry Zenz patted his arm. "Oh, you, Don—you'll always be a monk. But if you don't believe it, Fislinger, look at the statistics of the five thousand odd crimes committed by clergymen—that is those who got caught—since the eighties, and note the percentage of sex offenses—rape, incest, bigamy, enticing young girls—oh, a lovely record!"

Elmer was yawning, "Oh, God, I do get so sick of you fellows yammering and arguing and discussing. All perfectly simple—maybe we preachers aren't perfect; don't pretend to be; but we do a lot of good."

"That's right," said Eddie. "But maybe it is true that— The snares of sex are so dreadful that even ministers of the gospel get trapped. And the perfectly simple solution is continence—just take it out in prayer and good hard exercise."

"Oh, sure, Eddie, you bet; what a help you're going to be to the young men in your church," purred Harry Zenz.

Frank Shallard was meditating unhappily. "Just why are we going to be preachers, anyway? Why are you, Harry, if you think we're all such liars?"

"Oh, not liars, Frank—just practical, as Elmer put it. Me, it's easy. I'm not ambitious. I don't want money enough to hustle for it. I like to sit and read. I like intellectual acrobatics and no work. And you can have all that in the ministry—unless you're one of these chumps that get up big institutional outfits and work themselves to death for publicity."

"You certainly have a fine high view of the ministry!" growled Elmer.

"Well, all right, what's your fine high purpose in becoming a Man of God, Brother Gantry?"

"Well, I— Rats, it's perfectly clear. Preacher can do a lot of good—give help and— And explain religion."

"I wish you'd explain it to *me*! Especially I want to know to what extent are Christian symbols descended from indecent barbaric symbols?"

"Oh, you make me tired!"

Horace Carp fluttered, "Of course none of you consecrated windjammers ever think of the one *raison d'être* of the church, which is to add beauty to the barren lives of the common people!"

"Yeh! It certainly must make the common people feel awfully common to hear Brother Gantry spiel about the errors of supralapsarianism!"

"I never preach about any such a doggone thing!" Elmer protested. "I just give 'em a good helpful sermon, with some jokes sprinkled in to make it interesting and some stuff about the theater or something that'll startle 'em a little and wake 'em up and help 'em to lead better and fuller daily lives."

"Oh, do you, dearie!" said Zenz. "My error. I thought you probably gave 'em a lot of helpful hints about the *innasci-*

bilitas attribute and the *res sacramenti*. Well, Frank, why did you become a theologue?"

"I can't tell you when you put it sneeringly. I believe there are mystic experiences which you can follow only if you are truly set apart."

"Well, I know why I came here," said Don Pickens. "My dad sent me!"

"So did mine!" complained Horace Carp. "But what I can't understand is: Why are any of us in an ole Baptist school? Horrible denomination—all these moldly barns of churches, and people coughing illiterate hymns, and long-winded preachers always springing a bright new idea like 'All the world needs to solve its problems is to get back to the gospel of Jesus Christ.' The only church is the Episcopal! Music! Vestments! Stately prayers! Lovely architecture! Dignity! Authority! Believe me, as soon as I can make the break, I'm going to switch over to the Episcopalians. And then I'll have a social position, and be able to marry a nice rich girl."

"No, you're wrong," said Zenz. "The Baptist Church is the only denomination worth while, except possibly the Methodist."

"I'm glad to hear you say that," marveled Eddie.

"Because the Baptists and the Methodists have all the numbskulls—except those that belong to the Catholic Church and the henhouse sects—and so even you, Horace, can get away with being a prophet. There are *some* intelligent people in the Episcopal and Congregational Churches, and a few of the Campbellite flocks, and they check up on you. Of course all Presbyterians are half-wits, too, but they have a standard doctrine, and they can trap you into a heresy trial. But in the Baptist and Methodist Churches, man! There's the berth for philosophers like me and hoot-owls like you, Eddie! All you have to do with Baptists and Methodists, as Father Carp suggests—"

"If you agree with me about anything, I withdraw it," said Horace.

"All you have to do," said Zenz, "is to get some sound and perfectly meaningless doctrine and keep repeating it. You won't bore the laymen—in fact the only thing they resent is something that *is* new, so they have to work their brains. Oh, no, Father Carp—the Episcopal pulpit for actors that aren't good enough to get on the stage, but the good old Baptist fold for realists!"

"You make me tired, Harry!" complained Eddie. "You just want to show off, that's all. You're a lot better Baptist and a lot better Christian than you let on to be, and I can prove it. Folks wouldn't go on listening to your sermons unless they carried conviction. No, sir! You can fool folks once or twice with a lot of swell-sounding words but in the long run it's sincerity they look for. And one thing that makes me know you're on the right side is that you don't practise open communion. Golly, I feel that everything we Baptists stand for is threatened by those darn' so-called liberals that are beginning to practise open communion."

"Rats!" grumbled Harry. "Of all the fool Baptist egotisms, close communion is the worst! Nobody but people *we* consider saved to be allowed to take communion with us! Nobody can meet God unless we introduce 'em! Self-appointed guardians of the blood and body of Jesus Christ! Whew!"

"Absolutely," from Horace Carp. "And there is absolutely no Scriptural basis for close communion."

"There certainly is!" shrieked Eddie. "Frank, where's your Bible?"

"Gee, I left it in O.T.E. Where's yours, Don?"

"Well, I'll be switched! I had the darn' thing here just this evening," lamented Don Pickens, after a search.

"Oh, I remember. I was killing a cockroach with it. It's on top of your wardrobe," said Elmer.

"Gee, honest, you hadn't ought to kill cockroaches with a Bible!" mourned Eddie Fislinger. "Now here's the Bible, good and straight, for close communion, Harry. It says in First Corinthians, 11:27 and 29: 'Whoever shall eat this bread and drink this cup of the Lord unworthily shall be guilty of the body and the blood of the Lord. For he that eateth and drinketh unworthily eateth and drinketh damnation to himself.' And how can there be a worthy Christian unless he's been baptized by immersion?"

"I do wonder sometimes," mused Frank Shallard, "if we aren't rather impious, we Baptists, to set ourselves up as the keepers of the gates of God, deciding just who is righteous, who is worthy to commune."

"But there's nothing else we can do," explained Eddie. "The Baptist Church, being the only pure Scriptural church, is the one real church of God, and we're not setting ourselves up—we're just following God's ordinances."

Horace Carp had also been reveling in the popular Mizpah sport of looking up Biblical texts to prove a preconceived opinion. "I don't find anything here about Baptists," he said.

"Nor about your doggoned old Episcopalians, either—darn' snobs!—and the preachers wearing nightshirts!" from Eddie.

"You bet your life you find something—it talks about bishops, and that means Episcopal bishops—the papes and the Methodists are uncanonical bishops," rejoiced Horace. "I'll bet you two dollars and sixty-seven cents I wind up as an Episcopal bishop, and, believe me, I'll be high-church as hell—all the candles I can get on the altar."

Harry Zenz was speculating, "I suppose it's unscientific to believe that because I happen to be a Baptist practitioner myself and see what word-splitting, text-twisting, applause-hungry, job-hunting, medieval-minded second-raters even the biggest Baptist leaders are, therefore the Baptist Church is the worst of the lot. I don't suppose it's really any worse than the Presbyterian or the Congregational or Disciples or Lutheran or any other. But— Say, you, Fislinger, ever occur to you how dangerous it is, this Bible-worship? You and I might have to quit preaching and go to work. You tell the muttonheads that the Bible contains absolutely everything necessary for salvation, don't you?"

"Of course."

"Then what's the use of having any preachers? Any church? Let people stay home and read the Bible!"

"Well—well—it says—"

The door was dashed open, and Brother Karkis entered.

Brother Karkis was no youthful student. He was forty-three, heavy-handed and big-footed, and his voice was the voice of a Great Dane. Born to the farm, he had been ordained a Baptist preacher for twenty years now, and up and down through the Dakotas, Nebraska, Arkansas, he had bellowed in up-creek tabernacles.

His only formal education had been in country schools; and of all books save the Bible, revivalistic hymnals, a concordance handy for finding sermon-texts, and a manual of poultry-keeping, he was soundly ignorant. He had never met a woman of the world, never drunk a glass of wine, never heard a bar of great music, and his neck was not free from the dust of cornfields.

But it would have been a waste of pity to sigh over Brother Karkis as a plucky poor student. He had no longing for further knowledge; he was certain that he already had it all. He despised the faculty as book-adulterated wobblers in the faith—he could "out-pray and out-holler and out-save the whole lot of 'em." He desired a Mizpah degree only because it would get him a better paid job—or, as he put it, with the 1850 vocabulary which he found adequate for 1905, because it would "lead him into a wider field of usefulness."

"Say, don't you fellers ever do anything but sit around and argue and discuss and bellyache?" he shouted. "My lands, I can hear your racket way down the hall! Be a lot better for you young fellers if you'd forget your smart-aleck arguin' and spend the evening on your knees in prayer! Oh, you're a fine lot of smart educated swells, but you'll find where that rubbish gets you when you go out and have to wrestle with old Satan for unregenerate souls! What are you gasbags arguing about, anyway?"

"Harry says," wailed Eddie Fislinger, "that there's nothing in the Bible that says Christians have to have a church or preachers."

"Huh! And him that thinks he's so educated. Where's a Bible?"

It was now in the hands of Elmer, who had been reading his favorite book, "The Song of Solomon."

"Well, Brother Gantry, glad see there's one galoot here that's got sense enough to stick by the Old Book and get himself right with God, 'stead of shooting off his face like some Pedo-Baptist. Now look here, Brother Zenz: It says here in Hebrews, 'Forsake not the assembling of yourselves together.' There, I guess that'll hold you!"

"My dear brother in the Lord," said Harry, "the only thing suggested there is an assembly like the Plymouth Brotherhood, with no regular paid preachers. As I was explaining to Brother Fislinger: Personally, I'm so ardent an admirer of the Bible that I'm thinking of starting a sect where we all just sing a hymn together, then sit and read our Bibles all day long, and not have any preachers getting between us and the all-sufficient Word of God. I expect you to join, Brother Karkis, unless you're one of these dirty higher critics that want to break down the Bible."

"Oh, you make me tired," said Eddie.

"You make me tired—always twisting the plain commands of Scripture," said Brother Karkis, shutting the door—weightily, and from the outside.

"You all make me tired. My God, how you fellows can argue!" said Elmer, chewing his Pittsburgh stogie.

The room was thick now with tobacco fumes. Though in Mizpah Seminary smoking was frowned on, practically forbidden by custom, all of the consecrated company save Eddie Fislinger were at it.

He rasped, "This air is something terrible! Why you fellows touch that vile weed— Worms and men are the only animals who indulge in tobacco! I'm going to get out of here."

There was strangely little complaint.

Rid of Eddie, the others turned to their invariable topic: what they called "sex."

Frank Shallard and Don Pickens were virgins, timid and fascinated, respectful and urgent; Horace Carp had had one fumbling little greensick experience; and all three listened with nervous eagerness to the experiences of Elmer and Harry Zenz. Tonight Elmer's mind reeked with it, and he who had been almost silent during the ecclesiastical wrangling was voluble now. The youngsters panted as he chronicled his meetings with a willing choir-singer, this summer past.

"Tell me—tell me," fretted Don. "Do girls, oh—nice girls—do they really ever—uh—go with a preacher? And aren't you ashamed to face them afterwards, in church?"

"Huh!" observed Zenz, and "Ashamed? They worship you!" declared Elmer. "They stand by you the way no wife ever would—as long as they do fall for you. Why, this girl—Oh, well, she sang something elegant."

He finished vaguely, reminiscently. Suddenly he was bored at treading the mysteries of sex with these mooncalves. He lunged up.

"Going?" said Frank.

Elmer posed at the door, smirking, his hands on his hips, "Oh, no. Not a-tall." He looked at his watch. (It was a watch which reminded you of Elmer himself: large, thick, shiny, with a near-gold case.) "I merely have a date with a girl, that's all!"

He was lying, but he had been roused by his own stories, and he would have given a year of life if his boast were true. He returned to his solitary room in a fever. "God, if Juanita were only here, or Agatha, or even that little chambermaid at Solomon Junction—what the dickens was her name now?" he longed.

He sat motionless on the edge of his bed. He clenched his fists. He groaned and gripped his knees. He sprang up, to race about the room, to return and sit dolorously entranced.

"Oh, God, I can't *stand* it!" he moaned.

He was inconceivably lonely.

He had no friends. He had never had a friend since Jim Lefferts. Harry Zenz despised his brains, Frank Shallard despised his manners, and the rest of them he himself despised. He was bored by the droning seminary professors all day, the school-boyish arguing all evening; and in the rash of prayer-meetings and chapel-meetings and special praise-meetings he was bored by hearing the same enthusiasts gambol in the same Scriptural rejoicings.

"Oh, yes, I want to go on and preach. Couldn't go back to just business or the farm. Miss the hymns, the being boss. But—I can't do it! God, I am so lonely! If Juanita was just here!"

Chapter VII

THE Reverend Jacob Trosper, D.D., Ph.D., LL.D., dean and chief executive of Mizpah Theological Seminary, and Professor of Practical Theology and Homiletics, was a hard-faced active man with a large active voice. His cheeks were gouged with two deep channels. His eyebrows were heavy. His hair, now gray and bristly, must once have been rusty, like Eddie Fislinger's. He would have made an excellent top-sergeant. He looked through the students and let them understand that he knew their sins and idlenesses before they confessed them.

Elmer was afraid of Dean Trosper. When he was summoned to the dean's office, the morning after the spiritual conference in Frank Shallard's room, he was uneasy.

He found Frank with the dean.

"God! Frank's been tattling about my doings with women!"

"Brother Gantry," said the dean.

"Yes, sir!"

"I have an appointment which should give you experience and a little extra money. It's a country church down at Schoenheim, eleven miles from here, on the spur line of the Ontario, Omaha and Pittsburgh. You will hold regular Sunday morning services and Sunday School; if you are able to work up afternoon or evening services and prayer meeting, so much the better. The pay will be ten dollars a Sunday. If there's to be anything extra for extra work—that's up to you and your flock. I'd suggest that you go down there on a hand-car. I'm sure you can get the section-gang boss here to lend you one, as it's for the Lord's work, and the boss' brother does a lot of gardening here. I'm going to send Brother Shallard with you to conduct the Sunday School and get some experience. He has a particularly earnest spirit—which it wouldn't entirely hurt you to emulate, Brother Gantry—but he's somewhat shy in contact with sin-hardened common people.

"Now, boys, this is just a small church, but never forget that it's priceless souls that I'm entrusting to your keeping;

and who knows but that you may kindle there such a fire as may some day illumine all the world . . . providing, Brother Gantry, you eliminate the worldly things I suspect you of indulging in!"

Elmer was delighted. It was his first real appointment. In Kansas, this summer, he had merely filled other people's pulpits for two or three weeks at a time.

He'd show 'em! Some of these fellows that thought he was just a mouth-artist! Show 'em how he could build up church membership, build up the collections, get 'em all going with his eloquence—and, of course, carry the message of salvation into darkened hearts.

It would be mighty handy to have the extra ten a week—and maybe more if he could kid the Schoenheim deacons properly.

His first church . . . his own . . . and Frank had to take his orders!

II

In the virginal days of 1905 section gangs went out to work on the railway line not by gasoline power but on a hand-car, a platform with two horizontal bars worked up and down like pump-handles.

On a hand-car Elmer and Frank Shallard set out for their first charge. They did not look particularly clerical as they sawed at the handles; it was a chilly November Sunday morning, and they wore shabby greatcoats. Elmer had a moth-eaten plush cap over his ears, Frank exhibited absurd ear-muffs under a more absurd derby, and both had borrowed red flannel mittens from the section gang.

The morning was icily brilliant. Apple orchards glistened in the frost, and among the rattling weed-stalks by the worm-fences quail were whistling.

Elmer felt his lungs free of library dust as he pumped. He broadened his shoulders, rejoiced in sweating, felt that his ministry among real men and living life was begun. He pitied the pale Frank a little, and pumped the harder . . . and made Frank pump the harder . . . up and down, up and down, up and down. It was agony to the small of his back and shoulders, now growing soft, to labor on the up-grade, where the shining rails toiled round the curves through gravel cuts. But down-hill, swooping toward frosty meadows and the sound of cowbells in the morning sun, he whooped with exhilaration, and struck up a boisterous:

There is power, power, wonder-working power
In the blood
Of the Lamb—

The Schoenheim church was a dingy brown box with a toy steeple, in a settlement consisting of the church, the station, a blacksmith shop, two stores, and half a dozen houses. But at least thirty buggies were gathered along the rutty street or in the carriage-sheds behind the church; at least seventy people had come to inspect their new pastor; and they stood in gaping circles, staring between frosty damp mufflers and visored fur caps.

"I'm scared to death!" murmured Frank, as they strode up the one street from the station, but Elmer felt healthy, proud, expansive. His own church, small but somehow—somehow different from these ordinary country meeting-houses—quite a nice-shaped steeple—not one of these shacks with no steeple at all! And his people, waiting for him, their attention flowing into him and swelling him—

He threw open his overcoat, held it back with his hand imperially poised on his left hip, and let them see not only the black broadcloth suit bought this last summer for his ordination but something choice he had added since—elegant white piping at the opening of his vest.

A red-faced mustached man swaggered up to greet them, "Brother Gantry? And Brother Shallard? I'm Barney Bains, one of the deacons. Pleased to meet you. The Lord give power to your message. Some time since we had any preachin' here, and I guess we're all pretty hungry for spiritual food and the straight gospel. Bein' from Mizpah, I guess there's no danger you boys believe in this open communion!"

Frank had begun to worry, "Well, what I feel is—" when Elmer interrupted him with a very painful bunt in the side, and chanted with holy joy:

"Pleased meet you, Brother Bains. Oh, Brother Shallard and I are absolutely sound both on immersion and close communion. We trust you will pray for us, Brother, that the Holy Ghost may be present in this work today, and that all the brethren may rejoice in a great reawakening and a bountiful harvest!"

Deacon Bains and all who heard him muttered, saint to saint, "He's pretty young yet, but he's got the right idee. I'm sure we're going to have real rousing preaching. Don't think much of Brother Shallard, though. Kind of a nice-looking young fella, but dumm in the head. Stands there like a bump on a log. Well, he's good enough to teach the kids in Sunday School."

Brother Gantry was shaking hands all round. His sanctifying ordination, or it might have been his summer of bouncing from pulpit to pulpit, had so elevated him that he could greet them as impressively and fraternally as a sewing-machine agent. He shook hands with a good grip, he looked at all the more aged sisters as though he were moved to give them a holy kiss, he said the right things about the weather, and by luck or inspiration it was to the most acidly devout man in Boone County that he quoted a homicidal text from Malachi.

As he paraded down the aisle, leading his flock, he panted:

"Got 'em already! I can do something to wake these hicks up, where gas-bags like Frank or Carp would just chew the rag. How could I of felt so down in the mouth and so—uh—so carnal last week? Lemme at that pulpit!"

They faced him in hard straight pews, rugged heads seen against the brown wall and the pine double doors grained to mimic oak; they gratifyingly crowded the building, and at the back stood shuffling young men with unshaven chins and pale blue neckties.

He felt power over them while he trolled out the chorus of "The Church in the Wildwood."

His text was from Proverbs: "Hatred stirreth up strifes: but love covereth all sins."

He seized the sides of the pulpit with his powerful hands, glared at the congregation, decided to look benevolent after all, and exploded:

"In the hustle and bustle of daily life I wonder how many of us stop to think that in all that is highest and best we are ruled not by even our most up-and-coming efforts but by

Love? What is Love—the divine Love of which the—the great singer teaches us in Proverbs? It is the rainbow that comes after the dark cloud. It is the morning star and it is also the evening star, those being, as you all so well know, the brightest stars we know. It shines upon the cradle of the little one and when life has, alas, departed, to come no more, you find it still around the quiet tomb. What is it inspires all great men—be they preachers or patriots or great business men? What is it, my brethren, but Love? Ah, it fills the world with melody, with such sacred melodies as we have just indulged in together, for what is music? What, my friends, is music? Ah, what indeed is music but the voice of Love!"

He explained that hatred was low.

However, for the benefit of the more leathery and zealous deacons down front, he permitted them to hate all Catholics, all persons who failed to believe in hell and immersion, and all rich mortgage-holders, wantoning in the betraying smiles of scarlet women, each of whom wore silk and in her jeweled hand held a ruby glass of perfidious wine.

He closed by lowering his voice to a maternal whisper and relating a totally imaginary but most improving experience with a sinful old gentleman who on his bed of pain had admitted, to Elmer's urging, that he ought to repent immediately, but who put it off too long, died amid his virtuous and grief-stricken daughters, and presumably went straight to the devil.

When Elmer had galloped down to the door to shake hands with such as did not remain for Sabbath School, sixteen several auditors said in effect, "Brother, that was a most helpful sermon and elegantly expressed," and he wrung their hands with a boyish gratitude beautiful to see.

Deacon Bains patted his shoulder. "I've never heard so young a preacher hand out such fine doctrine, Brother. Meet my daughter Lulu."

And she was there, the girl for whom he had been looking ever since he had come to Mizpah.

Lulu Bains was a gray-and-white kitten with a pink ribbon. She had sat at the back of the church, behind the stove, and he had not seen her. He looked down at her thirstily. His excitement at having played his sermon to such applause was nothing beside his excitement over the fact that he would have her near him in his future clerical labors. Life was a promising and glowing thing as he held her hand and tried not to sound too insistently affectionate. "Such a pleasure to meet you, Sister Lulu."

Lulu was nineteen or twenty. She had a diminutive class of twelve-year-old boys in the Sunday School. Elmer had intended to sneak out during Sunday School, leaving Frank Shallard responsible, and find a place where he could safely smoke a Pittsburgh stogie, but in view of this new spiritual revelation he hung about, beaming with holy approbation of the good work and being manly and fraternal with the little boys in Lulu's class.

"If you want to grow up and be big fellows, regular sure-enough huskies, you just listen to what Miss Bains has to tell you about how Solomon built that wonderful big ole temple," he crooned at them; and if they twisted and giggled in shyness, at least Lulu smiled at him . . . gray-and-white kitten with sweet kitten eyes . . . small soft kitten who purred, "Oh, now, Brother Gantry, I'm just so scared I don't hardly dare teach" . . . big eyes that took him into their depths, till he heard her lisping as the voice of angels, larks, and whole orchestras of flutes.

He could not let her go at the end of Sunday School. He must hold her—

"Oh, Sister Lulu, come see the hand-car Frank and I—Brother Shallard and I—came down on. The *fun*-niest! Just laugh your head off!"

As the section gang passed through Schoenheim at least ten times a week, hand-cars could have been no astounding novelty to Lulu, but she trotted beside him, and stared prettily, and caroled, "Oh, hon-est! Did you come down on *that*? Well, I never!"

She shook hands cheerfully with both of them. He thought jealously that she was as cordial to Frank as to himself.

"He better watch out and not go fooling round *my* girl!" Elmer reflected, as they pumped back toward Babylon.

He did not congratulate Frank on having overcome his dread of stolid country audiences (Frank had always lived in cities) or on having made Solomon's temple not merely a depressing object composed of a substance called "cubits" but an actual shrine in which dwelt an active and terrifying god.

III

For two Sundays now Elmer had striven to impress Lulu not only as an efficient young prophet but as a desirable man. There were always too many people about. Only once did he have her alone. They walked half a mile then to call on a sick old woman. On their way Lulu had fluttered at him (gray-and-white kitten in a close bonnet of soft fuzzy gray, which he wanted to stroke).

"I suppose you're just bored to death by my sermons," he fished.

"Oh, nnnno! I think they're just wonderful!"

"Do you, honest?"

"Honest, I do!"

He looked down at her childish face till he had caught her eyes, then, jocularly:

"My, but this wind is making the little cheeks and the cute lips awful' red! Or I guess maybe some fella must of been kissing 'em before church!"

"Oh, no—"

She looked distressed, almost frightened.

"Whoa up!" he counseled himself. "You've got the wrong track. Golly, I don't believe she's as much of a fusser as I thought she was. Really is kinda innocent. Poor kid, shame to get her all excited. Oh, thunder, won't hurt her a bit to have a little educated love-making!"

He hastily removed any possible blots on his clerical reputation:

"Oh, I was joking. I just meant—be a shame if as lovely a girl as you weren't engaged. I suppose you are engaged, of course?"

"No. I liked a boy here awfully, but he went to Cleveland to work, and I guess he's kind of forgotten me."

"Oh, that is really too bad!"

Nothing could be stronger, more dependable, more comforting, than the pressure of his fingers on her arm. She looked grateful; and when she came to the sick-room and heard Brother Gantry pray, long, fervently, and with the choicest words about death not really mattering nor really hurting (the old woman had cancer) then Lulu also looked worshipful.

On their way back he made his final probe:

"But even if you aren't engaged, Sister Lulu, I'll bet there's a lot of the young fellows here that're crazy about you."

"No, honest there aren't. Oh, I go round some with a second cousin of mine—Floyd Naylor—but, my! he's so slow, he's no fun."

The Rev. Mr. Gantry planned to provide fun.

IV

Elmer and Frank had gone down on Saturday afternoon to decorate the church for the Thanksgiving service. To save the trip to Babylon and back, they were to spend Saturday night in the broad farmhouse of Deacon Bains, and Lulu Bains and her spinster cousin, Miss Baldwin, were assisting in the decoration—in other words doing it. They were stringing pine boughs across the back of the hall, and arranging a harvest feast of pumpkins, yellow corn, and velvety sumach in front of the pulpit.

While Frank and the spinster cousin of the Bainses discussed the artistic values of the pumpkins, Elmer hinted to Lulu:

"I want your advice, Lulu—Sister Lulu. Don't you think in my sermon tomorrow it might be helpful to explain—"

(They stood side by side. How sweet were her little shoulders, her soft pussy-cat cheeks! He had to kiss them! He had to! He swayed toward her. Damn Frank and that Baldwin female! Why didn't they get out?)

"—to explain that all these riches of the harvest, priceless though they are in themselves and necessary for grub—for the festal board, yet they are but symbols and indications of the— Do sit down, Lulu; you look a little tired. —of the deeper spiritual blessings which he also showers on us and not just at harvest time, and this is a very important point—"

(Her hand dropped against his knee; lay, so white, on the drab pew. Her breasts were young and undrained under her plaid blouse. He had to touch her hand. His fingers crept toward it, touched it by accident, surely by accident, while she looked devotion and he intoned sublimity.)

"—a very important point indeed; all the year round we receive those greater inner blessings, and it is for them more than for any material, uh, material gains that we should lift our voices in Thanksgiving. Don't you think it might be valuable to all of us if I brought that out?"

"Oh, yes! Indeed I do! I think that's a lovely thought!"

(His arms tingled. He *had* to slip them about her.)

Frank and Miss Baldwin had sat down, and they were in an intolerably long discussion as to what ought to be done about that terrible little Cutler boy who said that he didn't believe that the ravens brought any bread and meat to Elijah, not if he knew anything about these ole crows! Frank explained that he did not wish to rebuke honest doubt; but when this boy went and made a regular business of cutting up and asking foolish questions—

"Lulu!" Elmer urged. "Skip back in the other room with me a second. There's something about the church work I want to ask you, and I don't want them to hear."

There were two rooms in the Schoenheim church: the auditorium and a large closet for the storage of hymn-books, mops, brooms, folding chairs, communion cups. It was lighted by a dusty window.

"Sister Bains and I are going to look over the Sunday School lesson-charts," Elmer called largely and brightly.

The fact that she did not deny it bound them together in secrecy. He sat on an upturned bucket; she perched on a step-ladder. It was pleasant to be small in her presence and look up to her.

What the "something about church work" which he was going to ask her was, he had no notion, but Elmer was a very ready talker in the presence of young women. He launched out:

"I need your advice. I've never met anybody that combined common sense and spiritual values like what you do."

"Oh, my, you're just flattering me, Brother Gantry!"

"No, I'm not. Honest, I ain't! You don't appreciate yourself. That's because you've always lived in this little burg, but if you were in Chicago or some place like that, believe me, they'd appreciate your, uh, that wonderful sense of spiritual values and everything."

"Oh—Chicago! My! I'd be scared to death!"

"Well, I'll have to take you there some day and show you the town! Guess folks would talk about their bad old preacher *then*!"

They both laughed heartily.

"But seriously, Lulu, what I want to know is—uh— Oh! What I wanted to ask you: Do you think I ought to come down here and hold Wednesday prayer-meetings?"

"Why, I think that'd be awfully nice."

"But, you see, I'd have to come down on that ole handcar."

"That's so."

"And you can't know how hard I got to study every evening at the Seminary."

"Oh, yes, I can imagine!"

They both sighed in sympathy, and he laid his hand on hers, and they sighed again, and he removed his hand almost prudishly.

"But of course I wouldn't want to spare myself in any way. It's a pastor's privilege to spend himself for his congregation."

"Yes, that's so."

"But on the other hand, with the roads the way they are here, especially in winter and all, and most of the congregation living way out on farms and all—hard for 'em to get in, eh?"

"That's so. The roads do get bad. Yes, I think you're right, Brother Gantry."

"Oh! Lulu! And here I've been calling you by your first name! You're going to make me feel I been acting terrible if you rebuke me that way and don't call me Elmer!"

"But then you're the preacher, and I'm just nobody."

"Oh, yes, you are!"

"Oh, no, I'm not!"

They laughed very much.

"Listen, Lulu, honey. Remember I'm really still a kid—just twenty-five this month—only 'bout five or six years older'n you are. Now try calling me Elmer, and see how it sounds."

"Oh, my! I wouldn't dare!"

"Well, try it!"

"Oh, I couldn't! Imagine!"

"'Fraid cat!"

"I am not so."

"Yes, you are!"

"No, I'm not!"

"I dare you!"

"Well—Elmer, then! So there now!"

They laughed intimately, and in the stress of their merriment he picked up her hand, squeezed it, rubbed it against his arm. He did not release it, but it was only with the friendliest and least emphatic pressure that he held it while he crooned:

"You aren't really scared of poor old Elmer?"

"Yes, I am, a tiny bit!"

"But why?"

"Oh, you're big and strong and dignified, like you were lots older, and you have such a boom-boom voice—my, I love to listen to it, but it scares me—I feel like you'd turn on me and say, 'You bad little girl,' and then I'd have to 'fess. My! And then you're so terribly educated—you know such long words, and you can explain all these things about the Bible that I never can understand. And of course you are a real ordained Baptist clergyman."

"Um, uh— But does that keep me from being a man, too?"

"Yes, it does! Sort of!"

Then there was no playfulness, but a grim urgency in his voice:

"Then you couldn't imagine me kissing you? . . . Look at me! . . . Look at me, I tell you! . . . There! . . . No, don't look away now. Why, you're blushing! You dear, poor, darling kid! You *can* imagine me kissing—"

"Well, I oughtn't to!"

"'Shamed?"

"Yes, I am!"

"Listen, dear. You think of me as so awfully grown-up, and of course I have to impress all these folks when I'm in the pulpit, but you can see through it and— I'm really just a big bashful kid, and I need your help so. Do you know, dear, you remind me of my mother—"

V

Frank Shallard turned on Elmer in their bedroom, while they were washing for supper—their first moment alone since Lulu and Miss Baldwin had driven them to the Bains farm to spend the night before the Thanksgiving service.

"Look here, Gantry—Elmer. I don't think it looked well, the way you took Miss Bains in the back room at the church and kept her there—must have been half an hour—and when I came in you two jumped and looked guilty."

"Uh-huh, so our little friend Franky is a real rubber-necking old woman!"

It was a spacious dusky cavern under the eaves, the room where they were to stay the night. The pitcher on the black walnut washstand was stippled in gold, riotous with nameless buds. Elmer stood glaring, his big forearms bare and dripping, shaking his fingers over the carpet before he reached for the towel.

"I am not a 'rubber-neck' and you know it, Gantry. But you're the preacher here, and it's our duty, for the effect on others, to avoid even the appearance of evil."

"Evil to him that evil thinks. Maybe you've heard that, too!"

"Oh, yes, Elmer, I think perhaps I have!"

"Suspicious, dirty-minded Puritan, that's what you are, seeing evil where there ain't any meant."

"People don't hate Puritans because they suspect unjustly, but because they suspect only too darned justly. Look here now, Elmer. I don't want to be disagreeable—"

"Well, you are!"

"—but Miss Bains—she looks sort of cuddlesome and flirtatious, but I'm dead certain she's straight as can be, and I'm not going to stand back and watch you try to, uh, to make love to her."

"Well, smarty, suppose I wanted to marry her?"

"Do you?"

"You know so blame' much, you ought to know without asking!"

"Do you?"

"I haven't said I didn't."

"Your rhetoric is too complicated for me. I'll take it that you do mean to. That's fine! I'll announce your intentions to Deacon Bains."

"You will like hell! Now you look here, Shallard! I'm not going to have you poking your long nose into my business, and that's all there is to it, see?"

"Yes, it would be if you were a layman and I had no official connection with this outfit. I don't believe too much in going around being moral for other people. But you're the preacher here—you're an ordained minister—and I'm responsible with you for the welfare of this church, and I'm damned if I'm going to watch you seducing the first girl you get your big sweaty hands on— Oh, don't go doubling up your fists. Of course you could lick me. But you won't. Especially here in the deacon's house. Ruin you in the ministry. . . . Great God, and you're the kind we affably let into the Baptist ministry! I was saying: I don't propose to see you trying to seduce—"

"Now, by God, if you think I'm going to stand— Let me tell you right now, you've got the filthiest mind I ever heard of, Shallard! Why you should think I intend for one single second to be anything but friendly and open and aboveboard with Lulu—with Miss Bains— Why, you fool, I was in there listening about how she was in love with a fellow and he's gone off to Chicago and chucked her, and that was all, and why you should think—"

"Oh, don't be so fat-headed, Gantry! You can't get away with sitting in my room at the Sem boasting, you and Zenz boasting about how many affairs you've had—"

"Well, it's the last time I'll sit in your damned room!"

"Splendid!"

"Think what you want to. And go to the devil! And be sure and run tattling to Pop Trosper and the rest of the faculty!"

"Well, that's a good come-back, Gantry. I may do just that. But this evening I'll just watch Lulu—watch Miss Bains and you. Poor sweet kid that she is! Nice eyes!"

"Uh-huh, young Shallard, so you've been smelling around, too!"

"My God, Gantry, what a perfect specimen you are!"

VI

Deacon and Mrs. Bains—an angry-faced, generous, grasping, horsy, black-mustached man he was, and she a dumpling—managed to treat Frank and Elmer simultaneously as professors of the sacred mysteries and as two hungry boys who were starved at Mizpah and who were going to catch up tonight. Fried chicken, creamed chipped beef, homemade sausages, pickles, and mince pie in which Elmer suspected, and gratefully suspected, the presence of unrighteous brandy, were only part of the stout trencher-work required of the young prophets. Mr. Bains roared every three minutes at the swollen and suffering Frank, "Nonsense, nonsense, Brother, you haven't begun to eat yet! What's the matter with you? Pass up your plate for another helpin'."

Miss Baldwin, the spinster, two other deacons and their wives and a young man from a near-by farm, one Floyd Naylor, were present, and the clergy were also expected to be instructive. The theories were that they cared to talk of nothing save theology and the church and, second, that such talk was somehow beneficial in the tricky business of enjoying your sleep and buggy-riding and vittles, and still getting into heaven.

"Say, Brother Gantry," said Mr. Bains, "what Baptist paper do you like best for home reading? I tried the *Watchman Examiner* for a while, but don't seem to me it lambastes the Campbellites like it ought to, or gives the Catholics what-for, like a real earnest Christian sheet ought to. I've started taking the *Word and Way*. Now there's a mighty sound paper that don't mince matters none, and written real elegant—just suits me. It tells you straight out from the shoulder that if you don't believe in the virgin birth and the resurrection, atonement, and immersion, then it don't make no difference about your so-called good works and charity and all that, because you're doomed and bound to go straight to hell, and not no make-believe hell, either, but a real gosh-awful turble bed of sure-enough coals! Yes, sir!"

"Oh, look here now, Brother Bains!" Frank Shallard protested. "You don't mean to say you think that the Lord Jesus isn't going to save one single solitary person who isn't an orthodox Baptist?"

"Well, I don't perfess to know all these things myself, like I was a high-toned preacher. But way I see it: Oh, yes, maybe if a fellow ain't ever had a chance to see the light—say he was brought up a Methodist or a Mormon, and never *heard* a real dyed-in-the-wool Baptist explain the complete truth, then maybe God might forgive him 'cause he was ignorant. But one thing I do know, absolute: All these 'advanced thinkers' and 'higher critics' are going to the hottest pit of hell! What do you think about it, Brother Gantry?"

"Personally, I'm much inclined to agree with you," Elmer gloated. "But, anyway, we can safely leave it to the mercy of God to take care of wobblers and cowards and gas-bags like these alleged advanced thinkers. When they treacherously weaken our efforts at soul-saving out here in the field, and go in for a lot of cussing and discussing and fussing around with a lot of fool speculation that don't do anybody any practical good in the great work of bringing poor sufferin' souls to peace, why then I'm too busy to waste *my* time on 'em, that's all, and I wouldn't care one bit if they heard me and knew it! Fact, that's the only trouble with Brother Shallard here—I know he has the grace of God in his heart, but he will waste time worrying over a lot of doctrines when everything's set down in Baptist tradition, and that's all you need to know. I want you to think about that, Frank—"

Elmer had recovered. He enjoyed defying lightning, provided it was lightning no more dynamic than Frank was likely to furnish. He looked at Frank squarely. . . . It was perhaps half an hour since their talk in the bedroom.

Frank opened his mouth twice, and closed it. Then it was too late. Deacon Bains was already overwhelming him with regeneration and mince pie.

VII

Lulu was at the other end of the table from Elmer. He was rather relieved. He despised Frank's weakness, but he was never, as with Eddie Fislinger, sure what Frank would do or say, and he determined to be cautious. Once or twice he glanced at Lulu intimately, but he kept all his conversation (which, for Lulu's admiration, he tried to make learned yet virile) for Mr. Bains and the other deacons.

"There!" he reflected. "Now Shallard, the damned fool, ought to see that I'm not trying to grab off the kid. . . . If he makes any breaks about 'what are my intentions' to her, I'll just be astonished, and get Mr. Frank Shallard in bad, curse him and his dirty sneaking suspicions!"

But: "God, I've *got* to have her!" said all the tumultuous smoky beings in the lowest layer of his mind, and he answered them only with an apprehensive, "Watch out! Be careful! Dean Trosper would bust you! Old Bains would grab his shotgun. . . . Be careful! . . . *Wait!*"

Not till an hour after supper, when the others were bending over the corn-popper, did he have the chance to whisper to her:

"Don't trust Shallard! Pretends to be a friend of mine—couldn't trust him with a plugged nickel! Got to tell you about him. Got to! Listen! Slip down after the others go up t' bed. I'll be down here. Must!"

"Oh, I can't! Cousin Adeline Baldwin is sleeping with me."

"Well! Pretend to get ready to go to bed—start and do your hair or something—and then come down to see if the fire is all right. Will you?"

"Maybe."

"You must! Please! Dear!"

"Maybe. But I can't stay but just a second."

Most virtuously, most ministerially: "Oh, of course."

They all sat, after supper, in the sitting-room. The Bainses prided themselves on having advanced so far socially that they did not spend their evenings in the kitchen-dining-room—always. The sitting-room had the homeliness of a New England farm-house, with hectically striped rag carpet, an amazing patent rocker with Corinthian knobs and brass dragon's feet, crayon enlargements, a table piled with *Farm and Fireside* and *Modern Priscilla*, and the enormous volume of pictures of the Chicago World's Fair. There was no fireplace, but the stove was a cheery monster of nickel and mica, with a jolly brass crown more golden than gold, and around the glaring belly a chain of glass sapphires, glass emeralds, and hot glass rubies.

Beside the stove's gorgeous cheerfulness, Elmer turned on his spiritual faucet and worked at being charming.

"Now don't you folks dare say one word about church affairs this evening! I'm not going to be a preacher—I'm just going to be a youngster and kick up my heels in the pasture, after that lovely supper, and I declare to goodness if I didn't know she was a strict Mother in Zion, I'd make Mother Bains dance with me—bet she could shake as pretty a pair of heels as any of these art dancers in the theater!"

And encircling that squashy and billowing waist, he thrice whirled her round, while she blushed, and giggled, "Why, the very idee!" The others applauded with unsparing plow-hardened hands, cracking the shy ears of Frank Shallard.

Always Frank had been known as an uncommonly amiable youth, but tonight he was sour as alum.

It was Elmer who told them stories of the pioneer Kansas he knew so well, from reading. It was Elmer who started them popping corn in the parlor-stove after their first uneasiness at being human in the presence of Men of God. During this festivity, when even the most decorous deacon chuckled and admonished Mr. Bains, "Hey, who you shovin' there, Barney?" Elmer was able to evade publicity and make his rendezvous with Lulu.

More jolly than ever, then, and slightly shiny from buttered pop-corn, he herded them to the parlor-organ, on which Lulu operated with innocent glee and not much knowledge. Out of duty to the cloth, they had to begin with singing "Blessed Assurance," but presently he had them basking in "Seeing Nelly Home," and "Old Black Joe."

All the while he was quivering with the promise of soft adventure to come.

It only added to his rapture that the young neighboring farmer, Floyd Naylor—kin of the Bains family, a tall young man but awkward—was also mooning at Lulu, longing but shy.

They wound up with "Beulah Land," played by Lulu, and his voice was very soothing, very touching and tender:

O Beulah Land, sweet Beulah Land,
(You little darling!)
As on thy highest mount I stand,
(I wonder if I kinda looked pathetic, would she baby me?)
I look away across the sea,
(Oh, I'll be good—won't go too far.)
Where mansions are prepared for me,
(Her wrists while she plays—like to kiss 'em!)
And view the shining glory shore,
(Going to, by thunder! Tonight!)
My heav'n, my home for evermore.
(Wonder if she'll come down-stairs in a wrapper?)

"I just wish I knew," said the wife of one of the deacons, a sentimental and lively lady, "what you were thinking of while we sang, Brother Gantry?"

"Why— I was thinking how happy we'll all be when we are purified and at rest in Beulah Land."

"My, I knew it was something religious—you sang so sorta happy and inspired. Well! We must be going. It's been *such* a lovely evening, Sister Bains. We just don't know how to thank you and Brother Bains, yes, and Brother Gantry, too, for such a fine time. Oh, and Brother Shallard, of course. Come, Charley."

Charley, as well as the other deacons, had vanished into the kitchen after Brother Bains. There was a hollow noise, as of a jug mouth, while the ladies and the clergy talked loudly and looked tolerant. The men appeared at the door wiping their mouths with the hairy backs of their paws.

VIII

After the tremendous leave-taking, to a yawning host Elmer suggested, "If it won't bother you and Sister Bains, I'm going to stay down here by the fire a few minutes and complete my notes for my sermon tomorrow. And then I won't keep Brother Shallard awake."

"Fine, fine—eaaaaah—'scuse me—so sleepy. The house is yours, my boy—Brother. G'night."

"Good night! Good night, Brother Bains. Good night, Sister Bains. Good night, Sister Lulu. . . . Night, Frank."

The room was far more boisterous when he was left alone in it. It reeled and clamored. He paced, nervously smiting the palm of his left hand, stopping in fever to listen. . . . Time crawling forever. . . . She would not come.

Creep-mouse rustle on the stairs, reluctant tip-toe in the hall.

His whole torso swelled with longing. He threw back his arms, fists down by his side, chin up, like the statue of Nathan Hale. But when she edged in he was enacting the kindly burly pastor, an elbow on the corner of the parlor-organ, two fingers playing with his massy watch-chain, his expression benevolent and amused.

She was not in a dressing-gown; she wore her blue frock unaltered. But she had let down her hair and its pale silkiness shone round her throat. She looked at him beseechingly.

Instantly he changed his pose and dashed at her with a little boyish cry:

"Oh, Lu! I can't tell you how Frank hurt me!"

"What? What?"

Very naturally, as with unquestioning intimacy, he put his arm about her shoulder, and his finger-tips rejoiced in her hair.

"It's terrible! Frank ought to know me, but what do you think he said? Oh, he didn't dare come right out and say it—not to *me*—but he hinted around and insinuated and suggested that you and I were misbehaving there in the church when we were talking. And you remember what we were talking about—about my moth-er! And how beautiful and lovely she used to be and how much you're like her! Don't you think that's rotten of him?"

"Oh, I do! I think it's just dreadful. I never did like him!"

In her sympathy she had neglected to slip out from under his arm.

"Come sit down beside me on the couch, dear."

"Oh, I mustn't." Moving with him toward the couch. "I've got to go right back up-stairs. Cousin Adeline, she's suspicious."

"We'll both go up, right away. But this thing upset me so! Wouldn't think a big clumsy like me could be such a sensitive chump, would you!"

He drew her close. She snuggled beside him, unstruggling, sighing:

"Oh, I do understand, Elmer, and I think it's dandy, I mean it's lovely when a man can be so big and strong and still have fine feelings. But, honest, I *must* go."

"Must go, *dear*."

"No."

"Yes. Won't let you, 'less you say it."

"Must go, dear!"

She had sprung up, but he held her hand, kissed her finger-tips, looked up at her with plaintive affection.

"Poor boy! Did I make it all well?"

She had snatched away her hand, she had swiftly kissed his temple and fled. He tramped the floor quite daft, now soaringly triumphant, now blackly longing.

IX

During their hand-car return to Babylon and the Seminary, Elmer and Frank had little to say.

"Don't be such a grouch. Honest, I'm not trying to get funny with little Lulu," Elmer grumbled, panting as he pumped the hand-car, grotesque in cap and muffler.

"All right. Forget it," said Frank.

Elmer endured it till Wednesday. For two days he had been hag-ridden by plans to capture Lulu. They became so plain to him that he seemed to be living them, as he slumped on the edge of his cot, his fists clenched, his eyes absent. . . . In his dream he squandered a whole two dollars and a half for a "livery rig" for the evening, and drove to Schoenheim. He hitched it at that big oak, a quarter of a mile from the Bains farmhouse. In the moonlight he could see the rounded and cratered lump on the oak trunk where a limb had been cut off. He crept to the farmyard, hid by the corncrib, cold but excited. She came to the door with a dish-pan of water—stood sidewise in the light, her gingham work-dress molded to the curve from shoulder to breast. He whistled to her; she started; came toward him with doubtful feet, cried with gladness when she saw who it was.

She could not stay with him till the work was done, but she insisted that he wait in the stable. There was the warmth of the cows, their sweet odor, and a scent of hay. He sat on a manger-edge in the darkness, enraptured yet so ardent that he trembled as with fear. The barn door edged open, with a flash of moonlight; she came toward him, reluctant, fascinated. He did not stir. She moved, entranced, straight into his arms; they sat together on a pile of hay, taut with passion, unspeaking, and his hand smoothed her ankle.

And again, in his fancies, it was at the church that she yielded; for some reason not quite planned, he was there without Frank, on a week-day evening, and she sat beside him on a pew. He could hear himself arguing that she was to trust him, that their love partook of the divine, even while he was fondling her.

But— Suppose it were Deacon Bains who came to his whistle, and found him sneaking in the barnyard? Suppose she declined to be romantic in cow-barns? And just what excuse had he for spending an evening with her at the church?

But— Over and over, sitting on his cot, lying half-asleep with the covers clutched desperately, he lived his imaginings till he could not endure it.

Not till Wednesday morning did it occur to the Reverend Elmer Gantry that he need not sneak and prowl, not necessarily, no matter what his custom had been, and that there was nothing to prevent his openly calling on her.

Nor did he spend any two dollars and a half for a carriage. Despite his florid magnificence, he was really a very poor young man. He walked to Schoenheim (not in vision now, but in reality), starting at five in the afternoon, carrying a ham sandwich for his supper; walked the railroad track, the cold ties echoing under his heavy tread.

He arrived at eight. He was certain that, coming so very late, her parents would not stay up to annoy him for more than an hour. They were likely to ask him to remain for the night, and there would be no snooping Cousin Adeline Baldwin about.

Mr. Bains opened to his knock.

"Well, well, well, Brother Gantry! What brings you down to this part of the world this time of night? Come in! Come in!"

"I sort of thought I needed a good long walk—been studying too hard—and I took a chance on your letting me stop in and warm myself."

"Well, sir, by golly, Brother, I'd of been mad's a wet hen if you *hadn't* stopped! This is your house and there's always an extra plate to slap on the table. Yes, sir! Had your supper? Sandwich? Enough? Foolishness! We'll have the womenfolks fix you up something in two shakes. The woman and Lulu, they're still out in the kitchen. LU-lu!"

"Oh, I mustn't stop—so terribly far back to town, and so late—shouldn't have walked so far."

"You don't step your foot out of this house tonight, Brother! You stay right here!"

When Lulu saw him, her tranced eyes said, "And did you come all this way for me?"

She was more softly desirable than he had fancied.

Warmed and swollen with fried eggs and admiration, he sat with them in the parlor narrating more or less possible incidents of his campaigns for righteousness in Kansas, till Mr. Bains began to yawn.

"By golly, ten minutes after nine! Don't know how it got to be so late. Ma, guess it's about time to turn in."

Elmer lunged gallantly:

"Well, you can go to bed, but we young folks are going to sit up and tell each other our middle names! I'm no preacher on week days—I'm just a student, by Jiminy!"

"Well— If you call this a week day. Looks like a week night to me, Brother!"

Everybody laughed.

She was in his arms, on the couch, before her father had yawned and coughed up the stairs; she was in his arms, limp, unreasoning, at midnight; after a long stillness in the chilling room, she sat up hastily at two, and fingered her rumpled hair.

"Oh, I'm frightened!" she whimpered.

He tried to pat her comfortingly, but there was not much heart in him now.

"But it doesn't matter. When shall we be married?" she fluttered.

And then there was no heart in him at all, but only a lump of terror.

Once or twice in his visions he had considered that there might be danger of having to marry her. He had determined that marriage now would cramp his advancement in the church and that, anyway, he didn't want to marry this brainless little fluffy chick, who would be of no help in impressing rich parishioners. But that caution he had utterly forgotten in emotion, and her question was authentically a surprise, abominably a shock. Thus in whirling thought, even while he mumbled:

"Well—well— Don't think we can decide yet. Ought to wait till I have time to look around after I graduate, and get settled in some good pastorate."

"Yes, perhaps we ought," she said meekly to her man, the best and most learned and strongest and much the most interesting person she had ever known.

"So you mustn't mention it to anybody, Lu. Not ever to your folks. They might not understand, like you do, how hard it is for a preacher to get his first real church."

"Yes, dear. Oh, kiss me!"

And he had to kiss her any number of times, in that ghastly cold room, before he could escape to his chamber.

He sat on his bed with an expression of sickness, complaining, "Hell, I oughtn't to have gone so far! I thought she'd resist more. Aaah! It wasn't worth all this risk. Aaaaah! She's dumm as a cow. Poor little thing!" His charity, made him feel beneficent again. "Sorry for her. But, good God, she is so wishy-washy! Her fault, really, but— Aaah! I was a fool! Well, fellow has to stand right up and face his faults honestly. I do. I don't excuse myself. I'm not afraid to admit my faults and repent."

So he was able to go to bed admiring his own virtue and almost forgiving her.

Chapter VIII

THE ARDOR of Lulu, the pride of having his own church at Schoenheim, the pleasure of watching Frank Shallard puff in agony over the hand-car, all these did not make up to Elmer for his boredom in seminary classes from Monday to Friday—that boredom which all preachers save a few sporting country parsons, a few managers of factory-like institutional churches, must endure throughout their lives.

Often he thought of resigning and going into business. Since buttery words and an important manner would be as valuable in business as in the church, the class to which he gave the most reverent attention was that of Mr. Ben T. Bohnsock, "Professor of Oratory and Literature, and Instructor in Voice Culture." Under him, Elmer had been learning an ever more golden (yet steel-strong) pulpit manner, learning not to split infinitives in public, learning that references to Dickens, Victor Hugo, James Whitcomb Riley, Josh Billings, and Michelangelo give to a sermon a very toney Chicago air.

Elmer's eloquence increased like an August pumpkin. He went into the woods to practise. Once a small boy came up behind him, standing on a stump in a clearing, and upon being greeted with "I denounce the abominations of your lascivious and voluptuous, uh, abominations," he fled yelping, and never again was the same care-free youth.

In moments when he was certain that he really could continue with the easy but dull life of the ministry, Elmer gave heed to Dean Trosper's lectures in Practical Theology and in Homiletics. Dr. Trosper told the aspiring holy clerks what to say when they called on the sick, how to avoid being compromised by choir-singers, how to remember edifying or laugh-trapping anecdotes by cataloguing them, how to prepare sermons when they had nothing to say, in what books they could find the best predigested sermon-outlines, and, most useful of all, how to raise money.

Eddie Fislinger's note-book on the Practical Theology lectures (which Elmer viewed as Elmer's note-book also, before examinations) was crammed with such practical theology as:

Pastoral visiting:
No partiality.
Don't neglect hired girls, be cordial.
Guard conversation, pleasing manner and laugh and maybe one funny story but no scandal or crit. of others.
Stay only 15–30 minutes.
Ask if like to pray with, not insist.
Rem gt opportunities during sickness, sorrow, marriage.
Ask jokingly why husband not oftener to church.

The course in Hymnology Elmer found tolerable; the courses in New Testament Interpretation, Church History, Theology, Missions, and Comparative Religions he stolidly endured and warmly cursed. Who the dickens cared whether Adoniram Judson became a Baptist by reading his Greek New Testament? Why all this fuss about a lot of prophecies in Revelation—he wasn't going to preach that highbrow stuff! And expecting them to make something out of this *filioque* argument in theology! Foolish!

The teachers of New Testament and Church History were ministers whom admiring but bored metropolitan congregations had kicked up-stairs. To both of them polite deacons had said, "We consider you essentially scholarly, Brother, rather than pastoral. Very scholarly. We're pulling wires to get you the high honor that's your due—election to a chair in one of the Baptist seminaries. While they may pay a little less, you'll have much more of the honor you so richly deserve, and lots easier work, as you might say."

The grateful savants had accepted, and they were spending the rest of their lives reading fifteenth-hand opinions, taking pleasant naps, and drooling out to yawning students the anemic and wordy bookishness which they called learning.

But the worst of Elmer's annoyances were the courses given by Dr. Bruno Zechlin, Professor of Greek, Hebrew, and Old Testament Exegesis.

Bruno Zechlin was a Ph.D. of Bonn, an S.T.D. of Edinburgh. He was one of the dozen authentic scholars in all the theological institutions of America, and incidentally he was a thorough failure. He lectured haltingly, he wrote obscurely, he could not talk to God as though he knew him personally, and he could not be friendly with numbskulls.

Mizpah Seminary belonged to the right-wing of the Baptists; it represented what was twenty years later to be known as "fundamentalism"; and in Mizpah Dr. Zechlin had been suspected of heresy.

He also had a heathenish tawny German beard, and he had been born not in Kansas or Ohio but in a city ridiculously named Frankfort.

Elmer despised him, because of the beard, because he was enthusiastic about Hebrew syntax, because he had no useful tips for ambitious young professional prophets, and because he had seemed singularly to enjoy flunking Elmer in Greek, which Elmer was making up with a flinching courage piteous to behold.

But Frank Shallard loved Dr. Zechlin, him alone among the members of the faculty.

II

Frank Shallard's father was a Baptist minister, sweet-tempered, bookish, mildly liberal, not unsuccessful; his mother was of a Main Line family, slightly run to seed. He was born in Harrisburg and reared in Pittsburgh, always under the shadow of the spires—in his case, a kindly shadow and serene, though his father did labor long at family prayers and instruct his young to avoid all worldly pollution, which included dancing, the theater, and the libidinous works of Balzac.

There was talk of sending Frank to Brown University or Pennsylvania, but when he was fifteen his father had a call to a large church in Cleveland, and it was the faculty of Oberlin College, in Ohio, who interpreted and enriched for Frank the Christian testimony to be found in Plautus, Homer, calculus, basket-ball, and the history of the French Revolution.

There was a good deal of the natural poet in him and, as is not too rarely the case with poets, something of the reasoning and scientific mind. But both imagination and reason had been submerged in a religion in which doubt was not only sinful but, much worse, in bad taste. The flair which might have turned to roses and singing, or to banners and bravado, or to pity of hopeless toilers, had been absorbed in the terrible majesty of the Jew Jehovah, the brooding mercy of Our Lord, the tales of his birth—jeweled kings and the shepherds' campfire, the looming star and the babe in the manger; myths bright as enamel buds—and he was bemused by the mysteries of Revelation, an Alice in Wonderland wearing a dragon mask.

Not only had he been swathed in theology, but all his experience had been in books instead of the speech of toiling men. He had been a solitary in college, generous but fastidious, jarred by his classmates' belching and sudden laughter.

His reasoning had been introverted, turned from an examination of men as mammals and devoted to a sorrow that sinful and aching souls should not more readily seek the security of a mystic process known as Conviction, Repentance, and Salvation, which, he was assured by the noblest and most literate men he had ever known, was guaranteed to cure all woe. His own experience did not absolutely confirm this. Even after he had been quite ecstatically saved, he found himself falling into deep still furies at the familiarities of hobbledehoys, still peeping at the arching bodies of girls. But that, he assured himself, was merely because he hadn't "gone on to perfection."

There were doubts. The Old Testament God's habit of desiring the reeking slaughter of every one who did not flatter him seemed rather anti-social, and he wondered whether all the wantoning in the Song of Solomon did really refer to the loyalty between Christ and the Church. It seemed unlike the sessions of Oberlin Chapel and the Miller Avenue Baptist Church of Cleveland, Ohio. Could Solomon just possibly refer to relations between beings more mundane and frisky?

Such qualities of reason as he had, Frank devoted not to examining the testimony which his doubting sniffed out, but to examining and banishing the doubt itself. He had it as an axiom that doubt was wicked, and he was able to enjoy considerable ingenuity in exorcising it. He had a good deal of self-esteem and pleasure among the purple-broidered ambiguities of religion.

That he should become a minister had always been assumed. He had no such definite and ecstatic Call as came to Elmer Gantry, but he had always known that he would go on nibbling at theories about the eucharist, and pointing men the way to uncharted plateaus called Righteousness, Idealism, Honesty, Sacrifice, Beauty, Salvation.

Curly flaxen hair, clear skin, fine nose, setter eyes, straight back, Frank was a pleasant-looking young man at twenty-three, in his senior year at Mizpah Seminary.

He was a favorite of Dean Trosper, of the Professor of New Testament Interpretation; his marks were high, his manner was respectful and his attendance was perfect. But his master among the faculty was the stammering and stumbling Bruno Zechlin, that bearded advocate of Hebrew syntax, that suspected victim of German beer and German rationalism, and Frank was the only student of his generation whom Dr. Zechlin chose as confidant.

During Frank's first year in Mizpah, Zechlin and he were merely polite to each other; they watched each other and respected each other and remained aloof. Frank was diffident before Dr. Zechlin's learning, and in the end it was Zechlin who offered friendship. He was a lonely man. He was a bachelor, and he despised all of his colleagues whom he did not fear. Particularly did he dislike being called "Brother Zechlin" by active long-legged braying preachers from the bush.

At the beginning of Frank's second year in Mizpah he worried once in Old Testament Exegesis class, "Professor Zechlin, I wish you'd explain an apparent Biblical inconsistency to me. It says in John—some place in the first chapter, I think it is—that 'No man hath seen God at any time,' and then in Timothy it states definitely, about God, 'Whom no man hath seen nor can see,' and yet in Exodus xxiv, Moses and more than seventy others did see him, with pavement under his feet, and Isaiah and Amos say they saw him, and God especially arranged for Moses to see part of him. And there too—God told Moses that nobody could stand seeing his face and live, but Jacob actually wrestled with God and saw him face to face and did live. Honestly, professor, I'm not trying to raise doubts, but there does seem to be an inconsistency there, and I wish I could find the proper explanation."

Dr. Zechlin looked at him with a curious fuzzy brightness. "What do you mean by a proper explanation, Shallard?"

"So we can explain these things to young people that might be bothered by them."

"Well, it's rather complicated. If you'll come to my rooms after supper tonight, I'll try to make it clear."

But when Frank shyly came calling (and Dr. Zechlin exaggerated when he spoke of his "rooms," for he had only a book-littered study with an alcove bedroom, in the house of an osteopath), he did not at all try to make it clear. He hinted about to discover Frank's opinion of smoking, and gave him a cigar; he encased himself in a musty arm-chair and queried:

"Do you ever feel a little doubt about the literal interpretation of our Old Testament, Shallard?"

He sounded kind, very understanding.

"I don't know. Yes, I guess I do. I don't like to call them doubts—"

"Why not call 'em doubts? Doubting is a very healthy sign, especially in the young. Don't you see that otherwise you'd simply be swallowing instruction whole, and no fallible human instructor can always be right, do you think?"

That began it—began a talk, always cautious, increasingly frank, which lasted till midnight. Dr. Zechlin lent him (with the adjuration not to let any one else see them) Renan's "Jesus," and Coe's "The Religion of a Mature Mind."

Frank came again to his room, and they walked, strolled together through sweet apple orchards, unconscious even of Indian summer pastures in their concentration on the destiny of man and the grasping gods.

Not for three months did Zechlin admit that he was an agnostic, and not for another month that atheist would perhaps be a sounder name for him than agnostic.

Before ever he had taken his theological doctorate, Zechlin had felt that it was as impossible to take literally the myths of Christianity as to take literally the myths of Buddhism. But for many years he had rationalized his heresies. These myths, he comforted himself, are symbols embodying the glory of God and the leadership of Christ's genius. He had worked out a satisfying parable: The literalist, said he, asserts that a flag is something holy, something to die for, not symbolically but in itself. The infidel, at the other end of the scale, maintains that the flag is a strip of wool or silk or cotton with rather unesthetic marks printed on it, and of considerably less use, therefore of less holiness and less romance, than a shirt or a blanket. But to the unprejudiced thinker, like himself, it was a symbol, sacred only by suggestion but not the less sacred.

After nearly two decades he knew that he had been fooling himself; that he did not actually admire Jesus as the sole leader; that the teachings of Jesus were contradictory and borrowed from earlier rabbis; and that if the teachings of Christianity were adequate flags, symbols, philosophies for most of the bellowing preachers whom he met and detested, then perforce they must for him be the flags, the symbols, of the enemy.

Yet he went on as a Baptist preacher, as a teacher of ministerial cubs.

He tried to explain it to Frank Shallard without seeming too shameful.

First, he suggested, it was hard for any man, it was especially hard for a teacher of sixty-five, to go back on the philosophy he had taught all his life. It made that life seem too pitifully futile.

And he did love to tread theological labyrinths.

And, he admitted, as they plodded back through a winter twilight, he was afraid to come out with the truth lest he plain lose his job.

Man of learning he was, but too sorry a preacher to be accepted by a liberal religious society, too lumbering a writer for journalism; and outside the world of religious parasitism (his own phrase) he had no way of earning his living. If he were kicked out of Mizpah, he would starve.

"So!" he said grimly. "I would hate to see you go through all this, Frank."

"But—but—but— What am I to do, Dr. Zechlin? Do you think I ought to get out of the church? Now? While there's time?"

"You have lived the church. You would probably be lonely without it. Maybe you should stay in it . . . to destroy it!"

"But you wouldn't want it destroyed? Even if some details of dogma aren't true—or even all of 'em—think what a consolation religion and the church are to weak humanity!"

"Are they? I wonder! Don't cheerful agnostics, who know they're going to die dead, worry much less than good Baptists, who worry lest their sons and cousins and sweethearts fail to get into the Baptist heaven—or what is even worse, who wonder if they may not have guessed wrong—if God may not be a Catholic, maybe, or a Mormon or a Seventh-day Adventist instead of a Baptist, and then they'll go to hell themselves! Consolation? No! But— Stay in the church. Till *you* want to get out."

Frank stayed.

III

By Senior year he had read many of Dr. Zechlin's bootlegged books: Davenport's "Primitive Traits in Religious Revivals," which asserted that the shoutings and foamings and twitchings at revival meetings were no more sanctified than any other barbaric religious frenzies; Dods and Sunderland on the origin of the Bible, which indicated that the Bible was no more holy and infallible than Homer; Nathaniel Schmidt's revolutionary life of Jesus, "The Prophet of Nazareth," and White's "History of the Warfare of Science with Theology," which painted religion as the enemy, not the promoter, of human progress. He was indeed—in a Baptist seminary!—a specimen of the "young man ruined by godless education" whom the Baptist periodicals loved to paint.

But he stayed.

He clung to the church. It was his land, his patriotism. Nebulously and quite impractically and altogether miserably he planned to give his life to a project called "liberalizing the church from within."

It was a relief after his sophistries to have so lively an emotion as his sweet, clear, resounding hatred for Brother Elmer Gantry.

IV

Frank had always disliked Elmer's thickness, his glossiness, his smut, and his inability to understand the most elementary abstraction. But Frank was ordinarily no great hater, and when they went off together to guard the flock at Schoenheim, he almost liked Elmer in his vigorous excitement—beautiful earthy excitement of an athlete.

Frank considered Lulu Bains a bisque doll, and he would have cherished her like any ten-year-old in his Sunday School Class. He saw Elmer's whole body stiffen as he looked at Lulu. And there was nothing he could do.

He was afraid that if he spoke to Mr. Bains, or even to Lulu, in the explosion Elmer might have to marry her, and suddenly the Frank who had always accepted "the holy institution of matrimony" felt that for a colt like Lulu any wild kicking up of the heels would be better than being harnessed to Elmer's muddy plow.

Frank's minister father and his mother went to California for Christmas time, and he spent the holiday with Dr. Zechlin. They two celebrated Christmas Eve, and a very radiant, well-contented, extremely German *Weinachtsabend* that was. Zechlin had procured a goose, bullied the osteopath's wife into cooking it, with sausages for stuffing and cranberry pancake to flank it. He brewed a punch not at all Baptist; it frothed, and smelled divinely, and to Frank it brought visions.

They sat in old chairs on either side of the round stove, gently waving their punch glasses, and sang:

Stille Nacht, heilige Nacht,
Alles schläft, einsam wacht
Nur das traute hochheilige Paar,
Holder Knabe im lokkigen Haar
Schlaf in himm'lischer Ruh,
Schlaf in himm'lischer Ruh.

"Ah, yes," the old man meditated, "that is the Christ I still dream of—the Child with shining hair, the dear German Christ Child—the beautiful fairy tale—and your Dean Trospers make Jesus into a monster that hates youth and laughter—*Wein, Weib und Gesang. Der arme!* How unlucky he was, that Christ, not to have the good Trosper with him at the wedding feast to explain that he must not turn the water into wine. Chk! Chk! I wonder if I am too old to start a leetle farm with a big vineyard and seven books?"

V

Elmer Gantry was always very witty about Dr. Bruno Zechlin. Sometimes he called him "Old Fuzzy." Sometimes he said, "That old coot *ought* to teach Hebrew—he looks like a page of Yid himself." Elmer could toss off things like that. The applause of Eddie Fislinger, who was heard to say in hallways and lavatories that Zechlin lacked spirituality, encouraged Elmer to create his masterpiece.

Before Exegesis class, he printed on the blackboard in a disguised hand:

> "I am Fuzzy Zechlin, the gazabo that knows more than God. If Jake Trosper got onto what I really think about inspiration of the Scriptures, he'd fire me out on my dirty Dutch neck."

The assembling students guffawed, even ponderous Brother Karkis, the up-creek Calvin.

Dr. Zechlin trotted into the classroom, smiling. He read the blackboard inscription. He looked incredulous, then frightened, and peered at his class like an old dog stoned by hoodlums. He turned and walked out, to the laughter of Brother Gantry and Brother Karkis.

It is not recorded how the incident came to Dean Trosper.

He summoned Elmer. "I suspect it was you who wrote that on the blackboard."

Elmer considered lying, then blurted, "Yes, I did, Dean. I tell you, it's a shame— I don't pretend to have reached a state of Christian perfection, but I'm trying hard, and I think it's a shame when a man on the faculty is trying to take away our faith by hints and sneers, that's how I feel."

Dean Trosper spoke snappishly: "I don't think you need worry about anybody suggesting new possibilities of sin to *you*, Brother Gantry. But there is some justification to what you say. Now go and sin no more. I still believe that some day you may grow up and turn your vitality into a means of grace for many, possibly including yourself. Thaddeldo."

Dr. Bruno Zechlin was abruptly retired at Easter. He went to live with his niece. She was poor and liked bridge, and did not want him. He made a little money by translating from the German. He died within two years.

Elmer Gantry never knew who sent him thirty dimes, wrapped in a tract about holiness, nor why. But he found the sentiments in the tract useful in a sermon, and the thirty dimes he spent for lively photographs of burlesque ladies.

Chapter IX

THE RELATIONS of Brother Gantry and Brother Shallard were not ardent, toward Christmastide, even in the intimacy of pumping a hand-car.

Frank complained while they were laboring along the track after church at Schoenheim:

"Look here, Gantry, something's got to be done. I'm not satisfied about you and Lulu. I've caught you looking at each other. And I suspect you've been talking to the dean about Dr. Zechlin. I'm afraid I've got to go to the dean myself. You're not fit to have a pastorate."

Elmer stopped pumping, glared, rubbed his mittened hands on his thighs, and spoke steadily:

"I've been waiting for this! I'm impulsive—sure; I make bad mistakes—every red-blooded man does. But what about you? I don't know how far you've gone with your hellish doubts, but I've been listening to the hedging way you answer questions in Sunday School, and I know you're beginning to wabble. Pretty soon you'll be an out-and-out liberal. God! Plotting to weaken the Christian religion, to steal away from weak groping souls their only hope of salvation! The worst murderer that ever lived isn't a criminal like you!"

"That isn't true! I'd die before I'd weaken the faith of any one who needed it!"

"Then you simply haven't got brains enough to see what you're doing, and there's no place for you in any Christian pulpit! It's me that ought to go to Pop Trosper complaining! Just today, when that girl came to you worrying about her pa's giving up family-prayers, you let on like it didn't matter much. You may have started that poor young lady on the doubt-paved road that leads to everlasting Hell!"

And all the way to Mizpah Frank worried and explained.

And at Mizpah Elmer graciously permitted him to resign his place at Schoenheim, and advised him to repent and seek the direction of the Holy Spirit before he should ever attempt another pastorate.

Elmer sat in his room flaming with his evangelistic triumph. He was so sincere about it that not for minutes did he reflect that Frank would no longer be an obstacle to his relations with Lulu Bains.

II

A score of times before March, in her own house, in an abandoned log barn, at the church, Elmer contrived to have meetings with Lulu. But he wearied of her trusting babble. Even her admiration, since she always gushed the same things in the same way, began to irritate him. Her love-making was equally unimaginative. She always kissed and expected to be kissed in the same way. Even before March he had had enough, but she was so completely devoted to him that he wondered if he might not have to give up the Schoenheim church to get rid of her.

He felt injured.

Nobody could ever say he was unkind to girls or despised 'em, the way Jim Lefferts used to. He'd taught Lulu an awful lot; got her over her hick ideas; showed her how a person could be religious and still have a good time, if you just looked at it right and saw that while you ought to teach the highest ideals, nobody could be expected to always and exactly live up to 'em every day. Especially when you were young. And hadn't he given her a bracelet that cost five good bucks?

But she was such a darned fool. Never could understand that after a certain point a man wanted to quit love-making and plan his next Sunday's sermon or bone up on his confounded Greek. Practically, he felt resentfully, she'd deceived him. Here he'd thought that she was a nice, safe, unemotional little thing, whom it might be pleasant to tease but who'd let him alone when he had more serious matters to attend to, and then she'd turned out passionate. She wanted to go on being kissed and kissed and kissed when he was sick of it. Her lips were always creeping around, touching his hand or his cheek when he wanted to talk.

She sent him whining little notes at Mizpah. Suppose somebody found one of 'em! Golly! She wrote to him that she was just living till their next meeting—trying to bother him and distract his attention when he had a man's work to do. She mooned up at him with her foolish soft mushy eyes all through his sermons—absolutely spoiled his style. She was wearing him out, and he'd have to get rid of her.

Hated to do it. Always *had* been nice to girls—to everybody. But it was for her sake just as much as his—

He'd have to be mean to her and make her sore.

III

They were alone in the Schoenheim church after morning meeting. She had whispered to him at the door, "I've got something I have to tell you."

He was frightened; he grumbled, "Well, we oughtn't to be seen together so much but— Slip back when the other folks are gone."

He was sitting in the front pew in the deserted church, reading hymns for want of better, when she crept behind him and kissed his ear. He jumped.

"Good Lord, don't go startling people like that!" he snarled. "Well, what's all this you have to tell me?"

She was faltering, near to tears. "I thought you'd like it! I just wanted to creep close and say I loved you!"

"Well, good heavens, you needn't of acted as though you were pregnant or something!"

"Elmer!" Too hurt in her gay affection, too shocked in her rustic sense of propriety, for resentment.

"Well, that's just about how you acted! Making me wait here when I've got to be back in town—important meeting—and me having to pump that hand-car all alone! I do wish you wouldn't act like a ten-year-old kid *all* the time!"

"Elmer!"

"Oh, Elmer, Elmer, Elmer! That's all very well. I like to play around and be foolish jus' well's anybody, but all this—all this— All the *time*!"

She fled round to the front of the pew and knelt by him, her childish hand on his knee, prattling in an imitation of baby-talk which infuriated him:

"Oh, issums such cwoss old bear! Issums bad old bear! So cwoss with Lulukins!"

"Lulukins! Great John God!"

"Why, Elmer Gantry!" It was the Sunday School teacher who was shocked now. She sat up on her knees.

"Lulukins! Of all the damned fool baby-talk I ever heard that takes the cake! That's got 'em all beat! For God's sake try to talk like a human being! And don't go squatting there. Suppose somebody came in. Are you deliberately going to work to ruin me? . . . *Lulukins!*"

She stood up, fists tight. "What have I done? I didn't mean to hurt you! Oh, I didn't, dearest! Please forgive me! I just came in to s'prise you!"

"Huh! You *s'prised* me all right!"

"Dear! Please! I'm so sorry. Why, you called me Lulukins yourself!"

"I never did!"

She was silent.

"Besides, if I did, I was kidding."

Patiently, trying to puzzle it out, she sat beside him and pleaded, "I don't know what I've done. I just don't know. Won't you please—oh, *please* explain, and give me a chance to make up for it!"

"Oh, hell!" He sprang up, hat in hand, groping for his overcoat. "If you can't understand, I can't waste my time explaining!" And was gone, relieved but not altogether proud.

But by Tuesday he admired himself for his resolution.

Tuesday evening came her apology; not a very good note, blurry, doubtful of spelling, and, as she had no notion what she was apologizing about, not very lucid.

He did not answer it.

During his sermon the next Sunday she looked up at him waiting to smile, but he took care not to catch her eye.

While he was voluminously explaining the crime of Nadab and Abihu in putting strange fire in their censors, he was thinking with self-admiration, "Poor little thing. I'm sorry for her. I really am."

He saw that she was loitering at the door, behind her parents, after the service, but he left half his congregation unhand-shaken and unshriven, muttered to Deacon Bains, "Sorry gotta hurry 'way," and fled toward the railroad tracks.

"If you're going to act this way and deliberately *persecute* me," he raged, "I'll just have to have a good talk with you, my fine young lady!"

He waited, this new Tuesday, for another note of apology. There was none, but on Thursday, when he was most innocently having a vanilla milk-shake at Bombery's Drug Store, near the seminary, when he felt ever so good and benign and manly, with his Missions theme all finished and two fine five-cent cigars in his pocket, he saw her standing outside peering in at him.

He was alarmed. She looked not quite sane.

"Suppose she's told her father!" he groaned.

He hated her.

He swaggered out gallantly, and he did most magniloquently the proper delight at encountering her here in town.

"Well, well, well, Lulu, this *is* a pleasant surprise! And where's Papa?"

"He and Ma are up in the doctor's office—about Ma's ear-ache. I said I'd meet them at the Boston Bazaar. Elmer!" Her voice was like stretched quivering wire. "I've *got* to talk to you! You've got to— Walk down the street with me."

He saw that she had tried to rouge her cheeks. It was not customary in rural Midwest in 1906. She had done it badly.

The spring was early. These first days of March were soft with buds, and Elmer sighed that if she weren't such a tyrannical nagger, he might have felt romantic about her as they walked toward the court-house lawn and the statue of General Sherman.

He had expanded her education in boldness as well as vocabulary; and with only a little hesitation, a little of peering up at him, a little of trying to hook her fingers over his arm till he shook it free, she blurted:

"We've got to do something. Because I think I'm going to have a baby."

"Oh, good God Almighty! Hell!" said the Reverend Elmer Gantry. "And I suppose you've gone squealing to your old man and the old woman!"

"No, I haven't." She was quiet, and dignified—dignified as a bedraggled gray kitten could be.

"Well, that's good, anyway. Well, I suppose I'll have to do something about it. Damn!"

He thought rapidly. From the ladies of joy whom he knew in the city of Monarch he could obtain information— But—

"You look here now!" he snarled. "It isn't possible!" He faced her, on the brick walk through the court-house lawn, under the castiron wings of the rusty Justice. "What are you trying to pull? God knows I most certainly intend to stand by you in every way. But I don't intend to be bamboozled, not by anybody! What makes you think you're pregnant?"

"Please, dear! Don't use that word!"

"Huh! Say, that's pretty good, that is! Come across now. What makes you think so?"

She could not look at him; she looked only at the ground; and his virtuous indignation swooped down on her as she stammered her reasons. Now no one had taught Lulu Bains much physiology; and it was evident that she was making up what she considered sound symptoms. She could only mumble again and again, while tears mucked her clumsy rouge, while her bent fingers trembled at her chin, "Oh, it's— I feel so bad—oh, please, dear, don't make me go on explaining."

He had enough of it. He gripped her shoulder, not tenderly.

"Lulu, you're lying! You have a dirty, lying, deceitful heart! I wondered what it was about you that bothered me and kept me from marrying you. Now I know! Thank God I've found out in time! You're lying!"

"Oh, dear, I'm not. Oh, please!"

"Look here. I'm going to take you to a doctor's. Right now. We'll get the truth."

"Oh, no, no, no! Please, no! I can't."

"Why can't you?"

"Oh, please!"

"Uh-huh! And that's all you've got to say for yourself! Come here! Look up at me!"

They must have hurt, his meaty fingers digging into her shoulder, but then, he felt righteous, he felt like the Old Testament prophets whom his sect admired. And he had found something about which he really could quarrel with her.

She did not look at him, for all his pinching. She merely wept, hopelessly.

"Then you were lying?"

"Oh, I was! Oh, dearest, how can you hurt me like you do?" He released his grip, and looked polite. "Oh, I don't mean hurting my shoulder. That doesn't matter. I mean hurting *me*! So cold to me! And I thought maybe if we were married— I'd do everything to make you happy. I'd go wherever you did. I wouldn't mind if we had the tiniest little small house—"

"And you—*you*—expect a minister of the gospel to share *any* house with a liar! Oh, you viper that— Oh, hell, I won't talk like a preacher. I don't suppose I have done altogether right, maybe. Though I noticed you were glad enough to sneak out and meet me places! But when a woman, a Christian, deliberately lies and tries to deceive a man in his deepest feelings— That's too much, no matter what I did! Don't you ever dare to speak to me again! And if you tell your father about this, and force me into marriage, I'll—I'll— I'll kill myself!"

"Oh, I won't! Honest, I won't!"

"I'll repent my own fault in bitter tears and as for you, young woman— Go and sin no more!"

He swung round, walked away from her, deaf to her whimperings. She desperately trotted after his giant strides for a while, then leaned against the trunk of a sycamore, while a passing grocery clerk snickered.

She did not appear at church the next Sunday. Elmer was so pleased that he thought of having another rendezvous with her.

IV

Deacon Bains and his good wife had noticed how pale and absent-minded was their normally bouncing daughter.

"Guess she's in love with that new preacher. Well, let's keep our hands off. Be a nice match for her. Never knew a young preacher that was so filled with the power. Talks like a house afire, by golly," said the deacon, as they yawned and stretched in the vast billowy old bed.

Then Floyd Naylor came fretting to the deacon.

Floyd was a kinsman of the family; a gangling man of twenty-five, immensely strong, rather stupid, a poor farmer, very loyal. For years he had buzzed about Lulu. It would be over-romantic to say that he had eaten his faithful heart out in lone reverence. But he had always considered Lulu the most beautiful, sparkling, and profound girl in the universe. Lulu considered him a stick, and Deacon Bains held in aversion his opinions on alfalfa. He was a familiar of the household; rather like a neighbor's dog.

Floyd found Deacon Bains in the barnyard mending a whiffletree, and grunted, "Say, Cousin Barney, I'm kind of worried about Lulu."

"Oh, guess she's in love with this new preacher. Can't tell; they might get hitched."

"Yeh, but is Brother Gantry in love with her? Somehow I don't like that fella."

"Rats, you don't appreciate preachers. You never was in a real state of grace. Never did get reborn of the spirit proper."

"Like hell I didn't! Got just as reborn as you did! Preachers are all right, most of 'em. But this fella Gantry— Say, here 'long about two months ago I seen him and Lulu walking down the brick schoolhouse road, and they was hugging and kissing like all get-out, and he was calling her Sweetheart."

"Heh? Sure it was them?"

"Dead certain. I was, uh— Well, fact is, another fella and me—"

"Who was she?"

"Now that don't make no difference. Anyway, we was sitting right under the big maple this side of the schoolhouse, in the shade, but it was bright moonlight and Lulu and this preacher come by, near's I am to you, prett' near. Well, thinks I, guess they're going to get engaged. Then I hung around the church, once-twice after meeting, and one time I kinda peeked in the window and I seen 'em right there in the front pew, hugging like they sure ought to get married whether or no. I didn't say anything—wanted to wait and see if he'd marry her. Now it ain't any of my business, Barney, but you know I always liked Lulu, and strikes me we ought to know if this Bible-walloper is going to play straight with her."

"Guess maybe that's right. I'll have a talk with her."

Bains had never been very observant of his daughter, but Floyd Naylor was not a liar, and it was with sharpened eyes that the deacon stumped into the house and found her standing by the churn, her arms hanging limp.

"Say, uh, say, uh, Lu, how's things going with you and Brother Gantry?"

"Why, what do you mean?"

"You two engaged? Going to be engaged? He going to marry you?"

"Of course not."

"Been making love to you, ain't he?"

"Oh, never!"

"Never hugged you or kissed you?"

"Never!"

"How far'd he go?"

"Oh, he didn't!"

"Why you been looking so kind of peeked lately?"

"Oh, I just don't feel very well. Oh, I feel fine. It's just the spring coming on, I guess—" She dropped to the floor and, with her head against the churn, her thin fingers beating an hysterical tattoo on the floor, she choked with weeping.

"There, there, Lu! Your dad'll do something about it."

Floyd was waiting in the farmyard.

There were, in those parts and those days, not infrequent ceremonies known as "shotgun weddings."

V

The Reverend Elmer Gantry was reading an illustrated pink periodical devoted to prize fighters and chorus girls in his room at Elizabeth J. Schmutz Hall late of an afternoon when two large men walked in without knocking.

"Why, good evening, Brother Bains—Brother Naylor! This is a pleasant surprise. I was, uh— Did you ever see this horrible rag? About actoresses. An invention of the devil himself. I was thinking of denouncing it next Sunday. I hope you never read it—won't you sit down, gentleman?—take this chair— I hope you never read it, Brother Floyd, because the footsteps of—"

"Gantry," exploded Deacon Bains, "I want you to take your footsteps right now and turn 'em toward my house! You've been fooling with my daughter, and either you're going to marry her, or Floyd and me are going to take it out of your hide, and way I feel just now, don't much care which it is."

"You mean to say that Lulu has been pretending—"

"Naw, Lulu ain't said nothing. God, I wonder if I ought to *let* the girl marry a fellow like you? But I got to protect her good name, and guess Floyd and me can see to it you give her a square deal after the marriage. Now I've sent out word to invite all the neighbors to the house tonight for a little sociable to tell 'em Lulu and you are engaged, and you're going to put on your Sunday-go-to-meeting suit and come with us, right now."

"You can't bully me into anything—"

"Take that side of him, Floyd, but I get the first lick. You get what's left."

They ranged up beside him. They were shorter, less broad, but their faces were like tanned hard leather, their eyes were hard—

"You're a big cuss, Brother Gantry, but guess you don't get enough exercise no more. Pretty soft," considered Deacon Bains.

His fist was dropping down, down to his knee; his shoulder sloped down; his fist was coming up—and Floyd had suddenly pinioned Elmer's arms.

"I'll do it! All right! All right!" Elmer shrieked.

He'd find a way to break the engagement. Already he was recovering his poise.

"Now you fellows listen to me! I'm in love with Lulu, and I intended to ask her the moment I finish here—less than three months now—and get my first church. And then you two butt in and try to spoil this romance!"

"Hum, yes, I guess so," Bains droned, inexpressible contempt in his dragging voice. "You save all them pretty words for Lulu. You're going to be married the middle of May—that'll give time enough after the engagement so's the neighbors won't think there's anything wrong. Now into them clothes. Buggy waiting outside. We'll treat you right. If you use Lulu like you ought to, and honey her up and make her feel happy again, maybe Floyd and me won't kill you the night of your wedding. We'll see. And we'll always treat you fine in public—won't even laugh when we hear you preaching. Now git, hear me?"

While he dressed, Elmer was able to keep his face turned from them, able to compose himself, so that he could suddenly whirl on them with his handsomest, his most manly and winning smile.

"Brother Bains, I want to thank Cousin Floyd and you. You're dead wrong about thinking I wouldn't have done right by Lulu. But I rejoice, sir, *rejoice*, that she is blessed by having such loyal relatives!" That puzzled rather than captured them, but he fetched them complete with a jovial, "And such husky ones! I'm pretty strong myself—keep up my exercise lot more'n you think—but I guess I wouldn't be one-two-three with you folks! Good thing for ole Elmer you never let loose that darn' mule-kick of yours, Brother Bains! And you're right. No sense putting off the wedding. May fifteenth will be fine. Now I want to ask one thing: Let me have ten minutes alone with Lu before you make the announcement. I want to console her—make her happy. Oh, you can tell if I keep faith—the eagle eye of a father will know."

"Well, my father's eagle eye ain't been working none too good lately, but I guess it'll be all right for you to see her."

"Now, will you shake hands? Please!"

He was so big, so radiant, so confident. They looked sheepish, grinned like farmers flattered by a politician, and shook hands.

There was a multitude at the Bainses', also fried chicken and watermelon pickles.

The deacon brought Lulu to Elmer in the spare room and left her.

Elmer was at ease on the sofa; she stood before him, trembling, red-eyed.

"Come, you poor child," he condescended.

She approached, sobbing, "Honestly, dear, I didn't tell Pa anything—I didn't ask him to do it—oh, I don't want to if you don't."

"There, there, child. It's all right. I'm sure you'll make a fine wife. Sit down." And he permitted her to kiss his hand, so that she became very happy and wept tremendously, and went out to her father rejoicing.

He considered, meanwhile, "That ought to hold you, damn you! Now I'll figure out some way of getting out of this mess."

At the announcement of Lulu's engagement to a Man of God, the crowd gave hoarse and holy cheers.

Elmer made quite a long speech into which he brought all that Holy Writ had to say about the relations of the sexes—that is, all that he remembered and that could be quoted in mixed company.

"Go on, Brother! Kiss her!" they clamored.

He did, heartily; so heartily that he felt curious stirrings.

He spent the night there, and was so full of holy affection that when the family was asleep, he crept into Lulu's bedroom. She stirred on the pillow and whispered, "Oh, my darling! And you forgave me! Oh, I do love you so!" as he kissed her fragrant hair.

VI

It was usual for the students of Mizpah to let Dean Trosper know if they should become engaged. The dean recommended them for ministerial appointments, and the status of marriage made a difference. Bachelors were more likely to become assistants in large city churches; married men, particularly those whose wives had lively piety and a knowledge of cooking, were usually sent to small churches of their own.

The dean summoned Elmer to his gloomy house on the edge of the campus—it was a house which smelled of cabbage and wet ashes—and demanded:

"Gantry, just what is this business about you and some girl at Schoenheim?"

"Why, Dean," in hurt rectitude, "I'm engaged to a fine young lady there—daughter of one of my deacons."

"Well, that's good. It's better to marry than to burn—or at least so it is stated in the Scriptures. Now I don't want any monkey-business about this. A preacher must walk circumspectly. You must shun the very appearance of evil. I hope you'll love and cherish her, and seems to me it would be well not only to be engaged to her but even to marry her. Thaddeldo."

"Now what the devil did he mean by that?" protested Parsifal as he went home.

VII

He had to work quickly. He had less than two months before the threatened marriage.

If he could entangle Lulu with some one? What about Floyd Naylor? The fool loved her.

He spent as much time in Schoenheim as possible, not only with Lulu but with Floyd. He played all his warm incandescence on Floyd, and turned that trusting drudge from enemy into admiring friend. One day when Floyd and he were walking together to the hand-car Elmer purred:

"Say, Floydy, some ways it's kind of a shame Lu's going to marry me and not you. You're so steady and hard-working and patient. I fly off the handle too easy."

"Oh, gosh, no, I ain't smart enough for her, Elmer. She ought to marry a fella with a lot of book-learning like you, and that dresses swell, so she can be in society and everything."

"But I guess you liked her pretty well yourself, eh? You ought to! Sweetest girl in the whole world. You kind of liked her?"

"Yuh, I guess I did. I— Oh, well, rats, I ain't good enough for her, God bless her!"

Elmer spoke of Floyd as a future cousin and professed his fondness for him, his admiration of the young man's qualities and remarkable singing. (Floyd Naylor sang about as Floyd Naylor would have sung.) Elmer spoke of him as a future cousin, and wanted to see a deal of him.

He praised Lulu and Floyd to each other, and left them together as often as he could contrive, slipping back to watch them through the window. But to his indignation they merely sat and talked.

Then he had a week in Schoenheim, the whole week before Easter. The Baptists of Schoenheim, with their abhorrence of popery, did not make much of Easter as Easter; they called it "The Festival of Christ's Resurrection," but they did like daily meetings during what the heretical world knew as Holy Week. Elmer stayed with the Bainses and labored mightily both against sin and against getting married. Indeed he was so stirred and so eloquent that he led two sixteen-year-old girls out of their sins, and converted the neighborhood object-lesson, a patriarch who drank hard cider and had not been converted for two years.

Elmer knew by now that though Floyd Naylor was not exactly a virgin, his achievements and his resolution were considerably less than his desires, and he set to work to improve that resolution. He took Floyd off to the pasture and, after benignly admitting that perhaps a preacher oughtn't to talk of such things, he narrated his amorous conquests till Floyd's eyes were hungrily bulging. Then, with giggling apologies, Elmer showed his collection of what he called Art Photographs.

Floyd almost ate them. Elmer lent them to him. That was on a Thursday.

At the same time Elmer deprived Lulu all week of the caresses which she craved, till she was desperate.

On Friday Elmer held morning meeting instead of evening meeting, and arranged that Lulu and Floyd and he should have picnic supper in the sycamore grove near the Bains house. He suggested it in a jocund idyllic way, and Lulu brightened. On their way to the grove with their baskets she sighed to him, as they walked behind Floyd, "Oh, why have you been so cold to me? Have I offended you again, dear?"

He let her have it, brutally: "Oh, don't be such a damned whiner! Can't you act as if you had *some* brains, just for once?"

When they spread the picnic supper, she was barely keeping hold of her sobs.

They finished supper in the dusk. They sat quietly, Floyd looking at her, wondering at her distress, peeping nervously at her pretty ankles.

"Say, I've got to go in and make some notes for my sermon tomorrow. No, you two wait for me here. Nicer out in the fresh air. Be back in about half an hour," said Elmer.

He made much of noisily swaggering away through the brush; he crept back softly, stood behind a sycamore near them. He was proud of himself. It was working. Already Lulu was sobbing openly, while Floyd comforted her with "What is it, pretty? What is it, dear? Tell me."

Floyd had moved nearer to her (Elmer could just see them) and she rested her head on his cousinly shoulder.

Presently Floyd was kissing her tears away, and she seemed to be snuggling close to him. Elmer heard her muffled, "Oh, you oughtn't to kiss me!"

"Elmer said I should think of you as a sister, and I could kiss you— Oh, my God, Lulu, I do love you so terrible!"

"Oh, we oughtn't—" Then silence.

Elmer fled into the barnyard, found Deacon Bains, and demanded harshly, "Come here! I want you to see what Floyd and Lulu are doing! Put that lantern down. I've got one of these electric dinguses here."

He had. He had bought it for this purpose. He also had a revolver in his pocket.

When Elmer and the bewildered Mr. Bains burst upon them, saw them in the circle from the electric flashlight, Lulu and Floyd were deep in a devastating kiss.

"There!" bellowed the outraged Elmer. "Now you see why I hesitated to be engaged to that woman! I've suspected it all along! Oh, abomination—abomination, and she that committeth it shall be cut off!"

Floyd sprang up, a fighting hound. Elmer could doubtless have handled him, but it was Deacon Bains who with one maniac blow knocked Floyd down. The deacon turned to Elmer then, with the first tears he had known since boyhood: "Forgive me and mine, Brother! We have sinned against you. This woman shall suffer for it, always. She'll never enter my house again. She'll by God marry Floyd. And he's the shiftlessest damn' fool farmer in ten counties!"

"I'm going. I can't stand this. I'll send you another preacher. I'll never see any of you again!" said Elmer.

"I don't blame you. Try to forgive us, Brother." The deacon was sobbing now, dusty painful sobbing, bewildered sobs of anger.

The last thing Elmer saw in the light of his electric torch was Lulu huddled, with shrunk shoulders, her face insane with fear.

Chapter X

As he tramped back to Babylon that evening, Elmer did not enjoy his deliverance so much as he had expected. But he worked manfully at recalling Lulu's repetitious chatter, her humorless ignorance, her pawing, her unambitious rusticity, and all that he had escaped.

. . . To have her around—gumming his life—never could jolly the congregation and help him—and suppose he were in a big town with a swell church— Gee! Maybe he wasn't glad to be out of it! Besides! Really better for her. She and Floyd much better suited . . .

He knew that Dean Trosper's one sin was reading till late, and he came bursting into the dean's house at the scandalous hour of eleven. In the last mile he had heroically put by his exhilaration; he had thrown himself into the state of a betrayed and desolate young man so successfully that he had made himself believe it.

"Oh, how wise you were about women, Dean!" he lamented. "A terrible thing has happened! Her father and I have just found my girl in the arms of another man—a regular roué down there. I can never go back, not even for Easter service. And her father agrees with me. . . . You can ask him!"

"Well, I am most awfully sorry to hear this, Brother Gantry. I didn't know you could feel so deeply. Shall we kneel in prayer, and ask the Lord to comfort you? I'll send Brother Shallard down there for the Easter service—he knows the field."

On his knees, Elmer told the Lord that he had been dealt with as no man before or since. The dean approved his agonies very much.

"There, there, my boy. The Lord will lighten your burden in his own good time. Perhaps this will be a blessing in disguise—you're lucky to get rid of such a woman, and this will give you that humility, that deeper thirsting after righteousness, which I've always felt you lacked, despite your splendid pulpit voice. Now I've got something to take your mind off your sorrows. There's quite a nice little chapel on the edge of Monarch where they're lacking an incumbent. I'd intended to send Brother Hudkins—you know him; he's that old retired preacher that lives out by the brick-yard—comes into classes now and then—I'd intended to send him down for the Easter service. But I'll send you instead, and in fact, if you see the committee, I imagine you can fix it to have this as a regular charge, at least till graduation. They pay fifteen a Sunday and your fare. And being there in a city like Monarch, you can go to the ministerial association and so on—stay over till Monday noon every week—and make fine contacts, and maybe you'll be in line for assistant in one of the big churches next summer. There's a morning train to Monarch—10:21, isn't it? You take that train tomorrow morning, and go look up a lawyer named Eversley. He's got an office—where's his letter?—his office is in the Royal Trust Company Building. He's a deacon. I'll wire him to be there tomorrow afternoon, or anyway leave word, and you can make your own arrangements. The Flowerdale Baptist Church, that's the name, and it's a real nice little modern plant, with lovely folks. Now you go to your room and pray, and I'm sure you'll feel better.

II

It was an hilarious Elmer Gantry who took the 10:21 train to Monarch, a city of perhaps three hundred thousand. He sat in the day-coach planning his Easter discourse. Jiminy! His first sermon in a real city! Might lead to anything. Better give 'em something red-hot and startling. Let's see: He'd get away from this Christ is Risen stuff—mention it of course, just bring it in, but have some other theme. Let's see: Faith. Hope. Repentance—no, better go slow on that repentance idea; this Deacon Eversley, the lawyer, might be pretty well-to-do and get sore if you suggested he had anything to repent of. Let's see: Courage. Chastity. Love—that was it—love!

And he was making notes rapidly, right out of his own head, on the back of an envelope:

Love:
a rainbow
AM & PM star
from cradle to tomb
inspires art etc. music voice of love
slam atheists etc. who not appreciate love

"Guess you must be a newspaperman, Brother," a voice assailed him.

Elmer looked at his seatmate, a little man with a whisky nose and asterisks of laughter-wrinkles round his eyes, a rather sportingly dressed little man with the red tie which in 1906 was still thought rather the thing for socialists and drinkers.

He could have a good time with such a little man, Elmer considered. A drummer. Would it be more fun to be natural with him, or to ask him if he was saved, and watch him squirm? Hell, he'd have enough holy business in Monarch. So he turned on his best good-fellow smile, and answered:

"Well, not exactly. Pretty warm for so early, eh?"

"Yuh, it certainly is. Been in Babylon long?"

"No, not very long."

"Fine town. Lots of business."

"You betcha. And some nice little dames there, too."

The little man snickered. "There are, eh? Well, say, you better give me some addresses. I make that town once a month and, by golly, I ain't picked me out a skirt yet. But it's a good town. Lots of money there."

"Yes-sir, that's a fact. Good hustling town. Quick turnover there, all right. Lots of money in Babylon."

"Though they do tell me," said the little man, "there's one of these preacher-factories there."

"Is that a fact!"

"Yump. Say, Brother, this'll make you laugh. Juh know what I thought when I seen you first—wearing that black suit and writing things down? I thought maybe you was a preacher yourself!"

"Well—"

God, he couldn't stand it! Having to be so righteous every Sunday at Schoenheim—Deacon Bains everlastingly asking these fool questions about predestination or some doggone thing. Cer'nly had a vacation coming! And a sport like this fellow, he'd look down on you if you said you were a preacher.

The train was noisy. If any neighboring cock crowed three times, Elmer did not hear it as he rumbled:

"Well, for the love of Mike! Though—" In his most austere manner: "This black suit happens to be mourning for one very dear to me."

"Oh, say, Brother, now you gotta excuse me! I'm always shooting my mouth off!"

"Oh, that's all right."

"Well, let's shake, and I'll know you don't hold it against me."

"You bet."

From the little man came an odor of whisky which stirred Elmer powerfully. So long since he'd had a drink! Nothing for two months except a few nips of hard cider which Lulu had dutifully stolen for him from her father's cask.

"Well, what is your line, Brother?" said the little man.

"I'm in the shoe game."

"Well, that's a fine game. Yes-sir, people do have to have shoes, no matter if they're hard up or not. My name's Ad Locust—Jesus, think of it, the folks named me Adney—can you beat that—ain't that one hell of a name for a fellow that likes to get out with the boys and have a good time! But you can just call me Ad. I'm traveling for the Pequot Farm Implement Company. Great organization! Great bunch! Yes-sir, they're great folks to work for, and hit it up, say! the sales-manager can drink more good liquor than any fellow that's working for him, and, believe me, there's some of us that ain't so slow ourselves! Yes-sir, this fool idea that a lot of these fly-by-night firms are hollering about now, that in the long run you don't get no more by drinking with the dealers— All damn' foolishness. They say this fellow Ford that makes these automobiles talks that way. Well, you mark my words: By 1910 he'll be out of business, that's what'll happen to him; you mark my words! Yes-sir, they're a great concern, the Pequot bunch. Matter of fact, we're holding a sales-conference in Monarch next week."

"Is that a fact!"

"Yes-sir, by golly, that's what we're doing. You know—read papers about how to get money out of a machinery dealer when he ain't got any money. Heh! Hell of a lot of attention most of us boys'll pay to that junk! We're going to have a good time and get in a little good earnest drinking, and you bet the sales-manager will be right there with us! Say, Brother—I didn't quite catch the name—"

"Elmer Gantry is my name. Mighty glad to meet you."

"Mighty glad to know you, Elmer. Say, Elmer, I've got some of the best Bourbon you or anybody else ever laid your face to right here in my hip pocket. I suppose you being in a highbrow business like the shoe business, you'd just about faint if I was to offer you a little something to cure that cough!"

"I guess I would, all right; yes-sir, I'd just about faint."

"Well, you're a pretty big fellow, and you ought to try to control yourself."

"I'll do my best, Ad, if you'll hold my hand."

"You betcha I will." Ad brought out from his permanently sagging pocket a pint of Green River, and they drank together, reverently.

"Say, jever hear the toast about the sailor?" inquired Elmer. He felt very happy, at home with the loved ones after long and desolate wanderings.

"Dunno's I ever did. Shoot!"

> "Here's to the lass in every port,
> And here's to the port-wine in every lass,
> But those tall thoughts don't matter, sport,
> For God's sake, waiter, fill my glass!"

The little man wriggled. "Well, sir, I never did hear that one! Say, that's a knock-out! By golly, that certainly is a knock-out! Say, Elm, whacha doing in Monarch? Wancha meet some of the boys. The Pequot conference don't really start till Monday, but some of us boys thought we'd kind of get together today and hold a little service of prayer and fasting before the rest of the galoots assemble. Like you to meet 'em. Best bunch of sports *you* ever saw, lemme tell you that! I'd like for you to meet 'em. And I'd like 'em to hear that toast. 'Here's to the port-wine in every lass.' That's pretty cute, all right! Whacha doing in Monarch? Can't you come around to the Ishawonga Hotel and meet some of the boys when we get in?"

Mr. Ad Locust was not drunk; not exactly drunk; but he had earnestly applied himself to the Bourbon and he was in a state of superb philanthropy. Elmer had taken enough to feel reasonable. He was hungry, too, not only for alcohol but for unsanctimonious companionship.

"I'll tell you, Ad," he said. "Nothing I'd like better, but I've got to meet a guy—important dealer—this afternoon, and he's dead against all drinking. Fact—I certainly do appreciate your booze, but don't know's I ought to have taken a single drop."

"Oh, hell, Elm, I've got some throat pastilles that are absolutely guaranteed to knock out the smell—absolutely. One lil drink wouldn't do us any harm. Certainly would like to have the boys hear that toast of yours!"

"Well, I'll sneak in for a second, and maybe I can foregather with you for a while late Sunday evening or Monday morning, but—"

"Aw, you ain't going to let me down, Elm?"

"Well, I'll telephone this guy, and fix it so's I don't have to see him till long 'bout three o'clock."

"That's great!"

III

From the Ishawonga Hotel, at noon, Elmer telephoned to the office of Mr. Eversley, the brightest light of the Flowerdale Baptist Church. There was no answer.

"Everybody in his office out to dinner. Well, I've done all I can till this afternoon," Elmer reflected virtuously, and joined the Pequot crusaders in the Ishawonga bar. . . . Eleven men in a booth for eight. Every one talking at once. Every one shouting, "Say, waiter, you ask that damn' bartender if he's *making* the booze!"

Within seventeen minutes Elmer was calling all of the eleven by their first names—frequently by the wrong first names—and he contributed to their literary lore by thrice reciting his toast and by telling the best stories he knew. They liked him. In his joy of release from piety and the threat of life with Lulu, he flowered into vigor. Six several times the Pequot salesmen said one to another, "Now there's a fellow we ought to have with us in the firm," and the others nodded.

He was inspired to give a burlesque sermon.

"I've got a great joke on Ad!" he thundered. "Know what he thought I was first? A preacher!"

"Say, that's a good one!" they cackled.

"Well, at that, he ain't so far off. When I was a kid, I did think some about being a preacher. Well, say now, listen, and see if I wouldn't 've made a swell preacher!"

While they gaped and giggled and admired, he rose solemnly, looked at them solemnly, and boomed:

"Brethren and Sistern, in the hustle and bustle of daily life you guys certainly do forget the higher and finer things. In what, in all the higher and finer things, in what and by what are we ruled excepting by Love? What is Love?"

"You stick around tonight and I'll show you!" shrieked Ad Locust.

"Shut up now, Ad! Honest—listen. See if I couldn't 've been a preacher—a knock-out—bet I could handle a big crowd well's any of 'em. Listen. . . . What is Love? What is the divine Love? It is the rainbow, repainting with its spangled colors those dreary wastes where of late the terrible tempest has wreaked its utmost fury—the rainbow with its tender promise of surcease from the toils and travails and terrors of the awful storm! What is Love—the divine Love, I mean, not the carnal but the divine Love, as exemplified in the church? What is—"

"Say!" protested the most profane of the eleven, "I don't think you ought to make fun of the church. I never go to church myself, but maybe I'd be a better fella if I did, and I certainly do respect folks that go to church, and I send my kids to Sunday School. You God damn betcha!"

"Hell, I ain't making fun of the church!" protested Elmer.

"Hell, he ain't making fun of the church. Just kidding the preachers," asserted Ad Locust. "Preachers are just ordinary guys like the rest of us."

"Sure; preachers can cuss and make love just like anybody else. I know! What they get away with, pretending to be different," said Elmer lugubriously, "would make you gentlemen tired if you knew."

"Well, I don't think you had ought to make fun of the church."

"Hell, he ain't making fun of the church."

"Sure, I ain't making fun of the church. But lemme finish my sermon."

"Sure, let him finish his sermon."

"Where was I? . . . What is Love? It is the evening and the morning star—those vast luminaries that as they ride the purple abysms of the vasty firmament vouchsafe in their golden splendor the promise of higher and better things that—that— Well, say, you wise guys, would I make a great preacher or wouldn't I?"

The applause was such that the bartender came and looked at them funereally; and Elmer had to drink with each of them. That is, he drank with four of them.

But he was out of practise. And he had had no lunch.

He turned veal-white; sweat stood on his forehead and in a double line of drops along his upper lip, while his eyes were suddenly vacant.

Ad Locust squealed, "Say, look out! Elm's passing out!"

They got him up to Ad's room, one man supporting him on either side and one pushing behind, just before he dropped insensible, and all that afternoon, when he should have met the Flowerdale Baptist committee, he snored on Ad's bed, dressed save for his shoes and coat. He came to at six, with Ad bending over him, solicitous.

"God, I feel awful!" Elmer groaned.

"Here. What you need's a drink."

"Oh, Lord, I mustn't take any more," said Elmer, taking it. His hand trembled so that Ad had to hold the glass to his mouth. He was conscious that he must call up Deacon Eversley at once. Two drinks later he felt better, and his hand was steady. The Pequot bunch began to come in, with a view to dinner. He postponed his telephone call to Eversley till after dinner; he kept postponing it; and he found himself, at ten on Easter morning, with a perfectly strange young woman in a perfectly strange flat, and heard Ad Locust, in the next room, singing "How Dry I Am."

Elmer did a good deal of repenting and groaning before his first drink of the morning, after which he comforted himself, "Golly, I never will get to that church now. Well, I'll tell the committee I was taken sick. Hey, Ad! How'd we ever get here? Can we get any breakfast in this dump?"

He had two bottles of beer, spoke graciously to the young lady in the kimono and red slippers, and felt himself altogether a fine fellow. With Ad and such of the eleven as were still alive, and a scattering of shrieking young ladies, he drove out to a dance-hall on the lake, Easter Sunday afternoon, and they returned to Monarch for lobster and jocundity.

"But this ends it. Tomorrow morning I'll get busy and see Eversley and fix things up," Elmer vowed.

IV

In that era long-distance telephoning was an uncommon event, but Eversley, deacon and lawyer, was a bustler. When the new preacher had not appeared by six on Saturday afternoon, Eversley telephoned to Babylon, waited while Dean Trosper was fetched to the Babylon central, and spoke with considerable irritation about the absence of the ecclesiastical hired hand.

"I'll send you Brother Hudkins—a very fine preacher, living here now, retired. He'll take the midnight train," said Dean Trosper.

To the Mr. Hudkins the dean said, "And look around and see if you can find anything of Brother Gantry. I'm worried about him. The poor boy was simply in agony over a most unfortunate private matter . . . apparently."

Now Mr. Hudkins had for several years conducted a mission on South Clark Street in Chicago, and he knew a good many unholy things. He had seen Elmer Gantry in classes at Mizpah. When he had finished Easter morning services in Monarch, he not only went to the police and to the hospitals but began a round of the hotels, restaurants, and bars. Thus it came to pass that while Elmer was merrily washing lobster down with California claret, stopping now and then to kiss the blonde beside him and (by request) to repeat his toast, that evening, he was being observed from the café door by the Reverend Mr. Hudkins in the enjoyable rôle of avenging angel.

V

When Elmer telephoned Eversley, Monday morning, to explain his sickness, the deacon snapped, "All right. Got somebody else."

"But, well, say, Dean Trosper thought you and the committee might like to talk over a semi-permanent arrangement—"

"Nope, nope, nope."

Returned to Babylon, Elmer went at once to the office of the dean.

One look at his expression was enough.

The dean concluded two minutes of the most fluent description with:

"—the faculty committee met this morning, and you are fired from Mizpah. Of course you remain an ordained Baptist minister. I could get your home association to cancel your credentials, but it would grieve them to know what sort of a lying monster they sponsored. Also, I don't want Mizpah mixed up in such a scandal. But if I ever hear of you in any Baptist pulpit, I'll expose you. Now I don't suppose you're bright enough to become a saloon-keeper, but you ought to make a pretty good bartender. I'll leave your punishment to your midnight thoughts."

Elmer whined, "You hadn't ought—you ought not to talk to me like that! Doesn't it say in the Bible you ought to forgive seventy times seven—"

"This is eighty times seven. Get out!"

So the Reverend Mr. Gantry surprisingly ceased to be, for practical purposes, a Reverend at all.

He thought of fleeing to his mother, but he was ashamed; of fleeing to Lulu, but he did not dare.

He heard that Eddie Fislinger had been yanked to Schoenheim to marry Lulu and Floyd Naylor . . . a lonely grim affair by lamplight.

"They might have *ast* me, anyway," grumbled Elmer, as he packed.

He went back to Monarch and the friendliness of Ad Locust. He confessed that he had been a minister, and was forgiven. By Friday that week Elmer had become a traveling salesman for the Pequot Farm Implement Company.

Chapter XI

ELMER GANTRY was twenty-eight, and for two years he had been a traveling salesman for the Pequot Company.

Harrows and rakes and corn-planters; red plows and gilt-striped green wagons; catalogues and order-lists; offices glassed off from dim warehouses; shirt-sleeved dealers on high stools at high desks; the bar at the corner; stifling small hotels and lunch-rooms; waiting for trains half the night in foul boxes of junction stations, where the brown slatted benches were an agony to his back; trains, trains, trains; trains and time-tables and joyous return to his head-quarters in Denver; a drunk, a theater, and service in a big church.

He wore a checked suit, a brown derby, striped socks, the huge ring of gold serpents and an opal which he had bought long ago, flower-decked ties, and what he called "fancy vests"—garments of yellow with red spots, of green with white stripes, of silk or daring chamois.

He had had a series of little loves, but none of them important enough to continue.

He was not unsuccessful. He was a good talker, a magnificent hand-shaker, his word could often be depended on, and he remembered most of the price-lists and all of the new smutty stories. In the office at Denver he was popular with "the boys." He had one infallible "stunt"—a burlesque sermon. It was known that he had studied to be a preacher but had courageously decided that it was no occupation for a "real two-fisted guy," and that he had "told the profs where they got off." A promising and commendable fellow; conceivably sales-manager some day.

Whatever his dissipations, Elmer continued enough exercise to keep his belly down and his shoulders up. He had been shocked by Deacon Bains' taunt that he was growing soft, and every morning in his hotel room he unhumorously did calisthenics for fifteen minutes; evenings he bowled or boxed in Y.M.C.A. gymnasiums, or, in towns large enough, solemnly swam up and down tanks like a white porpoise. He felt lusty, and as strong as in Terwillinger days.

Yet Elmer was not altogether happy.

He appreciated being free of faculty rules, free of the guilt which in seminary days had followed his sprees at Monarch, free of the incomprehensible debates of Harry Zenz and Frank Shallard, yet he missed leading the old hymns, and the sound of his own voice, the sense of his own power, as he held an audience by his sermon. Always on Sunday evenings (except when he had an engagement with a waitress or a chambermaid) he went to the evangelical church nearest his hotel. He enjoyed criticizing the sermon professionally.

"Golly, I could put it all over that poor boob! The straight gospel is all right, but if he'd only stuck in a couple literary allusions, and lambasted the saloon-keepers more, he'd 've had 'em all het up."

He sang so powerfully that despite a certain tobacco and whisky odor the parsons always shook hands with extra warmth, and said they were glad to see you with us this evening, Brother.

When he encountered really successful churches, his devotion to the business became a definite longing to return to preaching; he ached to step up, push the minister out of his pulpit, and take charge, instead of sitting back there unnoticed and unadmired, as though he were an ordinary layman.

"These chumps would be astonished if they knew what I am!" he reflected.

After such an experience it was vexatious on Monday morning to talk with a droning implement-dealer about discounts on manure-spreaders; it was sickening to wait for train-time in a cuspidor-filled hotel lobby when he might have been in a church office superior with books, giving orders to pretty secretaries and being expansive and helpful to consulting sinners. He was only partly solaced by being able to walk openly into a saloon and shout, "Straight rye, Bill."

On Sunday evening in a Western Kansas town he ambled to a shabby little church and read on the placard outside:

This Morning: The Meaning of Redemption
This Evening: Is Dancing of the Devil?
FIRST BAPTIST CHURCH
Pastor:
The Rev. Edward Fislinger, B.A., B.D.

"Oh, Gawd!" protested Elmer. "Eddie Fislinger! About the kind of burg he would land in! A lot he knows about the meaning of redemption or any other dogma, that human wood-chuck! Or about dancing! If he'd ever been with me in Denver and shaken a hoof at Billy Portifero's place, he'd have something to hand out. Fislinger—must be the same guy. I'll sit down front and put his show on the fritz!"

Eddie Fislinger's church was an octagonal affair, with the pulpit in one angle, an arrangement which produced a fascinating, rather dizzy effect, reminiscent of the doctrine of predestination. The interior was of bright yellow, hung with many placards: "Get Right with God," and "Where Will You Spend Eternity?" and "The Wisdom of This World is Foolishness with God." The Sunday School Register behind the pulpit communicated the tidings that the attendance today had been forty-one, as against only thirty-nine last week, and the collection eighty-nine cents, as against only seventy-seven.

The usher, a brick-layer in a clean collar, was impressed by Elmer's checked suit and starched red-speckled shirt and took him to the front row.

Eddie flushed most satisfactorily when he saw Elmer from the pulpit, started to bow, checked it, looked in the general direction of Heaven, and tried to smile condescendingly. He was nervous at the beginning of his sermon, but apparently he determined that his attack on sin—which hitherto had been an academic routine with no relation to any of his appallingly virtuous flock—might be made real. With his squirrel-toothed and touching earnestness he looked down at Elmer and as good as told him to go to hell and be done with it. But he thought better of it, and concluded that God might be able to give even Elmer Gantry another chance if Elmer stopped drinking, smoking, blaspheming, and wearing checked suits. (If he did not refer to Elmer by name, he certainly did by poisonous glances.)

Elmer was angry, then impressively innocent, then bored. He examined the church and counted the audience—twenty-seven excluding Eddie and his wife. (There was no question but that the young woman looking adoringly up from the front pew was Eddie's consort. She had the pitifully starved and home-tailored look of a preacher's wife.) By the end of the sermon, Elmer was being sorry for Eddie. He sang the closing hymn, "He's the Lily of the Valley," with a fine unctuous grace, coming down powerfully on the jubilant "Hallelujah," and waited to shake hands with Eddie forgivingly.

"Well, well, well," they both said; and "What you doing in these parts?" and Eddie: "Wait till everybody's gone—must have a good old-fashioned chin with you, old fellow!"

As he walked with the Fislingers to the parsonage, a block away, and sat with them in the living-room, Elmer wanted to be a preacher again, to take the job away from Eddie and do it expertly; yet he was repulsed by the depressing stinginess of Eddie's life. His own hotel bedrooms were drab enough, but they were free of nosey parishioners, and they were as luxurious as this parlor with its rain-blotched ceiling, bare pine floor, sloping chairs, and perpetual odor of diapers. There were already, in two years of Eddie's marriage, two babies, looking as though they were next-door to having been conceived without sin; and there was a perfectly blank-faced sister-in-law who cared for the children during services.

Elmer wanted to smoke, and for all his training in the eternal mysteries he could not decide whether it would be more interesting to annoy Eddie by smoking or to win him by refraining.

He smoked, and wished he hadn't.

Eddie noticed it, and his reedy wife noticed it, and the sister-in-law gaped at it, and they labored at pretending they hadn't.

Elmer felt large and sophisticated and prosperous in their presence, like a city broker visiting a farmer cousin and wondering which of his tales of gilded towers would be simple enough for belief.

Eddie gave him the news of Mizpah. Frank Shallard had a small church in a town called Catawba, the other end of the state of Winnemac from the seminary. There had been some difficulty over his ordination, for he had been shaky about even so clear and proven a fact as the virgin birth. But his father and Dean Trosper had vouched for him, and Frank had been ordained. Harry Zenz had a large church in a West Virginia mining town. Wallace Umstead, the physical instructor, was "doing fine" in the Y.M.C.A. Professor Bruno Zechlin was dead, poor fellow.

"Whever became of Horace Carp?" asked Elmer.

"Well, that's the strangest thing of all. Horace's gone into the Episcopal Church, like he always said he would."

"Well, well, zatta fact!"

"Yes-sir, his father died just after he graduated, and he up and turned Episcopalian and took a year in General, and now they say he's doing pretty good, and he's high-church as all get-out."

"Well, you seem to have a good thing of it here, Eddie. Nice church."

"Well, it isn't so big, but they're awful' fine people. And everything's going fine. I haven't increased the membership so much, but what I'm trying to do is strengthen the present membership in the faith, and then when I feel each of them is a center of inspiration, I'll be ready to start an evangelistic campaign, and you'll see that ole church boom—yes-sir—just double overnight. . . . If they only weren't so slow about paying my salary and the mortgage. . . . Fine solid people, really saved, but they are just the least little bit tight with the money."

"If you could see the way my cook-stove's broken and the sink needs painting," said Mrs. Fislinger—her chief utterance of the evening.

Elmer felt choked and imprisoned. He escaped. At the door Eddie held both his hands and begged, "Oh, Elm, I'll never give up till I've brought you back! I'm going to pray. I've seen you under conviction. I know what you can do!"

Fresh air, a defiant drink of rye, loud laughter, taking a train—Elmer enjoyed it after this stuffiness. Already Eddie had lost such devout fires as he had once shown in the Y.M.C.A.; already he was old, settled down, without conceivable adventure, waiting for death.

Yet Eddie had said—

Startled, he recalled that he was still a Baptist minister! For all of Trosper's opposition, he could preach. He felt with superstitious discomfort Eddie's incantation, "I'll never give up till I've brought you back."

And—just to take Eddie's church and show what he could do with it! By God *he*'d bring those hicks to time and make 'em pay up!

He flitted across the state to see his mother.

His disgrace at Mizpah had, she said, nearly killed her. With tremulous hope she now heard him promise that maybe, when he'd seen the world and settled down, he might go back into the ministry.

In a religious mood (which fortunately did not prevent his securing some telling credit-information by oiling a bookkeeper with several drinks) he came to Sautersville, Nebraska, an ugly, enterprising, industrial town of 20,000. And in that religious mood he noted the placards of a woman evangelist, one Sharon Falconer, a prophetess of whom he had heard.

The clerk in the hotel, the farmers about the implement warehouse, said that Miss Falconer was holding union meetings in a tent, with the support of most of the Protestant churches in town; they asserted that she was beautiful and eloquent, that she took a number of assistants with her, that she was "the biggest thing that ever hit this burg," that she was comparable to Moody, to Gipsy Smith, to Sam Jones, to J. Wilbur Chapman, to this new baseball evangelist, Billy Sunday.

"That's nonsense. No woman can preach the gospel," declared Elmer, as an expert.

But he went, that evening, to Miss Falconer's meeting.

The tent was enormous; it would seat three thousand people, and another thousand could be packed in standing-room. It was nearly filled when Elmer arrived and elbowed his majestic way forward. At the front of the tent was an extraordinary structure, altogether different from the platform-pulpit-American-flag arrangement of the stock evangelist. It was a pyramidal structure, of white wood with gilded edges, affording three platforms; one for the choir, one higher up for a row of seated local clergy; and at the top a small platform with a pulpit shaped like a shell and painted like a rainbow. Swarming over it all were lilies, roses and vines.

"Great snakes! Regular circus lay-out! Just what you'd expect from a fool woman evangelist!" decided Elmer.

The top platform was still unoccupied; presumably it was to set off the charms of Miss Sharon Falconer.

The mixed choir, with their gowns and mortar-boards, chanted "Shall We Gather at the River?" A young man, slight, too good-looking, too arched of lip, wearing a priest's waist-coat and collar turned round, read from Acts at a stand on the second platform. He was an Oxonian, and it was almost the first time that Elmer had heard an Englishman read.

"Huh! Willy-boy, that's what he is! This outfit won't get very far. Too much skirts. No punch. No good old-fashioned gospel to draw the customers," scoffed Elmer.

A pause. Every one waited, a little uneasy. Their eyes went to the top platform. Elmer gasped. Coming from some refuge behind the platform, coming slowly, her beautiful arms outstretched to them, appeared a saint. She was young, Sharon Falconer, surely not thirty, stately, slender and tall; and in her long slim face, her black eyes, her splendor of black hair, was rapture or boiling passion. The sleeves of her straight white robe, with its ruby velvet girdle, were slashed, and fell away from her arms as she drew every one to her.

"God!" prayed Elmer Gantry, and that instant his planless life took on plan and resolute purpose. He was going to have Sharon Falconer.

Her voice was warm, a little husky, desperately alive.

"Oh, my dear people, my dear people, I am not going to preach tonight—we are all so weary of nagging sermons about being nice and good! I am not going to tell you that you're sinners, for which of us is not a sinner? I am not going to explain the Scriptures. We are all bored by tired old men explaining the Bible through their noses! No! We are going to find the golden Scriptures written in our own hearts, we are going to sing together, laugh together, rejoice together like a gathering of April brooks, rejoice that in us is living the veritable spirit of the Everlasting and Redeeming Christ Jesus!"

Elmer never knew what the words were, or the sense—if indeed any one knew. It was all caressing music to him, and at the end, when she ran down curving flower-wreathed stairs to the lowest platform and held out her arms, pleading with them to find peace in salvation, he was roused to go forward with the converts, to kneel in the writhing row under the blessing of her extended hands.

But he was lost in no mystical ecstasy. He was the critic, moved by the play but aware that he must get his copy in to the newspaper.

"This is the outfit I've been looking for! Here's where I could go over great! I could beat that English preacher both ways from the ace. And Sharon— Oh, the darling!"

She was coming along the line of converts and near-converts, laying her shining hands on their heads. His shoulders quivered with consciousness of her nearness. When she reached him and invited him, in that thrilling voice, "Brother, won't you find happiness in Jesus?" he did not bow lower, like the others, he did not sob, but looked straight up at her jauntily, seeking to hold her eyes, while he crowed, "It's happiness just to have had your wondrous message, Sister Falconer!"

She glanced at him sharply, she turned blank, and instantly passed on.

He felt slapped. "I'll show her yet!"

He stood aside as the crowd wavered out. He got into talk with the crisp young Englishman who had read the Scripture lesson—Cecil Aylston, Sharon's first assistant.

"Mighty pleased to be here tonight, Brother," bumbled Elmer. "I happen to be a Baptist preacher myself. Bountiful meeting! And you read the lesson most inspiringly."

Cecil Aylston rapidly took in Elmer's checked suit, his fancy vest, and "Oh. Really? Splendid. So good of you, I'm sure. If you will excuse me?" Nor did it increase Elmer's affection to have Aylston leave him for one of the humblest of the adherents, an old woman in a broken and flapping straw hat.

Elmer disposed of Cecil Aylston: "To hell with him! There's a fellow we'll get rid of! A man like me, he gives me the icy mitt, and then he goes to the other extreme and slops all over some old dame that's probably saved already, that you, by golly, couldn't unsave with a carload of gin! That'll do you, my young friend! And you don't like my check suit, either. Well, I certainly do buy my clothes just to please you, all right!"

He waited, hoping for a chance at Sharon Falconer. And others were waiting. She waved her hand at all of them, waved her flaunting smile, rubbed her eyes, and begged, "Will you forgive me? I'm blind-tired. I must rest." She vanished into the mysteries behind the gaudy gold-and-white pyramid.

Even in her staggering weariness, her voice was not drab; it was filled with that twilight passion which had captured Elmer more than her beauty. . . . "Never did see a lady just like her," he reflected, as he plowed back to his hotel. "Face kinda thin. Usually I like 'em plumper. And yet—golly! I could fall for her as I never have for anybody in my life. . . . So this darn' Englishman didn't like my clothes! Looked as if he thought they were too sporty. Well, he can stick 'em in his ear! Anybody got any objection to my clothes?"

The slumbering universe did not answer, and he was almost content. And at eight next morning—Sautersville had an excellent clothing shop, conducted by Messrs. Erbsen and Goldfarb—and at eight Elmer was there, purchasing a chaste double-breasted brown suit and three rich but sober ties. By hounding Mr. Goldfarb he had the alterations done by half-past nine, and at ten he was grandly snooping about the revival tent. . . . He should have gone on to the next town this morning.

Sharon did not appear till eleven, to lecture the personal workers, but meanwhile Elmer had thrust himself into acquaintanceship with Art Nichols, a gaunt Yankee, once a barber, who played the cornet and the French horn in the three-piece orchestra which Sharon carried with her.

"Yes, pretty good game, this is," droned Nichols. "Better'n barberin' and better'n one-night stands—oh, I'm a real trouper, too; play characters in tent-shows—I was out three seasons with Tom shows. This is easier. No street parades, and I guess prob'ly we do a lot of good, saving souls and so on. Only these religious folks do seem to scrap amongst themselves more'n the professionals."

"Where do you go from here?"

"We close in five days, then we grab the collection and pull out of here and make a jump to Lincoln, Nebraska; open there in three days. Regular troupers' jump, too—don't even get a Pullman—leave here on the day coach at eleven P.M. and get into Lincoln at one."

"Sunday night you leave, eh? That's funny. I'll be on that train. Going to Lincoln myself."

"Well, you can come hear us there. I always do 'Jerusalem the Golden' on the cornet, first meeting. Knocks 'em cold. They say it's all this gab that gets 'em going and drags in the sinners, but don't you believe it—it's the music. Say, I can get more damn' sinners weeping on a E-flat cornet than nine gospel-artists all shooting off their faces at once!"

"I'll bet you can, Art. Say, Art— Of course I'm a preacher myself, just in business temporarily, making arrangements for a new appointment." Art looked like one who was about to not lend money. "But I don't believe all this bull about never having a good time; and of course Paul said to 'take a little wine for your stomach's sake' and this town is dry, but I'm going to a wet one between now and Saturday, and if I were to have a pint of rye in my jeans—heh?"

"Well, I'm awful' fond of my stomach—like to do something for its sake!"

"What kind of a fellow is this Englishman? Seems to be Miss Falconer's right-hand man."

"Oh, he's a pretty bright fellow, but he don't seem to get along with us boys."

"She like him? Wha' does he call himself?"

"Cecil Aylston, his name is. Oh, Sharon liked him first-rate for a while, but wouldn't wonder if she was tired of his high-brow stuff now, and the way he never gets chummy."

"Well, I got to go speak to Miss Falconer a second. Glad met you, Art. See you on the train Sunday evening."

They had been talking at one of the dozen entrances of the gospel tent. Elmer had been watching Sharon Falconer as she came briskly into the tent. She was no high priestess now in Grecian robe, but a business-woman, in straw hat, gray suit, white shirt-waist, linen cuffs and collar. Only her blue bow and the jeweled cross on her watch-fob distinguished her from the women in offices. But Elmer, collecting every detail of her as a miner scoops up nuggets, knew now that she was not flat-breasted, as in the loose robe she might have been.

She spoke to the "personal workers," the young women who volunteered to hold cottage prayer-meetings and to go from house to house stirring up spiritual prospects:

"My dear friends, I'm very glad you're all praying, but there comes a time when you've got to add a little shoe-leather. While you're longing for the Kingdom—the devil does his longing nights, and daytimes he hustles around *seeing* people, *talking* to 'em! Are you ashamed to go right in and ask folks to come to Christ—to come to our meetings, anyway? I'm not at all pleased. Not at all, my dear young friends. My charts show that in the Southeast district only one house in three has been visited. This won't do! You've got to get over the idea that the service of the Lord is a nice game, like putting Easter lilies on the altar. Here there's only five days left, and you haven't yet waked up and got busy. And let's not have any silly nonsense about hesitating to hit people for money-pledges, and hitting 'em hard! We can't pay rent for this lot, and pay for lights and transportation and the wages of all this big crew I carry, on hot air! Now you—you pretty girl there with the red hair—my! I wish I had such hair!—what have you done, sure-enough *done*, this past week?"

In ten minutes she had them all crying, all aching to dash out and bring in souls and dollars.

She was leaving the tent when Elmer pounced on her, swaggering, his hand out.

"Sister Falconer, I want to congratulate you on your wonderful meetings. I'm a Baptist preacher—the Reverend Gantry."

"Yes?" sharply. "Where is your church?"

"Why, uh, just at present I haven't exactly got a church."

She inspected his ruddiness, his glossiness, the odor of tobacco; her brilliant eyes had played all over him, and she demanded:

"What's the trouble this time? Booze or women?"

"Why, that's absolutely untrue! I'm surprised you should speak like that, Sister Falconer! I'm in perfectly good standing! It's just— I'm taking a little time off to engage in business, in order to understand the workings of the lay mind, before going on with my ministry."

"Um. That's splendid. Well, you have my blessing, Brother! Now if you will excuse me? I must go and meet the committee."

She tossed him an unsmiling smile and raced away. He felt soggy, lumbering, unspeakably stupid, but he swore, "Damn you, I'll catch you when you aren't all wrapped up in business and your own darn-fool self-importance, and then I'll make you wake up, my girl!"

II

He had to do nine days' work, to visit nine towns, in five days, but he was back in Sautersville on Sunday evening and he was on the eleven-o'clock train for Lincoln—in the new brown suit.

His fancy for Sharon Falconer had grown into a trembling passion, the first authentic passion of his life.

It was too late in the evening for a great farewell, but at least a hundred of the brethren and sisters were at the station, singing "God Be with You Till We Meet Again" and shaking hands with Sharon Falconer. Elmer saw his cornet-wielding Yankee friend, Art Nichols, with the rest of the evangelistic crew—the aide, Cecil Aylston, the fat and sentimental tenor soloist, the girl pianist, the violinist, the children's evangelist, the director of personal work. (That important assistant, the press agent, was in Lincoln making ready for the coming of the Lord.) They looked like a sleepy theatrical troupe as they sat on their suit-cases waiting for the train to come in, and like troupers, they were dismayingly different from their stage rôles. The anemically pretty pianist, who for public uses dressed in seraphic silver robes, was now merely a small-town girl in wrinkled blue serge; the director of personal work, who had been nun-like in linen, was bold in black-trimmed red, and more attentive to the amorous looks of the German violinist than to the farewell hymns. The Reverend Cecil Aylston gave orders to the hotel baggageman regarding their trunks more like a quartermaster sergeant than like an Oxonian mystic.

Sharon herself was imperial in white, and the magnet for all of them. A fat Presbyterian pastor, with whiskers, buzzed about her, holding her arm with more than pious zeal. She smiled on him (to Elmer's rage), she smiled equally on the long thin Disciples-of-Christ preacher, she shook hands fervently, and she was tender to each shout of "Praise God, Sister!" But her eyes were weary, and Elmer saw that when she turned from her worshipers, her mouth drooped. Young she seemed then, tired and defenseless.

"Poor kid!" thought Elmer.

The train flared and shrieked its way in, and the troupe bustled with suit-cases. "Good-by—God bless you—God speed the work!" shouted every one . . . every one save the Congregational minister, who stood sulkily at the edge of the crowd explaining to a parishioner, "And so she goes away with enough cash for herself, after six weeks' work, to have run our whole church for two years!"

Elmer ranged up beside his musical friend, Art Nichols, and as they humped up the steps of a day-coach he muttered, "Art! Art! Got your stomach-medicine here!"

"Great!"

"Say. Look. Fix it so you sit with Sharon. Then pretty soon go out for a smoke—"

"She don't like smoking."

"You don't need to tell her what for! Go out so I can sit down and talk to her for a while. Important business. About—a dandy new town for her evangelistic labors. Here: stick this in your pocket. And I'll dig up s'more for you at Lincoln. Now hustle and get in with her."

"Well, I'll try."

So, in the dark malodorous car, hot with late spring, filled with women whose corsets creaked to their doleful breathing, with farmers who snored in shirt-sleeves, Elmer stood behind the seat in which a blur marked the shoulders of Art Nichols and a radiance showed the white presence of Sharon Falconer. To Elmer she seemed to kindle the universe. She was so precious, every inch of her; he had not known that a human being could be precious like this and magical. To be near her was ecstasy enough . . . almost enough.

She was silent. He heard only Art Nichols' twanging, "What do you think about us using some of these nigger songs—hand 'em a jolt?" and her drowsy, "Oh, let's not talk about it tonight." Presently, from Art, "Guess I'll skip out on the platform and get a breath of air," and the sacred haunt beside her was free to the exalted Elmer.

He slipped in, very nervous.

She was slumped low in the seat, but she sat up, peered at him in the dimness, and said, with a grave courtesy which shut him out more than any rudeness, "I'm so sorry, but this place is taken."

"Yes, I know, Sister Falconer. But the car's crowded, and I'll just sit down and rest myself while Brother Nichols is away—that is, if you'll let me. Don't know if you remember me. I'm— I met you at the tent in Sautersville. Reverend Gantry."

"Oh," indifferently. Then, quickly: "Oh, yes, you're the Presbyterian preacher who was fired for drinking."

"That's absolutely—!" He saw that she was watching him, and he realized that she was not being her saintly self nor her efficient self but a quite new, private, mocking self. Delightedly he went on, "—absolutely incorrect. I'm the Christian Scientist that was fired for kissing the choir-leader on Saturday."

"Oh, that was careless of you!"

"So you're really human?"

"Me? Good Heavens, yes! Too human."

"And you get tired of it?"

"Of what?"

"Of being the great Miss Falconer, of not being able to go into a drug-store to buy a tooth-brush without having the clerk holler, 'Praise God, we have some dandy two-bit brushes, hallelujah!' "

Sharon giggled.

"Tired," and his voice was lulling now, "of never daring to be tired, which same is what you are tonight, and of never having anybody to lean on!"

"I suppose, my dear reverend Brother, that this is a generous offer to let me lean on you!"

"No. I wouldn't have the nerve! I'm scared to death of you. You haven't only got your beauty—no! please let me tell you how a fellow preacher looks at you—and your wonderful platform-presence, but I kind of guess you've got brains."

"No, I haven't. Not a brain. All emotion. That's the trouble with me." She sounded awake now, and friendly.

"But think of all the souls you've brought to repentance. That makes up for everything, doesn't it?"

"Oh, yes, I suppose it— Oh, of course it does. It's the only thing that counts. Only— Tell me: What really did happen to you? Why did you get out of the church?"

Gravely, "I was a senior in Mizpah Theological Seminary, but I had a church of my own. I fell for a girl. I won't say she lured me on. After all, a man ought to face the consequences of his own foolishness. But she certainly did— Oh, it amused her to see a young preacher go mad over her. And she was so lovely! Quite a lot like you, only not so beautiful, not near, and she let on like she was mad about church work—that's what fooled me. Well! Make a long story short: We were engaged to be married, and I thought of nothing but her and our life together, doing the work of the Lord, when one evening I walked in and there she was in the arms of another fellow! It broke me up so that I— Oh, I tried, but I simply couldn't go on preaching, so I quit for a while. And I've done well in business. But now I'm ready to go back to the one job I've ever cared about. That's why I wanted to talk to you there at the tent. I needed your woman's sympathy as well as your experience—and you turned me down!"

"Oh, I am so, so sorry!" Her hand caressed his arm.

Cecil Aylston came up and looked at them with a lack of sanctity.

When they reached Lincoln, he was holding her hand and saying, "You poor, dear, tired child!" and, "Will you have breakfast with me? Where are you staying in Lincoln?"

"Now see here, Brother Gantry—"

"Elmer!"

"Oh, don't be ridiculous! Just because I'm so fagged out that it's nice to play at being a human being, don't try to take advantage—"

"Sharon Falconer, will you quit being a chump? I admire your genius, your wonderful work for God, but it's because you're too big to just be a professional gospel-shouter every minute that I most admire you. You know mighty good and well that you like to be simple and even slangy for a while.

And you're too sleepy just now to know whether you like me or not. That's why I want us to meet at breakfast, when the sleepiness is out of the wonderful eyes—"

"Um. It all sounds pretty honest except that last stuff—you've certainly used that before. Do you know, I like you! You're so completely brazen, so completely unscrupulous, and so beatifically ignorant! I've been with sanctimonious folks too much lately. And it's interesting to see that you honestly think you can captivate me. You funny thing! I'm staying at the Antlers Hotel in Lincoln—no use, by the way, your trying to get a room near my suite, because I have practically the whole floor engaged—and I'll meet you at breakfast there at nine-thirty."

III

Though he did not sleep well, he was up early and at his toilet; he shaved, he touched up his bluff handsomeness with lilac water and talcum, he did his nails, sitting in athletic underwear, awaiting his new suit, sent down for pressing. The new purpose in a life recently so dispirited gave vitality to his bold eyes and spring to his thick muscles as he strode through the gold-and-marble lobby of the Antlers Hotel and awaited Sharon at the restaurant door. She came down fresh in white crash bordered with blue. As they met they laughed, admitting comradeship in folly. He took her arm gaily, led her through a flutter of waitresses excited over the coming of the celebrated lady of God, and ordered competently.

"I've got a great idea," said he. "I've got to beat it this afternoon, but I'll be back in Lincoln on Friday, and how'd it be if you billed me to address your meeting as a saved business man, and I talked for half an hour or so on Friday evening about the good, hard, practical, dollars-and-cents value of Christ in Commerce?"

"Are you a good talker?"

"A knock-out."

"Well, it might be a good idea. Yes, we'll do it. By the way, what is your business? Hold-ups?"

"I'm the crack salesman of the Pequot Farm Implement Company, Sharon, and if you don't believe it—"

"Oh, I do. [She shouldn't have.] I'm sure you tell the truth—often. Of course we won't need to mention the fact that you're a preacher, unless somebody insists on asking. How would this be as a topic—'Getting the Goods with a Gideon Bible?'"

"Say, that would be elegant! How I was in some hick town, horrible weather, slush and rain and everything—dark skies, seemed like sun never would shine again—feet all soaked from tramping the streets—no sales, plumb discouraged—sat in my room, forgotten to buy one of the worldly magazines I'd been accustomed to read—idly picked up a Gideon Bible and read the parable of the talents—found that same day *you* were in town—went and got converted—saw now it wasn't just for money but for the Kingdom of Christ, to heighten my influence as a Christian business-man, that I had to increase sales. That bucked up my self-confidence so that I increased sales to beat the band! And how I owe everything to your inspired powers, so it's a privilege to be able to testify. And about how it isn't the weak skinny failure that's the fellow to get saved, but takes a really strong man to not be ashamed to surrender all for Jesus."

"Why, I think that's fine, Brother Elmer, I really do. And dwell a lot on being in your hotel room there—you took off your shoes and threw yourself down on the bed, feeling completely beaten, but you were so restless you got up and poked around the room and picked up the Gideon Bible. I'll feature it big. And you'll make it strong, Elmer? You won't let me down? Because I really will headline it in my announcements. I've persuaded you to come clear from Omaha—no, that's not far—clear from Denver for it. And if you do throw yourself into it and tear loose, it'll add greatly to the glory of God, and the success of the meeting in winning souls. You will?"

"Dear, I'll slam into 'em so hard you'll want me in every town you go to. You bet."

"Um, that's as may be, Elmer. Here comes Cecil Aylston—you know my assistant? He looks so cross. He is a dear, but he's so terribly highbrow and refined and everything and he's always trying to nag me into being refined. But you'll love him."

"I will not! Anyway, I'll struggle against it!"

They laughed.

The Rev. Cecil Aylston, of the flaxen hair and the superior British complexion, glided to their table, looked at Elmer with a blankness more infuriating than a scowl, and sat down, observing:

"I don't want to intrude, Miss Falconer, but you know the committee of clergy are awaiting you in the parlor."

"Oh, dear," sighed Sharon. "Are they as terrible as usual here? Can't you go up and get the kneeling and praying done while I finish my scrambled eggs? Have you told them they've got to double the amount of the pledges before this week is over or the souls in Lincoln can go right on being damned?" Cecil was indicating Elmer with an alarmed jerk of his head. "Oh, don't worry about Elmer. He's one of us—going to speak for us Friday—used to be a terribly famous preacher, but he's found a wider field in business—Reverend Aylston, Reverend Gantry. Now run along, Cecil, and keep 'em pious and busy. Any nice-looking young preachers in the committee, or are they all old stiffs?"

Aylston answered with a tight-lipped glare, and flowed away.

"Dear Cecil, he is so useful to me—he's actually made me take to reading poetry and everything. If he just wouldn't be polite at breakfast-time! I wouldn't mind facing the wild beasts of Ephesus, but I can't stand starch with my eggs. Now I must go up and join him."

"You'll have lunch with me?"

"I will not! My dear young man, this endeth my being silly for this week. From this moment on I'll be one of the anointed, and if you want me to like you— God help you if you come around looking pussy-catty while I'm manhandling these stiff-necked brethren in Christ! I'll see you Friday— I'll have dinner with you, here, before the meeting. And I can depend on you? Good!"

IV

Cecil Aylston was a good deal of a mystic, a good deal of a ritualist, a bit of a rogue, something of a scholar, frequently a drunkard, more frequently an ascetic, always a gentleman, and always an adventurer. He was thirty-two now. At

Winchester and New College, he had been known for sprinting, snobbishness, and Greek versification. He had taken orders, served as a curate in a peculiarly muddy and ancient and unlighted church in the East End, and become fanatically Anglo-Catholic. While he was considering taking the three vows and entering a Church of England monastery, his vicar kicked him out, and no one was ever quite certain whether it was because of his "Romish tendencies" or the navvy's daughter whom he had got with child.

He was ordered down to a bleak, square, stone church in Cornwall, but he resigned and joined the Plymouth Brethren, among whom, in resounding galvanized-iron chapels in the Black Country, he had renown for denunciation of all the pleasant sins. He came to Liverpool for a series of meetings; he wandered by the Huskinson docks, saw a liner ready for sea, bought a steerage ticket, took the passport which he had ready for a promised flight to Rio with the wife of an evangelical merchant in coals and, without a word to the brethren or the ardent lady of the coals, sailed sulkily off to America.

In New York he sold neckties in a department store, he preached in a mission, he tutored the daughter of a great wholesale fish-dealer, and wrote nimble and thoroughly irritating book-reviews. He left town two hours ahead of the fish-dealer's eldest son, and turned up in Waco, Texas, teaching in a business college, in Winona, Minnesota, preaching in a Nazarene Chapel, in Carmel, California, writing poetry and real-estate brochures, and in Miles City, Montana, as the summer supply in a Congregational pulpit. He was so quiet, so studious, here that the widow of a rancher picked him up and married him. She died. He lost the entire fortune in two days at Tia Juana. He became extra pious after that and was converted from time to time by Billy Sunday, Gipsy Smith, Biederwolf, and several other embarrassed evangelists, who did not expect a convert so early in the campaign and had made no plans to utilize him.

It was in Ishpeming, Michigan, where he was conducting a shooting-gallery while he sought by mail a mastership in Groton School, that he heard and was more than usually converted by Sharon Falconer. He fell in love with her, and with contemptuous steady resolution he told her so.

At the moment she was without a permanent man first assistant. She had just discharged a really useful loud-voiced United Brethren D.D. for hinting to delighted sons of Belial that his relations to her were at least brotherly. She took on the Reverend Cecil Aylston.

He loved her, terrifyingly. He was so devoted to her that he dropped his drinking, his smoking, and a tendency to forgery which had recently been creeping on him. And he did wonders for her.

She had been too emotional. He taught her to store it up and fling it all out in one overpowering catastrophic evening. She had been careless of grammar, and given to vulgar barnyard illustrations. He taught her to endure sitting still and reading—reading Swinburne and Jowett, Pater and Jonathan Edwards, Newman and Sir Thomas Browne. He taught her to use her voice, to use her eyes, and in more private relations, to use her soul.

She had been puzzled by him, annoyed by him, led meekly by him, and now she was weary of his supercilious devotion. He was more devoted to her than to life, and for her he refused a really desirable widow who could have got him back into the Episcopal fold and acquired for him the dim rich sort of church for which he longed after these months of sawdust and sweaty converts.

V

When Elmer descended from the train in Lincoln Friday afternoon, he stopped before a red-and-black poster announcing that Elmer Gantry was a power in the machinery world, that he was an eloquent and entertaining speaker, and that his address "Increasing Sales with God and the Gideons" would be a "revelation of the new world of better business."

"Jiminy!" said the power in the machinery world. "I'd rather see a sermon of mine advertised like that than sell steen million plows!"

He had a vision of Sharon Falconer in her suite in late afternoon, lonely and clinging in the faded golden light, clinging to him. But when he reached her room by telephone she was curt. "No, no, sorry, can't see you 'safternoon—see you at dinner, quarter to six."

He was so chastened that he was restrained and uncommenting when she came swooping into the dining-room, a knot-browed, efficient, raging Sharon, and when he found that she had brought Cecil Aylston.

"Good evening, Sister—Brother Aylston," he boomed sedately.

"Evening. Ready to speak?"

"Absolutely."

She lighted a little. "That's good. Everything else's gone wrong, and these preachers here think I can travel an evangelistic crew on air. Give 'em fits about tight-wad Christian business men, will you, Elmer? How they hate to loosen up! Cecil! Kindly don't look as if I'd bitten somebody. I haven't . . . not yet."

Aylston ignored her, and the two men watched each other like a panther and a buffalo (but a buffalo with a clean shave and ever so much scented hair-tonic).

"Brother Aylston," said Elmer, "I noticed in the account of last evening's meeting that you spoke of Mary and the anointing with spikenard, and you quoted these 'Idylls of the King,' by Tennyson. Or that's what the newspaper said."

"That's right."

"But do you think that's good stuff for evangelism? All right for a regular church, especially with a high-class rich congregation, but in a soul-saving campaign—"

"My dear Mr. Gantry, Miss Falconer and I have decided that even in the most aggressive campaign there is no need of vulgarizing our followers."

"Well, that isn't what I'd give 'em!"

"And what, pray, would you give them?"

"The good old-fashioned hell, that's what!" Elmer peeped at Sharon, and felt that she was smiling with encouragement. "Yes-sir, like the hymn says, the hell of our fathers is good enough for me."

"Quite so! I'm afraid it isn't good enough for me, and I don't know that Jesus fancied it particularly!"

"Well, you can be dead sure of one thing: When he stayed with Mary and Martha and Lazarus, he didn't loaf around drinking tea with 'em!"

"Why not, my dear man! Don't you know that tea was first imported by caravan train from Ceylon to Syria in 627 B.C.?

"No-o, didn't know just when—"

"Why, of course. You've merely forgotten it—you must have read in your university days of the great epicurean expedition of Phthaltazar—when he took the eleven hundred camels? Psaltazar? You remember!"

"Oh, yes, I remember his expedition, but I didn't know he brought in tea."

"Why, naturally! Rather! Uh, Miss Falconer, the impetuous Mr. Shoop wants to sing 'Just As I Am' for his solo tonight. Is there any way of preventing it? Adelbert is a good saved soul, but just as he is, he is too fat. Won't you speak to him?"

"Oh, I don't know. Let him sing it. He's brought in lots of souls on that," yawned Sharon.

"Mangy little souls."

"Oh, stop being so supercilious! When you get to heaven, Cecil, you'll complain of the way the seraphims—oh, do shut up; I *know* it's seraphim, my tongue just slipped—you'll complain of the kind of corsets they wear."

"I'm not at all sure but that you really do picture that sort of heaven, with corseted angels and yourself with a golden mansion on the celestial Park Lane!"

"Cecil Aylston, don't you quarrel with me tonight! I feel—vulgar! That's your favorite word! I do wish I could save some of the members of my own crew! . . . Elmer, do you think God went to Oxford?"

"Sure!"

"And you did, of course!"

"I did not, by golly! I went to a hick college in Kansas! And I was born in a hick town in Kansas!"

"Me too, practically! Oh, I did come from a frightfully old Virginia family, and I was born in what they called a mansion, but still, we were so poor that our pride was ridiculous. Tell me: did you split wood and pull mustard when you were a boy?"

"Did I? Say! You bet I did!"

They sat with their elbows on the table, swapping boasts of provincial poverty, proclaiming kinship, while Cecil looked frosty.

VI

Elmer's speech at the evangelistic meeting was a cloudburst.

It had structure as well as barytone melody, choice words, fascinating anecdotes, select sentiment, chaste point of view, and resolute piety.

Elmer was later to explain to admirers of his public utterances that nothing was more important than structure. What, he put it to them, would they think of an architect who was fancy about paint and clapboards but didn't plan the house? And tonight's euphuisms were full of structure.

In part one he admitted that despite his commercial success he had fallen into sin before the hour when, restless in his hotel room, he had idly fingered o'er a Gideon Bible and been struck by the parable of the talents.

In part two he revealed by stimulating examples from his own experience the cash value of Christianity. He pointed out that merchants often preferred a dependable man to a known crook.

Hitherto he had, perhaps, been a shade too realistic. He felt that Sharon would never take him on in place of Cecil Aylston unless she perceived the poetry with which his soul was gushing. So in part three he explained that what made Christianity no mere dream and ideal, but a practical human solvent, was Love. He spoke very nicely of Love. He said that Love was the Morning Star, the Evening Star, the Radiance upon the Quiet Tomb, the Inspirer equally of Patriots and Bank Presidents, and as for Music, what was it but the very voice of Love?

He had elevated his audience (thirteen hundred they were, and respectful) to a height of idealism from which he made them swoop now like eagles to a pool of tears:

"For, oh, my brothers and sisters, important though it is to be prudent in this world's affairs, it is the world to come that is alone important, and this reminds me, in closing, of a very sad incident which I recently witnessed. In business affairs I had often had to deal with a very prominent man named Jim Leff—Leffingwell. I can give his name now because he has passed to his eternal reward. Old Jim was the best of good fellows, but he had fatal defects. He drank liquor, he smoked tobacco, he gambled, and I'm sorry to say that he did not always keep his tongue clean—he took the name of God in vain. But Jim was very fond of his family, particularly of his little daughter. Well, she took sick. Oh, what a sad time that was to that household! How the stricken mother tiptoed into and out of the sick-room; how the worried doctors came and went, speeding to aid her! As for the father, poor old Jim, he was bowed with anguish as he leaned over that pathetic little bed, and his hair turned gray in a single night. There came the great crisis, and before the very eyes of the weeping father that little form was stilled, and that sweet, pure, young soul passed to its Maker.

"He came to me sobbing, and I put my arms round him as I would round a little child. 'Oh, God,' he sobbed, 'that I should have spent my life in wicked vices, and that the little one should have passed away knowing her dad was a sinner!' Thinking to comfort him, I said, 'Old man, it was God's will that she be taken. You have done all that mortal man could do. The best of medical attention. The best of care.'

"I shall never forget how scornfully he turned upon me. 'And you call yourself a Christian!' he cried. 'Yes, she had medical attention, but one thing was lacking—the one thing that would have saved her—I could not pray!'

"And that strong man knelt in anguish and for all my training in—in trying to explain the ways of God to my fellow business men, there was nothing to say. *It was too late!*

"Oh, my brothers, my fellow business men, are *you* going to put off repentance till it's too late? That's *your* affair, you say. Is it? Is it? Have you a right to inflict upon all that you hold nearest and dearest the sore burden of your sins? Do you love your sins better than that dear little son, that bonnie daughter, that loving brother, that fine old father? Do you want to punish them? Do you? Don't you love some one more than you do your sins? If you do, stand up. Isn't there some one here who wants to stand up and help a fellow business man carry this gospel of great joy to the world? Won't you come? Won't you *help* me? Oh, come! Come down and let me shake your hand!"

And they came, dozens of them, weeping, while he wept at his own goodness.

They stood afterward in the secluded space behind the white-and-gold platforms, Sharon and Elmer, and she cried, "Oh, it was beautiful! Honestly, I almost cried myself! Elmer, it was just fine!"

"Didn't I get 'em? Didn't I get 'em? Didn't I? Say, Sharon, I'm so glad it went over, because it was your show and I wanted to give you all I could!"

He moved toward her, his arms out, and for once he was not producing the false ardor of amorous diplomacy. He was the small boy seeking the praise of his mother. But she moved away from him, begging, not sardonically:

"No! Please!"

"But you do like me?"

"Yes, I do."

"How much?"

"Not very much. I can't like any one very much. But I do like you. Some day I might fall in love with you. A tiny bit. If you don't rush me too much. But only physically. No one," proudly, "can touch my soul!"

"Do you think that's decent? Isn't that sin?"

She flamed at him. "I can't sin! I am above sin! I am really and truly sanctified! Whatever I may choose to do, though it might be sin in one unsanctified, with me God will turn it to his glory. I can kiss you like this—" Quickly she touched his cheek, "yes, or passionately, terribly passionately, and it would only symbolize my complete union with Jesus! I have told you a mystery. You can never understand. But you can serve me. Would you like to?"

"Yes, I would. . . . And I've never served anybody yet! Can I? Oh, kick out this tea-drinking mollycoddle, Cecil, and let me work with you. Don't you need arms like these about you, just now and then, defending you?"

"Perhaps. But I'm not to be hurried. I am I! It is I who choose!"

"Yes. I guess prob'ly it is, Sharon. I think you've plumb hypnotized me or something."

"No, but perhaps I shall if I ever care to. . . . I can do anything I want to! God chose me to do his work. I am the reincarnation of Joan of Arc, of Catherine of Sienna! I have visions! God talks to me! I told you once that I hadn't the brains to rival the men evangelists. Lies! False modesty! They are God's message, but I am God's right hand!"

She chanted it with her head back, her eyes closed, and even while he quaked, "My God, she's crazy!" he did not care. He would give up all to follow her. Mumblingly he told her so, but she sent him away, and he crept off in a humility he had never known.

Chapter XII

TWO MORE series of meetings Sharon Falconer held that summer, and at each of them the power in the machinery world appeared and chronicled his conversion by the Gideon Bible and the eloquence of Sister Falconer.

Sometimes he seemed very near her; the next time she would regard him with bleak china eyes. Once she turned on him with: "You smoke, don't you?"

"Why, yes."

"I smelled it. I hate it. Will you stop it? Entirely? And drinking?"

"Yes. I will."

And he did. It was an agony of restlessness and craving, but he never touched alcohol or tobacco again, and he really regretted that in evenings thus made vacuous he could not keep from an interest in waitresses.

It was late in August, in a small Colorado city, after the second of his appearances as a saved financial Titan, that he implored Sharon as they entered the hotel together, "Oh, let me come up to your room. Please! I never have a chance to just sit and talk to you."

"Very well. Come in half an hour. Don't 'phone. Just come right up to Suite B."

It was a half-hour of palpitating, of almost timorous, expectancy.

In every city where she held meetings Sharon was invited to stay at the home of one of the elect, but she always refused. She had a long standard explanation that "she could devote herself more fully to the prayer life if she had her own place, and day by day filled it more richly with the aura of spirituality." Elmer wondered whether it wasn't the aura of Cecil Aylston for which she had her suite, but he tried to keep his aching imagination away from that.

The half-hour was over.

He swayed up-stairs to Suite B and knocked. A distant "Come in."

She was in the bedroom beyond. He inched into the stale hotel parlor—wall-paper with two-foot roses, a table with an atrocious knobby gilt vase, two stiff chairs and a grudging settee ranged round the wall. The lilies which her disciples had sent her were decaying in boxes, in a wash-bowl, in a heap in the corner. Round a china cuspidor lay faint rose petals.

He sat awkwardly on the edge of one of the chairs. He dared not venture beyond the dusty brocade curtains which separated the two rooms, but his fancy ventured fast enough.

She threw open the curtains and stood there, a flame blasting the faded apartment. She had discarded her white robe for a dressing-gown of scarlet with sleeves of cloth of gold—gold and scarlet; riotous black hair; long, pale, white face. She slipped over to the settee, and summoned him, "Come!"

He diffidently dropped his arm about her, and her head was on his shoulder. His arm drew tighter. But, "Oh, don't make love to me," she sighed, not moving. "You'll know it all right when I want you to! Just be nice and comforting tonight."

"But I can't always—"

"I know. Perhaps you won't always have to. Perhaps! Oh, I need— What I need tonight is some salve for my vanity. Have I ever said that I was a reincarnated Joan of Arc? I really do half believe that sometimes. Of course it's just insanity. Actually I'm a very ignorant young woman with a lot of misdirected energy and some tiny idealism. I preach elegant sermons for six weeks, but if I stayed in a town six weeks and one day, I'd have to start the music box over again. I can talk my sermons beautifully . . . but Cecil wrote most of 'em for me, and the rest I cheerfully stole."

"Do you like Cecil?"

"Oh, is a nice, jealous, big, fat man!" She who that evening had been a disturbing organ note was lisping baby-talk now.

"Damn it, Sharon, don't try to be a baby when I'm serious!"

"Damn it, Elmer, don't say 'damn it'! Oh, I hate the little vices—smoking, swearing, scandal, drinking just enough to be silly. I love the big ones—murder, lust, cruelty, ambition!"

"And Cecil? Is he one of the big vices that you love?"

"Oh, he's a dear boy. So sweet, the way he takes himself seriously."

"Yes, he must make love like an ice-cream cone."

"You might be surprised! There, there! The poor man is just longing to have me say something mean about Cecil! I'll be obliging. He's done a lot for me. He really knows something; he isn't a splendid cast-iron statue of ignorance like you or me."

"Now you look here, Sharon! After all, I *am* a college graduate and practically a B.D. too."

"That's what I said. Cecil really knows how to read. And he taught me to quit acting like a hired girl, bless him. But— Oh, I've learned everything he can teach me, and if I get any more of the highbrow in me I'll lose touch with the common people—bless their dear, sweet, honest souls!"

"Chuck him. Take me on. Oh, it isn't the money. You must know that, dear. In ten years, at thirty-eight, I can be salesmanager of the Pequot—prob'ly ten thousand a year—and maybe some day the president, at thirty thou. I'm not looking for a job. But— Oh, I'm crazy about you! Except for my mother, you're the only person I've ever adored. I love you! Hear me? Damn it—yes, damn it, I said—I worship you! Oh, Sharon, Sharon, Sharon! It wasn't really bunk when I told 'em all tonight how you'd converted me, because you *did* convert me. Will you let me serve you? And will you maybe marry me?"

"No. I don't think I'll ever marry—exactly. Perhaps I'll chuck Cecil—poor sweet lad!—and take you on. I'll see. Anyhow— Let me think."

She shook off his encircling arm and sat brooding, chin on hand. He sat at her feet—spiritually as well as physically.

She beatified him with:

"In September I'll have only four weeks of meetings, at Vincennes. I'm going to take off all October, before my winter work (you won't know me then—I'm *dandy*, speaking indoors, in big halls!), and I'm going down to our home, the old Falconer family place, in Virginia. Pappy and Mam are dead now, and I own it. Old plantation. Would you like to come down there with me, just us two, for a fortnight in October?"

"Would I? My God!"

"Could you get away?"

"If it cost me my job!"

"Then— I'll wire you when to come after I get there: Hanning Hall, Broughton, Virginia. Now I think I'd better go to bed, dear. Sweet dreams."

"Can't I tuck you into bed?"

"No, dear. I might forget to be Sister Falconer! Good night!"

Her kiss was like a swallow's flight, and he went out obediently, marveling that Elmer Gantry could for once love so much that he did not insist on loving.

II

In New York he had bought a suit of Irish homespun and a heather cap. He looked bulky but pleasantly pastoral as he gaped romantically from the Pullman window at the fields of Virginia. "Ole Virginny—ole Virginny" he hummed happily. Worm fences, negro cabins, gallant horses in rocky pastures, a longing to see the gentry who rode such horses, and ever the blue hills. It was an older world than his baking Kansas, older than Mizpah Seminary, and he felt a desire to be part of this traditional age to which Sharon belonged. Then, as the miles which still separated him from the town of Broughton crept back of him, he forgot the warm-tinted land in anticipation of her.

He was recalling that she was the aristocrat, the more formidable here in the company of F.F.V. friends. He was more than usually timid . . . and more than usually proud of his conquest.

For a moment, at the station, he thought that she had not come to meet him. Then he saw a girl standing by an old country buggy.

She was young, veritably a girl, in middy blouse deep cut at the throat, pleated white skirt, white shoes. Her red tam-o'-shanter was rakish, her smile was a country grin as she waved to him. And the girl was Sister Falconer.

"God, you're adorable!" he murmured to her, as he plumped down his suit-case, and she was fragrant and soft in his arms as he kissed her.

"No more," she whispered. "You're supposed to be my cousin, and even very nice cousins don't kiss quite so intelligently!"

As the carriage jerked across the hills, as the harness creaked and the white horse grunted, he held her hand lightly in butterfly ecstasy.

He cried out at the sight of Hanning Hall as they drove through the dark pines, among shabby grass plots, to the bare sloping lawn. It was out of a story-book; a brick house, not very large, with tall white pillars, white cupola, and dormer windows with tiny panes; and across the lawn paraded a peacock in the sun. Out of a story-book, too, was the pair of old negroes who bowed to them from the porch and hastened down the steps—the butler with green tail-coat and white mustache almost encircling his mouth, and the mammy in green calico, with an enormous grin and a histrionic curtsy.

"They've always cared for me since I was a tiny baby," Sharon whispered. "I do love them—I do love this dear old place. That's—" She hesitated, then defiantly: "That's why I brought you here!"

The butler took his bag up and unpacked, while Elmer wandered about the old bedroom, impressed, softly happy. The wall was a series of pale landscapes: manor houses beyond avenues of elms. The bed was a four-poster; the fireplace of white-enameled posts and mantel; and on the broad oak boards of the floor, polished by generations of forgotten feet, were hooked rugs of the days of crinoline.

"Golly, I'm so happy! I've come home!" sighed Elmer.

When the butler was gone, Elmer drifted to the window, and "Golly!" he said again. He had not realized that in the buggy they had climbed so high. Beyond rolling pasture and woods was the Shenandoah glowing with afternoon.

"Shen-an-doah!" he crooned.

Suddenly he was kneeling at the window, and for the first time since he had forsaken Jim Lefferts and football and joyous ribaldry, his soul was free of all the wickedness which had daubed it—oratorical ambitions, emotional orgasm, dead sayings of dull seers, dogmas, and piety. The golden winding river drew him, the sky uplifted him, and with outflung arms he prayed for deliverance from prayer.

"I've found her. Sharon. Oh, I'm not going on with this evangelistic bunk. Trapping idiots into holy monkey-shines! No, by God, I'll be honest! I'll tuck her under my arm and go out and fight. Business. Put it over. Build something big. And laugh, not snivel and shake hands with church-members! I'll do it!"

Then and there ended his rebellion.

The vision of the beautiful river was hidden from him by a fog of compromises. . . . How could he keep away from evangelistic melodrama if he was to have Sharon? And to have Sharon was the one purpose of life. She loved her meetings, she would never leave them, and she would rule him. And—he was exalted by his own oratory.

"*Besides!* There is a lot to all this religious stuff. We do do good. Maybe we jolly 'em into emotions too much, but don't that wake folks up from their ruts? Course it does!"

So he put on a white turtle-necked sweater and with a firm complacent tread he went down to join Sharon.

She was waiting in the hall, so light and young in her middy blouse and red tam.

"Let's not talk seriously. I'm not Sister Falconer—I'm Sharon today. Gee, to think I've ever spoken to five thousand people! Come on! I'll race you up the hill!"

The wide lower hall, traditionally hung with steel engravings and a Chickamauga sword, led from the front door, under the balcony of the staircase, to the garden at the back, still bold with purple asters and golden zinnias.

Through the hall she fled, through the garden, past the stone sundial, and over the long rough grass to the orchard on the sunny hill; no ceremonious Juno now but a nymph; and he followed, heavy, graceless, but pounding on inescapable, thinking less of her fleeting slenderness than of the fact that since he had stopped smoking his wind cer'nly was a lot better—cer'nly was.

"You *can* run!" she said, as she stopped, panting, by a walled garden with espalier pears.

"You bet I can! And I'm a grand footballer, a bearcat at tackling, my young friend!"

He picked her up, while she kicked and grudgingly admired, "You're terribly strong!"

But the day of halcyon October sun was too serene even for his coltishness, and sedately they tramped up the hill, swinging their joined hands; sedately they talked (ever so hard he tried to live up to the Falconer Family, an Old Mansion, and Darky Mammies) of the world-menacing perils of Higher Criticism, and the genius of E. O. Excell as a composer of sacred but snappy melodies.

III

While he dressed, that is, while he put on the brown suit and a superior new tie, Elmer worried. This sure intimacy was too perfect. Something would interrupt it. Sharon had spoken vaguely of brothers, of high-nosed aunts and cousins, of a cloud of Falconer witnesses, and the house was large enough to secrete along its corridors a horde of relatives. Would he, at dinner, have to meet hostile relics who would stare at him and make him talk and put him down as a piece of Terwillinger provinciality? He could see the implications in their level faded eyes; he could see Sharon swayed by their scorn and delivered from such uncertain fascination as his lustiness and boldness had cast over her.

"Damn!" he said. "I'm just as good as they are!"

He came reluctantly down-stairs to the shabby, endearing drawing-room, with its whatnot of curios—a Chinese slipper, a stag carved of black walnut, a shell from Madagascar—with its jar of dried cattails, its escritoire and gate-legged table, and a friendly old couch before the white fireplace. The room, the whole spreading house, was full of whispers and creakings and dead suspicious eyes. . . . There had been no whispers and no memories in the cottage at Paris, Kansas. . . . Elmer stood wistful, a little beaten boy, his runaway hour with the daughter of the manor house ended, too worshiping to resent losing the one thing he wanted.

Then she was at the door, extremely unevangelistic, pleasantly worldly in an evening frock of black satin and gold lace. He had not known people who wore evening frocks. She held out her hand gaily to him, but it was not gaily that he went to her—meekly, rather, resolved that he would not disgrace her before the suspicious family.

They came hand in hand into the dining-room and he saw that the table was set for two only.

He almost giggled, "Thought maybe there'd be a lot of folks," but he was saved, and he did not bustle about her chair.

He said grace, at length.

Candles and mahogany, silver and old lace, roses and Wedgwood, canvasback and the butler in bottle-green. He sank into a stilled happiness as she told riotous stories of evangelism—of her tenor soloist, the plump Adelbert Shoop, who loved crème de cocoa; of the Swedish farmer's wife, who got her husband prayed out of the drinking, cursing, and snuff habits, then tried to get him prayed out of playing checkers, whereupon he went out and got marvelously pickled on raw alcohol.

"I've never seen you so quiet before," she said. "You really can be nice. Happy?"

"Terribly!"

The roof of the front porch had been turned into an outdoor terrace, and here, wrapped up against the cool evening, they had their coffee and peppermints in long deck chairs. They were above the tree-tops; and as their eyes widened in the darkness they could see the river by starlight. The hoot of a wandering owl; then the kind air, the whispering air, crept round them.

"Oh, my God, it is so sweet—so sweet!" he sighed, as he fumbled for her hand and felt it slip confidently into his. Suddenly he was ruthless, tearing it all down:

"Too darn' sweet for me, I guess. Sharon, I'm a bum. I'm not so bad as a preacher, or I wouldn't be if I had the chance, but *me*— I'm no good. I have cut out the booze and tobacco—for you—I really have! But I used to drink like a fish, and till I met you I never thought any woman except my mother was any good. I'm just a second-rate traveling man. I came from Paris, Kansas, and I'm not even up to that hick burg, because they are hard-working and decent there, and I'm not even that. And you—you're not only a prophetess, which you sure are, the real big thing, but you're a Falconer. Family! Old servants! This old house! Oh, it's no use! You're too big for me. Just because I do love you. Terribly. Because I can't lie to you!"

He had put away her slim hand, but it came creeping back over his, her fingers tracing the valleys between his knuckles, while she murmured:

"You will be big! I'll make you! And perhaps I'm a prophetess, a little bit, but I'm also a good liar. You see I'm not a Falconer. There ain't any! My name is Katie Jonas. I was born in Utica. My dad worked on a brickyard. I picked out the name Sharon Falconer while I was a stenographer. I never saw this house till two years ago; I never saw these old family servants till then—they worked for the folks that owned the place—and even they weren't Falconers—they had the aristocratic name of Sprugg! Incidentally, this place isn't a quarter paid for. And yet I'm not a liar! I'm not! I *am* Sharon Falconer now! I've made her—by prayer and by having a right to be her! And you're going to stop being poor Elmer Gantry of Paris, Kansas. You're going to be the Reverend Dr. Gantry, the great captain of souls! Oh, I'm glad you don't come from anywhere in particular! Cecil Aylston—oh, I guess he does love me, but I always feel he's laughing at me. Hang him, he notices the infinitives I split and not the souls I save! But you— Oh, you will serve me—won't you?"

"Forever!"

And there was little said then. Even the agreement that she was to get rid of Cecil, to make Elmer her permanent assistant, was reached in a few casual assents. He was certain that the steely film of her dominance was withdrawn.

Yet when they went in, she said gaily that they must be early abed; up early tomorrow; and that she would take ten pounds off him at tennis.

When he whispered, "Where is your room, sweet?" she laughed with a chilling impersonality, "You'll never know, poor lamb!"

Elmer the bold, Elmer the enterprising, went clumping off to his room, and solemnly he undressed, wistfully he stood by the window, his soul riding out on the darkness to incomprehensible destinations. He humped into bed and dropped toward sleep, too weary with fighting her resistance to lie thinking of possible tomorrows.

He heard a tiny scratching noise. It seemed to him that it was the doorknob turning. He sat up, throbbing. The sound was frightened away, but began again, a faint grating, and the bottom of the door swished slowly on the carpet. The fan of pale light from the hall widened and, craning, he could see her, but only as a ghost, a white film.

He held out his arms, desperately, and presently she stumbled against them.

"No! Please!" Hers was the voice of a sleep-walker. "I just came in to say good-night and tuck you into bed. Such a bothered unhappy child! Into bed. I'll kiss you good-night and run."

His head burrowed into the pillow. Her hand touched his cheek lightly, yet through her fingers, he believed, flowed a current which lulled him into slumber, a slumber momentary but deep with contentment.

With effort he said, "You too—you need comforting, maybe you need bossing, when I get over being scared of you."

"No. I must take my loneliness alone. I'm different, whether it's cursed or blessed. But—lonely—yes—lonely."

He was sharply awake as her fingers slipped up his cheek, across his temple, into his swart hair.

"Your hair is so thick," she said drowsily.

"Your heart beats so. Dear Sharon—"

Suddenly, clutching his arm, she cried, "Come! It is the call!"

He was bewildered as he followed her, white in her night-gown trimmed at the throat with white fur, out of his room, down the hall, up a steep little stairway to her own apartments; the more bewildered to go from that genteel corridor, with its forget-me-not wallpaper and stiff engravings of Virginia worthies, into a furnace of scarlet.

Her bedroom was as insane as an Oriental cozy corner of 1895—a couch high on carven ivory posts, covered with a mandarin coat; unlighted brass lamps in the likeness of mosques and pagodas; gilt papier-mâché armor on the walls; a wide dressing-table with a score of cosmetics in odd Parisian bottles; tall candlesticks, the twisted and flowered candles lighted; and over everything a hint of incense.

She opened a closet, tossed a robe to him, cried, "For the service of the altar!" and vanished into a dressing-room beyond. Diffidently, feeling rather like a fool, he put on the robe. It was of purple velvet embroidered with black symbols unknown to him, the collar heavy with gold thread. He was not quite sure what he was to do, and he waited obediently.

She stood in the doorway, posing, while he gaped. She was so tall and her hands, at her sides, the backs up and the fingers arched, moved like lilies on the bosom of a stream. She was fantastic in a robe of deep crimson adorned with golden stars and crescents, swastikas and tau crosses; her feet were in silver sandals, and round her hair was a tiara of silver moons set with steel points that flickered in the candlelight. A mist of incense floated about her, seemed to rise from her, and as she slowly raised her arms he felt in schoolboyish awe that she was veritably a priestess.

Her voice was under the spell of the sleep-walker once more as she sighed "Come! It is the chapel."

She marched to a door part-hidden by the couch, and led him into a room—

Now he was no longer part amorous, part inquisitive, but all uneasy.

What hanky-panky of construction had been performed he never knew; perhaps it was merely that the floor above this small room had been removed so that it stretched up two stories; but in any case there it was—a shrine bright as bedlam at the bottom but seeming to rise through darkness to the sky. The walls were hung with black velvet; there were no chairs; and the whole room focused on a wide altar. It was an altar of grotesque humor or of madness, draped with Chinese fabrics, crimson, apricot, emerald, gold. There were two stages of pink marble. Above the altar hung an immense crucifix with the Christ bleeding at nail-wounds and pierced side; and on the upper stage were plaster busts of the Virgin, St. Theresa, St. Catherine, a garish Sacred Heart, a dolorous simulacrum of the dying St. Stephen. But crowded on the lower stage was a crazy rout of what Elmer called "heathen idols": ape-headed gods, crocodile-headed gods, a god with three heads and a god with six arms, a jade-and-ivory Buddha, an alabaster naked Venus, and in the center of them all a beautiful, hideous, intimidating and alluring statuette of a silver goddess with a triple crown and a face as thin and long and passionate as that of Sharon Falconer. Before the altar was a long velvet cushion, very thick and soft. Here Sharon suddenly knelt, waving him to his knees, as she cried:

"It is the hour! Blessed Virgin, Mother Hera, Mother Frigga, Mother Ishtar, Mother Isis, dread Mother Astarte of the weaving arms, it is thy priestess, it is she who after the blind centuries and the groping years shall make it known to the world that ye are one, and that in me are ye all revealed, and that in this revelation shall come peace and wisdom universal, the secret of the spheres and the pit of understanding. Ye who have leaned over me and on my lips pressed your immortal fingers, take this my brother to your bosoms, open his eyes, release his pinioned spirit, make him as the gods, that with me he may carry the revelation for which a thousand thousand grievous years the world has panted.

"O rosy cross and mystic tower of ivory—

"Hear my prayer.

"O sublime April crescent—

"Hear my prayer.

"O sword of undaunted steel most excellent—

"Hear thou my prayer.

"O serpent with unfathomable eyes—

"Hear my prayer.

"Ye veiled ones and ye bright ones—from caves forgotten, the peaks of the future, the clanging today—join in me, lift up, receive him, dread nameless ones; yea, lift us then, mystery on mystery, sphere above sphere, dominion on dominion, to the very throne!"

She picked up a Bible which lay by her on the long velvet cushion at the foot of the altar, she crammed it into his hands, and cried, "Read—read—quickly!"

It was open at the Song of Solomon, and bewildered he chanted:

"How beautiful are thy feet with shoes, O prince's daughter! The joints of thy thighs are like jewels, the work of the hands of a cunning workman. Thy two breasts are like two young roes. Thy neck is as a tower of ivory. The hair of thine head like purple; the king is held in the galleries. How fair and how pleasant art thou, O love, for delights!"

She interrupted him, her voice high and a little shrill: "O mystical rose, O lily most admirable, O wondrous union; O St. Anna, Mother Immaculate, Demeter, Mother Beneficent, Lakshmi, Mother Most Shining; behold, I am his and he is yours and ye are mine!"

As he read on, his voice rose like a triumphant priest's:

"I said, I will go up to the palm tree, I will take hold of the boughs thereof—"

That verse he never finished, for she swayed sideways as she knelt before the altar, and sank into his arms, her lips parted.

IV

They sat on the hilltop, looking down on noon in the valley, sleepily talking till he roused with: "Why won't you marry me?"

"No. Not for years, anyway. I'm too old—thirty-two to your—what is it, twenty-eight or -nine? And I must be free for the service of Our Lord. . . . You do know I mean that? I am really consecrated, no matter what I may seem to do!"

"Sweet, of course I do! Oh, yes."

"But not marry. It's good at times to be just human, but mostly I have to live like a saint. . . . Besides, I do think men converts come in better if they know I'm not married."

"Damn it, listen! Do you love me a little?"

"Yes. A little! Oh, I'm as fond of you as I can be of any one except Katie Jonas. Dear child!"

She dropped her head on his shoulder, casually now, in the bee-thrumming orchard aisle, and his arm tightened.

That evening they sang gospel hymns together, to the edification of the Old Family Servants, who began to call him Doctor.

Chapter XIII

NOT TILL December did Sharon Falconer take Elmer on as assistant.

When she discharged Cecil Aylston, he said, in a small cold voice, "This is the last time, my dear prophet and peddler, that I shall ever try to be decent." But it is known that for several months he tried to conduct a rescue mission in Buffalo, and if he was examined for insanity, it was because he was seen to sit for hours staring. He was killed in a gambling den in Juarez, and when she heard of it Sharon was very sorry—she spoke of going to fetch his body, but she was too busy with holy work.

Elmer joined her at the beginning of the meetings in Cedar Rapids, Iowa. He opened the meetings for her, made announcements, offered prayer, preached when she was too weary, and led the singing when Adelbert Shoop, the musical director, was indisposed. He developed a dozen sound sermons out of encyclopedias of exegesis, handbooks for evangelists, and manuals of sermon outlines. He had a powerful discourse, used in the For Men Only service, on the strength and joy of complete chastity; he told how Jim Leffingwell saw the folly of pleasure at the death-bed of his daughter; and he had an uplifting address, suitable to all occasions, on Love as the Morning and the Evening Star.

He helped Sharon where Cecil had held her back—or so she said. While she kept her vocabulary of poetic terms, Elmer encouraged her in just the soap-box denunciation of sin which had made Cecil shudder. Also he spoke of Cecil as "Osric," which she found very funny indeed, and as "Percy," and "Algernon." He urged her to tackle the biggest towns, the most polite or rowdy audiences, and to advertise herself not in the wet-kitten high-church phrases approved by Cecil but in a manner befitting a circus, an Elks' convention, or a new messiah.

Under Elmer's urging she ventured for the first time into the larger cities. She descended on Minneapolis and, with the support only of such sects as the Full Gospel Assembly, the

Nazarenes, the Church of God, and the Wesleyan Methodists, she risked her savings in hiring an armory and inserting two-column six-inch advertisements of herself.

Minneapolis was quite as enlivened as smaller places by Sharon's voice and eyes, by her Grecian robes, by her gold-and-white pyramidal altar, and the profits were gratifying. Thereafter she sandwiched Indianapolis, Rochester, Atlanta, Seattle, the two Portlands, Pittsburgh, in between smaller cities.

For two years life was a whirlwind to Elmer Gantry.

It was so frantic that he could never remember which town was which. Everything was a blur of hot sermons, writhing converts, appeals for contributions, trains, denunciation of lazy personal workers, denunciations of Adelbert Shoop for getting drunk, firing of Adelbert Shoop, taking back of Adelbert Shoop when no other tenor so unctuously pious was to be found.

Of one duty he was never weary: of standing around and being impressive and very male for the benefit of lady seekers. How tenderly he would take their hands and moan, "Won't you hear the dear Savior's voice calling, Sister?" and all of them, spinsters with pathetic dried girlishness, misunderstood wives, held fast to his hand and were added to the carefully kept total of saved souls. Sharon saw to it that he dressed the part—double-breasted dark blue with a dashing tie in winter, and in summer white suits with white shoes.

But however loudly the skirts rustled about him, so great was Sharon's intimidating charm that he was true to her.

If he was a dervish figure those two years, she was a shooting star; inspired in her preaching, passionate with him, then a naughty child who laughed and refused to be serious even at the sermon hour; gallantly generous, then a tight-fisted virago squabbling over ten cents for stamps. Always, in every high-colored mood, she was his religion and his reason for being.

II

When she attacked the larger towns and asked for the support of the richer churches, Sharon had to create several new methods in the trade of evangelism. The churches were suspicious of women evangelists—women might do very well in visiting the sick, knitting for the heathen, and giving strawberry festivals, but they couldn't shout loud enough to scare the devil out of sinners. Indeed all evangelists, men and women, were under attack. Sound churchmen here and there were asking whether there was any peculiar spiritual value in frightening people into groveling maniacs. They were publishing statistics which asserted that not ten per cent. of the converts at emotional revival meetings remained church-members. They were even so commercial as to inquire why a pastor with a salary of two thousand dollars a year—when he got it—should agonize over helping an evangelist to make ten thousand, forty thousand.

All these doubters had to be answered. Elmer persuaded Sharon to discharge her former advance-agent—he had been a minister and contributor to the religious press, till the unfortunate affair of the oil stock—and hire a real press-agent, trained in newspaper work, circus advertising, and real-estate promoting. It was Elmer and the press-agent who worked up the new technique of risky but impressive defiance.

Where the former advance-man had begged the ministers and wealthy laymen of a town to which Sharon wanted to be invited to appreciate her spirituality, and had sat nervously about hotels, the new salesman of salvation was brusque:

"I can't waste my time and the Lord's time waiting for you people to make up your minds. Sister Falconer is especially interested in this city because she has been informed that there is a subterranean quickening here such as would simply jam your churches, with a grand new outpouring of the spirit, provided some real expert like her came to set the fuse alight. But there are so many other towns begging for her services that if you can't make up your minds immediately, we'll have to accept their appeals and pass you up. Sorry. Can only wait till midnight. Tonight. Reserved my Pullman already."

There were ever so many ecclesiastical bodies who answered that they didn't see why he waited even till midnight, but if they were thus intimidated into signing the contract (an excellent contract, drawn up by a devout Chrstian Scientist lawyer named Finkelstein) they were the more prepared to give spiritual and financial support to Sharon's labors when she did arrive.

The new press-agent was finally so impressed by the beauties of evangelism, as contrasted with his former circuses and real estate, that he was himself converted, and sometimes when he was in town with the troupe, he sang in the choir and spoke to Y.M.C.A. classes in journalism. But even Elmer's arguments could never get him to give up a sturdy, plodding devotion to poker.

III

The contract signed, the advance-man remembered his former newspaper labors, and for a few days became touchingly friendly with all the reporters in town. There were late parties at his hotel; there was much sending of bell-boys for more bottles of Wilson and White Horse and Green River. The press-agent admitted that he really did think that Miss Falconer was the greatest woman since Sarah Bernhardt, and he let the boys have stories, guaranteed held exclusive, of her beauty, the glories of her family, her miraculous power of fetching sinners or rain by prayer, and the rather vaguely dated time when, as a young girl, she had been recognized by Dwight Moody as his successor.

South of the Mason and Dixon line her grandfather was merely Mr. Falconer, a bellicose and pious man, but far enough north he was General Falconer of Ole Virginny—preferably spelled that way—who had been the adviser and solace of General Robert E. Lee. The press-agent also wrote the posters for the Ministerial Alliance, giving Satan a generous warning as to what was to happen to him.

So when Sharon and the troupe arrived, the newspapers were eager, the walls and shop-windows were scarlet with placards, and the town was breathless. Sometimes a thousand people gathered at the station for her arrival.

There were always a few infidels, particularly among the reporters, who had doubted her talents, but when they saw her in the train vestibule, in a long white coat, when she had stood there a second with her eyes closed, lost in prayer for this new community, when slowly she held out her white nervous hands in greeting—then the advance-agent's work was two-thirds done here and he could go on to whiten new fields for the harvest.

But there was still plenty of discussion before Sharon was rid of the forces of selfishness and able to get down to the job of spreading light.

Local committees were always stubborn, local committees were always jealous, local committees were always lazy, and local committees were always told these facts, with vigor. The heart of the arguments was money.

Sharon was one of the first evangelists to depend for all her profit not on a share of the contributions nor on a weekly offering but on one night devoted entirely to a voluntary "thank offering" for her and her crew alone. It sounded unselfish and it brought in more; every devotee saved up for that occasion; and it proved easier to get one fifty-dollar donation than a dozen of a dollar each. But to work up this lone offering to suitably thankful proportions, a great deal of loving and efficient preparation was needed—reminders given by the chief pastors, bankers, and other holy persons of the town, the distribution of envelopes over which devotees were supposed to brood for the whole six weeks of the meetings, and innumerable newspaper paragraphs about the self-sacrifice and heavy expenses of the evangelists.

It was over these innocent necessary precautions that the local committees always showed their meanness. They liked giving over only one contribution to the evangelist, but they wanted nothing said about it till they themselves had been taken care of—till the rent of the hall or the cost of building a tabernacle, the heat, the lights, the advertising, and other expenses had been paid.

Sharon would meet the committee—a score of clergymen, a score of their most respectable deacons, a few angular Sunday School superintendents, a few disapproving wives—in a church parlor, and for the occasion she always wore the gray suit and an air of metropolitan firmness, and swung a pair of pince-nez with lenses made of window-glass. While in familiar words the local chairman was explaining to her that their expenses were heavy, she would smile as though she knew something they could not guess, then let fly at them breathlessly:

"I'm afraid there is some error here! I wonder if you are quite in the mood to forget all material things and really throw yourselves into the self-abnegating glory of a hot campaign for souls? I know all you have to say—as a matter of fact, you've forgotten to mention your expenses for watchmen, extra hymn books, and hiring camp-chairs!

"But you haven't the experience to appreciate *my* expenses! I have to maintain almost as great a staff—not only workers and musicians but all my other representatives, whom you never see—as though I had a factory. Besides them, I have my charities. There is, for example, the Old Ladies' Home, which I keep up entirely—oh, I shan't say anything about it, but if you could see those poor aged women turning to me with such anxious faces—!"

(Where that Old Ladies' Home was, Elmer never learned.)

"We come here without any guarantee; we depend wholly upon the free-will offering of the last day; and I'm afraid you're going to stress the local expenses so that people will not feel like giving on the last day even enough to pay the salaries of my assistants. I'm taking—if it were not that I abominate the pitiful and character-destroying vice of gambling, I'd say that I'm taking such a terrible gamble that it frightens me! But there it is, and—"

While she was talking, Sharon was sizing up this new assortment of clergy: the cranks, the testy male old maids, the advertising and pushing demagogues, the commonplace pulpit-job-holders, the straddling young liberals; the real mystics, the kindly fathers of their flocks, the lovers of righteousness. She had picked out as her advocate the most sympathetic, and she launched her peroration straight at him:

"Do you want to ruin me, so that never again shall I be able to carry the message, to carry salvation, to the desperate souls who are everywhere waiting for me, crying for my help? Is that your purpose—you, the elect, the people chosen to help me in the service of the dear Lord Jesus himself? Is that your purpose? Is it? Is it?"

She began sobbing, which was Elmer's cue to jump up and have a wonderful new idea.

He knew, did Elmer, that the dear brethren and sisters had no such purpose. They just wanted to be practical. Well, why wouldn't it be a good notion for the committee to go to the well-to-do church members and explain the unparalleled situation; tell them that this was the Lord's work, and that aside from the unquestioned spiritual benefits, the revival would do so much good that crime would cease, and taxes thus be lessened; that workmen would turn from agitation to higher things, and work more loyally at the same wages. If they got enough pledges from the rich for current expenses, those expenses would not have to be stressed at the meetings, and people could properly be coaxed to save up for the final "thank offering"; not have to be nagged to give more than small coins at the nightly collections.

There were other annoyances to discuss with the local committee. Why, Elmer would demand, hadn't they provided enough dressing-rooms in the tabernacle? Sister Falconer needed privacy. Sometimes just before the meeting she and he had to have important conferences. Why hadn't they provided more volunteer ushers? He must have them at once, to train them, for it was the ushers, when properly coached, who would ease struggling souls up to the altar for the skilled finishing touches by the experts.

Had they planned to invite big delegations from the local institutions—from Smith Brothers' Catsup Factory, from the car-shops, from the packing house? Oh, yes, they must plan to stir up these institutions; an evening would be dedicated to each of them, the representatives would be seated together, and they'd have such a happy time singing their favorite hymns.

By this time, a little dazed, the local committee were granting everything; and they looked almost convinced when Sharon wound up with a glad ringing:

"All of you must look forward, and joyfully, to a sacrifice of time and money in these meetings. We have come here at a great sacrifice, and we are here only to help you."

IV

The afternoon and evening sermons—those were the high points of the meetings, when Sharon cried in a loud voice, her arms out to them, "Surely the Lord is in this place and I knew it not," and "All our righteousness is as filthy rags," and "We have sinned and come short of the glory of God," and "Oh, for the man to arise in me, that the man I am may cease to be," and "Get right with God," and "I am not ashamed of the gospel of Christ, for it is the power of God unto salvation."

But before even these guaranteed appeals could reach wicked hearts, the audience had to be prepared for emotion, and to accomplish this there was as much labor behind Sharon's eloquence as there is of wardrobes and scene-shifters and box offices behind the frenzy of Lady Macbeth. Of this preparation Elmer had a great part.

He took charge, as soon as she had trained him, of the men personal workers, leaving the girls to the Director of Personal Work, a young woman who liked dancing and glass jewelry but who was admirable at listening to the confessions of spinsters. His workers were bank-tellers, bookkeepers in wholesale groceries, shoe clerks, teachers of manual training. They canvassed shops, wholesale warehouses, and factories, and held noon meetings in offices, where they explained that the most proficient use of shorthand did not save one from the probability of hell. For Elmer explained that prospects were more likely to be converted if they came to the meetings with a fair amount of fear.

When they were permitted, the workers were to go from desk to desk, talking to each victim about the secret sins he was comfortably certain to have. And both men and women workers were to visit the humbler homes and offer to kneel and pray with the floury and embarrassed wife, the pipe-wreathed and shoeless husband.

All the statistics of the personal work—so many souls invited to come to the altar, so many addresses to workmen over their lunch-pails, so many cottage prayers, with the length of each—were rather imaginatively entered by Elmer and the Director of Personal Work on the balance-sheet which Sharon used as a report after the meetings and as a talking-point for the sale of future meetings.

Elmer met daily with Adelbert Shoop, that yearning and innocent tenor who was in charge of music, to select hymns. There were times when the audiences had to be lulled into confidence by "Softly and Tenderly Jesus Is Calling," times when they were made to feel brotherly and rustic with "It's the Old-time Religion"—

> It was good for Paul and Silas
> And it's good enough for me—

and times when they had to be stirred by "At the Cross" or "Onward, Christian Soldiers." Adelbert had ideas about what he called "worship by melody," but Elmer saw that the real purpose of singing was to lead the audience to a state of mind where they would do as they were told.

He learned to pick out letters on the typewriter with two fingers, and he answered Sharon's mail—all of it that she let him see. He kept books for her, in a ragged sufficient manner, on check-book stubs. He wrote the nightly story of her sermons, which the newspapers cut down and tucked in among stories of remarkable conversions. He talked to local church-pillars so rich and moral that their own pastors were afraid of them. And he invented an aid to salvation which to this day is used in the more evangelistic meetings, though it is credited to Adelbert Shoop.

Adelbert was up to most of the current diversions. He urged the men and the women to sing against each other. At the tense moment when Sharon was calling for converts, Adelbert would skip down the aisle, fat but nimble, pink with coy smiles, tapping people on the shoulder, singing the chorus of a song right among them, and often returning with three or four prisoners of the sword of the Lord, flapping his plump arms and caroling "They're coming—they're coming," which somehow started a stampede to the altar.

Adelbert was, in his girlish enthusiasm, almost as good as Sharon or Elmer at announcing, "Tonight, you are all of you to be evangelists. Every one of you now! Shake hands with the person to your right and ask 'em if they're saved."

He gloated over their embarrassment.

He really was a man of parts. Nevertheless, it was Elmer, not Adelbert, who invented the "Hallelujah Yell."

Remembering his college cheers, remembering how greatly it had encouraged him in kneeing the opposing tackle or jabbing the rival center's knee, Elmer observed to himself, "Why shouldn't we have yells in this game, too?"

He himself wrote the first one known in history.

Hallelujah, praise God, hal, hal, hal!
Hallelujah, praise God, hal, hal, hal!
All together, I feel better,
Hal, hal, hal,
For salvation of the nation—
Aaaaaaaaaaa—*men!*

That was a thing to hear, when Elmer led them; when he danced before them, swinging his big arms and bellowing, "Now again! Two yards to gain! Two yards for the Savior! Come on, boys and girls, it's our team! Going to let 'em down? Not on your life! Come on then, you chipmunks, and lemme hear you knock the ole roof off! Hal, hal, hal!"

Many a hesitating boy, a little sickened by the intense brooding femininity of Sharon's appeal, was thus brought up to the platform to shake hands with Elmer and learn the benefits of religion.

V

The gospel crew could never consider their converts as human beings, like waiters or manicurists or brakemen, but they had in them such a professional interest as surgeons take in patients, critics in an author, fishermen in trout.

They were obsessed by the gaffer in Terre Haute who got converted every single night during the meetings. He may have been insane and he may have been a plain drunk, but every evening he came in looking adenoidal and thoroughly backslidden; every evening he slowly woke to his higher needs during the sermon; and when the call for converts came, he leaped up, shouted "Hallelujah, I've found it!" and galloped forward, elbowing real and valuable prospects out of the aisle. The crew waited for him as campers for a mosquito.

In Scranton, they had unusually exasperating patients. Scranton had been saved by a number of other evangelists before their arrival, and had become almost anesthetic. Ten nights they sweated over the audience without a single sinner coming forward, and Elmer had to go out and hire half a dozen convincing converts.

He found them in a mission near the river, and explained that by giving a good example to the slothful, they would be doing the work of God, and that if the example was good enough, he would give them five dollars apiece. The missioner himself came in during the conference and offered to get converted for ten, but he was so well known that Elmer had to give him the ten to stay away.

His gang of converts was very impressive, but thereafter no member of the evangelistic troupe was safe. The professional Christians besieged the tent night and day. They wanted to be saved again. When they were refused, they offered to produce new converts at five dollars apiece—three dollars apiece—fifty cents and a square meal. By this time enough authentic and free enthusiasts were appearing, and though they were fervent, they did not relish being saved in company with hoboes who smelled. When the half dozen cappers were thrown out, bodily, by Elmer and Art Nichols, they took to coming to the meetings and catcalling, so that for the rest of the series they had to be paid a dollar a night each to stay away.

No, Elmer could not consider the converts human. Sometimes when he was out in the audience, playing the bullying hero that Judson Roberts had once played with him, he looked up at the platform, where a row of men under conviction knelt with their arms on chairs and their broad butts toward the crowd, and he wanted to snicker and wield a small plank. But five minutes after he would be up there, kneeling with a sewing-machine agent with the day-after shakes, his arm round the client's shoulder, pleading in the tones of a mother cow, "Can't you surrender to Christ, Brother? Don't you want to give up all the dreadful habits that are ruining you—keeping you back from success? Listen! God'll help you make good! And when you're lonely, old man, remember he's there, waiting to talk to you!"

VI

They generally, before the end of the meetings, worked up gratifying feeling. Often young women knelt panting, their eyes blank, their lips wide with ecstasy. Sometimes, when Sharon was particularly fired, they actually had the phenomena of the great revivals of 1800. People twitched and jumped with the holy jerks, old people under pentecostal inspiration spoke in unknown tongues—completely unknown; women stretched out senseless, their tongues dripping; and once occurred what connoisseurs regard as the highest example of religious inspiration. Four men and two women crawled about a pillar, barking like dogs, "barking the devil out of the tree."

Sharon relished these miracles. They showed her talent; they were sound manifestations of Divine Power. But sometimes they got the meetings a bad name, and cynics prostrated her by talking of "Holy Rollers." Because of this maliciousness and because of the excitement which she found in meetings so favored by the Holy Ghost, Elmer had particularly to comfort her after them.

VII

All the members of the evangelistic crew planned effects to throw a brighter limelight on Sharon. There was feverish discussions of her costumes. Adelbert had planned the girdled white robe in which she appeared as priestess, and he wanted her to wear it always. "You are so queeeeenly," he whimpered. But Elmer insisted on changes, on keeping the robe for crucial meetings, and Sharon went out for embroidered golden velvet frocks and, at meetings for business women, smart white flannel suits.

They assisted her also in the preparation of new sermons.

Her "message" was delivered under a hypnotism of emotion, without connection with her actual life. Now Portia, now Ophelia, now Francesca, she drew men to her, did with them as she would. Or again she saw herself as veritably the scourge of God. But however richly she could pour out passion, however flamingly she used the most exotic words and the most complex sentiments when some one had taught them to her, it was impossible for her to originate any sentiment more profound than "I'm unhappy."

She read nothing, after Cecil Aylston's going, but the Bible and the advertisements of rival evangelists in the bulletin of the Moody Bible Institute.

Lacking Cecil, it was a desperate and coöperative affair to furnish Sharon with fresh sermons as she grew tired of acting the old ones. Adelbert Shoop provided the poetry. He was fond of poetry. He read Ella Wheeler Wilcox, James Whitcomb Riley, and Thomas Moore. He was also a student of philosophy: he could understand Ralph Waldo Trine perfectly, and he furnished for Sharon's sermons both the couplets about Home and Little Ones, and the philosophical points about will-power, Thoughts are Things, and Love is Beauty, Beauty is Love, Love is All.

The lady Director of Personal Work had unexpected talent in making up anecdotes about the death-beds of drunkards and agnostics; Lily Anderson, the pretty though anemic pianist, had once been a school teacher and had read a couple of books about scientists, so she was able to furnish data with which Sharon absolutely confuted the rising fad of evolution; and Art Nichols, the cornetist, provided rude but moral Maine humor, stories about horse-trading, cabbages, and hard cider, very handy for cajoling skeptical business men. But Elmer, being trained theologically, had to weave all the elements—dogma, poetry to the effect that God's palette held the sunsets or ever the world began, confessions of the dismally damned, and stories of Maine barn-dances—into one ringing whole.

And meanwhile, besides the Reverend Sister Falconer and the Reverend Mr. Gantry, thus coöperative, there were Sharon and Elmer and a crew of quite human people with grievances, traveling together, living together, not always in a state of happy innocence.

Chapter XIV

SEDATE as a long married couple, intimate and secure, were Elmer and Sharon on most days, and always he was devoted. It was Sharon who was incalculable. Sometimes she was a priestess and a looming disaster, sometimes she was intimidating in grasping passion, sometimes she was thin and writhing and anguished with chagrined doubt of herself, sometimes she was pale and nun-like and still, sometimes she was a chilly business woman, and sometimes she was a little girl. In the last, quite authentic rôle, Elmer loved her fondly—except when she assumed it just as she was due to go out and hypnotize three thousand people.

He would beg her, "Oh, come on now, Shara, please be good! Please stop pouting, and go out and lambaste 'em."

She would stamp her foot, while her face changed to a round childishness. "No! Don't want to evangel. Want to be bad. Bad! Want to throw things. Want to go out and spank a bald man on the head. Tired of souls. Want to tell 'em all to go to hell!"

"Oh, gee, please, Shara! Gosh all fishhooks! They're waiting for you! Adelbert has sung that verse twice now."

"I don't care! Sing it again! Sing songs, losh songs! Going to be bad! Going out and drop mice down Adelbert's fat neck—fat neck—fat hoooooly neck!"

But suddenly: "I wish I could. I wish they'd let me *be* bad. Oh, I get so tired—all of them reaching for me, sucking my blood, wanting me to give them the courage they're too flabby to get for themselves!"

And a minute later she was standing before the audience, rejoicing, "Oh, my beloved, the dear Lord has a message for you tonight!"

And in two hours, as they rode in a taxi to the hotel, she was sobbing on his breast: "Hold me close! I'm so lonely and afraid and cold."

II

Among his various relations to her, Elmer was Sharon's employee. And he resented the fact that she was making five times more than he of that money for which he had a reverent admiration.

When they had first made plans, she had suggested:

"Dear, if it all works out properly, in three or four years I want you to share the offerings with me. But first I must save a lot. I've got some vague plans to build a big center for our work, maybe with a magazine and a training-school for evangelists. When that's paid for, you and I can make an agreement. But just now— How much have you been making as a traveling man?"

"Oh, about three hundred a month—about thirty-five hundred a year." He was really fond of her; he was lying to the extent of only five hundred.

"Then I'll start you in at thirty-eight hundred, and in four or five years I hope it'll be ten thousand, and maybe twice as much."

And she never, month after month, discussed salary again. It irritated him. He knew that she was making more than twenty thousand a year, and that before long she would probably make fifty thousand. But he loved her so completely that he scarce thought of it oftener than three or four times a month.

III

Sharon continued to house her troupe in hotels, for independence. But an unfortunate misunderstanding came up. Elmer had stayed late in her room, engaged in a business conference, so late that he accidentally fell asleep across the foot of her bed. So tired were they both that neither of them awoke till nine in the morning, when they were aroused by Adelbert Shoop knocking and innocently skipping in.

Sharon raised her head, to see Adelbert giggling.

"How *dare* you come into my room without knocking, you sausage!" she raged. "Have you no sense of modesty or decency? Beat it! Potato!"

When Adelbert had gone simpering out, cheeping, "*Honest*, I won't say *anything*," then Elmer fretted, "Golly, do you think he'll blackmail us?"

"Oh, no, Adelbert adores me. Us girls must stick together. But it does bother me. Suppose it'd been some other guest of the hotel! People misunderstand and criticize so. Tell you what let's do. Hereafter, in each town, let's hire a big house, furnished, for the whole crew. Still be independent, but nobody around to talk about us. And prob'ly we can get a dandy house quite cheap from some church-member. That would be lovely! When we get sick of working so hard all the time, we could have a party just for ourselves, and have a dance. I love to dance. Oh, of course I roast dancing in my sermons, but I mean—when it's with people like us, that understand, it's not like with worldly people, where it would lead to evil. A party! Though Art Nichols *would* get drunk. Oh, let him! He works so hard. Now you skip. Wait! Aren't you going to kiss me good morning?"

They made sure of Adelbert's loyalty by flattering him, and the press-agent had orders to find a spacious furnished house in the city to which they were going next.

IV

The renting of furnished houses for the Falconer Evangelistic Party was a ripe cause for new quarrels with local committees, particularly after the party had left town.

There were protests by the infuriated owners that the sacred workers must have been, as one deacon-undertaker put it, "simply raising the very devil." He asserted that the furniture had been burned with cigarette stubs, that whisky had been spilled on rugs, that chairs had been broken. He claimed damages from the local committee; the local committee sent the claims on to Sharon; there was a deal of fervent correspondence; and the claims were never paid.

Though usually it did not come out till the series of meetings was finished, so that there was no interference with saving the world, these arguments about the private affairs of the evangelistic crew started most regrettable rumors. The ungodly emitted loud scoffings. Sweet repressed old maids wondered and wondered what might really have happened, and speculated together in delightful horror as to whether—uh—there could have been anything—uh—worse than drinking going on.

But always a majority of the faithful argued logically that Sister Falconer and Brother Gantry were righteous, therefore they could not do anything unrighteous, therefore the rumors were inspired by the devil and spread by saloon-keepers and infidels, and in face of this persecution of the godly, the adherents were the more lyric in support of the Falconer Party.

Elmer learned from the discussions of damages a pleasant way of reducing expenses. At the end of their stay, they simply did not pay the rent for their house. They informed the local committee, after they had gone, that the committee had promised to provide living quarters, and that was all there was to it. . . . There was a lot of correspondence.

V

One of Sharon's chief troubles was getting her crew to bed. Like most actors, they were high-strung after the show. Some of them were too nervous to sleep till they had read the *Saturday Evening Post*; others never could eat till after the meetings, and till one o'clock they fried eggs and scrambled eggs and burnt toast and quarreled over the dish-washing. Despite their enlightened public stand against the Demon Rum, some of the performers had to brace up their nerves with an occasional quart of whisky, and there was dancing and assorted glee.

Though sometimes she exploded all over them, usually Sharon was amiably blind, and she had too many conferences with Elmer to give much heed to the parties.

Lily Anderson, the pale pianist, protested. They ought all, she said, to go to bed early so they could be up early. They ought, she said, to go oftener to the cottage prayer meetings. The others insisted that this was too much to expect of people exhausted by their daily three hours of work, but she reminded them that they were doing the work of the Lord, and they ought to be willing to wear themselves out in such service. They were, said they; but not tonight.

After days when Art Nichols, the cornetist, and Adolph Klebs, the violinist, had such heads at ten in the morning that they had to take pick-me-ups, would come days when all of them, even Art and Adolph, were hysterically religious; when quite privately they prayed and repented and raised their voices in ululating quavers of divine rapture, till Sharon said furiously that she didn't know whether she preferred to be waked up by hell-raising or hallelujahs. Yet once she bought a traveling phonograph for them, and many records, half hectic dances and half hymns.

VI

Though her presence nearly took away his need of other stimulants, of tobacco and alcohol and most of his cursing, it was a year before Elmer was altogether secure from the thought of them. But gradually he saw himself certain of future power and applause as a clergyman. His ambition became more important than the titillation of alcohol, and he felt very virtuous and pleased.

Those were big days, rejoicing days, sunny days. He had everything: his girl, his work, his fame, his power over people. When they held meetings in Topeka, his mother came from Paris to hear them, and as she watched her son addressing two thousand people, all the heavy graveyard doubts which had rotted her after his exit from Mizpah Seminary vanished.

He felt now that he belonged. The gospel crew had accepted him as their assistant foreman, as bolder and stronger and trickier than any save Sharon, and they followed him like family dogs. He imagined a day when he would marry Sharon, supersede her as leader—letting her preach now and then as a feature—and become one of the great evangelists of the land. He belonged. When he encountered fellow evangelists, no matter how celebrated, he was pleased but not awed.

Didn't Sharon and he meet no less an evangelist than Dr. Howard Bancock Binch, the great Baptist defender of the literal interpretation of the Bible, president of the True Gospel Training School for Religious Workers, editor of *The Keeper of the Vineyard*, and author of "Fools Errors of So-Called Science"? Didn't Dr. Binch treat Elmer like a son?

Dr. Binch happened to be in Joliet, on his way to receive his sixth D.D. degree (from Abner College) during Sharon's meetings there. He lunched with Sharon and Elmer.

"Which hymns do you find the most effective when you make your appeal for converts, Dr. Binch?" asked Elmer.

"Well, I'll tell you, Brother Gantry," said the authority. "I think 'Just as I Am' and 'Jesus, I Am Coming Home' hit real folksy hearts like nothing else."

"Oh, I'm afraid I don't agree with you," protested Sharon. "It seems to me—of course you have far more experience and talent than I, Dr. Binch—"

"Not at all, my dear sister," said Dr. Binch, with a leer which sickened Elmer with jealousy. "You are young, but all of us recognize your genius."

"Thank you very much. But I mean: They're not lively enough. I feel we ought to use hymns with a swing to 'em, hymns that make you dance right up to the mourners' bench."

Dr. Binch stopped gulping his fried pork chops and held up a flabby, white, holy hand. "Oh, Sister Falconer, I hate to have you use the word 'dance' regarding an evangelistic meeting! What is the dance? It is the gateway to hell! How many innocent girls have found in the dance-hall the allurement which leads to every nameless vice!"

Two minutes of information about dancing—given in the same words that Sharon herself often used—and Dr. Binch wound up with a hearty: "So I beg of you not to speak of 'dancing to the mourners' bench!'"

"I know, Dr. Binch, I know, but I mean in its sacred sense, as of David dancing before the Lord."

"But I feel there was a different meaning to that. If you only knew the original Hebrew—the word should not be translated 'danced' but 'was moved by the spirit.'"

"Really? I didn't know that. I'll use that."

They all looked learned.

"What methods, Dr. Binch," asked Elmer, "do you find the most successful in forcing people to come to the altar when they resist the Holy Ghost?"

"I always begin by asking those interested in being prayed for to hold up their hands."

"Oh, I believe in having them stand up if they want prayer. Once you get a fellow to his feet, it's so much easier to coax him out into the aisle and down to the front. If he just holds up his hand, he may pull it down before you can spot him. We've trained our ushers to jump right in the minute anybody gets up, and say 'Now, Brother, won't you come down front and shake hands with Sister Falconer and make your stand for Jesus?'"

"No," said Dr. Binch, "my experience is that there are many timid people who have to be led gradually. To ask them to stand up is too big a step. But actually, we're probably both right. My motto as a soul-saver, if I may venture to apply such a lofty title to myself, is that one should use every method that, in the vernacular, will sell the goods."

"I guess that's right," said Elmer. "Say, tell me, Dr. Binch, what do you do with converts after they come to the altar?"

"I always try to have a separate room for 'em. That gives you a real chance to deepen and richen their new experience. They can't escape, if you close the door. And there's no crowd to stare and embarrass them."

"I can't see that," said Sharon. "I believe that if the people who come forward are making a stand for Christ, they ought to be willing to face the crowd. And it makes such an impression on the whole bunch of the unsaved to see a lot of seekers at the mourners' bench. You must admit, Brother Binch—Dr. Binch, I should say—that lots of people who just come to a revival for a good time are moved to conviction epidemically, by seeing others shaken."

"No, I can't agree that that's so important as making a deeper impression on each convert, so that each goes out as an agent for you, as it were. But every one to his own methods. I mean so long as the Lord is with us and behind us."

"Say, Dr. Binch," said Elmer, "how do you count your converts? Some of the preachers in this last town accused us of lying about the number. On what basis do you count them?"

"Why, I count every one (and we use a recording machine) that comes down to the front and shakes hands with me. What if some of them *are* merely old church members warmed over? Isn't it worth just as much to give new spiritual life to those who've had it and lost it?"

"Of course it is. That's what we think. And then we got criticized there in that fool town! We tried—that is, Sister Falconer here tried—a stunt that was new for us. We opened up on some of the worst dives and blind tigers by name. We even gave street numbers. The attack created a howling sensation; people just jammed in, hoping we'd attack other places. I believe that's a good policy. We're going to try it here next week. It puts the fear of God into the wicked, and slams over the revival."

"There's danger in that sort of thing, though," said Dr. Binch. "I don't advise it. Trouble is, in such an attack you're liable to offend some of the leading church members—the very folks that contribute the most cash to a revival. They're often the owners of buildings that get used by unscrupulous persons for immoral purposes, and while they of course regret such unfortunate use of their property, if you attack such places by name, you're likely to lose their support. Why, you might lose thousands of dollars! It seems to me wiser and more Christian to just attack vice in general."

"How much orchestra do you use, Dr. Binch?" asked Sharon.

"All I can get hold of. I'm carrying a pianist, a violinist, a drummer, and a cornetist, besides my soloist."

"But don't you find some people objecting to fiddling?"

"Oh, yes, but I jolly 'em out of it by saying I don't believe in letting the devil monopolize all these art things," said Dr. Binch. "Besides, I find that a good tune, sort of a nice, artistic, slow, sad one, puts folks into a mood where they'll come across both with their hearts and their contributions. By the way, speaking of that, what luck have you folks had recently in raising money? And what method do you use?"

"It's been pretty good with us—and I need a lot, because I'm supporting an orphanage," said Sharon. "We're sticking to the idea of the free-will offering the last day. We can get more money than any town would be willing to guarantee beforehand. If the appeal for the free-will offering is made strong enough, we usually have pretty fair results."

"Yes, I use the same method. But I don't like the term 'free-will offering,' or 'thank offering.' It's been used so much by merely second-rate evangelists, who, and I grieve to say there are such people, put their own gain before the service of the Kingdom, that it's got a commercial sound. In making my own appeal for contributions, I use 'love offering.'"

"That's worth thinking over, Dr. Binch," sighed Sharon, "but, oh, how tragic it is that we, with our message of salvation—if the sad old world would but listen, we could solve all its sorrows and difficulties—yet with this message ready, we have to be practical and raise money for our expenses and charities. Oh, the world doesn't appreciate evangelists. Think what we can do for a resident minister! These preachers who talk about conducting their own revivals make me sick! They don't know the right technique. Conducting revivals is a profession. One must know all the tricks. With all modesty, I figure that I know just what will bring in the converts."

"I'm sure you do, Sister Falconer," from Binch. "Say, do you and Brother Gantry like union revivals?"

"You bet your life we do," said Brother Gantry. "We won't conduct a revival unless we can have the united support of all the evangelical preachers in town."

"I think you are mistaken, Brother Gantry," said Dr. Binch. "I find that I have the most successful meetings with only a few churches, but all of them genuinely O.K. With all the preachers joined together, you have to deal with a lot of these two-by-four hick preachers with churches about the size of woodsheds and getting maybe eleven hundred a year, and yet they think they have the right to make suggestions! No, sir! I want to do business with the big down-town preachers that are used to doing things in a high-grade way and that don't kick if you take a decent-sized offering out of town!"

"Yuh, there's something to be said for that," said Elmer. "That's what the Happy Sing Evangelist—you know, Bill Buttle—said to us one time."

"But I hope you don't *like* Brother Buttle!" protested Dr. Binch.

"Oh, no! Anyway, *I* didn't like him," said Sharon, which was a wifely slap at Elmer.

Dr. Binch snorted, "He's a scoundrel! There's rumors about his wife's leaving him. Why is it that in such a high calling as ours there are so many rascals? Take Dr. Mortonby!

Calling himself a cover-to-cover literalist, and then his relations to the young woman who sings for him—I would shock you, Sister Falconer, if I told you what I suspect."

"Oh, I know. I haven't met him, but I hear dreadful things," wailed Sharon. "And Wesley Zigler! They say he drinks! And an evangelist! Why, if any person connected with me were so much as to take one drink, out he goes!"

"That's right, that's right. Isn't it dreadful!" mourned Dr. Binch. "And take this charlatan Edgar Edgars—this obscene ex-gambler with his disgusting slang! Uh! The hypocrite!"

Joyously they pointed out that this rival artist in evangelism was an ignoramus, that a passer of bogus checks, the other doubtful about the doctrine of the premillennial coming; joyously they concluded that the only intelligent and moral evangelists in America were Dr. Binch, Sister Falconer, and Brother Gantry, and the lunch broke up in an orgy of thanksgiving.

"There's the worst swell-head and four-flusher in America, that Binch, and he's shaky on Jonah, and I've heard he chews tobacco—and then pretending to be so swell and citified. Be careful of him," said Sharon to Elmer afterward, and, "Oh, my dear, my dear!"

Chapter XV

IT WAS NOT her eloquence but her healing of the sick which raised Sharon to such eminence that she promised to become the most renowned evangelist in America. People were tired of eloquence; and the whole evangelist business was limited, since even the most ardent were not likely to be saved more than three or four times. But they could be healed constantly, and of the same disease.

Healing was later to become the chief feature of many evangelists, but in 1910 it was advertised chiefly by Christian Scientists and the New Thoughters. Sharon came to it by accident. She had regularly offered prayers for the sick, but only absent-mindedly. When Elmer and she had been together for a year, during her meetings in Schenectady a man led up his deaf wife and begged Sharon to heal her. It amused Sharon to send out for some oil (it happened to be shotgun oil, but she properly consecrated it) to anoint the woman's ears, and to pray lustily for healing.

The woman screamed, "Glory to God, I've got my hearing back!"

There was a sensation in the tabernacle, and everybody itched with desire to be relieved of whatever ailed him. Elmer led the healed deaf woman aside and asked her name for the newspapers. It is true that she could not hear him, but he wrote out his questions, she wrote the answers, and he got an excellent story for the papers and an idea for their holy work.

Why, he put it to Sharon, shouldn't she make healing a regular feature?

"I don't know that I have any gift for it," considered Sharon.

"Sure you have! Aren't you psychic? You bet. Go to it. We might pull off some healing services. I bet the collections would bust all records, and we'll have a distinct understanding with the local committees that we get all over a certain amount, besides the collection the last day."

"Well, we might try one. Of course, the Lord may have blessed me with special gifts that way, and to him be all the credit, oh, let's stop in here and have an ice cream soda, I *love* banana splits, I hope nobody sees me, I feel like dancing tonight, anyway we'll talk over the possibility of healing, I'm going to take a hot bath the minute we get home with losh bath salts—losh and losh and losh."

The success was immense.

She alienated many evangelical pastors by divine healing, but she won all the readers of books about will-power, and her daily miracles were reported in the newspapers. And, or so it was reported, some of her patients remained cured.

She murmured to Elmer, "You know, maybe there really is something to this healing, and I get an enormous thrill out of it—telling the lame to chuck their crutches. That man last night, that cripple—he did feel lots better."

They decorated the altar now with crutches and walking-sticks, all given by grateful patients—except such as Elmer had been compelled to buy to make the exhibit inspiring from the start.

Money gamboled in. One grateful patient gave Sharon five thousand dollars. And Elmer and Sharon had their only quarrel, except for occasional spats of temperament. With the increase in profits, he demanded a rise of salary, and she insisted that her charities took all she had.

"Yuh, I've heard a lot about 'em," said he: "the Old Ladies' Home and the orphanage and the hoosegow for retired preachers. I suppose you carry 'em along with you on the road!"

"Do you mean to insinuate, my good friend, that I—"

They talked in a thoroughly spirited and domestic manner, and afterward she raised his salary to five thousand and kissed him.

With the money so easily come by, Sharon burst out in hectic plans. She was going to buy a ten-thousand-acre farm for a Christian Socialist colony and a university, and she went so far as to get a three months' option on two hundred acres. She was going to have a great national daily paper, with crime news, scandal, and athletics omitted, and a daily Bible lesson on the front page. She was going to organize a new crusade—an army of ten million which would march through heathen countries and convert the entire world to Christianity in this generation.

She did, at last, actually carry out one plan, and create a headquarters for her summer meetings.

At Clontar, a resort on the New Jersey coast, she bought the pier on which Benno Hackenschmidt used to give grand opera. Though the investment was so large that even for the initial payment it took almost every penny she had saved, she calculated that she would make money because she would be the absolute owner and not have to share contributions with local churches. And, remaining in one spot, she would build up more prestige than by moving from place to place and having to advertise her virtues anew in every town.

In a gay frenzy she planned that if she was successful, she would keep the Clontar pier for summer and build an all-winter tabernacle in New York or Chicago. She saw herself another Mary Baker Eddy, an Annie Besant, a Katherine Tingley. . . . Elmer Gantry was shocked when she hinted that, who knows? the next Messiah might be a woman, and that woman might now be on earth, just realizing her divinity.

The pier was an immense structure, built of cheap knotty pine, painted a hectic red with gold stripes. It was pleasant, however, on hot evenings. Round it ran a promenade out over the water, where once lovers had strolled between acts of the opera, and giving on the promenade were many barnlike doors.

Sharon christened it "The Waters of Jordan Tabernacle," added more and redder paint, more golden gold, and erected an enormous revolving cross, lighted at night with yellow and ruby electric bulbs.

The whole gospel crew went to Clontar early in June to make ready for the great opening on the evening of the first of July.

They had to enlist volunteer ushers and personal workers, and Sharon and Adelbert Shoop had notions about a huge robed choir, with three or four paid soloists.

Elmer had less zeal than usual in helping her, because an unfortunate thing had gone and happened to Elmer. He saw that he really ought to be more friendly with Lily Anderson, the pianist. While he remained true to Sharon, he had cumulatively been feeling that it was sheer carelessness to let the pretty and anemic and virginal Lily be wasted. He had been driven to notice her through indignation at Art Nichols, the cornetist, for having the same idea.

Elmer was fascinated by her unawakenedness. While he continued to be devoted to Sharon, over her shoulder he was always looking at Lily's pale sweetness, and his lips were moist.

II

They sat on the beach by moonlight, Sharon and Elmer, the night before the opening service.

All of Clontar, with its mile of comfortable summer villas and gingerbread hotels, was excited over the tabernacle, and the Chamber of Commerce had announced, "We commend to the whole Jersey coast this high-class spiritual feature, the latest addition to the manifold attractions and points of interest at the snappiest of all summer colonies."

A choir of two hundred had been coaxed in, and some of them had been persuaded to buy their own robes and mortar boards.

Near the sand dune against which Sharon and Elmer lolled was the tabernacle, over which the electric cross turned solemnly, throwing its glare now on the rushing surf, now across the bleak sand.

"And it's mine!" Sharon trembled. "I've made it! Four thousand seats, and I guess it's the only Christian tabernacle built out over the water! Elmer, it almost scares me! So much responsibility! Thousands of poor troubled souls turning to me for help, and if I fail them, if I'm weak or tired or greedy, I'll be murdering their very souls. I almost wish I were back safe in Virginia!"

Her enchanted voice wove itself with the menace of the breakers, feeble against the crash of broken waters, passionate in the lull, while the great cross turned its unceasing light.

"And I'm ambitious, Elmer. I know it. I want the world. But I realize what an awful danger that is. But I never had anybody to train me. I'm just nobody. I haven't any family, any education. I've had to do everything for myself, except what Cecil and you and another man or two have done, and maybe you-all came too late. When I was a kid, there was no one to tell me what a sense of honor was. But— Oh, I've done things! Little Katie Jonas of Railroad Avenue—little Katie with her red flannel skirt and torn stockings, fighting the whole Killarney Street gang and giving Pup Monahan one in the nose, by Jiminy! And not five cents a year, even for candy. And now it's mine, that tabernacle there—look at it—that cross, that choir you hear practising! Why, I'm the Sharon Falconer you read about! And tomorrow I become—oh, people reaching for me—me healing 'em— No! It frightens me! It can't last. *Make it last for me, Elmer!* Don't let them take it away from me!"

She was sobbing, her head on his lap, while he comforted her clumsily. He was slightly bored. She was heavy, and though he did like her, he wished she wouldn't go on telling that Katie-Jonas-Utica story.

She rose to her knees, her arms out to him, her voice hysteric against the background of the surf:

"I can't do it! But you— I'm a woman. I'm weak. I wonder if I oughtn't to stop thinking I'm such a marvel, if I oughtn't to let you run things and just stand back and help you? Ought I?"

He was overwhelmed by her good sense, but he cleared his throat and spoke judiciously:

"Well, now I'll tell you. Personally I'd never've brought it up, but since you speak of it yourself—I don't admit for a minute that I've got any more executive ability or oratory than you have—probably not half as much. And after all, you did start the show; I came in late. But same time, while a woman can put things over just as good as a man, or better, for a *while*, she's a woman, and she isn't built to carry on things like a man would, see how I mean?"

"Would it be better for the Kingdom if I forgot my ambition and followed you?"

"Well, I don't say it'd be better. You've certainly done fine, honey. I haven't got any criticisms. But same time, I do think we ought to think it over."

She had remained still, a kneeling silver statue. Now she dropped her head against his knees, crying:

"I can't give it up! I can't! Must I?"

He was conscious that people were strolling near. He growled, "Say, for goodness' sake, Shara, don't *holler* and carry on like that! Somebody might *hear!*"

She sprang up. "Oh, you fool! You fool!"

She fled from him, along the sands, through the rays of the revolving cross, into the shadow. He angrily rubbed his back against the sand dune and grumbled:

"Damn these women! All alike, even Shary; always getting temperamental on you about nothing at all! Still, I did kind of go off half cocked, considering she was just beginning to get the idea of letting me boss the show. Oh, hell, I'll jolly her out of it!"

He took off his shoes, shook the sand out of them, and rubbed the sole of one stocking foot slowly, agreeably, for he was conceiving a thought.

If Sharon was going to pull stuff like that on him, he ought to teach her a lesson.

Choir practise was over. Why not go back to the house and see what Lily Anderson was doing?

There was a nice kid, and she admired him—she'd never dare bawl him out.

III

He tiptoed to Lily's virgin door and tapped lightly.

"Yes?"

He dared not speak—Sharon's door, in the bulky old house they had taken in Clontar, was almost opposite. He tapped again, and when Lily came to the door, in a kimono, he whispered, "Shhh! Everybody asleep. May I come in just a second? Something important to ask you."

Lily was wondering, but obviously she felt a pallid excitement as he followed her into the room, with its violet-broidered doilies.

"Lily, I've been worrying. Do you think Adelbert ought to have the choir start with 'A Mighty Fortress Is Our God' tomorrow, or something a little snappier—get the crowd and then shoot in something impressive."

"Honest, Mr. Gantry, I don't believe they could change the program now."

"Oh, well, it doesn't matter. Sit down and tell me how the choir practise went tonight. Bet it went swell, with you pounding the box!"

"Oh, now," as she perched lightly on the edge of the bed, "you're just teasing me, Mr. Gantry!"

He sat beside her, chuckling bravely, "And I can't even get you to call me Elmer!"

"Oh, I wouldn't dare, Mr. Gantry! Miss Falconer would call me down!"

"You just let me know if *anybody* ever dares try to call *you* down, Lily! Why— I don't know whether Sharon appreciates it or not, but the way you spiel the music gives as much power to our meetings as her sermons or anything else."

"Oh, no, you're just flattering me, Mr. Gantry! Oh, say, I have a trade-last for you."

"Well, I—oh, let's see—oh, I remember: that Episcopalopian preacher—the big handsome one—he said you ought to be on the stage, you had so much talent."

"Oh, go on, you're kidding me, Mr. Gantry!"

"No, honest he did. Now, what's mine? Though I'd rather have *you* say something nice about me!"

"Oh, now you're fishing!"

"Sure I am—with such a lovely fish as you!"

"Oh, it's terrible the way you talk." Laughter—silvery peals—several peals. "But I mean, this grant opera soloist that's down for our opening says you look so strong that she's scared of you."

"Oh, she is, is she! Are you? . . . Huh? . . . Are you? . . . Tell me!" Somehow her hand was inside his, and he squeezed it, while she looked away and blushed and at last breathed, "Yes, kind of."

He almost embraced her, but—oh, it was a mistake to rush things, and he went on in his professional tone:

"But to go back to Sharon and our labors: it's all right to be modest, but you ought to realize how enormously your playing adds to the spirituality of the meetings."

"I'm so glad you think so, but, honest, to compare me to Miss Falconer for bringing souls to Christ—why she's just the most wonderful person in the world."

"That's right. You bet she is."

"Only I wish she felt like you do. I don't really think she cares so much for my playing."

"Well, she ought to! I'm not criticizing, you understand; she certainly is one of the greatest evangelists living; but just between you and I, she has one fault—she doesn't appreciate any of us—she thinks it's her that does the whole darn' thing! As I say, I admire her, but, by golly, it does make me sore sometimes to never have her appreciate your music—I mean the way it ought to be appreciated—see how I mean?"

"Oh, that is so nice of you, but I don't deserve—"

"But *I*'ve always appreciated it, don't you think, Lily?"

"Oh, yes, indeed you have, and it's been such an encouragement—"

"Oh, well, say, I'm just tickled to death to have you say that, Lily." A firmer pressure on her frail hand. "Do you *like* to have me like your music?"

"Oh, yes."

"But do you like to have me like *you*?"

"Oh, yes. Of course, we're all working together—oh, like sister and brother—"

"Lily! Don't you think we might ever be, uh, don't you think we could be just a little closer than sister and brother?"

"Oh, you're just being mean! How could you ever like poor little me when you belong to Sharon?"

"What do you mean? Me belong to Sharon? Say! I admire her tremendously, but I'm absolutely free, you can bet your life on that, and just because I've always been kinda shy of you—you have such a kinda flower-like beauty, you might say, that no man, no, not the coarsest, would ever dare to ruffle it—and because I've stood back, sorta feeling like I was protecting you, maybe you think I haven't appreciated all your qualities!"

She swallowed.

"Oh, Lily, all I ask for is the chance now and then, whenever you're down in the mouth—and all of us must feel like that, unless we think we're the whole cheese and absolutely *own* the gospel game!—whenever you feel that way, lemme have the privilege of telling you how greatly *one* fellow appreciates the loveliness that you scatter along the road!"

"Do you really feel that way? Maybe I can play the piano, but personally I'm nothing . . . nothing."

"It isn't true, it isn't *true*, dearest! Lily! It's so like your modesty to not appreciate what sunshine you bring into the hearts of all of us, dear, and how we cherish—"

The door shot open. In the doorway stood Sharon Falconer in a black-and-gold dressing-gown.

"Both of you," said Sharon, "are discharged. Fired. Now! Don't ever let me see your faces again. You can stay tonight, but see to it that you're out of the house before breakfast."

"Oh, Miss Falconer—" Lily wailed, thrusting away Elmer's hand. But Sharon was gone, with a bang of the door. They rushed into the hall, they heard the key in her lock, and she ignored their rapping.

Lily glared at Elmer. He heard her key also, and he stood alone in the hall.

IV

Not till one in the morning, sitting in flabby dejection, did he have his story shaped and water-tight.

It was an heroic spectacle, that of the Reverend Elmer Gantry climbing from the second-story balcony through Sharon's window, tiptoeing across the room, plumping on his knees by her bed, and giving her a large plashy kiss.

"I am not asleep," she observed, in tones level as a steel rail, while she drew the comforter about her neck. "In fact I'm awake for the first time in two years, my young friend. You can get out of here. I won't tell you all I've been thinking, but among other things you're an ungrateful dog that bit the hand that took you out of the slimy gutter, you're a liar, an ignoramus, a four-flusher, and a rotten preacher."

"By God, I'll show—"

But she giggled, and his plan of action came back to him.

He sat firmly on the edge of the bed, and calmly he remarked:

"Sharon, you're a good deal of a damn fool. You think I'm going to deny flirting with Lily. I won't take the trouble to deny it! If you don't appreciate yourself, if you don't see that a man that's ever associated with you simply couldn't be interested in any other woman, then there's nothing I can say. Why, my God, Shara, you know what you are! I could no more be untrue to you than I could to my religion! As a matter of fact— Want to know what I was saying to Lily, to Miss Anderson?"

"I do not!"

"Well, you're going to! As I came up the hall, her door was open, and she asked me to come in—she had something to ask me. Well, seems the poor young woman was wondering if her music was really up to your greatness—that's what she herself called it—especially now that the Jordan Tabernacle will give you so much more power. She spoke of you as the greatest spiritual force in the world, and she was wondering whether she was worthy—"

"Um. She did, eh? Well, she isn't! And she can stay fired. And you, my fine young liar, if you ever so much as look at another wench again, I'll fire you for keeps. . . . Oh, Elmer, how could you, beloved? When I've given you everything! Oh, lie, lie, go on lying! Tell me a good strong lie that I'll believe! And then kiss me!"

V

Banners, banners, banners lifting along the rafters, banners on the walls of the tabernacle, banners moving to the air that sifted in from the restless sea. Night of the opening of Waters of Jordan Tabernacle, night of the beginning of Sharon's crusade to conquer the world.

The town of Clontar and all the resorts near by felt here was something they did not quite understand, something marvelous and by all means to be witnessed; and from up and down the Jersey coast, by motor, by trolley, the religious had come. By the time the meeting began all of the four thousand seats were filled, five hundred people were standing, and outside waited a throng hoping for miraculous entrance.

The interior of the pier was barnlike; the thin wooden walls were shamelessly patched against the ravages of winter storms, but they were hectic with the flags of many nations, with immense posters, blood-red on white, proclaiming that in the mysterious blood of the Messiah was redemption from all sorrow, that in his love was refuge and safety. Sharon's pretentious white-and-gold pyramidal altar had been discarded. She was using the stage, draped with black velvet, against which hung a huge crystal cross, and the seats for the choir of two hundred, behind a golden pulpit, were draped with white.

A white wooden cross stood by the pulpit.

It was a hot night, but through the doors along the pier the cool breeze filtered in, and the sound of waters, the sound of wings, as the gulls were startled from their roosts. Every one felt an exaltation in the place, a coming of marvels.

Before the meeting the gospel crew, back-stage, were excited as a theatrical company on a first night. They rushed with great rapidity nowhere in particular, and tripped over each other, and muttered, "Say—gee—gee—" To the last, Adelbert Shoop was giving needless instructions to the new pianist, who had been summoned by telegraph from Philadelphia, *vice* Lily Anderson. She professed immense piety, but Elmer noted that she was a pretty fluffy thing with a warm eye.

The choir was arriving along with the first of the audience. They filtered down the aisle, chattering, feeling important. Naturally, as the end of the pier gave on open water, there was no stage entrance at the back. There was only one door, through which members of opera castes had been wont to go out to the small rear platform for fresh air between acts. The platform was not connected with the promenade.

It was to this door that Sharon led Elmer. Their dressing-rooms were next to each other. She knocked—he had been sitting with a Bible and an evening paper in his lap, reading one of them. He opened, to find her flaming with exultation, a joyous girl with a dressing gown over her chemise. Seemingly she had forgotten her anger of the night.

She cried, "Come! See the stars!" Defying the astonishment of the choir, who were filing into the chorus dressing-room to assume their white robes, she led him to the door, out on the railed platform.

The black waves glittered with lights. There was spaciousness and a windy peace upon the waters.

"Look! It's so big! Not like the cities where we've been shut up!" she exulted. "Stars, and the waves that come clear from Europe! Europe! Castles on a green shore! I've never been. And I'm going! And there'll be great crowds at the ship to meet me, asking for my power! Look!" A shooting star had left a scrawl of flame in the sky. "Elmer! It's an omen for the glory that begins tonight! Oh, dearest, my dearest, don't ever hurt me again!"

His kiss promised it, his heart almost promised it.

She was all human while they stood fronting the sea, but half an hour after, when she came out in a robe of white satin and silver lace, with a crimson cross on her breast, she was prophetess only, and her white forehead was high, her eyes were strange with dreaming.

Already the choir were chanting. They were starting with the Doxology, and it gave Elmer a feeling of doubt. Surely the Doxology was the end of things, not the beginning? But he looked impassive, the brooding priest, in frock coat and white bow tie, portly and funereal, as he moved magnificently through the choir and held up his arms to command silence for his prayer.

He told them of Sister Falconer and her message, of their plans and desires at Clontar, and asked for a minute of silent prayer for the power of the Holy Ghost to descend upon the tabernacle. He stood back—his chair was up-stage, beside the choir—as Sharon floated forward, not human, a goddess, tears thick in lovely eyes as she perceived the throng that had come to her.

"My dear ones, it is not I who bring you anything, but you who in your faith bring me strength!" she said shakily. Then her voice was strong again; she rose on the wave of drama.

"Just now, looking across the sea to the end of the world, I saw an omen for all of us—a fiery line written by the hand of God—a glorious shooting star. Thus he apprized us of his coming, and bade us be ready. Oh, are you ready, are you ready, will you be ready when the great day comes—"

The congregation was stirred by her lyric earnestness.

But outside there were less devout souls. Two workmen had finished polishing the varnished wooden pillars as the audience began to come. They slipped outside, on the promenade along the pier, and sat on the rail, enjoying the coolness, slightly diverted by hearing a sermon.

"Not a bad spieler, that woman. Puts it all over this guy Reverend Golding up-town," said one of the workmen, lighting a cigarette, keeping it concealed in his palm as he smoked.

The other tiptoed across the promenade to peer through the door, and returned mumbling, "Yuh, and a swell looker. Same time though, tell you how I feel about it: woman's all right in her place, but takes a real he-male to figure out this religion business."

"She's pretty good though, at that," yawned the first workman, snapping away his cigarette. "Say, let's beat it. How 'bout lil glass beer? We can go along this platform and get out at the front, I guess."

"All right. You buying?"

The workmen moved away, dark figures between the sea and the doors that gave on the bright auditorium.

The discarded cigarette nestled against the oily rags which the workmen had dropped on the promenade, beside the flimsy walls of the tabernacle. A rag glowed round the edges, worm-like, then lit in circling flame.

Sharon was chanting: "What could be more beautiful than a tabernacle like this, set on the bosom of the rolling deep? Oh, think what the mighty tides have meant in Holy Writ! The face of the waters on which moved the spirit of Almighty God, when the earth was but a whirling and chaotic darkness! Jesus baptized in the sweet waters of Jordan! Jesus walking the waves—so could we today if we had but his faith! O dear God, strengthen thou our unbelief, give us faith like unto thine own!"

Elmer, sitting back listening, was moved as in his first adoration for her. He had become so tired of her poetizing that he almost admitted to himself that he was tired. But tonight he felt her strangeness again, and in it he was humble. He saw her straight back, shimmering in white satin, he saw her superb arms as she stretched them out to these thousands, and in hot secret pride he gloated that this beauty, beheld and worshiped of so many, belonged to him alone.

Then he noted something else.

A third of the way back, coming through one of the doors opening on the promenade, was a curl of smoke. He startled; he almost rose; he feared to rouse a panic; and sat with his brain a welter of terrified jelly till he heard the scream "Fire—fire!" and saw the whole audience and the choir leaping up, screaming—screaming—screaming—while the flimsy door-jamb was alight and the flame rose fan-like toward the rafters.

Only Sharon was in his mind—Sharon standing like an ivory column against the terror. He rushed toward her. He could hear her wailing, "Don't be afraid! Go out slowly!" She turned toward the choir, as with wild white robes they charged down from their bank of seats. She clamored, "Don't be afraid! We're in the temple of the Lord! He won't harm you! I believe! Have faith! I'll lead you safely through the flames!"

But they ignored her, streamed past her, thrusting her aside.

He seized her arm. "Come here, Shara! The door at the back! We'll jump over and swim ashore!"

She seemed not to hear him. She thrust his hand away and went on demanding, her voice furious with mad sincerity, "Who will trust the Lord God of Hosts? Now we'll try our faith! Who will follow me?"

Since two-thirds of the auditorium was to the shoreward side of the fire, and since the wide doors to the promenade were many, most of the audience were getting safely out, save for a child crushed, a woman fainting and trampled. But toward the stage the flames, driven by the sea-wind, were beating up through the rafters. Most of the choir and the audience down front had escaped, but all who were now at the back were cut off.

He grasped Sharon's arm again. In a voice abject with fear he shouted, "For God's sake, beat it! We can't wait!"

She had an insane strength; she thrust him away so sharply that he fell against a chair, bruising his knee. Furious with pain, senseless with fear, he raged, "You can go to hell!" and galloped off, pushing aside the last of the hysterical choir. He looked back and saw her, quite alone, holding up the white wooden cross which had stood by the pulpit, marching steadily forward, a tall figure pale against the screen of flames.

All of the choir who had not got away remembered or guessed the small door at the back; so did Adelbert and Art Nichols; and all of them were jamming toward it.

That door opened inward—only it did not open, with the score of victims thrust against it. In howling panic, Elmer sprang among them, knocked them aside, struck down a girl who stood in his way, yanked open the door, and got through it . . . the last, the only one, to get through it.

He never remembered leaping, but he found himself in the surf, desperately swimming toward shore, horribly cold, horribly bound by heavy clothes. He humped out of his coat.

In the inside pocket was Lily Anderson's address, as she had given it to him before going that morning.

The sea, by night, though it was glaring now with flames from above, seemed infinite in its black sightlessness. The waves thrust him among the piles; their mossy slime was like the feel of serpents to his frantic hands, and the barnacles cut his palms. But he struggled out from beneath the pier, struggled toward shore, and as he swam and panted, more and more was the sea blood-red about him. In blood he swam, blood that was icy-cold and tumultuous and roaring in his ears.

His knees struck sand, and he crawled ashore, among a shrieking, torn, sea-soaked crowd. Many had leaped from the rail of the promenade and were still fighting the surf, wailing, beaten. Their wet and corpselike heads were seen clearly in the glare; the pier was only a skeleton, a cage round a boiling of flame, with dots of figures still dropping from the promenade.

Elmer ran out a little into the surf and dragged in a woman who had already safely touched bottom.

He had rescued at least thirty people who had already rescued themselves before the reporters got to him and he had to stop and explain the cause of the fire, the cost of the tabernacle, the amount of insurance, the size of the audience, the number of souls revived by Miss Falconer during all her campaigns, and the fact that he had been saving both Miss Falconer and Adelbert Shoop when they had been crushed by a falling rafter.

A hundred and eleven people died that night, including all of the gospel-crew save Elmer.

It was Elmer himself who at dawn found Sharon's body lying on a floor-beam. There were rags of white satin clinging to it, and in her charred hand was still the charred cross.

Chapter XVI

THOUGH to the commonplace and unspeculative eye Mrs. Evans Riddle was but a female blacksmith, yet Mrs. Riddle and her followers knew, in a bland smirking way, that she was instituting an era in which sickness, poverty, and folly would be ended forever.

She was the proprietor of the Victory Thought-power Headquarters, New York, and not even in Los Angeles was there a more important center of predigested philosophy and pansy-painted ethics. She maintained a magazine filled with such starry thoughts as "All the world's a road whereon we are but fellow wayfarers." She held morning and vesper services on Sunday at Euterpean Hall, on Eighty-seventh Street, and between moments of Silent Thought she boxed with the inexplicable. She taught, or farmed out, classes in Concentration, Prosperity, Love, Metaphysics, Oriental Mysticism, and the Fourth Dimension.

She instructed small Select Circles how to keep one's husband, how to understand Sanskrit philosophy without understanding either Sanskrit or philosophy, and how to become slim without giving up pastry. She healed all the diseases in the medical dictionary, and some which were not; and in personal consultations, at ten dollars the half hour, she explained to unappetizing elderly ladies how they might rouse passion in a football hero.

She had a staff, including a real Hindu swami—anyway, he was a real Hindu—but she was looking for a first assistant.

II

The Reverend Elmer Gantry had failed as an independent evangelist.

He had been quite as noisy and threatening as the average evangelist; to reasonably large gatherings he had stated that the Judgment Day was rather more than likely to occur before six A.M., and he had told all the chronic anecdotes of the dying drunkard. But there was something wrong. He could not make it go.

Sharon was with him, beckoning him, intolerably summoning him, intolerably rebuking him. Sometimes he worshiped her as the shadow of a dead god; always he was humanly lonely for her and her tantrums and her electric wrath and her abounding laughter. In pulpits he felt like an impostor, and in hotel bedrooms he ached for her voice.

Worst of all, he was expected everywhere to tell of her "brave death in the cause of the Lord." He was very sick about it.

Mrs. Evans Riddle invited him to join her.

Elmer had no objection to the malted milk of New Thought. But after Sharon, Mrs. Riddle was too much. She shaved regularly, she smelled of cigar smoke, yet she had a nickering fancy for warm masculine attentions.

Elmer had to earn a living, and he had taken too much of the drug of oratory to be able to go back to the road as a traveling-salesman. He shrugged when he had interviewed Mrs. Riddle; he told her that she would be an inspiration to a young man like himself; he held her hand; he went out and washed his hand; and determined that since he was to dwell in the large brownstone house which was both her Thought-power Headquarters and her home, he would keep his door locked.

The preparation for his labors was not too fatiguing. He read through six copies of Mrs. Riddle's magazine and, just as he had learned the trade-terms of evangelism, so he learned the technologies of New Thought: the Cosmic Law of Vibration; I Affirm the Living Thought. He labored through a chapter of "The Essence of Oriental Mysticism, Occultism, and Esotericism" and accomplished seven pages of the "Bhagavad-Gita"; and thus was prepared to teach disciples how to win love and prosperity.

In actual practise he had much less of treading the Himalayan heights than of pleasing Mrs. Evans Riddle. Once she discovered that he had small fancy for sitting up after midnight with her, she was rather sharp about his bringing in new chelas—as, out of "Kim," she called paying customers.

Occasionally he took Sunday morning service for Mrs. Riddle at Euterpean Hall, when she was weary of curing rheumatism or when she was suffering from rheumatism; and always he had to be at Euterpean to give spiritual assistance. She liked to have her hairy arm stroked just before she went out to preach, and that was not too hard a task—usually he could recover while she was out on the platform. She turned over to him the Personal Consultations with spinsters, and he found it comic to watch their sharp noses quivering, their dry mouths wabbling.

But his greatest interest was given to the Prosperity Classes. To one who had never made more than five thousand a year himself, it was inspiring to explain before dozens of pop-eyed and admiring morons how they could make ten thousand—fifty thousand—a million a year, and all this by the Wonder Power of Suggestion, by Aggressive Personality, by the Divine Rhythm, in fact by merely releasing the Inner Self-shine.

It was fun, it was an orgy of imagination, for him who had never faced any Titan of Success of larger dimensions than the chairman of a local evangelistic committee to instruct a thirty-a-week bookkeeper how to stalk into Morgan's office, fix him with the penetrating eye of the Initiate, and borrow a hundred thousand on the spot.

But always he longed for Sharon, with a sensation of emptiness real as the faintness of hunger and long tramping. He saw his days with her as adventures, foot-loose, scented with fresh air. He hated himself for having ever glanced over his shoulder, and he determined to be a celibate all his life.

In some ways he preferred New Thought to standard Protestantism. It was safer to play with. He had never been sure but that there might be something to the doctrines he had preached as an evangelist. Perhaps God really had dictated every word of the Bible. Perhaps there really was a hell of burning sulphur. Perhaps the Holy Ghost really was hovering around watching him and reporting. But he knew with serenity that all of his New Thoughts, his theosophical utterances, were pure and uncontaminated bunk. No one could deny his theories because none of his theories meant anything. It did not matter what he said, so long as he kept them listening; and he enjoyed the buoyancy of power as he bespelled his classes with long, involved, fruity sentences rhapsodic as perfume advertisements.

How agreeable on bright winter afternoons, in the gilt and velvet elegance of the lecture hall, to look at smart women, and moan, "And, oh, my beloved, can you not see, do you not perceive, have not your earth-bound eyes ingathered, the supremacy of the raja's quality which each of us, by that inner contemplation which is the all however cloaked by the seeming, can consummate and build loftily to higher aspiring spheres?"

Almost any Hindu word was useful. It seems that the Hindus have Hidden Powers which enable them to do whatever they want to, except possibly to get rid of the Mohammedans, the plague, and the cobra. "Soul-breathing" was also a good thing to talk about whenever he had nothing to say; and you could always keep an audience of satin-bosomed ladies through the last quarter-hour of lecturing by coming down hard on "Concentration."

But with all these agreeable features, he hated Mrs. Riddle, and he suspected that she was, as he put it, "holding out the coin on him." He was to have a percentage of the profits, besides his thin salary of twenty-five hundred a year. There never were any profits, and when he hinted that he would like to see her books—entirely out of admiration for the beauties of accountancy—she put him off.

So he took reasonable measures of reprisal. He moved from her house; he began to take for himself the patients who came for Personal Consultations, and to meet them in the parlor of his new boarding-house in Harlem. And when she was not present at his Euterpean Hall meetings, he brought back to Victory Thought-power Headquarters only so much of the collection as, after prayer and meditation and figuring on an envelope, seemed suitable.

That did it.

Mrs. Evans Riddle had a regrettable suspiciousness. She caused a marked twenty-dollar bill to be placed in the collection at vespers, a year after Elmer had gone to work for the higher powers, and when he brought her the collection-money minus the twenty dollars, she observed loudly, with her grinning swami looking heathenish and sultry across the room:

"Gantry, you're a thief! You're fired! You have a contract, but you can sue and be damned. Jackson!" A large negro houseman appeared. "Throw this crook out, will you?"

III

He felt dazed and homeless and poor, but he started out with Prosperity Classes of his own.

He did very well at Prosperity, except that he couldn't make a living out of it.

He spent from a month to four months in each city. He hired the ballroom of the second-best hotel for lectures three evenings a week, and advertised himself in the newspapers as though he were a cigarette or a brand of soap:

THE WORLD OWES YOU A MILLION DOLLARS!
WHY DON'T YOU COLLECT IT?

What brought millions to Rockefeller, Morgan, Carnegie? WILL POWER! It's within you. Learn to develop it. *You can!* The world-mastering secrets of the Rosicrucians and Hindu Sages revealed in twelve lessons by the renowned Psychologist

ELMER GANTRY, PH.D., D.D., PS.D.

Write or phone for FREE personal consultation

THE BOWERS HOTEL
MAIN & SYCAMORE

His students were school-teachers who wanted to own tearooms, clerks who wanted to be sales-managers, clergymen who wanted to be newspapermen, newspapermen who wanted to be real estate dealers, real estate dealers who wanted to be bishops, and widows who wanted to earn money without loss of elegance. He lectured to them in the most beautiful language, all out of Mrs. Riddle's magazine.

He had a number of phrases—all stolen—and he made his disciples repeat them in chorus, in the manner of all religions. Among the more powerful incantations were:

> I can be whatever I will to be; I turn my opened eyes on my Self and possess whatever I desire.
>
> I am God's child, God created all good things including wealth, and I will to inherit it.
>
> I am resolute—I am utterly resolute—I fear no man, whether in offices or elsewhere.
>
> Power is in me, encompassing you to my demands.
>
> Hold fast, O Subconscious, the thought of Prosperity.
>
> In the divine book of achievements my name is written in Gold. I am thus of the world's nobility and now, this moment, I take possession of my kingdom.
>
> I am part of Universal Mind and thus I summon to me my rightful Universal Power.
>
> Daily my Subconscious shall tell me to not be content and go on working for somebody else.

They were all of them ready for a million a year, except their teacher, who was ready for bankruptcy.

He got pupils enough, but the overhead was huge and his pupils were poor. He had to hire the ballroom, pay for advertising; he had to appear gaudy, with a suite in the hotel, fresh linen, and newly pressed morning coat. He sat in twenty-dollar-a-day red plush suites wondering where he would get breakfast. He was so dismayed that he began to study himself.

He determined, with the resoluteness of terror, to be loyal to any loves or associates he might have hereafter, to say in his prayers and sermons practically nothing except what he believed. He yearned to go back to Mizpah Seminary, to get Dean Trosper's forgiveness, take a degree, and return to the Baptist pulpit in however barren a village. But first he must earn enough money to pay for a year in the seminary.

He had been in correspondence with the manager of the O'Hearn House in Zenith—a city of four hundred thousand in the state of Winnemac, a hundred miles from Mizpah. This was in 1913, before the Hotel Thornleigh was built, and Gil O'Hearn, with his new yellow brick tavern, was trying to take the fashionable business of Zenith away from the famous but decayed Grand Hotel. Intellectual ballroom lectures add to the smartness of a hotel almost as much as a great cocktail-mixer, and Mr. O'Hearn had been moved by the prospectus of the learned and magnetic Dr. Elmer Gantry.

Elmer could take the O'Hearn offer on a guarantee and be sure of a living, but he needed money for a week or two before the fees should come in.

From whom could he borrow?

Didn't he remember reading in a Mizpah alumni bulletin that Frank Shallard, who had served with him in the rustic church at Schoenheim, now had a church near Zenith?

He dug out the bulletin and discovered that Frank was in Eureka, an industrial town of forty thousand. Elmer had enough money to take him to Eureka. All the way there he warmed up the affection with which a borrower recalls an old acquaintance who is generous and a bit soft.

Chapter XVII

FRANK SHALLARD had graduated from Mizpah Theological Seminary and taken his first pulpit. And now that he was a minister, theoretically different from all ordinary people, he was wondering whether there was any value to the ministry whatever.

Of what value were doggerel hymns raggedly sung? What value in sermons, when the congregation seemed not at all different from people who never heard sermons? Were all ministers and all churches, Frank wondered, merely superstitious survivals, merely fire-insurance? Suppose there were such things as inspiring sermons. Suppose there could be such a curious office as minister, as Professional Good Man; such a thing as learning Goodness just as one learned plumbing or dentistry. Even so, what training had he or his classmates, or his professors—whose D.D. degrees did not protect them from indigestion and bad tempers—in this trade of Professional Goodness?

He was supposed to cure an affliction called vice. But he had never encountered vice; he didn't know just what were the interesting things that people did when they were being vicious. How long would a drunkard listen to the counsel of one who had never been inside a saloon?

He was supposed to bring peace to mankind. But what did he know of the forces which cause wars, personal or class or national; what of drugs, passion, criminal desire; of capitalism, banking, labor, wages, taxes; international struggles for trade, munition trusts, ambitious soldiers?

He was supposed to comfort the sick. But what did he know of sickness? How could he tell when he ought to pray and when he ought to recommend salts?

He was supposed to explain to troubled mankind the purposes of God Almighty, to chat with him, and even advise him about his duties as regards rainfall and the church debt. But which God Almighty? Professor Bruno Zechlin had introduced Frank to a hundred gods besides the Jewish Jehovah, or Yahveh, who had been but a poor and rather surly relation of such serene aristocrats as Zeus.

He was supposed to have undergone a mystic change whereby it was possible to live without normal appetites. He was supposed to behold girls' ankles without interest and, for light amusement, to be satisfied by reading church papers and shaking hands with deacons. But he found himself most uncomfortably interested in the flicker of ankles, he longed for the theater, and no repentance could keep him from reading novels, though his professors had exposed them as time-wasting and frivolous.

What had he learned?

Enough Hebrew and Greek to be able to crawl through the Bible by using lexicons—so that, like all his classmates once they were out of the seminary, he always read it in English. A good many of the more condemnatory texts of the Bible—rather less than the average Holy Roller carpenter-evangelist. The theory that India and Africa have woes because they are not Christianized, but that Christianized Bangor and Des Moines have woes because the devil, a being obviously more potent than omnipotent God, sneaks around counteracting the work of Baptist preachers.

He had learned, in theory, the ways of raising money through church fairs; he had learned what he was to say on pastoral visits. He had learned that Roger Williams, Adoniram Judson, Luther, Calvin, Jonathan Edwards, and George Washington were the greatest men in history; that Lincoln was given to fervent prayer at all crises; and that Ingersoll had called his non-existent son to his death-bed and bidden him become an orthodox Christian. He had learned that the Pope at Rome was plotting to come to America and get hold of the government, and was prevented only by the denunciations of the Baptist clergy with a little help from the Methodists and Presbyterians; that most crime was caused either by alcohol or by people leaving the Baptist fold for Unitarianism; and that clergymen ought not to wear red ties.

He had learned how to assemble Jewish texts, Greek philosophy, and Middle-Western evangelistic anecdotes into a sermon. And he had learned that poverty is blessed, but that bankers make the best deacons.

Otherwise, as he wretchedly examined his equipment, facing his career, Frank did not seem to have learned anything whatever.

From Elmer Gantry's relations to Lulu Bains, from Harry Zenz's almost frank hint that he was an atheist, Frank perceived that a preacher can be a scoundrel or a hypocrite and still be accepted by his congregation. From the manners of Dean Trosper, who served his God with vinegar, he perceived that a man may be free of all the skilled sins, may follow every rule of the church, and still bring only fear to his flock. Listening to the celebrated divines who visited the seminary and showed off to the infant prophets, he perceived that a man could make scholarly and violent sounds and yet not say anything which remained in the mind for six minutes.

He concluded, in fact, that if there was any value in churches and a ministry, of which he was not very certain, in any case there could be no value in himself as a minister.

Yet he had been ordained, he had taken a pulpit.

It was doubtful whether he could have endured the necessary lying had it not been for Dean Trosper's bullying and his father's confusing pleas. Frank's father was easy-going enough, but he had been a Baptist clergyman for so many years that the church was sacred to him. To have had his son deny it would have broken him. He would have been shocked to be told that he was advising Frank to lie, but he explained that the answers to the ordination examination were after all poetic symbols, sanctified by generations of loving usage; that they need not be taken literally.

So Frank Shallard, pupil of Bruno Zechlin, said nervously to an examining cleric that, yes, he did believe that baptism by immersion was appointed by God himself as the only valid way of beginning a righteous life; that, yes, unrepentant sinners would go to a literal Hell; that, yes, these unrepentant sinners included all persons who did not go to evangelical churches if they had the chance; and that, yes, the Maker of a universe with stars a hundred thousand light-years apart was interested, furious, and very personal about it if a small boy played baseball on Sunday afternoon.

Half an hour after the ordination and the somewhat comforting welcome by veterans of the ministry, he hated himself, and ached to flee, but again the traditional "not wanting to hurt his father" kept him from being honest. So he stayed in the church . . . and went on hurting his father for years instead of for a day.

II

It was a lonely and troubled young man, the Frank Shallard who for his first pastorate came to the Baptist Church at Catawba, a town of eighteen hundred, in the same state with Zenith and the Mizpah Seminary. The town liked him, and did not take him seriously. They said his sermons were "real poetic"; they admired him for being able to sit with old Mrs. Randall, who had been an invalid for thirty years, a bore for sixty, and never ill a day in her life. They admired him for trying to start a boys' club, though they did not go so far in their support as to contribute anything. They all called him "Reverend," and told him that he was amazingly sound in doctrine for one so unfortunately well educated; and he stayed on, in a vacuum.

Frank felt well about his fifth sermon in Catawba; felt that he was done with hesitations. He had decided to ignore controversial theology, ignore all dogma, and concentrate on the leadership of Jesus. That was his topic, there in the chapel with its walls of glaring robin's-egg blue—the eager-eyed, curly-headed boy, his rather shrill voice the wail of a violin as he gave his picture of Jesus, the kindly friend, the unfailing refuge, the gallant leader.

He was certain that he had done well; he was thinking of it on Monday morning as he walked from his boarding-house to the post office.

He saw one Lem Staples, a jovial horse-doctor who was known as the Village Atheist, sitting on a decayed carriage seat in front of the Fashion Livery Barn. Doc Staples was a subscriber to the *Truth Seeker*, a periodical said to be infidel, and he quoted Robert Ingersoll, Ed Howe, Colonel Watterson, Elbert Hubbard, and other writers who were rumored to believe that a Catholic was as good as a Methodist or Baptist. The Doc lived alone, "baching it" in a little yellow cottage, and Frank had heard that he sat up till all hours, eleven and even later, playing cribbage in Mart Blum's saloon.

Frank disliked him, and did not know him. He was prepared to welcome honest inquiry, but a fellow who was an avowed atheist, why, Frank raged, he was a fool! Who made the flowers, the butterflies, the sunsets, the laughter of little children? Those things didn't just *happen*! Besides: why couldn't the man keep his doubts to himself, and not try to take from other people the religion which was their one comfort and strength in illness, sorrow, want? A matter not of Morality but of reverence for other people's belief, in fact of Good Taste—

This morning, as Frank scampered down Vermont Street, Lem Staples called to him, "Fine day, Reverend. Say! In a hurry?"

"I'm— No, not especially."

"Come sit down. Couple o' questions I'm worried about."

Frank sat, his neck prickling with embarrassment.

"Say, Reverend, old Ma Gherkins was telling me about your sermon yesterday. You figger that no matter what kind of a creed a fellow's got, the one thing we can all bank on, absolute, is the teaching of Jesus?"

"Why, yes, that's it roughly, Doctor."

"And you feel that any sensible fellow will follow his teaching?"

"Why, yes, certainly."

"And you feel that the churches, no matter what faults they may have, do hand out this truth of Jesus better than if we didn't have no churches at all?"

"Certainly. Otherwise, I shouldn't be in the church!"

"Then can you tell me why it is that nine-tenths of the really sure-enough on-the-job membership of the churches is made up of two classes: the plumb ignorant, that're scared of hell and that swallow any fool doctrine, and, second, the awful' respectable folks that play the church so's to seem more respectable? Why is that? Why is it the high-class skilled workmen and the smart professional men usually snicker at the church and don't go near it once a month? Why is it?"

"It isn't true, perhaps that's why!" Frank felt triumphant. He looked across at the pile of rusty horseshoes and plowshares among the mullen weeds beside the blacksmith's shop; he reflected that he would clean up this town, be a power for good. Less snappishly he explained, "Naturally, I haven't any statistics about it, but the fact is that almost every intelligent and influential man in the country belongs to some church or other."

"Yeh—belongs. But does he go?"

Frank plodded off, annoyed. He tried to restore himself by insisting that Doc Staples was a lout, very amusing in the way he mingled rustic grammar with half-digested words from his adult reading. But he was jarred. Here was the Common Man whom the church was supposed to convince.

Frank remembered from his father's pastorates how many theoretical church-members seemed blithely able month on month to stay away from the sermonizing; he remembered the merchants who impressively passed the contribution plate yet afterward, in conversation with his father, seemed to have but vague notions of what the sermon had been.

He studied his own congregation. There they were: the stiff-collared village respectables, and the simple, kindly, rustic mass, who understood him only when he promised Heaven as a reward for a life of monogamy and honest chicken-raising, or threatened them with Hell for drinking hard cider.

Catawba had—its only urban feature—a furniture factory with unusually competent workmen, few of whom attended church. Now Frank Shallard had all his life been insulated from what he gently despised as "the working class." Maids at his father's house and the elderly, devout, and incompetent negroes who attended the furnace; plumbers or electricians coming to the parsonage for repairs; railway men to whom he tried to talk on journeys; only these had he known, and always with unconscious superiority.

Now he timidly sought to get acquainted with the cabinet-makers as they sat at lunch in the factory grounds. They accepted him good-naturedly, but he felt that they chuckled behind his back when he crept away.

For the first time he was ashamed of being a preacher, of being a Christian. He longed to prove he was nevertheless a "real man," and didn't know how to prove it. He found that all the cabinet-makers save the Catholics laughed at the church and thanked the God in whom they did not believe that they did not have to listen to sermons on Sunday mornings, when there were beautiful back porches to sit on, beautiful sporting news to read, beautiful beer to drink. Even the Catholics seemed rather doubtful about the power of a purchased mass to help their deceased relatives out of Purgatory. Several of them admitted that they merely "did their Easter duty"—went to confession and mass but once a year.

It occurred to him that he had never known how large a race of intelligent and independent workmen there were in between the masters and the human truck-horses. He had never known how casually these manual aristocrats despised the church; how they jeered at their leaders, officers of the A. F. of L., who played safe by adhering to a voluble Christianity. He could not get away from his discoveries. They made him self-conscious as he went about the village streets trying to look like a junior prophet and feeling like a masquerader.

He might have left the ministry but for the Reverend Andrew Pengilly, pastor of the Catawba Methodist Church.

III

If you had cut Andrew Pengilly to the core, you would have found him white clear through. He was a type of clergyman favored in pious fiction, yet he actually did exist.

To every congregation he had served these forty years, he had been a shepherd. They had loved him, listened to him, and underpaid him. In 1906, when Frank came to Catawba, Mr. Pengilly was a frail stooped veteran with silver hair, thin silver mustache, and a slow smile which embraced the world.

Andrew Pengilly had gone into the Civil War as a drummer boy, slept blanketless and barefoot and wounded in the frost of Tennessee mountains, and come out still a child, to "clerk in a store" and teach Sunday School. He had been converted at ten, but at twenty-five he was overpowered by the preaching of Osage Joe, the Indian evangelist, became a Methodist preacher, and never afterward doubted the peace of God. He was married at thirty to a passionate, singing girl with kind lips. He loved her so romantically—just to tuck the crazy-quilt about her was poetry, and her cowhide shoes were to him fairy slippers—he loved her so ungrudgingly that when she died, in childbirth, within a year after their marriage, he had nothing left for any other woman. He lived alone, with the undiminished vision of her. Not the most scandalmongering Mother in Zion had ever hinted that Mr. Pengilly looked damply upon the widows in his fold.

Little book-learning had Andrew Pengilly in his youth, and to this day he knew nothing of Biblical criticism, of the origin of religions, of the sociology which was beginning to absorb church-leaders, but his Bible he knew, and believed, word by word, and somehow he had drifted into the reading of ecstatic books of mysticism. He was a mystic, complete; the world of plows and pavements and hatred was less to him than the world of angels, whose silver robes seemed to flash in the air about him as he meditated alone in his cottage. He was as ignorant of Modern Sunday School Methods as of single tax or Lithuanian finances, yet few Protestants had read more in the Early Fathers.

On Frank Shallard's first day in Catawba, when he was unpacking his books in his room at the residence of Deacon Halter, the druggist, the Reverend Mr. Pengilly was announced. Frank went down to the parlor (gilded cat-tails and a basket of stereopticon views) and his loneliness was warmed by Mr. Pengilly's enveloping smile, his drawling voice:

"Welcome, Brother! I'm Pengilly, of the Methodist Church. I never was much of a hand at seeing any difference between the denominations, and I hope we'll be able to work together for the glory of God. I do hope so! And I hope you'll go fishing with me. I know," enthusiastically, "a pond where there's some elegant pickerel!"

Many evenings they spent in Mr. Pengilly's cottage, which was less littered and odorous than that of the village atheist, Doc Lem Staples, only because the stalwart ladies of Mr. Pengilly's congregation vied in sweeping for him, dusting for him, disarranging his books and hen-tracked sermon-notes, and bullying him in the matters of rubbers and winter flannels. They would not let him prepare his own meals—they made him endure the several boarding-houses in turn—but sometimes of an evening he would cook scrambled eggs for Frank. He had pride in his cooking. He had never tried anything but scrambled eggs.

His living-room was overpowering with portraits and carbon prints. Though every local official board pled with him about it, he insisted on including madonnas, cinquecento resurrections, St. Francis of Assisi, and even a Sacred Heart, with such Methodist worthies as Leonidas Hamline and the cloaked romantic Francis Asbury. In the bay window was a pyramid of wire shelves filled with geraniums. Mr. Pengilly was an earnest gardener, except during such weeks as he fell into dreams and forgot to weed and water, and through the winter he watched for the geranium leaves to wither enough so that he could pick them off and be able to feel busy.

All over the room were the aged dog and ancient cat, who detested each other, never ceased growling at each other, and at night slept curled together.

In an antiquated and badly listed rocking-chair, padded with calico cushions, Frank listened to Mr. Pengilly's ramblings. For a time they talked only of externals; gossip of their parishes; laughter at the man who went from church to church fretting the respectable by shouting "Hallelujah"; local chatter not without a wholesome and comforting malice. Frank was at first afraid to bare his youthful hesitancies to so serene an old saint, but at last he admitted his doubts.

How, he demanded, could you reconcile a Loving God with one who would strike down an Uzza for the laudable act of trying to save the Ark of the Covenant from falling, who would kill forty-two children (and somewhat ludicrously) for shouting at Elisha as any small boy in Catawba today would shout? Was it reasonable? And, if it wasn't, if any part of the Bible was mythical, where to stop? How could we know if anything in the Bible was "inspired"?

Mr. Pengilly was not shocked, nor was he very agitated. His thin fingers together, far down in his worn plush chair, he mused:

"Yes, I'm told the higher critics ask these things. I believe it bothers people. But I wonder if perhaps God hasn't put these stumbling blocks in the Bible as a test of our faith, of our willingness to accept with all our hearts and souls a thing that may seem ridiculous to our minds? You see, our minds don't go far. Think—how much does even an astronomer know about folks on Mars, if there are any folks there? Isn't it with our hearts, our faith, that we have to accept Jesus Christ, and not with our historical charts? Don't we *feel* his influence on our lives? Isn't it the biggest men that feel it the most? Maybe God wants to keep out of the ministry all the folks that are so stuck on their poor minds that they can't be humble and just accept the great overpowering truth of Christ's mercy. Do you— When do you feel nearest to God? When you're reading some awful' smart book criticizing the Bible or when you kneel in prayer and your spirit just flows forth and you *know* that you're in communion with him?"

"Oh, of course—"

"Don't you think maybe he will explain all these puzzling things in his own good time? And meanwhile wouldn't you rather be a help to poor sick worried folks than write a cute little book finding fault?"

"Oh, well—"

"And has there ever been anything like the Old Book for bringing lost souls home to happiness? Hasn't it *worked*?"

In Andrew Pengilly's solacing presence these seemed authentic arguments, actual revelations; Bruno Zechlin was far off and gray; and Frank was content.

Equally did Mr. Pengilly console him about the intelligent workmen who would have none of the church. The old man simply laughed.

"Good Heavens, boy! What do you expect, as a preacher? A whole world that's saved, and nothing for you to do? Reckon you don't get much salary, but how do you expect to earn that much? These folks don't go to any Christian church? Huh! When the Master started out, wa'n't anybody going to a Christian church! Go out and get 'em!"

Which seemed disastrously reasonable to the shamed Frank; and he went out to get 'em, and didn't do so, and continued in his ministry.

He had heard in theological seminary of the "practise of the presence of God" as a papist mystery. Now he encountered it. Mr. Pengilly taught him to kneel, his mind free of all worries, all prides, all hunger, his lips repeating "Be thou visibly present with me"—not as a charm but that his lips might not be soiled with more earthly phrases—and, when he had become strained and weary and exalted, to feel a

Something glowing and almost terrifying about him, and to experience thus, he was certain, the actual, loving, proven nearness of the Divinity.

He began to call his mentor Father Pengilly, and the old man chided him only a little . . . presently did not chide him at all.

For all his innocence and his mysticism, Father Pengilly was not a fool nor weak. He spoke up harshly to a loud-mouthed grocer, new come to town, who considered the patriarch a subject for what he called "kidding," and who shouted, "Well, I'm getting tired of waiting for you preachers to pray for rain. Guess you don't believe the stuff much yourselves!" He spoke up to old Miss Udell, the purity specialist of the town, when she came to snuffle that Amy Dove was carrying on with the boys in the twilight. "I know how you like a scandal, Sister," said he. "Maybe 'tain't Christian to deny you one. But I happen to know all about Amy. Now if you'd go out and help poor old crippled Sister Eckstein do her washing, maybe you'd keep busy enough so's you could get along without your daily scandal."

He had humor, as well, Father Pengilly. He could smile over the cranks in the congregation. And he liked the village atheist, Doc Lem Staples. He had him at the house, and it healed Frank's spirit to hear with what beatific calm Father Pengilly listened to the Doc's jibes about the penny-pinchers and the sinners in the church.

"Lem," said Father Pengilly, "you'll be surprised at this, but I must tell you that there's two-three sinners in your fold, too. Why, I've heard of even horse-thieves that didn't belong to churches. That must prove something, I guess. Yes, sir, I admire to hear you tell about the kind-hearted atheists, after reading about the cannibals, who are remarkably little plagued with us Methodists and Baptists."

Not in his garden only but in the woods, along the river, Father Pengilly found God in Nature. He was insane about fishing—though indifferent to the catching of any actual fish. Frank floated with him in a mossy scow, in a placid backwater under the willows. He heard the gurgle of water among the roots and watched the circles from a leaping bass. The old man (his ruddy face and silver mustache shaded by a shocking hayfield straw hat) hummed "There's a wideness in God's mercy like the wideness of the sea." When Father Pengilly mocked him, "And you have to go to books to find God, young man!" then Frank was content to follow him, to be his fellow preacher, to depend more on Pengilly's long experience than on irritating questions, to take any explanation of the validity of the Bible, of the mission of the church, the leadership of Christ, which might satisfy this soldier of the cross.

Frank became more powerful as a preacher. He went from Catawba, via pastorates in two or three larger towns, to Eureka, a camp of forty thousand brisk industrialists, and here he was picked up and married by the amiable Bess.

IV

Bess Needham, later to be Bess Shallard, was remarkably like a robin. She had the same cheerfulness, the same round ruddiness, and the same conviction that early rising, chirping, philoprogenitiveness, and strict attention to food were the aims of existence. She had met Frank at a church "social," she had pitied what she regarded as his underfed pallor, she had directed her father, an amiable and competent dentist, to invite Frank home, for "a real feed" and bright music on the phonograph. She listened fondly to his talk—she had no notion what it was about, but she liked the sound of it.

He was stirred by her sleek neck, her comfortable bosom, by the dimpled fingers which stroked his hair before he knew that he longed for it. He was warmed by her assertion that he "put it all over" the Rev. Dr. Seager, the older Baptist parson in Eureka. So she was able to marry him without a struggle, and they had three children in the shortest possible time.

She was an admirable wife and mother. She filled the hot water bottle for his bed, she cooked corn beef and cabbage perfectly, she was polite to the most exasperating parishioners, she saved money, and when he sat with fellow clerics companionably worrying about the sacraments, she listened to him, and him alone, with beaming motherliness.

He realized that with a wife and three children he could not consider leaving the church; and the moment he realized it he began to feel trapped and to worry about his conscience all the more.

V

There was, in Eureka, with its steel mills, its briskness, its conflict between hard-fisted manufacturers and hard-headed socialists, nothing of the contemplation of Catawba, where thoughts seemed far-off stars to gaze on through the mist. Here was a violent rush of ideas, and from this rose the "Preachers' Liberal Club," toward which Frank was drawn before he had been in Eureka a fortnight.

The ring-leader of these liberals was Hermann Kassebaum, the modernist rabbi—young, handsome, black of eye and blacker of hair, full of laughter, regarded by the elect of the town as a shallow charlatan and a dangerous fellow, and actually the most scholarly man Frank had ever encountered, except for Bruno Zechlin. With him consorted a placidly atheistic Unitarian minister, a Presbyterian who was orthodox on Sunday and revolutionary on Monday, a wavering Congregationalist, and an Anglo-Catholic Episcopalian, who was enthusiastic about the beauties of the ritual and the Mithraic origin of the same.

And Frank's fretting wearily started all over again. He re-read Harnack's "What Is Christianity?" Sunderland's "Origin and Nature of the Bible," James's "Varieties of Religious Experience," Fraser's "Golden Bough."

He was in the pleasing situation where whatever he did was wrong. He could not content himself with the discussions of the Liberal Club. "If you fellows believe that way, why don't you get out of the church?" he kept demanding. Yet he could not leave them; could not, therefore, greatly succeed among the Baptist brethren. His good wife, Bess, when he diffidently hinted of his doubts, protested, "You can't reach people just through their minds. Besides, they wouldn't understand you if you *did* come right out and tell 'em the truth—as you see it. They aren't ready for it."

His worst doubt was the doubt of himself. And in this quite undignified wavering he remained, envying equally Rabbi Kassebaum's public scoffing at all religion and the thundering certainties of the cover-to-cover evangelicals. He who each Sunday morning neatly pointed his congregation the way to Heaven was himself tossed in a Purgatory of self-despising doubt, where his every domestic virtue was cowardice, his every mystic aspiration a superstitious mockery, and his every desire to be honest a cruelty which he must spare Bess and his well-loved brood.

He was in this mood when the Reverend Elmer Gantry suddenly came, booming and confident, big and handsome and glossy, into his study, and explained that if Frank could let him have a hundred dollars, Elmer, and presumably the Lord, would be grateful and return the money within two weeks.

The sight of Elmer as a fellow pastor was too much for Frank. To get rid of him, he hastily gave Elmer the hundred he had saved up toward payment of the last two obstetrical bills, and sat afterward at his desk, his head between his lax hands, praying, "O Lord, guide me!"

He leapt up. "No! Elmer said the Lord had been guiding *him*! I'll take a chance on guiding myself! I will—" Again, weakly, "But how can I hurt Bess, hurt my dad, hurt Father Pengilly? Oh, I'll go on!"

Chapter XVIII

THE Reverend Elmer Gantry was writing letters—he had no friends, and the letters were all to inquirers about his Prosperity Classes—at a small oak-desk in the lobby of the O'Hearn House in Zenith.

His Zenith classes here had gone not badly, not brilliantly. He had made enough to consider paying the hundred dollars back to Frank Shallard, though certainly not enough to do so. He was tired of this slippery job; he was almost willing to return to farm implements. But he looked anything but discouraged, in his morning coat, his wing collar, his dotted blue bow tie.

Writing at the other half of the lobby desk was a little man with an enormous hooked nose, receding chin, and a Byzantine bald head. He was in a brown business suit, with a lively green tie, and he wore horn-rimmed spectacles.

"Vice-president of a bank, but started as a school teacher," Elmer decided. He was conscious that the man was watching him. A possible student? No. Too old.

Elmer leaned back, folded his hands, looked as pontifical as possible, cleared his throat with a learned sound, and beamed.

The little man kept glancing up, rat-like, but did not speak.

"Beautiful morning," said Elmer.

"Yes. Lovely. On mornings like this all Nature exemplifies the divine joy!"

"My God! No business for me here! He's a preacher or an osteopath," Elmer lamented within.

"Is this—this is Dr. Gantry, I believe."

"Why, yes. I'm, uh, sorry, I—"

"I'm Bishop Toomis, of the Zenith area of the Methodist Church. I had the great pleasure of hearing one of your exordiums the other evening, Dr. Gantry."

Elmer was hysterically thrilled.

Bishop Wesley R. Toomis! For years he had heard of the bishop as one of the giants, one of the pulpit orators, one of the profound thinkers, exalted speakers, and inspired executives of the Methodist Church, North. He had addressed ten thousand at Ocean Grove; he had spoken in Yale chapel; he had been a success in London. Elmer rose and, with a handshake which must have been most painful to the bishop, he glowed:

"Well, well, well, sir, this certainly is a mighty great pleasure, sir. It sure is! So you came and listened to me! Well, wish I'd known that. I'd of asked you to come sit on the platform."

Bishop Toomis had risen also; he waved Elmer back into his chair, himself perched like a keen little hawk, and trilled:

"No, no, not at all, not at all. I came only as an humble listener. I dare say I have, by the chance and circumstance of age, had more experience of Christian life and doctrine than you, and I can't pretend I exactly in every way agreed with you, you might say, but at the same time, that was a very impressive thought about the need of riches to carry on the work of the busy workaday world, as we have it at present, and the value of concentration in the silence as well as in those happy moments of more articulate prayer. Yes, yes. I firmly believe that we ought to add to our Methodist practise some of the Great Truths about the, alas, too often occulted and obstructed Inner Divine Powers possessed in unconsciousness by each of us, as New Thought has revealed them to us, and that we ought most certainly not to confine the Church to already perceived dogmas but encourage it to grow. It stands to reason that really devout prayer and concentration should most materially effect both bodily health and financial welfare. Yes, yes. I was interested in what you had to say about it and— The fact is that I am going to address the Chamber of Commerce luncheon this noon, along much these same lines, and if you happen to be free, I should be very glad if—"

They went, Elmer and Bishop Toomis, and Elmer added to the bishop's observations a few thoughts, and the most caressing compliments about bishops in general, Bishop Wesley R. Toomis in particular, pulpit oratory, and the beauties of prosperity. Everybody had a radiant time, except possibly the members of the Chamber of Commerce, and after the luncheon Elmer and the bishop walked off together.

"My, my, I feel flattered that you should know so much about me! I am, after all, a very humble servant of the Methodist Church—of the Lord, that is—and I should not have imagined that any slight local reputation I might have would have penetrated into the New Thought world," breathed the bishop.

"Oh, I'm not a New Thoughter. I'm, uh, temporarily conducting these courses—as a sort of psychological experiment, you might say. Fact is, I'm an ordained Baptist preacher, and of course in seminary your sermons were always held up to us as models."

"I'm afraid you flatter me, Doctor."

"Not at all. In fact they attracted me so that—despite my great reverence for the Baptist Church, I felt, after reading your sermons, that there was more breadth and vigor in the Methodist Church, and I've sometimes considered asking some Methodist leader, like yourself, about my joining your ministry."

"Is that a fact? Is that a fact? We could use you. Uh—I wonder if you couldn't come out to the house tomorrow night for supper—just take pot-luck with us?"

"I should be most honored, Bishop."

Alone in his room, Elmer exulted, "That's the stunt! I'm sick of playing this lone game. Get in with a real big machine like the Methodists—maybe have to start low down, but climb fast—be a bishop myself in ten years—with all their spondulix and big churches and big membership and everything to back me up. Me for it. O Lord, thou hast guided me. . . . No, honest, I mean it. . . . No more hell-raising. Real religion from now on. Hurray! Oh, Bish, you watch me hand you the ole flattery!"

II

The Episcopal Palace. Beyond the somber length of the drawing-room an alcove with groined arches and fan-tracery—remains of the Carthusian chapel. A dolorous crucifixion by a pupil of El Greco, the sky menacing and wind-driven behind the gaunt figure of the dying god. Mullioned windows that still sparkled with the bearings of hard-riding bishops long since ignoble dust. The refectory table, a stony expanse of ancient oak, set round with grudging monkish chairs. And the library—on either side the lofty fireplace, austerely shining rows of calf-bound wisdom now dead as were the bishops.

The picture must be held in mind, because it is so beautifully opposite to the residence of the Reverend Dr. Wesley R. Toomis, bishop of the Methodist area of Zenith.

Bishop Toomis' abode was out in the section of Zenith called Devon Woods, near the junction of the Chaloosa and Appleseed rivers, that development (quite new in 1913, when Elmer Gantry first saw it) much favored by the next-to-the-best surgeons, lawyers, real estate dealers, and hardware wholesalers. It was a chubby modern house, mostly in tapestry brick with varicolored imitation tiles, a good deal of imitation half-timbering in the gables, and a screened porch with rocking-chairs, much favored on summer evenings by the episcopal but democratic person of Dr. Toomis.

The living-room had built-in book-shelves with leaded glass, built-in seats with thin brown cushions, and a huge electrolier with shades of wrinkled glass in ruby, emerald, and watery blue. There were a great many chairs—club chairs, Morris chairs, straight wooden chairs with burnt-work backs—and a great many tables, so that progress through the room was apologetic. But the features of the room were the fireplace, the books, and the foreign curios.

The fireplace was an ingenious thing. Basically it was composed of rough-hewn blocks of a green stone. Set in between the larger boulders were pebbles, pink and brown and earth-colored, which the good bishop had picked up all over the world. This pebble, the bishop would chirp, guiding you about the room, was from the shore of the Jordan, this was a fragment from the Great Wall of China, and this he had stolen from a garden in Florence. They were by no means all the attractions of the fireplace. The mantel was of cedar of Lebanon, genuine, bound with brass strips from a ship wrecked in the Black Sea in 1902—the bishop himself had bought the brass in Russia in 1904. The andirons were made from plow-shares as used by the bishop himself when but an untutored farm lad, all unaware of coming glory, in the cornfields of Illinois. The poker was, he assured you, a real whaling harpoon, picked up, surprisingly cheap, at Nantucket. Its rude shaft was decorated with a pink bow. This was not the doing of the bishop but of his lady. Himself, he said, he preferred the frank, crude, heroic strength of the bare wood, but Mrs. Toomis felt it needed a touch, a brightening—

Set in the rugged chimney of the fireplace was a plaque of smooth marble on which was carved in artistic and curly and gilded letters: "The Virtue of the Home is Peace, the Glory of the Home is Reverence."

The books were, as the bishop said, "worth browsing over." There were, naturally, the Methodist Discipline and the Methodist Hymnal, both handsomely bound Roycrofty in limp blue calfskin with leather ties; there was an impressive collection of Bibles, including a very ancient one, dated 1740, and one extra-illustrated with all the Hoffmann pictures and one hundred and sixty other Biblical scenes; and there were the necessary works of theological scholarship befitting a bishop—Moody's Sermons, Farrar's "Life of Christ," "Flowers and Beasties of the Holy Land," and "In His Steps," by Charles Sheldon. The more workaday ministerial books were kept in the study.

But the bishop was a man of the world and his books fairly represented his tastes. He had a complete Dickens, a complete Walter Scott, Tennyson in the red-line edition bound in polished tree calf with polished gilt edges, many of the better works of Macaulay and Ruskin and, for lighter moments, novels by Mrs. Humphry Ward, Winston Churchill, and Elizabeth of the German Garden. It was in travel and nature-study that he really triumphed. These were represented by not less than fifty volumes with such titles as "How to Study the Birds," "Through Madagascar with Camp and Camera," "My Summer in the Rockies," "My Mission in Darkest Africa," "Pansies for Thoughts," and "London from a Bus."

Nor had the bishop neglected history and economics: he possessed the Rev. Dr. Hockett's "Complete History of the World: Illustrated," in eleven handsome volumes, a second-hand copy of Hadley's "Economics," and "The Solution of Capitalism vs. Labor—Brotherly Love."

Yet not the fireplace, not the library, so much as the souvenirs of foreign travel gave to the bishop's residence a flair beyond that of most houses in Devon Woods. The bishop and his lady were fond of travel. They had made a six months' inspection of missions in Japan, Korea, China, India, Borneo, Java, and the Philippines, which gave the bishop an authoritative knowledge of all Oriental governments, religions, psychology, commerce, and hotels. But besides that, six several summers they had gone to Europe, and usually on the more refined and exclusive tours. Once they had spent three solid weeks seeing nothing but London—with side-trips to Oxford, Canterbury, and Stratford—once they had taken a four-day walking trip in the Tyrol, and once on a channel steamer they had met a man who, a steward said, was a Lord.

The living-room reeked with these adventures. There weren't exactly so many curios—the bishop said he didn't believe in getting a lot of foreign furniture and stuff when we made the best in the world right here at home—but as to pictures— The Toomises were devotees of photography, and they had brought back the whole world in shadow.

Here was the Temple of Heaven at Peking, with the bishop standing in front of it. Here was the Great Pyramid, with Mrs. Toomis in front of it. Here was the cathedral at Milan, with both of them in front of it—this had been snapped for them by an Italian guide, an obliging gentleman who had assured the bishop that he believed in prohibition.

III

Into this room Elmer Gantry came with overpowering politeness. He bent, almost as though he were going to kiss it, over the hand of Mrs. Toomis, who was a large lady with eye-glasses and modest sprightliness, and he murmured, "If you could only know what a privilege this is!"

She blushed, and looked at the bishop as if to say, "This, my beloved, is a good egg."

He shook hands reverently with the bishop and boomed, "How good it is of you to take in a homeless wanderer!"

"Nonsense, nonsense, Brother. It is a pleasure to make you at home! Before supper is served, perhaps you'd like to glance at one or two books and pictures and things that Mother and I have picked up in the many wanderings to which we have been driven in carrying on the Work. . . . Now this may interest you. This is a photograph of the House of Parliament, or Westminster, as it is also called, in London, England, corresponding to our Capitol in Washington."

"Well, well, is that a fact!"

"And here's another photo that might have some slight interest. This is a scene very rarely photographed—in fact it was so interesting that I sent it to the *National Geographic Magazine*, and while they were unable to use it, because of an overload of material, one of the editors wrote to me—I have the letter some place—and he agreed with me that it was a very unusual and interesting picture. It is taken right in front of the Sacra Cur, the famous church in Paris, up on the hill of Moant-marter, and if you examine it closely you will see by the curious light that it was taken *just before sunrise!* And yet you see how bully it came out! The lady to the right, there, is Mrs. Toomis. Yes, sir, a real breath right out of Paris!"

"Well, say, that certainly is interesting! Paris, eh!"

"But, oh, Dr. Gantry, a sadly wicked city! I do not speak of the vices of the French themselves—that is for them to settle with their own consciences, though I certainly do advocate the most active and widespread extension of our American Protestant missions there, as in all other European countries which suffer under the blight and darkness of Catholicism. But what saddens me is the thought—and I know whereof I speak, I myself have seen that regrettable spectacle—what would sadden you, Dr. Gantry, is the sight of fine young Americans going over there and not profiting by the sermons in stones, the history to be read in those historical structures, but letting themselves be drawn into a life of heedless and hectic gaiety if not indeed of actual immorality. Oh, it gives one to think, Dr. Gantry."

"Yes, it certainly must. By the way, Bishop, it isn't Dr. Gantry—it's Mr. Gantry—just plain Reverend."

"But I thought your circulars—"

"Oh, that was a mistake on the part of the man who wrote them for me. I've talked to him good!"

"Well, well, I admire you for speaking about it! It is none too easy for us poor weak mortals to deny honors and titles whether they are rightly or wrongly conferred upon us. Well, I'm sure that it is but a question of time when you *will* wear the honor of a Doctor of Divinity degree, if I may without immodesty so refer to a handle which I myself happen to possess—yes, indeed, a man who combines strength with eloquence, charm of presence, and a fine high-grade vocabulary as you do, it is but a question of time when—"

"Wesley, dear, supper is served."

"Oh, very well, my dear. The ladies, Dr. Gantry—Mr. Gantry—as you may already have observed, they seem to have the strange notion that a household must be run on routine lines, and they don't hesitate, bless 'em, to interrupt even an abstract discussion to bid us come to the festal board when they feel that it's time, and I for one make haste to obey and— After supper there's a couple of other photographs that might interest you, and I do want you to take a peep at my books. I know a poor bishop has no right to yield to the lust for material possessions, but I plead guilty to one vice—my inordinate love for owning fine items of literature. . . . Yes, dear, we're coming at once. Toojoor la fam, Mr. Gantry!—always the ladies! Are you, by the way, married?"

"Not yet, sir."

"Well, well, you must take care of that. I tell you in the ministry there is always a vast, though often of course unfair, amount of criticism of the unmarried preacher, which seriously cramps him. Yes, my dear, we are coming."

There were rolls hidden in the cornucopia-folded napkins, and supper began with a fruit cocktail of orange, apple, and canned pineapple.

"Well," said Elmer, with a courtly bow to Mrs. Toomis, "I see I'm in high society—beginning with a cocktail! I tell you I just have to have my cocktail before the eats!"

It went over immensely. The bishop repeated it, choking.

IV

Elmer managed, during supper, to let them know that not only was he a theological seminary man, not only had he mastered psychology, Oriental occultism, and the methods of making millions, but also he had been general manager for the famous Miss Sharon Falconer.

Whether Bishop Toomis was considering, "I want this man—he's a comer—he'd be useful to me," is not known. But certainly he listened with zeal to Elmer, and cooed at him, and after supper, with not more than an hour of showing him the library and the mementos of far-off roamings, he took him off to the study, away from Mrs. Toomis, who had been interrupting, every quarter of an hour, with her own recollections of roast beef at Simpson's, prices of rooms on Bloomsbury Square, meals on the French wagon restaurant, the speed of French taxicabs, and the view of the Eiffel Tower at sunset.

The study was less ornate than the living-room. There was a business-like desk, a phonograph for dictation, a card catalogue of possible contributors to funds, a steel filing-cabinet, and the bishop's own typewriter. The books were strictly practical: Cruden's Concordance, Smith's Dictionary of the Bible, an atlas of Palestine, and the three published volumes of the bishop's own sermons. By glancing at these for not more than ten minutes, he could have an address ready for any occasion.

The bishop sank into his golden oak revolving desk-chair, pointed at his typewriter, and sighed, "From this horrid room you get a hint of how pressed I am by practical affairs. What I should like to do is to sit down quietly there at my beloved machine and produce some work of pure beauty that would last forever, where even the most urgent temporal affairs tend, perhaps, to pass away. Of course I have editorials in the *Advocate*, and my sermons have been published."

He looked sharply at Elmer.

"Yes, of *course*, Bishop, I've read them!"

"That's very kind of you. But what I've longed for all these years is sinfully worldly literary work. I've always fancied, perhaps vainly, that I have a talent— I've longed to do a book, in fact a novel— I have rather an interesting plot. You see, this farm boy, brought up in circumstances of want, with very little opportunity for education, he struggles hard for what book-learning he attains, but there in the green fields, in

God's own pure meadows, surrounded by the leafy trees and the stars overhead at night, breathing the sweet open air of the pastures, he grows up a strong, pure, and reverent young man, and of course when he goes up to the city—I had thought of having him enter the ministry, but I don't want to make it autobiographical, so I shall have him enter a commercial line, but one of the more constructive branches of the great realm of business, say like banking. Well, he meets the daughter of his boss—she is a lovely young woman, but tempted by the manifold temptations and gaieties of the city, and I want to show how his influence guides her away from the broad paths that lead to destruction, and what a splendid effect he has not only on her but on others in the mart of affairs. Yes, I long to do that, but— Sitting here, just us two, one almost feels as though it would be pleasant to smoke—*Do you smoke?*"

"No, thanks be to God, Bishop. I can honestly say that for years I have never known the taste of nicotine or alcohol."

"God be praised!"

"When I was younger, being kind of, you might say, a vigorous fellow, I was led now and then into temptation, but the influence of Sister Falconer—oh, there was a sanctified soul, like a nun—only strictly Protestant, of course—they so uplifted me that now I am free of all such desires."

"I am glad to hear it, Brother, so glad to hear it. . . . Now, Gantry, the other day you said something about having thought of coming into the Methodist fold. How seriously have you thought about it?"

"Very."

"I wish you would. I mean— Of course neither you nor I is necessary to the progress of that great Methodist Church, which day by day is the more destined to instruct and guide our beloved nation. But I mean— When I meet a fine young man like you, I like to think of what spiritual satisfaction he would have in this institution. Now the work you're doing at present is inspiring to many fine young men, but it is single-handed—it has no *permanence*. When you go, much of the good you have done dies, because there is no institution like the living church to carry it on. You ought to be in one of the large denominations, and of these I feel, for all my admiration of the Baptists, that the Methodist Church is in some ways the great exemplar. It is so broad-spirited and democratic, yet very powerful. It is the real church of the people."

"Yes, I rather believe you're right, Bishop. Since I talked with you I've been thinking— Uh, if the Methodist Church should want to accept me, what would I have to do? Would there be much red tape?"

"It would be a very simple matter. As you're already ordained, I could have the District Conference, which meets next month at Sparta, recommend you to the Annual Conference for membership. I am sure when the Annual Conference meets in spring of next year, a little less than a year from now, with your credits from Terwillinger and Mizpah I could get you accepted by the Conference and your orders recognized. Till then I can have you accepted as a preacher on trial. And I have a church right now, at Banjo Crossing, that is in need of just such leadership as you could furnish. Banjo has only nine hundred people, but you understand that it would be necessary for you to begin at the bottom. The brethren would very properly be jealous if I gave you a first-class appointment right at the first. But I am sure I could advance you rapidly. Yes, we must have you in the church. Great is the work for consecrated hands—and I'll bet a cookie I live to see you a bishop yourself!"

V

He couldn't, Elmer complained, back in the refuge of his hotel, sink to a crossroads of nine hundred people, with a salary of perhaps eleven hundred dollars; not after the big tent and Sharon's throngs, not after suites and morning coats and being Dr. Gantry to brokers' wives in ballrooms.

But also he couldn't go on. He would never get to the top in the New Thought business. He admitted that he hadn't quite the creative mind. He could never rise to such originality as, say, Mrs. Riddle's humorous oracle: "Don't be scared of upsetting folks 'coz most of 'em are topsy-turvy anyway, and you'll only be putting 'em back on their feet."

Fortunately, except in a few fashionable churches, it wasn't necessary to say anything original to succeed among the Baptists or Methodists.

He would be happy in a regular pastorate. He was a professional. As an actor enjoyed grease-paint and call-boards and stacks of scenery, so Elmer had the affection of familiarity for the details of his profession—hymn books, communion service, training the choir, watching the Ladies' Aid grow, the drama of coming from the mysteries back-stage, so unknown and fascinating to the audience, to the limelight of the waiting congregation.

And his mother— He had not seen her for two years, but he retained the longing to solace her, and he knew that she was only bewildered over his New Thought harlequinade.

But—nine hundred population!

He held out for a fortnight; demanded a bigger church from Bishop Toomis; brought in all his little clippings about eloquence in company with Sharon.

Then the Zenith lectures closed, and he had ahead only the most speculative opportunities.

Bishop Toomis grieved, "I am disappointed, Brother, that you should think more of the size of the flock than of the great, grrrrrrrreat opportunities for good ahead of you!"

Elmer looked his most flushing, gallant, boyish self. "Oh, no, Bishop, you don't get me, honest! I just wanted to be able to use my training where it might be of the most value. But I'm eager to be guided by you!"

Two months later Elmer was on the train to Banjo Crossing, as pastor of the Methodist Church in that amiable village under the sycamores.

Chapter XIX

A THURSDAY in June 1913.

The train wandered through orchard-land and corn-fields—two seedy day-coaches and a baggage car. Hurry and efficiency had not yet been discovered on this branch line, and it took five hours to travel the hundred and twenty miles from Zenith to Banjo Crossing.

The Reverend Elmer Gantry was in a state of grace. Having resolved henceforth to be pure and humble and humanitarian, he was benevolent to all his traveling companions. He was mothering the world, whether the world liked it or not.

But he did not insist on any outward distinction as a parson, a Professional Good Man. He wore a quietly modest gray sack suit, a modestly rich maroon tie. Not just as a minister, but as a citizen, he told himself, it was his duty to make life breezier and brighter for his fellow wayfarers.

The aged conductor knew most of his passengers by their first names, and they hailed him as "Uncle Ben," but he resented strangers on their home train. When Elmer shouted, "Lovely day, Brother!" Uncle Ben looked at him as if to say "Well, 'tain't my fault!" But Elmer continued his philadelphian violences till the old man sent in the brakeman to collect the tickets the rest of the way.

At a traveling salesman who tried to borrow a match, Elmer roared, "I don't smoke, Brother, and I don't believe George Washington did either!" His benignancies were received with so little gratitude that he almost wearied of good works, but when he carried an old woman's suit-case off the train, she fluttered at him with the admiration he deserved, and he was moved to pat children upon the head—to their terror—and to explain crop-rotation to an ancient who had been farming for forty-seven years.

Anyway, he satisfied the day's lust for humanitarianism, and he turned back the seat in front of his, stretched out his legs, looked sleepy so that no one would crowd in beside him, and rejoiced in having taken up a life of holiness and authority.

He glanced out at the patchy country with satisfaction. Rustic, yes, but simple, and the simple honest hearts of his congregation would yearn toward him as the bookkeepers could not be depended upon to do in Prosperity Classes. He pictured his hearty reception at Banjo Crossing. He knew that his district superintendent (a district superintendent is a lieutenant-bishop in the Methodist Church—formerly called a presiding elder) had written the hour of his coming to Mr. Nathaniel Benham of Banjo Crossing, and he knew that Mr. Benham, the leading trustee of the local church, was the chief general merchant in the Banjo Valley. Yes, he would shake hands with all of his flock, even the humblest, at the station; he would look into their clear and trusting eyes, and rejoice to be their shepherd, leading them on and upward, for at least a year.

Banjo Crossing seemed very small as the train staggered into it. There were back porches with wash-tubs and broken-down chairs; there were wooden sidewalks.

As Elmer pontifically descended at the red frame station, as he looked for the reception and the holy glee, there wasn't any reception, and the only glee visible was on the puffy face of the station agent as he observed a City Fellow trying to show off.

"Hee, hee, there *ain't* no 'bus!" giggled the agent. "Guess yuh'll have to carry your own valises over to the hotel!"

"Where," demanded Elmer, "is Mr. Benham, Mr. Nathaniel Benham?"

"Old Nat? Ain't seen him today. Guess yuh'll find him at the store, 'bout as usual, seeing if he can't do some farmer out of two cents on a batch of eggs. Traveling man?"

"I am the new Methodist preacher!"

"Oh, well, say! That a fact! Pleased to meet yuh! Wouldn't of thought you were a preacher. You look too well fed! You're going to room at Mrs. Pete Clark's—the Widow Clark's. Leave your valises here, and I'll have my boy fetch 'em over. Well, good luck, Brother. Hope you won't have much trouble with your church. The last fellow did, but then he was kind of pernickety—wa'n't just plain folks."

"Oh, I'm just plain folks, and mighty happy, after the great cities, to be among them!" was Elmer's amiable greeting, but what he observed as he walked away was "I am like hell!"

Altogether depressed now, he expected to find the establishment of Brother Benham a littered and squalid crossroads store, but he came to a two-story brick structure with plate-glass windows and, in the alley, the half-dozen trucks with which Mr. Benham supplied the farmers for twenty miles up and down the Banjo Valley. Respectful, Elmer walked through broad aisles, past counters trim as a small department-store, and found Mr. Benham dictating letters.

If in a small way Nathaniel Benham had commercial genius, it did not show in his aspect. He wore a beard like a bath sponge, and in his voice was a righteous twang.

"Yes?" he quacked.

"I'm Reverend Gantry, the new pastor."

Benham rose, not too nimbly, and shook hands dryly. "Oh, yes. The presiding elder said you were coming today. Glad you've come, Brother, and I hope the blessings of the Lord will attend your labors. You're to board at the Widow Clark's—anybody'll show you where it is."

Apparently he had nothing else to say.

A little bitterly, Elmer demanded, "I'd like to look over the church. Have you a key?"

"Now let's see. Brother Jones might have one—he's got the paint and carpenter shop right up here on Front Street. No, guess he hasn't, either. We got a young fella, just a boy you might say, who's doing the janitor work now, and guess he'd have a key, but this bein' vacation he's off fishin' more'n likely. Tell you: you might try Brother Fritscher, the shoemaker—he might have a key. You married?"

"No. I've, uh, I've been engaged in evangelistic work, so I've been denied the joys and solaces of domestic life."

"Where you born?"

"Kansas."

"Folks Christians?"

"They certainly were! My mother was—she is—a real consecrated soul."

"Smoke or drink?"

"Certainly not!"

"Do any monkeying with this higher criticism?"

"No, indeed!"

"Ever go hunting?"

"I, uh— Well, yes!"

"That's fine! Well, glad you're with us, Brother. Sorry I'm busy. Say, Mother and I expect you for supper tonight, six-thirty. Good luck!"

Benham's smile, his handshake, were cordial enough, but he was definitely giving dismissal, and Elmer went out in a fury alternating with despair. . . . To this, to the condescension of a rustic store-keeper, after the mounting glory with Sharon!

As he walked toward the house of the Widow Clark, to which a loafer directed him, he hated the shabby village, hated the chicken-coops in the yards, the frowsy lawns, the old buggies staggering by, the women with plump aprons and wet red arms—women who made his delights of amorous adventures seem revolting—and all the plodding yokels with their dead eyes and sagging jaws and sudden guffawing.

Fallen to this. And at thirty-two. A failure!

As he waited on the stoop of the square, white, characterless house of the Widow Clark, he wanted to dash back to the station and take the first train—anywhere. In that moment he decided to return to farm implements and the bleak lonely freedom of the traveling man. Then the screen door was opened by a jolly ringleted girl of fourteen or fifteen, who caroled, "Oh, is it Reverend Gantry! My, and I kept you waiting! I'm terrible sorry! Ma's just sick she can't be here to welcome you, but she had to go over to Cousin Etta's—Cousin Etta busted her leg. Oh, please do come in. My, I didn't guess we'd have a young preacher this time!"

She was charming in her excited innocence.

After a faded provincial fashion, the square hall was stately, with its Civil War chromos.

Elmer followed the child—Jane Clark, she was—up to his room. As she frisked before him, she displayed six inches of ankle above her clumsy shoes, and Elmer was clutched by that familiar feeling, swifter than thought, more elaborate than the strategy of a whole war, which signified that here was a girl he was going to pursue. But as suddenly—almost wistfully, in his weary desire for peace and integrity—he begged himself, "No! Don't! Not any more! Let the kid alone! Please be decent! Lord, give me decency and goodness!"

The struggle was finished in the half-minute of ascending the stairs, and he could shake hands casually, say carelessly, "Well, I'm mighty glad you were here to welcome me, Sister, and I hope I may bring a blessing on the house."

He felt at home now, warmed, restored. His chamber was agreeable—Turkey-red carpet, stove a perfect shrine of polished nickel, and in the bow-window, a deep arm-chair. On the four-poster bed was a crazy-quilt, and pillow-shams embroidered with lambs and rabbits and the motto, "God Bless Our Slumbers."

"This is going to be all right. Kinda like home, after these doggone hotels," he meditated.

He was again ready to conquer Banjo Crossing, to conquer Methodism; and when his bags and trunk had come, he set out, before unpacking, to view his kingdom.

II

Banjo Crossing was not extensive, but to find the key to the First Methodist Church was a Scotland Yard melodrama.

Brother Fritscher, the shoemaker, had lent it to Sister Anderson of the Ladies' Aid, who had lent it to Mrs. Pryshetski, the scrubwoman, who had lent it to Pussy Byrnes, president of the Epworth League, who had lent it to Sister Fritscher, consort of Brother Fritscher, so that Elmer captured it next door to the shoemaker's shop from which he had irritably set out.

Each of them, Brother Fritscher and Sister Fritscher, Sister Pryshetski and Sister Byrnes, Sister Anderson and most of the people from whom he inquired directions along the way, asked him the same questions:

"You the new Methodist preacher?" and "Not married, are you?" and "Just come to town?" and "Hear you come from the City—guess you're pretty glad to get away, ain't you?"

He hadn't much hope for his church-building. He had not seen it yet—it was hidden behind the school-building—but he expected a hideous brown hulk with plank buttresses. He was delighted then, proud as a worthy citizen elected mayor, when he came to an agreeable little church covered with gray shingles, crowned with a modest spire, rimmed with cropped lawn and flower-beds. Excitedly he let himself in, greeted by the stale tomb-like odor of all empty churches.

The interior was pleasant. It would hold two hundred and ninety, perhaps. The pews were of a light yellow, too glaring, but the walls were of soft cream, and in the chancel, with a white arch graceful above it, was a seemly white pulpit and a modest curtained choir-loft. He explored. There was a goodish Sunday School room, a basement with tables and a small kitchen. It was all cheerful, alive; it suggested a chance of growth.

As he returned to the auditorium, he noted one good colored memorial window, and through the clear glass of the others the friendly maples looked in at him.

He walked round the building. Suddenly he was overwhelmed and exalted with the mystic pride of ownership. It was all his; his own; and as such it was all beautiful. What beautiful soft gray shingles! What an exquisite spire! What a glorious maple-tree! Yes, and what a fine cement walk, what a fine new ash-can, what a handsome announcement board, soon to be starred with his own name! His! To do with as he pleased! And, oh, he would do fine things, aspiring things, very important things! Never again, with this new reason for going on living, would he care for lower desires—for pride, for the adventure of women. . . . *His!*

He entered the church again; he sat proudly in each of the three chairs on the platform which, as a boy, he had believed to be reserved for the three persons of the Trinity. He stood up, leaned his arms on the pulpit, and to a worshiping throng (many standing) he boomed, "My brethren!"

He was in an ecstasy such as he had not known since his hours with Sharon. He would start again—*had* started again, he vowed. Never lie or cheat or boast. This town, it might be dull, but he would enliven it, make it his own creation, lift it to his own present glory. He would! Life opened before him, clean, joyous, full of the superb chances of a Christian knighthood. Some day he would be a bishop, yes, but even that was nothing compared with the fact that he had won a victory over his lower nature.

He knelt, and with his arms wide in supplication he prayed, "Lord, thou who hast stooped to my great unworthiness and taken even me to thy Kingdom, who this moment hast shown me the abiding joy of righteousness, make me whole and keep me pure, and in all things, Our Father, thy will be done. Amen."

He stood by the pulpit, tears in his eyes, his meaty hands clutching the cover of the great leather Bible till it cracked.

The door at the other end of the aisle was opening, and he saw a vision standing on the threshold in the June sun.

He remembered afterward, from some forgotten literary adventure in college, a couplet which signified to him the young woman who was looking at him from the door:

> Pale beyond porch and portal,
> Crowned with calm leaves she stands.

She was younger than himself, yet she suggested a serene maturity, a gracious pride. She was slender, but her bosom was full, and some day she might be portly. Her face was lovely, her forehead wide, her brown eyes trusting, and smooth her chestnut hair. She had taken off her rose-trimmed straw hat and was swinging it in her large and graceful hands. . . . Virginal, stately, kind, most generous.

She came placidly down the aisle, a hand out, crying, "It's Reverend Gantry, isn't it? I'm so proud to be the first to welcome you here in the church! I'm Cleo Benham—I lead the choir. Perhaps you've seen Papa—he's a trustee—he has the store."

"You sure are the first to welcome me, Sister Benham, and it's a mighty great pleasure to meet you! Yes, your father was so nice as to invite me for supper tonight."

They shook hands with ceremony and sat beaming at each other in a front pew. He informed her that he was certain there was "going to be a great spiritual awakening here," and she told him what lovely people there were in the congregation, in the village, in the entire surrounding country. And her panting breast told him that she, the daughter of the village magnate, had instantly fallen in love with him.

III

Cleo Benham had spent three years in the Sparta Women's College, specializing in piano, organ, French, English literature, strictly expurgated, and study of the Bible. Returned to Banjo Crossing, she was a fervent church-worker. She played the organ and rehearsed the choir; she was the superintendent of the juvenile department in the Sunday School; she decorated the church for Easter, for funerals, for the Halloween Supper.

She was twenty-seven, five years younger than Elmer.

Though she was not very lively in summer-evening front-porch chatter, though on the few occasions when she sinned against the Discipline and danced she seemed a little heavy on her feet, though she had a corseted purity which was dismaying to the earthy young men of Banjo Crossing, yet she was handsome, she was kind, and her father was reputed to be worth not a cent less than seventy-five thousand dollars. So almost every eligible male in the vicinity had hinted at proposing to her.

Gently and compassionately she had rejected them one by one. Marriage must, she felt, be a sacrament; she must be the helpmate of some one who was "doing a tremendous amount of good in the world." This good she identified with medicine or preaching.

Her friends assured her, "My! With your Bible training and your music and all, you'd make a perfect pastor's wife. Just dandy! You'd be such a help to him."

But no detached preacher or doctor had happened along, and she had remained insulated, a little puzzled, hungry over the children of her friends, each year more passionately given to hymnody and agonized solitary prayer.

Now, with innocent boldness, she was exclaiming to Elmer: "We were so afraid the bishop would send us some pastor that was old and worn-out. The people here are lovely, but they're kind of slow-going; they need somebody to wake them up. I'm *so* glad he sent somebody that was young and attractive— Oh, my, I shouldn't have said that! I was just thinking of the church, you understand."

Her eyes said that she had not been just thinking of the church.

She looked at her wrist-watch (the first in Banjo Crossing) and chanted, "Why, my gracious, it's six o'clock! Would you like to walk home with me instead of going to Mrs. Clark's— you could wash up at Papa's."

"You can't lose me!" exulted Elmer, hastily amending, "—as the slangy youngsters say! Yes, indeed, I should be very pleased to have the pleasure of walking home with you."

Under the elms, past the rose-bushes, through dust emblazoned by the declining sun, he walked with his stately abbess.

He knew that she was the sort of wife who would help him to capture a bishopric. He persuaded himself that, with all her virtue, she would eventually be interesting to kiss. He noted that they "made a fine couple." He told himself that she was the first woman he had ever found who was worthy of him . . . . Then he remembered Sharon. . . . But the pang lasted only a moment, in the secure village peace, in the gentle flow of Cleo's voice.

IV

Once he was out of the sacred briskness of his store, Mr. Nathaniel Benham forgot discounts and became an affable host. He said, "Well, well, Brother," ever so many times, and shook hands profusely. Mrs. Benham—she was a large woman, rather handsome; she wore figured foulard, with an apron over it, as she had been helping in the kitchen—Mrs. Benham was equally cordial. "I'll just bet you're hungry, Brother!" cried she.

He was, after a lunch of ham sandwich and coffee at a station lunch-room on the way down.

The Benham house was the proudest mansion in town. It was of yellow clapboards with white trim; it had a huge screened porch and a little turret; a staircase window with a border of colored glass; and there was a real fireplace, though it was never used. In front of the house, to Elmer's admiration, was one of the three automobiles which were all that were to be found in 1913 in Banjo Crossing. It was a bright red Buick with brass trimmings.

The Benham supper was as replete with fried chicken and theological questions as Elmer's first supper with Deacon Bains in Schoenheim. But here was wealth, for which Elmer had a touching reverence, and here was Cleo.

Lulu Bains had been a tempting mouthful; Cleo Benham was of the race of queens. To possess her, Elmer gloated, would in itself be an empire, worth any battling. . . . And yet he did not itch to get her in a corner and buss her, as he had Lulu; the slope of her proud shoulders did not make his fingers taut.

After supper, on the screened porch pleasant by dusk, Mr. Benham demanded, "What charges have you been holding, Brother Gantry?"

Elmer modestly let him know how important he had been in the work of Sister Falconer; he admitted his scholarly research at Mizpah Seminary; he made quite enough of his success at Schoenheim; he let it be known that he had been practically assistant sales-manager of the Pequot Farm Implement Company.

Mr. Benham grunted with surprised admiration. Mrs. Benham gurgled, "My, we're lucky to have a real high-class preacher for once!" And Cleo—she leaned toward Elmer, in a deep willow chair, and her nearness was a charm.

He walked back happily in the June darkness; he felt neighborly when an unknown muttered, "Evening, Reverend!" and all the way he saw Cleo, proud as Athena yet pliant as golden-skinned Aphrodite.

He had found his work, his mate, his future.

Virtue, he pointed out, certainly did pay.

Chapter XX

HE HAD two days to prepare his first sermon and unpack his trunk, his bags, and the books which he had purchased in Zenith.

His possessions were not very consistent. He had a beautiful new morning coat, three excellent lounge suits, patent leather shoes, a noble derby, a flourishing top hat, but he had only two suits of underclothes, both ragged. His socks were of black silk, out at the toes. For breast-pocket display, he had silk handkerchiefs; but for use, only cotton rags torn at the hem. He owned perfume, hair-oil, talcum powder; his cuff links were of solid gold; but for dressing-gown he used his overcoat; his slippers were a frowsy pulp; and the watch which he carried on a gold and platinum chain was a one-dollar alarm clock.

He had laid in a fruitful theological library. He had bought the fifty volumes of the Expositors' Bible—source of ready-made sermons—second-hand for $13.75. He had the sermons of Spurgeon, Jefferson, Brooks, and J. Wilbur Chapman. He was willing to be guided by these masters, and not insist on forcing his own ideas on the world. He had a very useful book by Bishop Aberman, "The Very Appearance of Evil," advising young preachers to avoid sin. Elmer felt that this would be unusually useful in his new life.

He had a dictionary—he liked to look at the colored plates depicting jewels, flags, plants, and aquatic birds; he had a Bible dictionary, a concordance, a history of the Methodist Church, a history of Protestant missions, commentaries on the individual books of the Bible, an outline of theology, and Dr. Argyle's "The Pastor and His Flock," which told how to increase church collections, train choirs, take exercise, placate deacons, and make pasteboard models of Solomon's Temple to lead the little ones to holiness in the Sunday School.

In fact he had had a sufficient library—"God's artillery in black and white," as Bishop Toomis wittily dubbed it—to inform himself of any detail in the practice of the Professional

Good Man. He would be able to produce sermons which would be highly informative about the geography of Palestine, yet useful to such of his fold as might have a sneaking desire to read magazines on the Sabbath. Thus guided, he could increase the church membership; he could give advice to errant youth; he could raise missionary funds so that the heathen in Calcutta and Peking might have the opportunity to become like the Reverend Elmer Gantry.

II

Though Cleo took him for a drive through the country, most of the time before Sunday he dedicated to refurbishing a sermon which he had often and successfully used with Sharon. The text was from Romans I:16: "For I am not ashamed of the gospel of Christ: for it is the power of God unto salvation to every one that believeth."

When he came up to the church on Sunday morning, tall and ample, grave and magnificent, his face fixed in a smile of friendliness, his morning coat bright in the sun, a Bible under his arm, Elmer was exhilarated by the crowd filtering into the church. The street was filled with country buggies and a Ford or two. As he went round to the back of the church, passing a knot at the door, they shouted cordially, "Good morning, Brother!" and "Fine day, Reverend!"

Cleo was waiting for him with the choir—Miss Kloof, the school-teacher, Mrs. Diebel, wife of the implement dealer, Ed Perkins, deliveryman for Mr. Benham, and Ray Faucett, butter-maker at the creamery.

Cleo held his hand and rejoiced, "What a wonderful crowd there is this morning! I'm so glad!"

Together they peeped through the parlor door into the auditorium, and he almost put his arm about her firm waist. . . . It would have seemed natural, very pleasant and right and sweet.

When he marched out to the chancel, the church was full, a dozen standing. They all breathed with admiration. (He learned later that the last pastor had had trouble with his false teeth and a fondness for whining.)

He led the singing.

"Come on now!" he laughed. "You've got to welcome your new preacher! The best way is to put a lot of lung-power into it and sing like the dickens! You can all make some kind of noise. Make a lot!"

Himself he gave example, his deep voice rolling out in hymns of which he had always been fond: "I Love to Tell the Story" and "My Faith Looks up to Thee."

He prayed briefly—he was weary of prayers in which the priest ramblingly explained to God that God really was God. This was, he said, his first day with the new flock. Let the Lord give him ways of showing them his love and his desire to serve them.

Before his sermon he looked from brother to brother. He loved them all, that moment; they were his regiment, and he the colonel; his ship's crew, and he the skipper; his patients, and he the loyal physician. He began slowly, his great voice swelling to triumphant certainty as he talked.

Voice, sureness, presence, training, power, he had them all. Never had he so well liked his rôle; never had he acted so well; never had he known such sincerity of histrionic instinct.

He had solid doctrine for the older stalwarts. With comforting positiveness he preached that the atonement was the one supreme fact in the world. It rendered the most sickly and threadbare the equals of kings and millionaires; it demanded of the successful that they make every act a recognition of the atonement. For the young people he had plenty of anecdotes, and he was not afraid to make them laugh.

While he did tell the gloomy incident of the boy who was drowned while fishing on Sunday, he also gave them the humorous story of the lad who declared he wouldn't go to school, "because it said in the Twenty-third Psalm that the Lord made him lie down in green pastures, and he sure did prefer that to school!"

For all of them, but particularly for Cleo, sitting at the organ, her hands clasped in her lap, her eyes loyal, he winged into poetry.

To preach the good news of the gospel, ah! That was not, as the wicked pretended, a weak, sniveling, sanctimonious thing! It was a job for strong men and resolute women. For this, the Methodist missionaries had faced the ferocious lion and the treacherous fevers of the jungle, the poisonous cold of the Arctic, the parching desert and the fields of battle. Were we to be less heroic than they? Here, now, in Banjo Crossing, there was no triumph of business so stirring, no despairing need of a sick friend so urgent, as the call to tell blinded and perishing sinners the necessity of repentence.

"Repentance—repentance—repentance—in the name of the Lord God!"

His superb voice trumpeted it, and in Cleo's eyes were inspired tears.

Beyond controversy, it was the best sermon ever heard in Banjo Crossing. And they told him so as he cheerily shook hands with them at the door. "Enjoyed your discourse a lot, Reverend!"

And Cleo came to him, her two hands out, and he almost kissed her.

III

Sunday School was held after morning service. Elmer determined that he was not going to attend Sunday School every week—"not on your life; sneak in a nap before dinner"—but this morning he was affably and expansively there, encouraging the little ones by a bright short talk in which he advised them to speak the truth, obey their fathers and mothers, and give heed to the revelations of their teachers, such as Miss Mittie Lamb, the milliner, and Oscar Scholtz, manager of the potato warehouse.

Banjo Crossing had not yet touched the modern Sunday School methods which, in the larger churches, in another ten years, were to divide the pupils as elaborately as public school and to provide training-classes for the teachers. But at least they had separated the children up to ten years from the older students, and of this juvenile department Cleo Benham was superintendent.

Elmer watched her going from class to class; he saw how naturally and affectionately the children talked to her.

"She'd make a great wife and mother—a great wife for a preacher—a great wife for a bishop," he noted.

IV

Evening services at the Banjo Crossing Methodist Church had normally drawn less than forty people, but there were a hundred tonight, when, fumblingly, Elmer broke away from old-fashioned church practise and began what was later to become his famous Lively Sunday Evenings.

He chose the brighter hymns, "Onward, Christian Soldiers," "Wonderful Words of Life," "Brighten the Corner Where You Are," and the triumphant pæan of "When the Roll is Called up Yonder, I'll be There." Instead of making them drone through many stanzas, he had them sing one from each hymn. Then he startled them by shouting, "Now I don't want any of you old fellows to be shocked, or say it isn't proper in church, because I'm going to get the spirit awakened and maybe get the old devil on the run! Remember that the Lord who made the sunshine and the rejoicing hills must have been behind the fellows that wrote the glad songs, so I want you to all pipe up good and lively with 'Dixie'! Yes, *sir!* Then, for the old fellows, like me, we'll have a stanza of that magnificent old reassurance of righteousness, 'How Firm a Foundation.'"

They did look shocked, some of them; but the youngsters, the boys and the girls keeping an aseptic tryst in the back pews, were delighted. He made them sing the chorus of "Dixie" over and over, till all but one or two rheumatic saints looked cheerful.

His text was from Galatians: "But the fruit of the Spirit is love, joy, peace."

"Don't you ever listen for one second," he commanded, "to these wishy-washy fellows that carry water on both shoulders, that love to straddle the fence, that are scared of the sternness of the good old-time Methodist doctrine and tell you that details don't mean anything, that dogmas and the discipline don't mean anything. They do! Justification means something! Baptism means something! It means something that the wicked and worldly stand for this horrible stinking tobacco and this insane alcohol, which makes a man like a murderer, but we Methodists keep ourselves pure and unspotted and undefiled.

"But tonight, on this first day of getting acquainted with you, Brothers and Sisters, I don't want to go into these details. I want to get down to the fundamental thing which details merely carry out, and that fundamental thing— What is it? What is it? What is it but Jesus Christ, and his love for each and every one of us!

"Love! Love! Love! How beauteous the very word! Not carnal love but the divine presence. What is Love? Listen! It is the rainbow that stands out, in all its glorious many-colored hues, illuminating and making glad again the dark clouds of life. It is the morning and the evening star, that in glad refulgence, there on the awed horizon, call Nature's hearts to an uplifted rejoicing in God's marvelous firmament! Round about the cradle of the babe, sleeping so quietly while o'er him hangs in almost agonized adoration his loving mother, shines the miracle of Love, and at the last sad end, comforting the hearts that bear its immortal permanence, round even the quiet tomb, shines Love.

"What is great art—and I am not speaking of ordinary pictures but of those celebrated Old Masters with their great moral lessons—what is the mother of art, the inspiration of the poet, the patriot, the philosopher, and the great man of affairs, be he business man or statesman—yes, what inspires their every effort save Love?

"Oh, do you not sometimes hear, stealing o'er the plains at dawn, coming as it were from some far distant secret place, a sound of melody? When our dear sister here plays the offertory, do you not seem sometimes to catch the distant rustle of the wings of cherubim? And what is music, lovely, lovely music, what is fair melody? Ah, music, 'tis the voice of Love! Ah, 'tis the magician that makes right royal kings out of plain folks like us! 'Tis the perfume of the wondrous flower, 'tis the strength of the athlete, strong and mighty to endure 'mid the heat and dust of the valorous conquest. Ah, Love, Love, Love! Without it, we are less than beasts; with it, earth is heaven and we are as the gods!

"Yes, that is what Love—created by Christ Jesus and conveyed through all the generations by his church, particularly, it seems to me, by the great, broad, democratic, liberal brotherhood of the Methodist Church—that is what it means to us.

"I am reminded of an incident in my early youth, while I was in the university. There was a young man in my class—I will not give you his name except to say that we called him Jim—a young man pleasing to the eye, filled with every possibility for true deep Christian service, but alas! so beset with the boyish pride of mere intellect, of mere smart-aleck egotism, that he was unwilling to humble himself before the source of all intellect and accept Jesus as his savior.

"I was very fond of Jim—in fact I had been willing to go and room with him in the hope of bringing him to his senses and getting him to embrace salvation. But he was a man who had read books by folks like Ingersoll and Thomas Paine—fool, swell-headed folks that thought they knew more than Almighty God! He would quote their polluted and devil-inspired ravings instead of listening to the cool healing stream that gushes blessedly forth from the Holy Bible. Well, I argued and argued and argued—I guess that shows I was pretty young and foolish myself! But one day I was inspired to something bigger and better than any arguments.

"I just said to Jim, all of a sudden, 'Jim,' I said, 'do you love your father?' (A fine old Christian gentleman his father was, too, a country doctor, with that heroism, that self-sacrifice, that wide experience which the country doctor has.) 'Do you love your old dad?' I asked him.

"Naturally, Jim was awful' fond of his father, and he was kind of hurt that I should have asked him.

"'Sure, of course I do!' he says. 'Well, Jim,' I says, 'does your father love you?' 'Why, of course he does,' said Jim. 'Then look here, Jim,' I said; 'if your earthly father can love you, how much more must your Father in Heaven, who created all Love, how much more must he care and yearn for you!'

"Well, sir, that knocked him right over. He forgot all the smart-aleck things he'd been reading. He just looked at me, and I could see a tear quivering in the lad's eyes as he said, 'I see how you mean, now, and I want to say, friend, that I'm going to accept Jesus Christ as my lord and master!'

"Oh, yes, yes, yes, how beautiful it is, the golden glory of God's Love! Do you not *feel* it? I mean that! I don't mean just a snuffling, lazy, mechanical acceptance, but a passionate—"

V

He had them!

It had been fun to watch the old fanatics, who had objected to the singing of Dixie, come under the spell and admit his power. He had preached straight at one of them after another; he had conquered them all.

At the end they shook hands even more warmly than in the morning.

Cleo stood back, hypnotized. When he came to her she intoned, her eyes unseeing, "Oh, Reverend Gantry, this is the greatest day our old church has ever known!"

"Did you like what I said of Love?"

"Oh . . . *Love* . . . yes!"

She spoke as one asleep; she seemed not to know that he was holding her hand, softly; she walked out of the church beside him, unspeaking, and of her tranced holiness he felt a little awe.

VI

In his attention to business, Elmer had not given especial heed to the collections. It had not been carelessness, for he knew his technique as a Professional Good Man. But the first day, he felt, he ought to establish himself as a spiritual leader, and when they all understood that, he would see to it that they paid suitably for the spiritual leadership. Was not the Laborer worthy of his Hire?

VII

The reception to welcome Elmer was held the next Tuesday evening in the basement of the church. From seven-thirty, when they met, till a quarter of eight, he was busy with a prodigious amount of hand-shaking.

They told him he was very eloquent, very spiritual. He could see Cleo's pride at their welcome. She had the chance to whisper, "Do you realize how much it means? Mostly they aren't anything like so welcoming to a new preacher. Oh, I am so glad!"

Brother Benham called them to order, in the basement, and Sister Kilween sang "The Holy City" as a solo. It was pretty bad. Brother Benham in a short hesitating talk said they had been delighted by Brother Gantry's sermons. Brother Gantry in a long and gushing talk said that he was delighted by Brother Benham, the other Benhams, the rest of the congregation, Banjo Crossing, Banjo County, the United States of America, Bishop Toomis, and the Methodist Episcopal Church (North) in all its departments.

Cleo concluded the celebration with a piano solo, and there was a great deal more of hand-shaking. It seemed to be the rule that whoever came or was pushed within reach of the pastor, no matter how many times during the evening, should attack his hand each time.

And they had cake and homemade ice cream.

It was very dull and, to Elmer, very grateful. He felt accepted, secure, and ready to begin his work.

VIII

He had plans for the Wednesday evening prayer-meeting. He knew what a prayer-meeting in Banjo Crossing would be like. They would drone a couple of hymns and the faithful, half a dozen of them, always using the same words, would pop up and mumble, "Oh, I thank the Lord that he has revealed himself to me and has shown me the error of my ways and oh that those who have not seen his light and whose hearts are heavy with sin may turn to him this evening while they still have life and breath"—which they never did. And the sullenly unhappy woman in the faded jacket, at the back, would demand, "I want the prayers of the congregation to save my husband from the sins of smoking and drinking."

"I may not," Elmer meditated, "be as swell a scholar as old Toomis, but I can invent a lot of stunts and everything to wake the church up and attract the crowds, and that's worth a whole lot more than all this yowling about the prophets and theology!"

He began his "stunts" with that first prayer-meeting.

He suggested, "I know a lot of us want to give testimony, but sometimes it's hard to think of new ways of saying things, and let me suggest something new. Let's give our testimony by picking out hymns that express just how we feel about the dear Savior and his help. Then we can all join together in the gladsome testimony."

It went over.

"That's a fine fellow, that new Methodist preacher," said the villagers that week.

They were shy enough, and awkward and apparently indifferent, but in a friendly way they were spying on him, equally ready to praise him as a neighbor or snicker at him as a fool.

"Yes," they said; "a fine fellow, and smart's a whip, and mighty eloquent, and a real husky *man*. Looks you right straight in the eye. Only thing that bothers me— He's too good to stay here with us. And if he is so good, why'd they ever send him here in the first place? What's wrong with him? Boozer, d'ye think?"

Elmer, who knew his Paris, Kansas, his Gritzmacher Springs, had guessed that precisely these would be the opinions, and he took care, as he handshook his way from store to store, house to house, to explain that for years he had been out in the evangelistic field, and that by advice of his old and true friend, Bishop Toomis, he was taking this year in a smaller garden-patch to rest up for his labors to come.

He was assiduous, but careful, in his pastoral calls on the women. He praised their gingerbread, Morris chairs, and souvenirs of Niagara, and their children's school-exercise books. He became friendly, as friendly as he could be to any male, with the village doctor, the village homeopath, the lawyer, the station-agent, and all the staff at Benham's store.

But he saw that if he was to take the position suitable to him in the realm of religion, he must study, he must gather several more ideas and ever so many new words, to be put together for the enlightenment of the generation.

IX

His duties at Banjo Crossing were not violent, and hour after hour, in his quiet chamber at the residence of the Widow Clark, he gave himself trustingly to scholarship.

He continued his theological studies; he read all the sermons by Beecher, Brooks, and Chapman; he read three chapters of the Bible daily; and he got clear through the letter G in the Bible dictionary. Especially he studied the Methodist Discipline, in preparation for his appearance before the Annual Conference Board of Examiners as a candidate for full conference membership—full ministerhood.

The Discipline, which is a combination of Methodist prayer-book and by-laws, was not always exciting. Elmer felt a lack of sermon-material and spiritual quickening in the paragraph:

The concurrent recommendation of two-thirds of all the members of the several Annual Conferences present and voting, and of two-thirds of all the members of the Lay Electoral Conferences present and voting, shall suffice to authorize the next ensuing General Conference by a two-thirds vote to alter or amend any of the provisions of this Constitution excepting Article X, § 1; and also, whenever such alteration or amendment shall have been first recommended by a General Conference by a two-thirds vote, then so soon as two-thirds of all the members of the several Annual Conferences present and voting, and two-thirds of all the members of the Lay Electoral Conferences present and voting, shall have concurred therein, such alteration or amendment shall take effect; and the result of the vote shall be announced by the General Superintendents.

He liked better, from the Articles of Religion in the Discipline:

The offering of Christ, once made, is that perfect redemption, propitiation, and satisfaction for all the sins of the whole world, both original and actual; and there is none other satisfaction for sin but that alone. Wherefore the sacrifice of masses, in the which it is commonly said that the priest doth offer Christ for the quick and the dead, to have remission of pain or guilt, is a blasphemous fable and dangerous deceit.

He wasn't altogether certain what it meant, but it had such a fine uplifting roll. "Blasphemous fable and dangerous deceit." Fine!

He informed his edified congregation the next Sunday that the infallibility of the Pope was "a blasphemous fable and a dangerous deceit," and they almost jumped.

He had much edification from these "Rules for a Preacher's Conduct" in the Discipline:

> Be Serious. Let your motto be, "Holiness to the Lord." Avoid all lightness, jesting, and foolish talking. Converse sparingly and conduct yourself prudently with women. . . . Tell every one under your care what you think wrong in his conduct and temper, and that lovingly and plainly, as soon as may be; else it will fester in your heart.

> As a general method of employing our time we advise you, 1. As often as possible to rise at four. 2. From four to five in the morning and from five to six in the evening to meditate, pray, and read the Scriptures with notes.

> Extirpate out of our Church buying or selling goods which have not paid the duty laid upon them by government. . . . Extirpate bribery—receiving anything, directly or indirectly—for voting at any election.

Elmer became a model in all these departments except, perhaps, avoiding lightness and jesting; conducting himself in complete prudence with women; telling every one under his care what he thought wrong with them—that would have taken all his spare time; arising at four; and extirpating sellers of smuggled goods.

For his grades, to be examined by the Annual Conference, he wrote to Dean Trosper at Mizpah. He explained to the dean that he had seen a great new light, that he had worked with Sister Falconer, but that it had been the early influence of Dean Trosper which, working somewhat slowly, had led him to his present perfection.

He received the grades, with a letter in which the dean observed:

"I hope you will not overwork your new zeal for righteousness. It might be hard on folks. I seem to recall a tendency in you to overdo a lot of things. As a Baptist, let me congratulate the Methodists on having you. If you really do mean all you say about your present state of grace—well, don't let that keep you from going right on praying. There may still be virtues for you to acquire."

"Well, by God!" raged the misjudged saint, and, "Oh, rats, what's the odds! Got the credentials, anyway, and he says I can get my B.D. by passing an examination. Trouble with old Trosper is he's one of these smart alecks. T' hell with him!"

X

Along with his theological and ecclesiastical researches, Elmer applied himself to more worldly literature. He borrowed books from Cleo and from the tiny village library, housed in the public school; and on his occasional trips to Sparta, the nearest sizable city, he even bought a volume or two, when he could find good editions secondhand.

He began with Browning.

He had heard a lot about Browning. He had heard that he was a stylish poet and an inspiring thinker. But personally he did not find that he cared so much for Browning. There were so many lines that he had to read three or four times before they made sense, and there was so much stuff about Italy and all those Wop countries.

But Browning did give him a number of new words for the notebook of polysyllables and phrases which he was to keep for years, and which was to secrete material for some of his most rotund public utterances. There has been preserved a page from it:

incinerate—burn up

Merovingian—French tribe bout A.D. 500

rem Golgotha was scene crucifixn

Leigh Hunt—poet—1840—n.g.

lupin—blue flower

defeasance—making nix

chanson (pro. Shan-song)—French kind of song

Rem: Man worth while is m. who can smile when ev thing goes dead wrong

Sermon on man that says other planets inhabited—nix. cause Bible says o of Xt trying to save THEM.

Tennyson, Elmer found more elevating than Browning. He liked "Maud"—she resembled Cleo, only not so friendly; and he delighted in the homicides and morality of "Idylls of the King." He tried Fitzgerald's Omar, which had been recommended by the literary set at Terwillinger, and he made a discovery which he thought of communicating through the press.

He had heard it said that Omar was non-religious, but when he read:

> Myself when young did eagerly frequent
> Doctor and Saint, and heard great argument
> About it and about: but evermore
> Came out by the same door wherein I went,

he perceived that in this quatrain Omar obviously meant that though teachers might do a whole lot of arguing, Omar himself stuck to his belief in Jesus.

In Dickens Elmer had a revelation.

He had not known that any literature published previous to the *Saturday Evening Post* could be thrilling. He did not care so much for the humor—it seemed to him that Mr. Dickens was vulgar and almost immoral when he got Pickwick drunk and caused Mantalini to contemplate suicide—but he loved the sentiment. When Paul Dombey died, Elmer could have wept; when Miss Nickleby protected her virtue against Sir Mulberry Hawk, Elmer would have liked to have been there, both as a parson and as an athlete, to save her from that accursed society man, so typical of his class in debauching youth and innocence.

"Yes, sir, you bet, that's great stuff!" exulted Elmer. "There's a writer that goes right down to the depths of human nature. Great stuff. I'll preach on him when I get these hicks educated up to literary sermons."

But his artistic pursuits could not be all play. He had to master philosophy as well; and he plunged into Carlyle and Elbert Hubbard. He terminated the first plunge, very icy, with haste; but in the biographies by Mr. Hubbard, at that time dominating America, Elmer found inspiration. He learned that Rockefeller had not come to be head of Standard Oil by chance, but by labor, genuis, and early Baptist training. He learned that there are sermons in stones, edification in farmers, beatitude in bankers, and style in adjectives.

Elmer, who had always lived as publicly as a sparrow, could not endure keeping his literary treasures to himself. But for once Cleo Benham was not an adequate mate. He felt that she had read more of such belles-lettres as "The Message to Garcia" than even himself, so his companion in artistic adventure was Clyde Tippey, the Reverend Clyde Tippey, pastor of the United Brethren Church of Banjo Crossing.

Clyde was not, like Elmer, educated. He had left high school after his second year, and since then he had had only one year in a United Brethren seminary. Elmer didn't think much, he decided, of all this associating and fellowshiping with a lot of rival preachers—it was his job, wasn't it, to get their parishioners away from them? But it was an ecstasy to have, for once, a cleric to whom he could talk down.

He called frequently on the Reverend Mr. Tippey in the modest cottage which (at the age of twenty-six) Clyde occupied with his fat wife and four children. Mr. Tippey had pale blue eyes and he wore a fourteen-and-a-half collar encircling a thirteen neck.

"Clyde," crowed Elmer, "if you're going to reach the greatest number and not merely satisfy their spiritual needs but give 'em a rich, full, joyous life, you gotta explain great literature to 'em."

"Yes. Maybe that's so. Haven't had time to read much, but I guess there's lot of fine lessons to be learned out of literature," said the Reverend Mr. Tippey.

"*Is* there! Say, listen to this! From Longfellow. The poet.

> Life is real! Life is earnest!
> And the grave is not its goal,

and this—just get the dandy swing to it:

> Lives of great men all remind us
> We can make our lives sublime,
> And, departing, leave behind us
> Footprints on the sands of time.

I read that way back in school-reader, but I never had anybody to show me what it meant, like I'm going to do with my congregation. Just think! 'The grave is NOT its goal!' Why, say, Longfellow is just as much of a preacher as you or I are! Eh?"

"Yes, that's so. I'll have to read some of his poetry. Could you lend me the book?"

"You bet I will, Clyde! Be a fine thing for you. A young preacher like you has got to remember, if you'll allow an older hand to say so, that our education isn't finished when we start preaching. We got to go on enlarging our mental horizons. See how I mean? Now I'm going to start you off reading 'David Copperfield.' Say, that's full of fine passages. There's this scene where— This David, he had an aunt that everybody thought she was simply an old crab, but the poor little fellow, his father-in-law— I hope it won't shock you to hear a preacher say it, but he was an old son of a gun, that's what he was, and he treated David terribly, simply terribly, and David ran away, and found his aunt's house, and then it proved she was fine and dandy to him! Say, 'll just make the tears come to your eyes, the place where he finds her house and she don't recognize him and he tells her who he is, and then she kneels right down beside him— And shows how none of us are justified in thinking other folks are mean just because we don't understand 'em. You bet! Yes, sir. 'David Copperfield.' You sure can't go wrong reading that book!"

"'David Copperfield.' I've heard the name. It's mighty nice of you to come and tell me about it, brother."

"Oh, that's nothing, nothing at all! Mighty glad to help you in any way I can, Clyde."

Elmer's success as a literary and moral evangel to Mr. Clyde Tippey sent him back to his excavations with new fervor. He would lead the world not only to virtue but to beauty.

Considering everything, Longfellow seemed the best news to carry to this surprised and waiting world, and Elmer managed to get through many, many pages, solemnly marking the passages which he was willing to sanction, and which did not mention wine.

> Ah, nothing is too late
> Till the tired heart shall cease to palpitate.
> Cato learned Greek at eighty; Sophocles
> Wrote his grand Œdipus, and Simonides
> Bore off the prize of verse from his compeers,
> When each had numbered more than fourscore years.

Elmer did not, perhaps, know very much about Simonides, but with these instructive lines he was able to decorate a sermon in each of the pulpits he was henceforth to hold.

He worked his way with equal triumph through James Russell Lowell, Whittier, and Ella Wheeler Wilcox. He gave up Kipling because he found that he really enjoyed reading Kipling, and concluded that he could not be a good poet. But he was magnificent in discovering Robert Burns.

Then he collided with Josiah Royce.

XI

Bishop Wesley R. Toomis had suggested to Elmer that he ought to read philosophy, and he had recommended Royce. He himself, he said, hadn't been able to give so much time to Royce as he would have liked, but he knew that here was a splendid field for any intellectual adventurer. So Elmer came back from Sparta with the two volumes of Royce's "The World and the Individual," and two new detective stories.

He would skip pleasantly but beneficially through Royce, then pick up whatever ideas he might find in all these other philosophers he had heard mentioned: James and Kant and Bergson and who was that fellow with the funny name—Spinoza?

He opened the first volume of Royce confidently, and drew back in horror.

He had a nice, long, free afternoon in which to become wise. He labored on. He read each sentence six times. His mouth drooped pathetically. It did not seem fair that a Christian knight who was willing to give his time to listening to people's ideas should be treated like this. He sighed, and read the first paragraph again. He sighed, and the book dropped into his lap.

He looked about. On the stand beside him was one of the detective stories. He reached for it. It began as all proper detective stories should begin—with the tap-room of the Cat and Fiddle Inn, on a stormy night when gusts of rain beat against the small ancient casement, but within all was bright and warm; the Turkey-red curtains shone in the firelight, and the burnished handles of the beer-pump—

An hour later Elmer had reached the place where the Scotland Yard Inspector was attacked from the furze-bush by the maniac. He excitedly crossed his legs, and Royce fell to the floor and lay there.

But he kept at it. In less than three months he had reached page fifty-one of the first volume of Royce. Then he bogged down in a footnote:

The scholastic text-books, namely, as for instance the *Disputations of Suarez*, employ our terms much as follows. *Being* (*ens*), taken quite in the abstract, such writers said, is a word that shall equally apply *both* to the *what* and to the *that*. Thus if I speak of the being of a man, I may, according to this usage, mean either the ideal nature of a man, apart from man's existence, or the existence of a man. The term "Being" is so far indifferent to both of the sharply sundered senses. In this sense Being may be viewed as of two sorts. As the *what* it means the Essence of things, or the *Esse Essentiæ*. In this sense, by the Being of a man, you mean simply the definition of what a man as an idea means. As the *that*, Being means the Existent Being, or *Esse Existentiæ*. The *Esse Existentiæ* of a man, or its existent being, would be what it would possess only if it existed. And so the scholastic writers in question always have to point out whether by the term Ens, or Being, they in any particular passage are referring to the *what* or to the *that*, to the Esse Essentiæ or to the Existentiæ.

The Reverend Elmer Gantry drew his breath, quietly closed the book, and shouted, *"Oh, shut up!"*

He never again read any philosophy more abstruse than that of Wallace D. Wattles or Edward Bok.

XII

He did not neglect his not very arduous duties. He went fishing—which gained him credit among the males. He procured a dog, also a sound, manly thing to do, and though he occasionally kicked the dog in the country, he was clamorously affectionate with it in town. He went up to Sparta now and then to buy books, attend the movies, and sneak into theaters; and though he was tempted by other diversions even less approved by the Methodist Discipline, he really did make an effort to keep from falling.

By enthusiasm and brass, he raised most of the church debt, and made agitation for a new carpet. He risked condemnation by having a cornet solo right in church one

Sunday evening. He kept himself from paying any attention, except for rollickingly kissing her once or twice, to the fourteen-year-old daughter of his landlady. He was, in fact, full of good works and clerical exemplariness.

But the focus of his life now was Cleo Benham.

Chapter XXI

WITH women Elmer had always considered himself what he called a "quick worker," but the properties of the ministry, the delighted suspicion with which the gossips watched a preacher who went courting, hindered his progress with Cleo. He could not, like the young blades in town, walk with Cleo up the railroad tracks or through the willow-shaded pasture by Banjo River. He could hear ten thousand Methodist elders croaking, "Avoid the vurry *appearance* of evil."

He knew that she was in love with him—had been ever since she had first seen him, a devout yet manly leader, standing by the pulpit in the late light of summer afternoon. He was certain that she would surrender to him whenever he should demand it. He was certain that she had every desirable quality. And yet—

Oh, somehow, she did not stir him. Was he afraid of being married and settled and monogamic? Was it simply that she needed awakening? How could he awaken her when her father was always in the way?

Whenever he called on her, old Benham insisted on staying in the parlor. He was, strictly outside of business hours, an amateur of religion, fond of talking about it. Just as Elmer, shielded by the piano, was ready to press Cleo's hand, Benham would lumber up and twang, "What do you think, Brother? Do you believe salvation comes by faith or works?"

Elmer made it all clear—muttering to himself, "Well, you, you old devil, with that cut-throat store of yours, you better get into Heaven on faith, for God knows you'll never do it on works!"

And when Elmer was about to slip out to the kitchen with her to make lemonade, Benham held him by demanding, "What do you think of John Wesley's doctrine of perfection?"

"Oh, it's absolutely sound and proven," admitted Elmer, wondering what the devil Mr. Wesley's doctrine of perfection might be.

It is possible that the presence of the elder Benhams, preventing too close a communion with Cleo, kept Elmer from understanding what it meant that he should not greatly have longed to embrace her. He translated his lack of urgency into virtue; and went about assuring himself that he was indeed a reformed and perfected character . . . and so went home and hung about the kitchen, chattering with little Jane Clark in pastoral jokiness.

Even when he was alone with Cleo, when she drove him in the proud Benham motor for calls in the country, even while he was volubly telling himself how handsome she was, he was never quite natural with her.

II

He called on an evening of late November, and both her parents were out, attending Eastern Star. She looked dreary and red-eyed. He crowed benevolently while they stood at the parlor door, "Why, Sister Cleo, what's the matter? You look kind of sad."

"Oh, it's nothing—"

"Come on now! Tell me! I'll pray for you, or beat somebody up, whichever you prefer!"

"Oh, I don't think you ought to joke about— Anyway, it's really nothing."

She was staring at the floor. He felt buoyant and dominating, so delightfully stronger than she. He lifted her chin with his forefinger, demanding, "Look up at me now!"

In her naked eyes there was such shameful, shameless longing for him that he was drawn. He could not but slip his arm around her, and she dropped her head on his shoulder, weeping, all her pride gone from her. He was so exalted by the realization of his own power that he took it for passion, and suddenly he was kissing her, conscious of the pale fineness of her skin, her flattering yielding to him; suddenly he was blurting, "I've loved you, oh, terrible, ever since the first second I saw you!"

As she sat on his knee, as she drooped against him unresisting, he was certain that she was very beautiful, altogether desirable.

The Benhams came home—Mrs. Benham to cry happily over the engagement, and Mr. Benham to indulge in a deal of cordial back-slapping, and such jests as, "Well, by golly, now I'm going to have a real live preacher in the family, guess I'll have to be so doggone honest that the store won't hardly pay!"

III

His mother came on from Kansas for the wedding, in January. Her happiness in seeing him in his pulpit, in seeing the beauty and purity of Cleo—and the prosperity of Cleo's father—was such that she forgot her long dragging sorrow in his many disloyalties to the God she had given him, in his having deserted the Baptist sanctuary for the dubious, the almost agnostic liberalisms of the Methodists.

With his mother present, with Cleo going about roused to a rosy excitement, with Mrs. Benham mothering everybody and frantically cooking, with Mr. Benham taking him out to the back-porch and presenting him with a check for five thousand dollars, Elmer had the feeling of possessing a family, of being rooted and solid and secure.

For the wedding there were scores of cocoanut cakes and hundreds of orange blossoms, roses from a real city florist in Sparta, new photographs for the family album, a tub of strictly temperance punch and beautiful but modest lingerie for Cleo. It was tremendous. But Elmer was a little saddened by the fact that there was no one whom he wanted for best man; no one who had been his friend since Jim Lefferts.

He asked Ray Faucett, butter-maker at the creamery and choir-singer in the church, and the village was flattered that out of the hundreds of intimates Elmer must have in the great world outside, he should have chosen one of their own boys.

They were married, during a half blizzard, by the district superintendent. They took the train for Zenith, to stop overnight on their way to Chicago.

Not till he was on the train, the shouting and the rice-showers over, did Elmer gasp to himself, looking at Cleo's rather unchanging smile, "Oh, good God, I've gone and tied myself up, and I never can have any fun again!"

But he was very manly, gentlemanly in fact; he concealed his distaste for her and entertained her with an account of the beauties of Longfellow.

IV

Cleo looked tired, and toward the end of the journey, in the winter evening, with the gale desolate, she seemed scarce to be listening to his observations on graded Sunday School lessons, the treatment of corns, his triumphs at Sister Falconer's meetings, and the inferiority of the Reverend Clyde Tippey.

"Well, you might pay a *little* attention to me, anyway!" he snarled.

"Oh, I'm sorry! I really was paying attention. I'm just tired—all the preparations for the wedding and everything." She looked at him beseechingly. "Oh, Elmer, you must take care of me! I'm giving myself to you entirely—oh, completely."

"Huh! So you look at it as a *sacrifice* to marry me, do you!"

"Oh, no, I *didn't* mean it that way—"

"And I suppose you think I don't intend to take care of you! Sure! Prob'ly I stay out late nights and play cards and gamble and drink and run around after women! Of course! I'm not a minister of the gospel—I'm a saloon-keeper!"

"Oh, dear, dear, dear, oh, my dearest, I didn't mean to hurt you! I just meant— You're so strong and big, and I'm—oh, of course I'm not a tiny little thing, but I haven't got your strength."

He enjoyed feeling injured, but he was warning himself, "Shut up, you chump! You'll never educate her to make love if you go bawling her out."

He magnanimously comforted her: "Oh, I know. Of course, you poor dear. Fool thing anyway, your mother having this big wedding, and all the eats and the relatives coming in and everything."

And with all this, she still seemed distressed.

But he patted her hand, and talked about the cottage they were going to furnish in Banjo Crossing; and as he thought of the approaching Zenith, of their room at the O'Hearn House (there was no necessity for a whole suite, as formerly, when he had had to impress his Prosperity pupils), he became more ardent, whispered to her that she was beautiful, stroked her arm till she trembled.

V

The bell-boy had scarcely closed the door of their room, with its double bed, when he had seized her, torn off her overcoat, with its snow-wet collar, and hurled it on the floor. He kissed her throat. When he had loosened his clasp, she retreated, the back of her hand fearfully at her lips, her voice terrified as she begged, "Oh, don't! Not now! I'm afraid!"

"That's damned nonsense!" he raged, stalking her as she backed away.

"Oh, no, please!"

"Say, what the devil do you think marriage is?"

"Oh, I've never heard you curse before!"

"My God, I wouldn't, if you didn't act so's it'd try the patience of a saint on a monument!" He controlled himself. "Now, now, now! I'm sorry! Guess I'm kind of tired, too. There, there, little girl. Didn't mean to scare you. Excuse me. Just showed I was crazy in love with you, don't you see?"

To his broad and apostolic smirk she responded with a weak smile, and he seized her again, laid his thick hand on her breast. Between his long embraces, though his anger at her limpness was growing, he sought to encourage her by shouting, "Come on now, Clee, show some spunk!"

She did not forbid him again; she was merely a pale acquiescence—pale save when she flushed unhappily as he made fun of the old-fashioned, long-sleeved nightgown which she timidly put on in the indifferent privacy of the bathroom.

"Gee, you might as well wear a gunny-sack!" he roared, holding out his arms. She tried to look confident as she slowly moved toward him. She did not succeed.

"Fellow *ought* to be brutal, for her own sake," he told himself, and seized her shoulders.

When he awoke beside her and found her crying, he really did have to speak up to her.

"You look here now! The fact you're a preacher's wife doesn't keep you from being human! You're a fine one to teach brats in Sunday School!" he said, and many other strong spirited things, while she wept, her hair disordered round her meek face, which he hated.

VI

The discovery that Cleo would never be a lively lover threw him the more into ambition when they had returned to Banjo Crossing.

Cleo, though she was unceasingly bewildered by his furies, found something of happiness in furnishing their small house, arranging his books, admiring his pulpit eloquence, and in receiving, as the Pastor's Wife, homage even from her old friends. He was able to forget her, and all his thought went to his holy climbing. He was eager for the Annual Conference, in spring; he had to get on, to a larger town, a larger church.

He was bored by Banjo Crossing. The life of a small-town preacher, prevented from engaging even in the bucolic pleasures, is rather duller than that of a watchman at a railroad-crossing.

Elmer hadn't, actually, enough to do. Though later, in "institutional churches" he was to be as hustling as any other business man, now he had not over twenty hours a week of real activity. There were four meetings every Sunday, if he attended Sunday School and Epworth League as well as church; there was prayer-meeting on Wednesday evening, choir practise on Friday, the Ladies' Aid and the Missionary Society every fortnight or so, and perhaps once a fortnight a wedding, a funeral. Pastoral calls took not over six hours a week. With the aid of his reference books, he could prepare his two sermons in five hours—and on weeks when he felt lazy, or the fishing was good, that was three hours more than he actually took.

In the austerities of the library Elmer was indolent, but he did like to rush about, meet people, make a show of accomplishment. It wasn't possible to accomplish much in Banjo. The good villagers were content with Sunday and Wednesday-evening piety.

But he did begin to write advertisements for his weekly services—the inception of that salesmanship of salvation which was to make him known and respected in every advertising club and forward-looking church in the country. The readers of notices to the effect that services would be held, as usual, at the *Banjo Valley Pioneer* were startled to find among the the Presbyterian Church, the Disciples Church, the United Brethren Church, the Baptist Church, this advertisement:

WAKE UP, MR. DEVIL!

If old Satan were as lazy as some would-be Christians in this burg, we'd all be safe. But he isn't! Come out next Sunday, 10:30 A.M. and hear a red-blooded sermon by Rev. Gantry on

WOULD JESUS PLAY POKER?
M. E. Church

He improved his typewriting, and that was a fine thing to do. The Reverend Elmer Gantry's powerful nature had been cramped by the slow use of a pen; it needed the gallop of the keys; and from his typewriter were increasingly to come floods of new moral and social gospels.

In February he held two weeks' of intensive evangelistic meetings. He had in a traveling missioner, who wept, and his wife, who sang. Neither of them, Elmer chuckled privily, could compare with himself, who had worked with Sharon Falconer. But they were new to Banjo Crossing, and he saw to it that it was himself who at the climax of hysteria charged down into the frightened mob and warned them that unless they came up and knelt in subjection, they might be snatched to hell before breakfast.

There were twelve additions to the church, and five renewals of faith on the part of backsliders, and Elmer was able to have published in the *Western Christian Advocate* a note which carried his credit through all the circles of the saints:

The church at Banjo Crossing has had a remarkable and stirring revival under Brother T. R. Feesels and Sister Feesels, the singing evangelist, assisted by the local pastor, Reverend Gantry, who was himself formerly in evangelistic work as assistant to the late Sharon Falconer. A great outpouring of the spirit and far-reaching results are announced, with many uniting with the church.

He also, after letting the town know how much it added to his burdens, revived and every week for two weeks personally supervised a Junior Epworth League—the juvenile department of that admirable association of young people whose purpose is, it has itself announced, to "take the *wreck* out of recreation and make it re-creation."

He had a note from Bishop Toomis hinting that the bishop had most gratifying reports from the district superintendent about Elmer's "diligent and genuinely creative efforts" and hinting that at the coming Annual Conference, Elmer would be shifted to a considerably larger church.

"Fine!" glowed Elmer. "Gosh, I'll be glad to get away. These rubes here get about as much out of high-class religion, like I give them, as a fleet of mules!"

VII

Ishuah Rogers was dead, and they were holding his funeral at the Methodist Church. As farmer, as store-keeper, as post-master, he had lived all his seventy-nine years in Banjo Crossing.

Old J. F. Whittlesey was shaken by Ishuah's death. They had been boys together, young men together, neighbors on the farm, and in his last years, when Ishuah was nearly blind and living with his daughter Jenny, J. F. Whittlesey had come into town every day to spend hours sitting with him on the porch, wrangling over Blaine and Grover Cleveland. Whittlesey hadn't another friend left alive. To drive past Jenny's now and not see old Ishuah made the world empty.

He was in the front row at the church; he could see his friend's face in the open coffin. All of Ishuah's meanness and fussiness and care was wiped out; there was only the dumb nobility with which he had faced blizzard and August heat, labor and sorrow; only the heroic thing Whittlesey had loved in him.

And he would not see Ishuah again, ever.

He listened to Elmer, who, his eyes almost filled at the drama of a church full of people mourning their old friend, lulled them with Revelation's triumphant song:

These are they that come out of the great tribulation, and they washed their robes, and made them white in the blood of the Lamb. Therefore are they before the throne of God; and they serve him day and night in his temple; and he that sitteth on the throne shall spread his tabernacle over them. They shall hunger no more, neither thirst any more; neither shall the sun strike upon them, nor any heat: for the Lamb that is in the midst of the throne shall be their shepherd, and shall guide them unto fountains of waters of life: and God shall wipe away every tear from their eyes.

They sang "O God, Our Help in Ages Past," and Elmer led the singing, while old Whittlesey tried to pipe up with them.

They filed past the coffin. When Whittlesey had this last moment's glimpse of Ishuah's sunken face, his dry eyes were blind, and he staggered.

Elmer caught him with his great arms, and whispered, "He has gone to his glory, to his great reward! Don't let's sorrow for him!"

In Elmer's confident strength old Whittlesey found reassurance. He clung to him, muttering, "God bless you, Brother," before he hobbled out.

VIII

"You were wonderful at the funeral today! I've never seen you so sure of immortality," worshiped Cleo, as they walked home.

"Yuh, but they don't appreciate it—not even when I said about how this old fellow was a sure-enough hero. We got to get on to some burg where I'll have a chance."

"Don't you think God's in Banjo Crossing as much as in a city?"

"Oh, now, Cleo, don't go and get religious on me! You simply can't understand how it takes it out of a fellow to do a funeral right and send 'em all home solaced. You may find God here, but you don't find the salaries!"

He was not angry with Cleo now, nor bullying. In these two months he had become indifferent to her; indifferent enough to stop hating her and to admire her conduct of the Sunday School, her tactful handling of the good sisters of the church when they came snooping to the parsonage.

"I think I'll take a little walk," he muttered when they reached home.

He came to the Widow Clark's house, where he had lived as bachelor.

Jane was out in the yard, the March breeze molding her skirt about her; rosy face darker and eyes more soft as she saw the pastor hailing her, magnificently raising his hat.

She fluttered toward him.

"You folks ever miss me? Guess you're glad to get rid of the poor old preacher that was always cluttering up the house!"

"We miss you awfully!"

He felt his whole body yearning toward her. Hurriedly he left her, and wished he hadn't left her, and hastened to get himself far from the danger to his respectability. He hated Cleo again now, in an injured, puzzled way.

"I think I'll sneak up to Sparta this week," he fumed, then: "No! Conference coming in ten days; can't take any chances till after that."

IX

The Annual Conference, held in Sparta, late in March. The high time of the year, when the Methodist preachers of half a dozen districts met together for prayer and rejoicing, to hear of the progress of the Kingdom and incidentally to learn whether they were to have better jobs this coming year.

The bishop presiding—Wesley R. Toomis, himself—with his district superintendents, grave and bustling.

The preachers, trying to look as though prospective higher salaries were unworthy their attention.

Between meetings they milled about in the large auditorium of the Preston Memorial Methodist Church: visiting laymen and nearly three hundred ministers.

Veteran country parsons, whiskered and spectacled, rusty-coated and stooped, still serving two country churches, or three or four; driving their fifty miles a week; content for reading with the Scriptures and the weekly *Advocate*.

New-fledged country preachers, their large hands still calloused from plow-handle and reins, content for learning with two years of high school, content with the Old Testament for history and geology.

The preachers of the larger towns; most of them hard to recognize as clerics, in their neat business suits and modest four-in-hands; frightfully cordial one to another; perhaps a quarter of them known as modernists and given to reading popular manuals of biology and psychology; the other three-quarters still devoted to banging the pulpit apropos of Genesis.

But moving through these masses, easily noticeable, the inevitable successes: the district superintendents, the pastors of large city congregations, the conceivable candidates for college presidencies, mission-boards, boards of publication, bishoprics.

They were not all of them leonine and actor-like, these staff officers. No few were gaunt, or small, wiry, spectacled, and earnest; but they were all admirable politicians, long in memory of names, quick to find flattering answers. They believed that the Lord rules everything, but that it was only friendly to help him out; and that the enrollment of political allies helped almost as much as prayer in becoming known as suitable material for lucrative pastorates.

Among these leaders were the Savonarolas, gloomy fellows, viewing the progress of machine civilization with biliousness; capable of drawing thousands of auditors by their spicy but chaste denunciations of burglary, dancing, and show-windows filled with lingerie.

Then the renowned liberals, preachers who filled city tabernacles or churches in university towns by showing that skipping whatever seemed unreasonable in the Bible did not interfere with considering it all divinely inspired, and that there are large moral lessons in the paintings of Landseer and Rosa Bonheur.

Most notable among the aristocrats were a certain number of large, suave, deep-voiced, inescapably cordial clerical gentlemen who would have looked well in Shakespearean productions or as floor-walkers. And with them was presently to be found the Reverend Elmer Gantry.

He was a new-comer, he was merely hoping to have the Conference recognize his credentials and accept him as a member, and he had only a tiny church, yet from somewhere crept the rumor that he was a man to be watched, to be enrolled in one's own political machine; and he was called "Brother" by a pastor whose sacred rating was said to be not less than ten thousand a year. They observed him; they conversed with him not only on the sacraments but on automobiles and the use of pledge envelopes; and as they felt the warmth of his handshake, as they heard the amiable bim-bom of his voice, saw his manly eyes, untroubled by doubts or scruples, and noted that he wore his morning clothes as well as any spiritual magnate among them, they greeted him and sought him out and recognized him as a future captain of the hosts of the Almighty.

Cleo's graciousness added to his prestige.

For three whole days before bringing her up to the Conference, Elmer had gone out of his way to soothe her, flatter her, assure her that whatever misunderstandings they might have had, all was now a warm snugness of domestic bliss, so that she was eager, gently deferential to the wives of older pastors as she met them at receptions at hotels.

Her obvious admiration of Elmer convinced the better clerical politicians of his domestic safeness.

And they knew that he had been sent for by the bishop—oh, they knew it! Nothing that the bishop did in these critical days was not known. There were many among the middle-aged ministers who had become worried over prolonged stays in small towns, and who wanted to whisper to the bishop how well they would suit larger opportunities. (The list of appointments had already been made out by the bishop and his council, yet surely it could be changed a little—just the least bit.) But they could not get near him. Most of the time the bishop was kept hidden from them at the house of the president of Winnemac Wesleyan University.

But he sent for Elmer, and even called him by his first name.

"You see, Brother Elmer, I was right! The Methodist Church just suits you," said the bishop, his eyes bright under his formidable brows. "I am able to give you a larger church already. It wouldn't be cricket, as the English say—ah, England! how you will enjoy going there some time; you will find such a fruitful source of the broader type of sermons in travel; I know that you and your lovely bride—I've had the pleasure of having her pointed out to me—you will both know the joy and romance of travel one of these days. But as I was saying: I can give you a rather larger town this time, though it wouldn't be proper to tell you which one till I read the list of appointments to the Conference. And in the near future, if you continue as you have in your studies and attention to the needs of your flock and in your excellence of daily living, which the district superintendent has noted, why, you'll be due for a *much* larger field of service. God bless you!"

X

Elmer was examined by the Conference and readily admitted to membership.

Among the questions, from the Discipline, which he was able to answer with a hearty "yes" were these:

Are you going on to perfection?

Do you expect to be made perfect in love in this life?

Are you earnestly striving after it?

Are you resolved to devote yourself wholly to God and his work?

Have you considered the Rules for a Preacher, especially those relating to Diligence, to Punctuality, and to Doing the Work to which you are assigned?

Will you recommend fasting or diligence, both by precept and example?

It was, the Conference members said, one to another, a pleasure to examine a candidate who could answer the questions with such ringing certainty.

Celebrating his renunciation of all fleshy devices and pleasures by wolfing a steak, fried onions, fried potatoes, corn, three cups of coffee, and two slices of apple pie with ice cream, Elmer condescended to Cleo, "I went through a-whooping! Liked to of seen any of those poor boobs I was with in the seminary answer up like I did!"

XI

They listened to reports on collections for missions, on the creation of new schools and churches; they heard ever so many prayers; they were polite during what were known as "inspirational addresses" by the bishop and the Rev. Dr. S. Palmer Shootz. But they were waiting for the moment when the bishop should read the list of appointments.

They looked as blank as they could, but their nails creased their palms as the bishop rose. They tried to be loyal to their army, but this lean parson thought of the boy who was going to college, this worried-faced youngster thought of the operation for his wife, this aged campaigner whose voice had been failing wondered whether he would be kept on in his well-padded church.

The bishop's snappy voice popped:

Sparta District:

Albee Center, W. A. Vance

Ardmore, Abraham Mundon—

And Elmer listened with them, suddenly terrified.

What did the bishop mean by a "rather larger town"? Some horrible hole with twelve hundred people?

Then he startled and glowed, and his fellow priests nodded to him in congratulation, as the bishop read out "Rudd Center, Elmer Gantry."

For there were forty-one hundred people in Rudd Center; it was noted for good works and a large pop factory; and he was on his way to greatness, to inspiring the world and becoming a bishop.

Chapter XXII

A YEAR he spent in Rudd Center, three years in Vulcan, and two years in Sparta. As there were 4,100 people in Rudd Center, 47,000 in Vulcan, and 129,000 in Sparta, it may be seen that the Reverend Elmer Gantry was climbing swiftly in Christian influence and character.

In Rudd Center he passed his Mizpah final examinations and received his Bachelor of Divinity degree from the seminary; in Rudd Center he discovered the art of joining, which was later to enable him to meet the more enterprising and solid men of affairs—oculists and editors and manufacturers of bath-tubs—and enlist their practical genius in his crusades for spirituality.

He joined the Masons, the Odd Fellows, and the Maccabees. He made the Memorial Day address to the G.A.R., and he made the speech welcoming the local representative home from Congress after having won the poker championship of the House.

Vulcan was marked, aside from his labors for perfection, by the birth of his two children—Nat, in 1916, and Bernice, whom they called Bunny, in 1917—and by his ceasing to educate his wife in his ideals of amour.

It all blew up a month after the birth of Bunny.

Elmer had, that evening, been addressing the Rod and Gun Club dinner. He had pointed out that our Lord must have been in favor of Rods and Guns for, he said, "I want you boys to notice that the Master, when he picked out his first disciples, didn't select a couple of stoop-shouldered, pigeon-toed mollycoddles but a pair of first-class fishermen!"

He was excited to intoxication by their laughter.

Since Bunny's birth he had been sleeping in the guest-room, but now, walking airily, he tiptoed into Cleo's room at eleven, with that look of self-conscious innocence which passionless wives instantly catch and dread.

"Well, you sweet thing, it sure went off great! They all liked my spiel. Why, you poor lonely girl, shame you have to sleep all alone here, poor baby!" he said, stroking her shoulder as she sat propped against the pillows. "Guess I'll have to come sleep here tonight."

She breathed hard, tried to look resolute. "Please! Not yet!"

"What do you *mean*?"

"Please! I'm tired tonight. Just kiss me good night, and let me pop off to sleep."

"Meaning my attentions aren't welcome to Your Majesty!" He paced the floor. "Young woman, it's about time for a show-down! I've hinted at this before, but I've been as charitable and long-suffering as I could, but, by God, you've gotten away with too much, and then you try to pretend—'Just kiss me good night!' Sure! I'm to be a monk! I'm to be one of these milk-and-water husbands that's perfectly content to hang around the house and not give one little yip if his wife don't care for his method of hugging! Well, believe me, young woman, you got another guess coming, and if you think that just because I'm a preacher I'm a Willie-boy— You don't even make the slightest smallest effort to learn some passion, but just act like you had hard work putting up with me! Believe me, there's other women a lot better and prettier—yet, and more religious!—that haven't thought I was such a damn' pest to have around! I'm not going to stand— Never even making the slightest effort—"

"Oh, Elmer, I have! Honestly I have! If you'd only been more tender and patient with me at the very first, I might have learned—"

"Rats! All damned nonsense! Trouble with you is, you always were afraid to face hard facts! Well, I'm sick of it, young woman. You can go to the devil! This is the last time, believe me!"

He banged the door; he had satisfaction in hearing her sob that night; and he kept his vow about staying away from her, for almost a month. Presently he was keeping it altogether; it was a settled thing that they had separate bedrooms.

And all the while he was almost as confused, as wistful, as she was; and whenever he found a woman parishioner who was willing to comfort him, or whenever he was called on important but never explained affairs to Sparta, he had no bold swagger of satisfaction, but a guilt, an uneasiness of sin, which displayed itself in increasingly furious condemnation of the same sin from his pulpit.

"O God, if I could only have gone on with Sharon, I might have been a decent fellow," he mourned, in his sorrow sympathetic with all the world. But the day after, in the sanctuary, he would be salving that sorrow by raging, "And these dance-hall proprietors, these tempters of lovely innocent girls, whose doors open to the pit of death and horror, they shall have reward—they shall burn in uttermost hell—burn literally—BURN!—and for their suffering we shall have but joy that the Lord's justice has been resolutely done!"

II

Something like statewide fame began to cling about the Reverend Elmer Gantry during his two years in Sparta—1918 to 1920. In the spring of '18 he was one of the most courageous defenders of the Midwest against the imminent invasion of the Germans. He was a Four-Minute Man. He said violent things about atrocities, and sold Liberty Bonds hugely. He threatened to leave Sparta to its wickedness while he went out to "take care of our poor boys" as a chaplain, and he might have done so had the war lasted another year.

In Sparta, too, he crept from timidly sensational church advertisements to such blasts as must have shaken the Devil himself. Anyway, they brought six hundred delighted sinners to church every Sunday evening, and after one sermon on the horrors of booze, a saloon-keeper, slightly intoxicated, remarked "Whoop!" and put a fifty-dollar bill in the plate.

Not to this day, with all the advance in intellectual advertising, has there been seen a more arousing effort to sell salvation than Elmer's prose poem in the *Sparta World-Chronicle* on a Saturday in December, 1919:

WOULD YOU LIKE YOUR MOTHER TO GO BATHING WITHOUT STOCKINGS?

Do you believe in old-fashioned womanhood, that can love and laugh and still be the symbols of God's own righteousness, bringing a tear to the eye as one remembers their brooding tenderness? Would you like to see your own dear mammy indulging in mixed bathing or dancing that Hell's own fool monkeyshine, the one-step?

Reverend Elmer Gantry

will answer these questions and others next Sunday morning. Gantry shoots straight from the shoulder.

POPLAR AVENUE METHODIST CHURCH

Follow the crowd to the beautiful times
At the beautiful church with the beautiful chimes.

III

While he was in Sparta, national prohibition arrived, with its high-colored opportunities for pulpit-orators, and in Sparta he was inspired to his greatest political campaign.

The obviously respectable candidate for mayor of Sparta was a Christian Business Man, a Presbyterian who was a manufacturer of rubber overshoes. It is true that he was accused of owning the buildings in which were several of the worst brothels and blind tigers in the city, but it had amply been explained that the unfortunate gentleman had not been able to kick out his tenants, and that he gave practically all his receipts from the property to missionary work in China.

His opponent was a man in every way objectionable to Elmer's principles: a Jew, a radical who criticized the churches for not paying taxes, a sensational and publicity-seeking lawyer who took the cases of labor unions and negroes without fee. When he consulted them, Elmer's Official Board agreed that the Presbyterian was the only man to support. They pointed out that the trouble with the radical Jew was that he was not only a radical but a Jew.

Yet Elmer was not satisfied. He had, possibly, less objection to houses of ill fame than one would have judged from his pulpit utterances, and he certainly approved the Presbyterian's position that "we must not try dangerous experiments in government but adhere courageously to the proven merits and economies of the present administration." But talking with members of his congregation, Elmer found that the Plain People—and the plain, the very plain, people did make up such a large percentage of his flock—hated the Presbyterian and had a surprised admiration for the Jew.

"He's awful' kind to poor folks," said they.

Elmer had what he called a "hunch."

"All the swells are going to support this guy McGarry, but darned if I don't think the Yid'll win, and anybody that roots for him'll stand ace-high after the election," he reasoned.

He came out boisterously for the Jew. The newspapers squealed and the Presbyterians bellowed and the rabbis softly chuckled.

Not only from his pulpit but in scattered halls Elmer campaigned and thundered. He was smeared once with rotten eggs in a hall near the red-light district, and once an illicit booze-dealer tried to punch his nose, and that was a very happy time for Elmer.

The booze-dealer, a bulbous angry man, climbed up on the stage of the hall and swayed toward Elmer, weaving with his fists, rumbling, "You damn' lying gospel-shark, I'll show you—"

The forgotten star of the Terwillinger team leaped into life. He was calm as in a scrimmage. He strode over, calculatingly regarded the point of the bootlegger's jaw, and caught him on it, exact. He saw the man slumping down, but he did not stand looking; he swung back to the reading-stand and went on speaking. The whole audience rose, clamorous with applause, and Elmer Gantry had for a second become the most famous man in town.

The newspapers admitted that he was affecting the campaign, and one of them swung to his support. He was so strong on virtue and the purity of womanhood and the evils of liquor that to oppose him was to admit one's self a debauchee.

At the business meeting of his church there was a stirring squabble over his activities. When the leading trustee, a friend of the Presbyterian candidate, declared that he was going to resign unless Elmer stopped, an aged janitor shrieked, "And all the rest of us will resign unless the Reverend keeps it up!" There was gleeful and unseemly applause, and Elmer beamed.

The campaign grew so bellicose that reporters came up from the Zenith newspapers; one of them the renowned Bill Kingdom of the Zenith *Advocate-Times.* Elmer loved reporters. They quoted him on everything from the Bible in the schools to the Armenian mandate. He was careful not to call them "boys" but "gentlemen," not to slap them too often on the back; he kept excellent cigars for them; and he always said, "I'm afraid I can't talk to you as a preacher. I get too much of that on Sunday. I'm just speaking as an ordinary citizen who longs to have a clean city in which to bring up his kiddies."

Bill Kingdom almost liked him, and the story about "the crusading parson" which he sent up to the Zenith *Advocate-Times*—the Thunderer of the whole state of Winnemac—was run on the third page, with a photograph of Elmer thrusting out his fist as if to crush all the sensualists and malefactors in the world.

Sparta papers reprinted the story and spoke of it with reverence.

The Jew won the campaign.

And immediately after this—six months before the Annual Conference of 1920—Bishop Toomis sent for Elmer.

IV

"At first I was afraid," said the bishop, "you were making a great mistake in soiling yourself in this Sparta campaign. After all, it's our mission to preach the pure gospel and the saving blood of Jesus, and not to monkey with politics. But you've been so successful that I can forgive you, and the time has come— At the next Conference I shall be able to offer you at last a church here in Zenith, and a very large one, but with problems that call for heroic energy. It's the old Wellspring Church, down here on Stanley Avenue, corner of Dodsworth, in what we call 'Old Town.' It used to be the most fashionable and useful Methodist church in town, but the section has run down, and the membership has declined from something like fourteen hundred to about eight hundred, and under the present pastor—you know him—old Seriere, fine noble Christian gentleman, great soul, but a pretty rotten speaker—I don't guess they have more than a hundred or so at morning service. Shame, Elmer, wicked shame to see this great institution, meant for the quickening of such vast multitudes of souls, declining and, by thunder, not hardly giving a cent for missions! I wonder if you could revive it? Go look it over, and the neighborhood, and let me know what you think. Or whether you'd rather stay on in Sparta. You'll get less salary at Wellspring than you're getting in Sparta—four thousand, isn't it?—but if you build up the church, guess the Official Board will properly remunerate your labors."

A church in Zenith! Elmer would—almost—have taken it with no salary whatever. He could see his Doctor of Divinity degree at hand, his bishopric or college presidency or fabulous pulpit in New York.

He found the Wellspring M.E. Church a hideous graystone hulk with gravy-colored windows, and a tall spire ornamented with tin gargoyles and alternate layers of tiles in distressing red and green. The neighborhood had been smart, but the brick mansions, once leisurely among lawns and gardens, were scabrous and slovenly, turned into boarding-houses with delicatessen shops in the basements.

"Gosh, this section never will come back. Too many of the doggone *hoi polloi.* Bunch of Wops. Nobody for ten blocks that would put more'n ten cents in the collection. Nothing doing! I'm not going to run a soup-kitchen and tell a bunch of dirty bums to come to Jesus. Not on your life!"

But he saw, a block from the church, a new apartment-house, and near it an excavation.

"Hm. Might come back, in apartments, at that. Mustn't jump too quick. Besides, these folks need the gospel just as much as the swell-headed plutes out on Royal Ridge," reflected the Reverend Mr. Gantry.

Through his old acquaintance, Gil O'Hearn of the O'Hearn House, Elmer met a responsible contractor and inquired into the fruitfulness of the Wellspring vineyard.

"Yes, they're dead certain to build a bunch of apartment-houses, and pretty good ones, in that neighborhood these next few years. Be a big residential boom in Old Town. It's near enough in to be handy to the business section, and far enough from the Union Station so's they haven't got any warehouses or wholesalers. Good buy, Reverend."

"Oh, I'm not buying—I'm just selling—selling the gospel!" said the Reverend, and he went to inform Bishop Toomis that after prayer and meditation he had been led to accept the pastorate of the Wellspring Church.

So, at thirty-nine, Cæsar came to Rome, and Rome heard about it immediately.

Chapter XXIII

HE DID NOT stand by the altar now, uplifted in a vow that he would be good and reverent. He was like the new general manager of a factory as he bustled for the first time through the Wellspring Methodist Church, Zenith, and his first comment was "The plant's run down—have to buck it up."

He was accompanied on his inspection by his staff: Miss Bundle, church secretary and personal secretary to himself, a decayed and plaintive lady distressingly free of seductiveness; Miss Weezeger, the deaconess, given to fat and good works; and A. F. Cherry, organist and musical director, engaged only on part time.

He was disappointed that the church could not give him a pastoral assistant or a director of religious education. He'd have them, soon enough—and boss them! Great!

He found an auditorium which would hold sixteen hundred people but which was offensively gloomy in its streaky windows, its brown plaster walls, its cast-iron pillars. The rear wall of the chancel was painted a lugubrious blue scattered with stars which had ceased to twinkle; and the pulpit was of dark oak, crowned with a foolish, tasseled, faded green velvet cushion. The whole auditorium was heavy and forbidding; the stretch of empty brown-grained pews stared at him dolorously.

"Certainly must have been a swell bunch of cheerful Christians that made this layout! I'll have a new church here in five years—one with some pep to it, and Gothic fixin's and an up-to-date educational and entertainment plant," reflected the new priest.

The Sunday School rooms were spacious enough, but dingy, scattered with torn hymn books; the kitchen in the basement, for church suppers, had a rusty ancient stove and piles of chipped dishes. Elmer's own study and office was airless, and looked out on the flivver-crowded yard of a garage. And Mr. Cherry said the organ was rather more than wheezy.

"Oh, well," Elmer conferred with himself afterward, "what do I care! Anyway, there's plenty of room for the crowds, and, believe me, I'm the boy can drag 'em in! . . . God, what a frump that Bundle woman is! One of these days I'll have a smart girl secretary—a good-looker. Well, hurray, ready for the big work! I'll show this town what high-class preaching is!"

Not for three days did he chance to think that Cleo might also like to see the church.

II

Though there were nearly four hundred thousand people in Zenith and only nine hundred in Banjo Crossing, Elmer's reception in the Zenith church-basement was remarkably like his reception in the Banjo basement. There were the same rugged, hard-handed brothers, the same ample sisters renowned for making doughnuts, the same brisk little men given to giggling and pious jests. There were the same homemade ice cream and homemade oratory. But there were five times as many people as at the Banjo reception, and Elmer was ever a lover of quantity. And among the transplanted rustics were several prosperous professional men, several well-gowned women, and some pretty girls who looked as though they went to dancing school, Discipline or not.

He felt cheerful and loving toward them—his, as he pointed out to them, "fellow crusaders marching on resolutely to achievement of the Kingdom of God on earth."

It was easy to discover which of the members present from the Official Board of the church were most worth his attentions. Mr. Ernest Apfelmus, one of the stewards, was the owner of the Gem of the Ocean Pie and Cake Corporation. He looked like a puffy and bewildered urchin suddenly blown up to vast size; he was very rich, Miss Bundle whispered; and he did not know how to spend his money except on his wife's diamonds and the cause of the Lord. Elmer paid court to Mr. Apfelmus and his wife, who spoke quite a little English.

Not so rich but even more important, Elmer guessed, was T. J. Rigg, the famous criminal lawyer, a trustee of Wellspring Church.

Mr. Rigg was small, deep-wrinkled, with amused and knowing eyes. He would be, Elmer felt instantly, a good man with whom to drink. His wife's face was that of a girl, round and smooth and blue-eyed, though she was fifty and more, and her laughter was lively.

"Those are folks I can shoot straight with," decided Elmer, and he kept near them.

Rigg hinted, "Say, Reverend, why don't you and your good lady come up to my house after this, and we can loosen up and have a good laugh and get over this sewing-circle business."

"I'd certainly like to." As he spoke Elmer was considering that if he was really to loosen up, he could not have Cleo about. "Only, I'm afraid my wife has a headache, poor girl. We'll just send her along home and I'll come with you."

"After you shake hands a few thousand more times!"

"Exactly!"

Elmer was edified to find that Mr. Rigg had a limousine with a chauffeur—one of the few in which Elmer had yet ridden. He did like to have his Christian brethren well heeled. But the sight of the limousine made him less chummy with the Riggses, more respectful and unctuous, and when they had dropped Cleo at the hotel, Elmer leaned gracefully back on the velvet seat, waved his large hand poetically, and breathed, "Such a welcome the dear people gave me! I am so grateful! What a real outpouring of the spirit!"

"Look here," sniffed Rigg, "you don't have to be pious with us! Ma and I are a couple of old dragoons. We like religion; like the good old hymns—takes us back to the hick town we came from; and we believe religion is a fine thing to keep people in order—they think of higher things instead of all these strikes and big wages and the kind of hell-raising that's throwing the industrial system all out of kilter. And I like a fine upstanding preacher that can give a good show. So I'm willing to be a trustee. But we ain't pious. And any time you want to let down—and I reckon there must be times when a big cuss like you must get pretty sick of listening to the sniveling sisterhood!—you just come to us, and if you want to smoke or even throw in a little jolt of liquor, as I've been known to do, why we'll understand. How about it, Ma?"

"You bet!" said Mrs. Rigg. "And I'll go down to the kitchen, if cook isn't there, and fry you up a couple of eggs, and if you don't tell the rest of the brethren, there's always a couple of bottles of beer on the ice. Like one?"

"*Would* I!" cheered Elmer. "You bet I would! Only—I cut out drinking and smoking quite a few years ago. Oh, I had my share before that! But I stopped, absolute, and I'd hate to break my record. But you go right ahead. And I want to say that it'll be a mighty big relief to have some folks in the church that I can talk to without shocking 'em half to death. Some of these holier-than-thou birds— Lord, they won't let a preacher be a human being!"

The Rigg house was large, rather faded, full of books which had been read—history, biography, travels. The smaller sitting-room, with its log fire and large padded chairs, looked comfortable, but Mrs. Rigg shouted, "Oh, let's go out to the kitchen and shake up a welsh rabbit! I love to cook, and I don't dast till after the servants go to bed."

So his first conference with T. J. Rigg, who became the only authentic friend Elmer had known since Jim Lefferts, was held at the shiny white-enamel-topped table in the huge kitchen, with Mrs. Rigg stalking about, bringing them welsh rabbit, with celery, cold chicken, whatever she found in the ice box.

"I want your advice, Brother Rigg," said Elmer. "I want to make my first sermon here something sen—well, something that'll make 'em sit up and listen. I don't have to get the subject in for the church ads till tomorrow. Now what do you think of some pacifism?"

"Eh?"

"I know what you think. Of course during the war I was just as patriotic as anybody—Four-Minute Man, and in another month I'd of been in uniform. But honest, some of the churches are getting a lot of kick out of hollering pacifism now the war's all safely over—some of the biggest preachers in the country. But far's I've heard, nobody's started it here in Zenith yet, and it might make a big sensation."

"Yes, that's so, and course it's perfectly all right to adopt pacifism as long as there's no chance for another war."

"Or do you think—you know the congregation here—do you think a more dignified and kind of you might say poetic expository sermon would impress 'em more? Or what about a good, vigorous, right-out-from-the-shoulder attack on vice? You know, booze and immorality—like short skirts—by golly, girls' skirts getting shorter every year!"

"Now that's what I'd vote for," said Rigg. "That's what gets 'em. Nothing like a good juicy vice sermon to bring in the crowds. Yes, sir! Fearless attack on all this drinking and this awful sex immorality that's getting so prevalent." Mr. Rigg meditatively mixed a highball, keeping it light because next morning in court he had to defend a lady accused of running a badger game. "You bet. Some folks say sermons like that are just sensational, but I always tell 'em: once the preacher gets the folks into the church that way—and mighty few appreciate how hard it is to do a good vice sermon; jolt 'em enough and yet not make it too dirty—once you get in the folks, then you can give 'em some good, solid, old-time religion and show 'em salvation and teach 'em to observe the laws and do an honest day's work for an honest day's pay, 'stead of clock-watching like my doggone clerks do! Yep, if you ask me, try the vice. . . . Oh, say, Ma, do you think the Reverend would be shocked by that story about the chambermaid and the traveling man that Mark was telling us?"

Elmer was not shocked. In fact he had another droll tale himself.

He went home at one.

"I'll have a good time with those folks," he reflected, in the luxury of a taxicab. "Only, better be careful with old Rigg. He's a shrewd bird, and he's onto me. . . . Now what do you mean?" indignantly. "What do you mean by 'onto me'? There's nothing to be onto! I refused a drink and a cigar, didn't I? I never cuss except when I lose my temper, do I? I'm leading an absolutely Christian life. And I'm bringing a whale of a lot more souls into churches than any of these pussy-footing tin saints that're afraid to laugh and jolly people. 'Onto me' nothing!"

III

On Saturday morning, on the page of religious advertisements in the Zenith newspapers, Elmer's first sermon was announced in a two-column spread as dealing with the promising problem: "Can Strangers Find Haunts of Vice in Zenith?"

They could, and with gratifying ease, said Elmer in his sermon. He said it before at least four hundred people, as against the hundred who had normally been attending.

He himself was a stranger in Zenith, and he had gone forth and he had been "appalled—aghast—bowed in shocked horror" at the amount of vice, and such interesting and attractive vice. He had investigated Braun's Island, a rackety beach and dance-floor and restaurant at South Zenith, and he had found mixed bathing. He described the ladies' legs; he described the two amiable young women who had picked him up. He told of the waiter who, though he denied that Braun's Restaurant itself sold liquor, had been willing to let him know where to get it, and where to find an all-night game of poker—"and, mind you, playing poker for keeps, you understand," Elmer explained.

On Washington Avenue, North, he had found two movies in which "the dreadful painted purveyors of putrescent vice" —he meant the movie actors—had on the screen danced "suggestive steps which would bring the blush of shame to the cheeks of any decent woman," and in which the same purveyors had taken drinks which he assumed to be the deadly cocktails. On his way to his hotel after these movies three ladies of the night had accosted him, right under the White Way of lights. Street-corner loafers—he had apparently been very chummy with them—had told him of blind pigs, of dope-peddlers, of strange lecheries.

"That," he shouted, "is what one stranger was able to find in your city—now *my* city, and well beloved! But could he find virtue so easily, could he, could he? Or just a lot of easy-going churches, lollygagging along, while the just God threatens this city with the fire and devouring brimstone that destroyed proud Sodom and Gomorrah in their abominations! Listen! With the help of God Almighty, let us raise here in this church a standard of virtue that no stranger can help seeing! We're lazy. We're not burning with a fever of righteousness. On your knees, you slothful, and pray God to forgive you and to aid you and me to form a brotherhood of helpful, joyous, fiercely righteous followers of every commandment of the Lord Our God!"

The newspapers carried almost all of it. . . . It had just happened that there were reporters present—it had just happened that Elmer had been calling up the *Advocate-Times* on Saturday—it had just happened that he remembered he had met Bill Kingdom, the *Advocate* reporter, in Sparta—it had just happened that to help out good old Bill he had let him know there would be something stirring in the church, come Sunday.

The next Saturday Elmer advertised "Is There a Real Devil Sneaking Around with Horns and Hoofs?" On Sunday there were seven hundred present. Within two months Elmer was preaching, ever more confidently and dramatically, to larger crowds than were drawn by any other church in Zenith except four or five.

But, "Oh, he's just a new sensation—he can't last out—hasn't got the learning and staying-power. Besides, Old Town is shot to pieces," said Elmer's fellow vinters—particularly his annoyed fellow Methodists.

IV

Cleo and he had found a gracious old house in Old Town, to be had cheap because of the ragged neighborhood. He had hinted to her that since he was making such a spiritual sacrifice as to take a lower salary in coming to Zenith, her father, as a zealous Christian, ought to help them out; and if she should be unable to make her father perceive this, Elmer would regretfully have to be angry with her.

She came back from a visit to Banjo Crossing with two thousand dollars.

Cleo had an instinct for agreeable furniture. For the old house, with its white mahogany paneling, she got reproductions of early New England chairs and commodes and tables. There was a white-framed fireplace and a fine old crystal chandelier in the living-room.

"Some class! We can entertain the bon ton here, and, believe me, I'll soon be having a lot of 'em coming to church! . . . Sometimes I do wish, though, I'd gone out for the Episcopal Church. Lots more class there, and they don't beef if a minister takes a little drink," he said to Cleo.

"Oh, Elmer, how *can* you! When Methodism stands for—"

"Oh, God, I do wish that just once you wouldn't deliberately misunderstand me! Here I was just carrying on a philosophical discussion, and not speaking personal, and you go and—"

His house in order, he gave attention to clothes. He dressed as calculatingly as an actor. For the pulpit, he continued to wear morning clothes. For his church study, he chose offensively inoffensive lounge suits, gray and brown and striped blue, with linen collars and quiet blue ties. For addresses before slightly boisterous lunch-clubs, he went in for manly tweeds and manly soft collars, along with his manly voice and manly jesting.

He combed his thick hair back from his strong, square face, and permitted it to hang, mane-like, just a bit over his collar. But it was still too black to be altogether prophetic.

The two thousand was gone before they had been in Zenith a month.

"But it's all a good investment," he said. "When I meet the Big Bugs, they'll see I may have a dump of a church in a bum section but I can put up as good a front as if I were preaching on Chickasaw Road."

V

If in Banjo Crossing Elmer had been bored by inactivity, in Zenith he was almost exhausted by the demands.

Wellspring Church had been carrying on a score of institutional affairs, and Elmer doubled them, for nothing brought in more sympathy, publicity, and contributions. Rich old hyenas who never went to church would ooze out a hundred dollars or even five hundred when you described the shawled mothers coming tearfully to the milk station.

There were classes in manual training, in domestic science, in gymnastics, in bird study, for the poor boys and girls of Old Town. There were troops of Boy Scouts, of Camp Fire Girls. There were Ladies' Aid meetings, Women's Missionary Society meetings, regular church suppers before prayer-meeting, a Bible Training School for Sunday School teachers, a sewing society, nursing and free food for the sick and poor, half a dozen clubs of young men and women, half a dozen circles of matrons, and a Men's Club with monthly dinners, for which the pastor had to snare prominent speakers without payment. The Sunday School was like a small university. And every day there were dozens of callers who asked the pastor for comfort, for advice, for money—young men in temptation, widows wanting jobs, old widows wanting assurance of immortality, hoboes wanting hand-outs, and eloquent book-agents. Where in Banjo the villagers had been shy to expose their cancerous sorrows, in the city there were always lonely people who reveled in being a little twisted, a little curious, a little shameful; who yearned to talk about themselves and who expected the pastor to be forever interested.

Elmer scarce had time to prepare his sermons, though he really did yearn now to make them original and eloquent. He was no longer satisfied to depend on his barrel. He wanted to increase his vocabulary; he was even willing to have new ideas, lifted out of biology and biography and political editorials.

He was out of the house daily at eight in the morning—usually after a breakfast in which he desired to know of Cleo why the deuce she couldn't keep Nat and Bunny quiet while he read the paper—and he did not return till six, burning with weariness. He had to study in the evening. . . . He was always testy. . . . His children were afraid of him, even when he boisterously decided to enact the Kind Parent for one evening and to ride them pickaback, whether or no they wanted to be ridden pickaback. They feared God properly and kept his commandments, did Nat and Bunny, because their father so admirably prefigured God.

When Cleo was busy with meetings and clubs at the church, Elmer blamed her for neglecting the house; when she slackened her church work, he was able equally to blame her for not helping him professionally. And obviously it was because she had so badly arranged the home routine that he never had time for morning Family Worship. . . . But he made up for it by the violence of his Grace before Meat, during which he glared at the children if they stirred in their chairs.

And always the telephone was ringing—not only in his office but at home in the evening.

What should Miss Weezeger, the deaconess, do about this old Miss Mally, who wanted a new nightgown? Could the Reverend Gantry give a short talk on "Advertising and the Church" to the Ad Club next Tuesday noon? Could he address the Letitia Music and Literary Club on "Religion and Poetry" next Thursday at four—just when he had a meeting with the Official Board. The church janitor wanted to start the furnace, but the coal hadn't been delivered. What advice would the Reverend Mr. Gantry give to a young man who wanted to go to college and had no money? From what book was that quotation about "Cato learned Greek at eighty Sophocles" which he had used in last Sunday's sermon? Would Mr. Gantry be so kind and address the Lincoln School next Friday morning at nine-fifteen—the dear children would be so glad of any Message he had to give them, and the regular speaker couldn't show up. Would it be all right for the Girls' Basket Ball team to use the basement tonight? Could the Reverend come out, right now, to the house of Ben T. Evers, 2616 Appleby Street—five miles away—because grandmother was very ill and needed consolation. What the dickens did the Reverend mean by saying, last Sunday, that hell-fire might be merely spiritual and figurative—didn't he know that that was agin Matthew V:29: "Thy whole body should be cast into hell." Could he get the proof of the church bulletin back to the printers right away? Could the officers of the Southwest Circle of Women meet in Mr. Gantry's study tomorrow? Would Reverend Gantry speak at the Old Town Improvement Association Banquet? Did the Reverend want to buy a secondhand motor car in A 1 shape? Could the Reverend—

"God!" said the Reverend; and, "Huh? Why, no, of course you couldn't answer 'em for me, Cleo. But at least you might try to keep from humming when I'm simply killing myself trying to take care of all these blame' fools and sacrificing myself and everything!"

And the letters.

In response to every sermon he had messages informing him that he was the bright hope of evangelicism and that he was a cloven-hoofed fiend; that he was a rousing orator and a human saxophone. One sermon on the delights of Heaven, which he pictured as a perpetual summer afternoon at a lake resort, brought in the same mail four comments:

i have got an idea for you verry important since hearing yrs of last sunday evening why do'nt you hold services every evning to tell people & etc about heven and danger of hell we must hurry hurry

hurry, the church in a bad way and is up to us who have many and infaliable proofs of heven and hell to hasten yes we must rescew the parishing, make everywhere the call of the lord, fill the churches and empty these damable theatre.

Yrs for his coming,
JAMES C. WICKES,
2113 A, McGrew Street.

The writer is an honest and unwavering Christian and I want to tell you, Gantry, that the only decent and helpful and enjoyable thing about your sermon last Sunday A.M. was your finally saying "Let us pray," only *you* should have said "Let me prey." By your wibbly-wabbly emphasis on Heaven and your fear to emphasize the horrors of Hell, you get people into an easy-going, self-satisfied frame of mind where they slip easily into sin, and while pretending to be an earnest and literal believer in every word of the Scriptures, you are an atheist in sheep's clothing. I am a minister of the gospel and know whereof I speak.

Yours,
ALMON JEWINGS STRAFE.

I heard your rotten old-fashioned sermon last Sunday. You pretend to be liberal, but you are just a hide-bound conservative. Nobody believes in a material heaven or hell any more, and you make yourself ridiculous by talking about them. Wake up and study some modern dope.

A STUDENT.

Dear Brother, your lovely sermon last Sunday about Heaven was the finest I have ever heard. I am quite an old lady and not awful well and in my ills and griefs, especially about my grandson who drinks, your wonderful words give me such a comfort I cannot describe to you.

Yours admiringly,
MRS. R. R. GOMMERIE.

And he was expected, save with the virulent anonymous letters, to answer all of them . . . in his stuffy office, facing a shelf of black-bound books, dictating to the plaintive Miss Bundle, who never caught an address, who always single-spaced the letters which should have been double-spaced, and who had a speed which seemed adequate until you discovered that she attained it by leaving out most of the verbs and adjectives.

VI

Whether or not he was irritable on week days, Sundays were to his nervous family a hell of keeping out of his way, and for himself they had the strain of a theatrical first night.

He was up at seven, looking over his sermon notes, preparing his talk to the Sunday School, and snarling at Cleo, "Good Lord, you might have breakfast on time today, at least, and why in heaven's name you can't get that furnace-man here so I won't have to freeze while I'm doing my studying—"

He was at Sunday School at a quarter to ten, and often he had to take the huge Men's Bible Class and instruct it in the more occult meanings of the Bible, out of his knowledge of the original Hebrew and Greek as denied to the laity.

Morning church services began at eleven. Now that he often had as many as a thousand in the audience, as he peeped out at them from the study he had stage-fright. Could he hold them? What the deuce had he intended to say about communion? He couldn't remember a word of it.

It was not easy to keep on urging the unsaved to come forward as though he really thought they would and as though he cared a hang whether they did or not. It was not easy, on communion Sundays, when they knelt round the altar rail, to keep from laughing at the sanctimonious eyes and prim mouths of brethren whom he knew to be crooks in private business.

It was not easy to go on saying with proper conviction that whosoever looked on a woman to lust after her would go booming down to hell when there was a pretty and admiring girl in the front row. And it was hardest of all, when he had done his public job, when he was tired and wanted to let down, to stand about after the sermon and be hand-shaken by aged spinster saints who expected him to listen without grinning while they quavered that he was a silver-plated angel and that they were just like him.

To have to think up a new, bright, pious quip for each of them! To see large sporting males regarding him the while as though he were an old woman in trousers!

By the time he came home for Sunday lunch he was looking for a chance to feel injured and unappreciated and pestered and put upon, and usually he found the chance.

There were still ahead of him, for the rest of the day, the Sunday evening service, often the Epworth League, sometimes special meetings at four. Whenever the children disturbed his Sunday afternoon nap, Elmer gave an impersonation of the prophets. Why! All he asked of Nat and Bunny was that, as a Methodist minister's children, they should not be seen on the streets or in the parks on the blessed Sabbath afternoon, and that they should not be heard about the house. He told them, often, that they were committing an unexampled sin by causing him to fall into bad tempers unbecoming a Man of God.

But through all these labors and this lack of domestic sympathy he struggled successfully.

VII

Elmer was as friendly as ever with Bishop Toomis.

He had conferred early with the bishop and with the canny lawyer-trustee, T. J. Rigg, as to what fellow-clergymen in Zenith it would be worth his while to know.

Among the ministers outside the Methodist Church, they recommended Dr. G. Prosper Edwards, the highly cultured pastor of the Pilgrim Congregational Church, Dr. John Jennison Drew, the active but sanctified leader of the Chatham Road Presbyterian Church, that solid Baptist, the Reverend Hosea Jessup, and Willis Fortune Tate, who, though he was an Episcopalian and very shaky as regards liquor and hell, had one of the suavest and most expensive flocks in town. And if one could endure the Christian Scientists' smirking conviction that they alone had the truth, there was the celebrated leader of the First Christian Science Church, Mr. Irving Tillish.

The Methodist ministers of Zenith Elmer met and studied at their regular Monday morning meetings, in the funeral and wedding chapel of Central Church. They looked like a group of prosperous and active business men. Only two of them ever wore clerical waistcoats, and of these only one compromised with the Papacy and the errors of Canterbury by turning his collar around. A few resembled farmers, a few stone-masons, but most of them looked like retail shops. The Reverend Mr. Chatterton Weeks indulged in claret-colored "fancy socks," silk handkerchiefs, and an enormous emerald ring, and gave a pleasant suggestion of vaudeville. Nor were they too sanctimonious. They slapped one another's backs, they used first names, they shouted, "I hear you're grabbing off all the crowds in town, you old cuss!" and for the manlier and more successful of them it was quite the thing to use now and then a daring "damn."

It would, to an innocent layman, have been startling to see them sitting in rows like schoolboys; to hear them listening not to addresses on credit and the routing of hardware but to short helpful talks on Faith. The balance was kept, however, by an adequate number of papers on trade subjects—the sort of pews most soothing to the back; the value of sending postcards reading "Where were you last Sunday, old scout? We sure did miss you at the Men's Bible Class"; the comparative values of a giant imitation thermometer, a giant clock, and a giant automobile speedometer, as a register of the money coming in during special drives; the question of gold and silver stars as rewards for Sunday School attendance; the effectiveness of giving the children savings-banks in the likeness of a jolly little church to encourage them to save their pennies for Christian work; and the morality of violin solos.

Nor were the assembled clergy too inhumanly unboastful in their reports of increased attendance and collections.

Elmer saw that the Zenith district superintendent, one Fred Orr, could be neglected as a creeping and silent fellow who was all right at prayer and who seemed to lead an almost irritatingly pure life, but who had no useful notions about increasing collections.

The Methodist preachers whom he had to take seriously as rivals were four.

There was Chester Brown, the ritualist, of the new and ultra-Gothic Asbury Church. He was almost as bad, they said, as an Episcopalian. He wore a clerical waistcoat buttoned up to his collar; he had a robed choir and the processional; he was rumored once to have had candles on what was practically an altar. He was, to Elmer, distressingly literary and dramatic. It was said that he had literary gifts; his articles appeared not only in the *Advocate* but in the *Christian Century* and the *New Republic*—rather whimsical essays, safely Christian but frank about the church's sloth and wealth and blindness. He had been Professor of English Literature and Church History in Luccock College, and he did such sermons on books as Elmer, with his exhausting knowledge of Longfellow and George Eliot, could never touch.

Dr. Otto Hickenlooper of Central Church was an even more distressing rival. His was the most active institutional church of the whole state. He had not only manual training and gymnastics but sacred pageants, classes in painting (never from the nude), classes in French and batik-making and sex hygiene and bookkeeping and short-story writing. He had clubs for railroad men, for stenographers, for bell-boys; and after the church suppers the young people were encouraged to sit about in booths to which the newspapers referred flippantly as "courting corners."

Dr. Hickenlooper had come out hard for Social Service. He was in sympathy with the American Federation of Labor, the I.W.W., the Socialists, the Communists, and the Nonpartisan League, which was more than they were with one another. He held Sunday evening lectures on the Folly of War, the Minimum Wage, the need of clean milk; and once a month he had an open forum, to which were invited the most dangerous radical speakers, who were allowed to say absolutely anything they liked, provided they did not curse, refer to adultery, or criticize the leadership of Christ.

Dr. Mahlon Potts, of the First Methodist Church, seemed to Elmer at first glance less difficult to oust. He was fat, pompous, full of heavy rumbles of piety. He was a stage parson. "Ah, my dear Brother!" he boomed; and "How are we this morning, my dear Doctor, and how is the lovely little wife?" But Dr. Potts had the largest congregation of any church of any denomination in Zenith. He was so respectable. He was so safe. People knew where they were, with him. He was adequately flowery of speech—he could do up a mountain, a sunset, a burning of the martyrs, a reception of the same by the saints in heaven, as well as any preacher in town. But he never doubted nor let any one else doubt that by attending the Methodist Church regularly, and observing the rules of repentance, salvation, baptism, communion, and liberal giving, every one would have a minimum of cancer and tuberculosis and sin, and unquestionably arrive in heaven.

These three Elmer envied but respected; one man he envied and loathed.

That was Philip McGarry of the Arbor Methodist Church.

Philip McGarry, Ph.D. of Chicago University in economics and philosophy—only everybody who liked him, layman or fellow-parson, seemed to call him "Phil"—was at the age of thirty-five known through the whole American Methodist Church as an *enfant terrible.* The various sectional editions of the *Advocate* admired him but clucked like doting and alarmed hens over his frequent improprieties. He was accused of every heresy. He never denied them, and the only dogma he was known to give out positively was the leadership of Jesus—as to whose divinity he was indefinite.

He was a stocky, smiling man, fond of boxing, and even at a funeral incapable of breathing, "Ah, sister!"

He criticized everything. He criticized even bishops—for being too fat, for being too ambitious, for gassing about Charity during a knock-down-and-drag-out strike. He criticized, but amiably, the social and institutional and generally philanthropic Dr. Otto Hickenlooper, with his clubs for the study of Karl Marx and his Sunday afternoon reception for lonely traveling-men.

"You're a good lad, Otto," said Dr. McGarry—and openly, in the preachers' Monday meetings: "You mean well, but you're one of these darned philanthropists."

"Nice word to use publicly—'darned'!" meditated the shocked Reverend Elmer Gantry.

"All your stuff at Central, Otto," said Dr. McGarry, "is paternalistic. You hand out rations to the dear pee-pul and keep 'em obedient. You talk about socialism and pacifism, and say a lot of nice things about 'em, but you always explain that reforms must come in due time, which means never, and then only through the kind supervision of Rockefeller and Henry Ford. And I always suspect that your activities have behind 'em the sneaking purpose of luring the poor chumps into religion—even into Methodism!"

The whole ministerial meeting broke into yelps.

"Well, of course, that's the purpose—"

"Well, if you'll kindly tell me why you stay in the Methodist Church when you think it's so unimportant to—"

"Just what are you, a minister of the gospel, seeking *except* religion—"

The meeting, on such a morning, was certain to stray from the consideration of using egg-coal in church furnaces to the question as to what, when they weren't before their congregations and on record, they really believed about the whole thing.

That was a very dangerous and silly thing, reflected Elmer Gantry. No telling where you'd get to, if you went blatting around about a lot of these fool problems. Preach the straight Bible gospel and make folks good, he demanded, and leave all these ticklish questions of theology and social service to the profs!

Philip McGarry wound up his cheerful attack on Dr. Hickenlooper, the first morning when Elmer disgustedly encountered him, by insisting, "You see, Otto, your reforms couldn't mean anything, or you wouldn't be able to hold onto as many prosperous money-grabbing parishioners as you do. No risk of the working-men in your church turning dangerous as long as you've got that tight-fisted Joe Hanley as one of your trustees! Thank Heaven, I haven't got a respectable person in my whole blooming flock!"

("Yeh, and there's where you gave yourself away, McGarry," Elmer chuckled inwardly. "That's the first thing you've said that's true!")

Philip McGarry's church was in a part of the city incomparably more run-down than Elmer's Old Town. It was called "The Arbor"; it had in pioneer days been the vineyard-sheltered village, along the Chaloosa River, from which had grown the modern Zenith. Now it was all dives, brothels, wretched tenements, cheap-jack shops. Yet here McGarry lived, a bachelor, seemingly well content, counseling pick-pockets and scrubwomen, and giving on Friday evenings a series of lectures packed by eager Jewish girl students, radical workmen, old cranks, and wistful rich girls coming in limousines down from the spacious gardens of Royal Ridge.

"I'll have trouble with that McGarry if we both stay in this town. Him and I will never get along together," thought Elmer. "Well, I'll keep away from him; I'll treat him with some of this Christian charity that he talks so darn' much about and can't understand the real meaning of! We'll just dismiss him—and most of these other birds. But the big three—how'll I handle them?"

He could not, even if he should have a new church, outdo Chester Brown in ecclesiastical elegance or literary messages. He could never touch Otto Hickenlooper in institutions and social service. He could never beat Mahlon Potts in appealing to the well-to-do respectables.

Yet he could beat them all together!

Planning it delightedly, at the ministers' meeting, on his way home, by the fireplace at night, he saw that each of these stars was so specialized that he neglected the good publicity-bringing features of the others. Elmer would combine them; be almost as elevating as Chester Brown, almost as institutional and meddling as Otto Hickenlooper, almost as solidly safe and moral as Mahlon Potts. And all three of them, in fact every preacher in town except one Presbyterian, were neglecting the—well, some people called it sensational, but that was just envy; the proper word, considered Elmer, was *powerful*, or perhaps *fearless*, or *stimulating*—all of them were neglecting a powerful, fearless, stimulating, and devil-challenging concentration on vice. Booze. Legs. Society bridge. You bet!

Not overdo it, of course, but the town would come to know that in the sermons of the Reverend Elmer Gantry there would always be something spicy and yet improving.

"Oh, I can put it over the whole bunch!" Elmer stretched his big arms in joyous vigor. "I'll build a new church. I'll take the crowds away from all of 'em. I'll be the one big preacher in Zenith. And then— Chicago? New York? Bishopric? Whatever I want! Whee!"

Chapter XXIV

IT WAS during his inquiry about clerical allies and rivals—they were the same thing—that Elmer learned that two of his classmates at Mizpah Seminary were stationed in Zenith.

Wallace Umstead, the Mizpah student-instructor in gymnastics, was now general secretary of the Zenith Y.M.C.A.

"He's a boob. We can pass him up," Elmer decided. "Husky but no finesse and culture. No. That's wrong. Preacher can get a lot of publicity speaking at the Y., and get the fellows to join his church."

So he called on Mr. Umstead, and that was a hearty and touching meeting between classmates, two strong men come face to face, two fellow manly Christians.

But Elmer was not pleased to learn of the presence of the second classmate, Frank Shallard. He angrily recalled: "Sure—the fellow that high-hatted me and sneaked around and tried to spy on me when I was helping him learn the game at Schoenheim."

He was glad to hear that Frank was in disgrace with the sounder and saner clergy of Zenith. He had left the Baptist Church; it was said that he had acted in a low manner as a common soldier in the Great War; and he had gone as pastor to a Congregational Church in Zenith—not a God-fearing, wealthy Congregational Church, like that of Dr. G. Prosper Edwards, but one that was suspected of being as shaky and cowardly and misleading as any Unitarian fold.

Elmer remembered that he still owed Frank the hundred dollars which he had borrowed to reach Zenith for the last of his Prosperity lectures. He was furious to remember it. He couldn't pay it, not now, with a motor car just bought and only half paid for! But was it safe to make an enemy of this crank Shallard, who might go around shooting his mouth off and telling a lot of stories—not more'n half of 'em true?

He groaned with martyrdom, made out a check for a hundred—it was one-half of his present bank-balance—and sent it to Frank with a note explaining that for years he had yearned to return this money, but he had lost Frank's address.

Also, he would certainly call on his dear classmate just as soon as he got time.

"And that'll be about sixteen years after the Day of Judgment," he snorted.

II

Not all the tenderness, all the serene uprightness, all the mystic visions of Andrew Pengilly, that village saint, had been able to keep Frank Shallard satisfied with the Baptist ministry after his association with the questioning rabbi and the Unitarian minister at Eureka. These liberals proved admirably the assertion of the Baptist fundamentalists that to tamper with biology and ethnology was to lose one's Baptist faith, wherefore State University education should be confined to algebra, agriculture, and Bible study.

Early in 1917, when it was a question as to whether he would leave his Baptist church or to be kicked out, Frank was caught by the drama of war—caught, in his wavering, by what seemed strength—and he resigned, for all of Bess' bewildered protests; he sent her and the children back to her father, and enlisted as a private soldier.

Chaplain? No! He wanted, for the first time, to be normal and uninsulated.

Through the war he was kept as a clerk in camp in America. He was industrious, quick, accurate, obedient; he rose to a sergeancy and learned to smoke; he loyally brought his captain home whenever he was drunk; and he read half a hundred volumes of science.

And all the time he hated it.

He hated the indignity of being herded with other men, no longer a person of leisure and dignity and command, whose idiosyncrasies were important to himself and to other people, but a cog, to be hammered brusquely the moment it made any rattle of individuality. He hated the seeming planlessness of the whole establishment. If this was a war to end war, he heard nothing of it from any of his fellow soldiers or his officers.

But he learned to be easy and common with common men. He learned not even to hear cursing. He learned to like large males more given to tobacco-chewing than to bathing, and innocent of all words longer than "hell." He found himself so devoted to the virtues of these common people that he wanted "to do something for them"—and in bewildered reflection he could think of no other way of "doing something for them" than to go on preaching.

But not among the Baptists, with their cast-iron minds.

Nor yet could he quite go over to the Unitarians. He still revered Jesus of Nazareth as the one path to justice and kindness, and he still—finding even as in childhood a magic in the stories of shepherds keeping watch by night, of the glorified mother beside the babe in the manger—he still had an unreasoned feeling that Jesus was of more than human birth, and veritably the Christ.

It seemed to him that the Congregationalists were the freest among the more or less trinitarian denominations. Each Congregational church made its own law. The Baptists were supposed to, but they were ruled by a grim general opinion.

After the war he talked to the state superintendent of Congregational churches of Winnemac. Frank wanted a free church, and a poor church, but not poor because it was timid and lifeless.

They would, said the superintendent, be glad to welcome him among the Congregationalists, and there was available just the flock Frank wanted: the Dorchester Church, on the edge of Zenith. The parishioners were small shopkeepers and factory foremen and skilled workmen and railwaymen, with a few stray music-teachers and insurance agents. They were mostly poor; and they had the reputation of really wanting the truth from the pulpit.

When Elmer arrived, Frank had been at the Dorchester Church for two years, and he had been nearly happy.

He found that the grander among his fellow Congregational pastors—such as G. Prosper Edwards, with his downtown plush-lined cathedral—could be shocked almost as readily as the Baptists by a suggestion that we didn't really quite *know* about the virgin birth. He found that the worthy butchers and haberdashers of his congregation did not radiate joy at a defense of Bolshevik Russia. He found that he was still not at all certain that he was doing any good, aside from providing the drug of religious hope to timorous folk frightened of hell-fire and afraid to walk alone.

But to be reasonably free, to have, after army life, the fleecy comfort of a home with jolly Bess and the children, this was oasis, and for three years Frank halted in his fumbling for honesty.

Even more than Bess, the friendship of Dr. Philip McGarry, of the Arbor Methodist Church, kept Frank in the ministry.

McGarry was three or four years younger than Frank, but in his sturdy cheerfulness he seemed more mature. Frank had met him at the Ministerial Alliance's monthly meeting, and they had liked in each other a certain disdainful honesty. McGarry was not to be shocked by what biology did to Genesis, by the suggestion that certain Christian rites had been stolen from Mithraic cults, by Freudianism, by any social heresies, yet McGarry loved the church, as a comradely gathering of people alike hungry for something richer than daily selfishness, and this love he passed on to Frank.

But Frank still resented it that, as a parson, he was considered not quite virile; that even clever people felt they must treat him with a special manner; that he was barred from knowing the real thoughts and sharing the real desires of normal humanity.

And when he received Elmer's note of greeting he groaned, "Oh, Lord, I wonder if people ever class me with a fellow like Gantry?"

He suggested to Bess, after a spirited account of Elmer's eminent qualities for spiritual and amorous leadership, "I feel like sending his check back to him."

"Let's see it," said Bess and, placing the check in her stocking, she observed derisively, "There's a new suit for Michael, and a lovely dinner for you and me, and a new lip-stick, and money in the bank. Cheers! I adore you, Reverend Shallard, I worship you, I adhere to you in all Christian fidelity, but let me tell you, my lad, it wouldn't hurt you one bit if you had some of Elmer's fast technique in love-making!"

Chapter XXV

ELMER had, even in Zenith, to meet plenty of solemn and whiskery persons whose only pleasure aside from not doing agreeable things was keeping others from doing them. But the general bleakness of his sect was changing, and he found in Wellspring Church a Young Married Set who were nearly as cheerful as though they did not belong to a church.

This Young Married Set, though it was in good odor, though the wives taught Sunday School and the husbands elegantly passed collection plates, swallowed the Discipline with such friendly ease as a Catholic priest uses toward the latest bleeding Madonna. They lived, largely, in the new apartment-houses which were creeping into Old Town. They were not rich, but they had Fords and phonographs and gin. They danced, and they were willing to dance even in the presence of the Pastor.

They smelled in Elmer one of them, and though Cleo's presence stiffened them into uncomfortable propriety, when he dropped in on them alone they shouted, "Come on, Reverend, I bet you can shake a hoof as good as anybody! The wife says she's gotta dance with you! Gotta get acquainted with these Sins of the World if you're going to make snappy sermons!"

He agreed, and he did dance, with a pretty appearance of being shocked. He was light-footed still, for all his weight, and there was electricity in his grasp as his hands curled about his partner's waist.

"Oh, my, Reverend, if you hadn't been a preacher you'd have been some dancing-man!" the women fluttered, and for all his caution he could not keep from looking into their fascinated eyes, noting the flutter of their bosoms, and murmuring, "Better remember I'm human, honey! If I did cut loose—Zowie!"

And they admired him for it.

Once, when rather hungrily he sniffed at the odors of alcohol and tobacco, the host giggled, "Say, I hope you don't smell anything on my breath, Reverend—be fierce if you thought a good Methodist like me could ever throw in a shot of liquor!"

"It's not my business to smell anything except on Sundays," said Elmer amiably, and, "Come on now, Sister Gilson, let's try and fox-trot again. My gracious, you talk about me smelling for liquor! Think of what would happen if Brother Apfelmus knew his dear Pastor was slipping in a little dance! Mustn't tell on me, folks!"

"You bet we won't!" they said, and not even the elderly pietists on whom he called most often became louder adherents of the Reverend Elmer Gantry, better advertisers of his sermons, than these blades of the Young Married Set.

He acquired a habit of going to their parties. He was hungry for brisk companionship, and it was altogether depressing now to be with Cleo. She could never learn, not after ten efforts a day, that she could not keep him from saying "Damn!" by looking hurt and murmuring, "Oh, Elmer, how can you?"

He told her, regarding the parties, that he was going out to call on parishioners. And he was not altogether lying. His ambition was more to him now than any exalted dissipation, and however often he yearned for the mechanical pianos and the girls in pink kimonos of whom he so lickerishly preached, he violently kept away from them.

But the jolly wives of the Young Married Set— Particularly this Mrs. Gilson, Beryl Gilson, a girl of twenty-five, born for cuddling. She had a bleached and whining husband, who was always quarreling with her in a weakly violent sputtering; and she was obviously taken by Elmer's confident strength. He sat by her in "cozy-corners," and his arm was tense. But he won glory by keeping from embracing her. Also, he wasn't so sure that he could win her. She was flighty, fond of triumphs, but cautious, a city girl used to many suitors. And if she did prove kind— She was a member of his church, and she was talkative. She might go around hinting.

After these meditations he would flee to the hospitality of T. J. Rigg, in whose cheerfully sloven house he could relax safely, from whom he could get the facts about the private business careers of his more philanthropic contributors. But all the time the attraction of Beryl Gilson, the vision of her dove-smooth shoulders, was churning him to insanity.

II

He had not noticed them during that Sunday morning sermon in late autumn, not noticed them among the admirers who came up afterward to shake hands. Then he startled and croaked, so that the current hand-shaker thought he was ill.

Elmer had seen, loitering behind the others, his one-time forced fiancée, Lulu Bains of Schoenheim, and her lanky, rugged, vengeful cousin, Floyd Naylor.

They strayed up only when all the others were gone, when the affable ushers had stopped pouncing on victims and pump-handling them and patting their arms, as all ushers always do after all church services. Elmer wished the ushers were staying, to protect him, but he was more afraid of scandal than of violence.

He braced himself, feeling the great muscles surge along his back, then took quick decision and dashed toward Lulu and Floyd, yammering, "Well, well, well, well, well, well—"

Floyd shambled up, not at all unfriendly, and shook hands powerfully. "Lulu and I just heard you were in town—don't go to church much, I guess, so we didn't know. We're married!"

While he shook hands with Lulu, much more tenderly, Elmer gave his benign blessing with "Well, well! Mighty glad to hear it."

"Yep, been married—gosh, must be fourteen years now—got married just after we last seen you at Schoenheim."

By divine inspiration Elmer was led to look as though he were wounded clear to the heart at the revived memory of that unfortunate last seeing. He folded his hands in front of his beautiful morning coat, and looked noble, slightly milky and melancholy of eye. . . . But he was not milky. He was staring hard enough. He saw that though Floyd was still as clumsily uncouth as ever, Lulu—she must be thirty-three or -four now—had taken on the city. She wore a simple, almost smart hat, a good tweed top-coat, and she was really pretty. Her eyes were ingratiatingly soft, very inviting; she still smiled with a desire to be friendly to every one. Inevitably, she had grown plump, but she had not yet overdone it, and her white little paw was veritably that of a kitten.

All this Elmer noted, while he looked injured but forgiving and while Floyd stammered:

"You see, Reverend, I guess you thought we played you a pretty dirty trick that night on the picnic at Dad Bains', when you came back and I was kind of hugging Lulu."

"Yes, Floyd, I was pretty hurt, but— Let's forget and forgive!"

"No, but listen, Reverend! Golly, 'twas hard for me to come and explain to you, but now I've got going— Lulu and me, we weren't making love. No, sir! She was just feeling blue, and I was trying to cheer her up. Honest! Then when you got sore and skipped off, Pa Bains, he was so doggone mad—got out his shotgun and cussed and raised the old Ned, yes, sir, he simply raised Cain, and he wouldn't give me no chance to explain. Said I had to marry Lu. 'Well,' I says, 'if you think *that's* any hardship—'"

Floyd stopped to chuckle. Elmer was conscious that Lulu was studying him, in awe, in admiration, in a palpitating resurgence of affection.

"'If you think that's any hardship,' I says, 'let me tell you right now, Uncle,' I says, 'I been crazy to marry Lu ever since she was so high.' Well, there was a lot of argument. Dad Bains says first we had to go in town and explain everything to you. But you was gone away, next morning, and what with one thing and another—well, here we are! And doing pretty good. I own a garage out here on the edge of town, and we got a nice flat, and everything going fine. But Lule and I kind of felt maybe we ought to come around and explain, when we heard you were here. And got two fine kids, both boys!"

"Honestly, we never meant—we didn't!" begged Lulu.

Elmer condescended, "Of course, I understand perfectly, Sister Lulu!" He shook hands with Floyd, warmly, and with Lulu more warmly. "And I can't tell you how pleased I am that you were both so gallant and polite as to take the trouble and come and explain it to me. That was real courtesy, when I'd been such a silly idiot! *That* night—I suffered so over what I thought was your disloyalty that I didn't think I'd live through the night. But come! Shall we not talk of it again? All's understood now, and all's right!" He shook hands all over again. "And now that I've found you, two old friends like you—of course I'm still practically a stranger in Zenith—I'm not going to let you go! I'm going to come out and call on you. Do you belong to any church body here in Zenith?"

"Well, no, not exactly," said Floyd.

"Can't I persuade you to come here, sometimes, and perhaps think of joining later?"

"Well, I'll tell you, Reverend, in the auto business—kind of against my religion, at that, but you know how it is, in the auto business we're awful' busy on Sunday."

"Well, perhaps Lulu would like to come now and then."

"Sure. Women ought to stick by the church, that's what I always say. Dunno just how we got out of the habit, here in the city, and we've always talked about starting going again, but— Oh, we just kinda never got around to it, I guess."

"I hope, uh, I hope, Brother Floyd, that our miscomprehension, yours and mine that evening, had nothing to do with your alienation from the church! Oh, that would be a pity! Yes. Such a pity! But I could, perhaps, have a—a comprehension of it." (He saw that Lulu wasn't missing one of his dulcet and sinuous phrases; so different from Floyd's rustic blurting. She *was* pretty. Just plump enough. Cleo would be a fat old woman, he was afraid, instead of handsome. He couldn't of married Lulu. No. He'd been right. Small-town stuff. But awful nice to pat!) "Yes, I think I could understand it if you'd been offended, Floyd. What a young chump I was, even if I *was* a preacher, to not—not to see the real situation. Really, it's you who must forgive me for my wooden-headedness, Floyd!"

Sheepishly, Floyd grunted, "Well, I *did* think you flew off the handle kind of easy, and I guess it did make me kind of sore. But it don't matter none now."

Very interestedly, Elmer inquired of Floyd, "And I'll bet Lulu was even angrier at me for my silliness!"

"No, by gosh, she never would let me say a word against you, Reverend! Ha, ha, ha! Look at her! By golly, if she ain't blushing! Well, sir, that's a good one on her all right!"

Elmer looked, intently.

"Well, I'm glad everything's explained," he said unctuously. "Now, Sister Lulu, you must let me come out and explain about our fine friendly neighborhood church here, and the splendid work we're doing. I know that with two dear kiddies—two, was it?—splendid!—with them and a fine husband to look after, you must be kept pretty busy, but perhaps you might find time to teach a Sunday School class or, anyway, you might like to come to our jolly church suppers on Wednesday now and then. I'll tell you about our work, and you can talk it over with Floyd and see what he thinks. What would be a good time to call on you, and what's the address, Lulu? How, uh, how would tomorrow afternoon, about three, do? I wish I could come when Floyd's there, but all my evenings are so dreadfully taken up."

Next afternoon, at five minutes to three, the Reverend Elmer Gantry entered the cheap and flimsy apartment-house in which lived Floyd and Mrs. Naylor, impatiently kicked a baby-carriage out of the way, panted a little as he skipped up-stairs, and stood glowing, looking at Lulu as she opened the door.

"All alone?" he said—he almost whispered.

Her eyes dropped before his. "Yes. The boys are in school."

"Oh, that's too bad! I'd hoped to see them." As the door closed, as they stood in the inner hall, he broke out, "Oh, Lulu, my darling, I thought I'd lost you forever, and now I've found you again! Oh, forgive me for speaking like that! I shouldn't have! Forgive me! But if you knew how I've thought of you, dreamed of you, waited for you, all these years— No. I'm not allowed to talk like that. It's wicked. But we're going to be friends, aren't we, such dear, trusting, tender friends . . . Floyd and you and I?"

"Oh, *yes!*" she breathed, as she led him into the shabby sitting-room with its thrice-painted cane rockers, its couch covered with a knitted shawl, its department-store chromos of fruit and Versailles.

They stood recalling each other in the living-room. He muttered huskily, "Dear, it wouldn't be wrong for you to kiss me? Just once? Would it? To let me know you really do forgive me? You see, now we're like brother and sister."

She kissed him, shyly, fearfully, and she cried, "Oh, my darling, it's been so long!" Her arms clung about his neck, invincible, unrestrained.

When the boys came in from school and rang the clicker bell downstairs, the romantics were unduly cordial to them. When the boys had gone out to play, she cried, wildly, "Oh, I know it's wrong, but I've always loved you so!"

He inquired interestedly, "Do you feel wickeder because I'm a minister?"

"No! I'm proud of it! Like as if you were different from other men—like you were somehow closer to God. I'm *proud* you're a preacher! Any woman would be! It's—you know. Different!"

He kissed her. "Oh, you darling!" he said.

III

They had to be careful. Elmer had singularly little relish for having the horny-handed Floyd Naylor come in some afternoon and find him with Lulu.

Like many famous lovers in many ages, they found refuge in the church. Lulu was an admirable cook, and while in her new life in Zenith she had never reached out for such urban opportunities as lectures or concerts or literary clubs, she had by some obscure ambitiousness, some notion of a shop of her own, been stirred to attend a cooking-school and learn salads and pastry and canapés. Elmer was able to give her a weekly Tuesday evening cooking-class to teach at Wellspring, and even to get out of the trustees for her a salary of five dollars a week.

The cooking-class was over at ten. By that time the rest of the church was cleared, and Elmer had decided that Tuesday evening would be a desirable time for reading in his church office.

Cleo had many small activities in the church—clubs, Epworth League, fancy-work—but none on Tuesday evening.

Before Lulu came stumbling through the quiet church basement, the dark and musty corridor, before she tapped timidly at his door, he would be walking up and down, and when he held out his arms she flew into them unreasoning.

He had a new contentment.

"I'm really not a bad fellow. I don't go chasing after women—oh, that fool woman at the hotel didn't count—not now that I've got Lulu. Cleo never *was* married to me; she doesn't matter. I like to be good. If I'd just been married to somebody like Sharon! O God! Sharon! Am I untrue to her? No! Dear Lulu, sweet kid, I owe something to her, too. I wonder if I could get to see her Saturday—"

A new contentment he had, and explosive success.

Chapter XXVI

IN THE AUTUMN of his first year in Zenith Elmer started his famous Lively Sunday Evenings. Mornings, he announced, he would give them solid religious meat to sustain them through the week, but Sunday evenings he would provide the best cream puffs. Christianity was a Glad Religion, and he was going to make it a lot gladder.

There was a safe, conservative, sanguinary hymn or two at his Lively Sunday Evenings, and a short sermon about sunsets, authors, or gambling, but most of the time they were just happy boys and girls together. He had them sing "Auld Lang Syne," and "Swanee River," with all the balladry which might have been considered unecclesiastical if it had not been hallowed by the war: "Tipperary" and "There's a Long, Long, Trail," and "Pack Up Your Troubles in Your Old Kit Bag and Smile, Smile, Smile."

He made the women sing in contest against the men; the young people against the old; and the sinners against the Christians. That was lots of fun, because some of the most firmly saved brethren, like Elmer himself, pretended for a moment to be sinners. He made them whistle the chorus and hum it and speak it; he made them sing it while they waved handkerchiefs, waved one hand, waved both hands.

Other attractive features he provided. There was a ukulele solo by the champion uke-player from the University of Winnemac. There was a song rendered by a sweet little girl of three, perched up on the pulpit. There was a mouth-organ contest, between the celebrated Harmonica Quartette from the Higginbotham Casket Factory and the best four harmonicists from the B.&K.C. railroad shops; surprisingly won (according to the vote of the congregation) by the enterprising and pleasing young men from the railroad.

When this was over, Elmer stepped forward and said—you would never in the world have guessed he was joking unless you were near enough to catch the twinkle in his eyes—he said, "Now perhaps some of you folks think the pieces the boys have played tonight, like 'Marching Through Georgia' and 'Mammy,' aren't quite proper for a Methodist Church, but just let me show you how well our friend and brother, Billy Hicks here, can make the old mouth-organ behave in a real highbrow religious hymn."

And Billy played "Ach Du Lieber Augustin."

How they all laughed, even the serious old stewards! And when he had them in this humor, the Reverend Mr. Gantry was able to slam home, good and hard, some pretty straight truths about the horrors of starting children straight for hell by letting them read the colored comics on Sunday morning.

Once, to illustrate the evils of betting, he had them bet as to which of two frogs would jump first. Once he had the representative of an illustrious grape-juice company hand around sample glasses of his beverage, to illustrate the superiority of soft drinks to the horrors of alcohol. And once he had up on the platform a sickening twisted motor-car in which three people had been killed at a railroad-crossing. With this as an example, he showed his flock that motor speeding was but one symptom of the growing madness and worldliness and materialism of the age, and that this madness could be cured only by returning to the simple old-time religion as preached at the Wellspring Methodist Church.

The motor-car got him seven columns of publicity, with pictures of himself, the car, and the killed motorists.

In fact there were few of his new paths to righteousness which did not get adequate and respectful attention from the press.

There was, perhaps, no preacher in Zenith, not even the liberal Unitarian minister or the powerful Catholic bishop, who was not fond of the young gentlemen of the press. The newspapers of Zenith were as likely to attack religion as they were to attack the department-stores. But of all the clerics, none was so hearty, so friendly, so brotherly, to the reporters as the Reverend Elmer Gantry. His rival parsons were merely cordial to the sources of publicity when they called. Elmer did his own calling.

Six months after his coming to Zenith he began preparing a sermon on "The Making and Mission of a Great Newspaper." He informed the editors of his plan, and had himself taken through the plants and introduced to the staffs of the *Advocate-Times*, its sister, the *Evening Advocate*, the *Press*, the *Gazette*, and the *Crier*.

Out of his visits he managed to seize and hold the acquaintanceship of at least a dozen reporters. And he met the magnificent Colonel Rutherford Snow, owner of the *Advocate*, a white-haired, blasphemous, religious, scoundrelly old gentleman, whose social position in Zenith was as high as that of a bank-president or a corporation-counsel. Elmer and the Colonel recognized in each other an enterprising boldness, and the Colonel was so devoted to the church and its work in preserving the free and democratic American institutions that he regularly gave to the Pilgrim Congregational Church more than a tenth of what he made out of patent medicine advertisements—cancer cures, rupture cures, tuberculosis cures, and the notices of Old Dr. Bly. The Colonel was cordial to Elmer, and gave orders that his sermons should be reported at least once a month, no matter how the rest of the clergy shouted for attention.

But somehow Elmer could not keep the friendship of Bill Kingdom, that peculiarly hard-boiled veteran reporter of the *Advocate-Times*. He did everything he could; he called Bill by his first name, he gave him a quarter cigar, and he said "damn," but Bill looked uninterested when Elmer came around with the juiciest of stories about dance-halls. In grieved and righteous wrath, Elmer turned his charm on younger members of the *Advocate* staff, who were still new enough to be pleased by the good-fellowship of a preacher who could say "damn."

Elmer was particularly benevolent with one Miss Coey, sob-sister reporter for the *Evening Gazette* and an enthusiastic member of his church. She was worth a column a week. He always breathed at her after church.

Lulu raged, "It's hard enough to sit right there in the same pew with your wife, and never be introduced to her, because you say it isn't safe! But when I see you holding hands with that Coey woman, it's a little too much!"

But he explained that he considered Miss Coey a fool, that it made him sick to touch her, that he was nice to her only because he had to get publicity; and Lulu saw that it was all proper and truly noble of him . . . even when in the church bulletins, which he wrote each week for general distribution, he cheered, "Let's all congratulate Sister Coey, who so brilliantly represents the Arts among us, on her splendid piece in the recent *Gazette* about the drunken woman who was saved by the Salvation Army. Your pastor felt the quick tears springing to his eyes as he read it, which is a tribute to Sister Coey's powers of expression. And he is always glad to fellowship with the Salvation Army, as well as with all other branches of the true Protestant Evangelical Universal Church. Wellspring is the home of liberality, so long as it does not weaken morality or the proven principles of Bible Christianity."

II

As important as publicity to Elmer was the harassing drive of finance.

He had made one discovery superb in its simple genius—the best way to get money was to ask for it, hard enough and often enough. To call on rich men, to set Sunday School classes in competition against one another, to see that every one received pledge-envelopes, these were all useful and he pursued them earnestly. But none of them was so useful as to tell the congregation every Sunday what epochal good Wellspring and its pastor were doing, how much greater good they could do if they had more funds, and to demand their support now, this minute.

His Official Board was charmed to see the collections increasing even faster than the audiences. They insisted that the bishop send Elmer back to them for another year—indeed for many years—and they raised Elmer's salary to forty-five hundred dollars.

And in the autumn they let him have two subordinates—the Reverend Sidney Webster, B.A., B.D., as Assistant Pastor, and Mr. Henry Wink, B.A., as Director of Religious Education.

Mr. Webster had been secretary to Bishop Toomis, and it was likely that he would some day be secretary of one of the powerful church boards—the board of publications, the board of missions, the board of temperance and morals. He was a man of twenty-eight; he had been an excellent basket-ball player in Boston University; he was tight-mouthed as a New England president, efficient as an adding machine, and cold as the heart of a bureaucrat. If he loved God and humanity-in-general with rigid devotion, he loved no human individual; if he hated sin, he was too contemptuous of any actual sinner to hate him—he merely turned his frigid face away and told him to go to hell. He had no vices. He was also competent. He could preach, get rid of beggars, be quietly devout in death-bed prayers, keep down church expenses, and explain about the Trinity.

Henry Wink had a lisp and he told little simpering stories, but he was admirable in the direction of the Sunday School, vacation Bible schools, and the Epworth Leagues.

With Mr. Webster and Mr. Wink removing most of the church detail from him, Elmer became not less but more occupied. He no longer merely invited the public, but galloped out and dragged it in. He no longer merely scolded sin. He gratifyingly ended it.

III

When he had been in Zenith for a year and three-quarters, Elmer formed the Committee on Public Morals, and conducted his raids on the red-light district.

It seemed to him that he was getting less publicity. Even his friend, Colonel Rutherford Snow, owner of the *Advocate-Times*, explained that just saying things couldn't go on being news; news was essentially a report of things done.

"All right, I'll *do* things, by golly, now that I've got Webster and Wink to take care of the glad hand for the brethren!" Elmer vowed.

He received an inspiration to the effect that all of a sudden, for reasons not defined, "things have gotten so bad in Zenith, immorality is so rampant in high places and low, threatening the morals of youth and the sanctity of domesticity, that it is not enough for the ministry to stand back warning the malefactors, but a time now to come out of our dignified seclusion and personally wage open war on the forces of evil."

He said these startling things in the pulpit, he said them in an interview, and he said them in a letter to the most important clergymen in town, inviting them to meet with him to form a Committee on Public Morals and make plans for open war.

The devil must have been shaken. Anyway, the newspapers said that the mere threat of the formation of the Committee had caused "a number of well-known crooks and women of bad reputation to leave town." Who these scoundrels were, the papers did not say.

The Committee was to be composed of the Reverends Elmer Gantry and Otto Hickenlooper, Methodists; G. Prosper Edwards, Congregationalist; John Jennison Drew, Presbyterian; Edmund St. Vincent Zahn, Lutheran; James F. Gomer, Disciples; Father Matthew Smeesby, Catholic; Bernard Amos, Jewish; Hosea Jessup, Baptist; Willis Fortune Tate, Episcopalian; and Irving Tillish, Christian Science reader; with Wallace Umstead, the Y.M.C.A. secretary, four moral laymen, and a lawyer, Mr. T. J. Rigg.

They assembled at lunch in a private dining-room at the palatial Zenith Athletic Club. Being clergymen, and having to prove that they were also red-blooded, as they gathered before lunch in the lobby of the club they were particularly boisterous in shouting to passing acquaintances, florists and doctors and wholesale plumbers. To one George Babbitt, a real estate man, Dr. Drew, the Presbyterian, clamored, "Hey, Georgie! Got a flask along? Lunching with a bunch of preachers, and I reckon they'll want a drink!"

There was great admiration on the part of Mr. Babbitt, and laughter among all the clergymen, except the Episcopal Mr. Tate and the Christian Scientific Mr. Tillish.

The private dining-room at the club was a thin red apartment with two pictures of young Indian maidens of Lithuanian origin sitting in native costumes, which gave free play to their legs, under a rugged pine-tree against a background of extremely high mountains. In Private Dining-room A, beside them, was a lunch of the Men's Furnishers Association, addressed by S. Garrison Siegel of New York on "The Rented Dress Suit Business and How to Run It in a High-class Way."

The incipient Committee on Public Morals sat about a long narrow table in bent-wood chairs, in which they were always vainly trying to tilt back. Their table did not suggest debauchery and the demon rum. There were only chilly and naked-looking goblets of ice water.

They lunched, gravely, on consommé, celery, roast lamb, which was rather cold, mashed potatoes, which were arctic, Brussels sprouts, which were overstewed, ice cream, which was warm; with very large cups of coffee, and no smoking afterward.

Elmer began, "I don't know who is the oldest among us, but certainly no one in this room has had a more distinguished or more valuable term of Christian service than Dr. Edwards, of Pilgrim Congregational, and I know you'll join me in asking him to say grace before meat."

The table conversation was less cheerful than the blessing.

They all detested one another. Every one knew of some case in which each of the others had stolen, or was said to have tried to steal, some parishioner, to have corrupted his faith and appropriated his contributions. Dr. Hickenlooper and Dr. Drew had each advertised that he had the largest Sunday School in the city. All of the Protestants wanted to throw ruinous questions about the Immaculate Conception at Father Smeesby, and Father Smeesby, a smiling dark man of forty, had ready, in case they should attack the Catholic Church, the story of the ant who said to the elephant, "Move over, who do you think you're pushing?" All of them, except Mr. Tillish, wanted to ask Mr. Tillish how he'd ever been fooled by this charlatan, Mary Baker Eddy, and all of them, except the rabbi, wanted to ask Rabbi Amos why the Jews were such numbskulls as not to join the Christian faith.

They were dreadfully cordial. They kept their voices bland, and smiled too often, and never listened to one another. Elmer, aghast, saw that they would flee before making an organization if he did not draw them together. And what was the one thing in which they were all joyously interested? Why, vice! He'd begin the vice rampage now, instead of waiting till the business meeting after lunch.

He pounded on the table, and demanded, "Most of you have been in Zenith longer than myself. I admit ignorance. It is true that I have unearthed many dreadful, *dreadful* cases of secret sin. But you gentlemen, who know the town so much better— Am I right? Are Conditions as dreadful as I think, or do I exaggerate?"

All of them lighted up and, suddenly looking on Elmer as a really nice man after all, they began happily to tell of their woeful discoveries. . . . The blood-chilling incident of the father who found in the handbag of his sixteen-year-old daughter improper pictures. The suspicion that at a dinner of war veterans at the Leroy House there had danced a young lady who wore no garments save slippers and a hat.

"I know all about that dinner—I got the details from a man in my church—I'll tell you about it if you feel you ought to know," said Dr. Gomer.

They looked as though they decidedly felt that they ought to know. He went into details, very, and at the end Dr. Jessup gulped, "Oh, that Leroy House is absolutely a den of iniquity! It ought to be pulled!"

"It certainly ought to! I don't think I'm cruel," shouted Dr. Zahn, the Lutheran, "but if I had my way, I'd burn the proprietor of that joint at the stake!"

All of them had incidents of shocking obscenity all over the place—all of them except Father Smeesby, who sat back and smiled, the Episcopal Dr. Tate, who sat back and looked bored, and Mr. Tillish, the healer, who sat back and looked chilly. In fact it seemed as though, despite the efforts of themselves and the thousands of other inspired and highly trained Christian ministers who had worked over it ever since its foundation, the city of Zenith was another Sodom. But the alarmed apostles did not appear to be so worried as they said they were. They listened with almost benign attention while Dr. Zahn, in his German accent, told of alarming crushes between the society girls whom he knew so well from dining once a year with his richest parishioner.

They were all, indeed, absorbed in vice to a degree gratifying to Elmer.

But at the time for doing something about it, for passing resolutions and appointing sub-committees and outlining programs, they drew back.

"Can't we all get together—pool our efforts?" pleaded Elmer. "Whatever our creedal differences, surely we stand alike in worshiping the same God and advocating the same code of morals. I'd like to see this Committee as a permanent organization, and finally, when the time is ripe— Think how it would jolt the town! All of us getting ourselves appointed special police or deputy sheriffs, and personally marching down on these abominations, arresting the blood-guilty wretches, and putting them where they can do no harm! Maybe leading our church members in the crusade! Think of it!"

They did think of it, and they were alarmed.

Father Smeesby spoke. "My church, gentlemen, probably has a more rigid theology than yours, but I don't think we're quite so alarmed by discovering the fact, which seems to astonish you, that sinners often sin. The Catholic Church may be harder to believe, but it's easier to live with."

"My organization," said Mr. Tillish, "could not think of joining in a wild witch-hunt, any more than we could in indiscriminate charity. For both the poverty-laden and the vicious—" He made a little whistling between his beautiful but false teeth, and went on with frigid benignancy. "For all such, the truth is clearly stated in 'Science and Health' and made public in all our meetings—the truth that both vice and poverty, like sickness, are unreal, are errors, to be got rid of by understanding that God is All-in-all; that disease, death, evil, sin deny good, omnipotent God, life. Well! If these so-called sufferers do not care to take the truth when it is freely offered them, is that our fault? I understand your sympathy with the unfortunate, but you are not going to put out ignorance by fire."

"Golly, let me crawl too," chuckled Rabbi Amos. "If you want to get a vice-crusading rabbi, get one of these smart-aleck young liberals from the Cincinnati school—and they'll mostly have too much sympathy with the sinners to help you either! Anyway, my congregation is so horribly respectable that if their rabbi did anything but sit in his study and look learned, they'd kick him out."

"And I," said Dr. Willis Fortune Tate, of St. Colomb's Episcopal, "if you will permit me to say so, can regard such a project as our acting like policemen and dealing with these malefactors in person as nothing short of vulgar, as well as useless. I understand your high ideals, Dr. Gantry—"

"Mr. Gantry."

"—Mr. Gantry, and I honor you for them, and respect your energy, but I beg you to consider how the press and the ordinary laity, with their incurably common and untrained minds, would misunderstand."

"I'm afraid I must agree with Dr. Tate," said the Congregational Dr. G. Prosper Edwards, in the manner of the Pilgrim's Monument agreeing with Westminster Abbey.

And as for the others, they said they really must "take time and think it over," and they all got away as hastily and cordially as they could.

Elmer walked with his friend and pillar, Mr. T. J. Rigg, toward the dentist's office in which even an ordained minister of God would shortly take on strangely normal writhings and gurglings.

"They're a fine bunch of scared prophets, a noble lot of apostolic ice-cream cones!" protested Mr. Rigg. "Hard luck, Brother Elmer! I'm sorry. It really is good stuff, this vice-crusading. Oh, I don't suppose it makes the slightest difference in the amount of vice—and I don't know that it ought to make any. Got to give fellows that haven't our advantages some chance to let off steam. But it does get the church a lot of attention. I'm mighty proud of the way we're building up Wellspring Church again. Kind of a hobby with me. But makes me indignant, these spiritual cold-storage eggs not supporting you!"

But as he looked up he saw that Elmer was grinning.

"I'm not worried, T. J. Fact, I'm tickled to death. First place, I've scared 'em off the subject of vice. Before they get back to preaching about it, I'll have the whole subject absolutely patented for our church. And now they won't have the nerve to imitate me if I do do this personal crusading stunt. Third, I can preach against 'em! And I will! You watch me! Oh, not mention any names—no come-back—but tell 'em how I pleaded with a gang of preachers to take practical methods to end immorality, and they were all scared!"

"Fine!" said the benevolent trustee. "We'll let 'em know that Wellspring is the one church that's really following the gospel."

"We sure will! Now listen, T. J.: if you trustees will stand for the expense, I want to get a couple of good private detectives or something, and have 'em dig up a lot of real addresses of places that *are* vicious—there must be some of 'em—and get some evidence. Then I'll jump on the police for not having pinched these places. I'll say they're so wide open that the police *must* know of 'em. And probably that's true, too. Man! A sensation! Run our disclosures every Sunday evening for a month! Make the chief of police try to answer us in the press!"

"Good stuff! Well, I know a fellow—he was a government man, prohibition agent, and got fired for boozing and blackmail. He's not exactly a double-crosser, lot straighter than most prohibition agents, but still I think he could slip us some real addresses. I'll have him see you."

IV

When from his pulpit the Reverend Elmer Gantry announced that the authorities of Zenith were "deliberately conniving in protected vice," and that he could give the addresses and ownerships of sixteen brothels, eleven blind tigers, and two agencies for selling cocaine and heroin, along with an obscene private burlesque show so dreadful that he could only hint at the nature of its program, when he attacked the chief of police and promised to give more detailed complaints next Sunday, then the town exploded.

There were front-page newspaper stories, yelping replies by the mayor and chief of police, re-replies from Elmer, interviews with everybody, and a full-page account of white slavery in Chicago. In clubs and offices, in church societies and the back-rooms of "soft-drink stands," there was a blizzard of talk. Elmer had to be protected against hundreds of callers, telephoners, letter writers. His assistant, Sidney Webster, and Miss Bundle, the secretary, could not keep the mob from him, and he hid out in T. J. Rigg's house, accessible to no one, except to newspaper reporters who for any Christian and brotherly reason might care to see him.

For the second Sunday evening of his jeremiad, the church was full half an hour before opening-time, standing-room was taken even to the back of the lobby, hundreds clamored at the closed doors.

He gave the exact addresses of eight dives, told what dreadful drinkings of corn whisky went on there, and reported the number of policemen, in uniform, who had been in the more attractive of these resorts during the past week.

Despite all the police could do to help their friends close up for a time, it was necessary for them to arrest ten or fifteen of the hundred-odd criminals whom Elmer named. But the chief of police triumphed by announcing that it was impossible to find any of the others.

"All right," Elmer murmured to the chief, in the gentleness of a boxed newspaper interview in bold-face type, "if you'll make me a temporary lieutenant of police and give me a squad, I'll find and close five dives in one evening—any evening save Sunday."

"I'll do it—and you can make your raids tomorrow," said the chief, in the official dignity of headlines.

Mr. Rigg was a little alarmed.

"Think you're going too far, Elmer," he said. "If you really antagonize any of the big wholesale bootleggers, they'll get us financially, and if you hit any of the tough ones, they're likely to bump you off. Darn' dangerous."

"I know. I'm just going to pick out some of the smaller fellows that make their own booze and haven't got any police protection except slipping five or ten to the cop on the beat. The newspapers will make 'em out regular homicidal gangsters, to get a good story, and we'll have the credit without being foolish and taking risks."

V

At least a thousand people were trying to get near the Central Police Station on the evening when a dozen armed policemen marched down the steps of the station-house and stood at attention, looking up at the door, awaiting their leader.

He came out, the great Reverend Mr. Gantry, and stood posing on the steps, while the policemen saluted, the crowd cheered or sneered, and the press cameras went off in a fury of flashlight powder. He wore the gilt-encircled cap of a police lieutenant, with a lugubrious frock coat and black trousers, and under his arm he carried a Bible.

Two patrol wagons clanged away, and all the women in the crowd, except certain professional ladies, who were grievously profane, gasped their admiration of this modern Savonarola.

He had promised the mob at least one real house of prostitution.

VI

There were two amiable young females who, tired of working in a rather nasty bread factory and of being unremuneratively seduced by the large, pale, puffy bakers on Sunday afternoons, had found it easier and much jollier to set up a small flat in a street near Elmer's church. They were fond of reading the magazines and dancing to the phonograph and of going to church—usually Elmer's church. If their relations to their gentlemen friends were more comforting than a preacher could expect, after his experience of the sacred and chilly state of matrimony, they entertained only a few of these friends, often they darned their socks, and almost always they praised Elmer's oratory.

One of the girls, this evening, was discoursing with a man who was later proved in court not to be her husband; the other was in the kitchen, making a birthday-cake for her niece and humming "Onward, Christian Soldiers." She was dazed by a rumbling, a clanging, a shouting in the street below, then mob-sounds on the stairs. She fluttered into the living-room, to see their pretty imitation mahogany door smashed in with a rifle butt.

Into the room crowded a dozen grinning policemen, followed, to her modest shame, by her adored family prophet, the Reverend Gantry. But it was not the cheerful, laughing Mr. Gantry that she knew. He held out his arm in a horrible gesture of holiness, and bawled, "Scarlet woman! Thy sins be upon thy head! No longer are you going to get away with leading poor unfortunate young men into the sink and cesspool of iniquity! Sergeant! Draw your revolver! These women are known to be up to every trick!"

"All right, sure, loot!" giggled the brick-faced police sergeant.

"Oh, rats! This girl looks as dangerous as a goldfish, Gantry," remarked Bill Kingdom, of the *Advocate-Times* . . . he who was two hours later to do an epic of the heroism of the Great Crusader.

"Let's see what the other girl's up to," snickered one of the policemen.

They all laughed very much as they looked into the bedroom, where a half-dressed girl and a man shrank by the window, their faces sick with shame.

It was with her—ignoring Bill Kingdom's mutters of "Oh, drop it! Pick on somebody your size!"—that Elmer the vice-slayer became really Biblical.

Only the insistence of Bill Kingdom kept Lieutenant Gantry from making his men load the erring one into the patrol wagon in her chemise.

Then Elmer led them to a secret den where, it was securely reported, men were ruining their bodies and souls by guzzling the devil's brew of alcohol.

VII

Mr. Oscar Hochlauf had been a saloon-keeper in the days before prohibition, but when prohibition came, he was a saloon-keeper. A very sound, old-fashioned, drowsy, agreeable resort was Oscar's Place; none of the grander public houses had more artistic soap scrawls on the mirror behind the bar; none had spicier pickled herring.

Tonight there were three men before the bar: Emil Fischer, the carpenter, who had a mustache like an ear-muff; his son Ben, whom Emil was training to drink wholesome beer instead of the whisky and gin which America was forcing on the people; and old Daddy Sorenson, the Swedish tailor.

They were discussing jazz.

"I came to America for liberty—I think Ben's son will go back to Germany for liberty," said Emil. "When I was a young man here, four of us used to play every Saturday evening—Bach we played, and Brahms—*Gott weiss* we played terrible, but we liked it, and we never made others listen.

Now, wherever you go, this jazz, like a St. Vitus's. Jazz iss to music what this Reverend Gantry you read about is to an old-time *Prediger*. I guess maybe he was never born, that Gantry fellow—he was blowed out of a saxophone."

"Aw, this country's all right, Pa," said Ben.

"Sure, dot's right," said Oscar Hochlauf contentedly, while he sliced the foam off a glass of beer. "The Americans, like when I knew dem first, when dere was Bill Nye and Eugene Field, dey used to laugh. Now dey get solemn. When dey start laughing again, dey roar dere heads off at fellows like Gantry and most all dese preachers dat try to tell everybody how dey got to live. And if the people laugh—oof!—God help the preachers!"

"Vell, that's how it is. Say, did I tell you, Oscar," said the Swedish tailor, "my grandson Villiam, he got a scholarship in the university!"

"That's fine!" they all agreed, slapping Daddy Sorenson on the back . . . as a dozen policemen, followed by a large and gloomy gentleman armed with a Bible, burst in through the front and back doors, and the gloomy gentleman, pointing at the astounded Oscar, bellowed, "Arrest that man and hold all these other fellows!"

To Oscar then, and to an audience increasing ten a second:

"I've got you! You're the kind that teaches young boys to drink—it's you that start them on the road to every hellish vice, to gambling and murder, with your hellish beverages, with your draught of the devil himself!"

Arrested for the first time in his life, bewildered, broken, feebly leaning on the arms of two policemen, Oscar Hochlauf straightened at this, and screamed:

"Dot's a damned lie! Always when you let me, I handle Eitelbaum's beer, the finest in the state, and since den I make my own beer. It is good! It is honest! 'Hellish beverage!' Dot *you* should judge of beer—dot a pig should judge poetry! Your Christ dot made vine, *he* vould like my beer!"

Elmer jumped forward with his great fist doubled. Only the sudden grip of the police sergeant kept him from striking down the blasphemer. He shrieked, "Take that foul-mouthed bum to the wagon! I'll see he gets the limit!"

And Bill Kingdom murmured to himself, "Gallant preacher single-handed faces saloon full of desperate gun-men and rebukes them for taking the name of the Lord in vain. Oh, I'll get a swell story. . . . Then I think I'll commit suicide."

VIII

The attendant crowd and the policemen had whispered that, from the careful way in which he followed instead of leading, it might be judged that the Reverend Lieutenant Gantry was afraid of the sinister criminals whom he was attacking. And it is true that Elmer had no large fancy for revolver duels. But he had not lost his delight in conflict; he was physically no coward; and they were all edified to see this when the raiders dashed into the resort of Nick Spoletti.

Nick, who conducted a bar in a basement, had been a prize-fighter; he was cool and quick. He heard the crusaders coming and shouted to his customers, "Beat it! Side door! I'll hold 'em back!"

He met the first of the policemen at the bottom of the steps, and dropped him with the crack of a bottle over his head. The next tripped over the body, and the others halted, peering, looking embarrassed, drawing revolvers. But Elmer smelled battle. He forgot holiness. He dropped his Bible, thrust aside two policemen, and swung on Nick from the bottom step. Nick slashed at his head, but with a boxer's jerk of the neck Elmer slid away from the punch, and knocked out Nick with a deliberately murderous left.

"Golly, the parson's got an awful wallop!" grunted the sergeant, and Bill Kingdom sighed, "Not so bad!" and Elmer knew that he had won . . . that he would be the hero of Zenith . . . that he was now the Sir Lancelot as well as the William Jennings Bryan of the Methodist Church.

IX

After two more raids he was delivered at his home by patrol wagon, and left with not entirely sardonic cheers by the policemen.

Cleo rushed to meet him, crying, "Oh, you're safe! Oh, my dear, you're hurt!"

His cheek was slightly bleeding.

In a passion of admiration for himself so hot that it extended even to her, he clasped her, kissed her wetly, and roared, "It's nothing! Oh, it went great! We raided five places—arrested twenty-seven criminals—took them in every sort of horrible debauchery—things I never dreamed could exist!"

"You poor dear!"

There was not enough audience, with merely Cleo, and the maid peering from the back of the hall.

"Let's go and tell the kids. Maybe they'll be proud of their dad!" he interrupted her.

"Dear, they're asleep—"

"Oh! I see! Sleep is more important to 'em than to know their father is a man who isn't afraid to back up his gospel with his very life!"

"Oh, I didn't mean—I meant— Yes, of course, you're right. It'll be a wonderful example and inspiration. But let me put some stickum plaster on your cheek first."

By the time she had washed the cut, and bound it and fussed over it, he had forgotten the children and their need of an heroic exemplar, as she had expected, and he sat on the edge of the bath-tub telling her that he was an entire Trojan army. She was so worshipful that he became almost amorous, until it seemed to him from her anxious patting of his arm that she was trying to make him so. It angered him—that she, so unappealing, should have the egotism to try to attract a man like himself. He went off to his own room, wishing that Lulu were here to rejoice in his splendor, the beginning of his fame as the up-to-date John Wesley.

Chapter XXVII

ELMER, in court, got convictions of sixteen out of the twenty-seven fiends whom he had arrested, with an extra six months for Oscar Hochlauf for resisting arrest and the use of abusive and profane language. The judge praised him; the mayor forgave him; the chief of police shook his hand and invited him to use a police squad at any time; and some of the younger reporters did not cover their mouths with their hands.

Vice was ended in Zenith. It was thirty days before any of the gay ladies were really back at work—though the gentlemanly jailers at the workhouse did let some of them out for an occasional night.

Every Sunday evening now people were turned from the door of Elmer's church. If they did not always have a sermon about vice, at least they enjoyed the saxophone solos, and singing "There'll be a Hot Time in the Old Town Tonight." And once they were entertained by a professional juggler who wore (it was Elmer's own idea) a placard proclaiming that he stood for "God's Word" and who showed how easy it was to pick up weights symbolically labeled "Sin" and "Sorrow" and "Ignorance" and "Papistry."

The trustees were discussing the erection of a new and much larger church, a project for which Elmer himself had begun to prepare a year before, by reminding the trustees how many new apartment-houses were replacing the run-down residences in Old Town.

The trustees raised his salary to five thousand, and they increased the budget for institutional work. Elmer did not institute so many clubs for students of chiropractic and the art of motion-picture acting as did Dr. Otto Hickenlooper of Central Methodist, but there was scarcely an hour from nine in the morning till ten at night when some circle was not trying to do good to somebody . . . and even after ten there were often Elmer and Lulu Bains Naylor, conferring on cooking classes.

Elmer had seen the danger of his crusading publicity and

his Lively Sunday Evenings—the danger of being considered a clown instead of a great moral leader.

"I've got to figure out some way so's I keep dignified and yet keep folks interested," he meditated. "The thing is sort of to have other people do the monkey-business, but me, I got to be up-stage and not smile as much as I've been doing. And just when the poor chumps think my Sunday evening is nothing but a vaudeville show, I'll suddenly soak 'em with a regular old-time hell-fire and damnation sermon, or be poetic and that stuff."

It worked, reasonably. Though many of his rival preachers in Zenith went on calling him "clown" and "charlatan" and "sensationalist," no one could fail to appreciate his lofty soul and his weighty scholarship, once they had seen him stand in agonized silent prayer, then level his long forefinger and intone:

"You have laughed now. You have sung. You have been merry. But what came ye forth into the wilderness for to see? Merely laughter? I want you to stop a moment now and think just how long it is since you have realized that any night death may demand your souls, and that then, laughter or no laughter, unless you have found the peace of God, unless you have accepted Christ Jesus as your savior, you may with no chance of last-minute repentance be hurled into horrible and shrieking and appalling eternal torture!"

Elmer had become so distinguished that the Rotary Club elected him to membership with zeal.

The Rotary Club was an assemblage of accountants, tailors, osteopaths, university-presidents, carpet-manufacturers, advertising men, millinery-dealers, ice-dealers, piano salesmen, laundrymen, and like leaders of public thought, who met weekly for the purposes of lunching together, listening to addresses by visiting actors and by lobbyists against the recognition of Russia, beholding vaudeville teams in eccentric dances, and indulging in passionate rhapsodies about Service and Business Ethics. They asserted that their one desire in their several callings was not to make money but only to serve and benefit a thing called the Public. They were as earnest about this as was the Reverend Elmer Gantry about vice.

He was extraordinarily at home among the Rotarians;

equally happy in being a good fellow with such good fellows as these and in making short speeches to the effect that "Jesus Christ would be a Rotarian if he lived today—Lincoln would be a Rotarian today—William McKinley would be a Rotarian today. All these men preached the principles of Rotary: one for all and all for one; helpfulness towards one's community, and respect for God."

It was a rule of this organization, which was merry and full of greetings in between inspirational addresses, that every one should, at lunch, be called by his first name. They shouted at the Reverend Mr. Gantry as "Elmer" or "Elm," while he called his haberdasher "Ike" and beamed on his shoe-seller as "Rudy." A few years before, this intimacy might have led him into indiscretions, into speaking vulgarly, or even desiring a drink. But he had learned his rôle of dignity now, and though he observed, "Dandy day, Shorty!" he was quick to follow it up unhesitatingly with an orotund "I trust that you have been able to enjoy the beauty of the vernal foliage in the country this week." So Shorty and his pals went up and down informing the citizenry that Reverend Gantry was a "good scout, a prince of a good fellow, but a mighty deep thinker, and a real honest-to-God orator."

When Elmer informed T. J. Rigg of the joys of Rotary, the lawyer scratched his chin and suggested, "Fine. But look here, Brother Elmer. There's one thing you're neglecting: the really big boys with the long pockets. Got to know 'em. Not many of 'em Methodists—they go out for Episcopalianism or Presbyterianism or Congregationalism or Christian Science, or stay out of the church altogether. But that's no reason why we can't turn their *money* Methodist. You wouldn't find but mighty few of these Rotarians in the Tonawanda Country Club—into which I bought my way by blackmailing, you might say, a wheat speculator."

"But—but—why, T. J., those Rotarians—why there's fellows in there like Ira Runyon, the managing editor of the *Advocate*, and Win Grant, the realtor—"

"Yeh, but the owner of the *Advocate*, and the banker that's letting Win Grant run on till he bankrupts, and the corporation counsel that keeps 'em all out of jail, you don't find *those* malefactors going to no lunch club and yipping about Service!

You find 'em sitting at small tables at the old Union Club, and laughing themselves sick about Service. And for golf, they go to Tonawanda. I couldn't get you into the Union Club. They wouldn't have any preacher that talks about vice—the kind of preacher that belongs to the Union talks about the new model Cadillac and how hard it is to get genuwine Eyetalian vermouth. But the Tonawanda— They might let you in. For respectability. To prove that they couldn't have the gin they've got in their lockers in their lockers."

It was done, though it took six months and a deal of secret politics conducted by T. J. Rigg.

Wellspring Church, including the pastor of Wellspring, bloomed with pride that Elmer had been so elevated socially as to be allowed to play golf with bankers.

Only he couldn't play golf.

From April to July, while he never appeared on the links with other players, Elmer took lessons from the Tonawanda professional, three mornings a week, driving out in the smart new Buick which he had bought and almost paid for.

The professional was a traditionally small and gnarled and sandy Scotchman, from Indiana, and he was so traditionally rude that Elmer put on meekness.

"Put back your divots! D' you think this is a church?" snapped the professional.

"Damn it, I always forget, Scotty," whined Elmer. "Guess it must be hard on you to have to train these preachers."

"Preachers is nothing to me, and millionaires is nothing to me, but gawf grounds is a lot," grunted Scotty. (He was a zealous Presbyterian and to be picturesquely rude to Christian customers was as hard for him as it was to keep up the Scotch accent which he had learned from a real Liverpool Irishman.)

Elmer was strong, he was placid when he was out-of-doors, and his eye was quick. When he first appeared publicly at Tonawanda, in a foursome with T. J. Rigg and two most respectable doctors, he and his game were watched and commended. When he dressed in the locker-room and did not appear to note the square bottle in use ten feet away, he was accepted as a man of the world.

William Dollinger Styles, member of the Tonawanda house

committee, president of the fabulous W. D. Styles Wholesale Hardware Company—the man who had introduced the Bite Edge Ax through all the land from Louisville to Detroit, and introduced white knickers to the Tonawanda Club—this baron, this bishop, of business actually introduced himself to Elmer and made him welcome.

"Glad to see you here, dominie. Played much golf?"

"No, I've only taken it up recently, but you bet I'm going to be a real fan from now on."

"That's fine. Tell you how I feel about it, Reverend. We fellows that have to stick to our desks and make decisions that guide the common people, you religiously and me commercially, it's a good thing for us, and through us for them, to go out and get next to Nature, and put ourselves in shape to tackle our complicated problems (as I said recently in an after-dinner speech at the Chamber of Commerce banquet) and keep a good sane outlook so's we won't be swept away by every breeze of fickle and changing public opinion and so inevitably—"

In fact, said Mr. William Dollinger Styles, he liked golf.

Elmer tenderly agreed with "Yes, that's certainly a fact; certainly is a fact. Be a good thing for a whole lot of preachers if they got out and exercised more instead of always reading."

"Yes, I wish you'd tell my dominie that—not that I go to church such a whole lot, but I'm church treasurer and take kind of an interest—Dorchester Congregational—Reverend Shallard."

"Oh! Frank Shallard! Why, I knew him in theological seminary! Fine, straight, intelligent fellow, Frank."

"Well, yes, but I don't like the way he's always carrying on and almost coming right out and defending a lot of these crooked labor unions. That's why I don't hardly ever hear his sermons, but I can't get the deacons to see it. And as I say, be better for him if he got outdoors more. Well, glad to met you, Reverend. You must join one of our foursomes some day—if you can stand a little cussing, maybe!"

"Well, I'll try to, sir! Been mighty fine to have met you!"

"H'm!" reflected Elmer. "So Frank, the belly-aching highbrow, has got as rich a man as Styles in his fold, and Styles doesn't like him. Wonder if Styles could turn Methodist—wonder if he could be pinched off Frank? I'll ask Rigg."

But the charm of the place, the day, the implied social position, was such that Elmer turned from these purely religious broodings to more esthetic thoughts.

Rigg had driven home. Elmer sat by himself on the huge porch of the Tonawanda Club, a long gray countryhouse on a hill sloping to the Appleseed River, with tawny fields of barley among orchards on the bank beyond. The golf-course was scattered with men in Harris tweeds, girls in short skirts which fluttered about their legs. A man in white flannels drove up in a Rolls-Royce roadster—the only one in Zenith as yet—and Elmer felt ennobled by belonging to the same club with a Rolls-Royce. On the lawn before the porch, men with English-officer mustaches and pretty women in pale frocks were taking tea at tables under striped garden-umbrellas.

Elmer knew none of them actually, but a few by sight.

"Golly, I'll be right in with all these swells some day! Must work it careful, and be snooty, and not try to pick 'em up too quick."

A group of weighty-looking men of fifty, near him, were conversing on the arts and public policy. As he listened, Elmer decided, "Yep, Rigg was right. Those are fine fellows at the Rotary Club; fine, high-class, educated gentlemen, and certainly raking in the money; mighty cute in business but upholding the highest ideals. But they haven't got the class of these really Big Boys."

Entranced, he gave heed to the magnates—a bond broker, a mine-owner, a lawyer, a millionaire lumberman:

"Yes, sir, what the country at large doesn't understand is that the stabilization of sterling has a good effect on our trade with Britain—"

"I told them that far from refusing to recognize the rights of labor, I had myself come up from the ranks, to some extent, and I was doing all in my power to benefit them, but I certainly did refuse to listen to the caterwauling of a lot of hired agitators from the so-called unions, and that if they didn't like the way I did things—"

"Yes, it opened at 73½, but knowing what had happened to Saracen Common—"

"Yes, sir, you can depend on a Pierce-Arrow, you certainly can—"

Elmer drew a youthful, passionate, shuddering breath at being so nearly in communion with the powers that governed Zenith and thought for Zenith, that governed America and thought for it. He longed to stay, but he had the task, unworthy of his powers of social decoration, of preparing a short clever talk on missions among the Digger Indians.

As he drove home he rejoiced, "Some day I'll be able to put it over with the best of 'em socially. When I get to be a bishop, believe me I'm not going to hang around jawing about Sunday School methods! I'll be entertaining the bon ton, senators and everybody. . . . Cleo would look fine at a big dinner, with the right dress. . . . If she wasn't so darn' priggish. Oh, maybe she'll die before then. . . . I think I'll marry an Episcopalian. . . . I wonder if I could get an Episcopal bishopric if I switched to that nightshirt crowd? More class. No; Methodist bigger church; and don't guess the Episcopalopians would stand any good red-blooded sermons on vice and all that."

II

The Gilfeather Chautauqua Corporation, which conducts week-long Chautauquas in small towns, had not been interested when Elmer had hinted, three years ago, that he had a Message to the Youth of America, one worth at least a hundred a week, and that he would be glad to go right out to the Youth and deliver it. But when Elmer's demolition of all vice in Zenith had made him celebrated, and even gained him a paragraph or two as the Crusading Parson, in New York and Chicago, the Gilfeather Corporation had a new appreciation. They came to him, besieged him, offered him two hundred a week and headlines in the posters, for a three-months tour.

But Elmer did not want to ask the trustees for a three-months leave. He had a notion of a summer in Europe a year or two from now. That extended study of European culture, first hand, would be just the finishing polish to enable him to hold any pulpit in the country.

He did, however, fill in during late August and early September as substitute for a Gilfeather headliner—the renowned J. Thurston Wallett, M.D., D.O., D.N., who had delighted thousands with his witty and instructive lecture, "Diet or Die, Nature or Nix," until he had unfortunately been taken ill at Powassie, Iowa, from eating too many green cantaloupes.

Elmer had planned to spend August with his family in Northern Michigan—planned it most uncomfortably, for while it was conceivable to endure Cleo in the city, with his work, his clubs, and Lulu, a month with no relief from her solemn drooping face and cry-baby voice would be trying even to a Professional Good Man.

He explained to her that duty called, and departed with speed, stopping only long enough to get several books of inspirational essays from the public library for aid in preparing his Chautauqua lecture.

He was delighted with his coming adventure—money, fame in new quarters, crowds for whom he would not have to think up fresh personal experiences. And he might find a woman friend who would understand him and give to his own solid genius that lighter touch of the feminine. He was, he admitted, almost as tired of Lulu as of Cleo. He pictured a Chautauqua lady pianist or soprano or ventriloquist or soloist on the musical saw—he pictured a surprised, thrilled meeting in the amber light under the canvas roof—recognition between kindred fine and lonely souls—

And he found it of course.

III

Elmer's metaphysical lecture, entitled "Whoa Up, Youth!" with its counsel about abstinence, chastity, industry, and honesty, its heaven-vaulting poetic passage about Love (the only bow on life's dark cloud, the morning and the evening star), and its anecdote of his fight to save a college-mate named Jim from drink and atheism, became one of the classics among Chautauqua masterpieces.

And Elmer better than any one else among the Talent (except perhaps the gentleman who played national anthems on water glasses, a Lettish gentleman innocent of English) side-stepped on the question of the K.K.K.

The new Ku Klux Klan, an organization of the fathers,

younger brothers, and employees of the men who had succeeded and became Rotarians, had just become a political difficulty. Many of the most worthy Methodist and Baptist clergymen supported it and were supported by it; and personally Elmer admired its principle—to keep all foreigners, Jews, Catholics, and negroes in their place, which was no place at all, and let the country be led by native Protestants, like Elmer Gantry.

But he perceived that in the cities there were prominent people, nice people, rich people, even among the Methodists and Baptists, who felt that a man could be a Jew and still an American citizen. It seemed to him more truly American, also a lot safer, to avoid the problem. So everywhere he took a message of reconciliation to the effect:

"Regarding religious, political, and social organizations, I defend the right of every man in our free America to organize with his fellows when and as he pleases, for any purpose he pleases, but I also defend the right of any other free American citizen to demand that such an organization shall not dictate his mode of thought or, so long as it be moral, his mode of conduct."

That pleased both the K.K.K. and the opponents of the K.K.K., and everybody admired Elmer's powers of thought.

He came with a boom and a flash to the town of Blackfoot Creek, Indiana, and there the local committee permitted the Methodist minister, one Andrew Pengilly, to entertain his renowned brother priest.

IV

Always a little lonely, lost in the ceaseless unfolding of his mysticism, old Andrew Pengilly had been the lonelier since Frank Shallard had left him.

When he heard that the Reverend Elmer Gantry was coming, Mr. Pengilly murmured to the local committee that it would be a pleasure to put up Mr. Gantry and save him from the scurfy village hotel.

He had read of Mr. Gantry as an impressive orator, a courageous fighter against Sin. Mr. Pengilly sighed. Himself, somehow, he had never been able to find so very much Sin about.

His fault. A silly old dreamer. He rejoiced that he, the mousy village curé, was about to have here, glorifying his cottage, a St. Michael in dazzling armor.

V

After the evening Chautauqua Elmer sat in Mr. Pengilly's hovel, and he was graciously condescending.

"You say, Brother Pengilly, that you've heard of our work at Wellspring? But do we get so near the hearts of the weak and unfortunate as you here? Oh, no; sometimes I think that my first pastorate, in a town smaller than this, was in many ways more blessed than our tremendous to-do in the great city. And what *is* accomplished there is no credit to me. I have such splendid, such touchingly loyal assistants—Mr. Webster, the assistant pastor—such a consecrated worker, and yet right on the job—and Mr. Wink, and Miss Weezeger, the deaconess, and *dear* Miss Bundle, the secretary—*such* a faithful soul, *so* industrious. Oh, yes, I am singularly blessed! But, uh, but— Given these people, who really do the work, we've been able to put over some pretty good things—with God's leading. Why, say, we've started the only class in show-window dressing in any church in the United States—and I should suppose England and France! We've already seen the most wonderful results, not only in raising the salary of several of the fine young men in our church, but in increasing business throughout the city and improving the appearance of show-windows, and you know how much that adds to the beauty of the down-town streets! And the crowds do seem to be increasing steadily. We had over eleven hundred present on my last Sunday evening in Zenith, and that in summer! And during the season we often have nearly eighteen hundred, in an auditorium that's only supposed to seat sixteen hundred! And with all modesty—it's not my doing but the methods we're working up—I think I may say that every man, woman, and child goes away happy and yet with a message to sustain 'em through the week. You see—oh, of course I give 'em the straight old-time gospel in my sermon—I'm not the least bit afraid of talking right up to 'em and reminding them of the awful consequences of sin and ignorance and spiritual sloth.

Yes, sir! No blinking the horrors of the old-time proven Hell, not in any church *I'm* running! But also we make 'em get together, and their pastor is just one of their own chums, and we sing cheerful, comforting songs, and do they like it? Say! It shows up in the collections!"

"Mr. Gantry," said Andrew Pengilly, "why don't you believe in God?"

Chapter XXVIII

HIS FRIENDSHIP with Dr. Philip McGarry of the Arbor Church was all, Frank Shallard felt, that kept him in the church. As to his round little wife Bess and the three respectable children, he had for them less passion than compassion, and he could, he supposed, make enough money somehow to care for them.

McGarry was not an extraordinary scholar, not especially eloquent, not remarkably virtuous, but in him there was kindness along with robust humor, a yearning for justice steeled by common sense, and just that quality of authentic good-fellowship which the Professional Good Fellows of Zenith, whether preachers or shoe-salesmen, blasphemed against by shouting and guffawing and back-slapping. Women trusted in his strength and his honor; children were bold with him; men disclosed to him their veiled sorrows; and he was more nimble to help them than to be shocked.

Frank worshiped him.

Himself a bachelor, McGarry had become an intimate of Frank's house. He knew where the ice-pick was kept, and where the thermos bottles for picnics; he was as likely as Frank to wash up after late suppers; and if he called and the elder Shallards were not in, he slipped up-stairs and was found there scandalously keeping the children awake by stories of his hunting in Montana and Arizona and Saskatchewan.

It was thus when Frank and Bess came home from prayer-meeting one evening. Philip McGarry's own prayer-meetings were brief. A good many people said they were as artificial a form of religious bait as Elmer Gantry's Lively Sunday Evenings, but if McGarry did also have the habit of making people sing "Smile, Smile, Smile" on all public events except possibly funerals, at least he was not so insistent about their shouting it.

They drifted down to the parsonage living-room, which Bess had made gay with chintzes, Frank studious with portentous books of sociology. Frank sat deep in a chair smoking a pipe—he could never quite get over looking like a youngish college professor who smokes to show what a manly fellow he is. McGarry wandered about the room. He had a way of pointing arguments by shaking objects of furniture—pokers, vases, books, lamps—which was as dangerous as it looked.

"Oh, I was rotten at prayer-meeting tonight," Frank grumbled. "Darn it, I can't seem to go on being interested in the fact that old Mrs. Besom finds God such a comfort in her trials. Mrs. Besom's daughter-in-law doesn't find Mrs. Besom any comfort in *her* trials, let me tell you! And yet I don't see how I can say to her, after she's been fluttering around among the angels and advertising how dead certain she is that Jesus loves her—I haven't quite the nerve to say, 'Sister, you tight-fisted, poison-tongued, old hellcat—' "

"Why, Frank!" from Bess, in placid piety.

" '—you go home and forget your popularity in Heaven and ask your son and his wife to forgive you for trying to make them your kind of saint, with acidity of the spiritual stomach!' "

"Why, *Frank!*"

"Let him rave, Bess," said McGarry. "If a preacher didn't cuss his congregation out once in a while, nobody but St. John would ever've lasted—and I'll bet he wasn't very good at weekly services and parish visiting!"

"*And*," went on Frank, "tomorrow I've got a funeral. That Henry Semp. Weighed two hundred and eighty pounds from the neck down and three ounces from the neck up. Perfectly good Christian citizen who believed that Warren G. Harding was the greatest man since George Washington. I'm sure he never beat his wife. Worthy communicant. But when his wife came to hire me, she wept like the dickens when she talked about Henry's death, but I noticed from the window that when she went off down the street she looked particularly cheerful. Yes, Henry was a bulwark of the nation; not to be sneered at by highbrows. And I'm dead certain, from something she said, that every year they've jipped the Government out of every cent they could on their income tax. And tomorrow I'm supposed to stand up there and tell his friends what a moral example and intellectual Titan he was, and how the poor little woman is simply broken by sorrow. Well, cheer up! From what I know of her, she'll be married again within six months, and if I do a good job of priesting tomorrow, maybe I'll get the fee! Oh, Lord, Phil, what a job, what a lying compromising job, this being a minister!"

It was their hundredth argument over the question.

McGarry waved a pillow, discarded it for Bess' purse, while she tried not to look alarmed, and shouted, "It is not! As I heard a big New York preacher say one day: he knew how imperfect the ministry is, and how many second-raters get into it, and yet if he had a thousand lives, he'd want to be a minister of the gospel, to be a man showing the philosophy of Jesus to mankind, in every one of 'em. And the church universal, no matter what its failings, is still the only institution in which we can work together to hand on that gospel. Maybe it's your fault, not the church's, young Frank, if you're so scared of your people that you lie at funerals! I don't, by Jiminy!"

"You do, by Jiminy, my dear Phil! You don't know it. No, what you do is, you hypnotize yourself until you're convinced that every dear departed was a model of some virtue, and then you rhapsodize about that."

"Well, probably he was!"

"Of course. Probably your burglar was a model of courage, and your gambler a model of kindness to everybody except the people he robbed, but I don't like being hired to praise burglars and gamblers and respectable loan-sharks and food-hounds like Henry Semp, and encourage youngsters to accept their standards, and so keep on perpetuating this barbarous civilization for which we preachers are as responsible as the lawyers or the politicians or the soldiers or even the school-masters. No, sir! Oh, I *am* going to get out of the church! Think of it! A *preacher*, getting religion, getting saved, getting honest, getting out! Then I'd know the joys of sanctification that you Methodys talk about!"

"Oh, you make me tired!" Bess complained, not very aggressively. She looked, at forty-one, like a plump and amiable girl of twenty. "Honestly, Phil, I do wish you could show Frank where he's wrong. I can't, and I've been trying these fifteen years."

"You have, my lamb!"

"Honestly, Phil, can't you make him see it?" said Bess. "He's—of course I do adore him, but of all the cry-babies I ever met— He's the worst of all my children! He talks about going into charity work, about getting a job with a labor bank or a labor paper, about lecturing, about trying to write. Can't you make him see that he'd be just as discontented whatever he did? I'll bet you the labor leaders and radical agitators and the Charity Organization Society people aren't perfect little angels any more than preachers are!"

"Heavens, I don't expect 'em to be! I don't expect to be content," Frank protested. "And isn't it a good thing to have a few people who are always yammering? Never get anywhere without. What a joke that a minister, who's supposed to have such divine authority that he can threaten people with hell, is also supposed to be such an office-boy that he can be cussed out and fired if he dares to criticize capitalists or his fellow ministers! Anyway— Dear Bess, it's rotten on you. I'd *like* to be a contented sort, I'd like to 'succeed,' to be satisfied with being half-honest. But I can't. . . . You see, Phil, I was brought up to believe the Christian God wasn't a scared and compromising public servant, but the creator and advocate of the whole merciless truth, and I reckon that training spoiled me—I actually took my teachers seriously!"

"Oh, tut, tut, Frank; trouble with you is," Philip McGarry yawned, "trouble with *you* is, you like arguing more than you do patiently working out the spiritual problems of some poor, dumm, infinitely piteous human being that comes to you for help, and that doesn't care a hoot whether you advocate Zoroastrianism or Seventh-day Adventism, so long as he feels that you love him and that you can bring him strength from a power higher than himself. I know that if you could lose your intellectual pride, if you could forget that you have to make a new world, better'n the Creator's, right away tonight—you and Bernard Shaw and H. G. Wells and H. L. Mencken and Sinclair Lewis (Lord, how that book of Lewis', 'Main Street,' did bore me, as much of it as I read; it just rambled on forever, and all he could see was that some of the Gopher Prairie hicks didn't go to literary teas quite as often as he does!—that was all he could see among those splendid heroic pioneers)! Well, as I was saying, if instead of starting in where your congregation has left off, because they never had your chance, you could draw them along with you—"

"I try to! And let me tell you, young fellow, I've got a few of 'em far enough along so they're having the sense to leave me and my evangelical church and go off to the Unitarians or stay away from church altogether—thus, Bess darling, depriving my wife and babes of a few more pennies! But seriously, Phil—"

"A man always says 'But seriously' when he feels the previous arguments haven't been so good yet!"

"Maybe. But anyway, what I mean to say is: Of course my liberalism is all foolishness! Do you know why my people stand for it? They're not enough interested to realize what I'm saying! If I had a successor who was a fundamentalist, they'd like him just as well or better, and they'd go back a-whooping to the sacred hell-fire that I've coaxed 'em out of. They don't believe I mean it when I take a shot at the fear of eternal punishment, and the whole magic and taboo system of worshiping the Bible and the ministry, and all the other skull-decorated vestiges of horror there are in so-called Christianity! They don't know it! Partly it's because they've been trained not to believe anything much they hear in sermons. But also it's my fault. I'm not aggressive. I ought to jump around like a lunatic or a popular evangelist, and shout, 'D' you understand? When I say that most of your religious opinions are bunk, why, what I mean is, they're *bunk!*' I've never been violently enough in earnest to be beaten for the sake of the Lord our God! . . . Not yet!"

"Hah, there I've got you, Frank! Tickles me to see you try to be the village atheist! 'For the sake of the Lord' you just said. And how often I've heard you say at parting 'God bless you'—and you meant it! Oh, no, you don't believe in Christ! Not any more than the Pope at Rome!"

"I suppose that if I said 'God damn you,' that would also prove that I was a devout Christian! Oh, Phil, I can't understand how a man as honest as you, as really fond of helping people—and of tolerating them!—can stand being classed with a lot of your fellow preachers and not even kick about it! Think of your going on enduring being a fellow Methodist preacher right in the same town with Elmer Gantry and not standing up in ministers' meeting and saying, 'Either he gets out or I do!' "

"I know! You idiot, don't you suppose those of us that are halfway decent suffer from being classed with Gantry, and that we hate him more than you do? But even if Elmer is rather on the swine side, what of it? Would you condemn a fine aspiring institution, full of broad-gauged, earnest fellows, because one of them was a wash-out?"

"One? Just one? I'll admit there aren't many, not *very* many, hogs like Gantry in your church, or any other, but let me give my loving fraternal opinions of a few others of your splendid Methodist fellows! Bishop Toomis is a gas-bag. Chester Brown, with his candles and chanting, he's merely an Episcopalian who'd go over to the Episcopal church if he weren't afraid he'd lose too much salary in starting again—just as a good share of the Anglo-Catholic Episcopalians are merely Catholics who'd go over to Rome if they weren't afraid of losing social caste. Otto Hickenlooper, with his institutions—the rich are so moved by his charities that they hand him money and Otto gets praised for spending that money. Fine vicious circle. And think of some poor young idiot studying art, wasting his time and twisting his ideas, at Otto's strictly moral art class, where the teacher is chosen more for his opinions on the sacraments than for his knowledge of composition."

"But, Frank, I've *said* all—"

"And the sound, the scholarly, the well-balanced Dr. Mahlon Potts! Oh, he's a perfectly good man, and not a fanatic. Doesn't believe that evolution is a fiendish doctrine. The only trouble with him—as with most famous preachers—is that he hasn't the slightest notion what human beings are like. He's insulated; has been ever since he became a preacher. He goes to the death-beds of prostitutes (but not very often, I'll bet!) but he can't understand that perfectly decent husbands and wives often can't get along because of sexual incompatibility.

"Potts lives in a library; he gets his idea of human motives out of George Eliot and Margaret Deland, and his ideas of economics out of editorials in the *Advocate*, and his idea as to what he really is accomplishing out of the flattery of his Ladies' Aid! He's a much worse criminal than Gantry! I imagine Elmer has some desire to be a good fellow and share his swag, but Dr. Potts wants to make over an entire world of living, bleeding, sweating, loving, fighting human beings into the likeness of Dr. Potts—of Dr. Potts taking his afternoon nap and snoring under a shelf of books about the doctrines of the Ante-Nicene Fathers!"

"Golly, you simply love us! And I suppose you think I admire all these fellows! Why, they regard me as a heretic, from the bishop down," said Philip McGarry.

"And yet you stay with them!"

"Any other church better?"

"Oh, no. Don't think I give all my love to the Methodists. I take them only because they're your particular breed. My own Congregationalists, the Baptists who taught me that immersion is more important than social justice, the Presbyterians, the Campbellites, the whole lot—oh, I love 'em all about equally!"

"And what about yourself? What about me?"

"You know what I think of myself—a man too feeble to stand up and risk being called a crank or a vile atheist! And about you, my young liberal friend, I was just saving you to the last in my exhibit of Methodist parsons! You're the worst of the lot!"

"Oh, now, Frank!" yawned Bess.

She was sleepy. How preachers did talk! Did plasterers and authors and stock-brokers sit up half the night discussing their souls, fretting as to whether plastering or authorship or stock-broking was worth while?

She yawned again, kissed Frank, patted Philip's cheek, and made exit with, "You may be feeble, Frank, but you certainly can talk a strong, rugged young wife to death!"

Frank, usually to be cowed by her jocose grumbling and Philip's friendly jabs, was tonight afire and unquenchable.

"Yes, you're the worst of all, Phil! You *do* know something of human beings. You're not like old Potts, who's always so informative about how much sin there is in the world and always so astonished when he meets an actual sinner. And you don't think it matters a hang whether a seeker after decency gets ducked—otherwise baptized—or not. And yet when you get up in the pulpit, from the way you wallow in prayer people believe that you're just as chummy with the Deity as

Potts or Gantry. Your liberalism never lasts you more than from my house to the street-car. You talk about the golden streets of Heaven and the blessed peace of the hereafter, and yet you've admitted to me, time and again, that you haven't the slightest idea whether there is any personal life after death. You talk about Redemption, and the Sacrament of the Lord's Supper, and how God helps this nation to win a war and hits that other with a flood, and a lot more things that you don't believe privately at all."

"Oh, I know! Thunder! But you yourself—you pray in church."

"Not really. For over a year now I've never addressed a prayer to any definite deity. I say something like 'Let us in meditation, forgetting the worries of daily life, join our spirits in longing for the coming of perpetual peace'—something like that."

"Well, it sounds like a pretty punk prayer to me, Frankie! The only trouble with you is, you feel you're called on to rewrite the Lord's Prayer for him!"

Philip laughed gustily, and slapped Frank's shoulder.

"Damn it, don't be so jocular! I know it's a poor prayer. It's terrible. Nebulous. Meaningless. Like a barker at the New Thought side-show. I don't mind your disliking it, but I do mind your trying to be humorous! Why is it that you lads who defend the church are so facetious when you really get down to discussing the roots of religion?"

"I know, Frank. Effect of too much preaching. But seriously: Yes, I do say things in the pulpit that I don't mean literally. What of it? People understand these symbols; they've been brought up with them, they're comfortable with them. My object in preaching is to teach the art of living as far as I can; to encourage my people—and myself—to be kind, to be honest, to be clean, to be courageous, to love God and their fellow-men; and the whole experience of the church shows that those lessons can best be taught through such really noble concepts as salvation and the presence of the Holy Ghost and Heaven and so on."

"Hm. Does it? Has the church ever tried anything else? And just what the dickens do you mean by 'being clean' and 'being honest' and 'teaching the art of living'? Lord, how we preachers do love to use phrases that don't mean anything! But suppose you were perfectly right. Nevertheless, by using the same theological slang as a Gantry or a Toomis or a Potts, you unconsciously make everybody believe that you think and act like them too."

"Nonsense! Not that I'm particularly drawn by the charms of any of these fellow sages. I'd rather be wrecked on a desert island with you, you old atheist!—you darned old fool! But suppose they were as bad as you think. I still wouldn't feel it was my duty to foul my own nest, to make this grand old Methodist Church, with its saints and heroes like Wesley and Asbury and Quayle and Cartwright and McDowell and McConnell—why, the tears almost come to my eyes when I think of men like that! Look here: Suppose you were at war, in a famous regiment. Suppose a lot of your fellow soldiers, even the present commander of the regiment himself, were rotters—cowards. Would you feel called on to desert? Or to fight all the harder to make up for their faults?"

"Phil, next to the humorous ragging I spoke of, and the use of stale phrases, the worst cancer in religious discussion is the use of the metaphor! The Protestant church is not a regiment. You're not a soldier. The soldier has to fight when and as he's told. You have absolute liberty, outside of a few moral and doctrinal compulsions."

"Ah-hah, now I've got you, my logical young friend! If we have that liberty, why aren't you willing to stay in the church? Oh, Frank, Frank, you are such a fool! I know that you long for righteousness. Can't you see that you can get it best by staying in the church, liberalizing from within, instead of running away and leaving the people to the ministrations of the Gantrys?"

"I know. I've been thinking just that all these years. That's why I'm still a preacher! But I'm coming to believe that it's tommyrot. I'm coming to think that the hell-howling old mossbacks corrupt the honest liberals a lot more than the liberals lighten the backwoods minds of the fundamentalists. What the dickens is the church accomplishing, really? Why have a church at all? What has it for humanity that you won't find in worldly sources—schools, books, conversation?"

"It has this, Frank: It has the unique personality and teachings of Jesus Christ, and there is something in Jesus, there is something in the way he spoke, there is something in the feeling of a man when he suddenly has that inexpressible experience of *knowing* the Master and his presence, which makes the church of Jesus different from any other merely human institution or instrument whatsoever! Jesus is not simply greater and wiser than Socrates or Voltaire; he is entirely *different.* Anybody can interpret and teach Socrates or Voltaire—in schools or books or conversation. But to interpret the personality and teachings of Jesus requires an especially called, chosen, trained, consecrated body of men, united in an especial institution—the church."

"Phil, it sounds so splendid. But just what *were* the personality and the teachings of Jesus? I'll admit it's the heart of the controversy over the Christian religion:—aside from the fact that, of course, most people believe in a church because they were *born* to it. But the essential query is: Did Jesus—if the Biblical accounts of him are even half accurate—have a particularly noble personality, and were his teachings particularly original and profound? You know it's almost impossible to get people to read the Bible honestly. They've been so brought up to take the church interpretation of every word that they read into it whatever they've been taught to find there. It's been so with me, up to the last couple of years. But now I'm becoming a quarter free, and I'm appalled to see that I don't find Jesus an especially admirable character!

"He is picturesque. He tells splendid stories. He's a good fellow, fond of low company—in fact the idea of Jesus, whom the bishops of his day cursed as a rounder and wine-bibber, being chosen as the god of the Prohibitionists is one of the funniest twists in history. But he's vain, he praises himself outrageously, he's fond of astonishing people by little magical tricks which we've been taught to revere as 'miracles.' He is furious as a child in a tantrum when people don't recognize him as a great leader. He loses his temper. He blasts the poor barren fig-tree when it doesn't feed him. What minds people have! They hear preachers proving by the Bible the exact opposites, that the Roman Catholic Church is divinely ordained and that it is against all divine ordinances, and it never occurs to them that far from the Christian religion—or any other religion—being a blessing to humanity, it's produced such confusion in all thinking, such secondhand viewing of actualities, that only now are we beginning to ask what and why we are, and what we can do with life!

"Just what are the teachings of Christ? Did he come to bring peace or more war? He says both. Did he approve earthly monarchies or rebel against them? He says both. Did he ever—think of it, God himself, taking on human form to help the earth—did he ever suggest sanitation, which would have saved millions from plagues? And you can't say his failure there was because he was too lofty to consider mere sickness. On the contrary, he was awfully interested in it, always healing some one—providing they flattered his vanity enough!

"What *did* he teach? One place in the Sermon on the Mount he advises—let me get my Bible—here it is: 'Let your light so shine before men that they may see your good works and glorify your Father which is in heaven,' and then five minutes later he's saying, 'Take heed that ye do not your alms before men, to be seen of them, otherwise ye have no reward of your Father which is in heaven.' That's an absolute contradiction, in the one document which is the charter of the whole Christian Church. Oh, I know you can reconcile them, Phil. That's the whole aim of the ministerial training: to teach us to reconcile contradictions by saying that one of them doesn't mean what it means—and it's always a good stunt to throw in 'You'd understand it if you'd only read it in the original Greek'!

"There's just one thing that does stand out clearly and uncontradicted in Jesus' teaching. He advocated a system of economics whereby no one saved money or stored up wheat or did anything but live like a tramp. If this teaching of his had been accepted, the world would have starved in twenty years after his death!

"No, wait, Phil, just one second and then I'm through!"

He talked till dawn.

Frank's last protest, as they stood on the steps in the cold grayness, was:

"My objection to the church isn't that the preachers are cruel, hypocritical, actually wicked, though some of them are that, too—think of how many are arrested for selling fake stock, for seducing fourteen-year-old girls in orphanages under their care, for arson, for murder. And it isn't so much that the church is in bondage to Big Business and doctrines as laid down by millionaires—though a lot of churches are that, too. My chief objection is that ninety-nine per cent. of sermons and Sunday School teachings are so agonizingly *dull!*"

Chapter XXIX

HOWEVER impatient he was with Frank, Philip McGarry's last wish was to set Elmer Gantry piously baying on Frank's trail. It was rather an accident. Philip sat next to Elmer at a dinner to discuss missionary funds; he remembered that Frank and Elmer had been classmates; and with a sincerely affectionate "It's too bad the poor boy worries so over what are really matters for Faith," he gave away to Elmer most of Frank's heresies.

Now in the bustle of raising funds to build a vast new church, Elmer had forgotten his notion of saving the renowned hardware impresario, Mr. William Dollinger Styles, and his millions from contamination by Frank's blasphemies.

"We could use old Styles, and you could get some fine publicity by attacking Shallard's attempt to steal Jesus and even Hell away from us," said Elmer's confidant, Mr. T. J. Rigg, when he was consulted.

"Say, that's great. How liberalism leads to atheism. Fine! Wait till Mr. Frank Shallard opens his mouth and puts his foot in it again!" said the Reverend Elmer Gantry. "Say, I wonder how we could get a report of his sermons? The poor fish isn't important enough so's they very often report his junk in the papers."

"I'll take care of that. I've got a girl in my office, good fast worker, that I'll have go and take down all his sermons. They'll just think she's practising stenography."

"Well, by golly, that's *one* good use for sermons. Ha, ha, ha!" said Elmer.

"Yes, sir, by golly, found at last. Ha, ha, ha!" said Mr. T. J. Rigg.

II

In less than a month Frank maddened the citizens of Zenith by asserting, in the pulpit, that though he was in favor of temperance, he was not for Prohibition; that the methods of the Anti-Saloon League were those of a lumber lobby.

Elmer had his chance.

He advertised that he would speak on "Fake Preachers—and Who They Are."

In his sermon he said that Frank Shallard (by name) was a liar, a fool, an ingrate whom he had tried to help in seminary, a thief who was trying to steal Christ from an ailing world.

The newspapers were pleased and explicit.

Elmer saw to it—T. J. Rigg arranged a foursome—that he played golf with William Dollinger Styles that week.

"I was awfully sorry, Mr. Styles," he said, "to feel it my duty to jump on your pastor, Mr. Shallard, last Sunday, but when a fellow stands up and makes fun of Jesus Christ—well, it's time to forget mercy!"

"I thought you were kind of hard on him. I didn't hear his sermon myself—I'm a church-member, but it does seem like things pile up so at the office that I have to spend almost every Sunday morning there. But from what they've told me, he wasn't so wild."

"Then you don't think Shallard is practically an atheist?"

"Why, no! Nice decent fellow—"

"Mr. Styles, do you realize that all over town people are wondering how a man like you can give his support to a man like Shallard? Do you realize that not only the ministers but also laymen are saying that Shallard is secretly both an agnostic and a socialist, though he's afraid to come out and admit it? I hear it everywhere. People are afraid to tell you. Jiminy, I'm kind of scared of you myself! Feel I've got a lot of nerve!"

"Well, I ain't so fierce," said Mr. Styles, very pleased.

"Anyway, I'd hate to have you think I was sneaking around damning Shallard behind his back. Why don't you do this? You and some of the other Dorchester deacons have Shallard for lunch or dinner, and have me there, and let me put a few questions to him. I'll talk to the fellow straight! Do you feel you can afford to be known as tolerating an infidel in your church? Oughtn't you to make him come out from under cover and admit what he thinks? If I'm wrong, I'll apologize to you and to him, and you can call me all the kinds of nosey, meddling, cranky, interfering fool you want to!"

"Well— He seems kind of a nice fellow." Mr. Styles was uncomfortable. "But if you're right about him being really an infidel, don't know's I could stand that."

"How'd it be if you and some of your deacons and Shallard came and had dinner with me in a private room at the Athletic Club next Friday evening?"

"Well, all right—"

III

Frank was so simple as to lose his temper when Elmer had bullied him, roared at him, bulked at him, long enough, with Frank's own deacons accepting Elmer as an authority. He was irritated out of all caution, and he screamed back at Elmer that he did not accept Jesus Christ as divine; that he was not sure of a future life; that he wasn't even certain of a personal God.

Mr. William Dollinger Styles snapped, "Then just why, Mr. Shallard, don't you get out of the ministry before you're kicked out?"

"Because I'm not yet sure— Though I do think our present churches are as absurd as a belief in witchcraft, yet I believe there could be a church free of superstition, helpful to the needy, and giving people that mystic something stronger than reason, that sense of being uplifted in common worship of an unknowable power for good. Myself, I'd be lonely with nothing but bleak debating-societies. I think—at least I still think—that for many souls there is this need of worship, even of beautiful ceremonial—"

"'Mystic need of worship!' 'Unknowable power for good!' Words, words, words! Milk and water! *That*, when you have the glorious and certain figure of Christ Jesus to worship and follow!" bellowed Elmer. "Pardon me, gentlemen, for intruding, but it makes me, not as a preacher but just as a humble and devout Christian, sick to my stomach to hear a fellow feel that he knows so blame' much he's able to throw out of the window the Christ that the whole civilized world has believed in for countless centuries! And try to replace him with a lot of gassy phrases! Excuse me, Mr. Styles, but after all, religion is a serious business, and if we're going to call ourselves Christians at all, we have to bear testimony to the proven fact of God. Forgive me."

"It's quite all right, Dr. Gantry. I know just how you feel," said Styles. "And while I'm no authority on religion, I feel the same way you do, and I guess these other gentlemen do, too. . . . Now, Shallard, you're entitled to your own views, but not in our pulpit! Why don't you just resign before we kick you out?"

"You can't kick me out! It takes the whole church to do that!"

"The whole church'll damn well do it, you watch 'em!" said Deacon William Dollinger Styles.

IV

"What are we going to do, dear?" Bess said wearily. "I'll stand by you, of course, but let's be practical. Don't you think it would make less trouble if you did resign?"

"I've done nothing for which to resign! I've led a thoroughly decent life. I haven't lied or been indecent or stolen. I've preached imagination, happiness, justice, seeking for the truth. I'm no sage, Heaven knows, but I've given my people a knowledge that there are such things as ethnology and biology, that there are books like 'Ethan Frome' and 'Père Goriot' and 'Tony-Bungay' and Renan's Jesus, that there is nothing wicked in looking straight at life—"

"Dear, I said *practical!*"

"Oh, thunder, I don't know. I think I can get a job in the Charity Organization Society here—the general secretary happens to be pretty liberal."

"I hate to have us leave the church entirely. I'm sort of at home there. Why not see if they'd like to have you in the Unitarian Church?"

"Too respectable. Scared. Same old sanctified phrases I'm trying to get rid of—and won't ever quite get rid of, I'm afraid."

V

A meeting of the church body had been called to decide on Frank's worthiness, and the members had been informed by Styles that Frank was attacking all religion. Instantly a number of the adherents who had been quite unalarmed by what they themselves had heard in the pulpit perceived that Frank was a dangerous fellow and more than likely to injure omnipotent God.

Before the meeting, one woman, who remained fond of him, fretted to Frank, "Oh, can't you understand what a dreadful thing you're doing to question the divinity of Christ and all? I'm afraid you're going to hurt religion permanently. If you could open your eyes and see—if you could only understand what my religion has meant to me in times of despair! I don't know what I would have done during my typhoid without that consolation! You're a bright, smart man when you let yourself be. If you'd only go and have a good talk with Dr. G. Prosper Edwards. He's an older man than you, and he's a doctor of divinity, and he has such huge crowds at Pilgrim Church, and I'm sure he could show you where you're wrong and make everything perfectly clear to you."

Frank's sister, married now to an Akron lawyer, came to stay with them. They had been happy, Frank and she, in the tepid but amiable house of their minister-father; they had played at church, with dolls and salt-cellars for congregation; books were always about them, natural to them; and at their father's table they had heard doctors, preachers, lawyers, politicians, talk of high matters.

The sister bubbled to Bess, "You know, Frank doesn't believe half he says! He just likes to show off. He's a real good Christian at heart, if he only knew it. Why, he was such a good Christian boy—he led the B.Y.P.U.—he *couldn't* have drifted away from Christ into all this nonsense that nobody takes seriously except a lot of long-haired dirty cranks! And he'll break his father's heart! I'm going to have a good talk with that young man, and bring him to his senses!"

On the street Frank met the great Dr. McTiger, pastor of the Royal Ridge Presbyterian Church.

Dr. McTiger had been born in Scotland, graduated at Edinburgh, and he secretly—not too secretly—despised all American universities and seminaries and their alumni. He was a large, impatient, brusque man, renowned for the length of his sermons.

"I hear, young man," he shouted at Frank, "that you have read one whole book on the pre-Christian mysteries and decided that our doctrines are secondhand and that you are now going to destroy the church. You should have more pity! With the loss of a profound intellect like yours, my young friend, I should doubt if the church can stagger on! It's a pity that after discovering scholarship you didn't go on and get enough of that same scholarship to perceive that by the wondrous beneficence of God's mercy the early church was led to combine many alien factors in the one perfection of the Christian brotherhood! I don't know whether it's ignorance of church history or lack of humor that chiefly distinguishes you, my young friend! Go and sin no more!"

From Andrew Pengilly came a scrawled, shaky letter begging Frank to stand true and not deliver his appointed flock to the devil. That hurt.

VI

The first church business meeting did not settle the question of Frank's remaining. He was questioned about his doctrines, and he shocked them by being candid, but the men whom he had helped, the women whom he had consoled in sickness, the fathers who had gone to him when their daughters "had gotten into trouble," stood by him for all the threats of Styles.

A second meeting would have to be called before they took a vote.

When Elmer read of this, he galloped to T. J. Rigg. "Here's our chance!" he gloated. "If the first meeting had kicked Frank out, Styles might have stayed with their church, though I do think he likes my brand of theology and my Republican politics. But why don't you go to him now, T. J., and hint around about how his church has insulted him?"

"All right, Elmer. Another soul saved. Brother Styles has still got the first dollar he ever earned, but maybe we can get ten cents of it away from him for the new church. Only— Him being so much richer than I, I hope you won't go to him for spiritual advice and inspiration, instead of me."

"You bet I won't, T. J.! Nobody has ever accused Elmer Gantry of being disloyal to his friends! My only hope is that your guidance of this church has been of some value to you yourself."

"Well—yes—in a way. I've had three brother Methodist clients from Wellspring come to me—two burglary and one forgery. But it's more that I just like to make the wheels go round."

Mr. Rigg was saying, an hour later, to Mr. William Dollinger Styles, "If you came and joined us, I know you'd like it—you've seen what a fine, upstanding, two-fisted, one-hundred-percent he-man Dr. Gantry is. Absolutely sound about business. And it would be a swell rebuke to your church for not accepting your advice. But we hate to invite you to come over to us—in fact Dr. Gantry absolutely forbade me to see you—for fear you'll think it was just because you're rich."

For three days Styles shied, then he was led, trembling, up to the harness.

Afterward, Dr. G. Prosper Edwards of Pilgrim Congregational said to his spouse, "Why on earth didn't *we* think of going right after Styles and inviting him to join us? It was so simple we never even thought of it. I really do feel quite cross. Why didn't *you* think of it?"

VII

The second church meeting was postponed. It looked to Elmer as though Frank would be able to stay on at Dorchester Congregational and thus defy Elmer as the spiritual and moral leader of the city.

Elmer acted fearlessly.

In sermon after sermon he spoke of "that bunch of atheists out there at Dorchester." Frank's parishioners were alarmed. They were forced to explain (only they were never quite sure what they were explaining) to customers, to neighbors, to fellow lodge-members. They felt disgraced, and so it was that a second meeting was called.

Now Frank had fancied a spectacular resignation. He heard himself, standing before a startled audience, proclaiming, "I have decided that no one in this room, including your pastor, believes in the Christian religion. Not one of us would turn the other cheek. Not one of us would sell all that he has and give to the poor. Not one of us would give his coat to some man who took his overcoat. Every one of us lays up all the treasure he can. We don't practise the Christian religion. We don't intend to practise it. Therefore, we don't believe in it. Therefore I resign, and I advise you to quit lying and disband."

He saw himself, then, tramping down the aisle among his gaping hearers, and leaving the church forever.

But: "I'm too tired. Too miserable. And why hurt the poor bewildered souls? And— I am so tired."

He stood up at the beginning of the second meeting and said gently, "I had refused to resign. I still feel I have an honest right to an honest pulpit. But I am setting brother against brother. I am not a Cause—I am only a friend. I have loved you and the work, the sound of friends singing together, the happiness of meeting on leisurely Sunday mornings. This I give up. I resign, and I wish I could say, 'God be with you and bless you all.' But the good Christians have taken God and made him into a menacing bully, and I cannot even say 'God bless you,' during this last moment, in a life given altogether to religion, when I shall ever stand in a pulpit."

Elmer Gantry, in his next sermon, said that he was so broad-minded that he would be willing to receive an Infidel Shallard in his church, providing he repented.

VIII

When he found that he liked the Charity Organization Society and his work in that bleak institution no better than his work in the church, Frank laughed.

"As Bess said! A consistent malcontent! Well, I *am* consistent, anyway. And the relief not to be a preacher any more! Not to have to act sanctimonious! Not to have men consider you an old woman in trousers! To be able to laugh without watching its effect!"

Frank was given charge, at the C.O.S., of a lodging-house, a woodyard at which hoboes worked for two hours daily to pay for lodging and breakfast, and an employment bureau. He knew little about Scientific Charity, so he was shocked by the icy manner in which his subordinates—the aged virgin at the inquiry desk, the boss of the woodyard, the clerk at the lodging-house, the young lady who asked the applicants about their religion and vices—treated the shambling unfortunates as criminals who had deliberately committed the crime of poverty.

They were as efficient and as tender as vermin-exterminators.

In this acid perfection, Frank longed for the mystery that clings to even the dourest or politest tabernacle. He fell in the way of going often to the huge St. Dominic's Catholic Church, of which the eloquent Father de Pinna was pastor, with Father Matthew Smeesby, the new sort of American, state-university-bred priest, as assistant pastor and liaison officer.

St. Dominic's was, for Zenith, an ancient edifice, and the coal-smoke from the South Zenith factories had aged the gray stone to a semblance of historic centuries. The interior, with its dim irregularity, its lofty roof, the curious shrines, the mysterious door at the top of a flight of stone steps, unloosed Frank's imagination. It touched him to see the people kneeling at any hour. He had never known a church to which the plain people came for prayer. Despite its dusky magnificence, they seemed to find in the church their home. And when he saw the gold and crimson of solemn high mass blazing at the end of the dark aisle, with the crush of people visibly believing in the presence of God, he wondered if he had indeed found the worship he had fumblingly sought.

He knew that to believe literally in Purgatory and the Immaculate Conception, the Real Presence and the authority of the hierarchy, was as impossible for him as to believe in Zeus.

"But," he pondered, "isn't it possible that the whole thing is so gorgeous a fairy-tale that to criticize it would be like trying to prove that Jack did not kill the giant? No sane priest could expect a man of some education to think that saying masses had any effect on souls in Purgatory; they'd expect him to take the whole thing as one takes a symphony. And, oh, I am lonely for the fellowship of the church!"

He sought a consultation with Father Matthew Smeesby. They had met, as fellow ministers, at many dinners.

The good father sat at a Grand Rapids desk, in a room altogether business-like save for a carved Bavarian cupboard and a crucifix on the barren plaster wall. Smeesby was a man of forty, a crisper Philip McGarry.

"You were an American university man, weren't you, Father?" Frank asked.

"Yes. University of Indiana. Played half-back."

"Then I think I can talk to you. It seems to me that so many of your priests are not merely foreign by birth, Poles and whatnot, but they look down on American *mores* and want to mold us to their ideas and ways. But you— Tell me: Would it be conceivable for an—I won't say an intelligent, but at least a reasonably well-read man like myself, who finds it quite impossible to believe one word of your doctrines—"

"Huh!"

"—but who is tremendously impressed by your ritual and the spirit of worship—could such a man be received into the Roman Catholic Church, honestly, with the understanding that to him your dogmas are nothing but symbols?"

"Most certainly not!"

"Don't you know any priests who love the Church but don't literally believe all the doctrines?"

"I do not! I know no such persons! Shallard, you can't understand the authority and reasonableness of the Church. You're not ready to. You think too much of your puerile powers of reasoning. You haven't enough divine humility to comprehend the ages of wisdom that have gone to building up this fortress, and you stand outside its walls, one pitifully lonely little figure, blowing the trumpet of your egotism, and demanding of the sentry, 'Take me to your commander. I am graciously inclined to assist him. Only he must understand that I think his granite walls are pasteboard, and I reserve the right to blow them down when I get tired of them.' Man, if you were a prostitute or a murderer and came to me saying 'Can I be saved?' I'd cry 'Yes!' and give my life to helping you. But you're obsessed by a worse crime than murder—pride of intellect! And yet you haven't such an awfully overpowering intellect to be proud of, and I'm not sure but that's the worst crime of all! Good-day!"

He added, as Frank ragingly opened the door, "Go home and pray for simplicity."

"Go home and pray that I may be made like you? Pray to have your humility and your manners?" said Frank.

It was a fortnight later that for his own satisfaction Frank set down in the note-book which he had always carried for sermon ideas, which he still carried for the sermons they would never let him preach again, a conclusion:

"The Roman Catholic Church is superior to the militant Protestant Church. It does not compel you to give up your sense of beauty, your sense of humor, or your pleasant vices. It merely requires you to give up your honesty, your reason, your heart and soul."

IX

Frank had been with the Charity Organization Society for three years, and he had become assistant general secretary at the time of the Dayton evolution trial. It was at this time that the brisker conservative clergymen saw that their influence and oratory and incomes were threatened by any authentic learning. A few of them were so intelligent as to know that not only was biology dangerous to their positions, but also history—which gave no very sanctified reputation to the Christian church; astronomy—which found no convenient Heaven in the skies and snickered politely at the notion of making the sun stand still in order to win a Jewish border skirmish; psychology—which doubted the superiority of a Baptist preacher fresh from the farm to trained laboratory researchers; and all the other sciences of the modern university. They saw that a proper school should teach nothing but bookkeeping, agriculture, geometry, dead languages made deader by leaving out all the amusing literature, and the Hebrew Bible as interpreted by men superbly trained to ignore contradictions, men technically called "Fundamentalists."

This perception the clergy and their most admired laymen expressed in quick action. They formed half a dozen competent and well-financed organizations to threaten rustic state legislators with political failure and bribe them with unctuous clerical praise, so that these back-street and backwoods Solons would forbid the teaching in all state-supported schools and colleges of anything which was not approved by the evangelists.

It worked edifyingly.

To oppose them there were organized a few groups of scholars. One of these organizations asked Frank to speak for them. He was delighted to feel an audience before him again, and he got leave from the Zenith Charity Organization Society for a lecture tour.

He came excitedly and proudly to his first assignment, in a roaring modern city in the Southwest. He loved the town; believed really that he came to it with a "message." He tasted the Western air greedily, admired the buildings flashing up where but yesterday had been prairie. He smiled from the hotel 'bus when he saw a poster which announced that the Reverend Frank Shallard would speak on "Are the Fundamentalists Witch Hunters?" at Central Labor Hall, auspices of the League for Free Science.

"Bully! Fighting again! I've found that religion I've been looking for!"

He peered out for other posters. . . . They were all defaced.

At his hotel was a note, typed, anonymous: "We don't want you and your hellish atheism here. We can think for ourselves without any imported 'liberals.' If you enjoy life, you'd better be out of this decent Christian city before evening. God help you if you aren't! We have enough mercy to give warning, but enough of God's justice to see you get yours right if you don't listen. Blasphemers get what they ask for. We wonder if you would like the feeling of a blacksnake across your lying face? The Committee."

Frank had never known physical conflict more violent than boyhood wrestling. His hand shook. He tried to sound defiant with: "They can't scare me!"

His telephone, and a voice: "This Shallard? Well this is a brother preacher speaking. Name don't matter. I just want to tip you off that you'd better not speak tonight. Some of the boys are pretty rough."

Then Frank began to know the joy of anger.

The hall of his lecture was half filled when he looked across the ice-water pitcher on the speaker's table. At the front were the provincial intellectuals, most of them very eager, most of them dreadfully poor: a Jewish girl librarian with hungry eyes, a crippled tailor, a spectacled doctor sympathetic to radical disturbances but too good a surgeon to be driven out of town. There was a waste of empty seats, then, and at the back a group of solid, prosperous, scowling burghers, with a leonine man who was either an actor, a congressman, or a popular clergyman.

This respectable group grumbled softly, and hissed a little as Frank nervously began.

America, he said, in its laughter at the "monkey trial" at Dayton, did not understand the veritable menace of the Fundamentalists' crusade. ("Outrageous!" from the leonine gentleman.) They were mild enough now; they spoke in the name of virtue; but give them rope, and there would be a new Inquisition, a new hunting of witches. We might live to see men burned to death for refusing to attend Protestant churches.

Frank quoted the Fundamentalist who asserted that evolutionists were literally murderers, because they killed orthodox faith, and ought therefore to be lynched; William Jennings Bryan, with his proposal that any American who took a drink outside the country should be exiled for life.

"That's how these men speak, with so little power—as yet!" Frank pleaded. "Use your imaginations! Think how they would rule this nation, and compel the more easy-going half-liberal clergy to work with them, if they had the power!"

There were constant grunts of "That's a lie!" and "They ought to shut him up!" from the back, and now Frank saw marching into the hall a dozen tough young men. They stood ready for action, looking expectantly toward the line of prosperous Christian Citizens.

"And you have here in your own city," Frank continued, "a minister of the gospel who enjoys bellowing that any one who disagrees with him is a Judas."

"That's enough!" cried some one at the back, and the young toughs galloped down the aisle toward Frank, their eyes hot with cruelty, teeth like a fighting dog's, hands working—he could feel them at his neck. They were met and held a moment by the sympathizers in front. Frank saw the crippled tailor knocked down by a man who stepped on the body as he charged on.

With a curious lassitude more than with any fear, Frank sighed, "Hang it, I've got to join the fight and get killed!"

He started down from the platform.

The chairman seized his shoulder. "No! Don't! You'll get beaten to death! We need you! Come here—come *here!* This back door!"

Frank was thrust through a door into a half-lighted alley.

A motor was waiting, and by it two men, one of whom cried, "Right in here, Brother."

It was a large sedan; it seemed security, life. But as Frank started to climb in he noted the man at the wheel, then looked closer at the others. The man at the wheel had no lips but only a bitter dry line across his face—the mouth of an executioner. Of the other two, one was like an unreformed bartender, with curly mustache and a barber's lock; one was gaunt, with insane eyes.

"Who are you fellows?" he demanded.

"Shut your damned trap and get t' hell in there!" shrieked the bartender, pushing Frank into the back of the car, so that he fell with his head on the cushion.

The insane man scrambled in, and the car was off.

"We told you to get out of town. We gave you your chance. By God, you'll learn something now, you God damned atheist—and probably a damn' socialist or I.W.W. too!" the seeming bartender said. "See this gun?" He stuck it into Frank's side, most painfully. "We may decide to let you live if you keep your mouth shut and do what we tell you to—and again we may not. You're going to have a nice ride with us! Just think what fun you're going to have when we get you in the country—alone—where it's nice and dark and quiet!"

He placidly lifted his hands and gouged Frank's cheek with his strong fingernails.

"I won't stand it!" screamed Frank.

He rose, struggling. He felt the gaunt fanatic's fingers—just two fingers, demon-strong—close on his neck, dig in with pain that made him sick. He felt the bartender's fist smashing his jaw. As he slumped down, limp against the forward seat, half-fainting, he heard the bartender chuckle:

"That'll give the blank, blank, blank of a blank some idea of the fun we'll have watching him squirm bimeby!"

The gaunt one snapped, "The boss said not to cuss."

"Cuss, hell! I don't pretend to be any tin angel. I've done a lot of tough things. But, by God, when a fellow pretending to be a minister comes sneaking around trying to make fun of the Christian religion—the only chance us poor devils have got to become decent again—then, by God, it's time to show we've got some guts and appreciation!"

The pseudo-bartender spoke with the smugly joyous tones of any crusader given a chance to be fiendish for a moral reason, and placidly raising his leg, he brought his heel down on Frank's instep.

When the cloud of pain had cleared from his head, Frank sat rigid. . . . What would Bess and the kids do if these men killed him? . . . Would they beat him much before he died?

The car left the highway, followed a country road and ran along a lane, through what seemed to Frank to be a cornfield. It stopped by a large tree.

"Get out!" snapped the gaunt man.

Mechanically, his legs limp, Frank staggered out. He looked up at the moon. "It's the last time I'll ever see the moon—see the stars—hear voices. Never again to walk on a fresh morning!"

"What are you going to do?" he said, hating them too much to be afraid.

"Well, dearie," said the driver, with a dreadful jocosity, "you're going to take a little walk with us, back here in the fields a ways."

"Hell!" said the bartender, "let's hang him. Here's a swell tree. Use the tow-rope."

"No," from the gaunt man. "Just hurt him enough so he'll remember, and then he can go back and tell his atheist friends it ain't healthy for 'em in real Christian parts. Move, you!"

Frank walked in front of them, ghastly silent. They followed a path through the cornfield to a hollow. The crickets were noisily cheerful; the moon serene.

"This'll do," snarled the gaunt one; then to Frank: "Now get ready to feel good."

He set his pocket electric torch on a clod of earth. In its light Frank saw him draw from his pocket a coiled black leather whip, a whip for mules.

"Next time," said the gaunt one, slowly, "next time you come back here, we'll kill you. And any other yellow traitor and stinker and atheist like you. Tell 'em all that! This time we won't kill you—not quite."

"Oh, quit talking and let's get busy!" said the bartender.

"All right!"

The bartender caught Frank's two arms behind, bending them back, almost breaking them, and suddenly with a pain appalling and unbelievable the whip slashed across Frank's cheek, cutting it, and instantly it came again—again—in a darkness of reeling pain.

X

Consciousness returned waveringly as dawn crawled over the cornfield and the birds were derisive. Frank's only clear emotion was a longing to escape from this agony by death. His whole face reeked with pain. He could not understand why he could scarce see. When he fumblingly raised his hand, he discovered that his right eye was a pulp of blind flesh, and along his jaw he could feel the exposed bone.

He staggered along the path through the cornfield, stumbling over hummocks, lying there sobbing, muttering, "Bess—oh, come—*Bess!*"

His strength lasted him just to the highroad, and he sloped to earth, lay by the road like a drunken beggar. A motor was coming, but when the driver saw Frank's feebly uplifted arm he sped on. Pretending to be hurt was a device of hold-up men.

"Oh, God, won't anybody help me?" Frank whimpered, and suddenly he was laughing, a choking twisted laughter. "Yes, I said it, Philip—'God' I said—I suppose it proves I'm a good Christian!"

He rocked and crawled along the road to a cottage. There was a light—a farmer at early breakfast. "At last!" Frank wept. When the farmer answered the knock, holding up a lamp, he looked once at Frank, then screamed and slammed the door.

An hour later a motorcycle policeman found Frank in the ditch, in half delirium.

"Another drunk!" said the policeman, most cheerfully, snapping the support in place on his cycle. But as he stooped and saw Frank's half-hidden face, he whispered, "Good God Almighty!"

XI

The doctors told him that though the right eye was gone completely, he might not entirely lose the sight of the other for perhaps a year.

Bess did not shriek when she saw him; she only stood with her hands shaky at her breast.

She seemed to hesitate before kissing what had been his mouth. But she spoke cheerfully:

"Don't you worry about a single thing. I'll get a job that'll keep us going. I've already seen the general secretary at the C.O.S. And isn't it nice that the kiddies are old enough now to read aloud to you."

To be read aloud to, the rest of his life . . .

XII

Elmer called and raged, "This is the most outrageous thing I've ever heard of in my life, Frank! Believe me, I'm going to give the fellows that did this to you the most horrible beating they ever got, right from my pulpit! Even though it may hinder me in getting money for my new church—say, we're going to have a bang-up plant there, right up to date, cost over half a million dollars, seat over two thousand. But nobody can shut *me* up! I'm going to denounce those fiends in a way *they'll* never forget!"

And that was the last Elmer is known ever to have said on the subject, privately or publicly.

Chapter XXX

THE Reverend Elmer Gantry was in his oak and Spanish leather study at the great new Wellspring Church.

The building was of cheerful brick, trimmed with limestone. It had Gothic windows, a carillon in the square stone tower, dozens of Sunday School rooms, a gymnasium, a social room with a stage and a motion-picture booth, an electric range in the kitchen, and over it all a revolving electric cross and a debt.

But the debt was being attacked. Elmer had kept on the professional church-money-raiser whom he had employed during the campaign for the building fund. This financial crusader was named Emmanuel Navitsky; he was said to be the descendant of a noble Polish Catholic family converted to Protestantism; and certainly he was a most enthusiastic Christian—except possibly on Passover Eve. He had raised money for Presbyterian Churches, Y.M.C.A. buildings, Congregational Colleges, and dozens of other holy purposes. He did miracles with card indices of rich people; and he is said to have been the first ecclesiastical go-getter to think of inviting Jews to contribute to Christian temples.

Yes, Emmanuel would take care of the debt, and Elmer could give himself to purely spiritual matters.

He sat now in his study, dictating to Miss Bundle. He was happy in the matter of that dowdy lady, because her brother, a steward in the church, had recently died, and he could presently get rid of her without too much discord.

To him was brought the card of Loren Latimer Dodd, M.A., D.D., LL.D., president of Abernathy College, an institution of Methodist learning.

"Hm," Elmer mused. "I bet he's out raising money. Nothing doing! What the devil does he think we are!" and aloud: "Go out and bring Dr. Dodd right in, Miss Bundle. A great man! A wonderful educator! You know—president of Abernathy College!"

Looking her admiration at a boss who had such distinguished callers, Miss Bundle bundled out.

Dr. Dodd was a florid man with a voice, a Kiwanis pin, and a handshake.

"Well, well, well, Brother Gantry, I've heard so much of your magnificent work here that I ventured to drop in and bother you for a minute. What a magnificent church you have created! It must be a satisfaction, a pride! It's—magnificent!"

"Thanks, Doctor. Mighty pleased to meet you. Uh. Uh. Uh. Visiting Zenith?"

"Well, I'm, as it were, on my rounds."

("Not a cent, you old pirate!") "Visiting the alumni, I presume."

"In a way. The fact is I—"

("Not one damn' cent. My salary gets raised next!")

"—was wondering if you would consent to my taking a little time at your service Sunday evening to call to the attention of your magnificent congregation the great work and dire needs of Abernathy. We have such a group of earnest young men and women—and no few of the boys going into the Methodist ministry. But our endowment is so low, and what with the cost of the new athletic field—though I am delighted to be able to say our friends have made it possible to create a really magnificent field, with a fine cement stadium—but it has left us up against a heart-breaking deficit. Why, the entire chemistry department is housed in two rooms in what was a cow-shed! And—"

"Can't do it, doctor. Impossible. We haven't begun to pay for this church. Be as much as my life is worth to go to my people with a plea for one extra cent. But possibly in two years from now— Though frankly," and Elmer laughed brightly, "I don't know why the people of Wellspring should contribute to a college which hasn't thought enough of Wellspring's pastor to give him a Doctor of Divinity degree!"

The two holy clerks looked squarely at each other, with poker faces.

"Of course, Doctor," said Elmer, "I've been offered the degree a number of times, but by small, unimportant colleges, and I haven't cared to accept it. So you can see that this is in no way a hint that I would *like* such a degree. Heaven forbid! But I do know it might please my congregation, make them feel Abernathy was their own college, in a way."

Dr. Dodd remarked serenely, "Pardon me if I smile! You see I had a double mission in coming to you. The second part was to ask you if you would honor Abernathy by accepting a D.D.!"

They did not wink at each other.

Elmer gloated to himself, "And I've heard it cost old Mahlon Potts six hundred bucks for his D.D.! Oh, yes, Prexy, we'll begin to raise money for Abernathy in two years—we'll *begin!*"

II

The chapel of Abernathy College was full. In front were the gowned seniors, looking singularly like a row of arm-chairs covered with dust-cloths. On the platform, with the president and the senior members of the faculty, were the celebrities whose achievements were to be acknowledged by honorary degrees.

Besides the Reverend Elmer Gantry, these distinguished guests were the Governor of the state—who had started as a divorce lawyer but had reformed and enabled the public service corporations to steal all the water-power in the state; Mr. B. D. Swenson, the automobile manufacturer, who had given most of the money for the Abernathy football stadium; and the renowned Eva Evaline Murphy, author, lecturer, painter, musician, and authority on floriculture, who was receiving a Litt.D. for having written (gratis) the new Abernathy College Song:

We'll think of thee where'er we be,
On plain or mountain, town or sea,
Oh, let us sing how round us clings,
Dear Abernathy, thoooooooooughts—of—thee.

President Dodd was facing Elmer, and shouting:

"—and now we have the privilege of conferring the degree of Doctor of Divinity upon one than whom no man in our honored neighboring state of Winnemac has done more to inculate sound religious doctrine, increase the power of the church, uphold high standards of eloquence and scholarship, and in his own life give such an example of earnestness as is an inspiration to all of us!"

They cheered—and Elmer had become the Reverend Dr. Gantry.

III

It was a great relief at the Rotary Club. They had long felt uncomfortable in calling so weighty a presence "Elmer," and now, with a pride of their own in his new dignity, they called him "Doc."

The church gave him a reception and raised his salary to seventy-five hundred dollars.

IV

The Rev. Dr. Gantry was the first clergyman in the state of Winnemac, almost the first in the country, to have his services broadcast by radio. He suggested it himself. At that time, the one broadcasting station in Zenith, that of the Celebes Gum and Chicle Company, presented only jazz orchestras and retired sopranos, to advertise the renowned Jolly Jack Gum. For fifty dollars a week Wellspring Church was able to use the radio Sunday mornings from eleven to twelve-thirty. Thus Elmer increased the number of his hearers from two thousand to ten thousand—and in another pair of years it would be a hundred thousand.

Eight thousand radio-owners listening to Elmer Gantry—

A bootlegger in his flat, coat off, exposing his pink silk shirt, his feet up on the table. . . . The house of a small-town doctor, with the neighbors come in to listen—the drug-store man, his fat wife, the bearded superintendent of schools. . . . Mrs. Sherman Reeves of Royal Ridge, wife of one of the richest young men in Zenith, listening in a black-and-gold dressing-gown, while she smoked a cigarette. . . . The captain of a schooner, out on Lake Michigan, hundreds of miles away, listening in his cabin. . . . The wife of a farmer in an Indiana valley, listening while her husband read the Sears-Roebuck catalogue and sniffed. . . . A retired railway conductor, very feeble, very religious. . . . A Catholic priest, in a hospital, chuckling a little. . . . A spinster school-teacher, mad with loneliness, worshiping Dr. Gantry's virile voice. . . . Forty people gathered in a country church too poor to have a pastor. . . . A stock actor in his dressing-room, fagged with an all-night rehearsal.

All of them listening to the Rev. Dr. Elmer Gantry as he shouted:

"—and I want to tell you that the fellow who is eaten by ambition is putting the glories of this world before the glories of Heaven! Oh, if I could only help you to understand that it is humility, that it is simple loving kindness, that it is tender loyalty, which alone make the heart glad! Now, if you'll let me tell a story: It reminds me of two Irishmen named Mike and Pat—"

V

For years Elmer had had a waking nightmare of seeing Jim Lefferts sitting before him in the audience, scoffing. It would be a dramatic encounter and terrible; he wasn't sure but that Jim would speak up and by some magic kick him out of the pulpit.

But when, that Sunday morning, he saw Jim in the third row, he considered only, "Oh, Lord, there's Jim Lefferts! He's pretty gray. I suppose I'll have to be nice to him."

Jim came up afterward to shake hands. He did not look cynical; he looked tired; and when he spoke, in a flat prairie voice, Elmer felt urban and urbane and superior.

"Hello, Hell-cat," said Jim.

"Well, well, well! Old Jim Lefferts! Well, by golly! Say, it certainly is a mighty great pleasure to see you, my boy! What you doing in this neck of the woods?"

"Looking up a claim for a client."

"What you doing now, Jim?"

"I'm practising law in Topeka."

"Doing pretty well?"

"Oh, I can't complain. Oh, nothing extra special. I was in the state senate for a term though."

"That's fine! That's fine! Say, how long gonna be in town?"

"Oh, 'bout three days."

"Say, want to have you up to the house for dinner; but doggone it, Cleo—that's my wife—I'm married now—she's gone and got me all sewed up with a lot of dates—you know how these women are—me, I'd rather sit home and read. But sure got to see you again. Say, gimme a ring, will you?—at the house (find it in the tel'phone book) or at my study here in the church."

"Yuh, sure, you bet. Well, glad to seen you."

"You bet. Tickled t' death seen you, old Jim!"

Elmer watched Jim plod away, shoulders depressed, a man discouraged.

"And that," he rejoiced, "is the poor fish that tried to keep me from going into the ministry!" He looked about his auditorium, with the organ pipes a vast golden pyramid, with the Chubbuck memorial window vivid in ruby and gold and amethyst. "And become a lawyer like him, in a dirty stinking little office! Huh! And he actually made fun of me and tried to hold me back when I got a clear and definite Call of God! Oh, I'll be good and busy when he calls up, you can bet on that!"

Jim did not telephone.

On the third day Elmer had a longing to see him, a longing to regain his friendship. But he did not know where Jim was staying; he could not reach him at the principal hotels.

He never saw Jim Lefferts again, and within a week he had forgotten him, except as it was a relief to have lost his embarrassment before Jim's sneering—the last bar between him and confident greatness.

VI

It was in the summer of 1924 that Elmer was granted a three-months leave, and for the first time Cleo and he visited Europe.

He had heard the Rev. Dr. G. Prosper Edwards say, "I divide American clergymen into just two classes—those who could be invited to preach in a London church, and those who couldn't." Dr. Edwards was of the first honorable caste, and Elmer had seen him pick up great glory from having sermonized in the City Temple. The Zenith papers, even the national religious periodicals, hinted that when Dr. Edwards was in London, the entire population from king to navvies had galloped to worship under him, and the conclusion was that Zenith and New York would be sensible to do likewise.

Elmer thoughtfully saw to it that he should be invited also. He had Bishop Toomis write to his Wesleyan colleagues, he had Rigg and William Dollinger Styles write to their Nonconformist business acquaintances in London, and a month before he sailed he was bidden to address the celebrated Brompton Road Chapel, so that he went off in a glow not only of adventure but of message-bearing.

VII

Dr. Elmer Gantry was walking the deck of the *Scythia*, a bright, confident, manly figure in a blue suit, a yachting cap, and white canvas shoes, swinging his arms and beaming pastorally on his fellow athletic maniacs.

He stopped at the deck chairs of a little old couple—a delicate blue-veined old lady, and her husband, with thin hands and a thin white beard.

"Well, you folks seem to be standing the trip pretty good—for old folks!" he roared.

"Yes, thank you very much," said the old lady.

He patted her knee, and boomed, "If there's anything I can do to make things nice and comfy for you, mother, you just holler! Don't be afraid to call on me. I haven't advertised the fact—kind of fun to travel what they call incognito—but fact is, I'm a minister of the gospel, even if I am a husky guy, and it's my pleasure as well as my duty to help folks anyway I can. Say, don't you think it's just about the loveliest thing about this ocean traveling, the way folks have the leisure to get together and exchange ideas? Have you crossed before?"

"Oh, yes, but I don't think I ever shall again," said the old lady.

"That's right—that's right! Tell you how I feel about it, mother." Elmer patted her hand. "We're Americans, and while it's a fine thing to go abroad maybe once or twice—there's nothing so broadening as travel, is there!—still, in America we've got a standard of decency and efficiency that these poor old European countries don't know anything about, and in the long run the good old U.S.A. is the place where you'll find your greatest happiness—especially for folks like us, that aren't any blooming millionaires that can grab off a lot of castles and those kind of things and have a raft of butlers. You bet! Well, just holler when I can be of any service to you. So long, folks! Got to do my three miles!"

When he was gone, the little, delicate old lady said to her husband:

"Fabian, if that swine ever speaks to me again, I shall jump overboard! He's almost the most offensive object I have ever encountered! Dear— How many times have we crossed now?"

"Oh, I've lost track. It was a hundred and ten two years ago."

"Not more?"

"Darling, don't be so snooty."

"But isn't there a law that permits one to kill people who call you 'Mother'?"

"Darling, the Duke calls you that!"

"I know. He does. That's what I hate about him! Sweet, do you think fresh air is worth the penalty of being called 'Mother'? The next time this animal stops, he'll call you 'Father'!"

"Only once, my dear!"

VIII

Elmer considered, "Well, I've given those poor old birds some cheerfulness to go on with. By golly, there's nothing more important than to give people some happiness and faith to cheer them along life's dark pathway."

He was passing the veranda café. At a pale green table was a man who sat next to Elmer in the dining salon. With him were three men unknown, and each had a whisky-and-soda in front of him.

"Well, I see you're keeping your strength up!" Elmer said forgivingly.

"Sure, you betcha," said his friend of the salon. "Don't you wanta sit down and have a jolt with us?"

Elmer sat, and when the steward stood at ruddy British attention, he gave voice:

"Well, of course, being a preacher, I'm not a big husky athalete like you boys, so all I can stand is just a ginger ale." To the steward: "Do you keep anything like that, buddy, or have you only got hooch for big strong men?"

When Elmer explained to the purser that he would be willing to act as chairman of the concert, with the most perspiratory regret the purser said that the Rt. Hon. Lionel Smith had, unfortunately, already been invited to take the chair.

IX

Cleo had not been more obnoxiously colorless than usual, but she had been seasick, and Elmer saw that it had been an error to bring her along. He had not talked to her an hour all the way. There had been so many interesting and broadening contacts; the man from China, who gave him enough ideas for a dozen missionary sermons; the professor from Higgins Presbyterian Institute, who explained that no really up-to-date scientist accepted evolution; the pretty journalist lady who needed consolation.

But now, alone with Cleo in the compartment of a train from Liverpool to London, Elmer made up for what she might have considered neglect by explaining the difficult aspects of a foreign country:

"Heh! English certainly are behind the times! Think of having these dingy coops instead of a Pullman car, so you can see your fellow-passengers and get acquainted. Just goes to show the way this country is still riddled with caste.

"Don't think so much of these towns. Kind of pretty, cottages with vines and all that, but you don't get any feeling that they're up and coming and forward-looking, like American burgs. I tell you there's one thing—and don't know's I've ever seen anybody bring this out—I might make a sermon out of it—one of the big advantages of foreign travel is, it makes you a lot more satisfied with being an American!

"Here we are, coming into London, I guess. Cer'nly is smoky, isn't it.

"Well, by golly, *so this* is what they call a depot in London! Well, I don't think much of it! Just look at all those dinky little trains. Why, say, an American engineer would be ashamed to take advantage of child-sized trains like them! And no marble anywhere in the depot!"

X

The page who took their bags up to their room in the Savoy was a brisk and smiling boy with fabulous pink cheeks.

"Say, buddy," said the Rev. Dr. Gantry, "what do you pull down here?"

"Sorry, sir, I don't think I quite understand, sir."

"Whadda you make? How much do they pay you?"

"Oh. Oh, they pay me very decently, sir. Is there anything else I can do, sir? Thank you, sir."

When the page was gone, Elmer complained, "Yuh, fine friendly kid *that* bell-boy is, and can't hardly understand the English language! Well, I'm glad we're seeing the Old Country, but if folks aren't going to be any friendlier than *he* is, I see where we'll be mighty darn glad to get back. Why, say, if he'd of been an American bell-boy, we'd of jawed along for an hour, and I'd of learned something. Well, come on, come on! Get your hat on, and let's go out and give the town the once-over."

They walked along the Strand.

"Say," Elmer said portentously, "do you notice that? The cops got straps under their chins! Well, well, that certainly is different!"

"Yes, isn't it!" said Cleo.

"But I don't think so much of this street. I always heard it was a famous one, but these stores—why, say, we got a dozen streets in Zenith, say nothing of N' York, that got better stores. No git up and git to these foreigners. Certainly does make a fellow glad he's an American!"

They came, after exploring Swan & Edgar's, to St. James's Palace.

"Now," said Elmer knowingly, "that certainly is an ancient site. Wonder what it is? Some kind of a castle, I guess."

To a passing policeman: "Say, excuse me, Cap'n, but could you tell me what that brick building is?"

"St. James's Palace, sir. You're an American? The Prince of Wales lives there, sir."

"Is that a fact! D'you hear that, Cleo? Well, sir, that's certainly something to remember!"

XI

When he regarded the meager audience at Brompton Road Chapel, Elmer had an inspiration.

All the way over he had planned to be poetic in his first London sermon. He was going to say that it was the strong man, the knight in armor, who was most willing to humble himself before God; and to say also that Love was the bow on life's dark cloud, and the morning and evening star, both. But in a second of genius he cast it away, and reflected, "No! What they want is a good, pioneering, roughneck American!"

And that he was, splendidly.

"Folks," he said, "it's mighty nice of you to let a plain American come and bring his message to you. But I hope you don't expect any Oxford College man. All I've got to give you—and may the dear Lord help my feebleness in giving you even that—is the message that God reigns among the grim frontiersmen of America, in cabin and trackless wild, even as he reigns here in your magnificent and towering city.

"It is true that just at the present moment, through no virtue of my own, I am the pastor of a church even larger than your beautiful chapel here. But, ah, I long for the day when the general superintendent will send me back to my own beloved frontier, to— Let me try, in my humble way, to give you a picture of the work I knew as a youth, that you may see how closely the grace of God binds your world-compelling city to the humblest vastnesses.

"I was the pastor—as a youngster, ignorant of everything save the fact that the one urgent duty of the preacher is to carry everywhere the Good News of the Atonement—of a log chapel in a frontier settlement called Schoenheim. I came at nightfall, weary and anhungered, a poor circuit-rider, to the house of Barney Bains, a pioneer, living all alone in his log cabin. I introduced myself. 'I am Brother Gantry, the Wesleyan preacher,' I said. Well, he stared at me, a wild look in his eyes, beneath his matted hair, and slowly he spoke:

"'Brother,' he said, 'I ain't seen no strangers for nigh onto a year, and I'm mighty pleased to see you.'

"'You must have been awfully lonely, friend,' I said.

"'No, sir, not me!' he said.

"'How's that?' I said.

"'Because Jesus has been with me all the time!'"

XII

They almost applauded.

They told him afterward that he was immense, and invited him to address them whenever he returned to London.

"Wait," he reflected, "till I get back to Zenith and tell old Potts and Hickenlooper *that!*"

As they rode to the hotel on the 'bus, Cleo sighed, "Oh, you were wonderful! But I never knew you had such a wild time of it in your first pastorate."

"Oh, well, it was nothing. A man that's a real man has to take the rough with the smooth."

"That's so!"

XIII

He stood impatiently on a corner of the Rue de la Paix, while Cleo gaped into the window of a perfumer. (She was too well trained to dream of asking him to buy expensive perfume.) He looked at the façades in the Place Vendôme.

"Not much class—too kind of plain," he decided.

A little greasy man edged up to him, covertly sliding toward him a pack of postcards, and whispered, "Lovely cards—only two francs each."

"Oh," said Elmer intelligently, "you speak English."

"Sure. All language."

Then Elmer saw the topmost card and he was galvanized.

"Whee! Golly! Two francs apiece?" He seized the pack, gloating— But Cleo was suddenly upon him, and he handed back the cards, roaring, "You get out of here or I'll call a cop!

Trying to sell obscene pictures—and to a minister of the gospel! Cleo, these Europeans have dirty minds!"

XIV

It was on the steamer home that he met and became intimate with J. E. North, the renowned vice-slayer, executive secretary of the National Association for the Purification of Art and the Press—affectionately known through all the evangelical world as "the Napap." Mr. North was not a clergyman (though he was a warm Presbyterian layman), but no clergyman in the country had more furiously pursued wickedness, more craftily forced congressmen, through threats in their home districts, to see legislation in the same reasonable manner as himself. For several sessions of congress he had backed a bill for a federal censorship of all fiction, plays, and moving pictures, with a penitentiary sentence for any author mentioning adultery even by implication, ridiculing prohibition, or making light of any Christian sect or minister.

The bill had always been defeated, but it was gaining more votes in every session. . . .

Mr. North was a tight-mouthed, thin gentleman. He liked the earnestness, uprightness, and vigor of the Reverend Dr. Gantry, and all day they walked the deck or sat talking—anywhere save in the smoking-room, where fools were befouling their intellects with beer. He gave Elmer an inside view of the great new world of organized opposition to immorality; he spoke intimately of the leaders of that world—the executives of the Anti-Saloon League, the Lord's Day Alliance, the Watch and Ward Society, the Methodist Board of Temperance, Prohibition, and Public Morals—modern St. Johns, armed with card indices.

He invited Elmer to lecture for him.

"We need men like you, Dr. Gantry," said Mr. North, "men with rigid standards of decency, and yet with a physical power which will indicate to the poor misguided youth of this awful flask-toting age that morality is not less but more virile than immorality. And I think your parishioners will appreciate your being invited to address gatherings in places like New York and Chicago now and then."

"Oh, I'm not looking for appreciation. It's just that if I can do anything in my power to strike a blow at the forces of evil," said Elmer, "I shall be most delighted to help you."

"Do you suppose you could address the Detroit Y.M.C.A. on October fourth?"

"Well, it's my wife's birthday, and we've always made rather a holiday of it—we're proud of being an old-fashioned homey family—but I know that Cleo wouldn't want that to stand in the way of my doing anything I can to further the Kingdom."

XV

So Elmer came, though tardily, to the Great Idea which was to revolutionize his life and bring him eternal and splendid fame.

That shabby Corsican artillery lieutenant and author, Bonaparte, first conceiving that he might be the ruler of Europe—Darwin seeing dimly the scheme of evolution—Paolo realizing that all of life was nothing but an irradiation of Francesca—Newton pondering on the falling apple—Paul of Tarsus comprehending that a certain small Jewish sect might be the new religion of the doubting Greeks and Romans—Keats beginning to write "The Eve of St. Agnes"—none of these men, transformed by a Great Idea from mediocrity to genius, was more remarkable than Elmer Gantry of Paris, Kansas, when he beheld the purpose for which the heavenly powers had been training him.

He was walking the deck—but only in the body, for his soul was soaring among the stars—he was walking the deck alone, late at night, clenching his fists and wanting to shout as he saw it all clearly.

He would combine in one association all the moral organizations in America—perhaps, later, in the entire world. He would be the executive of that combination; he would be the super-president of the United States, and some day the dictator of the world.

Combine them all. The Anti-Saloon League, the W.C.T.U., and the other organizations fighting alcohol. The Napap and the other Vice Societies doing such magnificent work in censoring immoral novels and paintings and motion pictures and plays. The Anti-Cigarette League. The associations lobbying for anti-evolution laws in the state legislatures. The associations making so brave a fight against Sunday baseball, Sunday movies, Sunday golfing, Sunday motoring, and the other abominations whereby the Sabbath was desecrated and the preachers' congregations and collections were lessened. The fraternities opposing Romanism. The societies which gallantly wanted to make it a crime to take the name of the Lord in vain or to use the nine Saxon physiological monosyllables. And all the rest.

Combine the lot. They were pursuing the same purpose—to make life conform to the ideals agreed upon by the principal Christian Protestant denominations. Divided, they were comparatively feeble; united, they would represent thirty million Protestant church-goers; they would have such a treasury and such a membership that they would no longer have to coax Congress and the state legislatures into passing moral legislation, but in a quiet way they would merely state to the representatives of the people what they wanted, and get it.

And the head of this united organization would be the Warwick of America, the man behind the throne, the man who would send for presidents, of whatever party, and give orders . . . and that man, perhaps the most powerful man since the beginning of history, was going to be Elmer Gantry. Not even Napoleon or Alexander had been able to dictate what a whole nation should wear and eat and say and think. That, Elmer Gantry was about to do.

"A *bishop*? *Me?* A Wes Toomis? Hell, don't be silly! I'm going to be the emperor of America—maybe of the world. I'm glad I've got this idea so early, when I'm only forty-three. I'll do it! I'll do it!" Elmer exulted. "Now let's see: The first step is to kid this J. E. North along, and do whatever he wants me to—until it comes time to kick him out—and get a church in New York, so they'll know I'm A 1. . . . My God, and Jim Lefferts tried to keep me from becoming a preacher!"

XVI

"—and I stood," Elmer was explaining, in the pulpit of Wellspring Church, "there on the Roo deluh Pay in Paris, filled almost to an intolerable historical appreciation of those aged and historical structures, when suddenly up to me comes a man obviously a Frenchman.

"Now to me, of course, any man who is a countryman of Joan of Arc and of Marshal Foch is a friend. So when this man said to me, 'Brother, would you like to have a good time tonight?' I answered—though truth to tell I did not like his looks entirely—I said, 'Brother, that depends entirely on what you mean by a good time'—he spoke English.

"'Well,' he said, 'I can take you places where you can meet many pretty girls and have fine liquor to drink.'

"Well, I had to laugh. I think I was more sorry for him than anything else. I laid my hand on his shoulder and I said, 'Brother, I'm afraid I can't go with you. I'm already dated up for a good time this evening.'

"'How's that?' he said. 'And what may you be going to do?'

"'I'm going,' I said, 'back to my hotel to have dinner with my dear wife, and after that,' I said, 'I'm going to do something that you may not regard as interesting but which is my idea of a dandy time! I'm going to read a couple of chapters of the Bible aloud, and say my prayers, and go to bed! And now,' I said, 'I'll give you exactly three seconds to get out of here, and if you're in my sight after that—well, it'll be over you that I'll be saying the prayers!'

"I see that my time is nearly up, but before I close I want to say a word on behalf of the Napap—that great organization, the National Association for the Purification of Art and the Press. I am pleased to say that its executive secretary, my dear friend Dr. J. E. North, will be with us next month, and I want you all to give him a rousing greeting—"

Chapter XXXI

FOR OVER a year now it had been murmured throughout the church-world that no speaker was more useful to the reform organization than the Rev. Dr. Elmer Gantry of Zenith. His own church regretted losing his presence so often, but they were proud to hear of him as speaking in New York, in Los Angeles, in Toronto.

It was said that when Mr. J. E. North retired from the Napap because of the press of his private interests (he was the owner of the Eppsburg, N.Y., *Times-Scimitar*), Dr. Gantry would be elected executive secretary of the Napap in his stead. It was said that no one in America was a more relentless foe of so-called liberalism in theology and of misconduct in private life.

It was said that Dr. Gantry had refused support for election as a bishop at the 1928 General Conference of the Methodist Church, North, two years from now. And it was definitely known that he had refused the presidency of Swenson University in Nebraska.

But it was also definitely known, alas, that he was likely to be invited to take the pastorate of the Yorkville Methodist Church in New York City, which included among its members Dr. Wilkie Bannister, that resolute cover-to-cover fundamentalist who was also one of the most celebrated surgeons in the country, Peter F. Durbar, the oil millionaire, and Jackie Oaks, the musical-comedy clown. The bishop of the New York area was willing to give Dr. Gantry the appointment. But— Well, there were contradictory stories; one version said that Dr. Gantry had not decided to take the Yorkville appointment; the other said that Yorkville, which meant Dr. Bannister, had not decided to take Dr. Gantry. Anyway, the Wellspring flock hoped that their pastor, their spiritual guardian, their friend and brother, would not leave them.

II

After he had discharged Miss Bundle, the church secretary—and that was a pleasant moment; she cried so ludicrously—

Elmer had to depend on a series of incapable girls, good Methodists but rotten stenographers.

It almost made him laugh to think that while everybody supposed he was having such a splendid time with his new fame, he was actually running into horrible luck. This confounded J. E. North, with all his pretenses of friendship, kept delaying his resignation from the Napap. Dr. Wilkie Bannister, the conceited chump—a fellow who thought he knew more about theology than a preacher!—delayed in advising the Official Board of the Yorkville Church to call Elmer. And his secretaries infuriated him. One of them was shocked when he said just the least little small "damn"!

Nobody appreciated the troubles of a man destined to be the ruler of America; no one knew what he was sacrificing in his campaign for morality.

And how tired he was of the rustic and unimaginative devotion of Lulu Bains! If she lisped "Oh, Elmer, you are so strong!" just once more, he'd have to clout her!

III

In the cue of people who came up after the morning service to shake hands with the Reverend Dr. Gantry was a young woman whom the pastor noted with interest.

She was at the end of the cue, and they talked without eavesdroppers.

If a Marquis of the seventeenth century could have been turned into a girl of perhaps twenty-five, completely and ardently feminine yet with the haughty head, the slim hooked nose, the imperious eyes of M. le Marquis, that would have been the woman who held Elmer's hand, and said:

"May I tell you, Doctor, that you are the first person in my whole life who has given me a sense of reality in religion?"

"Sister, I am very grateful," said the Reverend Dr. Gantry, while Elmer was saying within, "Say, you're a kid I'd like to get acquainted with!"

"Dr. Gantry, aside from my tribute—which is quite genuine—I have a perfectly unscrupulous purpose in coming and speaking to you. My name is Hettie Dowler—*Miss,* unfortunately! I've had two years in the University of Wisconsin. I've been secretary of Mr. Labenheim of the Tallahassee Life Insurance Company for the last year, but he's been transferred to Detroit. I'm really quite a good secretary. And I'm a Methodist—a member of Central, but I've been planning to switch to Wellspring. Now what I'm getting at is: If you should happen to need a secretary in the next few months—I'm filling in as one of the hotel stenographers at the Thornleigh—"

They looked at each other, unswerving, comprehending. They shook hands again, more firmly.

"Miss Dowler, you're my secretary right now," said Elmer. "It'll take about a week to arrange things."

"Thank you."

"May I drive you home?"

"I'd love to have you."

IV

Not even the nights when they worked together, alone in the church, were more thrilling than their swift mocking kisses between the calls of solemn parishioners. To be able to dash across the study and kiss her soft temple after a lugubrious widow had waddled out, and to have her whisper, "Darling, you were *too* wonderful with that awful old hen; oh, you are so dear!"—that was life to him.

He went often of an evening to Hettie Dowler's flat—a pleasant white-and-blue suite in one of the new apartment hotels, with an absurd kitchenette and an electric refrigerator. She curled, in long leopard-like lines, on the damask couch, while he marched up and down rehearsing his sermons and stopped for the applause of her kiss.

Always he slipped down to the pantry at his house and telephoned good-night to her before retiring, and when she was kept home by illness he telephoned to her from his study every hour or scrawled notes to her. That she liked best. "Your letters are so dear and funny and sweet," she told him. So he wrote in his unformed script:

Dearest ittle honeykins bunnykins, oo is such a darlings, I adore you, I haven't got another doggoned thing to say but I say that six hundred million trillion times. Elmer.

But—and he would never have let himself love her otherwise, for his ambition to become the chief moral director of the country was greater even than his delight in her—Hettie Dowler was all this time a superb secretary.

No dictation was too swift for her; she rarely made errors; she made of a typed page a beautiful composition; she noted down for him the telephone numbers of people who called during his absence; and she had a cool sympathetic way of getting rid of the idiots who came to bother the Reverend Dr. Gantry with their unimportant woes. And she had such stimulating suggestions for sermons. In these many years, neither Cleo nor Lulu had ever made a sermon-suggestion worth anything but a groan, but Hettie—why, it was she who outlined the sermon on "The Folly of Fame" which caused such a sensation at Terwillinger College when Elmer received his LL.D., got photographed laying a wreath on the grave of the late President Willoughby Quarles, and in general obtained publicity for himself and his "dear old Alma Mater."

He felt, sometimes, that Hettie was the reincarnation of Sharon.

They were very different physically—Hettie was slimmer, less tall, her thin eager face hadn't the curious long lines of Sharon's; and very different were they mentally. Hettie, however gaily affectionate, was never moody, never hysterical. Yet there was the same rich excitement about life and the same devotion to their man.

And there was the same impressive ability to handle people.

If anything could have increased T. J. Rigg's devotion to Elmer and the church, it was the way in which Hettie, instinctively understanding Rigg's importance, flattered him and jested with him and encouraged him to loaf in the church office, though he interrupted her work and made her stay later at night.

She carried out a harder, more important task—she encouraged William Dollinger Styles, who was never so friendly as Rigg. She told him that he was a Napoleon of Finance. She almost went too far in her attentions to Styles; she lunched with him, alone. Elmer protested, jealously, and she amiably agreed never to see Styles again outside of the church.

V

That was a hard, a rather miserable job, getting rid of the Lulu Bains whom Hettie had made superfluous.

On the Tuesday evening after his first meeting with Hettie, when Lulu came cooing into his study, Elmer looked depressed, did not rise to welcome her. He sat at his desk, his chin moodily in his two hands.

"What is it, dear?" Lulu pleaded.

"Sit down—no, *please*, don't kiss me—sit down over there, dearest. We must have an earnest talk," said the Reverend Dr. Gantry.

She looked so small, so rustic, for all her new frock, as she quivered in an ugly straight chair.

"Lulu, I've got something dreadful to tell you. In spite of our carefulness, Cleo—Mrs. Gantry—is onto us. It simply breaks my heart, but we must stop seeing each other privately. Indeed—"

"Oh, Elmer, Elmer, oh, my lover, *please!*"

"You must be calm, dear! We must be brave and face this thing honestly. As I was saying, I'm not sure but that it might be better, with her horrible suspicions, if you didn't come to church here any more."

"But what did she say—what did she *say*? I hate her! I hate your wife so! Oh, I won't be hysterical but— I hate her! What did she say?"

"Well, last evening she just calmly said to me— You can imagine how surprised I was; like a bolt out of the blue! She said—my wife said, 'Well, tomorrow I suppose you'll be meeting that person that teaches cooking again, and get home as late as usual!' Well, I stalled for time, and I found that she was actually thinking of putting detectives on us!"

"Oh, my dear, my poor dear! I won't ever see you again! You mustn't be disgraced, with your wonderful fame that I've been so proud of!"

"Darling Lulu, can't you see it isn't that? Hell! I'm a man! I can face the whole kit and boodle of 'em, and tell 'em just where they get off! But it's you. Honestly, I'm afraid Floyd will kill you if he knows."

"Yes, I guess he would. . . . I don't know's I care much. It would be easier than killing myself—"

"Now you look here, young woman! I'll have none of this idiotic suicide talk!" He had sprung up; he was standing over her, an impressive priestly figure. "It's absolutely against every injunction of God, who gave us our lives to use for his service and glory, to even think of self-slaughter! Why, I could never have imagined that you could say such a wicked, wicked, *wicked* thing!"

She crawled out after a time, a little figure in a shabby topcoat over her proud new dress. She stood waiting for a trolley car, alone under an arc-light, fingering her new beaded purse, which she loved because in his generosity He had given it to her. From time to time she wiped her eyes and blew her nose, and all the time she was quite stupidly muttering, "Oh, my dear, my dear, to think I made trouble for you—oh, my dear, my very dear!"

Her husband was glad to find, the year after, that she had by some miracle lost the ambitiousness which had annoyed him, and that night after night she was willing to stay home and play cribbage. But he was angry and rather talkative over the fact that whenever he came home he would find her sitting blank-faced and idle, and that she had become so careless about her hair. But life is life, and he became used to her slopping around in a dressing gown all day, and sometimes smelling of gin.

VI

By recommendation of J. E. North, it was Elmer who was chosen by the Sacred Sabbath League to lead the fight against Sunday motion pictures in Zenith. "This will be fine training for you," Mr. North wrote to Elmer, "in case the directors elect you my successor in the Napap; training for the day when you will be laying down the law not merely to a city council but to congressmen and senators."

Elmer knew that the high lords of the Napap were watching him, and with spirit he led the fight against Sunday movies. The State of Winnemac had the usual blue law to the effect that no paid labor (except, of course, that of ministers of the gospel, and whatever musicians, lecturers, educators, janitors, or other sacred help the ministers might choose to hire) might work on the Sabbath, and the usual blissful custom of ignoring that law.

Elmer called on the sheriff of the county—a worried man, whose training in criminology had been acquired in a harness-shop—and shook hands with him handsomely.

"Well, Reverend, it's real nice to have the pleasure of making your acquaintance," said the sheriff. "I've read a lot about you in the papers. Have a smoke?"

Elmer sat down impressively, leaning over a little, his elbow on the arm of the chair, his huge fist clenched.

"Thanks, but I never touch tobacco," he said grimly. "Now look here, Edelstein, are you the sheriff of this county?"

"Huh! I guess I am!"

"Oh, you guess so, do you! Well then, are you going to see that the state law against Sunday movies is obeyed?"

"Oh, now look here, Reverend! Nobody wants me to enforce—"

"Nobody? Nobody? Only a couple of hundred thousand citizens and church-members! Bankers, lawyers, doctors, decent people! And only an equal number of wops and hunkies and yids and atheists and papes want you to let the Sabbath be desecrated! Now you look here, Edelstein! Unless you pinch every last man, movie owners and operators and ushers and the whole kit and bilin' of 'em that are responsible for this disgraceful and illegal traffic of Sunday movies, I'm going to call a giant mass-meeting of all the good citizens in town, and I'm going to talk a lot less to 'em about the movie-proprietors than I am about *you*, and it's one fine, fat, nice chance you'll have of being re-elected, if two hundred thousand electors of this county (and the solid birds that take the trouble to vote) are out for your hide—"

"Say, who do you think is running this county? The Methodists and Baptists and Presbyterians?"

"Certainly!"

"Say, you look here now—"

In fact, upon warrants sworn to by the Reverend Dr. Elmer Gantry, all persons connected with the profanation of the Sabbath by showing motion-pictures were arrested for three Sundays in succession (after which the motion-pictures went on as before), and Elmer received telegrams of esteem from the Sacred Sabbath League, J. E. North, Dr. Wilkie Bannister of the Yorkville Methodist Church of New York City, and a hundred of the more prominent divines all over the land.

VII

Within twenty-four hours Mr. J. E. North let Elmer know that he was really resigning in a month, and that the choice for his successor lay between Elmer and only two other holy men; and Dr. Wilkie Bannister wrote that the Official Board of the Yorkville Methodist Church, after watching Elmer's career for the last few months, was ready to persuade the bishop to offer him the pastorate, providing he should not be too much distracted by outside interests.

It was fortunate that the headquarters of the Napap were in New York City and not, as was the case with most benevolent lobbying organizations, in Washington.

Elmer wrote to Dr. Bannister and the other trustees of the Yorkville Church that while he would titularly be the executive secretary of the National Association for the Purification of Art and the Press (and, oh! what a credit it would be to dear old Yorkville that their pastor should hold such a position!), he would be able to leave all the actual work of the Napap to his able assistants, and except for possibly a day a week, give all his energy and time and prayers to the work of guiding onward and upward, so far as might lie within his humble power, the flock at Yorkville.

Elmer wrote to Mr. J. E. North and the trustees of the Napap that while he would titularly be the pastor of the Yorkville Methodist (and would it not be a splendid justification of their work that their executive secretary should be the pastor of one of the most important churches in New York City?) yet he would be able to leave all the actual work to his able assistants, and except possibly for Sabbaths and an occasional wedding or funeral, give all his energy and time to the work of guiding, so far as might lie within his humble power, the epochal work of the National Association for the Purification of Art and the Press.

From both of these pious assemblies he had answers that they were pleased by his explanation, and that it would be a matter now of only a few days—

It was Hettie Dowler who composed these letters, but Elmer made several changes in commas, and helped by kissing her while she was typing.

VIII

It was too vexatious that at this climax of his life Elmer's mother should have invited herself to come and stay with them.

He was happy when he met her at the station. However pleasant it might be to impress the great of the world—Bishop Toomis or J. E. North or Dr. Wilkie Bannister—it had been from his first memory the object of life to gain the commendation of his mother and of Paris, Kansas, the foundation of his existence. To be able to drive her in a new Willys-Knight sedan, to show her his new church, his extraordinarily genteel home, Cleo in a new frock, was rapture.

But when she had been with them for only two days, his mother got him aside and said stoutly, "Will you sit down and try not to run about the room, my son? I want to talk to you."

"That's splendid! But I'm awfully afraid I've got to make it short, because—"

"Elmer Gantry! Will you hold your tongue and stop being such a wonderful success? Elmer, my dear boy, I'm sure you don't mean to do wrong, but I don't like the way you're treating Cleo . . . and such a dear, sweet, bright, devout girl."

"What do you mean?"

"I think you know what I mean!"

"Now you look here, Mother! All *right*, I'll sit down and be quiet, but— I certainly do not know what you mean! The way I've always been a good husband to her, and stood for her total inability to be nice to the most important members of my congregation— And of all the chilly propositions you ever met! When I have folks here for dinner—even Rigg, the biggest man in the church—she hasn't got hardly a thing to say. And when I come home from church, just absolutely tired out, and she meets me—does she meet me with a kiss and look jolly? She does *not!* She begins crabbing, the minute I enter the house, about something I've done or I haven't done, and of course it's natural—"

"Oh, my boy, my little boy, my dear—all that I've got in this whole world! You were always so quick with excuses! When you stole pies or hung cats or licked the other boys! Son, Cleo is suffering. You never pay any attention to her, even when I'm here and you try to be nice to her to show off. Elmer, who is this secretary of yours that you keep calling up all the while?"

The Reverend Dr. Gantry rose quietly, and sonorously he spoke:

"My dear mater, I owe you everything. But at a time when one of the greatest Methodist churches in the world and one of the greatest reform organizations in the world are begging for my presence, I don't know that I need to explain even to you, Ma, what I'm trying to do. I'm going up to my room—"

"Yes, and that's another thing, having separate rooms—"

"—and pray that you may understand. . . . Say, listen, Ma! Some day you may come to the White House and lunch with me and the *president*! . . . But I mean: Oh, Ma, for God's sake, quit picking on me like Cleo does all the while!"

And he did pray; by his bed he knelt, his forehead gratefully cool against the linen spread, mumbling, "O dear God, I am trying to serve thee. Keep Ma from feeling I'm not doing right—"

He sprang up.

"Hell!" he said. "These women want me to be a house dog! To hell with 'em! No! Not with mother, but— Oh, damn it, she'll understand when I'm the pastor of Yorkville! O God, why can't Cleo die, so I can marry Hettie!"

Two minutes later he was murmuring to Hettie Dowler, from the telephone instrument in the pantry, while the cook was grumbling and picking over the potatoes down in the basement, "Dear, will you just say something nice to me—anything—anything!"

Chapter XXXII

TWO EVENINGS after Elmer's mother had almost alienated him, he settled down in his study at home to prepare three or four sermons, with a hope of being in bed by eleven. He was furious when the Lithuanian maid came in and said, "Somebody on the 'phone, Doctor," but when he heard Hettie the ragged edges went out of his voice.

"Elmer? Hettie calling."

"Yes, yes, this is Dr. Gantry."

"Oh, you are so sweet and funny and dignified! Is the Lettish pot-walloper listening?"

"Yes!"

"Listen, dear. Will you do something for me?"

"You bet!"

"I'm so terribly lonely this evening. Is oo working hard?"

"I've got to get up some sermons."

"Listen! Bring your little Bible dictionary along and come and work at my place, and let me smoke a cigarette and look at you. Wouldn't you like to . . . dear . . . dearest?"

"You bet. Be right along."

He explained to Cleo and his mother that he had to go and comfort an old lady *in extremis*, he accepted their congratulations on his martyrdom, and hastened out.

II

Elmer was sitting beside Hettie on the damask couch, under the standard lamp, stroking her hand and explaining how unjust his mother was, when the door of her suite opened gravely and a thin, twitching-faced, gimlet-eyed man walked in.

Hettie sprang up, stood with a hand on her frightened breast.

"What d'you want here?" roared Elmer, as he rose also.

"Hush!" Hettie begged him. "It's my husband!"

"Your—" Elmer's cry was the bleat of a bitten sheep. "Your— But you aren't married!"

"I am, hang it! Oscar, you get out of here! How dare you intrude like this!"

Oscar walked slowly, appreciatively, into the zone of light.

"Well, I've caught you two with the goods!" he chuckled.

"What do you mean!" Hettie raged. "This is my boss, and he's come here to talk over some work."

"Yeh, I bet he has. . . . This afternoon I bribed my way in here, and I've got all his letters to you."

"Oh, you haven't!" Hettie dashed to her desk, stood in despair looking at an empty drawer.

Elmer bulked over Oscar. "I've had enough of this! You gimme those letters and you get out of here or I'll throw you out!"

Oscar negligently produced an automatic. "Shut up," he said, almost affectionately. "Now, Gantry, this ought to cost you about fifty thousand dollars, but I don't suppose you can raise that much. But if I sue for alienation of Het's affections, that's the amount I'll sue for. But if you want to settle out of court, in a nice gentlemanly manner without acting rough, I'll let you off for ten thousand—and there won't be the publicity—oh, maybe that publicity wouldn't cook your reverend goose!"

"If you think you can blackmail me—"

"Think? Hell! I know I can! I'll call on you in your church at noon tomorrow."

"I won't be there."

"You better be! If you're ready to compromise for ten thousand, all right; no feelings hurt. If not, I'll have my lawyer (and he's Mannie Silverhorn, the slickest shyster in town) file suit for alienation tomorrow afternoon—and make sure that the evening papers get out extras on it. By-by, Hettie. 'By, Elmer darling. Whoa, Elmer! Naughty, naughty! You touch me and I'll plug you! So long."

Elmer gaped after the departing Oscar. He turned quickly and saw that Hettie was grinning.

She hastily pulled down her mouth.

"My God, I believe you're in on this!" he cried.

"What of it, you big lummox! We've got the goods on you. Your letters will sound lovely in court! But don't ever think for one moment that workers as good as Oscar and I were wasting our time on a tin-horn preacher without ten bucks in the bank! We were after William Dollinger Styles. But he isn't a boob, like you; he turned me down when I went to lunch with him and tried to date him up. So, as we'd paid for this plant, we thought we might as well get our expenses and a little piece of change out of you, you short-weight, and by God we will! Now get out of here! I'm sick of hearing your blatting! No, I don't think you better hit me. Oscar'll be waiting outside the door. Sorry I won't be able to be at the church tomorrow—don't worry about my things or my salary—I got 'em this afternoon!"

III

At midnight, his mouth hanging open, Elmer was ringing at the house of T. J. Rigg. He rang and rang, desperately. No answer. He stood outside then and bawled "T. J.! T. J.!"

An upper window was opened, and an irritated voice, thick with sleepiness, protested, "Whadda yuh *want!*"

"Come down quick! It's me—Elmer Gantry. I need you, bad!"

"All right. Be right down."

A grotesque little figure in an old-fashioned nightshirt, puffing at a cigar, Rigg admitted him and led him to the library.

"T. J., they've got me!"

"Yuh? The bootleggers?"

"No. Hettie. You know my secretary?"

"Oh. Yuh. I see. Been pretty friendly with her?"

Elmer told everything.

"All right," said Rigg. "I'll be there at twelve to meet Oscar with you. We'll stall for time, and I'll do something. Don't worry, Elmer. And look here. Elmer, don't you think that even a preacher ought to *try* to go straight?"

"I've learned my lesson, T.J.! I swear this is the last time I'll ever step out, even look at a girl. God, you've been a good friend to me, old man!"

"Well, I like anything I'm connected with to go straight. Pure egotism. You better have a drink. You need it!"

"No! I'm going to hold onto *that* vow, anyway! I guess it's all I've got. Oh, my God! And just this evening I thought I was such a big important guy, that nobody could touch."

"You might make a sermon out of it—and you probably will!"

IV

The chastened and positively-for-the-last-time-reformed Elmer lasted for days. He was silent at the conference with Oscar Dowler, Oscar's lawyer, Mannie Silverhorn, and T.J. Rigg in the church study next noon. Rigg and Silverhorn did the talking. (And Elmer was dismayed to see how friendly and jocose Rigg was with Silverhorn, of whom he had spoken in most un-Methodist terms.)

"Yuh, you've got the goods on the Doctor," said Rigg. "We admit it. And I agree that it's worth ten thousand. But you've got to give us a week to raise the money."

"All right, T.J. See you here a week from today?" said Mannie Silverhorn.

"No, better make it in your office. Too many snooping sisters around."

"All right."

Everybody shook hands profusely—except that Elmer did not shake hands with Oscar Dowler, who snickered, "Why, Elmer, and us so closely related, as it were!"

When they were gone, the broken Elmer whimpered, "But, T.J., I never in the world could raise ten thousand! Why, I haven't saved a thousand!"

"Hell's big bells, Elmer! You don't suppose we're going to pay 'em any ten thousand, do you? It may cost you fifteen hundred—which I'll lend you—five hundred to sweeten Hettie, and maybe a thousand for detectives."

"Uh?"

"At a quarter to two this morning I was talking to Pete Reese of the Reese Detective Agency, telling him to get busy. We'll know a lot about the Dowlers in a few days. So don't worry."

V

Elmer was sufficiently consoled not to agonize that week, yet not so consoled but that he became a humble and tender Christian. To the embarrassed astonishment of his children, he played with them every evening. To Cleo he was almost uxorious.

"Dearest," he said, "I realize that I have—oh, it isn't entirely my fault; I've been so absorbed in the Work: but the fact remains that I haven't given you enough attention, and tomorrow evening I want you to go to a concert with me."

"Oh, Elmer!" she rejoiced.

And he sent her flowers, once.

"You see!" his mother exulted. "I knew you and Cleo would be happier if I just pointed out a few things to you. After all, your old mother may be stupid and Main-Street, but there's nobody like a mother to understand her own boy, and I knew that if I just spoke to you, even if you are a Doctor of Divinity, you'd see things different!"

"Yes, and it was your training that made me a Christian and a preacher. Oh, a man does owe so much to a pious mother!" said Elmer.

VI

Mannie Silverhorn was one of the best ambulance-chasers in Zenith. A hundred times he had made the street-car company pay damages to people whom they had not damaged; a hundred times he had made motorists pay for injuring people whom they had not injured. But with all his talent, Mannie had one misfortune—he would get drunk.

Now, in general, when he was drunk Mannie was able to keep from talking about his legal cases, but this time he was drunk in the presence of Bill Kingdom, reporter for the *Advocate-Times*, and Mr. Kingdom was an even harder cross-examiner than Mr. Silverhorn.

Bill had been speaking without affection of Dr. Gantry when Mannie leered, "Say, jeeze, Bill, your Doc Gantry is going to get his! Oh, I got him where I want him! And maybe it won't cost him some money to be so popular with the ladies!"

Bill looked rigorously uninterested. "Aw, what are you trying to pull, Mannie! Don't be a fool! You haven't got anything on Elmer, and you never will have. He's too smart for you! You haven't got enough brains to get that guy, Mannie!"

"Me? I haven't got enough brains— Say, listen!"

Yes, Mannie was drunk. Even so, it was only after an hour of badgering Mannie about his inferiority to Elmer in trickiness, an hour of Bill's harsh yet dulcet flattery, an hour of Bill's rather novel willingness to buy drinks, that an infuriated Mannie shrieked, "All right, you get a stenographer that's a notary public and I'll dictate it!"

And at two in the morning, to an irritated but alert court reporter in his shambles of a hotel room, Mannie Silverhorn dictated and signed a statement that unless the Reverend Dr. Elmer Gantry settled out of court, he would be sued (Emmanuel Silverhorn attorney) for fifty thousand dollars for having, by inexcusable intimacy with her, alienated Hettie Dowler's affections from her husband.

Chapter XXXIII

WHEN Mr. Mannie Silverhorn awoke at ten, with a head, he remembered that he had been talking, and with agitation he looked at the morning's *Advocate-Times.* He was cheered to see that there was no trace of his indiscretion.

But the next morning Mr. Silverhorn and the Reverend Dr. Gantry at about the same moment noted on the front page of the *Advocate-Times* the photostat of a document in which Emmanuel Silverhorn, atty., asserted that unless Dr. Gantry settled out of court, he would be sued for alienation of affections by Mr. Oscar Dowler, of whose wife, Dowler maintained, Dr. Gantry had taken criminal advantage.

II

It was not so much the clamor of the Zenith reporters, tracking him from his own house to that of T.J. Rigg and out to the country—it was not so much the sketches of his career and hints of his uncovered wickedness in every Zenith paper, morning and evening—it was not so much the thought that he had lost the respect of his congregation. What appalled him was the fact that the Associated Press spread the story through the country, and that he had telegrams from Dr. Wilkie Bannister of the Yorkville Methodist Church and from the directors of the Napap to the effect: Is this story true? Until the matter is settled, of course we must delay action.

III

At the second conference with Mannie Silverhorn and Oscar Dowler, Hettie was present, along with Elmer and T.J. Rigg, who was peculiarly amiable.

They sat around Mannie's office, still hearing Oscar's opinion of Mannie's indiscretion.

"Well, let's get things settled," twanged Rigg. "Are we ready to talk business?"

"I am," snarled Oscar. "What about it? Got the ten thou.?"

Into Mannie's office, pushing aside the agitated office-boy, came a large man with flat feet.

"Hello, Pete," said Rigg affectionately.

"Hello, Pete," said Mannie anxiously.

"Who the devil are you?" said Oscar Dowler.

"Oh—Oscar!" said Hettie.

"All ready, Pete?" said T.J. Rigg. "By the way, folks, this is Mr. Peter Reese of the Reese Detective Agency. You see, Hettie, I figured that if you pulled this, your past record must be interesting. Is it, Pete?"

"Oh, not especially; about average," said Mr. Peter Reese. "Now, Hettie, why did you leave Seattle at midnight on January 12, 1920?"

"None of your business!" shrieked Hettie.

"Ain't, eh? Well, it's some of the business of Arthur L. F. Morrissey there. He'd like to hear from you," said Mr. Reese, "and know your present address—and present name! Now, Hettie, what about the time you did time in New York for shop-lifting?"

"You go—"

"Oh, Hettie, don't use bad language! Remember there's a preacher present," tittered Mr. Rigg. "Got enough?"

"Oh, I suppose so," Hettie said wearily. (And for the moment Elmer loved her again, wanted to comfort her.) "Let's beat it, Oscar."

"No, you don't—not till you sign this," said Mr. Rigg. "If you do sign, you get two hundred bucks to get out of town on—which will be before tomorrow, or God help you! If you don't sign, you go back to Seattle to stand trial."

"All right," Hettie said, and Mr. Rigg read his statement:

I hereby voluntarily swear that all charges against the Reverend Dr. Elmer Gantry made directly or by implication by myself and husband are false, wicked, and absolutely unfounded. I was employed by Dr. Gantry as his secretary. His relations to me were always those of a gentleman and a Christian pastor. I wickedly concealed from him the fact that I was married to a man with a criminal record.

The liquor interests, particularly certain distillers who wished to injure Dr. Gantry as one of the greatest foes of the booze traffic, came to me and paid me to attack the character of Dr. Gantry, and in a moment which I shall never cease to regret, I assented, and got my husband to help me by forging letters purporting to come from Dr. Gantry.

The reason why I am making this confession is this: I went to Dr. Gantry, told him what I was going to do, and demanded money, planning to double-cross my employers, the booze interests. Dr. Gantry said, "Sister, I am sorry you are going to do this wrong thing, not on my behalf, because it is a part of the Christian life to bear any crosses, but on behalf of your own soul. Do as seems best to you, Sister, but before you go further, will you kneel and pray with me?"

When I heard Dr. Gantry praying, I suddenly repented and went home and with my own hands typed this statement which I swear to be the absolute truth.

When Hettie had signed, and her husband had signed a corroboration, Mannie Silverhorn observed, "I think you've overdone it a little, T.J. Too good to be true. Still, I suppose your idea was that Hettie's such a fool that she'd slop over in her confession."

"That's the idea, Mannie."

"Well, maybe you're right. Now if you'll give me the two hundred bucks, I'll see these birds are out of town tonight, and maybe I'll give 'em some of the two hundred."

"Maybe!" said Mr. Rigg.

"Maybe!" said Mr. Silverhorn.

"God!" cried Elmer Gantry, and suddenly he was disgracing himself with tears.

That was Saturday morning.

IV

The afternoon papers had front-page stories reproducing Hettie's confession, joyfully announcing Elmer's innocence, recounting his labors for purity, and assaulting the booze interests which had bribed this poor, weak, silly girl to attack Elmer.

Before eight on Sunday morning, telegrams had come in from the Yorkville Methodist Church and the Napap, congratulating Elmer, asserting that they had never doubted his innocence, and offering him the pastorate of Yorkville and the executive secretaryship of the Napap.

V

When the papers had first made charges against Elmer, Cleo had said furiously, "Oh, what a wicked, wicked lie—darling, you know I'll stand back of you!" but his mother had crackled, "Just how much of this is true, Elmy? I'm getting kind of sick and tired of your carryings on!"

Now, when he met them at Sunday breakfast, he held out the telegrams, and the two women elbowed each other to read them.

"Oh, my dear, I am so glad and proud!" cried Cleo; and Elmer's mother—she was an old woman, and bent; very wretched she looked as she mumbled, "Oh, forgive me, my boy! I've been as wicked as that Dowler woman!"

VI

But for all that, would his congregation believe him?

If they jeered when he faced them, he would be ruined, he would still lose the Yorkville pastorate and the Napap. Thus he fretted in the quarter-hour before morning service, pacing his study and noting through the window—for once, without satisfaction—that hundreds on hundreds were trying to get into the crammed auditorium.

His study was so quiet. How he missed Hettie's presence!

He knelt. He did not so much pray as yearn inarticulately. But this came out clearly: "I've learned my lesson. I'll never look at a girl again. I'm going to be the head of all the moral agencies in the country—nothing can stop me, now I've got the Napap!—but I'm going to be all the things I want other folks to be! Never again!"

He stood at his study door, watching the robed choir filing out to the auditorium chanting. He realized how he had come to love the details of his church; how, if his people betrayed him now, he would miss it: the choir, the pulpit, the singing, the adoring faces.

It had come. He could not put it off. He had to face them.

Feebly the Reverend Dr. Gantry wavered through the door to the auditorium and exposed himself to twenty-five hundred question marks.

They rose and cheered—cheered—cheered. Theirs were the shining faces of friends.

Without planning it, Elmer knelt on the platform, holding his hands out to them, sobbing, and with him they all knelt and sobbed and prayed, while outside the locked glass door of the church, seeing the mob kneel within, hundreds knelt on the steps of the church, on the sidewalk, all down the block.

"Oh, my friends!" cried Elmer, "do you believe in my innocence, in the fiendishness of my accusers? Reassure me with a hallelujah!"

The church thundered with the triumphant hallelujah, and in a sacred silence Elmer prayed:

"O Lord, thou hast stooped from thy mighty throne and rescued thy servant from the assault of the mercenaries of Satan! Mostly we thank thee because thus we can go on doing thy work, and thine alone! Not less but more zealously shall we seek utter purity and the prayer-life, and rejoice in freedom from all temptations!"

He turned to include the choir, and for the first time he saw that there was a new singer, a girl with charming ankles and lively eyes, with whom he would certainly have to become well acquainted. But the thought was so swift that it did not interrupt the pæan of his prayer:

"Let me count this day, Lord, as the beginning of a new and more vigorous life, as the beginning of a crusade for complete morality and the domination of the Christian church through all the land. Dear Lord, thy work is but begun! We shall yet make these United States a moral nation!"

DODSWORTH

TO
DOROTHY

Chapter 1

THE ARISTOCRACY of Zenith were dancing at the Kennepoose Canoe Club. They two-stepped on the wide porch, with its pillars of pine trunks, its bobbing Japanese lanterns; and never were there dance-frocks with wider sleeves nor hair more sensuously piled on little smiling heads, never an August evening more moon-washed and spacious and proper for respectable romance.

Three guests had come in these new-fangled automobiles, for it was now 1903, the climax of civilization. A fourth automobile was approaching, driven by Samuel Dodsworth.

The scene was a sentimental chromo—crisping lake, lovers in canoes singing "Nelly Was a Lady," all very lugubrious and happy; and Sam Dodsworth enjoyed it. He was a large and formidable young man, with a healthy brown mustache and a chaos of brown hair on a massive head. He was, at twenty-eight, assistant superintendent of that most noisy and unsentimental institution, the Zenith Locomotive Works, and in Yale (class of 1896) he had played better than average football, but he thought well of the most sentimental sorts of moonlight.

Tonight he was particularly uplifted because he was driving his first car. And it was none of your old-fashioned "gasoline buggies," with the engine under the seat. The engine bulked in front, under a proud hood over two feet long, and the steering column was not straight but rakishly tilted. The car was sporting and rather dangerous, and the lights were powerful affairs fed by acetylene gas. Sam sped on, with a feeling of power, of dominating the universe, at twelve dizzy miles an hour.

At the Canoe Club he was greeted by Tub Pearson, admirable in white kid gloves. Tub—Thomas J. Pearson—round and short and jolly, class-jester and class-dandy at Yale, had been Sam Dodsworth's roommate and chief admirer throughout college, but now Tub had begun to take on an irritable dignity as teller and future president of his father's bank in Zenith.

"It runs!" Tub marveled, as Sam stepped in triumph from the car. "I've got a horse all ready to tow you back!"

Tub had to be witty, whatever happened.

"Certainly it runs! I'll bet I was up to eighteen miles an hour!"

"Yeh! I'll bet that some day automobiles'll run forty!" Tub jeered. "Sure! Why, they'll just about drive the poor old horse right off the highway!"

"They will! And I'm thinking of tying up with this new Revelation Company to manufacture 'em."

"Not seriously, you poor chump?"

"Yes."

"Oh, my Lord!" Tub wailed affectionately. "Don't be crazy, Sambo! My dad says automobiles are nothing but a fad. Cost too much to run. In five years, he says, they'll disappear."

Sam's answer was not very logical:

"Who's the young angel on the porch?"

If she was an angel, the girl at whom Sam was pointing, she was an angel of ice; slim, shining, ash-blonde, her self-possessed voice very cool as she parried the complimentary teasing of half a dozen admirers; a crystal candle-stick of a girl among black-and-white lumps of males.

"You remember her—Frances Voelker—Fran Voelker—old Herman's kid. She's been abroad for a year, and she was East, in finishing-school, before that. Just a brat—isn't over nineteen or twenty, I guess. Golly, they say she speaks German and French and Italian and Woof-woof and all known languages."

Herman Voelker had brewed his way into millions and respectability. His house was almost the largest in Zenith—certainly it had the greatest amount of turrets, colored glass windows, and lace curtains—and he was leader among the German-Americans who were supplanting the New Englanders throughout the state as controllers of finance and merchandising. He entertained German professors when they came lecturing and looking, and it was asserted that one of the genuine hand-painted pictures which he had recently brought back from Nuremberg was worth nearly ten thousand dollars. A worthy citizen, Herman, and his tart beer was admirable, but that this beef-colored burgher should have fathered anything so poised and luminous as Fran was a miracle.

The sight of her made Sam Dodsworth feel clumsy as a St. Bernard looking at a white kitten. While he prophesied triumphs for the motor car, while he danced with other girls, he observed her airy dancing and her laughter. Normally, he was not particularly afraid of young women, but Fran Voelker seemed too fragile for his thick hands. Not till ten did he speak to her, when a partner left her, a flushed Corybant, in a chair near Sam's.

"Do you remember me—Dodsworth? Years since I've seen you."

"Remember! Heavens! I wondered if you were going to notice me. I used to steal the newspaper from Dad to get the news of your football heroisms. And when I was a nice young devil of eight, you once chased me out of your orchard for stealing apples."

"Did I? Wouldn't dare to now! Mavenex' dance?"

"Well—— Let me see. Oh. The next is with Levering Mott, and he's already ruined three of my two slippers. Yes."

If he did not dance with any particular neatness, a girl knew where she was, with Sam Dodsworth. He had enough strength and decision to let a young woman understand who was doing the piloting. With Fran Voelker, he was inspired; he waltzed as though he was proud of his shining burden. He held her lightly enough and, after the chaste custom of the era, his hands were gloved. But his finger-tips felt a current from her body. He knew that she was the most exquisite child in the world; he knew that he was going to marry her and keep her forever in a shrine; he knew that after years of puzzled wonder about the purpose of life, he had found it.

"She's like a lily—no, she's too lively. She's like a humming bird—no, too kind of dignified. She's—oh, she's a flame!"

They sat talking by the lake at midnight. Out on the dappled water, seen through a cloud of willow leaves, the youngsters in canoes were now singing "My Old Kentucky Home." Zenith was still in the halcyon William Dean Howells days;

not yet had it become the duty of young people to be hard and brisk, and knowing about radios, jazz, and gin.

Fran was a white shadow, in a lace shawl over her thin yellow dancing frock, as she drooped down on a newspaper which he had solemnly spread for her on the long grass. Sam trembled a little, and sounded very pompous, rather boyish:

"I suppose you went everywhere in Europe."

"More or less. France and Spain and Austria and Switzerland and—— Oh, I've seen the Matterhorn by moonlight, and Santa Maria della Salute at dawn. And I've been almost frozen to death in a mistral at Avignon!"

"I suppose you'll be bored in Zenith."

She laughed, in a small competent way. "I know *so* much about Europe—I'm no Cook's tripper!—that I know I don't know anything! All I can do in French is to order breakfast. Six months from now, all I'll remember of Germany is the names of nineteen towns, and how the Potsdamer Platz looks when you're waiting for a droschke. But you've *done* things. What are you doing now, by the way?"

"Assistant supe at the Locomotive Works. But I'm going to take a big gamble and—— Ever ride in an automobile?"

"Oh yes, several times, in Paris and New York."

"Well, I believe that in twenty years, say by 1923 or '4, they'll be as common as buggies are now! I'm going in on a new company here—Revelation Automobile Company. I'll get less salary, but it's a swell gamble. Wonderful future. I've been working on my mechanical drawing lately, and I've got the idea that they ought to get away from imitating carriages. Make a—it sounds highbrow, but I mean what you might call a new kind of beauty for autos. Kind of long straight lines. The Revelation boss thinks I'm crazy. What do you think?"

"Oh, splendid!"

"And I've bought me an automobile of my own."

"Oh, really?"

"Let me drive you home tonight!"

"No, sorry; Mama is coming for me."

"You've got to let me take you for a ride. Soon!"

"Perhaps next Sunday. . . . We must go back to the clubhouse, don't you think?"

He sprang up, meekly. As he lifted her to her feet, as he felt her slim hands, he murmured, "Certainly like to see Europe some day. When I graduated, I thought I'd be a civil engineer and see the Brazil jungle and China and all over. Reg'lar Richard Harding Davis stuff! But—— Certainly going to see Europe, anyway. Maybe I might run into you over there, and you might show me some of it."

"I'd love to!"

Ah, if she desired Europe, he would master it, and give it to her on a platter of polished gold!

There was the telephone call to her when he should have been installing machinery at the Revelation Automobile Company. There was the drive with her in his new car, very careful, though once he ventured on seventeen miles an hour. There was the dinner at the Voelkers', in the room with carved beams like a Hofbräuhaus, and Sam's fear that if Fran was kept on food like this, roast goose and stuffed cabbage and soup with Leberknödel, she would lose her race-horse slimness.

And there was even a moment when, recalling his vow made in Massachusetts Tech after graduating from Yale that he would cut loose from America and see the great world, he warned himself that between Fran and tying himself to the urgent new motor industry, he would be caught for life. The vision of himself as a Richard Harding Davis hero returned wistfully. . . . Riding a mountain trail, two thousand sheer feet above a steaming valley; sun-helmet and whipcord breeches; tropical rain on a tin-roofed shack; a shot in the darkness as he sat over a square-face of gin with a ragged tramp of Noble Ancestry. But his mind fled back to the excitement of Fran's image: her spun-glass hair, her tingling hands, her lips that were forever pursing in fantastic pouts, her chatter that fell suddenly into inexplicable silence, her cool sureness that made him feel foggy and lumbering.

In a slaty November drizzle, they were tramping the cliffs along the Chaloosa River. Fran's cheeks were alight and she was humming, but when they stopped to look at the wash of torn branches in the flooded river Sam felt that he must be protective. She was too slight and precious for such hardship as an autumnal rain. He drew the edge of his mackintosh over her woolly English topcoat.

"You must be soaked! I'm a brute to let you stay out!"

She smiled at him, very close. "I like it!"

It seemed to him that she had snuggled closer. He kissed her—for the first time, and very badly indeed.

"Oh, please don't!" she begged, a little shocked, her lively self-possession gone.

"Fran, you've got to marry me!"

She slipped from the shelter of his raincoat and, arms akimbo, said impishly, "Oh, really? Is that a new law?"

"It is!"

"The great Yale athlete speaks! The automobile magnate!"

Very gravely: "No, just a scared lump of meat that's telling you he worships you!"

Still she stared at him, among the autumn-bedraggled weeds on the river bank; she stared impudently, but quite suddenly she broke, covered her eyes with her hands, and while he clumsily dabbled at her cheeks with a huge handkerchief, she sobbed:

"Oh, Sam, my dear, but I'm so grasping! I want the whole world, not just Zenith! I *don't* want to be a good wife and mother and play cribbage prettily! I want splendor! Great horizons! Can we look for them together?"

"We will!" said Sam.

It was not till 1908, when he had been married for five years to Fran Voelker and they had had two babies, Emily and Brent, that Samuel Dodsworth came on his real struggle at the Revelation Automobile Company.

His superiors in the company had equally prized him for his steadiness and industry and fretted at him for being a dreamer. He was crazy as a poet, they said. Not only did he venture to blaspheme against the great Renault-Darracq dogmas of car-designing, not only did he keep on raving about long "stream-lines," but he insisted that the largest profits would lie in selling automobiles as cheaply as possible to as many customers as possible. He was only assistant manager of production in 1908, but he owned a little stock, and his father-in-law, portly old Herman Voelker, owned more. It was hard to discharge Sam, even when he growled at the president of the company, "If you keep the Rev looking like the one-horse-shay, we'll go bankrupt."

They tried to buy him out, and Sam, who had been absorbed in blue prints and steel castings, had to learn something about the tricks of financing: about bonds, transfer of stock, call loans, discounts to dealers. With Voelker's money behind him, he secured twenty-three per cent. of the stock, he was made vice president and manager of production, he brought out the first four-door model, and he saw the Revelation become the sensation of America for a season and one of its best-selling cars for a score of years.

And never, these twenty years, did he come nearer to the Brazilian jungle than Wall Street, nearer to the tinkling pagodas than the Revelation agency in Kansas City.

But he was too busy to be discontented; and he managed to believe that Fran loved him.

Chapter 2

SAMUEL DODSWORTH discovered that there was a snowstorm, nearly a blizzard, whirling about the house. He closed the windows with a bang and plumped back into bed till the room should be warm. He did not move so swiftly as he once had, and above the frogged silk pajamas which Fran insisted on buying for him, his hair was gray. He was healthy enough, and serene, but he was tired, and he seemed far older than his fifty years.

Fran was asleep in the farther of the twin beds, vast walnut structures with yellow silk draping. Sam looked about the bedroom. He had sometimes caught himself wondering if it wasn't too elaborate, but usually its floridness pleased him, not only as a sign of success but because it suited the luxurious Fran. Now he noted contentedly the chaise longue, with a green and silver robe across it; the desk, with monogrammed stationery very severe and near-English and snobbish; Fran's bedside table, with jeweled traveling-clock, cigarettes, and the new novels; the bathroom with its purple tiles.

Fran stirred, sighed and, while he chuckled at her resemblance to a child trying to slip back into dreams, she furiously burrowed her eyes into the little lacy pillow, which was crumpled with her determined sleeping.

"No use," he said. His rather heavy voice caressed her. "You know you're awake! Rise and shine! Face the problems of humanity and the grape fruit!"

She sat up, looking at him with the astonishment she had never quite lost at being married, breaking a yawn with a smile, tousling her bobbed hair that was still ash-blond, without gray. If Sam seemed older than his age, she was far younger. She was forty-one now, in 1925, but, rosy with sleeping, she seemed thirty-one.

"I'm going to have breakfast in bed you're smoking before breakfast again I haven't had breakfast in bed since yesterday," she yawned amiably, while he swung his thick legs over the edge of his lilac satin comforter and lighted a cigarette.

"Yes. Stay in bed. Like to, myself. Devil of a snowstorm," he said, paddling round to stroke her hair, to nuzzle his ruddy cheek against her soft fairness. "By the way, did I ever remember to tell you that I adore you?"

"Why—let me see—no, I don't believe so."

"Golly, I'm getting absent-minded! I'll have my secretary remind me to do it tomorrow." Seriously: "Realize that we finally wind up the old Revelation Company today? Sort of sorry."

"No! I'm not a bit sorry! I'm delighted. You'll be free for the first time in all these years. Let's run off some place. Oh, don't let yourself get tied up with anything new! So silly. We have enough money, and you go on stewing—'must change the design of the carburetor float—simply must sell more cars in the territory between Medicine Hat and Woolawoola.' So silly! What does it *matter*! Do ring for the maid, darling."

"Well, no, maybe it doesn't matter, but fellow likes to do his job. It's kind of a battle; fun to beat the other fellow and put over a thundering big sale. But I am rather tired. Wouldn't mind skipping off to Florida or some place."

"Let's!"

He had dutifully brought her heavy silver mirror, her brush and comb, her powder, her too-gorgeous lounging robe of Chinese brocade. When she had made herself a bit older by making herself youthful, she sat up in bed to read the Zenith *Advocate-Times.* If she looked fluffy and agreeably useless, there was nothing fluffy in her sharp comments on the news. She sounded like a woman of many affairs, many committees.

"Humph! That idiot-boy alderman, Klingenger, is going to oppose our playground bill. I'll wring his neck! . . . The D.A.R. are going to do another pageant. I will *not* be Martha Washington! You might be George. You have his detestable majesticness."

"Me?" as he came from his bath. "I'm a clown. Wait till you see me in Florida!"

"Yes. Pitching horseshoes. I wouldn't put it past you, my beloved! . . . Huh! It says here the Candlelight Club expect to have Hugh Walpole lecture, next season. I'll see our program committee pinches him off 'em."

He was slowly dressing. He always wore large grave suits, brown or gray or plain blue, expensively tailored and not very interesting, with decorous and uninteresting ties of dull silk and no jewelry save a watch-chain. But though you were not likely to see what he wore, you noted him as a man of importance, as an executive, tall, deep-chested, his kind eyes never truculent, but his mouth serious, with crescents of wrinkles beside it. His gray-threaded brown mustache, trimmed every week by the best barber at the best hotel, was fully as eccentric and showy as a doormat.

He made his toilet like a man who never wasted motions—and who, incidentally, had a perfectly organized household to depend upon. His hand went surely to the tall pile of shirts (Fran ordered them from Jermyn Street) in the huge Flemish armoire, and to the glacial nest of collars, always inspected by the parlor maid and discarded for the slightest fraying. He tied his tie, not swiftly but with the unwasteful and extremely unadventurous precision of a man who has introduced as much "scientific efficiency" into daily domesticity as into his factory.

He kissed her and, while she nibbled at sweetbreads and drank her coffee in bird-like sips and furiously rattled the newspaper in bed, he marched down-stairs to the oak-beamed dining-room. Over a second copy of the *Advocate*, and a Chicago paper, he ponderously and thoroughly attended to orange juice, porridge and thick cream, bacon, corn cakes and syrup, and coffee in a cup twice as large as the cup which Fran was jiggling in her thin hand as she galloped through the paper up-stairs.

To the maid he said little, and that amiably, as one certain that he would be well served. He was not extraordinarily irritable even when he was informed that Emily, his engaging daughter, had been up late at a dance and would not be down for breakfast. He liked Emily's morning gossip, but he never dreamed of demanding her presence—of demanding anything from her. He smiled over the letter of his son, Brent, now a junior in Yale.

Samuel Dodsworth was, perfectly, the American Captain of Industry, believing in the Republican Party, high tariff and, so long as they did not annoy him personally, in prohibition and the Episcopal Church. He was the president of the Revelation Motor Company; he was a millionaire, though decidedly not a multimillionaire; his large house was on Ridge Crest, the most fashionable street in Zenith; he had some taste in etchings; he did not split many infinitives; and he sometimes enjoyed Beethoven. He would certainly (so the observer assumed) produce excellent motor cars; he would make impressive speeches to the salesmen; but he would never love passionately, lose tragically, nor sit in contented idleness upon tropic shores.

To define what Sam Dodsworth was, at fifty, it is easiest to state what he was not. He was none of the things which most Europeans and many Americans expect in a leader of American industry. He was not a Babbitt, not a Rotarian, not an Elk, not a deacon. He rarely shouted, never slapped people on the back, and he had attended only six baseball games since 1900. He knew, and thoroughly, the Babbitts and baseball fans, but only in business.

While he was bored by free verse and cubism, he thought rather well of Dreiser, Cabell, and so much of Proust as he had rather laboriously mastered. He played golf reasonably well, and did not often talk of his scores. He liked fishing-camps in Ontario, but never made himself believe that he preferred hemlock boughs to a mattress. He was common sense apotheosized, he had the energy and reliability of a dynamo, he liked whisky and poker and pâté de foie gras, and all the while he dreamed of motors like thunderbolts, as poets less modern than himself might dream of stars and roses and nymphs by a pool.

A crisis in life had been forced on him, for his Revelation Company was being absorbed by the Unit Automotive Company—the imperial U.A.C., with its seven makes of motors, its body-building works, its billion dollars of capital. Alec Kynance, president of the U.A.C., was in Zenith, and today the final transfer of holdings was to be made.

Sam had wanted to fight the U.A.C., to keep independent this creation to which he had devoted twenty-two years, but his fellow directors were afraid. The U.A.C. could put on the market a car as good as the Revelation at a lower price, and drive them from the market. If necessary, the U.A.C. could sell below cost for a year or two. But they wanted the Revelation label and would pay for it. And the U.A.C. cossacks were good fellows. They did not treat Sam like a captive, but as a fellow warrior, to be welcomed to their larger army, so at the last Sam hid from himself the belief that the U.A.C., with their mass production, would cheapen and ruin the Revelation and turn his thunderbolt into a standardized cigar-lighter, and he had agreed to their generous purchase price.

He was not happy about it, when he let himself think abstractly. But he was extremely well trained, from his first days in Zenith High School, in not letting himself do anything so destructive as abstract thinking.

Sam clumped up-stairs and found Fran, very brisk, fairly cheerful, still in her brocade dressing-gown but crouching over her desk, dashing off notes: suggestions to partisans in her various clubs, orders to the secretaries of the leagues which she supported—leagues for the study of democracy, leagues for the blind, societies for the collection of statistics about the effect of alcohol on plantation-hands in Mississippi. She was interested in every aspect of these leagues except perhaps the purposes for which they had been founded, and no Indiana politician was craftier at soaping enemies, advising friends, and building up a political machine to accomplish nothing in particular.

She shone at Sam as he lumbered in, but she said abruptly, "Sit down, please. I want to talk to you."

("Oh, Lord, what have I done now?") He sat meekly in a chintz-covered overstuffed chair.

"Sam! I've been thinking lately. I didn't want to speak to you about it till you had the U.A.C. business all finished. But I'm afraid you'll get yourself tied up with some new job, and I want to go to Europe!"

"Well——"

"Wait! This may be our only chance, the only time you'll be free till we're so old we won't enjoy wandering. Let's take the chance! There'll be time for you to create a dozen new kinds of cars when we come back. You'll do it all the better if you have a real rest. A real one! I don't want to go just for a few months, but for a solid year."

"Good Heavens!"

"Yes, they are good! Think! Here's Emily going to be married next month. Then she won't need us. Brent has enough friends in college. He won't need us. I can chuck all these beastly clubs and everything. They don't mean anything; they're just make-believe, to keep me busy. I'm a very active female, Sam, and I want to do something besides sitting around Zenith. Think what we could do! Spring on the Italian Lakes! Motoring through the Tyrol! London in the Season! And I've never seen Europe since I was a girl, and you've never seen it at all. Let yourself have a good time for once! Trust me, can't you, dear?"

"Well, it would be kind of nice to get away from the grind. I'd like to look over the Rolls-Royce and Mercedes plants. And see Paris and the Alps. But a year—— That's a long time. I think we'd get pretty tired of Europe, living around in hotels. But—— I really haven't made any plans. The U.A.C. business was so sudden. I would like to see Italy. Those hill-towns must be very curious. And so old. We'll talk about it tonight. *Auf wiedersehen*, old lady."

He tramped out, apparently as dependable as an old Newfoundland and as little given to worrying about anything more complex than the hiding-places of bones. But he was fretting as he sat erect in his limousine, while Smith drove him into town.

These moments of driving were the only times when he was alone. He was as beset by people—his wife, his daughter, his son, his servants, his office-staff, his friends at lunch and on the golf course—as in his most frenziedly popular days at college, when it had been his "duty to old Yale" to be athletic and agreeable, and never to be alone, certainly never to sit and think. People came to him, swarmed about him, wanted his advice and his money and the spiritual support which they found in his ponderous caution. Yet he liked to be alone, he liked to meditate, and he made up for it on these morning rides.

"She's right," he worried. "I'd better not let her know how right she is, or she'll yank me off to London before I can pack my flask. I wonder—— Oh yes, of course, she does care for me, a lot. But sometimes I wish she weren't quite so good a manager. She just tries to amuse me by playing at being a kitten. She isn't one, not by a long shot. She's a greyhound. Sometimes when I'm tired, I wish she just wanted to cuddle up and be lazy with me. She's quicksilver. And quicksilver is hard, when you try to compress it!

"Oh, that's unfair. She's been the best wife—— I haven't given enough time to courting her, what with all this cursed business. And I'm tired of business. Like to sit around and chat and get acquainted with myself. And I'm tired of these streets!"

The limousine was laboring through a gusty snowstorm, skidding a bit on icy asphalt, creaking and lumbering as it climbed over drifts. The windows of the car were frost-emblazoned. Sam impatiently cleared a peep-hole with the heel of his glove.

They were creeping along Conklin Avenue, where the dreary rows of old red brick mansions, decayed into boarding houses, the cheap grocery shops and dirty laundries and gloomy little "undertaking parlors" and lunch-rooms with the blatant sign "Eats," not very entrancing at any time, were turned by the rags of blown snow into the bleakness of a lumber-camp, while the breadth of the street made it only the more shelterless and unintimate. On either side were streets of signboards advertising oil and cigarettes, of wooden one-story shacks between old-fashioned yellow brick tenement-houses gloomy in the sunless snow; a region of poverty without picturesqueness and of labor without hope.

"Oh, Lord, I'd like to get away from it! Be nice to see the Mediterranean and a little sunshine," Sam muttered. "Let's go!"

The General Offices of the Revelation Motor Company were in an immense glass and marble building on Constitution Avenue, North, above Court House Square, opposite the flashing new skyscraper of the Plymouth National Bank. The entrance to the floor given to executive offices was like the lobby of a pretentious hotel—waiting-room in brocade and tapestry and Grand Rapids renaissance; then something like an acre of little tables with typists and typists and typists, very busy, and clerks and clerks and clerks, with rattling papers; and a row of private offices resembling furniture showrooms, distinguished by enormous desks in imitation of refectory tables, covered with enormous sheets of plate glass, and fanatically kept free of papers and all jolly disorder.

The arrival of President Dodsworth was like that of a General Commanding. "Good morning!" rumbled the uniformed doorman, a retired sergeant. "Good *morning*!" chirped the girl at the inquiry desk, a charming girl whose gentleman-friend was said to be uncommonly high up in the fur business. "Good morning!" indicated the typists and clerks, their heads bowing like leaves agitated by a flitting breeze as he strode by them. "*Good* morning!" caroled Sam's private stenographer as he entered his own office. "GOOD MORNING!" shouted his secretary, an offensively high-pressure young slave-driver. And even the red-headed Jewish office boy, as he took Sam's coat and hung it up so that it would not dry, condescended "Mornin', boss."

Yet today all this obsequiousness, normally not unpleasant to the Great Man, annoyed him; all this activity, this proof that ever so many people were sending out ever so many letters about things presumably of importance, seemed to him an irritating fussiness. What did it matter whether he had another hundred thousand dollars to leave to Brent? What did it matter whether John B. Johnson of Jonesburg did or did not take the local Revelation agency? Why were all these hundreds of young people willing to be turned into machines for the purposes of rattling papers and bowing to the president?

The Great Man approached his desk, put on his eye-glasses, and graciously received a stock-report, as one accomplishing empires.

But the Great Man was thinking:

"They make me tired—poor devils! Come on, Fran! Let's go! Let's drift way round to China!"

Alec Kynance, president of the Unit Automotive Company, with his regiment of officers, lawyers, secretaries, was not coming for half an hour. Sam said impulsively to his stenographer, "Miss Rachman, skip down to the travel bureau at the

Thornleigh, won't you please, and bring me all the steamship folders and European travel information and so on that they have there. And round-the-world."

While he waited for her he turned over the papers in the wire basket which his secretary had reverently laid on the glass-topped vastness of his desk. These matters had seemed significant a few days ago, like orders given in battle, but now that the Revelation Company was no longer his——

He sighed, he shuffled the papers indifferently: The secret report on the dissipations of the manager of the Northwestern Division. The plans of the advertising agency for notices about the union of the U.A.C. and the Revelation, which was to be announced with glad, gaudy public rejoicing. What did they *matter*, now that he was turned from a bandit captain to a clerk?

For the first time he admitted that if he went to the U.A.C., even as first vice president, he would be nothing more than an office boy. He could make no daring decisions by himself. *They* had taken from him the pride in pioneering which was one of his props in life—and who *They* were, he didn't quite know. *They* were something more than just Alec Kynance and a few other officers of the U.A.C. *They* were part of a booming industrial flood which was sweeping over him. *They* would give him a larger house, a yacht, but *They* would not give him work that was really his own. He had helped to build a machine which was running away from him. He had no longer the dignity of a craftsman. He made nothing; he meant nothing; he was no longer Samuel Dodsworth, but merely part of a crowd vigorously pushing one another toward nowhere.

He wandered to the window. In that blast of snow, the shaft of the Plymouth National Bank Building was aspiring as a cathedral; twenty gray stories, with unbroken vertical lines swooping up beyond his vision into the snowy fog. It had nobility, but it seemed cruel, as lone and contemptuous of friendly human efforts as a forgotten tower on the Siberian steppes. How indifferently it would watch him starve and freeze!

With relief he looked at the travel brochures when his stenographer brought them in—a lively girl, shaking the snow from her little cloche hat, beaming at him, assuring him that he really did exist and was something of importance still. Then he was lost in the pictures. . . . Titanic walls of the Grand Canyon: scarlet pillars and pyramids of orange. A tawny road in Algiers, the sun baking, nodding camels, and drivers with dusky malign faces under their turbans. St. Moritz, shadowed by the mountains, and a pretty girl on a toboggan. A terrace at Cannes, where through fig-trees and palms and tumbling roses you looked on the sea with a lone felucca. A valley of colored patchwork fields seen from a harsh tor of Dartmoor. Japanese children rollicking among cherry trees beside a tiny temple. Dark wood of carven mediaeval houses looming over the Römerberg at Frankfort. The Grand Canal, with the fantastic columns of the piazzetta and the soft pink and cream of the ducal palace. The old sea-fronted walls of Ragusa. The streets of Paris—kiosks, impudent advertisements, a whisk of skirts, a whirligig of traffic, and little tables at which to loaf all day long.

"Wouldn't be so bad!" thought Sam. "I'd like to wander around a few months. Only I'm not going to let Fran coax me into being one of these wishy-washy expatriates, homeless, afraid of life, living on the Riviera as though they were in a sanatorium for neurotics. I'm going to go on doing something with life, and my place is here. We'll go abroad, only I'll make her fight for it or she'll feel she's running the whole show. Then I'll come back here, and I'll take Alec Kynance's show right away from him!"

"Mr. Kynance is here," announced his secretary.

Chapter 3

MR. ALEXANDER KYNANCE, president of the Unit Automotive Company, was a small bustling man with a large head, an abrupt voice, a lively mind, a magnificent lack of scruples, and a love for oratory and Corona-Coronas. He had been a section-hand and a railway superintendent, he had the best cellar of Burgundies in Detroit, and he made up for his runtiness by barking at people.

"Everything all ready? Everything all ready?" he barked at Sam Dodsworth, as the dozen representatives of the two companies settled down and rested their elbows on the gigantic mirror-surfaced table in the gold and oak directors'-room.

"I think so," Sam drawled.

"Just a few things left," said Kynance. "We've about decided to run the Revelation in between the Chromecar and the Highroad in class—drop it three hundred below your price—two-door sedan at eleven-fifty."

Sam wanted to protest. Hadn't he kept the price down to the very lowest at which his kind of car could be built? But suddenly—— What difference did it make? The Revelation wasn't his master, his religion! He was going to have a life of his own, with Fran, lovely loyal Fran, whom he'd imprisoned here in Zenith!

Let's go!

He was scarcely listening to Kynance's observations on retaining the slogan "You'll revel in a Revelation." Sam had always detested this battle-cry. It was the invention of a particularly bright and bounding young copy-writer who took regular exercise at the Y.M.C.A., but the salesmen loved it. As Kynance snapped, "Good slogan—good slogan—full o' pep," Sam mused:

"They're all human megaphones. And I'm tired."

When he had rather sadly signed the transfer of control to the U.A.C. and his lifework was over, with no chance for retreat, Sam shook hands a great deal with a number of people, and was left alone with Alec Kynance.

"Now to real business, old man," Kynance blatted. "You'll be tickled to death at getting hooked up with a concern that can control the world-market one of these days—regular empire, b' God!—instead of crawling along having to depend on a bunch of so-so assistants. We want you to come with us, of course. I haven't been hinting around. Hinting ain't my way. When Alec Kynance has something to say, by God he shoots! I want to offer you the second vice-presidency of the U.A.C., in general charge of production of all our eight cars, including the Rev. You've been getting sixty thousand salary, besides your stock?"

"Yes."

"We can offer you eighty-five, and your share in the managers' pool, with a good chance for a hundred thou in a few years, and you'll probably succeed me when the bootlegged hootch gets me. And you'll have first-class production-men under you. You can take it easy and just think up mean ideas to shove over. Other night you were drooling about how you'd like to make real Ritzy motor caravans with electric stoves and radios and everything built in. Try it! We've got the capital. And this idea you had about a motorized touring-school for boys in summer. Try it! Why, God, we might run all these summer camps out of business and make a real killing—get five hundred thousand customers—kid that hadn't gone on one of our tours, no class to him at all! Try it! And the U.A.C. getting into aeroplane manufacture. Go ahead. Draw up your plans. Yes sir, that's the kind of support we give a high-class man. When do you want to go to work? I suppose you'll have to move to Detroit, but you can get back here pretty often. Want to start right in, and see things zip?"

Sam's fantastic schemes for supercaravans, for an ambulatory summer school in which boys should see the whole country from Maine pines to San Joaquin wheat-fields, schemes which he had found stimulating and not very practical, were soiled by the lobster-faced little man's insistence on cashing in. No!

"First, I think I'll take a vacation," Sam said doubtfully. "Haven't had a real one for years. Maybe I'll run over to Europe. May stay three months or so."

"Europe? Rats! Dead's a doornail! Place for women and long-haired artists. Dead! Only American loans that keep 'em from burying the corpse! All this art! More art in a good shiny spark-plug than in all the fat Venus de Mylos they ever turned out. Naw! Go take a run through California, maybe grab a drink of good liquor in Mexico, and then come with us. Look here, Dodsworth. My way of being diplomatic is to come out flat. You necking around with some other concern? We can't wait. We got to turn out the cars! I can't keep this open, and I've offered you our pos-o-lutely highest salary. That's the way we do business. Yes or no?"

"I'm not flirting with any other company. I've had several offers and turned them down. Your offer is fair."

"Fine! Let's sign the contract right now. Got her here! Put down your John Hancock, and begin to draw the ole salary from this minute, with a month's vacation on pay! How's that?"

With the noisiness of a little man making an impression, Kynance slapped the contract on the glowing directors'-table, flourished an enormous red and black fountain pen, and patronizingly poked Sam in the shoulder.

Irritably Sam rumbled, "I can't tie myself up without thinking it over. I'll give you my answer as soon as I can. Probably in a week or so. But I may want to take a four-months rest in Europe. Never mind about the pay meanwhile. Rather feel free."

"My God, man, what do you think is the purpose of life? Loafing? Getting by with doing as little as you can? I tell you, what I always say is: there's no rest like a little extra work! You ain't tired—you're just fed up with this backwoods town. Come up to Detroit and see how we make things hum! Come sit in with us and hear us tell Congress where it gets off. Work! That's the caper! I tell you," with a grotesque, evangelical sonorousness, "I tell you, Dodsworth, to me, work is a religion. 'Turn not thy hand from the plow.' Do big things! Think of it; by making autos we're enabling half the civilized world to run into town from their pig-sties and see the movies, and the other half to get out of town and give Nature the once-over. Twenty million cars in America! And in twenty more years we'll have the bloomin' Tibetans and Abyssinians riding on cement roads in U.A.C. cars! Talk about Napoleon! Talk about Shakespeare! Why, we're pulling off the greatest miracle since the Lord created the world!

"Europe? How in hell would you put *in* four months? Think you could stand more'n ten art galleries? I *know*! I've seen Europe! Their Notre Dame is all right for about half an hour, but I'd rather see an American assembly-plant, thousand men working like a watch, than all their old, bum-lighted, tumble-down churches——"

It was half an hour before Sam got rid of Kynance without antagonizing him, and without signing a contract.

"I'd like," Sam reflected, "to sit under a linden tree for six straight months and not hear one word about Efficiency or Doing Big Things or anything more important than the temperature of the beer—if there is anything more important."

He had fallen into rather a rigid routine. Most days, between office and home, he walked to the Union Club in winter, drove to the golf course in summer. But tonight he was restless. He could not endure the fustiness of the old boys at the club. His chauffeur would be waiting there, but on his way to the club Sam stopped, with a vague notion of tasting foreignness, at a cheap German restaurant.

It was dark, quiet, free of the bouncing grandeur of Kynances. At a greasy oilcloth-covered table he sat sipping coffee and nibbling at sugar-crusted coffee-cake.

"Why should I wear myself out making more money for myself—no, for Kynance! He will like hell take my caravans away from me!"

He dreamed of a very masterwork of caravans: a tiny kitchen with electric stove, electric refrigerator; a tiny toilet with showerbath; a living-room which should become a bedroom by night—a living-room with a radio, a real writing desk; and on one side of the caravan, or at the back, a folding verandah. He could see his caravanners dining on the verandah in a forest fifty miles from any house.

"Kind of a shame to have 'em ruin any more wilderness. Oh, that's just sentimentality," he assured himself. "Let's see. We ought to make that up——" He was figuring on a menu. "We ought to produce those in quantities for seventeen hundred dollars, and our selling-point will be the saving in hotel bills. Like to camp in one myself! I will not let Kynance have my ideas! He'd turn the caravans out, flimsy and uncomfortable, for eleven hundred, and all he'd think about would be how many we could slam on the market. Kynance! Lord, to take his orders, to stand his back-slapping, at fifty! No!"

The German restaurant-keeper said, as one content with all seasons and events, "Pretty bad snow tonight."

"Yes."

And to himself: "There's a fellow who isn't worrying about Doing Big Things. And work isn't his religion. His religion is roast goose, which has some sense to it. Yes, let's go, Fran! Then come back and play with the caravan. . . . Or say, for an elaborate rig, why not two caravans, one with kitchen and toilet and stores, other with living-bedroom, and pitch 'em back to back, with a kind of train-vestibule door, and have a real palace for four people? . . . I would like to see Monte Carlo. Must be like a comic opera."

His desire for Monte Carlo, for palms and sunshine and the estimable fish of the Prince of Monaco, was enhanced by jogging through the snowstorm in his car, by being held up in drifts, and clutching the undercurving seat during a rather breathless slide uphill to Ridge Crest. But when he entered the warmth of the big house, when he sat in the library alone (Fran was not yet back from the Children's Welfare Bridge), with a whisky-soda and a volume of Masereel woodcuts, when he considered his deep chair and the hearth-log and the roses, Sam felt the security of his own cave and the assurance to be found in familiar work, in his office-staff, in his clubs, his habits and, most of all, his friends and Fran and the children.

He regarded the library contentedly: the many books, some of them read—volumes of history, philosophy, travels, detective stories; the oak-framed fireplace with a Mary Cassatt portrait of children above it; the blue davenport; the Biedermeyer rug from Fran's kin in Germany; the particularly elaborate tantalus.

"Pretty nice. Hotels—awful! Oh yes, I'll probably go over to the U.A.C. But maybe take six weeks or a couple of months in Europe, then move to Detroit. But not sell this house! Been mighty happy here. Like to come back here and spend our old days. When I really make my pile, I'll do something to help turn Zenith into another Detroit. Get a million people here. Only, plan the city right. Make it the most beautiful city in the world. Not just sit around on my chair in Europe and look at famous cities, but *make* one!"

Once a month, Sam's closest friends, Tub Pearson, his humorous classmate who was now the gray and oracular president of the Centaur State Bank, Dr. Henry Hazzard, the heart specialist, Judge Turpin, and Wheeler, the packing-house magnate, came in for dinner and an evening of poker, with Fran as hostess at dinner but conveniently disappearing after it.

Fran whisked in from her charity bridge as he was going up to dress. In her sleek coat of gray squirrel she was like a snow-sprinkled cat pouncing on flying leaves. She tossed her coat and hat to the waiting maid, and kissed Sam abruptly. She was virginal as the winter wind, this girl who was the mother of Emily about to be married.

"Terrible bore, the bridge. I won seventeen dollars. I'm a good little bridge-player, I am. We must hustle it's almost dinnertime oh what a bore Lucile McKelvey is with her perpetual gabble about Italy I bet I'll learn more Italian in three weeks than she has in three trips come on my beloved we are *late!*"

"We are going then?"

"Going where?"

"To Europe."

"Oh, I don't know. Think how nice it would be for you to 'pitch a wicked horseshoe,' as dear Tub would say, in Florida."

"Oh, quit it!"

As they tramped up-stairs he tucked his arm about her, but she released herself, she smiled at him too brightly—smile glittering and flat as white enamel paint—urbane smile that these twenty years had made him ashamed of his longing for her—and she said, "We must hurry, lamb." And too brightly she added, "Don't drink too much tonight. It's all right with people like Tub Pearson, but Judge Turpin is so conservative—I know he doesn't like it."

She had a high art of deflating him, of enfeebling him, with one quick, innocent-sounding phrase. By the most careless comment on his bulky new overcoat she could make him feel like a lout in it; by crisply suggesting that he "try for once to talk about *something* besides motors and stocks," while they rode to a formidable dinner to an elocutionary senator, she could make him feel so unintelligent that he would be silent all evening. The easy self-confidence which weeks of industrial triumphs had built up in him she could flatten in five seconds. She was, in fact, a genius at planting in him an assurance of his inferiority. Thus she did tonight, in her nicest and friendliest way, and instantly the lumbering Ajax began to look doubtfully toward the poker he had always enjoyed, to fear the opinion of Judge Turpin—an eye-glassed sparrow of a man who seemed to admire Sam, and who showed his reverence for the law by taking illicit drink for drink with him.

Sam felt unworthy and apologetic till he had dressed and been cheered by a glimpse of his daughter, Emily.

Emily, as a child, had been his companion; he had always understood her, seemed nearer to her than to Fran. She had been a tomboy, sturdy of shoulder, jolly as an old family dog out on a walk.

He used to come to the nursery door, lamenting:

"Milord, the Duke of Buckin'um lies wownded at the gate!"

Emily and Brent would wail joyously, "Not seriowsly, I trust," and he answer, "Mortually, I fear."

They had paid him the compliment of being willing to play with him, Emily more than the earnest young Brent.

But Emily had been drawn, these last five years, into the tempestuous life of young Zenith; dances, movie parties, swimming in summer, astonishingly unrestricted companionship with any number of boys; a life which bewildered Sam. Now, at twenty, she was to be married to Harry McKee, assistant general manager of the Vandering Bolt and Nut Company (considered in Zenith a most genteel establishment), ex-tennis-champion, captain during the Great War, a man of thirty-four who wore his clothes and his slang dashingly. The parties had redoubled, and Sam realized wistfully that Emily and he had no more of their old, easy, chuckling talks.

As he marched down to supervise the cocktails for dinner, Emily flew in, blown on the storm, crying at him, "Oh, Samivel, you old beautiful! You look like a grand duke in your dinner jacket! You sweet thing! Damn it, I've got to be at Mary Edge's in twenty minutes!"

She galloped up-stairs, and he stood looking after her and sighed.

"I'd better begin to dig in against the lonely sixties," he brooded.

He shivered as he went out to tell the butler-for-the-evening how to prepare the cocktails, after which, he knew, the butler would prepare them to suit himself, and probably drink most of them.

Sam remembered that this same matter of a butler for parties only had been the subject of rather a lot of pourparlers between Fran and himself. She wanted a proper butler in the house, always. And certainly they could afford one. But every human being has certain extravagances which he dare not assume, lest he offend the affectionate and jeering friends of his youth—the man who has ventured on spats dares not take to a monocle—the statesman who has ventured on humor dares not be so presumptuous as to venture on honesty also. Somehow, Sam believed that he could not face Tub Pearson if he had anything so effete as a regular butler in the house, and Fran had not won . . . not yet.

Tub Pearson—the Hon. Thos. J. Pearson, former state-senator, honorary LL.D. of Winnemac University, president of the Centaur State Bank, director in twelve companies, trustee of the Loring Grammar School and of the Zenith Art Institute, chairman of the Mayor's City Planning Commission—Tub Pearson was still as much the jester as he had been at Yale. He and his lively wife Matilde, known as "Matey," had three children, but neither viceregal honors nor domesticity had overlaid Tub's view of himself as a natural comedian.

All through the poker-game, at the large table in Sam's library, where they sat with rolled-up sleeves and loosened collars, gurgling their whisky-sodas with gratified sighs, Tub jabbed at Judge Turpin for sentencing bootleggers while he himself enjoyed his whisky as thoroughly as any one in Zenith. When they rested—that is to say, re-filled their glasses—at eleven, and Sam suggested, "May not have any more poker with you lads for a while, because Fran and I may trot over to Europe for six months or so," then Tub had an opportunity suitable to his powers:

"Six months! That's elegant, Sambo. You'll come back with an English accent: 'Hy sye, hold chappie, cawn't I 'ave the honor of raising the bloomin' pot a couple o' berries, dear old dream?'"

"Ever hear an Englishman talk like that?"

"No, but you will! Six months! Oh, don't be a damn' fool! Go for two months, and then you'll be able to appreciate getting back to a country where you can get ice and a bath-tub."

"I know it's a heresy," Sam drawled, "but I wonder if there aren't a few bath-tubs in Europe? Think I'll go over and see. My deal."

He did not show it; he played steadily, a rectangular-faced, large man, a cigar gripped in his mouth, cards dwarfed in his wide hand; but he was raging within:

"I've been doing what people expected me to, all my life. Football in college, when I'd as soon've stuck in the physics laboratory. Make money and play golf and be a good Republican ever since. Human cash-register! I'm finished! I'm going!"

But they heard from him only "Whoop you two more. Cards?"

Chapter 4

It was late when Sam yawned up to bed, for their poker-game had lasted till after one. The spacious chamber was half lighted from the bathroom. The dusky light caught the yellow silk curtains by her bed, the crystal on her wide dressing-table. She had left the windows closed, and the air was not unpleasantly stuffy with cold cream, powder, and steaminess lingering from a hot bath scented with bath-salts.

He was eager for her breathing presence. His determination to escape with her had made Fran seem nearer and more desirable than in months, but as he felt guilty about awakening her, he did not admit that he was doing anything so unkind—he merely dropped his shoes loudly.

She looked startled when she awoke. How many times she had looked startled, a little incredulous, when she had stirred to discover him beside her! She turned on her bedside light, she looked at him vaguely, as though she wasn't quite sure who he was, but, after all, one had to be polite. She was incredibly young and unmarked with wrinkles, a girl in a lace nightgown edged at the neck with white fur.

He plumped down on the bed beside her, kissed her shoulder. She suffered it, unresponding, and said, too cheerily, "Please no! Not now. Listen, dear, I want to talk. Ohhhhh, gee, I'm sleepy! I tried to stay awake till you came up, but I dozed off. So 'shamed! But pull up the big chair and listen."

"Don't you want me to kiss you?"

"Why do you always ask that? In that hurt way? You're so silly! You know you've had several drinks. Oh, I don't mind—though Tub and you, for men that are responsible citizens and don't really drink at all, always do manage to tuck away a lot too much! I don't mind. But don't you think it's a little icky, this sudden passion for embracing when you're—well, exhilarated?"

"Don't you *want* me to kiss you?"

"Good Heavens, my dear man, haven't I been your wife for twenty-two years? Oh, please, dear, don't be quarrelsome! Have I done something to hurt you? I'm so, so terribly sorry! I am, truly, dear. Kiss me!"

It was the coolest, most brief of kisses that she gave him and, that chore done, most briskly she rattled, "Now pull up the big chair and listen, dear. Or would you rather wait till tomorrow?"

She added, with the imitation of baby-talk which ordinarily tickled him, "Is mos' awful' important!"

He dragged the wing-chair to her bed and decorously sat down, wagging a varnished pump, but he said testily, "Good Lord, you don't need to coax. Let's have it."

"Oh, don't be such an old grump! Now I ask you: *is* that fair? Because I don't like the reek of whisky? Would you like it on my breath?"

"No. But I didn't take much. But—— Never mind. Listen, Fran. I know what you want. And I've decided. Kynance tried to tie me up with a contract to go to work right away, but I refused. So we'll go to Europe, and maybe for four-five months!"

"Oh. That."

With all his experience of her zig-zag incalculability, her shreds of knowledge that seemed to have no source, her ambitions and desires that seemed not worth the pains, her veiled resentment of hurts which he had not meant to inflict, her amiability when he had expected her to be angry, he was surprised now at her indifference.

"It's more fundamental than going to Europe. See here, Sam. Even if I didn't want to, oh, kiss you—— Sorry I don't seem to be more passionate. I wish I were, for your sake. But apparently I'm not. But even so, we have been happy, haven't we! We have built something pretty fine!"

"Yes, we have. What's worrying——"

"Even if we haven't been wild operatic lovers, I do think we mean something awfully deep and irreplaceable to each other. Don't we?"

His touchy ardor gave way to affection. He reached his long arm out and patted her slight, nervous fingers. "Yes. We differ on a lot of things, but I guess we've got something solid for each other that we can't find in anybody else."

"Something really permanent, Sam? Dependable? So we're like two awfully good friends backing each other in a terrible street fight?"

"Absolutely. But what's——"

"Listen. We've done the first part of our jobs. We've made enough money. We've brought up the children. You have something to show for your work—this really marvelous car that you've created. And yet we're still young, comparatively. Oh, let's not settle down into contentment with the dregs of life! Let's have a new life, all over, and not worry any more about duties (and I've had my own, young man—if you think it's easy to run a house like this, and entertain everybody!). Let's—oh, it's hard to express it, but I mean: let's not tie ourselves down to saying we'll come back from Europe (but it was sweet of you, dear, to consent without making me beg), but I mean: let's not insist that we *have* to be back from Europe in four months—yes, or four years! On the other hand, if we don't like it, let's not feel we have to stay; let's take the first boat back. But let's—— Oh, please now, get this! Let's start out of this stupid old town without one single solitary plan in our heads beyond landing in Europe, and coming back when we really want to, and going where we please when we please. Maybe we'll be back after two months on the Riviera, and then again, forty years from now, we may be living in a bamboo shack in Java and thumbing our noses at anybody who doesn't like it! Why, I'd almost like to sell this house, so we won't have anything to bind us."

"You're not serious? Good Lord, we couldn't do that! Why, it's our home! Wouldn't know what to do if we didn't have a safe harbor like this to come back to! Why, we've built ourselves into this old place, from the Radiola to the new garage doors. I guess I know every dahlia in the garden by its middle name! I love the place the way I do Emily and you and the boy. Only place where we can slam the door and tell everybody to go to hell and be ourselves!"

"But perhaps we'll get us some new selves, without losing the old ones. You'd—oh, you could be so magnificent, so tall and impressive and fine, if you'd let yourself be, if you didn't feel you had to be just an accessory to a beastly old medium-priced car, if you'd get over this silly fear that people might think you were affected and snobbish if you demanded the proper respect from them! There *are* great people in the world—dukes and ambassadors and generals and scientists and—— And I don't believe that essentially they're one bit bigger than we are. It's just that they've been trained to talk of world-affairs, instead of the price of vanadium and what Mrs. Hibbletebibble is going to serve at her Hallowe'en party. I'm going to be one of 'em! I'm not afraid of 'em! If you'd only get over this naïve passion for 'simplicity' and all those nice peasant virtues and let yourself be the big man that you really are! Not meekly say to His Excellency that though you look like a grand-duke, you're really only little Sammy Dodsworth of Zenith! He won't know it unless you insist on telling him! . . . And perhaps an ambassadorship for you, after you've been abroad long enough to learn the tricks. . . . Only to do all that, to grab the world, we must *not* be bound by the feeling that we're tied to this slow-pokey Zenith till death do us part from the fun of adventuring!"

"But to sell the house——"

"Oh, we don't need to do that, of course, silly—not at first. I just mean it as an example of how free we ought to be. Of course we wouldn't sell it. Heavens, we may be delighted to slink back here in six months! But don't let's plan to, that's what I mean. Oh, Sam, I'm absolutely not going to let my life be over at forty—well, at forty-one, but no one ever takes me for more than thirty-five or even thirty-three. And life would be over for me if I simply went on forever with the idiotic little activities in this half-baked town! I won't, that's all! You can stay here if you insist, but I'm going to take the lovely things that—I have a right to take them, because I understand them! What do I care whether some club of human, or half-human, tabby-cats in eye-glasses study dietetics or Lithuanian art next year? What do I care whether a pretentious bunch of young millionaire manufacturers have an imitation English polo team? . . . when I could have the real thing, in England! And yet if we stay here, we'll settle down to doing the same things over and over. We've drained everything that Zenith can give us—yes, and almost everything that New York and Long Island can give us. And in this beastly country—— In Europe, a woman at forty is just getting to the age where important men take a serious interest in her. But here, she's a grandmother. The flappers think I'm as venerable as the bishop's wife. And they *make* me old, with their confounded respectfulness—and their *charming* rejoicing when I go home from a dance early—I who can dance better, yes, and longer, than any of them——"

"Now, now!"

"Well, I can! And so could you, if you didn't let business sap every single ounce of energy you have! But at the same time—— I only have five or ten more years to continue being young in. It's the *dernière cartouche.* And I won't waste it. Can't you understand? Can't you understand? I mean it, desperately! I'm begging for life—no, I'm not!—I'm demanding it! And that means something more than a polite little Cook's trip to Europe!"

"But see here now! Do you actually mean to tell me, Fran, that you think that just moving from Zenith to Paris is going to change everything in your life and make you a kid again? Don't you realize that probably most people in Paris are about like most people here, or anywhere else?"

"They aren't, but even if they were——"

"What do you expect out of Europe? A lot of culture?"

"No! 'Culture!' I loathe the word, I loathe the people who use it! I certainly do not intend to collect the names of a lot of painters—and of soups—and come back and air them. Heavens, it isn't just Europe! We may not stay there at all. It's being free to wander wherever we like, as long as we like, or to settle down and become part of some community or some set if we like, and not feel that we have a duty to come back here. Oh, I could love you so much more if we weren't a pair of old horses in a treadmill!"

They sailed for Southampton in February, three weeks after Emily's wedding.

Sam was absorbed in completing the Revelation Company transfer, and in answering Fran when she complained, "Oh, work's become a disease with you! You go on with it when there's no need. Let the underlings finish up. Dear, it's because I do love you that—— Do you think you'll ever learn to enjoy leisure, to enjoy just being yourself and not an office? You're not going to make me feel guilty for having dragged you away, are you?"

"By God, I'll enjoy life if it kills me—and it probably will!" he grumbled. "You've got to give me time. I've started this business of being 'free' about thirty-five years too late. I'm a good citizen. I've learned that Life is real and Life is earnest and the presidency of a corporation is its goal. What would I be doing with anything so degenerate as enjoying myself?"

Chapter 5

THE S. S. *Ultima*, thirty-two thousand tons burden, was four hours out of New York. As the winter twilight glowered on the tangle of gloomy waves, Samuel Dodsworth was aware of the domination of the sea, of the insignificance of the great ship and all mankind. He felt lost in the round of ocean, one universal gray except for a golden gash on the western horizon. His only voyaging had been on lakes, or on the New York ferries. He felt uneasy as he stood at the after rail and saw how the rearing mass of the sea loomed over the ship and threatened it when the stern dipped—down, unbelievably down, as though she were sinking. But he felt resolute again, strong and very happy, as he swung about the deck. He had been sickish only for the first hour. The wind filled his chest, exhilarated him. Only now, the messy details of packing and farewells over, and the artificially prolonged waving to friends on the dock endured, did he feel that he was actually delivered from duty, actually going—going to strange-colored, exciting places, to do unknown and heroic things.

He hummed (for Kipling meant something to Sam Dodsworth which no Shelley could, nor Dante)—he hummed "The Gipsy Trail":

> Follow the Romany patteran
> North where the blue bergs sail,
> And the bows are gray with the frozen spray,
> And the masts are shod with mail.
> Follow the Romany patteran
> West to the sinking sun,
> Till the junk-sails lift through the houseless drift,
> And the East and the West are one.
> Follow the Romany patteran
> East where the silence broods
> By a purple wave on an opal beach
> In the hush of the Mahim woods.

"Free!" he muttered.

He stopped abruptly by the line of windows enclosing the music-room, forward on the promenade deck, as he fumbled for the memory of the first time he had ever sung "The Gipsy Trail."

It must have been when the poem was first set to music. Anyway, Fran and he had been comparatively poor. The money that old Herman Voelker had lent them had gone into the business. (A sudden, meaningless spatter of snow, out on that cold sea. How serene the lights in the music room! He began to feel the gallant security of the ship, his enduring home.) Yes, it was when they had gone off on a vacation—no chauffeur then, nor suites at the best hotels, but Sam driving all day in their shabby Revelation, with sleep in an earth-scented, wind-stirred tent. They had driven West—West, two thousand miles toward the sunset, till it seemed they must indeed come on the Pacific and junk-sails lifting against the misted sun. They had no responsibilities of position. Together they chanted "The Gipsy Trail," vowing that some day they would wander together——

And they were doing it!

Such exultation filled him, such overwhelming tenderness, that he wanted to dash down to their cabin and assure himself that he still had the magic of Fran's companionship. But he remembered with what irritable efficiency she had been unpacking. He had been married for over twenty years. He stayed on deck.

He explored the steamer. It was to him, the mechanic, the most sure and impressive mechanism he had ever seen; more satisfying than a Rolls, a Delauney-Belleville, which to him had been the equivalents of a Velasquez. He marveled at the authoritative steadiness with which the bow mastered the waves; at the powerful sweep of the lines of the deck and the trim stowing of cordage. He admired the first officer, casually pacing the bridge. He wondered that in this craft which was, after all, but a floating iron egg-shell, there should be the roseate music room, the smoking-room with its Tudor fire-place—solid and terrestrial as a castle—and the swimming-pool, green-lighted water washing beneath Roman pillars. He climbed to the boat deck, and some never realized desire for sea-faring was satisfied as he looked along the sweep of gangways, past the huge lifeboats, the ventilators like giant saxophones, past the lofty funnels serenely dribbling black woolly smoke, to the forward mast. The snow-gusts along the deck, the mysteriousness of this new world but half seen in the frosty lights, only stimulated him. He shivered and turned up his collar, but he was pricked to imaginativeness, standing outside the wireless room, by the crackle of messages springing across bleak air-roads ocean-bounded to bright snug cities on distant plains.

"I'm at sea!"

He tramped down to tell Fran—he was not quite sure what it was that he wanted to tell her, save that steamers were very fine things indeed, and that ahead of them, in the murk of the horizon, they could see the lanes of England.

She, in their cabin with its twin brass beds, its finicking imitations of gray-blue French prints on the paneled walls, was amid a litter of shaken-out frocks, heaps of shoes, dressing gowns, Coty powder, three gift copies of "The Perennial Bachelor," binoculars, steamer letters, steamer telegrams, the candy and the Charles & Company baskets of overgrown fruit and tiny conserves with which they were to help out the steamer's scanty seven meals a day, his dress-shirts (of which he was to, and certainly would not, put on a fresh one every evening), and French novels (which she was to, and certainly wouldn't, read in a stately, aloof, genteel manner every day on deck).

"It's terrible!" she lamented. "I'll get things put away just about in time for landing. . . . Oh, here's a wireless from Emily, the darling, from California. Harry and she seem to be standing the honeymoon about as well as most victims."

"Chuck the stuff. Come out on deck. I love this ship. It's so—— Man certainly has put it over Nature for once! I think I could've built ships! Come out and see it."

"You do sound happy. I'm glad. But I must unpack. You skip along——"

It was not often, these years, that he was kittenish, but now he picked her up, while she kicked and laughed, he lifted her over a pile of sweaters and tennis shoes and bathing-suits and skates, kissed her, and shouted, "Come on! It's our own honeymoon! Eloping! Have I ever remembered to tell you that I adore you? Come up and see some ocean with me. There's an awful lot of ocean around this ship. . . . Oh, damn the unpacking!"

He sounded masterful, but it was always a satisfaction, when he was masterful, to have her consent to be mastered. He was pleased now when she stopped being efficient about this business of enjoying life, and consented to do something for no reason except that it was agreeable.

In her shaggy Burberry, color of a dead maple leaf, and her orange tam o' shanter, she suggested autumn days and brown uplands. She was a girl; certainly no mother of a married daughter. He was cumbersomely proud of her, of the glances which the men passengers snatched at her as they swung round the deck.

"Funny how it comes over a fellow suddenly—I mean—this is almost the first time we've ever really started out like lovers—no job to call us back. You were dead right, Fran—done enough work—now we'll live! Together—always! But I'll have so much to learn, to keep up with you. You, and Europe! Hell, I'm so sentimental! D'you mind? Just come out of state prison! Did twenty years!"

Round and round the deck. The long stretch on the starboard side, filthy with deck chairs, with rug-wadded passengers turning a pale green as the sea rose, with wind-ruffled magazines, cups left from teatime, and children racing with toy carts. The narrow passage aft, where the wind swooped on them, pushing them back, and the steamer dipped so that they had to labor up-hill, bending forward, their limbs of lead. But, as they toiled, a glimpse of ship mysteries that were stirring to land-bound imaginations. They looked down into a hatchway—some one said there were half a dozen Brazilian cougars being shipped down there—and along a dizzy aerial gangway to the after deck and the wheel-house and a lone light in the weaving darkness. They saw the last glimmer of the streaky wake stretching back to New York.

Then, blown round the corner, released from climbing upward, a dash along the cold port side, blessedly free of steamer chairs and of lardy staring. Swinging at five miles an hour. The door of the smoking-room, with a whiff of tobacco smoke, a pleasant reek of beer, a sound of vocal Americans. The place where the deck widened into an alcove—thick walls of steel, dotted with lines of rivets smeared with thick white paint—and the door of the stewards' pantry from which, in the afternoon, came innumerable sandwiches and cakes and cups and pots of tea. The double door to the main stairway, where, somehow, a stewardess in uniform was always talking to a steward. The steel-gripped windows of the music room, with a glimpse of unhappy young-old women, accompanying their mothers abroad, sitting flapping through magazines. Where the deck was unenclosed, the yellow scoured rail and the white stanchions, bright in the deck light, brighter against the dark coil of sea. Always before them, the long straight lines of the decking planks, rigid as bars of music, divided by seams of glistening tar. Deck—ship—at sea!

Then forward, and the people along the rail—bold voyagers facing the midwinter Atlantic through glass windows—honeymooners quickly unclasping as the pestiferous deck-circlers passed—aged and sage gentlemen commenting on the inferiority of the steerage passengers who, on the deck below, altogether innocent of being condescendingly observed by the gentry-by-right-of-passage-money, jigged beside a tarpaulin-covered hatch to the pumping music of an accordion, and blew blithely on frosted fingers.

And round all over again, walking faster, turning from casual pedestrians into competitors in the ocean marathon. Faster. Cutting corners more sharply. Superior to thrusting wind, to tilting deck. Gaining on that lone, lean, athletic girl, and passing her. . . .

"That's the way to walk! Say, Fran, I wonder if sometime we couldn't get away from hotels and sort of take a walking-trip along the Riviera—interesting, I should think. . . . Darling!"

Gaining on but never quite passing that monocle-flashing, tweed-coated man whom they detested on sight and who, within three days, was to prove the simplest and heartiest of acquaintances.

A racing view of all their companions of the voyage, their fellow-citizens in this brave village amid the desert of waters: strangers to be hated on sight, to be snubbed lest they snub first, yet presently to be known better and better loved and longer remembered than neighbors seen for a lifetime on the cautious land.

Their permanent home, for a week; to become more familiar, thanks to the accelerated sensitiveness which is the one blessing of travel, than rooms paced for years. Every stippling of soot on the lifeboats, every chair in the smoking-room, every table along one's own aisle in the dining salon, to be noted and recalled, in an exhilarated and heightened observation.

"I do feel awfully well," said Sam, and Fran: "So do I. So long since we've walked together like this! And we'll keep it up; we won't get caught by people. But I must arise now and go to Innisfree and finish the unpacking of the nine bean rows oh *why* did I bring so many clothes! Till dressing-time—*my dear!*"

He was first dressed for dinner. She had decided, after rather a lot of conversation about it, that the belief that our better people do not dress for dinner on the first night out was a superstition. He sauntered up to the smoking-room for his first cocktail aboard, feeling very glossy and handsome and much-traveled. Then he was feeling very lonely, for the smoking-room was filled with amiable-looking people who apparently all knew one another. And he knew nobody aboard save Fran.

"That's the one trouble. I'm going to miss Tub and Doc Hazzard and the rest horribly," he brooded. "I wish they were along! Then it would be about perfect."

He was occupying an alcove with a semi-circular leather settee, before a massy table. The room was crowded, and a square-rigged Englishman, blown into the room with a damp whiff of sea air, stopped at Sam's table asking abruptly, "Mind if I sit here?"

The Englishman ordered his cocktail with competence:

"Now be very careful about this, steward. I want half Booth gin and half French vermouth, and just four drops of orange bitters, and no Italian vermouth, remember, no Italian vermouth." As the Englishman gulped his drink, Sam enjoyed hating him. The man was perfectly expressionless, like a square-headed wooden idol, colored like an idol of cedar wood. "Supercilious as the devil. Never would be friendly, not till he'd known you ten years. Well, he needn't worry! I'm not going to speak to him! Curious how an Englishman like that can make you feel that you're small and skinny and your tie's badly tied without even looking at you! Well, he——"

The Englishman spoke, curtly:

"Decent weather, for a February crossing."

"Is it? I don't really know. Never crossed before."

"Really?"

"You've crossed often?"

"Oh, perhaps twenty times. I was with the British War Mission during the late argument. They were always chasing me across. Lockert's my name. I'm growing cocoa down in British Guiana now. Hot there! Going to stay in London?"

"I think so, for a while. I'm on an indefinite vacation."

Sam had the American yearning to become acquainted, to tell all about his achievements, not as boasting but to establish himself as a worthy fellow.

"I've been manufacturing motor cars—the Revelation—thought it was about time to quit and find out what the world was like. Dodsworth is my name."

"Pleased to meet you." (Like most Europeans, Lockert believed that all Americans of all classes always said "Pleased to meet you," and expected so to be greeted in turn.) "Revelation? Jolly good car. Had one in Kent. My cousin—live with him when I'm home—bouncing old retired general—he's dotty over motors. Roars around on a shocking old motor bike—mustache and dignity flying in the morning breeze—atrocious bills for all the geese and curates he runs over. He's insanely pro-American—am myself, except for your appalling ice water. Have another cocktail?"

In twenty minutes, Sam and Major Clyde Lockert had agreed that the "labor turnover" was too high, that driving by night into the brilliance of headlights was undesirable, that Bobby Jones was a player of golf, and that they themselves were men of the world and cheery companions.

"I'll meet lots of people. And I like this ship. This is the greatest day of my life—next to my marriage, of course," Sam gloated, as the second dinner gong flooded the ship with waves of hysterical sound and he marched out to rouse Fran from her mysterious activities.

There was awaiting him in his cabin a wireless from Tub Pearson:

> BON VOYAGE STOP LONDON SURE SEE MY NEPHEW JACK STARLING AMERICAN EMBASSY LIVING GEORGIAN HOUSE STOP DONT RAISE ON BOBTAILED STRAIGHTS WISH WITH YOU TUB.

He wondered about introducing Major Lockert to Fran.

He was never able to guess how she would receive the people whom he found in the alley and proudly dragged in to her. Business men whom he regarded as upstanding and vigorous, she often pronounced dull; European visitors whom he found elegant, she was likely to call "not quite the real thing"; and men whom he had doubtfully presented to her as worthy but rather mutton-headed, she had been known to consider fine and very sensitive. And for all her theoretical desire to make their house a refuge for him and for whomever he liked to invite, she had never learned to keep her opinions of people to herself. When she was bored by callers, she would beg "Do you mind if I run up to bed now—such a headache," with a bright friendliness which fooled no one save herself, and which left their guests chilled and awkward.

Would she find Lockert heavy?

While they sat in the music room over after-dinner coffee, with a dance beginning in the cleared space, Lockert came ambling up to them.

"Mr. Lockert—my wife," Sam mumbled.

Lockert's stolidity did not change as he bowed, as he sat down in answer to a faint invitation, but Sam noted that his pale blue eyes came quickly alive and searched Fran with approval. . . . Fran's lovely pallor, in a *robe de style* such as only her slenderness could bear.

Sam settled back with his cigar and let them talk. To him, always, the best talk was no brilliance of his own, but conversation that amused Fran and drew her out of her silken sulkiness.

"You've been long in America, Mr. Lockert?"

"Not this time. I've been living in British Guiana—plantation—no soda for your whisky, and always the chance of finding a snake curled up in your chair on the verandah—nice big snakes, all striped, very handsome and friendly—don't seem to get used to 'em."

Lockert spoke to her not with such impersonal friendliness as he had for Sam, not with the bored dutifulness which most men in Zenith showed toward any woman over a flapperish eighteen, but a concentration, an eagerness in the presence of attractive women, an authentic need for women, which seemed to flatter Fran and to rouse her, yet make her timid. She had first looked at Lockert with metallic courtesy. "Here was another of those ponderous business men that Sam was always dragging around." Now she concentrated on him, she forgot Sam, and murmured youthfully:

"It sounds dreadful. And yet so exciting! I think I should be glad of a nice striped snake, for a change! I'm terribly fed up with the sound, safe American cities where you never find anything in your chair more thrilling than the morning paper. I think I'll go look for snakes!"

"Are you going East?"

"Don't know. Isn't it nice! No plans beyond London."

"You'll stay in London a bit?"

"Yes, if there aren't too many Americans there. Why *is* it that the travelling American is such a dreadful person? Look at those ghastly people at that second table there—no, just beyond the pillar—father with horn-rimmed spectacles, certain to be talking about either Coolidge or Prohibition—earnest mother in home-made frock out to hunt down Culture and terribly grim about it—daughter with a voice like a file. Why *is* it?"

"And why is it that you Americans, the nice ones, are so much more snobbish than the English?"

She gasped, and Sam awaited a thunderbolt, which did not come. Lockert was calm and agreeable, and she astonishingly bent to his domination with a puzzled: "Are we, really?"

"Appallingly! I know only two classes of people who hate their own race—or tribe or nation or whatever you care to call it—who travel principally to get away from their own people, who never speak of them except with loathing, who are pleased not to be taken as belonging to them. That is, the Americans and the Jews!"

"Oh, come now, that's idiotic! I'm as proud of being—— No! That's so. Partly. You're right. Why is it?"

"I suppose it's because your boosters go so much to the other extreme, talking about 'God's Country'——"

"But that expression is never used any more."

"It isn't? Anyway: 'greatest country on earth' and 'we won the war.' And your ghastly city-boosting tours and Elks' conventions—people like you hate this bellowing. And then I do think the English have, as you would say, 'put something over on you'——"

"I've *never* used the phrase!"

"——by sitting back and quietly assuming that we're the noblest and rightest people on earth. And if any man or any nation has the courage or the magnificent egotism to do that long enough, almost every one will accept it from him. Oh, the English are essentially more insufferable than the Americans——"

"But not so noisy about it," mused Fran.

Sam was not at all sure that he liked this discussion.

"Perhaps not," said Lockert; "though if there's anything noisier than the small even voice with which an Englishman can murmur, 'Don't be so noisy, my dear fellow——!' Physically, it may carry only a yard, but spiritually it rings clear up through the Heavens! And I'll be hearing it, now that I've become a Colownial. Even my cousin—I was speaking to your husband about him—absolute fanatic about motor transport—I'm to stay with him in Kent. And he'll be pleasant to me, and gently rebuking—— And he's rather a decent old thing—General Herndon."

"General *Lord* Herndon? Of the Italian drive?" said Fran.

"Yes. You see, my revered great-grandfather did so well out of cotton that he was rewarded with a peerage."

"And you're so proud of it! That's why you enjoy your mock humility. You had a quite American thrill in admitting that your cousin is a lordship. It's bunk—I mean, it's nonsense, the British assertion that only Americans take titles seriously. You have as much satisfaction out of not calling your cousin 'Lord' as——"

"As any charming American woman would out of calling him 'Lord'!"

She seemed helpless against Lockert's bland impertinence; she seemed to enjoy being bullied; she admitted, "Yes, perhaps," and they smiled at each other.

"But seriously," said Lockert, "you'll be more English than I am, after you've lived there a year. I've knocked about so much in South America and Colorado and Ceylon that I'm merely a tramp. Jungle rat."

"You really think so—that I'll become English?" She was unguardedly frank, she the ever-guarded.

"Quite. . . . I say, may I have this dance?"

Lockert, for all his squareness—he was as solid and ungraceful-looking as his favorite mutton-chop—danced easily. Sam drooped in his chair and watched them.

"Nice she has somebody to play with already," he insisted.

And within three days she had a dozen men to "play with," to dance and argue with, and race with around the deck. But always it was Lockert who assumed that he was her patron, who looked over her new acquaintances one by one, and was not at all shy about giving his verdict on them. She became helplessly angry at his assumptions, and he apologized so affably and so insincerely that she enjoyed quarreling with him for hours at a time, snuggled in a steamer robe on deck. And when Lockert and she found that they were both devoted to dogs and they became learned about wire-haired terriers, Sam leaned back listening as though she were his clever daughter.

Between times she was gayer with him and more affectionate than she had been for years; and day by day the casualness suitable to a manufacturer like Sam broke down into surprising, uncharted emotions.

Chapter 6

On their last day out—they were due in Southampton at noon, tomorrow—there was on the *Ultima* all the kindly excitement, all the anticipation and laughter, of the day before Christmas. When the Dodsworths came up to the smoking-room for their cocktail before dinner they were welcomed by the dozen people whom Lockert, the mixer of the voyage, had attracted to the round table in the center of the room.

What delightful people! Sam glowed; what a pleasure to travel with them: Lockert, the stolidly loquacious English adventurer; the jolly and vulgar little Jewish millinery buyer from Denver, who was quite the cleverest man aboard; Lechintsky, the pianist; Colonel Endersley, American military attaché at Constantinople; Sally O'Leary, the satiny movie actress, whose real name was Gwendolyn Alcovar; kindly and ruminating old Professor Deakins, the Assyriologist; Max Ristad, the Norwegian aviator; Pierce Pattison, the New York banker.

"Come on, you're late!" and "Sit down here; I've had mine," and "We missed you!" they cried. They were as friendly as a college reunion, as free of jealousy, and just as undiscriminating.

The Jewish buyer had two new anecdotes (against his own race, naturally), and they flowed down to dinner in a group.

The Captain's Dinner on the *Ultima* occurred on the last night of the voyage, and much was made of it. The dining salon was draped in scarlet, the stewards were in red hunting-coats, champagne was served at the expense of the Line. Even prohibitionists were betrayed into smiles which indicated that they wanted to keep up the friendships of this halcyon week. Toasts were drunk from table to table, with many bows, and the large Seattle contractor, who always overdid everything, threw confetti, and tonight no one minded his alcoholic philanthropy. The Comtesse de Val Montique, who had been born in Chicago, who owned nine million dollars, two châteaux, and part of a beautifully varnished husband, who crossed the ocean regularly twice a year and was so aristocratic that she had for friends only her servants, was moved tonight to look amiable as people passed her table. And the old captain, his beard like a whisk broom, went about the room patting shoulders and chuckling, "You cross again with Papa, eh?"

Sam was raised to a quivering sensitiveness toward all of them. He was not drunk, certainly, but after two cocktails, half a bottle of champagne, and a cognac or two, he was released from his customary caution, his habitual concentration on his own affairs. He was excited by their merriment at first; then it seemed to him pitiful that all of them, and he himself, should so rarely cease thus their indignant assertion of the importance of their own little offices and homes and learnings, and let themselves rejoice in friendliness. They seemed to him like children, excitedly playing now, but soon to be caught by weary maturity. He felt a little the *lacrimae rerum* of the whole world. He wanted to weep over the pride of the waiters as—the one moment on the voyage when they were important and beautiful and to be noticed—they bore in the platters of flaming ice cream. He wanted to weep over the bedraggled small-town bride who for the moment forgot that she had not found honeymooning quite so glorious, nor the sea so restful. And he saw as pitiful the fact that Fran expected to find youth again merely by changing skies.

All the while he looked as little sentimental as possible, the large, grave man plodding through the courses.

That was the great dance of the trip, with Japanese lanterns making the starboard deck curiously like the verandah of the Kennepoose Canoe Club, years and years ago, when he had found Fran. But he did not explain it to her. He couldn't. He said, "I adore you! You look mighty well in that gold and ivory dress." He had, indeed, little chance for sentimental explanations. No flapper aboard had more partners than Fran; certainly none danced so smoothly. Lockert was proprietorially about her, always, and to Sam he snapped, "Want to have you at Lord Herndon's for a week-end, if you'll come, and I'd like to show you a bit of London. We'll dine at Claridge's."

Sam was not at all sure that Lockert would do anything of the kind; he suspected that Lockert could forget people as quickly as he picked them up; yet it gave him a feeling of belonging a little to England. And there was Tub Pearson's nephew at the American Embassy, and of course Hurd, the manager of the London Revelation agency. He belonged!

He was emboldened to ask for a dance with Sally O'Leary, the movie queen who had made seduction famous.

"I'm not much good at this," he grumbled, as the steamer rolled and they struggled to dance up-hill. "You ought to be dancing with one of these young fellows."

"Don't be silly! You're a lovely partner. You're a man, not one of these gigolos, or whatever the damn' word is. If you didn't have such a lovely wife, I'd probably lay my head on your lovely big chest and ask you to go out to Hollywood and kill a coupla lovely beauty-parlor cowboys for me!"

He was pleased to believe that she meant it. His heightened sensitiveness, his wistful perception of the loneliness of the world, was gone in a boisterous well-being. When he danced with Fran and she dutifully pointed out his roughness, he laughed. Always she had a genius for keeping herself superior to him by just the right comment on his clumsiness, the most delicate and needle-pointed comparison of him with defter men. But tonight he chuckled, "I'm no Nijinsky, but I'm enjoying myself so much that even you can't make me mad!" He whirled her again, mercilessly; he slid gloatingly down the long deck, and marched her back to their table.

And, when Fran assured him they needed no more wine, there were joyful invasions of the smoking-room, where tablefuls of the shamelessly happy greeted him, "Come sit down!"

They liked him! He was Somebody! Not just as the president of the Revelation but in himself, in whatever surroundings!

He did sit down; he wandered from table to table in an ecstasy of friendliness . . . which became a little blurred, a little dizzy. . . . But they were the best company he'd ever known, everybody on board, all of 'em. . . . But he'd better watch out; he was slightly lit. . . . But they were the *best* folks——

He went out on deck, to clear his head; he swayed up to the boat deck. Then he stood fixed, and all his boisterousness vanished in a high, thin, clear ecstasy.

On the horizon was a light, stationary, *on land*, after these days of shifting waters and sliding hulls. He waited to be certain. Yes! It was a lighthouse, swinging its blade of flame. They had done it, they had fulfilled the adventure, they had found their way across the blind immensity and, the barren sea miles over, they had come home to England. He did not know (he never knew) whether the light was on Bishop's Rock or the English mainland, but his released imagination saw the murkiness to northward there as England itself. Mother England! Land of his ancestors; land of the only kings who, to an American schoolboy, had been genuine monarchs—Charles I and Henry VIII and Victoria; not a lot of confusing French and German rulers. Land where still, for the never quite matured Sammy Dodsworth, Coeur de Lion went riding, the Noir Faineant went riding, to rescue Ivanhoe, where Oliver Twist still crept through evil alleys, where Falstaff's belly-laugh discommoded the godly, where Uncle Ponderevo puffed and mixed, where Jude wavered by dusk across the moorland, where Old Jolyon sat with quiet eyes, in immortality more enduring than human life. And his own people—he had lost track of them, but he had far-off cousins in Wiltshire, in Durham. And all of them there—in a motor boat he could be ashore in half an hour! Perhaps there was a town just off there—— He saw it, from pictures in *Punch* and the *Illustrated London News*, from Cruikshank illustrations of his childhood.

A seaside town: a crescent of flat-faced houses, the brass-sheathed door of a select pub and, countrywards, a governess-cart creeping among high hedges to a village green, a chalky hill with Roman earthworks up to which panted the bookish vicar beside a white-mustached ex-proconsul who had ruled jungles and maharajahs and lost temples where peacocks screamed.

Mother England! Home!

He dashed down to Fran. He had to share it with her. For all his training in providing suitable company for her and then not interrupting his betters, he burst through her confidences as Lockert and she stood aloof from the dance. He seized her shoulder and rumbled, "Light ahead! We're there! Come up on the top deck. Oh, hell, never *mind* a coat! Just a second, to see it!"

His insistence bore Fran away, and with her alone, unchaperoned by that delightful Major Lockert, he stood huddled by a lifeboat, in his shirtsleeves, his dress coat around her, looking at the cheery wink of the light that welcomed them.

They had full five minutes of romancing and of tenderness before Lockert came along, placidly bumbling that they would catch cold . . . that they would find Kent an estimable county . . . that Dodsworth must never make the mistake of ordering his street-boots and his riding-boots from the same maker.

The smell of London is a foggy smell, a sooty smell, a coal-fire smell, yet to certain wanderers it is more exhilarating, more suggestive of greatness and of stirring life, than springtime hillsides or the chill sweetness of autumnal nights; and that unmistakable smell, which men long for in rotting perfumes along the Orinoco, in the greasy reek of South Chicago, in the hot odor of dusty earth among locust-buzzing Alberta wheatfields, that luring breath of the dark giant among cities, reaches halfway to Southampton to greet the traveler. Sam sniffed at it, uneasily, restlessly, while he considered how strange was the British fashion of having railway compartments instead of an undivided car with a nice long aisle along which you could observe ankles, magazines, Rotary buttons, clerical collars, and all the details that made travel interesting.

And the strangeness of having framed pictures of scenery behind the seats; of having hand straps—the embroidered silk covering so rough to the finger tips, the leather inside so smooth and cool—beside the doors. And the greater strangeness of admitting that these seats were more comfortable than the flinty Pullman chairs of America. And of seeing outside, in the watery February sunshine, not snow-curdled fields but springtime greenness; pollarded willows and thatched roofs and half-timbered façades——

Just like in the pictures! England!

Like most people who have never traveled abroad, Sam had not emotionally believed that these "foreign scenes" veritably existed; that human beings really could live in environments so different from the front yards of Zenith suburbs; that Europe was anything save a fetching myth like the Venusberg. But finding it actually visible, he gave himself up to grasping it as enthusiastically as, these many years, he had given himself to grinding out motor cars.

Chapter 7

NOT the charge and roaring of the huge red busses, not the glimpse of Westminster's towers beside the Thames, not the sight of the pale tall houses of Carlton House Terrace, so much delighted Sam and proved to him that incredibly he was in London as did a milk cart on its afternoon delivery—that absurd little cart, drawn by a pony, with the one big brassy milk container, instead of a truck filled with precise bottles.

"That certainly is old-fashioned!" he muttered in the taxicab, greatly content.

They planned to stay at the Berkeley, but when Sam stood at the booking-desk, making himself as large and impassive and traveled-looking as possible, and said casually, "I'd like a suite," the clerk remarked, "Very sorry, sir—full up."

"But we wirelessed for reservations!" snapped Fran.

"Come to think of it, I forgot all about sending the radio," said Sam, looking apologetically at the clerk, apologizing for the rudeness of Fran, his child.

She breathed quickly, angrily, but never yet had she quarreled with him in public.

"You might try the Savoy, sir. Or the Ritz—just across Piccadilly," the clerk suggested.

They drooped back to the taxicab waiting with their luggage, feeling unwelcome, and when they were safely inside the car, she opened up:

"I do think you might have remembered to send that wireless, considering that you had absolutely nothing else to do aboard—except drink! When I did all the packing and——Sam, do you ever realize that it really wouldn't injure your titanic industrial mind if you were occasionally just the least little bit thoughtful toward me, if you didn't leave absolutely everything about the house and traveling for me to do? I don't think it was very nice of you! And I'm so tired, after the customs and——"

"Hell! I suppose you got the tickets to Europe! I suppose you got our passports——"

"No. Your secretary did! I'm afraid you don't get any vast credit for that, my dear man!"

That was all the family scene for which they had time before they disembarked at the Ritz, but Fran was able to keep up quite a high level of martyrdom and bad temper, for the Ritz was nearly full, also, and they could not have a suite till the next day. Tonight, Fran had to endure a mere double bedroom with a private bath.

"I suppose," she stormed, "that I'm expected to spend my entire time in London packing and unpacking and moving and unpacking all over again! This awful room! Oh, I do think you might have remembered——"

All the gaiety was gone from Sam's large face. He held her arm, painfully, and growled, "Now that'll do! You ought to be ashamed of yourself! I always deny it, even to you, but you *can* be the nagging wife! Just the kind you hate! We've never had a better room than this, and tomorrow we'll have a suite, and you needn't unpack anything besides a toothbrush this evening—we needn't dress for dinner. You make me sick when you get this suffering, abused, tragedy fit. I know it's because you're tired and jumpy, but can't you ever be tired and jumpy without insisting that every one around you be the same way?"

"Is it necessary for you to shout at me, as a proof of *your* calmness—your superb masculine calmness—and is it necessary to break my arm? I am not a nagger! I've never nagged you! But the fact that you, who are so fond of talking about yourself as the great executive who never forgets a detail——"

"Never say anything of the kind!"

"——could forget to send that wireless, and then you're too self-satisfied even to be sorry about it——"

"Fran!" His arm circled her; he led her to the window. "Look down there! Piccadilly! London! I've always wanted to see it, just as much as you have. Are we going to quarrel now? Do you remember the very first evening I met you, after you'd come back from Europe, and I said we'd come here together? And we have. Togeth—— Oh, I guess I sound sentimental, but to be here in England, where all our people came from, with you——"

"I'm sorry. I was naughty. I'm sorry." Then she laughed. "Only my people didn't come from here! My revered ancestors galloped around the Bavarian mountains in short green pants, and yodeled, and undoubtedly they fought your ancestors on all possible occasions!"

But her laughter was not very convincing; her restoration to happiness not complete. She said, while she was unpacking her smaller bag, gliding in and out of the bathroom—she said, in rather a lonely, discouraged way:

"Same time, my dear, you aren't always thoughtful about me. American husbands never are. You're no worse than the rest, but you're just as bad. You think of nothing beyond business and golf. It never occurs to you that a woman, poor idiot, is lots more pleased when you remember to send her flowers, or when you 'phone to her at odd hours, just to say you love her, than she would be by a new motor car. Please don't think I'm nagging—maybe I was before, but I'm not now, really! I do so want us to be happy together! And now that you don't have to think about business, don't you think it might be nice to get acquainted with me? I'm really quite a nice person!"

"Nice? Oh, Lord!"

She was cheerfuller, after their long kiss, and he—he became very busy trying to be a thoughtful husband.

And she agreed that it was jolly that they needn't dress for dinner, and then she unpacked their evening clothes.

It was toward evening; he must make her first night in London exciting; and, like most American husbands, he assumed that the best way to do it was to invite some one, if possible some one a little younger and livelier than himself, to join them.

Major Lockert?

Oh, damn Major Lockert!

They'd seen too much of him on the ship—and the patronizing way in which he'd ambled into their compartment on the boat train and thrust a *Graphic* and a *Tatler* on them—— And the way he'd explained that you mustn't confuse a florin and a half-crown——

Still, Lockert was younger than himself—perhaps half a dozen years—and he could gabble about baccarat and Paris-Plage and other things that Fran seemed to find important——

"Let's get hold of somebody for dinner, honey," he said, "and then maybe we'll take in a show. How about it? Shall I try to get hold of Lockert?"

"Oh no!"

He was pleased; considerably less pleased when she went on, "He's been so kind to us, and so helpful, and we mustn't bother him on his first evening home. What about this young Starling, Tub's nevvy, at the American Embassy?"

"We'll try him."

The Embassy was closed, and at his bachelor apartment, Dunger, the porter, explained that Mr. Starling had gone to the Riviera for a fortnight.

"Do you remember any of the people you met here when you came abroad as a kid?" Sam asked.

"No, not really. And I haven't any relatives here—all in Germany. Hang it, I do think that after all these centuries my family might have provided me with one respectable English earl as kinsman!"

"What about Hurd, the Revelation agent? I think he came to our house once when he was in Zenith."

"Oh, he—he's a terrible person—absolute roughneck—how you ever happened to send an American like Hurd over here when you might have had a nice Englishman as London agent and—— Why, don't you remember I asked you not to write him we were coming? I *won't* be the 'president's little lady' to that awful bunch of back-slapping salesmen!"

"Now Hurd's a mighty good fellow! He's cocky, and I don't suppose he's read a book since he used to look at the lingerie ads. in the Sears-Roebuck catalogue as a kid, but he's a whirlwind at selling, and he tells mighty good stories, and he would know the best restaurants in London."

Softened, a bit motherly—or at least a bit sisterly—she comforted him, "You really would like to see him, wouldn't you? Well then, let's get him, by all means."

"No, this is your party. I want somebody that you'd like. Plenty of time to see Hurd; go call on him tomorrow, maybe."

"No, really, I think it would be lovely to have your Mr. Hurd. He wasn't so bad. I was exaggerating. Yes, do call him up—please do! I'd feel terrible if I felt that I'd kept you from seeing—— And perhaps you do owe it to the business. He may have some cables from the U.A.C."

"Well, all right. And if I don't get him, how about trying Colonel Enderley and his wife—I thought they were about the nicest people on the boat, and they may not have a date for tonight. Or that aviator, Ristad?"

"Splendid."

Hurd's office was closed.

Hurd's home address not in the telephone book.

Colonel and Mrs. Enderley not at the Savoy, after all.

Max Ristad not in.

Who else?

How many millions of American husbands had sat on the edges of how many millions of hotel beds, from San Francisco to Stockholm, sighing to the unsympathetic telephone, "Oh, not in?" ruffling through the telephone book, and again sighing, "Oh, not in?"—looking for playmates for their handsome wives, while the wives listened blandly and never once cried, "But I don't want any one else! Aren't we two enough?"

A little melancholy at having to struggle through their Second Honeymoon unassisted, they dined at the hotel and went to the theater. In the taxicab, he had a confused timidity—no fear of violence, no sense of threatened death, but a feeling of incompetence in this strange land, of making a fool of himself, of being despised by Fran and by these self-assured foreigners; a fear of loneliness; a fear that he might never be restored to the certainties of Zenith. He saw his club, the office, the dear imprisonment of home, against the background of London, with its lines of severe façades, its roaring squares, corners clamorous with newspaper vendors, and a whole nest of streets that irritated him because they weren't reasonable—he didn't know where they led! And a tremendous restaurant that looked bigger than any clashing Childs' in New York, which was annoying in a land where he had expected to find everything as tiny and stiff and unambitious as a Japanese toy garden.

And the taxi-driver hadn't understood his pronunciation—he had had to let the hotel porter give the name of the theater—and what ought he to tip the fellow? He couldn't ask Fran's advice. He was making up for his negligence about the radiogram for hotel reservations by being brusque and competent—a man on whom she could rely, whom she would love the more as she saw his superiority in new surroundings. God, he loved her more than ever, now that he had the time for it!

And what was that about not confusing a half-crown (let's see: that was fifty cents, almost exactly, wasn't it?) and a florin? Why had Lockert gone and mixed him all up by cautioning him so much about them? Curse Lockert—nice chap—awfully kind, but treating him as though he were a baby who would be disgraced in decent English society unless he had a genteel guide to tell him what he might wear and what he might say in mixed society! He'd managed to become president of quite a fair-sized corporation without Lockert's aid, hadn't he!

He felt, at the theater, even more forlorn.

He did not understand more than two-thirds of what the actors said on the stage. He had been brought up to believe that the English language and the American language were one, but what could a citizen of Zenith make of "Ohs rath, eastill in labtry"?

What were they talking about? What was the play about?

He knew that in America, even in the Midwestern saneness of Zenith, where the factories and skyscrapers were not too far from the healing winds across the cornfields, an incredible anarchy had crept into the family life which, he believed, had been the foundation of American greatness. People that you knew, people like his own cousin, Jerry Loring, after a decent career as a banker had taken up with loose girls and had stood for his wife's having a lover without killing the fellow. By God if he, Sam Dodsworth, ever found *his* wife being too friendly with a man——

No, he probably wouldn't. Not kill them. She had a right to her own way. She was better than he—that slender, shining being, in the golden frock she had insisted on digging out of a wardrobe trunk. She was a divine thing, while he was a clodhopper—and how he'd like to kiss her, if it weren't for shocking all these people so chillily calm about him! If conceivably she *could* look at another man, he'd just leave her . . . and kill himself.

But he must attend to the play, considering that he was being educated, and so expensively.

He concluded that the play was nonsense. In America there was a criminal amount of divorcing and of meriting divorce, but surely that collapse of all the decencies was impossible in Old England, the one land that these hundreds of years had upheld the home, the church, the throne! Yet here on the stage, with no one hissing, an English gentleman was represented as being the lover of a decent woman, wife of a chemist, and as protesting against running away with her because then they would be unable to continue having tea and love together at the husband's expense. And the English audience, apparently good honest people, laughed.

The queer cold bewilderment crept closer to him in the entr'acte, when he paced the lobby with Fran. The people among whom he was strolling were so blankly indifferent to him. In Zenith, he would have been certain to meet acquaintances at the theater; even in New York there was a probability of meeting classmates or automobile men. But here——He felt like a lost dog. He felt as he had on the first day of his Freshman year in college.

And his evening clothes, he perceived, were all wrong.

They went to bed rather silently, Sam and Fran. He would have given a great deal if she had suggested that they take a steamer back to America tomorrow. What, actually, she was thinking, he did not know. She had retired into the mysteriousness which had hidden her essential self ever since the night when he had first made love to her, at the Kennepoose Canoe Club. She was pleasant now—too pleasant; she said, too easily, that she had enjoyed the play; and she said, without saying it, that she was far from him and that he was not to touch her body, her sacred, proud, passionately cared-for body, save in a fleeting good-night kiss. She seemed as strange to him as the London audience at the theater. It was inconceivable that he had lived with her for over twenty years; impossible that she should be the mother of his two children; equally impossible that it could mean anything to her to travel with him—he so old and tired and aimless, she so fresh and unwrinkled and sure.

Tonight, she wasn't forty-two to his fifty-one; she was thirty to his sixty.

He heard the jesting of Tub Pearson, the friendliness of his chauffeur at home, the respectful questions of his stenographer.

He realized that Fran was also lying awake and that, as quietly as possible, her face rammed into her pillow, she was crying.

And he was afraid to comfort her.

Chapter 8

SAM had never, for all of Fran's years of urging that it was a genteel and superior custom, been able to get himself to enjoy breakfast in bed. It seemed messy. Prickly crumbs of toast crept in between the sheets, honey got itself upon his pajamas, and it was impossible to enjoy an honest cup of coffee unless he squared up to it at an honest table. He hated to desert her, their first morning in London, but he was hungry. Before he dared sneak down to the restaurant, he fussed about, trying to see to it that she had a proper breakfast. There was a room waiter, very morose, who spoke of creamed haddock and kippers. Now whatever liberalisms Samuel Dodsworth might have about politics and four-wheel brakes, he was orthodox about American breakfasts, and nothing could have sent him more gloomily to his own decent Cream of Wheat than Fran's willingness to take a thing called a kipper.

No, said Fran, after breakfast, she thought she would stay in bed till ten. But he needed exercise, she said. Why, she said, with a smile which snapped back after using as abruptly as a stretched rubber band, didn't he take a nice walk?

He did take a nice walk.

He felt friendly with such old-fashioned shops as were left on St. James's Street; brick shopfronts with small-paned windows which had known all the beaux and poets of the eighteenth century: a hat-making shop with antiquated toppers and helmets in the window; a wine office with old hand-blown bottles. Beyond these relics was a modern window full of beautiful shiny shotguns. He had not believed, somehow, that the English would have such beautiful shiny shotguns. Things were looking up. England and he would get along together.

But it was foggy, a little raw, and in that gray air the aloof and white-faced clubs of Pall Mall depressed him. He was relieved by the sign of an American bank, the Guaranty Trust Company, looking very busy and cheerful behind the wide windows. He would go in there and get acquainted but—— Today he could think of no reason; he had plenty of money, and there had been no time yet for mail to arrive—curse it!—how he'd like a good breezy letter from Tub Pearson, even a business letter from the U.A.C., full of tricky questions to be answered, anything to assure him that he was some one and meant something, here in this city of traditional, unsmiling stateliness, among these unhurried, well-dressed people who so thoroughly ignored him.

The next steamer back——

Too late in life, now, to "make new contacts," as they said in Zenith.

He realized that Fran's thesis, halfway convincing to him when they had first planned to go to Europe, her belief that they could make more passionate lives merely by running away to a more complex and graceful civilization, had been as sophomoric as the belief of a village girl that if she could but go off to New York, she would magically become beautiful and clever and happy.

He had, for a few days, forgotten that wherever he traveled, he must take his own familiar self along, and that that self would loom up between him and new skies, however rosy. It was a good self. He liked it, for he had worked with it. Perhaps it could learn things. But would it learn any more here, where it was chilled by the unfamiliarity, than in his quiet library, in solitary walks, in honestly auditing his life, back in Zenith? And just what were these new things that Fran confidently expected it to learn?

Pictures? Why talk stupidly about pictures when he could talk intelligently about engines? Languages? If he had nothing to say, what was the good of saying it in three languages? Manners? These presumable dukes and dignitaries whom he was passing on Pall Mall might be able to enter a throne-room more loftily, but he didn't want to enter a throne-room. He'd rather awe Alec Kynance of the U.A.C. than anybody who'd only inherited the right to be called a king!

No. He was simply going to be more of Sam Dodsworth than he had ever been. He wasn't going to let Europe make him apologetic. Fran would certainly get notions; want to climb into circles with fancy-dress titles. Oh, Lord, and he was so fond of her that he'd probably back her up! But he'd fight; he'd try to get her happily home in six months.

So!

He knew now what he'd do—and what he'd make her do!

He became happy again, and considered the Londoners with a friendly, unenvious, almost superior air . . . and discovered that his hat was just as wrong as his evening clothes. It was a good hat, too, and imported; a Borsalino, guaranteed by the Hub Hatters of Zenith to be the smartest hat in America. But it slanted down in front with too Western and rakish an air.

And, swearing that he'd let no English passers-by tell him what *he* was going to wear, he stalked toward Piccadilly and into a hat-shop he remembered having seen. He'd just glance in there. Certainly they couldn't *sell* him anything! English people couldn't sell like Americans! So he entered the shop and came out with a new gray felt hat for town, a new brown one for the country, a bowler, a silk evening hat, and a cap, and he was proud of himself for having begun the Europeanization which he wasn't going to begin.

For lunch he invited Hurd—Mr. A. B. Hurd, manager of the London agency of the Revelation Motor Company, an American who had lived in England for six years.

Fran was fairly amiable about meeting Mr. Hurd, for the hotel management had given her the suite which she had demanded, with a vast sitting-room in blue and gold.

"I was cross, last evening," she said to Sam. "I felt kind of lonely. I was naughty, and you were so sweet. I'll be good now."

But she couldn't help being a little over-courteous to Hurd when he came in.

Mr. Hurd was a round-faced, horn-spectacled, heavy-voiced man who believed that he had become so English in manner and speech that no one could possibly take him for an American, and who, if he lived in England for fifty years, would never be taken for anything save an American. He looked so like every fourth man to be found at the Zenith Athletic Club that traveling Middlewesterners grew homesick just at sight of him, and the homesicker when they heard his good, meaty, uninflected Iowa voice. He was proud of being able to say that the "goods vans with the motors were being shunted," though if he was in a hurry he was likely to observe that the "goods vans with the autos were by God being switched."

His former awe of Sam and of the elegance of Fran was lost now in his superiority as one who certainly did know his England and who could help these untraveled friends.

He bounded into their suite, shook hands, and crowed:

"Well, by Jove, d'you know you could've doggone near knocked me down with a feather when I found you folks were in town! I say, if you'd just told us you were coming, we'd've been down to the depot with the town brass band! By golly, d'you know, Chief, I'm almost sorry we're going in with the U.A.C. It's always been a pleasure to have a straight-shooter like you for boss, and all of us hope that you're going with the U.A.C. yourself. Say, maybe we aren't shoving over what we got left of the old Series V on the Britishers, too! Now I don't know what plans you folks have, and the one thing we learn here in England about handling our guests——"

(Sam wondered if Hurd noticed the sudden rigidity with which Fran received the suggestion that she could ever be considered a guest of Mr. A. B. Hurd.)

"——is not to bother 'em, like the Americans do, but let 'em alone when they want to be let alone. Now this noon you folks come grab lunch with me at the Savoy Grill—say, I've got the waiters there trained, and I'll tell 'em they're not to treat you like ordinary Americans—they all think I'm English; they think I'm kidding 'em when I tell 'em I'm a good Yank and proud of it! And then tomorrow evening I'll get Mrs. Hurd to come in from the country—we're living at Beaconsfield, got practically an acre there—and we might all take in a show. You folks will enjoy the English stage—real highbrow actors that know how to talk the English language, not a lot of these New York roughnecks. And then maybe next week-end you might like to come down and stay with us, and I'll drive you around and show you some real English landscape, and you'll meet some of the real sure-'nough English. There's a very high-class Englishman living right near us, in fact he's a knight, Sir Wilkie Absolom, the famous solicitor, that I know your good lady will fall for hard, Chief. Him and I play golf together right along, and I tell you he's a real democratic guy—he'll take you in and treat you just like you were English yourselves!"

"I *think*, Mr. Hurd," said Fran, "that we'd better be starting off and——" (So sweetly; as to a maid whom she was going to discharge come Saturday.) "——we can discuss plans on the way. You're very kind to bother with us, but I'm afraid that just these next few days we're going to be rather horribly busy. We've already, unfortunately, accepted a week-end invitation from some old friends—you see, I lived here a long time, before I was married—and tomorrow evening we're dining out. But now let's go and have lunch, and Sam and you will have such a nice chance to discuss all the details of the U.A.C. Just forget that I'm there."

And Hurd was unconscious that anything whatever had happened.

"Huh! Guess it'd be pretty hard to ever forget *you* were around, Mrs. Dodsworth! But I certainly would like to get the real, honest-to-God low-down on the combine. And maybe you'll be able to come out to us for the week-end after that. One American thing we do stick to—real central heating! Maybe won't be as swell as some of these castles, but lot more comfy all right!"

"Oh, I'm sure of it. Shall we go now?"

Sam raged within, "I'm not going to stand her highhatting him like that! He's being as polite as he can." And, as heartily as Hurd, he shouted, "Wait there! Hold your horses, Fran! If Hurd is buying us all this expensive food, we got to give him a cocktail first. He'll be our housewarming party here."

He stamped firmly across the floor, rang for a waiter, and ordered cocktails, ignoring her flashed fury, though he knew that he would have to pay for it afterward. But he did hope that Hurd wouldn't say, drinking, "Well, here's looking at you, Chief!"

Hurd didn't. He said, "Well, here's mud in your eye! Ha, ha, ha! Say, by golly, I guess it's a year since I've heard anybody get that off! But there's a few of the good old American expressions a fellow likes to keep up, even when he's lived as long among the English as I have. Well, let's go feed the old faces. Certainly is awful' nice to have you folks here. We must see a lot of each other."

Not that Fran said anything rude at lunch. It would have been better so. She merely knotted her brows and looked suffering. Fortunately Hurd did not seem to care; probably he did not look at her; probably he was one of the American men of whom Fran had complained that they never bothered to look at a woman of over nineteen.

Hurd was unflagging. "Guess you folks would like some American grub for a change. I do myself, after all these years here," he chuckled, and ordered clam chowder, fried chicken, and sugar corn. "You folks will do fine in this burg," he said. "You'll meet some of the best. I wouldn't wonder if quite a few men in the City (that's what we call the Wall Street Section, here) have heard of you, Chief. And your good lady ought to be able to get along fine with the ladies here. . . . Oh yes, you said you were here as a girl. Well, you'll find all that coming back to you before long. Shouldn't wonder if you took to English life quicker'n I did myself, and say, I took to it like a duck to water. Of course I'm a one-hundred-per-cent. American, but I do like English ways, and this damn' Prohibition—excuse me, Mrs. Dodsworth, but I'm agin Prohibition—I guess that's about the only subject where I haven't got any come-back when my English pals razz me about the States. And the wages for servants here—— Say, ain't it simply incredible, by Jove, what kitchen mechanics expect to get in America, and never do a lick of work for it! Sure, you'll like it here. But say, you must be sure to not make one mistake that even a lot of high-class Americans make when they first come over. Don't ever boast about how much money you make——"

(Surely Hurd must catch Fran's choke of rage.)

"——because the British think that's what they call putting on side. Not that you would do that, of course, but I mean—Surprise you how many of the real bon ton do. And of course I don't need to suggest to anybody with a social position like yours, Chief, that you can't just get to talking to fellows in a hotel bar here, like we would back home. Oh, you bet. I shouldn't wonder if you'd catch onto English ways even quicker than—— Well, as I was saying, I don't want to intrude on you folks, but it'd be a mighty great pleasure to give you any hints I can about the British slant on things, and to start you off with a genuine English bunch of acquaintances."

"It's frightfully kind of you, and it's been such a nice lunch," said Fran. "But do you mind if we run along now?

I'm afraid I'm a little late for my engagement at the hairdresser's."

When, quite wordless, they had walked through Trafalgar Square, he snarled at Fran, "Oh, *say* it!"

"Need I?"

"Better get it over!"

"You seem to be saying it to yourself, quite successfully!"

"I am. Only hurry the execution. I have too much imagination."

"Have you? If you had, would you have invited the charming and helpful and tactful Mr. A. B. Hurd to lunch with me? Couldn't you have enjoyed his highly British presence by yourself?"

"Fran, we've said all of this about so many different people—— Granted that I am a good deal of a fool about bringing the wrong kinds of people together——"

"You are, my beloved, and everybody gives you credit for being so loyal and hospitable!"

"Granted. And I admit Hurd likes himself a good deal. On the other hand, he's generous, he's honest, he's probably a man of very little home-training as a youngster. And that—— No, wait now! You *don't* know what I'm going to say! In that I've expressed all our whole row, if we went on with it all afternoon. You'd just go on saying that he's a fathead, and I'd just go on insisting that he's got a kind heart. Can't you ever forego the pleasure of catching me in an error? Here we are in London, with a free afternoon ahead of us and the job of lunching with Hurd done. Must you be sulky?"

"I am not sulky! Only you can't expect me to be very radiant after an experience like that! Oh, it doesn't matter." She achieved a half-smile. "Never mind. We'll be meeting some decent people here soon. No, don't—don't tell me that Hurd is decent. Probably he is. Probably he never beats his wife. I'm sure that his playmate, Sir Toppingham Cohen, is an adornment to any salon. . . . Oh, all right, Sam; I'll be good. Only damn it, damn it, damn it, to think of wasting time like—— Oh, let's go to Bond Street and buy lots of painfully expensive things."

*

When for two hours they had shopped up Regent Street and down Bond, Fran was in an expansive, youthful, rattling mood, and she cried, "Let's go back to the hotel—it really is a nice sitting-room—and have tea there by our own fireplace."

On the large table in their sitting-room was a box of roses.

"Oh, and you *thought* of me, this morning!" she rejoiced.

He had, but he had not thought of the flowers. They were from Major Lockert.

"Oh, it doesn't matter," she said, in a tone which suggested that it decidedly did matter, and while he was being over-solicitous about the kind of cakes she'd like with tea, Lockert himself was announced.

Lockert remarked, as though he had seen them five minutes before, "It's cost me almost a bob at the club telephone to find out where you were. I say Dodsworth my cousin says you're entirely wrong about hydraulic brakes I say won't you come down to his place for the week-end awf'ly modest country cot sort of place he'd like awf'ly to have you no no tea thanks must run along forgive informality General's a widower no Lady Herndon call on you do come."

"At the same time," Sam complained, "Hurd and your friend Lockert aren't essentially different. (Oh, I don't know whether we ought to go down to Lord Herndon's or not—no reason why he should care to see me, and it'll be one of these houses with forty servants.) Oh, Lockert talks more politely than Hurd, but at bottom they're both bullies—they both want to do things for you that you don't want done. I wish Tub Pearson were here!"

"You would! Of course we're going to Herndon's. And not because he's a General and a Lord but because—— Well. Yes. Because he's a General and a Lord. That's an interesting fact to discover about myself. Am I a snob? Splendid! I shall get on, if I can only be clear and resolute about it!"

Chapter 9

LOCKERT called for them in a long, sumptuous, two-seater Sunbeam which he drove himself. He insisted that there was plenty of room in the seat for the three of them, but it seemed to Sam that they were crowded, and that Fran, glossy in her gray squirrel coat and her small cloche hat, snuggled too contentedly against Lockert's shoulder.

He forgot it in the pleasure of driving from the lowering smoke of London to the winter sunshine of the country; gray fields beginning to stir with green, breathing a faint bright mist, above which, in the shining branches of the trees, the rooks were jubilant. Little villages he saw, with homely tea rooms and inn signs—"The Rose and Crown," "The Green Dragon," and "The Faithful Friend"; then thatched farmhouses, oasthouses—he could not understand what these domestic lighthouses might be—and on a ridge the splayed ruin of a castle, his first castle!

Knights in tourney; Elaine in white samite, mystic, wonderful—no, it was Guinevere who wore the white samite, wasn't it? must read some Tennyson again. Dukes riding out to the Crusades with minstrels playing on—what was it?—rebecks? Banners alive, and a thousand swords flashing. And these fairy stories really had happened, and around that wall up there, with its one broken lump of a tower! The cavalcade of knights—following this same road!—became more real to him than the motor, for he was bored by the talk of Fran and Lockert and lost the thread of it in ancient book-colored memories which returned as desirable and somehow tragic. The other two were chattering of cricket at Lord's, of polo at Hurlingham; they were spitefully recalling the poor old rustic banker on the *Ultima* who came to dinner every evening in prehistoric dress clothes with the top of his trousers showing like a narrow black scarf above the opening of his baggy white waistcoat. Their superciliousness shut Sam out in the darkness along with the kindly old banker.

He wanted to escape from the hotel-and-theater London of the tourist and see the authentic English—Dorset shepherds

—cotton operatives on the dole in Salford—collier captains in Bristol harbor—Cornish tin-miners—Cambridge dons—hop-pickers in Kentish pubs—great houses in the Dukeries. But they were too low or too high for Fran's attention, and was it probable, he sighed, that he would see anything that she did not choose?

A little incredulously he perceived that Fran was really attracted by Lockert—she who had not been given to even the flimsiest of tea-table flirtations, who had blushed and looked soft-eyed only at the attentions of the very best of visiting celebrities: a lecturing English novelist or a young Italian baron who was studying motor factories; she who had ever been rude with a swift cold rudeness to such flappers as were known to indulge in that midnight pawing known in Zenith as "necking." But Lockert seemed by his placid bullying to have broken her glistening shell of sexlessness. She, so touchy, so ready to take offense, accepted Lockert as though he were her oldest friend, to wrangle with, to laugh with.

"You drive much too fast," she said.

"It would be too fast for any one who wasn't as good a driver as I am."

"Oh, really! I suppose you've won races!"

"I have. With German shells. I was in the motor transport before they sent me to America. I've driven at night, on a road full of shell holes, without lights, at thirty miles an hour. . . . As I was saying, you're too American, Mrs. Dodsworth. Americans understand themselves less and are less understood by the world than any nation that's ever existed. You're excellent at all the things in which you're supposed to be lacking—lyric poetry, formal manners, lack of cupidity. And you're so timid and incompetent at the things in which you're supposed to excel—fast motoring, aviation, efficiency in business, pioneering—why, Britain has done more pioneering, in Canada and Africa and Australia and China, in any given ten years, than the States have in twenty. And you, who feel you're so European, you're so typically American! You have the most charming and childish misconceptions about yourself. You think you're an arrogant, self-contained, rational, ambitious woman, whereas actually you're warm-hearted and easily dazzled—you're simply an eager young woman, and it's only your shyness that keeps you going about doing the starry-eyed-wonder and trusting-little-niece sort of thing."

"My dear Major Lockert, I hope that the combination of your extraordinarily careful driving and your extraordinarily generous mind-reading isn't tiring you too much!"

But she didn't, Sam realized, succeed in making it nasty.

She had turned entirely toward Lockert. She no longer noticed Sam when he mumbled, "There's a lovely old stone church," or "Guess those are hop poles"; when he wanted to hold her hand and tell her with quick little pressures that they were sharing the English countryside.

"Oh, well——" he reflected.

He recalled "Pickwick Papers," and the coach with the jovial, well-warmed philosophers swaying down the frosty roads for Christmas in the country.

"Great!" he said.

They stopped for lunch at a village inn. To Sam's alert gratification they drove under an archway into a courtyard of coaching days. He was delighted by the signs on the low dark doors beneath the archway: Coffee Room, Lounge, Saloon Bar.

They stamped their feet and swung their arms as the Pickwickians had done when they had stopped, perhaps, at this same inn. If Fran had ignored him, she took him in again and warmed him with her smile, with an excited "Isn't this adorable, Sam! Just what we wanted!" She insisted, despite Lockert's ruddy and spinsterish protests, on going into the taproom and there, with authentic-looking low rafters, paneling of black oak, floor of cherry-red tiles, they sat at a long wooden table between benches, and Sam and Lockert warmed themselves with whisky while Fran sipped half a pint of bitter out of a pewter mug—Sam secretly bought it from the bar-maid afterward, and lost it in Paris.

The stairs to the dining-room were carpeted in warm dark red; the wall was plastered with Victorian pictures: Wellington at Waterloo, Melrose Abbey by Moonlight, Prince Collars and Cuffs, Rochester Castle; and on the landing was such a Cabinet of Curiosities as Sam had not seen since childhood: a

Javanese fan, carved chessmen, Chinese coins, and a nugget of Australian gold.

The dining-room was dominated by a stone fireplace on which were carved the Tudor rose and the high-colored arms of the local Earl. Near it, on the oak buffet, crowned with enormous silver platters, were a noble ham, a brown-crusted veal and ham pie, a dish of gooseberry tart; and at a table two commercial travelers were gorging themselves on roast beef with Yorkshire pudding.

"Great!" Sam rejoiced, and his glow continued even through watery greens and disconsolate Brussels sprouts.

Beyond Sevenoaks, Lockert played a lively tattoo with the horn, and shouted, "Almost there! Welcome to the Stately Homes of England!"

They came to an estate, high-walled, with deer to be seen through grilled gates, and the twisted Tudor chimneys of a great house visible beyond a jungle of pines.

"Oh, Lord, is this the place?" Sam privately wondered. "It'll be terrible! Ten footmen. I wonder if they do wear plush knee-pants? Whom does one tip?"

But the car raced past this grandeur, dipped into a red-brick hamlet, turned off High Street and into a rough lane gloomy between hedges, and entered a driveway before a quite new, quite unpretentious house of ten or twelve rooms. As with thousands of houses they had passed in crawling out of London, there was a glassed-in porch littered with bicycles, rubbers, and rather consumptive geraniums. At one side of the house was a tennis-court, an arbor, and the skeletons of a rose-garden, but of lawn there was scarcely a quarter-acre.

"I told you it was only a box," Lockert drawled, as he drew up with a sputter of gravel at the door.

There was a roar within. The door was opened by a maid, very stiff in cap and apron, but past her brushed the source of the roaring—a tiny, very slim image of a man, his cheeks almost too smoothly pink to be real, his mustache too precise and silvery, and his voice a parade-ground bellow too enormous to be credited in so miniature a soldier.

"How d'you do, Mrs. Dodsworth. Most awfully nice of you to come!" he thundered, and Lockert muttered, "This is the General."

If, in his quest for romance, the exterior of the house was a jar to Sam, the drawing-room was precisely what he had desired, without knowing that he had desired it. Here was definitely Home, with a homeliness which existed no longer in most of the well-to-do houses of Zenith, where, between the great furniture factories and the young female decorators with their select notions about "harmony" and "periods," any respectable living-room was as shiny and as impersonal as a new safety-razor blade. At Herndon's, blessedly, no two bits of furniture belonged to the same family or age, yet the chintzes, the fireplace, the brass fire-irons, the white paneling, belonged together. On a round table in a corner were the General's cups—polo cups, golf cups, the cup given him by his mess in India, a few medals, and a leering Siva; and through low casement windows the gray garden was seen sloping down to meadows and a willow-bordered pond. And the maid was wheeling in a tea-wagon with a tall old silver teapot, old silver slop-jar, mounds of buttered scones, and such thin bread and butter as Sam had never known could exist.

After a tea during which Herndon rumbled rather libelous stories about his fellow soldiers, they walked up the lane, across a common on which donkeys and embattled geese were grazing, past half-timbered shops with tiny windows containing a jar or two of sweets, to the fifteenth-century flint church, in itself a history of all Kent. The tower was square, crenelated, looking as though it would endure forever. In the low stone-paved porch were parish registers, and the names of the vicars of the parish since the Norman Gilles de Pierrefort of 1190. The pillars along the nave were ponderous stone; on the wall were brasses with epitaphs in black and red; in the chancel were the ancient stone shelf of the piscina of Roman Catholic days, and a slab commemorating Thos Siwickley, Kt.—all but the name and the florid arms had been worn away by generations of priestly feet.

While Herndon was lecturing them on the beauties of the church—with rather more than a hint about the iron-bound chest in which tourists, particularly American tourists, were permitted to deposit funds for the restoration of the roof—the vicar came in, a man innocent and enthusiastic at forty-five, tall, stooped, much spectacled, speaking an Oxonian English so thick that Sam could understand nothing beyond "strawdnerly well-proportioned arches," which did not much enlighten him.

As they ambled home he saw candles in cottage windows.

They stopped to greet a porcelain-cheeked little old woman with a wreck of a black hat, a black bag of a suit, and exquisite gloves and shoes, whom Herndon introduced as Lady Somebody-or-other——

"But," Sam reflected, "it isn't real! It's fiction! The whole thing, village and people and everything, is an English novel—and I'm in it! This is Chapter Two, and it's lovely. But I wonder about Chapter Twenty. Will there be the deuce to play? . . . Just because life is more easy and human here, I feel more out of it. So accustomed to having my office and the boys to boss around—— Now that I've quit, I've got nothing but myself—and Fran, of course—to keep me busy. These people, Lockert and Lord Herndon, they can live in themselves more. They don't need a movie palace and a big garage to be content. I've got to learn that, but—— Oh, I enjoyed seeing that church, and yet I feel lonely for old Tub making a hell of a racket."

The glow in him faded as he trudged with Lockert, both of them silent, behind the chattering Fran and Herndon.

And he was irritated when Herndon turned back to crow, in the most flattering way, "You know, I should never in the world have taken Mrs. Dodsworth and you for Americans. I should have thought you were an English couple who had lived for some time in the Colonies."

Sam grumbled within, childishly, "I suppose that's an Englishman's notion of the best compliment he can pay you!"

But Herndon was so cordial that he could not hint his resentment. He would, just that moment, have preferred rudeness and the chance of an enlivening row. But his loneliness, his uncharted apprehension, vanished with the whisky and soda which both Herndon and Lockert deemed it necessary for him to take before dinner, to ward off all possible colds and other ills. As he stalked up to their bedroom (the reddest red and the shiniest brass and the most voluble little fire), Sam fretted, "I'm getting to be as touchy and fanciful and changeable as an old maid. Yet I never was cranky in the office . . . never very cranky. Am I too old to learn to loaf? I will!" And he said, as he entered the room and was startled anew at Fran's shiningness in a combination of white glove silk, "Oh, honey, speaking of old churches, you fitted into that stone aisle as if you were the lady of the manor!"

"And you were so big and straight! Lockert and the General are sweet but—— Oh, you old sweet stone statue!"

He remembered for weeks their warm shared affection in the warm red room, as they laughed and dressed. His slight jealousies disappeared at the thought of Lockert off somewhere dressing alone, probably in a room as chill as the drafty corridor.

Chapter 10

THERE came in for dinner only a neighbor, whose name was Mr. Alls or Mr. Aldys or Mr. Allis or Mr. Hall or Mr. Aw or Mr. Hoss, with his wife and spinster sister. Because of the British fetish of unannotated introductions, Sam never did learn the profession of Mr. Alls (if that was his name) and naturally, to an American, the profession of a stranger is a more important matter than even his income, his opinion of Socialism, his opinion of Prohibition, or the make of his motor car. Listening to the conversation, Sam concluded at various times that Mr. Alls was a lawyer, an investment banker, a theatrical manager, an author, a Member of Parliament, a professor, or a retired merchant whose passions were Roman remains and race-track gambling.

For Mr. Alls was full of topics.

And all through the evening Sam kept confusing Mrs. Alls and Miss Alls.

They were exactly alike. They were both tall, thin, shy, pleasant, silent, and clad in lusterless black evening frocks of no style or epoch whatever. Against their modest dullness, Fran was a rather theatrical star in her white satin with a rope of pearls about her gesticulatory right arm . . . and she was also a little strident and demanding.

When Sam was introduced to Mrs. Alls (or it may have been Miss Alls), she said, "Is this your first visit to England? Are you staying long?"

Contrariwise, when he was introduced to Miss Alls (unless it was Mrs. Alls), she murmured, "How d'you do. How long are you staying in England? I believe this is your first visit."

So far as he could remember, they said nothing else whatever until they went home.

But Herndon, Lockert, Fran, and Mr. Alls made up for that silence. The General liked an audience, and considered Fran an admirable one. When she thought any one worth the trouble, she could be a clown, a great lady, a flirt, all in one. She was just irreverent enough to rouse Herndon, yet her manner hinted that all the while she really regarded him as greater than Napoleon and more gallant than Casanova. So he thundered out his highly contradictory opinions on Kaiser Wilhelm, the breeding of silver foxes, the improbabilities of Mr. Michael Arlen's "The Green Hat," the universal and scandalous neglect of the back-hand stroke in tennis, the way to cook trout, the errors of Winston Churchill, the errors of Lloyd George, the errors of Lord Kitchener, the errors of Ramsay MacDonald, the errors of Lord Birkenhead, the errors of Danish butter, and the incomparable errors of Lockert in regard to emigration and dog-feeding. Otherwise, the General said scarcely anything.

"The trouble with this country is," observed Herndon, "that there're too many people going about saying: 'The trouble with this country is——' And too many of us, who should be ruling the country, are crabbed by being called 'General' or 'Colonel' or 'Doctor' or that sort of thing. If you have a handle to your name, you have to be so jolly and democratic that you can't control the mob."

"We'll try to free you from that if you come to America," said Fran. "I'll introduce you as Mr. James Herndon, the pansy-grower, and I'll tell my butler that you're so fond of rude garden life that you'd be delighted to have him call you 'Jimmy.'"

"Am I expected, Ma'am, to say that I'd be charmed by anything that *your* butler might care to call me? As a matter of fact, I'd ask him not to be so formal, but call me 'Whiffins.' However, unfortunately, I am not named James."

"And unfortunately we haven't a butler, but only a colored gentleman who condescends to help us with the cocktails at parties, if he isn't too busy down in Shanty Town, preaching. But honestly—— Am I in bad taste? If I'm not, isn't it really rather pleasant to be known as Your Lordship?"

"Oh—— I inherited the handle while a subaltern—no great day of mourning for lost dear ones, you know—I inherited from a most gloomy old uncle. I'd never been able to rebuke my colonel—tried to, in my eager boyish way, but he'd never noticed it. When I inherited, he used to go quite out of his way to rebuke *me*, so I knew I'd made an impression. Fact, he was so stiff with me that I became popular with the mess. But of course you Yanks, roving your broad steppes, never dream of such puerile triumphs."

"Quite. They're too busy punching cattle," said Lockert; and Mr. Alls inquired, "Just how does one punch an unfortunate cow?"

"It's now done with automatic punching-machinery," explained Lockert. "Neat little hole right through the ear. Mrs. Dodsworth is an expert—punches six cattle simultaneously, while singing the 'Star Spangled Banner' and firing pistols."

"But my real achievement," asserted Fran, "is shooting Indians. I'd shot nine before I was five years old."

"Is it true," demanded Lord Herndon, "that the smarter American women always have girdles made of scalps?"

"Oh, absolutely—it's as *de rigueur* as for an Englishwoman to carry a bouquet of Brussels sprouts at a lawn-party, or——"

"Oh, what a hell of a way to talk!" fretted Sam Dodsworth. "If they can't talk sense, why don't they dry up? What's the use of talking, anyway, beyond 'Pass the salt' and 'How much do you want a ton?' Aren't these folks ever serious?"

Suddenly they were serious, and he was even less comfortable.

"Mr. Dodsworth," asked Mr. Alls (or Mr. Hoss), "why is it that America hasn't recognized Soviet Russia?"

"Why, uh—we're against their propaganda."

"But who is really responsible for the American policy? Congress or the Foreign Department?"

"I'm afraid I don't exactly remember."

It occurred to Sam that he hadn't the smallest information about Russian relations with America; only a thin memory of a conference about selling cars in Russia. He was equally shaky when they questioned him about the American attitudes toward the Allied war debt and toward Japan.

"Am I beginning to get old?" he wondered. "I used to keep up on things. Seems as though this last five years I haven't thought of anything but selling cars and playing golf."

He felt old—he felt older and older as Fran and Herndon slid over into a frivolous debate about lion hunting. He had never known that she could be so fantastic. Here she was telling some perfectly silly story about their having had a dear old lion for a pet; about Sam's kicking it downstairs one frosty night when he was in a bad temper; the poor lion slinking down the street, pursued by a belligerent black kitten, fleeing to the Zoo, and whimpering to be let into a cage. (And there wasn't even a Zoo in Zenith!)

Old! And out of it. He couldn't join in their talk, whether it was nonsense or the discussion of nationalization of mines presently set going by Herndon, who announced himself a Socialist as fervently as twenty minutes before he had announced himself a Die-Hard Tory. It was one of the few conversations in years in which Sam had not had an important, perhaps a commanding position. At dinner in Zenith, if he didn't feel authoritative when they talked of Stravinsky or the Algerian tour, soon or late the talk would return to motors and a mystery known as "business conditions," and then he would settle all debates.

He suddenly felt insecure.

As they walked to church next morning, he felt for the Kentish village a tenderness as for a shrunken, tender old grandmother. And when he noted a Revelation car parked across from the church, he was certain again that he was Somebody. But amid the politely interested, elegantly pious congregation at Morning Prayer, glancing at him over their celluloid-covered prayer books, he felt insecurity again. He was overgrown, clumsy, untutored. He wanted to flee from this traditional stillness to the anonymity and shielding clamor of London.

They rode, for the hour between church and luncheon, on ragged but sturdy horses from the village stable. Mrs. Alls had lent a wreck of a riding-habit to Fran, who looked disreputable and gay in her orange tam o' shanter—gayer than in her ordinary taut sleekness. They rode away from the village, through fields and shaggy woods, to the ridge of the North Downs.

For years Fran had ridden twice a week with an English ex-groom, turned gentleman teacher and trainer in America, his Cockney accent accepted in Zenith as the breath of British gentility. With her slim straightness she sat her aged nag like a young cavalry officer. Lockert and Lord Herndon looked at her more admiringly than ever, spoke to her more cheerily, as though she were one of their own.

Sam's riding had been a boyhood-vacation trifling; he was about as confident on a horse as he would have been in an aeroplane; he had never quite got over feeling, on a horse's back, that he was appallingly far up from the ground. Herndon had a shaky leg, and Sam and he rode slowly. Suddenly Lockert and Fran left them, in a gallop along the pleasant plateau at the top of the Downs.

"Don't you want to keep up with 'em? My leg's not up to much today," said Herndon.

"No, I'll trail," Sam sighed.

In a quarter-hour Fran and Lockert came cantering back. She was laughing. She had taken off her tam, and her hair was wild.

"Sorry we ran away, but the air was so delicious—simply had to have a scamper!" she cried and, to Sam, "Oh, was oo left alone! Poor boy!"

All the way back she insisted on riding beside him, consoling him.

A month ago he had felt that he had to protect her frailness. He was conscious now that his breath was short, that he had a corporation . . . and that Fran, turning to call back to Lockert, was bored by him.

Most insecure of all was Sam that afternoon when they motored for tea to Woughton Hall, the country place of Sir Francis Ouston, the new hope of the Liberals in Parliament. Here—so overwhelmingly that Sam gasped—was one of the great houses of which he had been apprehensive. Up a mile-long driveway of elms they came to a lofty Palladian façade, as stern as a court-house, with a rough stone wing at one end. "That's the old part, that stone—built about 1480," said Herndon.

In front was a terrace rimmed with clipped cypresses in the shape of roosters, crescents, pyramids, with old Italian wine-jars of stone. To the right, beyond a pair of tennis-courts, half a mile of lawn slipped in pale winter green toward rough meadows; to the left the stables were a red brick village.

There was about the whole monstrous palace a quietness dotted only with the sound of sparrows and distant rooks. To Sam, just now, the millionaire country houses he had seen on Long Island and the North Shore above Chicago—Tudor castles, Italian villas, French châteaux, elephantine Mount Vernons, mansions which he had admired and a little coveted—were raw as new factories beside a soft old pasture.

Through a vast entrance hall with tapestries on walls of carved stucco, and high Italian candle-sticks at the foot of a walnut stairway, they were shepherded to a carved oak drawing-room high as a church, and much noisier. After that Sam knew nothing but confusion and babble. First and last there must have been fifty people popping in for tea, people with gaudy titles and cheery manners, people so amiable to him that he could not hate them as he longed to. What they were all talking about, he never knew. They spoke of Sybil, who seemed to be an actress, and of politicians (he guessed they were politicians) to whom they referred as Nancy and F. E. and Jix and Winston and the P.M. One man mentioned something called the Grand National, and Sam was not sure whether this was the name of a bank, an insurance company, or a hotel.

What could he do when a lady, entirely unidentified, asked, "Have you seen H. G.'s latest?"

"Not yet," he answered intelligently, but who or what H. G. might be, he never did learn.

And through the bright-colored maelstrom of people, his heart aching with loneliness, he saw Fran move placidly, shiningly, man-conscious and man-conquering and at home. They were all one family; they took her in; but himself, how to get in he had no notion. He had addressed conventions of bankers; he had dragooned a thousand dancing people at a Union Club ball; but here—these people were so close-knit, so serenely sure, that he was an outsider.

He escaped from the lady who knew about H. G.; he crawled through the mass of suspended tea-cups and struggled to Fran's side. She was confiding (not very truthfully) to a man with a single eyeglass that she had a high, passionate, unresting interest in polo.

When Sam had the chance, he sighed to her, "Let's get out. Too darn' many people for me!"

"They're darlings! And I've made the most terrific hit with Lady Ouston. She wants us to come to dinner in town."

"Well—— I'd just like—— Thought we might get a little fresh air before dinner. I feel sort of out of it here. They all chirp so fast."

"You didn't seem to be doing so badly. I saw you in the corner with the Countess of Baliol."

"Was I? Which one? All the women I talked to just looked like women. Why the devil don't they wear their coronets? Honestly, Fran, this is too rich for my blood. I can stand meeting a couple hundred people at once, but not the entire British aristocracy. They——"

"My dear Sam, you are talking exactly like Mr. A. B. Hurd."

"I feel exactly like Mr. A. B. Hurd!"

"Are you going to demand that we take Zenith with us every place we go? Are you going to refuse to like anything that's the least bit different from a poker party at Tub Pearson's? And are you going to insist that *I* be scared and old, too, and not reach out for the great life that I can learn to master—oh, I can, I can! I'm doing it! Must I go back with you now and sit at Lord Herndon's select villa reading the *Observer* or else be punished by your sulking?"

And it was she who was sulky, though he had doubtfully urged her to stay as long as she liked—or as Herndon liked. She showed a gray sulkiness all evening, but not toward Herndon, decidedly not toward Lockert. They had only a cold ham and beef supper, with no other guests, and publicly Fran was frivolous. She played the piano, played and played, and since Herndon was seized with a passion to discuss motor headlights with Sam, Lockert hung about the piano. Herndon and Sam were at the other end of the drawing-room, before the fireplace, backs to the piano, but in the Venetian mirror over the fireplace Sam could watch the others, and he did, uneasily.

Only then was he certain that Lockert aspired to considerably more than a polite friendliness with Fran.

Lockert turned her music, he kept drawling amiable insults that were apparently more fetching than flattery. His hand touched her sleeve, once rested on her shoulder. She shrugged it off and shook her head, but she was not angry. Once Sam heard her: "——don't know *why* I like you—your perfectly disconcerting admiration of yourself——"

He felt, Sam, like a worthy parent watching his daughter and a suitor. He felt resigned. Then he began to feel angry.

"Damn it, was that why Lockert got us down here? To make love to Fran? Does he think I'm the kind that'll stand it? Does she?"

When they were going to bed, his accumulated anger came out in a chilly: "See here, my girl! All this His Lordship, Her Grace, Old England, palatial mansion stuff is fine—I've enjoyed it—but you're letting it dazzle you. You're letting Lockert be a whole lot too flirtatious. You're off your track. At home, you'd see that he doesn't just mean to pay you pretty little compliments——"

"My dear Mr. Dodsworth, do you mean to insinuate——"

"No, I'm saying it straight! Little good home bullying!"

"Do you mean to insinuate that I'd let Major Lockert, or anybody else, make the slightest improper advances toward me? I that never tolerated loose dancing at home, that have never in my life so much as held hands in a taxi? I that—oh, it's too beautifully ironical!—that you've practically accused, time and again, of being too sexless to suit your manly ardors! Oh, it's too much!"

"Yes, at home that has been so. Though I've never accused you of sexlessness—even when I've damn' well suffered from it! I've been patient. Waited. Waited a mighty long time. That's what makes it worse now, when you've been so little attracted by me, to see you falling for this man, or at least, I mean, being obviously attracted by him, just because he's——"

"Oh, *say* it! 'Just because he's the cousin of a Lord!' Say it! Try to make me seem as contemptible a little village greenhorn as you can!"

"I hadn't intended to say anything of—— Well, if I did, what I meant was: I mean, just because he's wandered enough so that he knows how to handle women by beating them. I can't. Never could beat you. Wouldn't if I could. . . . Oh, never mind. I don't mean anything serious. I just mean —— Even though you are naturally something of a European, you've got to remember that this is a pretty wise and dangerous old country. But of course you've got too much sense. Sorry I said anything."

She was standing, a little rigid, in her low-necked, lace-trimmed, yellow pajamas. He lumbered toward her, his hands out bumbling, "Sorry! Kiss me!"

She shuddered. She wailed, "No, don't touch me! Oh, don't you *ever* suggest things like that again! Lockert? I haven't the slightest interest in him. I'm ashamed of you! You ought to be ashamed of yourself!"

She resolutely said nothing more before they went to sleep; and in the morning she was queerly quiet and her eyes looked tired.

Lord Herndon, kindest of hosts and one of the few living men who were cheerful and full of ideas at breakfast, seemed hurt by their aloofness, but Lockert was inquisitive and slightly amused, and at the station (the Dodsworths were to return by train) he searched Fran's eyes interrogatively . . . most hopefully.

Sam was glad when the train was away, and she tried to pump up a friendly smile for him. But he was all abasement, all savage scorn of himself, that he should have spoiled the happy party of this, his child, by bucolic suspicions. She had been so innocently happy in discovering rural England, in sturdy friendship with Lockert, in chatter with Herndon, in a hair-blown race across the Downs, and then, he groaned, he had spoiled it all for her.

He took her hand, but it was lax—all strength gone out of the hand that yesterday had been so firm on the bridle.

Chapter 11

THE possessions of Sir Francis Ouston were numerous and very pretty. He owned thousands of acres of Welsh coal land, he owned Woughton Hall in Kent and a tall, bleak-faced house in Eaton Square, he owned the famous mare Capriciosa III, and he owned a position in the Liberal Party immediately after that of Asquith and Lloyd George.

He himself was owned by his wife.

Lady Ouston was a beautiful woman and very commanding. She had a high, quick, passionate voice and many resolute opinions. She was firm and even a little belligerent about the preferability of Jay's to Poiret in the matter of frocks, about the treachery of the Labor Party, about the desirability (entirely on behalf of the country) of Sir Francis's becoming Prime Minister, about the heinousness of beer-drinking among the working classes, about the scoundrelism of roast chicken without a proper bread sauce, and particularly about the bad manners, illiteracy, and money-grubbing of the United States of America.

She had been born—and her father and mother before her—in Nashville, Tennessee.

She was a formidable hostess. She had a salon, and while she did explorers and chemists and the few authors who understood morning coats, she had never stooped to fill her drawing-room by exhibiting cubist painters, Hindu nationalists, American cowboys, or any of the other freaks whereby rival professional hostesses attracted the right sort of people.

And her dinners were admirable. You could be sure of Napoleon brandy, the cousin of a duke, and the latest story about the vulgarity of New York.

It was not to one of Lady Ouston's very best dinners, with a confidential cabinet minister present, that Lockert persuaded her to invite the Dodsworths, but it was quite a good, upper-middle dinner, with Clos-Vougeot and the master of a Cambridge college.

Sam was quiet, extremely observant, not extremely jolly, as he surveyed that regiment of twenty people, all nibbling so delicately at their salmon and at other people's reputations. No one seemed to have any vulgarly decided opinions, and every one desired to know of him only two things: Was this his first visit to England? and How long would he stay? And they didn't seem to care so very much about either.

He wondered how many times he himself had asked foreign visitors to the Revelation plant—Britishers, Swedes, Germans, Frenchmen—whether this was their first visit to America, and How long did they plan to stay?

"I'll never say *that* again!" he vowed.

The dinner rather went on. Soup and a murmur about broadcasting and Bernard Shaw; salmon and a delicate murmur about Mussolini and influenza; roast mutton and an exchange of not very interested confidences about cat burglars. Sam was in a daze of gluttony and politeness when he realized that Lady Ouston was talking to him about America, and that every one at the table was beginning to pay attention. He did not know that she was born an American, and he listened to her with almost no comfort:

"——and of course none of us would ever think of classing your darling wife and you with the terrible, *terrible* sort of American tourists that one sees—or hears, rather—at the Cecil or in trains—where *do* you suppose such Americans come from! In fact, I'm quite sure you could both be mistaken for English, if you merely lived here a few years. So it's a quite impersonal question. But don't you feel, as we do, that for all our admiration of American energy and mechanical ingenuity, it's the most terrible country the world has ever seen? Such voices—like brass horns! Such rudeness! Such lack of reticence! And such material ideals! And the standardization—every one thinking exactly alike about everything. I give you my word that you'll be so glad you've deserted your ghastly country that after two years here, you'll never want to go home. Don't you already feel that a bit?"

Sam Dodsworth had never in his life boasted of being an American nor yet apologized for it. It was amazement which made him mutter, with what sounded like humility, "Why, never thought much about America, as a whole. Sort of taken it for granted——"

"You won't long! What a land! Such terrible politicians—positively the lowest form of animal life—even worse than Irish Republicans! And don't you rather feel ashamed of being an American when you think of America's making us pay the war debt when, after all, it was all you did contribute?"

"I do not!" Sam was suddenly and thoroughly angry; suddenly free of whatever diffidence he had before this formal society. "I never was much of a flag-waver. I don't suppose America is perfect, not by a long shot. I know we have plenty of fools and scoundrels, and I don't mind roasting them. But if you'll excuse me for differing with you——"

Lockert said pacifyingly, "You can't expect Mr. Dodsworth to agree, Lady Ouston. Remember he's——"

Sam snarled on, uncheckable: "——I suppose I have been sort of assuming that America is the greatest nation on earth. And maybe it is. Maybe because we have got so many faults. Shows we're growing! Sorry if it's bad manners not to be ashamed of being an American, but then I'll just have to be bad mannered!"

Behind his brusqueness he was saying to himself, and timidly, "Look at the dirty looks I'm getting! I've ditched things for Fran. What hell I'll get from her!"

But incredibly it was Fran herself who was attacking: "My dear Lady Ouston, out of a hundred and ten million Americans, there must be a few who have agreeable voices and who think of something besides dollars! Considering how many of us are a generation or less from England, we must have several nice people! And I wonder if every member of the British Parliament is a perfect little gentleman? I seem to have heard of rows—— We probably have more self-criticism at home than any other nation—our own writers call us everything from Main Streeters to the Booboisie. But curiously enough we feel we must work out our own fate, unassisted by the generous foreigners!"

"I think Mrs. Dodsworth is quite right," said Sir Francis. "We're not at all pleased here in England when the French and Italians call us barbarians—as they jolly well do!"

Suavely he said it, and stoutly, but Sam knew that thenceforth Fran and he would be as popular in the house of Ouston as a pair of mad dogs.

Fran developed a tactful headache at a quarter after ten.

Sir Francis and Lady Ouston were very cordial at parting.

Sam and Fran were silent in the taxi till he sighed, "Sorry, honey. I was bad. Awfully sorry I lost my temper."

"It doesn't *matter*! I'm glad you did! The woman's a fool! Oh, my dear——" Fran laughed hysterically. "I can see that the Oustons and us are going to be buddies! They'll insist on our yachting round the world with them!"

"And scuttling the yacht!"

"Haven't they a dear little daughter, so Brent can marry her?"

"Fran, I'm crazy about you!"

"*Du!* Old grizzly! I'm glad you *are* one! Sam, a terrible thought occurs to me. I'll bet you anything that fool woman was born an American! Convert! Professional expatriate! She's much too English to be English. Not that the real English love us any too much, but she's like an Irish critic living in London, or a Jewish peer—seven paces to the right of the King. Oh, my dear, my dear, and I might have fallen into expatriate—— Sam Dodsworth, if you ever catch me trying to be anything but a woolly American, will you beat me?"

"I will. But do I have to beat you very long at a time?"

"Probably. I'm rather a hussy. Only virtue is, I know it. And I did flirt with Clyde Lockert at Lord Herndon's! It flattered me to stir him out of that 'Damn your eyes' superiority of his. And I did stir him, too! But I'm so 'shamed!"

In their apartment she nuzzled her cheek against his shoulder, whispering, "Oh, I'd just like to crawl inside you and be part of you. Don't ever let me go!"

"I won't!"

The Ouston debacle considerably checked Fran's social career, though Lockert continued their mentor. He came to tea the next day, casual as ever, and drawled:

"Well, Merle Ouston was a bit of a public nuisance last night. So were you, Dodsworth!"

"Well, I couldn't sit there and listen to her——"

"You should've smiled. You Americans are always so touchy. No Englishman ever minds criticism of England. He laughs at it."

"Hm! I've heard that before—from Englishmen! I wonder if that isn't one of your myths about yourselves, like our belief that every American is so hospitable that he'll give any stranger his shirt. Well, I've never seen any of our New York bankers down at Ellis Island begging the Polack immigrants to come stay with them till they get jobs. Look here, Lockert! The Ouston woman said all our politicians were hogs. Suppose I started making nasty cracks about the King and the Prince of Wales——"

"That's quite different! That's a question of good taste! Never mind. Herndon and I are thoroughly pro-American."

"I know," said Fran. "You love America—except for the food, the manners, and the people."

"At least, there's one American that I esteem highly!" said Lockert, and his glance at her was ardent.

Sam waited for her to rebuke Lockert. She didn't.

Lockert took them to Ciro's, to dance; he had them made members of a rackety night club called "The Rigadoon," where there was friendliness and gin and a good deal of smell. Potentates of the English motor-manufacturing companies called on them and escorted Sam to their factories. They met three or four stout matrons at a dinner given by Lord Herndon in the women's annex of the Combined Services Club, and they were again admitted to the tedious perils of occasional dinner parties.

And all the while they were as unrelated to living English life as though they were sitting in a railway station waiting for the continental train. Lockert had gone off to the Riviera, a week after the Ouston dinner. Sam was relieved—then missed him surprisingly. And with Lockert away, their invitations were few.

"Well," said Sam, "till we get acquainted with more folks here, let's do the town. Historic spots and so on."

He had studied Mr. Karl Baedeker's philosophical volume on London, and he was eager to see the Tower, the Houses of Parliament, Kew Gardens, the Temple, the Roman bath, the National Gallery; eager to gallop up to Stratford and honor Shakespeare—not that he had honored Shakespeare by reading him, these twenty-five years past; and to gallop down to Canterbury—not that he had ever gone so far as to read Chaucer.

But Fran made him uncomfortable by complaining, "Oh, good Heavens, Sam, we're not trippers! I hate these post-card places. Nobody who really belongs ever goes to them. I'll bet Clyde Lockert has never been inside the Tower. Of course galleries and cathedrals are different—sophisticated people do study them. But to sit at the Cheshire Cheese with a lot of people from Iowa and Oklahoma, exclaiming over Dr. Johnson—atrocious!"

"I must say I don't get you. What's the idea of coming to a famous city and then not seeing the places that made it famous? You don't have to send souvenir cards about 'em if you don't want to! And I don't believe the people from Iowa will bite you unless you attack 'em first!"

She tried to make clear to him the beauties of snobbishness in travel. But, in her loneliness, she did consent to go with him, even to eat lark and oyster pie at the Cheese, though she was rather snappish with the waiter who wanted to show them the volumes of visitors' names.

Ambling through London with no duty of arriving anywhere in particular, Sam came to take its somber vastness as natural; felt the million histories being enacted behind the curtained windows of the million houses. On clear days, when rare thin sunshine caressed the gray-green bricks which composed the backs of London houses, even these ugly walls had for him, in relief at the passing of the mist-pall, a charm he had never found in the hoydenish glare of sunshine on bright winter days in Zenith. He loved, as he became familiar with them, even the absurd proud little shops with their gaudy glass and golden signs: chocolate shops with pictures of Royalty on the boxes of sweets, tobacco shops with cigarette-cases of imitation silver for Sunday-strolling clerks to flourish, even the ardors and fumes of fried fish shops. He was elated at learning the 'bus lines; saying judiciously, "Let's take a 92 and ride home on top." The virility of London, town of men back from conquering savages and ruling the lone desert, seemed akin to him. . . . But Fran began to speak of Paris, that feminine and flirtatious refuge from reality.

Between explorations they tasted a loneliness they had never known in their busy domination of Zenith.

Evening on evening they sat in their suite pretending that they were exhausted after a day's "sight-seeing"; that they were exhausted, and glad they were going to stroll out for dinner alone. All the while Sam knew that she was waiting, that he was waiting and praying, for the telephone to ring.

At their several party dinners they had met agreeable people who said, "You must come to us, soon!" and then forgot them blissfully. London's indifference to her charms depressed Fran, seemed to frighten her. She was wistfully grateful when he thought of ordering flowers, when he found some unexpected and cheery place to dine. Half the time he was pitiful that she should not be having her career; half the time he rejoiced that they had never been so close together as now, in their isolation.

She was almost timid when Jack Starling, the nephew of Tub Pearson and a secretary at the American Embassy in London, came bouncing back to town, called formally, inspected Fran's complexion and Sam's grammar, and adopted them with reserved enthusiasm. He was a pleasant, well-pressed young dancing-man, and full of ideas—not especially good ideas, but very lively and voluble. He called Sam "sir," which pleased Sam almost as much as it embarrassed him. In Zenith, no one except men who had served as officers in the Great War used "sir," save as a furious address to five-year-old boys whom they were about to beat.

And suddenly, after Starling's coming, Lockert was strolling in as though he had never been away, and Lord Herndon was in town for a month and, without any very traceable cause, the Dodsworths had more lunches, teas, dinners, dances, and theater parties than even a lady lion-hunter could have endured. Sam was so happy to see Fran excited and occupied that not for a fortnight did he admit privately that the only thing that bored him more than being an elephantine wallflower at dances was being a drowsy and food-clogged listener at dinner-parties; and that all these people whom they *must* call up, whom they simply *mustn't* forget to invite to their own small dinners, were persons whom he could with cheers never see again. Nor could he persuade himself that their own affairs (in a private room at the Ritz, with himself pretending to supervise the cocktails before dinner and Fran making a devil of a fuss about the flowers) were any livelier than other people's. The conversation was as cautious, the bread sauce quite as bready, and the dread hour from nine-thirty to ten-thirty passed on no swifter wings of laughter.

Mr. A. B. Hurd was a relief, now that Fran was busy enough so that Sam could slip away and revel with Mr. Hurd in shop gossip and motor prices and smutty stories and general American lowness.

Mr. Hurd had done his best to be hospitable, and as it had not occurred to him that there were people, like Fran, who did not wish to be hospitalitized, he had been bewildered and become shy—even his superb salesman's confidence had become shy. He had once, after innumerous telephone calls, been invited by Fran to tea, and he had brought his Oklahoma-born wife up from the country and put on his rather antiquated morning coat and very new spats.

He came into the Dodsworths' suite briskly enough, but when Mrs. Hurd crept in after her boisterous husband, Sam was so touched that he rose to the courtliness he could occasionally show. She was dressed in blue silk, with a skirt hiked up in back. Her hands looked the more rough because they had just been manicured, with rosy and pointed nails. Hurd's salary was adequate now, but Sam felt that Mrs. Hurd had for years washed dishes, diapers, muddy floors. Her lips were round with smiling, but her eyes were frightened as she shook Sam's hand in the small white-enameled foyer of the suite, and cried:

"My! I've heard so much about you, Mr. Dodsworth! Al is always talking about you and what a wonderful executive you are and what a lovely time he had with you folks when he was back in Zenith the last time and how much he enjoyed dining with you and—— It's just lovely that you're here in London now and I do hope Mrs. Dodsworth and you will find time to come down to the country and see us. I know how busy you must be with parties and all but——"

Sam ushered her into the sitting-room; he tried to catch Fran's eye to warn her to be good, while he was rumbling:

"Fran, this is Mrs. Hurd. Mighty great pleasure to meet her, after we've known her husband so long."

"How d'you do, Mrs. Hurd?" said Fran, and it was worthy of Lady Ouston at her politest and rudest. Fran pronounced it "Howj*duh*," and her voice rose at the end in a quiet brusqueness which finished Mrs. Hurd completely.

Mrs. Hurd fluttered, "I'm real pleased to meet you, I'm sure," then sat forward in her chair, refused the cake she most wanted, looked terrified while Fran purred about Paris. She did not venture on the invitation to the country which she had obviously come to deliver. Between Sam's heavy compliments to Hurd, Hurd's heavy compliments to Sam, and Fran's poisonously sweet manner of saying, "It was so *very* kind of you to come all this way in to see us, Mrs.—uh—Hurd," she was bewildered, and she ventured on no conversation beyond "My, you've got such lovely rooms here. I guess you know an awful lot of English folks—lords and everything, don't you?"

After that, Hurd resentfully gave up telephoning.

But when, with Lockert and Jack Starling returned, Fran found enough of the admiration natural to her, Sam was now and then able to sneak meanly out and get hold of Hurd for odd meals.

After a fortnight Hurd suggested, at luncheon:

"Say, Chief, I'd like to pull off a bachelor dinner for you one of these evenings—some of the high-class American business men here in London—just sit around and be natural and tell our middle names. Think you could duck your good lady and have an Old Home Week? What about next Saturday evening?"

"Fine. I'll see if my wife has anything on."

"Well, I hope she has. Strict lot of police in this ole town! Ha, ha, ha, ha, ha!"

Sam was not offended. Hurd was given to smutty limericks, to guffaws about young ladies of the night, yet there was a healthy earthiness about him which to Sam was infinitely cleaner than the suave references to perversions which he had increasingly been hearing in New York and in London, and which sickened him, made him glad to be normal and provincial and old-fashioned. Hurd—hang it, he liked Hurd! The man's back-slapping was real. He could do with a little back-slapping, these days! Why should it be considered a less worthy greeting than chilly hand-shakes and fishy "Howjduh's"?

When Sam returned to the hotel, Fran was having tea with Lockert.

"I can tell that you've been seeing one of your jocund American friends again," said Lockert.

"How?"

"You have a rather decent voice when you've been under our purely insular influences for a week or so. Color in it. But the moment you slip off to America again, it sharpens and becomes monotonous."

"'S too bad!" muttered Sam, leaning against the fireplace, very tall, wondering what would happen if he threw his tea—in the cup—at Lockert. Damn the fellow! Oh, of course he was friendly, he meant well, and probably he was right in his hints about the nice conduct of a clouded American barbarian in England. But still—— Hang it, there were some pretty decent people who seemed to like Sam Dodsworth the way he was!

He interrupted Fran's chronicle of shopping and Liberty silks to blurt, "Say, sweet, old Hurd wants to give me a bachelor dinner next Saturday evening—meet some of the American business men here. I think I ought to do it; he's tried so hard to be nice."

"And you'd like it? Be back in all the Rotarian joys of Zenith?"

"You bet your life I'd like it! We haven't a date for that evening, if I remember. Could you get up a hen party or go to the movies or something? I'd kind of like——"

"My dear, you don't have to ask permission to have an evening out!"

("The hell I don't!") "No, of course not, but I don't want you to feel stranded."

"I say, Fran," Lockert remarked, "would you care to dine with me that evening and go to the opera?"

"Well——" considered Fran.

"Fine," said Sam. "It's a go."

Jack Starling popped in just then, very cheery, and Sam was silent while the other three hilariously scoffed at America. Sam was thinking, almost impersonally. It was a new occupation for him, and he was a little confused. It had become a disease with both nations, he reflected, this discussion of Britain vs. America; this incessant, irritated, family scolding. Of course back in the cornfields of the Middlewest, people didn't often discuss it, nor did the villagers on the Yorkshire moors, nor Cornish fishermen. But the people who traveled and met their cousins of the other nation, the people who fed on newspapers on either side the water, they were all obsessed.

Fran and Lockert and Starling, chirping about it——

They found so much to laugh over——

Himself, he'd rather listen to Hurd's stories——

No. That wasn't true. He wouldn't. These Londoners (and Fran and Starling were trying to become Londoners) did talk better than the citizenry of Zenith. They were often a little silly, a little giggling, more than a little spiteful, but they found life more amusing than his business-driven friends at home.

Couldn't there be—weren't there people in both England and America who were as enterprising and simple and hearty as Mr. A. B. Hurd, yet as gay as Fran or Jack Starling, as curiously learned as Lockert, who between pretenses of boredom gave glimpses of voodoo, of rajahs, of the eager and credulous boy he had been in public school and through long riverside holidays at his father's vicarage in Berkshire?

Lockert—hang it, must Lockert always be in his thoughts?

It was true, the thing he had been trying to ignore. The beautiful intimacy which for a fortnight Fran and he had found in their loneliness, her contentment to be with him and let the world go hang, had thinned and vanished, and she was straining away from him as ardently as ever before.

Mr. Hurd's bachelor dinner for Sam was at eight-thirty. Lockert and Fran left the Ritz at seven, to dine before the opera. Sam saw them off paternally, and most filially Fran cried, "I hope you'll have a beautiful time, Sam, and do give my greetings to Mr. Hurd. I'm sure he's really quite a good soul, really." But she did not look back to wave at him as he watched them down the corridor to the lift. She had tucked her arm into Lockert's; she was chattering, altogether absorbed.

For an hour Sam tramped the apartment, too lonely to think.

Hurd's dinner was given in a private room at the Dindonneau Restaurant in Soho. There was a horseshoe table with seats for thirty. Along the table little American flags were set in pots of forget-me-nots. Behind the chairman's table was a portrait of President Coolidge, draped with red, white and blue bunting, and about the wall—Heaven knows where Hurd could have collected them all—were shields and banners of Yale and Harvard and the University of Winnemac, of the Elks, the Oddfellows, the Moose, the Woodmen, of the Rotarians, the Kiwanians, and the Zenith Chamber of Commerce, with a four-sheet poster of the Revelation car.

Fran would have sneered. . . .

Outside was the dark and curving Soho alley, with the foggy lights of a Singhalese restaurant, a French book-shop, a wig-maker's, an oyster bar. And the room was violently foreign, with frescoes by a sign-painter—or a barn-painter: Isola Bella, Fiesole, Castel Sant' Angelo. But Sam did not look at them. He—who but once in his life had attended a Rotary lunch—looked at the Rotary wheel, and his smile was curiously timid. There was no reason for it apparent to him, but suddenly these banners made him feel that in the chill ignobility of exile he was still Some One.

He felt the more Some One as he was introduced to the guests.

They had spent from a month to thirty years in England, and they were as different one from another as the exhibits at a Zoo, with the lion beside the monkey-cage. Yet in all of them was a hint of American heartiness and of that twang which is called "talking through the nose" because it consists in failing to talk through the nose. There was Stubbs of the Haymarket branch of the Pittsburgh and Western National Bank, a gray solid man of fifty, fanatic about golf. Young Ertman, the London correspondent of the Chicago *Register*, once a Rhodes scholar at Oxford, very select and literary. Young Suffern of the Baltimore *Eagle*, very red-faced and wide-shouldered and noisy. Doblin, manager of the English agency of the Lightfoot Sewing Machine Agency, old and thread-thin and gentle. Markart of the Orient Chewing Gum and Chicle Corporation; Knabe of the Serial Cash Registers; Fish of the American Forwarding Company; Smith of the Internation Tourist Agency; Nutthal of the Anglo-Peruvian Bank—he was Lancashire born but he had lived in Omaha for eighteen years and he was three hundred per cent. American. And a throng of American motor agents.

Each of them crunched Sam's hand and growled (only the Rhodes scholar's growl was more feline than canine): "Certainly is a mighty great pleasure to meet you. Staying over here long?"

Near the door was a side-table spread with Martini cocktails, Manhattan cocktails, Bronx cocktails, and bottles of Scotch, Canadian Club, American rye and Bourbon. Sam could not escape without four cocktails, and when he wavered to his seat beside A. B. Hurd, he had altogether forgotten that he had ever been lonely, that Fran was with Lockert.

There was a deal of noisy humor at the dinner; a deal of shouting the length of the table; a number of stories beginning "Jever hear the one about the two Jews——" And it must be said that Sam, privileged now to enjoy the suburbs of correct English society, enjoyed it more than any dinner this fortnight. He enjoyed it even when cognac and whisky sodas followed the dessert and some of the guests—free for only one evening a week from the American wives whom living in England had not weakened in their view of women's right to forbid men's rights—snatched the excuse to get quite reasonably drunk and to soar into American melody: "The Old Man Came Rolling Home," and "He Laid Jesse James in His Grave" and "Way Down on the Bingo Farm," with what they conceived to be a correct Cockney version of "She Was Poor but She Was Honest," all of them leading triumphantly up to:

My name is Yon Yonson,
I come from Visconsin,
I vork on a lumberyard dere,
Ven I go down de street
All de people I meet
Dey saaaaaaay,
"Vot's your name?"

And I sa-aaaaay:
My name is Yon Yonson,
I come from Visconsin——

It seemed a good song, at a certain stage of liquor, and they kept it up for ten minutes.

But between such high lights, Sam Dodsworth got in a seminar of inquiries about the question that to him, also, had become a disease: Is America the Rome of the world, or is it inferior to Britain and Europe? Or confusedly both?

Out of all the thirty, there were not ten whose speech showed that they had lived abroad. If occasionally they said "braces" instead of "suspenders," or "two bob" instead of "four bits," you would have supposed that they had been reading English fiction. There were not six who would ever have been taken for Englishmen by Americans, and not three who would have been taken for Englishmen by Englishmen.

Yet there were not more than six, Sam discovered incredulously, who wanted to return to America for the rest of their lives.

He had understood that hybrid cosmopolites with a fancy for titles and baccarat, eccentric artists who were fond of mistresses and chess, idlers who needed some one with whom to loaf, might prefer to live abroad. But that this should be true of the gallant thirty—good salesmen, up-and-coming authorities on cash registers and motor tires—was disturbing to him, and mystifying.

These men believed, and belligerently announced, that America was the "greatest country in the world," not only in its resources and increasing population and incomparable comforts of daily life, not only in its energy and mechanical ingenuity, but equally in its generosity, its friendliness, its humor, its aspiration for learning. Scarce one of them, Sam judged, but longed to see his own beloved quarter of America——

New York on a winter night, with the theaters blaring and the apartment-houses along Park Avenue vanishing up into the wild sky rosy from a million lights. Vermont on an autumn afternoon, with the maples like torches. Midsummer in Minnesota, where the cornfields talked to themselves, and across miles of rolling wheatland, dimpling to the breeze, you saw the tall red wheat-elevators and the spire of the German Catholic Church. The grave silence of the wilderness: plateaus among the scarred peaks of the Sierra Nevadas, painted buttes in Arizona, Wisconsin lakes caressing in dark waters the golden trunks of Norway pines. The fan-lights above serene old Connecticut doorways in Litchfield and Sharon. Proud cold sunsets in the last five minutes of the Big Game at Thanksgiving-time—Illinois vs. Chicago, Yale vs. Harvard—yes, and quite as aching with sentimental and unforgettable and lost sweetness, Schnutz College vs. Maginnis Agricultural School. Cities of a quarter of a million people with fantastic smoky steel works, like maniac cathedrals, which had arisen in twenty years upon unpeopled sand-barrens. The long road and a rather shaggy, very adventurous family in a squeaky flivver, the new Covered Wagon, starting out to see all the world from Seattle to Tallahassee, stopping to earn their bacon and bread and oil by harvesting; singing at night in tourist camps on the edge of wide-lawned towns——

"I certainly do like to get back to Alabama—mighty nice girls there, and you talk about your Georgia terrapin—say, listen, boy," said Stubbs of the Pittsburgh and Western National Bank, "we got the swellest food in the world in Alabama."

And Primble of the International Films Distributing Agency drawled, "Just about once a year I certainly got to get back to the Ozark Mountains and go fishing."

But except for half a dozen homesick souls, each of them admitted that he was going to go on loving, boosting, and admiring America, and remain in Europe as long as he could.

Their confessions could have been summed up in the ruminations of Doblin, pro-consul of sewing-machines, doyen of the American business-colony, old and thread-thin and gentle, who murmured (while the others listened, nodding, nervously shaking ashes from cigarettes, or holding their cigars cocked in the corners of their mouths):

"Well, I'll tell you the way I look at it personally. Strikes me that one-half or maybe two-thirds of the American people are the best fellows on earth—the friendliest and the most interested in everything and the jolliest. And I guess the remaining third are just about the worst crabs, the worst Meddlesome Matties, the most ignorant and pretentious fools, that God ever made. Male *and* female! I'd be tickled to death to live in America *if*. If we got rid of Prohibition, so a man could get a glass of beer instead of being compelled to drink gin and hootch. If we got rid of taking seriously a lot of self-advertising, half-educated preachers and editors and politicians, so that folks would develop a little real thinking instead of being pushed along by a lot of mental and moral policemen. If our streets weren't so God-awfully noisy. If there were a lot more cafés and a lot less autos—sorry, Mr. Dodsworth, you being a motor-manufacturer, but that slipped out and I guess I'll just have to stand by it.

"But the whole thing, the fundamental thing, is a lot harder to express than that. Nothing like so simple as just Prohibition. . . . Golly, the number of people who think they are getting profound when they talk about that one question! . . . The whole thing—— Oh, there's more ease in living here! Your neighbors don't spy on you and gossip and feel it's their business to tell you how to live, way we do at home. Not that I've got anything to hide. I haven't been drunk for thirty years. I've been true to my wife—unless you count one time when I kissed a little widow on the *Baltic*, and by golly that's as far as it went! But if there's one thing that would make me go out for all the vices I ever heard of, it would be the thought of a lot of morality hounds sneaking after me all the time, the way they do in the States. And you get better servants here—yes, and the servants themselves like their work a deuce of a sight better than our red-neck hired girls in America, because they're skilled, they're respected here, they're secure, they don't have the womenfolks nosing into their ice-boxes and love-letters all day long! And business—— Our greatest American myth is that we're so much more efficient than these Britishers and the folks on the Continent. All this high-pressure salesmanship bunk! Why say, I'll bet that stuff antagonizes more customers than it ever catches. And over here, they simply won't stand for it! An Englishman knows what he wants to buy, and he don't intend to be bullied into buying something else. And a Scotsman knows what he doesn't want to buy! Half our efficiency is just running around and making a lot of show and wasting time. I always picture the ideal 'peppy' American business man as a fellow who spends half his time having his letters filed away and the other half trying to find 'em again. And then—— Englishman don't feel he's virtuous because he spends a lot of extra time in his office not doing anything special. He goes home early and gets in some golf or tennis or some gardening. Might even read a book! And he's got a hobby, so that when he retires he has something to do; doesn't just waste away from being bored to death when he's old, the way we do.

"The Englishman will work, and work hard, but he doesn't fall for that nonsense that work—any kind of work for any purpose—is noble in itself. Why, when I go home—— Well, there's old Emmanuel White, president of my company. He's seventy-two years old, and he's never taken a vacation. He's worth two million dollars, and he gets to the office at eight, and sometimes he stays there till eleven at night and goes snooping around to see if anybody's left a light turned on. Maybe he gets some fun out of it, but he sure doesn't look like it. He looks like he lived on vinegar, and to have a conference with him is just about as pleasant as tending a sick tiger. And the fellows of forty and forty-five that never relax even when they do take an afternoon off—they drive like hell out to a golf course. Greatest myth in the world!

"But we're beginning to learn a little bit about leisure at home, I guess. That makes me hopeful that some day we may even get cured of optimism and oratory. But I don't expect it in my time, and you bet your sweet life I'm going to stay on here in England, even after I retire. Say! I've got a little place in Surrey, with an acre of ground and a rose garden. But I'm American, just's American as I ever was. And, thank God, there's enough Americans here so I can see a lot of 'em. I admire the English, but they make me feel kind of roughneck. But *live* here—you bet! Say, that's one of the best proofs that America is the greatest country in the world: Paris and London have become two of the nicest of American cities! Yes sir!"

Sam was rather bewildered. Doblin was the old-fashioned, Yankee, suramerican sort whom he preferred to all the strident new evangelists of business.

He was more bewildered when Fish of the American Forwarding Company—big jovial Fish, who had played center for the University of the Western Conference—chuckled:

"You bet! First year I was here, I was homesick all the time. I went home, and I intended to stay there. Well, I lasted just one year in that dear old Chicago! God, the Loop, the elevated, driving through that traffic out to Wilmette every evening, the eternal yow-yow-yow about investments and bridge! Didn't even enjoy golf! Golly, fellows worked at it! Felt guilty as hell if they were one stroke over yesterday! And most of 'em took up playing to get acquainted with possible customers at the club—sell 'em eighteen bonds in eighteen holes. I got transferred back here. I guess I'd enlist to fight for America against any blooming country in the world, but—— Maybe America will get civilized. I hope so. I'm going to send both my boys back home to American universities, and then let 'em decide whether they want to remain or come back here. Maybe we ought to stay home and fight the blue-noses, not let 'em exile us. But life's short. Want to be a good patriot, but—— Say! I wish you could see my house in Chelsea—twenty minutes from Trafalgar Square, even in one of these non-motorized London taxis, and yet it's as quiet as a hick town in Nebraska. Quieter! Because there's no kids drinking gin and hollering in flivvers, and no evangelist in the big tent raising hell. Yes *sir!*"

Sam was pondering.

He was coming to like England. Perhaps he really would live here. Take an interest in some motor agency. Have an Elizabethan black-and-white house in Kent, with ten acres. Join the American Club. These were good fellows—perhaps there were three or four who would even pass the censorship of Fran. He would not be lonely here. He would learn leisure. And think of getting old Tub to come over for a while in the summer! Trot all round England and Scotland with Tub in a car—play golf at St. Andrews——

Yes.

But he recalled the horrors of an arty tea to which Jack Starling had taken them in St. John's Wood. He recalled the tedium of dinner-parties—people dining solitarily in public. He recalled his discomfort in being unable to understand the violent differences between an Oxford man and a graduate of the University of London, between a public school man and one who abysmally was not. And yet—— There was *something* about life here——

He didn't feel that he had to hustle, when he walked the London streets. He didn't, just now, want to return to an office in Zenith and listen to vehement young men who made Patrick Henry orations about windshield-wipers; he didn't long again to study the schedules of a company which would provide seat-upholstery at .06774 cents cheaper a yard, or to listen to Doc Wimpole, the cut-up of the golf club, in his Swedish imitations or his celebrated way of greeting you: "Well, here's the old cut-throat! How many widows and orphans have you stuck with your rotten old Revs this week?"

No!

He went home, after tremendously cordial handshakings, more blissful about his new rôle of required adventurousness than ever before . . . and hoping that Fran would not say, "Did you have an agreeable time with the great American commercial intellects?"

She would! She'd wake up, no matter how softly he came into the bedroom, and she'd say—— (He had it all out, there in the taxicab.) She'd say, "Well, I hope you enjoyed yourself with Mr. Hurd and all the other hearty Rotarians!"

"Now you look here! I heard more good talk tonight, more talk that really got down to cases, than I've heard at any of your dinners where gentlemen try to talk like Members of Parliament and Members of Parliament try to talk like gentlemen——"

"Why, my dear Sam, we're becoming positively literary! The influence of dear Mr. Hurd is astonishing! Was his wife there? She'd do perfectly at a bachelor dinner!"

"Now you look here! I know what a profound scholar you are, and I know I'm a roughneck business man, but may I remind you that I did go to a quite well-known institution for young gentlemen in New Haven, and I have actually read several books, and furthermore——"

It was a complete triumph, there in the taxicab.

He came radiantly into their suite. On the couch, crushing her golden evening wrap, Fran lay sobbing.

He gaped from the doorway five full seconds before he chucked his opera hat at the table, dashed to her, plumped down on the couch, and cried:

"What is it? Sweet! What is it?"

She convulsively raised her face just enough to burrow it against his knee while she whimpered:

"I've always said—oh, damn!—I've always said it was really a compliment to a woman to be what they call 'insulted.' Well, maybe it is, but oh, Sam, I don't like it! I *don't!* Oh, I want to go home! Or anyway leave England. I can't face it. Probably it was my fault that——

"No, it wasn't! I swear it wasn't! I never gave him the slightest, littlest excuse to suppose that His Grace—— Oh, God, how I hate that man! He's so supercilious, and what about? I ask you, what about? What is the fool after all but a failure, an international hobo? Even if his cousin *is* the real thing! What is he? I ask you!

"It was like this. Oh, Sam, Sam darling, I hate to tell you, because I must have been at fault—partly. It was after the opera. I suggested to Clyde—to Major Lockert—that we might go somewhere and dance, but he said all the good places were so noisy—couldn't we just come up here and have a drink and talk. I didn't mind; I was a little tired. Well, at first, he was awfully nice. (Oh, I can see his line so clearly now, and it wasn't so bad, considering!) He sat—he sat right there in that chair—he sat there and he talked about his boyhood and how lonely he'd been. And you know what a fool I am about children—you know how I suffer at just the least little suggestion of anybody not having a happy childhood. Of course I almost cried. And then he said he was terribly inarticulate and shy (oh yes!) but he wanted to tell me how much it'd meant to know me—I'd been a sweet feminine influence—honestly, I think he used just those words!—of course he doesn't have a sweet feminine influence more than two or three times a week!—you can imagine the kind of Indian girls he tells that to on his plantation!—how I hate him!

"But anyway, he told me what a regular little sister I'd been to him, and—being seven kinds of a fool, as you know—I fell for it, and first thing I knew, he was sitting here on the couch beside me, holding my hand. And I confess—— Oh, I'm being terribly frank! If you ever are so beastly as to go and use this against me later, I'll *kill* you, I swear I will! . . . I didn't mind the hand-holding a bit. . . . Am I a hussy? I'm afraid I could become one! . . . But anyway—— I mean: He has some electricity about him; he's a very educated hand-holder; not too tight, and yet he sort of makes you shudder——

"But anyway, he held my hand as though it were some particularly sacred relic. And he went on telling me that my example had persuaded him that he must stop wandering and settle down with some glorious girl like me. And I believed it all! I felt like a Sister by a dying bedside!

"But anyway, he was going to cut out all this drifting and really do something with life. He *said* that! 'Do something with life!' I might have known!

"And then——

"Oh, you know what he said! I don't have to tell you. Probably you've said it to some cutie yourself! Only, if I ever catch you doing it, I'll *kill* you! You and I are the model monogamists from now on, d'you understand? Anyway, you can guess what he said. Where was he to find the admirable spouse who'd be exactly like me?

"And of course I made noises like a purr-pussy!

"And the next thing I knew, he'd thrown his arms around me, and he was trying to kiss me, and he was at the same time trying to inform me that I'd led him on—— Oh, I can sound funny about it, now, or try to, anyway. But it was pretty fairly ghastly. The idiot insisted on doing a real 'Woman, you have tempted me to perdition with your poisoned smile' sort of melodrama. Oh, Sam, Sam, Sam dear—you old darling! You're so *decent!* But I mean: When he found that I was most certainly not going to be embraced, he got awfully nasty. That's one thing he does do well! He said I'd led him on. He said that among 'civilized people' there were 'rules of the game,' and the way I'd let him kiss my shoulder—— Oh yes, he did that, too, in the taxicab going to dinner. Oh, I *am* being frank, probably disastrously frank! But, dear, don't treasure it up and use it against a pitiful fool that thought she was a woman of the world! And honestly, I really and truly did think, when he kissed my shoulder, that if I just ignored it he'd have sense enough to see that I wasn't taking any. 'Rules of the game among civilized people!' The fool! As if I didn't understand them just as well as he does, and maybe a lot better! But anyway——

"And maybe I *liked* his kissing my shoulder! Oh, I don't know! I don't know *anything*, after this ghastly evening! But anyway:

"He said it was my fault, and so on and so forth—you can imagine—and then he saw that he couldn't bully me, and he was terribly apologetic about 'showing his true feelings'—the swine hasn't got any true feelings! Anyway, he kissed my ear and my nose—a rotten marksman!—and he pleaded and—— Oh, I don't know why you should have to listen to all the ghastly details! Anyway, I kicked him out, and he—oh, he was charming, my dear!—he went back to his delightful assertion that all American women are bloodless rotters, who get a kick out of seeing men make fools of themselves and——

"Oh, oh yes, and he also said this. This really *was* pretty, and it'll interest you particularly! Though it certainly wasn't very consistent with his bleat about my being a bloodless siren! He said—he made it quite clear that he didn't merely expect a few consoling kisses, and he said that I didn't know how much sex passion there was concealed in me. He said that you—he was so kind as to indicate that you were a worthy motor-pedler and quite a nice kind friend, and probably you could defend yourself if you were attacked by bandits, but you had no sexual fire—'spiritual fire'—I think he said, to be exact—and I was what he called 'unawakened,' and he was willing—bless his dear, kind, neighborly soul!—he was willing to do the awakening.

"Oh, Sam, I'm trying to be funny about it, but actually I've never been so insulted, so hurt, so horribly misunderstood, so innocent——

"Or do *you* think I led him on, too?"

Through all her vehement chronicle, Sam had been sorry for her, most successfully; he had tried to agree with her, not very successfully; and, while he stroked her hair, he had studied a print on the wall.

He had not, till now, been very conscious of their sitting-room. But in these seconds he so concentrated on it that he could never forget one minutest detail: the walls, corn-flower blue; the ceiling, dull gold; a wing chair in cretonne with cabbage roses; the mahogany escritoire, with elegant books of

English memoirs, recently purchased by Fran, on the shelves above the writing tablet, on which she had made neat piles of the chaste Ritz stationery and the letters which were now beginning to come from home. The low table for tea, with the old silver tea-service which she had excitedly purchased on Bond Street. He was touched by the home-making which she was always doing in hotel suites. But most of all he had been inattentively absorbed by the colored print on the wall opposite him. It wasn't any print in particular. It was what any aged and semi-literate artist would do. Yet at this sensitive moment it was fascinating to Sam, this picture of a young gallant, rather leggy in tights, bent over a young woman with a smile and a flowery hat, against a background of towers and roses.

He roused himself from the study of it as he heard her demand, "Or do you think I led him on?"

"No. I'm sure you didn't, Fran. But still——"

Suddenly he had no control over what he was saying; no relation to the man who was saying it:

"Oh, God, I'm so tired! Tired!"

"If you don't think *I'm* tired!"

"Look here, Fran. I'm not awfully accustomed to dealing with little lovers in the home. I haven't had that sort of life. Oh, I know you never had any idea of Lockert's taking your friendliness for love-making. He was a swine. I suppose it's up to me to go out and shoot him."

"Oh, don't be silly!"

"Well, I would feel a good deal like a fool, but if you want me to——" He had been warning himself not to say what he thought. Suddenly he was saying it:

"But as a matter of fact, I don't entirely blame Lockert. You were flirting with him—you were doing it down at Lord Herndon's—even on the steamer you acted as if he was running the whole show for you. And he had some excuse for thinking he could grab you off. You have such a nice way of bawling me out right in his presence; you say, 'Do try to remember that Lady What's-her-name isn't used to Americans, and don't talk about Zenith,' and so on and so on, until you've got me as nervous as an ammeter, till I feel like a Middlewestern bull in a Bond Street china shop, and Lockert listens to it, and naturally he supposes that you think I'm a fool, while he's ace-high and——"

"Are there any other capital crimes that I've committed?"

"Yes. A few. You enjoy highhatting Hurd and decent fellows like that—you're so blame' courteous they feel like stable-boys—you play with 'em like a cat with a mouse—and Lockert's heard you doing it, and he sees you turning toward him for approval, and he thinks you think that he's so superior to me and my friends——"

"Now you listen to *me!* I deny everything you say! I have *never* nagged you! I have *never* said anything to embarrass you! I think even *you* will admit that in some things I have slightly more tact and patience than you have! And then out of pure friendliness, entirely for your own sake, I try to help you to understand people that you've misjudged, and you say I've bullied you! Oh, it's perfectly beastly of you! And idiotic! If you wouldn't fly off the handle so easily, if you'd listen and let me help you, perhaps you wouldn't make such perfectly appalling breaks as you did the night when you insulted Lady Ouston and made everybody so frightfully uncomfortable——"

"But you backed me up! You said I was right!"

"Naturally! I said it out of loyalty to you. I'm always loyal to you. I've never yet failed you in that—or in anything else!"

"Oh, haven't you! I suppose you call it loyalty to be constantly hinting and suggesting that I'm merely an ignorant business man, whereas anybody—*anybody!*—that has an English or French accent, any loafer living on women, is a gentleman and scholar! After all, I have managed to deal with a few European importers without feeling——"

"Go on! Explain that you're the great Herr Geheimrat General-direktor! That you invented and developed the entire motor industry! It's all so new and interesting! Oh, I've never wanted to say it, Sam, but you force me to! I have no question but that you've done well. There are very few more impressive people—in Zenith! But it happens that we are not in your dear Zenith, just now, but in England, and there are several things here that you don't know so much about, and that I do know! After all, this isn't my first trip to Europe! But you're too self-important to let me teach you! I certainly do not mean to hint that you're ill bred or common, but really—I hate to have to tell you this!—you certainly do seem vulgar and ill bred to people who don't understand you——"

"To Lockert, I suppose!"

"——and to people who venture to believe that the great tradition of Europe is slightly superior to the pep and hustle of Zenith! I could teach you that tradition, but you won't let me——"

"I suppose you're an authority!"

"I certainly am, comparatively! After all, I have been in Europe before! And my father's house was always full of Europeans. And I've read more French and German and British books, these twenty years, than you have detective stories! They accept me here. Oh, Sam, if you'd only let me help you——"

"My dear child, you can't at the same time pan me for my vulgarity and be the tender little mother! That's too damn' much to stand! And as a matter of fact, when it comes to vulgarity—— Now where the devil are all the cigarettes?"

Instantly it was more important to find the cigarettes without which no real smoker can be comfortable and emotional and quarrel actively than it was to enjoy the pain of hatred. They suspended battle to join in the hunt. He turned out his dinner-jacket, rammed his hands into the pockets of his overcoat, and yanked out bureau drawers, while she popped up from the couch to look triumphantly—then bleakly—into the black and scarlet Russian box which she had bought yesterday.

"And another thing—another thing—— But where *are* those cigarettes? I know I had half a package of Gold Flakes left, and some Camels," he muttered, as he searched.

It was she who thought of telephoning to the office; she who felt that she knew how to use servants, at no matter what time of night, while he would always be Americanishly shy of them.

She sat on the edge of the couch, she smoothed her skirt, she bent her head with irritating graciousness to receive a light from him when the cigarettes had come, and graciously, most irritatingly, she said:

"Sam, I hate to have to point it out again, but it really doesn't get you very far in a discussion to lose your temper and use big, strong, he-man words like 'damn' and 'the devil.' They aren't so awfully novel and startling to me! And as usual, you're merely missing the point. I'm neither 'panning' you, as you so elegantly put it, nor am I trying to mother you. I'm always willing to listen to your opinions on golf and how to invest my money. I merely expect you to admit that there may be a few things in which the poor ignorant female may know a little bit more than you do! Oh, you're like all the other American men! You speak no known language. You don't know Rodin from Mozart. You have no idea whether France or England controls Syria. You—you, the motor expert!—can never remember whether a lady should be on your right or your left in a car. You're bored equally by Bach and Antheil. You're bored by going with me to shop for the most divine Russian embroidery. You can't fence with a pretty woman at dinner. And—— But those are just symptoms! Separately, they don't matter. The thing is that you haven't the mistiest notion of what European civilization is, basically—of how the tradition of leisure, honor, gallantry, inherent cultivation, differs from American materialism. And you don't want to learn. You never *could* be European——"

"Fran! Stop sneering!"

"I am not sneer——"

"Stop it! Dear! I don't pretend to have any of these virtues. I guess it's perfectly true: I never could become European. But why should I? I'm American, and glad of it. And you know I never try to prevent your being as European as you want to. But don't take out your soreness at Lockert on me. Please!"

His encircling arms said more, and he nestled her head on his shoulder while she sobbed:

"I know. I'm sorry. But oh——"

She sat up, spoke resolutely.

"I'm terribly ashamed about this Lockert business. Shamed right down through me. I can't stand it! Sam, I want to leave England at once. I can't stand staying in this country with that man, thinking he's here laughing at me. Or else I *will* be asking you to go out and shoot him, and the law here is so prejudiced! I want to leave for France. *Now!*"

"But golly, Fran, I like this country! I'm getting to know London. I like it here. France'll be so foreign."

"Precisely! I want it to be! I want to start all over. I won't make a fool of myself again. Oh, Sam, darling, let's run away, like two school-children, hand in hand! And think! The joy of seeing blue siphons and brioches and kiosks and red sashes and red-plush wall-seats and fat lady cashiers! And hearing 'B'jour, M'sieu et Madame,' the way they say it when you're leaving a shop—like a little bell! Let's go!"

"Well, I did intend to see some aeroplane factories here. Fact I had a date——"

They went to Paris in four days.

The Channel steamer seemed to him like a greyhound—small, slim, power evident in its squat thick funnel. The delight of sea-faring which he had found on the Atlantic came to him again in the narrow gangways 'tween decks, suggesting speed in their sharp curve toward the bow. When he had established Fran in a chair on the boat deck, amid piles of snobbish blond luggage, he slipped down to the bar.

There is about a ship's bar, any bar of any ship, however small, a cheerfulness unknown elsewhere in life's dark and Methodist vale. It has the snug security of an English inn, with a suggestion of adventure as the waves flicker past the port-holes, as you speculate about the passengers—men coming from China and Brazil and Saskatchewan, men going to Italy and Liberia and Siam. As he clumped up to join Fran, Sam forgot, in waxing anticipation of the Continent, his regret for England, and he kept that anticipation even while he listened on deck to a proper cross-Channel conversation among a ripe Wiltshire vicar, his aunt, and his aunt's dear friend, Mrs. Illingworth-Dobbs:

"Oh yes, we shall stop in Florence most of the time."

"Shall you stop at the Stella Rossa *ancora una volta*?"

"No, I really think we shall stop at Mrs. Brown-Bloater's pension. You know we've always stopped at the Stella Rossa, but it's really too outrageous. Last year they began to charge extra for tea!"

"Extra? For *tea*?"

"Yes. And it used to be quite nice there! The guests were people one could know. But now it's filled with Jews and Americans and unmarried couples and even Germans!"

"Dreadful! But Florence is so lovely."

"Charming!"

"So artistic!"

"Yes, so artistic. And Sir William is taking a villa there for the season."

"I say, that will be jolly for you."

"*Sì, sì! Sarà una cosa veramente*—uh—really charming. Sir William is *so* fond of the artistic. It will be quite like home, having him there. *And I have heard definitely from Mrs. Brown-Bloater that she is not charging extra for tea!*"

Sam forgot the prospect of a Continent full of Mrs. Illingworth-Dobbses; he even forgot, in the zest of the steamer's speed, Fran's fretfulness that the boat was going up and down a good deal, for which she seemed to feel that he was to blame. The bow hit the waves like a mailed fist. There was just enough motion to show that he really was at sea, and as they left the English coast and cut into the fresh breeze, they plunged past foreign-looking craft: a French steam-trawler lurching up the Channel, with meaty little sailors in striped jerseys waving at them, a German coaster, a Dutch East Indiaman, rolling through the sun-crisped tide.

The sailors who passed their deck chairs, the officers on the bridge, they were all so sturdy, so mahogany-faced, so reliable, so British.

A man with a long blond mustache and a monocle strolled past. Fran insisted that he was Thomas Cook, of the Sons. And what was Karl Baedeker like? she speculated. Short and square, with a short square brown beard and double-thick spectacles through which he peered at menus and ruined temples and signs reading "Roma 3 chilometri."

"Yes, and what is Mr. Bass like? And the Haig Brothers? I wonder if they're like the Smith Brothers," said Sam, and, "Gosh, I'm enjoying this, Fran!"

Then he saw a pale line, which was the coast of France.

But he tramped aft, to look back toward England. He fancied that he could see the shadow of its cliffs. Doubtless it was a distant cloud-bank that he saw, but he imagined the cool and endearing hills, the welcoming crooked streets, the wholesome faces.

"England! Perhaps I'll never see it again. . . . Fran and Lockert, they've taken it from me. . . . But I love it. America is my wife and daughter, but England is my mother. And these fools talk about a possible war between Britain and America! If that ever came—— I thought Debs was foolish to go to jail as a protest against war, but I guess I understand better how he felt now. 'If I forget thee, O England, let my right hand forget her cunning, if I do not remember thee, let my tongue cleave to the roof of my mouth.' How did that go, in chapel? Oh yes: 'If I prefer not Jerusalem—London—above my chief joy'! Well. I never could prefer England above America. But next to America—— Oh, Lord, I'd liked to've stayed there! The Dodsworths were in England three thousand years, maybe, where they've been in America only three hundred.

"England!"

Then he turned eagerly toward France.

They crept into harbor, past the breakwater with its tiny lighthouses, bumped along a rough stone pier, saw advertisements of strange drinks in a strange language, and were flooded with small, shrieking, blue-bloused porters; heard children speaking French as though it were a natural language; and for the first time in his life Samuel Dodsworth was in the grasp of a real Foreign Land.

Chapter 12

SAM had remained calm amid the frenzy of a Detroit Automobile Show; he had stalked through the crush of a New Year's Eve on Broadway, merely brushing off the bright young men with horns and feather ticklers; but in the Calais customs-house he was appalled. The porters shrieked ferocious things like "attonshion" as they elbowed past, walking mountains of baggage; the passengers jammed about the low baggage platform; the customs inspectors seemed to Sam cold-eyed and hostile; all of them bawled and bleated and wailed in what sounded to him like no language whatever; and he remembered that he had four hundred cigarettes in his smaller bag.

The porter who had taken their bags on the steamer had shouted something that sounded like "catravan deuce"—Fran said it meant that he was Porter Number Ninety-two. Then Catravan Deuce had malignantly disappeared, with their possessions. Sam knew that it was all right, but he didn't believe it. He assured himself that a French porter was no more likely to steal their bags than a Grand Central red-cap—only, he was quite certain that Catravan Deuce had stolen them. Of course he could replace everything except Fran's jewelry without much expense but—— Damn it, he'd hate to lose his old red slippers——

He was disappointed at so flabby an ending when he found Catravan Deuce at his elbow in the customs room, beaming in a small bearded way and shouldering aside the most important passengers to plank their baggage down on the platform for examination.

Sam was proud of Fran's French (of Stratford, Connecticut) when the capped inspector said something quite incomprehensible and she answered with what sounded like "ree-an." He felt that she was a scholar; he felt that he was untutored and rusty; he depended on her admiringly. And then he opened the smaller bag and the four hundred cigarettes were revealed to the inspector.

The inspector looked startled, he gaped, he spread out his arms, and protested in the name of liberty, equality, fraternity, and indemnities. Fran tried to answer, but her French stumbled and fell, and she turned to Sam, all her airy competence gone, wailing, "I can't understand what he says! He—he talks patois!"

At her appeal, Sam suddenly became competent, ready to face the entire European Continent, with all appertaining policemen, laws, courts, and penitentiaries.

"Here! I'll get somebody!" he assured her, and to the customs inspector, who was now giving a French version of the Patrick Henry oration, he remarked, "Just a *mo*-ment! Keep your shirt on!"

He had a notion of finding the English vicar to whom he had listened on the Channel steamer. "Fellow seems to know European languages." He wallowed through the crowd as though he were making a touch-down, and saw on a cap the thrice golden words "American Express Company." The American Express man beamed and leaped forward at something in the manner with which Mr. Samuel Dodsworth of the Revelation Motor Company suggested, "Can you come and do a little job of interpreting for me?" . . . Sam felt that for a moment he was being Mr. Samuel Dodsworth, and not Fran Dodsworth's husband. . . . And for something less than a moment he admitted that he was possibly being the brash Yankee of Mark Twain and Booth Tarkington. And he could not successfully be sorry for it.

The American Express man saw them on the waiting train (a very bleak and tall and slaty train it seemed to Sam); he prevented Sam from tipping the porter enough to set him up in a shop. And so Sam and Fran were alone in a compartment, safe again till Paris.

Sam chuckled, "Say, I guess I'll have to learn the French for two phrases: 'How much?' and 'Go to hell.' But—— Sweet! We're in France—in Europe!"

She smiled at him; she let him off and didn't even rebuke him for his Americanism. They sat hand in hand, and they were more intimately happy than since the day they had sailed from America. They were pleased by everything: by the battery of red and golden bottles on their table at lunch, by the deftness with which the waiter sliced the cone of ice cream, by the mysterious widow who was trying to pick up the mysterious Frenchman who combined a checked suit and a red tie with a square black beard—such a beard, murmured Fran, as it was worth crossing the Atlantic to behold.

He was stimulated equally by the "foreignness" of the human spectacle flickering past the window of their compartment—women driving ox-carts, towns with sidewalk cafés, and atrocious new houses of yellow brick between lumpy layers of stone picked out in red mortar—and the lack of "foreignness" in the land itself. Somehow it wasn't quite right that French trees and grass should be of the same green, French earth of the same brown, French sky of the same blue, as in a natural, correct country like America. After the tight little fenced fields of England, the wide Picardy plains, green with approaching April, seemed to him extraordinarily like the prairies of Illinois and Iowa. If it was a little disappointing, not quite right and decent after he had gone and taken so long and expensive a journey, yet he was pleased by that sense of recognition which is one of the most innocent and egotistic of human diversions, that feeling of understanding and of mastering an observation. He was as pleased as a side-street nobody when in his newspaper he sees the name of a man he knows.

"I'm enjoying this!" said Sam.

He had been accustomed to "sizing up" American towns; he could look from a Pullman window at Kalamazoo or Titus Center and guess the population within ten per cent. He could and with frequency he did; he was fascinated by figures of any sort, and for twenty years he had been trying to persuade Fran that there was nothing essentially ignoble in remembering populations and areas and grade-percentages and the average life of tires. He had been able to guess not too badly at the size of British towns; he had not been too greatly bewildered by anything in England, once he was over the shock of seeing postmen with funny hats, and taxicabs with no apparent speed above neutral. But in Paris, as they bumped and slid and darted from the Gare du Nord to their hotel, he could not be certain just what it was that he was seeing.

Fran was articulate enough about it. She half stood up in the taxi, crying, "Oh, look, Sam, look! Isn't it adorable! Isn't it too exciting! Oh, the darling funny little *zincs*! And the Cointreau ads, instead of chewing gum! These bald-faced high white houses! Everybody so noisy, and yet so gay! Oh, I *adore* it!"

But for Sam it was a motion picture produced by an insane asylum; it was an earthquake with a volcano erupting and a telephone bell ringing just after he'd gone to sleep; it was lightning flashes and steam whistles and newspaper extras and war.

Their taxicab, just missing an omnibus, sliding behind its rear platform. A policeman, absurdly little, with an absurd white baton. Two priests over glasses of beer at a café. Silver gray everywhere, instead of London's golden brown. Two exceedingly naked plaster ladies upholding a fifth-story balcony. Piles of shoddy rugs in front of a shop, and beside them a Frenchman looking utterly content with his little business, instead of yearning at the department store opposite and feeling guilty as he would in New York or Chicago or Zenith. Fish. Bread. Beards. Brandy. Artichokes. Apples. Etchings. Fish. A stinking-looking alley. A splendid sweeping boulevard. Circular tin structures whose use he dared not suspect and which gave him a shocking new notion of Latin proprieties and of the apparently respectable and certainly bearded gentlemen who dashed toward them. Many books, bound in paper of a thin-looking yellow. An incessant, nerve-cracking, irritating, exhilarating blat-blat-blat of nervous little motor horns. Buildings which in their blankness seemed somehow higher than American skyscrapers ten times as high. A tiny, frowsy, endearing façade of a house which suggested the French Revolution and crazed women in red caps and kirtled skirts. A real artist (Sam decided), a being in red beard, wide black hat, and a cloak, with a dog-eared marble-paper-covered portfolio under his arm. Gossiping women, laughing, denouncing, forgiving, laughing. Superb public buildings, solid-looking as Gibraltar. Just missing another taxi, and the most admirable cursing by both chauffeurs——

"This certainly is a busy town. But not much traffic control, looks to me," said Samuel Dodsworth, and his voice was particularly deep and solemn, because he was particularly confused and timid.

It was at the Grand Hôtel des Deux Hémisphères et Dijon that he was able to reassume the pleasant mastery with which (he hoped) he had been able to impress Fran at the Calais customs. The assistant manager of the hotel spoke excellent English, and Sam had never been entirely at a loss so long as his opponent would be decent and speak a recognizable language.

Lucile McKelvey, of Zenith, had told Fran that the Hémisphères was "such a nice, quiet hotel," and Sam had wired for reservations from London. By himself, he would doubtless have registered and taken meekly whatever room was given him. But Fran insisted on seeing their suite, and they found it a damp, streaked apartment looking on a sunless courtyard.

"Oh, this won't do at all!" wailed Fran. "Haven't you something decent?"

The assistant manager, a fluent Frenchman from Roumania via Algiers, looked them up and down with that contempt, that incomparable and enfeebling contempt, which assistant managers reserve for foreigners on their first day in Paris.

"We are quite full up," he sniffed.

"You haven't anything else at all?" she protested.

"No, Madame."

Those were the words, but the tune was, "No, you foreign nuisance—jolly lucky you are to be admitted here at all—I wonder if you two really *are* married—well, I'll overlook that, but I shan't stand any Yankee impertinence!"

Even the airy Fran was intimidated, and she said only, "Well, I don't like it——"

And then Samuel Dodsworth appeared again.

His knowledge of Parisian hotels and their assistant managers was limited, but his knowledge of impertinent employees was vast.

"Nope," he said. "No good. We don't like it. We'll look elsewhere."

"But Monsieur has engaged this suite!"

The internationalist and the provincial looked at each other furiously, and it was the assistant manager whose eyes fell, who looked embarrassed, as Sam's paws curled, as the back of his neck prickled with unholy wrath.

"Look here! You know this is a rotten hole! Do you want to send for the manager—the boss, whatever you call him?"

The assistant manager shrugged, and left them, coldly and with speed.

Rather silently, Sam lumbered beside Fran down to their taxi. He supervised the reloading of their baggage, and atrociously overtipped every one whom he could coax out of the hotel.

"Grand Universel!" he snapped at the taxi-driver, and the man seemed to understand his French.

In the taxi he grumbled, "I *told* you I had to learn the French for 'Go to hell.'"

A silence; then he ruminated, "Glad we got out of there. But I bullied that poor rat of a clerk. Dirty trick! I'm sorry! I'm three times as big as he is. Stealing candy from a kid! Dirty trick! I see why they get sore at Americans like me. Sorry, Fran."

"I adore you!" she said, and he looked mildly astonished.

At the Grand Universel, on the Rue de Rivoli, they found an agreeable suite overlooking the Tuileries, and twenty times an hour, as she unpacked, Fran skipped to the window to gloat over Paris, the Casanova among cities.

Their sitting-room seemed to him very pert and feminine in its paneled walls covered with silky yellow brocade, its fragile chairs upholstered in stripes of silver and lemon. Even the ponderous boule cabinet was frivolous, and the fireplace was of lively and rather indecorous pink marble. He felt that it was a light-minded room, a room for sinning in evening clothes. All Paris was like that, he decided.

Then he stepped out on the fretted iron balcony and looked to the right, to the Place de la Concorde and the beginning of the Champs Elysées, with the Chamber of Deputies across the Seine. He was suddenly stilled, and he perceived another Paris, stately, aloof, gray with history, eternally quiet at heart for all its superficial clamor.

Beneath the quacking of motor horns he heard the sullen tumbrils. He heard the trumpets of the Napoleon who had saved Europe from petty princes. He heard, without quite knowing that he heard them, the cannon of the Emperor who was a Revolutionist. He heard things that Samuel Dodsworth did not know he had heard or ever could hear.

"Gee, Fran, this town has been here a long time, I guess," he meditated. "This town knows a lot," said Samuel Dodsworth of Zenith. "Yes, it knows a lot."

And, a little sadly, "I wish I did!"

There are many Parises, with as little relation one to another as Lyons to Monte Carlo, as Back Bay to the Dakota wheatfields. There is the trippers' Paris: a dozen hotels, a dozen bars and restaurants, more American than French; three smutty revues; three railroad stations; the Café de la Paix; the Eiffel Tower; the Arc de Triomphe; the Louvre; shops for frocks, perfumes, snake-skin shoes, and silk pajamas; the regrettable manners of Parisian taxi-drivers; and the Montmartre dance-halls where fat, pink-skulled American lingerie-buyers get drunk on imitation but inordinately expensive champagne, to the end that they put on pointed paper hats, scatter confetti, conceive themselves as Great Lovers, and in general forget their unfortunate lot.

The students' Paris, round about the Sorbonne, very spectacled and steady. The fake artists' Paris, very literary and drunk and full of theories. The real artists' Paris, hidden and busy and silent. The cosmopolites' Paris, given to breakfast in the Bois, to tea at the Ritz, and to reading the social columns announcing who has been seen dining with princesses at Ciro's—namely, a Paris whose chief joy is in being superior to the trippers.

There is also reported to be a Paris inhabited by no one save three million Frenchmen.

It is said that in this unknown Paris live bookkeepers and electricians and undertakers and journalists and grandfathers and grocers and dogs and other beings as unromantic as people Back Home.

Making up a vast part of all save this last of the Parises are the Americans.

Paris is one of the largest, and certainly it is the pleasantest, of modern American cities. It is a joyous town, and its chief joy is in its jealousies. Every citizen is in rivalry with all the others in his knowledge of French, of museums, of wine, and of restaurants.

The various castes, each looking down its nose at the caste below, are after this order: Americans really domiciled in Paris for years, and connected by marriage with the French noblesse. Americans long domiciled, but unconnected with the noblesse. Americans who have spent a year in Paris—those who have spent three months—two weeks—three days—half a day—just arrived. The American who has spent three days is as derisive toward the half-a-day tripper as the American resident with smart French relatives is toward the poor devil who has lived in Paris for years but who is there merely for business.

And without exception they talk of the Rate of Exchange.

And they are all very alike, and mostly homesick.

They insist that they cannot live in America, but, except for a tenth of them who have really become acclimated in Europe, they are so hungry for American news that they subscribe to the home paper, from Keokuk or New York or Pottsville, and their one great day each week is that of the arrival of the American mail, on which they fall with shouts of "Hey, Mamie, listen to this! They're going to put a new heating plant in the Lincoln School." They know quite as well as Sister Louisa, back home, when the Washington Avenue extension will be finished. They may ostentatiously glance daily at *Le Matin* or *Le Journal*, but the Paris editions of the New York *Herald* and the Chicago *Tribune* they read solemnly, every word, from the front page stories—"Congress to Investigate Election Expenses," and "Plans Transatlantic Aeroplane Liners" to the "News of Americans in Europe," with its tidings that Mrs. Witney T. Auerenstein of Scranton entertained Geheimrat and Frau Bopp at dinner at the Bristol, and that Miss Mary Minks Meeton, author and lecturer, has arrived at the Hôtel Pédauque.

Each of these castes is subdivided according to one's preference for smart society or society so lofty that it need not be smart, society given to low bars and earnest drinking, the society of business exploitation, or that most important society of plain loafing. Happy is he who can cleave utterly to one of these cliques; he can find a group of fellow zealots and, drinking or shopping or being artistic, be surrounded with gloriously log-rolling comrades.

But Sam Dodsworth was unfortunate, for his wife panted to combine smartness with an attention to Art, while he himself preferred business and the low bars.

For all of Fran's superiority to "sight-seeing," they were at first lonely in Paris, and Sam was able to drag her to all the places mentioned in the guide-books. They danced at Zelli's; they went up the Eiffel Tower and she came near to being sick in corners; thrice they went to the Louvre; and once he cajoled her into the New York Bar for a whisky and soda and spirited conversation with an unknown man about skiing and the Bronx. She showed even more zest than he in finding new small restaurants—he would have been content to return every night to the places in which he had conquered the waiters and learned the wine-list.

And, curiously, he enjoyed galleries and picture-exhibitions more than she.

Fran had read enough about art; she glanced over the studio magazines monthly, and she knew every gallery on Fifth Avenue. But, to her, painting, like all "culture," was interesting only as it adorned her socially. In story-books parroting the Mark Twain tradition, the American wife still marches her husband to galleries from which he tries to sneak away; but in reality Sam's imagination was far more electrified by blue snow and golden shoulders and dynamic triangles than was Fran's. Probably he would have balked at the blurs of Impressionism and the jazz mathematics of Cubism, but it chanced that the favorite artist just this minute was one Robinoff, who did interiors pierced with hectic sunshine hurled between the slats of Venetian blinds, or startling sun-rays striking into dusky woodlands, and at these (while Fran impatiently wanted to get on to tea) Sam stared long and contentedly, drawing in his breath as though he smelled the hot sun.

In every phase Fran was as incalculable about "sight-seeing" as about liking his business associates. One day she was brazen enough to be discovered with the tourists' badge, the red Baedeker, unconcealed; the next she wouldn't even sit with him at a sidewalk café—at the Napolitain or the Closerie-des-Lilas.

"But why not?" he protested. "Best place to see the world go by. Everybody goes to 'em."

"Smart people don't."

"Well, I'm not smart!"

"Well, I am!"

"Then you ought to be smart enough to not care what anybody thinks!"

"Perhaps I am. . . . But I don't care to be seen sitting with a lot of trippers in raincoats."

"But you sat in a café yesterday, and enjoyed it. Don't you remember the beggar that sang——"

"Exactly! I've had enough of it! Oh, if you want to go and yearn over your dear American fellow tourists, by all means go, my dear Samuel! I am going to the Crillon and have a decent tea."

"And yearn over the dear fellow American tourists that happen to be rich!"

"Is it necessary for you always to quarrel with me because I want to do what I want to do? I'm not keeping you from sitting on your sidewalks. Don't go to the Crillon! Go to one of your beloved American bars, if you want to, and scrape up acquaintance with a lot of drunken business men——"

They compromised on going to the Crillon.

He puzzled over her feeling that it was a duty to keep herself fashionable in the eyes of the choice people who did not know that she existed. He could understand that back in Zenith she might have a good human satisfaction in being more snobbish than the matron across the street, in the ancient sport of "putting it over on the neighbors." He had been unrighteously pleased when he had seen her better dressed than her dear friend and resented rival, Lucile McKelvey. "Good girl," he had crowed; "you were the best-dressed wench in the room!"

But why should it matter to Fran that a strange Parisian aristocrat passing in a carriage might some day see them sitting contentedly at a café and arch her brows at them?

He admitted that the serene and classic Place des Vosges with the Carnavalet Museum was perhaps more select than Pat's Chicago Bar; that *caneton pressé* might be a more elegant food than corn fritters at the Savannah Grill. "But," he fretted, "why can't you enjoy both—as long as you *do* enjoy 'em? Nobody's hired us to come here and be stylish!

We haven't got any duty involved! Back home there may have been a law against enjoying ourselves the way we wanted to, but there's none here!"

"My dear Sam, it's a matter of keeping one's self-respect. It's like the Englishman, all alone in the jungle, who always dresses for dinner."

"Yes, I've read about him! In the first place, he probably didn't do it, and in the second place, if he did he was a chump! That's how I've always figured it."

"You would! You couldn't understand what it meant to him——"

"Well, if all that stood between him and losing his self-respect was a hard-boiled shirt-front, I guess he might as well have let it slide! If I can't be self-respectful in a flannel shirt, I'm about ready to jump off the dock and——"

"Oh, you simply can't *understand!*"

They had never had much time in Zenith for a serious attention to quarreling and being domestically vulgar. All day he had been at the office; most evenings they had seen other people; on Sunday there had been golf and relatives. They had time a-plenty now, equally for quarreling and for intimate and adventurous happiness together. One day they wrangled—and endlessly, because they were not quarreling over any one thing in particular but over the differences in their philosophies of life; the next they went off (and sometimes she was simple and gay enough to let him carry sandwiches somewhat mussily in his pocket) to explore the Forest of Fontainebleau, and they laughed as they walked through groves shivering with April.

He was becoming acquainted with her and, sometimes, slightly, with himself.

He saw little enough of Frenchmen outside of hotel-servants, waiters, shopmen, but what he did see of them, what he saw of the surface of French life, puzzled him. Many travelers in like case take out their confusion in resentment, and damn the whole nation as trivial and mad. But there was in Sam a stubborn wish to get in behind any situation that he came across. He was not one to amuse himself by novelties, by making scenes, by collecting curious people, even overmuch by travel, but once he was dragged into something new he wanted to understand it, and he had a touch of humility, a deep and sturdy recognition of his own ignorance, whenever he could not understand.

And he could not understand these Frenchmen.

He watched them in cafés, at the theater, in shops, in trains to Tours and Versailles. How was it that they could sit, not restless, playing dominoes or chattering, over nothing more beguiling than glasses of coffee (and why was it that they drank coffee in glasses, anyway, instead of in cups)?

They liked talking so much. What the deuce did they find to talk about, hour on hour? How could they stand it without something to *do*?

Why were there so few grassy yards about the houses? How was it that the most respectable old couples, silvery old men and crouched little old women, were willing to be seen at ordinary cafés in the evening, when their counterparts back home considered the saloon, the café, as the final haunt of the abominable? He saw the French people being gracious in shops, beaming on the babies in the Luxembourg Gardens, laughing together as they paraded the streets, and he decided that they were the soul of kindliness. He saw a Frenchman scowl at American barbarians for daring to enter his quarter-filled railway compartment, he heard Fran being atrociously denounced by a recently smiling, buxom, clean, wholesome shop-woman when Fran insisted that she had been overcharged ten centimes for dry-cleaning a pair of gloves, and he decided that the French were rude and mean to a point of hatefulness . . . and that his Fran showed an enjoyment of squabbling which was a little disturbing to him.

He saw the Louvre, the silks in shops on the Place Vendôme, the trimness of their own apartment at the Grand Universel, and he decided that the French had the best taste in the world. He saw the department stores with their atrocious brass-fretted windows, their displays of fish and fowl and Marquise-in-a-garden chromos, of buffets carved with wooden blobs, of chairs that were even more violently high-colored than they were uncomfortable; he saw, in the haughty Parc Monceau, the imported ruins; he saw intelligent-seeming

Frenchmen snickering over smutty post-cards and the eternal, unchanging pictures of naked young women in *Vie Parisienne* and *Le Rire*; and he decided that the French had no taste whatever.

But behind all his decisions was the decision that Sam Dodsworth would never be anything save bewildered by foreign ways, while Fran might, perhaps, take to them so eagerly that their companionship would be smashed forever.

Chapter 13

SAM was used enough to New York hotels, and he had spent occasional fortnights at summer inns of Northern Michigan, Maine, the Berkshires. But he had never known the existence of the prosperous refugees from life who cling for years to hotels and pensions, who are mothered by chambermaids, fathered by concierges, befriended only by room-waiters—if they find any waiters kind enough and idle enough to be patient with their longing to gossip.

And he did not like it.

He felt as though he were living in an Old People's Home. The attention of the servants made him feel old; the elevator man infuriated him by placing a hand under his arm to help him out of an elevator which had stopped a whole inch above the floor; the page boy in the lobby infuriated him by spinning the revolving door—and usually spinning it so artfully that one blade just missed Sam's nose; the head waiter infuriated him by inquiring, as though Sam had never heard of menus, "A little soup this evening, Mr. Samuels?" and most of all he was infuriated by the room-waiters who were each morning astonished that he should desire eggs in addition to his Continental Breakfast, who fussed over knives and forks, who pushed up chairs and snatched away the pleasant litter of newspapers, and who held out his napkin as though he were too feeble to lift it for himself.

Yet he was dependent on them. Though Fran was making much now of reading the *Matin* daily and of knowing all about art exhibitions and the hours when theaters began, she had to turn to the tall and patronizing concierge for information about what train to take to Versailles—where to buy slippers—who was the best American dentist—how much one ought to pay for a lacquered Japanese cigarette case—why the deuce Mathilde et Cie. hadn't delivered the evening scarf they'd promised for this afternoon—and just what *was* the general reputation of Mathilde et Cie. for delivering things and for overcharging?

He sank heavily into accepting the hotel as his natural

dwelling, as a prisoner sinks into accepting a jail. Presently he was not bothered by the devious way from the elevator to their suite—to the right, sharp turning right again, turning left by that dusty old trunk with the red and green stripes which had apparently stood there in the corridor forever, then seventh door on the left—the door with the long scratch under the knob. He came to accept it as any other peasant accepts the long way to his hut, dark and meaningless and weary to tired legs. He was no longer annoyed by the too open-work and too generally brassy and light-minded appearance of the French elevator; he learned that the elevator was the "lift" or the "ascenseur" or indeed almost anything except the "elevator"; he learned that the room service-bell never worked and that the best way to get a waiter was to stand in the door and bellow "Gar-song"; and he learned that the Mr. Samuel Dodsworth who once had been received with a certain deference in the General Offices of the Revelation Motor Company in Zenith was fortunate here when the Greek boots nodded to him in the hall.

He even got used to living in a lack of privacy like that of a monkey in a Zoo. After a time he could without self-consciousness sit and read the Paris editions of the American papers in the old-fashioned lounge of the hotel—he went there daily, despite having a drawing-room of his own, in a sneaking, never-admitted hope that some day he would be recognized and picked up by a fellow American exile. The lounge was modern in its small and hideous tables covered with pebbled beaten brass, its fountain, with Neptune undistinguishable from any other marble tombstone, and the number of cocktails gulped daily at five o'clock by young ladies who spoke Chicagoese with a very fair imitation of a French accent. But the modernity of the lounge had not run to new chairs; they were of red and golden plush, made delicate and chaste with antimacassars, and looking rather as though they had been dedicated by Napoleon III.

It had not been easy for Sam to get used to reading in the lounge, to dressing his mind in public. He was accustomed to the communism of clubs, but there, no one paid attention to any one else. In the lounge, no one had very much to do except to pay attention. They stared, and always resentfully.

The English mother and daughter who were the most exclusive and the most resentful toward strangers were precisely the people who spent the most time in the lounge being exclusive and resentful. The French provincial magnate who had arrived just that morning was precisely the person who looked with the greatest irritation at a veteran like Sam, now settled here two whole weeks, when Sam annoyed him by taking the next chair and moving it two inches. And there were always elderly, slightly belching, very hairy couples who spent all their time catching his eye and then looking indignant because he had caught their eyes.

But after a fortnight he could enter the lounge, ignore the human furniture, and rustle his newspaper with almost as much relaxation as he had felt in his library in Zenith.

He was becoming accustomed to the home of the homeless.

He discovered slowly, and always with a little astonishment, that the French were human, even according to the standard of the United States of America.

He found that in certain French bathrooms one can have hot water without waiting for a geyser. He found that he needn't have brought two dozen tubes of his favorite (and very smelly) toothpaste from America—one actually could buy toothpaste, corn-plasters, New York Sunday papers, Bromo-Seltzer, Lucky Strikes, safety-razor blades, and ice cream almost as easily in Paris as in the United States; and a man he met at Luigi's Bar insisted that if one quested earnestly enough, he could find B.V.D.'s.

And he discovered that French chauffeurs drove better than Americans.

He meditated on it, alone with a cognac and soda (he had learned to say "Une fine à l'eau de seltz," and often the waiters understood him) in front of Weber's, during a not ungrateful hour of freedom when Fran was trying on hats.

"Just what did I expect in France? Oh, I don't know. Funny! Kind of hard to remember now just how I did picture it. Guess I thought there wouldn't be any comforts—no bathrooms, and everybody taking red wine and snails for breakfast, and no motor 'busses or comfortable trains, and no cocktails, and all the men wearing waxed mustaches and funny beards. And saying, 'Ze hired girl iz vun lofely girl—oo la la——'

"And then these young Frenchmen, in London clothes, driving Hispano-Suizas at a hundred kilometers an hour—— And you hear 'em at the Ritz, talking perfect English, talking about English stainless steel and about building bridges in the Argentine and the influence of the Soviets in China and——

"I suppose I felt that the entire known world revolved around the General Offices of the Revelation Motor Company, Constitution Avenue, Zenith, and all the time—— Towers and cathedrals and alleys, and Europe not caring what Sam Dodsworth thought about making the 1928 models a Delft blue——

"It seemed so important!

"But, mind you, I am glad I'm an American! But——

"Life was a lot simpler then. We knew we were It! We knew that all of Europe was unbathed and broke, and that America was the world's only bulwark against Bolshevism and famine. They lie so! These speakers at club meetings, and these writers in the magazines! They tell us that no European has ever played tennis or taught the Ten Commandments to his kids or built a railroad, and that the only thing that keeps Europe from reverting to the caveman is American cash.

"Rot!

"And yet, I'm never going to be European! Fran might—— Oh, Fran, my darling, are you going to drift away from me? Every day you get snootier about my poor old provincial Americanism! You're just waiting for some really slick European to come along—— And, by God, there's one thing I won't stand—her telling me how inferior I am to some gigolo——

"Fool! Of course the girl—— Say! That's what she still is; she's still a girl! Little older than Emily, but not so sensible. Of course she gets excited by Europe. She's done her job, hasn't she? She's run the house and brought Emily and Brent up, hasn't she? I've got to be patient.

"But falling for a feather-weight like Lockert——

"Hell! I wish Tub were here. Fran and I haven't got anybody——

"And you're still dodging the issue, my lad!

"What is Sam Dodsworth going to do about the fact that he's as provincial as a prairie-dog, and that he's only fifty-one, with a chance of another thirty years, and that he's discovered a world——

"Nothing, I guess! Too late. I'd be a pretty spectacle, now wouldn't I, as one of these American business-men that come over here and try to hide the fact that they made their coin out of soap or pork—— And so they collect first editions and apologize for being themselves! But just now and then I'll learn to sit still like this, and not feel I have to be efficient and hustle——

"My God! Five o'clock! I've got to hustle and meet Fran!"

But he had one comfort, given to him by his wife. He had been uncomfortably impressed by the fact that Mathieu, his customary room-waiter at the Grand Universel, a fat, curly-haired, and unctuous person with fascinatingly different spots on his dress-suit lapels every day, spoke English so perfectly.

According to the good American custom, Sam had said to him at his very first breakfast, "Where'd you learn your English?"

Mathieu chuckled, "I wass fife years in Tchicago."

Mathieu was rather more colloquially American than Sam in his suggestions for breakfast, or for lunch when it was too rainy for them to go out, or when there was a glorious American mail. "How about a nice little minute steak?" he would say, in the very accent of Chicago; or "Say, boss, there's some nice caviare just come in from Rooshia."

Whence it happened that Sam believed Mathieu spoke the American language.

But on the third day, at breakfast, Fran said, "Mathieu! Do you happen to know where these movie theaters are on the Left Bank that are putting on modernistic films?"

Mathieu stared.

"Pardon, Madame!" he said.

"Theaters—modern films—cinemas—oh, whatever you call 'em——!"

Fran slipped across the room to the bottle-green-and-golden dictionary on the flimsy desk.

"*Le—cinématograph moderne—est-ce qu'il y a*— I mean, are there any on the Left Bank?"

Mathieu looked at her with a most superior intelligence:

"Oh yez. You ask the concierge. He tell you! De veal steak iss fine today—just like Tchicago!"

When Mathieu had gone out to fetch the veal steak that was so fine today, Fran murmured, "I have made a great discovery! Aside from food-vocabulary, the Mathieus speak English no better than we do French! We're not so bad, my beloved!"

"You're not, of course. But I'm terrible!"

"Don't be silly! Yesterday you said *'A quelle heure est le Louvre fermé?'*—as a matter of fact, I think you did say *'est le Louvre closed?'* but the taxi-driver understood it perfectly, and I know you'd learn to speak a really splendid French, if you gave your mind to it."

"Honestly?" said Sam.

Chapter 14

THEY had ventured to the Left Bank for an evening at the Café Novgorod, the favorite of the more arty Americans. The café seemed to Sam less related to Paris than he was himself. . . . The French street: bourgeois fathers strolling with their brood; dark-eyed men jesting with girls in red kerchiefs; an old woman crawling along muttering to herself. But here, in the Café Novgorod, under the awning, a bumble of American voices:

"——get a little Citroen and tour Normandy——"

"——a complete meal for six francs, with lovely roast beef, though prob'ly it's horse-meat——"

"——that Elliot Paul is the only really distinguished essayist in——"

The young Americans there were so disposive. Sam heard them, at the tables about, dispose of Californian scenery, the institution of marriage, Whistler, corn fritters, President Wilson, cement roads, and the use of catsup. He became gloomier than at the thickest dinner-party in London, and he was thinking of bed when his gloom was interrupted by a voice like that of a female impersonator.

Lycurgus Watts (only he liked to be called "Jerry") was standing by their table and beaming in fondest affection.

Lycurgus (or Jerry) Watts was the professional amateur of Zenith. He was a large-faced man, as wide as a truck-driver, but he had a whiney, caressing voice, and he giggled at his own jokes, which were incessant and very bad. He was reputed to be fifty years old, and he looked anywhere from twenty-five to a hundred. He came from what was known as a "good family"—anyway, it was a wealthy family. His father had died when he was ten. He had lived and traveled with his widowed mother till he was forty-three, and he told every one that she was the noblest character he had ever known. Compared with her, all young women were such hussies that he would never marry. But he made up for it by a number of highly confidential friendships with men whose voices and matriolatry were like his own.

He wandered much, in Europe and Asia, but always he came back to the flat he kept in Zenith. It was so filled with his collections of lace, wrought-iron keys, and editions of Oscar Wilde, that there was scarcely room for his genuine Russian samovar and his bed with a cover of black and gold. He spent much of his time in Zenith in denouncing the tradesmen who manufactured soap and motor cars instead of collecting lace, and in checking up his profitable holdings in soap and motor cars. He got up the first exhibition of Slavic embroidery in the state, he read poetry aloud, and he talked a good deal about starting a new magazine of the new poetry and the new prose.

Whenever Sam had met Jerry Watts in Zenith, he had grumbled to Fran on the way home, "Why the devil did they invite that white grub? He makes me sick!" But as Jerry had invariably told Fran in three languages that she was the loveliest lady in town, she turned on Sam with "Oh, of course! Just because Jerry is really cultured, because he has brains enough to cultivate a fine leisure instead of grubbing in a dirty office, all you noble captains of industry look down on him as a dray-horse might look down on a fine race-horse!"

She even had Jerry for dinner. In fact, Sam had been led to hate Jerry with considerable heartiness.

But in the oppressive strangeness of Paris, any familiar face would have been exciting, and for five minutes Sam believed that he was glad to see Jerry Watts.

Jerry sat down; he giggled, "I *told* you you'd escape from that dreadful Middlewest, Fran, and come to a civilized country! Don't you just *adore* the Novgorod? Such darling roughnecks! Such delectable poses! Oh, my *dears*, I heard the best one here last evening! Tommy Troizka—he's the dearest Finn boy, and a great water-colorist, speaks English perfectly, oh, too simply divinely, and Tommy said, 'The trouble with your American intelligentsia is that most of you don't know how to *tell a gent* when you see him!' Isn't that precious! Oh, you'll adore being here in Paris! Don't you, Dodsworth?"

"Yeah, great town," said Sam.

"Have you been to the Lion d'Or yet?"

"Oh yes," said Fran.

"Have you tried the *rognons de la maison* at Emil's?"

"Yes."

"And of course you've been to the L'Ane Rouge and the Rendezvous des Mariniers?"

"Yes."

"And the Chemise Sale?"

"No, I don't think——"

"You haven't been to the Chemise Sale? Oh, Fran! Why, good Heavens! Don't you realize that the Chemise Sale is the duckiest little restaurant in Paris?"

Fran was annoyed.

It was not that she was given to ducky little restaurants or any other phase of synthetic Bohemianism, but that any other citizen of Zenith should know more about Paris than she was intolerable. She glared slightly when Jerry seized his advantage and laid down the rule that it was vulgar to go to Versailles but that they *must* see the exhibition of the Prismatic Internists. Sam felt patiently that she would presently despatch Jerry. Yet she looked pleased when Jerry piped:

"Have you met Endicott Everett Atkins? He's coming to tea at my place next Saturday afternoon—I have such a dusky little studio on the Rue des Petits-Champs. You and your husband must come."

"We'll be glad to," said Fran, to Sam's considerable discouragement.

Sam grunted, in the taxicab, "What do you want to go there for? Who's Endicott Everett Atkins? Sounds like a business college yell. He another lily like Watts?"

"No, he really is somebody. Dean of the American literary colony here—writes about French novelists and Austrian peasant furniture and Correggio and English hunting and Heaven knows what all."

"But I don't have to learn about peasant furniture, too, do I?" Sam said hopefully.

Mr. Endicott Everett Atkins was reputed to resemble Henry James. He had the massive and rather bald head, the portly dignity. He spoke—and he spoke a good deal—in a measured voice, and he had a small bright wife who was believed to adore him. He also was blessed, and furthered in his critical pursuits, by having no sense of humor whatever, though he knew so many sparkling anecdotes that one did not suspect it for hours. He came from South Biddlesford, Connecticut, and his father, to whom he often referred as "that dear and so classical a bibliophile," had been an excellent hat-manufacturer. He owned a real house in Paris, with an upstairs and down, and he spoke chummily of the Ambassador.

He did actually, against any expectation, keep his promise and appear at the tea in Mr. Jerry Watts's studio—an apartment with a scarlet-fever of Spanish altar-cloths, embroidered copes, and Mandarin robes. The only apparent reason for calling it a studio was that it had a north window, and that Mr. Jerry Watts naturally would call it a studio. "I just can't make love except by a north light!" he nickered to Fran.

On the refectory table was a small teapot, a small plate of limp cakes, and an enormous bowl of punch. After every one had had three glasses of the punch, the conversation became very agitated. There were massed about the table, screaming, some thirty people. Sam never remembered any of them, save Endicott Everett Atkins. The rest seemed to him as indistinguishable as separate mosquitoes in a swarm, and rather noisier. But there was nothing noisy about Mr. Endicott Everett Atkins. He had so developed poise, an appalling, reproving, Christian Science sort of poise, that Sam felt toward him as he once had toward the professor of Greek drama at Yale.

Mr. Atkins could purr at the thought of particularly pleasant and beautiful things—a Greek coin, a Javanese dancing girl, a check from his publisher—but in crowds he stood calm and expansive as an observation balloon in windless air. In the quietest corner of the apartment he held forth on the Italian Renaissance, the superiority of Parliament to Congress, the future of Anglo-Catholicism, the letters of Horace Walpole, and the perfection of anarchism as a theory—he had actually attended an anarchist meeting in Milan in 1890, as an ardent young traveler. You never remembered what he had said, but you felt that he had been tremendously sound, and you sighed, uneasily running your forefinger between collar and neck, "He has such a fund of knowledge——"

Mr. Atkins pounced on Fran, and if he did not also exactly pounce on Sam, he tolerated him. He took in Fran's shining hair, her freshness, her slim quickness. He brought her a cup of punch, bowing like Louis XIV. He won Sam by telling him of meeting Dr. Carl Benz, the father of the motor car, at Mannheim, back in 1885, and of seeing his first horseless carriage—it was, said Atkins, a wire-wheeled tricycle with a chain drive like a bicycle, a handle for steering, and under the seat a mass of machinery as wild-looking as a gutted alarm clock.

"Like to've seen it!" murmured Sam. "Happen to know what the horse-power was?"

Mr. Endicott Everett Atkins looked at him benevolently, his glossy baldness rose-hued in the red-shaded lamps. "It was three and a quarter," he said.

(It was not for sixty hours that, lying awake in the early morning, Sam realized that Atkins hadn't had the smallest notion what the horse-power of the Benz really was.)

With men, Mr. Endicott Everett Atkins rarely let down, but with slim and glistening women he came near to being human. He indicated to Fran that this was only a merry slumming prank of his to come to the studio of Mr. Lycurgus Watts—normally he moved only in the loftiest circles, among the loveliest ladies, the wittiest and bravest men, the rarest first editions, and he longed to introduce her to all of them.

She loved it.

He told her the delightful anecdote which he had heard from André Sorchon, who had it from E. V. Lucas, who had it from Henry James, who had it direct from Swinburne. He told her that her husband (Mr. Samuel Dodsworth) was extraordinarily like the late Duc de Malmaison, but that she was ever and ever so much nicer than the Duchesse. He told her that her ash-blond hair was astonishingly like that of Madame Zelie du Strom, the Swedish tragedienne who, Mr. Atkins agreed with himself, was greater than Bernhardt, Duse, and Modjeska put together——

Sam sat back, as so often he had sat back at directors' meetings, content to let others do the talking if he could do the plotting, and tried to make out the purposes of Mr. Endicott Everett Atkins.

"This fellow knows a lot. Well, at least he's read a lot. Well, if he hasn't read so much, he remembers all he has read. Here he's making love to Fran—telling her what a wonder she is—and she's lapping it up. Bless her! Let her have her fling—if the fling ain't any more dangerous than old Atkins! Wonder if I'll be as dry a bladder as he is in fifteen years? If I am, I'm going to retire to a log cabin and grow corn!"

"I really can't tell you," Mr. Endicott Everett Atkins was moaning at Fran, "how very, very much I admire your wisdom in coming to Europe in a really leisured pilgrimage. And I wonder if you realize you're doing a patriotic American duty—showing Europe that we have poised and exquisite creatures like yourself, if you'll permit the familiarity from an aged bookworm, as well as these Yankee tourist women—oh, these dreadful bouncing females, with their shrill voices, their ignorance of all gentle usages—and the way they frequent horrible American bars and dance in dreadful places——"

"Why shouldn't the 'Yankee tourist women' go and dance in Montmartre, if they enjoy it?" Sam meditated. "Does Atkins think the pretty buyer from Detroit comes here to please him? The American highbrow abroad is just like the Puritan back home—the Puritan says that if you drink anything at all, he'll disapprove of you, and the expatriate here says that if you drink anything but Château Haut Something-or-other at just the right temperature, *he'll* disapprove of you and——

"I will get back for my class reunion this June! Thirtieth reunion! Am I that old?

"Think of seeing Tub again and Poodle Smith and Bill Dyers and—— Now what the devil was the name of that big fellow with the red hair that played center? Florey—Floreau—Flaherty? Corking fellow!

"And Atkins goes on. I'd better listen and get what wisdom I can, because I think our 'really leisured pilgrimage to Europe' is drawing to a close!"

"——though I'm afraid, Mrs. Dodsworth, that you'll find our house too dreadfully bookish. Beautiful people like you are superior to books. You ought never to read anything—you ought only to live. You ought to exist imperishably on some Grecian isle amid the wine-dark sea, dancing in the sunshine. But if your husband and you will delight us by coming to lunch next Sunday, at least I may be able to show you one or two intaglios——"

At lunch at the Atkinses', on Sunday, Sam met his first Princess, Madame Maravigliarsi. Not that he knew at first that she was a Princess; in fact he supposed her to be a nice, rather shabby little Poor Relation. But Atkins revealed her princessity in a dramatic aside, and Sam was as impressed as any other proper democratic American.

And she was, Fran carefully ascertained, quite a good, high-ranking Princess, and only one-quarter American.

Sam sat next to her, at lunch in the tall cool room with its Venetian glass and the serene bust of Plato; and while he made a respectable show of not being humble, the boy who had read "Ivanhoe" and Shakespeare and "The Idylls of the King" was gloating, "I'm sitting next to a Princess!"

The Princess prattled of what she had said to Mussolini and what His Eminence the Secretary to the Pope had said to her, and for ten minutes Sam desired to know the renowned of the world. He remembered—what was it?—something that Fran had said to the effect that with his tall dignity and his experience as executive, he might become an ambassador, and be intimate with ever so many people who had said things to Mussolini and had Eminences say things to them——

But he wearied of Princess Maravigliarsi's chatter. It was *so* important that he see Trouville and Biarritz; it was *so* important that he properly hate the Bolsheviks; *so* important that he go to tea at Lady Ingraham's.

He dreaded these new obligations.

"So far as I can see," he brooded, "travel consists in perpetually finding new things that you have to do if you're going to be respectable."

Fran was polite to the Princess Maravigliarsi with a cold politeness which indicated to Sam that she was impressed. But it was to a certain Madame de Pénable that she gave most of her attention. Madame de Pénable was a red-headed, white-skinned, rather plump woman who seemed to specialize on knowing everybody of influence in every land. The Dodsworths never learned whether she was born in Poland, Nebraska, Africa, the Dordogne, or Hungary. They never learned just who Monsieur de Pénable was, if there ever had been a Monsieur de Pénable. They never learned whether she was in trade, living on alimony, or possessed of a family income. Sam suspected that she was an international spy. She was a pleasant woman, and very clever. She talked about herself constantly, and never told anything whatever about herself. She spoke English, French, German, and Italian perfectly, and at restaurants, with waiters as mysterious as herself, she went off into tongues which might have been Russian, Lancashire, or Modern Greek.

Apparently she fancied the Dodsworths as additions to her circle. Sam heard her inviting Fran and himself to lunch at the Ermitage.

"Fran is launched," he sighed. "At last we'll be gay and cosmopolitan! I wonder how much I'll be able to win from Tub at poker, now that I've had my style of playing perfected by European culture?"

Chapter 15

THEY ceased to be children exploring together, rather happy in their loneliness. They were dominated by Endicott Everett Atkins and Madame de Pénable and their smart groups. Madame de Pénable saw that because in her fresh, keen, naïve way Fran was different from European women, she was the more novel and attractive to the innumerable European men whom the De Pénable always had about her, running her errands, drinking her excellent Moselle, listening to her scandalous anecdotes; she saw also that Sam was likely to keep Fran from snatching such of these men as the De Pénable wanted to hold for her own.

She cultivated the Dodsworths enthusiastically.

Fran's life became hectic as life can be only in Paris: a ride in the Bois, lunch, shopping, tea, bridge, cocktails, dressing, dinner, the theater, dancing at such icily glittering haunts as the Jardin de Ma Soeur, cold cream and exhausted sleep. In between she managed to fit three hours a week of French lessons.

And Sam—he came along.

He enjoyed it, for a month. There was color to this life, and motion, like waves under the gray cliff that was Paris. There were pretty women who took him seriously, as one of the financial captains of America (he suspected, with an inward chuckle, that they thought him far richer than he was). There were gorgeous clothes and marvelous food. He learned something of the art of wine. He had long known that Rhine wines should be cold; that Burgundy is better than that womanish drink, champagne. But now, meeting people who took wine as seriously as he had motor engines, and listening to their reverent discussion of it, he learned the epochal differences between the several Burgundies—between Nuits St. Georges and Nuits-Prémeaux; the cataclysmic differences between vintages—between the lordly crop of 1911 and the mediocre product of 1912. He learned that it was a crime to dull the palate with a cocktail before a sacred bottle of good wine, and that it was bloody treason to heat Burgundy suddenly by plunging it in the hot water, instead of decently decanting it hours before drinking and letting—it—come—*slowly* (the connoisseurs breathed)—to—room—temperature.

It interested him, this cyclone of new excitements. And Fran was, for the first time in years, altogether satisfied.

Between them, Atkins and the De Pénable knew a dozen sets. Atkins fished for portrait painters, French critics, American ladies from the choicer portions of Back Bay and Rittenhouse Square, English poets who pretended to be biologists and English biologists who were flattered at being taken for poets. Madame de Pénable went in for assorted titles—a judicious mixture of Italians, French, Roumanian, Georgian, Hungarian—and she always had one sound, carefully selected freak: a delightfully droll pickpocket or a minor Arctic explorer.

The man out of all this boiling whom Fran most liked was an Italian aviator, Captain Gioserro, a bright-eyed, very smiling man, ten years younger than herself. He was dazzled by her; bewildered by her quick speech. He said that she was the Norse goddess, Freya, that she was an Easter lily, and a number of other highly elegant things, and she liked it and went riding with him.

Sam hoped that there was not going to be another Lockert explosion. He believed her when she insisted that she considered Gioserro a "mere boy." But alone, brooding, he was worried. He wondered if her rigid distaste for flirtation had existed only because she had not found American men attractive. She seemed softer, more relaxed, more lovely, and considerably less dependent on him. She was surrounded by amusing men, and warmed by their extravagant compliments. His conscious self declared that she couldn't possibly be tempted, but his sub-conscious self was alarmed.

And presently he became weary of their insane dashing. The voices—the voices that never ceased—the high thin laughter—the reference to Mike This and Jacques That and the amours of Lady the Other—the duty of being seen at every exhibition, every select tea, every concert——

Fran had sharply dropped for him the people they knew, all the low adventurers who sat about bars, the couples from Zenith whom they had met at the hotel, even the unfortunate Jerry Lycurgus Watts, once Jerry had served his biological purpose by producing Endicott Everett Atkins. And so Sam became exceedingly hungry for a good wholesome lowness; for poker, shirt-sleeves, sauerkraut, obscene vaudeville, and conversation about motor sales and Zenith politics.

Fran was having her portrait painted, glossily and very expensively, by a Belgian whose manner of serving tea and commenting on new frocks had enabled him to capture a number of rich American women. With him, painting was a social function; while he worked he was surrounded by the most decorative human parrots and peacocks, shrieking their admiration of his craftsmanship, which was excellent. He managed to add the muzziness of a Laurencin to the photography of a Sargent; he made his women look rich, and all alike.

Madame de Pénable had insisted on Fran's going to this good man, and when Sam learned that the De Pénable had also insisted on a number of other women benefiting by the Belgian's gifts, he wondered if possibly the lively De Pénable might not have some interest in the business. But Fran was magnificently offended when he made the hint.

"It may interest you to *know*," she raged, "that M. Saurier wanted to paint me for *nothing*, because he said I was the most perfect type of American beauty he had ever seen! But of course I couldn't let him do that. Of course you wouldn't have noticed that certain Europeans think I'm rather good-looking——"

"Don't," said Sam mildly, "be a damn' fool, my darling."

He went once to the orgy of her sittings; and he, the rock of ages in business crises, wanted to scream as he heard Madame de Pénable, and six women, who spoke all languages, except French, with a French accent, lilting that "le Maître" was at least a genius, and that he was particularly historic in the matter of "flesh tints."

He did not go again.

He came to like the affabilities of Endicott Everett Atkins even less than the expensive sunset-hues of Madame de Pénable. The De Pénable was surrounded by gay people. "Not so bad," Sam considered, "to have a cocktail with a pretty girl that tells you that you look like a cross between Sir Lancelot and Jack Dempsey." But Mr. Atkins had not yet heard of cocktails. And Mr. Atkins held forth. He had been everywhere, and he could make everywhere sound uninteresting. He would look at you earnestly and demand to know whether you had made a pilgrimage to Viterbo to see the Etruscan remains, and he made it sound so nagging a duty that Sam vowed he would never let himself be caught near Viterbo; he was so severe about American music that he made Sam long for the jazz which he had always rather irritably detested.

Toward the seven deadly arts Sam had had the inarticulate reverence which an Irish policeman might have toward a shrine of the Virgin on his beat . . . that little light seen at three of a winter's morning. They were to him romance, escape, and he was irritated when they were presented to him as a preacher presents the virtues of sobriety and chastity. He hadn't the training to lose himself in Bach or Goethe; but in Chesterton, in Schubert, in a Corot, he had been able to forget motors and Alec Kynance, and always he had chuckled over the gay anarchy of Mencken. But with rising stubbornness he asserted that if he had to take the arts as something in which he must pass an examination, he would chuck them altogether and be content with poker.

As Fran had both a sitting and a fitting that afternoon (to Sam they seemed much the same, except that Fran's costumer was more virile and less grasping than her portrait-painter) he had a whole afternoon off.

Secretly, a little guiltily, he reflected, "I've done Notre Dame right, with Fran. Now I think I'll sneak off and see if I really like it! You can't tell! I might! Even though old Atkins says I have to. . . . Hell! I wish I were back in Zenith!"

Solemnly, his Baedeker shamelessly in hand, Sam lumbered out of his taxi before Notre Dame, and quite as shamelessly slipped off across the river to a café facing the cathedral. There, quietly, without Fran's quivers of appreciation, he began to feel at home.

He admitted the cathedral's gray domination. There was strength there; strength and endurance and wisdom. The flying buttresses soared like wings. The whole cathedral expanded before his eyes; the work of human hands seemed to tower larger than the sky. He felt, dimly and disconnectedly, that he too had done things with his hands; that the motor car was no contemptible creation; that he was nearer to the forgotten, the anonymous and merry and vulgar artisans who had created this somber epic of stone, than was any Endicott Everett Atkins with his Adam's apple ecclesiastically throbbing as he uttered pomposities about "the transition in Gothic motifs." How those cheery artisans would have laughed—drinking their wine, perhaps, at this same corner!

He read in the Book of Words. (Did Ruskin and Cellini and Dante actually travel without Baedekers? How strange it seemed, and new!)

"Notre Dame . . . in early Roman times the site was occupied by a temple of Jupiter. The present church was begun in 1163."

He laid the book down and drifted into the pleasantest dreaming he had known for all the fatal weeks since he had been adopted by the Right People.

A temple of Jupiter. Priests in white robes. Sacrificial bulls with patient wondering eyes, tossing their thick garlanded heads. Chariots pounding across the square—right across the river there! The past, which had been to the young Sam Dodsworth playing football, to the man harassed by building motor cars, only a flamboyant myth, was suddenly authentic, and he walked with Julius Caesar, who in that moment ceased to be merely a drawing in a school-book, a ventriloquist's dummy talking the kind of overgrammatical rot that only school-masters could understand, and became a living, lively, talkative acquaintance, having a drink here with Sam, and extraordinarily resembling Roosevelt off-stage.

Heavy with meditation, happy in being unobserved and not having to act up to the splendors of Fran, he paid his bill and ambled across the bridge and into the cathedral.

It bothered him, as always, that there were no prim and cushioned pews such as he knew in Protestant churches in America; it made the cathedral seem bare and a little unfriendly; but beside a vast pillar, eternal as mountains or the sea, he found a chair, tipped a verger, forgot his irritation with people who buzzed up and wanted to guide him, and lost himself in impenetrable thoughts.

He roused himself to read, patiently, in Baedeker: "Geoffrey Plantagenet, son of Henry II of England, was buried beneath the high altar in 1186. In 1430 Henry VI of England was crowned king of France and in 1560 Mary Stuart (afterward Mary Queen of Scots) was crowned as queen-consort of Francis II. The coronation of Napoleon I and Josephine de Beauharnais by Pope Pius VII (1804) . . . was celebrated here with great ceremony."

(And in Saurier's studio brassy women were chattering about the races!)

Plantagenet! Rearing lions on scarlet banners edged with bullion. Mary Stuart and her proud little head. Napoleon himself—here, where Sam Dodsworth was sitting.

"Humph!" he said.

He stared at the Rose Window, but he was seeing what it meant, not what it said. He saw life as something greater and more exciting than food and a little sleep. He felt that he was no longer merely a pedler of motor cars; he felt that he could adventure into this Past about him—and possibly adventure into the far more elusive Present. He saw, unhappily, that the Atkins and De Pénable existence into which Fran had led him was not the realization of the "great life" for which he had yearned, but its very negation—the bustle, the little snobberies, the cheap little titles, the cheap little patronage of "art."

"I'm going to get out of this town and do something—— Something exciting. And I'll make her go with me! I've been too weak with her," he said weakly.

His longing for low and intelligent company could not be denied. He went to the New York Bar. Through the correspondent of a New York newspaper whom he had known as a reporter in Zenith, Sam had met a dozen journalists there, and he felt at home with them. They did not heap on him the slightly patronizing compliments which he had from the women in Madame de Pénable's den of celebrities. He was stimulated by what was to the journalists only commonplace shop-talk: how Trotsky really got along with Stalin—what Briand had said to Sir Austen Chamberlain—what was the "low-down" on the international battle of oil.

This afternoon he met Ross Ireland.

Sam had heard of Ireland, roving foreign correspondent of the Quackenbos Feature Syndicate, as one of the best fellows among the American journalists. The former Zenith reporter introduced Sam to him. Ross Ireland was a man of forty, as large as Sam, and in his over-sized rimless spectacles he looked like a surgeon.

"Pleased to meet you, Mr. Dodsworth," he said, and his voice still had all the innocence of Iowa. "Staying over here long?"

"Well, yes—some months."

"This your first trip across?"

"Yes."

"Say, I've just been driving one of your Revelation cars in the jungle in India. Great performance, even in rough going——"

"India?"

"Yes, just back. Real Kipling country. Oh, I don't know as I saw any Mowglis gassing with tigers and sixteen-foot snakes, and I heard more about jute and indigo than I did about Mrs. Hauksbees, but it certainly knocks your eye out! That big temple at Tanjore—tower eleven stories high, all carved. And the life there—everything different—*smells* different (and sometimes not so good!)—and the people still in masquerade costumes, and queer curry kind of grub, and Eurasian shops where the Babus will tell you grand lies—every one good for a mail-story. You ought to get out there, if you can take the time. And then beyond India, Burma—take a river-boat—regular floating market-place, with natives in funny turbans squatting all over the decks—go up the Irrawaddy to Mandalay and on to Bhamo. Or you can get steamers at Rangoon for Penang and Sandoway and Akyab and Chittagong and all kinds of fancy places."

(Rangoon! Akyab! Chittagong!)

"And then around to Java and China and Japan, and home by way of California."

"I'd like to do it," said Sam. "Paris is a lovely city, but——"

"Oh, Paris! Paris is nothing but a post-graduate course in Broadway."

"Looks good to me," said the ex-Zenith-newspaperman.

"It would! Paris is a town for Americans that can't stand

work," said Ross Ireland. "I'm keen to see America; tickled to death I'm going back in June. I've been away three years—first time I've ever been away. I'm homesick as the devil. But I like my America straight. I don't want it in the form of a lot of expatriates sitting around Paris cafés. And when I want to travel, I want to *travel*! Say, you land in Bangkok, with that big gold temple rising over the town, and the boat-men singing in—whatever it is that they *do* sing in—or you go to Moscow and see the moujiks in felt boots and sheepskin coats, with the church spires absolutely like white and gold lace-work against the sky—— Say, that's travel!"

Yes. That's the stuff! Sam was going to travel like that. He'd go—— Oh, to Constantinople, back through Italy or Austria, and home for his thirtieth class reunion—just time to do it now, if he hustled. Then Fran and he might start out again next autumn and see Egypt and Morocco—— Yes.

It is a favorite American Credo that "if the acting is good enough, you can enjoy a play in a language you don't understand as well as in English." Fran held to that credo. Sam urgently did not. He hated to sit through French plays, and when he returned to the hotel from the New York Bar and Ross Ireland—from the Irrawaddy River and Chittagong—he found Fran with tickets for "Le Singe qui Parle," a slightly bad temper, and the aviator Gioserro.

"You smell of whisky! Atrociously! Now please hurry and dress! Captain Gioserro and you and I are going to the theater. Now please hurry, can't you? I'll order the cocktails meanwhile. As you see, I'm all ready. After the theater, we'll meet Renée de Pénable and some other people and dance."

As he dressed, Sam fretted, "French play! Humph! I won't know which is the husband and which is the lover for at least the first two acts!"

If he slept at the play, he did it ever so modestly and retiringly, and he was unusually polite to Madame de Pénable. Fran was approving on their way home, and quite as easily as though they were back in Zenith, he asserted while they were undressing:

"Fran, I've got an idea that——"

"Just unfasten this snap on my shoulder-strap, would you mind? Thanks. You were so nice tonight. Much the best-looking man in the room!"

"That's——"

"And I'm so glad you've come to like Renée de Pénable. She's really a darling—so loyal. But, uh—— Sam, I do wish you hadn't brought up that question as to what right the French have in the Riff."

"But, my God, they talked about us in Haiti and Nicaragua first!"

"I know, but that's entirely different. This is an *ancient* question, and of course Renée was shocked, and so was that English woman, Mrs. What's-her-name. But it doesn't matter. I just thought I'd mention it."

And he'd thought he'd behaved so beautifully tonight!

"But," he went on heavily, becoming dimly irritated as he noted how little she heeded him while she brushed her hair, "I wanted to suggest that—— Look here, Fran, I've got kind of an idea. It's almost May, but we could get in a month or more on the Mediterranean and still have time to get home late in June, and then I could go to my class reunion—thirtieth——"

"Really? *Thirtieth?*"

"Oh, I'm not so old! But I mean: we haven't talked especially about when we would go home——"

"But I want to see a lot more of Europe. Oh, I haven't started!"

"Neither have I. I agree. But I just mean: there's several business things I ought to settle up at home, and there's this reunion, and I'd like to see Emily and her new home, and Brent——"

"But perhaps we could get them to come over here this summer. Would you mind handing me the cold cream that's in the bathroom—no—no—I think it's on the bureau—oh, thanks——"

"I thought we could go home for just a couple months, or maybe three, and then start out again. Say go West this time, and sail for China and Japan and round to Rangoon and India and so on."

"Yes, I'd like to do that sometime. . . . Oh, dear, how sleepy I am! . . . But not now, of course, now that we know nice people here."

"But that's just what I mean! I don't—— Oh, they're a lively bunch, and lots of 'em good families and so on, but I don't think they *are* nice."

"What do you mean?"

"I mean they're a bunch of wasters. All they do, Pénable and her whole gang, and Atkins's hangers-on aren't much better, all they do is just dance and chatter and show off their clothes. Their idea of a good time is just about that of a chorus-girl——"

Fran had been inattentive. She wasn't now. She snatched up a lace wrap, slapped it about her shoulders over her nightgown, and faced him, like a snarling white cat:

"Sam! Let's get this straight. I've felt you've been sulking, that you've been too afraid to——"

"Too polite!"

"——say what you thought. Well, I'm sick and tired of having to apologize, yes, to *apologize*, for the crime of having introduced you to some of the nicest and most amusing people in Paris, and for having backed you up when they were offended by your boorishness! Am I to understand that you regard Madame de Pénable and her whole *gang*, as you so elegantly call it, as simply rotters? May I point out to you that if I don't have quite so lively an appreciation of such nature's noblemen as Mr. A. B. Hurd——"

"Fran!"

"——yet possibly I may be a little better equipped to understand really smart, cosmopolitan people than you are! Kindly let me remind you that Renée de Pénable is the intimate friend of the most exclusive aristocracy of the *ancien régime* here——"

"But is she? And what of it?"

"Will you *kindly* stop sneering? You that are so fond of accusing *me* of sneering! And, my dear Samuel, you really don't do it so very well! Delicate irony isn't your long suit, my dear good man!"

"Damn it, I won't be talked to like a stable boy!"

"Then don't act like one! And if I may be permitted to go on and answer the charges which *you* brought up, not I—the whole subject is thoroughly distasteful to me—and oh, Sam, so vulgar, so beastly vulgar!" For a second she was dramatically mournful and hurt, but instantly she was a charging Cossack again: "But when you attack any one that's been as sweet to me as Renée, all I can say is—— Do you happen to realize that she is the dearest friend of the Duchesse de Quatrefleurs—she's promised to take me down to the Duchesse's château in Burgundy——"

"She's never done it!"

"As it *happens*, the Duchesse is ill, just at the moment! And your charming remark illustrates perfectly what I mean by your sneering! . . . Or, to take the example of Renée's friend, Mrs. Sittingwall. She's the widow of a very distinguished English general who was killed in the war——"

"He wasn't a general—he was a colonel—and now the woman is engaged to that old rip of a French stock-broker, Andillet."

"What of it? M. Andillet does dress too loudly, and he drives a car too fast, but he's a most amusing old dear, and he orders the best meal in Paris. And knows cabinet ministers—bankers—diplomats—everybody that's influential."

"Well, he looks to me like a crook. And what about the young gigolos that are always hanging around Mrs. Pénable?"

"I do think it's too gracious of you to take the word 'gigolo,' which I taught you in the first place——"

"You did not!"

"——and use it against me, my dear polylingual Sam! I suppose you are referring to boys like Gioserro and Billy Dawson. Yes, they're not at all like American business men, are they! They actually enjoy being charming to women, they enjoy sharing their leisure with women, they dance beautifully, they talk about something besides the stock-market——"

"Oh, they enjoy leisure, all right! Oh, now, Fran, I don't mean to be nasty about them, but you know they graft on women——"

"My dear man, Captain Gioserro (and he could call himself Count Gioserro, if he wanted to!) has a perfectly good family income, as his people have had before him, for generations——"

"Whoa now! Hold up! I question his having a very *good* family income. I notice that whenever he's with us, he always manages to let me pay. Not that I mind, but—— Why say, I've never seen him spend a cent except tonight, when he gave ten centimes to the fellow that opened the cab door. Now please listen, Fran, and don't go off into a tantrum. Don't you and Mrs. Pénable almost always pay the bills—for feeds, for taxis, for tips, for tickets—for Gioserro and young Dawson and most of these other slick young men that she has hanging around?"

"What of it? We can afford it. (The name, by the way, as I have remarked several hundred times before, is *Madame de Pénable*!) Or are you——" She became regally outraged and deliberate. "Are you perhaps hinting that because you so generously support me, you have the right to dictate on whom and for what I spend every cent? Do you desire me to give you a detailed account of my expenses, like an office boy? Then let me remind you—oh, this is *so* distasteful to me, but I must remind you that I have twenty thousand a year of my own, and now that I have a chance to be happy, with amusing people——"

She was sobbing. He caught her shoulders, and demanded, "Will you stop self-dramatizing yourself, my young lady? You know, and you know good and well, that I'm criticizing these young men for grafting just because I want to point out that they're no good; nothing but a lot of butterflies."

She broke away from his grasp and from her own sobs, and she was tart again: "Then thank God for the butterflies! I'm so tired of the worthy ants! . . . Sam, we might just as well have this out . . . if we're going on together."

The last five words chilled him. He was incredulous. She seemed a little to mean it, and she went on resolutely:

"Let's get it straight—just what we are up to; what we want. Now that we are meeting them, do you appreciate people with wit and elegance, or have you already had enough of them? Are you going to insist on returning to—oh, decent enough people, but people that can't see anything in life more amusing than poker and golf and motoring, that are afraid of suave manners, that think to be roughneck is to be strong? Does the accumulated civilization of two thousand years of Europe mean something to you or——"

"Oh, come off it, Fran! I'm not a roughneck and you know it. And I'm not uncivilized. And I like nice manners. But I like nice manners in people that are something more than amateur head-waiters and—— And after all, a rock takes a better polish than a sponge! These people, even Pénable herself, are parrots. What I'd like to meet—— Well, you take the colonial administrators and so on out in the British possessions. People that are doing something besides going night after night to these restaurants where your gigolos hang out——"

"Sam, if you don't mind, I think I've stood all the insults to my friends that I can for one night! You can think up a few new ones for tomorrow. I'm going to sleep. And now."

Whether she slept or not, she was rigidly silent, her face turned from him.

He expected her to be soft, fluttery, apologetic, in the morning. But, awakening at nine, she looked unrepentant as steel. He trundled out talk about breakfast, about the laundry, then he grumbled, "I don't know that I made myself quite clear last evening——"

"Oh yes, you did! Thoroughly! And I don't think I care to discuss it. Shall we not say anything more about it?" She was so brightly forgiving and superior that he was infuriated. "I'm going out now. I'll be back here about twelve. I'm lunching with Renée de Pénable, and if you think you can endure another hour with my degenerate friends, I should be glad to have you join us."

She vanished into the bathroom, to dress, and nothing more could he get out of her. When she was gone, he sat in bathrobe and slippers, over a second order of coffee.

She'd never before let a quarrel last overnight, at least when she'd been in the wrong——

Or was it possible that she had not been in the wrong in their controversy?

And (each second he was more confused) just what was the controversy about?

Anyway, she couldn't really have meant anything by her *"if we're going on together."* But suppose she had? Married couples did break up, quite incredibly, after years. Did he, in order to hold her, have to obey her, to associate forever with peacocks like this Mrs. Sittingwall and this fellow Andillet—

who was certainly a little more than friendly with the Pénable woman?

No, hanged if he would!

But if that meant losing Fran? Good God! Why, now that he had no work, he had nothing to absorb him save Fran, Emily, Brent, and three or four friends like Tub Pearson. Nor would he have anything new: he doubted if any other job could stimulate him like building up the Revelation Company; he doubted if he would make any new friends; he doubted if travel, pictures, music, hobbies, would ever be anything more than diversions interesting for an hour at a time. And of what he had left to keep life tolerable, Fran was first. She was the reason for everything! It was a second, a renewed Fran that he loved in his daughter Emily. His business and his making of money had been all for Fran—well no, maybe not all—hell! how hard it was to be honest about one's own self—maybe not all—fun putting business across, too—but she'd been the chief reason for it, anyway. As for his friends—— Why, he'd've chucked even Tub, if Fran hadn't liked him!

Fran! That just the other day had been a girl, cool and sparkling and strange, on the Canoe Club porch——

Good Lord, the Canoe Club had burned down twenty years ago.

In the radiant May of Paris, with the horse chestnuts out on the Champs Elysées, he sat huddled, feeling cold.

He went to lunch with Fran, Madame de Pénable, and Billy Dawson, a young American who was the airiest and most objectionable of the De Pénable's gentlemen valets. Sam was gravely polite. For two weeks he went with Fran and the De Pénable's court to all sorts of restaurants reeking with cigarette smoke and expensive perfume and smart scandal. Between times, he sneaked off, like a small boy going to the circus, to low places, looking particularly for the roving correspondent, Ross Ireland, and when he found that Ireland was sailing on June fifteenth on the *Aquitania*, which would arrive in time for Sam's thirtieth reunion at Yale, he anxiously engaged a stateroom for "self & wife." He liked Ross Ireland; he found particularly amusing, very like his own cultural pretenses, the fact that since Ireland was totally unable to learn any language save Iowan, he thundered that English was "enough to take anybody anywhere" and that "these fellows that talk about your having to know French if you're going to do political stuff in Europe are just trying to show what smart guys they are." And he liked the way in which Ireland mingled stories of Burmese temples with stories of Old Doc Jevons back t' home in Ioway.

This lowness Sam hid from his wife, and hid the fact that he was agonizingly bored by not having enough to do. Yet his devotion did not win her back. There was a courteous coolness about her, always.

When he had definitely to know about returning to America, she answered briskly:

"Yes, I've thought it over. I can understand that you need to go back. But I'm not going. I've practically promised Renée de Pénable to take a villa with her near Montreux for the summer. But I want you to go and see Tub and every one and thoroughly enjoy yourself, and then come back and join me in the late summer, and we'll think about the Orient."

But when she saw him off at the Gare St. Lazare she was suddenly softened.

She cried; she clung; she sobbed, "Oh, I didn't realize how much I'll miss you! Perhaps I'll come join you in Zenith. Do have the very best time you can, darling. Go camping with Tub—and give him my love—and tell him and Matey I hope they'll come over here—and try to get Em and Brent to come. Oh, my dear, forgive your idiotic, feather-brained wife! But let her have her foolish fling now! I did make a real home for you, didn't I? I shall again. Take care of yourself, my dear, and write me every day, and don't be angry with me—or do be angry, if it'll make you any happier! Bless you!"

And the first day out she sent him a radio: "You are a big brown bear and worth seventynine thousand gigolos even when their hair greased best butter stop did I remember to tell you that I adore you."

Chapter 16

WITH Ambrose Channel ahead of them, Sam Dodsworth and his friend Ross Ireland spent a considerable part of their time in the smoking-room of the *Aquitania* arguing with other passengers about the glories of America. Sam was appreciative enough, but Ross was eloquent, he was lyric, he was tremendous.

At praise of Paris, Cambodia, Oslo, Glasgow, or any other foreign pride, he snorted, "Look here, son, that's all apple-sauce, and I *know*! I've been hiking for three years. I've interviewed Count Bethlen and I've paddled up the Congo; I've done a swell piece about the Lena Gold Fields and I've driven three thousand miles in England. And believe me, I'm glad to be getting back to a real country, buddy!

"New York? Noisy? Say, why wouldn't it be noisy? It's got something going on! Believe me, they're remodeling all the old parts of Heaven after New York skyscrapers! Say, if we get past the perils of the deep and I have the chance to hang my hat up in Park Row again, you'll never get me farther away than an Elks' Convention at Atlantic City! And don't let anybody tell you that the Elks and the Rotarians and the National Civic Federation are any more grab-it-all than the English merchant, who hates our dollar-chasing so much that he wants to keep us from it by copping all the dollars there are to chase, or the elegant highbrow Frenchman who doesn't love the franc any more than he loves God. Why say, even about drinking—— I'll admit I like a sidewalk café better than I do a speak-easy, but once I round up my old bunch at Denny's and have a chance to stick my legs under the table with a lot of real home-baked he-Americans instead of these imitation-Frog Americans that loaf around abroad—— Boy!"

Sam discovered, dropping into Ross Ireland's stateroom, that Ross was guilty of secret intellectual practises. Except when, in morning clothes, he was interviewing Lord Chancellors and Generals Commanding, Ross felt that he must prove his sturdy independence by saying "Buddy," "Where d'you get that stuff," and "Oh, bologny." He was never, by any chance, "doing an analytical study"—at most he was "writing a little piece." He addressed English stewards as "Cap'n," he asked the Cockney smoking-room steward for his "check," and almost his only French expression was "viskey-soda." He announced, widely and loudly, that any newspaper-man who called himself a "journalist" was a Big Stiff, a Phoney High-brow, and an Imitation Limey. He said that any foreign correspondent who read history, went to concerts, or wore spats was "showing off."

But Sam discovered that Ross Ireland was guilty of reading vast and gloomy volumes of history; that he admired Conrad more than Conan Doyle; that he had a sneaking preference of chess to poker; and that he was irritably proud of having his evening clothes made in London.

That such a man, violently American yet not untraveled in distant coasts, should so rejoice at going back made Sam the more convinced about returning to his own. Of the vast and polished elegancies of the *Aquitania* he had little impression, none of the excitement about the steely resolution of ships which he had known on the *Ultima*, because all his excitement was focused on the blessed people he was going to see.

Tub Pearson——

He heard himself saying, "Well, you fat little runt! You horse-thief! Golly, I'm glad to see you!"

He stood forward on the promenade deck, fancying that his heart beat in rhythm with the rise and the fall of the prow, exulting as the ship slashed through the miles between him and home. He seemed a kindly but stolid figure there, a big man in a gray Burberry and a gray cap, a competent and unsentimental man. But he was boiling with sentiment. Once at night, when he saw the lights of a ship ahead, he pretended that they were the shore lights of Long Island, and he ardently imagined the dear familiarities—wide streets, clashing traffic, brick garages, the insolent splendor of skyscrapers and, toward the country, miles of white and green little houses where the sort of men he understood played games he understood, poker and bridge, and listened on the radio to the sort of humor and music that he understood. And before every other bungalow was a Revelation car.

"——and I'm going to *stay*!" he exulted.

All the way over, Ross Ireland and he had boasted to such passengers as had never seen America that they would not "be able to believe their eyes" when they steamed up North River. Ross chanted, "Greatest sight in the world—skyscrapers one after another—thirty, forty, fifty stories high, and beautiful—say! they make Cologne Cathedral look like a Methodist chapel and the Eiffel Tower look like an umbrella with the cover off!"

They both, indeed, made so many protestations about the sight of New York harbor that Sam began to wonder whether he really was going to be as thrilled as he was going to be thrilled. He remembered how, after the most conversational anticipation with Fran, he had been disappointed by his first sight of Notre Dame. It had seemed low and hulking—not half so impressive as the lath-and-plaster Notre Dame in the movie film. He managed to fret rather ardently. He hoped to be uplifted by New York as a young lover hopes to be enraptured by the sight of his lady.

They came through the Narrows, into New York harbor, early in the June morning. Sam was up at five, delighted by the friendly green of the lawn at Fort Hamilton, after the shifting sea. It was extraordinarily hot for early summer, a bit uncomfortable even on deck, and a fog hid the horizon. Sam was afraid that he was not to have his rediscovery of New York. After quarantine, as they trudged from Staten Island toward North River, he could see only anchored tramp steamers, and a huge water-beetle of a ferry boat, hoarse-voiced and insulting. Then the fog lifted, and he cried "My God!" High up shone the towers and spires of an enchanted city floating upon the mist, pyramids and domes glistening in the early sun, vast walls studded with golden windows, spellbound and incredible.

Ross Ireland, beside him, muttered "Gee!" and then, "Say, does it make you proud to be coming home to that?"

It is true that when they swaggered up North River, the debris of docks and warehouses and factories on the riverbank seemed rather littered. The thickening heat glared round them, and the river was greasy with swirls of fantastically colored oil films. But as they were cumbersomely warped into the dock, as Sam heard the good American shouts from the dark hedge of people waiting on the pier; "Attaboy!" and "Where'd you get the monocle?" and "How'd you leave Mary?" and "Oh, come on—have a heart!—sneak me *one* bottle ashore!"—he muttered over and over, "It's kind of nice to be home!"

Then there were the customs.

Not that the inspectors were so impolite as is fabled, but it is irritating to be suspected of smuggling liquor, particularly when, like Sam, you are smuggling liquor. He had a quart of pre-war Scotch among the suits in a wardrobe trunk, and the inspector found it, immediately.

"What's this? What d'you call this?"

"Why! It looks like a bottle!" said Sam, affably. "I can't imagine how it got there! Let me present it to you."

And they fined him five dollars. But what was worse was that being destitute of liquor caused in Sam a most indignant thirst—Sam Dodsworth, who had never in his life taken a drink before noon, except once after a certain football game in New Haven. He *had* to have——

The taxi-driver—Sam came to him after hours of paying customs-fees, of getting necessitous porters, in a high state of boredom, to trundle his luggage along the immensity of cement floor and through to freedom, of seeing it shot perilously down the most efficient and disconcerting moving belt, and of having it and himself thrown gasping into the lions' den of New York traffic—the taxi-driver gave Sam his first welcome to America.

"Wherejuh wanna go?" he growled.

It shocked Sam to find how jarred he was by this demonstration of democracy. Like most Americans in Paris, he had been insisting that all French taxi-drivers were bandits, but now they seemed to him like playful and cuddling children.

It was achingly hot in the side streets leading from the piers, and appallingly dirty. In front of warehouses and mean brick houses turned into tenements were flying newspapers, piles of bottles and rags and manure. Gritty clouds of ashes blew from open garbage cans, and tangled with the heat was New York's summertime stench of rotten bananas, unwashed laundry, ancient bedding, and wet pavements. In front of the taxicab, making Sam's heart stop with fear, darted ragged small boys (quite cheerful, and illogically healthy); and on the flimsy iron balconies of fire-escapes sat mothers with hair dragging across their eyes, nursing babies who in between sups wailed against the unjust heat. It was, Sam felt, a city nervous as a thwarted woman. (Sam still believed in male strength and female weakness.) It seemed so masculine in its stalwart buildings, but there was nothing masculine in its heat-shocked, clamor-maddened nerves. The traffic policemen raged at Sam's taxi-driver, the taxi-driver cursed all the truck-drivers, and, above the roaring of their engines, the truck-drivers cursed everybody on the street.

Ninth Avenue was insane with the banging of the Elevated; Eighth Avenue was a frontier camp of little shops; Seventh Avenue was a bedlam of traffic between loft buildings with enormous signs—"Löwenstein & Putski, Garments for Little Gents," and "The Gay Life Brassière, Rothweiser and Gitz"; Sixth Avenue combined the roar of Ninth with the nastiness of Eighth and the charging traffic of Seventh; and when in relief Sam saw the stateliness of Fifth Avenue, there was an inhuman mass of shiny cars from curb to curb.

The Sam Dodsworth who considered himself tireless was exhausted when he crawled into the cool refuge of his hotel. He sat by the window in his room, looking at the sullen stretch of the lofty office-building opposite, and longed for a drink.

"Conservatively, I'd give twenty-five dollars right now for the bottle of Scotch that the customs man took away from me. . . . Oh, Lord! . . . I don't like New York so well, in weather like this. I'll be glad to get out into the country. That's the real America. . . . I hope it will be! . . . I can see where I'm not going to complain about having too much leisure, the way I did in Paris! And I want that drink!"

It did not improve his opinion of Prohibition—it made the whole business seem the more imbecile and annoying and hypocritical—that after a telephone call, within half an hour he had a case of whisky in his room, and that he was taking a drink far earlier in the day than he would ever have done in Paris.

He had many people to see in New York before he went to New Haven for his class reunion. But he telephoned to no one—with the exception of the bootlegger. He had only the energy to sit by the window, getting what breeze there was, trying to ignore the ceaseless menace of the city roar, feeling more homeless than in Europe, trying to compose a lively cable to Fran and to get Brent, in New Haven, on the telephone.

He had not cabled Brent his date of sailing. "Boy's probably tied up with a lot of exams and things; when I land in New York I'll find out by 'phone when it's convenient for him to come down to New York." Brent was not to be found now by telephone. Sam sent him a telegram, and that was quite all that he felt like doing. He rested till one, till half-past. He had a small lunch, in his room, and the joy of having proper American sugar corn almost revived him, but afterward he sat by the window again till three, brooding. Lassitude bound him like a vast cobweb.

What was he doing here in New York? What was he doing anywhere? What reason had he for living? He was not necessary to Fran in Paris. And the motor-car industry seemed to be spinning on quite cheerily without him.

He faced his discovery—the incident had happened at his entrance to the hotel, but he had not admitted it to his consciousness till now. Alighting from his taxicab he had seen the new model Revelation car, as produced by the Unit Automotive Company, at three hundred dollars less than Sam's former price. He had wanted to hate it, to declare that it was tinny and wretched, but he had had to admit that it was a marvel of trimness, with the body swung lower, the windshield more raking. He felt antiquated. The U.A.C. had created this new model in six months; with his own organization he could not have produced it in less than a year. And he would have held it till the autumn motor shows and brought it out pompously, as though he were a priest grudgingly letting the laity behold his mysteries. Were the U.A.C. making light of seasons and announcement-dates—just tossing off new models as though they were cans of corn?

It came to him that he had not known when the new Revelation would be out. For the first months of his absence he had heard often from Alec Kynance, received all the gossip, with many invitations to return. He had heard but little the past three months. Was he out of it—perhaps forever?

He had come back to America feeling that the world of motors longed for him; he felt, this hot confused afternoon, that no one cared. . . . It was true that, to keep his time free, he had told no one he was arriving, but confound it, they might have found out somehow——

Come to think of it, not one of the reporters who had boarded the *Aquitania* and hunted down incoming celebrities—the Polish tennis champion, the famous radio-announcer who had been perfecting his art in Berlin, the latest New York–Paris divorcée—had paid attention to him. Yet when he had gone abroad, they had interviewed him as a Representative American Business Man——

He was frightened by his drop into insignificance.

At half-past three he was startled and cheered by a telephone-call:

"Hello? Dodsworth? This is Ross Ireland. Say, I'm in the same hotel. Doing anything? Mind if I run up for a minute?"

Ireland burst in, red, collar wilted, panting.

"Say, Dodsworth, am I crazy? Do I look crazy?"

"No, you look hot."

"Hot? Hell! I've been hot in Rangoon. But I sat back in a nice carriage, in my pretty little white suit and my sun helmet, and took it easy. I didn't feel as though I'd been in two hundred and twenty-seven train collisions, one right after another. Do you know what I've found out? I hate this damn' town! It's the dirtiest, noisiest, craziest hole I was ever in! I hate it—me that's been going up and down the face of the earth for the last three years, shooting my face off and telling everybody what a swell capital New York is.

"What you got to drink? Oh, God, only whisky? Well, let's have a look at it.

"Well, this morning I didn't even stop to unpack. I was going to see the dear old home town—the dear old neighbors, by heck, down on Park Row. I got down to the Quackenbos office, and the office boy hadn't ever heard my name—I've only been sending in three columns a week, signed, for three years! But he found a stenographer who thought she'd heard of me, and they actually let me in to see the old man—mind you, to get in to see him was sixteen times harder than it would be to see King George at Buckingham Palace, and when I did get in, there he was with his feet in a desk drawer reading the jokes in the *New Yorker*. Well, he was all right. He jumped up and told me I was the white-haired boy, and the sight of me'd just about saved him from typhoid, and we talked a whole half hour, and then made a date to finish up our business at lunch, tomorrow! Oh no, he didn't have one minute till then! Tonight—God, no, he had to help open up a new roof garden.

"Oh, I've been the boiled mutton-head! I've been going around Europe and Asia telling the heathen that the reason we hustle so in New York is because we get so much done. I never discovered till today that we do all this hustling, all this jamming in subways, all this elbowing into elevators, to keep ourselves occupied and keep from getting anything done! Say, I'll bet I accomplished more honest-to-God work in Vienna in three hours than I will here in three days! Those Austrian hicks don't have any bright office boys or filing-systems to prevent them from talking business. So they go home for two hours' lunch. Poor devils! No chance to ride on the subway! And only cafés to sit around in, instead of night clubs. Awful life!

"Well, when I'd got this whole half hour in with the boss—he took up most of it telling a swell new smutty story he'd just heard—one I used to tell back in Ioway in 1900—I drifted over to the *Chronicle* to see the bunch I used to work with. . . . I was city editor there once! . . . Half of the bunch were *aus*. Gone into politics, I guess. . . . The other half were glad to see me, so far as I could figure out, but they'd gone and got married or learned to play bridge or taken to teaching Sunday School or some immoral practise like that, and by golly not one of 'em could I get for dinner and a show tonight. By the way, you don't happen to be free for tonight, Dodsworth, do you? Grand! Tickled to death!

"Well, I went out to lunch with one of the fellows on the Sunday edition. He suggested some whisky, but I wanted something cool. He said he knew a place where we could get some real genuine Italian Chianti—and say, he called it 'genuwine Ytalian' too. As a joke. I believe he taught English in Harvard for a year. But being a hard-boiled newspaperman, of course he had to be a roughneck, to show he wasn't pedantic. . . . Like me, I guess. I've been pulling that same lowbrow pose myself.

"But anyway: we look up this genuwine Ytalian dump—I guess, from the smell, they used it as a laundry till it got too dirty—and the Wop brought on a bottle of something that was just about as much like Chianti as I'm like a lily of the valley. Honestly, Sam, it tasted like vinegar that'd been used on beets just once too often.

"And then—— Oh, I suppose, being just back after my first long hike, I felt I had a Chautauqua message for Young America—I suppose I felt I was a Peary bringing home the Pole under my arm. I tried to tell this chap how much I knew about Burma, and how chummy I was with Lord Beaverbrook, and all the news about the land problem in Upper Silesia, and was he interested? Say, he was about as much interested as I'd be in a chatty account of the advancement of Christian Science in Liberia! But he had a lot of important news for me. Golly! Bill Smith'd had a raise of twenty bucks a week! Pete Brown is going to edit the hockey gossip, instead of Mike Magoon! The Edam Restaurant is going to have a new jazz orchestra! The Fishback Portable Typewriter has gone up five dollars in price! Ellen Whoozis, the cocktail-party queen, who writes the Necking Notes, is going to marry the religious editor!

"Say, it was exactly like going back to the dear old Home Town in Ioway, after my first three years in New York! That time I wanted to tell the home-town boys all the news about the Brooklyn Bridge and immorality, and they wanted to talk about Henry Hick's new flivver!

"Well, I guess it's all about alike, really—Buddhism in Burma and Henry's flivver. It's all neighborhood gossip, with different kinds of neighbors. Only——

"But it isn't the same! I've seen—oh, God, Sam, I've seen the jungle at dawn, and these fellows have stayed here, stuck at little desks, and never drifted five steps away from their regular route from home, to the office, to the speak-easy, to the office, to the movie, to home. I was on a ship afire in the Persian Gulf——

"I know it's just vanity, Sam, but there *are* things outside America—— Whether they're ever going to have sense enough to make a Pan-Europa there—whether Britain is going to recognize Russia, and who's going to get Russian oil—what will become of Poland—what Fascism really means in Italy; things that ought to be almost as interesting as the next baseball game. But these lads that've stuck here in New York, they're so self-satisfied (like I was once!) that they don't care a hang for anything beyond the current price of gin! They don't know there is a Europe, beyond the Paris bars. Why even in my shop—I carry on in Europe as though I were the great, three-star, two-tailed special foreign correspondent but here (it's a fact!) the fellow that does the weekly cartoon about Farmer Hiram Winterbottom gets three times my salary—say, if *he* came into the office, old Quackenbos would give him the whole day!

"Well, now that I've told you what a nice, lace-collared, abused darling I am, let's——

"But this town, that I've been looking forward to—— (Man, do you realize we could sail back on the *Aqui* in a week? Think of that nice cool corner in the smoking-room!) I've found that the one and only up-to-date, new, novel, ingenious way of getting anywhere in this burg, if you want to *get* there, is to walk! It takes a taxi, in this traffic, ten minutes to make ten blocks. And the subway—— How many years since you've been in the subway? Well, don't! I thought I was a pretty big guy, and fairly husky, but say, the subway guard at the Grand Central just stuck his knee in the middle of my back and rammed me into a car that was already plumb-full like I was a three-year-old child! And I stood up as far as Brooklyn Bridge, with my nose in the neck of a garbage-wholesaler! Say, I feel like an anarchist! I want to blow up the whole town!

"Then, after lunch, I wanted to buy a few real first-edition suits of American athletic underwear, so I went to Mosheim's department store. Seen their new building? Looks like a twenty-story ice-palace. Windows full of diamonds and satins and ivory and antique Spanish furniture, and lingerie that would make a movie-actress blush. 'City of luxury—Europe beat a mile!' says I. 'Extra! Pleasure Capital of the World Discovered by H. Ross Ireland!' And then I tried to get into the store. Honestly, Sam, I'll be quite a husky fellow when I get my strenth. I used to play center and wrestle heavy-weight in the University of Iowa. But, by golly, I couldn't hardly wedge my way in through the doors. There was one stream of maniacs rushing out and another rushing in, as though it was a fire, and every aisle was jammed, and then when you got to the proper counter——

"Well, I've got good and plenty sore at the way the hired help treat you abroad. I've had a Turkish rug-vendor go crazy when I didn't want to pay more'n twice the price of a rug; I've had a hard-boiled Greek mate bawl hell out of me because he tripped over me on deck; I've had a gondolier say what he thought of my tip. But anyway, those fellows treated you as though you were almost their equals. It's like Chesterton says—if a fellow kicks his butler down-stairs, it doesn't show any lack of democracy; it's only when he feels too superior to his butler to touch him that he's really snooty. And that's how the nice bright young gent at the underwear-counter treated me. He had about six people to wait on, and unless I spoke quick and took what he gave me, he wasn't going to waste time on me, and he kept looking at me with a 'You big hick, don't try to fool me, that ain't no real New York suit you got on—back to Yankton.'

"Then I tried to get out of the store. One fellow elbowing you in the stomach and another jabbing you in the back, and the elevator man hollering 'Step lively, please,' till you wanted to sock him in the nose. Honestly, I felt like a refugee driven by the Cossacks—no, I didn't feel that human; I felt like I was one of a bunch of steers driven down the runway to the slaughter-house. God, what a town! Luxury! Gold! Everything but self-respect and decency and privacy!

"And what an oration! That's the longest speech I've made since I caught my No. 1 Boy in Burma wearing my best pants!"

"Well," Sam soothed, "it'll be better when you get out into the country."

"But I don't like the country! Being a hick by origin, I like cities. I had enough cornfields and manure-piles before I ran away, at fourteen. And from what I heard at lunch, all the other towns in America are becoming about as bad as New York—traffic jams and big movie theaters and radios yapping everywhere and everybody has to have electric dish-washers and vacuum cleaners and each family has to have not one car, by golly, but two or three—and all on the installment plan! But I guess any of those burgs would be better than this New York monkey jungle.

"And I thought I knew this town! Ten years I put in here! But honestly, it's sixteen times as bad as it was three years ago, seems to me. Ought to be lovely three years from *now*! And foreign—say, when you see a real old-fashioned American face on the street, you wonder how he got here. I think I'll go back to London and see some Americans!"

Ross, Sam felt, was exaggerating. But when Ross had gone and he had roused himself from his lassitude for a walk—for a hot crawl—he felt lost and small and alien in the immense conflict of the steaming streets.

And he had no place to go. He realized that this capital, barbaric with gold and marble, provided every human necessity save a place, a café or a plaza or a not-too-lady-like tea-shop, in which he could sit and be human. Well! He could go to the Metropolitan Art Gallery, the Aquarium, the dusty benches of Central Park, or sit gently in a nice varnished pew in a Protestant Church.

People running with suit-cases nicked his legs, small active Jews caromed into him, flappers with faces powdered almost purple looked derisively at his wandering and bucolic mildness, a surf of sweaty undistinguishable people swept over him, shop-windows of incredible aloof expensiveness stared at him, and at every street-crossing he was held up by the wave of traffic, as he crept over to Fifth Avenue, down to Forty-second, past leering cheap-jack shops and restaurants, over to Sixth and back again to the Grand Central Station.

He stood contemplatively (he who a year ago would never have stood thus, but would have rushed with the most earnest of them) on the balcony overlooking the shining acres of floor of the Grand Central Station, like a roofed-over Place de la Concorde. Why, he wondered, was it that the immensity of Notre Dame or St. Paul's did not dwarf and make ridiculous the figures of the worshippers as this vastness did the figures of travelers galloping to train-gates? Was it because the little people, dark and insignificant in the cathedrals, were yet dignified, self-possessed, seeking the ways of God, whereas here they were busy with the ludicrous activity of insects?

He fancied that this was veritably the temple of a new divinity, the God of Speed.

Of its adherents it demanded as much superstitious credulity as any of the outworn deities—demanded a belief that Going Somewhere, Going Quickly, Going Often, were in themselves holy and greatly to be striven for. A demanding God, this Speed, less good-natured than the elder Gods with their faults, their amours, their vanity so easily pleased by garlands and flattery; an abstract, faultless, and insatiable God, who once he had been offered a hundred miles an hour, straightway demanded a hundred and fifty.

And with his motor cars Sam had contributed to the birth of this new religion, and in the pleasant leisure of Europe he had longed for its monastic asperities! He blasphemed against it now, longing for the shabbiest bar on the raggedest side street of Paris.

He shook his great shaggy head as he looked down on traveling-salesmen importantly parading before bag-laden redcaps, on fagged brokers with clanking bags of golf sticks, on fretful women, contemptuous overdressed women, and sleek young men in white knickerbockers. They seemed to him driven to madness by the mad God of Speed that themselves had created—and Sam Dodsworth had created.

Sam and Ross Ireland foolishly tried to take a taxicab to the theater. When they were already half an hour late, they got out and walked the last six blocks. They saw a number of delightful and naked young women, as naked as they would have been at Folies-Bergère.

"From the breaths around us, I guess there's a few New Yorkers who haven't heard about Prohibition," sighed Ross, as they paced the street in the entr'acte. "Well, fortunately, the preachers haven't enough influence with God yet to keep the girls from being naked. They'll have to fix that up as soon as Prohibition really goes over—arrange to have the girls born with flannel nighties on. . . . Honestly, Sam, I don't get these here United States. We let librarians censor all the books, and yet we have musical comedies like this—just as raw as Paris. We go around hollering that we're the only *bona fide* friends of democracy and self-determination, and yet with Haiti and Nicaragua we're doing everything we accused Germany of doing in Belgium, and—you mark my word—within a year we'll be starting a Big Navy campaign for the purpose of bullying the world as Great Britain never thought of doing. We boast of scientific investigation, and yet we're the only supposedly civilized country where thousands of supposedly sane citizens will listen to an illiterate clodhopping preacher or politician setting himself up as an authority on biology and attacking evolution."

It was after the wearisome glare of the musical comedy, at a speak-easy which was precisely like an old-fashioned bar except that the whisky was bad, that Ross Ireland raged on:

"Yes, and to have a little more of our American paradox, we have more sentimental sobbing over poor de-uh mother in the movies, and more lynching of negroes, than would be possible anywhere else in the world! More space, and more crowded tenements; more hard-boiled pioneers, and more sickly discontented wives; more Nancies among young men; more highbrow lectures, and more laughing-hyena comic strips and more slang—— Well, take me. I'm supposed to be a newspaperman. I've seen a lot—and read a whale of a lot more than I ever admit. I have ideas, and I even have a vocabulary. But I'm so American that if I ever admit I'm interested in ideas, if I ever phrase a sentence grammatically, if I don't try to sound like a longshoreman, I'm afraid that some damned little garage-proprietor will think I'm trying to be pedantic! Oh, I've learned a lot about myself and my beloved America today!"

"Just the same, Ross, I prefer this country to——"

"Hell, so do I! Things I can remember, people I've talked to, knocking around this country, High Sierras to the Cape

Cod cranberry-bogs. Old Pop Conover, that used to be a Pony Express Rider, going lickety-split, risking his life among the Indians—I remember him at eighty, the whitest old man you ever saw; lived in a little shack in my town in Iowa, baching it—had an old chair made out of a flour-barrel. Say, he'd tell us kids stories by the hour; he'd put up a tramp for the night; and he'd've received a king just the same way. Never occurred to him that he was any better than the tramp or any worse than a king. He was a real American. And I've seen the bunch at football games—nice clean youngsters. But we're turning the whole thing into a six-day bicycle race. And with motor-cycles instead of the legs that we used to have once!"

With Ross Ireland talking always—assailing the American bustle .except at such times as Sam complained of it, whereupon Ross would defend it furiously—they ambled to a Broadway cabaret.

It was called "The Georgia Cabin," it specialized in Chicken Maryland and yams and beaten biscuit, and the orchestra played "Dixie" every half hour, to great cheering. Aside from Ross and Sam, everybody in the place was either a Jew or a Greek. It was so full of quaintness and expensiveness. The walls were in monstrous overblown imitation of a log cabin; and round the tiny fenced dancing-floor, so jammed that the dancers looked like rush-hour subway passengers moving in sudden amorous insanity, was the Broadway idea of a rail-fence.

The cover charge was two dollars apiece. They had two lemonades, at seventy-five cents each, with a quarter tip to the Hellenic waiter—at which he grumbled—and a quarter to the trim and cold-eyed hat-girl—at which she snapped, "Another pair of cheap skates!"

They said little as they marched toward their hotel. Over Sam, thick, palpable, like a shroud, was the lassitude he had felt in Paris. He was in a dream; nothing was real in all this harsh reality of trolley bells, furious elevated trains, swooping taxicabs, the jabbering crowds. The heat was churning up into a thunderstorm. Lightning revealed the cornices of the inhumanly lofty buildings. The whole air was menacing, yet he felt the menace indifferently, and heavily he said good night to Ross Ireland.

The storm exploded as he stood at the window of his hotel room. Every lightning flash threw into maniacal high relief the vast yellow wall of the building opposite, and its innumerable glaring windows; and in the darknesses between flashes he could imagine the building crashing over on him. It was terrifying as a volcanic eruption, even to Sam Dodsworth, who was not greatly given to fear. Yet terror could not break up the crust of dull loneliness which encased him.

He turned from the window with a lifeless step and went drearily to bed, to lie half awake. He muttered only, "This hustle of American life—regular battle—is it going to be too much for me, now I'm out of the habit?"

And, "Oh, God, Fran, I am so lonely for you!"

Chapter 17

BUT it was a pleasanter and more kindly America that he found the next evening, when he sat with Elon Richards, chairman of the board of the Goodwood National Bank, on the terrace at Willow Marsh, Richards' place on Long Island.

In the morning, Sam's son, Brent, telephoned from New Haven that he would finish his examinations in two days and be down for a real bender with his father. In the afternoon Sam labored mightily with Alec Kynance in the New York office of the U.A.C. He was again offered a vice presidency of the U.A.C. and again he refused.

He was vague about his refusal.

"Alec, it's hard to explain it—just feel that I've given most of my life to making motor cars, and now I'd like to sit around and visit with myself and get acquainted. Yes, I was lonely in Paris. I admit it. But it's a job I've started, and I'm not going to give it up yet."

Kynance was sharp.

"I don't know's I can ever make this offer again."

Sam scarcely heard him. He—of old-time the steadily attentive—was wool-gathering: "I'll never be good for anything *but* business, but why not have a little fun and try something new—big orange-grove in Florida, or real estate?"

When Sam telephoned to Richards of the Goodwood National, Richards insisted on his coming out to Long Island for the night.

Sam was relaxed and cheered by the drive, in the Hispano-Suiza which Richards' daughter, Sheila, had invited her father to buy the moment she had read the novels of Michael Arlen. They slipped through the vicious traffic of the Grand Central district, turned up First Avenue with its air of a factory village, crossed the superb arch of the Fifty-ninth Street Bridge, from which they looked down to towers looming over docks for steamers from Rio de Janeiro and Barbados and Africa.

They shot through a huddle of factories and workers' cottages, and fled along a road which followed the shore-line, with a salt breeze whispering through the open windows of the great car; they came into pleasant suburbs, and turned off on a country lane among real farms. Sam's slightly battered Americanism rose exultantly as he saw cornfields, pumpkin vines, white farm-houses with piles of poplar stove-wood.

And the talk was good.

Sam had never been such a fool as to assert that virile citizens talked only of bonds and prize-fighting, and that any one who pretended to an interest in Matisse or the Ca' d' Oro was an effeminate pretender. Only, he had pled with Fran, he himself had as much right to be interested in bonds and bored by Matisse as a painter had to be interested in Matisse and bored by bonds. Of course bonds had been important enough to Alec Kynance, that afternoon. Yet Alec's talk had not been good, because the little man could never keep his rôle of Napoleon of Commerce to himself, but insisted on treating every one he met as either a Faithful Guardsman whose ear he could tweak, or as a Faithful Field Marshal who was gaping to receive (from Alec) a new bâton.

But Elon Richards talked of consolidations and investments and golf and the more scandalous divorces of bankers with the simplicity and impersonality of a dairyman discussing cattle-feed. He announced (while the car slipped past the little farms and into a region of great estates) that the K.L. and Z. would be bankrupt within two months, that there really was something to this company that was going to grow 1,000,000 reindeer in Alaska, that Smith Locomotive Common wouldn't be such a bad buy, and that it was perfectly true that the Antelope Car was going to announce safety windshield glass as a standard accessory.

The great house at Willow Marsh stood on a bluff looking over marshes to Long Island Sound. They dined on a brick terrace, at a little table with quivering candles, round it three wicker chairs with Sam, Richards, and his daughter, Sheila. It was Sheila who six months ago had demanded the Hispano-Suiza, but this summer she was in a socialist stage. Sam was a little annoyed because all through dinner she kept asking why the workers should not take from Sam and her father all their wealth.

Richards, to Sam's incredulity, encouraged Sheila by teasing her:

"If you can get a really first-class leader, like Lenin, who's strong enough to take the money away from me in the first place and to construct a practical working state in the second, I shan't worry—just as soon work for him and his gang as for our stockholders. But if you think, my impudent young daughter, that because a lot of socialist journalists yap that maybe, possibly, some day, the working-class may get educated up to the point of running industry and therefore I ought to join 'em—well, let 'em *make* me!"

So for an hour.

After twenty-five years of big industry, Sam Dodsworth still believed, in an unformulated and hazy way, that socialism meant the dividing-up of wealth, after which the millionaires would get it all back within ten years. He still half believed that all Bolsheviks were Jews who wore bushy beards, carried bombs, and were hardly to be distinguished from anarchists. He didn't completely believe it, because in his office he had met suave and beardless Soviet agents who had talked competently about importing Revelation cars. But to take socialism seriously——

It annoyed him.

Why had he ever gone abroad? It had unsettled him. He had been bored in Paris, yet he liked crêpes Susette better than flapjacks; he liked leaning over the bridges of the Seine better than walking on Sixth Avenue; and he couldn't, just now, be very excited about the new fenders for the Revelation car. How was it that this America, which had been so surely and comfortably in his hand, had slipped away?

And here was the daughter of an Elon Richards, most safely conservative of bankers, contaminated with a lot of European socialism. Was life really as complicated as all that?

It was simpler when Sheila had left them. The June twilight was tender, and across the mauve ribbon of Long Island Sound unseen villages sprang to life in soft twinkling. On the cool terrace, after two choked days in New York, Sam relaxed in a wicker chair, shoulders moving with contentment. Richards' cigars were excellent, his brandy was authentic, and now that Sheila was away, driving her own car off to a dance, his talk was again reasonable.

But it came again——

"Curious, Richards," Sam pondered aloud. "Since I landed in New York yesterday, I've hated the whole rush and zip of it—till this evening, when I've had a chance to sit down in the country and feel human. Course it was probably just the hot weather. Only—— Do you know, I had a feeling of leisure in France and in England. I felt there as though people made their jobs work for them; they didn't give up their lives to working for their jobs. And I felt as though there was such a devil of a lot to learn about the world that we're too busy to learn here."

Richards puffed comfortably; then:

"Did you know I was reared in Europe, Sam?"

"No! Fact?"

"Yes. My father and mother were devoted to Europe. We wandered. I spent fourteen out of the first sixteen years of my life in schools in France and England and Switzerland, and I went back there every summer while I was in Harvard—except the last vacation, after Junior year. Then my father had a brain-wave, and sent me out to Oregon to work in a lumber camp. I was crazy about it! I was so sick of pensions and cafés and the general European attitude that, for an American, you weren't such a bad egg. In Oregon I got beaten up by the lumberjacks three times in seven days, but at the end of the summer I was ardently invited to stay on as straw boss of the camp. I loved it! And I've gone on loving it ever since. I know that plenty of French financiers are more elegant and leisurely than your flat-footed friend Alec Kynance, but I get more fun out of fighting Alec!

"Sam, it's a battle here, the way it is in Russia and China. And you, Sam, you old grizzly, can never be a contemplative gazelle. You've got to fight. And think of it! Maybe America will rule the world! Maybe in the end we'll be broken up by Russia. But isn't a world-fight like that better than sitting around avoiding conversational errors and meditating on the proper evening waistcoats? Life!"

Sam meditated, silently and long.

"Elon," said he, "there was a time when I knew my own mind. I didn't do whatever my latest stenographer suggested. But I've seen too many things, recently. If Fran were here—my wife—I'd probably be pro-Europe. You make me pro-America."

"Why be pro-anything? Why not dive head-first into whatever battle seems most interesting? You can be sure of this: the result won't mean anything. My girl, Sheila, informs me that a judicious use of eugenics, Karl Marx, and tennis would turn us all into a bunch of beneficent Apollos in five generations. God forbid! I have a sneaking suspicion that none of us poor vertebrates want perfection, really! But I mean: You're one of these kind-hearted, dutiful Americans who feels apologetic and inferior the moment he retires, and who'll spend the rest of his life trying to satisfy everybody he meets: his wife and his mistress——"

"Not yet!"

"Wait! ——and his friends. Sam, I'm such an idealist that I'd like to start an Association for the Hanging of All Idealists. For Heaven's sake decide whether you, your own self, are happier in America or in Europe, and then stick there! Me, I'm glad to have European bankers coming to me begging for loans instead of my going to European cafés and begging waiters for a table in the sun! Sam, this American adventure—— Because it is an adventure that we have here—the greatest in the world—and not a certainty of manners in an uncertainty of the future, like all of Europe. And say, do you know, our adventure is going to be the bigger because we *do* feel that Europe has a lot we need. We're no longer satisfied with the log cabin and the corn pone. We want everything that Europe has. We'll take it!"

"Um," said Sam.

That night he slept child-like, in a breeze from the Sound. He awoke at five, to sit on the edge of his bed, bulky in his rather touseled silk pajamas, meditating while he looked down on the marshlands smoking with morning, and the Sound, like whirls of cobweb over bright steel.

If he were fifty miles farther out on Long Island, perhaps he could see across to the Connecticut shore and New Haven.

He realized that this was grotesquely like a day in spring of his senior year in Yale when from East Rock he had looked across the Sound to Long Island, and in that distant shore beheld romantic harbors. He was separated from the boy who had sat on East Rock only by Long Island Sound, and thirty years, and that boy's certainty that he would "do something worth while." Today he could think of things far more interesting to attempt than in those solemn important days when he had been a football star weighed down with the monastic duties of an athlete. It was not, now, ridiculous to consider being a wanderer in Japan, a proponent of Sheila Richards' socialism or its crusading foe, or, twenty years hence, merely an old man with a pipe, content among apple trees on a hill above the Ohio River. But also it was obvious now that he was chained by people and strengths and weaknesses which he had not recognized in his young hour of vision on East Rock.

He could not return to a completely simple and secure life in America because of Fran's dislike for it, and without the habitual titillation of Fran's gaieties and bad temper, life was inconceivable. He could not become an elegantly lounging cosmopolitan because—his thought stumbled and growled—oh, because he was Sam Dodsworth!

He was chained by every friend who had made life agreeable—bound not to shock or lose them. He was chained by every dollar he had made, every automobile he had manufactured—they meant a duty to his caste. He was chained by every hour he had worked—they had left him stiff, spiritually rheumatic.

He still wanted the world . . . but there was nothing specific in the world that he wanted so much as, thirty years ago, he had wanted to be a Richard Harding Davis hero.

Then it came to him.

He marveled, "No, the trouble is that, aside from keeping in with Fran and the children and a few friends, I don't want anything enough to fight for it much. I've done about all I ever imagined—got position, made money, met interesting folks. I'd be a lot luckier if I were a hobo that hadn't done any of the things he wanted to. Oh, hang it, I don't much care. Maybe I didn't hitch my wagon to a high-enough star! This one don't look very good!

"Rats! When I get out of this crazy New York district and meet real, simple, hearty fellows back in Zenith—yes, sure, and at my re-union—I'll get over this grouch.

"But what's it all about, this business of life?

"I'd give my left leg if I could believe what the preachers say. Immortality. Serving Jehovah. But I can't. Got to face it alone——

"Oh, for God's sake, quit pitying yourself! You're as bad as Fran——

"Fran! She's never bad. Not really. Did I ever happen to remember to tell you that I adore you, Fran?"

Four hours later, at breakfast, he was an unsentimental Captain of Finance, attentive only to waffles.

He stood at a gate in the Grand Central Station watching his son lope up the inclined cement runway from the New Haven train.

"If there's anything finer than him at Oxford or in France——" he gloated, and "More Fran's boy than mine, though; got her good looks and quickness."

Brent was like a young race horse, his pale face and high thin forehead almost too bred-down, too refined. But there was health and buoyancy in his humorous eyes, his shout of "Hello, Dad! Swell to see you again. Good crossing?"

"Yes. Fair. Nice to see you, boy. How long can you stay?"

"Have to be back in the morning. Catch the milk-train."

"Too bad. Here, give your bag to a red-cap."

"And pay a quarter? Not a chance—not with corn whisky costing what it does."

"Um. I wouldn't drink much of that. But I guess you know that. Where'd you like to dine tonight? Ritz, or some hell-raising place?"

"I'll show you a real joint with real German beer."

"Fine. Uh——"

Sam looked shyly down at the shy boy, and blurted, "Mighty proud of you for making both Bones and Phi Beta Kappa."

"Oh, thanks. Gosh, you're looking fine, sir."

He found that though Brent would be in New York for only twelve hours, he had brought dinner clothes.

"Fran's boy, all right," he reflected, and somehow he was a bit lonely. He wished that he could give this nervous youngster something more than an allowance—some strength, some stability.

While they dressed, Brent recovered from his filial shyness enough to chatter about the miracles performed by Chick Budlong as a pole-vaulter, about the astounding fact that after being a perfectly good egg for over two years, Ogden Rose had turned literary and heeled the *Lit.*, about the "bum body job" of the new U.A.C. Revelation. He was emerging as the young elegant, slim in dinner clothes, and he belonged to a world which would resent Sam's intrusion, which desired no strength nor stability . . . even if, Sam considered, he had any to give.

The "German restaurant" to which Brent led him was altogether imitation: beer mugs made in Pennsylvania; beams stained to look old; colored glass windows which, if they could have been opened, would have been found to look on nothing but a plaster wall; and beer that was most deplorably and waterily imitation.

Against this soiled and tawdry background, against the soiled and insolent and rather pathetic Polish waiters, Brent was real as a knife-blade, and as shining.

Sam had had a notion that now, two men together, his son and he could be intimately frank. He would talk to Brent about drinking, gambling, the value of money as a means and its worthlessness as an end, and most of all, about women. Oh, he wouldn't snoop and paw—he'd just give his own notions of a life neither Puritanical nor licentious; be awfully frank about the danger of the daughters of the street, while admitting, like a man of the world, the compulsion of "sex"; and if Brent should be moved to give any confidences, he would treat them casually, sympathetically——

That warm rejoicing idea had been chilled the moment he saw Brent's self-confident figure. Why, the boy might think he was in Bad Taste, and next to the affection of Fran and Emily, he wanted Brent's affection and respect more than that of any one in the world. So, in parental fear, while he would have liked to expose his soul, he droned about Lord Herndon, Gioserro the aviator, the palace at Versailles——

But there was one intimate thing of which he could talk:

"Son, have you decided whether you'll go to Harvard Law School when you finish Yale?"

"I haven't quite decided, sir."

"Don't call me 'sir'! Look here, Brent; I have a notion—— If your Mother and I are still abroad when you graduate, how would it be for you to come and join us for a year or so? Maybe between us, we could get her to chase off to Africa and India and China and so on. Just now she's stuck on Paris. I've been finding out there's a devil of a lot to see in this world. There's no hurry about your getting down to earning money."

"But you went to work early, sir."

"Don't call me 'sir'—I'm still under the age for it—I hope! And I think that maybe I got to work too early. Rather wish, now, I'd bummed around the world a little first. And after all these years you've been studying, to go right on to your law books——"

"Well, you see, sir, I'm not sure I'll go out for law."

"Um. What you thinking of? Medicine? Motors?"

"No, I—— You know my roommate, Billy Deacon, his dad is president of Deacon, Iffley and Watts, the bond-house; and Billy wants me to come in with him selling bonds. I think probably I could be making twenty-five thousand a year in ten years, and in the law, if I went into a really tophole New York firm, I'd only be a clerk then. And some day I'll be in the hundred and fifty thousand a year class."

Brent said it with the modest confidence, the eager eyes, of a young poet announcing that he was going to write an epic.

Sam spoke doubtfully:

"May sound like a funny thing from a man that's always captured every dollar he could lay his hands on, but—— Brent, I've always wanted to build things; to leave something besides a bank balance. Afraid you wouldn't be doing that, just selling bonds. Not that I've anything against bonds, you understand! Nice handsome engravings. But are you going to need to make money so fast——"

"Life's a lot more expensive than when you started, Dad. Fellow has to have so many things. When I was a kid, a man with a limousine was a little tin god, but now a fellow that hasn't got a yacht simply isn't in it. If a fellow makes his pile, then he can lay off and have a hobby—see Europe and go out for public spirit and all that stuff. I believe I've got a swell chance with Bill Deacon and his bunch."

"Well. Course you've got to decide for yourself. But I wish you'd think it over—about really building things."

"Sure. I certainly will, sir."

Brent was bright with compliments about Sam's knowledge of Europe; he remarked that Sam's football glories were still remembered at Yale.

And Sam sighed to himself that he had lost the boy forever.

Chapter 18

SAM was packing, to go to New Haven for his thirtieth class reunion, when the mild little knock came at the door. He roared "Come in," and at first did not look to see who his visitor might be. The silence after the opening of the door made him turn.

Tub Pearson was on the threshold, grinning.

"Well, you fat little runt!" said Sam, which meant, "My dear old friend, I am enchanted to see you!" And Tub gave answer, "You big stiff, so they couldn't stand you in Yurrup any more, eh? So you had to sneak back here, eh? You big bum!" Which signified, to one knowing the American language, "I have been quite distressingly lonely for you in Zenith, and had you not returned, I should probably have given up the Reunion and gone to Europe to see you—I would, really."

"Well, you're looking fine, Tub." And they patted each other's arms, curtly.

"So are you. You look *ausgezeichnet.* I guess Europe agreed with you. Didn't bring me home a little of that swell French wine, did you?"

"Sure, I've got a whole case of it in my collar box."

"Well, bring it out. Let's not put off the fatal hour."

From behind a trunk (where, under the new American dispensation, all hotel guests hide the current bottle of whisky, to make it easier for the hotel servants to find it) Sam produced something, chuckling, "Now this may just look like plain Methodist bootlegged corn to you, Tub, but remember you ain't traveled expensively and got educated, the way I have. Say when. . . . Oh, say, Tub, I got a bottle of the real thing—pre-war Scotch—taken off me here at the docks."

"Oh, my God! What a sacrilege! Well now, tell me, what kind of a time d'you really have?"

"Oh, fine, fine! Paris is a fine city. Say, how's Matey and your kids?"

"Fine!"

"How's Harry Hazzard?"

"He's fine. He's got a grand-daughter. Say, they whoop it up all night long in Paris, don't they?"

"Yeh, pretty late. Have you seen Emily lately?"

"Just the other day at the country club. Looked fine. Oh, say, Sambo, can you explain one thing to me? Is there any chance the Bolsheviks will pay the Czarist debts to France? And what kind of a buy are French municipals?"

"Well, I didn't find out much about—— Oh, I met some high-class Frogs—fellow named Andillet, stock-broker, pretty well heeled I guess. But it isn't like with us. Hard to get those fellows down to real serious talk, out of the office. They want to gas about the theater and dancing and horse-racing all the time. But say, I did learn one mighty interesting thing: the Citroën people in France and the Opel people in Germany are putting up low-priced cars that'll give the Ford and the Chev a mighty hard run for their money in European territory and—— Oh! Say! Tub! Can you tell me anything about the rumors that Ford is going to scrap Model T and come out with an entirely new model? My God, I've tried and tried and I can't find out anything about it! I've asked Alec Kynance, and I've asked Byron Rogers of the Sherman, and I've asked Elon Richards, and if they know anything, they won't let it out and—— By golly, I'd like to find out something about it."

"So would I! So would I! And I can't find out a thing!"

They both sighed, and refilled.

"They finished the new addition to the country club?" asked Sam.

"Yes, and it's a beauty. They play much golf in France?"

"I guess so, on the Riviera. Been by my house recently? Everything look all right?"

"You bet. I stopped and spoke to your caretaker. Seems like a good reliable fellow. Say, just what does a fellow *do*, evenings in Paris? What kind of hang-outs do you go to? 'Bout like night-clubs here?"

"Well, a lot better wine—well no, at that, some of the places that are filled with Americans stick you and stick you good for pretty poor fizz. But on the whole—— Oh, I don't know; you get tired of racketing around. All these pretty women, talking all the time!"

"Didn't pick up a little cutie on the side, did you?"

"Did you say 'cutie' or 'cootie'?"

And they both laughed, and they both sighed, and of Sam's non-existent amorous affairs they said no more.

And they found that they had nothing else to say.

For years they had shared friends, games, secret business-reports. They had been able to talk actively about the man they had seen the day before, the poker they had played two days ago, the bank scandal that was going on at the moment. But in six months, most of the citizens of Zenith whose scandals and golf handicaps had been important had been dimmed for Sam; he could not visualize them, could think of nothing to ask about them. The two men fell into an uncomfortable playing at catch with questions and answers.

Sam said, mildly, "Kind of wish I'd started going abroad earlier, Tub—kind of interesting to see how differently they do things. But it's too late now."

He struggled to make clear what had interested him in England and France—the tiny, unchartable differences of dress, of breakfast bacon, of political parties, of vegetables in market places, of the ministers of God—but Tub was impatient. What he wanted was a gloating vicarious excursion into blazing restaurants full of seductive girls, marvelous food, wine unimaginably good at fifty cents a bottle, superb drunks without a headache, and endless dancing without short breath. Sam tried to oblige but——

"Funny!" He couldn't somehow picture the dancing rendezvous he had seen only a fortnight ago. He could see the musty cupboard where the patient chambermaid of their hotel floor had sat waiting, apparently all day and all night, knitting, smelling of herring and poverty; but of the Jardin de Ma Soeur he could see nothing but tables, smooth floor, and the too darkly enraptured eyes of Gioserro the aviator, dancing with Fran.

Sam dropped so low conversationally that he asked about the well-being of the Rev. Dr. Willis Fortune Tate of Zenith.

Then Ross Ireland banged in.

"Off to Mexico to do a story on oil, gimme a drink," he said, and all was liveliness again.

Sam was distressed that he should be relieved to have his

confidences with his oldest friend interrupted by this half-stranger, but he was pleased when Tub Pearson took to him. Half an hour later, when Ross had told his celebrated story of Doc Pilvins the veterinarian and the plush horse, the three of them went out to dinner, had cocktails, and became lively and content.

Only once in an evening of different night clubs, none of which were different, did Sam worry again:

"Good Lord, are all of us here in America getting so we can't be happy, can't talk, till we've had a lot of cocktails? What's the matter with our lives?"

But on the Yale campus next afternoon, with Tub, he was roaring with delight to see again the comrades of old days; the beloved classmates who stayed so unshakably in his mind that he had forgotten nothing about them save their professions, their present dwelling-places, and their names.

The 1896 division of the procession to the baseball game at Yale Field, in their blue coats and white trousers, was led by Tub Pearson, shaking a rattle and singing:

> Good morning, Mr. Zip, Zip, Zip,
> Got a hair-cut as short as mine?
> Good morning, Mr. Zip, Zip, Zip,
> I cer'n'ly am feeling fine.
> Ashes to ashes and dust to dust,
> If the army don't get you then the navy must——

Sam was moved to sadness and prayer by the sight of his classmates. It was one of the astonishments of the reunion how old many of them had become at fifty or fifty-two—Don Binder, for instance, in college a serious drinker, baby-faced and milky, now an Episcopalian rector who looked as though he were sixty-five and as though he carried the sins of the country on his stooped shoulders. The spectacle made Sam himself feel ancient. But as startling were the classmates who at fifty looked thirty-five, and who irritated a man like Sam, amiable about exercise but no fanatic, by shouting that everybody ought to play eighteen holes of golf a day.

But however sheepish Sam might feel, Tub was radiant, was again the class clown during the procession. He danced across the road from side to side, shaking his rattle, piping on a penny whistle, frightening a child on the sidewalk almost into epilepsy by kneeling down and trying to be chummy.

"He's fine. He's funny," Sam assured himself. "He's a great goat. Hell, he's an idiot! *Why* am I getting to be such a grouch on life? Better go back to the desk."

But whatever discomfort he had at playing the hobbledehoy, in the class reunion Sam found balm. They knew who he was! No one in Paris (except Fran, at times) knew that. But his classmates realized that he was Sambo Dodsworth, great tackle, Skull and Bones, creative engineer, president of a corporation, "prince of good fellows."

Except for a few professional alumni who at fifty could still tell what was the score in last year's Yale-Brown game, who at fifty had nothing with which to impress the world except the fact that they were Yale Men, the class had drifted far from the cheery loafing and simple-hearted idealism of college days. They were bank presidents and college presidents and surgeons and country school-teachers and diplomats; they were ranchmen and congressmen and ex-convicts and bishops. One was a major general, and one—in college the most mouse-like of bookworms—was the funniest comedian on Broadway. They were fathers and grandfathers, and most of them looked as though they overworked or overdrank. Not one of them had found life quite the amusing and triumphant adventure he had expected; and they came back wistfully, longing to recapture their credulous golden days. They believed (for a week) that their classmates were peculiarly set apart from the crooked and exasperating race of men as a whole.

And all of this Sam Dodsworth believed—for a week.

It was pleasant, on a clam bake at Momauguin, to loll in the sand with the general, a college president, and two steel kings, as though they were all of them nineteen again, to be hailed as "Old Sambo," to wrestle without thinking of dignity, and for a moment to be so sentimental as to admit that they longed for something greater than their surface successes. It was pleasant, in the rooms to which they were assigned in Harkness, to forget responsibilities as householders and company managers, and to loll puppy-like on window-seats, beside windows fanned by the elms, telling fabulous lies till one, till two of the morning, without thinking of being up early and on the job. It was pleasant at dinner in a private room to sing "Way Down on the Bingo Farm" and to come out with a long, clinging, lugubrious yowl in:

Here's to good old Yaaaaaaaaaaaale
She's so hearty and so hale——

Even the men who on the first day he had not been able to remember became clear. Why yes! That was old Mark Derby—always used to be so funny the way he played on a comb and never could remember his necktie.

He was nineteen again; in a world which had seemed barren of companionship he had found two hundred brothers; and he was home, he rejoiced—to stay!

So, with Tub Pearson, he rode westward from New York to Zenith, gratified as the thunderous slots of Manhattan streets gave way to the glowing Hudson, to tranquil orchards and old white houses and resolute hills.

The breakfast-room of Harry McKee, Sam's new son-in-law, was a cheery apartment with white walls, canary-yellow curtains at the French windows, and a parrot, not too articulate, in a red enamel cage. The breakfast set was of taffy-like peasant faïence from Normandy, and the electrical toaster and percolator on the table were of nickel which flashed in the lively Midwestern morning sunshine.

Sam was exultant. He had arrived late last evening, and as his own house was musty from disuse, he had come to Emily's. He had slept with a feeling of security, and this morning he was exhilarated at being again with her, his own Emily, gayest and sturdiest of girls. He had brought his presents for them down to breakfast—the Dunhill pipe and the Charvet dressing-gown for Harry, the gold and tortoise-shell dressing-table set and the Guerlain perfumes for Emily. They admired the gifts, they patted him in thanks, they fussed over his having real American porridge with real cream. In a blissful assurance of having come home forever to his own snug isle, after decades amid white-fanged seas, of having brought to his astounded tribe incredible tales of Troy and Circe and men with two heads, he began to expatiate on Paris, smiling at them, reaching out to take Emily's hand, launching into long-winded details.

"——now what I never understood about Paris," he was rumbling, "is how much of it is like a series of villages, with narrow streets and little bits of shops that don't hardly keep the proprietor busy. You always hear of the big boulevards and the wild dance halls, but what struck me was the simple little places——"

"Yes, that was so even in the war, when I was in Paris," said McKee. "But there must be a lot of difference since then. Say, Dad, I'm afraid I have to hustle to the office. Hope to sell a few million bolts to the Axton Car people today. But I want to hear all about Paris. Be home by six-thirty. Awful' good to have you back, sir. Good-bye, Emily of Emilies!"

After the kisses and flurry and engine-racings of McKee's departure, Emily beamed her way back and caroled, "Oh, don't eat that cold toast! I'll make you a nice fresh slab. You must try this lovely apricot jam. Now go on and tell me some more about Paris. Oh, it's perfectly ducky to be with you again! Harry is *next* to the nicest man living but you're the —— Oh, you *must* eat some more. Now tell me about Paris."

"Well," mildly, "I really haven't much to tell. It's hard to express how you feel about a foreign place. Something kind of different in the air. I'm afraid I'm not much on analyzing a thing like that. . . . Emily, uh—Harry doing pretty well financially?"

"Oh, splendidly! They've raised him another five thousand a year."

"You don't need a little check for yourself?"

"Oh, not a thing. Thanks, old darling. Drat him, Harry carried off the *Advocate* and I know you want to read it."

Sam did not hear her reference to the *Advocate*. Flushed, he was reflecting, "Am I trying to pay my daughter to be interested in me? Trying to buy her affection?" He scuttled away from the thought, into a hasty description of Les Halles at dawn, as he had seen them when the De Pénable menagerie, with himself as an attendant keeper, had had an all-night round of cafés. He had begun to care for his own narration; he was saying, "Well, I'd never tried white wine and onion soup for breakfast, but I was willing to try anything once," when the telephone began.

"Excuse me a second, Daddy," said Emily, and for five minutes she held a lively conversation with one Mona about a tennis tournament, knitted suits, Dick, speed boats, lobster salad, Mrs. Logan, and a Next Thursday mentioned with such italicized awe that Sam felt ignorant in not knowing how it might differ from any other Thursday. He realized, too, that he did not know who Mona, Dick, or Mrs. Logan were.

The importance of having eaten onion soup for breakfast had cooled by the time Emily whisked back to the table. Before Sam had warmed up and begun the story of Captain Gioserro's hiring a vegetable wagon to drive to the hotel, the sneering telephone called Emily again, and for three minutes she dealt with a tradesman who had apparently been sending bad meat. She dealt with him competently. She seemed to know everything about cuts of steak, the age of ducklings, and the trimming of a crown roast.

She was not his rollicking helpless girl. She was a Competent Young Matron.

"She doesn't need me any more," sighed Sam.

The Dodsworths had not rented their house but had left it tenantless, save for a caretaker who maintained a creeping ashen existence in a corner of the basement, spelling out old newspapers from garbage cans all day long. The caretaker, when he had admitted Sam after five minutes of ringing, wanted to show him through the house, but Sam said abruptly, "I'll go by myself, thanks."

The hall was dim as a tomb and as airless. His foot-fall on the carpetless floor was so loud that he began to tip-toe. There were presences which threatened him as an intruder in his own house. He stood in the door of the library. The room, once warm and tranquil, was bleakly unwelcoming. It was a dead room in a dead house. The rugs were rolled up, piled in a corner, their exposed under-sides drab and pebbly. The book-shelves were covered with sheets, and the deep chairs, swathed in gray covers, were as shapeless and distasteful as the wrapper of a slovenly housewife. The fireplace had a stingy cleanness. But in a corner of it clung a scrap of paper with Fran's hectic writing. He stooped slowly to pick it up, and made out the words "——call motor at ten and——" She seemed to dash into the room and flee away, leaving him the lonelier.

He climbed heavily up the stairway, steps clattering flatly, and shouldered into their bedroom. He looked about, silent.

The canopies of their two beds had been taken down, leaving the posts like bare masts; and the surfaces of those once suave and endearing retreats were mounds of pillows and folded blankets covered with coarse sheets.

He went to the drawn window blinds.

"Blinds getting cracked. Need new ones," he said aloud.

He looked about again, and shivered. He went to the bed in which Fran had always slept, and stood staring at it. He patted the edge of the bed and quickly marched out of the room—out of the house.

Brent was to have returned to Zenith for a fortnight, and Sam had a hundred plans for motoring with him, fishing with him. But Brent telegraphed, "Invited corking yachting party Nova Scotia mind if not return," and Sam, perfectly expressionless, wrote his answer, "By all means go hope have splendid time." As he walked out of the Western Union office he sighed a little, and stood with his hands in his pockets, looking up and down the street, a man with nothing to do.

He had thought of himself, when he had been the president of the Revelation Company, as a young man at fifty. To him, then, old age did not begin till seventy, perhaps seventy-five, and he would have another quarter-century of energy. But the completeness with which Emily, at twenty-one, had matured, become competent to run her own life, made Sam feel that he belonged to an unwanted generation; that, amazingly, he was old.

It was the afternoon of Elizabeth Jane's party which made Sam so conscious that he was a stranger, unable to mix with this brisk, luxurious Young Married Set, that he politely fled from Emily's house and holed-in at the Tonawanda Country Club.

Elizabeth Jane was Harry McKee's eleven-year-old niece. Like a surprising number of other successful youngish men of Zenith, hard-surfaced, glossy, ferociously driving in business, and outside of business absorbed only in sports and cocktail-lit dancing, McKee was fanatically interested in children. He was on the Zenith school-board and the Board of Visitors of St. Mark's Town and Country School. Emily and Harry McKee made Sam blush by the cheery openness with which they informed him that they intended to have only three children, but to have those with celerity and to have them perfect. (They apparently possessed more control of Providence than was understood by such an innocent as Sam.) While they awaited the arrival of the three, they were devoted to Elizabeth Jane, a sedate, bob-haired, bookish child, who reminded Sam of a boy minstrel in a Maxfield Parrish picture. (He had always admired Parrish's dream castles, despite Fran's scoffing.)

Sam liked Elizabeth Jane. "Real old-fashioned child," he said. "So innocent and demure."

And the next day Elizabeth Jane remarked placidly, when she had invited herself to tea with Sam and Emily, "Aunty, would it be awfully rude of me if I said my teacher is a damn' fool? Would it? She's started telling us about sex, and she's so scared and silly about it, and of course all of us kids know all about it already."

"My God!" said Samuel Dodsworth to himself.

McKee and Emily celebrated Elizabeth Jane's twelfth birthday with an afternoon party for forty children. Sam knew that there were to be many dodges of a rich nature; he was aware that a red and white striped pavilion was being erected on the McKee lawn, and orders in for such simple delights as Pêche Melba, Biscuit Tortoni, and Bombe Surprise, along with Viennese pastry, loganberry juice, imported ginger ale and lobster salad, and that the caterer was sending half a dozen waiters in dress suits. But he was still antiquated enough to picture the children playing Ring Around a Rosy, and Puss in the Corner, and Hide 'n' Go Seek.

He was lunching with Tub Pearson on the day of the party, and after lunch he excitedly went to the five and ten cent store and filled his pockets with dozens of pleasant little foolishnesses—false noses, chocolate cigars, tissue-paper hats—

and proceeded to McKee's, planning to set all the children at the party laughing with his gifts.

He was late. When he arrived the children were decorously sitting in four rows of chairs on the lawn, watching a professional troupe from the Zenith Stock Company perform an act from "Midsummer Night's Dream." And there was a professional magician afterward—though the young lordlings were bored by such kitchy banalities as rabbits out of silk hats—and a lady teacher from the Montessori School, who with a trained voice-for-children and trained gestures told ever such nice Folk Tales from Czechoslovakia, Serbia, Iceland, and Yucatan. Then, unherded but politely in order, the children filed past a counter at which Harry McKee, disguised as an Arab for no perceptible reason, gave each of them a present.

They each said, "Thank you very much," tolerantly, and unwrapped their presents, showing their trained social-mindedness by depositing the wrappers in a barrel therefor provided. Sam goggled at the presents. There were French perfume and packets of a thousand stamps, riding crops and portable phonographs, engraved stationery and a pair of love-birds.

He hastily pulled out the flaps of his coat pockets lest some one see the ludicrous little gifts he had bought.

And later, "I've got to get out of this. Too rich for my blood."

It took a week of tactful hinting about needing eight hours of daily golf, but in the end he escaped to one of the chintzy bedrooms at the Tonawanda Country Club and there, in an atmosphere of golf, gin-bottles in the locker room, small dinners followed by poker, and a reading-room full of magazines which on glossy paper portrayed country houses and polo teams, he made out a lotus-eating existence, with cold cauliflower and stringy lamb-chops and bootlegged whisky for lotuses.

He persuaded himself, for minutes at a time, that business affairs demanded his staying in Zenith, and he bleakly knew, for hours at a time, that they didn't.

His capital was invested in carefully diversified ventures—in U.A.C. stock, railroad and industrial and government bonds.

However often he conferred with his bankers and brokers, he couldn't find anything very absorbing to do in the way of changing investments.

But he also owned, as a more speculative interest, a share of a resort hotel near Zenith, and on his way to America he had persuaded himself that, with his newly educated knowledge of food and decoration and service, he would be able to improve this hotel.

It was quite a bad hotel, and very profitable.

He had a meal there, two days after arriving in Zenith, and it was terrible.

He told the manager that it was terrible.

The manager looked bored and resigned.

When Sam had persuaded him to stay, the manager explained that with the cost of materials and the salaries of cooks, he couldn't do a better meal at the price. It was all very well, the manager pointed out, to talk about the food in Paris. Only, this wasn't Paris. And furthermore, did Sam happen to know what chickens cost per pound at the present moment?

That was Sam's only achievement during his stay in Zenith. But weeks went by before he admitted, rather angrily, that business did not need him . . . just as Brent did not need him, Emily did not need him.

But certainly, he comforted himself, Fran needed him, and such friends as Tub Pearson.

Chapter 19

THOMAS J. PEARSON and Samuel Dodsworth had always been too well acquainted to know each other. They had been together since boyhood. Each was a habit to the other. It had been a habit for Tub to go once a week to Sam's for poker; a habit for Sam to telephone him for lunch every Tuesday or Wednesday. They analyzed each other, they considered each other as individuals, no more than a man considers the virtues of his own several toes, unless they hurt. Even Sam's absence from Tub at technical school, after college, had given them no understanding of each other. They were under the spell of the collegiate belief that one's classmates are the most princely fellows ever known in history.

But in Sam's six months abroad, Tub had grown into new habits. It was to the house of Dr. Henry Hazzard that Tub looked now for his weekly drug of poker. Sam saw that Hazzard was at least as necessary to Tub as himself, now, and sometimes he found himself allied against the two of them when the talk fell on labor or European alliances and they expressed the fat opinions which Sam himself had once accepted but about which he now felt shaky. He was slightly jealous, slightly critical. He noted that Tub wasn't quite so perfect as he had remembered. When Tub shrieked, during a game of poker, "'What ho' said the cat to the catamaran" or "Now is the time for all good men to come to the aid of the ante" Sam was not diverted. And he felt that Tub was as critical of him. If he hinted that the paving on Conklin Avenue was bad, or that the coffee at the country club left something to be desired, Tub scolded, "Oh, God, we expatriates certainly are a hard bunch to please!"

When Sam dined with them, he found himself turning oftener to Tub's bouncing goodwife, Matey, than to Tub.

Yet between times they played their nineteen holes happily, serene as a pair of old dogs out rabbit-hunting. If sometimes Sam found himself wishing for Ross Ireland's melodramatic talk about revolutions and lost temples, if sometimes

Tub seemed rather provincial, Sam was thoroughly scandalized, and rebuked himself, "Tub's the best fellow in the world!"

It is doubtful whether he was the more disturbed by finding that he could get along without Tub or by finding that Tub could get along without him.

Believing from Sam's first enthusiastic foreign letters that he would not return from Europe this year, Tub had planned with Dr. Hazzard a month's motoring-golfing expedition. They were excited about it. They were going to play over the best courses in Winnemac, Indiana, Illinois, Michigan, and Ohio. They spoke of the charms of stumbling over new varieties of bunkers, wild grass, and rosebushes. They raved over long shots across sand dunes, and disastrous ponds in which to lose dozens of golf balls.

They had planned to go by themselves, but now they invited Sam. He hesitated. He felt unwanted.

Of course they hadn't known he would be returning——

Of course they *had* urged him to come——

Only why couldn't they have waited to see whether he would return?

He compromised by going with them for two weeks out of the month.

It was a good jaunt. They laughed, and felt free of womenfolk and nagging secretaries, retold all the dirty stories they knew, drank discreetly, drove fast, and admired the golf courses on the North Shore, above Chicago. Sam enjoyed it. But he noted that when he left they seemed cheerful enough about going on by themselves.

Brent—Emily—business—now Tub and Hazzard—they didn't need him.

All thinking about matters less immediate than food, sex, business, and the security of one's children is a disease, and Sam was catching it. It made everything more difficult.

He thought about alcohol.

He noted that most of the men of the country club set, including himself, drank too much. And they talked too much about drinking too much. Prohibition had turned drinking from an agreeable, not very important accompaniment to gossip into a craze. They were jumpy about it, and as fascinated as a schoolboy peering at obscene posters.

And he began to meditate about his acquaintances, almost frankly.

He realized, almost frankly, that he was not satisfied now by Dr. Hazzard's best limericks, Tub's inside explanations about the finances of Zenith corporations, even Judge Turpin's whispers about the ashes upon the domestic hearths of their acquaintances.

Hang it, that *had* been good talk in Paris, even when he had not altogether understood it—Atkins' rumination on painters, the gilded chatter of Renée de Pénable's gang of pirates, and still more the stories of Ross Ireland. He had heard of Anastasia, who was declared to be the daughter of the Czar, of the Zinovieff letter which had wrecked the Labor Party of Britain, of the suicide of Archduke Rudolph, of the Empress Charlotte wandering melancholy mad through the haunted rooms of Castle Miramar, of systems to win at Monte Carlo, of Floyd Gibbons' plan to make a motor road from Tierra del Fuego to the Rio Grande, of Turkish women born in harems who now bobbed their hair and studied biology, of the Chinese "Christian general"—oh, a hundred stories touching great empires and hidden lands. And he had seen the King and Queen of England drive up Constitution Hill in an open motor, had seen Carpentier, the prize-fighter, dancing—a pale, solemn, unathletic-looking young man, seen Briand at the opera and Arnold Bennett at the theater.

It had been good talk and good seeing.

But even if he were articulate enough to bring home this booty to Tub and Dr. Hazzard and Judge Turpin, he felt—after a few stumbling trials he knew—that they would not be interested.

He saw that it was not a question of Ross Ireland being interested in kingdoms and of Tub being interested only in coupons and aces. He saw, slowly, that none of his prosperous industrialized friends in Zenith were very much interested in anything whatever. They had cultivated caution until they had lost the power to be interested. They were like old surly farmers. The things over which they were most exclamatory—money, golf, drinking—didn't fascinate them as brush-strokes or wood-winds fascinated the peering Endicott Everett Atkins; these diversions were to the lords of Zenith not pleasures but ways of keeping so busy that they would not admit how bored they were, how empty their ambitions. They had as their politics only a testy fear of the working class. (Why, Sam perceived uneasily, the whole country turned the dramatic game of politics over to a few seedy professional vote-wanglers!) To them, women were only bedmates, housekeepers, producers of heirs, and a home audience that could not escape, and had to listen when everybody at the office was tired of hearing one's grievances. The arts, to them, consisted only of jazz conducive to dancing with young girls, pictures which made a house look rich, and stories which were narcotics to make them forget the tedium of existence.

They did things, they rushed, they supervised, they contended—but they were not interested.

However difficult Fran might be at times, pondered Sam, however foolish Madame de Pénable with her false hair and her false gigolos, however pompous and patronizing Mr. Endicott Everett Atkins, they were fascinated by everything in human life, from their own amours to soup and aeroplanes.

He would like to be one of them. There was only one thing in the way. Could he?

Thus meditated Samuel Dodsworth, alone on the porch of the country club, awaiting the return of Tub Pearson.

What the devil was he doing here? He was as dead as though he were entombed. He had to "get busy"—either go back to work, at once, or join Fran.

Which?

Then, for a week or two, he became very busy peering into the Sans Souci Gardens development.

To the north of Zenith, among wooded hills above the Chaloosa River, there was being laid out one of the astonishing suburbs which have appeared in America since 1910. So far as possible, the builders kept the beauties of forest and hills and river; the roads were not to be broad straight gashes butting their way through hills, but winding byways, very inviting . . . if one could only kill off the motorists. Here, masked among trees and gardens, were springing up astonishing houses—considerably more desirable as residences than the gaunt fortified castles of the Rhine, the magnificent and quite untenantable museums of French châteaux. They were all imitative, of course—Italian villas and Spanish patios and Tyrolean inns and Tudor manor-houses and Dutch Colonial farmhouses, so mingled and crowding one another that the observer was dizzy. They were so imitative and so standardized that it was easy to laugh at them. But they were no more imitative of Munich than was Munich of Italy or than Italy of Greece, and like the rest of the great American Domestic Architecture of this era, they were probably the most comfortable residences in the world . . . for one who didn't mind it if his Venetian balcony was only ten feet from his neighbor's Swiss chalet, and if his neighbor's washing got slightly in the way of tea on his own lawn.

Driving through the Sans Souci Gardens, Sam was fascinated. He liked the energy with which roads were being dug, houses rising, stone fountains from Florence being set up in squares and circles designated by arty little swinging street signs as "Piazza Santa Lucia" and "Assisi Crescent" and "Plaza Reäl."

That there was something slightly ridiculous about mixing up Spain and Devon and Norway and Algiers, and transplanting them to the sandy hills of a Midwestern town, where of late the Indians had trapped rabbits and the rusty-bearded Yankees had trapped the Indians, did vaguely occur to Sam, but it was all a fantastic play to him, very gay and bright after the solemn respectabilities and the disapproving mansard roofs of the older residential avenues in Zenith.

Here, at least, he reflected, was all the color and irregularity he had gone abroad to seek; all the scarlets and yellows and frivolous pinks, all the twisty iron-work and scalloped tiles and striped awnings and Sicilian wine-jars he could swallow, along with (he thanked Heaven) all the mass-produced American electric refrigerators, oil furnaces, vacuum cleaners, garbage incinerators, over-stuffed chairs and built-in garages which, for all of Fran's scoffing and Mr. Atkins' expatriate distress, Sam still approved.

It came to him that now there was but little pioneering in manufacturing motors; that he hadn't much desire to fling out more cars on the packed highways. To create houses, perhaps less Coney-Island-like than these—noble houses that would last three hundred years, and not be scrapped in a year, as cars were——

"That'd be interesting," said Sam Dodsworth, the builder.

Of course he knew nothing about architecture. But he knew a good deal about engineering, about steel and wood and glass, about organizing companies, about getting along with labor.

"And say! Here's something that Fran would take an interest in! And she's an expert about decorations and all that stuff. . . . Might hold her here!"

In a leisurely way, apparently not much interested, Sam saw to it that he was introduced to the president of the Sans Souci Company and that they played golf together. He was invited to view the Gardens with the president, and afterward he spent a good deal of time walking through them, talking to architects, to carpenters, to gardeners. Otherwise he merely waited.

He was very good at waiting.

Twice a week letters from Fran had drawn him toward her and toward Europe. Her first letter had come on the day of his arrival in Zenith:

Villa Dorée,
Vevey,
Montreux,
La Suisse.

SAM DEAR, it's *too* glorious! Down the lake, the friendliest little steamers zipping by—peaks of the Dent de Midi—too perfectly *superb*—at sunset they're clouds of gold. And I've actually been walking! (Was Fran terribly bad in Paris, always galloping out to night clubs when you'd rather have gone walking? Well, you have your revenge—*awfully* lonely for your big bear growls and general dependability even though I am moved by beauty of this place and rather grateful for a little calm.) Walk up through vineyards to ducky little stone houses.

The villa is *charming*—not much ground but lawns and roses and terrace for tea, right on the lake. Renée de Pénable is just as glad as I am to be free for a while of all the noisy young dancing men. We've both sworn to let ourselves be old ladies with caps and knitting for a while, probably take to religion and camomile tea. I'm waiting for your letters, just had your steamer note, *so* glad you enjoyed crossing with Mr. Ireland, you probably had much more fun with him than with a bad sport like me—shouldn't have said that, looks mean, and I really and truly am glad you had a nice bachelorish time. Be sure and write *everything* about Brent and Emily and McKee. Give my regards to Tub and Dr. Hazzard. An astonishing big gull has just lighted on the lawn right in front of the window by which I write. We have the funniest pair of maids—one looks like a kewpie, and I suspect the purity of her intentions toward the postman, and cook is built like a Japanese wrestler—only more clothed, of course. I hope you will have a happy stay in Zenith. I do miss you. Come back soon and in early autumn we'll jaunt off together. I know you're a little fed up with Paris and personally I don't care if we don't get back there till spring, we might view Egypt, Italy, etc., for six months. Renée sends you her love and so do I, old grizzly!

Your FRAN.

Her next three letters were short, devoted to scenery and troubles. She always had troubles—always. They weren't very serious troubles, he thought: Renée had been cross, the cook had been cross—apparently Fran herself had never been cross. The dance at the Hôtel des Deux Mondes had been a bore, the rain had been wet, the English family next door had been rude, she had a toothache. Two of the letters were impersonal, almost chilling; in between was an affectionate cry for him so that he was confused and gave a good deal of his hours of meditation to wishing that she were a little less complicated.

The fourth letter was livelier:

Wouldn't you *know* it, Sam! After swearing that she never wanted to see a dancing man again, or anything in the way of a male more disturbing than a Father Confessor, Renée has already gathered about her (which unfortunately means more or less about me too) a brand-new horde of Apollos. How she does it *I* don't know! There'll be a nice young man of sixty staying with his venerable mamma at a hotel here; somebody in Paris asks him to call on us; he comes formally to tea; and the next day he's panting on the doorstep again, bringing a pack of males ranging from sixteen to eighty and from racing models to the latest thing in hearses. Of course she knows simply *everybody*—we can't go to the Deux Mondes for a cocktail without at least one gent swooping down on her with glad whoops of alcoholic welcome. So now the house is littered with fauns and Bacchuses, if that's the word.

There's an English hunting man named Randall who wears blue collars and shirts, and another Englishman picturesquely named Smith, and an Austrian baron who, as far as I can find out, sells clocks, and a man who seems to have leased the French Bourse, and a rich American Jew named Arnold Israel—he's about forty and very good-looking in a black-haired, black-eyed, beefy sort of way but a little too gaudily Oriental for my simple taste, when he kisses your hand he almost bites it, ugh! Of course it is nice to be able to dance again, but I really and truly did enjoy just mouching around and being quiet. Would you mind transferring five thousand (dollars) to my account at the Guaranty, Paris? Food here is more expensive than I had expected, and I've had to buy some more summer things—I found a shop in Montreux with simply *darling* hats, and while it's all very well to walk and to study the dear sweet smelly Common People by riding on trams, now that Renée has gone and dragged us into the Life Idiotic again we've had to hire a limousine and a chauffeur. I hope you're ever so happy, darling.

FRAN.

It was with her next letter that he began to fret. It reached him while he was motoring and golfing with Tub Pearson and Dr. Hazzard:

Such a lovely blue and golden day! The mountains are like the pillars of heaven. A bunch of us are taking a motor boat across to the French side of the lake. Arnold—Arnold Israel, an American here, I think I spoke of him—he has discovered a marvelous little inn where we can lunch—under the vine and fig tree sort of thing. He's really an awfully nice person, one of these extraordinary international Jews who can do everything and knows everything—rides like an angel, swims seven miles, tells the funniest living stories, knows more about painting than old Atkins and more about biology and psychology than sixteen college professors and I must say he dances like Maurice himself! And he is an American. It's funny, I know I'm playing into your hands but I must admit this, much though I admire Europeans, it *is* nice to rest one's self after even Renée's best cut-glass wit, etc., etc., by being simple and natural with a fellow countryman—one who will *understand* when you say, "She must have gotten that hat from the five and ten cent store," or even, "Attaboy." I find that with you away, you dear darling old vulgarian, I have positive joy in hearing somebody say, "Oh, hell." Makes me almost homesick. Oh yes, I guess I am American all right! Must hurry now, lots of love

F.

For ten days, no letter, then two together:

You would approve of your bad Fran thoroughly if you knew what a healthful life she is leading. Of course sometimes I do stay up a bit late at dances—we've met an awfully nice American Jewish family here named, of all things, Lee, friends of Arnold Israel—they have rented a wonderful old castle back from the lake above Glion, and they do give the most gorgeous parties. But otherwise I'm outdoors most of the time—riding, swimming, tramping, motoring, tennis—the Israel man has the most terrific cannon-ball in tennis. And then he'll read Shelley aloud, like a twenty-year-old Vassar girl! What a man! And to think that he's in the jute and hemp importing business! though it's true that he merely inherited the business from his hustling old father, and that he's able to leave it four or five months every year and loaf all through Europe.

Good Heavens, this whole letter seems to be about Arnold Israel! That's only because I thought he was the person here who would interest you most. I needn't tell you that he and I are merely the most impersonal kind of friends. Oh, I suppose he would get sentimental if I'd let him but I most certainly will not, and with all his Maharajah splendors, he has the most delicate and sensitive mind. I do appreciate what you say about Brent and Emily's having really grown up and hardly needing us. Madly though I adore them and long to see them, I'm almost afraid to, they'd make me feel so old, whereas now if you could see me in white blouse, shamelessly crimson skirt, white shoes and stockings, you would say I'm a flapper, and it's beautifully quiet here by the lake at night—getting in *quantities* of restful sleep.

Your FRAN.

Sam dear, this isn't really a letter but just a PS. to my note of yesterday. I feel as though I wrote so much about Mr. Israel that you'll think I think too much about him. That's the unfortunate thing about letters—one just chats along and often gives a wrong impression. If I have mentioned him several times it's only because most of the other people, no matter how well they may dance or swim, are really pretty dull, while he is a nice person to talk to, and of course—I needn't tell you, you old loyal darling, I have no other interest in him. Besides, Renée is crazy about him and wants to annex him for keeps, and as she's really the chef de bureau here, having found the villa, etc., even though she does pay only half the rent, if she wants her old Arnold she can certainly jolly well have him, for all I care. Hastily, F.

The next letter did not come for nearly a fortnight, and Sam realized, putting on his glasses to peer at the stamp, that it was not from Vevey, but from Stresa, in Italy:

Sam, the most dreadful thing has happened. Madame de Pénable and I had simply the most dreadful row, she said things I simply could not forgive, and I have left the villa and come here to Lake Maggiore. It's a lovely place, but as I don't know whether I shall stay, you'd better address me c/o Guaranty, Paris. And it was all about nothing.

I've written you about a Mr. Israel we met at Vevey and how crazy Renée was about him. One evening, I hate to say this about a woman who, after all, no matter how vulgar and unscrupulous she is has given me a good time, but I really must say she'd drunk more than was good for her and after the guests had gone she suddenly turned on me like a fish-wife and she used the most *dreadful* language and she accused me of carrying on an affair with Mr. Israel and of stealing him from her which was idiotic as well as false because I must say she never did have him so how could I have stolen him from her even supposing I had the slightest desire to! I've never had anybody talk to me the way she did, it was simply *dreadful!*

Of course I didn't condescend to stoop to her level and answer her, I simply said very politely, "My dear Madame de Pénable, I'm afraid you are hysterical and not altogether responsible for what you are saying and I would prefer not to discuss the matter any further certainly not till tomorrow morning." But that didn't stop her and finally I simply went to my room and locked the door and next day I moved to a hotel and then came down here—it really is lovely here, with the Borromean Isles including the famous Isola Bella lying out in the lake and across the lake, behind the nice village of Pallanza, the mountains rising, quite high and villages, etc., strung along the roads up the mountains. I feel awfully lonely here and that beastly toothache I had in London is returning but, after all, anything is better than living with a brawling vulgar fool like Mme. de Pénable.

I hate to 'fess up and I guess this gives you a lovely chance to crow over me, only I know you're too generous and understanding of your bad little girl to take such an advantage of her, but you certainly were completely right in what you said, or rather hinted, for you were too kind to come out and say anything rude, about the Pénable woman and her dreadful vulgar friends. I'm sorry. I hope I've learned something. Only I don't want you to think that Mr. Israel is in any way to blame, like the Pénable woman and her friends.

He was as innocent as I was, and he was good enough to see me off on the train at Vevey. He is a man I would like to have you meet, I think you would find in him all the nice, jolly, companionable, witty things you find in Ross Ireland and at the same time a subtlety and good taste that I'm sure you will admit with all his fine qualities Mr. Ireland lacks. Well, perhaps we will run into Arnold when you come back for I believe he is taking a whole year this time wandering around Europe.

Oh, do come soon, darling! I miss you so today! If you were here we'd take the little batello—aren't you proud of me, I've already learned ten words of Italian in one day; "Come in" is *avanti* and the bill is *le conto* or no, *il conto* I think it is—and we'd go scooting around the lake. If it's convenient you might send another couple of thousand, Guaranty Paris—of course I have to pay my share of the rent at the cursed villa at Vevey even though I'm not there. I suppose if I didn't, and I certainly would jolly well like not to, the De Pénable woman would go around saying that I was not only a libertine and a man-snatcher but also an embezzler!

How I'd like to have you spank her for me with your big beautiful strong hand! You'd do it so calmly and so thoroughly! So of course I have to pay my share of the rent and limousine hire there and as I also have to pay now for my rooms here or wherever I may be (you better not depend on this address reaching me but address c/o Guaranty) it will make things a little more expensive than I had hoped. Oh, dear, I did hope this would be a nice economical summer, and heaven knows I tried hard enough to make it so, but I didn't expect the unexpected to unexpect quite so disastrously. I feel better now after talking to you like this—I cried almost all last night—and I shall now live the life of a nun and devote myself to the study of the Italian language and people, as befits an old lady like me.

Your rumpled and repentant Fran.

That letter had come on the day when the president of the Sans Souci Gardens Company had invited Sam to lunch.

He was very frank, the president. He was a trained architect. He astonished Sam by admitting that he thought Sans Souci rather dreadful.

"There's too much mixture of styles, and the houses are too close together," he said. "But most Americans, while they'll pay a devil of a lot for a big impressive house, don't care enough for privacy so that they'll pay for a decent-sized plot of ground. And they *want* French châteaux in a Henry Ford section! But at least we've been educating them to be willing to come out toward the country instead of huddling together in the city. And I'm planning now, if Sans Souci doesn't ruin me, a much bigger development where we won't mix the styles. Oh, I suppose we'll have to go on cribbing from Europe and Colonial America. When a natural genius comes along and creates something absolutely new in houses, only a few people really like 'em. But I picture a new development—I hope with a less agonizing name than Sans Souci Gardens, which is the invention of that grand old Frenchman, one of my partners, Mr. Abe Blumenthal—in which, at least, we can keep the thing from looking like a world's fair. For instance, one section strictly confined to houses more or less in the Tudor style, and another all Dutch Colonial, or something not warring with Dutch Colonial. Or maybe the whole development in one style. Like Forest Hills on Long Island."

But—the Sans Souci president went on—he himself was too fanciful and too impatient. And as partner he needed some one (he hinted that it might be Sam) who would take the hundred or so notions for hotels and luxurious yachting tours and chain restaurants which he conceived every month, pick out the most practical, and control the financing, the selling.

He grinned. "Doesn't sound like much of an offer. It's based on the belief that I do have some new and interesting ideas along with quite a decent knowledge of architecture and building. But—— I'd like to see if it isn't possible for us to get together. While you'd been deciding that you were bored with selling cars and while you've been looking up my record for dependability——"

"Oh, you guessed that?" grunted Sam.

"Of course!"

"I'll think it over, I most certainly will," said Sam.

He returned to the country club, planning a dozen or so new kinds of real estate developments of his own, to receive Fran's distressed letter from Stresa.

It all seemed to fit in. He would bring her back; together they would look into the building of houses. He cabled her, "Too bad penable glad got rid her why don't you return zenith then abroad again in year or so."

She answered, "No want stay few more months suit self about joining."

And the great Samuel Dodsworth still had no more notion of what he was going to do than when, as a senior in college, he had sat on East Rock, looking at Long Island Sound, planning to be a bridge-builder in the Andes.

He wrote to her of the Sans Souci Gardens, and waited. He read about domestic architecture, and went to Cleveland and Detroit to inspect new developments.

Her next letter had been written some days before he had received her Stresa letter, before she had his cable. It informed him:

Yes, my dear Samivel, I am still at Stresa, though I may be off to Deauville immejit—I've always wanted to see one of those places where gloomy earls go to lose money at chemin de fer. But meantime I've been very happy here, after getting over my first hysterics at the De Pénable woman's beastliness. I've had such a nice girl here to give me Italian lessons daily and with her or other acquaintances made at the hotel I've explored all the divine villages about here—Pallanza and Baveno and Gignese, back in the hills and Cannobio, and Arona, etc. etc. I've taken a steamer clear up to Locarno, the Swiss end of the lake, and the tram up to the top of Monte Mottarone—Sam, it's so steep that when you look down at the lake below you the water seems absolutely to tip up like a tilted platter! So you're not to worry about me, I'm quite all right. I suppose I ought to tell you that Arnold Israel has come down here from Vevey, you remember the nice American I wrote you about, he's staying here at this same hotel.

I don't know that I ought to tell you this—even you, you old woofly-bear darling with your kind, decent, sympathetic mind might possibly misunderstand for, with all your virtues, after all you do have an American way of looking at things, but I'm afraid some gossip might come to you some day and I want you to understand. Needless to say, our relations are as innocent as though we were a boy and girl of eight and I do have such a nice happy clean time with him—Sam, Arnold drives a car even faster than you do, my heart almost stopped yesterday when he was driving 118 kilometers an hour, but he's such a superb driver that I usually feel quite safe. Now I must hurry and dress. Bless you. I hope you're well and happy. Best love to Emily and Harry.

F.

That afternoon he telephoned to the president of the Sans Souci Company that he was summoned abroad and could decide nothing for several months. He telegraphed to New York for a steamer reservation. He dashed to Emily, to Tub, to Hazzard, and said good-bye. But it was a week before he could sail, and meantime another letter had come from Fran—from Deauville:

Yes, here I am, and I don't like it much. This place is very gay but a little icky; lots of nice people but also *dreadful* ones, profiteers giving cocktail parties, race-track touts infesting the lounge. I wish I'd gone to the Lido instead. Perhaps I will. See here now, Samivel. In your letter, written to me at Vevey but received since I left, you said that you hoped I would, as you expressed it, "lay low" after my winter in Paris and "get to bed early for a while." I don't suppose you meant to be unpleasant but you couldn't realize how jumpy and hurt and bewildered I was after the horrible Pénable affair, like a lost child, and how your scolding would hurt me. Am I to spend the rest of my life growing old as gracefully *and as fast* as I can, which is apparently *your* ideal!

You talk as though I were some hell-raising flapper instead of a woman of the world who likes civilized amusements. There! I'm sure you didn't mean to be scolding, but can't you understand how it might hit me when I was in a very high-strung condition? Really, Sam, you must be a little more thoughtful! Do try to use a little imagination, now and then! Now that's off my chest and shall we just forget it? Only I must say—Sam, you may think I'm unjust, but really it was essentially your fault that I ever had the De Pénable trouble. If you hadn't insisted on running back to America for your class reunion, which wasn't so awfully necessary, after all, if you had stuck by me so that I wasn't in the anomalous and almost humiliating position of being without a husband, just like a lone adventuress, the De Pénable woman would never have dared act as though I *were* an adventuress and have turned on me the way she did. I hope you'll understand that I mean this only in the kindest and sweetest way, and we are, after all, aren't we, one of the few married couples who understand each other so well that we can be frank, and next time I hope you'll try to remember. There, that's over, and now for the news.

Yes, says the hussy defiantly, Arnold Israel *is* here with me, that is, as I'm sure you'll understand, he is in no sense *with* me, but he's here in Deauville. At first I wouldn't come along, but he was so thoughtful, so sweet, so understanding. He dug up somehow—I don't know how he does these things but he has what one might call the spiritual as well as the financial Midas touch, do you know that I've just discovered that while I thought he was merely loafing while he was away from his beastly old jute and hemp business, here in Europe, he's made about $40,000 by gambling in exchange and buying and selling a, well, a *reasonably* authentic Rembrandt and he wanted to give me some pearls but of course I wouldn't let him, but I'm drifting away from the thread of my story.

He found out at Stresa that a most respectable old Philadelphia couple, real Rittenhouse Square sort only fond of gaiety, were here, and he had them invite me to come here under their wing, which made it all right and prevents any of the nasty kind of gossip such as a beast like the De Pénable woman loves. After all, I thought, I'm silly about *not* coming with him. Sam will *never* misunderstand, he has imagination, and besides, I realized, I'm not a young flittergibbet or one of these horrible female Ponce de Leons like De Pénable, but a perfectly respectable matron who has brought up a son and a daughter now married, and no one would ever think of gossiping.

So here I am and while, as I say, I'm not crazy about the place, Arnold and I and his friends, a Mr. and Mrs. Doone, perfectly *darling* people and such wonderful sports though they're nearly seventy, we have gay little parties of our own and loaf around on the beach for hours nours nours at a time. Address me c/o Paris, though I'm certain to be here for at least three weeks more, as there is a magnificent costume ball coming off to which Arnold and I are going, most scrumptiously as the Sirocco and the North Wind, me with my nice pale Swede hair being naturally the North Wind. Lots of love,

F.

Sam cabled, "Sailing carmania meet you paris hotel universel september two." He added "Love," and crossed it out, and put it in again.

Twelve days later he was looking at the long fortifications at Cherbourg, watching the voluble little Frenchmen on the tender.

On deck, by night and day, he had walked out of his system all irritation at Fran, all hatred of Arnold Israel. When he had finished her letter from Deauville, he had suddenly grasped something which he had never completely formulated in their twenty-three years of marriage: that she was not in the least a mature and responsible woman, mother and wife and administrator, but simply a clever child, with a child's confused self-dramatizations. The discovery had dismayed him. Then it had made him the more tender. His other children, Brent and Emily, did not need him; his child Fran did need him! Something in life still needed him! He thought of her, awaiting him there in Paris, as he had thought of her in the uncomplicated days of their courtship.

Chapter 20

LATE of a cloudy afternoon, the Paris express slid through the thunderous gloom of the train shed, and Sam was jumpy with the excitement of arrival, looking down at the porters as though they were his friends, smiling at the advertisements of Cointreau and Fernet Branca, of Rouen and Avignon, on the station walls. He marched quickly out of the train, peering for Fran, anxious when he did not see her, and he felt utterly let down as he clumped after the porter with his bags.

She was at the end of the platform.

He saw her afar; he was startled to know how much lovelier she was than he had remembered. In a cool blue coat and skirt, with a white blouse, her hair, pale and light-touched as new straw, her slim legs so silken, her shoulders so confident, she was the American athletic girl, swift to dance, to play tennis, to drive like a cyclone. She was so vital, so *young*! His heart caught with admiration. But he was conscious that her face was unhappy, and that she looked at the approaching passengers only mechanically. Didn't she want him——

He came up to her shyly. He was confused by the rather polite smile that masked her face, but holding her by her shoulders, looming over her, he murmured, "Did I remember to write you that I adore you?"

"Why, no, I don't believe you did. Do you? That's very nice, I'm sure."

Her tone was as light and smooth and passionless, her laugh was as distant, as the banter of an actress in a drawing-room comedy.

They were strangers.

At the hotel she said hesitantly, "Uh, Sam—do you mind—I thought you'd be tired after the journey. I know I am, after coming from Deauville. So I got two single rooms instead of a double. But they're right next to each other."

"No, maybe better rest," he said.

She came with him into his room, but she hovered near the door, saying with a dreadful politeness, "I hope you will find the room all right. It has quite a nice bathroom."

He hesitated. "I'll unpack later. Let's not hang around here now. Let's skip right out and catch us a good old sidewalk café and watch the world go by again!" Wretchedly he noted that she looked relieved. He had given her but a tap of a kiss. She had demanded no further caress.

She was courteous, while he gossiped of Zenith; she laughed at the right moments; and she remained a stranger, forced to entertain the friend of a friend and wanting to get the duty over. She did ask questions about Emily and Brent, but when he talked of Tub, of golfing, she did not listen.

He could not endure it, but he said only, tenderly, "What's matter, honey? You seem kind of far off. Not feeling well? Glad to see me?"

"Of course! It's nothing. It's just—— I guess I didn't sleep very well last night. I'm a little nervy. But of course I'm glad to see you, dear old bear!"

And still they had not talked of Madame de Pénable, of Arnold Israel, of Stresa and Deauville. He had kept from it as much as she; he had said only, "Too bad you had your trouble with Mrs. Pénable, but I'm glad you had some fun after that. Your letters were great." He sounded provincial to himself as he maundered about Zenith, sounded rather dull and thick, but his senses were furiously awake. He noted how agitated she seemed. He noted that she drank three cocktails. He noted that he, Sam Dodsworth, was slowly massing for a battle, and that he dreaded it.

When they dressed for dinner, she closed the door between their two rooms.

"Let's go to Voisin's, where we can be quiet and talk," said he, when she came in to announce that she was ready.

"Oh, wouldn't you rather go some place a little more festive?"

"I would not!"

Then first was he brusque.

"I want to talk!"

She shrugged.

After the soup, he bumbled, "Well, I guess I've given you most of the news. Let's talk about plans. Where would you like to go, this fall? What about a good, long, easy hike through Italy and Spain and maybe over to Greece and Constantinople?"

"Why, I think that would be very nice, a little later on. But just now—— After all, I've had a dreadfully rustic summer—and of course you have, you poor thing! I think we both deserve a little gaiety here in Paris before we leave. After all, when you go traveling around to assorted places, you're frightfully detached from people."

Then, very blandly, as though it wasn't at all necessary to have his agreement, "I think we might stay here three months or so, and we might take a nice apartment up near the Etoile. I'm so sick of hotels."

"Well——" He stopped; then it came in a slow tidal wave. "I don't blame you for being sick of hotels. So am I! But I certainly don't intend to spend all fall, as I spent all spring, sitting on my rear in Paris——"

"Need you be vulgar?"

"Yes, I guess I need to. I don't intend to sit around here all fall, waiting for you to go. When we first started out, I was willing either to go on living in Zenith or travel, but if I'm going to travel, I want to *travel*—to see things, see different kinds of people and towns. I'd like to see Venice and Madrid; I'd like to have some German beer. I don't propose to go on being sacrificed to your ambition as a social climber——"

She flared, "That is a lie, and you know it's a lie! Do you think I have to *climb* to meet people like Renée de Pénable? Climb *down*, if anything! But I do find it rather more amusing to play with civilized people than to sit and soak at the New York Bar—yes, or go around gaping at ruins with a Baedeker! It's all very well for you, but I have to do the packing, I have to interpret for you. I have to plan the trip. Heavens, we'll *go* to Venice! But is there any need of our galumphing off like a Cook's tour when we could have a charming autumn here, with our own flat and servants, and all the friends that I have here now—quite independent of the De Pénable person? I'm sorry, Sam, but if you could just occasionally try to catch somebody *else's* point of view—— I should prefer to remain right here in Paris for——"

"Fran!"

"Well?"

He hesitated. While they talked, round them flowed the amenity of good service, and if they were two volcanoes, they kept their rumblings low, and to any observer they seemed merely a large and impassive man, probably English, and a woman with a quick-changing face who was a little angry but very much in control of her anger.

"Fran! You really would sacrifice me, to stay here?"

"Don't be so melodramatic! I can't see that it's any sacrifice to remain in the loveliest city——"

"Is Arnold Israel here in Paris?"

"Yes, he is! What of it?"

"When did you see him last?"

"This noon."

"He going to stay here in Paris some time?"

"I don't know. How should I know? Yes, I suppose he is."

"He give you any ideas about a flat near the Etoile?"

"See here, my dear Samuel! Have you been reading novels? Just what is the idea of this comic returned-husband-sternly-cross-examining-loose-wife pose——"

"Fran! How far did you go with this Israel?"

"Have you any idea how insulting you are?"

"Have you any idea how insulting I'm going to be, if you don't stop this injured-innocent business?"

"And have you any idea of how angry I'm going to be if you continue to act like a barroom bully—which is what you are, essentially! I've concealed it from myself, for years, but I knew all the time—— The great Sam Dodsworth, the football player, the celebrated bruiser, the renowned bully! Why, you belong in the kitchen, with the corner policeman, not among civilized——"

"You haven't answered! How far did you go with this Israel? I'm doing you the honor of asking you, not of snooping. And you haven't answered."

"And I most certainly do not intend to answer! It's an insult to be expected—— And it's an insult to Mr. Israel! He is a gentleman! I wish he were here! You wouldn't dare to talk to me as you've been talking, if he were here. He's quite as powerful as you are, my dear Samuel—and he has brains and breeding and manners as well. Aah! 'How far did you go in sin with your hellish lover!' After all the years I've tried to do something for you, you still have the vocabulary of a Laura Jean Libbey novel! Arnold, you will be shocked to learn, is so unregenerate that he prefers André Gide and Paul Morand to Laura Jean Libbey, and of course it's Black Guilt for me to have found a little pleasure in talking to him instead of discussing poker with your lovely friend Mr. Tub Pearson——"

While she raced on, quietly hysterical, he knew the answer to his question, and he was astonished that he was not more astonished, shocked that he was not more shocked. He did not greatly press her. When she stopped, shaking with muted sobs which he pitied, he said, gently:

"You found him very romantic?"

"Of course! He is!"

"Perhaps I can understand that—more or less."

"Oh, Sam, please *do* be human and understand! You do it so well, when you forget your Stern Man of Granite rôle and let yourself be sweet. Of *course* there was nothing wrong between Arnold and me—— Isn't it funny how—— I'm just as bad as I accused you of being! Using old cant phrases like that! 'Nothing wrong between Arnold and me!' After all, though, perhaps I was unjust to you; perhaps you didn't mean anything of the kind but merely—— You are kind, Sam, but if you don't mind my saying so, you're just the least little bit clumsy, now and then——"

She had checked her hysteria, had become amiable and prattling and self-confident again, and all the while he was reflecting, "She's lying. She never used to lie. She's changed. This fellow is her lover."

"——and what I suppose you were really hinting at was that I may have been handsomely kissed by my ardent Jewish friend, before I left Deauville. Well, I was! And I liked it! It doesn't matter if I never see him again—— Oh, Sam, if you could only *understand* how humiliating and infuriating it was of you to suggest that my desire to stay here had anything whatever to do with Arnold! But he was charming. If you could only have seen him, lolling among the sand dunes as though (I used to tell him) he were a Maharajah among gold cushions, with white flannels, and his hair wild and his shirt open at the throat—— It would've looked silly and pretentious with any other man, but on him it seemed natural. And all the while, with all his gorgeousness, talking so simply, so confidingly—really, it was touching. But haven't we talked enough of him? We must still make our plans——"

"Let's get him settled first. I've got——"

"Sam, the thing you never could realize about him, even if you met him, was how *touching* he was. Clever and handsome and rich and so on, and yet such a child! He needed some one like me to talk to. Oh, I was just an audience for him—nice old mother confessor. He was condescending enough to say that for a venerable dame of forty-two, I was still an excellent imitation of a pretty wench, and he'd supposed I was five years younger than himself, not two years older. And that I was the best dancer he'd found in Europe. But of course the bouquets were just preliminary to his talking about himself and his unhappy childhood, and you know what a fool I am about children—the least hint that anybody has had an unhappy childhood and I dissolve in tears! Poor Arnold! He suffered as a boy because he *was* clever and strong. Nobody could believe how sensitive he was. And his mother was a grim, relentless old dragon, who hated weakness of any kind, or what she thought was weakness, and when she'd find him day-dreaming, she'd accuse him of loafing—— Oh, it must have been hell, for so fine a spirit! And then in college, the usual trouble of the too clever and too handsome Jew—high-hatted by the stupidest, drabbest, meanest Yankees and Middlewesterners—they looked down on him, just the way a dray-horse might look down on a fine race-horse. Poor Arnold! Of course I was touched by so proud a person as he *caring* to tell me about his real self."

"Fran! You don't suppose that this is the first time your Mr. Israel has used the neglected-childhood approach? And apparently successfully!"

"Are you *again* hinting that I fell for him?"

"I am! It's rather important to know! Did you?"

"Well, then—yes. I did."

"Oh!"

"And I'm proud of it! I couldn't, once—under your heavy-handed tutelage, my dear Samuel!—have believed it possible to be an 'erring wife'! What blind hypocrites people are! And when it did happen, it all seemed so right, so natural and sweet——"

While she raced on he was incredulously admitting that this abominable thing, this newspaper-headline, divorce-court, sensational-novel degradation had actually happened to him—to her—to Emily and Brent. He had a fascinated desire to know details. He pictured this Arnold Israel, this black leopard of a man—no, too big for a black leopard, but that sort of gracefulness—returning to her Deauville hotel with her, shirt open at his too smooth throat—no, he'd be coming home with her in evening clothes, probably with a cape thrown back. He'd accompany her to her room at the hotel in Deauville; whisper, "Just let me come in for one good-night kiss." Then Fran became real. Since he had arrived, Sam's eyes had seen her but cloudily, his ears had heard her only as a stranger. Now he peered at her, was conscious of her, in black and silver, conscious of the curve from shoulder to breast; and he was raging at the thought of Israel.

All his long thinking and his wrath slid by in five seconds and he had not missed a word as she panted:

"You think it's an overwhelming attack on Arnold to suggest that he's used the same tactics before! Of course he has—of course he's had other affairs—perhaps lots of them! Thank Heaven for that! He's had some training in the arts of love. He understands women. He doesn't think they're merely business partners. Let me tell you, my dear Samuel, it would be better for you, and for me both, if you'd devoted a little of your valuable time to the despised art of rousing a woman to some degree of romantic passion—if you'd given some of the attention you've lavished on carburetors to me—and possibly even to other women—— I suppose you have been what is called 'faithful' to me since our marriage."

"I have!"

"Well, doubtless I ought to be highly gratified——"

"Fran! Do you want to marry this fellow Israel?"

"Heavens no! . . . Anyway, I don't think so."

"And yet you want to see him every day this fall."

"That's different. But not marry him. He's too much like plum cake—wonderful at a Christmas feast, but he'd bring indigestion. For a permanent diet I'd prefer good, honest, dependable bread—which you are—please don't think that's insulting; it's really a great compliment. No! Besides, he doesn't want to! I doubt if he'd care for any one woman for more than six months. Oh, I believe him when he says that he's almost morbidly faithful to the one woman while it lasts, but——"

"Has he got a wife some place?"

"I don't think so. I don't know! Heavens! Does it matter?"

"It may!"

"Oh, don't try to be melodramatic! It doesn't suit your Strong Calm Manly type! Anyway, Arnold wouldn't marry me, because I'm not a Jew. He's just as proud of being a Jew as you are of being a Nordic. He ought to be! He's more or less related to the Mendelssohns and the Rothschilds and all kinds of really significant people. A cousin of his in Vienna——"

"Fran! Have you any idea how serious this business is?"

"Well, rather more than you have, perhaps!"

"I doubt it! Fran, you'll either marry him or cut him out, absolutely and completely."

"My dear Samuel, he might have something to say about that! He's not one of your meek Revelation secretaries. And I won't be bullied!"

"Yes, you will! For the first time! God knows you're getting off easy. Oh, I'm not the kind that would grab a shotgun and start off to get you and your lover——"

"Well, I should hope not!"

"Don't be so sure! I could turn that way, if you just went on long enough! No, I'm not that kind, especially. But, by God, I'm still less of the complaisant husband who's going to sit around and watch his wife entertain her lover, as you've planned to, this fall——"

"I haven't admitted that I plan to do any——"

"You've admitted it and more! Now you'll either come away and travel with me, and chuck this fellow and forget him, or I'll divorce you—for adultery!"

"Ridiculous!"

"Worse than that! Horrible! You can imagine how Brent and Emily will feel!"

Very slowly: "Sam, I never till this moment suspected that—— I knew you were stupid and heavy and slow and fond of vulgar people, but I never knew you were simply a bullying rotten cad! No one has ever spoken so to me in all my life!"

"I know it. I've baby'd you. You regard yourself, young woman, as the modern American, with fancy European improvements. But I'm a lot more modern than you are. I'm a builder. I don't have to depend on any title or clothes or social class or anything else to be distinctive. And you've never seen it! You've just lambasted me because I *am* slow and clumsy, till you've stolen every bit of self-confidence I have. You've been the traitor to me in my own home. Criticizing! Not nagging, but just enjoying yourself by being so sweet and superior to me and humbling me. That was worse than your affair with this Israel."

"Oh, I haven't done that! Oh, I didn't mean to! I respect you so!"

"Do you respect me when you want me to sit around and be valet to your lover!"

"Oh no, no, no, I—— Oh, I can't think clearly. I'm all confused. I—— Yes, if you want, we'll leave for Spain tomorrow."

They did.

Chapter 21

SINCE the days of Alexander the Great there has been a fashionable belief that travel is agreeable and highly educative. Actually, it is one of the most arduous yet boring of all pastimes and, except in the case of a few experts who go globe-trotting for special purposes, it merely provides the victim with more topics about which to show ignorance. The great traveler of the novelists is tall and hawk-nosed, speaking nine languages, annoying all right-thinking persons by constantly showing drawing-room manners. He has "been everywhere and done everything." He has shot lions in Siberia and gophers in Minnesota, and played tennis with the King at Stockholm. He can give you a delightful evening discoursing on Tut's tomb and the ethnology of the Maoris.

Actually, the great traveler is usually a small mussy person in a faded green fuzzy hat, inconspicuous in a corner of the steamer bar. He speaks only one language, and that gloomily. He knows all the facts about nineteen countries, except the home-lives, wage-scales, exports, religions, politics, agriculture, history and languages of those countries. He is as valuable as Baedeker in regard to hotels and railroads, only not so accurate.

He who has seen one cathedral ten times has seen something; he who has seen ten cathedrals once has seen but little; and he who has spent half an hour in each of a hundred cathedrals has seen nothing at all. Four hundred pictures all on a wall are four hundred times less interesting than one picture; and no one knows a café till he has gone there often enough to know the names of the waiters.

These are the laws of travel.

If travel were so inspiring and informing a business as the new mode of round-the-world-tour advertisements eloquently sets forth, then the wisest men in the world would be deck hands on tramp steamers, Pullman porters, and Mormon missionaries.

It is the awful toil which is the most distressing phase of travel. If there is anything worse than the aching tedium of staring out of car windows, it is the irritation of getting tickets, packing, finding trains, lying in bouncing berths, washing without water, digging out passports, and fighting through customs. To live in Carlsbad is seemly and to loaf at San Remo healing to the soul, but to get from Carlsbad to San Remo is of the devil.

Actually, most of those afflicted with the habit of traveling merely lie about its pleasures and profits. They do not travel to see anything, but to get away from themselves, which they never do, and away from rowing with their relatives—only to find new relatives with whom to row. They travel to escape thinking, to have something to do, just as they might play solitaire, work cross-word puzzles, look at the cinema, or busy themselves with any other dreadful activity.

These things the Dodsworths discovered, though, like most of the world, they never admitted them.

More than cathedrals or castles, more even than waiters, Sam remembered the Americans he met along the way. Writers speak confidently, usually insultingly, of an animal called "the typical American traveling abroad." One might as well speak of "a typical human being." The Americans whom Sam encountered ranged from Bostonian Rhodes scholars to Arkansas farmers, from Riviera tennis players to fertilizer salesmen.

There were Mr. and Mrs. Meece from Ottumwa, Iowa, at a palm-smothered hotel in Italy. Mr. Meece had been a druggist for forty-six years, and his wife looked like two apples set one on top the other. They plodded at sight-seeing all day long; they took things exactly in the order in which the guide-book gave them; and they missed nothing—art galleries, aquariums, the King Ludwig monument in two shades of pink granite, or the site of the house in which Gladstone spent two weeks in 1887. If they enjoyed anything, they did not show it. But neither did they look bored. Their expressions showed precisely nothing. They returned to the hotel at five daily, and always dined in the grill at six, and Mr. Meece was allowed one glass of beer. He was never heard to say anything whatever to his wife except, "Well, getting late."

In the same hotel with them were the Noisy Pair: two New Yorkers who at all hours were heard, widely heard, observing that all Europeans were inefficient, that they could get no hot water after midnight, that hotel prices were atrocious, that no revue in Europe was as good as Ziegfeld's Follies, that they couldn't buy Lucky Strike cigarettes or George Washington coffee in this doggone Wop town, and that lil ole Broadway was good enough for *them*.

They were followed by other Americans: Professor and Mrs. Whittle of Northern Wisconsin Baptist University—Professor Whittle taught Greek and knew more about stained glass and the manufacture of Benedictine than any American living, and Mrs. Whittle had taken her doctorate at Bonn on the philosophy of Spinoza but really preferred fruit-ranching. The Whittles were followed by Percy West, the explorer of Yucatan; by Mr. Roy Hoops, who sold motor tires; by Judge and Mrs. Cady of Massachusetts—the Cadys had lived in the same house for five generations; by Mr. Otto Kretch and Mr. Fred Larabee of Kansas City, two oil men who were on a golfing tour of the world, to take three years; by the brass-bound heel-clicking Colonel Thorne; by Mr. Lawrence Simton, who dressed like a lily and spoke like a lady; by Miss Addy T. Belcher, who was collecting material for a new lecture trip on foreign politics and finance and who, off stage, resembled a chorus girl; and by Miss Rose Love, the musical comedy star, who off stage resembled a short-sighted school teacher.

Typical Americans!

Sam never lost the adventurousness of seeing on a railway car a sign promising that the train was going from Paris to Milan, Venice, Trieste, Zagreb, Vinkovci, Sofia and Stamboul. Though he became weary of wandering, so that one museum was like another, so that when he awoke in the morning it took a minute to remember in what country he was, yet the names of foreign towns always beckoned him.

To Avignon, they wandered, to San Sebastian and Madrid and Toledo and Seville. To Arles, Carcassonne, Marseilles, Monte Carlo. To Genoa, Florence, Sienna, Venice, with two months divided between Naples and Rome and a jaunt to Sicily. To Vienna, Budapest, Munich, Nuremberg. And so, late in April, they came to Berlin.

Sam might not tell of it when he went home, nor years later remember it, but he found that to him the real characteristic of

Making a Foreign Tour had nothing to do with towers or native costumes, galleries or mountain scenery. It was the tedium of almost every hotel, almost every evening, when they had completed their chore of sight-seeing. There was "nothing to do in the evening" save occasional movies, or cafés if they were not too far from the hotel in the foreign and menacing darkness.

Every evening the same. Back to the hotel, weary, a grateful cup of tea, and slow dressing. They never dared, after trying it once, to go down to dinner in tweeds and be stared at by the English tourists of the pay-in-guineas classes as though they were polluting the dining-room.

A melancholy cocktail in the bar. Dinner, always the same—white and gold dining-room, suavely efficient black-haired captain of waiters pulling out their chairs, a clear soup of parenthetic flavor, a fish not merely white but blanched, chicken with gloomy little carrots, crême caramel, cheese and fruit. The same repressed and whispering fellow-diners: the decayed American mother in silver with the almost equally decayed daughter in gold, staring pitifully at the large lone Englishman; the young intellectual Prussian honeymoon couple, pretending to read and ignore each other, and the fat mature Bavarian couple, wanting to be cheery but not daring. The aged Britons—he with a spurt of eyebrows and positive opinions on artichokes and the rate of exchange; she always glaring over her glasses at you if you laughed or asked the head-waiter about trains to Grasse. The vicar of the local English church, moistly friendly, the one person who came and spoke to you but who, by his manner of inquiring after your health, made you feel guilty because you weren't going to his service next Sunday.

Then the real tedium.

Sitting till ten in the lounge, listening to an orchestra mildly celebrating the centenary of Verdi, reading an old Tauchnitz, peeping up uneasily as you felt more and more the tightening of personal ties with these too well-known, too closely studied strangers.

It was worse when the hotel was half empty and the desert of waiting chairs in the lounge looked so lonely.

Always the same, except in a few cities with casinos and cabarets and famous restaurants—the same in Florence and Granada, in Hyeres and Dresden.

Every evening after such a siege of boredom Sam guiltily inquired of himself why they hadn't gone out and looked at what was called the "Native Life" of the city—at the ways of that inconspicuous 99/100 of the population whom tourists ignored. But—— Oh, they'd tried it. It wasn't a matter of dark-alley dangers; he would rather have liked a fight in a low bar. But foreign languages, the need of ordering a drink or asking a taxi fare in Italian or Spanish, was like crawling through a hedge of prickly thorns. And to go anywhere in dress clothes save to tourist-ridden restaurants was to be tormented by stares, comments, laughter. The frankness with which these Italians stared at Fran——

No, easier to stay in the hotel.

Once in a fortnight Sam was able to let himself be picked up in the bar by some American or English blade, and then he glowed and talked beamingly of motors, of Ross Ireland. And Fran welcomed and was gracious with such rescuers . . . whatever she said in the bedroom afterward about manners and vulgarity.

But it thrust them together, this aching tedium of marooned evenings, and they were often tender.

And Fran was getting tired of the isolation of travel. He gloated that before long, now, she would be content to go home with him, to *stay*, and at last, fed up on the syrupy marshmallows of what she had considered Romance, to become his wife.

Twilight in Naples, and from their room at Bertolini's they looked across the bay. The water and the mountains in the water were the color of smoke, and a few little boats, far out, were fleeing home before dark. In the garden below them the fronds of a palm tree waved slowly, and lemon trees exhaled an acrid sweetness. The lights at the foot of Vesuvius were flickering steel points. Her hand slipped into his and she whispered, "I hope the boats get safely home!" They stood there till palms and sea had vanished and they could see only the lights of Naples. Some one afar was singing "Sant Lucia." Sam Dodsworth did not know the song was hackneyed.

"Tee—ta—tah, tee de dee, tee—ta—tah, taaaa—da," he hummed. Italy and Fran! The Bay of Naples! And they would go on—to sun-bright isles, to the moon-hushed desert, pagoda bells, and home! "Tee—ta—tah, tee de dee—— Santaaaaa Lucia!" He had won her back to be his wife!

"And they still sing that horrible grind-organ garbage! Let's go eat," she said.

He startled and sighed.

They were again companions, as they had been in their first days of Paris, and sometimes they had whole afternoons that were gay, trusting, filled with the vigor of laughter and long walks. They had again the sweetness of depending on each other. But Sam was conscious that their relationship had become self-conscious.

Much of the time Fran was straining to be friendly. Getting into a rut of it, they quarreled more often over tinier things.

He knew that he had bruised her, humiliated her, by his bullying in Paris, but he could not, in all his hours of agonizing about it, see what else he could have done. He tried to win her with little gifts of flowers, of odd carved boxes, and he fretted over her being chilly at night, hot at noon, tired in galleries, till she wailed, "Oh, don't *fuss* so! I'm all *right*!"

"If I could only do things naturally and easily, the way that fellow Israel probably does," he sighed to himself . . . and fancied that she was sighing.

He caught himself being critical. For all his "trying to make it up to her," as he put it, he was testily aware of certain childishnesses in her which he had ignored.

In the matter of money she was a brat. She talked, always, of her thoughtfulness about economy; of jewing down a milliner from a thousand francs to seven hundred, of doing without a personal maid. But she took it for granted that they should have the best suite in the best hotel in every town, and she so used the floor maid and the hair-dresser and so had to tip them that a personal maid would have been cheaper.

Sam would have liked to economize a little. He still brooded on the Sans Souci Gardens—though he never subjected his dream to her brisk ridicule, for he guessed what she would say about the idiocy of Italian palaces in Zenith. If he could ever coax her back, he would try the gamble of building (if she permitted him!), and in it he could use all the capital he had.

But he never spoke to her of money, and she never suggested that an ordinary room would do them as well as the royal suite, and if she made any comment at all it was only on the inferiority of that suite.

For hours at a time he assured himself of Fran's beauty, gracefulness, wit, and her knowledge of European languages and customs. He convinced himself—except in Venice, when they were with Mrs. Cortright.

Edith Cortright had been born in Michigan, daughter of a banker who became Secretary of the Treasury of the United States. In Washington she had married Cecil R. A. Cortright of the British Embassy, and gone with him to the Argentine, to Portugal, to Rome, to Roumania, where he was minister, and on many vacations home to England. She was about the age of Fran, fortyish, and she had been a widow now for three years, wandering from England to Italy and back. A note from Jack Starling, Tub Pearson's nephew in London, sent her to call on the Dodsworths at the Danieli in Venice, and she invited them to tea at her flat, a floor of the Ascagni Palace; echoing rooms, stone floored, with tall windows on the Grand Canal, with the light from a marble fireplace on chests of smoky walnut and vast tables worn satiny with age.

Sam was at first not vastly taken with Edith Cortright. She was abrupt as she talked of diplomats, of villas on the Riviera, of Roman society, of painting. She was dressed in soft black, worn a little sloppily, and she was pale. But he saw how lovely her hands were, and realized that her quiet voice was soothing. He guessed that her intense eyes missed nothing.

Fran played up to Mrs. Cortright. She too talked of diplomats, she too had notions about villas and society and painting, and on their way home she informed Sam that her Italian accent was *much* better than Mrs. Cortright's. Suddenly, though resenting his own criticism as though some one else were daring to make it, he felt that Fran knew considerably less than he—and she—had always assumed. Her Italian! She knew a hundred words! Villas! They'd never seen a Riviera villa from a more intimate position than the outside wall!

He reflected that Fran had an unsurpassed show-window display but not much on the shelves inside.

Then he was angry with himself; then he pitied her; then loved her for her childish shrillness of make-believe, her eagerness to be noticed and admired.

He wished they were going to see more of Mrs. Cortright. He felt that she really belonged to this puzzling, reticent thing called Europe and that she might make it clear to him.

Sam was surprised, felt rather guilty, to find that he was becoming more a master of the nervous art of travel than Fran. In Paris she had been supreme; had taken to language and manners and food hectically, while he stood outside. And she still insisted that he couldn't understand Italian waiters and shopping and lace shawls and cathedrals as she could. But while she was daily becoming more uncertain, he was daily developing more of a sure purpose in travel.

He was going back to make some such a "development" as the Sans Souci Gardens, and contemplating it he was becoming conscious that there was such a thing as architecture. Details that once he would never have noticed became alive: hand-wrought iron balconies, baroque altars, tiled roofs, window shutters, copper pans in kitchens seen from the street. He began, shyly keeping it from Fran, to sketch doorways. He began, in the evenings of hotel tedium, to read stray notes on architecture—guide-book introductions, articles in copies of *Country Life* found in the hotel—instead of news-stand detective stories.

It made him increasingly eager to be out each morning and to see new things, to collect knowledge; and somehow, increasingly, it was he who planned where they should go, he who was willing to confer with concierges and guides, and it was Fran who followed him.

The contrast between Fran and Mrs. Cortright kept annoying him. He was not very well pleased to see that after twenty-four years of living with Fran he had not in the least come to know her.

Always, particularly when they had first come abroad, he had considered her clearly superior to other American women. Most of these others, he had grunted to himself, were machines. They sobbed about babies and dressmakers and nothing else. They were either hard-voiced and suspicious, or gushing. Their only emotion was a hatred of their men, with whom they joyously kept up a cat and mouse feud, trying to catch them at flirtation, at poker-playing. But Fran, he had gloated, had imagination and flair and knowledge. She talked of politics and music; she laughed; she told excited stories; she played absurd pleasant games—he was the big brown bear and she the white rabbit; he was the oak and she the west wind who ruffled his foliage—and she did it, too, until he begged mercy. She never entered a drawing-room—she made an entrance. She paused at the door, dramatic, demanding, stately in simple black and white, where other women hesitated into a room, fussy and tawdry. And they glowered, those other women, when Fran gathered in the men and was to be heard talking with derisive gaiety about tennis, Egyptian excavations, Bolshevism—everything in the world.

He had been so proud of her!

And in Paris, at first—how different her devouring of French life from the flatness of the American women whom he heard in restaurants croaking, in tinny, Midwestern voices, "Mabel says she knows a place in Paris where she can buy Ivory Soap, but I've found one where I can get Palm Olive Soap for seven cents a cake!"

Ah, he had rejoiced, not of these was his Fran—swift silver huntress, gallant voyager, shrewd critic, jubilant companion!

And now, however he cursed himself for it, he could not down the wonder whether she really was any of these poetic things—whether she didn't merely play at them. He could never root out suspicion, planted when he had read her letter about Deauville and Arnold Israel, that she was in heart and mind and soul an irresponsible child. And the minute he was pleased with the bright child quality in her, the irresponsibility annoyed him. . . . Bobbing at cherries is not so pretty a sport at forty-three.

A child.

Now she was ecstatic—a little too demandingly ecstatic for his unwieldiness to follow her—over a moonlit sea, a tenor solo, or a masterpiece of artichoke cookery. Half an hour later she was in furious despair over a hard bed, a lukewarm bath, or a missing nail-file; and Sam was always to blame, and decidedly was to be told about it. He was to blame if it rained, or if they could not get a table by the window in a restaurant; it was not her tardy dressing but his clumsiness in ordering a taxi which made them late for the theater.

She was a child in her way of preening herself over every attractive man who looked interestedly at her along the journey—now that she had been converted to salvation by passion. And she was equally a child in laughing at, in forgetting, the older and less glittering men who were kind to them on trains and friendly at hotels. She forgot so easily!

Sam was certain that she had forgotten Arnold Israel. He identified certain Paris letters, with a thick, black, bold script, as Israel's. At first she was jumpy and secretive about them; then, in a month, she let them lie unopened. And once, apropos of a gesticulating operatic baritone, she began making fun of Israel's ardors. . . . He would almost have been gladder, Sam sighed, if she had enough loyalty to remember Arnold longer.

She was lovely quicksilver, but quicksilver is hard for a thick hand to hold.

A child!

He noted, too, her pretentiousness when she was with people like Mrs. Cortright. Fran let it be known that she herself was of importance. She rebuked people who—never having seen her before—failed to know that she was an expert at tennis, French and good manners. She didn't exactly say it, but she spoke as though ruddy old Herman Voelker, her respectable sire, had been at least a baron, and she was forever laughing at this fellow-traveler as being "common" and approving that other as being of "quite a good family—quite decent." She was like a child boasting to a playmate of her father's wealth.

But he felt it with a brooding pity that made him the fonder—made it the harder for him to fight his way free from her capricious domination of his life.

So, after months given more to exploring themselves than to exploring Europe, they came in April to Berlin.

Chapter 22

THE GOOD Herr Rechtsanwalt Biedner was giving a dinner, at his flat just off the Tiergarten, to his second cousin, Fran Dodsworth, and to Fran's husband. Herr Dr. Biedner was very Prussian, with close-cropped head, small eyes, hard jaw, and sausage rolls at the back of his neck, and he was probably the kindest and pleasantest man the Dodsworths had ever met, and the most international-minded.

Now, in the spring of 1927, Berlin looked prosperous again; also Herr Biedner had an excellent law practise, and his home was as thick with comfort as a coffee cake with sugar. In the hallway was an armoire of carved oak, and the horns of a stag; in the living-room, about a monumental stove of green porcelain, was a perfect auction-room of old easy chairs, and what seemed like hundreds of portraits of the Kaiser, Bismarck, Von Moltke, Beethoven, and Bach clustered behind the grand piano.

Sam was edified to discover that a porcelain stove really could heat a room, and that the pianist of the family was not Frau Biedner or some unrevealed daughter but Herr Biedner himself, though he seemed to be a perfectly worthy and successful lawyer. He was also gratified by the sight of three wine glasses at each plate, and of slim green bottles of Deidesheimer Auslese, 1921.

But the conversation appalled him.

They were so kind, these half dozen German business men and their wives whom Herr Biedner had assembled to greet his American cousins, and they all spoke English. But they talked of things which meant nothing in the world to Sam—of the Berlin theater, of the opera, of a Kokoschka Austellung, of Stresemann's speech at the League of Nations Council, of the agrarian situation in Upper Silesia——

"Golly, this is going to be heavy going," sighed Sam. "I wish somebody would tell a funny story."

And with weighty politeness he answered the weightily polite queries of the woman next him: Was this his first trip to

Germany? Was he going to stay long in Berlin? Was it really true that since Prohibition it was difficult to get wine in America?

The one light was the man beside Fran at dinner. With apparent gratification, Biedner had introduced him as Count Obersdorf, taking Sam aside to explain that Kurt von Obersdorf was the present head of one of the greatest Austrian families. His ancestors had owned castles, towns, thousands of acres, whole counties; they had had power of life and death; kings had bargained for their support. But the family had steadily grown poor the past two hundred years, and been finally ruined by the Great War, in which the Graf Kurt had served as major of Austrian artillery. Though his mother kept up a pretense of state, with two slew-footed peasant servants in a ruined old house in the Salzkammergut, Kurt was working in the Berlin bureau of the Internation Tourist Agency (the famous I.T.A.). He could not afford to marry. He had a reasonable salary; he was head of the I.T.A.'s banking department; but he had to "punch the time-clock," said Herr Dr. Biedner, obviously proud of this Americanism. "He is a fine sport about it. And he uses not much his title. His ancestors probably hanged my ancestors for shooting rabbits, but now he is like one of us here in my household, and he says that nowhere else in Berlin can he get a proper Suppe mit Leberknödel."

Being impressed by the title of count and by a vision of hard-riding ancestors in armor, Sam assured himself that he wasn't in the least impressed by title or ancestors, and he studied the family hero attentively.

Kurt von Obersdorf was perhaps forty. He was a tall, loose, lively man, with thick black hair. He had dignity enough, but he was full of laughter, and you felt that by choice he would like to be a clown. He made love to every woman and made friends with every man. Fran blushed when he kissed her hand, and Sam felt less disconsolate, less swamped by foreigners, when Kurt shook his hand and babbled in an Oxford accent with occasional tumbles into comic-paper diction, "I know so much about your Revelation car. Herr Dr. Biedner tells me you were responsible for it. I am enchanted to see you here in Berlin. Since six years I have driven a Revelation, the same car, it belongs to a friend, it is very shabby but the other day I drove it to Wild Park at a hundred and fifty kilometers an hour. I was arrested!"

Kurt demanded to see the Biedner grand-child (rather a nasty child, Sam thought, but Kurt chittered at it boisterously); then he played the piano; then he mixed the cocktails which Herr Biedner regarded as suitable to Americans and which the good burgher guests tasted with polite and beaming anxiety.

"Lively fellow, that count. Shows off too much. Never sits still," Sam meditated, with a sound American disapproval of foreign monkey-tricks, and all the while he liked Kurt better than any one he had met since Paris.

All through dinner, Kurt concentrated on Fran.

Sam became restive as he overheard Kurt dashingly tell Fran just what her "type" was, and cheerfully insult her by announcing what he liked and what he detested about that type.

"Yes," Sam caught, "you regard yourself as very European, Mrs. Dodsworth, but you are altogedder American. You are brilliant. You are an automobile's head-light. You learn quick. But you hurry right out and use all you learn. You never have fun out of not letting anybody know you know something. You are very beautiful. I suppose, especial, you have the most beautiful hair I ever have seen. But you would be discontented if there came anybody who did not—*wie sagt man?*—who did not acknowledge it. You are a play—author and heroine and actor, every one together. A great play. But you could never just cook for some man."

"Why should I?" demanded Fran.

It came to Sam that he had heard this before.

Major Lockert, telling Fran about herself, delighting her by talking about her, stirring her to a desire for men who desired her.

Yes. Lockert had started this biological process which had set Fran alight, changed her into something altogether different from the Fran who had sailed with him—— Or had he? Perhaps her first romance had uncovered the real, the essential Fran, whom neither he nor herself had known in the chill polite years of Zenith.

Damn Lockert!

And that aviator fellow, that Italian, Gioserro, had carried on the process. Damn Gioserro!

And Arnold Israel had really broken the delicate coating of ice over her. Damn Arnold Israel!

And now Kurt von Obersdorf, a man who could laugh, was going to lure her—— Oh, damn Kurt!

Or should he damn Fran instead? Fran to whom life was a fashion-show.

Or damn the Sam Dodsworth who had thought carburetors more fascinating than the souls and bodies of women?

Anyway, he wouldn't have another Arnold Israel affair. Nipitinthebud. Certainly would!

He worked up a good sound rage at Kurt von Obersdorf, and had it ruined the moment Kurt came to him, with Fran in tow, after dinner.

"Mr. Dodsworth," said Kurt, "I have behaved outrageously to your wife. She thinks I have insulted her because I say that she is only making believe when she thinks herself European—she is lovely, really, because she *is* American! But I am so pro-American! I admire all things American so much—huge buildings and central heating and adding-machines and Fords. Can I please take you about Berlin? I would be very happy!"

"Oh, we mustn't trouble you."

"But it would be a pleasure! Your cousins, the Biedners, they were so very kind to me when I first came from Vienna, and I have had so little chance to repay. And the Herr Doctor is so busy with legal t'ings—*aber fabelhaft!* I have much more time. Let me have the pleasure of doing something for the Herr Doctor!"

But from the way in which Kurt looked at Fran, Sam wondered if he might not have a livelier reason.

"Tomorrow—Sunday—are you free? May I take you out to a funny place for lunch?"

"That would be very kind of you," Sam said unenthusiastically.

"Splendid! I call for you at twelve."

Their suite in the Hotel Adlon looked on the eighteenth-century Pariser Platz, smacking of royal coaches and bewigged footmen, and beyond the Branderburger Tor, at the end of Unter den Linden, they could see the thick woods and little paths of the Tiergarten. This Sunday morning, after the party at Herr Biedner's, was flooded with spring, such exultant and surprised reawakening as only Northern cities know. Sam bullied Fran out of bed at eight-thirty, whistled while he shaved, devoured eggs in defiance of Fran's daily objection to American breakfasts in Europe (but she always managed to eat them if they were ordered for her), and lured her into the Tiergarten. The statues of portentous armored Hohenzollerns along the Sieges Allee they admired—neither of them had yet been properly told that the statues were vulgar and absurd—and they followed paths beside brooks, over little bridges, along a lake, to the Coney Island minarets which leered at them over the wall about the Zoo. Quite lost, they rounded the Zoo, stumbled on the Bräustübl and had a second breakfast of Rostwürstchen and Munich beer thick as molasses. After the more languid airs of Italy, their northern blood was roused by the spring breeze, and they came back to the Adlon chattering, smiling, content, just in time to meet Graf Obersdorf in the Adlon lobby.

He bounced toward them as though he had known them a dozen years. "It is a good thing that I shall take you away today! It is such a beautiful weather and if you are not dragged off where you can only loaf, then conscientious tourists like you would go see museums and palaces and all kind of dreadful things!"

"I am *not* a conscientious tourist!" protested Fran.

Kurt shook his head. With his experience at the Internation Tourist Agency, he could not imagine an American who was not a collector of sights, who did not work at travel as though it were a tournament with the honors to the person who could last out the largest number of museums. He was as convinced that all Americans mark down credits for themselves in their Baedekers as are Americans that all Germans drink beer every evening.

He called a taxi. Sam was rather glad that Kurt had not wasted money on an apparently private limousine. If he were going to the country by himself, Sam fancied, Kurt would go quite gaily in a motor 'bus, and be friendly with the driver before they got there. Already he had seen Kurt plunge into lively conversations with the Adlon concierge, the news-stand man, two pages, and the taxi-driver; and most of the way out to the rustic haven disastrously named Pichelsberg, Kurt told riotously of how frightened he had been all through the war, of how he had been captured by a very small Italian with a very large rifle, and of how he had won a debate about the plays of Pirandello with the Italian major who had him in for questioning.

The driver stopped by the road to tighten the fan-belt, and Kurt skipped out to watch him.

"Kind of like an American, this fellow—this count," said Sam. "Got a sense of humor, and don't take himself too seriously."

"Oh no, it's a very different thing," Fran insisted. "He's completely European. Americans are humorous to cover up their worry about things. They think that what they do is immediately important and the world is waiting for it. The real European has a sense of a thousand years of ancestors like himself behind him; he knows that his love affairs or his politics or his tragedies aren't very different from a hundred that have gone before. And they aren't so violently ambitious for success—they want to fit into life as they find it rather than to move it about—and they'd rather retire to a little cottage hidden among trees than to build a big stucco house on a hill for strangers to admire. Count Obersdorf doesn't take himself seriously—but he takes Obersdorfs in general and Austrians in general and Europe in general seriously. And he *is* rather a lamb, isn't he! I'll be glad, though, when he feels easier with us and becomes his own real thoughtful self—when he understands that we're not his 'conscientious tourists'—imagine!—but the sort that——"

"Yeah, nice fella," said Sam.

He was irritated by her self-election to superiority; he was bothered by her desire to have this new suitor consider her superior. When Kurt had scrambled back into the taxi she looked at him as fondly, as though he were a bright boy whom she wanted to amuse.

Sam sighed.

They left the taxicab at a path leading into thick scrub pines, and in the lazy warm day they ambled over pine needles to a shining river, the Havel, and along it to an immense waste of outdoor restaurant, the Erster Schildhorn, a block of tables set under trees by the river, attended by hysterically flying waiters. For all the haste of the waiters, it took a full hour and a half to lunch. And they liked it. In the spell of spring air, of rustling water, of good heavy stultifying food, they grew relaxed, content to sit and drink beer forever, to forget cities and hotel lobbies and motors and the social items in the *New York Herald*. Marinierte Herring and beer—noodle soup and beer—ham knuckle and butter-dripping mashed potatoes and beer—Apfel Strudel and whipped cream and coffee—the stolid Sam, the fiery Fran, the mercurial Kurt, they all gorged equally, and sat in the sun by the water, in a pleasant and anti-social coma, so deep a coma that Fran and Kurt did not talk and Sam was only mildly aroused by the fabulous spectacle of a man solemnly riding out on the Havel in a boat propelled like a bicycle, sausage legs revolving—a procedure as sacrilegious to Sam as rowing an automobile.

Without inquiring their desires—he was always a benevolent despot of a host—Kurt led them, when their eyes were cleared of the haze of food, on a walk of miles along the river and into Potsdam.

Here, Kurt explained, lived a small colony of the old Junkers, the court circle of before-the-war, ex-ministers and generals and their proud ladies, dispossessed by the republic. He was taking them to tea at the house of his aunt, the old Princess Drachenthal, whose husband, killed by the misery of the war which he had labored to prevent, had been an ambassador.

"The Crown Prince often comes in for tea. You will like my aunt. She is a dear old thing," said Kurt.

"Speak English?" Sam muttered uneasily.

Kurt looked at him curiously. "She was brought up in England. Her mother was the daughter of the Duke of Wessex."

Sam marched on tireless. Fran, in coat and skirt smart as a cavalry uniform, walked with the swift nervousness of a tennis player, while Kurt loped ahead and behind and to the side like an Airedale.

They passed country houses, square blocks of white, set in immense lawns; they passed beer gardens, festive and vocal;

and came to the decorous gray flat-fronted houses of Potsdam, sedate as Gramercy Park or a crescent in Bath. It was a clean, homelike, secure kind of country, and Sam found himself liking its orderliness better than the romantic untidiness of Italy. And found himself not only liking but feeling at one with the Germans.

He still had a war psychosis. He had expected to find in Germany despotic and "sabre-clanking" officials and hateful policemen; had worked up an adequate rage in anticipation. He was nearly disappointed when he found the customs officials friendly, when he asked questions of a Berlin policeman and was answered with a salute and directions in English, and when their room waiter at the Adlon remembered having seen them at the Blackstone Hotel in Chicago! Now he admitted that in all of Europe, however interesting other nationals, however merry the Italians and keen the French, he found only the British and the Germans his own sort of people. With them alone could he understand what they thought, how they lived, and what they wanted of life.

He liked this Sunday stream of Berliners on excursion—vast families with babies and rye bread and pickles and cold ham; eager young men and girls, hatless, the cropped girls rather masculine as far down as the neck but thoroughly feminine below; and occasional strayed Bavarians faithful to green hats with feathers and deer-horn ornaments, green jackets, green leather shorts, and rucksacks—the rucksacks not necessarily containing anything but a handkerchief, since to a true Bavarian a rucksack is worn not so much for portage as for elementary modesty; as some races conceal the face and some the chest so the Bavarians conceal the small of the back.

Fran protested against the infrequency of "native costumes"; she pointed out that despite the occasional Bavarians, most of these excursioners could not be told from a crowd in America. But that, after months of constantly eating the plum pudding of novelty, was precisely what Sam liked about them, and he was less homesick this afternoon than for weeks; he developed a liking for Count Obersdorf; he felt that the walk was "taking the kinks out of his legs"; he was glad that Fran had a lively companion in Kurt; and he came cheerfully up to the gloomy brown mansion of the Princess Drachenthal.

*

She was a fragile old lady, like a porcelain cup, and she seemed translucent as porcelain. She called Fran "my dear," and she welcomed Sam to Germany. Apparently Kurt had telephoned about the Dodsworths; she said that she was glad to have a "great American industrialist" see Germany first hand.

"My poor stricken country needs the co-operation of America. We look to you—and if you do not give back the glance we shall have to look to Russia."

She was apparently convinced that Sam had come in a limousine; she asked whether he had sent his chauffeur round back for his tea; and when she learned that Kurt and these visiting dignitaries had actually lunched at a low Volk Lokal and walked into Potsdam, she shook her head, as one not understanding. There were so many things the little old Princess did not understand in these machine-devoured days, she who as a girl had known the security of an old cow-smelling country house in Silesia and of a rose-red Tudor mansion in Wiltshire, in a day when counts did not work in tourist agencies, and America was a wilderness to which rebellious peasants ran off, quite unaccountably and naughtily. But there was the reality of breeding in her, and she tried to understand this bulky "great American industrialist" who was so silently pleasant, this vivacious American woman with the marvelous ruffled blouse peeping from her little blue jacket, the ageless American girl whose gay poise reduced the Count Obersdorf to the position of rattle-headed boy.

Sam perceived the worn elegance of the Princess, took pride in Fran's deference, and found restfulness in the drawing-room, which had very bad gilt chairs, an over-ornamented porcelain stove with very bad plaques of bounding shepherdesses, very bad pictures of stag-hunting and moonlight, far too many glass cases with Prince Drachenthal's decorations, far too many faded cabinet photographs of the '80's and '90's and yet, bad in all its details, was suggestive of aristocratic generations.

A retired German general came in for tea, with a refugee Russian colonel-baron, a Frau von Something who was apparently so distinguished that no one thought of explaining her, and a handsome fervent boy, the Princess's grand-son, who was taking his examinations in law at the University of

Bonn and who wanted, he said, to go to America. They were free of Renée de Pénable's pretentiousness, as simple as a group at Tub Pearson's, decided Sam. No, they were simpler, for Tub would have to be humorous for the benefit of the ladies and gentlemen, no matter how it hurt. Kurt von Obersdorf had dropped all of the slight skittishness into which he fell when he pranced for Fran's benefit, and he was discussing Bolshevism with the Russian ex-colonel.

They somehow lured Sam into talking. He discovered himself being eloquent about chrome steel and General Motors stock, while Fran, in a corner, was deferentially lively with Princess Drachenthal.

"Sort of like coming home—no, it's more like coming home than coming home will be, because Fran is satisfied here. Oh, Lord, *will* she be satisfied in Zenith when—— Oh, quit fussing! Course she will!" reflected the inner Sam, while the outer Mr. Dodsworth sagely informed them, "——and in my opinion the greatest fallacy in world-marketing today is a competition between American, German, French, English and Italian cars in South America, instead of all of us combining to educate the South Americans to use more motors and especially to help them to build more through highways that would tap every square mile of the continent——"

He wondered why Fran had been uneasy, in Venice, with Edith Cortright, when she was suavely at ease with Princess Drachenthal, far more of a personage.

"Because she was jealous? Because Mrs. Cortright, an American, has a position and a flat in a palace and everything? Or because she felt Mrs. Cortright could catch her easier when she was bluffing? No! That's unfair! Fran is no bluffer! Look how lovely she is to the old Princess, and how the Count and the General and everybody falls for her!"

They rode back to Berlin in the train, rather quietly. Sam hinted that Kurt must have an engagement for the evening, but Kurt protested, almost childishly, "Oh no! Are you bored with me? You must let me take you to dinner!"

"Of course, we'd be *enchanted*," said Fran, and Sam, prodded with a look, achieved, "Mighty nice of you, Count."

"If you really like, I will show you a nice restaurant, and maybe later—if you are not too tired, Madame—we could go a little while to some place to dance. You dance, I know, like an angel."

"Next to Carry Nation and Susan B. Anthony," said Fran gravely, "I am probably the best dancer in America."

"They are famous dancers?" said Kurt.

"Yes, they're so good they're known in America as the Gold Dust twins," explained Sam.

"Really? And you dance like them, Madame? I shall have to be very good!" said Kurt.

While Fran dressed for dinner, Sam and Kurt had side-car cocktails in the Adlon Bar. Sam liked the scarlet Chinese Chippendale walls, with little Burmese figures; the somewhat obese Bacchanalians in the painting over the bar; the corners with settees comforting to a drinking man; and the fact that here was one place in Europe where no foreign language—i.e., any language save American, with traces of English—was ever heard.

At the bar were always half a dozen of the American business men stationed in Berlin—shipping-men, bankers, representatives of the movies, and for the American journalists it was a club, where they exchanged tips on Russia and Roumania, Breitscheid's coming speech and the Zentrum Party's capture of the schools.

"I like this; I see myself sneaking in here pretty often," Sam promised himself.

He forgot the bar in attention to Kurt's confidences. He had never known any one so frankly emotional about his friends as Kurt, nor one so eager to be liked.

"Shall I be rude if I talk about Mrs. Dodsworth?" urged Kurt. "She is so lovely! A kind of Arctic beauty, shining like ice. And yet so very warm-hearted and gracious and fun-ny. And such gallantry—an explorer—but very elegant—like in a *Roman*, with many bearers and dressing for dinner in the jungle. One feels she could do anything she wanted to enough. Forever young. She is—perhaps thirty-five?—one would say she was twenty-eight. Our European women are very *gemütlich*, they are easy to be with, they wait on us, but not many among them have a sword-like quality like Mrs. Dodsworth and such high spirits—— Oh, I hope I am not rude! She is lucky to be accompany with a great red Indian like you—a chief, *sagt man*?—who can guide and protect her!"

Sam made the most awkward sound—something between "Thanks" and "Like hell!"

"As I said once, I admire America very much, and it is so kind of you two to come and *bummel* with me! And meet my friends."

"Kindness all yours, Count. Good Lord! Mighty nice of you to let us meet such nice people as the Princess and——"

"Oh, don't call me 'Count.' I am not a count—there aren't any more counts—the republic has come to stay—I am just a clerk for the I.T.A.! If I am only something with a title, then I would better be nothing! I shall be glad if you call me 'Kurt.' We Austrians are almost like you Americans in our fondness to call by the first name among people we like. Yes."

"Well, that's mighty nice of you——"

Sam wished that he could warm up. But he was conscious of waiting for Fran—of Kurt's waiting. He was annoyed at the prospect of again being admitted as Fran's patient escort, as he had been in Madame de Pénable's gang. Yet he felt that Kurt was honest in professing admiration for both of them, and he forced himself to sound amiable:

"I guess one of the things we Americans fool ourselves about is claiming that we're the only really hospitable race in the world. Don't believe any stranger in America ever was received in a more friendly way than Mrs. Dodsworth and—than Fran and I have been here and in England. Mighty nice!"

Then Fran was upon them, in amethyst velvet, and with velvet she had put on a patronizing grandeur. The simple-hearted Kurt was confused; it took him ten minutes to understand that she was not showing displeasure in dropping her jollity, but merely playing a different rôle. Entreated to join them in a cocktail, she condescended. "It would be ever so amusing to have an aperitif in the bar, but do you really think one *could*?"

"Oh yess, it is quite proper . . . almost!" Kurt begged.

Sam said nothing. He had seen Fran enjoying too many drinks in too many bars, and not calling them "aperitifs," either.

She was full of high life amid the upholstery and expensive food of Horcher's, and she generously commended the Rheinlachs. But somehow she came out of it—somehow, sometime, Kurt began calling her "Fran," and she admitted him with "Kurt"; she laughed without admiring her own laughter, and, permitting them an entr'acte during her personal drama of The Sophisticated American Lady Abroad, she allowed them to be human and cheerful again. Kurt talked, less flamboyantly now, more naturally, and Sam realized that however Kurt might insist that he was no nobleman now but only a tourist-agency clerk, Kurt belonged to the once powerful of the earth and, but for the war, would be magnificence in a castle. His father had been gentleman in waiting and friend to the Emperor, his great-uncle, the field-marshal, had organized the war against Prussia, and he himself, as a boy, had played with the Archduke Michael.

Sam wondered whether, however genuine his family, Kurt was one of these fictitional adventurers who would be likely to borrow money, and to introduce swindlers to a rustic from the Middle West. He rejected it. No. If he knew anything about people, this man was honest, unselfishly fond of entertaining people. And the Biedners vouched for him, and to Fran's father, the canny old brewer, a Biedner had been almost as beautiful and dependable and generally Biblical as stock in a national bank.

Obviously Fran had no doubts whatever about Kurt von Obersdorf. In the glow of his stories about the frivolous days of old Vienna, she forgot her own charms. She consented when Kurt proposed that they go to the Königin and dance; she consented when he proposed that they leave that decorative but packed haunt of the more sporting Junkers and venture to the vulgar Cabaret von Vetter Kaspar.

The wit there was devoted chiefly to the water-closet, and Sam was astonished to hear Fran shamelessly joining in Kurt's whooping laughter. Of course he laughed himself; but still —— Well, this fellow Obersdorf, he enjoyed things himself so much that he made you feel like laughing at—well, at things that people didn't talk about in Zenith, anyway not in mixed company—— But still——

They came out of the cabaret at one in the morning.

"Now just one more place!" Kurt demanded. "Such a place as I do not think you will see in America. *Shrecklich!* Such curious men hang out there and dance with one another. But you must see it once."

"Oh, it's pretty late, Kurt. I think we'd better be getting home," said Sam. An evening of stories, and a bottle of champagne, had warmed him to a point where it seemed natural to call Kurt by his first name, but not to a point where he forgot the joys of a good soft pillow.

"Yes, it *is* late," said Fran, but vaguely.

"Oh no!" Kurt begged. "Life is so short! To waste it in sleeping! And you are here a so small time. Then you will wander on and perhaps I shall never see you again! Oh, you did enjoy today, did you not? We are good friends, *nicht*? Let us not be serious! Please! Life is so short!"

"Oh, of course we'll come!" rippled Fran; and, though Sam grumbled to himself, "Life'll be a damn' sight shorter if I don't get some sleep once in a while!" he looked agreeable as they heaved themselves into a taxicab.

Their new venture in restaurants was called "Die Neuste Ehe"—"The Latest Style in Marriage"—and after two minutes' view of it, Sam concluded that he preferred the old style. Here, in a city in which, according to the sentiment of the American comic weeklies, all males were thick as pancakes and stolid as plow-horses, was a mass of delicate young men with the voices of chorus girls, dancing together and whispering in corners, young men with scarves of violet and rose, wearing bracelets and heavy symbolic rings. And there was a girl in lavender chiffon—only from the set of her shoulders Sam was sure that she was a man.

As they entered, the bartender, and a very pretty and pink-cheeked bartender he was, waved his towel at them and said something in a shrill playful German which Sam took to signify that Kurt was a charming person worthy of closer acquaintance, that he himself was a tower of steel and a glory upon the mountains.

It was new to Sam.

He stood gaping. His fists half clenched. The thick, reddish hair on the back of his hands bristled. But it was not belligerence he felt—it was fear of something unholy. He saw that Fran was equally aghast; proudly he saw that she drew nearer his stalwartness.

Kurt looked at the jocund bartender; quickly he looked at Fran and Sam; and he murmured, "This is a silly place. Come! Come! We go some place else!"

Already the manager was upon them, smirking, inviting them in two languages to give up their wraps. Kurt said something to him in a rapid, hissing German—something that made the manager sneer and back off—something so hateful and contemptuous that Sam reflected, "This Kurt is quite a fellow, after all. Wouldn't be such a bad guy to have with you in a scrap!"

As Kurt lifted the heavy brocade curtain before the street door to usher them out, the bartender, in a cat-call voice, shouted something final. Kurt's jaw tightened. It was a good jaw-line. But he did not turn and, out on the pavement, his face was full of an apology that was almost suffering as he begged of Fran:

"I am so sorry. I had never been there. I had just heard of it. I did not think they would be so dreadful. Oh, you will never forgive me!"

"But I didn't mind them!" Fran protested. "I think it would have been amusing to watch them, for a little while."

Kurt insisted, "Oh no, no, no! Of course you were shocked! Come! There is another place I do know, over the street. You will show me you forgive me by coming——"

They danced till three, at which hour every one in the café was sleepy except Kurt. The orchestra went home and, to the cheers of the grimly merry groups who were left slumbering over their champagne, Kurt trotted forward and played the piano like a vaudeville performer, and they all obediently awakened for the last dregs of joviality. A monocled officer-like German begged Fran to dance, and Sam was able to snatch three minutes of secret sleep.

He was gratified when, after he had grumbled, "Now we've *got* to go home," Fran and Kurt took him seriously enough to consent.

It was raining, and the street was like the inside of a polished steel cylinder. A late taxicab cruised up, but the doorman and his faithful big umbrella had gone home. Kurt whipped off his coat, wrapped it about Fran and, in shirt-sleeves, stood waiting till Sam was inside the cab. . . . And he *would* sit on the little folding seat and he wouldn't let them take him home, but escorted them to the Adlon, babbling, "It was fun, wasn't it! You do forgive me for the Neuste Ehe, don't you! It was a von-derful day, wasn't it! And you will come by me Wednesday evening for a little dinner to meet some friends? Oh, you must!"

Yes, they would, thank you very much——

In the extreme drowsiness of their room, Fran hinted, "You enjoyed it, didn't you, darling?"

"Yes, everything except the last hour or so. Got pretty sleepy."

"Kurt is a darling, don't you think?"

"Yes, he's a nice fellow. Mighty kind."

"But Heavens, what a bossy person he is! He simply demanded that I be shocked at that Den of Vice, and I had to do my best to please him—and you too, you pure-minded males! Well, he's a nice boy, and so are you, and I'm going to sleep till noon. I *like* Berlin!"

Chapter 23

THREE DAYS of museums, of art galleries, of palaces, of the Zoo. They went to Sans Souci, where Fran talked of Voltaire (she really had read "Candide") and Sam thought in a homesick way of the Sans Souci Gardens development in Zenith and snapped at himself that it was time to clinch with Fran, to make her come home and begin a new life of "making things."

They saw nothing of Kurt von Obersdorf—he merely telephoned to them eight or ten times and made them go out and see things. He so insisted that they see Molnar's "Spiel im Schloss" that they sulkily went, though by now Sam had convinced himself that he was right in thinking he didn't care greatly for plays in a language he didn't understand, and though Fran, exhausted by the florid endearments which had been poured upon her at a women's tea given by Frau Dr. Biedner, for once in her life wanted to go to bed.

She said that she understood every word of "Spiel im Schloss."

Sam said that he guessed it was pretty fine acting all right, and he thought he'd just slip down-stairs and have a nightcap in the bar.

He fell to talking with an American journalist who knew Ross Ireland; he had several nightcaps; and in general he enjoyed himself. When he slipped into their room, Fran was asleep. So, as he put it, he had got away with it, and he felt as exultant as a boy who has played hooky and discovers afterward that teacher has been sick all day.

In England Fran had learned to say Lift for Elevator, Zed for Zee, Labóratory for Láboratory, Schenario for Scenario, and Shi for Ski. And before she had ever left America she had been able to point her Europeanism by keeping her fork in her left hand. But now she added to her accomplishments the ability to make a European 7 by crossing it, and ardently she crossed every 7, particularly in letters to friends in Zenith, who were thus prevented from knowing what figure she was using.

*

The four great mysteries of life in post-war Berlin, not to be explained by the most diligent searching of history and economics and Lutheran theology, are all connected with apartment-houses, and thus are they: Why can no visitor get into an apartment-house after eight in the evening without protocols? Why are the automatic elevators kept locked, so that no visitor can use them? Why does no Berlin landlord provide modern locks, but always compel his tenants to carry a bunch of keys comparable in size to those used in the Middle Ages for closing cathedrals? Why does a landlord who has spent a hundred thousand marks on a marble staircase (with neat gilt edgings and mosaic inserts) refuse to spend a mark a night to provide lights in the hallways? They are dark. They are very dark. A light may be had by pressing a button, which provides illumination for a time, but in all the history of Berlin that time of illumination has never been known to last while a visitor climbed from the ground floor to the top.

On the top floor of an apartment house on the Brücken Allee lived Kurt von Obersdorf, and on the vertiginous way up to it Sam pointed out these four mysteries, and was pleased to have Fran agree with him.

They were received by Kurt's maid. She was an ancient thing, rusty and feeble and in some doubt as to what to do with Sam's hat and stick. While she puttered, Sam looked about. The apartment had a narrow corridor, the drab plaster rather flaked, and adorned with a yellow-stained engraving of St. Stefan's Dom in Vienna. Over a doorway were two crossed swords.

Suddenly Kurt bounced out on them, slimmer and looser than ever in dinner clothes, took Fran's wrap himself, spoke to the creeping servant with that mixture of scolding and family fondness which only a European can manage, and prattled:

"I am so glad! I was afraid you would be angry with me for my clumsiness about Die Neuste Ehe the other evening and punish me by not coming. Let me tell you who are the other guests. There are your cousins, Dr. and Frau Biedner, and the Baroness Volinsky—she is such a pretty girl, a Hungarian; her husband is a Pole, a terrible fellow; he is not coming, thank

God!; and Theodor von Escher, the violinist—he is such a *von-derful* violinist!—and his wife, Minna—you will fall in love with her, and Professor and Frau Braut—he is professor of economics in Berlin University, such a brain, he knows more America than *anybody*—he will prove to you that in two hundred years America will be a wilderness again, you will like him so much! They are a funny mix' lot, but all speak English, and I wanted you to meet different kinds. Fran, you look like a heaven's angel in ivory! *Kom' mal!*"

He ushered them, as though they were royalty, into a small, shabby, friendly apartment in which three people seemed a crowd. The chairs of old brown leather were hollowed and listed; the couch was covered with what Sam viewed as "some kind of yellow silk," though Fran whispered later that it was "perfectly priceless old damask." The pictures were largely photographs of friends, officers in Austrian uniform. But there were shelves of wildly disarranged books, and Sam noted later that they were in German, English, Italian, and French. He observed a dozen ponderous and dismaying volumes on American law and banking and history, the sort of tomes which he had always admired in libraries and shunned in the home.

When the door to the right was opened for a moment, Sam saw a narrow bedroom with a mean camp bedstead, racks of gorgeous ties, a picture of a beautiful girl, a crucifix, and nothing much else. That, with the little dining-room and a mysterious kitchen somewhere and a bathroom old enough to be historic, seemed to make up the domain of the head of the house of Obersdorf.

There were cocktails, agitatedly mixed by Kurt in a glass pitcher, and there was dinner (not very good) and conversation (tremendous). Under Kurt's hectic captaincy, there was none of the timid burgher decorum of dinner at the Biedners'; also there was more to drink, including an Assmannshauser champagne which made Sam determined to explore the Rhine Valley. Any one who didn't shout from time to time received Kurt's worried attention. Kurt was convinced that a person who was silent in his house had either ceased to like him—and probably for good reasons, for some hideous sin he had unconsciously committed against them—

or else was suffering from a hidden malady which ought to be treated out of hand.

But between the shouts, most of the conversation was carried on by Professor Braut.

When he first surveyed that learned man, who left with you the impression that he had whiskers even in his eyes, Sam had decided, "This bearded beauty may know something about economics in Germany, but I'll bet he doesn't know anything about the land of the safety-razor!"

Professor Braut turned to him. His accent was much thicker than Kurt's. "Please," he said, "I vonder if you coult tell me something I am trying to learn about agrarian movements in America."

"I don't know very much about them," said Sam. "Have you been in America?"

"Oh, a liddle—before the war. I was a professor in Harvard for a year, and in Leland Stanford a year, and I traveled maybe a year, but of course that is nothing to get any real knowledge of your great country."

Then, at Kurt's suggestion, Professor Braut gave a minute history of the Non-partisan League in North Dakota.

Through it he turned constantly to Sam for confirmation, and Sam—who knew very little about North Dakota and precisely nothing about the Non-partisan League—nodded blandly. At the end, Sam addressed himself strongly:

"He knows more about your own country than you do! Sambo, you know nothing. Ignorant! I wish I hadn't given up thirty years to motor-cars. And I haven't really learned much here in Europe. A tiny bit about architecture and a little less about wine and cooking and a few names of hotels. And that's all!"

While Kurt chattered of the adventures of Archduke Michael as a chauffeur to a Hungarian Jew, Sam had a vision of learning and of learned men, of men who knew things with precision, without emotional prejudice, and who knew things which really affected the broad stream of human life; who considered the purposes of a thousand statesmen, the function of a thousand bacteria, the significance of a thousand Egyptian inscriptions, or perhaps the pathology of a thousand involved and diseased minds, as closely as he himself had considered the capacities of a hundred salesmen and engineers and clerks in the Revelation Company. He saw groups of such learned men, in Berlin, in Rome, in Basle, in both Cambridges, in Paris, in Chicago. They would not be chatterers. Oh, he pondered, probably some of them would be glib and merry enough over a glass of beer, but when it came to their own subjects, they would speak slowly, for to any given question there would be so many answers among which to select. They would not vastly please Fran; they would not all of them be dancers of elegance, and perhaps they would fail to choose quite the right waistcoats. They would look insignificant and fuzzy, like Professor Braut, or dry and spindling. And he would be proud to have their recognition—beyond all recognitions of wealth or title.

How was it that he had not known more of them? In Yale, teachers had been obstacles which a football-player had to get past in order to carry out his duty of "doing something for old Yale." New York was to him exclusively a city of bankers, motor dealers, waiters, and theater employees. On this European venture which was to have opened new lives to him, he had seen only more waiters, English spinsters marooned in hotels, and guides with gold teeth.

Scholars. Men who knew. Suddenly he felt that he might have been such a man. What had kept him from it? Oh, he had been cursed by being popular in college, and by having a pretty wife who had to be surrounded with colored lights——

No, he rebuked himself. He couldn't get away with excuses like that! In the first place, he was a dirty dog to be ungrateful for having been popular and for having had such a glorious girl as his Fran—look at her now, laughing about the sanctity of the sausage in the German social scheme—look at her, reducing the Count of Obersdorf, kin of princesses and maybe kings, to bouncing admiration! No, he'd been lucky.

Besides! A fellow did not become things—anyway not after five or six or seven years of age. He simply was things! If he had had the capacity to be a savant, nothing would have prevented.

Or——

Suddenly he felt better about it. Was it possible that in some involved, unelucidated way, he himself was a savant in fields not admitted by the academicians as scholarship? He told himself that in the American motor-world he was certainly not known merely as a pedler and as a financial acrobat, but as the authority on automobile-designing, as the first man to advocate four-wheel brakes. Hm. *Did* that constitute him a scholar, or——

Or possibly an artist? He had created something! He had no pictures in the academies, no books to be bound in levant, no arias nor flimsy furniture named after him, but every one of the twenty million motors on the roads of America had been influenced by his vision, a quarter of a century ago, of long, clean streamlines!

Yes! And it didn't hurt a man to be a little proud of some honest thing he had done! It gave him courage to go on. Especially with a wife like Fran, who was always criticizing——

Good God, had he really become confirmed, since the case of Arnold Israel, in this habit of seeing Fran not as his loyal companion but as a dreaded and admired enemy, to placate whom was his object in life? Was this the truth about his wanderings, all his future?

He hastily got out of that torturing wonder by sending his mind back to scholarship, while he looked intelligent and placidly ate *Backhuhn* and seemed to listen to Theodor von Escher on his own superiority to Kreisler.

Could he ever attain scholarship now? Was it too infantile a fancy to think of becoming the first great historian of motors, historian of something which was, after all, more important in social evolution than twenty Battles of Waterloo? Or could he learn something of architecture? For he really was a little tired of motors. They meant, just now, sitting at a desk in the Revelation offices. Could he really make better Sans Souci Gardens?

Anyway, he wasn't going on just being a Cook's tourist, rather less important to Fran than concierges and room-waiters. He'd do *something*——

Or was this inner glow, so exciting and so rare—was it merely a reflection of drinking champagne and being warmed by Kurt's hospitality? Was his formless determination to "do something" and his belief that he still could "do something" only, in essence, like the vows of a drunkard?

"No, by God," swore Samuel Dodsworth.

"It isn't that. A drink or two, and a jolly bunch, do loosen me up. I'm slow at starting—— Hm! Very slow! Here I am fifty-two years old, and just this last year or so I've wanted to be more than a money-coining machine. . . . To be *something*. Though God knows what! . . . Eh?" (He answered furiously a chorus of accusers.) "I have been a good citizen! And I have brought up my children! And I have paid my debts! And I have done the job that was first at hand! And I have loved my friends! And now I'm not going to stand back the rest of my life and be satisfied and dead—dead on my feet—dead!

"I wish I'd known Kurt before. I'd like to've gone off for a few weeks with him and Ross Ireland. Only I ought to've done it ten years ago, and now it's—— But I won't *let* it be too late!

"Hm! *You* let! It's what Fran will let her dear husband do——

"Why is it I always go back to that—as though it was she that cramped my style, instead of my own lack of brains?"

And, annoyed by the way in which thoughts scamper around in circles if you once let them loose, Sam came abruptly out of his meditation and was again the large and prosperous American husband of a lovely American wife, a worthy husband listening with meekness to the conversation of her European friends.

Sam had noted, and been rather surprised at it, that Kurt von Obersdorf did not condescend to a mere university professor, as any American of good family would have done. For all his love of gossiping, Kurt listened humbly when Professor Braut really got going, like a liner towed out through little ripples of talk, tugs yanking at its sulky ponderousness, but finally plunging into the long rollers of conversation.

Braut was lecturing Fran as though she were a rather small seminar. He did violence, while he talked, to the English W and V and T, yet in his earnestness, his was no comic dialect:

"Emotionally, as a Prussian, with the symbols of blood and iron, of Bismarck and Luther and *der alte Fritz*, I detest the prostituted elegance of Paris and the Italians, like children playing at Empire. Yet all the time I think of myself—most people like me think of themselves—more as Europeans than as German or French or Polish or Hungarian; we think of ourselves, whatever family differences we may have, as standing together against the Russians (who are certainly not European but Asiatic), against the British, the Americans—however we admire them—the Latin Americans, the Asiatics, the colonists. The European culture is aristocratic. I do not mean that boastfully; I do not speak of famous old families, like that of our friend Graf Obersdorf here. I mean that we are aristocratic, as against democratic, in that we believe that the nation is proudest and noblest and most exalted which has the greatest number of really great men—like Einstein and Freud and Thomas Mann—and that ordinary, undistinguished people (who may be, mind you, counts or kings, as well as servant maids) are happier in contributing to produce such great men than in having more automobiles and bath-tubs.

"And by the aristocratic tradition of the real Europe I do not mean any hauteur. I think perhaps I have seen more rudeness to servants—as well, of course, as more rudeness to masters—in America than anywhere in Europe. Servants here are not so well paid, but they have more security and more respect. An American thinks of a good cook as a low person; a European respects him as an artist.

"The European, the aristocrat, feels that he is responsible to past generations to carry on the culture they have formed. He feels that graciousness, agreeable manners, loyalty to his own people, are more important than wealth; and he feels that to carry on his tradition, he must have knowledge—much knowledge. Why, think of what the young European must learn, if he is not to be ashamed of himself!

"He must know at least two languages, and if he does not know them, his friends are sorry that he is so poor a linguist. He must have—even though he may plan to be a stock-broker or an importer, or sell your automobiles, Mr. Dodsworth—he must have some understanding of music, painting, literature, so that he will really enjoy a concert or an exhibition of pictures, and not go there to make an impression. His manners must be so good that he can be careless. He must know the politics of all the great countries—I would bet you, Mrs. Dodsworth, that my four grandsons, though they have never been in America or England, know as much about President Coolidge and Secretary Hoover and Governor Smith as most Americans of their age.

"They must know cooking and wines. They themselves may prefer to live on bread and cheese, but they must be able to give their guests good dinners, and at not much cost—oh, so terribly little cost most of us can afford now since the war! And most of all, they must understand women, and the beginning of that—I t'ink Mrs. Dodsworth will agree—is really to like women, and to like them to *be* women, and not imitation men!

"That is a small bit of the required training of the real European—German or Swiss or Dutch or whatefer! And that training helps to keep us together, understanding each other, no matter how foolish we are and suicide with Great Wars! However we may oppose it, we are all at heart Pan-Europeans. We feel that the real Continental Europe is the last refuge of individuality, leisure, privacy, quiet happiness. We think that good talk between intelligent friends in a café in Vienna or Paris or Warsaw is more pleasant and important than having septic tanks or electric dish-washing machines.

"America wants to turn us into Good Fellows, all provided with the very best automobiles—and no private place to which we can go in them. When I think of America I always remember a man who made me go out to a golf club and undress in a locker room, where quite uninvited men came up and made little funny jokes about Germany and about my being a professor! And Russia wants to turn us into a machine for the shaving off of all the eccentricities which do not belong to the lowest common denominator. And Asia and Africa do not t'ink that human life and the sweetness of human life matter. But Europe, she believes that a Voltaire, a Beethoven, a Wagner, a Keats, a Leuwenhoeck, a Flaubert, give drama and meaning to life, and that they are worth preserving—they and the people who understand and admire them! Europe! The last refuge, in this Fordized world, of personal dignity. And we believe that is worth fighting for!

We are menaced by the whole world. Yet perhaps we shall endure . . . . perhaps!

"Some of us think that perhaps we shall prevail even against Americanization—which I may venture to define as a theological belief that it is more important to have your purchases tidily rung up on a cash-register than to purchase what you want. (And mind you—I am not so anti-American as I seem—I quite understand that the mystic process of 'Americanization' is being carried on as much by German industrialists and French exporters and English advertising-men as it is by born Yankees!) I think the *echt* Europe may be able to endure. For I remember always of Greece and Rome. Rome was the America of ancient history; Greece the perhaps over-cultured Continental Europe. *Vi et armis*, Rome conquered. Yet it was Greek architecture, Greek philosophy, and its gracefulness of body which revivified Europe in the Renaissance, more than Roman law.

"So! I deliver a lecture. *Hässlich!* Yet I must finish. To be clear, when I speak of the European you must understand that I speak of a very small, select, special class, which is far nearer to other members of that class in foreign nations than it is to most of its own countrymen. The beer-sodden peasant in a Gastzimmer at a country inn, or here in Berlin dancing in masses at Die Neue Welt, is not a European in that special sense. Neither is the bustling young business man on the Friedrichstrasse, or on the Rue de Rivoli, who is trying to sell vulgar porcelain or shoddy silk so fast as he can. Both of them would gladly emigrate to America and change leisure for automobiles. And also there are a few people born in America who *do* belong to what I call 'Europeans'—your author Mrs. Edith Wharton, I imagine, must be so. But wherever they were born, there is this definite class, standing for a definite aristocratic culture—and most Americans who think they have 'seen Europe' go home without any idea at all of its existence and what it stands for, and they perceive of Europe just loud-tongued guides, and passengers in trains looking unfriendly and reading *Uhu* or *Le Rire*. They have missed only everything that makes Europe!"

Sam was surprised to find himself answering:

"Yes, that's about true. America thinks of the Europeans as a bunch of restaurant cashiers trying to do us on exchange—thinks of Europe as dead—nothing but pictures by men that lived three hundred years ago. We forget your Freud and Einstein—yes, and European aeroplane constructors, and this Youth movement in Germany, and the French tennis players that beat us. But you have just as untrue an idea of America. All over Berlin, in the book-stores, I see books about America; titles like 'The Dollar Land.' Well, I'll bet the French peasant that sticks the centimes away in the sock, and the German farmer, love the dollar ten times as much as the average American. We love to make money, but we love to spend it. We're all like sailors on a spree. We have to have every parrot that's on sale on the waterfront. And——

"Why do you suppose so many hundreds of thousands of Americans come to Europe? Not more than one out of a hundred Europeans who do go to America ever goes there to learn, to see what we have. And after all, a Woolworth Building or a Chicago Tribune Building or a Ford plant or a Grand Canyon or a Sharon, Connecticut—and incidentally a mass of 110,000,000 people—might be worth studying. You of all people, Professor, know that most Europeans go to America just to make money. But why are the Americans here? Oh, a few of 'em to get social credit for it, back home, or to sell machinery, but most of 'em, bless 'em, come here as meekly as school-boys, to admire, to learn!

"What most Europeans think of America! Because we were a pioneer nation, mostly busy with farming and cod-fishing and chewing tobacco, a hundred years ago, Europe thinks we still are. The pictures of Americans in your comic papers indicate to me that Europe sees all Americans as either money-lenders who lie awake nights thinking of how they can cheat Europe, or farmers who want to spit tobacco on the Cathedral of St. Mark, or gunmen murdering Chicagoans in their beds. My guess is that it all comes from the tradition that Europeans started a hundred years ago. Here a few weeks back, when we were in Vienna, I picked up 'Martin Chuzzlewit' and waded through it. Funny, mind you, his picture of America a hundred years ago. But he shows a bunch of people along the Ohio River and in New York who were too lazy to scratch, who——"

"Sam!" warned Fran, but he strode on unregarding.

"——were ignorant as Hottentots and killed each other with revolvers whenever they felt like it, with no recourse. In fact, every American that Dickens shows in the book is a homicidal idiot, except one—and he wanted to live abroad! Well! You can't tell me that a degenerate bunch like that could have taken the very river-bottom swamps that Dickens describes, and in three generations have turned 'em into the prosperous cement-paved powerful country that they are today! Yet Europe goes on reading hack authors who still steal their ideas from 'Martin Chuzzlewit' and saying, 'There, I told you so!' Say, do you realize that at the time Dickens described the Middlewest—my own part of the country—as entirely composed of human wet rags, a fellow named Abe Lincoln and another named Grant were living there; and not more than maybe ten years later, a boy called William Dean Howells (I heard him lecture once at Yale, and I notice that they still read his book about Venice *in* Venice) had been born? Dickens couldn't find or see people like that. Perhaps some European observers today are missing a few Lincolns and Howellses!

"The kind of pride that you describe, Professor, as belonging to the real aristocratic Europeans, is fine—I'm all for it. And I want to see just that kind of pride in America. Maybe we've gone too fast to get it. But as I wander around Europe, I find a whale of a lot of Americans who are going slow and quiet, and who are thinking—and not all of 'em artists and professors, by a long shot, but retired business men. We are getting a tradition that—— Good Lord! You said you'd been lecturing. I'm afraid I have, too!"

Kurt cried "To America!" and adumbrated "Yes, America is *the* hope of—— And of course the paradise of women."

Fran exploded:

"Oh, that is the one most idiotic fallacy about America—and it's just as much believed in America as in Europe—and it's just as much mouthed by women as by men—and deep down they don't believe a word of it! It's my profound conviction that there's no woman living, no real normal woman, who doesn't want a husband who can beat her, if she deserves it—no matter though she may be president of a college or an aviator. Mind you, I don't say she wants to be beaten, but she wants a man who *can* beat her! He must be a man whom she respects! She must feel that his work, or his beautiful lack of work, is more important than she is."

Sam looked at her in mild astonishment. If anything had been certain about their controversies, it had been that Fran ought to be more important to him than his work. He tried to remember just where she had got this admirable dissertation on feminism. Certain of the phrases he traced to Renée de Pénable.

"And that's just what you do have in Europe, and what we don't have in America. Mind you, I'm not speaking of Sam and myself—he's awfully competent at beating me when I deserve it!"

Her jocular glance at Sam was admiringly observed by all assembled.

"I'm just speaking generally. Oh, the American wife of the prosperous classes—sometimes even among people who have no money visible to the naked eye—has privileges for which the European woman would envy her. She doesn't have to beg her husband for money. She has a joint bank-account. If she wants to study singing or advocate anti-vivisection or open a tea-room or dance with nasty young men at hotels, it never occurs to him to object. And so she's supposed to be free and happy. Happy! Do you know why the American husband gives his wife so much freedom? Because he doesn't *care* what she does—because he isn't sufficiently interested in her to care! To the American man—except darlings like Sam, here—a wife is only a convenience, like his motor, and if either one of them breaks down, he takes it to a garage and leaves it and goes off whistling!"

This time her glance at Sam told him what she need not have told him, but she went on with an admirable air of impersonality:

"Whereas the European husband, if I understand it, feels that his wife is a part of him—or at least of his family honor—and he would no more permit her this fake 'freedom' than he would permit one of his legs to go wandering off cheerfully without the other! He *likes* women! And another thing. Any real woman is quite willing, no matter how clever she is, to give up her own chances of fame for her husband, *providing* he is doing something she can admire. She can understand sacrificing herself for the kind of civilized aristocracy that Professor Braut speaks of; she can sacrifice for a great poet or soldier or scholar; but she isn't willing to give up all her own capabilities for the ideal of industrial America—which is to manufacture more vacuum-cleaners this year than we did last!"

Sam caught her eye. He said, very slowly, "Or more motor cars?"

She laughed. . . . What a jolly, pioneering, affectionate American couple they were!

She said affectionately:

"Yes, or more motors, darling!"

"And you're probably right, at that!" he said.

Every one laughed.

"When people talk about the American wife and the American husband," Fran went on, "they always make the mistake of trying to find out which sex is 'to blame.' One person will tell you with great impressiveness that the American husband is to blame, because he's so absorbed in his business and his men friends that he never pays any real attention to his wife. Then the next will explain that it's the wife's fault—'The trouble is that when the American husband comes home all tired out after the awful rush of our business competition, he naturally wants some attention, some love from his wife, but she expects him to hustle and change his clothes and take her out to the theater or a party, because she's been bored all day with not enough to do.' And they're both wrong. There's no *blame*—it isn't the fault of either. I am convinced that the fault belongs to our American industrial system, with its ideal of forced selling—which isn't a big enough ideal to satisfy any really sensitive woman. No! She prefers the European culture and tradition of which you spoke, Professor Braut."

"That's kind of hard on me, as one of the promoters of the American industrial system," said Sam.

"Oh, you, you old darling, you're not really an industrialist at heart—you're a researcher."

And again she looked at him so appreciatively that every one was edified at the sight of one happy American couple.

There was, at table and over coffee in the drawing-room, ever so much more conversation. Sam listened to it heartily, while within he was in a panic of realization that Fran, his one security in life now that work and children and friends were lost, had this evening definitely given the challenge that she was bored by him, that she desired a European husband, that the interlude with Arnold Israel, who was more European than Europe, had not been an accident but a symptom.

He watched her turning toward Kurt. He could not ignore her jealousy of Kurt's pretty little friend, the Baroness Volinsky.

The Baroness was a slim, slight girl with beautiful ankles and curly shingled hair. She had nothing much to say. Throughout dinner, Kurt had turned to her with a hundred intimate approaches—"Do you remember Colonel Gurtz?" and "Vot a first night that was at 'The Patriot.'" Fran had concentrated on the Baroness Volinsky that chilling inquiring courtesy which is the perfection of hatred; had asked abrupt questions about Hungary—questions which somehow suggested that Hungary was an inferior land where the women wore wooden shoes—and had not listened to the answers.

When they chattered their way into the drawing-room and Kurt sat on the arm of the Baroness's chair, Sam noted that within five minutes Fran was sitting on the other arm of the chair, and that she insisted on speaking French, which Kurt spoke admirably and the Baroness not at all. And shortly thereafter the Baroness went home, followed by the Biedners and the Brauts, then by the violinist, Von Escher, who said almost obsequiously to his wife, "Could you possibly find your way home in safety alone? I must go practise with my pianist—tonight is his only free time."

Minna von Escher, with a snippishness which surprised Sam, remarked to her husband that she had often found her way home alone!

During the agitated German adieux, Sam murmured to Fran, "We better go too, eh?" but she insisted, "Oh, let's stay a little while—best part of the evening, don't you think?"

He didn't think. He merely looked passive.

Thus there were four together, Sam and Fran, Kurt and Minna von Escher, in that pleasant quiet after the gabble of conversation. In a corner of the room Kurt was showing Fran an enormous, very old-fashioned album of pictures of his boyhood home—apparently a castle in the Tyrol. Fran was in a leather chair; Kurt sat on the floor beside her, constantly bolting up to kneel and point out this old servant, that old schoolroom. They were locked in intimacy, forgetful of every one else.

Sam talked to Minna von Escher. She had a clown-like face, a Brownie-face, with a snub nose and too wide a mouth, but her eyes opened in such surprised roundness, there was such vitality in her speech, her hands and her ankles were so fine, that she was more attractive than most pretty women. She lay on the couch, full-length, rather petulant, and Sam sat by her, leaning over with his elbows on his legs, like an old man smoking on a fence rail.

"Your wife—she praises European husbands!" said Minna. "If she had one! Oh, they can be charming; they *küss d' Hand*, they remember your birthday, they send flowers. But I get so very much tired of having my good Theodor make love to every woman he meets! Just now—of course he had to go practise with a man pianist, at midnight—well, he is by this time at the apartment of Elsa Emsberg, and if Elsa is a pianist or a man, she has changed much this past week—and she was *my* friend in the first place! Oh, I am a European, but I wish once I had an American husband who would not sacrifice me to music and lof-affairs!"

She looked at him in a lively, appraising way, and suddenly Sam knew that she considered him an interesting big animal, that he could make love to her if he liked, and as much as he liked, and he was frightened by it.

He had always been monogamic. Now and then he had been attracted by some other woman, but he had been as shocked as though he were a priest. Perhaps the fact that his intimate life with Fran had not been very passionate had made him feel that the whole matter of sex stimulation was something rather shameful, to be avoided as far as possible. Certainly, when he tried to think about it, he escaped from thought with a gruff,

"Oh, a fellow's got to be loyal to his wife, and not go getting mixed up in a lot of complications."

But just now he seemed insufficiently afraid of "getting mixed up." He caught himself noting that Minna had an exquisite body. He thought, "I ought to give Fran a dose of her own medicine." He looked away from Minna, and growled, "Oh, I guess most husbands in all countries are 'bout equally selfish; just take different ways of showing it." He looked away, but his look was drawn back to her, and he wanted to take her hand.

"Oh no, you would not be selfish!"

"Sure would!"

"No! I know you better! Big, terrifically strong men like you are always gentle and kind!"

"Hm! I wish you could have met some of the kind, gentle, big fellows from Harvard and Princeton that used to sit on my chest when I played football!"

"Oh, in sports it is different. But with women—— You would be so gentle. But brave. Do you go hunting and camping much, and all those thrilling things, in your great American wilderness?"

"Well yes, I used to. I did quite a long canoe trip once, in Canada."

"Oh, *tell* me about it!"

No one since he had left Zenith had shown so comforting an interest in him. He was not looking away from her now; he was swallowed by her expanding, flattering eyes as he labored:

"Well, it was nothing especial. Went with a friend of mine. We made about a thousand miles, with sixty-four portages, and the last five days we lived on tea, without sugar or condensed milk, and fish, and our tent got burnt up, and we slept under the canoe when it rained. Yes, that was good going. Hm! Like to do it again."

"Why don't you? Why don't you? I can imagine you wonderful in that wilderness."

"Oh, Fran—Mrs. Dodsworth—she doesn't care much for that kind of hiking."

"Hiking? Hiking?"

"Oh, you know." He made a vast circular gesture. "Going. Traveling."

"Oh yes. And she does not like it? Oh, I would!"

"Would you? I'll have to take you camping!"

"Oh, you must!" She seized his sleeve, excitedly shook it. "Don't make a joke! Do it!"

And he was certain that he could—and more certain that between Fran and Kurt, so innocently looking at pictures in their corner, was being woven a spider-web of affection. He felt helpless, he felt irritated, and that irritation submerged his rising fascination in Minna von Escher. No! He wasn't going to encourage Fran by giving her an example!

For a moment, while Minna was sputtering an account of her own courage and ingenuity on a North Sea voyage, Sam checked his suspicions. But he saw Fran blush at some remark of Kurt too low to overhear, saw her glance joined to his, and suddenly Sam was angry.

He grumbled at Minna, "Yes, must have been a mighty nice trip—never done much yachting, myself—say, my Lord, it's getting late!"

He poured across the room: "Fran! Know what time it is? It's almost one!"

"Yes? What of it?"

"Well. . . . Pretty late. We were going out to see Brandenburg tomorrow."

"We don't *have* to go tomorrow! Good Heavens! We're not on a Cook's tour!"

"Well . . . Kurt has to be on the job."

"Oh no-o!" begged Kurt. "It does not matter. I shall be so unhappy if you run away early!"

"Of course if you *insist*——" said Fran.

She sounded vicious. Kurt looked at them miserably, as though he was wondering what he could do to reconcile them.

"No, no! Just didn't want you to tire yourself out. And here's Mrs. Escher pretty near asleep," Sam crowed jovially. And everybody laughed, and everybody looked relieved, and everybody said that Yes, wasn't it much more fun to be together, just the Family, after the others had gone.

But Sam had poisoned their moment. They looked self-conscious, and talked about music. Minna von Escher, not at all pleased by Sam's coyness, made yawning signs of going home, and the party broke up in fifteen minutes, with effusive announcements of what a good time they had had.

And so, in the taxicab, when they had dropped Minna at a residence which was confoundedly out of their way, Sam and Fran again started the battle.

Chapter 24

AFTER Fran had cried, "Good night—such a happy evening—*auf Wiedersehen!*" to Minna von Escher, she was silent for a minute, and it was a minute of sixty-thousand seconds, each weighted with fury, like the minute of suspense before a thunder-shower, in a meadow land where the grass turns poison-green with fear. Sam waited, trying to think of something to think.

She spoke in the manner of a school-teacher who has endured too much but who is still trying to keep her temper:

"Sam, Heaven knows I don't ask much of you in the way of social graces. But I do think I have a right to ask you not to be so selfish that you spoil not only all my pleasure but that of everybody else! I really don't see why you should always and unfailingly demand that everybody do what *you* want!"

"I didn't——"

"We were all perfectly happy, sitting there and talking so cheerfully. And I didn't notice that you were being so neglected—certainly that dog-faced Von Escher woman was flattering you and your pioneer hardihood sickeningly enough, and you simply lapping it up! And it wasn't even very late—I don't suppose you'll ever learn that Berlin and Paris are not exactly like Zenith, and that sometimes people do manage to keep awake here after ten o'clock! Count Obersdorf was telling me all about his family, and it was frightfully interesting, and suddenly you feel sleepy and—bang! The great Samuel Dodsworth is sleepy! The great industrial leader wants to go home! Everything must break up immediately! Nobody else must be considered! The great I Am has spoken!"

"Fran! I'm not going to lose my temper and let you enjoy a row tonight. . . . At least I hope not!"

"Go on! Lose it! It wouldn't be such a novel and shocking sensation! I'm quite used to it!"

"You are like hell! You've never seen me lose it properly! The last fellow that did—— Well, I paid the hospital bills!"

"Oh, the wonderful great hero that can knock people's heads off! That has all the charming virtues of a drunken lumberjack! That——"

"This is a little beside the point, Fran. I wasn't boasting—I was regretting. Listen, darling; now that you've blown off steam, can't you be reasonable a little while?"

Thus they reached the Adlon, bowed to the doorman as though they were in the best of humor, crossed the marble lobby, a fine, substantial, dignified couple, went serenely up in the elevator, and fell to it again:

"Fran, we've got to come down to cases. We've been drifting, without any plans, and I wanted to talk plans. . . . Maybe you were right about tonight. I didn't mean to sound grouchy when I suggested going home, and if I did, I'm sorry."

"It doesn't matter. As a matter of fact, it was probably a good thing. I have a slight headache, from too much cigarette smoke in that tiny place—I do wish you wouldn't always take your own cigars along and smoke them—it looks so pretentious. But let's not talk plans tonight. Heavens, if you were in such a mad passion to get away and get to bed, it's a little too much for you to want to stay up half the night talking about plans, when——"

"But I'm in a mood for it!"

"But I'm not! My dear man, is there any hurry?"

"But we'll put it off, the way we've *been* putting it off, if we wait till tomorrow."

"Does it matter?"

"It certainly does! By God, I'm going to be a little stubborn myself, for once!"

"For once! Oh, Sam, as if you were ever anything else!"

"All right. Have it your way. If I'm always stubborn, you won't be surprised——"

"*And—please—don't—shout!*"

"I am not shouting! Fran, please quit playing the cat-and-mouse with me. Look here. It's getting to be time for us to go home, and I do like Von Obersdorf, but he's the kind of fellow that's always so surrounded with people that if we stay here we'll find ourselves mixed up with a whole lot of folks, and we won't get away for weeks."

"What of it? Isn't that what we want? Isn't it worth while really knowing *one* European city? Not that Kurt has anything to do with it. It's really my cousins, the Biedners."

"But it is Kurt that counts! He's a mighty nice kind chap, but he isn't satisfied unless everybody is having a party all the time, unless he sees you every day, and especially as he's sort of attracted to you——"

"Sam, are you hinting that he and I—— Oh, this is too much! Just because I did like one man besides your high and mighty and sacred self, I can see that you're going to have the pleasure forever more of throwing it up to me, and of hinting the most outrageous things if I so much as have a polite talk with a man!"

"*Fran, for God's sake stop acting!*"

"And for God's sake stop cursing! Oh, I don't know what's gotten into you! A few years ago, even a few months ago, you would never have dreamed of talking to me the way you do. And every day you're getting worse. You have no idea of the kind of language you use——"

"Stop acting! I know perfectly well that so far this Obersdorf fellow and you have been as innocent as babes. But I also know that you could get too fascinated by him——"

"Nonsense! All we have is the polite interest that any European gentleman and lady have in each other. It's just exactly what I was saying tonight! The American male is totally unable to think of any woman as an agreeable teatime companion—if I hadn't been too polite and wanted to protect you, I could have told them a lot more about American wives and husbands! You never think of any woman except as a potential mistress, or as too unattractive to interest you. Whereas Kurt—— 'Innocent as babes!' Why, of course we have been, and we'll go on being so!"

"You sure will! And if only for the reason that I'm not going to have another Arnold Israel affair!"

She did not flare back as he expected. She stood fixed, looking at him reproachfully, tears coming. She was suddenly young and helpless and pitiful, and she spoke slowly:

"Oh, Sam, that wasn't kind of you! I never remember things and throw them up at you, as you do with me. You never understood about Arnold. I didn't defend myself when you were angry about him. But he was Romance—probably my last—and certainly my first! You were always so good; I've admired you and respected you; but you've always been so sound, so cautious, whereas with Arnold there was danger and excitement and madness and—— Just for once in a whole lifetime, I let myself risk danger! And I found I had a talent for it, too! And then, for you, I gave it up; I obediently settled down to plodding around from hotel to hotel, wherever you wanted to go. Arnold kept writing me, and I scarcely ever answered him, and now, of course, I've lost him for ever—for your sake! And then you insult me about him! Oh, Sam, that *wasn't* generous!"

She cried a little, sitting twisted in a big chair, her cheek against the back of it.

Sam felt that there was something wrong, something self-dramatizing, about her version, but his sulkiness at being beguiled was less than his fondness of her. He stroked her hair; he said, more tenderly and intimately than for a long while:

"I was beastly. Forgive me. And besides, of course I know your friendship for Kurt is something quite different." He heard an inner, testy voice: "It isn't, and you know it, fool!" But he went on urgently, drawing a small gilt chair, ridiculous beneath his bulk, to her side, and holding her hand as he talked:

"Fran, I want to go home and get to work. I'm naturally an active sort of fellow. I can't stand this loafing any more. And I don't want to manufacture cars. Maybe I half agree with you in what you said about industrialized America, tonight. What I want to do—— Oh, I suppose there'd be a lot of industrialization to it; certainly have to use modern methods in production and sales and advertising if we're going to meet competition. But there would be a kind of individual achievement, I'd hope, and a lasting—— This is something I've been figuring on for nine-ten months now, but I haven't said anything about it because I wanted to be sure. And for once, it would be something you could take part in——"

She sat up with a bounce, tears dried, and demanded, "Oh, *say* it! Don't make a speech! Forgive me, darling, for being rude, but you *do* take such a time——"

"Well, I want to have this clear, especially to myself. I never did pretend to be especially quick on the trigger!"

"As a matter of fact, you do think very quickly, once you have your facts, but you have a superstition—— I fancy it started back in college, when you had to play up to Silent Hero rôle. You have some kind of a childish idea—oh, I know you so *much* better than you do yourself!—you have an idea that it's somehow ridiculous for so big and solid a man as you are to speak quickly, and you've always suffered from it——"

"We're getting away from the point. Let me finish. As I say, this is a project that you could do as much with, and have as much fun with, as I could, and maybe more. Here's the idea:"

And, rather lumberingly, much interrupted, he outlined his notion of a better Sans Souci Gardens.

He had scarcely finished when she volleyed, "Oh, it's too utterly impossible!"

"Why?"

"You haven't the taste for that sort of thing—domestic architecture and decoration and so on. Why, Sam, I bet you can't tell me what the color of the last curtains we had in the drawing-room at home was!"

"They were—well, they were a kind—— Now let's see. They were pale red."

"They were a sort of beige, with so little red in it that it didn't matter. Dear, I do see the fun of a new venture like that, but for *you*——"

"Well, I personally attended to picking out the body colors and upholstery of the Revelation, the last five years, and I think it's generally admitted that they were the swellest——"

"You didn't, really. You depended on that awful lizzie, Willy Dutberry, that you had in the designing shop."

"Well, anyway, I picked out Willy, didn't I? And I had sense enough to follow his steer, didn't I?—even if he did wear side-whiskers and a pink tie! And for my development, I'll pick out—— Hell, Fran, I do know how to pick men! I don't pretend to know everything, even about autos. I don't need to. But I can——"

"And another thing, Sam. I do love you for wanting to produce something individual and lasting. But an American garden suburb—— Phooey! Nasty, jammed-together huddle of World's Fair exhibition buildings, with pretentious street-names——"

"Then make one that isn't pretentious or jammed! People have to live somewhere! And I'd depend on you a lot for suggestions about good taste and all that——"

"It's awfully flattering of you, my dear, but I certainly do not intend—or certainly not till I'm a lot older—I don't intend to give all my days and nights to being sweet to a lot of horrible parvenus who want Touraine châteaux with Frigidaire furnishings and all at mail-order prices!"

They argued for an hour. Fran had recovered from her Duse rôle, and was alternately airy and pityingly maternal. Sam felt that he had somehow not made clear his plan, but she blocked his each new effort at being articulate, and they went to bed at three with nothing clear except that, while she might condescend to go home with him in a vague four or five or six months, she was not going to help him "build stone castles of cement, and brick manor houses of linoleum," and that she was refraining entirely on account of her artistic ethics.

Remumbling the whole talk again as he lay awake, Sam could not get quite straight how it had happened that he had again failed to lure her home.

"And she says I'm a bully. Well, as a bully, I class about 1/2 h.p., 2 m.p.h.," he sighed, as he fell asleep.

He dreamed that Fran had fallen from a cliff and lay dead below him, and that Minna von Escher had come to smirk temptingly at him. He awoke to revile himself, then to rejoice that it wasn't so. In the dawn, he sat up in bed to look at Fran, and she was so childish, even her little nose hidden under the sheets, that he could think of no slogan of deliverance from her power.

Dining with Kurt—at Hiller's, Borchardt's, Peltzer's, at the Bristol and Kaiserhof, at the simpler Siechen's and Pschorrbräu. Dining at the Winter Garten, on the terrace, watching the vaudeville performance. Dining at outdoor places round about the Tiergarten, as the weather grew warmer and the beer more refreshing. A motor flight to the country house of a friend of Kurt, where all one glorious Sunday afternoon they loafed in the garden or bathed in the Havel.

But the point was that they were always with Kurt.

And Kurt, though he liked Sam, admired him, yet had conceived that Sam and Fran, like so many other American couples he had seen squabbling into and out of the Internation Tourist Agency, were on the point of breaking. And to him, the Viennese, accustomed to tempestuous strays from the bitter mountains and gray plains to Eastward and the North, this cool eager American woman was more exotic, more stimulating, than any Russian or Croatian or Zingara. . . . And she had a useful income of her own. . . . And there was, in all honor, no reason why he should not be there when the break-up came, nor why Fran should not have the privilege of buttressing the ancient house of Obersdorf.

At least, so Sam guessed at Kurt's opinion, and he could not protest that the chart was altogether in error.

It was a slow task for Sam to admit that he, with the training of an executive and the body of a coal-heaver, could not bully or coax his slim wife into reasonableness when her romanticizing ran away with her and she disclosed a belief that she was so superior that he ought to accompany her wherever she cared to stroll, or to stand acquiescent while she beamed at Kurt.

It was impossible, but it was so.

Sam tried all the recognized methods of bullying her. Their naked and wretched squabble after Kurt's party was repeated. He insisted that she was "coming home to America and coming right now!" But what was he to do when she reminded him that she had an income, and when she asserted (she really believed it) that she could always earn her own living?

What, still less, could he do when, after a night when he had lain awake ribbing up righteous anger, they awakened to a sparkling, growing day, and they walked along the Canal, lunched well, drove to the Wannsee and back, and watched sunset over the Tiergarten; when she stopped, twitched his sleeve, and said gravely, "Oh, Sam darling, will you let me thank you for all the lovely places you've taken me? I'm so heedless and silly that often I don't speak of it, but all the while, inside of me, dear——"

Her eyes were wet.

"——I'm terribly grateful. Venice! Rome! Paris! And this quiet sunset. Thank you, dear. . . . And thank you for not being a Tartar husband—for understanding that I can be excited and friendly with nice little people like Kurt without being a hussy!"

Just what was he to do? Except perhaps to mutter, "Have I ever remembered to say I adore you?"

Nor could he turn on Kurt von Obersdorf, since Kurt was—after much doubting Sam believed it—quite as fond of him as of Fran; since Kurt seemed eager to bring them together again, whatever it might cost himself in a chance at Fran's favors and fortune.

With the Dodsworths' isolation in Berlin, Kurt's ability to fall headlong in friendship, and Fran's liking for the glories of a Count, however dimmed, they three became a family, and as one of the family Kurt sought to soothe them. He was curiously impartial; with all his emotionalism he was a fair umpire. When Fran snapped at her husband for his inability to learn any German beyond "Zweimal dunkles," Kurt begged, "Oh, do not speak so crossly—that is not nize," and when Sam growled that he'd be damned if he'd sit till two A.M. watching her dance, Kurt would represent, "But you ought to be happy to see her so happy! Forgive me! But she is so lovely when she is happy! And she is fragile. She is easily broken by things and moods that we do not mind."

Kurt said—he really seemed to mean—that he too was lonely in Berlin, and though he very much did not want to intrude, he would be glad if he might play about with the Dodsworths every day that they remained. . . . And whatever his comparative poverty might be, he always paid his share of the bills.

"Be so much easier too if he weren't so damn' fair and square!" Sam sighed.

He had no proof, no proof whatever, that there was between Kurt and Fran anything more than this family affection.

Once or twice, as when the Berlin agent for the Revelation

car looked Sam up and took him to a luncheon of the American Club, Kurt and Fran slipped away by themselves. He spent a conversational evening in the Adlon Bar while they went learnedly to the opera. After these outings, Fran looked rosy and content.

In London, thanks to the attentions of Mr. A. B. Hurd, Sam had retained something of a position as an industrialist. Since then, progressively, he had become merely the Husband of the Charming Mrs. Dodsworth. He saw it, though he could not see precisely how it had happened. In Berlin, he felt that no one considered him as anything save her attendant—even after the unfortunate incident of Herr Dr. Johann Josef Blumenbach.

Herr Blumenbach's card was brought up to Sam as he was about to change for dinner. "Don't know who he is. Still, name does sound kind of familiar. Probably some friend of *hers*," Sam decided, and grumbled to the page, "Let him come up."

When he informed Fran, who was sewing a snap on an evening frock in her bedroom, she protested that she knew no Blumenbachs. She followed him to their sitting-room, and sniffed. A square, bullet-headed, bristle-headed, swollen-nosed man was Herr Dr. Johann Josef Blumenbach, with ancient and absurd spats.

"Excuse me that I call on you, Herr Dodtswort'," he sputtered, "and please to excuse my English, it is I guess owful bad English that I speak. But I have some liddle interest in a motor factory and from the motor magazines, besides my cousin lives in America, in St. Louis, I know moch about your development of the streamline in owtomobeelz. I vould be very pleast if Frau Dodtswort' and you would care to look over our factory."

Very suavely Fran eliminated Herr Blumenbach with, "That's very kind of you, Herr Uh, but we're leaving in just a couple of days, and I'm afraid we're going to be *frightfully* busy. You will excuse us, I'm sure."

He looked at her with a most active dislike; he snorted, "Oh, t'ank you very moch," and disappeared with quite ludicrous haste.

"His nerve! Probably hoped to get money out of you for

some horrible gamble," she said placidly as Sam trailed her back to the significant business of sewing on the snap. "*Horrid* man! And *you*'d have taken an hour to get rid of him!"

When Kurt inevitably came in to pick them up for dinner, Sam inquired, "Ever hear of a man named Blumenback, Johann Blumenback or some such a name—something to do with motors?"

"But of course!" said Kurt.

"Horrid man," offered Fran.

"Oh no-o-o! He iss a very fine man. Very public spirited. And he is one of the two or three big men in the motor industry in Germany. He controls the Mars company—I suppose the Mars is the finest motor in Europe——"

"Of course! That's where I'd heard the name," muttered Sam.

"——and I wish you could meet him. He would give you everything inside on motor industry here. But I have not the honor to know him. I have just seen him in a *Gesellschaft*."

"We must hurry!" said Fran.

And Sam said nothing at all.

He thought, many times, that if he telephoned to Herr Dr. Blumenbach, he might be accepted and entertained in Berlin as the Samuel Dodsworth he once had been—might thus again become that Samuel Dodsworth.

And he did nothing at all.

They had expeditions with the Baroness Volinsky and Minna von Escher, until Kurt, wounded to his little heart, as he could so often and so piteously be wounded, was convinced that no amount of advertising the merits of the pretty little baroness would make Fran like her. As to why Sam and Minna did not get along, he never understood, so he looked hurt and gave it up.

To Sam, Frau von Escher was a reminder that there were women who did not find him clumsy and cold, and he wanted to escape from that reminder. He could well enough picture falling into the entertaining distress of passion. He could even question whether it wasn't merely emotional indolence and fear of getting "mixed up," not morality, which had kept him "pure." Wasn't it because he did want to kiss Minna's wide derisive mouth that he was chilly to her, and contradicted everything she said . . . and gave Fran a chance to point out that he *was* rude and that it had been only her influence which had kept him amiable all these years?

"Hell!" said Sam Dodsworth wearily, and for all his searching he never found a more competent way of expressing it.

So he groped through the fog, and there was no path to be found. In the distance was the sound of menacing waters, and always he stumbled over unseen roots in a trance less real than any dream.

Chapter 25

IT SEEMED a singularly undistinguished morning. Sam looked forward only to a vague dinner with Kurt and a friend from Vienna, and as Kurt had said nothing more ecstatic about his friend than that he was "soch a good fellow and he speaks seven languages and is so fonny," Sam knew that the fellow couldn't be up to much. For the afternoon they planned to see the exhibit of Kolbe's sculptures at Cassirer's and the French impressionists at the Gallerie Tannhäuser, and Sam hoped (not very optimistically) to lure Fran out to Charlottenburg to inspect factories and tenements for laborers. . . . She liked to discuss what she called the Lower Classes with every one save members of the Lower Classes.

He lolled in the sitting-room of their suite, rather slovenly in dressing-gown and ancient slippers, which Fran was always going to replace by new elegance and never did. When he had finished reading the Paris American papers and had exclaimed over the fact that Mr. T. Q. Obelisk of Zenith had just landed in Europe and was going to squander an entire three weeks in Paris, he had nothing more to do. He thought of answering Henry Hazzard's last letter. But—oh, thunder, there was no news—— He thought of having a drink, and answered that it was much too early in the day. He thought of going for a walk but—oh, he'd walked all over the inner city.

He mouched. He prowled through the sitting-room, turning over tourist agency folders about Java—the North Cape—Rio de Janeiro.

He peeped into the bedroom. Fran, in nightgown and fluffy pink knitted bed jacket, was still abed, but over her chocolate she was furiously trying to read the *Vossische Zeitung* and the *Tageblatt* with the aid of a dictionary, imagination, and discreet skipping. He looked admiringly at her display of scholarship, he said that it was going to be a swell day, and returned to the sitting-room to stare out at the Pariser Platz and wish he were home.

At a knock, he said "Come IN!" indifferently. It would be the room-waiter, to clear away.

It was a boy with a cable.

For a time Sam put off opening it. It pleased him to think that even in his insignificance here in Berlin, he was the sort of man who received cables. Then he read:

"congratulate us birth nine pound son stop emily splendid shape cheers stop your first grandchild harry mckee."

Sam stood glorying. He was not finished, after all—something of him had been carried on with this new life! And Emily would be so happy! How he loved her! And *now*, by golly, Fran would want to go home! They'd catch the next steamer and see the baby, Emily, Harry, Brent, Tub, Henry Hazzard—— In maybe two weeks——

He paraded into the bedroom, trying to play-act, trying to sound unemotional as he remarked, "Um, uh, Fran—lil cable from Zenith."

"Yes?" sharply. "Anything wrong?"

"Well—— Fran!" He went to kiss her; he ignored her slight impatience. "We're granddaddy and grandmammy! And the devils never let us know youngster was coming—prob'ly spare us worry. Emily has a son! Nine pounds!"

"And how——"

"She's fine, apparently. So Harry wires." In her quick, happy look he felt more secure and married and real than for weeks. "My God, I wish they had the transatlantic 'phone working from here, way they have from London now. We'd 'phone 'em, if it cost a hundred a minute. Wouldn't that be great, to hear Emily's voice! Tell you what I am going to do! I'll 'phone Kurt Obersdorf and tell him about our grandson. I've got to holler——"

Her face tightened. "Wait!"

"What's the idea?"

"I'm delighted. Of course. Dear Emily! She'll be so happy. But, Sam, don't you realize that Kurt—oh, I don't mean Kurt individually, of course; I mean all our friends in Europe—— They think of me as young. Young! And I am, oh, I *am!* And if they know I'm a grandmother—— God! A grandmother! Oh, Sam, can't you *see*? It's horrible! It's the end, for me! Oh, please, please, please try to understand! Think! I was so young when I married. It isn't *fair* for me to be a grandmother now, at under forty." With swiftness he calculated that Fran was now forty-three. "A grandmother! Lace caps and knitting and rheumatism! Oh, please try to understand! It isn't that I'm not utterly happy for Emily's sake, but—— I have my own life, too! You mustn't tell Kurt! Ever!"

He knew then, well enough.

He was too hard hit to dare be angry. "Yes, I see how you mean. Yes, I—— Well, I'll go cable to Emily and Harry."

It was that evening, before they went out to dinner with Kurt, that he noticed her new habit of perfuming the back of her right hand, and reflected, "I wonder if it has anything to do with his kissing her hand? Wonder? You don't wonder; you know!"

He saw further that she faintly perfumed the inside of her arm to the elbow, and he was a little sickened as he stalked out to the sitting-room and tried to divert himself by reading the list of Circular Tours in Great Britain and France in the "European Travel Guide" of the American Express Company, while waiting for her to finish dressing. It didn't altogether absorb him. He looked about the room. There were roses—sent by Kurt. There was Feuchtwanger's "Jud Süss"—sent by Kurt.

Then there was Kurt himself, knocking, coming in gaily, crying, "Is that wife of ours late again? Sam, I have brought you a box of real Havana cigars smuggled through without duty! Oh, my roses came! I am glad. Sam, haf you any idea how thankful a lonely poor man—and to a *Wiener* like me, Berlin is just as foreign as it is to you!—so thankful to have Fran and you tolerate me while you are here! You are so good! . . . Fran! Are you not dressed? You are keeping your poor children waiting! If I were Sam, I would beat you! And my friend probably waiting in the lobby."

"Coming, Kurt!" she sang, lark-like.

And Kurt was kissing the back of her hand. And Sam Dodsworth said nothing at all.

But it was down in the bar, where they went to have cocktails and to wait for Kurt's friend, that the new and almost honestly analytic Sam Dodsworth caught himself in a situation more shameful and enfeebling than anything that had happened in their apartment. An American motor salesman, whom Sam had met at the American Club luncheon, stopped at their table to nod his greetings, and Sam caught himself saying, a little proudly, "Mr. Ashley, I don't think you've met my wife. And this is the Count Obersdorf."

"Mighty pleased to meet you, Count," said the motor man, after kissing Fran's hand in what he considered a European manner.

Sam sharply cross-examined himself. "Look here, Sambo. Were you flattered to be able to introduce a Count? This tourist agency clerk! How long will it be before you become the kind of rotten soak that sits around boasting that his wife has a count for a lover? No! I'm not that bad, not yet. But I guess my mind is kind of sick, now. What the devil was it that hit me? I don't understand. Emily, my darling, with a son! Doesn't Fran want——"

Coolly, quite prosaically, he interrupted Kurt to demand of Fran, "Say, uh, remember I told you about that young lady—that cousin of mine—that's just had a baby? Wouldn't you like to skip back to America and see her?"

"Oh, I'd love to. But I don't suppose we'll see her till next autumn," said Fran placidly.

"Here comes my friend. *Soch* a lovely fellow," said Kurt.

The second message from Zenith, from home, came in a letter which was handed to Sam at the desk, three evenings later, as they were going out to dinner with Kurt.

"From old Tub!" he chuckled, and tucked it into his pocket. When they were at table he suggested, "Mind if I glance at my letter?"

Tub wrote, in schoolboyish script:

> How are you and how's all the lovely femmes in Europe? Well, you're not going to get away with hogging them much longer. Matey and I have finally decided about time we ran over and had a look at the old country and get a decent drink. She's a grand wife and likes her likker. We sail on May tenth, on the *Olympic*, arrive London probably 16th, and Paris the 21st—stay Savoy

London and Continental Paris. In Paris about a week, then Holland, Belgium, Switzerland, Italy, south France, and sail from Cherbourg again on June 20th. Some fast trip, eh, but I bet we don't miss much, your last post card, and a hell of a tightwad you are about writing say you're going to Germany but don't see what you find there, can only get beer there and it's the bubbles that cure all your trouble that I want to taste again, you remember old song, champagne.

Now if you're too busy to remember old friends all right, but would be awfully glad if you could manage meet us London or Paris, or if along route afterwards send me schedule c/o Equitable Trust, 23 rue de la Paix.

Don't take any wooden money.

Sincerely, Your friend

THOS. J. PEARSON.

The letter had followed Sam from Paris to Rome to Berlin; Tub was already in London and would be in Paris in three days.

It was one of the few holograph letters Sam had received from Tub. Usually his laconic messages were dictated, typed on banking-house paper as stiff and luxuriously engraved as a bond. In it Sam felt an unfamiliar urgency; Tub was prepared to be angry, to consider himself deliberately slighted, if the Dodsworths did not appear in Paris to greet him and his jolly wife Matilde, otherwise Matey.

He interrupted Kurt—("Damn it! Seems at though, these days, I always have to interrupt that fellow in order to be able to speak to my own wife!") He crowed, "Say, who d'you think's in London and going to Paris? Tub and Matey!"

"Oh, really?" she said politely. She showed considerably more warmth in explaining to Kurt, "Tub is an old friend of Sam—quite a prosperous banker. If they come to Berlin, they'd be awfully happy to meet you. Oh! You said one day you wished you could get into a bank in America. Tub—Mr. Pearson his name is—might be able——"

"But we'll see him in Paris," Sam interrupted again. "Not coming to Berlin. And we ought to skip right down and be there to welcome 'em. Remember they've never been abroad before. I'll wire him in London tonight—might even see if I can get him on the 'phone—and we can probably get reservations for the Paris train for tomorrow evening."

Surely when Fran heard good old Matey gossip of their friends, when she scented Zenith again—— The miracle had happened!

"But, Sam dear," Fran protested, "I don't see any reason under Heaven why we *should* go down! And you complaining of how tired you were of Paris when we left it! I know how fond you are of your friends, but I don't see why you should let them use you!"

"But don't you want to see Tub and Matey?"

"Don't be silly! Of course, I'd be very glad to see them. But to trot all the way to Paris——"

"But don't you *want*—I can't imagine your not wanting——"

"Well, if you must know, I think your good friend Mr. Tub Pearson is a little heavy in the hand. He always works so hard at being humorous. And you yourself have admitted that Matey is dreadfully uninteresting. And fat! Good Heavens, I've had them for twenty years! No, you can do what you'd like, but I'm not going."

"But I wouldn't be much good to 'em as a guide. I can't speak French."

"Exactly! Then why go? They can get along as every one else does."

"But you could make it so much pleasanter for them——"

"It's all very well to be friendly and that sort of thing, but I'm not going to travel fifteen hours in a dirty train for the pleasure of acting as an unpaid Cook's guide to Mr. and Mrs. Tub Pearson!"

"Well, all right. Then I'll go by myself."

"As you wish!"

She turned briskly to Kurt, and with excessive sweetness discoursed on the state of the theater in Central Europe. Kurt looked at Sam, troubled, wishing to say something soothing. Sam was very quiet all that evening.

It was she who opened the engagement when they were alone, at the hotel.

"I'm sorry about Tub, and I'll go down there—a beastly journey!—if you absolutely insist——"

"I never insist on anything."

"——but I do think it's too ridiculous to be expected to be a guide—and of course your beloved Tub will want to go to the most obvious and stupid and Americanized places in Paris——"

"No, I've decided you'd better not come. You're probably right. Tub will want to get drunk on Montmartre."

"For which charming occupation, my dear Samuel, you'll be a much better collaborator than I, I'm afraid!"

"Look here, Fran: I wonder if you have any idea how dangerous it might be for you, one of these days, if you go on being so airy and insulting with me? I'd stood——"

"'S the truth!"

"——a good deal. I can understand your not thinking Tub is any Endicott Everett Atkins, but how you can fail to enjoy giving a good time to a neighbor that we've known as long and as closely as we have Tub—— Why you don't, just for once, forget what *you're* going to get out of it and think what you could *give*——"

"Oh, put in the Beatitudes, too!"

"——is simply beyond me! I used to think you were loyal!"

"I am! The way I've refused to stand any one ever criticizing you——"

"Will you listen! Don't be so damned *perfect*, just for once! I used to think you were loyal, but between this business about Tub, and your lack of interest in Emily's boy——"

"Now I've had enough! You've quite sufficiently indicated that I'm an inhuman monster! Why, after I heard the news about Emily, I cried half the night, wanting to see her and the baby. But—— Oh, if I could only make you understand!" She had thrown off her flippancy and was naked and defenseless in her seriousness. "I do rejoice that she has a child. I do love her. But—oh, I've tried to use my brains, such as they are, which I admit isn't very much, except that I do have common sense. I've tried not to be sentimental, and ruin myself, yes, and you, without doing Emily or anybody else any good! What good would it do if I were there? Could I help her? I could not! I'd just be in the way. Heavens, any trained nurse would be of more value than a dozen me's, and she's surrounded with only too much love and solicitude. I'd be just another burden, at a time when she has plenty. On the other hand, as it would affect me——

"When the world hears the word 'grandmother,' it pictures an old woman, a withered old woman, who's absolutely *hors de combat*. I'm not that and I'm not going to be, for another twenty years. And *yet*, most people are so conventional-minded that even if they know me, see me, dance with me, once they hear I'm a grandmother that label influences them more than their own senses, and they put me on the side-lines immediately. I won't be! And yet I love Emily and——

"Let me tell you, young man, when there *was* something I could do for her, and for Brent, I did it! I'm not for one second going to stand any hints from you that I'm not a good mother—*and* loyal! For twenty years, or anyway till Brent went off to college, there wasn't one thing those children wore that I didn't buy. There wasn't a thing they ate that I didn't order. You—oh yes, you came grandly home from the office and permitted Em to ride on your shoulders and thought what a wonderful parent you were, but who'd taken her to the dentist that day? I had! Who'd planned her party and written the invitations? I had! Who'd gotten down on her knees and scrubbed Em's floor when the maids had the 'flu and the nurse was away junketing? I did! I've done my work, I've earned the right to play, and I'm not going to be robbed of it just because you're so slow and unimaginative that you've lost the power of enjoyment and can't conceive any occupation beyond selling motors and playing golf!"

"Yes. I guess—I guess maybe there's a good deal to what you say," he sighed. "Well, it works out all right. I'll trot off and welcome Tub and then come back."

"Yes, and you'll probably enjoy it more if I'm not there. Men ought to get off by themselves now and then, away from the dratted women. Take my advice and get rid of Matey as much as you can—get her interested in buying a lot of clothes and you and Tub knock around together. You'll probably have a wonderful time. You do see now that I wasn't merely being beastly and unselfish, don't you?"

And she kissed him, fleetingly, and was cheerfully off to bed.

Even of such kisses there had not been over many, since the affair of Arnold Israel. The change in their intimacy was never admitted, but it was definite. It was not that Fran was less attractive to him; indeed more than ever he valued her sleek smoothness; but she had become to him a nun, taboo, and any passion toward her was forbidden. She seemed relieved by it; and they had drifted into a melancholy brother and sister relationship which left him irritable and hopeless.

They said nothing, neither then nor next day, of the fact that when Sam went to Paris, Fran and Kurt von Obersdorf would be left together. And these two, Fran and Kurt, very cheery and affectionate, saw him off on the evening train for Paris, and Kurt brought him as *bon voyage* presents a package of American cigarettes, a cactus plant, and a copy of the *Nation*, under the misconception that it was one of the most conservative of American magazines and especially suitable to the prejudices of a millionaire manufacturer.

Sam had to share his sleeping compartment with a small meek German who insisted, with apologetic gestures, on taking the undesirable upper berth, to which Sam was billeted. So when the German wanted to keep on the night-light, Sam could not object, and he lay in his berth staring up into a narrow vault made gloomier by that sepulchral blue glimmer which took away the oblivion of darkness and revealed the messy crowdedness of the compartment: the horribly life-like trousers swaying against the wall, the valises wedged under the little folding table by the window, the litter of newspapers and cigarette butts. The train was loud with fury; it carried him on powerless; life carried him on powerless. Without Fran, he felt small, callow, defenseless. Why was he venturing to Paris, alone? He knew no French, really; he knew little of anything in Europe. He was marooned.

She had let him go off so casually. Was he going to lose her, to whom he had turned with every triumph and every worry these twenty-four years; whose hand had always been there, to let him warm and protect it, that he might himself be warmed and protected?

Or already lost her?

He brooded, a lumpy blanketed mound in the mean blue ghost-light.

What could he *do*?

The train seemed to be running with such abnormal speed. Surely even the Twentieth Century had never raced like this. Anything wrong?

It would be nice if it were Fran in the upper berth; if her hand were drooping over the edge, so that he could see it, perhaps touch it by pretended accident——

Not that she'd be in the upper, though, if they were together!

When he awoke at three, his first loneliness for her had passed, and he worked up a good deal of angry protest.

This "adventurous new life" they'd been going to find—— Rats! Might be for her, but he himself had never been so bored. All came of trying to suit himself to her whims. And then lose her, after all——

What would Kurt and she be doing while he was away?

And this business of her having been such a devoted mother! Ever been a time when the children hadn't had a nurse or a governess, with plenty of maids? If she ever did "get down on her knees and scrub a floor" it'd never happened more than once.

Oh, she'd meant it; she really did believe she'd been a sacrificing mother. Chief trouble with her. Never could see herself as she was. Never!

Yes, he'd have to rebel against her—or against his worship of her. Not been a go, his trying to be happy in her way. Make a life for *himself*. Be pretty darn' lonely for a while. Sure. But not impossible to make a new life——

There were women, to say nothing of men friends——

Suddenly he was taut with desire for Minna von Escher. He felt her lips; he saw her too clearly.

Well, there were gorgeous girls in Paris—— Hang it, he was no washed-out Sir Galahad, like he'd read about in Tennyson! He'd been patient and sacrificing. Lot of good it'd done him! Why should Fran have all the love? He'd go out——

Then Fran's face, hovering in the wan blue dusk, a hurt,

reproving face, very pale, very pure. He could not wound her, even by thought. And so he tossed, helpless in the rushing train, turning from the desire to serve Fran to the desire for Minna's warm arms, and back ever to Fran . . . and back ever to Minna.

He breakfasted well in the restaurant carriage, and if he missed Fran, it was a relief to have a man's proper ration of bacon and eggs without having her chronic complaint that real Europeans don't take horrid heavy breakfasts. When he had lighted a cigar, Sam felt a faint exciting flavor in traveling alone, in going where he would.

He heard an American woman, at breakfast, say to her companion, "But the play I really liked was 'They Knew What They Wanted.'"

He heard no more. He pondered, "That's been the trouble with me, my entire life. It isn't simply that I've never got what I wanted. I've never known what I wanted. There are women who are better sports than Fran. Not so selfish. More peace. If I find them——

"Be funny if now I really were starting that 'adventure in new life' that we've talked so much rot about! Yes, I have known what I wanted—Fran! But probably as a kid wants the moon. (That's what she's like too—the moon on a still November night!) And if I can't have her—well, I hope I have the sense to find something else, and to take it. . . . But I won't!"

Chapter 26

HE WAS going to surprise Tub and Matey at the station. He had gone to the Continental Hotel, at which Tub had reservations. From Berlin, he had merely wired Tub in London, "Be in Paris day or two after you arrive delighted see you"; from Paris he had telephoned to Mr. A. B. Hurd, of Revelation Motors in London, asking him to snoop about and find out from the Savoy porter what train Tub was taking.

Sam waited in the Gare du Nord, excited but pleasantly superior. *He* was no American tourist, embarrassed by the voluble Parisians! He knew 'em! He could say to a porter, "*Apportez le bagage de Monsieur à un taxicab*" just as well as old Berlitz—almost as well as Fran. He swung his stick, strolled along the platform, and nodded to the gathering porters, feeling much as he had on the evening after the last game of the football season. When the lean swift French locomotive flashed in, hurling its smoke up to join the ghosts of smoke-palls that lurked under the vast roof of the train shed, he chuckled aloud.

"Old Tub! And Matey! First time in Paris!"

He looked over the heads of the crowd and saw Tub handing his bags out of the car window to a porter, saw him and the plump Matey hustle out of the car, saw him, with the blank worried nervousness of a man who doesn't expect to be met and who feels that the labors of travel are too much for him, wave his arms in the effort of explaining in Zenith French—dealcoholized French, French Hag—where he wanted to go.

Swift, looming, Sam thrust through the crowd toward the Pearsons. He saw that Tub himself was carrying a small suitcase—probably with Matey's famous and atrocious jewelry. He swooped on Tub, grasped his shoulder, and snarled (with one of the exceedingly few impersonations in his unhistrionic life), "Here, you, fella! Not allowed carry y' own baggage!"

Tub looked up with all the rage of an honest American who has been enfeebled by rough seas, doubted by customs officials, overcharged by waiters, overinformed by guides, misunderstood by French conductors; who has suddenly by thunder had enough and who is going to expose and explode the entire continent of Europe. He looked up, he looked bewildered, and then he said slowly, "Well, you damned old horse-thief! Well, you big stiff!"

They banged each other's shoulders, Sam kissed the suddenly beaming Matey, and they went down the platform together, Sam with one arm about Tub's shoulder and one about Matey's. He said sharply to the porter, "*Un taxi, s'il vous plait*"—just as the porter was waving to a taxi on his own—and Tub clamored, "Well, I'm a son of a gun! Say, you've certainly learned to parley-vous like a native, Sambo!"

They asked after Fran.

It hurt him that they seemed content to miss her, willing to believe that she "had a touch of 'flu and had to lie low a couple weeks, so she couldn't come down to welcome you." But he resented it only for a moment. There were so many exciting places to show Tub! It was delightful to have the Tub who had always been cleverer and more fashionable than he now regarding him as a sophisticated European and turning to him, admiring his dash and flavor.

And it was pleasant to be Tubbish and foolish and noisy without Fran's supercilious inspection.

Matey Pearson was a good soul. She was fat and pleasant. As a girl she had been the gayest and maddest of her set in Zenith; the fastest skater, the most ecstatic dancer, the most reckless flirt. Now she had three children—one was Brent's classmate in Yale—and she cultivated the Episcopal Church, a rare shrewd game of poker, and the choicest dahlias in Zenith. Fran said that she was vulgar. She said that Fran was lovely.

At the hotel she kissed Sam again, and cried, "Say, my heavens but it's nice to see a human being that's *human* again! Now you boys get to thunder out of here and let me unpack, and you go off and get decently drunk, but do try to be sober enough for dinner, which gives you two hours, if we dine at eight, and enough time too, sez I. Get out of here! I love you both. With reservations!"

To be alone with Tub Pearson, on Tub's first afternoon on the continent of Europe!

They had leapt over the barriers that had been erected between them since college—different vocations, rivalry as to the splendor of their several children, rivalry as to social honors, and this last flagrancy of Sam in living abroad while Tub stayed true at home. They were today the friends who had shared dress-shirts and speculations in Senior year.

From time to time they looked at each other and muttered, "Awful' good to be here with you, you old devil!"

Sam did not see that Tub was completely gray, that he was podgy, that round his eyes were the lines of a banker who day after day sharply refuses loans to desperate men. He saw the lively Tub whom he had protected in fights with muckers and whom he had admired for his wit; and while he held to his temporary superiority as the traveled man and tutored gourmet, he anxiously showed Tub all his little treasures.

He took Tub to the New York Bar, and impressed Tub as an habitué by casually asking whether anybody had heard from Ross Ireland. He took Tub to Luigi's, introduced him to Luigi, and recommended the scrambled eggs. He took Tub to the Chatham Bar; he was so fortunate as to find Colonel Kelly, the famous soldier of fortune; and he felt expansive and philanthropic; he felt, after this third highball, as though his European agonies really had been worth while, when he observed Tub's respectful attention to Colonel Kelly.

He felt that Tub was the finest and most lovable man living; that he was beyond belief lucky to have such a friend; and they returned to the Continental in a high state of philanthropy and Yalensianism.

Matey looked them over and sighed, "Well, you aren't much drunker than I thought you'd be, and now you better go in and wash your little faces in the bathroom and have a coupla Bromo Seltzers—believe me, Sam, traveling with *that* man, I never fail to have some real genuine American Bromo along—and then if you can both still walk, we'll go out and have the handsomest dinner in Paree."

He took them to Voisin's, but when they were seated Tub looked disappointed.

"Not such a lively place," he said.

"No, I know it isn't, but it's a famous old restaurant, and perhaps the best food and wine in town. What kind of a place would you like? Find it for you tomorrow."

"Well, I don't know. I don't know exactly what I did think a Paris restaurant would be like but—— Oh, I thought there'd be a lot of gilt, and marble pillars, and a good orchestra, and lots of dancing, and a million pretty girls, regular knock-outs, and not so slow either. I better watch meself, or I'll be getting Matey jealous."

"Hm," said Matey. "Tub has a good, conscientious, hard-working ambition to be a devil with the ladies—our fat little Don Juan!—but the trouble is they don't fall for him."

"That's all right now! I'm not so bad! Say, can you dig us up a place like that, tomorrow?"

"I'll show you a good noisy dance place tonight," said Sam. "You'll see all the pretty chickens you want—and they'll come and tell you, in nine languages, that you're a regular Adonis."

"They don't need to tell me that in more than one language—the extrabatorious language of clinging lips, yo ho!" yearned the class-wit.

"You're wrong, Sam," said Matey. "He *doesn't* make me sick—not very sick—not worse'n a Channel crossing. And you're wrong about thinking that I secretly wish he would go out with one of these wenches and get it out of his system. Not at all. I can get much more shopping money out of the brute while he's in this moon-June-spoon-loon mood. And when his foot does slip, how he'll come running back to his old Matey!"

"I don't know whether I will or not! Say, do we eat?"

The head waiter had been standing at attention the while. Sam was aching to show off his knowledge of restaurant French, and he held out his hand for the menu, but Tub seized it and prepared to put into the life of Voisin's all the liveliness and wit and heartiness he felt lacking.

"Do you *sprechen Sie* pretty good English?" he demanded of the head waiter.

"I think so, sir."

"Attaboy! Been in England, son?"

"Sixteen years, sir."

"Um, not so bad—not so bad for a Frog! Well now, look

here, Gooseppy, we want Mrs. Voisin to shake us up something tasty, and you take the orders from me, François, and you bring me the check afterwards, too, see, and don't have anything to do with that big stiff there. He's a Scotch Jew. If you let him order, he'd stick us with stew, and then he'd make you take ten per cent. off the check. Now listen. Have you got any nice roast elephant ears?"

Tub winked at Sam, tremendously.

The head waiter said patiently, but not too patiently, "May I recommend the *canard aux navets*?"

But Tub was a conscientious Midwestern Humorist—he was a Great Little Kidder—he had read "Innocents Abroad" and had seen "The Man from Home," and he knew that one of the superbest occupations of an American on the grand tour was "kidding the life out of these poor old back numbers of Europeans." He tried again:

"Not got any elephants' ears, Alberto? Well, well! I thought this was a first-class hash-house—right up to the Childs class. And no elephants' ears?" The head waiter said nothing, with much eloquence. "How about a nice fricassee of birds' nests?"

"If the gentleman wishes, I can send to a Chinese restaurant for it."

"Tub," Matey observed, "the comedy isn't going over so big. You give Sam that menu now, and let him order, *hear me*?"

"Well, it was kind of a flop," Tub said morosely. "But I *told* you this was a dead hole. I may not be the laddie buck that locks up the Bullyvards every evening, but I know a live joint from a dead one when it comes up and bites me. Well, shoot the works, Sam."

With a quiet superiority for which he would have deserved to be flogged, except that with Fran's monopolization of that pleasure he rarely had a chance at it, Sam swiftly ordered foie gras, consomé, frogs' legs, gigot of mutton, asparagus, and a salad, with a bottle of Châteauneuf-du-Pape, and though he ordered in French, so well trained were the head waiter and the sommelier that they understood him perfectly.

And again the luxurious inquiries about Home—*was* Emily

really well?—how was Harry Hazzard's Lincoln sedan standing up?—what was this business about building a new thirty-story hotel?

They had dined at nine. It was eleven when Sam took them to Montmartre, to the celebrated "Caverne Russe des Quarante Vents," where Tub was satisfied in finding the Paris he had pictured. The Caverne was so large, so noisy, with such poisonously loud negro jazz-bands, such cover-charges, such incredible coat-room charges, such abominable champagne at such atrocious prices, such a crowded dancing floor, such a stench of cigarette smoke and perfume and perspiration, such a sound of the voices of lingerie-buyers from Fort Worth and Milwaukee, such moist girls inviting themselves to one's table, such rude Hellenic waiters and ruder Hebraic managers, that it was almost as good as Broadway. A Frenchman had once entered the place, in 1926, but he had had to go as courier to a party from Birmingham, Alabama, and he resigned and utterly gave up the profession of courier the next day.

"Gee, this is some place!" exulted the Hon. Thomas J. Pearson (president of the Centaur State Bank, trustee of the Fernworth School for Girls, vice president of the Zenith Chamber of Commerce, vestryman of St. Asaph's P. E. Church), and straightway he was dancing with a red-headed girl like a little brass and ivory statue.

"Well——" philosophized Matey. "Eh? Heavens no, I don't want to dance in this stock exchange! Well, I might just as well *pretend* I don't mind Tub's chasing after all these little goldfish, because he'll do it anyway, and I might as well get the credit for being broad-minded. Which I ain't! You old darling, Sambo, I was sorry Tub felt he had to uphold the banner of American Humor by making a goat of himself with that snooty waiter at that place—wh'd' they call it?—there tonight."

"Oh, good Lord, Matey, he's just like a——"

"You're going to say, 'He's just like a kid let out of school, and he's got to kick up his heels,' which if I remember the rhetoric that that old Miss Getz drummed into my mutton head in finishing school, is both a cliché and a mixed metaphor. Oh, I adore the fat little devil! He's awfully sweet when you can get him tied down at the domestic hearth, with no audience. But once that animal smells applause—— Honestly, I think that the sense of humor of the people that *talk* about having a 'sense of humor' is a worse vice than drinking. Oh, well, it might have been worse. He might have turned out religious, or a vegetarian, or taken to dope. The little monkey! And he's drinking too much, tonight. I just hope he won't take enough so he'll wake up with a perfectly fierce head tomorrow, and feel so conscience-stricken that I'll have to give him the devil just to relieve him. Oh, I can do it—and probably will!—but I want to enjoy myself, too, while I'm here, and I'm going to take home a great, big, expensive boule cabinet, if I have to forge a check for it!"

She consented, later, to dance with Sam, though it was more like charging a mob than dancing. She was nimble, for all her plumpness; and as she did not, like Fran, point out his every clumsy step, his every failure to follow the music, he danced rather well with her, and enjoyed it, and recovered some of the high spirits with which he had met them at the train—spirits too high and romantic to last forever.

Tub dug out, somewhere, probably in the bar, a quite respectable fellow-banker from Indiana, and two Irish girls, whose art was commercialized but pretty, and everybody danced—everybody drank a good deal—everybody laughed.

Tub himself had so good a time that he showed the highest sign of pleasure known to an American: he wanted to "go on some place else."

They did—to another Caverne or Taverne or Palais or Câve or Rendezvous, with the same high standard of everything except wine and music and company and then, too brightly lit to waste any more time in dancing or flirtation or anything save sitting and really attending to drinking and humor, Tub insisted that they go back to the New York Bar, where, he assured Matey, they would "meet reg'lar fell's."

They did. In a corner table of the bar, under the sketches of Parisian celebrities, they were picked up by an American navy officer who had magnificent lies about the China coast, and somehow there was added to their party a free-lance journalist and a lone English corn-merchant, who talked a good deal, and very spiritedly, about the admitted fact that Englishmen never talk much and then shyly.

Tub, in one day, was a warmer habitué of the New York Bar than was Sam Dodsworth after a year. It was not merely that Sam was dogged by a sense of dignity, by a feeling that a Prominent Manufacturer ought not to be seen about bar rooms, but also that he had a certain judicious timidity which suggested that there was no reason why the keen, hard-minded journalists who frequented the bar and exchanged gossip of kings and treaties should be interested in him. But Tub was a Professional Good Fellow—when he was away from the oak-panel and gold velvet vestry of St. Asaph's, the trustees' room at the Fernworth School, or the marble and walnut office at the Centaur State Bank, where he put on a pair of horn-rimmed spectacles which somehow prevented his eyes from twinkling or looking slyly humorous.

He hadn't forgotten one of the men he had met at the bar that afternoon. He called two of the journalists by their first names, and he was in general so full of prankishness that the lone naval officer broke into tears of relief and told them all about his most recent fight with his wife.

But there was one flaw in the joviality. Tub had drunk Burgundy at dinner, Napoleon brandy afterward, champagne all evening, and now he decided (in spite of the earnest counsel of Sam, Matey, the naval officer, the Englishman, the journalist, the waiter, and a few by-sitters) to show his loyalty to America and the Good Old Days by drinking real American rye whisky—and it was a very copious loyalty that he showed.

In the middle of the commander's story about his wife, Tub began to look listless, with fine lines of sweat-drops on his upper lip—and it was only two in the morning and he had been drinking steadily for only twelve hours, which is not even par for a representative of Prohibition America on his first day in Paris.

Matey cried to Sam, "He's passing out! Can you take him off and kill him or something?"

In the seclusion of the wash-room, usefully close at hand, Sam washed Tub's face, fed him aspirin, scolded him, and they started home and——

All of Sam's romantic exultation was gone, the glow was gone, the childish belief that he had suddenly achieved freedom was gone, in a leaden light of reality. He was not angry with Tub. But he had felt warmth and assurance, he had felt—he admitted it—a protection against Fran in Tub's comradeship, and that was not enhanced in the unromantic service of holding up a man retching and swaying in a barroom toilet.

They got Tub into a taxicab, while he protested that he was all right now and desired to return to his friends. Sam had to roar at him a good deal, and lift him in. During this knockabout scene, an open motor passed, and Sam saw that looking disgustedly out of it was Endicott Everett Atkins, with his high nose, his Roman imperial, and his Henry Jamesian baldness. Atkins turned to say something to the lady beside him.

Sam shivered. He fancied Atkins getting the information to Fran. He heard her saying, "Now was I right about your dear friend Tub!" He felt cold and irritated. He was less gentle with Tub than he had meant to be.

Not till Matey and he had Tub in bed did it come fully to Sam that he might do well to forget himself and think of her.

"Hard luck!" he whispered. "But we all slip now and——"

"Oh, you can talk as loud as you want," she said placidly. "Gabriel with an augmented trumpet band wouldn't wake the little monkey now! But I do want to talk to you, and if he did wake up and want to go out again—— Oh, well, there's no place to go but the bathroom. Heigh! Scandal in Zenith society! I guess this is that new American Jazzmania you read about!"

They sat absurdly in the bathroom, she on a white straight chair, he precariously on the cold edge of the tub, while she went on:

"No, I don't mind. Honestly! Tub doesn't get really potted more than once a year, and I never did think much of the females who lay for their menfolks and try to get an advantage over 'em when they have a chance like that. Life's too short!—too short to raise hell about anything except some real vice, like his being humorous and making speeches. Rather be friendly and—— Sam! You old dear thing! When are you going to chuck Fran and let yourself be happy again?"

"Why, Matey, honestly, she and I are on the best terms——"

"Don't lie to me, Sam darling (you know how Tub and I *do* love you!). Rather, don't lie to yourself! I know. Fran has written to me, now and then. Awful clever and jolly and uninterested. And you don't propose to sit there and tell me that if she wouldn't come home last summer and wouldn't come down from Berlin to see us, she isn't about ready to cut out Zenith entirely! And there's no reason why she shouldn't! She never was very much Zenith anyway . . . or she *thought* she wasn't! Only, Sam darling, *only*, if she is going to cut out Zenith, she's going to cut out you, for even if you are kind of a Lord High Chancellor, still, same time, you *are* Zenith, and in the long run, after you've had your fling, you'd rather see the sunshine on a nice, ragged, old Middlewestern pasture than on the best formal Wop garden in the world!"

"Well—yes—I guess that's more or less true, Matey, but——"

He wanted to tell her of the Sans Souci Gardens dream; he dismissed the matter and struggled on:

"But that doesn't mean Fran doesn't appreciate Zenith and her friends and all that. Course she does! Why, she's always talking about Tub and you——"

"Yeah, I'll bet she is! 'My dear Samuel, *is* it necessary for women like your dear Mrs. Pearson to use such vulgarisms as "I'll bet she is" all the time?'"

Though Matey's hearty and slightly brassy voice could never mimic Fran's cool melodies, there was enough accuracy in the impersonation to make Sam grin helplessly, and with that grin he was lost. Matey took advantage of it to pounce:

"Sam darling, I do know it's none of my business, and you can tell me so whenever you want to, but I figured that probably you've been so alone here, seeing nobody but the kind of folks that Fran wants, and—— Sam, I've seen you change a lot, more than you know, this last ten years. You never were a chatterbox, but you did used to enjoy an argument or telling a nice clean smutty story, and you've been getting more silent, more sort of scared and unsure of yourself, while Fran has been preening herself and feeling more and more that it was only her social graces and her Lady Vere de Vere beauty that kept up your position, because you were so slow and clumsy and so fond of low company and so generally an undependable hick! And you have more brains in your little finger than—— And you're kind! And humble—too damn' humble! And you want to know a fact twice before you say it once, and she—well, she wants to say it twice before she's learned it at all!

"Oh, golly, I guess I'm defying the thunderbolt. Shoot, Jupiter. . . . Now mind you, I *liked* Fran. I admire her. But when I think of how she's treated you, as though she were the silver-shod Diana of the outfit—and especially the way she shows it in public by being so pizen polite to you—well, I just want to wallop her! Now tell me to go to the dickens, darling. . . . Listen to that man Tub snoring in there! *There's* an aristocratic, college-bred consort for you! The poor lamb! How sick and righteous he'll be tomorrow—up to about noon!"

Sam laboriously lighted a cigar, searched through a perfectly blank mind for something to say, and then, for the first time in months, he was talking candidly about something that really mattered to him.

"Yes, Matey, I'll admit there is something to what you say. I suppose I ought to be highty-tighty and bellow, 'How dare you talk about *my* wife!' But—— Hell, Matey, I am so sick and tired and confused! Fran is a lot kinder and more appreciative than you think. A lot of what you imagine is snootiness is just her manner. She's really shy, and tries to protect——"

"Oh, I am so tired, Sam, of hearing and reading about these modern folks—you get 'em in every novel—these sensitive plants that go around being rude and then stand back complacently and explain that it's because they're so *shy*!"

"Shut up, now! Listen to me!"

"That sounds better!"

"Well, I mean—— It *is* true with Fran. Partly. And partly she enjoys it—gets a kick out of it—feels she's a heroine in a melodrama. . . . Damn this bathtub—coldest arm-chair I've found in Europe." Without a smile he laid the bath-mat on the edge of the tub, heavily sat down again, and went on:

"And she really thinks that having a social position is worth sacrificing for. And that it still matters to have a title. And I do know she makes me clumsy. But—— Well, first place, I really am an old-fashioned believer in what we used to call the Home. I hate to see all the couples busting up the way they are. Think of the people we know that've separated or gotten divorced, right in our own bunch at home—Dr. and Mrs. Daniels—think of it, married seventeen years, with those nice kids of theirs. And then, and I guess this is more important, Fran has got a kind of charm, fascination, whatever you want to call it, for me that nobody else has. And when she likes something—it may be meeting somebody she likes, or a good party, or a sunset, or music—well, she's so wrought up about it that it seems as if she had a higher-powered motor in her, with better ground cylinders, than most of us.

"Even when she's snooty—oh, she's trying to have some *form* in life, some standards, not just get along anyhow, sloppily, the way most of us do; and then we resent her demanding that we measure up to what she feels is the highest standard. And her faults—oh, she's a child, some ways. To try to change her (even if a fellow could do it!) would be like calling in a child that was running and racing and having a lovely time in the sunshine, and making her wash dishes."

"And so she leaves you to wash the dishes! Oh, Sam, it's a thankless job to butt in and tell a man that in *your* important opinion, his wife is a vampire bat. But it makes your friends sore to see you eternally apologetic to your wife, when she ought to thank her lucky stars she's got you! I swear she never, for one moment, with anybody, thinks what she can give, but only what she can get. She thinks that nobody on earth is important except as they serve her or flatter her. But—— You've never been interested in any other woman, have you?"

"Not really."

"I wonder if you won't be? I'm making a private bet with myself that after another six months of carrying Fran's shawl, you'll begin to look around. And if you do, you'll be surprised at the number of nice women that'll fall for you! Tell me, Sam. Could you fall for them?"

"Well, I don't know. I don't believe in being deliberately unhappy for the sake of sticking to a bad bargain. If Fran and I did drift apart and I couldn't find some kind of security elsewhere, I wouldn't regard it as any virtue, but simply as an inability to face things as they are——"

"Ah hah! A year ago you wouldn't have admitted that! A year ago, if I'd dared even to thumb my nose at Fran, you'd've bitten me! Sam, you old darling, I never have criticized Fran before, have I?—not in all these years. Now I feel that the bust-up has happened, and all that's needed is for you to see it, and then you'll be nice and heart-broken and sulky and unhappy, and after that you'll find some darling that'll be crazy about you and spoil you proper, and then all will be joyous tra-la—curse it, that sounds like Tub! And I'm going to bed. G'night, Sam dear. Like to ring us up about eleven?"

As he plowed down the vast corridors of the hotel to his room, too sleepy to think, Sam felt that this saint of unmorality had converted him, and opened a door upon a vista of tall woods and dappled lawns and kind faces.

Chapter 27

WHAT Tub and Matey and Sam did during their week together may be deduced by studying a newspaper list of "Where to Lunch, Dine, and Dance in Paris," the advertisements of dress-makers, jewelers, perfumers, furniture-dealers, and of revues; and by reprinting for each evening the more serious features of Tub's first night in Paris.

It was a fatiguing week, but rather comforting to Sam.

Through it, the pious admonitions of Matey, along with the thought of Minna von Escher and his own original virtue, prepared him to yield to temptation—only he saw no one who was tempting.

The Pearsons begged him to go on to Holland with them, but he said that he had business in Paris; he spoke vaguely of conferences with motor agents. Actually, he wanted a day or two for the luxury of sitting by himself, of walking where he would, of meditating in long undisturbed luxurious hours on what it was all about.

He had two hasty, stammering notes from Fran, in which she said that she missed him, which was all very pleasant and gratifying, but in which she babbled of dancing with Kurt von Obersdorf till three A.M.—of a day with Kurt in the country—of an invitation from Kurt's friends, the Von Arminals, to spend the next week-end at their place in the Hartz Mountains. "And of course they'd be enchanted to have you also if you get back in time, asked me tell you how sorry they are you aren't here," her pen sputtered.

"Hm!" said Sam.

Suddenly he was testy. Oh, of course she had a "right" to be with Kurt as much as she liked. He wasn't a harem-keeper. And of course it would be puerile to rage, "If she has a right to be loose, then I have the same right." There was no question of "rights." It was a question of what he wanted, and whether he was willing to pay for it—whether he wanted new, strange loves, whether he could find them, and whether he was willing to pay in dignity, in the respect that Fran had for him despite her nervous jabbings.

When he had seen the Pearsons off for Amsterdam, with mighty vows to meet them in Zenith within six months, when he had for an hour sat outside the Café des Deux Magots, brooding on the Franocentric universe which had cataclysmically replaced the universe of business and creating motors and playing golf, then sharply, gripping the marble top of the little table with his huge hand, he admitted with no more reservations that he was hungry as a barren woman, hungry for a sweetheart who should have Fran's fastidiousness, Minna von Escher's sooty warmth, and Matey Pearson's shrewd earthiness.

He dined alone in a little Montparnasse restaurant filled with eager young couples: a Swedish painter with an Italian girl student, an American globe-trotter with his Polish mistress, pairs of white Russians and Italian anti-fascists. They all twittered like love-birds and frankly held hands over the *vin ordinaire* and horse-meat. And here, as it was very cheap, there were actually French people, all in couples except when they belonged to enormous noisy family parties, and the couples stroked each other's hands, unabashedly nuzzled each other's cheeks, looked into each other's eyes, the world well lost.

It was spring—spring and Paris—scent of chestnut blossoms, freshness of newly watered pavements, and Sam Dodsworth was almost as lonely as though he were at the Adlon with Kurt and Fran.

When he thought of Fran's cool, neat politeness to him, he was angry. When he looked about him at youth in love, he was angrier. This passion, ungrudging and unabashed, Fran had never given him. He had been robbed—— Or robbed her? All wrong, either way. Had *enough*——

Oh, he was lonely, this big friendly man, Sam Dodsworth, and he wanted a man to whom he could talk and boast and lie, he wanted a woman with whom he could be childish and hurt and comforted, and so successful and rich was he that he had neither, and he sought them, helpless, his raw nerves exposed. So searching, he strolled after dinner to the Select, which was rivaling the Café du Dôme as the resort of the international yearners in Paris.

A man alone at a café table in the more intellectual portions of Paris, and not apparently expecting some one, is always a man suspect. At home he may be a prince, a successful pickpocket, or an explorer, but in this city of necessitous and over-friendly strollers, this city where any one above the rank of assassin or professional martyr can so easily find companions, the supposition is that he is alone because he ought to be alone.

But it is also a rule of this city of spiritual adventurers which lies enclosed within the simple and home-loving French city of Paris, this new Vanity Fair, of slimier secrets, gallanter Amelias and more friendly Captain Dobbinses than Thackeray ever conceived, that if such a solitary look prosperous, if he speak quietly to the waiters, not talk uninvited to the people at the next table, and drink his fine à l'eau slowly, he may be merely a well-heeled tourist, who would be gratified to be guided into the citadel of the arts by a really qualified, gently tourist-despising, altogether authentic initiate of the Parisian Hobohemia—a girl who has once had a book-review printed, or a North Dakota 'cellist who is convinced that every one believes him to be an Hungarian gipsy.

So it happened that when Samuel Dodsworth sat melancholy and detached at a table before the Select, four young people at another table commented upon him—psychoanalytically, biologically, economically; cleverly, penetratingly, devastatingly.

"See that big dumbbell there by himself?" remarked Clinton J. Gillespie, the Bangor miniaturist. "I'll bet he's an American lawyer. Been in politics. Fond of making speeches. He's out of office now, and sore about it."

"Oh, hell!" said the gentleman next. "In the first place he's obviously an Englishman, and look at his hands! I don't suppose you have room for mere hands in your rotten little miniatures! He's rich and of good family, and yet he has the hands of a man who works. Perfectly simple. He's the owner of a big country estate in England, crazy about farming, and prob'ly he's a baronet."

"Grand!" said the third, smaller, sharper-nosed man. "Perfect—except for the fact that he is obviously a soldier and—— I'm not quite sure about this, but I think he's German!"

"You all," said the fourth, a bobbed-haired girl of twenty with a cherubic face, rose-bud mouth, demure chin, magazine-cover nose, and the eyes of a bitter and grasping woman of forty, "make me very sick! You know so much that isn't so! I don't know what he is, but he looks good for a bottle of champagne, and I'm going over and grab it."

"What the devil good, Elsa," complained Clinton J. Gillespie, "is it for you to come to Paris if you always go talking to Babbitts like that fellow? You never *will* become a novelist!"

"Won't that be fierce—when I think over some of the novelists that hang around this joint!" rasped Elsa, and she tripped to Sam's table, she stood beside him, warbling, "I *beg* your pardon, but aren't you Mr. Albert Jackson of Chicago?"

Sam looked up. She was so much like the edifying portrait of "Miss Innocence" on the calendar which the grocer sends you at New Year's that he was not irritated even by this most ancient of strategies. "No, but I wish I were. I am from Chicago, but my name is Pearson, Thomas J. Pearson. Loans and banking. Won't you sit down? I'm kind of lonely in Paris."

Elsa did not seat herself precipitately. It was impossible to say just when it was that she did sit down, so modestly did she slip into a chair, looking as though she had never had so unmaidenly an encounter, as though momently she would take fright and wing away. She murmured, "That was *too* silly of me! You must have thought I was a terribly bold little creature to speak to you, but you did look so much like Mr.—Mr. Jackson, who is a gentleman that I met once at my aunt's house in New Rochelle—my father is the Baptist minister there—and I guess I felt lonely, too, a wee bit—I don't know many people in Paris myself, though I've been here three months. I'm studying novel-writing here. But it was awfully kind of you not to mind."

"Mind? It was a privilege," Sam said gallantly . . . and within himself he was resolving, "Yes, you cute little bitch-kitty, you lovely little gold-digger, I'm going to let you work me as much as you want to, and I'm going to spend the night with you!"

And he was triumphant, after so much difficulty, at having been at last able to take the first step toward sin.

"And now, young lady, I hope you're going to let me buy you a little drink or something, just to show you think I'm as nice and respectable as if you'd met *me* in your aunt's house, too. What would you like?"

"Oh, I—I—— I've scarcely ever tasted alcohol." Sam had seen her flip off two brandies at the other table. "What *does* one drink? What would be safe for a young girl?"

"Well—— Of course you wouldn't touch brandy?"

"Oh no!"

"No, of course not. Well, what would you most like?"

"Well—— Oh, you won't think it's awfully silly of me, Mr. Uh——"

"Mr. Thomas—Pearson J. Thomas."

"Of course—how silly of me! You wouldn't think it was awfully silly of me, Mr. Thomas, if I said I've often heard people speaking about champagne, and always wanted to taste some?"

"No, I wouldn't think that was a bit silly. I'm told it's a very nice innocent drink for young girls." ("I will! And tonight! She picked on me first!") "Is there any particular brand of champagne you'd like to try?"

She looked at him suspiciously, but she was reassured by his large and unfanciful face, and she prattled more artlessly than ever:

"Oh, you must think I'm a *terrible* little silly—just a regular little *greenhorn*—but I don't know the name of one single brand of any kind of wine! But I did hear a boy that I know here—he's such a hardworking boy, a student—but he told me that Pol Roger, Quinze, I mean 1915, was one of the nicest vintages."

"Yes, I'm told it's quite a nice little wine," said Sam, and as he ordered it, his seemingly unobservant glance noted that one of Elsa's young men shrugged in admiration of something and handed another of the three a five-franc note, as though he were paying a bet.

"Am I going to have collaboration in my first seduction?" he wondered. "I may need it! I'll never go through with it! I'd like to kiss this little imp half to death but—— Oh, God, I can't pick on a kid younger than my daughter!"

While he talked ardently to Elsa for the next half hour—about Berlin and Naples, about Charles Lindbergh, who had just this week flown from New York to Paris, and, inevitably, about Prohibition and the novels that she hadn't yet quite started to write—his whole effort was to get rid of scruples, to regain his first flaunting resolve to forget the respectable Samuel Dodsworth and be a bandit.

He was helped by jealousy and champagne.

After half an hour, Elsa started, ever so prettily, and cried, "Why! There's some boys I know at the second table over. As you are alone in Paris—— Perhaps they might be willing to take you around a little, and I'm sure they'd be delighted to meet you. They're *such* nice boys, and so talented! Do you mind if I call them over?"

"B' d'lighted——"

She summoned the three young men with whom she had been sitting and introduced them as Mr. Clinton Gillespie, late of Bangor, miniaturist, Mr. Charley Short, of South Bend, now in the advertising business but expecting shortly to start a radical weekly, and Mr. Jack Keipp, the illustrator—just what Mr. Keipp illustrated was forever vague. Unlike Elsa, they did not need to be coaxed to sit down. They sat quickly and tight, and looked thirsty, and exchanged droll sophisticated glances as Sam meekly ordered two more bottles of Pol Roger.

While taking his champagne, they took the conversation away from him. They discussed the most artistic of topics—the hatefulness of all other artists; and now and then condescendingly threw to that Philistine, Mr. Pearson J. Thomas, a bone of explanation about the people of whom they gossiped. After half a bottle each, they forgot that they thought of Elsa only as nice young men should think of a Baptist minister's daughter. They mauled her. They contradicted her. One of them—the sharp-nosed little man, Mr. Keipp—held her hand. And after an entire bottle, Elsa herself rather forgot. She laughed too loudly at a reference to a story which no Christmas-card cherub would ever have heard.

So jealousy and a very earnest dislike of these supercilious young men came to help kill Sam's reluctance.

"Hang it," he informed himself, "you can't tell me she hasn't been a little more than intimate with this Keipp rat! In any case, old Granddaddy Sambo would be better for her than this four-flusher. Give her a much better time. I *will!*"

His resolution held. Once he had accomplished the awful struggle of winning himself, once he turned from it to winning her, he began to see her (through a slightly champagne-colored haze) as wondrously desirable.

"Probably I'll kick myself tomorrow. I don't care! I'm glad I'm going to have her! Now to get rid of these young brats! Stop brooding, Sam, and speak your little piece! . . . I'll take her to the Continental, too, by thunder!"

Fran would have marveled to hear her taciturn Samuel chattering. Early he discovered a way of parrying these young geniuses—by admitting, before they hinted it, that he was a lowbrow, but that he ranked higher among the lowbrows than they among the highbrows.

This attack disorganized them, and enabled him to contradict them with cheerful casualness. He heard himself stating that Eddie Guest was the best American poet, and a number of other things which he had heard from Tub Pearson and which he did not believe. His crassness was so complete that they were staggered, being accustomed to having gentlemen as large and as rich as Mr. Pearson J. Thomas deprecate their own richness and largeness, and admire the sophistication of Mr. Gillespie, Mr. Short, and Mr. Keipp.

Elsa agreed with him in everything; made him ardent by taking his side against them; encouraged him till (with a mild astonishment at his own triumphs of asininity) he heard himself asserting that vacuum cleaners were more important than Homer, and that Mr. Mutt, of the comic strips, was a fuller-blooded character than Soames Forsyte.

And meantime, he was buying.

Mr. Gillespie, Mr. Short, and Mr. Keipp never refused another drink. After the champagne, Elsa suggested brandies (she had forgotten that it was a beverage of which she had scarcely heard) and there were many brandies, and the pile of saucers, serving as memoranda of drinks for which he would have to pay, rose and rose in front of Sam, while the innocent pioneer part of the table in front of Mr. Gillespie, Mr. Short, and Mr. Keipp was free of anything save their current brandies.

But Sam was craftily delighted. Could anything better show Elsa that he was a worthier lover than the sharp-nosed Mr. Keipp?

He was talking, now, exclusively to Elsa, ignoring the young men. He was almost beginning to be honest with her, in his desire to have sympathy from this rosy child. He decided that her eyes weren't hard, really, but intelligent.

He finally dared to grope under the table, and her hand flew to his, so warm, so young, so living, and answered his touch with a pressure which stirred him intolerably. He became very gay, joyous with the thought of the secret they were sharing. But a slight check occurred to the flow of his confidences.

Elsa cooed, "Oh, excuse me just a moment, dear. There's Van Nuys Rodney over there. Something I have to ask him. 'Scuse me a moment."

She flitted to a table at which sat a particularly hairy and blue-shirted man and he saw her drop all her preening in an absorbed conversation.

He sat neglected by his guests at his own table.

In three minutes, Mr. Jack Keipp lounged to his feet, muttered, "Pardon me a moment," and Sam saw him join Elsa and Van Nuys Rodney and plunge into talk. Then Mr. Gillespie yawned, "Well, I think I'll turn in," Mr. Short suggested, "Glad met you, Mr. Oh," and they were gone. Sam watched them stroll down the boulevard. He wished that he had been pleasanter to them—even Shorts and Gillespies would be worth having in this city of gaiety and loneliness.

When he looked back, he saw that Elsa, Mr. Keipp, and Mr. Rodney had vanished, complete.

He waited for Elsa to come back. He waited an hour, with the monstrous pile of saucers before him as his only companion. She did not come. He paid the waiter, he rose slowly, unsmilingly beckoned to a taxicab, and sat in it cold and alone.

Some time in the night—and he was never quite sure whether he had been dreaming or half-awake—he heard Fran saying coldly, "My dear Samuel, don't you see at last—isn't it exactly what I told you?—that you have less knowledge of women than a European like Kurt would have at eighteen? You American men! Fussing and fuming and fretting over the obvious question of whether or not you'll seduce that little harlot! And then unable to accomplish it! What a spectacle! But

Kurt—in the first place, of course, Kurt would have taken Elsa away from there, away from her little parasite friends——"

It was Fran's very voice, and he had nothing to answer.

He awoke again to hear not Fran but himself jeering, "And the rottenest part of the whole thing was the cheap superiority you felt to those three little rats of would-be artists. Poor kids! Of *course* they have to be conceited and supercilious, to keep their courage up, because they're failures."

And again, "Yes, that's all true, but I'll find Elsa again, and this time——"

Chapter 28

HE SLEPT badly; he rose at six and rang for breakfast. But at breakfast everything was gratefully clear to him.

He was so thankful that he had not gone astray with Elsa that he did not think of it for more than a second. All his thoughts blazed about Fran.

Why had he let the dissensions, the blame and impatience, all the nothings, grow into a barrier unreal but thwarting as a wall seen in a nightmare? All that was needed was a really frank talk with her! And this trip to Paris, confessing to Matey, being idiotic with Elsa, just being alone and away from Fran, had made it possible for him to be frank.

He'd been stupid. Fran was a child. Why not treat her as one, a lovely and much beloved child; be more patient, not be infuriated by her passing tantrums? A child. A lake mirroring sunny clouds and thunder squalls.

Just go back and say, "Look here, dear——"

He wasn't sure what he was to say after "Look here, dear," but he would be ever so affectionate and convincing. He did love her! Fran, with her eager eyes——

But what about Kurt von Obersdorf?

Well—belligerently—what *about* it! Either she was still innocent, and did not understand her danger, or she had fallen, and would regret it. In either case, when he had paternally explained the danger of free-lance lovers like Kurt, she would come to her senses and laugh with him at this make-believe enmity between them—yes! that was it—all a make-believe, an exciting game, like so many things in her secret and dramatic life! And they would go home together.

He would hasten to her. Now! If possible he would fly! He would see her late this very afternoon!

He had never been in an aeroplane, for all his professional interest in aviation engines. Like most sound people, he had always been slightly afraid of flying, but in his ardor now he despised his fear.

Then there rose such a hubbub of efficiency as he had not experienced since the most critical days of Revelation Motors.

A demand that the porter find at what time the Berlin 'plane flew—it went at nine, two hours from now. Telephoning to demand a ticket. The room-waiter rushing down for Sam's bill. The *valet de chambre* packing. A motor ordered to take him to the flying-field.

Driving out, he felt a slight agitation. His much motoring had not hardened him to flying. But his apprehension was overcome by the prospect of seeing Fran in a few hours, and when he dismounted at the flying field, when he saw the great 'plane, its metal body and thick crimped metal wings as solid-looking as a steamer, when he saw how casually the pilot took his place in front and the attendants loaded luggage, all nervousness vanished in exultation. He climbed up a tiny step-ladder, walked across the left-hand wing, and entered the little door like a child taken on a boat ride.

The cabin was like that of a very large limousine or a rather small omnibus. The seats were of leather, deep and easy as chairs in a club; the cabin walls were covered with stamped leather; the pilot was to be seen, with his intricacy of instruments before him, only through a tiny window forward. Save when he glanced out of the window beside him, Sam had no sense of being in anything so fantastic and fragile as an aeroplane. His half-dozen fellow passengers seemed casual about the whole thing. One of them, as soon as he was seated, opened a book and did not look up for an hour.

Sam was vastly ashamed that he had been diffident. He almost hoped for a little danger.

They started with no ceremonies—just at a gesture from the official in charge. They trundled along the ground for so long a time that Sam wondered whether they were overloaded, unable to rise. Suddenly a little qualm came—oh, it would be all right of course when they were high in air, going a steady course, but wouldn't it be rather nasty to leave the ground, to spin and toss as they climbed?

Actually, he never did know when they left the ground. They were bumping along the turf, very noisily, the propeller draft blowing the grass stalks backward; then, magically, they were ten feet up in the air, they were above the hangar roofs, they were as high up as the distant Eiffel Tower, and as for sensations, there were none save the lively inquiry as to why he didn't have any sensations.

He noted that the country below him was like a map; he told himself that he was thrilled when they passed over something like a fog bank—and rather more like a wash of soap suds—and he realized that it was a cloud and that they must be nearly a mile high in air. But he had read of the country looking like a map, of passing over clouds. In fact he experienced nothing of which he had not read many times—until he noted, and this was something he had never read, that aeroplane travel, in calm weather, is the most monotonous and tedious form of journeying known to mankind, save possibly riding on a canal boat through flat country. How tired he got of looking at maps, hour on hour! He had less relationship to the country than in the swiftest motor, the most violent train.

It was so monotonous and safe-seeming that he laughed to remember his nervousness; laughed the more when a French business man took out his portable typewriter, set it on a suitcase on his knees and, a mile up in the air, began placidly to type a letter.

He forgot, then, all about aviating and, just glancing out occasionally at distant green hills, he gave himself up to the thought of Fran. Oh, he would do anything for her . . . he would make her understand it . . . surely such devotion would bring her to his arms!

They had left Paris at nine; they were due to alight in Germany, at Dortmund, at twenty minutes to three. Before one they ran into a thunder-shower, and all the commonplace dullness of their flight was instantly snatched away.

Their little cabin seemed gruesomely insecure as the lightning glared past them, as they quivered in a blast of wind, as they ran into a dark cloud and for two minutes seemed lost in midnight, as they came out of the cloud into rain which crashed against the windows. Sam, who had cheerfully enough driven with motor racers at a hundred and ten miles an hour, was distinctly bothered. He was helpless! There was no ground to step out on, not even a sea to swim in, only the treacherous and darkened air.

The man across the little aisle from Sam—and Sam never did find out what was the snarly language he spoke—looked over, laughed deprecatingly, took out a bottle of cognac, drank long and gurglingly and, without a word, handed it over. Without hesitation Sam drank from the bottle and bowed his gratitude.

He tried to think of Fran again, and she remained a floating pale young face that outside his window kept pace in mid-air with the 'plane. But for a time she was only that.

They ran through the thunder-shower into rough air. They swooped upward, they fell a hundred feet—the sensation was precisely as in a dropping express elevator, which leaves one's stomach two floors above—they rocked and quivered like a dory in high seas.

The business man, who had uninterestedly kept up his typing all through the storm, quietly rose and was very sick in a little paper bag. At the sight, the agreeable philanthropist with the cognac was sicker, much sicker. And Sam Dodsworth wanted to be sick, and was distressed because he couldn't be.

For an hour and more they were shaken thus, helpless as dice in a box, and when with ineffable gratitude they circled down toward the flying field at Dortmund, Sam saw that there was another thunder-shower coming.

Had Fran or Tub Pearson been there to observe him, he might not have had the courage to admit that he hadn't the courage to go on to Berlin by 'plane, and it was hard enough in the presence of that rather demanding censor, Sam Dodsworth, but as they delicately touched the ground and taxied along—the aeroplane as innocent and demure as though it had never thought of such insane capering a mile in air—Sam determined, "Well, we'll call that enough for a starter, and go on by train!"

Though he reeled a little with land-sickness when he stepped out, he beamed with idiotic bliss on the recovered earth, the beautifully safe and solid earth.

There were taxicabs waiting at the flying-field, but it came to Sam that he did not know the German for even "station" or "train." In Berlin, he had depended on Fran. He looked disconsolately at the driver of the taxi in which a porter had set his bag, and grunted, "Berlin? Vagon? Berlin?"

"Surest t'ing you know, boss," said the taxi-driver. "Train for Berlin. Well, how's the folks back in the States?"

Sam said the inevitable.

"Was I *there*? Say, don't make me laugh! I was born in Prussia but I was twenty-six years in Philly and K.C., and then I come back here, like a boob, and I got caught by the army, and don't let nobody tell you that was any nice, well-behaved war, either! Jump in, boss."

On the Berlin train, Sam forgot Fran for three minutes, in anger at himself for having failed to go on by aeroplane. It betrayed him as irresolute and growing old. Was he soft? He determined that the coming autumn, with Fran or without, he would make another canoe trip in Canada; he would live sparsely, sleep on the ground, carry on the portage, paddle all day long, and make himself shoot the worst rapids. Yes! With Fran or without——

But it must be *with*! Surely Fran could not withstand the new passion he was bringing to her from his Paris venture.

His train reached Berlin just before midnight.

At the hotel he seized his suit-case without waiting for the doorman, and pounded into the lobby.

"My wife in?—Mr. Dodsworth, suite B7," he demanded, at the desk.

"I think the lady must be out, sir. The key is here," said the clerk.

Dismally, Sam followed the boy with his bag to the elevator.

He sent the key back to the desk. He told himself that he did so because he was tired and might be asleep before she returned.

She was not in the suite. It smelled of her, shouted of her. She had spilled a little pink powder on the glass cover of her toilet-table; on the turned-back bed was her nightgown with the Irish lace; a half-finished letter to Emily was on the desk in the sitting-room; and these shadows of her made her absence the more glaring. From midnight till half-past two he sat waiting for her, reading magazines, and all his furious and simple-minded excitement grew cold minute by minute.

At half-past two he heard laughter in the corridor. Hating himself for it, yet quite unable to resist, he sprang up, turned off the lights in the sitting-room, and stood in the dark bedroom, just beyond the door.

He heard the door opening; heard Fran bubbling, "Yes, you can come in for a moment. But not long. Poo' lil Fran, she is all in! What an orchestra that was! I could have danced till dawn!"

And Kurt: "Oh, you darling—*darling!*"

"Good evening," said Sam, from the bedroom door, and Fran sobbed, once, quickly.

"Just got back from Paris." Sam strode into the sitting-room, turned on the lights, stood there feeling clumsy and thick, wishing he had not been melodramatic.

"Oh, Sam, I am so glad you got back safe!" cried Kurt. "Fran and I have been dancing. Now I vill go home, and tomorrow I ring you up about luncheon."

He glanced at Fran, hesitated as though he wanted to say something, bowed, and was gone. Fran glared at Sam with lip-biting hatred. Sam begged:

"Dear, I came back so quickly—listen, dear, I *flew*—because I couldn't live without you! I'm not angry that Kurt and you were out so late——"

"Why should you be!" She tossed her gold and crimson evening wrap on the couch.

"Dear! Listen! This is serious! I've come back to you, willing to do everything I can to make you happy. I adore you. You know that. You're everything I have. Only we've got to cut out this nonsense of being homeless adventurers and go home——"

"And that's your idea of 'making me happy'! And now *you* listen—to repeat your favorite phrase! I love Kurt, and Kurt loves me, and I'm going to marry him! No matter what it costs me! We decided it tonight. And all I can say is I'm glad Kurt was too much of a gentleman to punch your head, as he probably wanted to, when you played that sweet, provincial trick of hiding in the bedroom to listen to us——"

"Fran, Fran!"

"Now don't play the injured and astonished small boy! You have no complaint. You've never known me. You've never known anything about me. You've never known what I wore, what flowers I put in your study, what sacrifices I made to cover up your awkwardnesses and help you keep your dull friends and your dull work and your dull reputation!"

"Fran!"

"Oh, I know! I'm being beastly. But I was so happy with Kurt—till two minutes ago. And then I find you here, a prowling elephant—oh yes, the great Mr. Dodsworth, the motor magnate, who has a right to commandeer my soul and my dreams and my body! I can't *stand* it! Poor—yes, Kurt and I will be poor. Only, thank God, we'll have my twenty thousand a year! But that will be poverty among the sort of people he knows——"

She was altogether hysterical; she was tearing at her evening frock; and he was as appalled as a man witnessing a murder. He said timidly, "All right, dear. Just one thing. Does he want to marry you?"

"Yes!"

"Then I'll go away." He had a vision of such loneliness as he had known in Paris at the Select. "Can you get a divorce here in Germany?"

"Yes. I believe so. Kurt says so."

"You'll stay in Berlin?"

"I think so. A friend of the Biedners has a nice flat to let, overlooking the Tiergarten."

"All right. Then I'll go away. Tomorrow. 'Fraid it's too late tonight. I'll sleep on the couch here in the parlor, if you don't mind."

"Very well. . . . Oh, you *would* play the rôle of the patient, suffering martyr at a time like this! You have just enough native instinct to guess that's the one way you can put me hopelessly in the wrong, and make me feel as if I'd been a dirty dog in not appreciating you—as if I must go back and be the dutiful dull consort. Well, I won't! Understand that!" He felt as though he were being driven into a corner. "Kurt has everything I've always wanted—real culture, learning, manners, even his dear, idiotic, babyish clownishness. Yes—I'll hurry and get it in before you graciously throw it up at me—yes and position. I *admit* I'd like to be a countess. Though how unimportant that part is, a man like you could never understand. Yes, and physically Kurt has—oh, he hasn't your lumbering bull strength, but he rides, he fences, he dances, he swims, he plays tennis—oh, perfectly. And he has a sense of romance. But you'll go around telling all the dear dull people in Zenith that I didn't appreciate your sterling——"

"Stop it! I warn you!"

"——virtues, and that I'm a silly tuft-hunting American woman, and you'll enjoy sneering that for all his rank, the Count Obersdorf is only a clerk and probably a fortune-hunter, and that will make you feel so justified for all your dullness! Oh, I can see what a sweet time you'll have spreading scandal about me——"

"God!" Fran shrank at something in his face. He was standing by the center table. He had cooled his huge right hand by grasping a vase of roses. That hand slowly closed now, his shoulder strained, and the vase smashed, the water dripped through his fingers. He threw the mess, glass fragments and crushed flowers, into a corner, and wiped his bleeding fingers. The hysterical gesture relieved him.

She looked frightened, but she quavered gallantly, "don't be mel——"

He broke in with a very hard, business-like: "We'll have no more melodrama on either side. I warned you that I'd fly off the handle. If you enjoy your little game of picking at me any more, it won't be a vase next time. Now there's just a couple of things to settle. That I go is decided. But—— You're quite sure that Kurt wants to marry you?"

"Quite!"

"Been anything more than——"

"No, not yet—I'm sorry to say! There might have been if you hadn't come tonight. Oh, I'm sorry! Please! I don't mean to be quite as nasty as I sound! But I'm a little hysterical, too. Don't you suppose I know what people will think about me—what even Brent and Emily will think! Oh, I'll pay——"

"You will. Now will you promise me: see as much as you want to of Kurt, but promise me that you'll wait a month before you decide to sue for divorce. To be sure."

"Very well."

"I'll instruct my bank to send you ten thousand a year, on top of your own money. That seems to end everything."

"Oh, Sam, if I could only make you see that it was your ignorance, your impotence, and not my fault——"

Suddenly he had seized an astonished and ruffled Fran, thrust her into the bedroom, growled, "We've talked enough tonight," locked the door on her infuriated protests . . . berated himself for that ruffianism . . . sighed that he would lie awake all night . . . and, with no bedtime preparations save removing his coat and shoes, dropped on the couch and gone instantly and blindly asleep.

Chapter 29

IN THE MORNING he was cool, determined to clear off as soon as possible. She was no less cool. When he unlocked the bedroom door, at eight, she was already dressed, in crisp blue coat and skirt and plain blouse, and she looked at him as though he were a servant whom she had resolved to discharge for insolence. She said quietly:

"Good morning. You know, of course, that your mauling me and threatening me last evening made finally impossible any rapprochement between us."

"Eh? That's fine."

"Oh. Oh, I see. Very well, that makes everything so *much* easier. At last we know where we are. Now I suppose you'll return to Paris, at least for a while."

"I suppose so. I'll take the evening train."

"Then you'll have a lot to do. I'm sorry to trouble you, but I'm afraid we'll have to make a number of agreements—about our house in Zenith, about finances, and so on—it's very generous of you to go on sending money, though I certainly should not take it unless I felt that, after all, running your house, entertaining your business acquaintances and all, perhaps I've earned it. And you'll have to pack—be something of a job to divide up the luggage, of course, now our things are all mixed up together in the trunks. So we must get busy. If you'll be so good as to order breakfast for us—and to shave!—which you decidedly need, if you'll permit me to say so!—I'll go down and have the concierge get your *wagon lit* and ticket. And I'll telephone to Kurt. I assume you will want to abuse him for a while—oh, he won't mind! And I think it might be good for my reputation here, so long as I'm in an anomalous position, which I can't expect you to understand or appreciate, if Kurt and I saw you off together on the train tonight."

"Fran, I'm not planning to get out any shotgun, but I most certainly will not see Von Obersdorf again, any time, under any considerations. For both my sake and his, I'm afraid you'll have to give up your idea of having your cake and eating it—of kicking me out and yet of having every one suppose you're a devoted and deserted wife. That's flat. *Understand?*"

"Quite. Very well. And I should be glad if you'd find it possible not to yell at me any more, just this last day, so that I'll have a little pleasanter memory of you! Please order some orange juice for me. I'll be back by the time breakfast is here. You'll find your blue suit freshly pressed in the closet—I had it done while you were away."

At eleven, while Sam was packing and Fran was out buying another suit-case, into the sitting-room, into the bedroom, without knocking, came Kurt von Obersdorf, and Sam looked up to see him standing in the door, his fingers nervous on his palms.

"I know you did not want to see me. Fran telephoned me so. But you do not understand, Sam. I am not a gigolo or a Don Juan. I do love Fran; I would beg her to marry me if she were free. But if I told you how much I like and admire you, you would think I was a sentimental fool. I have kep' telling her she does not appreciate you. If I could bring you two together—oh, *don't* run off and desert her; she needs your steadiness! If I could bring you two together again, and keep you both for my ver' dear friends, *I* would go away, instead—yes, I would go today!"

Sam rose from the wardrobe trunk, dusted his hands, stood gravely in his shirt-sleeves:

"Suppose I just called your bluff, Von Obersdorf? Suppose I said, 'All right, you leave Berlin today, for good, and I'll stay.'"

"I would do it! I will! If in turn you promise me to be always more tender with Fran! Oh, I do not mean I can go forever, and hide myself. I am a poor man. I support partly my mother. But I can be called for business to Budapest, for three weeks. We organize now a new branch there. Shall I go?"

He looked the zealot, he said it like a crusader.

But Sam realized hastily, dismayingly, that he wanted to go; that he wanted to be free of Fran's play-acting; he realized that he was afraid to be left alone with her fury if Kurt should desert them.

"No," he said. "And I apologize. I believe you. Here's what we've got to do. Of course I have no way of knowing just how fond you are of Fran. But it certainly doesn't look as if Fran and I could ever get together again. Don't even know it would be a good thing, for either of us. What we have to do is to do nothing; let things take their course. I'm going. She stays. You stay. You see how you feel, and I'll see how I feel, and if you do love the girl—as I by God have and as I suppose I still do!—don't let any consideration for me stand in your way. I wouldn't, I guess, if the shoe was on the other foot. Not that I'm going to say any 'Bless you my children.' I feel more like saying, 'Damn you both!' But I can't see where you're to blame. No. Now I've got to finish packing. Good-bye, Obersdorf. Don't see me off tonight—definitely don't want it. And I guess I ought to tell you that I'm afraid she's right. Guess you can make the girl happier than I can."

"But *you*—going alone——"

"Now hell's big bells on a mountain! Don't worry about me! I'm free, white, and twenty-one! Everybody's had too much considerateness for everybody else in this business! I figure that maybe it would have been a lot clearer-cut if one of us had been out-and-out hoggish and known what he wanted and just grabbed it. No. I'll be all right. Good-bye."

Kurt shook the proffered hand hesitatingly. Sam turned his back. When he looked up, Kurt was gone.

If Fran knew that Kurt had called, she gave no sign. All day she was courteous, brisk, and harder than enamel.

To pack for his journey—the journey to nowhere which might last forever—it was necessary to unpack the rather large number of trunks and bags which these spoiled children of new wealth had found necessary. Their baggage had for months been their only home. To divide it was like the division of property after a funeral.

But she was efficient about it, and horribly kind.

When she came to the shawl he had bought as a surprise for her that exciting day in Seville, she looked at it slowly, stroked it, started to speak, then firmly put it away in a drawer of the bureau. But it was harder when she came to the silly shell-box.

It brought back a day on the Roman Campagna, a windy radiant day of fast walking. They had found a tomb old as the Caesars, forgotten amid long grass, and had lunched in a palm-thatched outdoor booth at a peasant trattoria. A pedler came whining to their table with a tray of preposterous shell-boxes, and Fran seized one, crying, "Oh, *darling*, will you look at this adorably awful thing?" It was a masterpiece; a wooden box with cheap red velvet glued round the sides, and on top a scurf of tiny gilded sea-shells about a small streaky mirror. "Look! All my life—— When I was a little girl, we had a maid (only I think we called her a hired girl!) that had a box *exactly* like this, and I thought it was the most beautiful thing in the world. I used to sneak up to her little room, under the eaves, to worship it. And I've always wanted one like it. And here it is! But of course one couldn't buy the horrible thing!"

"Why not?"

"Oh, could we? It would make me remember—— Oh, of course not! Perfectly silly, with us traveling——"

But he rose to her fancy; he demanded of the old pedler, "How much liras? Eh?" and interrogatively held up five fingers.

After much conversation which neither Sam nor the pedler understood, and at which Fran giggled helplessly, Sam bought the object for seven lire, and that night Fran surrounded it with a pearl necklace and burned a candle in front of it. Then she had forgotten it—but not quite thrown it away. It had made its way into one of those neglected drawers of a wardrobe trunk, one of those old attics of traveling, which contain bathing suits, walking shoes, solid histories intended to make journeying educational, and all the other useful staples which one surely will use, and never will.

Fran dove into this attic drawer busily; she drew out the shell-box, and stood holding it. Her eyes were deep, pitiful, regretful, and all their defense was gone. He looked back at her, helpless. And neither of them found anything to say, and suddenly she had snatched out of the attic drawer a never-used thermos bottle and their moment was gone.

A minute later when, after desperate groping for speech, he felt that it would be an ingratiating thing to say, "If I happen to go to Spain, would you like me to get you any lace or embroidery or anything?" she answered suavely, "Oh, thanks, thanks no. I fancy I may run down to the Balkans before long, and I believe there's some very decent embroidery there. I say, will you please notice that I'm putting these dress collars not with your day collars but with your evening shirts? Heavens, we must hurry!"

When a man straggles on the short death-walk from his cell through the little green door, into the room where stands the supreme throne, does he, along with his incredulous apprehension, along with trying to believe that this so-living and eternal-seeming center and purpose of the universe, himself—this solid body with its hard biceps, its curiously throbbing heart that ever since his mother's first worry has in its agonies been so absorbing, this red-brown skin that has glowed after the salt sea at Coney Island and has turned a sullen brick after wild drinking—the astonishment that this image of God and Eternity will in five minutes be still and stiff and muck—is he at that long slow moment nonetheless conscious of a mosquito bite, of a toothache, of the smugness of the messages from Almighty God which the chaplain gives him, of the dampness of the slimy stone corridor and the echo of their solemn march? Is he more conscious of these little abrasions than of the great mystery?

So busy were Sam and Fran at the station—buying magazines, looking over the new Tauchnitzes, seeing that his extra trunks were registered through to Paris—that they had no time to question whether this might be their last parting. They had dined in the crowded bar of the Adlon, too close to others to have the luxury of mourning; she had said nothing more emotional than "If you should decide to go to America, when you see Emily and the boy tell them that I'll come back and see them in a few months now . . . no matter what happens . . . unless they'd like to come over to Europe. Of course I'd like that. . . . I put some new tooth-powder in the bottle in your fitted case."

She was as attentive as a courier at the station; it was she who with her quick inaccurate German persuaded the conductor to change Sam to a one-berth compartment, who prevented his giving the hotel porter, who met them with their hand luggage and registered the trunks through, more than four marks as tip.

By general, it had been he, these months, who had borne the duties of tickets, luggage, reservations, while she sat back in cool elegance and was not shy about criticizing him for his errors. But tonight she led the expedition, she thought of everything, and he felt helpless as a maiden aunt. He had a new respect for her. . . . Perhaps, with Kurt, she wouldn't be a child any longer, but grasp reality. That made him the more disconsolate, the more hopeless of some future miraculous reconciliation. He saw her a woman reborn. It seemed to him that she was grasping the intricacies of daily life in Europe as deftly as she managed everything from the cook's salary to the women's club program in America. He could not imagine her, just now, going back to Zenith. Kurt von Obersdorf and the Princess Drachenthal and Europe had utterly defeated and put in their place Sam Dodsworth and Tub and Matey Pearson and Ross Ireland and the Midwest.

Thus his thoughts blundered and writhed while he ambled after her through the station—to the news-stand, to the cigar-stand, to the train-gate—feeling himself no closer to her polished and metallic briskness than he was to the bundle-lugging third-class passengers who plodded through the echoing immensity of the train-shed; and thus, with everything necessary and unnecessary accomplished and overaccomplished, they stood together beside his sleeper, his luggage stored, his ticket taken by the guard, and suddenly they tumbled like the falling Lucifer from the paradise of keeping busy to the inferno of feeling. She put it off a moment. She sighted the boy trundling his little platform wagon of wine and sandwiches and fruit; she cried, "Oh, you might want something to drink," and darted off to bring him back a flask of cognac.

There was nothing else.

The train took another diabolic three minutes to start. They walked up and down—a tall, well-tailored pair, obviously complacent and not much interested, not very emotional.

He took her arm, as he had so many times at so many railroad stations, but dropped it with hot guiltiness.

"No, *please*," she said, tucking her arm into his. "It is

going to be a little hard to realize, isn't it, old thing! Oh, Sam darling, you and I can't get along together. And I do love Kurt. I stand by that! But we have been partners, good partners, in this funny business of life. . . . We've had so many happy times, just you and I together!" Her voice lost its confidence. "Shall I ever see you again? And—oh, my blessings, my dear——"

"*Eeeeeein-steigen—bitte einsteigen!*" cried the mourning voice of the guard.

"That means 'all aboard'?" croaked Sam.

"Yes. Quick!"

The train was starting as he climbed up to the vestibule. Fran stood alone. He saw her with a strange, impersonal pity. She seemed so slim and young and defenseless, so alone in the gray city. He realized that she was crying.

His heavy mature voice became young and shaky as he cried, "Dear, did I remember to tell you today that I adore you?"

The guard slammed the vestibule door, and as through an open window he craned to look back at her, he saw Kurt von Obersdorf running down the platform, he saw Fran droop into Kurt's arms, and he walked slowly into the roaring loneliness of his compartment.

Chapter 30

KALEIDOSCOPE. Scarlet triangles and azure squares, crystalline zigzags and sullen black lines. Meaningless beauty and distortions that were the essence of pain. Such were the travels of Samuel Dodsworth, those summer months.

He longed to go home to Zenith, to have the solace of Tub and Matey, of Emily and Brent, of streets and corners and offices that respected him and did not sneer at him as an ignorant tourist. But to face the derision that would be his if he came back without Fran, to hear in every corner the delighted whispering which was the vicarious vengeance of men who wanted to be free of their own wives and took out their timorous hatred in snickering and twilight gossiping about the marital troubles of others—that he could not endure. And to face a gloating, damp, pawing pity, to face the morons who would suppose that he was so little that he would be gratified by their libeling Fran, his Fran, and by cumbersomely congratulating him on losing her, who was his very soul—that was not to be borne.

If he had had a job at home, he would probably have plunged back into it, and in a fury of papers and secretaries and telephone-calls have concealed himself from the scandal. But he hadn't. Just now the Sans Souci Gardens plan seemed to him as preposterous as his lifelong belief that he was man enough to hold his wife.

Yet twice, in Paris, he reserved passage to America, and twice he frugally went to the Cunard office and got back his passage money.

He crept over to London to hear the one language he knew, and fled from it because he did know the language, because some one might recognize him and pity him. He went on a German tour to the North Cape and the Baltic, got off at Riga, and fled from it because he did not know the language.

He returned to England, rented a motor, and toured along the old Roman road through Kent, stopping in villages of half-timbered houses and cottages covered with red tile shingles; into Sussex villages secret in still wooded valleys beneath the shining downs. He might have been seen, a very large man alone in a rather small car; a lone figure sitting on the sky-cut rim of a hill, hour on hour, clasping his knees, apparently brooding; a man alone in a public bar, listening to everything that was said—surprised and pleasant when some one spoke to him.

He felt the peace and security of the English valleys and farmsteads—and it made him the more restless because he was so definitely an outsider. He returned to Paris, and night after night he sat in American bars, and was put down as one of the beachcombers who have been something once but who have gone bankrupt—financially or nervously or alcoholically—and of whom one must pityingly beware.

He understood. So it came to pass that he spent most of his time alone, in his room in the Grand Universel. (It gave him a curious mean pleasure, now, to have a cheap single bedroom instead of a suite.) He drank a good deal. Sometimes he had a cognac instead of breakfast. But between blurred drowsinesses, he saw with clarity that he was utterly a man alone, that his work, his children, his friends, his habitual routine of life, and at last his wife, all the props and crutches with which he had been enabled to hobble through life as a Good Fellow, were gone, and that he had nothing upon which to depend except such solaces as he might find in his own brain. No one really needed him, and he was a man who had never been able to depend on any one to whom he could not give.

In childish, absurd ways he managed to kill time, day on day, in a fog which now and then mercifully concealed from him the needs of Samuel Dodsworth. Till noon he loafed in his room at the Grand Universel, frowsy in dressing-gown, taking an hour to read the Paris *Tribune* and *Herald*, taking half an hour to shave. He managed, once a fortnight, to spend an hour in having his hair cut, and though he tried to give the appearance of being a busy and important man, he was glad when he had to wait at the barber's; when he could, without looking ridiculous, spend that time in turning over *Sketch* and the *Graphic*. He took to having manicures—he had despised the practise. He never admitted it to himself, but he neglected giving a hotel address to the Guaranty

Trust, so that he might have a reason to plod to the bank for his mail every day.

He was grateful to the doormen and the mail clerks at the Guaranty Trust for treating him like some one who still mattered; and when he had a letter—they were few now, and most of them were from Fran, who seemed to desire to keep up a sisterly friendship with him—he took it with fatuous dignity and retired to a table in front of a café on the Boulevard des Italiens to read it, to re-read it, though the most that he gathered was that she had found a charming new restaurant in Berlin.

Once a man who was asking for his mail at the Guaranty Trust said, "Aren't you Mr. Dodsworth of the Revelation Company? Met you, sir, at the motor show in New York."

Sam was so pleased that he asked the man to lunch, and telephoned to him often, to the end that the man, who had regarded Sam as one of his gods, saw that he was merely a solitary and common human being, and despised him and was uninterested.

And always Fran was with him, scolding at his weakness; always he saw her face. At twilight, and at three in the morning, when he could sleep no longer and rose to smoke a cigarette, he heard her saying, "Oh, Sam, I couldn't have *believed* that you could ever become a dirty drunk like this!" He nestled his head on her shoulder and weepingly confessed his failure as a human being and thereafter was racked with pity for her mad and gallant effort to be more than herself, so that he would gladly have done what he could to help Kurt to win her. . . . Samuel Dodsworth, so abnormally flushed that no friend of his hearty triumphant days would have recognized him, sitting on the edge of his bed, his hair wild and his pajamas wrinkled, smoking cigarettes, longing to telephone from Paris to Berlin and tell Fran that he hoped she would be the Countess Obersdorf, and kept from it chiefly by the thought that she wouldn't like it at all and would be very tart about it if he awoke her at three in the morning.

He had known unhappiness often enough, but never complete suffering like this—a suffering so vague and directionless and unreasonable that he raged at himself for his moody weakness—a suffering so confusing that he would have preferred any definite pain of the body. Fran was to him a madness. Now he cursed her for disloyalty and in long unmoving silences reviewed her superciliousnesses, but the result was no stout resolution to be free, but sudden pity for her—a fear that she would be slighted by Kurt's family—a picture of her alone and friendless, crying at twilight. He remembered in jagged reminiscences the most grotesquely assorted things—a white fur evening cape she had once had, and how she had prepared a lunch of coffee and salad and cold partridge on the roadside, when they had motored to Detroit; her way of saying "I am a very sleepy young woman," and a funny slatternly pair of pink wool bedroom slippers which she had loved. He glowed in these relivings and came bolt out of them to ache the more, till she was to him a spiritual virus from which he had to be free.

He found Nande Azeredo; and he was rather completely untrue to Fran, and while he liked Nande, he could not persuade himself to like being untrue.

He had gone back to the Café Select, hoping to see Elsa and by some magic to take her away from the sharp-nosed Mr. Keipp. There was no question now of willingness to be what he still called "disloyal," there was only a question of keeping from going insane. The moralities with which comfortably married clergymen concern themselves did not exist for him now.

He did not see Elsa, and as he sat alone a tall, rather handsome girl, with a face as broad between the cheek bones as a Tartar ambled up, sat down uninvited, and demanded, in an English that sounded as though it were played on a flute, "Vot's the trouble? You look down in the mout'."

"I am. What would you like to drink?"

"Grand Marnier. . . . Did she die, or run away from you?"

"I'd rather not talk about it."

"So bad as that? Good. I talk about this place here. I will give imitations of the people here."

And she did, merrily, not badly. She seemed to him quite the brightest light he had found since Berlin. His guess was that she was an artists' model; there were few professional prostitutes to be found at the Dôme or the Select, no matter how competent were some of the amateurs.

She told him that she was Nande Azeredo, as though he ought to know who she was.

Fernande Azeredo (he discovered presently) was half Portuguese, half Russian, and altogether French. She was twenty-five and she had lived in nine countries, been married three times, and once shot a Siberian wolf. She had been a chorus girl, a dress mannequin, a masseuse, and now she scratched out a thin living by making wax models for show-window dummies and called herself a sculptress. She boasted that though she had had fifty-seven lovers ("And, my dear, one was a real Prince—well, pretty real"), she had never let one of them give her anything save a few frocks.

And he believed her.

This alley-kitten—or alley-tigress—read him as such geniuses as Elsa and Keipp and Gillespie and Short had never done. She knew by divination that he was an American, a business man, graduate of a university; she knew that he had lost at love; she knew that essentially he was kindly and solid and not to be diverted by the obscenities with which she had amused other traveling Americans.

"You are a nize man. Maybe you buy me a dinner. Or I don't care a damn—you come to my little flat and I cook you a shop. I have not got no man, now. The last—oh, the dirty hound—I threw him out because he stole my fur coat and pawned it!"

And he believed her.

Her flushed vitality pleased him. Though she said nothing of importance, she uttered her little, profane, sage comments on the warfare between men and women with such vigor, she so assured him that he was large and powerful and real and that she preferred him to all of the limp poetasters about the place, that he was warmed by her companionship. And without mentioning Berlin or Kurt, without making it quite clear whether Fran had been sweetheart or wife, he forgot his "I'd rather not talk about it," and told her rather frankly of his illness.

Then he returned to his hotel, packed a bag, and spent three nights and days in the flat of Nande Azeredo.

She astonished him by the casual, happy, utterly proud way in which she served her Man. He had not known that any women save spinster secretaries could be happy in serving. She darned his socks and made him drink less cognac, she cooked snails for him so that he actually liked them, she taught him new ways of love, and when she found that he did not know them, she laughed at him, but affectionately. For the first time in his life he began to learn that he need not be ashamed of the body which God had presumably given him but which Fran had considered rather an error. He found in himself a power of intense passion such as, all his life, he had guiltily believed himself to lack; and sometimes Nande's flat seemed to him the Bower of Eden.

It was an insane little flat: three rooms, just under the roof, looking on a paved courtyard which smelled of slops and worse, and was all day clamorous with quarreling, children playing, delivery of charcoal, and the banging of garbage cans. Her dishes were cracked, her cups were chipped; the plaster walls were rain-streaked and Sam's roses she set out in a tin can; but on a couch covered with gold brocade lolled horribly a number of powdery-faced dolls, very elongated and expensive. Her clothes were in heaps and there was no concealment of sanitary appliances. And everywhere were instruments for the making of noise: a phonograph which by preference she turned on at three in the morning, rattles and horns left over from the last carnival, a very cheap radio—fortunately out of order—and seven canaries.

He could not, for a time, believe that Nande, whatever her virtues, was not calculating on what she would get out of him. When they were ambling the Rue de la Paix together (that street which Fran had seemed to know so well, but which Nande made living by telling the most scandalous tales about the shop-keepers and their favorites among the women clerks) he buzzed, "What'd you like me to buy you, Nan? Some pearls or——"

She stopped before him, planted her arms akimbo, and spoke furiously. "I am not vot you call a gold-digger! I am not lady enough! If when you get tired of me, you vant to give me a hundred dollars—or fifty—fine. But you must, by God, understand, when Nande Azeredo takes a man, it iss because she likes him! Pearls? What would I do with pearls? Can I eat pearls?"

She worked daily—though not for very many hours daily—at her atrocious modeling, and somehow she managed to bring him in precisely the sorts of English books he wanted: Shelley, for the vanity of remembering that he had been a University Man before he became a beachcomber, and detective stories, which he really read.

"Lord!" he reflected, "what a wife she'd make for a pioneer! She'd chuck this Parisian show like a shot, if she loved somebody. She'd hoe the corn, she'd shoot the Indians, she'd nurse the babies—and if she couldn't get Paris lingerie, she'd probably spin it."

But it was just her admirable vigor which after three days wearied him.

It was amusing, the first time, to see Nande, arms akimbo, in a shawl or a chemise, denouncing the grocer's boy for an overcharge of thirty centimes, denouncing him with so many applications of the epithet "Camel" that he blanched and fled. But it was much less amusing, the twentieth time she quarreled with tradesmen, waiters, taxi-drivers, and motorists—who, she believed, were in a conspiracy to run her down—and with Sam himself, for not eating more. She was so shrill: her conversations started with a shriek and ended with a howl. He longed for a decent quiet. And always he saw Fran watching Nande and himself in mockery.

Whenever he stoutly convinced himself that Nande was beautiful as a young tigress and a miracle of loyal kindness, the cool wraith of Fran appeared, and Nande seemed then a blowsy gutter-looper. To his angry defense of Nande, Fran answered with the look she gave rude servants. She watched while Nande scrubbed the floor, bawling indecent lyrics; she slipped through the room just as Nande cheered Sam by slapping his rear; and he was turned into a schoolboy caught with the kitchen maid.

So he told Nande that business called him to Italy. She pretended to believe him; she begged him to be careful of cognac and women; she casually accepted a present of a hundred dollars; she saw him off.

As the train was starting, she slipped into his hand a little package.

He looked at it an hour or two afterward. It contained a gold cigarette case which must have cost her all of his hundred dollars.

Nande Azeredo!

He never wrote to Nande. He wanted to, but she was not one to whom you could say anything on paper.

She seemed to him a character in a play; a rather fantastic and overacted character; but she had definitely done something to him. She had, along with the glances of Minna von Escher, broken down all the celibacy which had plagued him, and however much he still fretted over Fran, imagined her loneliness in Berlin, let himself be wrung by pity for her self-dramatizing play at romance which was bound to turn into tragedy, he no longer felt himself her prisoner, and he began to see that this world might be a very green and pleasant place.

He was more conscious of the *wagon lit* than he had ever been, for he was wondering if he might not spend much of his life, now, in those homes for people who flee from life. . . . Blue upholstered seat, rather hard, with hard cylindrical cushions. Above the blue velvet, yellow and brown florid stamped leather, rough to a speculative touch. The Alarm Signal to stop the train, all labeled nicely in four languages for the linguistic instruction of tourists, which he always longed to pull, even if it cost him five hundred lire. The tricky little cabinet in the corner which turned into a wash-stand when one let down the folding shelf. And the detached loneliness of which he rid himself now and then by poking out into the corridor, to lean against the brass rail across the broad low windows, or to sit on the tiny folding seat. And outside, mountains; stations with vacant-faced staring loungers; plains which seemed to him altogether like the American Middlewest till suddenly the sun, revealing a high and distant castle on an abrupt cliff, restored to him the magic of foreignness.

Till now, Sam Dodsworth had never greatly heeded fellow passengers, except Americans who looked as though they might be good fellows with whom to gossip and have a drink. Of most of them, had you demanded a description from him after the journey, he would have said, "Oh, they looked about like anybody else, I guess—why?" He saw them not as trees walking but as clothes sitting.

But the incredible jar of being dismissed by Fran, the opening of his eyes to the possibilities of misery in the world, made him feel the universal pathos of things more sensitively than he had even on the exalted night when he had first beheld the lights of England. He felt—no doubt sentimentally—akin to everything that was human; he saw—no doubt often without reason—a drama, tragic or comic, behind all the face-masks of travelers, behind surly faces, stupid faces, mean faces, common faces. He a little forgot himself—and Fran and Kurt and Nande Azeredo—as he wondered whether that tight-mouthed woman had recently been burying her husband, whether that overdressed young salesman had a nagging wife at home, whether that petulant and snarling old man had lost his fortune. He studied the railroad workmen who stood back to let the train pass, and speculated as to which of them was about to be married, which was an ecstatically religious communist, which was longing to murder his wife.

Thus brooding, hour-long, not having to hasten back to the compartment and entertain Fran. Thus slowly and painfully perceiving a world vaster than he had known. Thus considering whether he was so badly beaten, so enfeebled by Fran's scorn, that he could never find the Not Impossible She and, with her, experience the not impossible self-confidence and peace.

He poked about Rome for a week, trying to persuade himself that he was studying architecture. It was hot, and he fled to Montreux, with a notion of swimming and cool mountains. Daily he examined schedules of sailings for New York and surmised that one of these days would find him fleeing aboard a steamer. He drifted to Geneva, solemnly viewed the League of Nations building, and in his hotel wondered which of the not very exciting-looking gentlemen with top hats were famous ministers of state. Then, in a small restaurant, he heard, like an angelic trump, the voice of Ross Ireland, the correspondent: "Well, Sam, you old devil, where did you come from!"

They had many drinks.

With Ross he tramped for a week, rucksack on shoulders, through the Bernese Oberland. He felt rather foolish, at first, to be carrying a sack and walking dustily past large hotels, for he had been trained to feel that it was undignified for him to walk, except on a duck pass or a golf course. But he enjoyed seeing a view without the need, as a rich, busy, and motorized tourist, of having to hustle past it; he found himself breathing deeper, sleeping better, brooding less, and drinking beer instead of cognac. In fact he believed that he had discovered walking, and wrote enthusiastic recommendations of it on post cards to Fran, Tub, and Dr. Hazzard. He came to feel superior to large, plushy hotels. Ross and he ate dumplings and pig's knuckle; they rested at tiny tables in front of inns when they had panted into a village, sweaty and shoulders aching.

Ross insisted that whenever they "saw church-steeples and heard the bright prattle of children," those were the signs certain and indivisible of the proximity of beer, and however much they enjoyed the mountain-side lanes, they cheered up and hastened their step and began to listen for the bright prattle as soon as they saw a church steeple.

And Sam decided what he would do with the wreckage of his life.

He had not known that wandering could be so satisfying as it was with Ross Ireland, who never complained and became superior like Fran, or felt bound to be funny like Tub, or noisy like Nande; who was interested in everything from pig-pens to cloisters; and who enjoyed erecting theories of life more than anything save tearing them down.

Ross was going to the Orient again, after summer in Europe. He invited Sam to come along and Sam accepted, with more tingling anticipation than he had known since he had first sailed for England. . . . Turkestan, Borneo, Siam, Pekin, Penang and the sight of Java Head!

Ross was called to Paris, but that city meant for Sam, now, only too much loneliness and too much Nande, and he squatted in Gstaad, trying to be very healthy and full of fresh air.

And before Ross had been gone forty-eight hours, Sam was thrown back into as much fidgety fretting as he had ever known.

He cursed himself for his weakness; he sought to sink himself in an enormous volume on English Gardens and Domestic Architecture of the Eighteenth Century; he sought to recapture a longing for the Orient; and it was in vain.

Bluntly, he could not go off to the Far East and leave Fran unprotected.

Oh, he told himself she did not need protection. His presence irritated her more than it soothed her, and he was a fool, and a puerile and whining fool, not to be able to cut loose from his mother's apron strings, now inconveniently worn by a wife. But—— If anything went wrong there in Berlin—— If Fran wanted to run to him for help, and he should be ten thousand miles away——

He couldn't do it.

He wondered, occasionally, if he wasn't confusing the need to serve Fran with the need of women in general, that basic need which he had just consciously discovered; he wondered whether, if it were a woman with some of Ross Ireland's sportsmanship and inquiring mind who had invited him to come along, he would not have found it possible to go, armored with a good, round, satisfying cliché like "Fran made her bed; let her lie in it."

No! He swore to himself that his care for Fran was authentic; was to him what prayer was to a hermit, and honor to a soldier; and always he wound up his fretful meditations with, "Oh, hell, I can't analyse it, but I'm not going to desert her! Only wish I could!"

He wrote Ross not to count on his company this coming autumn, and again fled from himself, but with himself, to Venice, because the current news photographs from the Lido, the pictures of gay companies on the beach, made it seem a place to divert a solitary man. And perhaps one of these exquisite gold and ivory Englishwomen——

No! He didn't want that sort. He wanted some one with Fran's fineness but with Nande's sturdiness, Ross Ireland's brains.

He was able to laugh at himself: "If there were such a woman anywhere, what would she want with you?"

But as, in the too-familiar blue-velvet and stamped leather *wagon lit* compartment, he clanked on toward Venice, he was not quite free of the pictures of lovely ladies on Lido beach; not quite sure that he had in life any purpose beyond the quest of the Not Impossible She.

Chapter 31

SAM was not particularly enlivened by the Lido in season. The hotels seemed to him to smack of the Chicago World's Fair of 1893 with the added flavor of a Turkish bath; and the intimacy with which two-thirds of this basking, bathing, lunching, dancing society knew one another, whether they were Italian, English, American, or Austrian, made him feel utterly the outsider. He moved back into Venice, to the Bauer-Grünwald which, despite a German atmosphere which too readily reminded him of his Berlin débâcle, was more welcoming than the Royal Danieli.

Venice is the friendliest city in the world. There are other cities in which friendlier people may be found, but in Venice it is the city itself, the spectacle of the Piazza San Marco, the cozy little streets, the open-fronted shops of the coppersmiths, the innumerable churches that are always open, the alternately effusive and quarrelsome gondoliers, the greedy but amiable pigeons, the soft sky, the rustling water of the Grand Canal, the cafés thrusting their tables halfway across the Piazza, the palaces so proud in their carved balconies and so cheerfully poverty-stricken in their present inhabitants, the crowd with nothing to do save stroll and wait for the band concerts, which are so amiable that here less than anywhere else in the world does the stranger miss the warm gossip of people whom he knows.

Sam found the waiting into which all his life had turned now more tolerable than it had been at any time save when he had been drugged with fatigue on his walking tour with Ross, or save when that rather soiled Salvationist, Nande Azeredo, had stooped to save him. He lay abed till nine, content with the sound of the Grand Canal outside his windows, the squabbles of gondoliers. He rose to lean placidly on the sill and look at the wonders of Santa Maria della Salute and San Giorgio Maggiore, seeming, on their tiny islands, to be floating out to sea; to watch the panorama of vegetable scows, brick scows, cement scows, wangling their way into side canals, while the bargees quarreled magnificently with the more aristocratic gondoliers and with the uniformed drivers of motor boats belonging to officials. He had a meager cup of coffee, and, buying the latest Paris *Daily Mail*, *Chicago Tribune*, and *New York Herald* on the way, ambled to the Piazza for his real breakfast.

In the afternoon, Florian's and the Aurora were the accepted haunts, shaded then from the biting sun, but in the morning it was the Quadri and Lavena's which were sheltered, and at one of these cafés he drank his coffee, nibbled at croissants smeared with clouded honey from Monte Rosa, and read the papers, excited at the news from Washington and New York, excited when he saw that some one he knew, Ross Ireland or Endicott Everett Atkins, had dined with a Celebrity at Ciro's. . . . And once, in the Berlin news, he saw that Mrs. Samuel Dodsworth had been the guest of honor at a dinner given by the Princess Drachenthal and that among those present had been the Count of Obersdorf, the Baroness de Jeune, Sir Thomas Jenkins of the Allied Commission, and the newly made Geheimrat, Dr. Biedner. He sat for a long time, looking vacantly across the Piazza, at the spate of tourists whose wives were kodaking them in the act of feeding the pigeons of St. Mark.

He worked at his new game of architecture. With Ruskin's "Stones of Venice" under his arm, he saw daily a new church, a new palace, and now and then he made sketches, not very bad, and was not displeased when loudly commenting tourists mistook him for an authentic artist. He lunched simply; he slept for an hour afterward, and betook himself then to the one real duty of a wise visitor in Venice—to spend most of the afternoon and evening sitting in the Piazza and doing nothing whatever save watch the spectacle.

It had been agreeable in Paris or on Unter den Linden to watch the parade, but there the motors, the horses, the brisk policemen had made it a hard and somewhat nervous spectacle. Here, where there was no traffic, where the marble-walled piazza was like a stage with the chorus of an incredibly elaborate comic opera, there was only a lazy and unharassed contentment. The crowd changed every second. Now two Fascist officers paced by, trim in black shirts, olive-green uniforms, and gold-badged and tasseled service caps. Now it was two carbinieri with the cocked hats of Napoleon and the solemn manner of judges. Now a tourist steamer vomited a rush of excited novices—inquiring Germans or stolid English, golden-haired Scandinavians, or Americans of whom the women were thrilled and the males cocked up their cigars and announced, very publicly, that if *this* was Venice, they didn't think it was so doggone much!

The guides, slightly less numerous but much more insistent than the cloud of pigeons, attacked every one who was not entirely engaged in the sacred act of being photographed, and yammered, "Me gide spik fine English, show you San Marco." The children fell under everybody's feet. The gatherers of cigarettes swooped on each butt as it fell. The English couples went by amiably contemptuous. And at last the sunset turned the dark leaded glass behind the horses of San Marco into gold.

He was content, by comparison with his active agonizing in Paris. But he was also lonely, despite the show of the Piazza. He had to have some one to talk to, and never did he meet any one whom he knew.

It was not easy for him to pick up acquaintances. Once he sat at a table next to a party of Americans. They did not seem very complex and difficult; they looked like small town merchants and professional men with their wives; and Sam took the chance. He leaned toward the nearest, a spectacled little man, and drawled, "On a tour?"

The little man looked scornfully cautious. *He'd* read the papers! *He* wasn't going to be taken in by any of your slick international crooks!

He sniffed "Yes," and he did not embroider it.

"Uh—enjoying Italy?"

"Yes, thanks!"

The little man turned his back, and Sam was flushed and shamed and much lonelier than before.

He was grateful when he was picked up by a large and lugubrious and green-hatted Bavarian who was apparently even more desolate than himself, and though they had in common only a hundred words of English, twenty of German, and ten of Italian, they were both strong men who could endure a lot of gesturing. They gave each other confidence in battling with gondoliers, and together they lumbered to the Colleoni and SS. Giovanni e Paolo, gaped at the glass-makers at Murano, and visited the Armenian monastery on the peaceful isle of San Lazzaro. Sam saw the Bavarian friend off at the station as regretfully as he had seen Ross Ireland off at Interlaken, and all that evening he clung to his favorite table at Florian's as though it was his only home.

He heard regularly from Fran, but where once her letters had been festal, now he hesitated to open them.

She complained a good deal. It had been rainy—it had been hot. She had gone to the Tyrol for a week (she did not say that Kurt had come along but he guessed it) and the hotels had been crowded. She had suffered unparalleled misfortune in having to stay at a small hotel where the food was heavy and the guests heavier. She had met a cousin of Kurt, an Austrian ambassador, and though she had showered blessings of wit and courtesy on the fellow, he had not appreciated her.

As to whether Sam himself was any happier, she never inquired.

Her letters left him always a little blue. And they did not suggest that she would like to see him.

He was in the Piazza, meditating on one of these letters, a little after four of a blazing afternoon. He saw a familiar-looking woman pass his table. She was perhaps forty; she was slim, rather pale. She wore black crêpe, without ornament, and a wide black hat with a tiny brooch of brilliants. Her hands were as fine as lace.

He remembered. It was Mrs. Cecil R. A. Cortright, Edith Cortright, American-born widow of the British minister to Roumania (or was it Bulgaria?) who, on a hint from Tub's nephew, had asked them to tea at her flat in the Palace Ascagni in Venice, months ago. He darted up, to welcome the first recognizable face he had seen in weeks; he hesitated—Mrs. Cortright was not the sort of woman one greeted carelessly. He ventured again. He tossed a ten lira note on the table for the waiter, and, circling the square with his long stride, so arranged it that he met her as she was passing through the Piazzetta dei Leoni and entering the Calle di Canonica.

"Oh, how d'you do," he observed. "Do you remember having my wife and me to tea last spring—friends of Jack Starling——"

"Oh, but of course! Mr. ——?"

"Samuel Dodsworth."

"You and Mrs. Dodsworth *have* come back here soon."

"Oh, she's, uh, she had to stay in Berlin."

"Really? You're here alone? You must come to tea again."

"Be awfully glad to. You walking this way?" Quite fatuously, rather eagerly.

"Just a bit of shopping. There's a rabbit-warren of a pastry shop down here—— Perhaps you'd like to come along, and come home for a cup of tea this afternoon, if you haven't friends waiting for you."

"I don't know a soul in town."

"In that case, you must come, surely."

He rolled beside her, bumbling, "Must be an awful lot of people you know at the Lido now, with the season on."

"Yes. Unfortunately!"

"Don't you like the rotogravure set?"

"Oh, that is a nice thing to call them!" she said. "I've been looking for a phrase. Some of them are extremely agreeable, of course; nice simple people who really like to dance and swim, and don't go to the Lido just to be seen and photographed. But there's an international, Anglo-American-French set—smart women, just a little ambiguous, and men with titles and tailors and nothing much else, and sharp couples that play bridge too well, and three-necked millionaires that—well, they seem to me like a menagerie. There's a dreadful woman named Renée de Pénable——"

"Oh, you know her?"

"How can any one help it! The woman contrives to be simultaneously in Paris, the Lido, Deauville, Cannes, New York, and on all known trains and steamers! You know her? Do you like her?"

"Hate her," remarked Sam. "Oh, I don't know's I ought to say that. She's always been awfully decent to us. But I feel she's a grafter."

"No, she's subtler than that. She is quite generous to ninety-nine out of a hundred of her group—tramps in gold-foil!—so that she can get the dazzled hundredth to set her up in a gown shop or a charity society or something else that mysteriously collapses in two months. She's—oh, she's very amusing, of course."

"Neither do I!" roared Sam.

They smiled at each other, to the approval of seven youthful Venetians engaged in doing nothing and choosing the dimmest and smelliest Sottoportico to do it in.

Sam rejoiced that Edith Cortright might prove to be human, patient with large lost men. He was surer of it as he heard her bartering with the owner of the minute pastry shop for a dozen cakes. The proprietor demanded five lire, Mrs. Cortright offered two, and they compromised on three, which were their probable value.

Often enough Sam had seen Fran chaffering, but she was likely to lose her temper, more likely to make the shop-keeper lose his. With Mrs. Cortright, the baker shook his fingers, agonized over the insult to his masterpieces, asserted that his nine children and grand-mother would starve, but she only laughed, and all the while he laughed back. He took the three lire with the greatest cheerfulness, and cried after them, "Addio!" as though it were a blessing.

"The good soul!" said Mrs. Cortright as they returned to the Piazza. "We do that every week. That's really the reason why I go to him myself, instead of sending a maid, who gets them for twenty centesimi less than I do, probably, and pockets ten. But this pâtissier is an artist, and like all artists, a conservative. He tries to keep up the good old days when buying and selling in Italy really was an adventure, because everybody made a game of bargaining—the days that Baedeker wrote of when he tells you to 'keep a calm and pleasant demeanor, when haggling.' But that's all passing, I'm afraid. Between the regulations of the Fascists, and the efficient business of impressing tourists, the shops are becoming as dependable as Swan and Edgar's or a Woolworth's, and about as appealing. I think I'll go back and end my few declining years on Mulberry Street, in New York. That's about the only part of Italy, now, that hasn't been toured and described and painted and guided to death; the only part that hasn't been made safe for the vicar's aunt."

In the presence of Fran and her aggressive smartness, Edith Cortright had been abrupt, hiding her heart behind dutiful courtesy as she hid her taut frailness of body beneath frocks of soft, non-committal black. But now, as they tramped to the Palazzo Ascagni, avoiding the sun in arcades and under vast walls above tiny streets, as they climbed the sepulchral marble stairs to her flat, and sighingly relaxed in the coolness of the vast rooms behind blinds streaked with poisonous sun, she was easy; in a subdued silvery manner, she was gay. It was as though she found everything in life amusing and liked to think about it aloud. And she seemed younger. He had thought her forty-five; now she seemed forty.

The stone floor of her drawing-room, laid in squares waxed to ivory smoothness, the old walnut of a Sixteenth Century armoire, suggested quietness, a feeling of civilization grown secure and placid through generations. The formal monastic chairs which had dignified the room when Sam had seen it in the spring—as well as the shameless over-stuffed Americanized arm-chairs with which Mrs. Cortright had eased the rigor of Venetian stateliness—had been replaced by wicker with chintz cushions.

Sam's spirit was refreshed here, his hot body was refreshed, and when Mrs. Cortright showed herself so superior to Expatriate Americanism that she dared to be American and to offer iced tea, he rejoiced in her more than in the mosaics of St. Mark's, which he had taught himself to admire with a quite surprising amount of sincerity. Mrs. Cortright and the room which illustrated her seemed to him quite as traditional as the faded splendors of the Princess Drachenthal at Potsdam; but he could reach Mrs. Cortright, understand her, not feel with her like an inanely smirking boy invited to tea by the schoolmaster's wife. He was a little afraid of her, a little afraid that behind her pallid restraint there might be comment on such a stumbling tourist as himself. But it was a fear that he could understand and answer, not a bewildering midnight strangeness.

He saw that in an age of universal bobbing, when no Fran would have dared be so eccentric, Mrs. Cortright kept her hair long, parted simply and not too neatly. And he saw again the lovely hands moving like white cats among the cups of taffy-colored majolica.

She did not talk, this time, of diplomats and Riviera villas and painting. She said:

"Tell me—— Really, I'm not impertinent; I ask myself the same thing, and perhaps I'm looking for an answer for myself. What do you find in Europe? Why do you stay on?"

"Well, it's kind of hard to say." He sipped his iced tea, appreciative of the thin tart taste against his tongue. "Oh, I guess—— Well, to be absolutely frank, it's because of my wife. I've enjoyed coming abroad. I've learned a lot of things—not only about pictures and all that, but in my own line—I'm a motor manufacturer, if you remember. For instance, I went to the Rolls-Royce works in England, and it was a perfect revelation to me, the way they were willing to lose money by going on having things like polishing done by hand instead of by machinery, as we'd do them, because they felt they were better done by hand. But—oh, I can understand how the artists that hang around places like Florence, and that don't care whether the government is monarchial or communist as long as the tea and the sunsets are good, can be perfectly content to stay there for years. But me—I'm getting restless at being so much of an outsider. I feel like the small boy that's never consulted about where the picnic will be held. I suppose I'm awfully lowbrow not to care for any more galleries and ruins but—oh, I want to go home and *make* something! Even if it's only a hen-coop!"

"But couldn't you make that here? In England, for example?"

"No, I'd feel the English chickens wouldn't understand my speaking American, and probably go and die on me."

"Then you don't want to stay? Why do you?"

"Oh, well, my wife still feels——"

Swiftly, as though she were covering a blunder, Mrs. Cortright murmured, "And of course she is lovely. I remember her with such pleasure. She must be an enchanting person to wander with. . . . And please don't feel that I'm one of those idiots who regard painting as superior to manufacturing—I neither regard it as inferior, as do your Chambers of Commerce who think that all artists are useless unless they're doing pictures for stocking advertisements, nor do I regard it as superior, as do all the supercilious lady yearners who suppose that a business man with clean nails invariably prefers golf to Beethoven."

It was not brilliant talk, nor did it dazzle Sam by novelty. In both Europe and America he had encountered all the theories about modern business men: that they were the kings and only creators in the industrial age: that they were dull and hideous despots. He had hacked out his own conclusion: that they were about like other people, as assorted as cobblers, labor leaders, Javanese dancers, throat specialists, whalers, minor canons, or asparagus-growers. Yet in the talk of Edith Cortright there was a sympathy, an apparent respect for him, a suggestion that she had seen many curious lands and known many curious people, which inspirited him. Incredulously, he found himself trying to outline his philosophy of life for her; more incredulously, found himself willing to admit that he hadn't any. She nodded, as in like confession.

He urged: "I've enjoyed talking with you. Look here: Would I be rude if I asked you to go for a gondola ride, now it's getting cooler, and possibly dine with me on the Lido this evening, if you're free? I've been, uh—kind of lonely."

"I should be glad to, but I can't. You see my friends here are mostly the rather stuffy, frightfully proper, very sweet old Italian family sort who haven't yet got over being shocked by Colleoni. I'm afraid I couldn't go out in a gondola with you unless I were chaperoned—bedragoned—which would be a frightful bore. But won't you come here to dinner tomorrow evening—eight-thirty, black tie?"

"Be pleased to. Eight-thirty. . . . But why do you stay in Europe?"

"Oh . . . I suppose America terrifies me. I feel insecure there. I feel everybody watching me, and criticizing me unless I'm buzzing about Doing Something Important—uplifting the cinema or studying Einstein or winning bridge championships or breeding Schnauzers or something. And there's no privacy, and I'm an extravagant woman when it comes to the luxury of privacy."

"But look here! In America you could certainly go gon-doling—well, motoring—as you liked. Here you have to be chaperoned to avoid criticism!"

"Only with one class—the formal people that I've chosen (wisely or foolishly) to live with. My grocer and my dentist and my neighbor on the floor below (amiable-looking person—I rather fancy he's a gambler)—they don't feel privileged to help me conduct my affairs, or rather, they wouldn't if I were so adventurous as to be conducting any! At home, they would. It's only in Europe that you can have the joy of anonymity, of being lost in the crowd, of being yourself, of having the dignity of privacy!"

"You try New York! Get lost enough there!"

"Oh, but *New York*—— Self-conscious playing at internationalism! Russian Jews in London clothes going to Italian restaurants with Greek waiters and African music! One hundred per cent. mongrels! No wonder Americans flee back home to Sussex or Somerset! And never, day or night or dawn, any escape from the sound of the Elevated! New York—no. But I am sure that there is still a sturdy, native America—and not Puritanical, either, any more than Lincoln or Franklin were Puritanical—that you know. But tell me (to get away from my lost, expatriate, awfully unoriented and unimportant self), tell me frankly: what have you seen in Europe—I mean that you'll remember ten years from now?"

He slumped in his chair, he rubbed his chin, and sighed:

"Well, I guess about as much as I'd get out of reading the steamship and hotel ads in a New York Sunday paper! I know a little less than when I started. Then, I knew that all Englishmen were icicles, all Frenchmen chattered, and all Italians sat around in the sun singing. Now I don't even know that much. I suspect that most Englishmen are friendly, most Frenchmen are silent, and most Italians work like the devil—pardon me!"

"Exactly!"

"I've learned to doubt everything. I've learned that even a fairly successful executive—and I *was* that, no matter how much of a loafer I seem now——"

"Oh, I know!"

"I've learned that even a fairly good garage boss like myself isn't much good at deciding between Poiret and Lanvin, or between Early English and Decorated. No American business man ought to go abroad, ever, except to a Rotary convention, or on a conducted tour where he's well insulated from furriners. Upsets him. Spoils his pleasure in his own greatness and knowledge! . . . What have I learned? Let's see: The names of maybe fifty hotels, of which I'll remember five, in a few years. The schedules of half a dozen de luxe trains. The names of a few brands of Burgundy. How to tell a Norman doorway from Gothic. How to order from a French menu—providing there's nothing unusual on the bill. And I can say 'How much' and '*Too* much' in English, French, German, Italian, and Spanish. And I think that's about all I've learned here. I guess they caught me too late!"

Chapter 32

WITH his second drink, at Florian's, after dinner, he recaptured a rare exhilarating glow at the thought of travel, alone and fast. He could go as he would: North, South—the very names had magic: *North* and snow-drifts among silent pines; *South* and bamboo huts in the jungle; *East* and a cranky steamer jogging up a purple strait; *West* and a bench by a log cabin in the Rockies, with a lake two thousand feet below, and himself, strong and deep-breathing as he had been at thirty, smelling the new-cut chips, the frosty air. Yes! He would see them all! He wouldn't go back to an office!

He had twenty, perhaps thirty years more. He would have a second life; having been Samuel Dodsworth he would go on and miraculously be some one else, more ruthless, less bound, less sentimental. He could be a poet, a governor, an explorer. He'd learned his faults of commercial-mindedness, of timidity before women. Correct 'em! He'd seen the gaps in his knowledge. Fill 'em!

Twenty years more!

Start right now. Tomorrow he would take up Italian. Tomorrow he would write to Ross Ireland about that jaunt to the Orient. Yes!

After the comfort of tea with Edith Cortright, he had been lonelier than ever. For five minutes he had planned to flee to Fran. But fried scampi and a drink solaced him; a second drink set his imagination dancing. Then he wanted another drink—and didn't want it.

No! He shook himself. He hated this flabby, easy escape through alcohol into a belief in his own power and freedom. He wasn't (proudly) one of the weaklings who took refuge from problems in the beautiful peace of the gutter, where the slime covered one's ears from the nasal voices of the censors who were always demanding of a tired man a little more than he could do.

But was that true? Was anything he had thought true—even this easy disgust at easy escape? Was it possible that he was unable to fall permanently into drunkenness, to disintegrate, to scorn all decent scorn and be content with a Nande Azeredo in a stinking garret, not because he was too strong but because he was too weak—too weakly afraid of what Fran, Tub, Matey, strangers like Mrs. Cortright, would say? Was it possible that it took more courage to be a hobo, deliberate, out and out, than to go on living like a respectable manufacturer while he ached like a Verlaine? Was dry rot really braver than a moist and dripping rage of defiance?

He gave it up.

He was so tired of dragging out his little soul and worrying over it! If he could only be laughing, unthinking, with Tub Pearson. Or if Mrs. Cortright had been willing to dine with him——

Mrs. Cortright. Now there was a woman! As proper as Fran and as worldly, yet as indifferent to titles and luxury as Nande.

"Mighty sweet woman!"

He thought again about that third drink, then vehemently didn't want it, vehemently retired into the respectability from which for a moment he had thought he might escape. For at the next table was an American party, full of merriment and keeping their brother from falling by setting an edifyingly bad example.

There were three men, three women. Apparently some of them were married to some of the others, but they seemed confused as to who was married to whom.

They noted Sam, and one of the men staggered over to shout, "American, ain't you? Well, say, why the lone fiesta? Come over and join a live bunch!"

Rather pleased, Sam went over and joined.

"Just arrived?" he asked, as was proper.

"You bet. Landed at Naples, yesterday," said his host. "Came over on a Wop ship—elegant boat too—and say, boy, that was some trip, too, I'll tell the cock-eyed world! Say, I've heard about wet voyages, but this trip—say, I bet I never went to bed before three G.M. once, the whole way over! And the girls—say, they were just as good as the men. Dorine here, she drank two bols champagne in two hours, and the whole bunch were so crazy about the Italian officers—say, the officers had to brush 'em off the bridge every time they wanted to do any fancy navigating! And that gave us boys a chance to get in a little petting ourselves! Some trip! Say, if you could have seen the nightshirt parade the last night out! Boy! Some trip!"

One of the women—and save for her damp eyes a most spinsterish and unaphrodisiac lady she appeared—cried, "Some trip is right! And I've got a date to meet the second officer in Paris. He's going to lay off one trip. And maybe I'll just keep him laid off. Maybe I'll decide to buy me a nice little boy friend. Some baby! Oh, those Or-i-ental eyes! Say, Pete, for the love o' Gawd, ain't you going to buy our little friend here"—she pointed at Sam with a thin, chaste, overmanicured, and rather wobbly forefinger—"a lil drink?"

But Sam declined. His vision of the beauties of the gutter had vanished with haste and a ludicrous squawking. He was grimly again the Sam Dodsworth who was proud of keeping in shape. He accepted, with irritating signs of pleasure, a lemonade (it was the first he had tasted in months) and sat wondering about these fellow-countrymen.

He could not place them. In age they seemed to run from thirty to forty. They were not so vulgar nor so vicious as at first they seemed. Once in a while they were betrayed by alcohol into revealing that they did have vocabularies and had perhaps read a book. He suspected that two out of the three men were university graduates; that all six of these loud-mouthed libertines were, at home, worthy deacons and pall-bearers. He had known in Zenith of "young married couples," theoretically responsible young doctors and lawyers and salesmen, who turned dances at country clubs into a combination of brothel and frontier bar. But he had not gone to such dances. These people were none of his! Then, shocked, he realized that perhaps they were. Were these oafs anything but younger and gayer and slightly more amorous Tub Pearsons?

They were not altogether to blame. They were the products of Prohibition, mass production, and an education dominated by the beliefs that one goes to college to become acquainted with people who will later be useful in business, and that the greatness of a university is in ratio to the number of its students and the number of its athletic victories.

Or so Sam brooded.

He had heard much of the "sexually cold American woman." Heaven knows, he raged, he had felt it in Fran! Yet with these riotous women, it was the lack of chill which he resented. The amiable lady who was going to "buy her" a second officer had, during Sam's stay at the table, kissed one of the men, held the hand of another, and was now turning her withered excitement on himself: "Say, you're some husk! Gee, I bet you hurt the lil ole golf ball's feelings when you slam it one!"

He smiled bleakly.

He thought of seeing Mrs. Cortright next evening. He had recalled her only as a pleasant, unexciting, worthy person, but now he saw her as a Grecian vase, he saw her as a bowl of alabaster within which a fire could be lighted.

"A finish to her—like a European," he reflected. "Yet she's American, thank God! I couldn't fall for a real European. Has to be somebody that could look at an old gray New England barn with the frost on it, in October, and get a kick out of it, without my having to explain."

His long, ambling thoughts were interrupted by his original host's inquiring:

"You been here in Venice some time?"

"Yes. Several times."

"Well, maybe you can explain—— Hope I'm not stepping all over anybody's feet, but me—— Well, this is the first time I've ever been abroad, and I'd always thought Venice would be kinda like a musical comedy. But of all the darn' slow places—— Why, there isn't a first-class cabaret in town! Nothing but a lot of run-down tenements with a lot of carvin's on 'em and a bunch of Chicago Drainage Ditches in between!"

"Well, I like it!"

"But what do you like about it?"

"Oh, lots of things. Especially the architecture."

But what his mind saw, as he blurted out something about being tired and took his leave, was no vision of arching bridges, of secret alleys and the quivering reflection of airy towers; it was the memory of Edith Cortright serene in her Venetian palace.

"She couldn't possibly go out and grab things, like Fran," he reflected, as he clumped toward the Bauer-Grünwald. "She's definitely a 'great lady.' Yet I'll bet that at heart she's lonely. She wouldn't mind cooking for her man any more than Nande would. Oh, damn it, Sam, why are you so simple? Why do you insist on thinking everybody else is lonely, merely because you are?"

It was a small and placid dinner at Edith Cortright's, on Thursday evening. The only guests besides Sam were an English couple who were vaguely and politely something important—very politely but very vaguely. If Sam did not find them cheery, he was amused by the pleasant carelessness of Mrs. Cortright's household.

The Fran who liked to quote poems about Gipsies and Villon and the Brave Days When We Were Twenty-one was, in private life, a sergeant major. Theoretically, she was the mother confessor and breezy confidante of all her servants and of the plumber, the postman, and the bootlegger. Practically she was always furious at their incompetence. She was chummy with them only when they assured her of her beauty and power; when the seamstress gurgled that Fran had the most exquisite figure in Zenith, or when the corner druggist asked her if his new hat was really correct English style.

Or so Sam brooded.

Edith Cortright seemed to have no discipline, no notion as to her servants' duties. They argued with her. They contradicted her. The butler said that she *had* ordered broccoli; and the maid came in with clacking slippers. They were always chattering. They seemed to be sharing some secret joke with her; and when she smiled at Sam, in her tired way, after a voluble colloquy with the butler, he wished he could be admitted to their tribal companionship.

A stone floor the dining-room had, and walls of hard plaster, with strips of Syrian embroidery. About the walls were chairs, stately, uncomfortable, inhuman. The windows, giving on the Grand Canal, were immensely tall. It was an apartment for giants to live in. Sam felt that into this room had strode men in armor who with gigantic obscene laughter had discussed the torture of pale protestants against the Doge, and that they, not so unlike Edith Cortright for all her gentleness, had guffawed here with servants purple-uniformed, slatternly, and truculent.

The English couple crept away early. After their flutter of good-bye's, Sam lumbered to his feet and sighed, "I guess I'd——"

"No. Stay half an hour."

"If you'd really—— And how I have come to hate hotels!"

"You really liked having a home."

"I certainly did!"

"Why do you stay away from it? Isn't it——"

Then she laughed, lighted a cigarette, held it with arching fingers. "I suppose it's rather ludicrous, my trying to give advice—and my own life such a mess that I endure it only by getting rid of all ambition, all purpose, and just floating, trying to get along with as little complication as possible."

They talked slowly, and mostly they talked in silence. It was tranquil in that vast cool room above the Grand Canal. Out on the harbor, bands of singers in gondolas chanted old Italian ballads. They were, actually, rather commercialized, these singers; not for romance and the love of moonlight were they warbling, and between bursts of ecstasy they passed the hat from listening gondola to gondola, and were much rewarded by sentimentalists from Essen, Pittsburgh, and Manchester. The songs were conscientiously banal—"Donna è Mobile" and "Santa Lucia" for choice. Yet the whole theatric setting and the music across the water lured Sam into a still excitement.

"I can't imagine you in any complications," he wondered.

"I shouldn't use that word, perhaps. All the complications are inside myself. It's just that certain conditions of life have rather taken my confidence in myself away from me, and I'm so afraid of doing the wrong thing that it's easier to do nothing."

"That's how I feel myself! Though with you, I can't imagine it—you're sure of yourself."

"Not really. I'm like a man learning a new language—he can do it beautifully as long as he can introduce the subjects of conversation and use the words he knows—he can talk splendidly about Waiter, bring two more coffees, or What is the next train for Turin, but he's lost if somebody else asks the questions and insists on talking about anything beyond page sixty in the Hugo Method! Here, in my own flat, with my own people, I'm safely on this side of Page Sixty, but I'd be horribly fluttered if I stepped out on Page Sixty-one! . . .

By the way, I shall be very happy if you're bored by your hotel here and care to come in for tea now and then."

"Awfully good of——"

Without much consciousness of rising, he had strolled to the open window. "I do appreciate it. . . . Feel rather at loose ends."

"Why don't you tell me about it? If you care to. I'm a good confidante!"

"Well——"

He flung out with a suicidal defiance.

"I don't like to whine—I don't think I do, much—and I don't like admitting I'm licked. But I am. And I'm getting a little sick of not being able to sleep nights, brooding about it. Too damn much brooding probably!" He tramped out to the narrow balcony, above the canal and the sound of splashing water. On this balcony once (though Sam did not know it) Lord Byron had stood, snarling to a jet-bright lady a more pitiful and angry tale.

Edith Cortright was beside him, murmuring—oh, her words were a commonplace "Would you like to tell me about it?" but her voice was kind, and curiously honest, curiously free of the barriers between a strange man and a strange woman. And with her Venice murmured, and the songs of love.

"Oh, I suppose it's a very ordinary story. My wife is younger than I am, and livelier, and she's found a man in Berlin, and I guess I've lost her. For keeps. . . . Oh, I know I oughtn't to undress in public like this. But I swear I haven't before! Am I rotten to——"

She said quickly, "Don't! Of course you're not. I'd be glad if I could tell my own story."

"Please!"

"And I haven't told people, either, not even my friends, though I suppose they guess—— Perhaps you and I can be franker with each other because we are strangers. I do understand how you feel, Mr. Dodsworth. I suppose the people I know here and in England and at home believe that I lead such a nun-like existence because I had an idolatrous worship of the late Honorable Cecil R. A. Cortright. Such a charming man! Perfect manners, and too perfect a game of bridge! Wonderful war record—M.C., D.S.O. Actually my husband was—— He was a dreadful liar; one of these hand-kissing, smiling, convincing liars. He was a secret drunkard. He humiliated me constantly as a backwoods American; used to apologize to people, oh, so prettily, when I said 'I guess' instead of the equally silly 'I fancy.' And his dear mother used to congratulate me on my luck in having won her darling. Oh, I'm sorry! Beastly of me! Fatal Venetian night!"

Her quick breath was not a sob but a sound of anger. Her hand gripped the thin fluted railing of the balcony. He patted it shyly and said, as he would to his daughter Emily, "Maybe it's good for both of us to tell our troubles a little. But—— I wish I could *hate* my girl. I can't. And I imagine you can't hate Cortright. Might be good for us!"

"Yes," dryly. "It would. But I'm beautifully beginning to be able to. I—— Have you ever seen Malapert's etchings? Let me show you a book of them I received today."

He dutifully looked at etchings for fifteen minutes, and said farewell rather pompously.

Trudging home, along dark pavements which hung like shelves above swarthily glittering rios, through perilous-looking unlighted archways, he was by turns guilty over having talked of Fran, impatient with himself for having too touchy a conscience, raging at the late Cecil Cortright as a scoundrel, and joyous that behind her fastidious reticence Edith Cortright could be blunt.

It was the guiltiness which persisted when he awoke. Edith would be hating him for having blatted about Fran, for having led her to talk. When for half an hour he had been trying to compose a note of apology, a note came from her:

> No, you did not say anything you should not have, and I don't believe I did. I write this because I think I know how remorseful all Americans are after we have said something we really think. Put it down to Santa Lucia who, though I don't really know my hagiology, is probably the patroness of sentimentalists like you and me. Would you like to come in for tea at five today?
>
> EDITH CORTRIGHT.

Chapter 33

DAILY, for a fortnight, he saw Edith Cortright—at tea, at dinner, at lunch on the Lido. She apparently forgot her discomfort at being unchaperoned, and went architecture-coursing with him, went with him to the summer opera, sailed with him to Torcello and Malamocco—sailing gondola with orange lateen sail, from which they looked back to Venice floating on the dove-colored water.

He talked, of Zenith and Emily, of motors and the virtues of the Revelation car, of mechanics and finance. He had never known another woman who was not bored when he tried to make clear his very definite, not unimportant notions on the use of chromium metal. And she, she talked of many things. She was a reader of thick books, with a curiosity regarding life which drifted all round its circumference. She talked of Bertrand Russell and of insulin; of Stefan Zweig, American skyscrapers, and the Catholic Church. But she was neither priggish nor dogmatic. What interested her in facts and diagrams was the impetus they gave to her own imagination. Essentially she was indifferent whether the world was laboring toward Fascism or Bolshevism, toward Methodism or atheism.

He followed her through all her mazed reflections. He was not rebuffed by her ideas as so often he had been by Fran's pert little learnings. (For Fran wore her knowledge as showily as she wore her furs.)

Of themselves they talked rarely, and they believed that they talked but little of Fran and Cecil Cortright. Yet, lone sentence by sentence, they told their married lives so completely that Sam began to speak of "Cecil" and Edith of "Fran," as though they four had always been together. When she realized it, Edith laughed.

"We ought to make an agreement that I shall be allowed to speak of Cecil for just as many minutes as you do of Fran. Or we might compose a sort of litany—

'Oh, Lord, Cecil was irritable before breakfast,
'And Lord, Thou knowest Fran did not appreciate
streamline bodies'!"

And once she got below the surface and told him that subconsciously he had *wanted* to lose Fran to Kurt, or to any other available suitor.

Yet there was always between them a formality, even when they used each other's first names as well as those of their eternally problematic mates.They did not discuss their souls. They did not discuss why it was that they seemed to like each other. The nearest they came to intimacy was in planning, almost childishly, their "futures."

He said abruptly, at coffee after dinner in Edith's flat, "What shall I do? Shall I go back to America, without Fran? And shall I do the job I've been trained to, or play with some experiments? Let me tell you of a couple of silly ideas I have."

He outlined his plans for caravan building, and for venturing on Sans Souci Gardens villages.

"Why not do both?" suggested Edith. She seemed to take his desired experiments more seriously than had Fran. "I like your idea of trying to make a suburb that would be neither stuffy nor too dreadfully arty—no grocery clerks coaxed to dance on the green. And the caravans would be fun. Cecil and I had one for two months in England."

"Do you mean to say you did the cooking?"

"Of course I did! I'm an excellent cook! I babble of Freud and Einstein, but I know nothing about psycho-analysis, nothing about mathematics. But I do know garlic and taragon vinegar! I really love housekeeping. I should have stayed in Michigan and married a small-town lawyer."

"Could you like a town like Zenith? After Venice?"

"Yes, if I had a place of my own there. Here, everything decays—lovely decay, but I'm tired of being autumnal. I'd like hot summer growing and spring budding for a change—even if the corn-stalks were ugly!"

Then, first, did it occur to him that it was not quite ludicrous to think that Edith and he might some day return together to Zenith, to work and to life. He said little to himself, nothing at all to her, of what seemed dimly to be growing as a secure and healing love, yet a day or two after he seized the impulse and showed Edith the letter from Fran.

Fran's letter revealed more of herself and of her relation to Kurt than anything she had written:

> I haven't heard from you for a week, old man, I admit I haven't been much on correspondence either but I haven't been feeling any too merry and bright, I think too much city I really *must* get out into the country and Kurt and I—you really are an old *darling* and awfully generous I realize it to let me talk so frankly about him and still be friends with me—we're going to try to go to the Harz Mountains for a week.
>
> It's been a funny thing—you always think I have no meekness but honestly I have shown quite biblical humility in trying to fit myself to his so-different life. He's let me fuss over his funny *pathetic* little flat—oh, Sam, it just breaks my heart the way that flat reveals how *poor* the poor man is, that ought to be a great nobleman like his ancestors and I suppose would have been if it hadn't been for the war which after all was not his fault. At first I was irritated by the complete sloppiness etc. etc. of his dear funny old servant then I thought maybe it was because she has such an *elementary* kitchen equipment, honestly it was about what you would expect in Kurt's native wilds a *frightful* old coal stove that she has to stoke up all the time and the flues do not draw. I wanted to give him a jolly new electric range and he finally consented, though not readily, honestly—*please*, pretty please, I hope this won't hurt your feelings and as I say I know how *generous* you are, but you can't have any idea how proud he is! But it was the cook who balked. No! She wouldn't have a nice new electric range or an electric dish-washing machine! She *preferred* their own familiar things! She's truly feudal—isn't that almost as hard as "truly rural" that we used to say in school!—and so is Kurt. I think perhaps I realized that with a chauffeur, of course Kurt can't afford his

own chauffeur or even car yet though I do believe with his real genius for finance he will be a very rich man on his own inside another ten years but he can't afford one now but whenever he can get him he uses an Austrian chauffeur at a hire garage near here that was a private in Kurt's own regiment during the war and that really is almost practically like Kurt's own chauffeur.

Well, at first do you know I was shocked by their chumminess. The chauffeur would tell the Herr Graf that the Herr Graf was wearing lovely new gloves today, and Kurt would ask him about his sweetheart and they would joke about it and Kurt would tell him he ought to make his sweetheart an honest woman and the chauffeur would waggle his finger in a knowing way that made me angry, and so one day I jumped on Kurt about it and my dear! the way he turned on me!

He said, "You are a bourgeoise! I am feudal! We who are feudal can be familiar with our servants because we know they cannot ever be impertinent!"

Sam laid down the letter, and it was of Edith and her way with servants that he was thinking.

I find myself settling, dear old man, no matter if we have apparently busted up for keeps and it *is* rather tragic if one suffers one's self to think about it after the many, many happy years we *did* have together, *didn't* we, but if we did break up, I do know you will go on being my *friend* and be glad to know that I *do* find myself settling down to my job of being a European. It hasn't been easy and I can't expect you to understand the pains, the almost agony I have given to it. Sometimes I am frankly lonely—for whatever you may say about me to Tub and your *dear* Matey, oh, Sam, I suspect you talked about me to her in Paris far more than you ever admitted—but I mean, whatever you may say about me, perhaps with a lot of justice, at least you must admit that one of my probably few virtues has been a rather rare *frankness* and *honesty*, and frankly at times I have been very lonely, have wished you were here so I could tousle your funny old thick hair. And sometimes I have been frightened by the spectacle of one lone femme Americaine facing all of censorious Europe. And sometimes—you know his dear childish enthusiasm without very much discrimination—I have been a little bored by some of Kurt's Dear Old Friends. Yet I love and I think I am coming to really understand the *thickness* of European life. Our American life is so thin, so without tradition.

Sam laid down the letter and thought of the tradition of pioneers pushing to the westward, across the Alleghenies, through the forests of Kentucky and Tennessee, on to the bleeding plains of Kansas, on to Oregon and California, a religious procession, sleeping always in danger, never resting, and opening a new home for a hundred million people. But with no comment he read on:

I have learned, and I must say with some surprise which has probably been good for my little ego that Kurt thinks much more of a violinist or a chemist than of the nicest prince with the most quarteriest quarterings living. And—for whatever you may think about me you must admit that I *do* understand the Europeans and I really *am* European!—and do grasp it—I haven't had too much difficulty following him. Oh, my dear, do forgive me if this hurts you, but he is what the romantic novelists call *my man*! I have some stunning plans for him. I think I see the way, I can't of course give away any details even to you, but I think I see a way of getting a certain great American bank to establish a branch in Berlin, and making Kurt the head of it.

You would probably be amused you certainly wouldn't know your wild Fran how meek she is if you saw her letting Kurt boss her in all sorts of little things yes and I suppose big ones too but still he *is* so dear—he always notices what I wear, honestly he bullies me really dreadfully about my clothes but at the same time is always willing to go shopping with me which you must admit, for all your gorgeous bigness you never were. Oh my dear I suppose it is unpardonable to write to *you* about *him* this way and if I stop to think about it and re-read this letter probably I never shall mail this letter that I'm writing in my ducky little coloraturo (or is it coloratura) flat on an evening that if I must confess is a little lonely and makes me feel like a lost lorn tourist *American* but we are friends aren't we—— phone ringing must answer bless you F.

He had the letter at ten in the morning. At twelve he was ringing at Edith's flat. He thrust Fran's letter at her without a word. When Edith had read it she sighed, and suggested:

"It's so hot here. I've been thinking of going down to Naples—to Posilipo, out on the point, where it's cool—and taking a little house on the estate of the Ercoles. Baron Ercole has a big place, but he's frightfully poor. He's an ex-diplomat; he teaches law in the University of Naples; and the poor darlings live mostly by renting villas on their place. Why don't you come down with me? I don't think there's much more to be said about your Fran, after this letter. It might be good for you to swim and sail at Naples, instead of sitting here brooding. Would you like to come?"

"Decidedly! But what about your friends who are so eager to be scandalized——"

"Oh, not the Ercoles. They'll believe I'm having an affair with you, and be delighted—they've lived in too many countries, in the diplomatic corps, to have many morals. They'll like you. Edmondo Ercole and you will have such a good time being silent together! Oh, that sounds like Fran, I imagine! I'm sorry!"

In the sunset an Italian hilltown, battlements and a shaggy tower on a rock abrupt amid the sloping plain. The windows of the town took the low sunlight and blazed one after another as the train passed. "As though the houses were full of gay people," said Edith. He looked at it with still pleasure. He felt that her presence had unlocked his heart; had enabled him, for the first time, to see Italy.

He had, theoretically, been in Naples before, but as they drove from the station to the Villa Ercole he realized that all he had seen—all he had seen anywhere in Europe—had not been the place itself but Fran's hectic and demanding attitudes; her hysteria of delight over a moonlight, or her hysteria of annoyance over bad service. In Edith's quiet presence he perceived that Naples was not, as he had remembered it, a rather grim, very modern barricade of tall apartment houses, but a series of connected villages extending for miles along the bay, between blue water and hills into which human beings had burrowed like gophers.

The driver of their taxi, being Neapolitan, was in a rage so long as any vehicle was on the road ahead of him, and as that was always, their journey was a series of escapes from death. Yet even in this chariot race, Sam expanded and nestled into contentment, as in the old days of overwork and brief vacations he had relaxed into delight on his holidays in a canoe.

He patted Edith's hand in an effort to express his happiness, as he saw Vesuvius roll up, with its trail of smoke—toward Naples, now, promising good weather; saw Capri with the dots of white houses on the lofty plateau between the ruin-dotted mountains; saw sun-washed Sorrento at the foot of its giant promontory; saw the villas of Posilipo below the cliff up which their taxi was racing.

The taxi passed a yellow plaster gatehouse, with a bobbing concierge—a smiling, life-loving, plump Italian woman, with innumerous children about her—and instantly they were free of the roaring thoroughfare, free of banging traffic, ejaculatory drivers, shouldering trams, suicidal children, and cluttered little shops for the sale of charcoal and wine. The park of the Villa Ercole dropped from that high-lying thoroughfare down to the bay, with a roadway twisting and redoubling on itself like a mountain trail. They sped among enormous pines, between whose framing trunks he saw, across the suave bay, the bulk of Vesuvius, as absolute in its loneliness as Fujiyama. They passed half a dozen plaster villas, yellow as old gold, very still, remembering glories not quite past. In a modern stone wall, supporting a stretch of the corkscrew road, was a patch of thin ancient Roman brick set in a herring-bone pattern and above it the fragment of a marble bust, the head of a warrior whose villa may have stood here two thousand years ago.

There was no sound, even of birds, no sound from the street above—a minute away yet inconceivably far.

"Lord, how quiet it is here!" said Sam.

"That's why I wanted to come here—that and the Ercoles."

On the last sweeping curve of the driveway, just before it came to an end before the tall château in which the Ercoles themselves still dwelt, Edith bade the driver halt at a tiny wooden bridge which led across to what seemed to be the top story of a yellow plaster tower whose lower stages were hidden beneath the cliff beside them.

"There's our house!" she said. "It's the funniest house in the world! It's on three levels. The garden is so steep that you can enter it from any floor. And there are really only about two rooms to a floor."

She led him, across the bridge and along a toy-house hallway, to the simplest of bedrooms. The floor was of shining stone; on the walls there were no pictures, but only a majolica Virgin and Child. The high narrow bed, with neither headboard nor footboard, had four slender posts at the corners. It was covered with a gold encrusted brocade, rather worn. There was a naked-looking white steel washstand, a fine oval mirror, two heavy brocade chairs, a heavy oak table set out with pens and stationery, a brazier for charcoal, and nothing else whatever—yet there was everything, for outside the French windows was a terrace, apparently the roof of a room below, which gave on the bay, so that the room was filled with the sparkle of southern sun on southern waters and with the image of Mount Vesuvius and its distant indolence of smoke.

"This is your room, I suppose," said Edith. "But, good heavens, there's no wardrobe, no place even for your brushes and razor! Bianca—Baroness Ercole—probably hasn't been able to afford them yet—wrote me she was just refurnishing this house, hoping to rent it."

"I don't mind. Keep my stuff in wardrobe trunk," said Sam. He was glad of the simplicity, glad that the room was free of the stuffiness of much furniture. He could see himself rejuvenated here, in this cool shrine, with the sweet air and the beaming sea outside, and with Edith's unsentimental friendship to make him believe in himself.

They went on the balcony-terrace and Sam cried out. The shore-line from Posilipo to Naples, which had been below them and hidden from them on their drive to the villa, was romantic enough for a Christmas calendar—and no amount of Fran's scolding had kept Samuel Dodsworth from liking chromo art. The bay was edged with cliffs, eaten into vast caves. Mysterious stairways climbed from the rocks at the edge of the water, disappearing into holes in the cliffs. Sam reflected how excited he would have been as a boy to find these vanishing stairways, after reading in Stevenson and Walter Scott of secret passageways, of smugglers and underground chambers.

To a tiny beach at the foot of a cliff a fisher-boy, barefoot and singing, was drawing up his unwieldy boat. His skin was golden in the sunlight.

It is true that just then shot into sight a four-oar shell, rowed by members of a club fostered by the Fascists, but this spectacle, contemporary as though it were on the Thames, Sam ignored. It did not suit his romantic private vision of the Bay of Naples.

The villas along the bay were white and imposing upon the cliff-tops, at the head of sloping canyons filled with vines and mulberries, or, set lower, mediaeval palaces of arcaded and yellowed marble with their foundations in the water. It was late in the afternoon, and the mellowed glow lay on distant Naples, vast tawny pyramid rising to the abrupt bastions of Castel Sant' Elmo, a city enchanted, asleep these hundreds of years in the lazy light.

He muttered, "This place—this place——"

"Yes. Isn't it!" she said.

For hours they seemed to have been absorbed in the kindly radiance but it was probably three minutes since they had entered the house. No servant had answered her knock on entering, none had disturbed them since. They continued exploring; went down the rough stone staircase of the tower-cottage, found her bedroom, as primitive as his; and down to the ground floor. They came into a drawing-room, floored with waxed and polished tiles of old dark red, a room large enough to tolerate fifteen-foot windows hung with damask, full-blooming camellia trees in tall stone wine-jars, and a long table of rosewood decorated with bronze, a table over-decorated yet curiously elegant. Sam scarcely noticed two women, in calico and dust-caps, who were on their knees finishing the polishing of the floor. He gaped when the younger and more slender sprang up, fled to Edith Cortright, and kissed her.

Edith said, smiling, brisker than he had ever known her, "Bianca, this is my friend Mr. Dodsworth—Sam, your hostess, Baroness Ercole."

And, altogether unabashed at being caught in the crimes of poverty and work, the Baroness Ercole made him welcome with her smile, gave him her wax-crusted hand to kiss, and invited them to dinner.

Chapter 34

HE FOUND a new Edith Cortright, a surprisingly vigorous and outdoor Edith, once she was away from Venetian proprieties. She gave up soft black for a linen sailor-blouse and a shocking skirt; she showed a talent for swimming, sailing, tennis, and managing the house. The Ercole estate, with its half a dozen villas, was like a private village, and a hectic village life it was into which Sam had come. The smiling Italian servants walked without warning into any room, at any time—embarrassed him by bouncing into his bedroom when he was shaving, cheerfully conducted the fish-pedler into the drawing-room at tea-time, and at all hours, under all windows, squabbled and laughed and gabbled and made love and sang. And there were so many of them belonging to the various villas. Sam was always discovering some new cottage—half-dug in the cliffs, or atop a coach house, or mysteriously under it with its door opening on another level—filled with gardeners or gatekeepers or maids, with their children, their goats, their puppies, their rabbits, and long-faced Italian cats.

The Baron and Baroness Ercole and their friends—officers who came out from the barracks, navy officers, young professors from the university—were as gay and welcoming as any American country club set priding itself on hospitality. They played tennis, they organized dances, they motored (at appalling speed) to festivals in distant mountain villages, and in everything they made Edith and Sam a part of their own. Half of them did not speak English, but their smiles recognized him as an old friend.

Alone, Edith and Sam explored Capri and Sorrento and Pompeii; were drawn up to the terror and fumes of Vesuvius; crept through the back alleys of old Naples, where one street is given up to fish, one to vegetables, one to the most cheerfully lugubrious artificial funeral wreaths and to votive pictures depicting the escape of pious persons from shipwreck, runaway horses, and falling bricks through the intervention of the saints.

Fran, who insisted that she "despised sight-seeing," had yet been so ejaculatory, so insistent that he should realize to the full whatever most struck her, that he had had to work hard at travel, and had been conscious only of collecting unrelated impressions. Edith was lazily indifferent to his liking things. With her, he let his mind loaf, and slowly some sense of the real Italy came to him, some feeling that it was not a picturesque show but a normal and eager life.

They came home, dusty from Naples, for tea in the dim huge room looking on the bay. The late-afternoon glow over the piled hill of Naples faded to misty blue. The last high light in the scene was the smoke of Vesuvius, a fabulous flamingo hue in the vanishing sunlight. As the bay turned to a blue fabric woven with silver threads, the lights of braziers came out cheerfully in the little fishing boats. And in the twilight hush, Edith's voice was quiet, not pricking him with demands for admiration of her cleverness, her singular charms, but assuring him (though actually she talked only of the Ercoles, perhaps, or politics, or antipasto) that she was happy to be with him, that she took strength from him by giving him strength.

He assumed that he was strong and primitive as the west wind, that she was sophisticated and fragile, utterly a creature of indoors, and he was the more startled on the day when they rested on the stone wall by the orange grove. It was an ancient, crumbly, slatternly stone wall, lizards darting from the crevices, moss and tiny weeds like a velvet cushion along the top. Below, in the hollow, was a tile and plaster house of three irregular flat-roofed and terraced stories, apparently not connected, entered by doorways above crazy stone flights of steps, all curiously like a New Mexican pueblo. The grove climbed from the hollow to the highway above—orange trees, lemons, a palmetto or two, with vines stretched upon the elongated branches of mulberry trees. Where a group of boulders intruded on the slope, the earth between rocks had been painfully turned into tiny vineyards, a yard or two square, protected by little stone walls. The grove suggested centuries of minute and patient labor, yet it was disorderly, the ground rough and littered, the trees a tangle, with no straight lines.

"You wondered," said Edith, perched on the wall, "whether I could stand a canoe trip, sleeping on the ground. What do you think of this orchard?"

"Don't quite see the connection."

"What do you think of it? How does it strike you—as an efficient person?"

"Well, the fruit looks all right, but it seems kind of higgledy-piggledy. And it's darned hot, here on this wall!"

"Exactly! Well, the Italian peasant loves the heat, and he loves just the bare ridged ground—the earth, earthy earth! He loves earth and sun and wind and rain. He's a mystic, in the highest sense of that badly escorted word. The European is the same everywhere, in that. The Tyrolese love the sharp smell of the glaciers, the ragged mountain-slopes that almost frighten me, so that they die of homesickness abroad. The Prussian loves that thick sandy waste and the bleak little pines. The French villager doesn't mind the reality of manure piles and mud puddles in front of his house. The English farmer loves his bare downs with their sharp little furze bushes. They love earth and wind and rain and sun. And I've learned it from them. You wonder if I could 'stand' sleeping on the ground! I'd love it so much more than you! I'm so much more elementary. Here, we may have ruins and painting, but behind them we're so much closer to the eternal elements than you Americans. You don't love earth, you don't love the wind——"

"Oh, look here now! What about our millions of acres of plowed fields? Nothing *like* it, outside of maybe Russia! What about our most important men, that get out in the fresh air and motor and golf——"

"No. Your farmers want to get away from their wash of acres to the city. Your business men drive out to the golf club in closed sedans, and they don't want just bare earth—they want the earth of the golf course all neatly concealed by lawn. And I—you think of me as sitting in drawing-rooms, but here you've seen me reveling in sea water and running on the beach. And often and often when you think I'm napping in my room, I sneak out to that little bit of walled-off garden just above the house and lie there in the hot sun, in the wind, smelling of the reeking earth, finding life! That's the strength of Europe—not its so-called 'culture,' its galleries and neat voices and knowledge of languages, but its nearness to earth. And that's the weakness of America—not its noisiness and its cruelty and its cinema vulgarity but the way in which it erects steel-and-glass skyscrapers and miraculous cement-and-glass factories and tiled kitchens and wireless antennae and popular magazines to insulate it from the good vulgarity of earth!"

He wondered about it. He admitted that he had seen only an indoor Europe. With hotel lounges, restaurants, bedrooms, train coupés, even galleries and cathedrals and a few authentic homes, he was familiar enough. But he realized that he had but little sense of the smell of earth in the changing countries. He could remember St. Stefan's Kirche in Vienna, but he could not remember the colors of the Austrian Alps, the sound of mountain streams, the changing smell of the crowded and musty pines at dawn, at noon, and in the dusk. He had talked with Spanish waiters but he had not been silent with Spanish peasants.

Perhaps, as she said, it was he who was the decadent and ephemeral flower of an imperiled civilization and she who was the root, not to be killed; he saw that she had more essential lustiness than he, more endurance than the lively but glass-encased Fran, vigorous enough in joy but wilting and whimpering under trials. The Ercoles, Kurt von Obersdorf, Lord Herndon, they were not to be crushed. In humility he turned to the eternal earth, and in the earth he found contentment. He had daily less need to "buzz out and look at things," as Fran put it. He sat for hours with Edith, or alone by the bay, staring at the miraculously involved branches of a cypress, discovering the myriad minute skyscrapers in a patch of moss. And he began to desire to have—with Edith—a farm at home, and not a gentleman's show-place, to increase social credit, but an authentic farm, smelling of horses and cattle and chickens, with cornfields baking at noon, mysterious in their jungle-like alleys. This simple-hearted ambition stirred him more, gave him more feeling that he had something secret and exciting to live for, than any of the business plans which were rousing him again to self-respect. . . . But it must be with Edith. . . . He smiled a little to think of himself, this bucolic lump, drawn back to earth by her thin unearthen hands. Edith! He understood better the slim starry Virgins before whom sun-black peasants bowed in Italian chapels.

He asked himself, then, "Am I in love with Edith—whatever this 'being in love' means?"

He had never so much as kissed her; only three or four times had he even patted her hand. He felt, sometimes, that behind her reticence there could be an honest passion, uncramped by the desire to make an impression, but he drifted on in a curious contented languor, willing to wait for exaltation. He found that when she was away, he missed her—had every moment some idea or observation he desired to share with her. But that was to him a lesser hint of what Edith Cortright had done to him than his increase in self-confidence.

It took him a time to perceive that perhaps he really was accepted by Edith, by the Ercoles and the various Captain Counts and Professores Dottores whom the Ercoles knew, as something more than the provincial, insensitive, Midwestern manufacturer whom Fran had pitied. Baron Ercole did not explain with bored patience when Sam asked elementary questions about Fascismo. Edith was not tart with him when he grumbled that he did not like the Narcissus in the Naples Museum.

They did not expect him to be an authority on sculpture, Chianti, Roman history, or the ranks of Italian nobility. Apparently they not only expected him to be precisely what he was, but admired him for it. He was at first embarrassed, made rather suspicious, by the Baroness Ercole's admiration of him as a strong oarsman, a kindly companion, a frank talker, a sound financier, but day by day he saw that she meant it. In this most Italian Italy he might without apology still be a most American American. Light seemed to be woven into the very texture of his face that these months past had been heavy and lifeless and unhealthily flushed; and his eyes flickered as of old they had in talk with his daughter Emily.

"You are real," they all said, in one way or another, and "I *am* real!" he began to gloat.

He slept tranquilly, conscious in his sleep of the security of Edith's presence on the floor below, shielding him against terror. He did not awake now at three, for a cigarette and brooding about Fran.

But once, late at night, he thought that he heard Fran calling, a sharp, beseeching "Sam—oh, *Sam!*" and he sprang up, stood swaying, bewildered as he realized that she was not with him, probably never would be again.

And the time, which he forgot as soon as possible, when Edith came into the room when he was writing and he raised his head, smiling, with "my Fran!"

Edith's only effort to correct his provincial ways was in a gentle urging, "Let yourself enjoy life, Sam! You're typically American in being burdened with a sense of guilt, no matter what you do or you don't do."

This may conceivably have had some connection with the fact that when he appeared with Edith, when they went to dinner with one of the Ercoles' friends or to the Excelsior for tea, more people looked interestedly at him, standing casually beside her, than in the days when he had been anxious to make an impression for Fran's sake. He no longer minded meeting strangers or having to listen to their foreign accents. He took them as they came.

He awoke one morning to lie looking at the bay and to realize that he was definitely and positively happy.

He had written to Fran a good deal about Edith. Fran was polite in her comments; she sent her greetings to "Mrs. Cortright"; and she was still politer, almost effusively jolly, when she wrote to him from Berlin that she was at last suing for divorce. With the term of residence she already had, the process would take three months. She was very pleasant about the fact that the grounds would be desertion, and the affair free of scandal.

He remembered how excited they had been when they had gone to Chicago together and he had bought her first little string of pearls; how proud she had been of them, and how grateful. . . . Then he felt curiously free.

When he reluctantly brought this decisive letter to Edith, she read it slowly, and ventured, "Do you mind awfully?"

"Oh yes, a little."

"But it does clear things up, doesn't it! And—— I hope it won't break your beautiful new calm!"

"I won't let it!"

"But I've seen you so badgered by her letters!"

"Yes, but—— I say! Could you ever possibly consider going to a place like Zenith to live?"

"Of course. Do places differ so much?"

"Would it amuse you to work on a plan like these garden suburbs?"

"I don't know. It might."

It was an hour afterward, when they had pretended to keep placidly busy with books and writing letters, that Edith burst out:

"Sam! About your suburbs. Something could be done—not just Italian villas and Swiss chalets—for a town with a tradition of Vermont Yankees and Virginians in buckskin. Why shouldn't one help to create an authentic and unique American domestic architecture? Our skyscrapers are the first really new thing in architecture since the Gothic cathedral, and perhaps just as beautiful! Create something native—and not be afraid to keep in all the plumbing and vacuum-cleaners and electric dishwashers! Dismiss the imitation châteaux. The trouble with the rich American is that he feels uncouth and untraditional, and so he meekly trots to Europe to buy sun-dials and Fifteenth Century mantelpieces and refectory tables—to try to buy aristocracy by buying the aristocrats' worn-out coats. I like my Europe in Europe; at home I'd like to watch people make something new. For example, your motor cars."

"Then you would like a place like Zenith, that's growing?"

"How can I tell? I'd certainly like the adventure of trying it."

He felt that her hesitation was more promising than the enthusiasms of Fran. Suddenly a horde of Ercoles were trouping in, planning a swim, and no more that day, nor the next, did they speak of Fran, of Zenith, of themselves. But when they said good night, he kissed her hands, and her eyes dwelt upon him.

They were dining at Bertolini's, high above Naples, looking out toward Capri, and he was talking of possible schemes: a two-story caravan with a canvas-sided collapsible upper floor, so that the caravan could pass under arches en route; a caravan that could turn into a house boat, carrying its own hull along, collapsed; a summer resort entirely for children whose parents were going abroad; a dozen fantastic, probably practical plans. She was amused by them, suggested improvements, and Sam was lustily content.

But after his second cognac the orchestra played selections from the Viennese operettas which Fran loved, and he remembered how happy he had been with Fran in Berlin, at first. It came to him that if Kurt failed to marry her, she would be a bewildered and lonely exile; and through the music, through the darkness beyond the music, he saw her fleeing, a desolate wraith; and while Edith gossiped most amiably, Sam's heart was heavy with pity for the frightened and bewildered child Fran, who once had laughed so eagerly with him.

But, back at the Villa Ercole, he stood with Edith on the terrace and across the whispering darkness of the bay, he saw the cone of Vesuvius with a thin line of fire.

"Don't worry it too much!" said Edith suddenly, and he was grateful that she understood his cloudy thoughts without making him wrap them in cloudier words.

Chapter 35

FOR DAYS they drifted in perfect calm, and he was proud that the enervating thought of Fran was gone from him. All one morning they explored the ridge above Posilipo, found fragments of a Roman emperor's villa and the carp-pond in which he used to drown his slaves as the best fish-food, and discovered the mausoleum which, history asserts, was the tomb of Vergil, or of some one else. They straggled home, up the long street which was a wilderness of children and carts, and sank down sighing in the cool drawing-room.

"*Collatzione, Teresa,*" he ordered, then: "Curious, Edith, but this house that you've rented, and that belongs to an Italian I never saw till the other day, is the first that I ever felt was really mine. I actually dare give an order!"

"But I'm sure your Fran never *meant* to be a domestic dictator. . . ."

The gardener had left the mail on the table, but Sam did not pick it up till after lunch, and then but carelessly. On top was a letter from Fran. He pretended, not very skillfully, that he had to go to his room, and he read Fran's letter alone:

> I haven't much excuse, probably I've been a fool and not appreciated you but anyway, maybe with no right to, I am turning to you rather desperately. Kurt's mother finally came up from Austria. She was pretty rude to me. She indicated, oh quite clearly that for the Catholic and Highly Noble Kurtrl to marry a female who was (or soon would be) heinously divorced, who was an American, and who was too old to bear him heirs, would be disastrous. And she didn't spare me very much in putting it that way, either. Not a pretty scene—me sitting there smoking in Kurt's flat and trying to look agreeable while she wailed at Kurt and ignored me. And Kurt stood by her. Oh, his nice little sentimental heart bled for me, and since then he's such a good time being devastated and trying to take both sides at once. But he "thought ve had better put off the marriage for

maybe a couple of years till ve von her over." God! Is he a man or a son? There ain't going to be no vinning over, and no marriage! I'm sick of his cowardice, when I risked so much, but why go into that.

If you still care to bend your Olympian head and forgive the probably wicked and unforgivable Magdalene or however it's spelled, I should be glad to join you again, anyway I've stopped divorce proceedings. Of course I realize that in saying this so honestly, without efforts to protect myself as most women would, I risk another humiliation at your hands such as I had from Kurt. Of course I don't know how far you have committed yourself in the rather strange relations with this Mrs. Cortwright in which you have apparently had so much pleasure and relief from my aggravating self, though how you could be willing to take snubs from the highly proper Italians by thus living with her openly instead of concealing things is beyond——

Oh forgive me, forgive me, dear Sambo darling, forgive me, your bad child Fran! I sound so beastly and snotty when in my heart I'm desolated and scared and lost and I turn to you as the Rock of Ages! I wrote so abominably and unjustly because I'm so wretched, so desperate, and I won't even tear it up—I want you to know that if you do let your bad Fran come back, she probably hasn't learned as much as she should in her mediocre little tragedy, she'll probably be just as snobbish and demanding as ever, though God knows I don't want to be, I am so tired of thread-bare grandeurs now and want so much to be simple and honest.

I think you will credit me with not trying to come back just because you are rich and strong, and Kurt poor and honest. It's just—— Oh, you know what it is! I venture to turn to you because I do know that once, anyway, you loved me a great deal. And if we could manage to stick together, it will be so much better for Brent and Emily—oh, I know, probably it's shameless of me to speak of that so late, but it is true.

I find there is a boat leaving Hamburg September 19, Cherbourg the next day, the *Deutschland* and if you

> *care* to join me on it, or meet me in Paris, I should be—— Oh Sam, if you still do love me, you mustn't be proud, you mustn't take this chance to punish me, but come, because otherwise—— Oh, I don't know what I *will* do! I've been so proud! Now I feel the world is jeering at me! I don't dare leave my flat, don't dare answer the phone and hear their pitying laughter, I have my maid answer it for me, and usually it is still Kurt, but I'll never see him again, never, he talks of killing himself but he won't—his Mamma wouldn't let him!
>
> As soon as you get this, won't you please telephone me here, from Naples.
>
> If you feel like coming, I hope this will not inconvenience your hostess, Mrs. Cortright, whom I remember so agreeably in Venice, kindly give her my regards. But I hope that my appeal may be somewhat more important to you than even your social duty to that doubtless most charming lady who is I am sure much less irritating than I.

Her whole handwriting changed then; he felt that the rest of the letter had been written hours later:

> Oh, Sam, I do need you so, did I ever tell you that I adore you?
>
> Your shamed and wretched little Fran.

He blundered down to the drawing-room, snorting, "Got to run into Naples. May be late for tea. Don't wait."

"What is it?"

"Oh, it's nothing."

He fled from her.

All the way down, on the tram, he asked himself whether he wanted to have Fran again, and whether he was really going to join her, and to both he answered with perfect blankness. But when he asked whether he wanted to leave Edith, he denied it, sharply, with fury, reflecting wretchedly how good she had been, how honest, how understanding, and perceiving there was rising in him a passion for her greater than the mystic vexation with which Fran had fascinated him.

And he was going to desert Edith, going to be weak enough to betray her?

"Oh, probably," he sighed, when for an hour, at the American Express Company, he had been waiting for the telephone call to Berlin.

He seemed to wait forever.

He was as conscious of the scene in the express office as though he had sat there for years. A picture of a big New York Central locomotive. Racks of pamphlets about spicy places—Burma and Bangkok and São Paulo—he would never see them now, because Fran would find them crude and unfashionable. A tourist lady writing letters and between sentences boasting to her mother of the *won-derful* corals she had found on the Piazza dei Martiri——

Then startlingly, "Your Berlin call!"

He heard Fran's voice, quicksilver voice, eagerness of the wildly playing child in its lifting mutations:

"Oh, Sam, it really is you? You really are coming, dearest? You do forgive poor Fran?"

"Sure. Be on the boat. *On the boat.* Yes, the nineteenth, yes, sure, we'll talk over everything, good-bye, honey, you better get the tickets as you're there in Germany. *Get the steamer tickets*, good-bye, honey, I'll wire you a confirmation."

He walked back most of the way, looking old and slow and sweaty, laboring over the coming scene with Edith. She would be very polite but surprised, contemptuous of him for returning to the servitude of Fran's witchery.

He slunk in a few minutes after six.

She was reading by the great window in the drawing-room. She glanced up, then, wondering, "What is it? What's happened?"

"Well——"

He stood by the window, making much of clipping and lighting a cigar, and he did not look at her as he grumbled, "Fran's lover, this Count Obersdorf, has turned her down. His mother thought she was kind of déclassé—divorce and all that. Poor kid, that must've been hard on her. She's given up the idea of divorce, and she's sailing for home. She'll be kind of—— Oh, people'll talk a lot, I guess. I'm afraid I'll have to go with her. Fact, I'll have to catch the midnight for Rome, tonight. . . . I wish there were some way of telling you all that you've——"

"Sam!"

She had sprung up. He was astonished by the fury in her quiet eyes.

"I won't let you go back to that woman! And I won't see you killed—yes, killed!—by her sweet, gay, well-mannered, utter damned selfishness! Her only thought about anybody is what they give her! The world offers you sun and wind, and Fran offers you death, fear and death! Oh, I'd seen how you've aged five years in five minutes, after one of her complaining letters! And you won't be helping her—you'll just make her feel all the more that she can do any selfish, cruel thing she wants to and come out of it unscathed! Think of Peking and Cairo! No! Think of the farm you could have in Michigan, among the pines! Think of how natural and contented you'd be—yes, *we'd* be—back there——"

"I know, Edith; I know every bit of it. I just can't help it. She's my child. I've got to take care of her."

"Yes. Well." The passion did not fade from her eyes, but snapped out, as though one should turn off a light, and she said dully, "Sorry. I was impertinent. At least let me help you pack."

Throughout the packing, dinner, and the rather dreadful waiting afterward, when he could not find two civil words to put together, she was a little abrupt of speech, very courteous. She asked questions about Zenith. She politely hoped that she might see him "and Mrs. Dodsworth" some distant day. Only once was she near to intimacy, when, after a torturing pause, she blurted, "There really isn't much to say, is there! But I do want you to know that because you've seemed to like me, you've given me a new assurance."

When he tried to counter with florid compliments, she bustled out to the kitchen.

The sound of the coming taxicab released him from the eternity of sitting dead in a tomb. While the servants straggled out with his luggage, he held her hand, patting it.

"It is all ready, Signore," said the maid. She received the highly expected tip, and with a "Com' beck soon!" which sounded sincere, she vanished.

In the twilight outside the tree-shadowed door, he awkwardly shook hands with Edith, but while he was trying to say something agreeable, she cried:

"It's too late now. But I thought that some day—— I thought it would be easy for me to talk, and I would tell you all sorts of things about how I feel and think. That it's been pleasant to be with you. That you're bigger than you know, not smaller, like celebrities. That you've made me willing to stop being afraid of the world, and to attack it again. I've felt——" She seized his rough sleeve. "That curious feeling, always a surprise every time I was with you, of 'Why it's *you*!' That feeling that you were different from any other living person—not necessarily one bit finer but—oh, different! I shouldn't say any of this, but before it's quite too late—too late!—I want to try to be reckless. But I can't say any of the things I thought. Bless you, my dear! And God keep you through the wickedness of this Happy Ending!"

He kissed her, a terrible clinging kiss, and lumbered over to the roadway and his taxicab. He looked back. She seemed to start toward him, then closed the door quickly. Through a window he heard her voice, weary and spiritless: "Only one for breakfast, Teresa."

He was alone with a yawning taxi-driver, as a breeze came up from the bay in the Southern darkness.

Chapter 36

FRAN was lovely, very young, in a gray-squirrel mantle.

"I got it for almost *nothing*, at the summer sales in Berlin," she said. "Why is it most women never can seem to economize? I'll bet your wonderful flame, Mrs. Cost—Cortright? funny, I never *can* seem to remember her name—she's frightfully clever, I'm sure, but I'll bet she'd have paid twice as much for it."

The late September was cold even for mid-Atlantic. Fran smoothed the fur, draped it closer in her steamer-chair. She seemed to him like a leopard with its taut limbs hidden by a robe.

Now, after tea hour on the S.S. *Deutschland*, a raging sunset smeared the waves with a frightening crimson. They smelled a storm. The ship ducked before the attacking waves. But Fran was full of liveliness and well-being. As she talked, she nodded every instant to people they had met aboard, the men who were always in a knot about her at the dances, the matrons who talked of "that charming Mrs. Dodsworth—she told me she was much younger than her husband—he's a little slow, don't you think—but she's so fond of him—looks after him like a daughter."

Fran cuddled down in her richness of fur.

"Oh, it's nice to be *going* somewhere!" she said. "I bet we'll both be crazy to start off somewhere, maybe back to Paris, when we've been home a few months. (What an *atrocious* hat that woman has on and my *dear*, will you regard her shoes! Why they *allow* people like that in the first cabin?) And you can't know how tired I got of sticking around Berlin forever 'n' ever! Oh, you were so right about Kurt, Sam dear. I don't know how you guessed it! You'd be the first to admit you aren't usually so *awfully* good at judging character, except in the case of business men, but you were right with—— Oh, he was so *bossy*! He was furious if I so much as suggested I'd like to run down to Baden-Baden by myself. And where he got the idea that he was so important—— Oh, his family may be as old as the Coliseum—the Coliseo—but when I saw his mother, my *dear*, the most awful old country frump——"

"Don't!" said Sam. "Don't know why, but I kind of hate to hear you riding Kurt and his mother that way. They were probably hurt, too."

Most graciously, quite forgivingly, "Yes, you're right. Sorry, M'sieu! I'll be a good girl. And of course everything is all right now. After all, it's such a wonderful Happy Ending to our wild little escapades! We've both learned lots, don't you think? and now I won't be so flighty and you won't be so irritable, I'm sure you won't."

There was dancing in the verandah café. Young Tom Allen, the polo player—young Tom, all black and ivory and grin—came to ask her to dance. She smiled up at him, airily patted Sam's arm, and scampered away, while Tom seemed to be holding her hand under shelter of her squirrel robe.

The sunset was angry now, the color of port wine.

Sam staggered around and around the slanting deck, alone, and alone he stood aft, looking back in the direction of Europe. But there was only foggy gray.

He awoke, bewildered, at two in the morning. The storm had come; the steamer was pitching abominably. In his half sleep he heard Edith whimpering in her sleep in the twin bed beside him. Smiling, glad to comfort her who had been all comfort to him here in sun-bright Naples, he stretched out his arm, sleepily stroked her thin wrist.

He startled, he sat up and gasped, at the astonishment of hearing the voice of Fran.

"Oh, thank you! Nice of you to wake me up. Having a kind of nightmare. My, it's rough!"

In his agitation he tightened his fingers on her wrist.

"Oh, Sam, *don't*—— Oh, don't be *ardent*! Not yet. I must get used—— And I'm so sleepy!" Very brightly: "You don't mind, do you? Nighty-night!"

He lay awake. In the watery light from the transom he saw the sheen of her silver toilet things on the dresser. He thought of this tremendous steamer, pounding the waves. He thought of the modern miracle of the radio, up above, of the automatic electric steering apparatus. Yet on the bridge were sailors, unautomatic, human, eternal. The ship, too, was eternal, as a vehicle of man's old voyaging. Its creaking seemed to him like the creaking of an ancient Greek trireme.

But while his thoughts reached out thus for things heroic, he heard her placid breathing and he smelled not the sea gale but perfume that came from little crystal vials among her silver toilet-things that were vaster than the hull of the steamer, stronger than the storm.

He felt that he would never sleep again.

He closed his great fist, tight. Then it relaxed, and he was asleep.

He roused to hear her bubbling, in a stormy dawn:

"Are you awake? Don't let me disturb you. Horrid morning! Let's get up some bridge. We'll get Mr. Ballard and Tom Allen. He's a dear boy, isn't he! Though I feel like a mother toward him. Oh, Sam, if you aren't too sleepy—— Oh. While we're in New York, I think I'll see if I can't pick up a really nice Chinese evening wrap. Tom told me about a shop. Of course I have those others, but they're getting so shabby, and after all, you don't expect me to look a fright, like Matey Pearson, do you! I'll make her eyes start out of her head with the Marcel Rochas frock I got in Paris, and think, I only had two days to get it in! Zenith will simply foam at the mouth! Oh, after all, it *is* kind of nice to be going home—for a while—after all we've gone through—and Sam, I wonder if you understand that *I* understand probably you were just as brave and honest as I was, even with the hideous suffering I had to face in Berlin! And—— Oh, I don't know what reminded me of it, but you must be careful with the Ballards. I'm afraid you bored them last evening, talking about Italian motors. You must remember that they have a villa in Florence, and they're used to the real Italy, and artists and the nobility and so on. But of course it doesn't matter. And—— Do you mind ringing for coffee? That's an old dear!"

The scent of her perfumes seemed stronger than by night, in the sleep-thickened air of the stateroom.

He slowly raised himself to ring for the steward. He had said nothing whatever.

She blissfully dropped off to sleep again, and he bathed, dressed, swayed out on deck. The open portion of the promenade dock was protected by canvas against which the water crashed, sending streams between the lashings to trickle along the deck. He labored forward, stood solemnly at a window looking ahead at the bow plunging into the waves, at the foam hurled over the forepeak, at a desolate immigrant in a tattered old raincoat trying to keep a footing on the forward deck.

It was black ahead. To a landsman it was menacing. Yet there was strength in the stormy air and, after a long breath, stretching out his great arms, Sam began to plow around the deck.

His eyes seemed turned inward; his lips moved a little in his meditation.

After half an hour, breakfastless, he suddenly climbed the stairs from A Deck to the Boat Deck and, down a narrow corridor, past the tiny florist-shop, came to the wireless bureau—a narrow desk across a small room, like a telegraph office in a minor hotel.

Emotionlessly, he wrote and handed in a message to Edith Cortright: "Will you be Naples three weeks from now?"

He went down to breakfast. All morning and half the afternoon he played bridge, watching Fran flirt with the ebullient Tom Allen.

The answer to his radio came just before tea-time: "No but shall be venice for couple months bless you edith."

For an hour, while Fran made much of tea with half a dozen men, Sam sat alone in the smoking-room, pretending to read whenever any lone and necessitous drinker came in to look for a drinking companion.

At the dressing-hour, he said mildly to Fran, "I wonder if we mightn't have dinner here in our stateroom tonight? I want to talk about things. We've sort of avoided it."

"Good Heavens, Sambo, what's come over you? Do you regard it as particularly cheerful to dine in this beastly little hole of a room on a rough night like this? Besides! I promised the Ballards we'd join them in the grill for dinner—such a common, stupid commercial crowd in the salon."

"But we must talk."

"My dear man, I think we'll manage it, with four full days ahead of us on this steamer! I'm really not going off to the Riviera or any place, you know!"

It was not till late in the evening that he had his chance. As they came down to the stateroom at bedtime, Fran very lively after a session in the smoking-room, he said, without prelude:

"Not much use trying to do it tactfully. Wanted to, but—— Fran, we can't make a go of it, and I'm going back and join Edith Cortright."

"I don't quite understand. What have I done now? Oh, my God, if you haven't learned—— You haven't learned anything, not one single thing, out of all our sorrows! Still criticizing me, and such a kind sweet way of springing something beastly cruel on me just when I've been happy, as I have tonight!" She faced him, hands clenched. "Will you *kindly*, Mr. Dodsworth, be a little less mysterious and tell me just what it is I've done to hurt your tender little feelings *this* time?"

"Nothing. We just can't make a go of it. You don't get me. I'm not making a scene. I'm not trying to bully you. I meant just what I said. I'm going back to Italy, from New York, on the first ship. I'm not blaming or criticizing——"

She sat abruptly on the chair before her dressing-table. She said quietly, with fear edging her voice, "And what is to become of me?"

"I don't know. If I did, I wouldn't have met you on the ship."

She moaned. "Oh! You do manage to hurt! I congratulate you! You see, I've been flattering myself you really wanted to come back to me!"

He started to say something comforting, then held it back in panic, as if in danger. "I'm not going to be polite, Fran. You know how awfully I've loved you, a good many years. You tampered with it. . . . What's going to become of you? I don't know. But I guess it'll be just the same thing that's been becoming of you this past couple of years. You haven't needed me. You've found people to play with, and plenty of beaux. I suppose you'll go on finding them——"

"And this is the man that 'loved me awfully'——"

"Wait! For the first time in all our arguments, I'm going to think of what would become of *me*! I can't help you. I'm just your attendant. But me—you can kill me. I didn't used to mind your embarrassing me and continually putting me in my place. Didn't even know you were doing it. But I do now, and I won't stand it!"

"Was it your dear Mrs. Cortright who taught you that lovely theory? about embarrassing you? After the years when I've never allowed one single soul to criticize you——"

"Understand? I'm *finished*!"

He did not, unfortunately, leave her in any heroic and dignified way. He flounced out of the stateroom like a child in a tantrum. And that was because he knew that only by childish violence could he escape from her logic, and because he knew that he must escape, even over the side of the lurching ship. For she was indeed perfectly logical and sound. She knew what she wanted!

It was misery for him to look out at her from the taxicab which he was taking to the Italian Line dock, after three days in New York; to see her standing in front of the hotel, alone, deserted, her eyes pitiful, and to realize that he might never see her again. The look in her eyes had been the meaning of life for him, and he was deserting it.

They were dining at the Ritz in Paris, Edith and Sam, feeling superior to its pretentiousness, because that evening they had determined to return to America, when his divorce should be complete, and to experiment with caravans. They were gay, well dined and well content.

But after his second cognac the orchestra played selections from Viennese operettas, and he remembered how happy Fran and he had been in Berlin. He remembered the wretchedness of the letter he had received from her that day. She was staying with Emily in Zenith; she said that she was seeing no one; that his "*dear* friends Tub and Matey" were a little too polite; and that she was thinking of going, in a few days, to Italy——

Through the darkness beyond the music, he saw her fleeing, a desolate wraith, and his heart was heavy with pity for the frightened and bewildered child who once had laughed so eagerly with him.

He came out of his silence with a consciousness that Edith was watching him. She said lightly, "You enjoy being sad about her! But hereafter, every time there is a music, I shall also think of Cecil Cortright. How handsome he was! He spoke five languages! How impatient I was with him! How I failed him! How virtuous it makes me feel to flay myself! What a splendid, uncommon grief I have! Dear Sam! . . . What a job it is to give up the superiority of being miserable and self-sacrificing!"

He stared, he pondered, he suddenly laughed, and in that laughter found a youthfulness he had never known in his solemn youth.

He was, indeed, so confidently happy that he completely forgot Fran and he did not again yearn over her, for almost two days.

CHRONOLOGY

NOTE ON THE TEXTS

NOTES

Chronology

1885 Born Harry Sinclair Lewis on February 7, third son of Dr. Edwin J. Lewis and Emma Kermott Lewis, in Sauk Centre, Minnesota. (Father, born 1848 on farm in Westville, Connecticut, moved with family in 1857 to Lisburn, Pennsylvania, where grandfather established match factory. When the business failed the family moved in 1866 to a farmstead just outside of Elysian, Minnesota. Father taught school and on December 28, 1873, married fellow teacher Emma Kermott, born 1849 in London, Ontario. They moved 60 miles to Redwood Falls, where father studied medicine with local doctor before enrolling in Rush Medical College, Chicago. Father received M.D. in 1877 and set up practice in Ironton, Wisconsin, then moved family to Sauk Centre in 1883.) Older brothers are Fred, born 1875, and Claude, born 1878. Father is strict, inflexible, and methodical; his word is law with sons. ("*Hoc pater meus dixit*," Lewis writes in diary as a teenager.) Town is 28 years old, with population of about 1,200, unpaved streets, wooden sidewalks, false storefronts, eight churches, eight liquor licenses, and is surrounded by wheat-covered prairie dotted with 30 lakes within a ten-mile radius.

1888 Mother has pleuritic attack and develops consumption.

1889–90 Mother spends winter in New Mexico.

1890–91 Mother spends winter in California and Texas. Father brings mother back from El Paso in May after learning that her health is worsening. Mother dies June 25, 1891. Lewis admires Claude and follows him around. ("For sixty years," Lewis will write in 1947, "I have tried to impress my brother Claude.") Accompanies father in buggy or sleigh on calls to patients in surrounding countryside.

1892 Father marries Isabel Warner, daughter of Chicago family with whom he lodged when studying medicine, on July 7. She becomes active in local Congregational Church and in social and cultural clubs, and persuades town to build restroom for farmers' wives. (Lewis will remember her as "more mother than stepmother.")

1895–96 Rescued from drowning while swimming in Sauk Lake by Claude. Brother Fred tries dental school in New York, drops out, and begins working in Sauk Centre flour mill (will be a miller all his life). Stepmother helps organize and becomes leader of the Gradatim Club, a self-improvement and civic-good-deeds group of 30 women. Its affiliation with Minnesota Federation of Women's Clubs takes her on trips; Lewis frequently goes along, and also accompanies her when she visits relatives in Chicago. Grades in sixth grade are uneven; deportment poor, fails every period in music and drawing, as well as several in penmanship.

1896–97 Claude enters University of Minnesota. Father and brothers enjoy hunting and fishing. Lewis is solitary, plays on barn workbench with numerous keys. Starts Robin Hood Club and becomes its leader, but then is expelled by other boys because of his temper and the intensity of his fantasies. Spends hours talking and arguing about politics and literature with Dr. J. A. Dubois, an amateur poet and political progressive.

1898 Attempts to run away in April to enlist as a drummer boy in Spanish-American War. Father catches him at railroad station in Melrose, ten miles from home. Nicknamed "Doodle" after Yankee Doodle for escapade (other nicknames later in life are Hal and Red, for his red hair). Stands 17th in class of 18 in eighth grade and does poorly in sports.

1900–1 Enters eleventh grade. Elected president of the Delphian, school literary society. Starts keeping a diary in November, writing in a code he invents. Reads Anthony Hope's *Rupert of Hentzau*, Kirk Monroe's *Under the Dog Star*, Hall Caine's *The Christian*, and works by Thackeray, George Eliot, and Victor Hugo. (Further high school reading will include Dickens' *Nicholas Nickleby*, Kipling's *Kim*, and Scott's *Kenilworth*; later names these three writers as favorites of his young years.) Begins to do well in school; gets 90s in all subjects except Cicero. Deportment marks are still poor; diary entries include "general depravity this morning," "had some fun," "raised hell in the junior room," "was sent out," "got sent home," "got fired from school today." Writes poems that are rejected by *Youth's Companion*, *Harper's*, *Outlook*, and *The New England Magazine*; tells himself "persistancy is the great element of success."

1901–2 Enters twelfth grade. Is tall, uncoordinated, and weighs 120 pounds. Attends public lectures, elocutionists' performances, band concerts, amateur theatricals, and village dances. Tutored in German by a Catholic priest and in Greek by an Episcopal minister. Fred marries Winnie Hanson, the daughter of a Swedish immigrant farmer, in October 1901. Lewis plays lead in senior play, *Class Day*. Works without pay for a few days in June 1902 at *The Herald*, a local paper, setting type, covering his high school graduation, and writing short news column. Takes Yale entrance examinations in St. Paul; passes 11 of 13 subjects, but is advised to spend a year at a preparatory school. Works for two weeks as night clerk in new Palmer House hotel in Sauk Centre.

1902–3 Enters Oberlin Academy, in Oberlin, Ohio. Works hard and does well in studies, but does not get along with roommate, who finds Lewis too "fresh." Joins Young Men's Christian Association and is swept up in fervor of "positive earnest muscular Christianity" fostered by nearby Oberlin College. Pledges himself to become a missionary, preferably in Africa. Travels with a few other students by railroad handcar to nearby town of Nickel Plate to teach young girls in Sunday school. Feels disliked by other students and describes himself in diary: "Tall, ugly, thin, red-haired but not, methinks, especially stupid." During Christmas holidays, visits stepmother's family in Chicago. Sees Claude, who is studying at Rush Medical College, and visits various churches. Lewis has eyes checked and gets glasses. Learns that no course in geometry will be available the next term; desperately homesick, he asks his father to let him come home at the end of March and study for Yale exams on his own. Father agrees, and saves four cords of ironwood for him to split. At home, studies geometry, the *Iliad* and *Anabasis*, and finishes splitting the wood by late April. Passes all eight exams in St. Paul in June and is admitted to Yale in July.

Meets and likes published poet Arthur Wheelock Upson, eight years his senior, who is working at a St. Paul bookstore. Suffers from worsening acne.

1903–4 Travels to New Haven in September by way of New York City, which he finds overwhelming and savagely impersonal. Enters Yale, rooming alone in a boarding house before moving to 79 South Middle College on campus in mid-October. Joins Freshman Union debating society. Finds friendships difficult to establish; nicknamed "God Forbid" after remark made during a debate. Befriended by first-year English instructor, Chauncey B. Tinker, who goes for long walks with him and finds him the most interesting student in his class. Enjoys good relationships with other professors. Undergoes X-ray treatments for acne during year. Attends lecture by William Butler Yeats in November and is deeply impressed. Begins sporadic reporting for city newspaper *Journal and Courier* in December. Finishes term in top fifth of his class. Teaches Sunday-school classes for Y.M.C.A. but gradually loses zeal. In March becomes first freshman to place poem in *Yale Literary Magazine* (*Lit*) and has several other poems published in the *Courant*, another college literary publication. Short of money because of a decline in father's income, abandons student Commons, eating lunch and dinner at cheap restaurants and making breakfast in his room. Moves in with students across the hall in April to save more money. Reviews plays as freelance drama critic of the *Journal.* Grades fall. Takes summer job waiting on tables at Randall Hall at Harvard. Quits after less than three weeks and sails for Portland, Maine, as crewman on British ship *Georgian*, which is carrying 650 head of cattle to Liverpool. Finds tending the livestock exhausting, the living conditions filthy, and considers much of the crew to be "profane, dirty, and vile" runaway criminals, but does become friends with three fellow crewmen, including M. Wayne Womer, a Methodist minister. Ship arrives in Liverpool July 27 and Lewis explores the area, with only $3 to spend. Returns to the United States on August 13 as crewman on the *Georgian* with "great store" of literary material.

1904–5 Takes temporary rooms in New Haven. Works at odd jobs, tutors, and reports for the *Courier* for a few days.

Moves on September 23 into room at 232 Durfee on campus. Acquires a cane, white waistcoat, derby, and spectacles hanging from silk cord. Neglects his studies, cuts classes, receives poor grades, and feels "very blue." Begins reading Whitman and takes long solitary walks. Starts smoking and drinking regularly. Reads constantly, including Maeterlinck, Shaw, Wharton, Wells, and London. Worries about money and continues to get tutoring and newspaper work. Makes his first friends at Yale, Frederick Kinney Noyes and, in particular, Allan Updegraff, who introduces him to writings of Ernest Haeckel and Max Nordau. Helps Updegraff with Greek translations. Though Lewis continues to teach Sunday school, he becomes a skeptic ("Christian religion is a crutch") and begins proselytizing for socialism. Has one story and three poems printed in *Lit* and four stories and seven poems printed in *Courant.* Begins to send manuscripts to commercial publishers, using the name Sinclair Lewis; article "Did Mrs. Thurston Get the Idea of 'The Masqueraders' from Mr. Zangwill?" (on possible plagiarism) is accepted by *The Critic* for $20. Visits Upson in Minneapolis before going home for summer. Writes little but reads widely, including Hamlin Garland's *Main-Travelled Roads* and Tolstoy's *War and Peace.* Finds social life easy, has friends, including Paul Hilsdale (who will soon enter Yale), and newcomer lawyer Charles T. Dorion, with whom he enjoys long conversations, but grows restless and describes Sauk Centre as "a hell for dullness." Conceives novel, *The Village Virus,* about small-town life ("how it getteth into the veins of good men & true").

1905–6 Enters junior year at Yale. Protests against compulsory daily chapel and argues before the student union against proposal to levy an $18 athletic tax on all students. Sells "kid verse" to *The Housekeeper.* First commercially published fiction, "Matsu-No-Kata: A Romance of Old Japan," appears in December *Pacific Monthly.* Outraged when Yale students boo and laugh at Jack London during lecture in January. Elected to editorial board of *Lit* in February. Contributes to "The Editor's Table," including "Unknown Undergraduates," plea for understanding of unconventional students. Turns down election to *Courier* editorial board in March (position taken by runner-up William Rose Benét). In summer goes to England on cattle boat *Philadelphia*, accompanied by Yale acquaintance Robert Pfeiffer; finds conditions better than on previous trip. Travels around England for a month, visiting Oxford and London. Returns in steerage on passenger ship *Lucania*.

1906–7 Lewis and Updegraff drop out of Yale without telling parents and take jobs as janitors at Upton Sinclair's utopian community, Helicon Home Colony, on the Palisades near Englewood, New Jersey, populated by dozens of socialists, anarchists, syndicalists, single-taxers, spiritualists, and New Thoughtists. Meets and falls in love with Edith Summers, whom he nicknames Cherub. Quits Helicon Home Colony after a month, is hospitalized for jaundice, then rents room with Updegraff at 239 Avenue B on Lower East Side of New York City. Intending to live by freelance writing, he sells some children's verses and stories to five-cent magazines, and has three poems accepted by *Smart Set*. Earns $15.34 in January and $27.75 in February. In March begins translating French and German stories for *Transatlantic Tales*, earning $20 a week. Reads Thoreau during lunch breaks. Updegraff leaves because of health in spring to take job in Yellowstone National Park. Lewis proposes marriage to Edith Summers in late spring, but in November records "final letter from Cherub." When Updegraff returns in October, Lewis gives him his translating job and begins freelancing again, but market dries up after financial panic in autumn 1907. Moves to 576 Fox Street in the Bronx. Earns $242.69 for the year. In November, goes by steerage to Panama, where the canal is being dug, in search of a job and literary material. Crosses the isthmus and back but cannot find work. Decides to return to Yale, delighting his family; father sends $50 (will continue to do so every month until he graduates). Takes room in boarding house at 14 Whalley Avenue.

1908 Readmitted to Yale by special faculty vote. Welcomed by Chauncey Tinker and befriended by Professor William Lyons Phelps. Updegraff marries Edith Summers. Undergraduate friends include Paul Hilsdale from Sauk Centre and Leonard Bacon. Does full year's work in half a year. Develops kidney trouble in April and is terrified of imaginary burglars. Corresponds with William Rose Benét about Bohemian life in New York. Graduates in June, by special faculty courtesy, as a member of the class of 1907. Goes home to Sauk Centre, stopping en route to visit family in Chicago, where he meets Anna Louise Strong, with whom he has long corresponded after reading her work in the Oberlin college magazine. Visits Claude, now a surgeon, and his wife, Mary, for three weeks in St. Cloud, Minnesota. Continues to write and now sends all manuscripts to literary agent, Flora May Holly, in New York. Works for eight weeks for Waterloo, Iowa, *Daily Courier*, writing editorials until he is fired for his radical views and ignorance of Iowa politics. Learns in August that Arthur Upson has died in a boating accident. Goes to New York, where Updegraff gets him a job interviewing derelicts for two charitable organizations. Plans novel *Ecce Homo* in which Christ is reincarnated as a political radical. In December sells a story to *Red Book* for $75 and leaves for California. Works on novel about a clerk named Wren.

1909 Offered job as part-time secretary to Grace MacGowan Cooke, who had earlier been at Helicon Home Colony. Spends six months in art colony at Carmel founded in 1905 by San Francisco poet George Sterling. Visitors include Anna Strunsky, Jack London, Mary Austin, James Hopper, and Arnold Genthe. Writes story "The Smile Lady" for New Thought magazine *Nautilus.* Owing Cooke money, Lewis leaves with Benét in June and stays until mid-August with his family in army post at Benicia on San Francisco Bay, where Benét's father is commanding officer. Completes serial for *Nautilus* and sells story to *Sunset* magazine in July (it appears in January 1910). Moves to 1525 Scott St. in San Francisco and after a month of hunting for work, gets a rewrite job for *Evening Bulletin* for $35 a week, but is fired two months later. Falls in love with painter Eugenia (Gene) Baker. Hired as night-desk wire editor by Associated Press in December for $20 a week. Enjoys visits to Benét family. Plans *The Fathers*, novel about fathers and sons.

1910 Quits AP February 18 on learning that he is about to be fired. Returns to Carmel for three weeks. Has accumulated trunkful of notes, clippings, and file of more than 100 story plots. Sells 14 of them to Jack London for $70 (will later sell him 12 more). In March goes to Washington, D.C., for job as subeditor and clerk for *Volta Review*, a magazine for teachers of the deaf edited by Yale friend Kinney Noyes, at $15 a week. Rooms with Noyes in boarding house for $24 a month. Resents Noyes's cynicism. Moves to New York City in October to work for Frederick A. Stokes Co., book publishers, at $15 a week. Becomes friends with George Soule, an acquaintance from Yale, who also works there. Works under editorial direction of William Morrow. Lives at 10 Van Nest Place in Greenwich Village, where William Rose Benét, George Soule, and "tramp poet" Henry Kemp also have rooms (dislikes Kemp). Attends Anarchists' Ball at Christmas, where he sits next to Theodore Dreiser—"about the biggest realist in America"—and witnesses an argument between him and Emma Goldman.

1911–12 Joins the Socialist Party in January 1911 and remains a member until April 1912. Works hard and does well at Stokes, gradually getting into publicity department. Worried about having time for writing, takes off a week without pay in April (salary is now $25 a week). Given two months off in summer and $200 to write boys' adventure story for Stokes (receives three percent royalty when book is published). Goes to Provincetown, Massachusetts, and completes *Hike and the Airplane* in three weeks (published summer 1912 under pseudonym Tom Graham). Returns to New York in September. Likes and sees Rose and Anna Strunsky, Edna Kenton, Frances Perkins, Edna Ferber, Sonya Levien, and Mary Heaton Vorse, whose aphorism he will quote all his life: "The art of writing is the art of applying the seat of your pants to the seat of your chair." Makes acquaintance of other young men in publishing, including Alfred Harcourt, B. W. Huebsch, Harry Maule, and Harrison Smith. Returns to Provincetown in July 1912 and finishes draft of novel *Our Mr. Wrenn.* On September 12 meets Grace Livingston Hegger, a young woman who works for *Vogue*, in the office freight elevator. (Grace, born in New York to English parents, was convent-educated. Her father, who had owned a gallery of paintings and carbon photographs on Fifth Avenue, died when she was 15 and left the family in reduced circumstances. She lives with her mother and brother in a small apartment on W. 70th St. near the Hudson River.) Lewis soon and often proposes marriage to her; she demurs. In October Lewis quits Stokes and goes to work for $30 a week at pulp magazine *Adventure*, edited by Arthur Sullivant Hoffman, who had earlier employed him at *Transatlantic Tales*.

1913 Continues courtship of Grace Hegger, who likes his humor and ambition, taking her on picnics, explorations of the city, and to the opera, concerts, and plays. Helps form The Adventurers' Club, an informal dinner club made up of contributors to *Adventure*, as well as non-writing professional explorers. Manuscript of *Our Mr. Wrenn* is turned down by Macmillan, Century, and Holt, but on May 6 Harper & Brothers accepts it on the advice of Elizabeth Jordan, who will become his editor. Goes to work in August for Publishers' Newspaper Syndicate at $60 a week, writing book reviews for subscribing newspapers. Moves with Soule and Harrison Smith to 2469 Broadway in October.

1914 February, engagement to marry Grace is announced and *Our Mr. Wrenn* is published to generally favorable reviews; it sells 3,000 copies. Lewis and Grace are married on April 15 in the Ethical Culture Lecture Room. They honeymoon on Chesapeake Bay, then move to bungalow in Port Washington, Long Island; also living there are William Rose Benét and his wife, Theresa Thompson, and Kathleen and Charles Norris. Lewis sells plots to Albert Payson Terhune and writes several chapters for Terhune's serial *Dad*. When Publishers' Syndicate goes out of business in the summer, Lewis goes to work for publisher George H. Doran; earns $75 a week. Takes part in suffragist marches.

1915 Walks the length of Cape Cod with Grace in July, and writes a story at Wellfleet that becomes his first to appear in *The Saturday Evening Post*; it earns him $500. Returns to New York and writes three more stories for the *Post*. Novel *The Trail of the Hawk* is published in September and is widely praised, selling 6,500 copies. With $2,500 in savings and confidence that earning money from magazines will not be difficult, quits Doran in November.

1916 Lewis and Grace visit the Benéts on January 1 in Augusta, Georgia, then continue to St. Augustine, Florida, where they stay six weeks. Writes serial tale *The Innocents*, about an old married couple. Lewis meets William Dean Howells. Goes in March to Chicago to do research on real-estate offices for *The Job* (will do extensive research for his novels for the remainder of his career). Meets Carl Sandburg, and visits Margaret Anderson and others. After they are rejected by *The Saturday Evening Post*, Lewis sells *The Innocents* to *Woman's Home Companion* for $1,000 and "I'm a Stranger Here Myself," a satire of Midwestern tourists, to *Smart Set* for $75. Lewises arrive in Sauk Centre on April 24 for three-month visit; Lewis sees the town from Grace's perspective. Works on *The Job*, novel about an office worker. Buys a Model T Ford and leaves with Grace for a four-month trip to the West. They spend one month in Seattle and visit with Anna Louise Strong, then drive down the coast to Carmel, where they stay two months. Though relations with old friends are strained, Lewis writes four stories, including "Young Man Axelbrod."

1917 Lewises visit Santa Barbara, Los Angeles, San Diego, the Grand Canyon, Sante Fe, and New Orleans before sailing to New York, where they rent an apartment at 309 Fifth Avenue until June. *The Job* published in February to mixed reviews; sells close to 5,000 copies. Lewises sublet a house in Spuyten Duyvil near Alfred Harcourt. On July 26, Grace gives birth by cesarean section to son Wells (named for H. G. Wells). Novel *The Innocents* published in September. Family moves to St. Paul, Minnesota, where they rent a large house at 516 Summit Avenue.

1918 Writes play, *Hobohemia*, adapted from earlier *Saturday Evening Post* story satirizing Greenwich Village. Returns to New York in March. Moves with Grace to Chatham on Cape Cod in May and makes the first of several tries at starting *Main Street*. Becomes depressed and sets it aside to write short stories and four film scenarios, one of which he sells. Goes to New York in July for five weeks. Drives to Minneapolis in October, where he is joined by wife, son, and mother-in-law. They move to 1801 James Avenue South. Lewis finishes two magazine serials, *Free Air* (accepted by *Saturday Evening Post* in January 1919) and *For Sale Cheap*, which is rejected by six magazines.

1919 February, goes to New York for opening of *Hobohemia*; *The New York Times* calls it "preposterous," but it runs for 11 weeks. Rents house at 315 Broad St., Mankato, Minnesota, hometown of Carol Kennicott, the heroine of *Main Street*, in June. Household includes Grace's mother, nurse, and cook. Encourages Harcourt to start his own publishing house (Lewis will invest some of his own money in it). Sells screen rights to *Free Air* for $3,000 and, at Harcourt's urging, expands it to book length. Brings parents to visit in July, and takes them on drive to Elysian, Minnesota, where father's parents are buried. Takes summer tour with Grace to Chicago, through Indiana, Kentucky, Tennessee, Virginia, and Pennsylvania. Visits James Branch Cabell, who reads and comments on an incomplete manuscript of *Main Street*. In September they rent a house in Washington, D.C., at 1814 16th St. N.W. (will later move to 1639 19th St.). *Free Air* is published in October by Harcourt, Brace, & Howe, to mixed reviews, and sells over 8,000 copies.

1920 Rents office on 17th Street and works ten and twelve hours a day on *Main Street*, completing first draft on February 27. Joins Cosmos Club, meets Clarence Darrow, Hendrik Willem Van Loon, Dean Acheson, and Elinor Wylie (urges Harcourt to publish her poetry). Protests suppression of James Branch Cabell's *Jurgen*. In July submits *Main Street* manuscript to Alfred Harcourt, who calls it "the truest book I have ever read" and thinks it might sell 20,000 copies. Spends rest of summer with family at Kennebago Lake in Maine, working on proofs and resting. *Main Street* published October 23 and sells 180,000 copies in just over six months. Receives excellent reviews and letters of praise from F. Scott Fitzgerald, Sherwood Anderson, H. L. Mencken, Upton Sinclair, Willa Cather, Zona Gale, Fannie Hurst, and John Galsworthy.

1921 In January works in New Jersey for two weeks with Harriet Ford and Harvey O'Higgins on stage version of *Main Street*. Goes on lecture tour of Midwest in February. Researches novel about businessman named Pumphrey (later renamed Babbitt). Lectures in April at Town Hall, New York City, and at Princeton University. Learns that Pulitzer Prize jury had chosen *Main Street*, but that they were overruled by Columbia University trustees, who award the prize to Wharton's *The Age of Innocence.* Lewis, wife, son, and mother-in-law sail to England in May. Stepmother dies June 14. Leads busy social life; meets Rebecca West and becomes friends with Frazier "Spike" Hunt, American foreign correspondent for the Hearst papers. Spends July in Mullion, South Cornwall, working on *Babbitt.* Moves into rented house in Bearsted, near Maidstone, Kent, in August. Introduced to George Bernard Shaw by Mary Austin. After two weeks in Paris, where they meet Edith Wharton, Lewises go to Pallanza on Lake Maggiore. Stage version of *Main Street* opens in New York, October 5 (closes December 17). November, Lewis goes to Rome alone and finds rooms in the Grand Hotel de Russie. Grace goes to Florence for a week before joining Lewis in Rome. Infatuated with young American woman, Lewis takes room on opposite side of the hotel from those he reserves for his wife. Quarrels with Grace, who forms friendship with an Italian professor. Sees Edna St. Vincent Millay several times (recommends to Harcourt that they publish her, Evelyn Scott, and Mary Austin). Works on *Babbitt.* Screen rights to *Main Street* sold for $40,000, though Lewis receives under $10,000 because of terms of the contract with play company.

1922 Returns to London in January, leaving Grace in Rome; takes rooms at 10 Bury St., where he finishes first draft of *Babbitt.* Meets many writers and publishers, including Lytton Strachey, Somerset Maugham, and Jonathan Cape (who will become his British publisher). Declines election to National Institute of Arts and Letters. Troubled by skin disease, has a number of epithelioma cauterized. Grace rejoins him in May and after a trip to Glasgow they sail to New York. Met by reporters on arrival, Lewis attacks English culture and writers for their complacency and lack of "pep." Completes work on galleys of *Babbitt* on Long Island. On June 18 attends class reunion at Yale; tells classmates, to their amusement, "When I was in college, you fellows didn't give a damn about me, and I'm here to say that now I don't give a damn about you." July, drives out in his new Cadillac to spend ten days in Sauk Centre. Rents large house at 25 Belknap Road in Hartford, Connecticut, but leaves at once for

Chicago and Elmhurst, Illinois, to meet Eugene Debs, whom he has long admired and envisions as the hero of a novel about the American labor movement. Visits Debs several times with Carl Sandburg. In Chicago, meets with Dr. Morris Fishbein, editor of the *Journal of the American Medical Association*, and Paul De Kruif, a bacteriologist and medical journalist; Lewis gets from them the beginning of the idea for *Arrowsmith*. *Babbitt*, published September 14, receives enthusiastic praise in America and England and sells 141,000 copies by December 31. November, screen and dramatic rights to *Babbitt* sold to Warners for $50,000. December, agrees with Paul De Kruif to split royalties 75-25 percent on novel about bacteriologist. Begins long friendship with Carl Van Doren.

1923 Visits H. L. Mencken in Baltimore in January, then leaves New York with De Kruif for two-month cruise of the Caribbean, stopping in St. Thomas, Barbados, Curacao, Colombia, Panama, Venezuela, and Trinidad before sailing to England. During voyage De Kruif educates Lewis in bacteriology and epidemiology, and together they plan a novel involving an episode of plague on a tropical island. Lewis arrives in London in March and moves into Bury St. flat. De Kruif introduces him to medical researchers and takes him to laboratories. Meets Bertrand Russell. Learns that Cather's *One of Ours* has won Pulitzer Prize (an admirer of Cather's work, Lewis had earlier written Mencken that he found the novel "damnably disappointing"). Grace joins him in May, and they spend a weekend at H. G. Wells' country house. Meets Arnold Bennett at London theater and John Maynard Keynes and Virginia Woolf at dinner at Keynes' house. In July the Lewises take house in France, near Fontainebleau; they see Edith Wharton several times. Lewis finishes first draft of *Arrowsmith* by September. De Kruif reads it and "is wildly enthusiastic," Lewis writes. Travels with Grace in Italy. Sees Fascist parades in Siena, and again in Florence, where Mussolini is present. Returns to London with Grace in November and takes a house at 58 Elm Park Gardens, Chelsea. Revises novel; Harcourt sells serial rights to *The Designer* for $50,000. Campaigns for Bertrand Russell, who is standing for Parliament as Labour candidate for Chelsea.

1924 Lewis argues frequently with Grace and gets drunk more often. Goes with her to Spain in March, then returns to London while Grace goes on by herself to Biarritz. Finishes *Arrowsmith*, returns to New York in May; Grace follows in June, but they remain separated. Writes articles on presidential election for *The Nation*; supports Progessive candidate Senator Robert La Follette. Visits Sauk Centre in June, then sets out on canoe trip in Saskatchewan wilderness with brother Claude as part of annual expedition of the Canadian Department of Indian Affairs; quits it after six weeks. In September De Kruif requests line on title page or next page giving notice of his collaboration on *Arrowsmith*; Lewis instead drafts acknowledgment of his debt to De Kruif for his help, which De Kruif accepts, though friendship ends. Advises Walter White, assistant secretary of the NAACP, on his novel *The Fire in the Flint*. Lewises sail in October for England.

1925 *Arrowsmith* published March 5 and is widely praised as Lewis's best book. Lewis travels with Grace on the French and Italian Riviera, then goes on to Austria and Germany, researching novel about a retired American industrialist touring Europe. Writes Harcourt (referring to *Arrowsmith* by its hero's first name), "Any thoughts on pulling wires for *Martin* for Nobel Prize?" Leaves wife and son in Paris and goes to London, staying in Bury St. flat, then returns to America with them in late May. Rents country house in Katonah, N.Y. Sees family in Sauk Centre and St. Cloud on trip to Midwest, and visits with Dr. Fishbein and Carl Sandburg in Chicago. Returns to Katonah and starts *Mantrap*, short novel based on Saskatchewan trip. Sells Famous Players–Paramount Company scenario of a film on 300th anniversary of New York City for $10,000. (Father comments: "It is certainly marvelous how such a bundle of nerves can pull in the money.") Finishes first draft of *Mantrap* in late August. After summer of friction, leaves Grace and moves to the Great Northern Hotel in New York City. Hires Louis Florey as secretary. Writes Grace that because of her "bullying" and "bossing," and because she wanted a "settled life with intelligent but definitely respectable neighbors," and he wanted an "unsettled life with unrespectable neighbors," they must separate for an indefinite time. *Collier's* buy serial rights to *Mantrap* in October for

$42,500. Lewis goes to the Hotel Frascati in Bermuda with Florey and writes a play. Grace takes apartment in New York. Lewis returns to New York to the Shelton Hotel in December.

1926 Travels in January to Kansas City, where he meets with William Stidger, a conservative clergyman, and with the Rev. L. M. Birkhead, an agnostic Unitarian, as part of his research for a novel about a minister. Visits Mary Austin in Santa Fe before leaving for California in February. Buys car and hires secretary in San Francisco (fires him after a few weeks). Visits with George Sterling. Hears evangelist Aimee Semple McPherson preach in Los Angeles. Meets Ramon Guthrie (who later becomes close friend) in Tucson. Grace joins him there for tour through Arizona and New Mexico. After return to Kansas City, Grace finds him an apartment and then goes back to New York. Lewis visits churches and speaks from pulpits himself; on one occasion, he attacks the idea of a vindictive God who strikes down agnostics, then takes out a watch and notes after 15 minutes that he is still standing (press reports that Lewis had dared God to strike him dead). Meets for lunch every Wednesday with 15 clergymen, including a Roman Catholic priest and a rabbi. Refuses Pulitzer Prize for *Arrowsmith*, arguing that it should be awarded on literary merit and objecting to the official terms of the prize, which state that it is to be given to the American novel that best presents "the wholesome atmosphere of American life, and the highest standards of American manners and manhood." Leaves Kansas City in mid-May to spend summer with Birkhead family on Lake Pelican in Pequot, Minnesota, working on *Elmer Gantry*. Makes trips to Indiana to visit Eugene Debs, and to New York to see Grace before she goes to Switzerland and Austria for the summer. *Mantrap*, with film rights sold for $50,000, is published on June 3, to mild reviews. Father dies August 29; Lewis goes to Sauk Centre for the funeral. Falls in love with Maude Child, estranged wife of Richard Child, a writer and former ambassador to Italy. Grace returns from Europe in September, and after taking Wells to a school in Deerfield, Massachusetts, they take a house at 3028 Q St., N.W., in Washington, D.C. Works steadily on *Elmer Gantry*, using room in Hotel Lafayette as office. Marriage deteriorates; Lewis drinks heavily after Child rejects him.

Accepts invitation in late November from old friend Charles Breasted to stay with him at the Grosvenor in New York. Hands novel in to publisher and returns to Washington on Christmas Eve to be with Wells and nephew Freeman. Leaves Washington on December 27 and returns to New York. Drinking heavily and exhausted after finishing novel, is persuaded by Harcourt to recover at Bill Brown's Training Camp on the Hudson.

1927 Corrects proofs, goes to parties, sees old friends, then enters a sanitarium for three days in late January. Convinces Earl Blackman, a young Presbyterian clergyman he had befriended in Kansas City, to accompany him to Europe. Visits London, Paris, Zurich, and northern Italy. *Elmer Gantry* is published on March 10 in first printing of 138,000 copies. Harcourt cables Lewis: "Reviews violent either way. Clergy hot." (Evangelist Billy Sunday denounces Lewis as "Satan's cohort.") Lewis travels with Ramon Guthrie to Venice, then goes on alone to Dubrovnik, Corfu, Athens, Vienna, and Munich. Returns to Paris, drinks heavily, then begs Guthrie to accompany him on walking trip in Alsace. Goes to Berlin and is introduced by H. R. Knickerbocker, Hearst reporter, to foreign correspondent Dorothy Thompson on July 8; proposes marriage to her on July 9 at party for her 33rd birthday, and repeats the proposal each time he sees her. Travels with her on assignment to Vienna, flying in an airplane for the first time, and then with her to England for a month's walking trip. Continues walking with the Guthries in the Rhineland. Settles in Berlin and starts *Dodsworth*, then sets it aside. Quickly writes *The Man Who Knew Coolidge*. Goes to Paris in October to consult with Melville Cane, his New York lawyer, about obtaining a divorce (Lewis will give $50,000 to a trust fund for Wells and $50,000 to Grace). Meets Ernest Hemingway in Berlin in November. Joins Dorothy Thompson in Moscow, where she is covering the tenth anniversary of the Bolshevik revolution.

1928 Dorothy Thompson resigns her position as Berlin correspondent for the New York *Evening Post*. In March, she and Lewis take villa, where Gorky had once lived, in Posillipo, outside Naples. *The Man Who Knew Coolidge*, published on April 5, receives dismal reviews and sells poorly. On April 16, Grace is granted a divorce in Reno, Nevada. Lewis and Dorothy are married on May 14 in a civil ceremony at St. Martin's Registry Office, and immediately afterward in a Church of England ceremony with invited guests at the Savoy Chapel, London. They take three-month honeymoon, traveling through England in car and trailer, and on foot. Dramatization of *Elmer Gantry* by Patrick Kearney opens in New York August 9; Lewises return to the United States in time to see performance before it closes on September 15. They buy 300-acre farm near Barnard, Vermont, with two houses ("Twin Farms"), and spend peaceful autumn there. Visitors include son Wells and young journalist friend Vincent Sheean. In November they move to New York apartment at 37 W. 10th St.

1929 Exhausted and drinking heavily after finishing *Dodsworth*, Lewis takes Dorothy to Florida in mid-February. Begins writing monthly series of stories for *Cosmopolitan*. *Dodsworth* published on March 14 to mixed reviews. Lewis remains in Florida until the end of March. Returns to Vermont with Dorothy in May. Lewis enlists Marxian theorist Ben Stolberg and other advisers to help with the labor novel, but is dissatisfied with their theoretical approach. Gives drunken speech at Bread Loaf Writers' Conference at Middlebury, Vermont. Goes to Marion, North Carolina, in early October to report on textile-mill strike for Scripps-Howard papers, then travels to Toronto to report on American Federation of Labor conference for United Press. Meets and hires Carl Haessler, labor news reporter, for $150 a week to advise him on labor novel, and plans to go back to version with Debs as hero. Together they visit factories and attend labor meetings in Boston, New Jersey, Pennsylvania, and Washington, D.C. Lewis is disappointed by weak state of organized labor.

1930 Unable to continue work on novel, terminates contract with Haessler. En route to California, stops in Reno, Nevada, and successfully petitions to reduce alimony to Grace from $1,000 to $200 a month until his income increases. Rents house in Monterey, California, for two months. Talks with Lincoln Steffens and Tom Mooney (labor agitator imprisoned in San Quentin for 1916 bombing) about the labor novel, but his interest in it again wanes. Dorothy, who is pregnant, is unhappy in Monterey and returns to New York. Lewis drinks heavily. Returns to New York and Vermont in April. Argues with Harcourt about Harcourt's resistance to publishing a uniform edition of Lewis's works and considers changing publishers. Son Michael born in New York on June 20. The family settles at Twin Farms; Lewis, unable to bear the noise and crying, moves baby and nurse to the smaller farmhouse. Son Wells, soon to enter Phillips Academy at Andover, spends summer at Twin Farms. Lewises take journalist Franklin P. Adams's house in Westport, Connecticut, in October for the winter. Learns on November 5 that he has become the first American to be awarded the Nobel Prize for literature. Has face cleared of epithelioma by electric needles, then sails with Dorothy for Stockholm. Receives the prize on December 10, and two days later delivers address on the atrophied gentility of "official" academic American culture while praising writers such as Dreiser, Cather, Sherwood Anderson, and Eugene O'Neill. Receives extended applause. Newspapers in America print garbled version of address, and it is widely attacked; New York *Herald Tribune* writes of Lewis's "hour of awful nakedness in Stockholm." Calvin Coolidge says, "No necessity exists for becoming excited." Lewises go to Berlin where Dorothy is rushed to hospital on December 25 with ruptured appendix.

1931 After ten days' rest together in the Thuringian mountains in Germany, Lewis leaves Dorothy in Berlin and goes to Bury St. flat in London. Breaks with Alfred Harcourt, feeling, in addition to earlier problems, that the publisher did not support him sufficiently during the controversy over his Nobel Prize speech and did not use the publicity to sell more of his books. Depressed about death of closest English friend, C. B. Thomson (killed in the 1930 crash of the airship R101), and break with Harcourt. Meets Thomas Wolfe, whom he had earlier publicly praised, and gets drunk with him. Sails with Dorothy to New York at the end of February and goes directly to Westport. At dinner at New York Metropolitan Club on March 19, Lewis accuses Dreiser of having "stolen three thousand words" from his wife's book on Russia; Dreiser slaps Lewis twice. Incident is reported—sympathetically toward Dreiser—in papers across the United States. A few days later, in lecture delivered in Toledo, Ohio, Lewis praises Dreiser's work. After receiving offers from numerous publishers, Lewis signs with Doubleday, Doran in return for a $30,000 advance and the promise of extensive advertising. En route to Vermont in May, Lewis and Harrison Smith, drunk and dressed in country clothes, stop at Yale, where Lewis tries to present his Nobel medal to university, but he becomes enraged when a young library assistant doubts his identity and declines to accept it. Spends summer in Vermont; visitors include son Wells, H. L. Mencken and his wife, Sara Haardt, Phil and Lily Goodman, and Christian Gauss of Princeton. Grace publishes *Half a Loaf,* novel inspired by her marriage to Lewis. Lewises moves to 21 E. 90th St. in New York. Dorothy goes to Europe in November, interviews Hitler, and returns home for Christmas. Lewis enjoys film of *Arrowsmith,* starring Ronald Colman and Helen Hayes. Works on novel *Ann Vickers.*

1932 Spends most of January at Twin Farms. Dorothy returns to Europe in March. Lewis, drinking heavily, goes to stay with friends in East Setauket, Long Island. Fearful that Dorothy is abandoning him, sails for Europe on April 15. After he promises to stop drinking they are reconciled and return to New York together on May 26. Works with Sidney Howard in Vermont on stage version of *Dodsworth.* After Yale prepares library exhibition of his works, gives Nobel medal to university and attends 25th class reunion. Takes two rooms at 66 Park Avenue in August, where with help from secretary-stenographer Louis Florey he finishes *Ann Vickers* (serialized August to November in *Redbook*). Lewises sail for Europe with Michael on the *Europa* August 24. Rent villa in Semmering, Austria, two hours away from Vienna; Lewis travels alone to Germany and Italy. Takes small apartment as office in Vienna. Gives huge Christmas party that lasts ten days; Dorothy falls in love with one of the guests, Christa Winsloe, author of *Mädchen in Uniform.*

1933 *Ann Vickers,* published on January 25, is reviewed favorably and eventually sells 133,000 copies. Lewis destroys furniture in Vienna apartment while drunk. Goes to London in early February, where he sees his new publisher, Nelson Doubleday. Dorothy goes to Munich and

Portofino with Christa Winsloe. Lewis returns to New York on February 25 and takes large penthouse apartment at the Hotel New Yorker. Rehires Florey as secretary. Grace Hegger Lewis marries longtime suitor, Telesforo Casanova. Lewis travels to California with Florey in late March, studying management of hotels on way in preparation for new novel, *Work of Art*. Returns to Twin Farms in late April; Dorothy joins him there on May 15, accompanied by Christa Winsloe. Lewis buys large house at 17 Wood End Lane in Bronxville, N.Y. Turns in novel and makes two trips to Chicago with Florey, during which he collaborates with Lloyd Lewis (no relation) on a play, *Jayhawker*, about the Kansas-Missouri border raids before and during the Civil War. Learns from his German publisher Ernst Rowohlt that German booksellers have stopped selling his books because Klaus Mann had included his name on the masthead of an anti-Nazi periodical. Lewis responds that Mann had acted without his permission, but asks that his books no longer be published in Germany as protest against Nazi censorship.

1934 Drinks heavily. *Work of Art* published; it receives poor reviews and sells 50,000 copies. Attends rehearsals of play *Dodsworth*, which opens on February 24, starring Walter Huston and Fay Bainter, and is very successful. Goes to Bermuda in mid-February to rewrite *Jayhawker*. Dorothy goes to Europe in early summer. Lewis travels to the Midwest with Florey and sees brother Claude; together they visit brother Fred and Sauk Centre. Returns to Vermont, where Carl Van Doren comes to keep him company. Takes rooms at the Berkshire Hotel in New York in August for rehearsals of *Jayhawker*. Dorothy becomes first American writer expelled from Germany by the Nazi regime. *Jayhawker* opens in New York on November 5 and closes on November 24. Late in November, Dorothy writes him during her lecture tour: "more and more your life becomes nothing at all except work and drinking and—recovering from drinking."

1935 In January Lewis is again invited to join the National Institute of Arts and Letters; writes he is "delighted to accept." Puts together a collection of short stories (published in June, *Selected Short Stories* sells only 3,308 copies). Lewises visit Wells in Boston and then go to Falmouth,

Jamaica, in February; Lewis drinks heavily, flirts with another woman, argues with Dorothy, and leaves in a rage for another part of the island. In a few days asks her to join him; she writes, "Why do you think you have to go on surpassing yourself? And mourning your lost youth?" Returns to Dorothy and Michael in Falmouth, where they remain until they go back to Bronxville at the end of March. In May, starts a new novel about the threat of fascism in the United States. Works on it steadily for long hours, seven days a week, and completes it early in August. Begins drinking heavily again; completes proofreading with help of nephew Freeman. Sails for Europe with Dorothy on August 31; they return separately after six weeks. Lewis, still drinking heavily, enters hospital on return. *It Can't Happen Here* is published October 21 and sells 94,000 copies (sales eventually reach 320,000). Attends dinner given in his honor by the left-wing League of American Writers; after hearing his novel repeatedly praised on political grounds, he criticizes its literary merit and asks guests to sing "Stand Up, Stand Up, for Jesus." A Dartmouth undergraduate and student of Ramon Guthrie, Budd Schulberg, invites Lewis to speak to leftist students, who bait him for lacking firm political commitments; he shouts, "You young sons of bitches can all go to hell," and walks out. Gives large dinner party for H. G. Wells when he lectures in America. Film rights to *It Can't Happen Here* sold to Metro-Goldwyn-Mayer.

1936 Lewis weeps when he learns on January 18 of the death of Rudyard Kipling. During this year, makes continued effort—with several lapses—to stop drinking. Dorothy begins writing column "On the Record" for the New York *Herald Tribune*, becoming the first woman commentator on public affairs for a major newspaper. Lewises go to Washington, D.C., for six weeks. Metro-Goldwyn-Mayer abandons *It Can't Happen Here*; Lewis believes studio fears its films will be banned in Germany and Italy and calls move a blow to free expression. Sails with Florey for Bermuda on March 1 without telling Dorothy, intending to write a play about anti-Semitism. Meets James Thurber in Bermuda. (Thurber later writes: "You couldn't always tell at seven in the morning whether he was having his first drink of the day or his last one of the night.") Goes to Vermont in April. Tours factories in May with Ramon

Guthrie in unsuccessful attempt to revive his labor novel. Awarded honorary degree by Yale in June. Dorothy returns to New York to prepare coverage of the national political conventions, rejoining him at Twin Farms later in the summer. Wells spends the summer with him. Dorothy's success increases marital tension. At the invitation of the Federal Theatre Project of the Works Progress Administration, collaborates with screenwriter J. C. Moffitt on play based on *It Can't Happen Here.* Moves into Essex House during rehearsals and participates in casting and staging of New York production. Quarrels with Moffitt. Play opens simultaneously in 18 cities on October 27, playing before packed theaters. Dorothy goes to Europe. Again drinking heavily, Lewis enters rest home in the Catskills.

1937 Continues to try to write play on anti-Semitism. Spends time with playwright S. N. Behrman and Lawrence Langner, head of the Theatre Guild. Begins work on short anticommunist novel, *The Prodigal Parents.* Leaves Bronxville on April 28; tells Dorothy their marriage is over. When Dorothy hears that Lewis and Florey have disappeared from New York, she tracks them down in an inn in Old Lyme, Connecticut, and finds Lewis in the throes of delirium tremens, with three broken ribs from a fall. She takes him to the Austen Riggs Center, in Stockbridge, Massachusetts, and fires Florey. Lewis stops drinking, rents house in Stockbridge, and finishes *The Prodigal Parents.* Hires John Hersey, a recent Yale graduate, as his secretary. Works on *Publish Glad Tidings*, a play about communism in Kronland, an imaginary Balkan country (is unable to find producer for it). Elected to the American Academy of Arts and Letters. Returns to New York in the autumn and moves into an apartment at the Wyndham, 42 W. 58th St.; begins writing another play. In October, starts writing "Book Week" column for *Newsweek*, lets Hersey go, and begins a countrywide lecture tour (lasts through February 1938).

1938 *The Prodigal Parents*, published January 19, receives bad reviews and sells 50,000 copies (eventually will sell nearly 100,000). Struggles for months with play *Queenie and the Jopes*, but is unable to get it produced. Donates working notes, manuscripts, and proofs of novels, as well as letters, to Yale in May. Persuaded to play Doremus Jessup in a summer-stock production of *It Can't Happen Here*, takes house for the summer in Cohasset, Massachusetts; house guests include Wells, who is working on a novel. Lewis enjoys learning to act; courts young actresses unsuccessfully. Told that son Michael is very ill with pneumonia, goes to Twin Farms and stays until crisis has passed. Production opens August 22 to a sell-out audience and is held over an extra week. Returns to New York and takes rooms in the Plaza Hotel. Writes, with help from actress Fay Wray, play *Angela Is Twenty-Two*. Reads and is pleased with Wells's novel (published as *They Still Say No* in 1939). Moves to apartment in the Lombardy on East 56th St. in October. Joins Actors Equity, with Helen Hayes as sponsor. Directs and stars in *Angela*, playing a widower his own age who marries a very young woman. Production opens in Columbus, Ohio, on December 30.

1939 Finds role too exhausting and drops out of production on January 23 (play closes in Chicago April 1 after successfully touring more than 20 cities). Goes to Hollywood to write screen adaptation of *Angela*. Stays at the Beverly Hills Hotel for a month. Asks Dorothy to divorce him; she responds that while she will not oppose a divorce, it is up to him to obtain one. Starts new novel, *Bethel Merriday*, about theater life. Returns to New York in May. Spends two weeks at Twin Farms. Plays the stage manager in production of Thornton Wilder's *Our Town* in Ogunquit, Maine, August 7–12. Goes to Provincetown, August 13, to take the role of Nat Miller in Eugene O'Neill's *Ah, Wilderness!* and is assigned an 18-year-old apprentice, Rosemary Marcella Powers, to cue him as he learns his lines. (Powers' father had died when she was nine; her mother, Katherine, supported the family by taking in boarders. After graduating from high school in South Orange, New Jersey, she had worked in a series of small stock companies.) Lewis advises her to use name Marcella and spends week constantly in her company. Leaves for Clinton, Connecticut, to repeat role in *Our Town*, then meets Marcella for weekend in Boston before taking her to Skowhegan, Maine, where he is scheduled to act in *Angela Is Twenty-Two*. Returns to New York and rents separate apartment for Marcella in the Lombardy. Introduces her to his friends as his niece. She is kind to him and impressed by his friends. Finishes *Bethel Merriday* and leaves with Marcella on October 22 for a long vacation. Goes to Florida by train, buys a Buick convertible in Jacksonville, and drives to St. Augustine, then to the Gulf Coast and New Orleans, where they stay at 1536 Nashville Avenue for two months. Hires Joseph Hardrick as cook, chauffeur, and valet.

1940 In New Orleans acts with Marcella in Paul Vincent Carroll's *Shadow and Substance*, taking the role of Canon Skerritt while Marcella plays Brigid, the servant. Goes to California and rents house at 724 North Linden Drive in Beverly Hills where he writes play *Felicia Speaking* (never produced). *Bethel Merriday* published on March 22 and sells only 30,000 copies. Alexander Korda buys the film rights for $50,000 (never produces it). Michael, who has been attending a small boarding school in Arizona, comes with his nurse to visit. Returns to the Northeast to act with Marcella in seven summer-stock theaters. Accepts invitation to teach at the University of Iowa and is angry when the Iowa State Board of Education withdraws offer (grounds are that he is a drunkard, though he is still not drinking). Unhappy with Doubleday, Lewis changes publishers when his friend and editor Harry Maule moves to Random House. Still interested in teaching, drives west with Hardrick and arranges appointment at the University of Wisconsin with "no pay, no tenure, and no official rank." Rents large house at 1712 Summit Avenue, Madison; Marcella comes for a two-week visit. Lewis quits after five classes and returns to New York, taking penthouse apartment in the Middletowne on E. 48th St., where Marcella has a small apartment. En route to Cuba in December for vacation with Marcella, meets Ernest Hemingway and his wife, journalist Martha Gellhorn, in Key West and travels with them to Cuba.

1941 After a brief trip back to New York, drives to Miami to act in *Angela Is Twenty-Two*. Leaves at the end of the production in a jealous rage over Marcella's interest in other men and drives to St. Augustine, where he sees James Branch Cabell. Drinking again, Lewis returns to New York and shatters furniture, including his beloved Capehart record player; the hotel management wants to throw him out of apartment and calls his friend Dr. Cornelius

Traeger, who calls Dorothy. Together with two male nurses, they take him to Doctors Hospital in a strait jacket. Recovers and forgives Marcella, resuming his patronage and now urging her to see men her age. Lewis hires James S. Hart to do research on philanthropic and propaganda organizations for a projected novel (*Gideon Planish*), and renews friendship with the Rev. Birkhead, now in New York as director of Friends of Democracy. Becomes one of four judges of the Readers Club, which is responsible for the monthly republication of a book that had not received proper attention on its first appearance. Duties also include writing prefaces (Lewis will write eight in two years). Recommends, among others, that works by Ramon Guthrie and Edith Summers Kelley and Hemingway's *The Sun Also Rises* be published. Rents country house in Lakeville, Connecticut, in May and entertains a stream of visitors before leaving to act and direct in summer stock in Stony Creek, Connecticut. Puts up the money to produce, and directs Marcella in *The Good Neighbor* by Jack T. Levin. Play opens on Broadway October 21; critics agree that it is "immensely dull," and it closes after one night. Joins America First Committee in opposition to American entry in World War II (Dorothy Thompson is a leading advocate of American aid to Britain). Goes on extensive cross-country debating tour with old acquaintance Rabbi Lewis Browne; topics include "Has the Modern Woman Made Good?" "The Country Versus the City," and "Can Fascism Happen Here?" Dorothy files for divorce in Vermont on November 12 (decree granted January 2, 1942). Lewis is in Cleveland when Japan attacks Pearl Harbor on December 7.

1942 Wartime blackouts prevent debates in San Diego and San Francisco. Holds last debate with Browne in Portland, Oregon, and then goes to Minneapolis. Returns to New York for two months, takes Marcella to plays, and has "face operation" at the end of March. Takes a house on Lake Minnetonka west of Minneapolis and starts writing *Gideon Planish*. Dismisses Hart. Marcella and her mother visit. Takes excursions into the country, including graveyard in Elysian where his grandparents are buried; visits Sauk Centre and takes camping trip with Michael to Hungry Jack Lake, near the Canadian border. Starts writing short stories for *Cosmopolitan*. Rents large house at

1500 Mount Curve Avenue in Minneapolis; briefly visits Wells, now an army second lieutenant stationed at Camp Sheridan, in Chicago. Teaches writing at the University of Minnesota in Minneapolis. Enjoys teaching, works on his novel, has open-house parties for students on Sundays and does not drink. Leaves for New York December 10 to deliver novel to Random House, where he works with his new editor, Saxe Commins.

1943 Writes short stories, one of which, "Green Eyes: A Handbook of Jealousy," is bought for a film to star Ann Sheridan. *Gideon Planish* is published April 19; reviews are mixed. Trade sales are 50,000 copies (eventually sells nearly 100,000). Rents a huge duplex at 300 Central Park West, gets Marcella to furnish it, and rewards her with a mink coat. Takes up chess. Leaves for Minnesota with Hardrick on May 11, but soon returns to New York and then goes to Williamstown, Massachusetts. Dorothy Thompson announces her engagement to the painter Maxim Kopf on June 13. Lewis goes to Hollywood on June 23 to collaborate with Dore Schary on scenario for anti-Nazi film *Storm in the West* (never produced). Takes rooms at the Chateau Marmont on Sunset Boulevard. Makes many friends in the film world, including Katharine Hepburn (whose parents had been friends during his stay in Hartford in 1922) and Spencer Tracy. Becomes unhappy with the "taboos" in Hollywood: "all really stirring issues, political, racial, biological, must be sidestepped or not even approached." Returns to New York on September 7, and on October 4 begins two-month debating tour with Rabbi Lewis Browne. Sees Michael twice. Learns that Wells has been awarded the Silver Star for bravery in Sicily.

1944 Now vice-president of the National Institute of Arts and Letters, urges American Academy to give its Award of Merit Medal to Dreiser and writes the letter that will accompany it. Writes short stories for *Cosmopolitan*, then an essay for *Good Housekeeping* on an obsession of his, "There's No Excuse for Lateness." Helps get Marcella minor editorial job at *Good Housekeeping* when she gives up stage career. Angered by attack on the alleged anti-Americanism of 1920s writers in Bernard DeVoto's *The Literary Fallacy*, writes reply, "Fools, Liars, and Mr. DeVoto," which appears in *Saturday Review* on April 15. *This Is the Life*, film version of *Angela Is Twenty-Two*, released; *The New York Times* calls it "a nice winsome, unpretentious show." Lewis leaves for Minneapolis on May 5. Begins research for novel with a judge as hero. Rents a large house in Duluth at 2601 E. Second St., with five bedrooms and a bowling alley in the basement. Becomes close friends with circuit judge Mark Nolan. Lewis attends his court every morning, and follows him on the circuit, driven by Asa ("Ace") Lyons, the owner of a local taxi fleet (Hardrick is in the army). Marcella and her mother visit Duluth in late July; Lewis sets up social engagements for them with the help of novelist Margaret Culkin Banning, but then castigates his Duluth friends for condescending to them. Returns to New York duplex on August 28. Helps with doctors and a lawyer when Carl Van Doren is hospitalized (his brother Mark Van Doren writes, "He was pure, simple, blazing goodness and affection"). Lieutenant Wells Lewis is killed by a German sniper in Alsace on October 29; Lewis learns of his son's death in Chicago on November 14, where he is on another debating tour with Rabbi Browne. In late November, Lewis seconds Bernard DeVoto for membership in National Institute of Arts and Letters. Sees Michael, now attending the Valley Forge Military School, during Christmas holidays.

1945 On January 1 buys Duluth house (which had cost $100,000 to build) for $15,000, as well as three neighboring lots. Buys seven landscapes by Childe Hassam. Works with Saxe Commins on completion of novel about Minnesota judge, *Cass Timberlane*. Begins writing a monthly literary essay for *Esquire* (first piece appears in June, series continues for seven months) and plans a novel on the consequences of a white man discovering that he is 1/32 black. Sets Marcella up as a literary agent. Leaves for Duluth with Lyons on April 20, preceded by Katherine Powers, who will act as housekeeper. Has regular discussions at his home with several Duluth African-Americans as part of research for *Kingsblood Royal*; occasionally invites them, along with his white friends, to his parties. Lectures at nearby colleges. Michael visits for five days in late June. Returns to New York in September. Checks into the Algonquin and enters hospital for another "face operation." *Cass Timberlane* published on October 3 (it will sell 1,140,000 copies, and with serial, film, book club, and royalty income, will earn Lewis nearly $600,000). Driven by Lyons, tours South in November for research on southern black life. Returns to Duluth on December 9; Marcella visits for Christmas holidays.

1946 Joseph Hardrick returns from army. Lewis goes to Minneapolis January 9 to do research at Urban League and in city's black community. Learns of the death of brother Fred from a heart attack on January 15, and goes to Sauk Centre for funeral. (Writes to a friend on January 20 that, because his brother was so much older and different from him, "the only sad thing about it to me was the thought of how many amusing things and pleasant places he has missed in his life . . . Sauk Centre seemed so small.") Sells Duluth house to a bank president for $20,000, staying on for two months to work on *Kingsblood Royal.* Drives east with Lyons on March 21. In April, rents Thorvale Farm, a spacious house on 750 acres of land with a view of Mount Greylock, near Williamstown, Massachusetts (will later buy it for $45,000 and spend $70,000 refurbishing it, purchasing latest farm equipment, rebuilding swimming pool, and acquiring archery set, tennis equipment, and fishing and hunting gear). Hires Alma and Wilson Perkins, friends of Hardrick, as servants. Unsuccessfully tries to get teaching position at Williams College. Writes draft of *Kingsblood Royal* in five weeks. Briefly employs Russell Lembke as secretary. Receives many house guests from New York, including George Jean Nathan, Carl Van Doren, Louis Untermeyer, the Bennett Cerfs, and the Harry Maules. Commins arrives in late September to go over novel line-by-line. Marcella visits occasionally. In the autumn Lewis is shocked when Marcella announces her intention to marry young writer Michael Amrine, but does not object and tells her to come back to him if the marriage fails. Turns again for a short time to the labor-novel idea. Accepts invitation in late December to go to Hollywood.

1947 Taking Hardrick with him, arrives in Los Angeles mid-January and checks into the Ambassador Beach Club in Santa Monica. Works with director Leo McCarey on screenplay, *Adam and Eve*, after writer St. Clair McKelway abandons it, then quarrels with McCarey and quits. Works on play, *The Responsible Man*, using labor theme (never produced). Learns that Marcella will definitely marry Michael Amrine. Moves to Santa Barbara in February for six weeks. Writes Marcella in March: "I send you every most affectionate, admiring, and earnest hope for your great happiness. . . . To have known you is the one distinguished event of my life." As agent, she introduces him to a young writer, Barnaby Conrad, and Lewis invites him to come to Williamstown as his secretary. Renews friendship with Alfred Harcourt, now living with his wife, Ellen Eayrs, in Santa Barbara. Returns to New York and then Thorvale Farm in April. *Kingsblood Royal*, published the first week of May, is a Literary Guild selection and eventually sells nearly 1,500,000 copies; receives sharply divided reviews. Lewis attends his 40th reunion at Yale. Receives many house guests at Thorvale Farm. At first enjoys Conrad's company, but then lets him go early in September. Now planning a novel on early years of Minnesota, goes to Minneapolis and hires graduate student James Roers to help with the research. Drives with Hardrick to Sauk Centre (his last visit). Returns to Thorvale Farm in November. Roers arrives on December 9; Lewis soon finds him irritating and sends him to New York (will pay him $250 a month until Roers returns to graduate school in March 1948). Film of *Cass Timberlane*, starring Spencer Tracy and Lana Turner, is a success.

1948 Goes to New York in January to persuade Katherine Powers to join him in Williamstown. Takes her with him on walks and trips to Maine and Quebec. Visitors include F. P. Adams, the Cerfs, Daniel Aaron, and Norman Mailer. Lewis works intensely on Minnesota historical novel, *The God-Seeker*. Goes in early August to Peterborough, New Hampshire, and is delighted with his son Michael's performance in summer stock. Redraws his will, leaving half his estate to Michael, dividing a quarter among Marcella Powers Amrine, agent Edith Haggard, Carl Van Doren, and Joseph Hardrick, and reserving income from a quarter for Katherine Powers during her lifetime. Takes manuscript of *The God-Seeker* to New York in September, then returns to Williamstown. Claude and Mary visit. Sails for Italy on October 19 with Katherine Powers on the *Saturnia*. Hardrick misplaces two of her bags, and though they are eventually found, Lewis fires, and disinherits, him.

Hires car and driver and sees sights in Naples, Pompeii, and Capri. Takes suite in Ambassador Hotel in Rome. Writes articles on Italy for the Bell Syndicate. Travels by train to Florence on December 15 and takes rooms in the Excelsior.

1949 Finishes newspaper assignment. Changes English publisher after Jonathan Cape criticizes *The God-Seeker* (Cape had also not liked *Kingsblood Royal*); arranges with old friend A. S. Frere for Heinemann to become his publisher. Resumes drinking. Introduced by a friend to Bernard Berenson at his villa, I Tatti; they become friends, continually playing word games. With car and driver, tours Umbria, the Marches, Veneto, and the northern lakes with Katherine Powers. Begins novel *Over the Body of Lucy Jade* in Assisi on March 3. *The God-Seeker*, final reworking of themes from the labor novel and from *The Fathers*, is published in New York on March 4 to unfavorable notices and sells only 30,000 copies. Arrives in Venice and takes rooms at the Gritti Palace; encounters Hemingway and his fourth wife, former journalist Mary Welsh, and spends some time with them. (In his novel *Across the River and Into the Trees*, published in 1950, Hemingway describes a character, identifiable as Lewis, who suffers from a grotesque skin condition and whose appearance is compared to that of Nazi propaganda minister Joseph Goebbels.) Tours the Italian Riviera in late April, then returns to America, drinking heavily. Goes to Thorvale Farms and convinces Katherine Powers to join him there. Shortly after her arrival, Lewis comes down with pneumonia. During illness, Claude visits and Lewis persuades him to accompany him to Italy in the autumn. Studies Italian. At the end of May, goes to New York with Claude and puts house on the market for $75,000. Finishes *Lucy Jade* in July; Bennett Cerf criticizes it and Herbert Mayes of *Cosmopolitan* rejects it. Drinks heavily, develops delirium tremens, and is treated with sedatives at direction of Dr. Traeger. Receives welcome visit from old friend Vincent Sheean, who drives up with Michael from Twin Farms. Sails with Claude to Italy September 7 on the *Nieuw Amsterdam*. Befriends Harvard professor Perry Miller during voyage. Tours England with Claude, then visits the Millers in Holland. Lewis goes on to Bellagio on

Lake Como and then to Venice, Ravenna, and Assisi, where, drinking alone in his hotel, he meets travel agency clerk Alexander Manson, a former sergeant-major in the British army. Hires Manson as secretary-companion. Rents Villa La Costa, at 124 Via del Pian' dei Giullari, a large villa built in 1939 by a Fascist official. Becomes friends with Lady Una Troubridge (the inspiration for the heroine of Radcliffe Hall's *The Well of Loneliness*). Takes long drives with her through the countryside in a Studebaker he has bought. Sees Berenson only rarely. Works on *World So Wide*, new version of *Lucy Jade*. Continues to drink heavily. Has heart attack in December. Una Troubridge calls in Dr. Vincenzo Lapiccirella, a leading cardiologist.

1950 Sees Dr. Lapiccirella regularly; he urges Lewis to stop drinking. Manages to limit drinking to wine; continues smoking. Sees a dermatologist who diagnoses his skin condition as *acne necrotica seborrhoeica* and prescribes treatment that is temporarily effective. Works intensively on *World So Wide* and starts to write poetry. Finishes the novel in April (published March 1951). Learns in early May that old friend William Rose Benét has died of a heart attack. Travels with Manson and his wife, Tina Lazzerini, in northern Italy and France before going to Zurich, where he stays for July and August. Learns in July that closest friend Carl Van Doren has died of a heart attack. Suffers two heart attacks himself. Visited by Williamstown friend Ida Kay, tells her that he will not return to America. Goes back to Italy and responds to medical treatment in Turin. Gives up plans for trip to Sicily and goes to Rome, where Manson finds a large apartment for him overlooking the Tiber. Suffers from bronchial pneumonia. Becomes totally dependent on Manson; visitors suspect Lewis is being given narcotics. Michael comes to see him for Christmas, but arrives late for dinner, and is told by Manson that Lewis is angry and wants Michael to return to London; they see each other only to say good-bye. Grows feverish and delirious on morning of December 31. Doctor is summoned and diagnoses Lewis as suffering from "acute delirium tremens"; he is taken in the evening to the Clinica Electra, a hospital specializing in psychiatric and nervous disorders.

1951 Suffers heart attack on January 9. Dies at 7:40 A.M., January 10. Body is cremated and the ashes sent to Minnesota. The funeral ceremony is held at Sauk Centre High School on January 28, and then, with the temperature at −22°, Claude pours ashes into a hole two feet square in the Lewis family plot.

Note on the Texts

This volume contains three novels by Sinclair Lewis: *Arrowsmith* (1925), *Elmer Gantry* (1927), and *Dodsworth* (1929). The texts printed here are taken from the first American editions.

Lewis began working on *Arrowsmith* in August 1922 after a series of conversations with Dr. Morris Fishbein, managing editor of the *Journal of the American Medical Association*, and Dr. Paul De Kruif, a bacteriologist and medical journalist. Lewis and De Kruif agreed to collaborate on a novel about an outbreak of bubonic plague on a tropical island and signed a contract giving De Kruif a 25 percent share of the book's royalties. In January 1923 the two men traveled to the Caribbean to conduct research for the novel, then tentatively titled "The Barbarian." Their tour included visits to hospitals and almshouses in Barbados and a bacteriological laboratory in Panama. In a letter to H. L. Mencken, Lewis praised De Kruif for having "as much synthetic fictional imagination as he has synthetic imagination, and that's one hell of a lot. It's going to be my best book—though it isn't just *mine* by a long shot." Writing to the staff at Harcourt, Brace and Company, his publisher, Lewis described the collaboration: "When I'm compiling notes into a coherent whole, De Kruif is preparing more data—clear, sound, and just the stuff for dramatic purposes"; in the same letter, he wrote, "There are hundreds of notes, schedules, maps; and the actual skeleton from which I write the book is well under way." After finishing their research in the Caribbean, Lewis and De Kruif went to London, where they met with medical researchers and toured laboratories. Lewis worked on the manuscript while in England and France during the spring and summer of 1923 and completed the first draft, now titled "Martin Arrowsmith," on September 30. Both De Kruif and Grace Hegger Lewis read the typescript and wrote suggestions for revisions in the margins.

In October, Alfred Harcourt wrote Lewis of an offer to serialize "Martin Arrowsmith" in *The Designer and the Woman's Magazine* for $50,000. Lewis responded that although he disliked serialization, "it seemed foolish to lose fifty thousand"; but he insisted that neither he nor Sewell Haggard, the editor of *The Designer*, would "change the thing into a sweet sunny tale." Nevertheless, the periodical version omits philosophical passages, references to venereal disease, satirical commentary about subjects other than medicine, and critical remarks regarding religious practices. Although the periodical version of the novel was substantially cut, Lewis also added passages, mostly to ensure the coherence of the narrative. None of these revisions were incorporated into the book version. The serial version appeared as "Dr. Martin Arrowsmith" in eleven installments between June 1924 and April 1925.

Arrowsmith was published by Harcourt, Brace and Company on March 5, 1925. Lewis dedicated the book to De Kruif, although he rejected De Kruif's request to be credited as a collaborator on the title page. De Kruif accepted the dedication with the condition that Lewis change the phrase "for his suggestions" to "for his help," which he agreed to. An autographed edition of 500 copies was published simultaneously with a "trade edition" of more than 50,000 copies. Both of these "editions" were set from the same plates, with the "trade edition" described on its copyright page as "Second printing [first trade edition], January, 1925," the date referring to the date of copyright registration. The novel was published in England by Jonathan Cape in 1925 as *Dr. Martin Arrowsmith* (the title was changed because there was a British publisher named Arrowsmith). Lewis made no changes to the novel after the publication of the first edition. The text of the 1925 Harcourt, Brace and Company trade edition of *Arrowsmith* is printed here.

Lewis conducted research for what he described as "the big religious novel I've planned so long" early in 1926. During two visits to Kansas City, he spoke with more than 15 members of the clergy, mostly Protestant ministers but also a Roman Catholic priest and a rabbi, at weekly lunchtime meetings. In May 1926, while living at Lake Pelican in Pequot, Minnesota, he began writing the novel, using the provisional title "Sounding Brass." Working from his research notes, detailed character biographies, and a full outline, Lewis wrote more than half of the novel's first draft during the spring and summer of 1926. He submitted the typescript of a revised draft to Harcourt, Brace and Company shortly before Christmas 1926. Alfred Harcourt called the novel "amazingly good, even for you" and suggested a number of changes, especially at the end of the narrative; Lewis then made substantial revisions to the galley proofs. *Elmer Gantry* was published by Harcourt, Brace and Company on March 10, 1927; an English edition was published by Jonathan Cape in 1927. Lewis did not subsequently revise the novel, and he was not involved in Patrick Kearney's stage adaptation, which ran for six weeks in New York in 1928. The text printed here is that of the 1927 Harcourt, Brace and Company first printing of *Elmer Gantry*.

While living in Berlin in the summer of 1927 Lewis began working on a novel called "The Yearner," a story about the breakup of a marriage that he had wanted to write for several years. Lewis used several titles, including "Blind Giant," "Sunset," "Exile," "Home," and "A Man Alone," before choosing *Dodsworth.* He wrote about 50,000 words of the first draft by the end of November 1927, when he set it aside to travel to the Soviet Union. He resumed working on *Dodsworth* in March 1928 while staying at a villa outside Naples and completed the novel's first draft shortly after his marriage to journalist Dorothy Thompson in May. Lewis revised the draft as he traveled through England during the summer and finished the novel in New York City in December 1928. *Dodsworth* was published by Harcourt, Brace and Company on March 14, 1929. The British edition, published by Jonathan Cape, also came out in 1929. Lewis made no changes to the book after the 1929 Harcourt, Brace and Company first printing, the text of which is printed here.

This volume presents the texts of the original printings chosen for inclusion here without change except for the correction of typographical errors; it does not attempt to reproduce nontextual features of their typographic design. Spelling, punctuation, and capitalization are often expressive features and are not altered, even when inconsistent or irregular. The following is a list of typographical errors corrected, cited by page and line number: 24.22, c'mmerialism; 31.23, Cliff; 40.10, tickelish; 92.22, Cliff; 108.16, hunted; 283.15, Pickerbaughs; 359.15, stores; 405.22, almhouse; 509.7, permillennial; 532.32, it she; 622.26, Lot's; 715.22, Rogers; 776.31, Ishua; 816.22, high.; 879.25, And—; 966.24–25, luglage; 1077.33, Ridge; 1111.16, San; 1158.23, noon I.

Notes

In the notes below, the reference numbers denote page and line of this volume (the line count includes chapter headings). No note is made for material included in standard desk-reference books such as Webster's *Collegiate, Biographical,* and *Geographical* dictionaries. Biblical references are keyed to the King James Version. For further biographical background, see: Richard Lingeman, *Sinclair Lewis: Rebel from Main Street* (New York: Random House, 2002); Mark Schorer, *Sinclair Lewis: An American Life* (New York: McGraw-Hill Book Company Inc., 1961); *From Main Street to Stockholm: Letters of Sinclair Lewis, 1919–1930*, ed. Harrison Smith (New York: Harcourt, Brace and Company, 1952); Grace Hegger Lewis, *With Love from Gracie. Sinclair Lewis: 1912–1925* (New York: Harcourt, Brace and Company, 1955); Vincent Sheean, *Dorothy and Red* (Boston: Houghton Mifflin Company, 1963).

ARROWSMITH

2.1 *Paul H. DeKruif*] De Kruif (1890–1971) was a Michigan-born bacteriologist and the author of *Microbe Hunters* (1926) and other books of popular science.

6.18 Zenith] City invented by Lewis, which first appears in *Babbitt* (1922).

19.7 G.U.] Gastrointestinal upset.

21.5–6 Back Bay] Upper-class neighborhood in Boston.

35.29 Korpsbrüder] Brother students, i.e., fellow members of a student society.

35.30 *Die goldene Zeit!*] The golden age.

41.20 *Die Wacht am Rhein*] "The Watch on the Rhine," German patriotic song with words by Max Schneckenburger (1840) and music by Carl Wilhelm (1854).

41.22 *Kerl*] Chap, fellow.

68.35 *Cimex lectularius*] Bedbug.

82.32 *Town Topics*] A weekly New York magazine, edited from 1891 to 1920 by Colonel William d'Alton Mann (1839–1920), that purveyed society gossip.

90.33 Baumanometer] Brand name of a wall-mounted mercury sphygmomanometer (instrument for measuring blood pressure).

93.5 Charley and Will] Charles Mayo (1865–1939) and William Mayo (1861–1939), co-founders of the Mayo Clinic in Rochester, Minnesota.

140.31 dieners!] Lackeys.

140.31 *Du Heiliger!*] O Holy One!

150.38 putting on lugs.] Borrowing money.

177.7 "The Golden Bowl"] Novel by Henry James, published in 1904.

182.10 Spirits Frumentus] Grain alcohol.

191.12–13 'Der Graf von Luxemburg'] Operetta (1909) by Franz Lehár with libretto by Robert Bodanzky and Alfred Maria Willner.

191.14 'Die Meistersinger,'] *Die Meistersinger von Nürnberg* (1868), opera by Richard Wagner.

191.17 Cosmos Club] Elite men's club in Washington, D.C.

205.35–36 Chum Frink] T. Cholmondeley Frink, fictitious advertising man and syndicated newspaper poet who appears in *Babbitt.*

235.22 Raymond Pearl's] Pearl (1879–1940) was a professor of biology and medical statistics at Johns Hopkins University and a close friend of H. L. Mencken.

270.2 D.B.'s] Deadbeats.

318.15 Oberst] Colonel.

320.1 Lüchow's] German restaurant formerly in New York City.

422.29–30 *Versteh' nicht*] *Verstehe nicht:* I don't understand.

425.20 anti-Shiga] Shiga bacillus causes dysentery.

446.29–30 *capitus enlargatus*] Swelled head (pseudo-Latin).

451.27 *ops terrara*] *Orbis terrarum:* the globe of the world.

ELMER GANTRY

477.6 "The Good . . . Time"] "In the Good Old Summer Time" (1902), popular song by Ren Shields and George Evans.

479.10 the *Ewigkeit*] Eternity.

480.10–11 "The world . . . early and soon"] "The world is too much with us; late and soon," sonnet by William Wordsworth, first published in 1807.

485.13 E. P. Roe] Edward Payson Roe (1838–88), Presbyterian minister who became a popular novelist after the success of *Barriers Burned Away* (1872), inspired by the Chicago fire.

485.18–19 "Some Mistakes of Moses,"] Lecture by Robert G. Ingersoll (1833–99), who was known as "the great agnostic," that critically examined the first five books of the Bible. It was first published in 1879

485.19 "The Age of Reason."] Book by Thomas Paine (1737–1809), published in two volumes in 1794 and 1795, attacking the authority of the Bible and promoting deism.

502.6 McGuffey's Reader] *McGuffey's Eclectic Readers,* a series of six primers for schools, published between 1836 and 1857 and compiled by William Holmes McGuffey (1800–73), president of Cincinnati College (1836–39) and Ohio University (1839–43) and professor at Woodward College (1843–45) and the University of Virginia (1845–73).

502.6–7 boy . . . burning deck] A reference to the first line of "Casabianca" (1829) by English poet Felicia Dorothea Hemans (1793–1835). The poem tells how the son of a French admiral remained at his post on the *L'Orient* until the ship exploded during the battle of the Nile in 1798.

502.8 Nick Carter Series] Popular series of dime novels and pulp magazine stories about the detective Nick Carter. The first Nick Carter story appeared in 1886 and was followed by more than 1,500 titles written by dozens of authors.

502.32 "Nicæa"] Hymn, also known as "Holy! Holy! Lord God Almighty," with words by Reginald Heber (1783–1826) set to music composed in 1861 by John Bacchus Dykes (1823–76).

502.35–36 "Throw Out the Lifeline,"] Hymn (1888) with words and music by Edwin Smith Ufford.

502.38 "Onward, Christian Soldiers,"] Hymn with words (1864) by Sabine Baring-Gould (1834–1924) and music (1871) by Sir Arthur Sullivan (1842–1900).

510.20 sabellianism] An anti-Trinitarian Christian heresy associated with Sabellius, who was excommunicated c. 220 for his belief in the indivisibility of God.

511.39 bottle-pool] A billiards game in which players try to knock over a bottle in the center of the table with a ricocheting cue ball.

515.30 Bulls of Bashan] See Psalm 22:12.

521.16–17 "When the Roll . . . Yonder"] Hymn (1893) with words and music by James Milton Black (1856–1938).

521.24 "Shall We Gather at the River?"] Hymn (1864) with words and music by Robert Lowry (1826–99).

522.20 "Rejoiceth . . . a race,"] Psalm 19:5.

527.6–7 Draw me nearer . . . side.] From the hymn "I Am Thine, O Lord" (1875), words by Frances (Fanny) J. Crosby (1820–1915), music by William Howard Doane (1832–1915).

553.8 "Ben Hur"] *Ben-Hur: A Tale of the Christ* (1880), novel by Lew Wallace (1827–1905).

559.30 "What a Young Man Ought to Know,"] Book (1897) by Lutheran clergyman Sylvanus Stall (1847–1915) instructing young men on sexual topics, including the dangers of masturbation.

560.7–8 "Les Miserables"] Novel (1862) by Victor Hugo (1802–85).

560.9 "The Scarlet Letter"] Novel (1850) by Nathaniel Hawthorne (1804–64).

560.22–23 "Pippa Passes,"] Drawing (1854) by Elizabeth Siddal (1829–62), inspired by the dramatic poem published in 1841 by Robert Browning.

560.28 "Imitation of Christ,"] Devotional work (c. 1427) attributed to Thomas Á Kempis (c. 1380–1471), a German monk.

564.33 supralapsarianism] Doctrine held by some Calvinists that God decreed both election and reprobation before decreeing the Fall.

564.40–565.1 *innascibilitas* attribute] The attribute of being independent of birth.

565.1 the *res sacramenti*] The reality of the sacrament.

573.6–8 There is power . . . Lamb—] From the hymn "There is Power in the Blood" (1899) by Lewis Ellis Jones (1865–1936).

574.32 "The Church in the Wildwood."] Hymn (1857) by William S. Pitts (1830–1918).

595.16 Adoniram Judson became a Baptist] The American missionary Adoniram Judson (1788–1850) was ordained as a Congregational minister in 1812 shortly before he sailed for India, but his study of the Greek New Testament during his voyage to Calcutta persuaded him to become a Baptist. In 1813 Judson began working in Burma, where he survived harsh imprisonment by Burmese authorities during the Anglo-Burmese war (1824–26) and translated the Bible into Burmese.

595.19–20 *filioque* argument] Doctrine that the Holy Spirit proceeds from both the Father and the Son.

596.22 Main Line] Upper-class Philadelphia suburbs situated along the main railroad line west of the city.

602.17 *Weinachtsabend*] Christmas Eve celebration (literally, "eight wine evening," and a pun on *Weihnachtsabend*, Christmas Eve).

602.24 Stille Nacht, heilige Nacht] German Christmas carol with words (1816) by Joseph Mohr (1792–1848) and music (1818) by Franz Gruber (1787–1863); later translated as "Silent Night, Holy Night."

602.34 *Wein, Weib und Gesang. Der arme!*] Wine, women and song. The poor fellow!

603.11 gazabo] Fellow, guy.

639.6–7 'Jerusalem the Golden'] Hymn (1861) with music (1853) by Alexander Ewing (1830–95) and words by John Mason Neale (1818–66) taken from his 1849 translation of the poem "De Contemptu Mundi" (c. 1140) by Bernard of Cluny.

661.25 Chickamauga] Civil War battle fought near Chickamauga Creek in northwestern Georgia, September 19–20, 1863, ending in a Confederate victory.

676.40 "Softly and Tenderly Jesus Is Calling,"] Hymn (1880) with words and music by Will L. Thompson (1847–1909).

677.1–2 "It's the Old-time Religion"] American folk hymn from the 19th century.

677.5 "At the Cross"] Hymn (1885) with words (1707) by Isaac Watts (1674–1748) and music (1885) by Ralph E. Hudson (1843–1901), who also wrote the refrain.

681.6 Ralph Waldo Trine] New Thought philosopher (1866–1958); author of the 1897 best seller *In Tune with the Infinite, or, Fullness of Peace, Power, and Plenty.*

708.38 "Kim,"] Novel (1901) by Rudyard Kipling (1865–1936).

730.27 spondulix] Money.

732.29 Elizabeth of the German Garden] The English writer Elizabeth von Arnim (1866–1941), born Marie Annette Beauchamp, published her first novel *Elizabeth and Her German Garden* anonymously. Her subsequent books were signed "By the author of Elizabeth and Her German Garden" and "By Elizabeth."

746.11–12 Pale beyond . . . she stands.] From "The Garden of Proserpine" (1866) by Algeron Swinburne (1837–1909).

754.8 "Wonderful Words of Life,"] Hymn (1874) with words and music by Philip Bliss (1838–76).

754.8–9 "Brighten the Corner Where You Are,"] Hymn (1913) with words by Ina D. Ogdon (1877–1964) and music by Charles H. Gabriel (1856–1932).

754.20–21 'How Firm a Foundation.'] Hymn (1787) with words by John Rippon (1751–1836) that is sung to several different tunes.

762.36 Fitzgerald's Omar] *The Rubaiyat of Omar Khayyam,* a free translation (1859) by Edward FitzGerald (1809–83) of quatrians by the Persian poet (d. ?1132).

763.38–39 "The Message to Garcia"] "A Message to Garcia," inspirational magazine essay (1899) by Elbert Hubbard (1859–1915).

764.23–29 Life is real! . . . sands of time.] From "A Psalm of Life" (1839).

765.31–36 Ah, nothing . . . fourscore years.] From "Morituri Salutamus" (1875).

777.6 "O God, Our Help in Ages Past,"] Hymn with words (1719) by Isaac Watts (1674–1748) and music (1708) by William Croft (1678–1727).

785.15 Four-Minute Man] "Four-Minute Men" were speakers who gave short talks, about four minutes in length, at public gatherings urging listeners to buy war bonds or enlist in the armed forces.

795.7 badger game] Extortion scheme in which a woman lures a man into a compromising situation before being interrupted by her male accomplice, who pretends to be an outraged husband and demands money.

822.5 "Ach Du Lieber Augustin."] A German folk song.

834.37 *Gott weiss*] God knows.

835.3 *Prediger*] Preacher.

843.39 Pierce-Arrow] Luxury car made by the Pierce-Arrow Motor Car Company between 1903 and 1938.

864.18–19 'Ethan Frome' . . . Renan's Jesus] *Ethan Frome* (1911), novella by Edith Wharton; *Père Goriot* (1834), novel by Honoré de Balzac; *Tono-Bungay* (1909), novel by H. G. Wells; *Life of Jesus* (1863), study by Ernest Renan.

865.26 B.Y.P.U.] Baptist Young People's Union.

871.12 Dayton evolution trial] The widely publicized July 1925 trial in Dayton, Tennessee, of John T. Scopes, a high school biology teacher, who violated a state law barring the teaching of evolution in order to make a test case. Scopes was convicted, but his sentence was later set aside on appeal on technical grounds.

890.27–28 Lord's Day Alliance] Religious society devoted to promoting observance of the Sunday Sabbath and supporting "blue laws" that close business and entertainment facilities on Sunday.

890.28 Watch and Ward Society] Boston organization, founded in 1876, that reviewed books, plays, and magazines for obscenity.

DODSWORTH

916.2 DOROTHY] Dorothy Thompson (1894–1961), a journalist and author, Lewis's second wife.

920.18 droschke] Hackney carriage.

921.18 Leberknödel] Liver dumpling.

926.14 Jermyn Street] Street in London noted for shirtmakers' shops.

938.26 Masereel] Frans Masereel (1889–1972), Belgian painter and illustrator best known for his satiric, expressionist woodcuts.

947.8 *dernière cartouche*] Last cartridge (i.e., bullet).

956.7 BOBTAILED STRAIGHTS] In poker, four cards to a straight, open at both ends.

956.32 *robe de style*] A style of evening dress, with a full skirt and fitted bodice, fashionable in the 1920s.

963.17–18 Coeur de Lion . . . Noir Faineant] Lion-heart, sobriquet of King Richard I (1157–99). In the historical romance *Ivanhoe* (1819) by Sir Walter Scott, Richard I returns to England disguised as a knight known as "Le Noir Faineant" ("The Black Sluggard").

963.20 Uncle Ponderevo] Character who sells worthless patent medicines in *Tono-Bungay* (1909) by H. G. Wells.

963.21 Jude] Jude Hawley, hero of *Jude the Obscure* (1895) by Thomas Hardy.

963.22 Old Jolyon] Jolyon Forsyte, character in *The Forsyte Saga* (1922) by John Galsworthy.

963.27 *Punch*] British humorous weekly founded in 1841.

963.27–28 *Illustrated London News*] Illustrated weekly magazine founded in 1842.

1024.31 *ancora una volta*] Yet another time.

1025.7 *Si, si! Sarà una cosa veramente*] Yes, yes! That will be something.

1025.32 Mr. Bass] Michael Thomas Bass (1799–1884), English brewer who made Bass Ale internationally popular.

1025.32 Haig Brothers] Haig & Haig, distillers of Scotch whisky.

1025.33 Smith Brothers] Manufacturers of cough lozenges; their bearded faces are depicted on the box.

1026.7 Debs] Eugene Debs (1855–1926), labor leader and Socialist Party presidential candidate from 1904 through 1920, was convicted of sedition in 1918 for making an anti-war speech and sentenced to ten years in prison. He was pardoned in 1921 by President Warren G. Harding.

1029.35 Gare du Nord] Paris train station.

1030.1 *zincs*] Bars.

1036.37 *caneton pressé*] Pressed duck, i.e., a young male duck cooked in a sauce made from juices pressed out of the carcass.

1047.40 *rognons de la maison*] Kidneys of the house.

1056.31 "le Maître"] The master.

1062.9 Riff] The Rif Mountains in northeastern Morocco, center of a revolt against the Spanish protectorate from 1921 until 1926, when the rebellion was defeated by French and Spanish troops.

1069.19 Park Row] Street in lower Manhattan near City Hall where many newspapers had their offices.

1092.9 heeled the *Lit.*] Tried out for the *Yale Literary Magazine.*

1095.19 *ausgezeichnet*] First-rate.

1109.14 Anastasia] Anastasia Nikolayevna (1901–18), youngest daughter of Czar Nicholas II, was murdered by the Bolsheviks along with her family. In the 1920s a woman known as Anna Anderson attracted wide public attention with her claim to be Anastasia.

1109.15 Zinovieff letter] On October 25, 1924, two British newspapers printed a letter, allegedly written by Grigory Yevseyevich Zinoviev (1883–1936), president of the Comintern (Communist International), instructing British Communists to engage in subversive activity within the armed forces. The publication of the letter contributed to the defeat of the Labour government by the Conservatives in the general election held on October 29.

1109.16 Archduke Rudolph] Crown prince of Austria (1858–89), who died in an apparent love suicide pact at Mayerling, the royal hunting lodge.

1109.17–18 Empress Charlotte . . . Castle Miramar] Charlotte (1840–1927), a Belgian princess, was the wife of Maximilian (1832–67), Austrian archduke and emperor of Mexico (1864–67) until his overthrow and execution. Castle Miramar was their home in Trieste.

1109.19 Floyd Gibbons'] Gibbons (1887–1939) was an American foreign correspondent who won fame for his dispatches in World War I.

1143.30 Kokoschka Austellung] Kokoschka exhibition. Oskar Kokoschka (1886–1980), German expressionist painter.

1144.24–25 Suppe mit Leberknödel.] Soup with liver dumpling.

1145.25 *wie sagt man?*] How do you say it?

1146.28 *aber fabelhaft*] But wonderfully.

1153.39 *gemütlich*] Genial, jolly.

1154.9 *bummel*] Stroll.

1156.5 *Shrecklich*] *Schrecklich:* dreadful, frightful.

1159.3 Sans Souci] Palace of Frederick the Great in Potsdam.

1161.9 *Kom' mal!*] Come in!

1164.23 *Backhuhn*] Fried chicken.

1168.11 *echt*] Real, authentic.

1168.14 *Vi et armis*] By force of arms.

1168.18 *Hässlich*] Unpleasant.

1168.37–38 *Uhu* or *Le Rire*] *Uhu* was a German satirical magazine, *Le Rire* a French satirical magazine.

1182.30 lizzie] Homosexual.

1187.19 *Gesellschaft*] Social gathering.

1197.17 *Nation*] Liberal American political weekly magazine.

1204.10 *canard aux navets*] Duck with turnips.

1258.26 Colleoni] Bartolomeo Colleoni (1400–75), Italian soldier of fortune notorious for changing sides in wars between Venice and Milan.

Cataloging Information

Lewis, Sinclair, 1885–1951.
Arrowsmith, Elmer Gantry, Dodsworth.

(The Library of America ; 133)
I. Title: Arrowsmith. II. Title: Elmer Gantry.
III. Title: Dodsworth. IV. Series.

PS3523.E94 2002
813'.52—dc21
ISBN 1-931082-08-1 (alk. paper)
2002019451

THE LIBRARY OF AMERICA SERIES

The Library of America fosters appreciation and pride in America's literary heritage by publishing, and keeping permanently in print, authoritative editions of America's best and most significant writing. An independent nonprofit organization, it was founded in 1979 with seed money from the National Endowment for the Humanities and the Ford Foundation.

1. Herman Melville, *Typee, Omoo, Mardi* (1982)
2. Nathaniel Hawthorne, *Tales and Sketches* (1982)
3. Walt Whitman, *Poetry and Prose* (1982)
4. Harriet Beecher Stowe, *Three Novels* (1982)
5. Mark Twain, *Mississippi Writings* (1982)
6. Jack London, *Novels and Stories* (1982)
7. Jack London, *Novels and Social Writings* (1982)
8. William Dean Howells, *Novels 1875–1886* (1982)
9. Herman Melville, *Redburn, White-Jacket, Moby-Dick* (1983)
10. Nathaniel Hawthorne, *Collected Novels* (1983)
11. Francis Parkman, *France and England in North America*, vol. I (1983)
12. Francis Parkman, *France and England in North America*, vol. II (1983)
13. Henry James, *Novels 1871–1880* (1983)
14. Henry Adams, *Novels, Mont Saint Michel, The Education* (1983)
15. Ralph Waldo Emerson, *Essays and Lectures* (1983)
16. Washington Irving, *History, Tales and Sketches* (1983)
17. Thomas Jefferson, *Writings* (1984)
18. Stephen Crane, *Prose and Poetry* (1984)
19. Edgar Allan Poe, *Poetry and Tales* (1984)
20. Edgar Allan Poe, *Essays and Reviews* (1984)
21. Mark Twain, *The Innocents Abroad, Roughing It* (1984)
22. Henry James, *Literary Criticism: Essays, American & English Writers* (1984)
23. Henry James, *Literary Criticism: European Writers & The Prefaces* (1984)
24. Herman Melville, *Pierre, Israel Potter, The Confidence-Man, Tales & Billy Budd* (1985)
25. William Faulkner, *Novels 1930–1935* (1985)
26. James Fenimore Cooper, *The Leatherstocking Tales*, vol. I (1985)
27. James Fenimore Cooper, *The Leatherstocking Tales*, vol. II (1985)
28. Henry David Thoreau, *A Week, Walden, The Maine Woods, Cape Cod* (1985)
29. Henry James, *Novels 1881–1886* (1985)
30. Edith Wharton, *Novels* (1986)
31. Henry Adams, *History of the U.S. during the Administrations of Jefferson* (1986)
32. Henry Adams, *History of the U.S. during the Administrations of Madison* (1986)
33. Frank Norris, *Novels and Essays* (1986)
34. W.E.B. Du Bois, *Writings* (1986)
35. Willa Cather, *Early Novels and Stories* (1987)
36. Theodore Dreiser, *Sister Carrie, Jennie Gerhardt, Twelve Men* (1987)
37. Benjamin Franklin, *Writings* (1987)
38. William James, *Writings 1902–1910* (1987)
39. Flannery O'Connor, *Collected Works* (1988)
40. Eugene O'Neill, *Complete Plays 1913–1920* (1988)
41. Eugene O'Neill, *Complete Plays 1920–1931* (1988)
42. Eugene O'Neill, *Complete Plays 1932–1943* (1988)
43. Henry James, *Novels 1886–1890* (1989)
44. William Dean Howells, *Novels 1886–1888* (1989)
45. Abraham Lincoln, *Speeches and Writings 1832–1858* (1989)
46. Abraham Lincoln, *Speeches and Writings 1859–1865* (1989)
47. Edith Wharton, *Novellas and Other Writings* (1990)
48. William Faulkner, *Novels 1936–1940* (1990)
49. Willa Cather, *Later Novels* (1990)
50. Ulysses S. Grant, *Memoirs and Selected Letters* (1990)

51. William Tecumseh Sherman, *Memoirs* (1990)
52. Washington Irving, *Bracebridge Hall, Tales of a Traveller, The Alhambra* (1991)
53. Francis Parkman, *The Oregon Trail, The Conspiracy of Pontiac* (1991)
54. James Fenimore Cooper, *Sea Tales: The Pilot, The Red Rover* (1991)
55. Richard Wright, *Early Works* (1991)
56. Richard Wright, *Later Works* (1991)
57. Willa Cather, *Stories, Poems, and Other Writings* (1992)
58. William James, *Writings 1878–1899* (1992)
59. Sinclair Lewis, *Main Street & Babbitt* (1992)
60. Mark Twain, *Collected Tales, Sketches, Speeches, & Essays 1852–1890* (1992)
61. Mark Twain, *Collected Tales, Sketches, Speeches, & Essays 1891–1910* (1992)
62. *The Debate on the Constitution: Part One* (1993)
63. *The Debate on the Constitution: Part Two* (1993)
64. Henry James, *Collected Travel Writings: Great Britain & America* (1993)
65. Henry James, *Collected Travel Writings: The Continent* (1993)
66. *American Poetry: The Nineteenth Century*, Vol. 1 (1993)
67. *American Poetry: The Nineteenth Century*, Vol. 2 (1993)
68. Frederick Douglass, *Autobiographies*, (1994)
69. Sarah Orne Jewett, *Novels and Stories* (1994)
70. Ralph Waldo Emerson, *Collected Poems and Translations* (1994)
71. Mark Twain, *Historical Romances* (1994)
72. John Steinbeck, *Novels and Stories 1932–1937* (1994)
73. William Faulkner, *Novels 1942–1954* (1994)
74. Zora Neale Hurston, *Novels and Stories* (1995)
75. Zora Neale Hurston, *Folklore, Memoirs, and Other Writings* (1995)
76. Thomas Paine, *Collected Writings* (1995)
77. *Reporting World War II: American Journalism 1938–1944* (1995)
78. *Reporting World War II: American Journalism 1944–1946* (1995)
79. Raymond Chandler, *Stories and Early Novels* (1995)
80. Raymond Chandler, *Later Novels and Other Writings* (1995)
81. Robert Frost, *Collected Poems, Prose, & Plays* (1995)
82. Henry James, *Complete Stories 1892–1898* (1996)
83. Henry James, *Complete Stories 1898–1910* (1996)
84. William Bartram, *Travels and Other Writings* (1996)
85. John Dos Passos, *U.S.A.* (1996)
86. John Steinbeck, *The Grapes of Wrath and Other Writings 1936–1941* (1996)
87. Vladimir Nabokov, *Novels and Memoirs 1941–1951* (1996)
88. Vladimir Nabokov, *Novels 1955–1962* (1996)
89. Vladimir Nabokov, *Novels 1969–1974* (1996)
90. James Thurber, *Writings and Drawings* (1996)
91. George Washington, *Writings* (1997)
92. John Muir, *Nature Writings* (1997)
93. Nathanael West, *Novels and Other Writings* (1997)
94. *Crime Novels: American Noir of the 1930s and 40s* (1997)
95. *Crime Novels: American Noir of the 1950s* (1997)
96. Wallace Stevens, *Collected Poetry and Prose* (1997)
97. James Baldwin, *Early Novels and Stories* (1998)
98. James Baldwin, *Collected Essays* (1998)
99. Gertrude Stein, *Writings 1903–1932* (1998)
100. Gertrude Stein, *Writings 1932–1946* (1998)
101. Eudora Welty, *Complete Novels* (1998)
102. Eudora Welty, *Stories, Essays, & Memoir* (1998)
103. Charles Brockden Brown, *Three Gothic Novels* (1998)
104. *Reporting Vietnam: American Journalism 1959–1969* (1998)
105. *Reporting Vietnam: American Journalism 1969–1975* (1998)
106. Henry James, *Complete Stories 1874–1884* (1999)
107. Henry James, *Complete Stories 1884–1891* (1999)

108. *American Sermons: The Pilgrims to Martin Luther King Jr.* (1999)
109. James Madison, *Writings* (1999)
110. Dashiell Hammett, *Complete Novels* (1999)
111. Henry James, *Complete Stories 1864–1874* (1999)
112. William Faulkner, *Novels 1957–1962* (1999)
113. John James Audubon, *Writings & Drawings* (1999)
114. *Slave Narratives* (2000)
115. *American Poetry: The Twentieth Century*, Vol. 1 (2000)
116. *American Poetry: The Twentieth Century*, Vol. 2 (2000)
117. F. Scott Fitzgerald, *Novels and Stories 1920–1922* (2000)
118. Henry Wadsworth Longfellow, *Poems and Other Writings* (2000)
119. Tennessee Williams, *Plays 1937–1955* (2000)
120. Tennessee Williams, *Plays 1957–1980* (2000)
121. Edith Wharton, *Collected Stories 1891–1910* (2001)
122. Edith Wharton, *Collected Stories 1911–1937* (2001)
123. *The American Revolution: Writings from the War of Independence* (2001)
124. Henry David Thoreau, *Collected Essays and Poems* (2001)
125. Dashiell Hammett, *Crime Stories and Other Writings* (2001)
126. Dawn Powell, *Novels 1930–1942* (2001)
127. Dawn Powell, *Novels 1944–1962* (2001)
128. Carson McCullers, *Complete Novels* (2001)
129. Alexander Hamilton, *Writings* (2001)
130. Mark Twain, *The Gilded Age and Later Novels* (2002)
131. Charles W. Chesnutt, *Stories, Novels, and Essays* (2002)
132. John Steinbeck, *Novels 1942–1952* (2002)
133. Sinclair Lewis, *Arrowsmith, Elmer Gantry, Dodsworth* (2002)
134. Paul Bowles, *Novels 1949–1955* (2002)
135. Paul Bowles, *Collected Stories & Later Writings* (2002)
136. Kate Chopin, *Complete Novels & Stories* (2002)

This book is set in 10 point Linotron Galliard, a face designed for photocomposition by Matthew Carter and based on the sixteenth-century face Granjon. The paper is acid-free Domtar Literary Opaque and meets the requirements for permanence of the American National Standards Institute. The binding material is Brillianta, a woven rayon cloth made by Van Heek-Scholco Textielfabrieken, Holland. The composition is by The Clarinda Company. Printing and binding by R.R.Donnelley & Sons Company. Designed by Bruce Campbell.